The
Sea
of
Tranquility

The
Sea
of
Tranquility

a novel

KATJA MILLAY

ATRIA PAPERBACK

New York   London   Toronto   Sydney   New Delhi

ATRIA PAPERBACK
A Division of Simon & Schuster, Inc.
1230 Avenue of the Americas
New York, NY 10020

First Atria Paperback edition June 2013

ATRIA PAPERBACK and colophon are trademarks of Simon & Schuster, Inc.

For information about special discounts for bulk purchases, please contact Simon & Schuster Special Sales at 1-866-506-1949 or business@simonandschuster.com.

The Simon & Schuster Speakers Bureau can bring authors to your live event. For more information or to book an event, contact the Simon & Schuster Speakers Bureau at 1-866-248-3049 or visit our website at www.simonspeakers.com.

Designed by Nancy Singer

Manufactured in the United States of America

10 9 8 7 6 5 4 3 2 1

Library of Congress Cataloging-in-Publication Data has been applied for.

ISBN 978-1-4767-3094-3
ISBN 978-1-4767-3093-6 (ebook)

In memory of my father
Because he said so

The
Sea
of
Tranquility

I hate my left hand. I hate to look at it. I hate it when it stutters and trembles and reminds me that my identity is gone. But I look at it anyway, because it also reminds me that I'm going to find the boy who took everything from me. I'm going to kill the boy who killed me, and when I kill him, I'm going to do it with my left hand.

Chapter 1

Nastya

Dying really isn't so bad after you've done it once.
And I have.
I'm not afraid of death anymore.
I'm afraid of everything else.

—

August in Florida means three things: heat, oppressive humidity, and school. *School.* I haven't been to school in over two years. Not unless you count sitting at the kitchen table being homeschooled by your mom, and I don't. It's Friday. My senior year starts on Monday, but I haven't registered. If I don't go in today, I won't have a schedule on Monday morning, and I'll have to wait at the office for one. I think I'd rather skip the bad 1980s movie scene where I walk in late on the first day and everybody has to stop what they're doing to stare at me, because while that wouldn't be the worst thing that would ever happen to me, it would still suck.

My aunt pulls into the parking lot of Mill Creek Community High School with me in tow. It's a cookie cutter high school. Except for the putrid color of the walls and the name on the sign, it's an exact replica of the last one I attended. Margot—she made me drop the aunt part because it makes her feel old—turns down the radio she's been blaring the entire way here. Thankfully it's a short ride, because loud sounds make me edgy. It's not the sound itself that bothers me; it's just the fact that it's loud. The loud sounds make it impossible to hear the soft ones, and the soft sounds are the ones you have to be afraid of. I can handle it now because we're in a car, and I usually feel safe in cars. Outside is a different story. I never feel safe outside.

"Your mother expects a phone call when we're done here," Margot tells me. My mother expects a lot of things she's never going to get. In the scheme of things, a phone call is not much to ask, but that doesn't mean she'll get one. "You could at least text her. Four words. *Registered. All is well.* If you're feeling really generous, you could even throw one of those little happy faces on the end."

I look sideways at her from the passenger seat. Margot is my mother's younger sister by a good ten years. She is the opposite of my mother in almost every way. She doesn't even look like her, which means that she doesn't look like me either, because I am a carbon copy of my mother. Margot is dirty blond with blue eyes and a perpetual tan that she easily maintains by working nights and napping by the pool during the day, even though she's a nurse and she should know better. I have pale white skin, dark brown eyes, and long, wavy, just-this-side-of-black hair. She looks like she belongs in a Coppertone ad. I look like I belong in a coffin. People would have to be stupid to believe we're related, even if it is one of the only things about me that's true.

She's still got that cocky smile on her face, knowing that even if she hasn't convinced me to placate my mother, then at least she's planted a little guilt. It's impossible to dislike Margot, even when you really, really try, which makes me hate her a little, because I'll never be one of those people. She took me in, not because I don't have anywhere else to go, but because I don't have anywhere else I can stand to be. Luckily for her, she really only has to see me in passing, because once school starts, we'll rarely ever be home at the same time.

Even so, I doubt taking in a sullen, bitter, teenage girl is at the center of the vision board for a single woman in her early thirties. I wouldn't do it, but then I'm not a very good person. Maybe that's why I ran like hell from the people who love me the most. If I could be alone, I would. Gratefully. I'd rather be alone than have to pretend I'm okay. But they won't give me that option. So I'll settle for being with someone who at least doesn't love me as much. I'm thankful for Margot. Not that I tell her this. Not that I tell her anything. I don't.

When I walk in, the main office is a mass of commotion. Phones ringing, copiers running, voices everywhere. There are three lines leading up to the front counter. I don't know which one to get into, so I pick the one closest to the door and hope for the best. Margot sweeps in behind me and immediately pulls me around the side, past all of the lines, and up to the receptionist. She's lucky I saw her coming, or the second her hand was on my arm, she would have found herself facedown on the ground with my knee in her back.

"We have an appointment with Mr. Armour, the principal," she says authoritatively. Margot, the responsible adult. She's playing my mom's part today. This is a side of her I don't usually see. She prefers the cool aunt role. She doesn't have any kids of her own, so this is a little out of her depth. I didn't even realize we had an appointment, but I see the sense in it now. The receptionist, a fiftyish, unpleasant-looking woman, motions us to a couple of chairs next to a closed, dark wood door.

We only have to wait a few minutes, and no one notices or acknowledges me at all. The anonymity is nice. I wonder how long it will last. I look down at myself. I didn't get decked out for the visit today. I expected to come in, fill out some paperwork, hand over some immunization records, and be done with it. I wasn't expecting the swarms of students crowding the office. I'm wearing jeans and a black V-neck T-shirt, both a little—okay, a lot—tighter than they need to be, but otherwise completely nondescript. The shoes are where I made the effort. Black stilettos. Four-and-a-half inches of insanity. I'm not using them so much for the height, even though I seriously need it, as for the effect. I wouldn't have bothered with them today, except I needed the practice. My balance on them has gotten better, but I figured a dress rehearsal wouldn't hurt. I'd prefer to avoid eating ass on my first day of school.

I look at the clock on the wall. The second hand is bouncing back and forth inside my head, even though I know I can't possibly hear the ticking over everything else going on. I wish I could tune out the noise in this room. It's disconcerting. There are too many sounds at once and my brain is trying to separate them, to sort them out into neat little piles, but it's almost impossible with all of the machines and voices melting together. I open and close my hand in my lap and hope we get called in soon.

A few minutes that seem like an hour later, the heavy wooden door opens, and we're ushered inside by a fortysomething man in an ill-fitting shirt and tie. He smiles warmly before sliding back behind his desk into an oversized leather chair. The desk is imposing. Too big for this office. Obviously the furniture is meant to intimidate, because the man does not. Even before he's said much, I peg him as soft. I hope I'm right. I'm going to need him on this.

I settle back into one of two matching burgundy leather chairs opposite Mr. Armour's desk. Margot sinks into the chair next to me and launches into her spiel. I listen for a few minutes as she explains my "unique situation" to him. *Unique situation, indeed.* As she goes into detail, I see him glance over at me. His eyes widen just slightly as he looks closer, and I catch the glimmer of recognition in them. *Yes, that's me.* He remembers me. If I had gotten farther away, this might not even be necessary. The name wouldn't mean much of anything. The face would mean even less. But I'm only two hours from ground zero, and if even one person puts it together, I'll be right back where I was there. I can't take the chance, so here we sit, in Mr. Armour's office, three days before the start of my senior year. Nothing like last minute. Though this, at least, is not my fault. My parents fought the move until the end, but they finally relented. I may have Margot to thank for some of that. Though I think the fact that I broke my father's heart helped the cause a little, too. And, probably, they were all just tired.

I'm completely zoned out on the conversation now and I'm busy checking out Armour's office. There's not much to distract; a couple of houseplants that look like they need to be watered, along with a few family pictures. The diploma on the wall is from the University of Michigan. His first name is Alvis. *Huh.* What kind of crap name is Alvis? I don't even think it means anything, but I'll definitely check later. I'm running through possible origins in my head when I see Margot pulling out a file and handing it to him.

Doctor's notes. Lots of them.

As he looks over the paperwork, my eyes are drawn to the old-school metal hand-crank pencil sharpener on his desk. It strikes me as odd. The desk is a rich, fancy cherry number, nothing like the crap industrial ones teachers get. Why anyone would mount such an ancient pencil sharpener on it is beyond me. It's a complete contradiction. I wish I could ask about it. Instead, I focus on the ring of adjustable pencil holes and wonder idly if my pinky finger would fit into any of them. I'm contemplating how much it would hurt to sharpen it, and how much blood there might be, when I hear Mr. Armour's tone shift.

"Not at all?" He sounds nervous.

"Not at all," Margot confirms. She's got her put-on, no-nonsense demeanor in full swing.

"I see. Well, we'll do what we can. I'll make sure her teachers are informed before Monday. Has she filled in a class request form?" And like clockwork, we've gotten to the part where he's started to talk about me like I'm not in the room. Margot hands him the form and he peruses it quickly. "I'll get this to the guidance department so they can have a schedule drawn up by Monday morning. I can't promise she'll get these electives. Most classes are already full at this point."

"We understand. I'm sure you'll do whatever possible. We appreciate your cooperation and, of course, your discretion," Margot adds. It's a warning. Go, Margot. I think it's kind of wasted on him, though. I do get the feeling he genuinely wants to help. Plus, I think I make him uncomfortable, which means he probably hopes to see as little of me as possible.

Mr. Armour walks us to the door, shaking Margot's hand and nodding almost imperceptibly at me with a strained smile that I think might be pity, or possibly, disdain. Then, just as quickly, he looks away. He follows us back into the chaos of the front office and asks us to wait a moment while he heads down a hallway to the guidance office with my paperwork.

I look around and see that several of the same people I saw earlier are still waiting in line. I thank whatever god still believes in me for appointments. I'd rather clean the inside of a Port-O-Let with my tongue than spend another minute in this cacophony. We stand against the wall as far out of the way as we can get. There are no empty chairs now.

I glance to the front of the line where a dirty-blond Ken doll is tossing his most panty-dropping smile in the direction of Ms. Unpleasant on the other side of the counter. Ms. Unpleasant is now positively glowing in the aura of this boy's flirtations. I don't blame her. He's the kind of good-looking that transforms once self-respecting females into useless puddles of dumbass. I struggle to separate out their conversation. Something about an office aide position. *Aahh, lazy bastard.* He cocks his head to the side and says something that makes Ms. Unpleasant laugh and shake her head in resignation. He's won whatever it is he came here for. I watch the slight shift in his eyes. He knows it too. I'm almost impressed.

While he's waiting, the door opens again and a psychotically cute girl walks in and scans the room until her eyes land on him.

"Drew!" she yells over the commotion and everyone turns. She seems oblivious to the attention. "I'm not going to sit in the car all day! Come *on!*" I check her out while she glowers at him. She's blond, like him, though not exactly; her hair is lighter, like she spent the whole summer in the sun. She's attractive in the most obvious way possible, wearing a pink, well-filled-out halter top and carrying an obsessively color-coordinated, pink Coach purse. He seems mildly amused by her displeasure. Must be his girlfriend. A matching set, I think. *Panty-Combusting Ken comes complete with Piqued Princess Barbie: unachievable measurements, designer purse, and annoyed scowl included!*

He holds up a finger to her to convey that he'll just be a minute. If I were him, I'd choose a different finger. I smirk at the thought and glance up to see him smirking right back at me, his eyes alight with mischief.

Behind him, Ms. Unpleasant quickly scrawls something on his form and signs the bottom. She passes it back to him, but he's still looking at me. I point to her and raise my eyebrows at him. *Aren't you going to get what you came for?* He turns and takes the form from her hands, thanks her, and winks. He winks at the menopausal office lady. He's so blatantly obvious, it's almost inspired. *Almost.* She shakes her head again and shoos him toward the door. *Well played, Ken, well played.*

While I've been amusing myself with the office drama,

Margot's been whispering with a woman who I assume is the guidance counselor. Drew, who I desperately want to keep calling Ken, is still standing near the door, talking to a couple other guys who are waiting at the back of the line. I wonder if he's purposely trying to piss off Barbie. It seems easily done.

"Let's go." Margot reemerges, ushering me toward the front doors.

"Excuse me!" a woman's raised voice shrills, before we make it to the exit. Everyone in line turns in unison, watching the woman hold up a file folder in my direction. "How do you pronounce this name?"

"NAH-stee-ya," Margot enunciates, and I inwardly cringe, acutely aware of the audience around us. "Nastya Kashnikov. It's Russian." She tosses the last two words off over her shoulder, obviously pleased with herself for some reason, before we head out the door with everyone's eyes on our backs.

When we reach the car, she lets out a sigh and her demeanor noticeably shifts back to the Margot I know. "Well, that hurdle's cleared. For now," she adds. Then she smiles her dazzling, all-American-girl smile. "Ice cream?" she asks, sounding like she might need it more than me. I smile back, because even at ten thirty in the morning, there's only one answer to that question.

Chapter 2

Josh

Monday, 7:02 AM. Pointless. That's what today is going to be, along with the 179 school days that come after it. I'd contemplate the waste of it all now if I had the time, but I don't. I'm gonna be late as it is. I head to the laundry room and yank some clothes out of the still-running dryer. I forgot to turn it on last night, but I don't have time to wait; so now I'm stuck pulling on a pair of damp jeans while I walk and trying not to trip over myself. Whatever. It's not like I'm surprised.

I grab a coffee mug out of the cabinet and attempt to fill it without spilling it all over the counter and burning myself in the process. I put it on the kitchen table, next to a shoe box full of prescription bottles, in time to see my grandfather coming out of his room. His white hair is so disheveled that he momentarily reminds me of a mad scientist. He walks alarmingly slow, but I know better than to offer to help him. He hates that. He used to be so badass and now he's not, and he feels every bit of that loss.

"Coffee's on the table," I say, grabbing my keys and heading for the door. "I laid out your pills and logged them already. Bill's coming in an hour. You sure you'll be okay until then?"

"I'm not an invalid, Josh," he practically growls at me. I try not to smile. He's pissed. Pissed is good. It makes things seem a little bit normal.

I'm in my truck and down the driveway in seconds, but I'm not sure it'll be enough. I don't live far from school, but the backup to get into the parking lot on the first day is always a bitch. Most teachers will look the other way today, but I wouldn't have to worry about it anyway; no one's going to give me a detention, late or not. I floor it, and a couple of minutes later I'm waiting to get into the lot. The line of cars snakes out onto the road, but at least it's moving periodically.

I'm running on four hours of sleep and only one cup of coffee. I wish I had had time to grab another one for myself, but I didn't, and it probably would have ended up in my lap by the time I got to school anyway.

I pull out my schedule while I'm idling and check it again. Shop isn't until fourth period, but at least it's not all the way at the end of the day. The rest of it I don't give a shit about.

When I finally make it onto campus, Drew is out front with his usual followers, regaling them with any number of BS stories about his summer. I know they're all BS because he spent most of the summer hanging out with me, and I know for a fact that we didn't do crap. Apart from the time he spent disappearing with whatever girl he was hooking up with, he was on my couch.

Looking at him now, I don't think there's anyone happier to be back at school. I'd roll my eyes if it didn't seem such a chick thing to do, so instead, I just stare blankly ahead and keep walking. He nods in my direction as I pass, and I return the gesture. I'll talk to him later. He knows I won't go near him when he's surrounded. No one else acknowledges me, and I pass through the rest of the crowd into the main courtyard, just as the first bell rings.

My first three classes could all be the same. All I do is listen to rules, pick up syllabi, and try to stay awake. My grandfather was up five times last night, which means I was up five times last night, too. I really have to start getting more sleep. *In a week you will*, I think bitterly, but I won't dwell on that now.

10:45 AM. First lunch. I'd rather just head straight to shop. Eating this early sucks. I make my way to the courtyard and park myself on the back of the bench farthest from the center, the same one I've sat at for the past two years. No one bothers me because it's easier to pretend I don't exist. I'd rather spend the half hour sweeping sawdust than sitting here, but there isn't any sawdust to sweep yet. At least it's early enough that the metal benches aren't scorching under the sun. Now I just have to wait out the next thirty minutes, which will probably be the longest of the day.

Nastya

Surviving. That's what I'm doing now, and it hasn't been quite as horrible as I expected. I get a lot of sideways looks, probably because of the way I'm dressed, but other than that no one really talks to me. Except for Drew, the Ken doll. I did run into him this morning, but mostly it was a nonevent. He talked. I walked. He gave up. I've made it to lunch and this is the test. No one's really had much of an opportunity for socializing yet, so I've been able to skate below the surface, but lunch is just a highly unsupervised hell dimension. Avoidance seems the best option at first, but I have to face the looks and the comments at some point. Personally, I'd rather shove a cactus up my ass, but apparently that option isn't on the table, so I might as well just rip the Band-Aid off now and get it over with. Then, I'll find an empty restroom and check my hair and fix my lipstick, or as we cowards like to call it, hide.

I try to surreptitiously check out my clothes and make sure nothing's where it shouldn't be and that I'm not flashing more than I'd originally planned. I've got on the same stilettos as Friday, but this time I went with a low-cut black tank top and a nearly nonexistent skirt that my ass doesn't look half bad in. I left my hair down so it falls past my shoulders and covers the scar on my forehead. My eyes are rimmed with thick black eyeliner. It's slutty and probably only attractive to the basest of human creatures. *Drew.* I smile to myself as I recall him looking me up and down in the hallway this morning. Barbie would be pissed.

I don't dress this way because I like it so much or because I want people to stare at me in general. But people are going to stare at me for the wrong reasons anyway, and if they are going to stare at me for the wrong reasons, then at least I should get to pick them. Plus, a little unwelcome staring is a small price to pay for scaring everyone off. I don't think there's a girl in this school who will want to talk to me, and any boy who's interested probably won't be much for conversation. And so what? If I'm going to get unwanted attention, better it be for my ass than for my psychosis and my effed-up hand.

Margot hadn't gotten home by the time I left for school this morning or she might have tried to talk me out of it. I wouldn't have blamed her. I think my first period teacher wanted to nail me on a dress code violation when I first walked in, but once he checked my name on his roster, he ushered me to a seat and didn't look at me again for the rest of the class.

Three years ago, my mother would have had a fit, cried, lamented her shortcomings as a parent, or possibly just locked me in my room if she saw me at school like this. Today, she'd look disappointed but would ask if it made me happy and I'd nod my head and lie so we could pretend it wasn't a problem. The clothes probably wouldn't even be the biggest issue, because I'm not sure she would mind the streetwalker uniform nearly as much as the makeup.

My mother loves her face. It's not out of arrogance or con-ceit; it's out of respect. She's grateful for what she was born with. She should be. It's an awesome face, a perfect face, an ethereal face. The kind people write songs and poems and suicide notes about. It's that exotic kind of beauty that men in romance nov-els obsess over, even if they have no idea who you are, because *they must possess you.* That kind of beauty. That's my mom. I grew up wanting to look just like her. Some people tell me I do, and maybe it's true, under there somewhere. If you scrape off the makeup and dress me to look like a girl as opposed to what I look like now—a profanity-spewing guttersnipe being dragged out of a crack house on *Cops.*

I imagine my mother shaking her head and giving me the disappointed look, but she chooses her battles these days and I'm not sure this one would make the cut. Mom's beginning to believe I may be a lost cause and that's a good thing, because I am, and I left her house so she could accept it. I was a lost cause a long time ago. That thought makes me sad for my mother, because she didn't ask for any of this. She thought she'd gotten her miracle, and I was the only one who knew she hadn't, no matter how much I wanted to give it to her. Maybe I was the one who took it away.

Which brings me back to the courtyard where I am still wait-ing on the outskirts like a guest on an episode of *Extreme Avoid-ance: High School Edition.* I planned to get here early enough to make it across before lunch was in full swing, but I got sidelined by my history teacher, and that three minutes meant the differ-ence between a half-empty courtyard and the one teeming with students that I'm staring at right now. I'm focused, at the moment, on the brick pavers covering the entirety of said courtyard and se-riously questioning the wisdom of my four-and-a-half-inch stilet-tos. I'm gauging my odds of making it across with both my ankles and my dignity intact when I hear a voice to my right call out.

I turn instinctively, but I know immediately that it's the

wrong thing to do. Sitting on a bench, a couple feet away, is the owner of that voice, and he's looking right at me. He's leaning back casually with his legs spread farther apart than they need to be in a blatant display of wishful thinking. He smiles, and I can't deny that he knows he's good-looking. If self-adoration were cologne, he would be the boy you couldn't stand next to without choking. Dark hair. Dark eyes. Like me. We could be brother and sister or one of those really creepy couples who look like they should be brother and sister.

I'm pissed at myself for looking. Now, when I turn and ignore him to make my way across the battlefield, I can be certain that his eyes—as well as every other set of eyes on that bench with him—are going to be trained on my back. And when I say my back, I mean my ass.

I recontemplate the unstable surface of the pavers. No pressure or anything. I avert my eyes back to the task at hand in time to hear him add, "If you're looking for someplace to sit, my lap is free." And there it is. It's not even clever or original, but his equally wit-free friends laugh anyway. There go my hopes for our bourgeoning sibling kinship. I step off the ledge and start walking, keeping my eyes trained straight ahead as if I have some purpose outside of simply surviving this walk.

I'm not even halfway through the day. I still have four of the seven classes left on the schedule that shit gave birth to.

—

I got to school early enough this morning to stop in the office and pick up my schedule. Of course, if I'd known at the time what I'd find on it, I might have put off the inevitable. It was crazy in there again, but Ms. Marsh, the guidance counselor, had given instructions for me to go to her office and pick up my schedule from her personally—just another one of the many perks of being me.

"Good morning, Nastya, Nastya," she said, repeating my

name with two different pronunciations and absentmindedly looking to me for confirmation, which I didn't give her. She was far too cheery for the first day of school or for seven o'clock in the morning in general. It was definitely unnatural. There's probably a class for guidance counselors only—*How to Emit Inappropriate Joy in the Face of Adolescent Horror.* I'm fairly certain they don't make teachers take it, because they don't even bother to pretend. Half of them are as miserable as I am.

She motioned for me to sit. I didn't. My skirt was way too short for sitting in a chair that didn't have a desk obscuring it. She handed me a map of campus and my schedule. I scanned it, mostly looking for the electives, because I knew what all the required courses were going to be. *You've got to be kidding me.* For a minute I was convinced that she must have handed me the wrong schedule, so I checked the top of the paper. *No, that's me.* I wasn't sure what the right reaction was in that situation. You know the one, where the universe decides to put its steel-toed boot up your ass yet again. Crying was out of the question and a screaming hissy-fit laced with maniacal laughter and profanity was, most definitely, off the table, which left me with my only other option: stunned silence.

Ms. Marsh must have caught the look on my face, and I'm betting it was pretty expressive, because she immediately launched into a detailed explanation involving graduation requirements and overfilled electives. She sounded almost like she was apologizing to me, and maybe she should have been, because it seriously sucked, but I almost wished I could have told her it was okay so she'd stop feeling bad. I'd survive it. It would take more than a few shitty classes to break me. I took my schedule, my map, and my abject horror and made my way to class, reading it again and again as I went. Unfortunately, it stayed the same every time.

—

At this point, I've made it almost to the halfway mark. It hasn't been so bad, relatively speaking, and everything in my life is relative. My teachers aren't horrible. My English teacher, Ms. McAllister, actually looks me in the eye like she's daring me to expect her to treat me differently. I like her. But the worst is yet to come, so I won't start pouring the champagne just yet.

Plus, I still have to navigate the trail of tears that is this court-yard. I'm nothing if not a coward, but I can't put it off much longer. I'm about six feet in and not doing so badly. I'm focused on my goal—the beacon that is the double-door entrance to the English wing—on the opposite side of my brick-lined square nemesis.

I take in everything I can with my peripheral vision. It's packed out here. And loud. So unbearably loud. I try to let all of the separate conversations and voices melt together into what I imagine is one continuous hum.

There are small groups around all of the benches, piled on top of them and standing next to them. Some students sit on the outer edges of the garden boxes that are placed incremen-tally throughout. Then there are the smart ones who sit on the ground in the shade of the walkway that runs around the perim-eter. There aren't enough places to sit, there's barely any reprieve from the sun, and it's hotter than hell out here. I can't imagine the utter craphole the cafeteria must be that this many people would rather sweat their asses off out here to avoid it. My old high school was the same way, but I never had to deal with the lunch period madness or any of the decisions that came along with it, like where to sit and who to sit with. I spent every lunch period practicing in the music room and that was the only place I wanted to be.

By now, I'm almost there. So far I've only seen a few faces I recognize: a boy who was in my history class, sitting by himself reading a book, and a couple of girls from math, who are gig-gling with angry Barbie of front office tirade fame. I can feel some of the looks I'm getting, but other than the ego-addled asshole with the free lap seating, no one else has spoken to me.

There are two more benches I have to pass to get to the doors, and it's the one on the left that catches my attention. It's empty, save for one boy, sitting right in the middle. It might not seem strange except for the fact that every other bench in this place—in truth every other place where a person could justifiably put their ass—is filled. Yet there is no one sitting on that bench, except him. When I look more closely, there's no one even hanging around in the immediate vicinity. It's like there's an invisible force field surrounding this space and he's the only one inside it.

Curiosity claims me, and I momentarily forget my purpose. I can't help but look at the boy. He's perched on top of the backrest, his worn-out brown work boots planted firmly on the seat. He's leaning over with his elbows resting on his knees in a pair of faded jeans. I can't see his face very well. His light brown hair hangs tousled over his forehead, and his eyes are cast downward at his hands. He's not eating; he's not reading; he's not looking at anyone. Until he is. And then he's looking at me. *Crap.*

I turn away instantly, but it's still too late. It wasn't like I just glanced at him. I was at a dead stop, in the middle of the courtyard, full-on staring. I'm only steps away from the asylum beyond those double doors and I take the risk of quickening my walk as much as I can without drawing attention. I make it to the relative obscurity of the building's overhang and reach for the door handle and pull. *Nothing.* It doesn't give. And I repeat, *crap.* It's locked. It's the middle of the day. Why would they lock the doors from the outside?

"It's locked," a voice from below me says. *No shit.* I look down. I hadn't even noticed the boy with the sketchbook, sitting on the ground right next to the doors. Where he's positioned, he's blocked by a large planter box, invisible from the main courtyard. Smart kid. His clothes are a mess, and his hair looks like it hasn't seen a brush in a week. He's sitting shoulder to shoulder with a brown-haired girl wearing sunglasses in the shade and holding a camera. She looks up at me briefly before turning her attention back to her camera. Other than the sunglasses, she's entirely nondescript. I wonder if I should have gone that route, but it's too late to second guess now.

"They don't want anyone sneaking in to smoke in the bathrooms during lunch," sketchbook boy with holes in his concert T-shirt tells me.

Oh. I wonder what happens if you're late to class. I guess you're just SOL. I glance across to the swarm of girls hovering around the courtyard restroom door. No thanks. I'm trying to figure out some other escape route, when I notice he's still craning his neck up and looking at me. It's a good thing I'm not a couple of steps closer or I'm quite sure he could see right up my almost imaginary skirt. At least I'm wearing cute underwear; they're the only thing on me that isn't black.

I glance at the sketchbook he's holding. His arm is draped over the top so I can't see what he's drawing. I wonder if he's any good. I can't draw for crap. I nod my head in thanks to him and turn to see if I can find somewhere else to go. Before I can walk away, two girls come barreling out of the door, almost running me down and knocking me off my awesome shoes. They're talking a mile a minute and don't even notice me there, which is fine, because I'm able to slip through the doors just past them. I wander into the cool, empty reprieve of the English building and remember how to breathe.

Chapter 3

Josh

Fourth hour can't come soon enough. I'm sweating already from sitting out in the sun at lunch, but there won't be much in the way of air-conditioning in the workshop. When I walk in, I immediately feel at home, even though the space looks entirely different than it did in June. There aren't tools and pieces of lumber on every surface. No carpet of sawdust covering the floor. No machines running. It's the quiet that's initially unnerving. It's not supposed to be quiet in here, and this is the only time of year when it is.

The first couple weeks are a rehash of rules for equipment usage and safety procedures that I could recite verbatim if anybody asked. Nobody asks. Everybody knows I know them. I could teach this class if I wanted to. I throw my books down on the far corner worktable where I sit every year, at least during the time we're expected to sit. Before I can pull the stool out from under the table, Mr. Turner calls me over.

I like Mr. Turner, but he doesn't care whether I like him or not. He wants my respect and he has that, too. What he tells me to do, I do. He's one of the few people who don't mind expecting things from me. At this point, I think I've learned as much from Mr. Turner as I did from my dad.

Mr. Turner's been running this program for as long as anyone can remember, years before I got here, when it wasn't anything more than a cop-out elective. Now it's one of the premier programs in the state. He runs it like a business wrapped around a master class in craftsmanship. In the advanced classes, our work raises the money for the materials and the equipment. We take orders and fill them, and that money gets filtered back into the program.

You don't get into the advanced classes without going through the introductory levels first, and even that isn't a guarantee. Mr. Turner only takes the students who live up to his expectations in terms of work ethic and ability. That's how he keeps the upper level classes so small. You need his approval to get in, and in a school with overflowing electives around every corner, he's still able to get away with it because he's that good.

When I get to his desk, he asks about my summer. He's trying to be polite but he knows me well enough that he doesn't have to bother. I've been in one of his classes every year since ninth grade. He knows my shit and he knows me. All I really want to do is build stuff and be left alone and he allows me both. I answer in as few words as possible and he nods, knowing we're done with the pretense.

"Theater department wants shelving built in their prop storage room. Can you head over there, take the measurements, plan it out, and make a list of what we need? You don't need to be here for all this." He picks up a stack of papers, which I assume are handouts on rules and procedures, with a measured amount of boredom and resignation. He just wants to build, too. But he also doesn't want someone losing a finger. "Bring me what you come up with at the end of class and I'll get you what you need. You can probably have it finished up in a week or so."

"No problem." I hold back a smile. The preliminary crap is the only part of this class I don't like and I've just been freed from it. I get to build, even if it is just shelves. And I get to do it away from everybody else.

I scrawl my signature across the bottom of the waivers and hand them back to him. Then I grab my books in time to see a couple other kids coming in. There shouldn't be many—probably only about a dozen or so students—in this section. I know everybody who's come in so far, except for one person; the girl from the courtyard, the one who was watching me. She can't possibly be in this class. She must agree, judging by the look on her face as she scans the room, taking in everything from the high ceilings down to the industrial power tools. Her eyes narrow just slightly with curiosity, but that's all I see of her because this time she turns and catches me looking.

I watch people a lot. Normally it's not an issue because no one really looks at me, and if they do, I'm pretty adept at looking away fast. Very fast. But damn if that girl wasn't faster. I know she's new here. If not, she's made some drastic, unfortunate transformation over the summer, because I'm more than aware of most of the people on this campus, and even if I wasn't, I'd remember the girl who comes to school looking like an undead whore. Regardless, I'm out the door about ten seconds later and I'm pretty sure they'll have worked out her schedule before I get back.

I hole up in the theater prop room for all of fourth period, measuring and drawing up plans and material lists for the shelving they need. There's no clock in here and I'm not ready when the bell rings. I shove the legal pad with my notes on it into my backpack and head out toward the English wing. I get to Ms. McAllister's room and walk past everyone still milling around in the hallway, eking out every last second to socialize before the bell rings. The door is propped open, and Ms. McAllister looks up when I walk in.

"Aah, Mr. Bennett. We meet again." I had her last year. They must have moved her up from junior to senior English.

"Yes, ma'am."

"Polite as always. How was your summer?"

"You're the third person who's asked."

"Nonanswer. Try again."

"Hot."

"Still loquacious." She smiles.

"Still ironic."

"I suppose we are both nothing if not consistent." She stands up and turns to pick up her roster, and three stacks of papers off the top of the file cabinet behind her.

"Can you bring that desk up to the front for me?" She points at a lopsided desk in the corner of the room. I drop my things on a desk in the back and walk over to pick up the broken one to move it to the front. "Just put it there." She motions in front of the whiteboard. "I just need something to put all of this on so I can talk." She drops the stacks of papers onto the desk as the warning bell rings.

"You need a podium."

"Josh, I'm lucky to have a desk with a working drawer," she notes with forced exasperation, walking over to the open classroom door without missing a beat. "You fools better get in here before that bell rings, because I do believe in giving detention on the first day of school and I give morning detention, not afternoon." She singsongs the last couple of words as a mass of students barrels into the room just before the tardy bell goes off.

Ms. McAllister doesn't do bullshit. She's not intimidated by the popular kids or the ones with the rich parents, and she doesn't want to be your friend. Last year, she managed to convince me that there was actually something here that might be worth learning without ever once making me talk in class.

Generally, I have two types of teachers. There are the ones

who ignore me completely and pretend I don't exist and there are the ones who call me out and force attention on me because they think it's good for me—or maybe just because it gives them some sort of control-freakish thrill to know that they can. Ms. McAllister isn't either of those. She leaves me alone without ignoring me, so as teachers go, she's damn near perfect.

She pulls out the doorstop just as Drew slips through the opening.

"Hey, Ms. McAllister." He smiles and winks because he has no shame.

"Immune to your charms, Mr. Leighton."

"Someday, we'll recite poetry to one another." He slides into the only empty desk, right in the front of the room.

"That we will. But the poetry unit isn't until next semester, so you'll have to stow your sonnets until then." She retreats to her desk and pulls a yellow slip of paper out of the drawer and walks back to him. "Don't be too disappointed. We do have a date tomorrow morning. Six forty-five AM. In the media center." She winks back at him as she lays the detention slip on his desk.

Nastya

Fourth hour shop class wasn't so horrible. Mr. Turner didn't pay much attention to me at all, which in a class of fourteen is pretty hard to do. He did check my schedule right off the bat to make sure I was in the right place and then asked me why they put me there. I shrugged. He shrugged. Then he handed it back, telling me I wouldn't be up to speed with everyone else, but if I really wanted to stay, he could let me be an assistant or something like that. It's obvious he doesn't really want me participating, but I think I'll stay. It's a small class where I can probably be left alone, which is as much as I'm prepared to ask on day one.

I make it all the way through to fifth period before being faced with one of those inane get-to-know-you games in my suckfest of a music class—a class which I will soon be clawing my way out of by any means necessary. The teacher, Miss Jennings, a cute, twentysomething woman with a blond bob, pale skin, and hatefully perfect piano-playing hands, makes us sit in a circle. An elementary school, duck-duck-goose-style *circle*. This affords each of us the best possible vantage point for studying, and subsequently, dissecting one another. Oh, and getting to know each other, of course. That too.

As get-to-know you games go, this isn't the worst I've endured. Everyone has to say three things about themselves and one of those things has to be a lie. Then the class tries to figure out which one is the lie. It's kind of sad that I'm not actually going to take part in the game, because if I was going to play, it would be fairly awesome. I'm pretty sure I would hand over large quantities of cash to listen to my classmates and the adorable blond pixie teacher debate the possible veracity of each of my responses:

My name is Nastya Kashnikov.

I was a piano-playing prodigy who doesn't belong anywhere near an Intro to Music class.

I was murdered two and a half years ago.

Discuss.

Instead, when they get to me, I sit stone-faced and silent. Ms. Jennings looks at me expectantly. *Check your roster.* She's still looking at me. I'm looking at her. We have a weird staring thing going on between us. *Check your roster. I know they told you.* I'm trying to will her telepathically now, but I am sadly lacking in the superpower department.

"Would you like to share three things about yourself?" she asks as if I am simply a moron with no clue what's going on around me.

I finally throw her a bone and shake my head as slightly as I can. *No.*

"Come on. Don't be shy. Everyone's done it so far. It's easy. You don't have to reveal your darkest secrets or anything," she says lightly.

That's a good thing, because my darkest secrets would probably give her nightmares.

"Can you at least tell everyone your name?" she finally asks, obviously not one to engage in a battle of wills. Her patience is running low and she's covering.

Again, I shake my head. I have not broken eye contact with her, and I think it's starting to freak her out a little bit. I kind of feel sorry for her, but she should have read her paperwork before class. All the other teachers did.

"O-kaaay." She drags the word out and her tone changes. She's really starting to get annoyed now, but then, so am I. I check out the dark brown roots coming through in her hair because it gives me something to focus on while her head is down, scanning what I assume is the class roster on a clipboard in front of her. "We'll use process of elimination. You must be"—she pauses, her smile wavers just a little, and I know this is where it clicks because she's all sorts of aware when she looks back up at me and says—"I am so sorry. You must be Nastya."

This time I nod.

"You don't talk."

Chapter 4

Nastya

Every choice I've made since my life spontaneously combusted has been questioned. There has never been a shortage of people standing by, waiting to pass judgment on the way I choose to deal with things.

People who have never been through any sort of shit always assume that they know how you should react to having your life destroyed. And the people who have been through shit think you're supposed to deal with it the exact same way they did. As if there's a playbook for surviving hell.

—

By the time I pull into Margot's driveway at just after three o'clock, I'm literally drenched in relief, or maybe it's just sweat because the humidity here is ridiculous. Either way I'll take it, because for the first time today I feel like I can breathe. All in all, it could have been worse. Word traveled fairly quickly after fifth hour, but at least the day was almost done. I figure by tomorrow it will all be out in the open and then we can just get on with it.

Even seventh hour, the cruel joke that is my Speech and Debate elective, went as well as could be expected, which is saying a lot, seeing as how I'm at a disadvantage with the whole speech part. We got to do the infinitely cool circle thing again, but by that point I was desensitized to both my dread and the whispers that had already begun to follow me.

My good pal, Drew, was also there. He didn't sit next to me, which I was glad for, because his comments were amusing enough and easily ignorable, but I was afraid I might have to fend off his hands, too. My relief only lasted so long before I realized that he had positioned himself directly across the circle from me so that every time I lifted my head I couldn't help but see him and his I-can-make-you-a-woman eyes and his I-know-what-you-look-like-under-your-clothes smirk. I bet he practices in the mirror. I think he could teach a class. I looked down at my desk and traced the names carved in the surface to keep myself from smiling, not because I found him attractive, which he undeniably was, but because he was entertaining as all hell.

I'm actually kind of thankful that he's there. He's something to focus on other than the things about that class that suck; for example, *everything*. I should also mention that *everything* includes the dark-eyed, dark-haired, refreshingly charm-free jackhole from the courtyard, whose name is, apparently, Ethan. Fortunately, there were plenty of free desks in the room, so I didn't have to take him up on his enormously appealing lap offer. Not so fortunately, one of those free desks was next to mine, so that's where he sat. He didn't make any more comments, but he smirked a lot, and he wasn't nearly as good at it as Drew.

I get inside and throw my backpack on the kitchen table and pull out everything that needs a signature so Margot can sign it. Before I can get it all unpacked, my phone vibrates and I have to stop to dig it out. I don't bother keeping it accessible. It's not like I need it that often. It can only be one of two people. My mother or Margot. No one else uses the number; not even my dad anymore.

I only keep the phone for the most necessary of communication—texts, mostly one-way, from them to me. When I have to, I'll use it to let Margot know where I am or if I'm going to be late. That was part of the deal for me staying here. It's understood that that's all the information I'll part with. No *How was your day?* No *Did you make any friends?* No *Have you looked for a therapist yet?* Just basic logistical facts. Talking has never been the issue. Communication is the issue.

The message is from Margot. *Went to grab takeout for your first day. Back in a few.* I'm still trying to get used to eating at four o'clock. Margot works the night shift, which means we eat dinner early so she can shower and get to work. Then again, apparently lunch here is at ten forty-five in the morning, so I guess it all works out.

I kick off the torture devices and change into running clothes so I can go after the early bird special. I'd go now, but it's hot, and I make sure never to be outside at this time of day when the sun has a way of stalking me, searing memories into my skin. I won't even go out to check the mail if I don't have to. My phone vibrates again. I look at the screen. Mom. *Hope your first day was good. Love you. M.* I put the phone back on the table. She doesn't expect a reply.

Margot gets back with all manner of Chinese food. We won't need to cook for a week. That's a good thing, because I can't cook real food to save my life and I get the feeling, from the drawer full of takeout menus, that Margot can't either. I've been here for five days and I don't think the kitchen's been used once. At least meals aren't awkward with Margot. She has no problem talking enough for both of us. Whatever I fail to bring to the conversation, she dutifully makes up for. I'm not even sure she needs me sitting here.

After less than a week, I know who she's dated for the past three years and who she's dating now. I know all of her workplace gossip, even though I have no idea who any of the people she mentions are. I'm sure Andrea would not appreciate the fact that Margot is telling me about her financial problems and Eric would not want me to know that his girlfriend cheated on him and Kelly would be appalled to learn that I am aware of her bipolar disorder and every medication she takes for it. But the more Margot talks, the less awkward it is that I don't, and I prefer conversations about people I don't care about. The times she brings up my family are worse because I don't want to think about them, and I can't tell her to shut the hell up.

After we eat, she rushes to shower off a day's worth of sweat and suntan oil and I pack up container after container of leftovers and wait for the sun to fade so I can run.

I never even make it out the front door because the sky turns black before sunset and opens up in torrential rain. I don't mind running in rain, but this is even a bit much for me. It's too difficult to see and impossible to hear anything through this kind of downpour. When I look out the sliding glass door at the back of the house, it seems like it might be raining horizontally, and even I'm not desperate enough to go out in this kind of lightning. I kick off my sneakers and sit and then stand and then sit and then stand again. My brain is on the spin cycle right now.

I have no treadmill here, so I do jumping jacks in place until I get bored, switch to alternating sets of chest presses and mountain climbers, move on to weighted squats and lunges, and then do as many push-ups as I can before my arms give out and I drop my face into the carpet. It's not the kind of soul-sucking exhaustion I'm looking for, but for tonight it will have to do.

I pull out clothes for tomorrow and pack up all of the signed paperwork and shove it into my backpack. I almost wish I had homework, but I don't, so I wander around the living room. Margot's got a stack of newspapers piled up next to the front door, and I realize that I haven't checked the birth announcements for nearly two weeks.

I grab the papers and sift through them until I find the right sections. The first one is disappointing. Nothing new. All of the overused classics and the same trendy crap that I wouldn't saddle a cat with, much less a kid. My name, of course, is never there, but it's not my name I'm looking for. I scan four papers; there are three Alexanders, four Emmas, two Sarahs, a crapload of names ending in -den (Jaden, Cayden, Braden, *gag*), a bunch I don't remember, and one worthy of going on my wall. I cut it out and grab my laptop. I pull up the internet and wait for my start page to load. Within seconds, I'm staring at the lovely, pink-and-blue-splat-tered baby name website that greets me every time I get online.

I type in my newfound query, Paavo, which turns out to be nothing but the Finnish version of Paul. It's kind of a letdown.

I like names. I collect them: names, origins, meanings. They're an easy thing to collect. They don't cost anything and they don't really take up any space. I like to look at them and pretend that they mean something, and maybe they don't, but the pretend-ing is nice. I keep most of them on the walls of my bedroom at home—home where I used to live. I keep the ones that echo. Good names with significance. Not the crap everyone seems to be using these days. I like foreign names too; the unusual ones that you rarely see. If I ever had a baby, I'd pick one of those, but babies aren't really something I see in my future, even the far off one.

I fold up the papers to put them away, glancing down one more time. Out of the corner of my eye, I catch one of the Sarahs again, and I smile. It reminds me of the one amusing part of my day.

I was running to my locker between classes and had to duck around the corner and wait when I saw Drew in a heated exchange with Barbie, two lockers down from mine. I decided that if I had to choose between being tardy to class or walking into the middle of that verbal smackdown, tardiness was the lesser of the evils. It wasn't that difficult dodging Drew's not-so-subtle come-ons when I ran into him by myself, but I certainly didn't want to take the chance that he'd proposition me in front of his girlfriend. That would definitely make my ever-growing list of things I do not need. So I leaned against the wall and waited for them to move on.

"Give me twenty bucks." I heard Drew say to her.

"Why?" Apparently *annoyed* is the only quality her voice possesses.

"Because I need twenty bucks." His tone indicated that this should be enough of a reason.

"No." Then, what must have been the sound of her slamming her locker. Hard.

"I'll pay you back." *No, you won't.*

"No, you won't." *Smart girl.*

"You're right. I won't." I peered around and caught him flash that cocky smile at her. "What? At least I'm honest."

"Why don't you go ask one of your whores?" *Damn.*

"Because none of them love me as much as you do."

"That stupid grin might work on every other female in this school, but you know it won't work with me, so forget it."

"Sarah, you know you're going to give it to me, so come on."

Sarah. I smiled. I couldn't help but appreciate the absolute perfection of the name; bland, common, and wholly unoriginal. Best of all, it means *princess.*

She exhaled loudly and I leaned around to see her digging in her purse. *Seriously?* She's going to give him money? He's better than I gave him credit for. Maybe I just gave her too much credit. My self-respect may not be off the charts, but hers must be nonexistent. She took out a twenty-dollar bill and shoved it at him.

"Here. Just so I can get you to leave me alone." He grabbed it and started walking away, but not before she yelled after him, "If you don't pay me back, I am so telling Mom!"

Mom? *Oh.*

That little revelation was fun, though it does make me wonder if my observation skills are failing me. Did I really miss that? My brother, Asher, and I used to bicker with the best of them, but our animosity threshold was several levels lower than theirs.

I toss the last of the newspapers back on top of the pile and return to the computer, trying to come up with anything else I can do online to kill time. I'm not on Facebook or anything else anymore, so there's no point in that. I could torture myself by using Asher's name and password to check up on people I used to be friends with, but I decide against it. There's isn't anything I want to know.

The lightning is flashing incessantly outside the window, taunting me every time it lights up the sky. My phone is on my bed, whispering in my ear like a bottle of scotch to a recovering alcoholic, while the rain continues cackling at me through my window. I may actually be desperate enough to go out in this weather. I need to run that badly.

More jumping jacks. Lift some weights. More push-ups. Lift more weights. I may not be able to get a treadmill in here, but a punching bag I think I can manage, even if it's just one of those portable ones. I don't think Margot will let me hang a heavy bag in her living room, but I'm not that picky. I'll take anything I can hit right now.

Cookies. I need to bake cookies. It's the next best thing to running. Not really, but I do love cookies and I don't like the shit they sell in packages, which is what Margot buys. Oreos are acceptable. Because they're Oreos and no matter what you do, you can't replicate them. Trust me on this one. I've spent more than a few days in my kitchen, trying to do just that. It's never going to happen. So Oreos get a pass, but factory-sealed chocolate chip cookies that are shelf-stable for up to six months are another story. Life really is too short for that. Believe me, I know.

I rummage through Margot's kitchen, and I have no idea why I'm surprised that she doesn't own any flour or baking soda or baking powder or vanilla or just about any ingredient that could possibly be required for baking. I do locate some sugar and salt, and miraculously, a set of measuring cups, but that won't get me very far. I resolve to head to the grocery store this weekend. I won't make it long without cookies. Or cake.

I give up, eat half a bag of jelly beans, leaving the black ones because they suck, and head to the shower to wash the shit that was this day off of me. I have a riveting conversation with myself while letting the conditioner set in my hair. I talk about my crap schedule. I tell myself about the unfortunate irony that is my music class and wonder if that tops the ridiculousness of Speech and Debate. I ponder, out loud, whether any female in the school, student or teacher, is immune to the charms of a certain blond named Drew. Then I answer: ME. Oh, and Sarah of course, though he seems to be able to badger her into submission.

I have these conversations periodically, just to make sure my voice still works in case I ever want to use it again. Returning to the world of the vocal was always the plan, but some days I wonder if I ever will. Most of the time, I don't have much exciting news, so I repeat names or random words, but today was noteworthy so it warranted full sentences. Sometimes I even sing, but I save that for the days when my self-loathing is at peak levels and I want to hurt myself.

I crawl into my bed, which is covered in a sage-green floral-print comforter just like the one in my bedroom at home. It was probably more my mother's doing than Margot's. I think she has trouble grasping the concept that I was trying to get away from that place, not bring it with me. I lift up the mattress and pull out the composition book I've hidden there. I'll have to find a better place for it soon. The rest of them are in the back of my closet, packed in a cardboard box, underneath old paperbacks and my middle school yearbooks. The one in my hands is black and white with the word *Trig* written in red marker across the cover. Like all of the others, the first few pages are filled with fake class notes. I grab a pen and I write. Exactly three and a half pages later, I slide the book back to its hiding place and turn off the light, wondering what fresh hell tomorrow will bring.

Chapter 5

Nastya

I live in a world without magic or miracles. A place where there are no clairvoyants or shapeshifters, no angels or superhuman boys to save you. A place where people die and music disintegrates and things suck. I am pressed so hard against the earth by the weight of reality that some days I wonder how I am still able to lift my feet to walk.

—

On Friday morning, the first thing I do is pick up my amended schedule from the guidance office. Ms. McAllister signed off on my teacher aide position for fifth hour, so I have now officially dropped Intro to Music, which means I get to spend that period making photocopies and handing out papers instead of wanting to bleed myself dry.

At this point, I've gotten better on the shoes, even though they're too cramped at the front and my toes unleash a string of expletives at me when I put them on. I chose my second most appalling outfit for today's endeavors—more black on black, because that's really all I have anyway. I keep the thick black eyeliner, the red lipstick, and the black nail polish. The stilettos, as always, are the exclamation point on an ensemble that screams *Hideous!* I am a slutty horror show. I think of pearl buttons and white eyelet skirts and wonder what Emilia would be wearing if she were alive today.

I've been successfully hiding in hallways and bathrooms during lunch all week. The disheveled artist boy, whose name I have since learned—by surreptitiously glancing at the cover on his sketchbook—is Clay, was kind enough to give me an unsolicited short list of my best bets for solitude when he caught me trying the doors to the English wing again on the second day. I've checked out most of them. Give me a few more days and I'll probably be able to draw a map and star the best places for disappearing. Then I can sell it to other losers like me.

I find, from my daily walks, that the layout here stays pretty much the same. You would think there was a designated seating chart for the courtyard because no one strays from the place they planted themselves the day before. I recognize more of the faces at this point, but even the ones I know don't acknowledge me. I am left blissfully alone. I've scared, offended or made everyone uncomfortable enough to stay away. Mission accomplished. It's even worth all of the discomfort of the shoes. If I don't do anything wrong, it should stay this way.

I'm considering in which direction to head today, when I pass the boy in the force field. I wonder how he does that. Maybe I can find out his secret, because I would love to get one of those for myself. Sometimes I think he's invisible and I'm the only one who sees him, but I guess that's not the case, because if it was, I'm sure someone would have grabbed that bench by now. Maybe he's a ghost and no one goes near the bench because he haunts it.

He always sits in the same position and he's completely motionless. Ever since he caught me on Monday, I've been trying not to stare more than a couple of seconds each day. He hasn't looked up at me again. I still get the feeling he's watching, but maybe I just kind of want him to be. I shake that off quickly. The last thing I need is anyone's attention.

Still, he is extremely nice to look at. Nice arms. Not douche-bag workout arms, just *work* arms. I saw him on the first day in my shop class, but only for a second, and then he left and never came back. Now the only time I ever see him is at lunch. That handful of seconds I spend crossing the courtyard becomes the most intriguing part of my day. If I'm being honest with myself, those precious seconds are the only reason I still walk across this damn thing every day.

I walked it on the first day to make a point. I walked it on the second day to see if he was still there and still alone. I walked it on the third and the fourth to see if he'd look up at me again. He didn't. Today, I just wanted to look. So that's what I'm doing when the pointed end of the heel of my shoe ends up lodged in the crack between two brick pavers. Beautiful.

Fortunately, since I was walking pathetically slowly to make the most of my stalking experience, I don't end up face-first on the ground. Not so fortunately, I am now stuck directly between his bench and that of Princess Sarah and her ladies in waiting. I try to nonchalantly wiggle my heel out from where it's ensnared, but it won't budge. I'll have to maneuver my way down to kneeling and try to pull it out with my hands, which will be a feat of balance, but bending over in this dress is so not an option.

I kneel down slowly and slip my foot out of the shoe. Then I grab the heel with my right hand and yank it. It comes out easier than I expect and I stand up and slip my foot back into it. I glance to my left and see that statue boy still hasn't moved. He seems utterly oblivious to my shoe debacle. It's a small miracle, but small miracles are the only kind I can hope for right now, so I'll take it. Too bad I haven't gone completely unnoticed, because the next thing I hear—

"I think those are made for street corners, not school." *Sarah.* This is followed by giggles and then another female voice—

"Yeah, does your dad know you left Hell dressed like that?"

"I thought her dad was in Transylvania." More giggles. Seriously.

The insults here are really subpar. At least they could throw something mildly entertaining at me if they're going to make me turn around. I look to my right to find the fountain of wit that spewed that gem at me. Several girls surround Sarah and are looking at me and, yes, still giggling. I guess I congratulated myself a minute or two too soon. I mentally run through my options: A) hurl said shoe at them, B) hurl insults at them, C) ignore them and walk away, D) smile my most demonic and unhinged smile at them. I've chosen D, the only real option of the bunch. I won't ignore this, at least not in the slink-away-with-my-tail-between-my-legs way. Besides, since I'm apparently the spawn of Satan, or possibly Dracula, depending on who you ask, it can never hurt to throw a little crazy out there just to drive the message home before the weekend.

I stare them down for a few more seconds, debating whether to unleash the smile all at once or just let it subtly drift across my face, when I'm interrupted by a voice behind me.

"Enough, Sarah."

Sarah's mouth, which was open in what I suspect was the formation of another display of her scathing wit, clamps shut so fast I think I hear her teeth clash. I turn around, even though I kind of know that the only person in that general vicinity is the last one I would expect to be all knight-in-shining-armor. Not that the situation even called for it. It was hardly an attack. It was more like a sort of lame insult version of karaoke. A performance by amateurs. Something you mock rather than fear. I can tell these girls wouldn't have stopped there, and if I was the type to care it might have hurt my feelings, but I don't care and my feelings haven't been hurt in a very long time.

At this point, I'm completely turned around and mine aren't

the only eyes on the boy in the bubble. In fact, there are quite a few sets of eyes watching him now, waiting to see if anything else comes out of his mouth. I feel like I've found myself in the middle of a *Twilight Zone* episode where everything around me has frozen and I'm the only one who can move. But I don't.

The boy's eyes are trained on Sarah, giving her a look that matches the don't-fuck-with-me tone in his voice. His glance flicks to me for a second and then he's back to staring at his hands like nothing at all happened. I'm contemplating moving now, but I can't seem to find my legs just yet. I turn away from the boy and catch Sarah staring at me now. The look on her face isn't carved out of jealousy or even bitterness, which is what I kind of expect; it's forged out of one hundred percent pure, rock solid WTF. As much as I'm trying to keep my face blank, I have a feeling that my expression quite possibly looks a lot like hers, but probably for very different reasons.

She seems perplexed as all hell that he said something. I don't really know this kid well enough to know if his interference is the most surprising element of this whole situation. If you ask me, the weird part about it is how everybody reacted. They all shut up. They didn't question him, didn't laugh or ask why, they didn't ignore him and continue with the ridicule, and they didn't turn their derision on him. They just *stopped*. He said *Enough* and that was that. *Because I said so. End of story. Don't make me have to tell you twice.*

In the mere seconds that I have been standing here, everyone else has gone back to what they were doing, and maybe it's my imagination, but the decibel level seems to have dropped just a bit, as if no one wants to be heard discussing what just happened. What *did* just happen?

I'll think about it in a few minutes, or after school, or maybe never, but right now I want to get the hell out of the middle of this courtyard. I make it across without any more shoe malfunctions, and someone has mercifully stuck a book in the door to the English building so I'm able to walk right in. I glance down as I push through the door and see that it's an art history book and that sitting next to it is a smirking Clay, sketchbook, as always, in hand. I really want to ask if he knows what that was about, but I can't, so I slip into the building. I make it halfway down the corridor and turn off into the stairwell and lean up against the wall, grateful to be alone in the quiet.

Before I can turn recent events over in my mind, I hear the door open again. I press my back to the wall of the stairwell, trying to make myself as inconspicuous as possible. If I press hard enough, maybe I can make myself disappear.

I concentrate on the direction of the footsteps, which are getting louder by the second. The cadence is slow, and one foot falls ever so slightly heavier than the other. The steps are solid, but soft. They aren't clumsy or awkward. It's a graceful walk. Whoever it is, they're taller than me; it doesn't take them nearly as many steps to get to the alcove where I'm loitering. I wait for the footsteps to pass, but they don't. They turn right at me and now I'm just hoping that whoever it is will simply ignore me. I look down at the floor so I won't have to make eye contact, and I wait for it to be over.

And then, before I can remember to hold my breath, a set of well-worn work boots stops in front of me. Steel-toed, if I'm not mistaken. I don't need to look up to know who they belong to. I've been looking at those boots on the seat of an industrial metal bench for five days now. Apparently confusion and curiosity have turned me momentarily stupid, because against my better judgment I do look up, and it's the closest I've ever been to him.

"I won't do that again," he says, impaling me with his sickeningly perfect blue eyes like he wishes I didn't exist. But the way he says it isn't angry. It's just matter-of-fact. He's completely calm. There's almost no inflection in his voice at all. He doesn't wait for any sort of acknowledgment or response, even though right now I just might be pissed off enough to give him one, and it certainly wouldn't be a thank you. Then he's crossed the alcove and walked out the door on the other side of the stairwell, as if he were never here at all.

I won't do that again? No one asked you to do it this time, asshole. Does he honestly think he just did me a favor? That, by calling attention to me and pissing off a bunch of vanity-obsessed girls on my behalf, girls who will no doubt be seeking to save face when he is not around, he has helped me? He's more delusional than I am. I'd like to tell him so. Too bad I don't even know his name. And if I had a list of questions right now, *"What's your name?"* probably wouldn't even make the cut.

What I want to know is why anyone listened to him. They shut up like they were being reprimanded by an angry dad, because that's exactly what he sounded like. It's the same tone of voice he used with me just now. I'm almost surprised he didn't throw a *young lady* on the end of it for good measure. Clearly, I'm the only one here who doesn't understand why I'm supposed to listen to him. It's as if he commands some sort of respect or reverence. Maybe his dad is like the principal or the mayor or a mob boss and no one wants to piss him off. Who knows? All I know is that *I'm* pissed off.

Chapter 6

Josh

I've gotten through the rest of the day without seeing the girl again. I've mentally flogged myself for opening my stupid mouth at lunch. If there was a reason for it, I might cut myself some slack, but the girl really didn't seem like the helpless type. Maybe I was just trying to stop her from making enemies of those bitches. Maybe I just wanted Sarah to shut the hell up because I know she's better than that. Maybe I just wanted the girl to look at me again.

The halls are already emptying out as I push my way toward the back of the school, against the flow of the rest of the students. I want to get to the theater wing before they lock the doors so I can pick up my level. I left it there earlier and I need it this afternoon. Plus, I won't leave it overnight, anyway. It's mine. It was my father's. It's old and wooden and archaic but I won't use another one, and I won't take the chance that it'll disappear if I leave it here; so I go back to get it.

When I get there, it's sitting where I left it on one of the unfinished shelving units I've been working on all week. I check my progress and run my hands along the edges. I'll be done with the whole thing by next Wednesday. I could drag it out until Friday, but I'm hoping Mr. Turner will be done with the preliminary procedural crap before that. I'd like to get back to shop and work on something more interesting than shelves. I grab the level and head back out to the parking lot.

I'm almost to my car when I hear my name.

"Bennett! Josh!" Drew corrects himself almost instantly because he knows he sounds like an asshole calling me by my last name. He's standing in the next row of cars and he's not alone. He rarely is, so it's not surprising to see a girl standing next to him as he leans against his car in the pose I have grown accustomed to seeing, the one where he tries to look casually indifferent while he works out the most direct route into a girl's pants or down her shirt or up her skirt. Whatever the case may be.

What's surprising is the girl he's talking to. It doesn't take more than a glance to know who she is: crazy-long black hair, tight black dress that barely covers her ass or her chest, black spike heels, black shit all over her eyes. Eyes that are turning to glare at me right now. As I get closer, the blank expression she usually wears changes. It's subtle, and I doubt most people would notice, because the change is mostly in the eyes, but I can see the difference. It's not blank. She's pissed, and if I'm not mistaken, she's pissed at me. I don't get much of an opportunity to examine it because she's walking away before I even reach them.

"Call me!" Drew yells over his shoulder to her, laughing as if this is some sort of joke.

"You know her?" I ask, laying my books and my level on the hood of his car. Most of the parking lot has emptied out by this point; for as slow as the traffic moves into this place in the morning, the afternoon exodus takes no time at all.

"I plan to," Drew responds, not looking at me. He's still watching the girl walk away. I ignore the innuendo. If I had to acknowledge every thinly veiled sexual suggestion that comes from his mouth, we'd talk of nothing else, which would probably make him happy.

"Who is she?"

"Some Russian chick. Nastya something I haven't learned to pronounce. I was starting to worry that I was losing my appeal because she'd never talk to me, but apparently she doesn't talk to anybody."

"Are you surprised? She kind of screams antisocial." I pick the level up off the car and turn it over in my hands watching the water shift from one side to the other.

"Yeah, but it's not that. She doesn't talk, period."

"At all?" I look at him skeptically.

"At all." He shakes his head, smiling with warped satisfaction.

"Why not?"

"Don't know. Maybe she doesn't speak English. But then I guess she could still say yes and no and shit." He shrugs as if it's of no consequence.

"How do you even know?"

"Because she's in my Speech and Debate class." He smirks at the irony of that fact. I don't respond. I'm trying to process the information, and Drew can keep this conversation going on his own. "I'm not complaining. Gives me a chance to work on her every day."

"Not a very good sign if you have to work on her. Maybe you *are* losing your appeal," I reply dryly.

"Don't be ridiculous," he says in all seriousness, looking down at his watch. His smile returns. "It's three o'clock. Better get your ass home." And with that, he hops in his car and drives off, leaving me standing in the parking lot, thinking of pissed-off Russian girls and black dresses.

Chapter 7

Nastya

I feel like I'm waiting here. Waiting for something that hasn't happened yet. Something that isn't yet. But that's all I feel and nothing else. I don't know if I even exist. And then someone flips a switch and the light is gone, the room is gone, the weightlessness is gone. I want to ask to wait, because I wasn't finished yet, but I don't have a chance. There is no gentle pulling. No coaxing. No choice. I'm wrenched out. Yanked, as if my head is being snapped back. I'm in the dark and everything is pain. There are too many sensations at once. Every nerve ending is on fire. Like the shock of being born. And then, there are flashes of everything. Colors, voices, machines, harsh words. The pain doesn't flash. The pain is constant, steady, never-ending. It's the only thing I know.

I don't want to be awake anymore.

—

I made it through my second Monday at school. You'd think I'd be drained just from the constant suck of it all, but apparently not, because I still can't sleep. I've been in bed for two hours now; I know it's after midnight, but I can't see the clock from here so I'm not sure exactly what time it is. I think about the composition book tucked under the mattress beneath me. I reach down and shove my hand under to touch it. My three and a half pages are done, every word accounted for, but still no sleep. Maybe writing them again would help, but it won't bring me the soul-sucking exhaustion my body is begging for, so I pull my hand back and rest it on my stomach, opening and closing it to the rhythm of my breathing.

I can hear that the hard rain has stopped, so I peel off the covers and look out the window. My window faces into the back-yard, and it's too dark to see if it's still pissing rain, so I head to the front of the house and peer into the beam cast by a nearby street lamp. There's no rain visible in the yellow glow reflecting off the wet sidewalk below, and I'm stripping out of my makeshift pajamas before I even get back to my bedroom, giddy with the thought of running out the past few days, pounding my aggres-sion into the sidewalk and leaving it behind me as I go. It takes no time to slip on a pair of running shorts and a T-shirt and throw on my shoes. My feet love me again. I glance at the clock. 12:30. I hook a canister of pepper spray onto my hip and grip the kubotan that holds my keys in my right hand, even though it's annoying as all hell to run with. It's my security blanket. Clutched in my fingers, offering me the illusion of a security that doesn't exist.

I lock the door behind me and force myself to ease into a jog, down the driveway and into the rain-drenched streets, but it's not easy. I want to tear down the road until I can't breathe, until there is not enough oxygen left in the world to keep me from suffocating. The humidity is brutal, especially paired with the late summer temperatures, but I can't care. It'll only mean more sweat, and I can handle that. Every drop is the stress leach-ing out of me, taking with it all of my anxiety and energy so I can collapse into sleep tonight or this morning or whenever the hell I crawl into bed. Maybe I'll stay out until it's time to go to school and then sleepwalk through the day. All the better.

My feet disobey me and break into a full-throttle run only seconds after I hit the road. My legs will hate me later, but it will be worth it. I run fast and far the way I've become accustomed to running. I wish I was on one, long, straight expanse of highway so I could just keep going without having to turn or think or make decisions of any kind. Instead, I head right and follow my feet without thinking. I don't pay any attention to the houses or the cars. My body and my mind have missed this over the past couple of weeks: first through the drama of the move to Margot's house, and then with the constant nightly rain that traps me indoors. If this is what I have to do every night—wait until the weather clears, even in the dregs of night—then I will. I won't go this long without it again.

The first night I ever ran, I ended up throwing up all over my shoes. It was one of the best nights of my life. It didn't start out that way. It started out with me fighting with my parents. Followed by me listening to my parents fight about me. I sat in that room and sat in that room and sat in that room on the comforter that looks exactly like the one I sleep on here. I sat in that room until I couldn't sit there anymore. I couldn't be in that house, listening to another fight that I caused. My father would ask my mother why she kept blaming herself and my mother would ask my father why it didn't bother him and my father would tell my mother that it killed him inside but that he didn't see the point in drowning in it and my mother would tell my father that as long as I was drowning in it, she would be, too. It was always the same fight on an endless loop.

It was nine o'clock at night and the first shoes I could find were a pair of sneakers, so I shoved my feet into them without socks and ran down the stairs, flinging the door open and not bothering to close it. It was my very unsophisticated, very literal version of running away. I ran and ran and ran. There was no slow warm-up. There was no pace or purpose. There was only *away*.

I don't even know how far I made it that night, probably not very, before I was gasping and my lungs ached and my stomach convulsed and I puked right where I was standing. And it was awesome. It was cathartic and constructive and destructive and perfect. Then I sat on the ground and cried—the ugly kind of crying where you keep sucking breaths in all at once and it makes that horrible sound as the air scrapes against your throat. Then I got up and went home.

I ran every night after that. I learned to control myself and to warm up and pace myself, but I always ended up pushing too far, running too hard, running too long. My therapist told my parents it was healthy. Maybe not the vomiting so much, but the running in general. It was a *healthy outlet.* My parents love the word *healthy.*

My dad tried to come with me a couple of times. He tried, he did. But I wouldn't hold back for him and he couldn't keep up. I don't think pushing himself to the point of heaving was as appealing for him as it was for me. The only reason I ran was to suck every ounce of energy out of myself so that there was nothing left to use for regret or fear or remembering. It takes much more to exhaust me now. I run longer every day. It's gotten harder to achieve the body-draining fatigue that I love, because if I'm going to run, I want to feel like I've been wrung out and spun dry, but it still does the trick. It's the only therapy I get now.

My lungs feel okay, but my stomach is teetering. I've been out of commission for a little while lately, so hopefully I can tap myself out easily tonight. With every step, I stomp out the shit in my head until it's all but gone. It will come back in the daylight, when I'm replenished enough to think, but for now it's away and for now that's enough. My thoughts drift off with the last vestiges of my energy and adrenaline, leaving me with the all too familiar feeling of nausea I've come to know well. I slow to a jog and then a walk, trying to lull my stomach into submission, but it's not working.

My feet stop, giving me a minute to scan the street for a gutter or well-placed hedge to throw up in, and for the first time since I tore through the door, I take note of my surroundings. I haven't been on this street before. I'm not sure how far I've run, but it's unfamiliar. It's late. Most of the houses are dark now, and I try to slow my already rapid breathing. I bolt for the nearest hedge to heave into. I miscalculate the distance and end up running straight into it. Thorns. Of course. Insult to injury. The thorns slash my legs every time I move, but I'm too busy puking to extricate them just yet. When my stomach has been thoroughly emptied, I lift my legs out as carefully as possible, trying to minimize the damage, but it's already been done. I can see blood just beginning to seep through the torn skin on my calves, but it's the least of my worries right now.

I close my eyes, then lift them open again. I force myself to take in my surroundings and to remind myself where I am, and more importantly, where I am not.

The sickness in my stomach is replaced by a new kind of dread. The houses are the same, all the same. I can't find a street sign, but I know I ran fast and I ran far and I didn't pay attention to anything. I broke every rule that I have and I've gotten what I deserve for it. It's the middle of the night and I am alone and lost and drenched in darkness.

I instinctively pat my pocket, feeling for my phone so I can use the GPS. Empty. Of course I didn't bring it. I ran out the door so fast I forgot, because I'm careless and impatient and I didn't think of anything beyond air and sneakers.

I follow the sidewalk. I must be on the outer edge of the community against the preserve that walls it in. I know that this sidewalk probably circles the whole neighborhood, which can give me some bearings and I should stay on it. But I can't help it. I want to get the hell away from all of those trees. I can't see past them and I can't control what comes out of them and there are too many sounds to process.

There are no street lamps where I'm standing now, but I can see the faint yellow glow of one up ahead. The houses along the other side of the street are shadowed in dark and sleep. Like all sane people at this hour. The churning in my stomach is still there, but it's being overshadowed by the fear of being lost.

My kubotan is swinging at my side until my keys are nothing but a blur. I listen to the quiet that settles around me. I can hear everything: the hum of the street lamps from overhead, crickets chirping, unintelligible voices coming from a television somewhere, and a sound I can't place right away. It's rhythmic and coarse. Following the direction of the sound, I glance down into the darkness and see light coming from one house at the end of the road. It's brighter than what could be given off by the front lamps alone. I head toward the house, not knowing what I expect to find there. Maybe someone awake who can give me directions. *Directions you can't ask for, idiot.* In the distance the rhythmic scratching sound continues. Soft and almost musical and I follow it. The house is close and the sound is louder now, though I still can't tell what it is, until a moment later when I'm there.

I stop at the end of the driveway in front of a pale yellow house with a brightly lit open garage. I want to look in to see if anyone is inside before I get too close, but my feet won't stop. The sight of it pulls me in. As soon as I reach the threshold, I am frozen, only one thought forming in my mind. *I know this place.* I take a tentative step closer, looking around, remembering details of a place I know I have never been. *I know this place.* The thought invades my brain repeatedly, and as it does, I finally take note of the rhythmic sound, still humming in my ears. There is a figure sitting at a workbench on the far wall of the garage, his hand moving back and forth, sanding down the narrow edge of a wooden beam. My eyes are fixed on those hands as if they're hypnotizing me. I pull my gaze away to follow the dust falling to the floor, catching the light as it goes. *I know this place.* The thought comes at me again and I suck in my breath all at once and I just need a second. One more second to process what it means. *I know this place.* But before I can think, the hands have stopped, the sound has stopped, and the person in the garage has turned around to face me.

And I know him, too.

Chapter 8

Nastya

Lit up by the fluorescent lights, Josh Bennett studies me across the garage. I haven't moved or looked away. I don't see any recognition in his eyes, and I wonder if he knows who I am. I'm just now remembering that I probably look like a different person. My hair is pulled back in a ponytail, and I don't have a trace of makeup on my sweat-covered, and probably very flushed, face. I'm in running clothes and sneakers. I'm not sure I would recognize myself if I didn't already know what I was supposed to look like under the crap I cover myself in at school. I'm beginning to wish I at least had the makeup on because I'm feeling very exposed under the fluorescent lights with this boy staring at me. He's skewering me with those eyes. I know I'm being assessed somehow, but I'm not sure on what criteria.

"How did you know where I live?" He's annoyed and he doesn't bother hiding the accusation in his words.

Obviously I didn't, because it would have been the last place on earth I would have come, but I guess now he thinks I'm a stalker. My right hand tightens around the kubotan, even though I don't feel like I'm in any real danger, and my left hand matches it, even though it's holding nothing. I probably look crazy or confused or both.

His eyes drop down to my legs, which are crisscrossed by the bloody tendrils that infernal shrub left in its wake, and then they return to my face, and I wonder what he sees there. I wonder if he senses how defeated I feel. I did not plan for anyone to see me like this, much less Josh Bennett, who apparently I am supposed to fear or revere, though I don't know why. Is he wearing a ring? Is he waiting for me to kneel down and kiss it?

One of us is going to have to blink first, so I take a tentative step back as if I'm trying to evade a predator, hoping he won't notice that I'm moving until I'm already gone. I lift my foot to take another step.

"Do you want a ride home?" He looks away before he says it, and his tone loses some of its edge. My foot comes down harder than I mean it to. If I had a list of the things Josh Bennett might say to me in this situation, asking me if I want a ride wouldn't have made the top fifty. His voice is devoid of any emotion as usual. For the record, no, I do not want a ride home, but I think I need one. And it sucks to need something from someone who so clearly detests you, but I'm not proud enough to say no.

I nod, opening and closing my mouth quickly because I really want to say something, even if I don't know what it is I want to say. He stands and walks to the door that leads into the house, opening it enough to reach in and grab a set of keys that must have been hanging on the inside wall. He turns to close the door but looks back in and pauses a moment as if he's listening for something. I imagine he must be checking to see if his parents are awake, but they probably aren't. They're probably asleep at this hour along with the rest of the civilized world. Except for me. And Josh Bennett, who apparently likes to do woodworking in the dead of night in his garage. I look around to try to figure out what exactly he was working on, but it all just looks like a bunch of wood and tools to me and I can't tell. I glance at the garage one more time, memorizing it, and as much as I hate to admit it, I know I'm coming back here.

I walk out and wait in the driveway next to a truck. It's the only car here, so I guess he doesn't have his own. It's a beautiful truck. Even I can admit that, and I'm not a big truck person. His father must take good care of it. I wish my car was that shiny, but I hate to wash it, so I'm lucky you can even tell what color the paint is at this point.

Josh stops at a small refrigerator that sits on the floor under one of the workbenches and pulls a bottle of water out of it. He walks up and hands it to me, wordlessly, before unlocking my door and opening it. I take the bottle out of his hand and look at it, suddenly aware of just how much I must be sweating. I turn to climb into the truck and I'm glad I'm not in a skirt, because I'm seriously short and I have to take a pretty big step up to get into it. He closes the door behind me, then walks around and climbs in the driver's side. He seems a lot more graceful doing it than me, like he was born climbing in and out of this truck. I'm wondering if I'm allowed to hate Josh Bennett, because I'm thinking I might start.

And then we sit. He doesn't look at me, but he doesn't start the car, either. I wonder what the hell he's waiting for and maybe wandering lost in the dark might not be the worst thing after all. Everything feels endless right now. My stupidity hits me upside the head a moment later when I realize that he's not sitting here to make me uncomfortable, he just doesn't know where to go. Looking around the car for something to write on is futile. There isn't a damn thing in here. It's the cleanest car I've ever seen. When I get in my car tomorrow morning, it's going to feel like a slum compared to this. Before I can do the eye-pleading thing with him and hope he understands, he reaches across the dashboard and pulls the GPS down and hands it to me so I can type in the address.

The ride is ridiculously short. It takes only minutes to get back to Margot's and I feel stupid for having him drive me. I paid attention to everything on the way. I tell myself it's so I won't get lost again, but really I need to find my way back there.

I should say thank you, but he won't expect it and I get the feeling he's more comfortable with the silence anyway. When he pulls into the driveway, I reach for the door almost before he's put the truck in park, determined to put us both out of our misery. I jump down onto the ground and turn to close the door. I don't say thank you. He doesn't say good night, but he does speak.

"You look different," he says, and I shut the door in his face.

Chapter 9

Nastya

Josh Bennett walks in and heads straight for my table in shop and I try not to look, but I really, really want to. I just don't want him to know that I'm looking. Soon I have no choice in the matter because he's standing in front of me, staring at my face. I stare back at him and I want to scream *What?!* I can almost see the word, interrobang and all, floating up from my lips in unspoken fervor, because he's the only person I know who can appear seriously put out with no expression at all on his face. Does everyone irritate him so much, or is it just a special gift I have? He seems immensely disturbed by the fact that I even exist, much less occupy the same space in his precious shop class.

"I sit here," he finally says, and again, he doesn't sound pissed, just matter-of-fact, like that's the way things are and I should know it like everyone else. Does this mean I'm supposed to get up? Move? Where? This is where Mr. Turner put me and I'm trying to decide if I want to have a stare-down with Josh Bennett or get up and move because our near silent dispute already has an audience. Before I can make my decision, Mr. Turner calls Josh over to his desk. He leaves his books on my—his?—table in an obvious show of ownership and refusal to concede and walks to the front of the room. I see Mr. Turner look in my direction and back to Josh, and I assume he's telling him that he told me to sit here. I don't know if Josh is going to get his way or not, but the way things seem to go around here, that's usually what happens. I'm not going to give him a chance to be smug about it, so before he turns to come back, I move myself.

There aren't any other empty tables. The one I was sitting at was the last one. There are empty seats at the others but I don't want to sit next to anyone; it becomes too awkward for me and for the person stuck sitting with me. Plus, I like sitting in the back so I know no one is behind me.

There's a counter built around the perimeter of the room with storage cabinets underneath, so I take my books and place them on it and hope like hell I can sit up here without flashing the world. I push myself up on the counter and turn to face the front. As I do, I see Josh walking back. He doesn't look at me but he does speak. His back is turned to the rest of the class and his voice is low, so I'm pretty sure no one but me can hear it.

"I wasn't going to make you move."

I'm not sure if I should be annoyed that he assumes he had the power to make me move or if I should feel bad for misinterpreting him. I'm thinking I'll never understand Josh Bennett and then I'm wondering why I try.

—

"There's a party tonight at Trevor Mason's. Want to go?"

I look at Drew. We're sitting in Debate. It's almost two thirty and I'm trying to pull the last five facts I need to finish my assignment off the internet before the bell so I don't have to deal with it tonight or any other time this weekend. I don't know what Drew's working on, other than me, because I don't think he's accomplished a thing this entire period. He'll no doubt pro-

cure an A for whatever nonwork he did. That's how things operate for Drew around here.

What did he just ask me? It was pretty straightforward and
shockingly innuendo-free, so I'm momentarily dumbfounded.
Go to a party tonight? Not what I was expecting. He's been
tossing all of his sexually charged material my way since the
first day of school. I'd call it banter, but it's really not, since my
contribution is nothing more than pointed looks and hand gestures, and even those are few and far between. He tried to get
me to resort to note writing a few days ago but I shut that down
quickly enough. Note writing is for fact-based, pertinent information only, not conversations.

Go to a party with Drew? Why not? I surprise even myself,
but really, why not? Okay, there are probably about a hundred
reasons why not. Because let's face it, he's probably not asking
me for my sparkling wit and entertaining anecdotes. But much
to my chagrin, Drew is actually one of the few things in my day
that I don't completely dread, because at least with him, I feel a
certain sense of control. I can handle Drew. He doesn't scare me,
and right now that may just be enough. I find that, in spite of
his blatant man-whorishness and put-on cocky smolder, I like
him. Not *like him, like him*. But I do like him, and I wonder what
that says about me. He's entertaining, and I am sorely in need
of entertainment. I nod to him. *Sure, party, of course.* He looks
surprised for a moment. Hell, I'm kind of surprised myself. Then
the surprise is gone and the self-assured, of-course-you-said-yes
smile spreads across his face.

"I'll pick you up at nine?" he asks.

I nod, digging a notebook out of my backpack and ripping
a page out of it. I grab the pen he's been holding out of his hand
and write down the address, because addresses are acceptable
note material.

"You should probably wear black," he mocks as I write the

address. I've worn nothing but black in the past two weeks. I hand the paper to him, seeing that conquering gleam lingering in his eyes. I tilt my head to the side and look him up and down in all his preppy hotness until my eyes rest back on his face. Then I shrug and walk away.

Chapter 10

Josh

Drew pulls into my driveway just after midnight, and I know immediately that no good can come of this. I put down the pencil I've been using to mark down measurements with and watch him get out of the car and walk toward the garage.

"Dude, I need a favor."

"Of course you do."

"I need you to take Nastya." *Take Nastya?* At first I wonder where he wants me to take her, until I glance down the driveway and see what he means.

"What? No way." I look past him to the dark figure slumped over in the front seat of the car. "What did you do to her? Is she even conscious?"

"Nothing. No," he says defensively, following my eye line back to the car. So now we're both standing in my garage, his arms crossed, my hands shoved in my pockets, watching through the windshield of his car for signs of movement. "She just drank too much."

"Too much of what?"

"Flamethrowers." He avoids my eyes when he says it.

"What asshole gave her flamethrowers?" He looks at me

without answering, which is answer enough. He's an idiot. A flamethrower is grain alcohol mixed with cherry Kool-Aid. He might as well have chloroformed her. "What were you thinking? She weighs like twenty-five pounds."

"Yeah, okay, Dad. Thanks for the lecture, but it's not really solving the problem. Besides, how was I supposed to know she couldn't handle it? She looks like a badass."

"A twenty-five-pound badass." It's true. She does look like a badass. I've seen her arms, and she's ripped, which is kind of weird and scary all at once because it just seems all wrong on her. She's really small and fragile-looking, and at the same time, it's like she's some exotic teenage mercenary, all rock solid, dressed in black, ready to take somebody down. None of it makes any sense. It's kind of disconcerting. She's like an optical illusion. You look at it from one angle and you see the picture and you think you've got a lock on it and then it shifts and the image changes to something entirely different and you can't even find the original picture anymore. It's a serious mindfuck.

"Josh, seriously. I can't take her home like this, and if I miss curfew again my mom will rip my balls off." He's not really making his case with that point. I'd pay good money to watch Drew finally get nailed for something. Drew's mom is the sweetest woman ever, but there's one person who can piss her off like no one else and he's standing in front of me, begging for a stay of execution, or maybe just a stay of castration. I won't say no. He knew it when he came here. The asking is just a formality. I never say no to Drew.

I walk over to the car and open the passenger door. I try to wake her up and ask if she can walk into the house. She stirs a little and opens her eyes. I'm not even sure they focus on me, and then her head drops forward onto her chest like it's too heavy for her to hold up and I know there's no way she'll be walking anywhere. She barely even moves when I drag her out of the seat and pick her up to carry her into the house.

"Shit, Drew," I mutter.

He leans against his car and exhales. "True story."

Nastya

When I pry my eyes open, it takes me a minute to try to figure out where I am. And I do try, really try, to figure out where I am and I have no freaking clue and that seriously scares the crap out of me. I reach up to brush my hair back out of my eyes so I can look around and attempt to determine what the hell is going on. The only three things that I know for certain took place last night are that one, small elves climbed up my body and tied my hair into a mass of tiny knots; two, I must have slept with my mouth open because something crawled into it and died; and three, I was sucked through a vortex into some animated world where an anvil was dropped on my head.

I lift my hand to my forehead and press, trying to relieve some of the pounding as I attempt, not without effort, to sit up. I'm on someone's couch. Someone's couch. *Someone's couch.* And as soon as I remember, I'm wishing I could forget.

"Good morning, Sunshine!" Josh Fucking Bennett. By now, I'm pretty sure that if I was to find his birth certificate, that is exactly what it would say. I don't have time to figure out why I'm here or what he's playing at with the fake, overwrought cheeriness, because he doesn't even take a breath, and I wonder if the real Josh Bennett has been abducted by aliens, or maybe the elves carted him off after they got done with my hair. "I'm glad you're awake. I was starting to worry about you. You know, with all the projectile vomiting last night." I wince, from either physical pain or embarrassment, I'm not sure which. He sees my discomfort but it doesn't stop him. I think he might actually be encouraged. "No, don't you worry your pretty little head over it," he says with mock sincerity, then pauses, looking me over. "Well, today, maybe not so pretty, and last night, definitely not so pretty, but still, don't worry about it. It only took four or five towels to soak it up and I think the smell will go away after a day or two. Hopefully it won't stick that badly to your hair. I did what I could, but a ponytail probably would have been helpful."

Josh Bennett cleaned up my puke. Fabulous. He's getting even now and having far too much fun doing it. I can't decide which is worse, angry dad Josh Bennett or sarcastic, mocking Josh Bennett. I'd like to punch them both in the throat right now but I'm not sure I can lift my arm.

Why the hell am I here? The last I knew, I was with Drew at an overcrowded party, drinking something that tasted suspiciously not like alcohol. I look down at myself, eternally grateful for the fact that I am still wearing the same clothes I was in last night, even if they have what I am now sure is throw up splattered on them. At least Josh Bennett didn't have to strip me and let me wear his boxer shorts. The thought gives me little comfort. Maybe because I'm just now realizing that, while my clothes are still on, my bra is suspiciously MIA. I try to look around to see if it's lying on the floor or something, but it really hurts to move my head.

He hasn't stopped talking, but I have no idea what he's saying, even though his voice seems to be inside my skull. He's still on the ponytail thing. Something about them being a requirement for drunk girls. He's doing nothing to lower his voice. In fact, he might actually believe he's on a stage somewhere projecting to the back of a theater, because that's how loud he's being.

I shift my eyes up to him. He looks like hell, and I wonder if he's slept at all. He's obviously annoyed and why shouldn't he be? It's the ass-crack of dawn on a Saturday morning and he's up with a strange girl on his couch—the same strange girl who projectile vomited in his bathroom last night while he tried to hold back her hair. I think I may just have to cut him some slack—like a whole crapload of slack—especially when he goes into the kitchen and returns with a glass of ice water, which I desperately need right now. I look at the glass in his hand as he offers it to me. It's a pathetic, short glass tumbler. Is he some sort of conservationist? I'm going to need about eighteen of those right now. I take it, gratefully bringing it up to my lips and immediately gulping it down. The liquid is at the back of my throat before it's coming right back up again. *What the hell?* Vodka. I spit it out, not even conscious of where it goes, and start retching. My stomach clenches and convulses but nothing else comes up. I glare at Josh Bennett, who is staring at me now with a look of what? Disbelief? Repentance? Fear?

"Shit! I didn't think you'd actually drink it." He grabs the glass out of my hand. What did he think I was going to do with it? Bathe? "I thought you'd be able to tell." He looks at me with apology. "It was a joke. Obviously a shitty one," he mutters under his breath as he runs back to the kitchen and returns with yet another towel. This boy will be doing laundry all day. I wonder how he's going to explain this to his parents. It's a miracle they aren't out here already, wanting to know what's going on. I yank the towel out of his hands and get down on the floor to clean up my own mess. Even if this one was his fault, I'd rather not owe him anything else. He stands over me while I mop up what remains of the vodka I sprayed across the floor. I realize what I must look like, down on all fours, my hair, my face, my clothes a reflection of the cruel joke that has been this night.

I look up and glower at him, angry just for the fact that he has witnessed my utter humiliation and that, as much as he's glorying in my downfall, I owe him some debt of gratitude. Drew, on the other hand, is another story. I owe him a fate worse than death. I think I may have preferred to have him dump me on my front porch for my aunt to find rather than put me at the mercy of Josh Bennett. As soon as the thought crosses my mind, I know that maybe it's not so true. But it feels like it should be. I realize I've been glaring at him through my entire thought process, and I wonder what my face must have betrayed, because he's smiling at me now. *Smiling.* And it's almost a real smile, though I can't be positive, because I've never really seen him smile. At school he wears the same unchanging expression, day in and day out, like nothing in the world touches him on any level. And that brings me back to my alien abduction theory, which I'm starting to consider as a real possibility, when he speaks.

"You really want to tell me to fuck off right now don't you, Sunshine?" He's not done playing with me yet. I narrow my eyes when he calls me Sunshine again, which is a tactical error because now he knows it annoys me and I have a feeling he's enjoying annoying me. "What? Sunshine fits you. It's bright and warm and happy. Just. Like. You."

And that's when I lose it. I can't help it. As shitty as I feel right now, as stupid as I look, as angry as I am at myself, at Drew, at Josh Fucking Bennett, and drinks that taste deceptively like cherry Kool-Aid and nothing else. The ridiculousness of this whole situation slams into me all at once, and for the first time in forever I laugh. Maybe it's not even real laughter. Maybe it's just the deranged cackling of a very unstable girl, but I don't care, because it feels good and I don't think I could control it now if I tried. Now the smile is gone from his face. Moved from his to mine, and he's wearing my confusion. He's looking at me like the insane girl I am. I may have actually surprised him. You win, Josh Bennett. You earned it.

When my hysterics subside, he takes the vodka-laden towel from me and goes back into the kitchen. I study the room for the first time. It's simple. There isn't much in it that's modern. Almost everything in here, except for the couch, is made out of wood, which shouldn't surprise me. None of it goes together.

I don't think any two pieces of furniture in this room match. Every piece is a different style, a different type of wood, a different finish. I wonder if he built any of it.

The oddest thing is that there are no fewer than three coffee tables in here. The one in front of the couch I'm sitting on is really nothing to look at. It's all square edges and plain and the finish is wearing off across the surface where people probably spent years putting down glasses without using coasters. It might not seem out of place, if not for the fact that there are two more across the room, and they are anything but plain. The pair of them are from another world and I walk over to get a closer look at them. They don't even appear to be coffee tables in the traditional sense, but I don't know what else to call them. They look old. Ornate and understated at the same time. I have no idea why they would be shoved, unceremoniously, against the wall on the far side of the room. I kneel down and reach out to run my fingers along one of the curved legs of the table closest to me, but then I hear Josh coming and I head back over to the couch. I don't need him thinking I'm . . . thinking I'm what? Fondling his furniture? I don't know. I just don't want him thinking anything.

When Josh comes back, he's carrying one of those huge plastic hospital mugs. I have a whole collection of them at home. Mine are white with teal lettering. The one he's holding is red on white. He hands the mug to me. "Water." I look at him skeptically. "For real this time. I promise."

I manage to get all of the water down in addition to the ibuprofen he hands me with it. Then he takes the mug, without a word, and goes back into the kitchen, returning a moment later with it refilled. He makes me drink that one, too, which I'm none too happy about, because I really just want to get out of here. I look like crap, I feel like crap, and I have no idea how all of this is going to play out on Monday. But I'll deal with that thought later, when my head isn't exploding and I'm not on Josh Bennett's couch.

I stand up to leave, looking down at myself and wondering if I should even ask.

"It's on the bathroom floor." He's smiling at the carpet, not at me, when he says it. "You seemed really disgusted by it for some reason. Ripped it out from under your shirt, through your sleeve, in one fluid motion and flung it across the room. It was pretty impressive." Wonderful. Last night's dinner, the charred remains of my dignity, and apparently, now, my undergarments, too. What else did I leave on Josh Bennett's bathroom floor? I have to admit that, even in the midst of such utter degradation, I think it's funny that he can't seem to say the word bra.

He points me in the direction of the bathroom and I walk as gingerly as I can. Every step sends shock waves rippling from my feet up into my brain. When I get there, my bra mocks me from the tile floor in the corner between the bathtub and the toilet. At least it was a cute black lacy one, because ugly underwear is the only thing that could make this morning any worse. I kneel down to retrieve it, and in the process wonder if I can possibly scrape up the discarded dregs of my self-respect. I may need them.

Josh doesn't need any directions this time. He says nothing at all on the way home, and I can't decide if I'm grateful for that or not. He drops me off at Margot's with thirty minutes to spare before she gets home from work. It's just enough time for me to shower and change and pretend all is well before she walks in the door.

"Feel better, Sunshine." He's not looking at me, but I can still see one side of his mouth turned up when I shut the door.

I think about the fact that he let me sleep on his couch

when Drew obviously dumped me there. He held back my hair, cleaned up massive amounts of puke, brought me painkillers, and stood over me while he forced me to drink a half-gallon of water so I wouldn't get dehydrated. There's nothing sunny or shiny about me, but after last night, he's earned the right to mock me this morning. So yes, I think, at least for a little while, Josh Bennett can call me whatever the hell he likes.

Chapter 11

Josh

At 4:00 PM on Sunday the doorbell rings. When I open it, I find Drew's mom on my porch with a plastic container in her hands.

"It's Sunday. I made sauce. Drew said you weren't coming for dinner, so I wanted to drop it by." She knows I can't make spaghetti sauce to save my life and it pisses me off, so she always brings me some.

"Thanks." I step aside and push the door open so she can come in. "You could have had Drew bring it to me. You didn't have to come all the way over here."

"Drew disappeared somewhere this afternoon. Probably to see whichever girl he's chasing now." She raises her eyebrows questioningly at me and I keep my expression blank, wondering if I know exactly which girl that is. I take the container from her and turn to put it in the refrigerator, while she sits down on a bar stool at the kitchen counter in front of the plate of cookies that appeared at my front door earlier today. "Besides, you know I like to check on you and interrogate you on your life every now and then. Even if I know you won't answer." She smiles, picking up a cookie.

"Thanks," I say for the second time in as many minutes, not

sure what I'm thanking her for: coming by, checking on me, not expecting me to answer. Any of a number of things. I could probably thank Mrs. Leighton all day long, but she wouldn't expect me to.

"You could make it easy on me and just move in with us." She doesn't even try to hide the smirk on her face. She's asked me to move in with them every week since I found out my grandfather was leaving. She always gets the same response, but she never stops asking. I'm not sure how I'd feel if she did.

"Thanks," I say again, and now we're up to three. I don't need to refuse anymore.

"I'm just being selfish, you know. I need you to be a good influence on Drew. Someone has to save that boy from himself. I'm not old enough to be a grandmother." She looks knowingly at me.

"I think you give me too much credit."

"Josh, I love my son, but some days I think you may be the only good thing about him. You are, quite possibly, the only reason I keep him." She shakes her head and I know she's not being serious. Drew is a mama's boy, through and through. He just also happens to be a huge pain in her ass most days. "You've been holding out on me. When did you start baking?" She turns the half-eaten cookie over in her hand, examining it.

"I didn't." I pause, looking at the plate. Now that part of the bottom is visible, I can see the blue paisley pattern around the edges. I wonder if it's part of a set and if I should return it. "Someone else gave me those."

"Someone else?" she says suspiciously. I can tell her interest is piqued. She got tired of asking Drew about the girls in his life because they come and go so fast that there's never any point. But she's never stopped questioning me, waiting for the day when she might actually get an answer. "Well." She takes another bite of the cookie. "*Someone else* can bake. These are delicious."

"I'm not being evasive." I smile, answering the question she asked without asking. "I don't know who it was. They were on my porch this morning."

"Oh," she says, pulling the cookie away from her mouth, her smile gone.

"I have a good idea who it was. I think you're safe." Her expression softens to slight relief. I do have a good idea who it was, but I can't know for sure. There was no note with them when the cookies showed up, but I couldn't help the feeling that they were a thank-you of sorts. And really, there just isn't anybody else it could have been. "Besides, I've eaten like six of them already. If someone wanted to poison me, I think we'd know by now."

We talk for a few more minutes before she gets up to leave, asking me one more time if I'm sure I won't come to dinner. I won't and she already knows that. I'm still pissed at Drew for Friday night and I don't feel like dealing with his shit yet.

"I waited for her in the parking lot this morning," Drew says when I run into him before the warning bell Monday morning. He called me last night but I didn't pick up and I deleted the message without listening to it. I haven't spoken to him since he showed up on Saturday afternoon, wondering what happened with Nastya after he dumped her there. I could say he dropped her off, but we both know that's not what happened. It would be one thing if he was actually concerned about whether or not she made it home okay or how she was feeling, but his primary concern was finding out how pissed she was at him, and I didn't do anything to try to ease his mind. I hope she's pissed at him. She should be.

"She won't talk to me," he laughs as we make our way to first period. "Well, you know, she won't make distinctive facial expressions at me. She did make one expression involving a finger but it could have just been a tic or some sort of muscle spasm."

"Of course," I reply.

"Are you still pissed at me, too?"

"I'm over it."

"You should be. Come on, I dropped a really hot drunk girl, who doesn't talk, off at your house. That's like a gift."

I stop walking and look at him, wondering, yet again, why we are friends. I know him well enough to know that he's not being serious. Drew is an ass and a whore but he's not a complete douche bag. Still, I can't help but call him on it. He deserves it this time.

"Sorry," I apologize with an utter lack of conviction and keep walking. "I thought you were just asking me to clean up your mess. I didn't realize you were being a friend and giving me an unresponsive drunk girl to rape. Next time, be a little clearer so I don't miss such a golden opportunity." I can't hide the sarcasm in my tone and I don't try.

"You know I was kidding." He has the grace to at least sound like he feels bad. "I left her with you because I knew you wouldn't do anything." Now he makes me sound like some sort of monk, and I don't think I like that any better.

"She doesn't know that. She probably thinks you did exactly what you said you did. Dumped her with some strange guy without thinking twice about what would happen."

"What did happen? You were so pissed at me on Saturday you wouldn't tell me shit."

"Maybe because I was up half the night cleaning up vomit and the other half watching to make sure she didn't choke on any more." I stop walking and look at him so he realizes that I'm not joking. There is nothing at all funny about the amount of puke I faced on Friday night. I may never be the same again. "You want to know what happened? She threw up. A lot. She passed out. She woke up. I took her home. That's it."

"Dude, I so owe you," he says, still cringing from the discussion of vomit.

"You have no idea."

Nastya

When I get to shop on Monday, Margot's blue paisley plate is sitting on the counter in the back of the room where I usually sit. Josh isn't at his regular table but he must have put it here. I see him on the other side of the shop where all the power tools are. I don't want to stare at him long enough to figure out what he's doing, so I shove the plate in my backpack before he gets back to his seat. The bell rings and he slides onto his stool without a glance in my direction and things are normal again. The normalcy doesn't last long, which shouldn't surprise me. I don't think anything is normal where Josh Bennett is concerned. Though, I really shouldn't be judging him on normalcy, especially when I'm watching him from the confines of my own, very precarious glass house.

"Hey, Bennett! Is it true you got emancipated?" *Emancipated?* I look around to see who's asking the question. It's some punk-ass skater kid whose name, I think, is Kevin, but I haven't paid enough attention to know for certain. Mostly what I've picked up is that his hair is overlong in the front, his pants are always baggy, and he thinks he's pretty awesome. I really don't care who asked the question, but I'm definitely interested in the answer.

Josh nods, but says nothing. He's looking down, working on the scale drawing we were assigned Friday. He doesn't bother to lift his head and acknowledge Kevin or anyone else whose attention is now on him.

"So that means you're, like, free to do whatever the hell you want?"

"Apparently so." He turns the ruler and traces a line along the edge of it with a pencil. "Of course, I can't murder anyone, so it has its limits," he adds dryly, still not looking up. I have to stifle my own smile, especially when Kevin soldiers on, completely oblivious to the innuendo.

"Man, that's awesome. I'd be having parties every night."

Kevin doesn't seem to take the hint that Josh has nothing to say to him and keeps pushing. I'm kind of wishing Josh would give this kid the fuckuppance he so richly deserves, but I think that's more my style than Josh Bennett's.

I hear someone tell Kevin, in a hushed voice, to shut up. The kids around him look anywhere from curious to uncomfortable to downright astonished by his line of questioning. I'm in the curious camp myself, but I'm trying to act disinterested. I can tell Mr. Turner's picked up on it, too, because he keeps glancing in that direction. He's not going to interfere, but he damn sure wants to know what's being said. He looks almost disgusted. I know that I'm missing some vital piece of information here, and I can't ask anyone what it is. Why has he been emancipated? Are his parents abusive? Dead? In jail? Out of the country? Maybe there's a top secret spy mission involved.

My mind turns while their conversation continues. I'm still trying to figure out why Josh has been emancipated and what it has to do with the fact that everyone stays the hell out of his way. We've been sitting here for all of forty-five seconds and yet I almost feel like the air in the room has gotten heavier.

Josh

I can see their expressions without looking. Usually everyone ignores me, but the times when they don't are worse. Like now. You either get the ignorant crap spewed by morons like Kevin Leonard or you get the sucks-to-be-you stares. Especially from the girls. The girls are the worst. Drew says I should use it to my advantage; that I waste the shitty cards I've been dealt and that I should at least get something out of being such a tragic figure. But there's something about being pity-fucked that just doesn't sit well. It's hard to want a girl who looks at you like you're a lost puppy she wants to take home and feed or a dejected child who needs to curl up in her lap and be coddled. There's nothing at all hot about a girl feeling sorry for me. Maybe if I was desperate, but probably not even then.

The adults are even worse because they love to make their dumbass comments about how well I'm doing; how well adjusted I've become; how well I handle everything. As if they have any clue. The only thing I've learned to do well is avoid, but everyone would rather believe it's all good. That way they can crawl back under the shelter of that rock they live under. The one they think death can't see them through.

It's even the same with the teachers. I can get out of almost any assignment I want if I play the death card. It makes everyone uncomfortable, so they'll do just about anything you want to get you to go away so they can pretend it doesn't happen. They get to convince themselves that they empathize and that they've done their good deed for the day. When I'm lucky, they just ignore me because that's easier for all of us anyway. Easier than having to acknowledge death.

One death card might be more than enough to play for a missed assignment or copping a feel on some girl, but I'm racking up a full deck at this point, and I can probably get away with almost anything. People started looking the other way a long time ago. Maybe I did, too.

When I was eight I went to a spring training game with my dad. Once a month my parents would split up and each take either my sister, Amanda, or me out for the day. One month I'd go with my dad and Amanda would go with my mom. The next month we'd switch. It was March and it was my turn to go with my mom, but since that's when the game was, I begged to go with my dad instead. I told my mom she could have me April and May to make up for it. Because I was such a fucking prize.

My mom said it sounded like a good deal to her and made me shake on it.

My dad and I got home at six o'clock. I had fallen asleep in the car on the way home. He woke me up when we pulled in but ended up carrying me into the house anyway because my ass was not crawling out of that car. We ate too much, laughed too much, yelled too much. My stomach hurt. My face was sunburnt. I lost my voice and I couldn't keep my eyes open. It was the last happy day of my life.

When I woke up, I didn't have a mom or a sister anymore, but apparently it would all work out, because we'd end up having more money than we would ever need. The trucking company's lawyers said it was a generous settlement. My dad's lawyers said it was fair. Fair compensation for my mother's life. Fair compensation for my dead sister. They didn't consider the fact that I really lost my father, too, that day. That something in him broke, shattered, melted, combusted, disintegrated like the car my mother was driving when an eighteen-wheeler delivering soda drove right over it. But I'm sure if they had considered that, too, they would have determined that it was also more than fair. Generous, even. I don't have a sister to bitch about or a mother to talk to or a father to build things with. But I have millions of nearly untouched dollars in bank accounts and brokerage funds and life is so very fucking fair.

"It's completely awesome," I reply, hoping my agreement will get Kevin to turn back around and impress someone else with his ignorance and talk of legendary partying. "Nobody gives a shit what I do." It's true in more ways than one. I look up and focus my eyes on his, hoping he understands.

I go back to finishing the scale drawing I've been working on, glad that everyone's attention has shifted back to more important things, like math tests and hot girls. Mr. Turner is making his way around the room, looking over everyone's shoulders to check their progress. He passes my table and glances behind me.

"Nastya, you can't draw sitting up there. Why don't you move over and sit at the empty seat next to Kevin?" He sounds almost apologetic for asking her to move. I'm surprised he's even expecting her to do the assignment. So far he's been acting like she's not even in the class, which we both know she shouldn't be. But I guess he got stuck with her, because she's still here. I think she makes people as uncomfortable as I do. Mr. Turner's never been awkward with me, but he sure as hell is around her. Maybe it's the clothes, or lack thereof, because he always seems kind of scared to look at her. I had forgotten she'd been behind me this whole time, and that she must have heard the entire exchange earlier. She starts picking up her things and Mr. Turner shifts his attention back to me.

"Looks good," he says, checking out the sketch in front of me. "What are you going to use?"

"European ash, probably. Natural finish," I reply. He nods, but stands there a second longer.

"Everything okay?" he asks and I know he's referring to the Kevin situation, which is stupid, because I don't let that crap bother me anymore.

"Everything's good," I tell him, turning the ruler on my paper as he walks back up to his desk. Behind me, I hear Nastya hop down off the counter, the click of her heels hitting the floor. She passes behind me, moving around my table to the one where Kevin Leonard is laughing his self-congratulatory ass off. Everyone's working on their own now, and the noise level has kicked up considerably, so I'm not sure if I'm imagining things, or maybe I'm just crazy, when I hear the words.

You lie. They aren't even a whisper. They drift into my consciousness so soft they almost have no form, as if they're made of air and longing, but I swear I hear them anyway. When I look up, the only person who could have said them is settling down on a stool next to Kevin Leonard and I kick myself for being ridiculous, because I know they can't be real, and that the longing those words were born from is mine.

I make it to Art just under the wire, slipping in and sitting at an empty table in the back, behind Clay Whitaker. I'm not much for art, but there were no course numbers left to sign me up for an extra shop class. I'd taken them all, so I needed another elective to fill my schedule. Preferably one without homework or thought involved. The path of least resistance is well worn by my boots. Mrs. Carson lets me get by with turning in sketches of furniture that I love and whatever I'm designing to build at some point. Sometimes I draw stuff I see in antique stores. Things I wish I had the talent to make. Maybe one day. I'm not that great when it comes to the drawing. I'm okay. Not terrible, not amazing. I glance at the table in front of me. Clay Whitaker is amazing. He can do with a sketchbook and charcoal what I wish I could do with lumber and tools. I pull out my backpack and rummage through it for the picture I printed off the internet last night. I barely get started when Clay turns around.

"What are you drawing?" He inclines his head to get a better view of the picture in front of me.

It's a mid-eighteenth-century George the Second–style marble-topped console table. Our assignment was to bring in a photograph to re-create so that's what I picked.

"Table," I say.

"One day you should try drawing something with two legs instead of four."

Drawing people doesn't interest me; plus, I suck at it. "What are you drawing?" I ask.

"Who, not what," he corrects. Clay rarely draws anything other than people. He's obsessed with human faces. If I'm forever drawing furniture, he's forever drawing people. He's damn good at it, too. It's almost creepy how realistic his drawings look. There is some arcane quality about his sketches; some way he makes you see past the face itself and into it. I've seen him make even the plainest, most uninspiring face interesting in ways I don't have words for. I'm jealous of his talent. If I didn't have something of my own to love like that, I'd be insanely jealous. As it is, I can appreciate his ability without hating him for it, but I know there are a few people in this class who can't. Sometimes I think Mrs. Carson herself is one of them. It must be kind of depressing to have to teach someone who surpasses your abilities on every level.

My attention shifts back to Clay as he drags a four-by-six photograph off his table and passes it back to me with a shit-eating grin on his face like he knows something I don't. I take the picture out of his hands and look down at it. I'm not sure who I expected it to be, but it certainly wasn't the girl whose face I'm looking at now. Even so, I can't say I'm surprised. If there's an interesting face in this school, it's Nastya Kashnikov's; maybe just because she never opens her mouth to take away from the mystery. I stare at the picture a second longer than I should. She's looking in the general direction of the lens, but not directly facing it. The camera must have been zoomed in on her, because it's not that well focused, and it's obvious that she didn't know the picture was being taken.

"Why her?" I ask, reluctantly handing it back.

"Her face is insane, even with all that shit she covers it up with. If I can do that justice, I'll never need to draw another girl again." He's staring at the photograph like he's picturing how she looks without the makeup. I want to tell him he's right. What she looks like in that picture is nothing compared to what she looks like without a trace of makeup on and her hair pulled off her face. That's what I'd like a picture of, instead of having to rely on my memory of her, lost and dripping sweat in my garage at one in the morning.

"I wouldn't think she was your type." I yank my attention away from thoughts I shouldn't be having and put the focus back on him so maybe he won't notice, but Clay always notices. Clay's as much of an outcast here as anybody and I know he's a watcher, too. I've seen enough of his drawings to know how many people he studies when they don't know he's looking. And when Clay looks, he sees, and that's the most disconcerting thing of all.

"My dick doesn't have to want her. Just my pencil." He smiles at me again, like he's got some secret of mine. He probably does. He's always watching me like he never got the message to leave me the hell alone. For some reason, I don't mind. He stays in the fringes, and other than the shit he still occasionally takes for coming out, he flies under the radar. I go back to my own crappy drawing and then kick myself when my mouth opens again.

"How did you get the picture?"

"Michelle." The name is an answer in itself. Yearbook Michelle. Clay's the only one who doesn't throw the word *yearbook* in front of her name when he says it. She sits with him every day at lunch, camera all but surgically attached to her hands. "I got her to take it in the courtyard one day when Nastya wasn't looking." He shrugs, looking a little guilty, though not at all apologetic. He uses her name like he knows her, and I wonder how well.

"She'd kick your ass if she knew you took it." It's a dumbass thing to say. I don't know her well enough to know what she'd do, and I'm talking about her like I do. She's ripped enough to kick his ass, and mine, too. Really, she should have kicked my ass for handing her a glass of vodka when she was hung over, but she laughed in my face instead, so what the hell do I know?

"There are a lot of people who want to kick my ass," he responds nonchalantly, as if it's just a fact of life. It's true that a lot of the assholes in this school want to kick the crap out of him, but wanting and doing are two different things. They still talk shit about him, but nobody's laid a hand on Clay since eighth grade, and he and I both know why.

When my mom died, I went through the angry phase. It's okay, of course, because anger is acceptable when you're grieving, especially when you're an eight-year-old boy. People will make a lot of excuses for you. I dealt with my acceptable anger by doing unacceptable things like beating the crap out of other kids who pissed me off. Pissing me off didn't take much. I was pretty liberal about what would be enough to set me off. Turned out, even the unacceptable things I did with my fists were considered acceptable and brushed under the carpet.

I punched Mike Scanlon in the face, twice, because he said my mom was in the ground getting eaten by maggots. I don't think there was even enough of her body left after the crash to feed a maggot, but I didn't argue with him. I just nailed him in the face. Gave him a black eye and a split lip. He told his dad. His dad came to my house and I hid around the corner, listening and wondering how much trouble I was going to get in. But he wasn't even mad. He told my dad it was okay. He said he understood. He didn't understand crap, but I didn't get in trouble. And that's the way it always went.

The only time I really had to answer for it at all was the one time it happened at school. I punched Jake Keller on the soccer field during PE and I thought I was in for it. The principal called me in, which had never happened in my life. Lucky for me, he also understood and I got off with a warning and a few trips to the school psychologist. All the kids I beat up learned that no one was going to touch me for anything I did. I could hit them in broad daylight with ten witnesses and even their own dads would tell them to give me a break.

My angry phase had ended by the time I got to eighth grade, just in time for my dad to have a heart attack. By that time, almost everybody left me alone. No one would give me an excuse to get angry at them. Then one day I was walking home from school and ran into three shits beating the crap out of Clay Whitaker. I didn't even know him at the time, but they were kicking him good and I needed an excuse to kick someone back. I had a lot of healthy, acceptable anger built up and they were good therapy. There were three of them and I wasn't the biggest kid around. They should have been able to grind me into the sidewalk without breaking a sweat. But they had only garden-variety cruelty to fuel them. I had pure unadulterated rage.

Clay was sitting on the ground when the other kids finally ran off. I was hurt and out of breath so I sat down, also, because I didn't know where to go and I didn't care if anyone else came looking for me. No one did. I probably would have hit them, too. Clay didn't say thank you, or anything else to me for that matter, which was good, because I didn't deserve any thanks. I didn't do it for him. There weren't any noble intentions.

I didn't care if I got in trouble. I didn't care about Clay Whitaker, sitting a couple feet away, bloody and crying. I just didn't care. That was the last time I hit anyone. After that day, I decided to wait until someone gave me a good reason. But it didn't matter, because everyone had already learned that I'd get away with it if I did. I wasn't even sure what a good reason would be, but I figured I'd know when the time came. And maybe it never would.

I didn't say a word to Clay before I finally got up and walked home and we never spoke about what happened. I was used to people not bothering me, but after that day, nobody bothered Clay Whitaker, either.

"I'm starting to understand the feeling," I mutter, and he

knows I'm not serious but he throws his hands up and takes the hint.

"Fine. I'll leave you to your very compelling table. I'm going to draw a girl," he says smugly, and turns around to open his sketchbook.

Chapter 12

Nastya

I used to spend excessive amounts of time thinking about what I'd be doing over the next twenty or so years. It usually had something to do with playing the piano in concert halls all over the world. Which would mean lots of world travel that would include stays at fabulously glamorous hotels with fabulously fluffy towels and fluffier bathrobes. There would also be the unbelievably hot, musically gifted, swoon-worthy princes who would tour with me and inevitably fall obsessively in love with me. Because that happens. I would be revered for the talent that came from my father's side of the family and the beauty that came from my mother's. I'd wear elegant gowns in colors that haven't even been imagined yet and everyone would know my name.

Now I spend my time thinking about what I'll be doing over the next twenty or so hours and hoping it involves something resembling sleep.

—

I've been able to run every night for a week now. The weather has cooperated. My legs are coming back. I push myself harder than I should but I haven't thrown up again since the first night. My body is remembering. The best part is that I can exhaust myself, drain everything the day dredges up, so I can sleep. I still can't do without the notebooks, but the running helps. It gives me something, or maybe more accurately, it takes something away. I don't care. I know I depend on it too much but it's one of the only things I can depend on.

Exercise, notebooks, hate. The things that do not let me down.

I know my way around the streets now. I can pay attention without paying attention. I've memorized the ambient sound. I know what belongs and what doesn't. I know where the sidewalks are uneven, where the pavement has been pushed up by the roots of an angry tree. My mind has learned what to expect from the night I run in. I leave around the same time every evening but I don't run the same route twice. I can get myself home a dozen different ways from any direction if I need to. I am not comfortable. I'll never be comfortable leaving the house again, but I feel prepared, and that's better than I was the last time, and the most I can expect to be.

For the past six nights, I have purposely avoided the pale yellow stucco house on Corinthian Way. The one with the perpetually open garage. I run past the street every night, but I can't ignore the pull I feel to at least glance down the road from the turn off. I can tell by the pattern of the lights whether or not the garage door is up, and it hasn't disappointed yet. It hasn't been closed once, no matter what time it is. I always wonder what he might say if I were to show up there again. I know it wouldn't be much, but I wonder what the words would be anyway. Would he say anything? Would he ignore me and keep working as if I wasn't there? Would he tell me to leave? Ask me to stay? No, I know he wouldn't do that. Josh Bennett doesn't ask anybody to stay. I could come up with a hundred possibilities, but I really can't figure out which of them would be the closest to possible.

Then, for a just a moment, I lose focus. I stop thinking about what he would say to me and start pondering what I would say to him. That's the moment I push my feet hard and fast in the opposite direction and I run far away from Corinthian Way and my absurd, self-destructive thoughts.

I get back to Margot's house at 9:25 and head straight for the shower. I talk more to myself in that shower than I have in months. Within the safety of an empty house, under the muting of the running water, I remind myself of all the complications that will come from opening my mouth. I try to get all of the words out of my system. I tell Ethan Hall that he's a douche while I visualize administering a perfectly executed palm heel strike to his face. Or a fork to his eye, which is equally appealing. I tell Ms. Jennings that, contrary to popular belief, Bach was not more prolific than Telemann; he's just better remembered. I tell Drew which of his pick-up lines works the best and who I think he should really use them on instead of wasting them on me. I tell my Dad that he can still call me Milly because, even though it's a sucky nickname, it makes him happy and that makes me happy in a way I don't know how to be anymore. I tell my therapists thank you, but that nothing they do or say or try to make me say will help. I talk until the water runs cold and my voice feels hoarse from overuse. I hope it's enough to help me keep my mouth shut. I haven't said a word to another living person in 452 days. I write my three and a half pages, tuck away my composition book, and crawl into bed, knowing how close I came to not making it to 453.

—

I've been doing a decent job avoiding Josh at school. Other than fifth hour, the only time I have to see him is in shop, which is always a humbling experience since everyone in that class knows their way around lumber and power tools and I'm lucky I can identify a hammer, maybe not even that. The other day this kid named Errol asked me to hand him one, and when I did, he looked at me like I was an idiot. Apparently there are like four hundred kinds of hammers and I didn't give him the right one. Now nobody even asks me to get them stuff.

I could have tried to drop the class, but I decided to choose my battles with the guidance department and Shop was the lesser of the evils when compared to Speech and Debate and Intro to Music. Between the two of those, I figured I could survive Speech since Mr. Trent had told me I could earn my grade doing research and finding interpretation material. Plus, I had crash-hot sexy Drew to amuse me and I'll take all the amusement I can get. And if I'm being completely honest with myself, which I usually endeavor to avoid, I knew from day one that I needed the hell out of Intro to Music. That class was a fault line running just beneath the surface of my unstable mind. I'd rather avoid it. I'm good at avoiding.

And besides, being the teacher's aide in Ms. McAllister's fifth hour has been more entertaining than I could have hoped for. It's like the school equivalent of watching *Big Brother*; I get to eavesdrop on the drama and it's not mentally taxing in the least. Drew is in there, along with Josh, dirtbag Ethan, fuckwad Kevin Leonard, and this badass girl named Tierney Lowell who Drew argues with nonstop. I don't think she's my biggest fan, either. She hasn't told me outright, but she glares at me like I spend my free time murdering puppies, so it's an educated guess.

Shop really isn't so bad, either, even if it does make me feel inept and useless most of the time. No one bothers me, and Mr. Turner doesn't expect me to do much of anything. Josh is apparently some sort of god there. He walks around like he built the place. They should give him a dedicated phone line in the workshop, because every time the phone rings, the same thing happens: Turner answers, Turner summons Josh, Josh leaves. He gets sent out a lot. Shelves need fixing? Call Josh Bennett. Drawers stuck? Get Josh. Need an exquisitely crafted, custom-built dining room set? Josh Bennett is your man.

Just don't ask him to talk. He hasn't said anything to me at school since the day he told me he wasn't going to make me relinquish my seat at his table, benevolent despot that he is. I, obviously, have not said anything to him.

Chapter 13

Josh

Drew walks in at about ten after eleven on Sunday morning. I forgot to lock the door when I went out to get the newspaper, so he walks right in. I have to cancel the stupid thing. I don't read it. It's another remnant from my grandfather living here. I tried to convince him to read it online but he wouldn't have it. He said he liked the feel of it in his hands and the smell of the paper. I hate the way newspaper feels and I like the way it smells even less. I make a note to call today and have them stop delivery. I don't want to have to see another one in my driveway.

"What's up?" I ask while he makes himself at home.

"Sarah. House. Girls. Too many," he sighs, collapsing prone onto the couch and staring up at the ceiling.

"I didn't think there was such a thing as too many girls in your world."

"When it comes to Sarah's friends, I make exceptions."

"You never make exceptions."

"Okay. True story. But I should."

I don't blame him. Sarah's friends are painful. They're nice to look at, but they all know it, which kind of diminishes the appeal. They're all the things about the girls at school that I can't stand, and Sarah's becoming just like them. I guess I'm lucky I intimidate them, because after they try their flirting thing once, they usually realize they're not going to get a reaction and they don't come back for more.

"You've already hit at least three of them. Finally learn your lesson?"

"Think they finally learned theirs. Plus, Sarah put her foot down and said no more with the friends. Off-limits."

"Does she really think you're going to listen?"

"She put her foot down to them. *I'm* off-limits."

"How deprived they must feel."

"Don't mock. It's true. I'm like a rite of passage."

"Why are you here?" I ask.

"Told you. Can't be in the house. I feel my testosterone levels dropping by the second in there."

"Yeah, but why are you *here*?" My house is usually not the first resort for escape when Drew needs to get away from his. It used to be a few years ago, but not anymore. I think it might have something to do with my possession of a Y chromosome.

"Nowhere else to go."

"You could pick up some grain alcohol. Go make a peace offering."

"I'm not going over there alone. They might never find my body."

"Giving up so soon?" There are a hundred other girls he could go after; this one I just don't get.

"No. Just have to switch tactics. Ideas?"

I don't have any ideas and if I did I wouldn't help him out. I do have questions, though, and I seem to come up with more every day. "Why do you think she doesn't talk?"

"Nobody knows. I hit her with some of my favorite material, and judging by the look I got, she has no problem grasping the English language. I'm voting no vocal cords."

I know for a fact that's not true. She laughed when she was here—full-on laughed. I looked it up. You need vocal cords to produce sound like that, so I know that's not it. Maybe it's still a physical thing. I don't know shit about anything like that, but something tells me it's not physical, and that makes me wonder even more. What reason does someone have to not talk? Did she ever talk? Maybe she's never uttered a single word. I don't know. I do know that she pays attention; she's watching everything all the time, even when she's not even looking. I don't think she misses a damn thing. It might creep me out if I didn't kind of get it. I wonder if she sees things that I don't, but it's not like she'd tell me and I would never ask anyway.

"She doesn't seem like your type," I say. With rare exception, Drew tends to go the vapid, cute, and popular route. He's all about the path of least resistance when it comes to girls, and fortunately for him, that path seems to lead to almost any girl in school. I don't think he's ever been turned down, even though they all know his reputation and he's never done anything to sugarcoat it. He's never pulled out the love card and pretended to have any sort of feelings for a girl to get her to sleep with him. He doesn't have to. They do it anyway without any emotional persuasion from him. They provide that all on their own.

Most girls think they'll be the one he ends up staying with, but it never happens. You'd think at least one of them would publicly call him out for it. Try to make him take responsibility and own up, but none of them do, because at the end of the day they know that Drew did exactly what Drew does, and most of them realize they probably shouldn't have bought into the reform-the-asshole fantasy.

I'd like to blame him, but it's hard when he doesn't deny or make excuses or apologies. He is what he is. Take it or leave it. I couldn't do what he does, not that there isn't a certain appeal. I'd be lying if I said it wasn't something I've thought about, but it's way too much responsibility for me. There are too many feelings coming off those girls, and I'm not good at deflecting them. They seem to roll right off Drew. The tears and the name-calling and the bitterness don't even faze him. I have enough responsibility, and I don't need anyone's feelings to worry about. I banished my own a long time ago, and I'll be damned if I have to deal with someone else's.

"She's female. She's hot. Requirements met," he says bluntly.

"She seems to hate you." She seems to hate everyone but I don't bother to say that. I'm really trying to figure out why he's wasting his time with this girl. It's out of character. He should have given up on this a while ago.

"So, it's a challenge."

"Exactly. Doesn't exerting effort go against your personal philosophy?"

"It does, but maybe I'm entering a personal growth phase. Trying to improve myself."

I stifle a laugh or a gagging sound. I'm not sure which.

"Your lack of faith is insulting. Besides, not all of us have a sure thing in our back pockets with no strings and no effort required." He looks deliberately at me. I can't dispute it. There's no point in acting all high and mighty when I don't ever have to worry about getting a girl to have sex with me.

I've got Leigh, even though she's not around as much as she used to be now that she's in college, but that just makes it easier. She's only a couple of hours away and she comes by whenever she's home for weekends and holidays. Then she leaves again. She doesn't tell me she loves me. She doesn't ask if I love her. I don't and I never will. We have an easy, nonemotional arrangement: we use each other and go home. It's about as perfect as a situation gets. Even if I didn't have Leigh, I don't think I'd be desperate enough to sink to Drew's level. I like getting laid well enough, but knowing me, I'd still feel like a prick and end up dating the girl for months out of guilt.

"You don't get to judge me. In fact, in light of my newfound self-improvement goals, I'm going to conquer my fear of being flayed alive and go over to her house right now." He jumps up off the couch and heads for the door.

"Good luck with that," I say, not meaning it in the least.

I spend the rest of the afternoon involved in varying degrees of avoidance. I finally did pick up the phone and cancel the newspaper, which I wasn't sure I'd actually do. Then I figured as long as I was dealing with things, I'd call the hospice and have them come take away the hospital bed they delivered for my grandfather two months ago. He's been gone for two weeks, but it feels like forever. If there weren't so many phone calls to make, I might wonder if he was ever here at all.

When I hang up with the hospice, I look at the phone and think about calling my grandfather. I thought about calling yesterday and the day before and the day before that. But I haven't actually called. I spoke to him last week and it sucked. He's a hundred times worse since he left here. His mind isn't his anymore. It belongs to oxycodone and morphine and every other painkiller they can pump into him to make it easier. Talking to him isn't even talking to him anymore. He's a body on the other end of the phone; the mind is all but gone. I can almost hear his brain struggling to process the words as I speak to him. He can't make sense of it and I know it frustrates him, and if there is any part of my heart left to break, it breaks with his confusion. Still, I get selfish sometimes and call him anyway. For me. And I talk. I tell him things I wouldn't tell another living person, because I know that when I hang up, it will be like I never told anyone at all.

Even the last real conversation we had, on the Saturday night before my great-uncle and his wife came to pick him up, was tainted by the drugs. He sat me down to give me the advice he thought I still needed. He told me to sit on the couch, and he sat in the recliner across from me the way he had for years when he was imparting whatever piece of wisdom he felt I needed at that point in my life. I never really listened because I didn't think I needed his wisdom. That night I sat. And I listened. I'd listen to anything he wanted to say. I was greedy for it, desperate for whatever words he had left to give me, even if they were delivered through a drug-addled haze.

He told me a lot of things that night and I remember them all. There was talk of women and unforgivable things, porch swings and red brick houses and memories that didn't exist yet.

I have to be at Drew's for dinner at six, which means I need to get in the shower now and find some better clothes to put on. Drew's mom likes it when you dress for Sunday dinner. It's not any fancy thing, but according to Mrs. Leighton, dressing nicely makes it special, so that's what we do. I tried to get out of going, but she wouldn't let me. I haven't gone to Sunday dinner in three weeks. I don't hate it. It's actually fun most of the time. I get to eat real food that I don't have to cook and Drew doesn't act like such a douche around his family. It's just that, when I go there, I feel like I'm in an episode of *Sesame Street,* stuck in the upper quadrant of the TV screen while they sing that one of these things just doesn't belong here. The normalcy of it reminds me, in detail, of how fucked my life actually is. I could stand here all day thinking of all of the reasons not to go, but I know I'm not getting out of it, so I suck it up, pull some decent clothes out of the closet, and jump in the shower.

Chapter 14

Nastya

There are twenty-seven bones in your hand and wrist. Twenty-two of mine were broken. Relatively speaking, my hand is kind of a miracle. It's full of plates and screws, and even after several surgeries, it still doesn't look quite right. But it works better than they thought it would. And it's not like it can't do anything; it just can't do the one thing I want it to. The thing that made me, me.

—

I never had much of a social life, even before. After school, I passed my hours in the music lab or in private instruction, and my Saturdays were spent playing the piano at weddings. There were times during wedding season that I'd hit three in a day. I'd run out of one church, jump in the car my mom would be sitting in out front, and rush to the next. It got crazy sometimes, and I rarely had a free weekend, but the money was awesome, the time commitment minimal, and it was easy.

Most wedding coordinators and brides aren't very original. I had about five pieces of music that were rotated through: the standards that you tend to hear at every wedding. I took it for granted that I could sleepwalk through those things. I had three dresses that got rotated just like the music; all conservative and girly with varying degrees of formality depending on the wedding itself. I wonder what they would have done if I walked in dressed like I do today.

When I wasn't playing weddings, I played at upscale malls and restaurants. I was a pretty little novelty in the beginning. I was everybody's pet. I don't know if anyone really knew my name; they mostly just called me the Brighton Piano Girl, which was fine, because that's who I was. Once I got older, everybody was used to seeing me here or there, but back when I started, around eight years old, people usually did a double take. I'd wear my frilly little dresses and my hair would always be tied back out of my face with a matching ribbon. I'd smile and play my Bach or Mozart or whatever overused pieces of music they asked me to play. Everyone knew me and people would always clap when I got done and say hi whenever they saw me. I loved every second of it.

By the time I was forced to stop, I had quite a bit of money put away. I was saving it to pay for the summer music conservatory in New York that I had been drooling over for three years and was finally old enough, at fifteen, to apply to. My parents said if I wanted to go I had to work for the money, but that was a joke, because work meant play and playing was never work. Between that and school and private instruction and recitals, it hadn't left much time for a social life, but it was a small sacrifice. Plus, if I'm being honest, it probably wasn't any sacrifice. I didn't go to parties and I was too young to drive. I liked Nick Kerrigan but mostly we just looked at each other and looked away a lot.

I didn't have a bunch of girlfriends to go hang out at the mall with and my mom bought most of my clothes anyway. Even at fifteen, I was younger than fifteen. My style was Sunday school chic. The couple of friends I had were like me. We spent all of our free hours practicing because that's who we were. Piano girls. Violin girls. Flute girls. That was normalcy. My grades weren't awesome and I was the polar opposite of popular, but it was okay. It was better than being normal. I never gave two shits about normal. I wanted extraordinary.

Normal people had friends. I had music. I wasn't missing anything.

These days I'm missing everything. I'm haunted by music; music I can hear, but never play again. Melodies that taunt me note by note, mocking me with the simple fact that they exist.

I still have all of the money that I saved for the conservatory. I had more than enough, but I never did get to go. I spent that summer in and out of hospitals, recovering, in physical therapy, learning to pick up quarters off a table, and with therapists talking about why I was mad.

At this point I've regained enough control in my hand that I could probably bang something out on the piano if I tried, but it would never be what it used to be, what it should be. Music should flow so that you can't tell where one note ends and the next begins; music should have grace, and there is no grace left in my hand. There are metal screws and damaged nerves and shattered bones, but there isn't any grace.

Today is Sunday and I have nowhere to be. I never had weddings to do on Sundays, but I usually spent the mornings filling in at the Lutheran church if they needed me. I wasn't religious; it was just a favor to one of my mom's friends, so I did it. Afternoons were usually spent at the grand piano upstairs in the mall outside Nordstrom. Then I'd actually practice the real stuff in the evenings, and once in a while I did my homework.

Now homework is about the only thing I have to do, so miraculously it's been getting done. But I'm still kind of crap at it.

Margot spends the afternoons next to the pool until she has to get ready for work. I can't sunbathe. It doesn't work so well with the translucent skin, plus, I suck with the sitting still. I will douse myself with sunscreen on occasion, braid my hair and swim laps until my limbs won't move. I can't run in the afternoons, so it's a good alternative.

I'm only on lap twenty-five when I lift my head out of the water to see Margot standing at the edge of the pool next to the perpetually smirking Drew Leighton. I'm momentarily dumbfounded, wondering how he knew where I lived, when I remember that he picked me up for that ill-fated party last week.

I look down at myself through the surface of the water and realize that I won't be escaping anytime soon. I am so not about to pull myself up and out of this pool dripping wet and nearly naked in front of him. I might go to school half-naked, but half-naked and nearly naked are two entirely different things, and I'm not planning to define the difference for him in a very small bikini. It's bad enough that I have no makeup on, but there isn't anything I can do about that now, so I've got to let it go. I grab the sunglasses I left at the edge of the pool and compensate by staying as far away from him as possible.

"I'm Nastya's aunt," Margot introduces herself to Drew. "I assume you two know each other." She turns and smiles knowingly in my direction. Since the first day of school she's been pushing me to make friends and have some sort of social life, so this must be thrilling her to no end. Drew is putting on the boyish charm in a way that I'm sure has won over many a suspicious mother. He'll probably need to work a little harder on Margot. She's younger and cute and used to being flirted with. She isn't oblivious to what he's playing. Still, that suspicion is being tempered by her desire for me to get some sort of life. She walks away, leaving me to him, and goes back to her chair and a copy of *Cosmopolitan*. She's not fooling me, though. I know she's straining to hear every word.

If I wasn't trapped in the pool by my state of undress, I could fully enjoy the situation a bit more. Drew can't use his arsenal of sexual innuendos on me now, while he's being chaperoned. He kicks off his shoes and sits down at the edge of the pool, dangling his feet in the water.

"I feel I've done my penance. You should forgive me now."

I just stare at him. I don't even bother changing my expression. He's going to have to exert a little effort to get me to waste facial expressions on him.

"You haven't even looked at me in a week. It's killing my reputation."

I have a feeling a nuclear bomb couldn't kill his reputation at this point, much less a week without my attention, but I appreciate him giving me the credit.

"Let me make it up to you. Come to dinner at my house. Tonight."

This makes me suspicious and I'm pretty sure it shows. Innocence does not become Drew. It doesn't gel with the pure unadulterated sex that drips from his pores. I meet his eyes and wait for the catch.

"You won't even have to be alone with me. My whole family will be there."

Perhaps he thinks this is a selling point. It isn't. I don't mind parents. I actually used to do quite well with parents. Now, probably not so much, but it's not the parents that concern me. It's the sister I'm not going anywhere near. I'm already on her radar. I was even before the unwanted courtyard heroics of a certain Josh Bennett, and I'm not rushing to put myself in the eye of that storm again by showing up to a family dinner on her brother's arm. No way. Not happening. Not ever.

"I'm sure she'd love to go," Margot chimes in over her magazine. So much for pretending she's not eavesdropping. My defiant convictions lasted all of three seconds. "I have to work. There's no point in you sitting here eating dinner alone." *Thanks,*

Margot. I flash her the smile I save for my mortal enemies. She looks at me, face full of innocence, eyes full of mischief. She knows I'm cornered. Damn self-inflicted mutism. Is that even a word? Irrelevant. I shake my head but I can't offer an excuse and I don't have one anyway, though I'm sure I could easily come up with something believable: homework, emptying bedpans at the local nursing home, cholera. Alas, they all stay trapped in my throat as I look on helplessly while my evening's fate is decided by my meddling aunt and a cocksure teenage boy. Margot knows I have nothing to do and Drew isn't about to give me a chance to get out of it anyway. He's on his feet in an instant, bolting before the plans can be rescinded.

"Dinner's at six. I'll pick you up at five forty-five. Dress nice. My mom likes to pretend we're civilized once a week." He smiles conspiratorially in Margot's direction. He knows he has her to thank for this. It's no mystery that, given a choice, I never would have agreed. I'm angrier at myself. I dug my own grave on this one. You give up talking and you give up free will. I wonder what Margot would think if she knew the truth of Drew Leighton, the sex volcano she just sacrificed me to.

"Don't get up. I'll just walk around the house. Nice meeting you." He turns back to me. "See you later."

It sounds like a threat.

If only Margot hadn't heard the doorbell, I could be blissfully, comfortably alone this evening, just like I should be. I wouldn't be in the predicament I'm in now, at five o'clock, staring at my closet and wondering what one wears to Sunday dinner at the home of one's non-boyfriend. I spent the afternoon alternately putting off the decision and coming up with self-inflicted injuries that might get me out of it.

Once I'd accepted my fate, I killed most of the day in the kitchen, baking and frosting a three-layer chocolate cake. My mom would have several choice words for me if I were to show up to dinner as a guest empty-handed, and desserts are about the only thing in my repertoire. I've avoided the inevitable as long as possible, but unless I'm planning to wear the towel I've got wrapped around myself, I need to pick something soon. I'm running out of time.

True to his word, Drew knocks on the door at exactly five forty-five. I'm kind of surprised that he didn't just beep the horn and expect me to come running. Okay, I'm really not. As much as it pains me to say so, he actually possesses surprisingly good manners. The better to get into girls' pants, I suppose. I won't give him too much credit.

I pick up the cake and hold it in front of my body as if it can actually shield me, preventing Drew from seeing what I'm wearing. It's a simple sleeveless shift dress with a very subtle scoop neck and a slight A-line skirt that hits just barely above my knee. It's the most conservative thing in my closet. My mother bought it for me before I left, along with a bunch of other dresses I never wore. I kept it because it was black, but that's about the only reason. I feel like I'm going on a job interview. I don't think I'll look even remotely right at a Sunday dinner, but I guess it's better than the stuff I wear to school.

He opens my car door and I slide in with the cake on my lap. "You didn't have to do that." Drew inclines his head toward the cake. I shrug. I didn't mind. I like excuses to bake and I don't get them very often these days, which means that I still bake, but I end up eating most of it myself. Sugar has a very special, oversized place on my food pyramid. "You'll get points with my mom, though. She's pregnant. Again," he adds pointedly. "And she loves chocolate."

We pull into Drew's driveway about ten minutes later. He lives in a development a few miles down the road from Margot's. He parks the car and kills the engine, but he doesn't move to get out. He looks uncomfortable, which makes me uncomfortable. I'm really hoping he doesn't hit on me in the car in front of his parents' house, because I'll have to get pissed and the cake will probably not survive. He turns to me and takes a breath. He's not smiling, and when he speaks, the tone of voice is completely different from what I'm used to with him. The cocky self-assuredness is gone and that makes me nervous. I'm accustomed to his brash overconfidence. I'm prepared for it and it puts us on even footing, like neither of us is real.

"I really am sorry." The sincerity in his words catches me off-guard. I would have been ready for a full-on assault of charm and creative come-ons, but I'm completely unprepared for the utterly guileless apology I'm getting. Maybe this is his new angle. He turns his eyes to the windshield, and I'm glad, because I'm more at ease with him not looking right at me. "You were okay with Bennett, you know. Josh is the best person I know. I wouldn't have left you anywhere else. I know it was shitty and I probably should have taken you home and taken care of you myself since it was kind of my fault in the first place. If there are two choices, I'm usually going to pick the wrong one, but I really didn't do it to be an asshole. Just comes naturally." He stops talking and is quiet for a minute before looking back at me again.

"We good?"

I tilt my head and study him. Are we? Yes, I think we are. As much as I'd like to question his motives, I also kind of want to believe he's not a completely awful person. Then at least I'll have an excuse for why I can't seem to dislike him.

"Good enough?" he tries.

I nod. *Yes, good enough.*

"Good enough," he repeats, without question this time, and the telltale flirt comes back into his voice. His posture loosens and he seems to relax. He's back in familiar territory. "Let's go inside before I give in to the fantasy I'm having of covering you in that cake and licking the frosting off."

I glare at him. I'm kind of glad to have this Drew back. I roll my eyes and shake my head. He shrugs, resigned.

"Sorry. Nature's a bitch. Can only fight it for so long." He comes around to open the car door and offers to take the cake for me, but I shake my head. I need to hold it. I cling to the cake like a lifeline as I walk up to the house, hoping my left hand doesn't choose now to stutter and make me drop it. A three-layer cake with scratch fudge frosting, adorned with piles of shaved curls of dark chocolate, was probably overkill, but I'm hoping it does its job and that they'll notice the cake instead of me.

We walk into a high-ceilinged foyer that opens up into an exquisitely furnished living room. It's pristine. I feel like I should take my shoes off so my heels don't tear into the carpet but that would probably be weird. Plus, as much as the shoes hurt my feet, they give me comfort. I used to perform in front of audiences, now I hide behind cake and high heels. Drew leads me back through a formal dining room. The table must seat at least ten people. It's already set with china and fabric napkins that are folded to look like swans. Drew must notice me gaping at it.

"Told you my mom likes to pretend we're civilized once a week." Civilized is one thing. This is something different entirely. "It's usually not this bad. I think she went a little overboard because I told her I was bringing you. Usually it's just us and Josh. And he doesn't count as company." What the crap? I'm not sure which part of that little explanation I'm supposed to panic about first: either the part where his mother appears to have prepared for the coming of the queen because of me, or the part where Josh Bennett is expected. Both are equally appalling but I think I'm giving the edge to Josh. As much as I fear the scrutiny of Drew's mother, it's a little worse to imagine eating a meal across the table from the boy who mopped up my vomit and watched me strip my bra off and throw it across the room. I spent most of the afternoon freaking out about what to wear and dreading having to face Drew's sister. The thought that Josh Bennett might be here never even entered my mind. I don't have any more time to get used to the idea because the doorbell rings, and then the door opens before anybody could possibly have gotten there. Josh isn't company here. Of course he doesn't wait to be let in.

Before I know what's happening, Drew's mother is coming toward me, taking the cake out of my hands. I want to hold onto it, keep it in front of me just a little longer, but it's not an option, so I relinquish it to her. My hands feel very empty.

"You must be Nastya!" Her smile comes from every part of her face. There isn't a question where Drew and Sarah came by their looks. Their mother is beautiful. I can't help glancing down at her stomach. She must not be very pregnant because I can't even tell. I wonder how old she is. She has to be at least forty, I imagine. It's weird to me why anyone would want another baby at that age, but I guess if you can, why not? She's shifting things in the refrigerator now to make room for the cake. I didn't ask her to, but I'm glad. The heat and humidity already started doing a number on the frosting on the way over here.

"Honey, it is so sweet of you to bring dessert. It's beautiful," she says, shutting the refrigerator door and turning toward me. She closes the gap between us a moment later, and before I can comprehend what she's doing, she hugs me. I don't do hugging. I don't like people touching me even when there's no threat involved. It's too intimate and it bothers me. She doesn't seem to notice how stiff my arms are at my sides, and she lets me go a second later when Drew starts talking.

"How come you call her *honey* and never use terms of endearment on me?" he fake whines.

"I do," Mrs. Leighton says, patting him on the cheek as she walks by. "Just last week I called you the bane of my existence."

"That's right," he says. "That was a good day."

It's hard not to want to smile watching them. It's hasn't been so long that I don't remember what it was like when my family was happy, too.

It's only seconds before Josh Bennett finds us. Judging by the look on his face, he didn't know I was going to be here any more than I was expecting him. I think he literally took a step back when he saw me.

Mrs. Leighton steps between us before excessive awkwardness sets in. She hugs him and he actually hugs her back. It looks wrong to me. I'm used to seeing Josh separated by a six-foot radius from all human contact, so to see him here, looking warm and alive and touchable with Drew's mom, takes me a minute to process. I hope my mouth isn't hanging open. I'm going to have ten miles' worth of thoughts to sort through when I run tonight. Not only do I have unexpectedly sincere Drew to process, but now I've got not-so-untouchable Josh Bennett as well.

Sarah's in the kitchen a moment later. She obviously knew I was coming because there's no surprise on her face. Only disdain.

"I guess you all already know each other," Mrs. Leighton says, saving us from friendly pretense. "Dinner will be ready in ten minutes. Sarah, you pour drinks. Drew, take Josh and check on your dad at the grill. Make sure he doesn't overcook the steaks again. Nastya, you can help me bring in the food from the kitchen." I nod, thankful that she's given me something to do so I don't have to stand around feeling not only out of place, but useless, as well. I follow her to the stove, and she hands me a couple of trivets to put out on the table. There's something at once comforting and unsettling about being asked to help. Like I'm not being treated like an outsider. This morning, my plans consisted of eating Fun Dip while watching misguided fame whores choke down buffalo testicles on old reruns of *Fear Factor*. Now I'm standing in black stiletto heels in the middle of a

Norman Rockwell painting. More thoughts to process for later. I should start writing a list so I won't forget anything.

Dinner is actually the most enjoyable thing I've done in months. For all the pomp and circumstance of the table, Drew's parents are completely down to earth. His father is self-deprecating and funny. His mother is sharp as a tack and doesn't take crap from any of them. Drew turned up the well-bred charm and turned down the suggestiveness as soon as we walked into the house. He sits next to me and Josh is on the other side of him, so I really can't even see Josh at all throughout the meal. I make a note to count that particular blessing tonight. Sarah is seated across from me so I can't avoid seeing her. She says nothing to me and remarkably little to everyone else, but with all the talking going on at the table, it seems to have gone unnoticed. I do catch her looking at me a lot, and I can't figure out if she's angry or uncomfortable. Maybe she's afraid it will come out how she's treated me at school and she doesn't want her parents to find out that she's such a stereotypical bitch. They must have some clue. I've seen the way she acts with Drew and she can't hide that all the time. Maybe sibling rivalry is acceptable here, but treating other people like garbage isn't.

Once dinner is finished and we've all helped clear the dishes, Mrs. Leighton brings the cake over to the table along with an apple pie. Sarah follows behind her with a stack of plates and forks and a container of vanilla ice cream and helps her serve it.

"This is delicious, Nastya. Where did you order it from? I need dessert for a dinner party in a couple of weeks and I'd love to bring one of these."

I shake my head and point to myself.

"You?" She doesn't sound shocked so much as intrigued. I nod. "From scratch?" I nod again. I only bake from scratch. I don't have anything against mixes, they just seem like cheating, and I don't feel like I can take credit for them. It's just a cake. It's not music, but it's something.

"I can't bake at all," she says. I'm sure she could. It's not that hard; you just need to know the ratios, and once you get those down you can play with it. It mostly comes down to math and science, which is funny, because I suck at math and science. "Josh knows someone who can bake. Don't you?" She looks over at him and I get the feeling the question isn't entirely innocent. I look down and push the cake around my plate into a pool of melting ice cream.

"Just someone from school." He sounds as uncomfortable as I feel. I mentally will everyone to drop it, and I think Josh may be doing the exact same thing. I really don't want him to explain the circumstances surrounding how those cookies ended up on his porch. He obviously didn't have any trouble figuring out they were from me, which means he knew exactly why they were there.

"Who?" Drew asks around a mouthful of chocolate cake. Interesting, though not entirely surprising. He didn't tell Drew. I wonder how his mom knows. Josh is waiting just a little too long to answer, and I see Mrs. Leighton's gaze flick from him to me. She seems satisfied. She got her answer.

"Drew, talk with your mouth full again and you'll be serving at my next book club meeting." She points her fork in his direction and his mouth clamps shut. Obviously this is a threat of monumental proportions. He holds his hands up in surrender to his mother.

Once we finish cleaning up the dessert dishes, Mrs. Leighton makes coffee and we all sit on the oversized white couches in the living room. I decline the coffee. I don't drink it, because no matter how much sugar I put into it, it still tastes like ass-water to me. Maybe it's just because my taste buds are so desensitized to sweet that anything not comprised of at least ninety percent sugar tastes wrong. Even if I was addicted to caffeine, in a dystopian future where coffee was an illegal controlled substance and I hadn't gotten my hands on any in three days, I still would have refused it. I never would have overcome my horror if my hand decided to lose its grip while holding a full cup of coffee on one of those white brocade sofas. Sarah doesn't drink any, either, so I guess it doesn't seem strange. Josh drinks three cups of it, not that I'm counting.

I listen to everyone talk until the conversation dwindles and the coffee pot is empty. The phone rings, giving Sarah an escape she must have been desperate for, judging by how fast she jumps off the couch at the sound. Drew walks over to his mother and takes her empty cup. Josh takes Mr. Leighton's and follows Drew back to the kitchen. I don't have a coffee cup to use as an excuse to bolt, so I sit in awkward silence, hoping they don't stay in the kitchen too long. I study the coffee table, not really wanting to make eye contact with either of Drew's parents. It looks familiar to me. I tilt my head to study the legs and I realize that it's almost identical in style to the one I had seen in Josh's living room on the morning we shall not mention. The similarities in the design are clear, but this table is obviously newer. The surface of the wood and the finish are flawless. I don't even realize that I'm leaning over and running my fingers along the curved wood of the table leg when Drew's father speaks.

"Beautiful, isn't it? Josh made it." He's staring, with pride, at the table, and thankfully not at my face. My hand stops moving, but I don't look away from the table. I pull my arm in and settle back onto the sofa in time to see Josh standing in the doorway from the kitchen, watching us. Mr. Leighton looks up. "What was it, Josh? A Christmas gift?"

"Mrs. Leighton's birthday." Josh's hands are shoved in his pockets and he's looking past us at the table. He doesn't step any further into the room until Drew comes in behind him, forcing him to move.

"Your big-ass truck is blocking me in," he says, slapping Josh on the back. "Sorry, Mom." He turns, looking halfway contrite about his language. I've heard a lot worse than that out of his mouth. I wonder if he thinks his mother is even remotely fooled, because I'm betting she knows his act pretty well.

"Book club," she taunts, holding up her hand as if balancing a tray.

"Noted," he responds, shifting his attention back to Josh. "Can you please move your truck so I can take Nastya home?" he begs with sarcasm.

"Didn't you say she lives in Josh's neighborhood?" Mrs. Leighton asks. I think I actually hear her loading the bullets into that question.

Oh no. No, no, no, no, no, no, no. Please no.

"Josh, can you drop her off? It's silly for you both to go in the same direction when Josh is going there anyway." She seems to look at all of us at once. How does she do that? We aren't even standing next to one other. It's more than unnerving.

Between Josh and me, I don't know which one of us looks the most horrified. We're both on equal ground with this one. Josh nods in resignation, and I try to look like I think this is a good plan. A good, logical, practical, not-at-all-awkward plan.

Drew and his parents walk us out to the driveway. Sarah never reemerged after the phone call, which is fine with me. Josh unlocks the car with his remote and Drew opens the door for me, while I try to figure out how high I have to hike my dress up to step into the truck without tearing it. I really don't want to end the evening by flashing my pink heart polka dot underwear at Drew's dad. Once I manage to get in, Drew's mom comes over to the passenger side. Thankfully I'm already up and seated so I don't have to worry about being hugged again, but what comes next is almost worse.

"Thank you for coming. It was so nice to meet you. We'll see you next Sunday at six?" It's a question without much question involved. She tilts her head sideways to look past me at Josh. "You can pick her up on your way, right?" She did it again. She's good. I try to shake my head. I could write a note for this. This would be noteworthy. I look around frantically for a piece of paper, but the truck is as barren as it was the first time I rode in it. Nothing. At this point I'm hoping Josh might save me, save us both. Maybe he has plans and will have to decline and I can nod in unison. No such luck.

"No problem. Thanks for dinner, Mrs. Leighton, Mr. Leighton." He nods at Drew's father.

"One day we'll get you to call us Jack and Lexie," he laughs, shaking his head as if he knows this will never happen. "Maybe when you're thirty."

"Good night, Mr. Leighton," Josh responds.

Drew waves from the front porch, already on his cell phone, as Josh backs the truck down the long driveway. Ten minutes in a car with Josh Bennett feels much longer than ten minutes in a car with Drew. Drew fills all the silence without ever realizing that he's doing it. Josh melts into the silence like he's part of it. He doesn't say a word on the way home until he pulls into Margot's driveway for the third time now.

"You can get out of it if you want, you know. But you should go. She likes you."

I nod and open the door to the truck. I can't step down and reach the ground, and trying to jump in these shoes, no matter how short the distance, is not going to end with my ankles intact. I bend over and slide my left shoe off, followed by my right, and hop out onto the driveway, turning to shut the door.

"You're going to need better shoes if you want to get near the tools. Mr. Turner will never let you in the construction area in those things." He shakes his head as if he can't believe he's telling me this. I think it might physically hurt him to talk to me. I don't know what the right response to that is. I don't think Mr. Turner is planning to let me near the tools no matter what shoes I'm wearing. I nod again and close the door.

It's almost ten at this point. Normally I would be throwing on sneakers and running clothes right about now. I'm torn in half between needing to run and knowing it can't serve its whole purpose tonight. For the first time in two weeks, I'm not really sure I want to run. I think better when I'm moving and I have plenty to think about tonight, but that's the problem. I don't have a treadmill to run on here so I have to go out, but when I'm running outside I have to fragment my mind. I have to keep part of it constantly, acutely aware of every sound, every echo, every movement going on around me. It makes it hard to figure out the things I need to figure out. It's the same way I have to split my focus every time I'm around other people so I don't accidentally respond to something or someone. It's natural to want to talk and I have to remain constantly on alert so that I don't slip. I thought it would get easier. It should have been harder when I first stopped. But it's the opposite. When I first stopped I had absolutely nothing I wanted to say. I wasn't tempted at all. Now, more and more, I find things I'm desperate to say. They constantly bombard my mind and I have to choke them back. It's exhausting.

I decide against braving the assault on my senses and I stay in. This whole night has been draining enough.

Chapter 15

Josh

"Party at Kara's Friday night. You in?"

I look at Drew as if this is a rhetorical question. It should be.

"At some point I'll get you to come with me." *No, you won't.* "Fine. I have a backup plan. And there she is." I look up to see Nastya coming down the hall toward us. She's still wearing those shoes. We'll be starting actual construction soon, and it's true what I told her. Mr. Turner won't let her near the workshop unless she's got on decent shoes that will protect her feet. She obviously doesn't care.

"Shouldn't I have been the backup plan?"

"You probably shouldn't be any plan, but I'll break you eventually."

"You get her wasted again, she can throw up on your couch."

"Are you never going to get over that?"

"No." It's true. I think the things I saw that night will haunt me forever.

"Hey, Nastypants!" Drew picks up his pace and breaks away from me to reach Nastya just before she gets to the shop door. I half-expect the look she impales him with to kill him on contact. "What?" I hear him cajole her as I get closer. "It's a term of endearment." If this is his new tactic, I'm afraid for him. Before I can worry too much for his safety, her face subtly changes. I think she's fighting it, but she loses, because she actually half smiles at him. Maybe it's not even a smile. Her lips just barely turn up at the corners, but on her face it stands out because of the rarity of it. I'd be disappointed that his crap is actually working on her but I don't think it is. I think she's amused. The smile is gone in seconds, and she walks into the room, leaving Drew in the hall just as I catch up. He didn't even ask her about the party.

"That worked out well for you."

"She didn't hurt me." He smiles, seemingly satisfied with the outcome.

"She should." Tierney Lowell is closing her locker across the hall and turning towards us. Really she's turning towards Drew. I don't know that she sees me at all. Her jeans are so tight that I wonder if they're cutting off her circulation, and she's wearing a black bra under a white T-shirt that rides up above the waist to show just enough of her skin to tease. She's got the body to pull it off and she isn't shy about it. The two of them hooked up some time last year, and the aftermath wasn't particularly pretty. Tierney didn't take too well to being discarded. That didn't surprise me. What surprised me was the fact that it had happened in the first place. She's hard-core and he's Drew. It never added up to me. Drew didn't even tell me that it had happened until after it got out, and by that time it was done. Drew was moving on to another girl; Tierney was pissed and people were talking about how clueless she was for being surprised. I don't think she ever seemed surprised, just disappointed.

Drew doesn't respond to her and she walks away without another word.

"That one was a mistake from the beginning," he says. Most of them are mistakes if you ask me. The constant drama doesn't seem worth the trouble. I head in to Shop and Drew takes off toward the office, where he gets to spend the next period running passes around the school, flirting in the halls, and generally avoiding any responsibility whatsoever.

Nastya is sitting next to Kevin Leonard at the table Mr. Turner moved her to a week ago. I'm glad she stayed there because it made me nervous having her behind me all the time. I like being able to watch everyone else without them watching me. Most people know better than to look at me anyway, but Nastya hasn't been most people since the day she got here.

When the bell rings, Mr. Turner does a visual roll check. Then he tells one person from each table to go up to the front and pick up a materials box. I'm the only one at my table so I head up. All of the other tables have two people, except for Nastya's, where there are three: Nastya, Kevin, and Chris Jenkins. She doesn't move to get up, and Chris goes to get the box. Inside are several pieces of wood, a hammer, different size nails, sandpaper and a few other items that seem to vary in each box. Kevin grabs the box out of Chris's hands and turns it over on the table. The box of nails opens when it hits the surface and they go rolling in every direction. This gets everyone's attention but no one moves to pick them up.

"Clean it up, Leonard," Mr. Turner calls over to him, not seeming the least bit surprised with his idiocy. I know why Mr. Turner signed him in to this class. As much as I'd like to ignore the fact, Kevin's pretty good when it comes to building. He doesn't have much of a sense of artistry or style, but he has an innate understanding of construction and balance. Too bad he's such an asshole.

Nastya is kneeling down on the floor, picking up nails and loading them up in her left hand. Chris is gathering up the ones on the table and sweeping them back into the container. Kevin is laughing. Nastya has most of the nails off the floor and her hand is close to full. I think she's about to stand back up and then the nails are all over the floor again. I'm not even sure what happened. It's like she just let go of them. She doesn't even seem surprised. She just starts picking them up again. I think I'm the only one who noticed. Nobody helps her. Not even me.

Mr. Turner goes on to explain the assignment. We'll have today, plus the next three periods, to design, plan, and construct something that's either useful or aesthetically pleasing with whatever materials we find in the box we picked up. We're allowed to add up to two additional items of our choosing but nothing else. I've already studied what's in mine and I know what I'm going to build. I spend the rest of the period measuring, sketching, and planning while everyone else sits around arguing about whose idea is better and what they should make. Tomorrow I'll start construction. The rest of them will probably still be fighting.

—

I've spent the past hour going through every drawer of every tool cabinet in my garage and I still can't figure out where I put my stud finder. I slam the bottom drawer on the last cabinet shut and look at the clock on the wall. Ten thirty. Too late to go buy another one, not that I really need it tonight, but I have nothing else on my plate right now and it's something to do.

I stand back up and turn around, looking for something to occupy my time, and she's standing at the top of my driveway, just outside the threshold of my garage. I'm glad I don't gasp or anything equally pathetic because if I did, I'd probably have to cut off my balls and hand them to her. I wouldn't deserve them anymore.

She looks almost exactly the same as the first time she showed up here, except she's not lost or scared. She came here on purpose. We look at each other for a minute and I realize that I'm waiting for her to say something, which obviously isn't going to happen. I'm not sure what I'm supposed to say to her, so in a bold and unprecedented move, I do nothing. I turn around and continue looking for the stud finder I know isn't here. I pretend not to care what she's doing, but I'm hyperaware of every breath she takes. I can tell the second she decides to stop standing there. Only she doesn't turn and leave like I expect her to; she steps into the garage.

I can't pretend I'm not noticing her now. I watch to see what she's going to do. She's looking around again, like she did the night she showed up all sweaty and lost and amazing. She's not looking at me at the moment; she's much more interested in the surroundings. It's just a garage with a lot of wood and tools. I don't know what's so mesmerizing about it but I'm not arguing, because while she's preoccupied with studying the room, I can study her. The makeup is gone again tonight and her hair is up, so I can see her face. Even when she went to dinner at Drew's house, she still had all of the makeup on: black eyeliner, dark red lips, the works. It's horrible and it makes no sense when you see what's underneath it.

She's not as drenched or out of breath as before, but she still must have been running. I wonder if she runs every night. Her legs are all muscle, just like her arms. It still doesn't look right with her face. Her face reminds me of the porcelain dolls that are still lining the shelves in my sister's room. Childlike. Smooth and hard and flawless and fragile.

She walks around, running her hands along the counters, stopping at the vise attached to the end of one of the workbenches. She turns it a few times, watching it close, before sliding her hand in between the plates and continuing to tighten it. I can't even move because I'm wondering what's going on, but the more it turns, the tighter the hold gets on her hand, and I don't know how much longer I can ignore it before I have to jump up and ask her if she's batshit crazy. I get the feeling I'm actually standing in my garage, watching this girl decide whether or not to crush her hand. She stops just shy of that point and loosens the vise just enough to where it releases her hand, and then she continues her surveying of the room.

My eyes shift away before she sees me looking, and I start rifling through the same drawers I've already searched twice tonight before I start working my way around the counters. The workbench my father and I built together years ago lines the perimeter of the garage. According to Mark Bennett, you could never have enough work surfaces. The more the better. So we built in as much as the garage could handle. I think maybe it was just something to do.

I hear her move while my back is to her, and when I turn around she's sitting on the workbench on the other side of the garage. She's just planted herself there and made herself comfortable. *Okay.* It's kind of freaking me out to have her sitting in my garage, watching me. Because that's what she's doing now. She's watching me and she's not even bothering to try and conceal the fact that she's doing it. I kind of want to scream at her to get the hell out, but I also kind of want her to stay. Which makes me the dumbass I am.

I eventually sit down and work on checking cut lines on some beams I need for a job I have and then planing them. It's quiet work so I can do it at night, plus I have to stay busy, or I'm going to end up in a staring contest with this girl in a lame attempt to read her mind or something. At midnight she jumps off the counter and heads back down the driveway without a word or any sort of acknowledgment, just the way she came.

—

I don't pay much attention in my first three classes and no one notices. At lunch I watch for her, wondering if she'll look at me.

I never do see her cross the courtyard, but when I get up to head in to the shop wing just before the bell, she's leaning against the wall with Clay Whitaker. I walk in the other direction.

I pick up the material box from Monday's class, bring it to my table, and pull out my plans. She walks in and heads to the back counter behind my table to retrieve the box she's working out of with Kevin and Chris, neither of whom has shown up yet.

"Good morning, Sunshine." I don't even bother to think before the words leave my mouth, but at least I don't say it loud enough for anyone but her to hear. I probably shouldn't have done it, shouldn't have reacted to last night at all, but I couldn't help it. I feel like she was messing with me last night and I want to mess with her back. I don't like her thinking she can just show up at my house to play a game of mystery mindfuck whenever she pleases.

She's behind me, but I can almost feel her stiffen at the words. Good. Maybe if she doesn't want to be reminded of the night she coughed up her intestines in my bathroom, she'll think twice about coming back to my house again like she belongs there. I wonder what it will take for her to pick up on the fact that she lives in the same world as everybody else, and in that world, people leave me the fuck alone.

She recovers quickly enough and goes back to her table without looking back at me. Kevin and Chris show up a minute later and the bell rings. Mr. Turner sets us all to work and the room gets loud almost immediately. It's amazing the amount of noise fourteen students can produce when coupled with the sound of sawing and hammering.

Halfway through the class, Nastya hasn't moved from her seat, but she can't feign disinterest. She's been watching everything Chris and Kevin are doing. At one point, she reaches out and slides the scale drawing Chris had done over in front of her, studying it for a few minutes before pushing it back toward them. They don't say anything to her, but I do notice Kevin look down her shirt when she leans over, and I want to punch him in the face.

Kevin gets out of his seat a few minutes later and goes over to Mr. Turner's desk. Mr. Turner scribbles something on a pass and hands it to him, and Kevin walks out of the room, leaving Chris with Nastya. It's obvious Chris needs another set of hands, and he keeps glancing up at her as if he's not sure he can ask her to help. Finally, frustration gets the better of him and I hear him ask her to hold the pieces he's working on in place so he can nail them together. He shows her where to put her hands and she nods, placing them on either side, the way he demonstrates to her. Once he gets them in position, they move on to the next set. It looks like he has four identical pieces he's putting together the same way. I scan over what they've done so far. I can't see what's on the drawing and I'm trying to figure out what they're making. It looks cool.

At that moment, Kevin walks back in, crumpling up the hall pass and tossing it into the trash can in the corner.

"Better not have been slacking while I was gone," he says, not even bothering to look at Chris before he slaps him on the back. I wish I could say that what happens next takes place in slow motion, like when something catastrophic happens in a movie, where it all slows down so you can see exactly what happened and how. Nothing slows down, but I see it anyway. Kevin's hand hits Chris's back. Chris was already midmovement with the hammer and the momentum he's already got going, coupled with the slap on his back, sends the hammer down even harder. Just not where it's supposed to go. The hammer hits the ring finger on Nastya's left hand, which had been splayed flat against the table with her thumb bracketing the wood in place.

I'm focused on her face. I catch her eyes widen almost imperceptibly with the initial shock of pain before they narrow again. Water slips into her eyes and they turn glassy with tears that don't escape. How the hell is she not crying? I saw how hard that hammer hit her. I heard how hard that hammer hit her. I think even I might have cried. I would have felt stupid after, but it probably would have happened anyway. It had to hurt that much. She doesn't even move. Neither do Chris or Kevin. They're just staring at her, her hand still on the table. *Get the girl some fucking ice.* Chris looks horrified. Kevin looks like he has no idea what just happened. She moves now to look down at her hand but she keeps it in place, staring at it. I'm really hoping someone gets up and gets her some ice soon or I'm going to have to go do it. I should have done it already, but for some reason I'm frozen here, too. I can't stop watching her. Why won't she cry? Chris finally seems to break out of his trance and runs to the freezer that's kept in the shop area solely for the purpose of having ice on hand. Mr. Turner is already over at the table checking her fingers. I watch her just barely flinch as he checks for movement, but otherwise her face is like stone. Or maybe porcelain.

Chris comes back with an ice pack and offers it to her. She looks surprised and almost like she's about to refuse it. It reminds me of the vise again, and I wonder if she's insane. Then I watch her mind change and she accepts it without any acknowledgment or thanks. I'm glad she doesn't thank him. He looks guilty as hell. Looking at his face, you'd think he's in more pain than she is, but he still hasn't apologized. Kevin is the one who should be begging for forgiveness, but I won't hold my breath for that one. Mr. Turner comes back from his desk with a clinic pass and sends Valerie Estes, the only other girl here, with Nastya, to hold her books.

It couldn't have been more than a matter of seconds that passed between the hammer coming down on her fingers and when Chris brought her the ice, but it felt longer. Maybe time does slow down. It's not until she's left the room and everything has calmed back down that I replay the whole scene in my head. It's then that I realize that even when the hammer came down, even when the full force of the blow landed on her fingers and the pain had to be excruciating, she never made a sound.

You've got to be shitting me.

That's my initial thought as I watch her walk back into my garage for the second night in a row. My eyes go to her hand immediately and I see that two of her fingers are splinted together. She doesn't hesitate tonight. I initially think she's going to perch herself back up on the counter where she sat last night. For a minute it looks like she thinks so, too. Then she sinks down, cross-legged, onto the floor and leans her back against the cabinets behind her. She doesn't seem to mind the layer of sawdust carpeting the ground, but I still wonder why she'd choose to sit there. It's not like the counter is particularly clean, but it's not as bad as the floor out here. Then I realize that she probably couldn't push herself up onto the counter with one hand.

I go back to what I was doing before and we remain like this, in silence, for at least half an hour. Me working, her watching.

"Didn't it hurt?" I finally ask, because I want to know, even though she won't respond. She turns her hand over in front of her as if she's trying to decide if it hurt or not. She shrugs. Good answer. What did I expect? I wait a few more minutes, trying to concentrate on recalibrating my table saw, and then I ask the real question.

"What do you want?" It comes out nastier than I mean it to, but it's probably for the best. Nothing. It's driving me insane, wondering what it is that possesses her to keep coming here. It's not like I'm particularly friendly. Maybe tonight she'll get the hint and she won't come back. I try to convince myself that I'm relieved by that possibility, but I'm not convinced. I shove the thought aside and try to focus on the saw.

The silence persists. I don't know how long she plans to stay, hovering, watching. It's like having a ghost in my garage. I feel like I'm being haunted. With all of the dead people I've got in my corner, you'd think one of them would be the one hanging around. In fact, I used to hope for that. Being haunted seemed like a gift. I prayed for it. My mother, my sister, my father, my grandmother. After every one of them died I would hope that they'd come back, even once, and let me see them again. Give me a sign. Let me know that there was something else and it was good and they were good, but none of them ever came back for me. My grandfather assured me before he left that there was an afterlife, one he'd seen if only briefly, a long time ago. I listened but I didn't believe him. It was a story born of disease and painkillers, not memories and truth. He'll be dead any day now and I won't be waiting for a sign. I'll just be relieved that I have no one left to lose.

At ten thirty the ghost girl gets up and brushes the sawdust off her pants with her good hand and then she's gone again.

Chapter 16

Nastya

Josh shows up at five forty-five on Sunday, right on schedule. I run to the refrigerator as he pulls into the driveway. I made tiramisu for dessert since everybody seems to like coffee, except for Sarah, and I couldn't care less about her. My fingers are still splinted, so I've got to get the dish out with one hand, which is proving difficult. Margot put it in the fridge for me this morning, but she left for work early so I'm on my own. It's awkward, but I manage to stretch my hand over the edge and get a good enough grip on it. The doorbell rings just as I get there, but now I have the dish in my right hand and can't grab the doorknob with my left, so I'm just standing there for a minute, holding the tiramisu and looking at the door. Finally I have to put the dish on the floor so I can use my right hand to turn the knob.

Josh is standing on the porch, hands in his pockets, looking as if he's picking me up for a date. His hair, as usual, hangs over his forehead, just a little longer than it needs to be. Like a kid who doesn't have a mother nagging him to get it cut. I hate to admit how well he cleans up, dressed in a burgundy polo shirt and khaki dress pants, not that I mind the worn-out jeans he's usually in. I'm still surprised to see that he's not wearing work boots. I was beginning to think they were physically attached to him.

We're going to have to hurry to beat the rain. I can see the storm forming in the sky behind him. I've been in the kitchen all day so I hadn't noticed. Usually I like to sit at the front window and watch the clouds roll in and the sky turn because it happens so quickly here that you can see it change in a matter of minutes.

Today I was too busy making tiramisu, kicking myself for not going to the mall to buy a new dress, and ultimately trying to think of a brilliant plan to get out of this dinner. Dysentery was topping my excuse list today. It would have been far easier if Drew's parents had looked down their noses at me and the whole affair last week had been uncomfortable and forced, but they didn't and it wasn't. I won't ever fit in there the way they're pretending I do. I'm not even sure why she invited me back. The only thing I contributed to the evening was cake. Though, according to Drew, one could never underestimate the power of cake to his mother. I imagine they're accepting me for Drew's sake. And if that's the case, they probably don't expect me to be around for long. I wonder how many girls have passed through the Leighton Sunday Dinner, one time, never to be seen again.

I ended up not bothering with the pretense of a nice, conservative, innocent dress. I figured the sooner we got to the truth of it, the sooner we could cut our losses and walk. I'm wearing a low-cut black halter top and a black miniskirt—emphasis on the mini—paired with knee-high, spike-heeled leather boots. If I looked out of place last Sunday, it will be nothing compared to this. After tonight, things can go back to normal. Drew can find himself a nice girl who will have uncommitted sex with him and I can go back to a comfortable, expectation-free existence.

Josh studies me for a minute, taking in my appearance as if he's looking for an answer to an unspoken question. His greeting consists of one word: "Sunshine." Mine consists of no words.

I kneel down to retrieve the tiramisu from the foyer floor but I can't get my fingers under it for leverage. I find myself silently cursing hammers and clueless boys. I'm about to try to use the palm of my left hand to push it into my right when Josh steps inside and kneels down, far too close to me, and picks it up. He doesn't smell like sawdust and there's nothing right about that. No matter how good he looks right now, Josh Bennett without work boots and the smell of sawdust is all sorts of wrong.

We pull into the driveway at the Leighton house and have just enough time to jump out and run as the sky opens up. I wrap my arm around the dish and reinforce it against my chest. Somehow both the tiramisu and my ankles survive the jump intact. When I hit the ground, Josh is next to me and he takes the dish out of my hands and runs to the shelter of the porch overhang. We manage to make it without getting completely drenched. Before he opens the door, he hands me back the tiramisu and then reaches up and frames my face with his hands, gently running his thumbs across the skin below both of my eyes. I think my mouth might be hanging open because I have no idea what the hell he's doing.

"Black shit," he says, by way of explanation, and I realize that my eye makeup must be running. Then he opens the door for me without another word.

When we get inside, everything happens almost precisely as it did the week before. The table isn't set quite as fancy, which I'm happy about, because it means I'm not such a novelty this week. But then I have to face that, if I'm not a novelty, it means I have a place here and I don't want that at all.

We walk into the kitchen, past the dining room, where I notice there's an extra place setting at the table, and I wonder who else is coming. Drew is fighting with the stereo because apparently it's his turn to pick the dinner music tonight, and I can't imagine what that's going to be.

When I walk into the kitchen I brace myself for the repulsed look I know I'll get once Mrs. Leighton sees my clothes, but it never comes. She simply smiles and proceeds to rearrange the refrigerator to make room for the dish while telling me that I didn't have to go to the trouble. I have a monstrous case of déjà vu, and I know that in a minute I'm getting hugged whether I like it or not.

Sitting on two bar stools at the granite breakfast bar off the kitchen are Sarah and a girl I recognize from school. I'm pretty sure she's the one who accused me of being sired by Dracula. They're laughing and attempting to knot their hair together. It's the height of immature teenage girlishness. I want to mock them for it, but I'm appalled by the fact that it makes me sad.

For a moment I feel like a survivor in some postapocalyptic world, looking through a window, imagining a part of my life that's gone now. I wonder what it would be like to have even one girlfriend. I used to have a couple, but they weren't like this either. They were single-mindedly music-obsessed like I was. It was our link. Other girls compared nail polish colors and crushes; we compared audition pieces. Our friendships with each other never came first because music was always more important. Take the music out of the equation, and I don't know if I had anything in common with them at all. Even if I did, I still would have cut them off afterward. It hurt too much to be around them.

My friend Lily continued calling me for months, but the only things she ever had to talk about were auditions and recitals and practice. I tried to be happy for her, but I wasn't. I was jealous and pissed. It was like watching my best friend blissfully dating my ex-boyfriend who I was still madly in love with, watching her have everything I loved but couldn't have anymore. In other words, painful, depressing, and unhealthy. And I'm nothing if not healthy.

Even if I was talking—because let's face it, the silent thing is definitely a barrier in terms of making friends—I probably still wouldn't have any. I lost almost the entirety of my sixteenth year. While other girls my age were thinking about homecoming dances, driving lessons, and losing their virginity, I was thinking about physical therapy, police lineups, and psychiatric counseling. I left the house to go to doctors' offices, not football games. I interviewed with police detectives, not the manager at Old Navy.

Eventually, my body healed as much as it was going to. My mind started getting put back together, too. I think it's just that the pieces got put back a little out of order. It seems like the more my body healed, the more fractured my mind became, and there aren't enough wires and screws to fix the breaks in it.

So I didn't do the normal stuff I was supposed to be doing at fifteen and sixteen. At the age when most kids are trying to figure out *who* they are, I was busy trying to figure out *why* I was. I didn't belong in this world anymore. It's not that I wanted to be dead, I just felt like I should be. Which is why it's hard when everyone expects you to be grateful simply because you're not.

It left me lots of time to think, lots of time to get angry and feel sorry for myself. To ask, *Why me?* To ask, *Why?* period. I have a black belt in self-pity. I was an expert in the field. Still am. It's a skill you never forget. Needless to say, all the thinking and all the questions didn't accomplish much. That's when I started focusing on the anger. I stopped worrying about being polite, about hurting people's feelings and saying what I was supposed to say, healing the way I was supposed to heal so that everyone could believe I was okay again and move on with their lives. My parents needed to believe I was okay, so for a long time I tried to convince them that I was. I tried to convince myself, too, but I was a much tougher sell because I knew the truth. I was so very not okay. I realized that I was going to feel shitty either way. I was probably going to feel shitty for the rest of my life, a life I should not even still be living. A life that should have let me go. So I got angry. Then I got very angry. Then I got angrier still. But you can only go so long being angry before you learn to hate. I stopped feeling so sorry for myself and started hating instead. Whining was pathetic, but hate got things done. Hate strengthened my body and shaped my resolve and what I resolved to do was to get revenge. Hate seemed pretty damn healthy to me.

Nonetheless, I've learned that although hatred is good for some things, it won't make you a lot of friends. I turn away from Sarah and the girl who has since been introduced as Piper. *Piper.* I roll it around in my head. It's a pointless name, a meaningless name (unless you count pipe player as a meaning, and that thought makes me laugh, because well, you know, *pipe player*), a name for someone like her. As I walk toward the dining room, I'm not at all confused as to why I have no friends.

Despite the presence of Sarah and Piper, dinner is fun again. We—okay, *they*—talk about college applications, building the homecoming float, drama auditions, and how drastically the tax laws are changing. That last one is courtesy of Mr. Leighton, who is a CPA. I kind of tune out at that point because the intricacies of tax law are a little outside my sphere of comprehension, but then the conversation starts turning toward debate.

"We've got a tournament two Saturdays from now," Drew tells his parents.

"What are you arguing?" his dad asks, refilling his wineglass. Mrs. Leighton stares at it like she'd like to rip it out of his hand, but I guess she's not allowed. Pregnancy must put a crimp in the whole wine-drinking thing. I can't blame her, though. I'd kind of like to rip it out of his hand, too.

"I'm not sure exactly. Something centering on the importance of the conservation of fabric." He looks in my direction, focusing on my clothes, or lack thereof, while he bullshits them.

"Mr. Trent assigned Nastya to help me with the research, so I wanted to pick something she was passionate about."

At that point Sarah chokes on whatever she has in her mouth. Mr. Leighton continues swirling his wine around in his glass as if he's actually giving credence to what Drew said and considering the relevant arguments on the topic. Piper doesn't even seem to have gotten the joke. I watch Josh's jaw twitch out of the corner of my eye, the only sign at all that he's sitting at the same table with the rest of us, listening to this conversation. I'm still watching him struggle to remain stoic and unaffected when I hear the sound of Mrs. Leighton's shoe connecting with Drew's shin.

Chapter 17

Josh

My father started teaching me how to build after my mother and sister died when I was eight. I don't know if he necessarily wanted to, or if he had no choice because I just kept following him. He was holed up in the garage all the time, and if I wanted to see him I had to come out here. He never really talked, but I took what I could get. In the beginning, I mostly watched him. I picked up on a lot just by paying attention, but once I got the tools in my hands, I realized how little I knew. The first thing I built was a lopsided birdfeeder. I ended up making four of them before I got it right. I've been at this for almost ten years and some days I still feel like I don't know shit.

I wonder how much Nastya picks up on. She watches everything that goes on in shop, though she hasn't touched so much as a nail since the hammer incident. She's been watching me here at night for the past two weeks. I haven't been successful in getting her to leave, so I've given up. Last night I tried being outright rude. I figured if telling her to get the fuck out didn't do the trick, nothing would, so that's what I told her. She didn't get the fuck out, at least not until she felt like it an hour later.

She's sitting in her normal spot on the counter again, watching me right now, so I guess that's my answer. Her legs are ceaselessly swinging back and forth, taunting me as if to say, *Ha, ha, we're here and you can't make us leave, so suck it.* I think they're using a mocking, singsong, playground voice when they do it. I want to tell them to shut up. I'm pulling the battery off my drill and putting it on the charger and trying to figure—

"Why do you have so many saws?"

You would think I would spin around at this moment in some sort of shocked frenzy, but it's almost like I've been expecting her to talk to me since the day we met and I've just been wondering what she was going to say. I can tell you that I've run through more than a couple of scenarios in my mind, and in not one of them did she ask me about the number of saws I own. I do turn around because I need to see her right now, but it's a lot slower and more controlled than even I planned.

"They're all designed for different purposes, for different jobs, for different kinds of wood. It's complicated. It would take me hours to go through them all." Okay, it's not really complicated. It would just take a very lengthy, tedious, boring explanation, and right now I don't want to think about saws. I can't believe this is what we're talking about. The word *surreal* does not suffice.

"I don't think I want anything, but I'll leave if you want me to." It takes me a minute to switch gears and realize that she's answering the question that I asked her more than a week ago. Is she calling my bluff? I look around the floor for the gauntlet she's thrown down because she's obviously waiting to see if I'll pick it up. I have to decide if I really do want her gone, because if I tell her to leave this time, I have no doubt that she'll take my word for it.

I should say yes. Hell, yes. I've been trying to get rid of you since you showed up, but that's a lie and we both know it. I'm not ready to give her an answer yet, so I answer her with another question. She's talking; I want to keep it that way. Part of me knows that there's a very real possibility that when she walks out of here tonight, she may not come back no matter what I tell her and I may never hear her speak again. It hits me, once more, just how much she reminds me of a ghost and how at any moment she might just fade away.

"Who else knows you talk?" I ask, and not just to keep her talking, but because I really do want to know. Does Drew know and he hasn't told me? Does she talk to her family? Drew said she lived with an aunt—actually he said a hot aunt—but that's all I really know.

"No one."

"Did you ever talk? Before now?"

"Yes."

"Are you going to tell me why you've taken this vow of silence?"

"No," she says, looking right into my eyes. Neither of us will break eye contact. "And you're never going to ask. Ever."

"Okay. I'm never going to ask. Check," I say matter-of-factly. "And why have I agreed to this?"

"You haven't."

"And why should I?"

"I don't know that you should."

"So I haven't agreed to keep your secret and you can't give me any reason why I should. You're not really making a strong case for yourself. What makes you think I won't tell anyone?"

"I don't think you want to." And this is where she wins even if she doesn't know it yet. She's right. I don't want to tell anyone. I want her secret all to myself, but she has no way of knowing that.

"That's a big gamble on your part."

"Is it?" She cocks her head to the side and studies me.

"You have no reason to trust me."

"No, but I trust you anyway," she says, walking out toward the driveway.

"And I'm supposed to trust you?" I say to her back. This girl really is crazy if she thinks she's walking in here, out of nowhere, and expecting me to do that.

She stops, turning to level her eyes at me before she goes.

"You don't have to trust me. I don't have any of your secrets."

She leaves before I can respond. She barely even sat down, but in the few minutes that she was here, everything shifted. Maybe she's giving me time to decide if I want this, whatever this is. Her secret? Her friendship? Her story? Maybe I don't want it. I do know that I *shouldn't* want it, and that may make my decision right there.

I know something about her that no one else does. I haven't had a secret in years. Everybody knows my story. Mother and sister killed in a car accident. *Tragic.* Father has a heart attack. *Dies.* Grandmother fights ovarian cancer. *Loses.* A year later grandfather picks up the cancer baton. I don't know if I'm supposed to die now, too, or if I'm just supposed to be the last one left.

Some days, I can't help wondering if my name will ever mean anything else.

I won't tell anyone about her. I know that much. I still have a hundred questions formulating in my mind but only one that keeps coming back again and again. *Why me?* It's the obvious question, the question that still plagues me even hours after she's left. It's the one question I don't ask, because no matter what the answer is, I don't want it. I just don't care.

——

It's been days since she spoke to me. I expected her to show up the next night, but she didn't. Or the night after. Or the night after that. I've seen her at school every day, but she hasn't so much as looked in my direction once. I'm beginning to think I imagined the entire encounter. Maybe I'm the batshit one in this scenario. I've spent the last several days trying to make myself believe that I was glad she had stopped coming and that I couldn't care less. After all, it was what I wanted. I made several arguments to myself. I wasn't very convincing.

I hadn't even had the excuse of seeing her at Drew's on Sunday. Leigh was here for the weekend and I was with her. It should have made things easier, but I think it might have made them worse.

"You don't have an accent."

When she finally shows up, exactly one week after she spoke to me, this is the first thing I say.

"No."

"I thought you would. The name." I can't stand the name. It doesn't fit. But then maybe nothing about her does. She considers this and for a minute I think she might say something, but she doesn't. She just keeps walking around my garage and touching tools and running her hands across half-built pieces of furniture, and it's starting to piss me off.

"Are you Russian?" I ask, hoping to distract her.

"You got to ask the questions last time. Tonight's my turn." She didn't answer the question, but at least it seems to have temporarily shifted her focus away from all my stuff.

"I don't remember agreeing to that."

"I don't remember giving you the choice." And she's back to wandering around my garage again. Studying. I feel like grabbing my crotch and checking to see if my balls are still there, because I think they may be in her pocket and I need to get them back. This was fun or different or intriguing for a little while but not anymore. It's one thing to have her sitting and watching, but if she wants to start with the interrogation and the inevitable teenage girl psychoanalysis, I'm out.

"You know who likes to talk? Drew. Why don't you head over there and make his day?" I need to walk away. I pretend I have to get something out of the tool chest across the room. She settles back on the workbench and the legs start swinging immediately.

"I think there are other things he'd rather I did with my mouth." There's nothing coy or suggestive in her tone. She says it like she's talking about helping him study for trig.

"Did you really just say that?"

"Believe so," she says blandly.

"Well, if you do that you might make his week."

"I could make his year if I wanted to." Confident girl. Makes me wonder if she can back that up, and I shouldn't be thinking about that at all. The legs are still swinging and it's driving me crazy.

"Do you want to?" Not what I planned to ask. I wonder how much it would hurt to cut out my tongue.

"I'm asking the questions."

"Not to me you're not." *There.*

"Do you live here alone?" That lasted a while.

"Yes."

"Why were you emancipated?"

"Necessity."

"Is it hard?"

"*What?*"

"Is it hard to get emancipated?" I knew that's what she was asking. Really, I did.

"No. It's embarrassingly easy."

She doesn't speak right away, which, ironically, is now unusual. I look at her and she's studying me.

"What?"

"I'm trying to figure out if you're being sarcastic."

"No, it really is embarrassingly easy. It basically comes down to two things. Age and money. And, really, it's the money that's the most important. I think the state would cut you loose at twelve as long as they knew it wouldn't cost them a dime to support you."

"So, what did you have to do?" If these are the questions she's going to ask, then I can deal with it. As long as she's far away from anything personal, I'll tell her what she wants to know. She lives with her aunt. Maybe she wants to be emancipated, though she's got to be almost eighteen so there doesn't seem to be much of a point to it now. My grandfather and I took care of it a year ago as soon as he found out he was sick.

"You fill out some paperwork, provide documentation that you're at least sixteen and have the financial means to support yourself. Then your guardian signs it, quick hearing, and you're on your own."

She nods as if the explanation is acceptable to her. She doesn't ask about the money. Maybe she has some social graces.

"Who was your legal guardian?" Interesting question, but I'm not opening that door. She could ask anyone else. Everyone knows the story, but I don't think I'm in danger there just yet. She'll find out sooner rather than later. I'm not deluded enough to think it won't come out somehow, but it's nice to have one person exist who doesn't know all my tragic bullshit. At least for a little while.

"Why do you care?"

"I just wondered if that's who was visiting you on Sunday. Drew said you had company; that's why you weren't at dinner." I did have company and it most definitely wasn't my grandfather, but I'm not getting anywhere near the Leigh situation with this girl. Not now or ever.

"A friend was in town." I'm expecting another onslaught of questions, but no more come. I have quite a few for her, but she seems to be done talking right now, and I'm afraid if I invite any more conversation tonight, I'll probably be the one regretting it.

After about ten minutes of leg swinging and silence, she starts asking questions again. They aren't what I expect, but nothing with this girl is. And these questions, I don't mind. She asks about tools and wood and furniture building. I don't know how many questions she asks but I know that my voice is hoarse by the end of the evening.

When she jumps down from the counter—her universal sign for *I'm leaving now*—I say the one thing that I've been thinking all night.

"You're not what I expected you to be like." I catch her eye, and she actually looks a little surprised and a lot curious, which I think she tries to hide.

"How did you expect me to be?"

"Quiet."

Chapter 18

Nastya

My mother's voice. It's the first thing I remember after I opened my eyes.

My beautiful girl. You came back to us.

But she was wrong.

⎯

If Edna St. Vincent Millay was right and childhood is the kingdom where nobody dies, then my childhood ended when I was fifteen. Which I guess is more than Josh got, because according to what I've picked up on from Drew, his ended at eight. I don't know more than that, because I don't ask Josh questions I'm not prepared to answer myself.

I have to go home this weekend. My mom expected me to visit a month ago. I'm surprised she hasn't shown up here. It isn't like Charlotte Ward to wait for anything she wants.

I don't really have much I need to pack. I left most of my old clothes there. I won't see anyone except my family and a therapist, so I'm leaving my Hollywood Boulevard attire at Margot's, which means my feet will be happy for a couple days at least. I have to miss school on Friday so I can get to Brighton early enough to make the therapy appointment my mom made. I thought about telling Josh I was going, but I didn't end up mentioning it for a lot of reasons, mostly because I'm not responsible to him. I could probably make it back by six o'clock on Sunday to get to dinner, but it might be for the best if I skip it this week.

When I walk through the front door of the very out of place Victorian-style house I grew up in, I feel home. The feeling only lasts a moment. It's not real. It's just a knee-jerk reaction; an echo of a feeling that used to exist. Just once, I'd like to go home and have home be what it used to be. Then again, maybe I'm just imagining some sort of halcyon days that exist more in my memory than they ever did in real life.

My mother is at the dining room table we have never used except for holidays. She has proofs spread all over the surface. My mother is a photographer, which is kind of funny, because she's drop-dead gorgeous, but she's never actually in any pictures because she's always the one taking them. She works freelance and is never without an assignment because she's really good, which means she can make her own rules, take the jobs she wants, come and go as she pleases. My bedroom walls upstairs used to be covered with her photographs. All of my favorite ones. I'd sit at the table and look at her proofs with her and pick the ones that jumped out at me. There was always one photo that resonated above the others, and I'd point it out and she'd make me a copy. It was our ritual. I don't even remember the last picture I picked. I didn't know it was going to be the last one. I could walk over to her, sit down at the table, and point one out right now, but I don't. My walls are covered with new wallpaper.

As soon as she sees me, she's out of her chair. I don't think it takes her more than three steps to reach the entryway and wrap her arms around me. I hug her back because she needs it, even if I don't. It's different from hugging Mrs. Leighton but not in the way that you would think. Hugging my mother is far more awkward. She pulls back and I see the expression in her eyes; the one I have gotten so used to; the one I have seen a thousand times in the last three years. The look of person staring out a window, waiting for someone they know is never coming home.

I'm not the only one who isn't the same person anymore. None of us are. I wish I could have made that different for them, given them everything they believed they had gotten back that day when they found me alive and not dead. Who knows what we would be like now, if my mother had been allowed to watch me fade away from her? She would have lost the little girl anyway, just later and gradually. Not the way it happened—in one big-ass fell swoop. Even if everything hadn't occurred the way it did, that child part of me would still have disappeared. Imperceptibly over time. I just got too old, too fast. All at once.

And she wasn't ready to say goodbye.

I'm saved by the appearance of my brother, Asher, who comes bounding down the stairs. He's a year younger than me and what seems like two feet taller. He grabs me in a bear hug and lifts me off the ground. He's gotten the memo that I don't like being touched about fifty times, but either he hasn't bothered to read it yet or he just doesn't care. He refuses to adhere to any rules or suggested boundaries where I'm involved. It upsets my parents and pisses the crap out of me in a way that only a brother can. Asher calls bullshit on me and I let him. He's the only one. He's not afraid of losing me or pushing me away, because he knows that right now is about as far away as I can get, and he figures he has nothing to lose.

I have an hour before I have to be at therapy. Asher says he'll drive me. I shrug. I can drive myself, but my appointment is at three thirty, which is the witching hour as far as I'm concerned, so I'll take the company, and besides, I miss him. Asher might be my younger brother, but I don't think he realizes it. He would beat the world down for me if it would make things better, and I think he feels like a failure because it won't.

On the drive, he regales me with stories from school. He's a junior and a popular one. Playing baseball as opposed to the piano will do that for you. He's dating a girl named Addison. I'd like to tell him that her name has the misfortune of meaning *Adam's son.* He wouldn't care anyway, because according to him, she's *smokin' hot,* though I have a feeling that's not the whole story. He can say what he wants, to save face, but I know Asher well enough to know that *smokin' hot* will only get a girl so far and then she'll have to have some substance. He doesn't have to worry. I won't call him out for failure to be a douche. There are enough douches in the world. I'm glad my brother isn't one of them. He's got two AP classes this year, which is two more than I have, and he's taking the SATs in a few weeks, so he's been cramming like hell and I'm invited to help him this weekend if I want to. I don't know what helping would entail, but I have a feeling it would be hindered by my silence, so he's on his own. During the fifteen-minute ride, I get caught up on the last seven weeks in the uncomplicated world of Asher Ward. No wonder his name means blessed.

I sit through my therapy appointment, even though I don't say anything, because everyone cuts me more slack when I go. I'm not sure what good inconsistent therapy sessions even do, but showing up apparently demonstrates that I'm making an effort. I'm not. The only effort I'm making is to do just enough to be left alone.

I am an expert in all manners of therapy. The only thing I'm not an expert in is getting them to work. My parents had me in therapy before I even left the hospital, which is the recommended course of action when the devil finds your fifteen-year-old and the afterlife spits her back out.

I stayed in therapy long enough to know that nothing that happened to me was my fault. I didn't do anything to invite it or deserve it. But that just makes it worse. Maybe I don't blame myself for what happened, but when they tell you that something was completely and utterly random, they're also telling you something else. That nothing you do matters. It doesn't matter if you do everything right, if you dress the right way and act the right way and follow all the rules, because evil will find you anyway. Evil's resourceful that way.

The day evil found me, I was wearing a pink silk blouse with pearl buttons and a white eyelet skirt that came all the way down to my knees and was walking to school to record a Haydn sonata for my conservatory audition. The sad thing is that I didn't even need it. I'd already recorded it once, along with a Chopin étude and a Bach prelude and fugue, but I wasn't happy with the sonata and wanted to record it again. Maybe if I could have lived with that slight imperfection, I wouldn't be living with such a huge one now.

Either way, I still wasn't doing anything wrong. I was out in the sunlight in the middle of the day, not lurking in the dark. I wasn't skipping school or sneaking out. I was going exactly where I was supposed to be going, exactly when I was supposed to be going there. He wasn't after me. He didn't even know who I was.

They tell you it was random to make you feel blameless. But all I hear them telling me is that I have no control, and if I have no control, then I'm powerless. I would have preferred being blamed.

I've done the support group thing, too, but I hated it even before I stopped talking. I never understood how hearing everyone else's shit stories was supposed to make me feel better about mine. Everyone sits around and laments the crap hands they've been dealt. Maybe I'm just not a sadist. It doesn't comfort me to see other people as annihilated as I am. There isn't any safety in these numbers. Just more misery and I have enough of my own.

Plus, support groups get a little antagonistic when you don't talk. It's like you're pilfering everyone else's pain, taking, but not offering anything in return. They regard me like I'm some sort of thief. One time, a blond girl named Esta—a name I couldn't find a meaning for unless you count the fact that it's the Spanish word for *this*—told me I needed to "put up or shut up," and I wasn't sure how to react to that, but it kind of would have been worth talking just to ask her what the hell she was smoking. Then I found out that she had been stabbed by her mom and making fun of her wasn't quite so funny anymore.

I got to hear about rapes and gunshot wounds and hate crimes, people who knew their attackers, people who didn't, people whose assailants were punished and those who weren't. There isn't any comfort in it. If eavesdropping on someone else's nightmares is supposed to make me feel better, I'd rather stay feeling like shit. I don't think telling them about my horror story would do me any good. And besides, I'm not even supposed to have a story to tell.

So that's what it was like every week. I'd sit in a circle and a bunch of people who'd been through as much shit as I had would look at me like I snuck into the club without paying the cover. And I'd feel like screaming and telling them that I had paid it the same as everyone else in the room, I just didn't feel like waving around my receipt.

Today my therapist doesn't talk to me about blame. She talks to me about talking. I wish I could say that I listen, but I spend most of the time thinking about how to tweak my angel food cake recipe and proper kickboxing techniques.

On the way home, I get what I knew was coming.

"Mom still thinks you might come back." Asher won't look at me when he says it. I don't even know if he's talking about back home or just back. "You're not going to." He doesn't even bother to make it sound like a question. Then it gets even better.

"They want you to talk to Detective Martin again." Of

course Ash would be the designated bomb dropper. I know he hates being put in this position, but somehow Asher has become the path of least resistance to me. "She'll come to the house if you want, so you don't have to go to the station, but they want to show you some pictures. They know you don't remember anything, but they want you to look anyway, in case something jogs your memory."

I stare out the window so I don't have to look at his face when I lie to him with my silence. I don't need my memory jogged. My memory jogs me. I remember everything.

Every detail.

Every night.

For the past 473 days.

On Saturday, I meet with Detective Martin. I look at the pictures. Check out the drawings. Shake my head. He isn't there. He never is. They have no idea what they're looking for. She gives us another business card. I'm not sure how many we have now.

I should tell. I know I should. But he's mine. I don't want him getting the chance to walk away. I want him to pay and I want to be the one who decides how.

On Sunday morning, my dad makes pancakes for breakfast like we always used to. I come downstairs to the smell of bacon frying and I know that in two days you'll still be able to smell the lingering aroma of bacon grease in the house. I won't still be here in two days to smell it, but it will be here even if I'm not.

Asher comes down wearing swim trunks and no shirt and is promptly sent back upstairs by my mother to get one. He groans at the request but goes anyway. He's on his way to the beach with the famous Addison Hartley, who is picking him up in less than an hour. I'm actually excited to meet the girl who has my brother trying to act like he's not acting like a lovesick fool. I'm happy for him, because going to the beach with someone you're stupidly in love with is such an awesomely normal thing to do. He invites me to go with them, but I shake my head no for all the good it does me.

"Come with us. It'll be fun," he tries to convince me. I'm quite sure it would be fun, if it was only Asher and his girlfriend going. Even though I'm freakishly pale, I still might have considered it if not for all of the other kids who I knew would be there. I may be gone, but around Brighton I am never forgotten. I shake my head again.

"Go with him. All of your old friends will be there," my mother says hopefully. It's hard to see hope in your mother's face when you know you're going to kill it. I don't know what she's more misguided about, thinking this is a selling point or thinking that I actually have old friends. The only old friends I had are probably spending their Sunday with a musical instrument, not running around half naked on the beach.

"There's nothing stopping you from going, Mil—" my dad says, catching himself before finishing. *Right, Dad,* nothing but the fact that I have to wear a shirt the whole time to hide the scars and field a thousand questions I wouldn't want to answer even if I did talk. Getting impaled with a railroad spike would be less painful.

If I had to decide who, out of all of us, this whole shit situation was the hardest on, I'd say it was my father. My father is a quiet badass. Gentle, protective, and if need be, murderous to protect his children. Like all fathers should be. The problem is he didn't protect me. Because he couldn't. No one could. But I don't think he sees it that way.

"You have to rejoin the world sometime," he starts. I feel the *no excuses* lecture. Asher and I have never been allowed to make excuses about anything, even now. I have a feeling he's talking about more than going to the beach. "You didn't get a choice in what happened to you. Neither did we. But *you* have a choice in what happens now. We don't. You're the one in control, and all we can do is sit on the sidelines and watch, even if you keep making the wrong calls over and over again." We're obviously veering into sports metaphor territory. "We're not going to force you to do anything you aren't ready to do. You've had enough forced on you. But you have to make a decision about how long you're going to let this define your life."

Now I think my parents realize that they've parented themselves into a corner with their insistence that Asher and I make our own choices growing up and that we stand behind them and live with the consequences. Because they can't take it back. Now they're stuck letting me make all of my own decisions, wrong or not, and watching me live with them because that's what they taught me to do.

It was fine when being the Brighton Piano Girl defined my life. When I was making the *right* choices. When all of my choices were influenced by what my parents wanted me to choose. I let their current steer me, let it smooth and shape me like a stone pushed along the sand until I was perfect. And as soon as I was, I was ripped out of the water and thrown and smashed into a thousand pieces that I can't put back together. I don't know where they go. And there are so many missing that the ones that are left don't fit together anymore.

I think I'll stay in pieces. I can shift them, rearrange, depending on the day, depending on what I need to be. I can change on a whim and be so many different girls and none of them has to be me.

We sit down at the table and eat pancakes made from a box mix. Even Asher doesn't say anything else. After breakfast I go to my room and look for more names to add to the walls. I see Addison arrive from my window, but I don't go downstairs. I never do get to meet her, but Asher's right; she does look smokin' hot.

—

I get in my car just after five on Sunday afternoon. Everyone walks me out. My mom reminds me to text her when I get back to Margot's so she knows I arrived safely. My dad hugs me and closes the door of my now very clean car, which he made Asher help him wash yesterday. I lock the doors as soon as I'm in, turn off the radio, and leave.

Going home is like culture shock. Different house, different face, different clothes, different name. Same comforter. Sometimes I think I wouldn't mind wrapping Asher up in a box and taking him back to Margot's with me. But then he'd see the way I am there. That I've probably gotten worse instead of better and I'd have to face the very disappointments and lost hopes I ran away from in the first place. Plus, once he did the requisite double-take and recognized me, he'd probably beat the crap out of any guy who looked at me in all my Snow White meets Frederick's of Hollywood glory.

By the time I get back to Margot's, it will be after seven o'clock. I planned it that way on purpose so I wouldn't have to decide whether or not to go to Drew's. I'm starting to feel guilty about the fact that neither Josh nor I have made any move to tell him about the amount of time we spend together. It's not that I really mind Drew knowing; I think he's finally accepted the fact that there is not enough alcohol in the world to get me to have sex with him, so that's not the issue. The problem is that he would inevitably start to wonder how Josh and I spend so much time together with no talking involved, and even if his suspicions are unconfirmed, they're still suspicions I'd rather avoid. Plus, if I'm being honest, the hours I spend in that garage with Josh, apart from school and Margot and everything else, are mine. I just don't want to share it yet. Apparently Josh hasn't said anything, either.

Chapter 19

Josh

"Nastya can't make it to dinner. She asked me to drop this off on my way to work." The blond woman at the door hands me a really tall, elaborately iced cake. I can see the blue paisley pattern around the edge of the plate. The last time I saw that plate, it was on my front porch covered with cookies.

"She asked you?" I say skeptically. Does she talk to other people and she's lying to me? I don't know why, but that bothers me. A lot.

"She wrote down this address under the words *Drop off, Sunday,* and *5:45.* At the bottom she tacked on the word *please.* It's the most communication I've gotten from her in years." She sounds aggravated at having to explain herself to me.

"Okay. Thanks." I take it out of her hands, and she looks at me like she's waiting for something.

"Who are you?" she asks.

"Josh Bennett." *Who are you?*

"Can I come in?"

I'm kind of dumbfounded by the request, but I don't want to be rude. I look at her again. She's really thin and tan and blond and doesn't remotely resemble any serial killers in my mind. She doesn't resemble Nastya either, but I've got to assume she's the aunt Drew talked about, so I push the door back and let her step inside. I really don't know what she wants from me, unless Nastya's messing with me in more ways than I imagine and this woman knows things I don't.

"Margot Travers. Nastya lives with me." She holds out her hand. I hold up the cake in response.

"Listen, I'm not going to beat around the bush because I have to be at work soon, and frankly it's just not my thing." *Okay.* "Even if I didn't have to drop the cake off, I would have been over here this weekend anyway to find out what's going on." I can't decide if I'm more nervous or curious now, but I'm definitely listening. "There's a tracker on Nastya's phone." She pauses for a second. I guess she's giving me a minute to react. I don't. "I check it periodically, and a few weeks ago this address came up, so I started checking it more often, and do you know what I found?" Of course I do, and you know that I do. You just want to ask for dramatic effect and then you're going to tell me anyway. "This address came up again and again and again—at nine o'clock, ten o'clock, eleven o'clock. Sometimes midnight." Sounds about right. I don't confirm or deny. I'll let her keep talking until she asks me something outright.

"Is there something you want to tell me?" she asks expectantly.

"Is there something you want to know?" I feel like I'm in the middle of a seventh-grade stare-down.

"What's going on?"

"Why aren't you asking her?"

She looks at me as if to say *Yeah, right.* "She doesn't talk to me."

Every time she pauses, her eyes scan the room like she's looking for my porn collection or the entrance to my hidden meth lab. I'm getting a little insulted at the fact that this woman nearly pushes Nastya out the door with Drew, of all people, but she's here giving me the third degree. Maybe because Drew shows up, knocks on the door, and asks her to be a guest at a well-chaperoned dinner on a Sunday evening, while I let her covertly hole up in my garage, late at night, with no adult supervision anywhere.

"Then why should I?" I respond, because now I'm just being a child. But then I realize what she's really asking, what she really wants to know. And it's not my first suspicion. Because this woman isn't trying to figure out if her niece is sneaking over here and having sex with me. She wants to know if she's *talking* to me. I take a breath because now I want this over, and if I give her some sort of answer, maybe it'll be enough to get her off my case. Plus, I'm getting the feeling she's going to start issuing rules or threats and I don't really handle either of those well. I may not know if I want Nastya hanging around all the time or not, but I don't like the idea of someone else making that decision for me. I can give her an answer, but I'm doing it for my benefit, not hers. "She's in my shop class. She's really behind everyone else, so she comes over here at night when she goes running and watches me work."

She looks at me long enough to make me wonder how she's going to respond.

"That's it?" She sounds disappointed. Her eyes narrow again. "Your parents don't mind that she's here all the time?"

"Doesn't bother them at all." It's not really a lie. Not really.

"Where's Nastya?" I'm greeted by Drew's dad almost as soon as I walk in the door for dinner. The comment brings his mom around the corner a second later. The music's already playing, and I can tell it's Sarah's. I'd rather listen to a circular saw, but we're not allowed to insult anyone's music when it's their week.

"Nastya's not coming?" Mrs. Leighton asks, taking the cake out of my hands and sounding genuinely disappointed. "Then where did this come from?"

"Her aunt dropped it off this afternoon and said she wanted you to have it."

"She is the sweetest thing!" she exclaims, carrying it into the kitchen. I don't know if there's another person on Earth who would refer to Nastya as the sweetest thing, and I wonder if she sees something the rest of us don't.

Dinner at Drew's ends up being just the five of us, like so many dinners I've eaten at this table before. We don't talk about Nastya at all until dessert comes and the cake gets brought out.

"She's a freak," Sarah says, glad to finally have the chance to talk behind her back. She looks at me when she says it and I look away because she's pissing me off.

"Sarah, not everyone has such an easy life. Some people have problems, and you need to learn to empathize, not judge." Mrs. Leighton is skewering her with the look that has kept all three of us in line for years, four of us if you count Mr. Leighton.

"Is that why you invite her?" Shit. I wonder if my voice sounds as pissed off as I think it does.

"No, we really like her." She sounds surprised by the question. Her response is sincere, but it's the sincerity that pisses me off. Before I get a chance to respond, Sarah opens her bitchy mouth and saves me from myself, if only for a moment.

"Speak for yourself."

"Shut up, Sarah," Drew counters with the phrase that must leave his mouth a hundred times a day.

"Drew!" Mrs. Leighton lays her fork down next to her plate, and it's obvious that it pains her not to slam it onto the table.

"What? She can be a bitch, but I can't tell her to shut up?" Drew stands up and pushes his chair back from the table.

"Sit down, Drew." The forced calm in his mother's voice is

a warning, and he sits. He's readying for his comeuppance, but I'm not done yet.

"How can you like her? You don't even know her." I should drop it. I know I should, but I don't get it. It's like she's a novelty or a pet. *Look at the troubled, misguided mute girl we've taken in. Aren't we amazingly generous and understanding?* I hate it and I don't want it coming from Drew's mom.

"I don't know how well you can really know a girl who can't talk," she says sympathetically.

Doesn't talk, I silently correct. *Can, just won't.* I know that one thing.

Mrs. Leighton's attention is on me now. She's trying to explain it for me as well as for herself. She wants to convince me, but she doesn't need to. I already know. The answer is *You can't.* You can't know her at all, at least not Nastya, because she won't give you anything, and what she gives you isn't real. She may talk to me, but I don't know her either.

"So how can you say you like her?" I'm not as angry now, but I want to know.

"She's obviously a nice girl. She has manners. She never comes to dinner empty-handed." I don't know how manners and nice are equal, but I keep my mouth shut because being mad at Sarah is one thing, but being mad at Drew's mom is something else. I don't think she's ever done anything to piss me off before. The feeling sucks. I don't even know where it comes from. "Clearly, there's something going on in her life and we can't judge—"

"So what is it? You invite her because you feel sorry for her or because you're using her to teach Sarah how to be a better person?" I had to cut her off. It was getting way too close to the point where the psychoanalysis was going to start, and I didn't want to let it happen. I didn't want to hear it. It would feel too much like I was being psychoanalyzed, letting them tear me open and pick apart every action and choice and motivation, so they can feel superior and sane. I didn't want them to do it to her while she wasn't even here. Of course, I feel like I've just ripped myself open for them, spared them the trouble and dumped out my feelings so they can lay them across the dining room table and poke around in them with a stick.

"Josh." She says a lot with that word. Like I'm being called out and judged and questioned and pitied. Everyone's looking at me. I can't blame them. I invited it by being the stupid bastard who couldn't keep my mouth shut. It's not even an outburst. I never even raised my voice. I don't even think my tone changed at all, but they still aren't used to it. It's the Josh Bennett equivalent of tattooing her name across my chest. Regrettable, moronic, and really fucking embarrassing.

"I'm sorry," Mrs. Leighton continues, and now I can tell she thinks I'm deluding myself. But I'm not the one taking in strays. I'm not trying to save anyone.

"She's not a sideshow." I cut her off again because I don't want Mrs. Leighton's apologies. She doesn't owe them to me. I should quit while I'm ahead, but that would be smart, and I'm not being smart tonight.

"She dresses like one." Obviously Sarah isn't being smart either.

"I like the way she dresses." I don't know if Drew is trying to get everyone back on track by reminding us all what an idiot he is, or if he really is just an idiot.

"Less work for you," she retorts.

"What is your problem Sarah?" I demand.

"What's yours? My parents aren't allowed to be nice to her and I'm not allowed to not be nice. You're the one with the issue." Sarah has no problem raising her voice. The worst part about it is that she's right. I am the one with the issue and I don't even know what the issue is.

I don't know how this whole dinner devolved into the mess we're in now, but I have a feeling I'm to blame for it. I could have kept my mouth shut, listened to them play a nice game of *Solve Sunshine* and let it go. But I didn't.

Mrs. Leighton manages to corner me at my truck before I can leave, and I wish she'd just leave me alone like everyone else. Apparently I've been claimed by this woman whether I like it or not.

"Which one of you is dating that girl?"

"I don't think either of us is." Maybe Drew is, but I don't think so. At least dating wouldn't be the word for it, but I don't want to think about that so much. "Drew, I guess."

"I doubt that." She looks knowingly at me.

"Then why ask?"

"Josh." I wish she would stop saying my name like that. Soft and tentative, like she's licking broken glass. "Look at the way she dresses, the way she covers her face with that makeup and the fact that she doesn't speak. She might be silent, but she is screaming for help."

I feel like I'm watching an episode of *General Hospital*.

"So why doesn't someone give it to her?"

"Maybe nobody knows how. Sometimes it's easier to pretend nothing is wrong than to face the fact that everything is wrong, but you're powerless to do anything about it." I wonder if she's talking about me and she thinks she's being subtle.

"Why are you telling me this? Shouldn't you be talking to Drew?"

"Drew doesn't care."

Her accusation is clear and I answer it.

"Neither do I."

Chapter 20

Nastya

I hate my left hand. I hate to look at it. I hate it when it stutters and trembles and reminds me that my identity is gone. But I look at it anyway, because it also reminds me that I'm going to find the boy who took everything from me. I'm going to kill the boy who killed me, and when I kill him, I'm going to do it with my left hand.

—

Clay Whitaker is chasing me on my way to first period on Thursday, hair as disheveled as his clothes, looking every bit a refugee from the Island of Misfit Boys. His sketchbook is closed up and tucked under his arm the way it always is, like it's attached to him or something. I would still love to see what's in it. I wonder how many of those he goes through and how fast he fills them up. It can't be the same book all the time. Maybe he goes through as many sketchbooks as I do black-and-white composition books. His closet probably has a stack of them from floor to ceiling, and I bet if you flipped through them you wouldn't find the exact same picture on every page. Not like in my notebooks. His are probably like a photo album of memories, where he can look back and know exactly what place he was at in his mind when he drew the picture. Mine aren't like that. I can't flip the pages and read what I wrote and tell you what was happening in my life, in my mind, at that time. I can only tell you what happened on one particular day, and it's the one I'm not supposed to remember.

"Hey, Nastya!" He's panting when he reaches me, smiling through heavy breaths. I stop and step off to the side so we aren't standing in the middle of the hallway. I'm curious because Clay will say hello to me if I run into him, but he never seeks me out.

"I wanted to ask a favor, and I figured since you kind of owe me, you'd say yes."

Really? I'm not worried about whatever favor he wants, but I am trying to figure out what I owe him for. I narrow my eyes at him, and his smile is still there.

"How many times have you gotten into the English wing at lunchtime because a certain book has been propping the door open? A book which, by the way, is dented to hell and I'm probably going to have to pay for, so you kind of owe me double."

I'll concede that. *Come on. Bring it.* I motion with my hand.

"I want to draw you." Not what I was expecting, but I hadn't really stopped to think about what I was expecting. It's not such an unusual request, considering that it's coming from Clay Whitaker, but I don't know why he wants me. I hope he doesn't think I'd pose naked for him because that's not happening. I tap on his sketchbook and motion for him to open it. I've been dying to see what he does, and he couldn't have handed me a more perfect excuse. If it's possible, his smile gets even wider, but now it's genuine, too. He's not trying to sell me something anymore, even though that's exactly what his drawings are going to do.

We've been facing each other, but he moves over to stand next to me, leaning his back against the wall so he's shoulder to shoulder with me. He drops his backpack to the ground and opens the sketchbook. The first drawing is of a woman, older, with a lined face and thin lips. Her eyes are sunken, and it's horribly depressing. I look over to him and he's waiting for my reaction. I don't know what reaction to give him, so I motion for him to turn the page. The next picture is of a man's face. He looks like an older version of Clay, and it must be his father, unless it's some sort of future self-portrait. Just like the first drawing, it's jarringly real. I swear I can look at the eyes and tell what they were thinking. It isn't just inspired; it's almost frightening. The next one is a woman with eyes I can tell are bloodshot even though the drawing is black and white, and my reaction is almost visceral. I can feel it. I want to touch her and find out what's wrong. But it's nothing compared to the feeling I get when I see the page he flips to next.

I'm staring at myself. The picture is me but not me. It's a me he's never seen. My face looks younger and my eyes are clear. There isn't a trace of makeup on me, and my hair is smoothed back in a ponytail pulled over my right shoulder. This one I do touch. I can't help it. My hand just goes there. I pull it away as soon as my fingers meet the paper. I wish he hadn't shown this to me here. I can't look at it anymore. I close the book and shove it back at him.

Now I'm not so certain that the second picture wasn't actually a future self-portrait after all. I'm sure he could easily look at a face and age, not only the skin, but the person behind it. It's what he did to me in reverse. He regressed me. Took the age and the days and the years and everything that happened in them away and drew me the way I used to be.

When I turn to face him, I don't know what's in my expression. It could be any of a thousand emotions I don't want to try to sort out right now in the hallway before first period. The bell is going to ring soon and the corridor is filling up around us.

Clay is staring at me. He's waiting and he's not smiling anymore. He must have been watching the entire time I was looking at the book, gauging my reactions while he showed me his soul. No matter how proud he may be, I know that showing me his work still has to be like ripping off his clothes, spinning around in front of me naked, and waiting for judgment. I used to feel the same way when I played anything I had composed.

"So?"

I pull a spiral notebook out of my backpack. The first of two preschool warning bells just blasted through the hall and I have to get to class. *Time and place?* I write, and hand it to him just as Yearbook Michelle comes running up and grabs his arm, pulling him away.

"Come on! We're gonna be late!" I don't think she even noticed that he was talking to me.

"Find me at lunch!" he yells over his shoulder as I walk off in the opposite direction, haunted by my own face.

⁓

"To the right. Just a little. Back more. Forget it. The light in here sucks. Let's go back downstairs. The kitchen is the only room in this house with enough decent natural light." Clay picks up his sketchpad, charcoal pencils, and some other art crap, and I follow him back down the stairs of the townhouse I've spent the past several days in. He's obsessed. I can't blame him. I recognize it. I know the overwhelming need to create something. I watch him draw and hate him a little bit for it. I don't feel bad about it. I feel justified. I miss it. I want it back so badly that I would break my hand apart all over again just to give myself something else to feel. Sometimes the wanting almost kills me again.

It's a little bit devastating being surrounded by people who can do what you can't anymore. People who create. People whose souls no longer live in their bodies because they've leached so much of themselves into their work. Josh. Clay. My mother. I want to steal from them to let myself live.

"Back downstairs?" Maddie Whitaker has been here every day that I've come. She works doing data entry from home, so Clay says she's always around. He sees his dad on the weekends on the other side of town, which is why he's been having me sit for him during the week.

"Crap light," he says, and it's enough of an answer for her.

I smile as I walk by and then remember I'm not wearing any makeup and instinctively look down. The minute I walked in on the first day, Clay promptly sent me to the bathroom to wash "that stuff" off of my face. He didn't ask. He just told. Apparently I owe him that too. I could have argued, but I've seen exactly what Clay's hands can do and I won't stand in their way.

I sit for the next hour, watching Clay, charcoal in hand, with his eyebrows pulled together the way they get when he's concentrating. He hasn't let me see anything he's done yet. I don't even know how many he's drawn. I thought I was agreeing to one picture, maybe two, but we seem to have gone beyond that. By like eighty.

He finally takes pity on me and lets me up to use the bathroom.

How many more? I write down on a pad of sticky notes I find on the kitchen counter, because I'm stalling before I have to sit again.

"I don't know. I'll know when I've got them all, but I won't know how many that is until I'm done."

Cryptic, much? I scribble back. Because if I'm going to be spending this much time with him, I have to at least be able to communicate a little. Plus, Clay won't sell me out.

"Not trying to be. Some people I can capture in one picture. For most, it's two or three. For you, it's more."

Now he's got me. I'm in. *Why does it take so many pictures to capture one face?*

"I'm not trying to capture one face. I'm trying to capture all the faces." He stops to see if I'm getting this. "Most people have more than one. You have more than most."

He tears apart faces and puts them back together whole, like I would a piece of music. I could play it a hundred ways, imbue it with a different emotion every time and try to find the truth of it. He does that with faces, except he's not putting the truth in, he's drawing it out. He's looking for the truth of me. I wonder if he'll find it, and if he does, maybe he can show me where it is again.

Chapter 21

Josh

My router is acting up for the second night in a row. I thought I had it back in working order last night, but now it's pissing me off again. I wanted to finish this chair by the end of the week because I have three more projects waiting that all should have taken priority over this. But I wanted to build the chair and I couldn't get it out of my head. So now I'm behind and I'll be living out here for the next couple of weeks, trying to get back to even. I don't mind. There are worse places to be.

The quiet out here is strange. It shouldn't be. I'm used to the quiet, but it only took me a matter of days without her to feel it. It's unsettling. Years of working out here by myself undone by less than two months of her company. And now she hasn't been here for days. Maybe it's a good thing, because I obviously need a reality check. I try to work with the garage door down as much as possible, just so I know that I can. I'm not going to let myself get used to anyone again. She can come here. She can sit in my garage, hand me tools, ask me questions. She can use me to get the talking out of her system. I can handle the company as long as I don't come to expect it too much. And I won't. I don't know when she's coming back, but I wonder how long I can keep the garage closed before I start to suffocate.

Nastya

I've been clocking more miles this week than I have for the past several. A lot of my running time has been being spent in a certain garage, and I'm trying to rein it in. But I miss him. It's not like going without seeing a friend for a few days. He's the be-all and end-all of my friends right now. I have Drew, and I seem to have acquired Clay somewhere along the way, but Josh is my escape. He's my hiding place.

It's been days since I've been to Josh's house. I've spent the whole week sitting in a chair at Clay's, feeling antsy and ridiculous and just wanting to get up and move. I hate the sitting still. When you spend months in a bed letting your body heal and then sitting in a chair, trying to make your hand work, you get sick of it fast and you want to run away. So every day when I get done at Clay's, I have to run. It's the only thing that keeps the frayed edges of my sanity intact. And since Margot caved a few weeks back and let me get a portable punching bag, I have something to hit now, and I spend a good amount of time doing that, too.

By Friday night, I can't help it. I don't even know if he'll be home, but my feet take me there anyway. I wonder if he missed me, too. I slow myself down before I reach the driveway. He's in the back, adjusting one of his saws, and he's turned away from me. I look around for someplace to climb up on the counter, but there isn't one. Every inch of space on the workbench is occupied. Piles of wood scraps, random tools and boxes covering the whole thing. It's never this overrun in here. Josh is meticulous, which means this is on purpose, and I wonder if it's a message. Maybe he realized how much he enjoyed not having me all over his space. He got reacquainted with his solitude and found that he'd missed it.

I'm not ready to leave yet. If I'm going to be rejected, I'd like it to come complete with humiliation. I'm hoping he'll come out from behind that stupid saw and say something to me, but he doesn't look like he's rushing to do so. Out of the corner of my eye, in front of the side door where the workbench ends, is the chair I'd seen him working on last week. I recognize the legs on it, the design he had painstakingly routed on all four of them. He must have finished it this week, and I wonder if he made it on order or if he did it for himself. It's exquisite, and every time I see something he's made, I hate him a little more for it. My jealousy is a living thing. Shifting, changing, growing. Like my rage and my mother's regret.

I run my hands along the arc of the backrest and kneel down to examine the legs. The armrests are wide and curved to match the lines of the back. I wonder if he's started another one yet, because it should be part of a matching set. My fingers are still tracing their way down the other side, and before I've thought better of it, I slide into the seat, and that's when the perfection of it strikes me. Because this chair should not be comfortable, but I may never want to leave it. My arms are resting on the sides and I lean back and look up to find Josh watching me. It's unnerving the way he's staring, no matter how much I may have gotten used to him, and I kind of wish he wasn't so damn good-looking because it makes it hard to look away.

The expression on his face is almost anxious, but there's something like mischief in it as well. It's the same look Clay had when he showed me the picture he'd drawn of me. He's waiting for a reaction, for approval. I look down at the chair I'm sitting in and then back up at him, but he's not looking at me anymore.

He's gone back to adjusting the saw as if everything has returned to the way it should be, and that's when it hits me. He made sure there was no place for me to sit on the counter so I'd be forced to notice it. Because the chair was meant for me.

The realization is enough to propel my ass straight up and out of that chair. He looks up, jarred by the sudden movement, and for a moment we just stare at one other. I must look like a crazed animal, ready to bolt like the first night I walked in here. I can say what I'm thinking, but I don't need to. He already knows.

"It's only a chair." He's talking me down off a ledge.

"I can't take it." I try to make it sound like he's the unreasonable one for giving it to me.

"Why not?"

"You should sell it."

"I don't need to."

"I won't take it. Give it to someone else."

"You need someplace to sit. I'm tired of you moving everything around and getting in my way whenever I'm working. Now you have a place to sit. So sit." He motions me down into the chair with a tilt of his head and I sit, and it feels more perfect than it did a few moments ago. He leans over me and places his hands on top of mine on the armrests and looks straight into my eyes, which flays me a little bit.

"It's a chair. Stop overanalyzing it. I'm not selling it and I'm not giving it to someone else. I made it for you. It's yours." He pulls away and stands up straight. When his hands are gone from mine, I realize that it's the first time he's ever really touched me, and I wish he'd put them back. "Besides, it already has your name on it."

"Where?"

"Look underneath. I was going to put it on the back where you could actually see it, but it didn't work."

I slide down out of the chair and get as low as I can to the ground so I can twist my head around and see what he's talking about. And I do and it's unmistakable. There, on the underside of the seat, is an engraving of the sun.

I know at that moment what he's given me and it's not a chair. It's an invitation, a welcome, the knowledge that I am accepted here. He hasn't given me a place to sit. He's given me a place to belong.

Chapter 22

Nastya

It amazes me how people are so afraid of what can happen in the dark, but they don't give a second thought about their safety during the day, as if the sun offers some sort of ultimate protection from all the evil in the world. It doesn't. All it does is whisper to you, lulling you with its warmth before it shoves you facedown into the dirt. Daylight won't protect you from anything. Bad things happen all the time; they don't wait until after dinner.

—

I've never been to Josh's house during the day. It looks different in the afternoon. I wouldn't be here now if my car battery hadn't been unjumpably dead when I left school today. I live close enough to the campus to walk, but I don't walk anywhere in the afternoon. Mornings I can deal with, but there's a period of time in the afternoon when I hate being outside. Even nighttime doesn't bother me so much. The dark doesn't breed fear in me the way the daytime does. The afternoon sun has a way of following me, burning memories onto my back. Josh always offers me rides home from his house. He thinks it should make me nervous, running alone at night, and it does. I'm not stupid enough to think I'm ever safe outside, anywhere, at any time of day. It's just that I'm more nervous during the daytime.

So now I'm here, on Josh Bennett's couch at three fifteen in the afternoon, watching *General Hospital*. Josh spent the last commercial break patiently filling me in on as much of the past decade's worth of story lines as he could in three and a half minutes while I ate as many Twizzlers as I could. When the commercials were over, he stopped abruptly and told me he'd tell me the rest during the next break. I don't think I've spent much time actually watching the television. Mostly I've been looking at Josh and trying to figure out who the hell he is. I've developed a theory that, perhaps, Josh is really twins and that there are two of him, because I'm convinced, from day to day, that he's not the same person. It's like that Christian Bale movie where the twin brothers share the same life and you never know which one you're with. That's how I feel with him.

I crumple up the empty cellophane wrapper and walk into the kitchen. "Where's your trash?" With as much time as I spend at this house, I never actually come inside. We pretty much live in the garage.

"Under the sink," he says, not looking away from the TV. "Do you ever eat anything other than sugar?"

I mentally tally what I've eaten today: two protein bars, two bags of peanut M&M's (but they were the small bags so it's really like eating only one), plus the recently consumed Twizzlers. "Sometimes," I answer. Really, I wouldn't even bother with the protein bars if I didn't need them after working out. When I lived with my parents, we actually sat down and ate meals, real ones, like the way we eat at Drew's on Sundays. Margot doesn't cook, plus we always have to eat early so she can get to work, and I'm usually not in the mood. Maybe when I'm eighty I'll like eating dinner at four o'clock in the afternoon, but now, not so much.

I sit back down on the couch next to him and we watch the rest of the show. By four o'clock I know more than I ever cared to know about Quartermaines and Spencers. I shouldn't mock. While I was stuck recovering all those months, I watched my share of bad soap operas. And bad game shows. And bad talk shows. I was an expert in all things daytime television. I just didn't watch *General Hospital*. After today, I know enough that I can pretend like I did.

When it's over, we climb into Josh's truck so he can take me to buy a car battery. We have to stop back at the school parking lot on the way, because I know the make and model of my car, but that's the extent of my knowledge. Apparently that's not enough information to tell me what kind of battery I need.

Josh looks at my car, writes something down, and then takes my keys and pops the hood. I'm still holding onto my backpack with all my books, so I jump out to throw it in my car so I won't have to keep carrying it. As soon as I do, I wish I wasn't so lazy, because that's when I see Tierney Lowell walking toward us in the parking lot. She's not the only one. There are quite a few students exiting the building, and I realize that it's just after four and most of the practices and club meetings are finishing up. She's the one I notice though, because for some reason she seems to hate me. Okay, most of the girls don't like me and I'm an easy target because of the clothes. I get that. But she shoots daggers at me like she just caught me feeding chocolate to her dog. Normally, that's cool, because it's all easily ignorable and I can avoid her without much effort. However, right now I'm jumping out of Josh Bennett's truck and he's standing next to my car and in a minute we'll be leaving together, and that's an act of exhibitionism I wasn't planning to put on just yet.

We get back in the truck immediately, with the shared, unspoken need to get out of there as quickly as possible. Once we've driven away, I look out the window, scanning the cars around us. Josh's windows are tinted, but I still won't take any chances. When I feel safe enough that we're not being watched, I ask the question I've been holding onto since we left his house.

"You watch *General Hospital*?" I don't really need confirmation. I know for a fact that he watches it. He doesn't look at me, but I see his lips turn up in the half-smile he gets when he's embarrassed about something, which is really just a real smile he's trying to drown.

"Yes," he says. Okay, he did answer my question, but what I really wanted to know was why or how or something that will explain it to me because *come on*. But if there's anything more surprising to me than the newfound knowledge that he's a closet soap opera addict, it's the fact that he actually keeps talking and offers me an explanation, one I didn't have to ask for. "My mom used to watch it. Religiously. Never missed an episode. My dad and I made fun of her all the time. When she died, I kept thinking that maybe she'd come back, and when she did, I wanted to be able to tell her everything that had happened so she wouldn't have missed anything. So I watched it. Every day. After a while I realized she wasn't coming back, but I was pot-vested by that point. I just never stopped." He shrugs like he's accepted this fact, only I'm not sure if he's accepting the fact that his mother isn't coming back or that he watches *General Hospital*. Maybe he's not sure either.

"How old were you?"

"I was eight, which I guess is old enough to get it. I just didn't really want to . . . I don't know . . . My dad tried to make it make sense for me, but there really isn't a way to explain how a person you've seen every day of your life just *isn't* anymore. Someone just hit Delete and she's gone. I had a hard time grasping that I could come home one night and find that the person who was laughing and hugging me that morning just stopped existing. I didn't believe it was possible. I didn't want to believe it was possible . . . so, yeah, *General Hospital*."

I didn't look away from him once while he was telling that story. It's the first real thing he's ever told me. It makes me feel ashamed because I've never told him anything real. Not even my name.

He turns and looks at me for a second with what is almost a look of apology on his face. Resignation, maybe? Then he shifts his attention back to the road, and we pull into the store parking lot a minute later.

I have one of Josh Bennett's secrets now. He gave it to me. I wish I could give it back.

Chapter 23

Josh

Whenever someone knocks on my door, there's a part of me that still kind of expects them to be carrying some sort of food. In the days and weeks after my mom and my sister died, I got a crash course in grieving. I learned the way it works: some of it was about how I was expected to react, but most of it was about how other people were expected to react. I don't think there's a written set of rules, but there might as well be, because everyone seems to do the same things. A lot of it has to do with food. My grandmother explained the psychology of this to me at one point, but I didn't really listen because I didn't really care. People must know that just because you need to eat doesn't mean you want them coming by your house nonstop, using casserole dishes and coffee cakes as an excuse to eavesdrop on your grief.

I was indoctrinated into all of the pointless condolence rituals at age eight, and I came to realize that they never really change. I could always count on an onslaught of food and sympathy that I had no use for.

Sometimes people will try to tell you some funny thing they remember, which usually isn't funny at all, just sad. Then you stare at each other uncomfortably until they finally get up to leave, and you thank them for coming, even though they just made you feel worse.

Then you get the people who just want an excuse to come by to see how ripped up your face looks from crying, see if you've cracked yet so they can talk about it with the neighbors. *Did you see poor Mark Bennett and the boy? What a tragedy. It's just so sad.* Or something equally lame. But they brought you some food, so they're entitled.

Ten minutes later the doorbell rings again and we start all over. It goes on like this for days. Too many apologies and a crapload of food. Mostly lasagna.

Maybe some people find comfort in obligatory words and reheatable food; my dad and I just weren't those people. We thanked everybody anyway. Took their foil pans and condolences. Then we threw it all away and ordered pizza. I wonder if there is a person on Earth who is consoled by a casserole.

Then I think about Leigh, and I know that, sometimes, someone shows up at your door offering something better than words and food. Sometimes, somebody brings you something you really need, and it's not a fucking coffee cake.

The first time I met Leigh, she was standing on my front porch, holding the telltale foil-covered dish. My grandmother had died two days earlier, and at that point I had about six of them in the refrigerator and a couple more on my counter. I was fifteen, and I think I visibly exhaled with disgust at the sight of it. But not at the sight of her. She was wearing a really short green sundress and she was seriously hot. Those are the only real details I recall. I recognized her from school, but she was two grades ahead of me and we never spoke. I didn't even know her name until that day.

I took the dish from her, which was actually from her mom, who knew my grandmother. I invited her in because I had learned that that's what you were supposed to do. My grandfather wasn't home, so I did the grieving host thing. We went through the required conversation, making sure to hit all the main points and platitudes. After a few minutes of standing in the kitchen, vying for the title of most uncomfortable, she asked if anyone was home and if I wanted to go into my bedroom. I think it was her way of saying she was sorry and my way of saying thanks for the casserole.

That was the first time Leigh came over. But it wasn't the last. We never dated. Never hung out. She'd come over and sneak into my room at night or we'd end up in her car somewhere, but that was the extent of our involvement, and it's been the extent for close to three years now. Even now that she's at college, we manage to keep up a regular schedule. Sometimes we talk but never about anything real.

Maybe it was wrong. Maybe it is wrong. Wrong or not, I don't feel bad about it. I was up to four deaths by the time she showed up, with only one more to go. I needed one normal thing and Leigh gave me that, and it didn't cost me any emotions or feelings or commitment. I didn't have to love her. I like her, though I'm not sure if that would have been a deal breaker, either. I don't even think it mattered to her if I cared. We still employ a policy of equal-opportunity using, no questions asked. She's sweet and laid-back and good-looking as hell. But if she walked away tomorrow, I wouldn't miss her. People disappear all the time. I might not even notice.

—

It's not a coffee cake Nastya's carrying when she walks into my garage just after eight o'clock. Though if it was, I'm sure it would have been homemade, covered with cinnamon and unbelievably awesome. She is carrying two plastic grocery bags. She walks past me without a word and reaches up with one hand to awkwardly open the door to the inside of the house without letting go of the bag.

"Sunshine?" She doesn't respond, so I follow her in and find her opening the freezer and shoving no fewer than four half-gallon containers of ice cream into it. "What are you doing?"

"What does it look like?" she snaps.

"You get knocked up?"

She whirls around on me. "*What?*" Guess not. I hold my hands up, palms out in surrender. She's obviously not in the mood.

"Sorry, just"—I motion toward the open freezer, her hand still inside on one of the containers—"a lot of ice cream."

"Right, because I'd have to be pregnant to want ice cream. Next you'll be saying that I must have my period because that's the only reason girls have for getting pissed, but of course since you're a guy, you won't actually say *period*, but something prick-ish like *on the rag*." She slams the freezer door shut. Now might be the moment to swear profusely that I had no intention of bringing up her period in any manner, much less one containing the word *rag*, but I feel safer keeping my mouth shut right about now and letting her play this out.

With any other girl I could probably pull out the classic guy fail-safe of walking over and wrapping my arms around her and letting her put her head on my shoulder. It's cheap, but it works. Drew swears by it. But I'm afraid that in this particular instance it would result in one of two things: a string of innovative new expletives or her knee in my balls. My money's on the knee.

"I like ice cream. You never have any. Bad things happen when I go too long without ice cream," she says, sounding slightly calmer.

"Are you sure you got enough?"

"Fuck off."

"Maybe you should open one of those now," I suggest.

So that's what we do. Except that we don't open one, we open all four of them and eat straight out of the containers at the crap coffee table in front of my couch. I keep this one in front of the couch because it's shit and I don't care what happens to it. I don't have to worry about coasters or Drew putting his shoes on it. I figure I'll keep it here until he leaves for college, or some girl finally kills him.

Nastya doesn't eat from the middle of the container like a normal person. A normal person who doesn't eat ice cream out of a bowl, that is. She waits until it starts melting and scrapes away the melted part from around the edge of the container. According to her, half-melted ice cream tastes better than fully frozen ice cream. I can't tell if she's right because she makes me eat the more frozen stuff from the center and threatens me if I try to eat from the edges. We put a pretty big dent in every one of those containers, and she's definitely more Sunshine and less Nasty afterward. I make a mental note for the next time she gets pissy that, in lieu of mood stabilizers, ice cream will do the trick.

We're both on a sugar high after all the ice cream, and we end up back in the garage because I have a list of projects to finish. I figure she's going to go running because that's usually her MO when she's carb-loaded, but she doesn't leave.

"Give me something to do," she says, with just the barest hint of wariness.

"What do you want to do?" I ask, assessing her.

"Nothing with power tools or anything like that. Something I can do with my right hand."

"You want to sand?" I offer. "It sucks, but—"

"I'll sand. Just show me what to do."

I grab a sheet of sandpaper and demonstrate how to attach it to the sanding block.

"We have to sand with the grain on this." I pick up her hands to show her how much pressure to use, and they're so soft that I hate to put sandpaper anywhere near them.

"How do I know when it's done?" she asks, starting to work.

"My dad's rule was always that when you think you're done, you're probably halfway there."

She tilts her head and looks at me like I'm useless. "So, how do I know when it's done?"

I smile. "Just show it to me when you think it's ready. You'll start to know after you've done it a few times."

She keeps her eyes on me for just a second longer than she needs to before turning back to the wood. I know the questions are there. I saw them in her eyes as soon as I mentioned my father. How? When? What happened? But she doesn't ask. She just keeps sanding and I won't stop her. I despise sanding.

It's after midnight by the time we call it quits. I don't know how her hands even held up this long. She sanded the hell out of everything I gave her. I never did ask her what was wrong earlier.

Chapter 24

Nastya

When I get to his house at 7:40, Josh is in his driveway, leaning against the side of his truck. As soon as he sees me, he unlocks the doors and comes around to open mine.

"About time, Sunshine," he says. "I was about to give up on you."

"I didn't know you had a field trip planned," I reply once I've settled into the truck and shut the door.

"I have to get to Home Depot before they close."

"You didn't have to wait for me." He really didn't. It's not like I was going to be sad to miss the weekly hardware store stock-up.

"No. But I knew you'd be showing up sooner or later and my garage would be closed and you'd feel abandoned and then I'd feel guilty and I hate feeling guilty. So it was just easier to wait." One side of his mouth turns up.

"Your life is so hard," I say dryly.

"You are the only person who would even think to say something like that to me." He sounds weirdly pleased.

"Force field hasn't kept me out yet."

"What's that supposed to mean?"

I give him a pointed look because I'm sure he can figure it out. He keeps staring at me, so finally I shrug and then throw in a sigh so he knows that I'm exasperated at having to explain this to him.

"At school, no one comes near you. When I first saw you on the bench in the courtyard, I wondered if you were surrounded by some sort of force field. I kind of wanted to get one for myself. You can hide in plain sight. It's pretty awesome."

"Force field," he repeats, somewhat amused. "Might as well be. People used to call it the dead zone," he adds, but he doesn't elaborate. "Maybe you have special powers." I assume he's commenting on my ability to breach his force field, but I don't respond.

I don't have any special powers. I'm certain of that, because I've spent a lot of time lamenting my lack of them. I do have an uncanny capacity for bitterness and misdirected rage, but I don't think that counts. I feel a little misled. I spent a crapload of time over the past couple years reading books and watching movies, and in all of them, when you die and they bring you back to life, supernatural abilities are just part of the deal. *Sorry you didn't win the grand prize of eternal peace, but you're not walking away empty-handed!* You may come back broken and wrong, but at least you get some cosmic consolation prize, like the ability to read minds or speak to the dead or smell lies. Something cool like that. I can't even manipulate the elements.

Of course if I were to take the books at their word, I'd also have to believe that all teenage boys go around calling girls *baby,* because apparently that's the express train to romance. He was an asshole a minute ago, but then he drops the baby on you and it's all over. Uncontrollable swooning and relinquishment of all self-respect activated. *Ooooh, he called me* baby. *My panties are wet and I luuuuuuv him.* Do real boys actually call girls *baby*? I don't have enough experience to know. I do know that if a guy ever called me *baby*, I'd probably laugh in his face. Or choke him.

Josh pulls the truck into the parking lot and waits for me to get out before leading the way in through the automatic doors to the store. I follow him down one aisle after another. He's almost as comfortable here as he is in his garage. It's like he's being pulled around by an invisible string that leads him to everything he's looking for. He's on autopilot, not even thinking. He must spend half his life in this store.

"I'll get the wood next time," he says. "I don't feel like dealing with it tonight. Plus, I think we're going to have to hit the lumber yard for what I need anyway." The *we're* part of that sentence sticks in my head.

"What are you making?" I ask, glancing down the aisle to make sure it's empty before speaking.

"I have a job for one of the teachers at school. Then I have two Adirondack chairs to make."

"You sell everything you build?"

"Some of it I give away. Some of it I sell. It's how I pay for the wood and the tools."

"Is that why you haven't applied to college?"

"Huh?" he says, putting two more cans of finish in the cart.

"I heard Mrs. Leighton talking to you. You haven't applied yet. You don't want to go?"

"I never really got into the whole school thing."

"Did your parents want you to go?"

"I don't know. We never really got that far."

"So what are you going to do?"

"Probably the same thing I'm doing now. Just more of it."

I get that. I used to think the exact same way, but he can actually do it.

"You can afford that?" I ask. We're in front of a display of little drawers full of every size screw you can imagine, and he's pulling them out without even looking.

"I can afford just about anything I'm willing to pay for." I'm not sure exactly what he means by that, but the way he says it is bitter, and if there's something that makes him sound that way, I don't want to get into it.

We get up to the self-checkout and I start taking things out of the cart and handing them to him one at a time as he runs them over the scanner. It strikes me how utterly domestic this all seems. He could have come without me because I really haven't served any purpose here at all. I could have used the time to run, which is probably what I should have been doing. It's what I would have done if I had shown up at his house and he wasn't there. I would have run myself into exhaustion. He's right about one thing, and I wonder if he knew just how right he was and if that's why he waited. If I had gotten to his house and seen that closed garage, I would have felt abandoned and I may never have gone back.

When we get back to his house just after nine o'clock, I help him carry the bags into the garage and watch him put everything away. He is all grace and fluid in this place; there isn't one wasted movement. Everything he does has purpose. I don't feel uncomfortable about watching. He watches me, too. We have an unspoken agreement. I let him watch me. He lets me watch him. We never call each other on it. It's a gift we give one another. No strings, no expectations, no reading between the lines. We're like mysteries to one another. Maybe if I can solve him and he can solve me, we can explain each other. Maybe that's what I need. Someone to explain me.

When everything has been put away, he closes the garage door and goes into the house, waiting for me to follow before he shuts the door.

"Did you eat?" he asks.

"Yeah, before I came over. You?"

"Yeah. I would have heated you up something if you were hungry. So, you actually cooked tonight?" He regards me skeptically.

I snort. Because snorting is attractive. "No."

"What'd you eat for dinner?"

"Peanut butter cookies."

"I don't need to ask if you're serious, do I? I don't know how you exercise so much with the way you eat."

"Peanut butter has protein in it," I say, full of false indignation. "Besides, I was messing with the recipe. I had to eat a bunch of them to see when I got it right."

"Did you?" he asks, pulling a bottle of water out of the refrigerator and drinking half of it before handing it to me.

"I don't know. I'll bring you some and you can tell me."

"I'll eat your cookies, but you let me feed you real food first."

"You're going to cook for me?" I almost choke on the water before passing the bottle back.

"I cook anyway. What's the difference if you're here?"

"Don't put yourself out."

"I won't." He smiles as I walk around the counter and pick up the MP3 player that's sitting next to the phone.

"What are you listening to?" I ask, turning it on.

"Nothing. I took it out for you. It just sits here. I thought you might want to use it when you run."

Oh. I flip it off without looking and put it back down. "That's okay. I don't need one, but thanks."

"How come? You're the only person I've ever seen running without music. Doesn't it get boring?" he asks. It's a valid question, but it doesn't get boring. It's never quiet enough to get boring and I certainly don't plan to stick shit in my ears like a written invitation for someone to jump me. I shrug, pushing it back farther on the counter and turning away.

"Not really. I heard you and my aunt had a nice chat," I say sarcastically, moving to the sofa. I kick my shoes off and tuck my feet underneath me.

"I was wondering if she'd mention that."

"Why didn't you?"

He shrugs. Between the two of us we do a lot of shrugging. Maybe that's why I finally started talking to him. My shoulders just got tired.

"What did she say?" he asks, sinking down next to me.

"She said she wasn't stupid and that I shouldn't treat her like she is."

"So are you not supposed to be here right now?"

"No. She's okay. She just expects me to let her know where I am from now on. As long as I text her it's fine." It's true. Margot did sit me down and lecture me. She made sure I felt the full measure of my lack of consideration for her and that I understood that if anything happened to me, she would be the one dealing with the wrath of my mother, a five-foot-three woman who could strike fear in a berserker. But God bless Margot, because she wasn't going to force me into a corner with rules and ultimatums, either, which was good, because I would have ignored them. Not because I wanted to rebel against her or because I didn't want anyone telling me what to do, but because I wasn't going to give up sitting in that garage.

"Look, Em," she said, "I'm not naïve. I was young, too. I'm thirty-two years old and I still have a list of stories I will never tell my mother, and if Charlotte was my mother, that list would be even longer, so believe me, I understand. But you also need to understand that you are my responsibility, and beyond that I love you." I think I cringed at that part but she ignored me and kept going. "You'll be eighteen years old soon and I know exactly how futile it will be to forbid you to do anything, but I need you to respect me enough to let me know where you are and who you're with and what you're doing. If you do, we'll be fine. If you don't, I will not hesitate to throw you under the bus with your mother."

She made sure to tack on that she knew I was a smart girl and that smart girls often do the stupidest things and then she hugged me and told me I could tell her anything and she wouldn't judge me. I think it was her version of a sex talk.

I hugged her back because it was my only way to say thank you for letting me keep him without a fight. She wasn't going to make it difficult for me to see him and I desperately needed something in my life that wasn't difficult.

Chapter 25

Josh

"How'd you learn to cook?" The legs are swinging from my kitchen counter, not my workbench, tonight. She eats here all the time now. Sometimes she helps. Sometimes she watches. She always talks.

I reach up and open the cabinet over the refrigerator where my mother stored all of her cookbooks. She looks up at the overfilled shelf. I really only use a few of the ones in the front, but the cabinet goes pretty far back and the books are three rows deep.

"You learned to cook by reading cookbooks?" She raises her eyebrows.

"Isn't that how most people do it?"

"Not most seventeen-year-old boys."

"I don't think many seventeen-year-old boys learn to cook at all."

No response to this one. I didn't say it to make her feel bad, but I think she does, because that quiet sets in. The quiet everyone thinks they should fill but they can't because they're busy trying to figure out what to say. So while they sit and think about it, the silence stretches out until there aren't any words left that wouldn't make everything more uncomfortable. All the okay things to say dissolved in the silence while they were busy thinking.

"If it sucks, can we order pizza?" she asks. Silence can't win against her. It doesn't intimidate her at all. When you spend over a year not talking to another living person, I guess you learn to manipulate the voids.

"It won't suck," I respond.

"Confident, aren't we?" she mocks.

"Have I starved you yet?"

"Surprisingly, no. But that looks questionable." She glances at the cutting board in front of me.

"Vegetables?"

"Apparently."

"How old are you? Eight?" I ask

"How old are *you*? Forty?" she retorts.

"It won't suck," I repeat. "Trust me. I've been cooking a while."

"How long?"

"Three years, give or take." It was right around the time when my grandmother got too sick to do it anymore. About the same time I had to learn to use the washing machine and empty the vacuum cleaner.

"Since you were fourteen? Why?"

"I got tired of eating dry cereal out of the box for dinner every night, so one day I pulled out the books and started reading."

"I can't cook for shit."

"You can bake." Damn, can she bake. She brought those peanut butter cookies over last week covered in sugar with a crisscross pattern across the top. As soon as I looked at them, I remembered that my mother used to make them, too, but I had completely forgotten. And it made me wonder how many other things about her I had forgotten.

"Not the same thing."

"You could learn to cook if you wanted to. I'll even loan you a cookbook if you want," I say half-sarcastically. She doesn't seem too enthusiastic about that. "It's not that hard."

"Maybe not for you. We can't all be awesome at everything like Josh Bennett." She makes me sound like a renowned jackass.

"You know how many meals awesome Josh Bennett effed up in the beginning?" Now I'm making myself sound like a renowned jackass.

"Enlighten me."

"Let's just say I didn't quit eating cereal for the first few months. And even then, my grandfather and I ate a lot of dry, overcooked food."

"You could have eaten at Drew's house every night."

"Yeah, if I wanted to put up with Drew every night." I'm not that much of a glutton for punishment, but she's right: I was always invited.

"He *is* your best friend. Not that I have any clue how that happened."

"We were in Little League together. When everybody started dying and everybody else started ignoring me, he didn't. He just kept coming back and coming back, even when I tried to get rid of him. Eventually I realized he wasn't going anywhere."

"Sounds like Drew."

Sounds like you, too, Sunshine.

"Little League?" she asks, smirking.

"Didn't last," I say. "Once I realized that I was more interested in figuring out how to make a bat than how to swing one, I quit."

She's watching me chop vegetables, but I know she won't offer to help with anything involving hands and sharp knives.

"I messed up everything I baked in the beginning, too," she tells me, switching back to our last conversation. I find that hard to believe. I imagine she came out of the birth canal holding a cupcake and a spatula.

"When did you start?"

"When I was fifteen." She looks down at her left hand, turning it over and staring. I assume she's done talking, because I'm used to being answered with a bare minimum of information from her. Intentionally vague is about as good as it usually gets, but she surprises me and keeps going. "My hand got messed up and I had to do a lot of physical therapy. They suggested that I knead bread dough to build strength back. At some point, I figured that if I was going to spend so much time kneading the dough, I might as well bake the bread." She coughs out a laugh.

"Easier said than done, I take it."

"Understatement." She smiles unguardedly, and it's at war with everything I'm used to from her. "The first time, I don't think it rose at all. It was just this flat, hard, disk-shaped thing. My dad ate it anyway and said it wasn't that bad. You should have seen his face trying to chew it. I don't know how he did it." She hasn't stopped smiling while she tells me this. I'm watching the memory play across her face, and I realize that I've completely stopped chopping the vegetables and I'm just staring at her. I force myself to start chopping again before she notices. "I tried again and again and again. It was always one issue or another. I just couldn't get it right. It pissed the crap out of me."

"Did you finally give up?" I ask, and she looks at me as if the thought is outrageous.

"There was no way I was being brought down by a stupid loaf of bread. I went through so much flour. My mom had to start buying yeast in bulk. Once, I got so pissed, I threw the dough at the ceiling. I thought my mom was going to ban me from the kitchen when she found me on a stepladder, trying to clean it off with a bench scraper. But I finally did it. It took months, but I eventually ended up with a decent loaf of bread."

She shrugs, looking back down at her palm and folding her fingers over. "Hand got stronger, too."

I watch her study her hand and I wonder what she means when she says it got messed up. If you look closely, her fingers aren't exactly straight and sometimes her hand will jerk or she'll drop things. Neither of us acknowledges it when it happens. And there are the scars, some fainter than others. But I know them all. I spend so much time staring at her hands, I could map every one of those scars at this point.

"Do you still bake it? Bread?" I ask.

"Hell no." She snorts as if this is the most absurd question I could ever ask. "It's a pain in the ass. Takes too much time and it's a bitch to get it to work with the humidity here. I just had to know that if I wanted to, I could. I like the stuff that's full of sugar better anyway."

She tilts her chin toward the cutting board in front of me. "I think you chopped those into submission."

I glance down at the red peppers I've annihilated while listening to her talk.

"Not my fault that you're distractingly pretty." I have to take a minute to confirm to the pissed off part of my brain that still works that, yes, in fact, I did just say that. And I don't know if distractingly is even a word. If it is, it's stupid. Like me. Ignoring it and pretending it never happened seems like the best possible plan at the moment and I'm hoping she'll go with it, but she does the next best thing.

"Drew says I'm sexy as fuck." She shrugs blandly and lets me off the hook.

"That, too," I smile, not meeting her eyes as I scrape together what's left of the red peppers. I pour oil into the bottom of a sauté pan and line up the vegetables on the counter. "Turn the front burner on to eight." I point at the stove, and she reaches over to do it just as the front door opens, which shuts us both up.

"Hey, what's go—" Drew stops midsentence when he sees Nastya. I don't know if the shock registering on his face is from the fact that she's here, sitting on the counter like she owns the place, or the fact that she's almost unrecognizable to him. She's wearing white denim shorts and a pink T-shirt and the makeup is long gone from her face, which you can actually see because her hair is pulled back and braided. She looks younger, like she always does like this, and running along her hairline, you can see the jagged scar that she's constantly trying to cover up. I'm used to this Nastya, but I know Drew's never seen her looking even remotely like a real girl, and I've never once mentioned it to him.

I don't know if not telling him was a betrayal. If it was, I should feel guilty, and there's a part of me that does. But I feel justified, too. Even if it is selfish. He can be pissed if he wants. It would still be worth it.

Nastya slides down from the counter and I think she's going to leave me to deal with explanations, but she doesn't. She steps across the kitchen, opens the upper cabinet where I keep the dishes, and pulls out another dinner plate. Then she grabs an extra set of silverware from the drawer and places it on the table. Drew walks to the table, pulls out a chair, and lowers himself into it. He hasn't taken his eyes off her yet. Like he's trying to work out the truth of her. It's the optical illusion again. My eyes have adjusted to it, but he's still trying to find the focus.

"So, you want to introduce me to your girlfriend?" he asks, looking directly at me now. There's more curiosity than malice in the question. He might also be just a little bit impressed.

"Not my girlfriend." With one hand I pass Nastya the trivets to put on the table and keep stirring with the other. I don't look at her face on purpose.

"Well, in that case"—he reaches out and pulls Nastya onto his lap as she places the trivets on the table—"what's for dinner?"

Chapter 26

Josh

"How do you know there's not a God?" Tierney Lowell spits out at Drew, twenty minutes into a debate that's been raging since the fifth period bell rang. It started with a discussion about a short story we'd read last week and somehow devolved into a full-scale back-and-forth on the existence of God.

"How do you know there *is* one?" Drew retorts. He isn't even trying. This is laziness, or just apathy. I've seen him practicing for Debate, and this is nothing for him. He's just baiting Tierney for fun.

"I never said I *knew*. Faith isn't about knowledge. That's why it's called faith, jackass. Thus, the expression *leap of faith*."

"Ms. Lowell?"

"Moron, mule, idiot, fool, Drew," Tierney tosses out. It's Ms. McAllister's rule. You use an unacceptable word, you have to come up with five to replace it. She lets the Drew part slide.

"When did you turn all religious?" Drew doesn't miss a beat. Everyone is paying attention, heads whipping back and forth like the audience at a tennis match. Immoral people debating the existence of God is always a crowd pleaser. Especially with palpable sexual tension thrown in. The only other sound in the room is the periodic slam of the stapler Sunshine is using in the corner. She's been collating papers since class started. Her back is turned but I can almost see her listening.

"I hate religion. I believe in God."

"Believing in God is for weak people." Drew almost sounds bored, but it's obvious he's enjoying this.

"Then it's a mystery why you don't." She leans back in her chair but Drew doesn't take the bait.

"People believe in God because they don't believe in themselves. They need something else to depend on or to blame instead of taking responsibility for their own shit—crap, excrement, waste, mistakes, faults."

"That's rich coming from a person who takes responsibility for nothing."

"I've never denied my actions."

"Which makes you such a moral paragon."

"Morals?" Drew chokes out the word, which probably burns on his tongue. "Isn't that the pot smoker calling the kettle black?" Kevin Leonard and the other stoners in the room think this is the greatest thing they've ever heard. "Don't lecture me, T. I take responsibility for everything I do."

"Not everything."

"If you're going to make accusations, back it up. Give me some support. Otherwise your arguments mean nothing."

"We're not in Debate, Drew." She doesn't look cowed by him. She looks betrayed.

"We might as well be. Same rules. You want to say something, support it. Otherwise, don't throw it out there, because you just make your argument weak. Kind of like people who believe in God."

Ms. McAllister changes the subject and effectively ends the discussion. It's surprising that she let it go on as long as she did. The conversation might be over, but the glaring between Drew and Tierney continues until the end of class, and I wonder if they might start ripping each other's clothes off right here.

Nastya

"Go sit. I've got it." Josh nudges me away from the sink after we've cleared the dishes from dinner. I eat here more often than not now. It's the only time I ever consume an actual meal. He makes me real food and I keep him in desserts.

"You cooked. I can wash the dishes."

"No. You can't." He pulls the sponge out of my hands and turns off the tap while I go clear off the rest of the table and dump the dishes in the sink. We've fallen into an oddly domestic pattern and it's kind of pathetic when you stop to think about why.

"I can't wash the dishes?" I ask, disbelieving.

"No." He shakes his head.

"Why not?"

"Because you suck at it."

"I suck at it?" Who sucks at washing dishes? It's not brain surgery. It's cleaning the food out of a pan.

"Yes. How can you not know this? I have to rewash the dishes every night after you leave."

"You do not." *Does he?*

He looks at me and I know it's true.

"You're anal-retentive."

"Yes, I like to eat off clean dishes. I have issues," he deadpans.

I think of how low I've sunk. I don't even have the ability to clean a dish properly. He cooks, he cleans up the dishes, he builds freaking furniture. I feel useless around here. The dryer buzzes and I figure I can do something.

"Fine. I'll go fold the clothes." I turn to head into the laundry room.

"No, you won't. Just sit."

"I can't fold clothes, either?"

"You are *not* folding my underwear."

"You're kidding."

"No. It's weird." He reaches across me and pulls open a drawer full of dish towels with a dripping wet hand. "Here. Dry." He snaps the towel at my chest, splattering me with water in the process.

I grab it out of his hands. "Maybe I'll just go get a pair of your boxer shorts and dry the dishes with those." Childishness is not beneath me.

"How do you know I wear boxer shorts?"

"Just hoping." The alternative is so unappealing.

He shrugs, handing me a plate. "Go ahead. You're the one who has to eat off them."

"No one likes you," I reply, because muttering under my breath, like a surly teenager, is cool.

I end up using the towel and Josh is right. He does wash the dishes better than I do. Mostly because I'm lazy when it comes to any kind of cleaning, but he doesn't need to know that.

"What was with Drew and Tierney today in English?" I ask.

"What? The God thing? Drew and Tierney always argue. Drew would argue the merits of celibacy if Tierney were against it."

"Maybe. It just seemed personal."

"Drew likes to piss her off. He was just messing with her today. He could have argued her into the ground if he wanted."

"I'm surprised he didn't. He'll destroy anyone in Debate." It's impressive. If he feels like it, he'll verbally assault someone to the point where they can barely stand when it's over. He won every round at the tournament we attended a few weeks ago, and he didn't even pull out the full arsenal of charm.

"He didn't have to. She has no chance up against him. It

wasn't even worth his effort." It's true. That's just Drew. He does it for fun until he gets bored. He's like a cat batting a lizard around until it's too maimed to play with anymore.

"Why does Ms. McAllister let it go? It wasn't even what you were supposed to be discussing."

"That's how she gets to know everyone. She can figure you out a lot easier if she just lets you go and listens. Finds out how you think. Learns your strengths and weaknesses." It's like recon. I'm impressed. But it's not the most efficient when you only have two people arguing.

"No one else even got involved," I say.

"No one else is stupid enough to want to debate the existence of God. It's an unwinnable argument." He finishes putting the last of the clean dishes back into the cabinets.

"On which side?"

"Either."

"Do you believe in God?"

"Yes," he answers definitively. My expression must betray me because he asks, "What?"

"I'm just surprised. I didn't think you would."

"Because I'm cursed and everyone around me dies?" he asks unemotionally.

I don't want to give him affirmation, but it is what I was thinking.

"I believe in God, Sunshine. I've always believed that God exists," he says.

And what he says next isn't self-pity or angst or melodrama. It's truth.

"I just know that he hates me."

Maybe what he says should floor me, but it doesn't even make me blink. Maybe I should jump in immediately and tell him that he shouldn't think that way. That, of course, God doesn't hate him. That it's a ridiculous thing to believe. Except, it's not. Nothing about it is ridiculous. When you watch every person you love systematically removed from your life until at seventeen years old there is no one left, how can you think anything else? It makes such perfect sense that the only thing that surprises me is that I didn't think of it myself.

Chapter 27

Josh

"You look ridiculous."

Sunshine is already in my garage at eight o'clock, dressed to go to a party with Drew. She hates the parties, but he gets her to go every time.

Our routine has become, well, routine. We do homework, make dinner, and then hang out in the garage. Sometimes she leaves for a while to run before she ends up back here sanding down wood or looking over my shoulder and asking a hundred questions about every single thing I'm doing. She'll sand down anything and everything, but she won't go near any of the power tools because she doesn't trust her hand.

"What? You don't think it works? I may not change them back." She looks down at the old worn-out work boots she's borrowed from me. They're enormous on her feet, and she has them pulled and laced as tightly as possible to hold them on. She walked in earlier in the most torturous black dress imaginable and open-toed shoes. I have too many tools going today, so she only got to stay if she changed the shoes. Part of me hoped she'd choose the leaving option so I wouldn't have to keep looking at her in that dress and struggling to keep my dick in check, but she didn't put me out of my misery. Weeks ago, when I finally accepted the fact that she wasn't going away, I promised myself I wouldn't go anywhere near her. I'm not that self-destructive. But on days when she walks in wearing tight black dresses and my work boots, I wonder how long I can keep that promise.

"You sure you won't come?" she asks. She always asks when she's going out with Drew. But I won't subject myself to that, even to be close to her. Drew pulls into the driveway and saves me from having to answer.

"Nice boots. I like it. Maybe I'll let you keep those on."

She flips him off but it means nothing.

"You should come," he says to me. "I can hook you up."

"Hook yourself up. I'm good."

"Yeah, we know." He looks at Nastya. "I'm good, too. I have my own personal Sunshine to keep me warm."

Something in me snaps with that. He goes out with her; he touches her; he says shit no one should be allowed to get away with to her. But he cannot call her Sunshine. I'm nailing a board down over my anger so I don't blow up. They'll be out of here in a minute and it'll be over. I wish they'd get out of here now.

"Call me Sunshine again, and I will murder you, cocksucker."

I don't know whose head spins faster, mine or Drew's, but I'm the speechless one in this garage right now. Once I register the words, my shock has to compete with my amusement, and I fight the smile because, obviously, she doesn't like him calling her Sunshine any more than I do.

I'm not sure when she made the decision to speak to him, but I know it wasn't at this moment. I may not have figured out much about her, but I have picked up on the fact that everything she does is a choice. She considers the repercussions for every action she takes. The girl does not understand the word *spontaneous*. She plans every breath.

"You talked? You talked! She talked!" He looks at me for my reaction, but there isn't one. I'm surprised, but I'm not shocked. I'm still trying to stifle a smile.

If it's at all possible, I think his eyes get wider.

"You fucker! You knew!" He's going back and forth between Sunshine and me, unable to decide who to look at. Neither of us is looking at him.

He's regaining his composure, and I remember myself enough to walk over and close the garage. My house is all the way down at the end of the street, so nobody can really see in, but Drew is being obnoxiously loud right now and we don't need an audience.

"Well, well, well." Now he's pleased with himself but there's no reason for it. Drew can find a way to make anything his own personal triumph. Obviously his charms are so irresistible that he can make a not-quite-mute girl talk. Or maybe he just thinks he's figured something out.

"How long?" he asks, and I'm not sure what he means until he motions between Nastya and me. "You two? How long?"

"Us two nothing. We talk—that's it." I look across to where she's leaning against the workbench. She keeps glancing over at me. I can't tell if she wants me to know something or if there's something she wants from me. I feel a mixture of relief and resentment. I'm glad to be done keeping this from Drew, but I can't help feeling that I've lost something irretrievable and that she's the one who gave it away without asking.

"That's it? She hasn't talked to anyone since she's been here. Not one word. Except apparently to you. And that's it?"

"Didn't mean to let you down." I think I'm the one who's disappointed. I know that she's just a little bit less mine than she was a few minutes ago.

"She doesn't even have an accent." He turns his attention back to Nastya.

"Disappointed?" Her voice comes out like arsenic-laced honey. It sounds nothing like the one she uses with me.

"Extremely. I thought it would be hot. I've never had someone scream my name with an accent before. I was looking forward to it."

"You're vile." There's more amusement than disgust there.

"You've been waiting a while to say that to me, haven't you? Feel good?"

"Not as good as I thought it would." She scrunches up her nose as she thinks about it, and she looks unbearably cute. She's obviously done because she walks to the back of the garage to hit the button and open the door back up.

"Hey," Drew calls before she can press it, as if he's just remembered something monumental. "Did you just call me a cocksucker?" he asks.

Her eyes light up for him and one side of her mouth quirks into the faintest hint of a smile. "True story."

The mischief in his eyes matches hers and his smile is a mixture of pride and disbelief, and I get why she chose to speak to him.

"Welcome to the party, Sunshine."

Chapter 28

Nastya

The party at Jen Meadows's house is lame, and we know when we get there that we probably won't stay. It's a relief, because even though it's inside, the noise at these things always gets to me. It's too hard to filter out the sounds and where they're coming from. I've gotten to the point where I can relax a little indoors with people around, but given a choice, I'd prefer the quiet.

Drew keeps me attached to his side more diligently than usual. Normally, he drapes his arm over my shoulders as we walk in, in a clichéd display of ownership, and then once that's established, I'm released. He never lets me get far and I never venture more than a couple feet from him, but tonight he doesn't want to let me go at all.

He keeps looking at me sideways and smiling like we're coconspirators in something. I should regret what I did, but I don't—even though he did spend the whole ride over here trying to get me to tell him why I don't talk, until I finally explained to him, in vivid detail, the fate that would befall him if he asked again. He didn't. I think it had something to do with the love he has for his boy parts.

His arm snakes around my waist, and he backs me against a wall just in time for me to look over his shoulder and see Tierney Lowell walk in the door. Chris Jenkins has a cup in her hand and is talking in her ear before she makes it through the living room.

Drew slides his hand down my arm and laces his fingers through mine, pulling me toward the stairs in direct view of the rest of the room. I have two choices: I can stop him in front of everyone, which would consist of me standing still and refusing to budge while he tries to lead me up the stairs, or I can go with him. Option A is the one that will draw more attention. Drew and I disappearing upstairs to a bedroom at a party isn't going to raise any eyebrows. Apparently we've been screwing for weeks. It doesn't bother me. Drew has had every opportunity to try to take advantage of me and he never has. Other than the arm around my shoulders and occasionally holding my hand, he doesn't touch me at all. No surreptitious feel-copping whatso-ever. Drew keeps me around for some reason, but whatever it is, I'm fairly certain it isn't sex.

"Why do you want everyone to think we're together?" I whisper when he pulls me through the door of an empty bed-room and shuts it behind me. He reaches down and turns the lock. The only light is coming in under the door and from a street lamp outside the window. It's a guest room with a bed that's obviously already been occupied once tonight. The music is still so loud that I don't have to worry about anyone hearing us, but I keep my voice down anyway and Drew follows suit.

"Because we should be." He leans back against the door and closes his eyes. He's delivering a line but he doesn't mean a word of it.

"You don't do together. You do one-offs."

"I could make an exception." He looks me up and down but his heart isn't in it and I don't know why he's bothering.

"You could, but if you did, it wouldn't be for me."

"What would you do if I kissed you right now?"

"I'd probably let you, just to see what all the fuss is about. Then I'd rip your lips off and feed them to you, which would be kind of hard because, you know, you'd have no lips."

He nods, not looking at me. "You're scary."

"So you're not going to kiss me?"

"No. But not because of the lip-ripping thing, though that is compelling."

"You must have a good reason to tank your reputation over it."

"I don't have to tank anything. What do you think we're doing right now? Talking? You don't even speak, so that limits the options. Everyone downstairs knows I'm screwing you right now." He pulls out his shirt and rumples his clothing.

"Am I enjoying it?"

"I'm the best you've ever had," he says hypnotically, like he's using Jedi mind tricks on me.

"Undoubtedly. So why not just do what we're doing anyway?"

"I could call your bluff, you know." He opens one eye to look at me.

"But you won't." I might be a little disappointed if I wasn't so relieved. "You should at least tell me why. I showed you mine."

"If I showed you mine, you'd probably rip that off, too." He won't give me anything, even though there's obviously something there to give.

"So what was the point of the past couple months if you never had any intention of following through?"

"People think I'm hooking up with you, they won't expect me to be screwing everything else on two legs."

"But isn't that what you do?" I never really bought the whole of his image, at least not to assume that it was all of him. But he was the one selling it. I was led to believe that if you look up *moral turpitude*—or maybe just *man-whore*—the definition is Drew Leighton. This is shattering that image.

"I liked you so much better when you didn't talk."

"Yeah, I know. Can't unring a bell. Don't know what you got till it's gone. Hindsight's a bitch. Answer the question."

He rolls his eyes and exhales, making sure I experience the full weight of his annoyance.

"It's what I'm supposed to do. If I stop, everyone will want to know why. Then they'll start speculating. Subterfuge is much easier."

"Why me?"

"I figured you'd never tell anyone the truth." He shrugs, and if Drew Leighton could do sheepish, I'd say he was trying, but it's a little out of his depth. "Sorry. It didn't start out that way. If it makes you feel better, I really did plan to pull the same shit with you as always. If you would have gone for it, we'd have hooked up at the first possible opportunity and we would not be here right now. But you just seemed to take it all as a joke, and it was a relief. I was relieved to not have to follow through on it, and the more I chased you, the less you took me seriously. So the real question is, why did *you* put up with it?"

"Same reason as you. People smell your piss all over me, they assume I'm off the table. Other than Ethan the Arrogant, I get left alone. Win-win." I don't really care what people say about me. I'm fine with lies and rumors. It's the truth I don't want being told.

"Where does Josh fit into this?" he asks, finally meeting my eyes.

"We're not talking about Josh."

"Aren't we?" he probes.

"Josh is screwing someone else." Add that to the fact that he doesn't want to have to give a crap about anyone ever again and he's kind of an impossible dream.

"So? Josh Bennett has a fuck buddy." He shrugs like he's just told me that Josh wears pants. It's the same tone he used when he dropped it on me the first time, and it sucks just the same to hear it. "How do you think he's managed to keep his hands off you this whole time? Doesn't mean anything." The look I give him says otherwise. "Don't get all judgmental. He's a good guy, not a saint."

"What is she to him?" I try not to sound jealous or like I'm fishing for information, but I am on both counts.

"She," he says, looking at my chest, because he is still Drew, before pulling his gaze up to my eyes, "is a poor man's Sunshine."

I have a seriously hard time believing that, because Josh never comes anywhere near me.

"He doesn't even look at me sideways much less try to touch me."

"You're right. He doesn't look at you sideways. He looks right at you and doesn't even try to hide it. The only thing I've ever seen him drool over as much has four legs and is made of mahogany, but I don't think he's planning to ask it out any time soon."

"Don't let him do that, Drew. Not with me. He'll listen to you."

"No. He won't." He pauses to look up at me from the floor. "I think that beam's been cut, Nastya."

"Beam's been cut?"

"Yeah, like that time has passed, that ship has sailed, that cherry's been popped. I was just trying to put it in building terms, but my frame of reference is limited. Didn't work, huh?"

"Not really."

"Don't worry. Josh likes to keep his life free of unnecessary complications. I think you're safe for a while." He reaches up and tousles his hair purposefully.

"How long do we have to stay in here?" I'm done with the

Josh conversation. Some things are better left alone, and this is the definition of one of those things. I look at the tangled sheets on the bed and decide against it. I slide down the wall onto the floor next to Drew and cross my ankles. He pulls my head onto his shoulder, letting me lean against him.

"At least another twenty minutes. I have a reputation to uphold."

Chapter 29

Josh

"Shit!" The saw blade slices through my hand, and in seconds I've got blood soaking my pants where I'm pressing down on it with the palm of my other hand. I'm not good with blood. In fact, I am absolutely horrible when it comes to blood, so this situation pretty much sucks for me.

I sink down to the ground and lean against the cabinets. I need to stop the bleeding, but sitting is taking priority because I think I might pass out.

"What the hell, Josh?" Nastya is picking up my hand, and I want to tell her to stop because there's so much blood, but I just end up cursing again.

"Here." She's got pressure on the cut now and I'm trying to reach up with my right arm to grab the towel that's on the counter. She shoves it away.

"That's covered with grease and sawdust. Crap!" she says as my blood starts running down her arm while her hand stays clamped over the gash. "Hold this!" She grabs my right hand back and presses it over the blood-gushing split across my left palm.

I make the mistake of looking before she presses my hand

down over it again, and I get seriously light-headed. Blood is my kryptonite. Massive amounts of puke I can handle, but I can't do blood. Especially my own.

"A lot of blood," I breathe out.

"No, it's not," she says, pressing her hand down on top of mine.

"Yes, it is," I manage, because I'm right on this one. If I'm sitting on the floor like a pussy because of some blood, then I'm going to insist that it's an awful lot of blood.

"No," she says emphatically, and there's no room left for discussion when she looks right in my eyes, forcing me to focus on her. "It's really not."

She keeps glancing around for something to stop the bleeding.

"Can you get up?" she asks.

Fuck. I'm gonna pass out in front of her if she makes me stand right now. Before I can fully absorb the humiliation of that thought, she diverts my attention. By taking off her shirt. She has it off in one motion and is wrapping it around my hand before I can ask her what the hell she's doing. It's almost more impressive than the bra maneuver.

"Shouldn't I be the one taking off my shirt?" I ask to lighten the moment. At least for me. She doesn't seem at all affected.

"If I thought you could get it off before you lost another pint of blood, believe me, I would have gone that route." She pulls the shirt tight around my hand and holds it down. "Besides, I have to focus, and looking at you shirtless might cause me to hyperventilate. Then we'd both be passed out." Sarcastic smartass.

"I haven't passed out." *Yet*.

"Yet"—she smiles, lifting my hand and checking out her work—"now at least you won't bleed all over the carpet. Inside," she commands, but I'm too busy staring at her chest in a pink lace bra. I'm not sure if I'm more shocked by the fact that I'm staring at her tits or by the fact that it's pink, not black, but at least it's got my mind off the blood. And then, before I can even move to stand, my traitorous dick jerks. I'm bleeding out in the middle of my garage. Ten seconds ago, my worst fear was that I would pass out in front of her. That's not my worst fear anymore. It does it again and I'm in the midst of an undeniable hard-on. Now I *try* to think about the blood, but she's right in front of me, offering to help me up, and it's far too late for that. She glances down. *Of course* she glances down.

"You're kidding me, right?" She looks back to my face, and if I had any blood to spare, it would probably turn red. Fortunately, between my dick and my hand, all of my blood is spoken for. "Seriously? Right now? At this moment? *Seriously?*" She shakes her head and laughs and it's almost worth all of the embarrassment. "It must so suck to be a guy."

"Your fault. You're the one who took off your shirt."

"If you get your ass into the house, I can put on another one." She's gently pulling on my upper arm.

I push myself up as slowly as possible. Thankfully the shirt is knotted tight enough around my hand that the bleeding is under control, and I'm able to make it inside without sacrificing what's left of my Y chromosome.

A few minutes later, she comes out of my bedroom wearing one of my T-shirts, and it might almost be worse than seeing her in no shirt at all. She sets the first aid kit on the table in front of us.

"Is this the only thing you have? I think I'm going to need more."

"Guest bathroom. Under the sink."

Now we have a huge bottle of peroxide and extra gauze, and she looks at me nervously before unwrapping the shirt.

"Don't watch. Okay?"

"I thought it wasn't that bad."

"It's not. But I think a paper cut might do you in, so just close your eyes or look over there or something."

I pick *or something*. I reach out with my good hand and lift up the hem of the T-shirt she's wearing and trace my thumb up one of the scars on her abdomen that I was too busy staring at her chest earlier to really study. Her breath hitches almost imperceptibly at the contact, before she swats my hand away and I drop the shirt.

"You haven't lost so much blood that I'm above hitting you. And if I hit you, it will hurt."

I don't doubt that for a second. "What's it from? The scar?"

"Surgery."

"No shit, Sunshine. What about the one by your hair?" I've wanted to ask about this one for ages. The other one, I just discovered tonight, along with a pink lace bra and a set of abs that is just insane.

"Catfight."

"That I can believe."

"Good. Quit talking. I'm afraid you're going to pass out as it is."

"Then you talk to me." I lean my head back and close my eyes while she starts on my hand.

"About what?"

"I don't know. Anything other than blood. Tell me a story."

"What kind of story would you like?" She cajoles me like a five-year old, which is exactly what I'm acting like right now. I blame blood loss.

"The real one."

"You said you didn't want to hear about blood."

I don't know what that means, but I know it means something. It's just another piece of the puzzle she is. But the more she gives me, the more abstract she gets. It's like pieces to three different puzzles. You try to put them together but they never fit, and when you force them, the picture comes out all wrong.

She's got my hand unwrapped, and I watch her face while she's cleaning it. She doesn't look bothered at all. Once some of the blood is gone, I can't help checking it out. The gash runs from the base of my thumb diagonally across my palm towards my wrist. It hurts like a bitch. She covers it with some antibiotic crap and wraps it with gauze because there aren't any bandages big enough to cover it.

She disappears into the kitchen and I hear her open the fridge and dig through the cabinets. When she comes back, she hands me a can of soda and a chocolate bar. In addition to the ice cream, she has taken to stashing candy here, too. I wonder how long it'll be before she has a shelf in the medicine cabinet and a drawer in my dresser. And once that happens, I wonder how long it'll be before she's gone.

"Am I dying?" I ask.

"I think you'll live. Why?" She's amused.

"Because giving up your sugar is like giving up your life's blood. I figure I must be dying."

"Consider it a transfusion. You're as pale as me right now. It's scary."

"I didn't think anything scared you."

"Not the sight of blood. Unlike some people." She smirks at me.

"I owe you a shirt. You didn't have to do that."

"You were bleeding like a son of a bitch. I didn't have time to fight with yours. Besides, you know how many people have seen me without my clothes? Doesn't bother me."

I'm not touching that last part. I like thinking about her without her clothes, but I don't like thinking about anybody else seeing it. "I thought you said it wasn't that much blood."

She tightens the gauze and puts my hand back on the table. "Relatively speaking, it wasn't."

"Relative to what? Being shanked?"

"You should probably still get stitches." The look I give her tells her that is not happening. "It'll heal faster. Plus, you need to get it looked at to see if you sliced a tendon or something."

I wince at the *sliced a tendon* comment and I catch her smirk at me again. She's getting to do a lot of smirking at my expense tonight.

"The longer it takes to heal, the longer you won't be able to play with your tools," she singsongs. I'm not oblivious to the double entendre, and I could probably make some lame comeback about still having my right hand, but she knows she's hitting home right now and I'm listening. "Compromise," she says, grabbing her phone and shooting off a text. "Margot's off tonight. If she's home, you let her look." The phone beeps a few seconds later and she holds it up. *Come on over.*

An hour later, we're back at my house. My hand is treated and wrapped, and I've been sworn off tools for at least a week, depending on how it heals.

"Your left hand sucks now, too." She picks up my bandaged hand and turns it over in hers. "You're going to go crazy, aren't you?"

"High probability." The thought of a week or more of not being able to work is more depressing than I want to admit.

"You won't even be able to wash the dishes." She's loving this.

"We'll use paper plates," I respond dryly.

"I sit with you for your therapy," she says, and it takes me a minute to realize what she's talking about. The garage, the tools, the wood, the work. My therapy. The thing that keeps me sane. "Want to come along for mine?"

Her therapy turns out to be nightly running. Not jogging. Not a leisurely stroll. Hard-ass running. She's been kicking my ass for three days in a row like a tiny, porcelain drill instructor. It's miserable and exhausting. I've thrown up every time. I wish I could say I hate it.

I haven't been able to keep up with her, at least not for any real distance. My legs are longer and I can take her in a sprint, but I have no stamina. She can go hard for miles, but the way she does it, nothing about it is for exercise. She runs like something is chasing her.

"You won't keep throwing up. It gets easier," she says, standing several feet away while I purge in the bushes at some unfortunate stranger's house.

"Only if I keep doing it," I respond, thinking I should start running with a bottle of mouthwash. Or at least gum.

"You're not going to?" Not surprised or curious. Disappointed.

I don't do well with disappointment. Especially not hers. If she wants me to run with her, I will. Maybe she'll eventually get tired of waiting for me to keep up and she'll send me home where I can hide in my garage. Running away is her thing. Hiding is mine.

When we get back to my house, I jump in the shower immediately and offer to drive her home when I get out. I have to yank myself out of the water because I could probably stay in there all night. Every part of my body aches.

When I get out to the family room, there's a note on the coffee table.

Had to run—no pun intended. Couldn't trust myself knowing you were wet and naked in the next room. Didn't want to tempt fate. See you tomorrow.

P.S. I folded your laundry. Don't worry. I didn't touch your panties.

On the bottom, it's signed with a little drawing of the sun with a smiley face in it, which has to be the most out-of-character thing I've ever seen from her.

I head over to the utility room, and there's a perfectly folded pile of my clean laundry on top of the washer. When I open the dryer door, there's nothing left in it but my abandoned boxer shorts.

Chapter 30

Nastya

"Ice cream."

I know those words. I like those words. I look up from the Physics textbook that has been my close companion for the past three hours. I will never pass this test. I should never have even signed up for the class. I was reaching from the beginning. Josh is standing next to me and leans over, shutting the book. I have a feeling this may have something to do with the frustrated barrage of profanity that left my mouth moments ago.

Academics have never been my forte. I'm not very smart, a fact that I have no trouble proving to myself several times a day. Asher is the smart one. He checked off that box on the family rubric. Asher has baseball and school. I had the piano. Now I don't have anything.

"You need it. We're getting it. Now." Angry dad voice again.

"Now?"

"Now. Remember when you said that bad things happen when you don't get enough ice cream? Bad things are happening. You're all stressed out and cranky like a teenage boy who's not getting laid."

"Nice analogy." *Do they get cranky?*

"Sorry, it's true. And nobody likes a cranky Sunshine. It goes against the laws of nature." He pulls my chair away from the table with me in it.

"You make me sound like a petulant four-year-old." *Petulant—sulky, crabby, peevish, moody, sullen.* Picked that one up from Asher while he was studying for the SATs.

"You're acting like one. With a more colorful vocabulary. Get your ass in the truck. We're going." He grabs his keys and stands in the entryway, holding the door open and waiting.

We pull up to a strip mall a couple miles away at eight o'clock and I follow him into an ice cream parlor that's tucked away in the back corner of the plaza. If you didn't know it was there, you'd probably never find it. It's a Tuesday, and it's mostly empty except for a family at a corner table with a little boy whose clothes seem to have seen more chocolate ice cream than his mouth. I haven't been in here before. I prefer to eat my ice cream out of the container at the kitchen counter where no one can watch me. Ice cream makes me happy. I like to concentrate on the joy.

This place is a little pastel paradise. It's small and screams CUTE! at the top of its lungs from every direction. Six glass-top tables are scattered around the front of the shop. It must be a nightmare to keep them clean in a place full of melting sugar. The chairs have silver metal frames that match the table bases and padded vinyl seat cushions in pastel pink, yellow, blue, and lavender. I look down at myself in black on black. I look like teenage Elvira walking into a Bonne Bell commercial.

There's a girl I don't recognize wiping down the tables in the front and a girl behind the counter who I do. She's a senior named Kara Matthews from my ex–music class. She stares at us when we walk in. Then she must realize that she's doing it, because she looks away, but it's pretty obvious what she's thinking. *Nastya Kashnikov and Josh Bennett walk into an ice cream parlor together on a Tuesday night.* It's like the beginning of a bad joke. Or the Apocalypse.

"What do you want?" Josh asks, knowing I can't answer him here. I raise my eyebrows impatiently. He holds his hands out in surrender at the look I give him. "I didn't want to be accused of being a chauvinist, but if you don't tell me what you want, I'm just going to have to guess." There's mischief there and I don't trust him. I shrug. I'm an excellent shrugger. It's rivaled only by my ability to nod.

There's nothing I can do. I sit down, facing the front windows, so I don't have to look at Kara Matthews or let her look at me. I'm thankful that I'm still in my school clothes. Josh walks back to the counter and I can hear his voice but I can't figure out what he's saying. I do hear Kara.

"Seriously?" she laughs. I wonder what he's said, but he spoke too low for me to hear. The thought of Josh Bennett flirting with Kara Matthews is outside the realm of possibility for my imagination. I trace my fingers around the beveled edge of the glass table and try to predict what kind of concoction he's going to walk back with just to taunt me. Probably lime sorbet and peanut butter cup ice cream or some equally vile combination.

The wait lasts forever. It shouldn't take this long to order ice cream, and I almost cave and turn around when I hear him walking back to the table with the uneven footfalls I have memorized by now.

"Dinner," Josh says, coming around from behind with what can only be described as a trough of ice cream. He sets it down in front of me. He must have gotten every kind of ice cream they have. It reminds me of something my dad would do. Something so utterly ridiculous that I would have no choice but to be cheered up from whatever tragedy had befallen my young life. Back before I knew what real tragedy was. When the hard things were the fact that Megan Summers had better clothes or that I had messed up during a performance. Charles Ward was the master of cheer-ups when I was little. Better than a barrel full of puppies. Maybe even better than melty ice cream.

"I didn't know what kind you wanted so I got them all." He's not lying. I look at the trough, and I'm fairly certain the only ice cream flavors not in there are the ones they haven't invented yet. He sits down across from me and leans his elbows on the table, unsuccessfully trying to stifle the shit-eating grin on his face.

I don't have a pen and talking here is out, so I grab my phone from my purse and text the boy sitting across the table from me. His phone beeps a second later and he pulls it out to read the two-word message I sent him.

Where's yours?

And then he does something that shocks even me. Josh Bennett, king of the brooding stoics, laughs. Josh Bennett laughs, and it's one of the most natural, uninhibited, beautiful sounds I've ever heard. I know Kara Matthews is watching us and people will talk tomorrow. But right now I can't even care. Josh Bennett laughs, and for one minute, everything is right in the world.

"We're going on vacation over Thanksgiving," my mother tells me on the phone when I get home from Josh's.

It's ten o'clock and there were three messages from her, along with a text that simply read *Please call*. Ten o'clock is never too late for my mother. Not anymore. She pores over pictures until all hours. Before the attack, I never remember her working through the nights like she does now. But after, it was all she seemed to do. My mother went through the most prolific period in her life while I was recovering. She'd say she stayed up because she wanted to be awake if I woke up and needed anything, but I don't think she could sleep. It was easier to crawl into a computer full of her photographs than a bed full of her nightmares. I'd sit up with her sometimes, because I couldn't sleep, either. I'd watch her, amazed at just how much a person could accomplish fueled by tea and regret.

"We're staying in a beautiful house. We'd like you to come." She waits for a reaction. She always waits. There's a hope my mother never loses that, one day, I'll fill that pause. She probably wouldn't even care what the words were at this point, just that they were there.

"We thought it would be fun to go skiing." *Skiing? Seriously, Mom? With the hand?* I don't want to go on vacation. I certainly don't want to go skiing. I'd rather be hit in the face with a dodge-ball. Repeatedly.

"I already talked to Dr. Andrews. We can make an appointment to have your hand looked at again before we go. She thinks it should hold up fine as long as it isn't for too long a period. If it starts to bother you, we can go in and sit by the fire and drink coffee." I hate coffee. I can't ski. I'm from Florida. I have no sense of balance or coordination, and I have a hand that likes to randomly lose its grip at inopportune times. Not to even mention the fact that it's so full of plates and screws that it will set off every metal detector in the airport.

My brother is the athlete. He must be in heaven. I don't want them not to go because of me, but I don't think that's an issue. They'll go whether I do or not. And I'm not going. I'll be miserable and then everyone will be miserable and it'll be my fault. Again. I'm tired of being responsible for other people's misery. I can't even put up with my own.

My mom keeps talking. She's not afraid of being interrupted, but she wants to get all her selling points made. Like the faster she gets them out, the more convincing they'll be.

"The house is big. It belongs to Mitch Miller, your father's boss, and he's not using it this year, so he offered it to us. Addison is coming, too." *Addison is coming? It fits. Morals were* never the big issue with my mother, just excellence. Asher and I could probably screw half the country under her roof as long we didn't lose focus. I wonder if it would still apply to me now that I'm not good at anything anymore. Knowing Asher, he probably isn't even sleeping with the girl yet, but it's an easy thing to judge my mother on, so I use it.

I tap the phone three times which means I'm hanging up.

"Please at least think about it. Margot's going to come, too, and I don't want you to be alone on Thanksgiving." I hang up before she can tell me that she loves me. Not because I don't want to hear that she says it, but because I don't want her to hear that I don't.

—

My life outside of school has become virtually unrecognizable, but almost nothing between the hours of 7:15 and 2:45 has changed. Josh and I barely acknowledge one another, Drew flings sex-bombs at me at every turn, and I try to sidestep dress code violations. The rest of my time, I spend avoiding whatever it is that needs avoiding that day. Nasty looks from Tierney Lowell. Being propositioned by Ethan Hall. Everyone at lunch.

I'm passing through the courtyard on my way to my favorite empty bathroom where I can get twenty-five minutes of uninterrupted angst before heading to Shop. I look at Josh before I start across. He's already there. His third period is right off it so he usually gets here first. I only let myself look at him now because he's far enough away that no one will notice. When I get closer, I always make sure to avert my eyes because I'm afraid if I glance at him for even a second, the whole world will know everything that goes on in my head. I'm just walking by, and out of the corner of my eye I can see that he's looking down at his hands in the exact same position he was in the first time I saw him, and I start wondering if he sits like that because he knows how amazing it makes his arms look.

"Sunshine."

It's so quiet that I almost don't hear it, and thankfully, no one else can, but I know it's real. He doesn't look up until I stop and stare at him, wondering what the hell he's thinking. Then he's staring back at me like he couldn't care less who sees.

"Sit."

I walk over to him so at least I'm no longer standing in the middle of the courtyard. My back is to everyone else when I face him and narrow my eyes. *What are you doing?*

"Kara Matthews must have been on the phone half the night," he says flatly. I already know this. At this point I've learned that Josh and I have been secretly screwing for weeks, but that now, he and Drew are just passing me back and forth. I guess he's heard it, too, but I don't have to answer to it. I just play dumb and walk away. I doubt Josh has to answer to it, either. I'm surprised anyone even got close enough for him to hear what they were saying. Most of them are usually terrified that they'll drop dead from being too near him, or worse, that they'll have to acknowledge that he exists. I don't know what this has to do with him calling me over in the middle of the courtyard. Giving them more ammunition is not usually his MO.

"Sit," he repeats, and it's gentle. Not a command. Not a request. Just the only thing left to do. "There's no reason to keep hiding in the bathroom. Hide here. There's a force field, you know." He lowers his voice when he says it, like he's telling me a secret, and then just barely hints at a smile that no one but me would catch before he puts it away and sobers, adding quietly, "No one will bother you."

So I sit. He's on the backrest and I'm on the seat. We don't touch. We don't speak. We aren't even at eye level with one another. And today, for the first time since I came to this school, the courtyard isn't nearly so horrible after all.

Chapter 31

Josh

My grandfather died this morning. Nothing changed.

I thought that when he died I would crack and cry and get drunk and throw shit because it was over, because he was the last one. But I didn't. I didn't break down. I didn't punch holes in the wall. I didn't start fights with every asshole in school. I just kept going like nothing even happened. Because it was all so incredibly normal.

—

"Where are we going?" Sunshine asks when she climbs into my truck. I don't feel like being here. The garage doesn't offer me anything today. That workshop is the only thing in the world that I count on, and I don't want to think that it's powerless for me right now. I'd rather just leave it for a little while so I don't have to be afraid that I've lost that, too. I don't really know where we're going. I just want to go.

We drive for a long time. I haven't said anything since we got in the truck. I never even answered her question. Sunshine is good with silence. She leans her head against the window and looks outside and she just lets me drive.

We end up stretched out in the bed of the truck, staring up at the sky in the parking lot of a closed-down car dealership.

I haven't started counting yet. I wonder if it's just me or if it's like that for everybody; that every time someone dies you start counting how much time has passed since they've been gone. First you count it in minutes, then in hours. You count in days, then weeks, then months. Then one day you realize that you aren't counting anymore, and you don't even know when you stopped. That's the moment they're gone.

"My grandfather's dead," I say.

"If we had a telescope, I could show you the Sea of Tranquility." She points up at the sky. "See? Up there on the moon. You can't really tell from here."

"Is that why you have a picture of the moon in your bedroom?" At this point I'm an expert at going along with her tangents.

"You noticed that?"

"It was the only thing on the wall. I thought you were into astronomy."

"I'm not. I keep it there to remind me that it's bullshit. I thought it sounded like this beautiful, peaceful place. Like where you'd want to go when you die. Quiet and water everywhere. A place that would swallow you up and accept you no matter what. I had this whole image of it."

"Doesn't sound like a bad place to end up."

"It wouldn't be, if it were real. But it's not. It's not a sea at all. It's just a big, dark shadow on the moon. The whole name is a lie. Doesn't mean anything."

Her left hand is resting on her stomach, opening and closing. She does that all the time, but I don't think she realizes it.

"So your warped fascination with names extends beyond people?"

"They're all lies, really. Your name could mean *to excel* and you could be useless and crap at everything. You can put a name on anything, call it whatever you want, doesn't make it real. Doesn't make it true." She sounds bitter. Or just disillusioned.

"So if they're all such meaningless crap, why are you so obsessed?" I can't count how many mutilated newspapers she's left on my kitchen table once she's cut her way through the birth announcements. At first, I thought she was one of those girls who takes prenaming her future children to the extreme, but apparently it's just some weird hobby.

"Because it's good when you find one that does mean something. Makes all the empty ones worthwhile." The faintest smile crosses her face, and I wonder what she's thinking, but she doesn't give me the chance to ask.

"Where do you think he is?" she asks, still staring at the sky.

"Someplace good, I guess. I don't know." I wait and she does too. "I asked him once if he was afraid. Of dying. Then I realized it was kind of a shit thing to ask someone who's dying, because if they weren't thinking about it before, they definitely would be after."

"He was upset?"

"No. He laughed. Said he wasn't afraid at all. But he was on a lot of drugs by then, so he wasn't all there. He told me he already knew where he was going because he'd been there before." I stop because I think that's all of my grandfather's craziness that I want to share. He wasn't always like that. Just at the end, with the drugs and the pain. But then she's looking at me with the curiosity of a hundred questions in her eyes and I feel like I have to answer her. "When he was like twenty, he was working construction and he fell and his heart stopped, so I guess he was technically dead for like a minute or something. He told the story a thousand times."

"Then why would you think it was the drugs talking if you'd heard it before?"

"Because he said he didn't remember. Everyone asked him if there was a light and all that bullshit, but he always said he couldn't remember any of it once he woke up. Then the night before he left, he sat me down and said he had two things he wanted to give me—one final piece of advice and his last secret. And that's when he told me that he always remembered it, where he went when he died. He said he remembered exactly what it was like."

"What did he say?"

"He said there wasn't really any form or sense to it. That it was like feeling without knowing. Like a fever dream. Like the dream of second chances. He said the only part of it that had definition was a porch swing in front of a red brick house, but he didn't know what it meant at the time, so he didn't say anything about it to anyone. Then he showed me this old picture of him sitting with my grandmother on a porch swing in front of the red brick house she lived in when they met."

"That's sweet," she says, but there's almost something like disappointment there, and I wish I was allowed to reach over and touch her face or her hand or anything.

"Yeah, it's sweet," I say, not meaning it. "Except he didn't actually meet her until three years after he had that accident; that's why he didn't get it at the time. But once he saw that swing and that house, then he knew. He knew he wasn't supposed to die. He was supposed to come back so he could meet her because his heaven was where she was, even if he didn't know it at the time. And that's why he wasn't scared." I turn to see her watching the moon, the ghost of a smile playing on her lips where the disappointment was a minute ago. I look up at the sky to see what she sees, and she moves closer and rests her head on my chest. I don't care if it's only because she's cold or the metal truck bed is hard as hell. I don't question it; I just close my arm around her and pull her into me like I've been doing it for years. "Like I said. Lots of painkillers."

—

"Was it good advice?" she asks on the drive home. Her head is resting against the window, and she's watching the road go by.

"What?"

"You said your grandfather gave you one last piece of advice. Was it good advice?" She's sitting up now and facing me.

"No." I laugh when I think about it. "I'm fairly certain it was the worst piece of advice ever. But I'm going to blame that on the drugs, too."

"Now you have to tell me. I have to know what qualifies as the worst advice ever." She twists her body toward me and tucks one of her legs under the other.

"He said"—and I'm almost embarrassed telling her this—"that every woman has one unforgivable thing, one thing that she'll never be able to get past, and for every woman it's different. Maybe it's being lied to, maybe it's being cheated on, whatever. He said the trick in relationships was to figure out what that unforgivable thing was, and to not do it."

"That was advice?"

"I warned you. He also told me there was a raccoon in the kitchen that night. So . . ."

"Do you believe it?"

"About the raccoon or the advice?"

She looks at me and tilts her head impatiently, and I glance at her before turning back to the road.

"You tell me. You're a girl. You're not one of those girls who wants to be called a woman, right? Even though you're almost eighteen? That just seems weird."

"Please don't," she says dryly.

"So what's yours?" I ask.

"My advice?"

"No, your unforgivable thing. Apparently you must have one."

"Never thought about it." She turns back to the window. "I'm guessing murder is out."

"Murder is out. You'd be dead, so the forgiveness would be a moot point."

"Not necessarily, but we'll say so for the sake of argument. I guess I'd go with loving me too much."

"Loving you too much would be unforgivable? I'm going to pull a McAllister on you and require supporting details."

"Too many obligations. People like to say love is unconditional, but it's not, and even if it was unconditional, it's still never free. There's always an expectation attached. They always want something in return. Like they want you to be happy or whatever, and that makes you automatically responsible for their happiness because they won't be happy unless you are. You're supposed to be who they think you're supposed to be and feel how they think you're supposed to feel because they love you, and when you can't give them what they want, they feel shitty, so you feel shitty, and everybody feels shitty. I just don't want that responsibility."

"So you'd rather no one loved you?" I ask. I wish I wasn't driving so I could look at her for more than a second.

"I don't know. I'm just talking. It's an unanswerable question." She pulls her foot out from under her and puts her head back down against the glass.

"Worst advice ever," I say.

I'm used to being alone, but tonight I feel more alone. Like I'm not just alone in my house, I'm alone in the world. And maybe that's its own blessing, because now I never have to do this again.

Tonight when I climb into bed, I don't even bother to count.

Chapter 32

Nastya

I didn't stop talking immediately. I talked right up until the day I remembered everything that happened, more than a year later. That was the day I went silent. It wasn't a ploy or a tactic. It wasn't psychosomatic. It was a choice. And I made it.

I just knew that suddenly I had answers. I had all the answers to all the questions, but I didn't want to say them. I didn't want to release them out into the world and make them real. I didn't want to admit that such things happened and that they happened to me. So I chose the silence and everything that came along with it because I wasn't a good enough liar to speak.

I always planned to tell the truth. I just wanted to give myself a little time. A chance to find the right thing to say and the courage to say it. I didn't take a vow of silence. I wasn't suddenly struck mute. I just didn't have the words. I still don't. I never found them.

—

I don't feel any different when I wake up on my eighteenth birthday. I don't feel older or mature or free. I feel inadequate, if anything, because I know what I was supposed to be at eighteen and it's not what I am. My dad's brother, my uncle Jim, got really down with himself when I was fourteen and he came to stay with us for a while to "reevaluate." My mom said that it just happens sometimes when you get older. You get halfway through with your life and you realize you haven't done the things you wanted to do or become what you thought you'd become, and it's disheartening. I wonder if she knows how disheartening it is when you get to that place at eighteen.

Margot's car isn't in the driveway when I get home from school. Normally she's sleeping at this hour, either in bed or in a chair by the pool. I know she made sure she had the night off because Margot loves birthdays and she's been more excited than me about this one.

I toss my backpack on my bed and barely make it to the kitchen when the doorbell rings. Standing on the other side of the door are Margot, my mother, my father, Asher, and Addison. My mother is holding a cake, and her smile just barely falters before she catches it. I'm in the doorway in my school clothes and makeup. My mother has never seen me like this. She's seen glimpses of it, but not the full effect all at once, and I think it devastates her a little. Margot looks like Margot, my brother looks resigned, my father barely looks, and Addison doesn't know what to look like. I think she wonders what she's doing here as much as I do.

They've done the "Surprise! Happy birthday!" thing in the doorway, so I step out of the way and they come in—cake, presents and all. My parents suggest going to a restaurant, but I don't want to go out. It's three thirty and there's too much of a chance of running into people from school, so Margot calls for pizza and puts the cake in the refrigerator while everyone crashes in the family room to wait for the food.

"We could probably still get you a ticket if you want to come with us for Thanksgiving," my mom throws out. It took exactly forty-three seconds from the time she got into the house to bringing it up.

"The house is sick. You should see it, Em. Three fireplaces. A balcony. *Hot tub*." Addison's face turns pink, and my brother looks at her apologetically. Bringing up the hot tub in front of the parents is really an amateur move.

"You could bring someone, too, if you want." That comes out of left field. I wish she would stop trying. My mother's hope is a weapon. I see Margot watching me from the kitchen. I wonder what, if anything, she's told them about my extracurricular activities. "Margot says you eat dinner with a boy's family every Sunday. What's his name?" She turns to Margot.

"Drew Leighton." Margot's still looking at me. No mention of Josh Bennett, and I wonder why she's kept that to herself but told them about Drew.

"Drew," my mother repeats. "That's right. Why don't you call him now? He can celebrate with us. We'd love to meet him. You know him from school?"

I nod.

"They're in Debate together," Margot answers for me.

"Addison's on Debate," Asher interjects, and maybe we can turn the conversation on her, because Drew Leighton is too close to Josh Bennett and my family isn't getting anywhere near Josh Bennett.

"Debate Drew Leighton?" It's the first time I've heard Addison's voice. It's all soft and feminine like her. She's sitting next to Asher, holding his hand, and it kind of pisses me off. "I know him! He's—" She cuts herself off before she continues, and I smile at her. I can't help it. We both know what she was about to say. "He's a really good debater. Everyone knows him."

"Really?" Asher looks at her dubiously and then over at me, and I know he plans to find out the truth of it later.

I nod, and she stifles her own smile and continues in a more appropriate direction.

"He came in third in state last year and everyone knows he's the biggest threat in Extemp and LD. No one wants to go up against him this year." She sounds almost reverential. It's understandable when you've seen Drew debate, and she obviously has, or at least she's aware enough of it. I'm almost proud to hear someone talk about Drew for what he should be talked about, but it's a rare thing. I find myself smiling at her for real, and maybe I'm not so pissed about Addison holding my brother's hand after all.

We eat pizza and everyone relaxes and I find myself missing my family and wondering if maybe I didn't exaggerate everything. Maybe it wasn't so forced and awkward. Then again, maybe it's just not awkward because I'm watching from the outside right now. It may be my birthday that brought them here, but they're in their own element and I'm just looking in. Even Addison has a place, in this picture, with my family. I'm the outsider.

Asher goes on about school and baseball and homecoming. Margot talks about nurse shortages at work and how the schedule is starting to kill her a little bit. My dad doesn't say much. He just glances at me every once in a while, and I try to work out what he's seeing when I look at his eyes, but they tell me nothing, and I wonder if they're just a reflection of my own. Ever since the day I told him to stop calling me Milly, and then stopped telling him anything else at all, there's been very little between us. My mother still tries, but my father has lost all hope. Maybe he's the smart one. Though it doesn't make me feel any better. My father has shut down and it's worse than any anger or disappointment he could level at me. The man who was the source of all my smiles can't even conjure one himself now. I'm a coward and a fraud and I murdered his spirit. There's something about knowing that I broke my father's heart that makes me hate myself a little more than I already do.

We get done with dinner, but we all ate so much pizza that no one can even think about cake yet. Except maybe me. I can always think about cake.

My mother and Margot move a pile of presents from the counter to the table in front of me. There are way too many of them, but I wish there weren't any, because I don't want to feel grateful and there's nothing they can give me that I need anyway.

I open them all and feel like I'm under a microscope where my every facial expression is being studied. It makes me want to scream, but I can't, so I just swallow it like dirt and blood.

The last present is the smallest box, and I should know to be scared by the anxious expression on my mother's face. Or maybe my father's face tells the real story, because he looks like he thinks this is a really bad idea and he's probably said as much to my mother a hundred times. I rip open the paper and I'm holding a brand-new, jacked-up iPhone.

My mother starts extolling the virtues of the phone as if I don't know everything it can do, for example, reveal my exact whereabouts at any given moment. I don't need to listen to the sales spiel, but I'm right back in the room when I hear the kicker.

"You can keep the phone and we'll pay the bills. The only condition is that you call and *talk* to us on it at least once a week."

I smile. I can't help it. Up until two and a half minutes ago, I was genuinely enjoying this day. I had actually chastised myself for being upset that they had come and let myself think that maybe this would be a turning point. But it's not a turning point. It's an ambush.

My family has taken my birthday and turned it into an intervention. They all trade off explaining to me how my behavior is hurting them. I find out, in great detail, how my failure to speak affects each and every member of my family. I listen to all of it. They haven't tied me to the chair so I can't escape or enlisted the help of an objective third party to impart the proper amount of guilt while keeping us all focused on the problem at hand. *Me.* There's no reason I have to stay here and listen to this, but I do, until every one of them has spoken.

Except Addison. She just looks uncomfortable. I think they pulled a bait and switch on her, too, with the whole birthday party idea. She looks like she wants to bolt as much as I do, and I feel kind of sorry for her. I wonder if we could make a run for it together.

When they've all finished, I smile. I love them and they love me, and we all know this. I hug my brother. I nod to Addison and Margot. I kiss my mother and father on the cheek. I leave my awesome iPhone on the table and I walk out the door.

My mother's camera is still sitting on the counter, untouched. She didn't take one picture.

I walk into Josh's garage and climb up onto the workbench, crossing my ankles. Josh wanted to put another coat of finish on my chair, so it's out of commission right now. I thought it looked fine, but he kept pointing out why it didn't until I gave up and let him do it.

"My mother turned my birthday party into an intervention," I say. As soon as it's out of my mouth, I cringe, realizing that it's probably pretty crappy to complain about your parents to someone who doesn't have any. It's like bitching that your shoes are too tight to someone who's walking across broken glass barefoot.

That's the irony of Josh and me, and it shames me every time I think about it. He has no family. No one to love him. I'm surrounded by love and I don't want any of it. I piss all over what he would thank God for, and if I needed more proof that I have no soul, then there it is.

"When was your birthday?" He looks up at me.

"Today."

"Happy birthday." He smiles, but it's sad.

"Yeah."

"You didn't tell me," he says, walking over to put his drill on the charger before turning back around.

"People who go around advertising their birthdays are douche bags. It's a fact. You can look it up on Wikipedia."

"So, intervention?" He tilts his head.

"Yep."

"I wasn't aware of your drug problem. Should I hide the silver?"

"I think it's safe."

"Heavy drinking?"

"No. But you might beg to differ."

"True. I've seen the ugly side of your drinking and I hope never to go there again." He comes around and climbs up on the workbench next to me. Close enough that his leg touches mine, and it's grounding. "So what are we intervening?"

"Silence." He looks at me skeptically when I answer. "They want me to talk."

"If you spent every night in their garage they might rethink that."

"Jackass."

"There's my Sunshine," he says, kicking my foot.

"They gave me an iPhone with the condition that I call and speak to them on it once a week." I brush the sawdust into a pile next to my leg and poke a hole in it so it looks like a volcano.

"Not what you wanted, huh?"

"I was hoping for implants."

He nods thoughtfully. "Always helpful with the job search after college."

We sit for a minute without talking. My legs start swinging out of instinct and he reaches over and stills them with his hand, but he doesn't say anything and then finally—

"Was the cake at least good?" He knows where my heart lies.

"Didn't even get to it."

"That's the real tragedy. Forget the intervention."

"I'm not hungry anyway."

"I'm not talking about the cake," he says, taking my hand and pulling me down from the counter before I can protest. "I'm talking about the wish."

He makes me wait while he goes back into the house, and a few minutes later we're driving away in his truck with a red plastic beach pail full of pennies on the seat between us.

It's not even dark yet when he pulls into the parking garage of an outdoor shopping center. The bucket of pennies is so full that he has to struggle to get it out of the truck without spilling it. He picks up the handle with one hand and slides the other underneath for support so it won't snap off and then kicks the door shut with his foot.

The sun is just starting to set and the plaza lights have kicked on. It's one of those high-class places with stores no real person ever shops at and restaurants with overpriced food you'd never want to eat anyway. But the fountain is amazing. Right in the middle of all the pretense, it's an even more pretentious spectacle. Every few minutes, the spray pattern shifts and the lights change color from below. There's a walkway that forms a bridge across it and the fountain spray arcs overhead, splitting in two on either side so you can pass underneath it without getting wet. It feels like magic and I'm a little girl. I wish I had my mother's camera.

I follow Josh halfway through the walkway, where he stops and curses under his breath at the pennies when he sets them down at his feet. The fountain obscures us and I don't think anyone from school would be out here anyway, but I still worry about being seen or, more problematically, heard in public. It's one of the reasons I never go anywhere, but it's not the only one.

"Have at it," he says.

"What?"

"Wishes. You only get one with a cake, and even that you only get if you blow out all the candles, which is kind of shitty because it's your birthday and there shouldn't be a contingency on a wish. Pennies are a sure thing and you can have as many as you want."

I stare down at the pail. "I don't think I can think of that many things to wish for." There's only one thing I really want.

"Sure you can. It's easy. Watch." He leans over and grabs a handful of pennies in his left hand and picks one up with his right. He thinks for a second and then tosses it into the fountain. "See? You don't even need good aim." He turns to me expectantly. "Here."

I can smell the sawdust on him as he takes my left hand and pours a fistful of pennies into it. My hand stutters and he steadies it with his, for a moment, before letting go. "Your turn."

I look at the pennies and up to the fountain and wonder if there is such a thing as magic or miracles. Josh is watching me as I make the same wish I always do. It's the one that won't come true, but I wish it anyway, so maybe I haven't totally given up after all. I toss the penny into the air and watch it fall into the water while the lights below switch from pink to purple.

"What'd you wish?"

"I can't tell you that!" I say indignantly.

"Why not?"

"Because it won't come true." Do I really need to say this? I'm pretty sure it's a given in wish situations.

"Bullshit."

"It's the rule," I insist.

"It's only the rule with birthday cakes and shooting stars, not pennies in fountains."

"Who says?" I ask, sounding like a first grader.

"My mom."

That shuts me up quick. I look at the pennies and the fountain and anywhere but at him because I don't want to scare him away, and I'm hoping he'll say something else. Then he does, and I wish he hadn't.

"Then again, I doubt many of her wishes actually came true, so maybe she didn't know what she was talking about after all."

For just one moment, I see an eight-year-old boy glued to a television set, waiting for his mother to come home.

"Maybe she just made the wrong ones," I say quietly.

"Maybe."

"You talk about your mom more than your dad."

"My dad was around longer. I remember him. I remember what he was like. I've forgotten almost everything about my mom, so I try to make myself think about her more. Otherwise, I'm afraid one day I'll wake up and I won't remember her at all." He tosses a penny into the fountain and I watch it sink. "If you asked me now about my sister, the only word I'd be able to come up with is *annoying*. I remember that she bugged the hell out of me and that's about it. If I didn't have pictures, I don't even think I could tell you what she looked like." He looks at me. "Your turn."

I'm not sure if he's referring to the wishing or the confessions, but I go with the pennies. I don't even wish. I just throw one.

"I'm sorry." The two easiest and emptiest words to say and I say them.

"Because I don't remember my mom or because you asked?"

"Both. But mostly the asking."

"No one ever asks. Like they think they're doing me a favor. That if they don't bring it up, I won't have to think about it. I never stop thinking about it. Just because I don't talk about it doesn't mean I forget. I don't talk about it because no one ever asks." He stops and looks at me again, and I wonder if I'm supposed to say something, but I don't want to, because if I say something I'm afraid I might say everything. He turns back to the fountain so his eyes aren't on me anymore, but I think he's still watching. "I'd ask you, you know. If I was allowed. I'd ask you a thousand times until you'd tell me. But you won't let me ask."

We manage to find the laughter in the evening again, and we wish ourselves through most of the bucket of pennies. At one point, a mother with two little girls passes through, and Josh gives them each a handful of pennies and begs them to help us because we're running out of things to wish for. They take the affair very seriously, as if each wish is so precious that they can't afford to waste it. They squeeze their eyes shut and concentrate, making sure they do it just right. And I wish for every one of their wishes to come true.

Toward the end, we start making mega wishes and fortifying them with handfuls of pennies. One of those wishes results in the clasp of my bracelet coming undone, causing it to fly off into the fountain along with my wish-imbued pennies. Josh rolls up the bottoms of his jeans and pulls off his boots. I just have to take off my shoes because I'm still in the skirt I wore to school and it's plenty short. We look around, hoping there aren't any security guards in the area before we step in. Thankfully the water is shallow, because it's freakishly cold and my legs are ice the second I get in.

"Where did it go?" he asks. I point off in the direction I threw the pennies. I don't think it could have gotten very far. We head off in that direction, but it's impossible to see anything because the entire fountain floor is carpeted with coins. Half of them probably came from us. It's a tapestry of silver and copper and colored light. Every time I see something I think might be my bracelet, I have to reach down and submerge my arm into the water, which is what I'm doing when Josh decides to push my leg with his foot just enough to knock me off balance and send me face-first into the ice-cold water. The splash is followed by laughter from him and a death glare from me. I plan to grab him and pull him in after me, but I don't have to, because he tries to step away from my grasp too quickly and falls in all on his own.

"Karma's a bitch, Bennett."

His pants and half his shirt are soaked, but he managed to keep his head out of the water, unlike the drowned rat that is me. When he looks at my face, he starts laughing all over again and I finally give up and dissolve in it, too. "Don't do the last-name bullshit. I hate it," he says, pulling me to my feet

"Not really caring what you hate right now," I say, trying to force some venom into my voice, but it's hard when I'm fighting what I am quite certain are the early stages of hypothermia. I feel like one of those insane polar bear people who jump in the freezing cold ocean every year, and I mentally put that on my list of things I will never do.

"Screw the bracelet. It's not worth it," I say, climbing out of the water with Josh right behind me. He doesn't argue.

We split up the rest of the pennies between the two little girls, whose mother gives us a dirty look because I think she's had enough wishing for the night. Or maybe because we're soaking wet and just climbed out of the fountain. I pick up the empty pail and swing it back and forth between us while we walk to the parking garage, leaving the fountain, my bracelet, a crapload of pennies, and two giggling girls behind us. Josh reaches over to take the pail from me. He stops my hand and opens my fingers, retrieving the handle with his left hand and holding mine open with his right. His hand is no warmer than my own, but it feels good anyway, and I wait for him to let go, but he doesn't.

When we reach his truck in the parking garage, he tosses the bucket into the back and then reaches up and cradles my face in his hands the way he did that day on the Leightons' front porch.

"Black shit," he says, letting one side of his mouth turn up as he wipes the streaks away with his thumbs. Then, he moves away and opens my door. "Happy birthday, Sunshine."

"I wished that my hand would work again," I tell him when he climbs in after me. It was my first wish and the only one that mattered.

"I wished my mother was here tonight, which is stupid, because it's an impossible wish." He shrugs and turns to me, drowning the smile that cracks me every time.

"It's not stupid to want to see her again."

"It wasn't so much that I wanted to see her again," he says, looking at me with the depth of more than seventeen years in his eyes. "I wanted her to see you."

Chapter 33

Josh

"There are clean towels in the guest bathroom. I'm going to shower in the master."

"I hope you have a big hot-water heater, because I may never come out," Sunshine yells from the hall. She's still shivering because she has almost no body fat on her, and I kind of feel like shit for the whole fountain thing.

"I'm going to put water on for tea. You want some?" I call from the kitchen where I'm filling the teakettle.

"You drink hot tea?"

"So?"

"So, you're not old. Or British. I can count on one finger the number of teenage boys who drink hot tea."

"I used to make it for my grandfather. I got used to it. Shut up." I finish filling the kettle and put it on top of the stove before I head into the bathroom. "You want it or not?"

"Not. Tea sucks. I'll be out in an hour. Maybe two." The bathroom door slams.

I'm out of the shower ten minutes later and the water is still running in the guest bathroom, so maybe she wasn't lying. I throw my wet clothes in the empty washer then head into the kitchen to turn the stove burner on. Maybe tea does suck, but I heat the water anyway. She won't turn down hot chocolate.

The doorbell rings and I figure it has to be Drew, because other than the girl using all the hot water in my bathroom, he's the only person who would come over here. He's got a key, so I don't know why he doesn't just come in.

"What?" I open the door, ready to hear about whatever minor irritation has sent him fleeing from his house this time, but it isn't Drew. It's a kid I've never seen before, and he's staring at me so intensely that I feel like he's checking me out. Not like he wants me, but like he wants to know who the hell I am, except that he's the one knocking on my door.

"Can I help you?" I finally ask because the kid isn't talking.

"Is my sister here?" *Sister?* "Margot said she'd probably be here. Nastya." He spits out her name like it tastes bad in his mouth.

"She's your sister?" There's not much of a resemblance unless you really, really look. He actually looks a lot like Margot.

"Yeah. She left. Is she here?"

I push back the door and let him in. The water in the shower is still running and there's no ignoring it. *Damn it, Sunshine.* He's not looking relieved and I can guess why as I stand in front of him in a T-shirt and sweatpants, still wet from the shower, while we listen to the water continue running two doors down.

"She's in the shower," I say, because it's not like I can hide the fact. I need to warn her before she comes out. "I'll go let her know you're here."

"Why is my sister showering in your house?" he demands before I can get away. He's pissed. I'm getting the full overprotective brother treatment and I kind of respect him for it, but I don't like the way he's talking to me in my own house, like I'm some sort of scumbag. It's the same thing Margot did when she came over. I don't think I'm particularly threatening and it's not as if Nastya comes across like some delicate flower.

"Your sister is eighteen years old. She can do more than shower here if she wants."

"My sister is emotionally stunted at fifteen." He levels his eyes at me. This is not really a conversation I anticipated having tonight. I don't even know how to respond to that.

"So you're saying she's immature?" It's the only thing I can come up with. And I can't decide which side I'm on anyway. Some days she seems older than anyone I've ever met and others she's like a little girl.

"I'm saying she's messed up." He exhales and he looks tired, like he's said this a thousand times before and he doesn't want to be here, saying it now.

"I don't agree." I do agree. I just don't know why or how or anything that might matter.

"I know my sister."

"I know your sister." I know what she tells me. The fragments of a life she gives me glimpses of on the days she's feeling particularly generous or maybe just reckless.

"Did you even know today was her birthday?" he asks. I don't answer. "I didn't think so. From the look on your face earlier, you didn't know she had a brother, either. You ever wonder what else you don't know?" *Always.* "She's got issues and she doesn't need another one. Leave it alone."

I don't appreciate being referred to as an issue.

"If there's something you want me to know, why don't you tell me? Otherwise you can take the condescending attitude and get out of my house."

He doesn't answer. He won't betray her, and as much as I want to know what the hell is going on, I can respect that. Still, I'm not letting him make me the villain here. I want to like this kid, but he's starting to piss me off.

"You like taking advantage of messed-up girls? Is that your thing?" he asks.

"What's yours? Pointless accusations and intimidation?"

The water stops running and I'm ready to bolt down the hall to intercept her before she comes out, but the door opens before I can get there. I didn't even have a chance to leave her a dry change of clothes. She comes out of the hallway, dripping wet with a towel wrapped around her, and all the blood drains down from my brain and my stupid dick twitches because that's what it does when beautiful, wet, towel-clad girls come out of my shower. I wish I could enjoy the view because, *seriously*. But this isn't the time, and fortunately my dick gets the message that her extremely pissed-off-looking brother is standing next to me and stays down.

She opens her mouth but sees him before any words make it out. I don't know whose eyes are wider. Something unspoken goes on between the two of them. I can't tell if she looks frightened or ashamed, but it looks like she's gotten younger just seeing him. The teakettle whistles, and we're so on edge that I think we all might piss our pants right here. Except for Nastya, because right now, she's not wearing any. I look between the two of them and settle on her.

"Got company, Sunshine. Anyone want tea?"

Her brother eventually leaves once he accepts that she isn't going back with him. I wonder how much hell she's going to catch for that. Answering to people isn't something I ever have to worry about, so it never crosses my mind, but she has a family and I don't know how she gets away with just not going home, even if she is eighteen. She made a comment once that her parents are afraid to discipline her, but she didn't elaborate. I wonder if they're scared of her, too. She spends most of her time here already, but how much of that information gets back to her parents is beyond me. If her family didn't think we were screwing before, they do now.

"You're not sleeping on the couch," I tell her when she pulls the pillow and blanket she's used before out of the linen closet.

"All right. Sorry." She puts them down and starts looking around for her keys.

"You don't have to leave."

"But you said—"

"I just meant that the couch is seriously uncomfortable. You can take my bed. I'll sleep on the couch."

"I am not taking your bed. I don't mind the couch. I've slept on it before."

"So you know it sucks."

"It's better than always going back to Margot's and being alone. I don't want you giving up your bed." She sits down on the couch and clutches the pillow in her lap.

"So sleep with me."

"What?" Her eyes go wide and I laugh.

"Not that kind of sleep with me. Just sleep. It's a king-size bed—you won't even know I'm there."

"Somehow I doubt that." She looks around like she's trying to figure something out. "How is it possible that you only have one bed in this house, anyway?"

"There's a twin bed in Amanda's room but you can't find it anymore because I started storing everything in there and it's underneath a bunch of crap. I got rid of the one in my old room when they needed to bring in the hospital bed for my grandfather. So now I just have the one in the master." She doesn't look at me like she feels bad, just like she understands.

"It can't really be that bad," she says, walking down to Amanda's room. The door is always closed and she's never gone in before, but she does now.

She steps inside to the almost nonexistent pathway of visible carpet, and scans the room. There are boxes and piles of old clothing folded on the bed. A couple of random pieces of furniture I built, but wasn't happy with, are shoved here and there; things I would keep in the garage, but don't, because I need the space out there more than I need it here.

"Okay, it is that bad," she laughs, before her eyes narrow with curiosity, and I turn to see what she's looking at. "You have a piano," she says softly, stepping over to it. "Why is it in here?"

"Amanda was taking lessons. I never did. I rolled it in here a couple years ago when I needed the space in the living room for one of the tables."

She runs her fingers along the top of the keys so lightly that I'm not sure she even touches them at all. There's a reverence in the way she does it.

"Do you play?" I ask, because she's never mentioned it.

"No," she says. It takes her a second to look up at me because she's still staring at the keys. "Not even a little."

When I crawl into bed with her later, it doesn't matter how huge the mattress is—I'm not completely brain dead. I know that this is a monumentally bad idea with repercussions written all over it. But she's right. It's just nice not being alone. And the couch is hellishly uncomfortable.

"Is it just me, or is this really strange?" she finally asks after about twenty minutes of awkward silence, because neither of us is sleeping.

"It's not just you," I agree.

"Do you want me to go?" she asks.

"No." I don't even need to do anything with her. Not that I don't want to, because I want to touch her more than I probably should. But it really isn't that. I just like her here.

She reaches over and finds my arm, just below my shoulder and follows it until she reaches my hand. It reminds me of the way she touched the piano keys earlier, and I can feel the trail her fingers leave all the way down my arm. There's a comfort that wasn't here a moment ago. Then, without a word, she curls up next to me and that's how we fall asleep. Her hand in mine. Together.

——

On Wednesday in art class, Clay Whitaker shows me the portfolio he's been working on, and I want to hit him. He's always updating, adding, deleting, based on whatever competition he's entering it in or the college he's applying to, and then he'll show it to me, even though I never ask to see it and I don't know shit about art. I don't want to hit him for the portfolio itself, but for showing it to me here, in the middle of class, where it's nearly impossible to keep my face blank. I think it's a test. I look at Clay watching me, and I know it's a test.

Every last drawing is of Sunshine. He has her face from every angle. Every emotion I can imagine anyone ever feeling is in her eyes in these pictures. I forgive him for every minute he stole her from my garage.

"Draw one for me." The words are out of my mouth before I can bitch slap them into submission.

"You want me to draw you?" He's annoyed or disappointed. I haven't given him the reaction he was expecting.

"No. I want you to draw her. For me."

Clay looks a little more pleased with that.

"How?" he asks.

"What do you mean, how?" I sound pissed and I mean to, but it's me I'm pissed at. I just spilled my guts all over the floor in art class and now he's going to kick them around a little bit for fun.

"How do you see her? If you want me to draw her for you, it should be how you see her. Not how I see her."

"You've drawn a hundred pictures of her. Just draw another one or give me one of those." I motion toward the portfolio.

"When you look at her what do you feel?"

"Are you fucking serious? Forget it." He can kiss my ass if he wants to start talking feelings with me.

"You obviously want it for a reason."

"I want a picture to jack off to. What do you care?" I keep drawing so I don't have to look at him, but I'm mutilating the sketch I'm working on. I'll have to start over, but I don't care.

"Joy, fear, frustration, longing, friendship, anger, need, despair, love, lust?"

"Yes."

"Yes, what?"

"All of it," I reply, because I'm all in now whether I like it or not.

"I can have it to you in a couple of days."

True to his word, Clay walks into class two days later and hands me an oversized cardboard folder and tells me not to open it until I get home. There's a part of me that almost hoped he had forgotten or that it was a bad dream and I had never really asked. Then he shows me another drawing he's added to his portfolio, and now I know where Sunshine has been for the past two days.

"You're obsessed," I tell him, handing it back.

"Am I the only one?"

"Yes." He's looking at me skeptically, and I know this was a huge mistake, but it's one I can't take back now. "I just wanted a picture. I wouldn't have asked if I knew you were going to be such a dick about it."

"Don't worry," he says, and for a moment, smug Clay is gone. "I'm not going to tell her."

I accept this and we don't speak for a minute during which time my brain leaves my body and deserts me.

"What are you doing tonight?" I ask him.

"You asking me out?"

"Dinner at Drew's at six." I've officially gone batshit crazy. Drew's parents are out of town this weekend, but his mom made a ton of food and insisted that we still do Sunday dinner. Then they decided to come home early, so Drew moved it to tonight.

"You're out of your mind," Clay responds. "First the picture and now this? I will not be a victim in whatever self-destruction you have planned."

"You can stalk the object of your obsession some more." I tilt my head toward his sketchbook. "Bring Yearbook Michelle if you want."

"You do realize Drew will shit if Michelle and I show up at his house."

"Yep."

"Six o'clock?"

"Six o'clock."

Chapter 34

Nastya

I'll take control any way I can get it now. I may not be able to prevent some random psychotic from finding me in some random location at some random time, but I can control what I do to him when he gets there.

I've taken enough self-defense classes over the past two years to know that there were several things I could have done that day. I'm no martial arts expert. Not even close. All I really know are a couple of difficult but seriously awesome takedown maneuvers, along with some key dirty street-fighting moves, but even those may have been enough. I could have gouged his eyes or crushed his windpipe or boxed his ears or kneed him in the groin or employed the always classic gold standard: scream and run like hell. I didn't do any of those things. Know what I did? I smiled and said hi. Because I was polite. And stupid.

—

Drew's driveway is empty when Josh and I pull up. Josh picks up the cupcake carrier—a gift to me from Margot for no particular reason—and carries it into the house while I follow. It's hard not to smile, because I'm used to seeing him carrying lumber, so a pink plastic cupcake carrier is something different entirely.

Drew and Sarah are in the kitchen where Mrs. Leighton would usually be. I can smell dinner immediately. Italian.

"Josh," Sarah bites out as soon as we walk in. "Aren't you supposed to reheat food no higher than three hundred fifty degrees?"

"It'll heat faster at four fifty," Drew argues.

"It'll dry out," Sarah lilts. It seems like this argument has been going on for a while. She glances in my direction, and I get the disgusted look she seems to save just for me.

"Depends on what it is, but yeah, it'll probably dry out," Josh says, moving around them to put the cupcakes on the counter. The kitchen is stifling from the heat coming off both compartments of the double oven, and I wonder if the meticulously piped Swiss meringue buttercream on those cupcakes can survive. My hand didn't freak out at all while I was doing it, so they look perfect.

"See!" Sarah says in Drew's face, triumphantly walking over to the oven to lower the temperature. I guess Josh's word holds when it comes to reheating food as well.

"Suck it," Drew says.

"Your girlfriend's here. Ask her." Sarah smiles overly sweetly at me before disappearing down the hall toward her bedroom.

"I hate her," Drew says, but he lets the girlfriend comment go.

I look around the kitchen at the number of bowls and dishes littering the countertop. Mrs. Leighton must have known it would end up being more than the four of us because she made enough food for an army.

Within the next fifteen minutes, the doorbell rings four more times. Piper walks in first, dressed in an outfit she must have coordinated with Sarah. She says hi to Drew and Josh before she heads to Sarah's room without acknowledging me. Her arrival is followed by Damien Brooks and Chris Jenkins. Chris I know from hammer-wielding shop fame. He looks at me awkwardly and says hi. Ever since the hammer incident, he's tried to ignore me even more. I wasn't sure that was even possible, but he's been doing an admirable job. Damien I've seen around but never met. He looks at my chest but doesn't say anything. Chris has a case of beer in each hand. Damien has a twelve-pack in his left and a bottle of tequila in his right. Clearly Drew gave them a very different description of Sunday dinner, and now I get why he moved it up to Friday. Of course, I may also have been a little more creative with the invitation I issued to Tierney Lowell in the bathroom a few days ago. When the doorbell rings for the third time, I'm the only one who's expecting her.

—

I was in the girls' restroom at the far end of the foreign language hallway on Wednesday. Tierney must have seen me and followed me in, because she obviously wasn't using the facilities. When I got done washing my hands, she handed me a paper towel with a gesture so full of menace that I had to respect her, because anyone who can make handing you a paper towel look like a threat is impressive. Of course, she still hadn't stopped glaring at me, and I didn't want to seem rude, so I glared back. It was so completely absurd that I wanted to laugh. It took a serious amount of throat clenching to keep from erupting, but I had invested myself in that particular starefest and I don't like to lose. She obviously had something to say, so I wished she would just get on with it, because she wasn't going to intimidate me no matter how many rumors I had heard about her: drug dealing, illegal abortions, knife wielding. I even heard she brings glass to the beach.

I didn't believe any of it and was kind of hoping she would stop looking at me like I poisoned her grandmother. I really kind of like Tierney and I wish she'd like me too, because to be honest it would be nice to have a female friend to not talk to sometimes.

"You must know a lot of tricks for him to keep you around this long." Mystery solved. *Drew.* I'd say, *of course,* like I should have gotten it all along, except I couldn't have known, because even now, I'm just not seeing it. If she and Drew had, in fact, hooked up like Josh said—and with Drew anything is possible—she doesn't seem like the type who would be much for sticking around, either. I don't see Tierney Lowell being the kind of person who's going to let anyone, much less Drew Leighton, take advantage of her. I so wished I was more in the loop on things because I wanted the rest of that story. Badly.

Crap. I was going to have to write a note. It was rule breaking, but I chalked it up to absolute necessity: life-threateningly unavoidable because otherwise my curiosity would kill me. I grabbed the notebook she was holding and pulled a pen out of my purse. I decided to jump off a cliff with this one because there was only one reason this girl was cornering me in the bathroom, and it was pure, undiluted jealousy. *Do you still love him?* I wrote on the paper and shoved it at her, feeling seriously melodramatic.

She gaped at me, her eyes narrowing and her voice laced with forced venom. "I *never* loved him."

She didn't laugh like it was the most absurd suggestion on Earth, so I grabbed the paper back and scribbled down the invitation. *Bunch of us hanging out at Drew's Sunday at 6.* That was a logistical note, so it was totally acceptable.

She read it and looked back at me with unveiled skepticism, clearly familiar with the Leighton family tradition. "They do Sunday dinner."

I shook my head and pointed back down at the note again, hoping that would convince her. I knew she wasn't totally buying the fact that I wasn't trying to lure her into some plot involving pig's blood and public humiliation, but I could tell she was interested, too. I walked out wondering which part of her would win out.

—

Unlike everyone else so far, Tierney is the only one who waits to be let in. I wasn't sure she'd show; I shoved another note in her locker yesterday after Drew changed the plans, but I didn't know if she'd even seen it. When Josh opens the door, she looks almost nervous, standing on the porch, wearing a short denim skirt and two purple spaghetti strap camisoles layered one on top of the other. She really is a pretty girl; she just always looks mad, but maybe that's just when she's looking at me.

"Tierney?" Josh asks, because it's not like he doesn't know who she is, but he's certainly wondering why she's here. I watch to see how he reacts, but it's Josh, and as usual he gives nothing away. He could have opened the door to two hyenas having sex and he wouldn't have changed his expression.

I would have pressed him for more details about Drew and Tierney the other day, but he gets weird when I ask questions about Drew, so I figured I'd have to be patient and wait until tonight.

"I was invited," she says, not wanting to look pathetic, like she just showed up at Drew's house hoping to see him because his parents were out of town, and I feel kind of shitty for putting her in this position. Josh doesn't say anything else. He just opens the door further and lets her walk in. She catches me watching from the dining room but does nothing more than check out my outfit before heading back to the kitchen. Tierney knows exactly where she's going in this house.

I try to nonchalantly catch up with her before she gets to the kitchen. I want to see Drew's reaction. As soon as she walks through the doorless entryway, I hear Damien Brooks yell, "T-Lo in the house!" removing all doubt as to his immense douchery. "What's up, sexy? Didn't know you'd be here."

"Neither did I." She shifts her attention as Drew returns from putting the rest of the beer in the garage refrigerator.

"Tierney," Drew says, tamping down his initial surprise.

"Drew."

"Were we expecting you?"

"Your"—she pauses and motions toward me—"she invited me."

I knew that was coming. Drew walks over and puts his arm around my waist and pulls me up against him. I'm used to his possessive displays by now, so I just go with it. Josh's eyes shift to Drew's hand around my waist before he walks away.

"Funny, she didn't mention it," Drew says, but it doesn't sound like he thinks it's funny. His fingers tighten just slightly against the bare skin on my stomach where my shirt's ridden up. I push him away and flip him off, trying to play it off like this is just something we do, which I guess it kind of is, but he still needs to watch it and I make sure my expression tells him so.

"Later, Nastypants. I promise." He's talking to me but he's still looking at Tierney. "Right now I have a dinner to host!" He claps his hands dramatically to get everyone's attention which he already has anyway. "You know the rules. Everybody helps!" Within moments, this mishmashed group of us, from preppy and prissy to slutty and scandalous, is doing just that. We are all pulling out dishes, pouring drinks, and making trips back and forth between the kitchen and the dining room. Damien Brooks is standing at the counter, slicing loaves of garlic bread, and Tierney Lowell is hovering over the dining room table, making flawless napkin fans. It's surreal. Mrs. Leighton would be proud.

By the time Clay and Yearbook Michelle show up, no one is shockable anymore.

"Something you want to tell me?" Josh whispers so only I

can hear as we walk side by side into the dining room, carrying plates and silverware. Is he angry? I can't tell. I know I was out of line with the Tierney thing, but if anything Drew is the one who should be upset about that. I don't answer, grateful for the fact that we're surrounded by other people so I don't have to respond. Who knows how this whole evening is going to turn out anyway? It's like *The Breakfast Club* in a powder keg in here and I'm wondering who's going to light the match.

Josh

Everyone ends up on the couches in the family room once dinner has been cleaned up. The beer already has a good dent in it, and the bottle of tequila that piece of shit Damien Brooks brought is looming over the coffee table like a bad omen.

Sarah drank two beers during dinner and she's already acting ridiculous. Two more and she'll be face-down on the carpet. The good thing about Sarah drinking is that, when she does, she stops being such a bitch for a few minutes, and I remember why I actually liked her once and why I hate how she's become.

I look around for Sunshine and see her coming out from the kitchen, passing Damien, who grabs her arm for some reason to stop her. I don't even know what happens, except that about one point five seconds later, Damien is face-first on the ground with her knee pressed into his back. Then, just as quickly, she's off him.

"What the fuck was that?" he whines, pushing himself up from the ground and acting like nothing hurts, but it's obvious that something does. I'd think it was funny if I hadn't seen her face. But I did, and I know there's nothing funny about it. She's backed against the wall, and I can't tell if she's terrified or enraged. I try to catch her eye to see if she's okay, but I think she's purposely not looking at me. I'm wondering if there's a way for me to get her out of here for a few minutes, but I don't even get a chance to come up with anything.

"You have got to teach me how to do that!" Sarah's eyes go wide and she looks at Nastya for the first time with something other than disgust. It's pure awe. I'm kind of in awe myself. Damien is bigger than all of us and everyone is bigger than Sunshine.

Tierney looks sideways at Drew. "I'd like to get in on that, too."

The next hour becomes an impromptu self-defense demonstration. All the furniture is pushed against the walls and we've padded the floor down as well as possible.

I get to play the role of predator and get the crap kicked out of me while Sunshine points out every vulnerable spot on my body, from eyeballs to lower ribs to groin—which I like the idea of having her hands on, but I won't even let her pretend to hurt—to feet. There's no doubt that I got the shit end of the stick here. Thankfully, she doesn't really want to hurt me, but she does seem extremely serious about making sure they get what she's showing them to do. There's no question that she doesn't think it's a joke.

"I'm afraid I might break you," I say when she makes me come at her again. Really I'm afraid she's going to break me. She's freakishly strong.

She snatches a piece of paper from the counter, scribbles on it, and shoves it at me. Her eyes are narrowed in challenge and I try not to smile.

You'll have to try harder than that to break me. Quit being a pussy!!!!!

She's daring me because she thinks I'm not really trying to hurt her. She's right; I'm not. Every time, I plan to go at her full force, but I can't and I pull back some. She has to be mad if she's actually writing it down, so I try harder. Finally, I go at her like I really want to take her down. The only person who ends up down is me. She must have practiced this move a thousand times; I have no idea how she even did it. The sad part is, I think that time *she* pulled back for *me*.

Then, before everyone scatters, she picks up the paper and starts writing again. I think she's writing something to me, because it's odd for her to be writing at all. But when she's done, she hands it to Sarah and the other girls, then immediately turns away to start picking up the pillows off the floor.

We try to put the room back together, but it's a half-assed job. Once the couches are back in place, we figure it's good enough. Sarah lays Sunshine's note down on an end table when she goes back to the kitchen for another beer, and I finally get a look at it. She's written the name of the martial arts studio she goes to and then underneath that, only a few words, written in all caps—

RUN FIRST AND RUN FAST.

Drew sits down on one end of the couch and pulls Nastya into the seat next to him. I settle on the other side of her. My leg presses up against hers when I sit, but she doesn't pull away and I don't either. I've spent the last hour with her hands all over me; you would think that would be enough. But it's not even close to enough. It never is. Not like it matters, she'll probably be in Drew's lap by the end of the night anyway.

"I know," Sarah slurs, putting another empty beer bottle on the counter and throwing herself onto the love seat. "Let's play Truth or Dare."

"Lame," Damien yells from the kitchen, where he's opening every cabinet looking for shot glasses.

"That game sucks ass," Chris seconds.

"I'd play Truth or Dare," Drew says, running his fingers down Sunshine's arm and making me want to punch him.

"You would?" Sarah perks up, already too far down the road to plastered to be skeptical.

"Yeah, if I were thirteen and a loser."

Before Sarah can tell Drew to shut up, Tierney leans over the counter from the kitchen. "Afraid of a game, Drew?"

"Fear is coursing through my veins, T. Remind me again why you're here." He picks up Nastya's hand and kisses the back of it and then puts it down on his leg. I'm hyperaware of every time he puts his hands on her and it's making me feel like some sort of obsessed stalker.

"To play Truth or Dare," she contends matter-of-factly, coming around the counter and grabbing the shot glasses from Damien's hands. She puts them on the table and fills them with tequila. "Everyone plays. You cop out, you do a shot. Simple." She tops the last glass off and rights the bottle without losing a drop.

I'd half expect Clay and Yearbook Michelle to be a little shell-shocked, but they look more amused than anything. I imagine if you're just a spectator here, this whole evening would be pretty damn entertaining.

—

"Okay, Drew. Truth or Dare?" We're four rounds in, and this one comes from Chris. Things started getting ugly after the first round and the tension in this room is starting to wear on me. I'm ready to go home.

Sunshine is three shots down and way past half-lit. She picked truth every time and wouldn't even write the answers to anything. They asked her how many guys she'd had sex with, how old she was when she lost her virginity, and the strangest place she's ever had sex. She took the shot every time. By the last round, when Piper switched off the sex topic and got bold enough to ask why she doesn't talk, I stood up and took the shot for her.

"Truth," Drew answers.

"How long did it take to get her to—" Chris looks in Nastya's direction and cuts himself off.

"To what? Why ask the question if you can't even say it?" Piper laughs mockingly.

"I think he's scared." Sarah giggles. "He knows she can kick his ass."

"That's such a waste of a question anyway. Everyone knows she screwed him. Who cares when?" Damien says.

"Doesn't matter," Tierney counters. "Question was asked. Answer it or shoot."

Drew looks at Nastya, and if I wasn't paying attention I might miss the exchange that goes on between the two of them, but I know that there was something unspoken happening that no one else picked up on. The whole thing bothers me, and that bothers me even more.

"Trevor Mason's party. Second week of school."

"That was a couple months ago. Isn't that like a record, Drew?" Tierney asks, but she can't seem to force the hostility she's going for into her tone.

Everyone is still talking, but I'm not listening anymore. Trevor Mason's party is the one Drew got Sunshine so shit-faced at that she spent most of the night on my bathroom floor, and I got so scared that she had alcohol poisoning that I almost took her to the hospital. He fucked her and I cleaned up her puke.

There's a part of me that wanted to believe that he had never touched her, at least not *really* touched her. But I didn't ask, because only a part of me believed that. The other part of me knew that there was still a possibility that it had happened, and if it had, I didn't want the confirmation.

"Drew," I say, not giving a shit how pissed I sound. "Truth."

"Drew just went and you have to give him a choice anyway," Piper whines, but no one else gets on the rule-enforcing train because they all want to know what the hell this is about. Except for Drew and Nastya, who look like they want to tell me to shut the hell up. It would be good advice. Too bad I don't listen.

"Truth, Drew." I haven't taken my eyes off him, and I can feel the tension rolling off Nastya. She pulls her hand away from Drew and subtly presses her leg against mine, but I don't want any part of it.

"Fine," Drew says.

"Did you fuck her before or after the party?" He knows exactly why I'm asking.

"Pour the shot, T," he says, not looking away. Maybe I'm an idiot for thinking he wouldn't screw her when she was that drunk.

"Hey!" The voice breaks me out of the standoff I've got going on with Drew, and I freeze, watching Leigh walk in. None of us even heard the front door open. I start racking my brain. Was I supposed to meet her? Did I even know she was coming? All of a sudden this room is a hundred times smaller and I feel very trapped. There's something about having Leigh and Sunshine in a room together that makes me imagine two planets colliding. World-ending destruction. I reached my drama threshold hours ago. This is the reason I avoid this kind of crap.

Leigh smiles, completely clueless about what she's walking into. It was bad before she got here, and this is just worse. I stand, out of instinct, as she approaches me. I can see Drew pull Nastya into his lap and whisper something in her ear. Her eyes just barely shift, and I haven't forgotten that I want an answer from him before I leave here.

"What's going on?" I ask, trying not to sound as annoyed as I am, because Leigh hasn't done anything wrong, but I really, really don't want her here.

"I came down last minute," she explains. "I stopped by your

house but you weren't there. Home Depot is closed"—she smiles knowingly at me— "so I figured you had to be here."

"You don't have to cover for the fact that you wanted to see me, Leigh, but subtlety is always appreciated." If Drew thinks he's lightening the mood, he's an idiot.

"You haven't changed at all, have you?" She smiles at Drew.

"You have. I think your tits got bigger." He lifts his chin toward her and then switches gears before she can respond. "Too bad you missed an awesome game of Truth or Dare. We just finished." Maybe he's not such an idiot. His survival skills are kicking in. Leigh's arrival gave him an out and he's taking it.

"I haven't played Truth or Dare since I was in middle school," Leigh laughs, sitting on the couch with Drew and Nastya and pulling me down with her so that there's not an inch of space between us. Nastya's eyes keep darting to Leigh, but she won't look at me.

"Wish we could say the same," Damien groans.

"You didn't seem to mind when you were daring Piper to jerk you off in the closet," Sarah spits back.

"What-the-fuck-ever." Tierney lets out an exaggerated breath. "There's way too much drama in this room. Enough with the tequila; it's just making you people worse." She tosses a bag of weed onto the coffee table and turns to Drew. "I need a two-liter soda bottle, something to cut through plastic, a screen, and a pitcher of water."

Dalí has nothing on the scene that unfolds next in the Leighton living room. People who were trying to sabotage one another thirty minutes ago are now collaborating on a bong-making scavenger hunt. They keep bringing things to Tierney for approval like she's their ant queen or something. She checks out the pile of stuff in front of her. "There isn't a screen."

"I didn't know where to get one," Sarah says.

Tierney leaves the room and disappears down the hall.

When she comes back a few minutes later, she's holding a small, round screen in her hand.

"Where'd you get that?"

"Bathroom faucet," she answers, kneeling down in front of the coffee table and setting to work on building a gravity bong.

Halfway through, Piper eyes Tierney's progress suspiciously. "I'm not putting my mouth on that thing."

"You'll put your hands on Damien's dick, but you won't put your mouth on this?" Tierney looks almost disgusted by the waste and we get treated to another exasperated exhalation. "Your loss. You get a bigger hit, but whatever." She looks around and her eyes settle on Damien. "Here." She throws some rolling papers at him and tells him to roll Piper a joint, but he doesn't get far before she pushes him away because he's destroying it.

"If you can't roll a joint, don't try," Tierney snaps.

"It's not like it's that hard," he says defensively, but he doesn't fight her when she repos the papers.

"It's an art, jackass. Get out of my way." Tierney proceeds to roll the tightest joint I've ever seen. She's right about it being an art, and she's more than talented. I suck at rolling joints, not that it's something I do all the time, but it might be nice to have the skill.

"Everybody's gotta be able to do something with their hands," Drew says, idly running his fingers through Sunshine's hair while Tierney glowers at him before resuming bong construction.

It's hard to watch her and not be impressed. She's completely focused, as if this is a high-tech operation she's in charge of, and she has total respect for it. Clay hasn't left her side and is making her explain the entire process. He kind of reminds me of Sunshine in my garage. Tierney talks him through every step, instructing him not only on what she's doing but the science of it as well. It's like watching the illegal substance version of physics class.

I try to focus on watching their progress so I don't obsess over the fact that Leigh is running her fingers up and down my thigh, and Sunshine is sitting right next to her with a front row seat.

When Tierney gets done, she hands the bong to Clay and looks almost proud of him. "You go first. You worked for it." Then she turns to the rest of the room and tells us we better lighten up because she's sick of all the angst and she's not wasting good weed on assholes.

Leigh leans over and whispers something in my ear about finding a bedroom and then we're up and walking down the hall before I know what's going on. I make the mistake of turning back around to fortify myself with the picture of Drew all over Sunshine on the couch, but when I do, she's watching me. Unflinching. Making sure I have to answer for what I'm about to do. Drew looks from her to me and tightens his arm around her waist so that she looks away just before I'm out of her line of vision.

Chapter 35

Josh

I walk Leigh out and return to the family room, wishing I was drunk or high like everyone else here. Sarah and Piper are gone, which means they're probably passed out in her room. Through the sliding glass door, I can see Michelle lying on the grass, staring at the sky. Or sleeping. I can't tell from here. The gravity bong is abandoned on the coffee table and Damien and Chris are still half-baked, trying to kill each other on the PlayStation. Across the room, Tierney is giving Clay a lesson on joint rolling, and I hear him say something about wanting to draw her, which she laughs hysterically at. Drew is on the couch, staring at her. He looks up when he hears me, and I can see the disgust take over his face. I don't need his. I have enough of my own.

"Where is she?" I ask.

"Do you care?" He's making sure I know I'm an asshole.

"What?" I'm tired and I want to go home, and my tolerance for Drew's bullshit was running dangerously low hours ago.

"It's a simple question," he continues. My fist is tightening with every word and I force myself to loosen my hand. "Do you *care* where she is? Did you *care* when you were in my guest room screwing another girl?" I can't believe he has the balls to say any of this to me. It's not like Sunshine and I are together, and he obviously knows that better than anyone.

Tierney is completely blitzed and struggling for clarity while she watches this play out.

"Not here, Drew."

"Fine. Outside then." He gets up and he's surprisingly sober, and I realize I haven't seen him touch anything since dinner hours ago. He never did take the shot he made Tierney pour when he refused to tell me whether Sunshine was drunk or not when they had sex.

"Answer my question." I lean up against the side of my truck and shove my hands in my pockets because I need something to do with them.

"I took her home," he says. "Now answer mine." He's not fucking around. He's pissed.

"That's not the question I meant."

"I know. Answer mine first."

"Yes, I *care* where she is," I mock his tone.

"Is that what you were doing in the bedroom with Leigh? *Caring*?" The sarcastic condescension is getting on my nerves. I don't *care* if I deserve it or not.

"I was ending it," I tell him, even though I don't owe him an explanation. And the whole time I was wondering what the hell I was doing. I sat on the bed and looked at her green eyes and blond hair and the perfect body that was mine whenever I wanted it, no strings attached. It was simple, convenient, un-complicated. And I didn't want it anymore. Okay, I wanted it, but wanting it had never involved a choice before today.

I leaned over and kissed her, hoping it would make every other thought go away. I closed my eyes, and for the first time since I had been with Leigh, it wasn't her face I was picturing.

I didn't see blond hair and green eyes and simple and uncomplicated. I saw dark hair, dark eyes, dark, complicated, frustrating, messed-up everything. And the moment I broke away and opened my eyes to look at the girl pulling my shirt up over my head, I knew what I would lose if I did this. There was never a price before, but now there was and it wasn't worth it.

When I backed away, she looked at me and it was like she already knew. Like she had been waiting for it, knowing it was going to happen at some point, just not how or when or why. And I didn't even think I could tell her why.

"Sorry," I said because I didn't know what else to say to a girl who was taking my clothes off when I was about to reject her out of nowhere for what seemed like no reason. We sat there like that, not touching each other and not really knowing how to talk and I realized how different the silence sounded with her.

"The girl on Drew's lap," she finally said.

"Yeah." It came out before I could think to lie.

She narrowed her eyes and just barely pursed her lips and I noticed the way her lipstick was smeared around the edges of her mouth and I wondered how much of it I was wearing.

"She doesn't talk much."

"You don't know the half of it."

"Does *she* know the half of it?"

I didn't answer and I doubted Leigh expected me to.

"Josh," she said, resting her head on my shoulder and half-laughing the way people do when they're sad but they're trying to cover it. "What are we going to do with you?" I felt like telling her it was a good question and asking if she had the answer.

She didn't make any move to leave the room so I didn't either. Mostly because I didn't know the etiquette. If there was a right thing to do in that situation I wasn't sure what it was. Was

I supposed to get up and leave her there? Kiss her goodbye? Were we supposed to "break up"?

Then Leigh did something she hadn't done since the day I met her; she surprised me. She lay back on the bed and looked up at the ceiling and started to tell me about school. Random things, really. How she walks around campus instead of through it to get to class because it's quieter and there are oak trees and there aren't enough oak trees in Florida. She told me how her roommate has perfected a way of entering and leaving a room in the loudest manner possible and how she took a Postmodern Fiction class just to fill a course requirement and discovered that she really loved it.

It was all just details. Mundane and real and what her everyday life was made of, and I realized how much we didn't know each other and what a shame that was.

Three years of memories with Leigh hit me and every one of them looked the same. I watched her unflawed hands toying with a button on her shirt and I tried to remember if they were soft because I'd already forgotten, or maybe I just never noticed in the first place. And I started to think that maybe I was the perfect example of a dick. But when she stopped talking, she looked at me and smiled.

"I always thought we'd actually have a conversation one day," she said. "I just figured we should do that. Even if it was a little one-sided."

I smiled at that point too. I said I was sorry again and she said maybe she would stop by sometime to say hi. I figured she probably wouldn't and I think she figured she wouldn't either, but neither of us said that.

She wasn't even upset. No drama. No questions or tears. Just the same as I would have been if it had been the other way around. Ending things with Leigh was just like everything else had always been with Leigh—easy.

Even when I walked her out, I kept thinking how simple it would be to change my mind and take it back. And then screw her in the backseat of her car so that it would make it impossible for me to ever take anything back again.

"That changes things," Drew says.

I don't really know what it changes for Drew. I know that I just gave up getting laid because I felt guilty about a girl I don't even have.

"Why didn't you tell me you slept with her?" I ask, and I still want to know if he waited until she was wasted, because if he did, I'll seriously hurt him.

"Because I didn't." Not the answer I was expecting.

"You said you did."

"I guess I didn't take the truth part of Truth or Dare literally." He shrugs.

"She didn't disagree." I think back to the look exchanged between the two of them. He was asking her for permission, but I don't get why she gave it to him.

"We have an agreement."

"Break it," I tell him, even though I have no right.

"Why?"

"Because you're all over her all the time. You make her look like a whore."

"First, I hardly think I'm the only thing making her look like a whore. Second, if she asks me to stop, I'll stop. Otherwise, why should I?"

"Because I'm asking you to stop."

"She and I have a mutually beneficial relationship. Kind of like you and Leigh but we don't have sex. It works. Why would I give that up?" He's not hiding the subtext.

"Because it doesn't mean anything to you."

"Why does it mean anything to you?"

"Because she's mine and I don't want you touching her." I'm a five-year-old fighting over a toy. I feel like an idiot as soon as I say it, but it's said and it's true. And I don't want it to be.

"I know," he says arrogantly.

"You *know*?"

"I'm not stupid, Josh. The two of you have been eye-fucking each other since the beginning of school. I wasn't going to do anything with her and she was never going to do anything with me."

"Then why all the bullshit tonight?"

"Just wanted to hear you say it." He smiles and heads back toward the house. I'm too relieved to be pissed at him.

"What's with you and Tierney?" I ask when he gets to the porch.

"Trying not to screw each other. Trying not to kill each other. Same thing that's always with me and Tierney."

I'm at Nastya's house at nine o'clock the next morning. We're supposed to have plans, but after last night I'm not sure if we still do. I wait in the driveway because Margot probably just went to bed and I don't want to knock and wake her up.

When the door opens, Sunshine comes out wearing a pink, flowered sundress and flat white sandals and I wonder who she is today. She gets in the truck and shuts the door.

"Shut up. It was a birthday present," she says before I can even comment.

"Doesn't mean you had to wear it." *But I'm glad you did.*

"I figured I should get something out of the intervention since I didn't take the phone. Besides, I spend so much time doing your laundry that I haven't gotten to any of mine." She buckles her seat belt and we're off without a word about last night.

We hit three antique stores by noon, and I still haven't found anything remotely like the console table I'm looking for. If she's true to form, Sunshine will start complaining around store number five. That's where her antiquing patience tends to run out. Store number four is a high-end one, two towns west of us, and I have to promise her ice cream after this one to get her to leave the truck.

"Wouldn't it be easier to just find what you're looking for on the internet?"

"Where's the fun in that?" I ask. She's right. It would be much easier, but I like the looking.

"Where's the fun in this?" She pulls open the door and exaggeratedly drags her feet inside.

"You know you like it."

"I do?"

"You do."

"And you know this, how?"

"Because I know you, and no one makes you do anything you don't want to do. If you didn't want to come, you wouldn't come. And if you didn't come, you wouldn't be here. So it follows that if you didn't want to come, you would not be here right now. But you are here, so by the transitive property of Sunshine, you want to be here."

"I hate you."

"I know that too," I say nonchalantly, and one side of her mouth turns up in response.

"It was worth coming just to hear that many words leave your mouth at one time. That may never happen again."

"Probably not."

"So remind me again why you can't join modern society and use the internet."

I shrug because it'll probably sound stupid. "I like finding things no one else is looking for. Things that got lost or forgotten, shoved in a corner. Stuff I never knew existed. I don't even need to buy it. I just like to find it and know that it's there. That's the part I like."

"But this stuff is all old."

"They're antiques. That's kind of the point."

"So why not just buy something new?" She stops and turns her head to face me.

"I like old things," I say, putting my hand on her back and pushing her further into the store. They've been around for years. They stay.

"Is any of this even worth what they're charging for it?" She looks at the price tag on an ornate mahogany sideboard.

"Depends on how badly you want it. It's worth whatever you're willing to pay for it."

"Can you even afford any of it?"

"Yes."

"You sell that much furniture?" She looks impressed.

"No." I do okay with selling the furniture, but not even close to this well. I don't have enough time.

"Oh." She doesn't ask anything else, but I tell her anyway, even though it's the thing I hate mentioning the most.

"I have a lot of money."

"How much is a lot?"

"Millions." I watch her face. *Millions.* It sounds absurd. I've never told anyone before. The only people who know are the ones who have always known. It feels weird to even say it out loud. I don't talk about the money. I try not to even think about the money. I have a lawyer, two accountants, and a financial adviser who worry about it for me. If they handed it all over to me tomorrow, I wouldn't know what to do with it. I'd probably end up hiding it under the bed.

"No wonder you didn't have a problem getting emancipated," she says dryly.

"No wonder."

Her eyes narrow. "You're not lying." She studies my face and I shake my head.

"You don't spend any of it." It's not a question.

"My dad never wanted to touch it so I try not to as much as possible. I use what I have to for paying the bills because I can't make enough to live on while I'm in school." I can't say I hate that it's there, because I do need it. But I hate what it means, and I'll never let myself be happy about it.

"Did you buy anything with it?"

"I bought my truck last year when my dad's old one finally kicked it. And I bought an antique table."

"Which one?"

"The dark one on the far wall of the living room near the sliding glass door."

"The dark one? That's it?"

"What do you mean?"

"Usually you get all flowery and descriptive talking about the curves of the wood and the symmetry of the lines and the marriage of form and function." She puts on a pretentious tone and waves her hand around in the air.

"I talk like that?"

"When you talk about wood and furniture you do."

"I sound like a pompous ass."

"If the shoe fits."

She moves on to the back of the store where they keep the shelves with all of the ceramics and vases and lamps. "I have to be home by five," she says, turning over the three-thousand-dollar price tag on a hideous lamp with a base that looks like a harlequin. "I need this," she adds sarcastically.

"Why five?"

"I have to meet Drew to do debate research. There's another tournament coming up. State possession of nuclear weapons. Exciting stuff."

I haven't thought about Drew since this morning, and I don't really want to bring him into this now; knowing him, though, he's probably going to say something to her tonight and I have to do preemptive damage control.

"About last night," I start, and I realize how clichéd that sounds. Now I know why. She doesn't stop her intense examination of an ugly-ass vase, but I know she's listening. She's always listening. "I told Drew to keep his hands off you."

"Why would you do that?" This must interest her more than the vase because she turns around.

"Because everyone talks shit about you because of it." And I'm jealous, which is the real reason, because neither of us really cares about the crap people say. "But it's not my business, so I'm sorry."

"And he agreed?" She looks a combination of shocked and amused.

"Not without persuasion."

"What kind of methods do you have that would work on Drew?" She laughs.

"I lied," I say, even though I'm lying now. "I told him you were mine."

No response, so I keep talking. "Sorry. I didn't mean to act like you were an action figure or something."

I wait for some sort of reaction, but there is none. She turns the price tag around on a jewelry box so it's facing the right way and puts it back.

"As long as it's Lara Croft, we're good."

"Of course." I smile, but it's weak. "Anatomically correct, too."

"Come on," she says, heading back up to the front of the store. "If you're not going to buy me the three-thousand-dollar clown lamp, we need to get going. You promised me ice cream."

After the ice cream, I drag her to one more hole-in-the-wall antique store in the old part of town and then we head back. The iridescent painted cat she insisted I buy her is between us on the seat, and I can't wait to get home because it's scaring the crap out of me. I think she saw the fear in my eyes when she picked it up at the store, and after that, there was no way she was walking out without it. I told her I'd rather buy her a bracelet to replace the one she lost on her birthday, because I really did feel shitty about that, but she said no. She said it would be inappropriate, whatever that means. I guess nightmarish ceramic cats are acceptable because that's what she's got. Every time she looks at it she smiles and it's worth ten times what I paid for it.

"Thanks for coming," I say, just to have something to say while she's digging her keys out of her purse.

"Thanks for the cat." She smiles again, picking it up and holding it up to her face. "I named him Voldemort." She puts it in her lap like it's a real cat and for a minute I'm afraid it might actually bite her.

"My pleasure," I say, and I mean it, even if it sounds dumb.

She cradles the cat under her arm and reaches for the door handle, stopping to look at me before she jumps out.

"Just so you know," she says, her smile fading as her eyes lock onto mine. "You didn't lie."

Chapter 36

Nastya

Josh's garage is open when I drive by on my way home from Drew's. He's on a stool, hand sanding a piece of wood. He must be desperate to get whatever it is done, because he usually leaves the sanding for me.

"Done?" he asks when I take the sandpaper out of his hand to check the grit before handing it back. I pull another sheet of it from the cabinet and sit down next to him.

"For tonight." I hold a piece of wood up to him. "With or against?"

"With the grain on all of these." He motions to the wood pieces between us on the work bench.

"What's it going to be?" I tilt my head toward the pile of cut wood while I attach the paper to a sanding block.

"Bookshelf. For Sarah's birthday."

I nod and start working on one of the shelf pieces.

"You changed," he says, after a few minutes of listening to nothing but the lullaby of sandpaper on wood.

I look down at the jeans and black T-shirt I put on after he dropped me off and shrug.

"Probably a good idea. Drew would never have been able to concentrate with you in that dress."

"Can you blame him? I am distractingly pretty," I deadpan, just to get him off the subject of Drew and me. It never ends well. Besides, the dress was for Josh, not Drew.

"You're not going to forget about that, are you?"

"Why would I want to?" I have a list of things I'd like to forget, but that isn't on it. I've replayed it in my head a thousand times. Maybe because he didn't say *beautiful* or *stunning* or *gorgeous* or any crap like that. He said *pretty*, and *pretty* I might actually be able to believe.

"Because it's the stupidest thing I've ever said and I'd like you to," he half-snaps, and it slingshots my mind back to the picture of him disappearing down the hall last night with one of the most beautiful girls I've ever seen. Blond, tan, all lit up and everything I'm not.

"Consider it forgotten." I finish sanding one side of the shelf I had been working on and place it back on the counter. I stand up and brush the dust off my pants and I can feel him watching. "It's late. I should go." I didn't stay here after last night and I'm sure as hell not staying here tonight.

"See you tomorrow?" he says as I walk toward my car.

I wave over my shoulder, but I don't look back.

Josh

I'm in her driveway before she can get her key in the door. I left my house as soon as she was off my street, because fuck if I can do this anymore.

"Can I come in?"

She opens the door and steps inside, and I follow her.

"Don't say things if you don't mean them. I'm not that pathetic that I need empty compliments." She locks the door behind me and throws her purse onto the front table along with a can of pepper spray and that baton key holder thing she always carries around.

"I did mean it. It was just stupid."

"Wow. Even better. You're on a roll. Keep going."

"You're not going to make this easy, are you?"

"That was the nicest thing anyone's said to me since I've been here and you took it away. So, no."

"I didn't mean to."

"But you did."

I know I did. I can tell. She can't cover the hurt in her expression even though I know she's trying.

"You know I meant it. I am human. And male. And not remotely blind. Do you want me to say it again? You are distractingly, even-if-that-is-not-a-real-word, pretty. You are so pretty that I bullied Clay Whitaker into drawing me a picture of you so I could look at you when you aren't around. You are so pretty that one of these days I'm going to lose a finger in my garage because I can't concentrate with you so close to me. You are so pretty that I wish you weren't so I wouldn't want to hit every guy at school who looks at you, especially my best friend." I stop to catch my breath. "More? I can keep going." I *can* keep going, but even as I say all of this, I know it's not quite true. She's not just distractingly pretty. She's the most beautiful girl I've ever seen, and I want to touch her so badly right now that it's almost impossible to keep my hands from reaching out and doing it.

"How?" Her eyes are searching mine like she doesn't quite believe me, and they're so wide that I think I could walk right into them if she'd let me. "I've changed my clothes at your house a hundred times. You never try to look. I sleep in your bed. You never come near me."

"I didn't know I was allowed."

"You were waiting for permission?" She looks at me like I'm insane, and I wonder if I am.

"I said I was male. I didn't say I was an asshole." The silence that used to be so comfortable is torture right now, so I fill it. "I'm not Drew."

She picks up the baton thing and starts swinging it around, and I realize that it's a weapon. Her keys are attached to one end of it and they're spinning so fast that they're nothing but a blur. I want to reach out and still it, but I think if it hit me it would seriously hurt. "Drew's not really an asshole—he just plays one on TV," she says, shaking her head and wincing. "Sorry. That wasn't even remotely funny."

"Not even a little." I smile. "But you're right. He's really not an asshole." I don't know why it makes me happy that she sees that about him, but it does.

"Why are we talking about Drew?" *Good question, Sunshine.* Because it's easy. Because if we stop, we're going to have to deal with what we're doing here and neither of us knows how. We suck at this.

"Will you have dinner with me tomorrow night?" I spit the words out before I can talk myself out of them.

"It's Sunday. We always have dinner together."

"No. Just us."

"You don't want to go to Drew's?" She looks confused.

"No." I definitely do not want to go to Drew's.

"Why not? Are you still pissed about the sex thing? He said he told you it wasn't true."

"I'm trying to ask you out, and you're making it really impossible."

She stops spinning the baton. "Why would you ask me out?"

"Isn't that what people do? Go on dates?" People still do that, right? Leigh never expected movies and dinner first, so I really don't have a clue.

"I don't know. I've never been on a date." And it's swinging again.

"Never?"

"Sorry, no. Never really had a chance. My life hasn't exactly been what you'd classify as normal. How many dates have you been on?" Her defensiveness is kicking in.

"None." My life hasn't been quite normal, either. "Guess we're both freaks."

"I think we established that a while ago."

"So let's pretend. One night. We'll go out and pretend we're normal." We never even left the foyer, so I'm still right next to the door, but I'm not ready to open it yet. She looks scared. Like she thinks this is a very bad idea and that at any second now she's going to say so. I put my hands on either side of her face so she has to look at me. "One night," I repeat, not giving her a chance to formulate an excuse. "I'll pick you up tomorrow." I press my lips to her forehead, even though that's not where I want them at all.

"Are you still with her?" she whispers, and I can't believe I didn't think to tell her. Actually, I can, because I've never discussed Leigh with her. Not once. I wonder if it's been in her head this whole conversation.

"No," I say.

"Not even just for—" She stops and looks uncomfortable and I kind of want to laugh, because some of the conversations she has with Drew would make a porn star blush, but she can't spit this out. Looking at her now, I'm forced to admit to the vulnerability that she's always been hiding behind every sexual innuendo and under every tight black dress.

"Not for anything. I promise." I trace my thumb under her bottom lip and back away before I let myself kiss her, because I've been waiting to kiss her for months and I don't want to do it standing in the foyer while she has a weapon in her hand and we just got done talking about Leigh.

She nods and looks embarrassed for asking, but she shouldn't be. I would have needed to know if it was the other way around.

"So, tomorrow. You and me. Normal. All right?"

"All right." She smiles, but it's not even a real smile, just the vague idea of one.

I turn toward the door, but she stops me.

"What am I supposed to wear?"

I shrug because I don't even know where we're going yet.

"Wear something normal."

I pull up to my house just in time to see Clay Whitaker walking back to his car in my driveway. He looks nervous when he sees me.

"What's up?" I ask. I didn't even know he knew where I lived.

"You never told me what you thought of the picture." Nice try, Clay, but that's not why you're here.

"Picture was perfect, Clay. You know it was. What do you want? Because you don't do subtle well."

"Why'd you have me draw it?"

I feel like every single person I know wants a confession from me tonight.

"I'm going to walk in that house right now and give you your picture back so I never have to hear a fucking word about it again." I start toward the front porch, and the motion sensors kick the lights on.

"You didn't see her face." He's not talking about the picture anymore. He's talking about at Drew's when I walked away with

Leigh and he's wrong. I did see her face and it was awful and it would be nice if everyone would let me forget it.

"What is it about that girl that makes everyone think they have some sort of ownership or obligation to protect her?" Me, included. "In case you haven't noticed she should probably be the one protecting all of us."

"Drew and I maybe. Not sure about you." He's kicking an invisible rock back and forth with his foot and I start looking around for one of my own.

"Fine, Clay. Tell me what to do."

"You're asking me?" He's shocked. So am I. "You do realize that gay teenage boys and straight teenage girls are not inter-changeable, right? Same strategies don't really work."

"I get it. I've never done this before." I'm trying to figure out how I got to the point where I'm standing in my driveway, asking Clay Whitaker for advice. How is it that with everything that's happened in my life, this girl is going to be the thing that undoes me?

"You've never done this before?" he asks with more than a little disbelief.

I look at him like the insulting idiot that he is, especially in light of what he thinks I was doing last night with Leigh. "I've done *that* before. I just haven't done *this* before." I motion back and forth between myself and the direction of Nastya's house even though he probably has no idea what I'm doing.

"You've never just gone out with a girl?" He laughs but I'm not seeing the humor, and I make sure my expression tells him so. "Okay, not funny. Seriously, why don't you just ask Drew for advice?" He considers that for a moment. "Scratch that. Never mind." He walks over and leans up against the door of his car. "Okay, then. What does she like?"

"Running and ice cream. And hitting things. And names."

"Names?"

"Don't ask."

"Well, the whole sweat and adrenaline rush from the running might be nice for foreplay, but I don't think it's going to play well on a first date. You'd be better off going with ice cream. Very chaste. Like her." He smirks.

"I thought you were going to be serious."

"I was being serious." He stops and I can tell he's trying to decide something. "How do you know so much about her anyway? She doesn't even talk." It's almost like what I said to Mrs. Leighton, but Clay's intentions are different.

"Already did the ice cream thing." I ignore his question.

"Then it looks like you're down to hitting things."

Chapter 37

Nastya

Is it sad to be going on a first date at eighteen years old? I thought about texting Josh to cancel at least six times today. At one point I finally did text him that I couldn't go because I had nothing to wear. He texted me right back—

Nothing sounds good c u at 4

So now I'm stuck. The only thing that makes me feel better is that Josh seems to be as socially inept as me. Except that he talks. So I guess he gets the edge. But still. I really need him. I don't want to mess this up. It's bad enough that my brain is a cesspool; I can't imagine the hellhole my heart would be if he wasn't in it.

Since wearing nothing isn't really a viable option, I'm back to square one. I have absolutely no idea what to wear. My fashion sense isn't lacking. It's nonexistent. I went from recital clothes to recovery clothes to repulsive clothes. I've never done normal. I don't even know what that is. This is where the female friend thing would come in. I would have sucked it up and written a note asking Margot to help me, but the whole idea was kind of last-minute and she had plans this afternoon so she's not even home. Which means my closet and I are on our own.

My closet is of no use to me. It may actually be laughing at me. It's true. I hear it. Other than the sundress I wore yesterday, I'm out of options in the normal department. I look at my clothes. Black, black, some more black. I don't want to wear any of it. I don't want to look like Nastya Kashnikov tonight. I don't want to be a Russian whore. I don't want to look like Emilia, either. Maybe for tonight I could just be someone else. Some third girl I haven't met yet.

I realize with a craptastic amount of horror that I am going to have to go to the mall. I throw on one of the eight variations of tight black T-shirts I own and a pair of jeans and head out.

Only I don't end up at the mall. I end up at Drew's. The God that I have recently come to think might hate me is smiling on me today because Sarah isn't home. But then neither is Drew. Mrs. Leighton opens the door. I look at her stomach, which seems to have grown exponentially since the last time I saw her.

"Hey, sweetie," she says, and she's the only person on Earth I don't have the urge to smack for calling me sweetie. She lets me in after explaining that Drew and Sarah went out on a friend's boat with Mr. Leighton. She pours lemonade, and we sit at the breakfast bar and stare at each other.

"Oh!" she says after a few minutes, and I'd gotten so accustomed to the quiet that I almost fall off the stool. She grabs for my hand and I yank it back out of instinct before I can think about it. I feel like a fool but she ignores it. "I just wanted you to feel the baby kick," she says, reaching for my hand and letting me meet her halfway. She places it on her stomach and it's the weirdest feeling in the world. I almost expect an alien to burst through her abdomen at any moment.

"Feel it?" She looks at me expectantly. I pull my hand back. I can't help but see the hurt on her face, but I'm too afraid I might start crying and I can't keep my hand there anymore. "Sorry," she says. "I just get a little excited. You'd think the third time around it wouldn't be a big deal, but it never gets old. It's my favorite part." It would probably be mine, too, but I won't ever get to find out. Maybe I never would have wanted one anyway, but the deciding would have been nice. The piece of shit who took my hand took that, too.

All I wanted was to figure out what to wear on a date I probably shouldn't even be going on, and I don't know how I ended up with my hand on Mrs. Leighton's stomach, feeling her baby kick and fighting back tears.

Mrs. Leighton doesn't do well with the silence. She's a space filler. "It's a girl," she says. "We just found out."

There's a pad of paper and a pen next to the phone on the counter. I pick it up and write.

Name?

"Catherine," she says. "After Jack's mother."

I smile because I know that one. *Pure, unsullied* I scrawl and hand it to her.

She returns the smile. "Drew said you had a thing with names. What does mine mean? Lexie, well, Alexa, really. Do you know?"

Defender I scribble and underneath *You.* Then, before she asks, I give her Drew's—*masculine, manly* and Sarah's—*princess.* She rolls her eyes and laughs. "Self-fulfilling prophecies, you think?" The quiet returns and then she asks, "What about Josh?" I think there's more to that question than she's letting on but she's testing the waters.

Salvation I write. She looks at the word and nods. And for a minute she looks as sad as I feel.

"That fits, I think."

I'm not sure what she means so I put down the pen. I've written too much for one day already.

"Did you need something?" she asks. "You came over?"

I think about asking her for help with the dress situation.

She could help me. She would help me. But I can't ask for it. I shake my head and climb off the stool. I still have time to make it to the mall and pull something together.

She walks me to the door but doesn't open it. When she turns, her eyes are soft like her.

"You know, people always think it's the girls who are desperate to change the boys, to make them a better person, to be the thing they need." She's looking at me like I must understand what she's talking about, but maybe I'm just dense because I have no freaking clue. "Josh may seem like a very old man sometimes. But at the end of the day, he's still a teenage boy and he wants what all teenage boys want." She stops when I narrow my eyes at her and then laughs. "Not that. Get your mind out of the gutter. No. To be the hero. To save the girl. To save you." She pauses to heighten the effect of the fact that she's casting me as the damsel in distress in this particular scenario. "But for Josh, he doesn't just want that, he needs it. He needs to be able to fix things and make it all better; to believe that you're okay so that he can believe that he's okay. And if he can't . . ." She raises her eyebrows and leaves the thought hanging in the air like a guilt trip, and I really don't know the point of this speech. Anyone who wants to save me is going to need a time machine because that dream is dead. No one was there to save me last time, and if I end up needing to be saved from anything else, I'll do it myself, thank you very much.

I turn to leave and she opens up the door. I'm thinking I'm going to give her a pass due to pregnancy hormones and then—

"I think you and I both know it's Josh who needs saving. Have a good time tonight."

You've got to be freaking kidding me.

Josh knocks on the door at exactly four o'clock. I still don't know why we're leaving so early. We can't be having dinner at this hour because Josh hates eating early as much as I do. He's dressed in a dark blue polo shirt and belted khaki pants. He looks exactly like he does when he goes to dinner on Sundays. It pisses me off how easy it must be for guys to get dressed. He seems to have no trouble pulling off normal and looking entirely too beautiful doing it.

I try not to look as uneasy as I feel while he stands in the entryway, taking me in. I ended up in a pale-blue sleeveless dress with a dark-blue Greek-inspired design running in a band around the very bottom. It's definitely not on the cutting-edge of awesome, but it's simple. I thought it looked good and it felt like what I thought normal should feel like. I twisted all of my hair back in a loose knot at the nape of my neck. I know the scar at my hairline is probably all sorts of obvious, but he's seen it so many times already, I just don't care.

"You look different," he says, repeating the same words he used the first night I ended up at his house, and I smile because it's exactly how I'd like to look tonight. "And distractingly pretty," he adds softly, his lips turning up just slightly.

"Are you going to tell me where we're going now?" I ask. It's been driving me crazy all day. I hate not knowing things. I'm a planner and a control freak, which is hard for a person who usually has very little control over anything.

"No," he says simply, taking my hand and helping me into the truck.

And then we drive. And we drive. And we drive.

"Seriously, Josh. What the hell?" No wonder he picked me up so early. We're on a freaking road trip.

"You've said that four times since we left."

"Yeah. Because *seriously*, Josh. *What the hell*? Where are we going?"

"Close your eyes. Relax. I'll let you know when we're there."

—

"Sunshine? We're here." I open my eyes and look at the clock on the dashboard. 6:10. *Seriously, Josh. What the hell?*

"Where are we?" I ask, trying to figure out what the point of this two-hour drive was.

"Dinner."

We're in a parking lot. I look out the window and see the sign for an Italian restaurant I know far too well and I know that this is not happening. Through the glass on the side of the building I can see a man in a suit playing the piano, but it's not him I'm seeing anymore.

"What are you staring at?" Josh asks.

Me, in an alternate universe, I think.

"We're in *Brighton*?" I ask, trying to control the near hysteria in my voice.

"Yes." He's wary now. I think I'm scaring him a little, which is fine, because he's scaring me.

"*Why* are we in Brighton?" I force some calm into my demeanor, because freaking out isn't going to get me anywhere right now, and when I say anywhere, I mean the hell out of Brighton.

"Because we have reservations." His voice is tentative. He's eyeing me like at any moment I might completely lose my mind.

I don't say anything. I can't say anything.

"You like Italian food and I looked at the ratings for like fifty places in a two-hour radius and this was the best one, plus I was able to get us in. What's wrong?" He's confused and I can't blame him for it.

"Josh, there are like five hundred Italian restaurants at home. You could have taken me to any of them. Why did we drive two hours to have dinner?"

"I wanted to talk to you."

I wanted to talk to you. He says it like it's the most obvious answer in the world. He drove us two hours away for dinner, to a place where no one would know us, so that we could have a conversation. I want to laugh and cry and hug the living crap out of him. I kiss him instead. As soon as my lips are on his, his hand is at the back of my neck and he's pulling me against his chest like he's been waiting for this forever and he's not going to let me get away. But I don't want to get away, and if the steering wheel wasn't there, I would climb into his lap just to be closer to him.

Then he shifts just slightly and I'm not kissing him anymore. He's kissing me. And when he does, part of me is lost. But it's the part that's twisted and mangled and wrong, and for just that moment, with his hands in my hair and his lips on my mouth, I can pretend that it never existed.

"I thought you were pissed," he says when I pull away. "Not that I'm complaining."

"I am, but not at you." My hands are still wrapped around his upper arms, and I really don't want to let go.

"At what, then?" he asks, brushing the hair that came loose out of my eyes.

"Everything else."

He did all of this so that we would be able to go out and actually talk to one another and he brought me to the one place where we can't do that. He's just staring at me now like he doesn't know what that means and he's not sure where we go from here. I'd like to just go home and sit in his garage, where everything is comfortable and I can sand down wood and watch piles of sawdust grow around my feet and feel like I'm okay for however long I stay there.

There's something in the way he's looking at me that freaks me out, but I can't look away. He leans in again and I don't move at all until I feel his lips on mine. There's a reverence in the way he kisses me that frightens me, because it's the most wonderful thing I've ever felt.

"Sorry," he says. "I've been wanting to do that for a really long time, I just wanted to do it again."

"How long?"

"Since the first night you walked into my garage."

"I'm glad you didn't," I confess.

"Why?"

"I had just thrown up. I think it would have ruined the moment."

"As opposed to this moment, which is now full of romance." He smiles and I let go of his arms and sit back, trying to figure out what to say.

"Do you want to go in?" he asks finally.

I shake my head. "We can't stay here."

"Why not?" he asks, and I feel terrible for taking this away from him. Just another thing that I can add to the list of disappointments I've leveled at people I care about. I don't want Josh Bennett's disappointment, too. I don't think I can handle it. But I don't have a choice right now. There's no amount of disappointment that can get me into that restaurant. I look at Josh and wish I could just kiss him again instead of having to answer, but I know I'm not getting out of this one.

"Because it's where I'm from."

Our attempt at normalcy ends up being bad pizza at a hole-in-the-wall we found somewhere on the road between Brighton and home, and there's nothing about it that's normal. It's not even extraordinary. It's perfect and I want it to stay perfect, but nothing ever does. People like Josh Bennett and I don't get perfect. Most of the time, we don't even get remotely tolerable. And that's why it scares me. Because, even if there was such a thing to begin with, perfect never lasts.

—

We pull in to Margot's driveway just before eleven, and I look at Josh, because I don't know why he brought me here instead of back to his house.

"I had a good time tonight," he says.

"Shouldn't I be saying that to you?"

"I don't know. Is there a rule?" he asks.

"I don't know," I concede. "I had a good time, too. It was fun. All things considered." I still feel bad for ruining his plans.

"No things considered," he says gently, lifting his hand to my cheek before leaning over to kiss me. Just once. And it isn't perfect. It's soft and warm and true and real. "It was fun. Nothing else matters."

Nothing else matters. If I had a penny right now, I'd wish that were true; I want to believe it more than I've ever wanted to believe anything.

"Then why are you bringing me back here?" I ask.

He shrugs sheepishly. "I thought it would be kind of presumptuous to expect you to sleep with me on the first date."

I yawn before he even finishes speaking. "If all you're expecting is sleep, then I'm a sure thing."

"Well" —he smiles— "far be it from me to turn down a sure thing."

And with that, he backs his truck out of the driveway, and we go home.

Chapter 38

Nastya

My first therapist's name was Maggie Reynolds. She talked to me like a kindergarten teacher would. Soft and patient and unthreatening. Coddling. It made me want to smack her in the face and I really wasn't a smack-someone-in-the-face kind of person at that time. Not like I am now, when pretty much everybody makes me want to smack them in the face.

Every time I asked her why I couldn't remember what happened, she told me it was natural. Because, isn't everything? She said it was my brain's way of protecting me from something I wasn't ready to face yet. That my mind would never give me more stress than I could handle, and that when I was strong enough, I would remember. We just had to be patient. But it's hard to be patient when no one else is.

Everyone might have agreed that it was natural to forget, but it didn't mean they would stop asking. The question was always the same, from the police, from my family, from my therapists. *Do you remember anything?* The answer was always the same, too. No. I don't remember anything. Not one single thing about what happened that day.

Then one day I guess my mind decided I was ready, because

that was the day I remembered everything and then I stopped answering the questions altogether. I think maybe my brain made a mistake about how strong I was, but it didn't let me send the memories back.

I never even had one nightmare until after my memory returned. Once the vision of what had happened was back in my head, it wouldn't be ignored. It came at me with a vengeance, night after night, like it was making up for lost time. I would wake up sweating and shaking in a state of remembered terror, and I couldn't tell anyone why.

So I wrote. I spit every detail out of my head and onto paper so that the memory wouldn't have any hold over me. I felt like a criminal. Like I was perpetrating some crime by not telling, and every night I was waiting for the nightmares to call me on it, to turn me in. So I took away their leverage. I confessed myself. Every night into the notebooks. The words were the sacrifice I offered up daily in exchange for dreamless sleep.

They have never failed me.

—

It's the second night this week that Josh and I are headed to the Leightons' for dinner. We spent Thanksgiving here, also. I think we both would have been happy to have stayed at his house and ordered pizza and worked in the garage like the antisocialites that we are, but you don't say no to Mrs. Leighton. It wasn't a request. It was a requirement. And it was nothing like Sunday dinner. It was grandparents and cousins and aunts and uncles and strays like Josh and I. We hid in Drew's room for the most part, because Josh hates hugging ambushes as much as I do, and these people were huggers. *All of them.*

When we got to the table, with the china and the centerpiece and the napkin swans, I took a picture with my phone and sent it to my mom so she would know I wasn't alone. I don't know if it made her feel better. Seeing a table covered with food and surrounded by somebody else's family might not have been the type of comfort I was trying to send.

We didn't have school at all this week, so aside from Thanksgiving, we've had the past nine days to do nothing but build. The weather's been beautiful and the humidity is low, so I've been in the driveway finishing. We've finally found something I'm better at than Josh, and he doesn't care, because the only thing he likes less than sanding, is finishing.

Other than Drew's house, we haven't gone anywhere except the grocery store and the hardware store. We work on furniture most of the day, come in at three o'clock for Josh's *GH* fix, cook dinner, build some more, go running, and sleep.

It's been a perfect week. I hate that it's already Sunday.

"Dad's turn for music tonight." Mrs. Leighton has a tray full of twice-baked potatoes balancing on one hand and a water pitcher in the other.

"Isn't it Drew's turn?" Sarah asks, putting the last of the silverware on the table.

"Nice try. Drew's got next week. It's mine." Mr. Leighton laughs maniacally to taunt her and I smile because it reminds me of something my dad would do. He opens a cabinet full of CDs and scans through them before pulling one out and turning on the stereo.

It takes me three notes to recognize the Haydn sonata he's put on. It's the one I know by heart. The one I practiced a thousand times to play for my audition that day at school. The one that became the theme song for my murder, instead. That's what we're listening to over Sunday dinner. The soundtrack to my death.

I haven't heard it since that day, since the last time I played it before I left my house that afternoon, since I heard myself humming it while I walked to school. I don't hear it now. I also don't do anything hopelessly dramatic like drop dishes or freak out and run from the room. I stop breathing instead.

I'm walking and humming and practicing every note in my head. I'm not nervous because it's just a recording and if I mess up I can redo it as many times as I want until I'm happy. Nick Kerrigan is recording it for me in the music lab and he likes me and he'll stay as long as I need. He told me. I like him too so that works for me. I'm checking out my hands because I want them to look good and I don't want my nails chipped and then there's a boy in front of me. He smiles but he looks wrong. Wrong in his eyes. But I smile and say hi and walk past him. And then his hand is on my arm so tight that it hurts and I turn but I can't say anything because he hits me in the face and then I'm facedown on the ground and he's dragging me somewhere. Then I'm not on the ground anymore because he yanks me up by my hair. He says it's my fault. He calls me a Russian whore and tells me to stand up but I don't know why because he just knocks me down again. There's blood and dirt in my mouth and I don't remember how to scream anymore. I don't even remember how to breathe. I wonder if I'm Russian but I don't think so and I don't know why this boy hates me. He's pulled my hair so hard so many times that it's ripped part of my scalp off and the blood runs into one of my eyes and I can't see out of it anymore. He must be tired of picking me up because he just leaves me on the ground and starts kicking me instead. I don't know how many times in my stomach and my chest. A couple of times between my legs. I think I hear my ribs cracking. I don't know how long he kicks me. Maybe forever. I don't feel any of it anymore. Nothing even hurts. I can still see out of my left eye. On the ground, I can't tell how far away, is one of my pearl buttons. The sun is hitting it and it looks like it's changing colors and it's so beautiful and I want to hold it. If I can reach it everything will be okay. I think he's still kicking and my hand reaches out for it but I can't get there. Everything stops except his breathing. I see his boots next to my hand. Then I can't see anything anymore because everything is black and I can't feel my body. The last thing I hear is the sound of the bones in my hand being crushed and then there isn't anything anymore.

"Nastya?"

"Nastya?"

I don't know that name.

When I open my eyes, I can see again. I'm on Drew Leighton's white brocade sofa and there's no blood anywhere and nothing hurts except my soul. I can see the coffee table Josh Bennett made. I can see Josh Bennett, sitting on the floor next to the couch, holding my hand and staring at me. I can see all of the questions he isn't asking. Everyone here looks scared, even Sarah, and I wonder if I look scared, too. Because I have no idea what just happened.

Mrs. Leighton makes me drink water even though I try to refuse because I'm freaked out, not dehydrated. Apparently I stopped breathing long enough that I passed out and she wants to call my aunt. I shake my head and look at Josh, imploring him with every *please* I can force into my eyes. He says he'll take me home, and I hope he's talking about his home, because that's where I want to be, even if I don't like the look on his face. The look people give you when they're afraid that one wrong word will cause you to break. But if I didn't break before, I'm sure as hell not doing it on the white brocade sofa at Drew Leighton's house.

I have remembered what happened to me every day for nearly two years. I've seen it in nightmares. I've written it in notebooks every night for hundreds of days. But I have never relived it until now. I know that I'm safe here. But I know what dirt and blood taste like, too.

I'm sleeping at Josh's again, because somewhere along the line, that became the norm. The more time I spend here, the more I hate being at Margot's by myself. I make sure she always knows where I am, and even if she doesn't like it, I think she understands, or maybe I just need to believe that she does. I feel more at home at Josh's than anywhere else in the world, and right now, I need a home.

I have to hide in the bathroom to write my three and a half pages, even though tonight I feel like I already did. I write them anyway and then slip the composition book into my backpack, behind my trig book, like it's homework.

"Don't," I say, when I climb into bed in the dark, because even in pitch black silence, I can see and hear and feel the question all around me.

"You have to tell me sometime," he says softly as if someone in the house might hear us.

"But I don't have to tell you tonight," I whisper back.

He takes my left hand like he knows it guards all my secrets and he thinks maybe he can learn them just by holding it.

"You were awake, but it was like you weren't even there." He pulls me against him and kisses the scar on my forehead, keeping his arm wrapped tightly around me, pulling my head onto his chest and pressing my body to his. "It scared the hell out of me and you won't tell me why it happened."

I have to tell him something, so I tell him what I know is true.

"Sometimes I just forget how to breathe."

Chapter 39

Josh

"Damn, your girlfriend can bake." Drew shoves yet another cookie in his mouth. He's eating them as fast as Sunshine can pull them out of the oven.

"Not my girlfriend," I say, because, according to her, she's not, and that's fine because I hate the term anyway. Saying *girlfriend* somehow puts us in an official relationship, and if she is an official part of my life, she will probably be officially gone very soon. So if she doesn't want to be called my girlfriend, I'm okay with that.

"Fine," Drew counters. "Your wife." He walks up to her and pulls a cookie off the tray, burning his fingers in the process. "No wonder you always smell like brown sugar and"—he stops, picking up a bottle off the counter and reading the label—"pure vanilla extract."

He's right. She does smell like brown sugar and vanilla, but I thought I was the only one who noticed.

He flips the cap open on the bottle and inhales it. "Seriously, they should sell this as perfume." Sunshine is just staring at him with a slightly disgusted look on her face.

"You *smell* me?"

"You don't have to make it sound so creepy. It's not like I sneak into your room and watch you sleep." He walks over and slaps me on the back. "Josh does that."

Sunshine throws an oven mitt at him, and he pretends to be wounded. "Watch it, woman. Since you're not taken, I can throw you down on the floor and make love to you right now."

She gags loudly and Drew looks mock offended. "The idea of having sex with me is that distasteful?"

"No, the idea of having sex with you is, as always, the pinnacle of dreams. It's the *make love* part that's repulsive. I hate that expression. I could be sixty years old and I'd still rather say *fuck* than *make love*. Ichth." She shudders.

"Good," he says, confidence restored. "Then since you're not taken, I can throw you down on the floor and fuck you right now."

"Do me a favor," I say. "Either screw each other and get it over with or quit acting like you're going to." I turn the TV off because I can't hear it anyway and toss the remote on the couch. I sound like a jealous bastard. I am a jealous bastard. Just because I know there's nothing going on between them doesn't mean it doesn't piss me off.

"Are those our only two options?" Drew asks. "Because I know which one I'm going with."

Sunshine shoves another cookie in Drew's mouth and tells him to quit while he's ahead.

"You know I've gained like ten pounds since I met you. How do you eat all this shit and not get fat?" he asks, wiping crumbs off his hands.

"I run," she says. "A lot."

Drew looks repulsed. "Well I'm not doing *that*."

"Don't worry." She smiles. "You have enough testosterone to keep your metabolism going for a while."

"True story," he says cockily.

"Speaking of true stories and testosterone, is anyone ever going to tell me what the deal is with Tierney Lowell?" Sunshine asks.

Drew stiffens. "No."

She arches one eyebrow at him, and he groans exaggeratedly like a kid who just had his video games taken away.

"Fine. But only because I'm fragile and you scare me."

Drew moves over on the couch so she can sit next to him, but she sits down in my lap instead, and I really have no problem with the fact that she's not my girlfriend.

"It's an age-old story," he says flatly. "Boy meets girl. Boy asks girl to touch him inappropriately. Girl dazzles boy with her impressive knowledge and proper use of profanity. Boy and girl end up in detention together. Love blossoms. In secret. For four months."

Sunshine looks at me for confirmation. "True story," I deadpan. I always knew they had hooked up, but I thought it was a one-time deal. I actually just found out the rest of the story. He didn't tell me until I laid into him the week after the infamous Truth or Dare dinner. But I remember there was something up with Drew during that time period and now it all makes sense.

"And?" she asks.

"And nothing. That's all you're getting." He turns the TV back on.

"You suck," she mutters.

"So do you, no doubt."

Somehow I didn't find that nearly as funny as the two of them.

Chapter 40

Nastya

Drew and I have spent the past three hours at his dining room table with dueling laptops, pulling up research and precedents for the most boring argument ever on term limits. I guess it's better than gas taxes, which we could have gotten stuck with. The county debate tournament is in two weeks. I don't have to compete, but I have to attend, and my grade comes from doing prep work.

So far I've gotten away with being designated as Drew's researcher. No one else really has researchers, but I'm there, and I can't compete for myself, so he gets to use me. If he wasn't so good it never would have flown, but he performs. When Drew does well, the team does well, and when the team does well, Mr. Trent looks good, so he'll give Drew just about anything he asks for. Which works for me, because it keeps me out of the claws of Ethan Hall, who still thinks asking me for blow jobs in the guidance office, while pretending to harmlessly flirt, is romantic.

I hand Drew the printouts and my notes, and we split up the rest of the work so we can finish it tonight. I haven't quit badgering him about Tierney yet.

"Why can't you guys at least be friends? Wouldn't that be

better than nothing?" I'm not an expert on relationships. Not any of them. Not familial, not romantic, not friendly. Relationships require communication, which is not really my thing, so it's a weak subject for me. I just don't get why he has to act like he hates her when he so obviously doesn't.

"No, it would *not* be better than nothing. It would absolutely be *worse* than nothing."

"That's such a cop-out. Guys always say that because it's easy."

"And girls always want to change the rules in the middle of the game. You can't change the rules and think everyone else is just going to keep playing. I know what her hair smells like, but I can't get close enough to press my face into it. I know how soft her skin is on every part of her body, but I can't touch it. I know what she tastes like, but I can't kiss her. I'm not allowed anymore. So why should I torture myself with being around her, just so I can say we're still friends?"

"Still doesn't make any sense."

"It's the only thing that makes sense, and if you'd stop to think about it for one minute, you'd realize it. If you and Josh were suddenly not together, do you think you could still hang out with him all the time? Be in his house, but not touch him? Act happy for him when he's going out with some other girl and she's going to know all the things about him that you know, but that all of a sudden you're not supposed to know anymore? You couldn't do it, either."

"Josh isn't in love with me and I'm not in love with him."

"Sell it to someone who's buying, Sunshine. Have you seen the way he looks at you?" I've seen the way he looks at me, but I don't know what it means. "Like you're a seventeenth-century, hand-carved table in mint condition."

"So he looks at me like I'm furniture."

"Exactly. See? You know what I'm talking about."

"Nobody likes a smart-ass."

"Fallacy. Everybody likes a smart-ass. Especially you." He fixes his eyes on mine, and it's obvious he won't be done proving his theories until I concede. "Friends is bullshit, and you'll know it, too, when it happens to you. When the two of you break up, you'll know exactly what I mean."

"We can't break up if we aren't together." I enunciate every word in my most exasperated voice, but it doesn't deter him.

"Semantics. It's going to happen and everyone"—he gestures around the room to the audience that isn't there—"knows it but you. One day, you're going to get drunk and screw the shit out of each other and then you're going to realize how incredibly, stupidly in love you are, or maybe vice versa, knowing you two. Could happen. But anyway, you'll be *together*. And then one day, you *won't*. And when that day comes, I can promise you, you won't be friends. You'll hate each other before you'll ever just be friends."

"I don't want him to love me." Why I say this out loud is beyond me, but it's true. I don't want the obligations and the expectations. I don't want to be the source of disappointment in another person's life.

"He doesn't want to love you either, so I guess you're on the same page."

Talking about Josh is starting to feel like a very bad idea. "We're supposed to be talking about Tierney."

"We're supposed to be talking about government term limits."

"All right, I'll accept your impossible friendship theory if you tell me what happened. Maybe if I know how it ended, I'll agree with you." I actually am starting to agree with him, but I'm not telling him yet. I want the story.

"I was an asshole."

"That's a given. Quit stalling."

"We got together. *Together, together*," he clarifies. "Not just my version of together. Tierney didn't want anyone to know because she refused to have people thinking she was another name on a very long and undistinguished list. She said she was better than that. And she was better than that. She never would have hooked up with me if it was nothing. But dickhead Trevor Mason kept giving me shit, so I told him. Except I didn't tell him we were together. I just told him we were screwing. She got pissed. Broke up with me. Everybody acted like she was a loser for thinking I gave a crap about her."

"Did you give a crap about her?"

He nails me with a look that says that I know the answer and he's not saying it. I think his throat might close up if he tried to say the word *love*.

"You guys don't even have anything in common. What's the attraction? And please refrain from listing body parts or anything involving the word *oral*."

"She's Tierney. She gives me shit, but she won't take mine. She makes me laugh, but she laughs more. She argues with me about everything, even when she knows she'll never win. Plus, she's hot as hell and she can't stand me. Is there anything else that could possibly make her more attractive?"

"It sounds like you're giving a speech. Bottom line it, Drew."

"Damn, you're annoying," he groans, but that's what he always does when he's going to answer anyway. "Listen, I know what I look like and I know how smart I am. Shut up. Don't look at me like that. I know it and you know it. But I know I'm a pretty shit human being, too," he says, sounding momentarily sincere. "Tierney made me feel like I wasn't completely worthless as a person."

"But you treat her like she's worthless. You hurt her feelings all the time. I know she's all hard-core and everything, but you do know she has feelings, right?"

"Of course I know she has feelings. Do you know how smart that girl is? No. Nobody does, because she doesn't want you to know. She doesn't want you to know she's funny and sweet either—yes, I used the word *sweet*, and if you ever mention it again there will be consequences." He shoots me the look-into-my-eyes-and-feel-my-wrath glare before continuing. "You know who knows those things? I do. So, yes, Nastya, I know she has feelings, and I know how to hurt every one of them."

"So that's what you do? You feel guilty for hurting her so you make up for it by hurting her more? You're the definition of a jackhole. Why wouldn't you have just apologized to her right after it happened? Told people the truth?" I close the laptop and push it aside.

"Because she was so pissed. She broke up with me and said I was everything she ever knew I was and that people were right, that she was pathetic for believing anything else."

"And that was it?"

Apparently that wasn't even close to it. He proceeds to tell me that the night Tierney laid all of that on him, he went to a party and had sex with Kara Matthews.

"Why the hell would you do that?" Nothing Drew does should surprise me at this point, but this does.

"Because I was depressed and pissed and I lost her because I was a prick so I figured I might as well act like one."

"You know, for someone who thinks he's such an awesome debater, your logic is seriously flawed. You hadn't lost her. You didn't lose her until you screwed Kara Matthews. It was a test."

"First of all, I am an awesome debater. Second of all, it was not a test. She broke up with me for real. She hated me."

"That's *why* it was a test." How is it that an inexperienced social loser like me can grasp this and Drew Leighton cannot? "She handed you a golden opportunity to prove her wrong. Instead, you stuck your dick in Kara Matthews and proved that Tierney meant absolutely nothing and that every bad thing she ever thought about you was true."

I can't pretend not to know why I adore Drew Leighton. He's as fucked up and emotionally stunted as I am, just in a different way. But, right now, I kind of hate him for being so astronomically clueless. I walk over and wrap my arms around him and put my head on his shoulder, because I know what self-loathing looks like, and if I want there to be hope for me I need there to be hope for him.

"You really are an asshole," I say.

He sighs and rests his chin on the top of my head. "That's what I've been trying to tell you."

I end up staying long enough that Mr. and Mrs. Leighton and Sarah get home and I'm roped into having dinner with them, which isn't such a dreadful thought now that Sarah is not my mortal enemy anymore.

Sometime after the dinner party from hell, Sarah decided she didn't completely despise me. That whole night may have been the definition of a bad idea, but if one good thing came out of it, it's that somehow the tension between the two of us has dissipated. It's not like we're swapping sex stories and bra shopping together, but still. If I knew that teaching her how to knock a guy on the ground would endear her to me, I would have done it months ago. Nevertheless, things have gotten easier, maybe almost nice.

"You'd look a lot better without all that makeup," she tells me, and I think it's her idea of a compliment. I don't know if I'd look better, or just different, but I'm not ready to give it up. "If you looked normal, you could have more friends. You know, even with the not talking. People are kind of scared of you."

Good. That's the plan. The conversation is pretty one-sided, but it's better than being scowled at, insulted, and generally treated like a pariah, which is what I'm used to from Sarah.

"Not everybody can be as socially blessed as you, Sarah," Drew chimes in. "It's a gift being related to me."

"No, it's a curse," she says, and it's genuine.

"Right. As if you'd have half as many friends or go on half as many dates if I weren't your brother." I think Drew is joking, but it sets her off, and when I hear what she says, I don't blame her. I feel sorry for her instead.

"You're absolutely right! That's the fucking problem, Drew! Girls all want to be friends with me because they think it's a free pass *to you*. Guys want to go out with me because they figure I'm a cheap slut *like you*. You want to take credit for my social life? Go ahead. You *are* responsible for it." She pauses because she's so worked up, and I can tell Drew is wishing he never said anything because he didn't see this coming at all. I don't even want to be in the room anymore. I wonder if anybody here has an invisibility cloak I could borrow, because that would be awesome right now.

"I *hate* being your sister!" Sarah hisses. "I would do *anything* to not be related to you!"

Drew doesn't say anything else. No cocky comebacks. No derision. He just walks out and leaves me with Sarah, who starts to cry. I'm seriously hoping they have some ice cream here, because without words it's pretty much the only thing I've got to work with.

"I hate him," she says through tears, and I know that she doesn't, but I can't tell her that.

Later that night, we push all the furniture to the side of the room again and offer to give Mr. and Mrs. Leighton a demonstration of Sarah's up-and-coming self-defense skills. I drag Drew back into the room and offer him up as an assailant and then refresh

Sarah's memory on how to cause him bodily harm. And Drew lets her do it as many times as she needs to, even when she doesn't pull back enough and it's really starting to hurt. Then the last time he comes at her from behind, he whispers, "I'm sorry," before wrapping his arms around her. There's a part of me that's hoping she'll press her arms up and out before dropping straight down out of his grasp, driving her elbow back into him and then running like I taught her, but I'm glad she doesn't when he apologizes again and she turns in his arms and hugs him back.

Just as he loosens up, she stomps on his instep for real, then mock knees him in the groin and Mrs. Leighton applauds.

Chapter 41

Nastya

"You're destroying your hands," Josh tells me, picking them up and turning them over to look at my palms. I pull them back, but I can't help smiling because it's a compliment. It's even better than being called distractingly pretty.

"I like it," I tell him, examining them myself. "Means they're doing something." I may not be able to use them the way I'd like—unless one-handed piano playing becomes all the rage, I'm SOL—but at least I can do something. Josh hates sanding. It's his least favorite thing to do, because according to him, it's boring. He keeps trying to get me to use a belt sander when it's feasible, but there's just no satisfaction in that. I like sanding because it's mindless and repetitive and it lets me think. I can smooth out all the rough edges. And at the end of the night, I can look at what I've done and see a pile of sawdust and feel like I've accomplished something. When I look at my hands, I don't see scrapes and scratches; I don't see injuries; I see healing.

I think I'm still smiling at my hands like an idiot, and when I look back up he's watching me with something like respect, and that look is definitely better than being called distractingly pretty.

"They used to be soft, but the sandpaper is killing them," he says. "They're turning into my hands." I wonder if he thinks that's an insult. His hands are miracles. I can watch them for hours, transforming wood into something it never dreamed of being.

"So I won't touch you and then and you won't notice."

"No need to be rash," he jokes, picking my hands up again and running his thumb along one of the scars on my left one. The plastic surgeons worked miracles, but they still couldn't get it perfect. You can still see all the wrong about it when you look. "I just like your hands," he continues, not taking his eyes off them. "Sometimes I think they're the only real thing about you."

He says things like that a lot. Like he's reminding me that just because he doesn't ask the questions, it doesn't mean he forgets they exist.

"You want to test that theory?" I ask, smiling at him. He keeps his grip on my hands and pulls me back toward the wall.

"Not with the garage door open."

—

I spend half of Saturday morning sitting cross-legged on a flatbed at Home Depot with Josh pushing me up and down the lumber aisles, telling me about how every kind of wood varies. I learn which to use for furniture, which are better for floors, which are the best for finishing, and so on. Finally he kicks me off the flatbed and I have to walk because he needs it to actually put wood on. I might complain about having to get up if it didn't mean that I get to spend the next twenty minutes watching him load up lumber, and complaining about that would be wrong on so many levels. It's worth the standing any day.

When we get home, we plan to spend the afternoon finishing, but it starts to pour and we can't work with the garage closed and the finish will get cloudy anyway from the humidity. At this point, I could tell you this and then some. Between Josh and shop class, I'm getting quite an education.

We spend the afternoon in the kitchen and I figure if he can teach me about lumber, I can teach him how to bake a decent cookie. I scold him for packing the flour into a measuring cup, and he keeps doing it just to annoy me until I take it away and do it myself.

"Why do I have to learn how to make them when I have you here to do it for me?"

"You know," I say, pushing a bag of brown sugar and another measuring cup at him since he wants to pack things so badly, "one day I may not be here, and then you'll be cookieless and sad." As soon as the words are out of my mouth, I regret them. I mentally kick the thought in the groin, and when it doubles over, I knee it in the face so it will never rear its ugly head again. Unfortunately, it's too late for that.

"It's okay," he says gently, with just a whisper of a smile. "I'm not that sensitive about it. Everyone just assumes I am. Don't be everyone, okay?"

"Why aren't you angry about it?"

"What's the point?"

"So you're just okay with it?"

"I said I wasn't angry. I didn't say I was okay with it. I understand all the crap people say. It's natural. It's inevitable. It's a part of life. Still doesn't make it okay that someone can just disappear like they never existed. But being pissed all the time doesn't make it okay, either. I know. I used to be pissed all the time. It gets old."

"If I were you I'd be the angriest person in the world."

"I think you already are."

There isn't any point in arguing with that, so I step over to show him how hard to pack down the brown sugar, but I still feel shitty.

"After we're done with this, maybe you can help me move the coffee table over from the wall. I think I'm going to get rid of the piece of crap in front of the couch," he says, changing the subject and letting me off the hook.

"You're going to move the love of your life into the middle of the room where Drew can violate it with his shoes any time he likes?" This is genuinely surprising because I know how Josh feels about that table.

"Since when did it become the love of my life?" He sounds bemused.

"You talk about it like it's a girl."

"What can I say?" He shrugs. "That table makes me want to be a better man. Jealous?"

"You know it'll kill Drew not to be able to put his feet on it. Unless you've decided to allow that."

He looks mildly horrified. I think he's imagining it happening. "Maybe it's fine where it is."

"Just so you know," I inform him, "one day, I'm going to get tired of sharing your affection with that coffee table and I'm going to make you choose."

"Just so you know," he mimics me, "I would chop that table up and use it for firewood before I would ever choose anything over you." It's a ridiculous thing to say, but he nails me with those eyes, making sure I know he's serious and I wish he wouldn't do that.

"That would be a waste." I take the bag of brown sugar he's still holding and put it back so I can have an excuse to turn away, because I'm not in the mood for serious, and for some reason, this conversation keeps veering back toward places I don't want to go. "You don't even have a fireplace."

"You make it impossible to say anything nice to you."

"Not impossible. Just difficult," I say lightly, hoping he'll change his tone, too. I figure maybe I can distract him, and I lift myself up on my tiptoes to kiss him. I can tell he knows what I'm doing and he hesitates just a second before lifting his hand to the back of my neck and leaning into me, letting his mouth move against mine, soft and searching, coaxing out my secrets. His eyes are on me when I pull away, and I walk over to turn on the mixer, hoping the noise of it will effectively kill any conversation.

"Tell me where you got the scar." It comes out of nowhere and from everywhere.

"No," I whisper. He can't hear it over the mixer, but he knows I said it. The worst thing is that there's a part of me that's starting to want to tell him, and that scares the living crap out of me. Josh makes me feel safe, and safe is something I never thought I'd feel again.

He pulls me back against him and holds me there. I can feel the warmth of his fingers imprinting the skin at my waist. His mouth is next to my ear, and for just one second I expect him to call me a Russian whore.

"Please."

"I don't even know which one you're asking about," I say, and I'm thankful not to have to see his face. There's something in the way he says please that won't let me laugh this off or lie to him. There's a desperation in it that I don't want to acknowledge.

"Any. Just one. Just something. Tell me something true." His arms are solid, wrapping around me, pressing my back against his chest, and it feels more like truth than anything has in such a long time. But I still have nothing to give him.

"I don't even know what that is anymore."

—

"Do you live here anymore?" Margot asks me one afternoon when I get back from school. I wish I could say it's not a valid question, but I'm at Josh's more often than not. I come home in the mornings before she gets back from work just so I can shower and change for school. Sometimes not even that. Little by little, my clothes seem to be making it to his house, also.

I can shrug or shake my head or play dumb and act like I don't know what she's saying, but I owe her more than that. There's a part of me that almost opens my mouth, but I just can't make myself do it. If I say something, I'll have to say everything and that isn't happening today. I pull some notebook paper out of one of my school folders and write.

If I say no will you make me come back?

"Sit, Em." She pulls out a chair at the kitchen table and I do the same, keeping the pencil and paper in my hand.

"I know you're an adult now." She puts the word adult in air quotes, and I want to shake my head at her and beg her not to make me lose respect. "But you're not all grown-up," she continues. She's not telling me anything I don't know.

Point? I write, and turn the paper toward her. I'm not trying to give her attitude, actually. I just want to know if I'm going to be fighting to keep the one thing that's been keeping me sane. And, really, it's not even as much Josh as it is that garage.

"Does it help? Being there?"

My instinct is to say that nothing helps, because that's always my instinct, but it's not true this time. Everything about being there helps. It's a place to be and something to do and a person who doesn't compare me to Emilia. I don't just nod. I write *Yes* on the paper.

"I won't pretend to like it. But you're alone here all the time and I don't like that, either." She hesitates and I don't know if I should write something or just see if she says anything else. And she does. "Are you sleeping with him?"

Well, yes, I am, in fact, sleeping with him, but I'd put money on the fact that that's not what she's asking. I shake my head no, because it's true, even though I'm not sure for how long.

"Really?" she asks, and I don't know if she's disappointed or relieved or just skeptical.

Really.

"I still want to know where you are."

I nod. I don't blame her for that and it doesn't matter anyway, because I know she can track my phone. It's just courtesy and courtesy I can do.

"He's really cute." She smiles conspiratorially.

And I nod to that, too.

Chapter 42

Josh

"How many miles did you run?" I ask when she walks back into the garage just after ten and strips the can of pepper spray from her waist and the heart monitor off her wrist.

"Didn't track it. Just ran," she pants while the sweat drips down her face. She grabs a bottle of water and comes up next to me, looking over my shoulder. "How far did you get?"

"Almost done. I was about to quit. It'll be ready to finish tomorrow, if it's not raining."

"I can help when I get done at Clay's." She's been at Clay's at least twice a week for a month. He's doing some sort of freaky layered montage thing. I don't get it. I like the ones where I can just see her face.

"Tell him he's monopolizing you and I'm starting to get jealous."

"I'll let him know." She smiles. "He's got that competition next month and I can't sit this weekend, so I said I'd do it after school." Between researching with Drew, sitting for Clay, running, school, and building with me she never stops for a second. She just signed up for some Krav Maga class, too, whatever that is. She's not good with down time.

"Is that the one you're going to with him?"

She nods, tilting back the rest of the bottle of water. "It's at some art gallery in Ridgemont. They use it every year for the state competition and they display all the finalists' work."

"Still going home this weekend?" I wish she wasn't because I'm used to her now. I realized how much it sucks to cook alone and eat alone and watch TV alone and generally be alone.

"I said I would."

She never sounds happy about going home, and I have absolutely no clue why, except that it has something to do with all the scars she has and the stories she won't tell me. Whenever she comes back from there, it's like she's out of focus for a few days, like a hologram that keeps blurring in and out. She's always been like that, like music and lyrics to two different songs. It's just worse after she's been back to Brighton.

"You don't talk to anyone in your family?"

"You know I don't." She's getting the *where-are-you-going-with-this?* tone in her voice that I'm so familiar with now.

"Why not?"

"Because I can't tell them what they want to hear. If I talk to them, I'll have to lie and I don't want to." It's more information than she's ever given me before, and it's still not enough. It doesn't tell me shit.

"You stopped talking just so you wouldn't have to lie?"

"I didn't plan to. I just wanted a day and then I just wanted one more day and then one more after that and that turned into a week, which turned into a month and you get the idea."

"They just let you stop? They didn't care?"

"They cared, but it's not like they could do anything about it. What were they going to do? Shake me? Yell at me and insist? Ground me? I never left the house anyway. They didn't really have a lot of options. Plus, according to my impressive collection of therapists, it was a very *natural* response, whatever that means." *Natural response to what, Sunshine? Please keep talking.* But she doesn't. Just another random piece in a puzzle made of all the wrong pieces.

"Wouldn't lying have been easier than silence?"

"No. I'm crap at it. I don't believe in doing something if you can't excel at it." She's back to sarcasm and we're effectively done with this conversation. I know how it works, and I wonder how long I'll let her get away with it.

I start cleaning up and she walks over to crash in the chair while she waits, finally noticing the bag I put there earlier.

"You don't want my ass on your counters but you're putting crap on my chair," she jokes, picking it up to put it on the ground next to her.

"Open it."

She looks in the bag and pulls out the shoe box, then narrows her eyes at me. I watch because I want to see her face when she opens the box. I know it's a stupid present, probably not the thing girls want to get. I'm not really an expert on the whole thing.

And then maybe I am, because her face lights up when she sees them.

"You bought me boots?" she says, like I just gave her diamonds.

"I didn't get to give you anything for your birthday. I hope they fit. I looked at your shoes one day and they said seven, so that's what I got." I shove my hands in my pockets.

She's already taking off her running shoes and trying them on.

"Steel-toed?" she asks.

I nod.

"And black." She smiles and I love that smile more because I think I put it there.

"And black," I confirm.

"You didn't wrap them," she scolds.

"Yeah, I was hoping you wouldn't call me on that."

"I'm kidding," she laughs, and I could listen to it forever. She stands and examines the boots on her feet. "They're perfect."

"Now you can get around the good stuff in Shop."

Her smile fades. "I can't use any of it."

"You can use some of it," I say, because I want the smile back and because it's true. She can do more than she thinks she can. For some reason, she just won't try. "And I can be your other hand when you need it."

She's walking around the garage and flexing her feet to break them in, and I realize that there really is nothing sexier than this girl in black work boots. "You'll have to bring them to school to change into."

"Screw that," she says, and I get the smile back tenfold. "I'm wearing these to school."

"So I did okay?" I ask, just because I want to hear her say it.

"Almost better than the pennies." She pushes herself up on her toes and kisses me, and she's salty and sweaty and awesome.

"You didn't kiss me for the pennies," I say.

"I didn't know I was allowed."

She refuses to go inside once she's got those boots, so we spend another hour in the garage, where she helps me start measuring and marking for a side table she designed for a shop assignment. It's a really cool design with Queen Anne–style legs. I wish she could build the whole thing herself, but the hand does make some of it impossible and she doesn't have the expertise for all of it yet, anyway. I've been at this for ten years and I still have trouble with a lot of things. I do walk her through every step, though. She yells at me if I do something without explaining, because even if she can't do it herself, she wants to at least know how.

I don't get nearly as much done as I used to out here, but I think it might be worth it, because there's something seriously hot about her bossing me around in my garage with a hammer in her hand. I haven't been bossed around in a while, and she's really cute when she's determined and pissed, so I don't mind so much.

I've lived and breathed sawdust for as long as I can remember. I think she does now, too.

Chapter 43

Josh

Expected. That's what we've become, and it's scarier than anything else.

We're in the courtyard at lunch every day. We don't touch each other or laugh, and of course we don't talk, but we're together. No one bothers us. Other than an occasional visit from Clay, the force field stays intact.

I'm trying to finish reading the story Ms. McAllister assigned, because there's a quiz fifth hour today and I haven't gotten through it yet. Sunshine leans over to see what I'm reading and tilts her head enough so that it just barely grazes my shoulder, and even the slightest contact from her makes me feel home. It's instinctual. I turn toward her and kiss her hair before I realize what I've done in a courtyard full of people. For us, it's a version of PDA on par with ripping each other's clothes off and performing a live sex show right here.

I wait for the world to implode, or at least for the looks and comments to start, but there's nothing. No distinguishable change in the atmosphere at all. And I wonder if the impossible has happened. That this, us, she and I, we have become normal. As soon as the word enters my mind, I know it's the

wrong one. We haven't become normal; we've become expected. And not just by everyone at school. I've come to expect
us, too. I expect her. I expect her here. I expect her at home. I
expect her in my life.

And it's terrifying.

Chapter 44

Nastya

"I like to talk, so I'm just going to imagine our conversation here," Clay says while he's drawing me on his back porch after school. I smile and he yells at me to put my face back, which isn't easy, because Clay yelling at me is even funnier.

"Normally you'd hit all the gay questions first because that's what people like to do," he says while he draws, and I don't know how he can concentrate on both things at once. I'm a one-thing-at-a-time type of person, which is why I have so much trouble keeping my mouth shut. Silence takes a serious amount of discipline. Because when you *can* talk but you just *don't,* part of your mind is constantly occupied with concentrating on making sure you don't open your mouth. Some days I wonder if it would be easier if I physically couldn't speak, because then I wouldn't have to think about it all the time.

"First question is always the classic *Did you always know you were gay?* That's a good one," he says, looking at me without really looking. "Answer? I don't know. I don't really think so, because I didn't really know what gay was till I was like ten. So I'm not sure. When I knew, I knew and I didn't really try to figure it out but people always ask that one."

He picks up a gray squishy eraser thing and rubs it against the paper.

"Next one is usually *Have you ever been with a girl, and if you haven't, then how can you be sure you're gay?* Answer? Not telling. None of your business. Next." He puts the eraser down and looks at the picture like he's not happy with something.

"Then there's the one I don't mind answering. *Were your parents pissed?*" The eraser is back again. "Not really. I don't think they were pissed. They didn't tell me if they were. Disappointed? Maybe. But if so, they didn't outright say that either. I got the *It may not be the path we would have chosen for you, but we just want you to be happy* speech. It's a classic. I think it's on a website or something so parents can just print it out and read it, because both of them said the exact same thing, like they coordinated it or something. They haven't been together since I was two, so I had to do the coming out thing twice with them. I think Janice, my dad's wife, was a little freaked out, but I didn't care what she thought so much. And she's been cool since." Damn, this boy can talk. I don't think he took a breath once. I wonder if I should be embarrassed that I wanted to ask him every one of those questions, and if I talked, I probably would have by now.

Clay is looking happier with the picture now. His face is relaxed. When he's frustrated, his face tenses and he twists the bottom of his shirt around. I spend a lot of time staring at him, too. Not much else to do.

"But enough about me. Let's talk about you. What first? I bet your classic is *Why don't you talk?* I'm right, aren't I? But I'm going to skip that one. I think there are far more interesting questions to ask."

He asks his questions. Lots of them. But he doesn't get any answers from me so he comes up with his own. He takes pleasure in telling me how the world is coming to an end because Josh Bennett lets me sit with him at lunch and has been seen not only having unsolicited conversations with people but also, *gasp,* smiling. And that thought makes me smile, which Clay seems to appreciate.

According to Clay, the prevailing explanation for my foray into the Josh Bennett Dead Zone is that I must already be dead. That one amuses me because they think it's funny, but I think it's kind of true. Other people are sure I'm in a cult and I'm brainwashing him. That theory is my favorite. I'll have to let Josh know.

"At least you shouldn't have to worry about that shitdick Ethan after today," Clay continues.

I look at him, confused.

"You didn't hear about that?" His eyes are wide, but I don't know why, because he knows no one really speaks to me. "This afternoon, Ethan was walking down the hall and bragging about you blowing him in the bathroom."

I shrug. This isn't anything new. Ethan spews this crap all the time, especially since he's figured out that I don't dispute it. The only three people at school that I care about know it's not true, and I have a feeling that everyone who knows Ethan knows it's not true also. Clay must see my lack of shock, and it makes him almost giddy at the fact that he gets to tell me the rest of this story.

"Yeah, okay, not a big deal, right? But this time he did it with Josh walking behind him. It was awesome. Michelle and I had a front row seat. Josh nailed Ethan to the wall and Ethan's like, 'You don't scare me, Bennett.' and Josh is like, 'Good. Then you won't run the next time you see me coming, because if you ever say her name again, I'll make it possible for you to suck your own dick.' The best part was that Josh never even raised his voice. Just flat, scary freaking calm. Then he let Ethan go and walked away like nothing happened." He raises his eyebrows at me. "See? Awesome."

I don't really think it's so awesome. I know how much Josh hates to call attention to himself, and I wish he didn't think he had to do it for me.

Clay finishes the drawing, and when he starts cleaning up, I go grab my stuff. At this point, I've paid my debt for his door holding ten times over. I figure he owes me something now. When he's done, I pull the photograph I've been holding for days out of my backpack and hand it to him. Then I grab a sheet of paper and a pen and ask for what I want.

Chapter 45

Nastya

I didn't remember what actually happened to me until over a year after it did. For days, then weeks, then months, I knew what everyone else knew. I knew that I left home to walk to school to record my last audition piece. I had gone home to change and get ready first, before heading back to campus. I agonized over every aspect of my appearance that day, especially my hands. I meticulously painted my nails to perfection. I wore a pale pink blouse with pearl buttons and a white eyelet skirt and everyone knew what I was wearing because they found me in it, even if the buttons were torn off.

I knew exactly where I was found in a heavily wooded section of the preserve that separated the park I cut through that day from the subdivision behind it. I knew that they didn't find me until late that night because a thunderstorm had rolled in, making the search nearly impossible. By that time, the Amber Alert had been running all over the state for hours. My name, my picture, my description. Everywhere. Even after they found me, the morbid curiosity didn't stop. People never can get enough of tragic stories about pretty little girls. I was good entertainment for a while, especially during the *will she or won't she* period, when they didn't know if I'd live.

I knew that when they got me to the hospital I was taken into surgery immediately, and my heart stopped on the table for ninety-six seconds before they were able to restart it.

I knew that I woke up with a hand that wasn't even a hand anymore and that I would never play the piano again because a few days later, they told me so. And then, when they thought I had gotten strong enough, they told me I would never be able to have children. I guess they thought losing the ability to create a child would be harder for me to handle than losing the ability to create music, but I'm not so sure they were right.

I knew what had happened to me by piecing together an extensive list of injuries. For months, that's what I felt like. A list of injuries. A sum total of hurts. My entire body was made of pain.

One day I overheard one of my many doctors talking to a police detective when he didn't know I could hear. *Have you caught that monster yet?* he asked. The detective told him that they hadn't. *You should string him up when you get him. He ruined that poor girl.* I guessed he was right, because that was exactly how I felt, and when you hear your doctor saying that you're ruined, you figure he knows what he's talking about.

—

"Did you always sleep with a shirt on? Before me?" I ask Josh when we get into bed. Asher hates sleeping in a shirt. He insists that all guys hate sleeping in clothes, but I don't know if it's true. Josh always sleeps in a T-shirt and boxer shorts, which is usually what I'm sleeping in, too. Josh won't let me fold his underwear, but apparently he doesn't have a problem with my wearing them.

"Before you, I didn't sleep with anything on," he says, and I can hear the smile in his voice, even if I can't see it.

"Oh." I feel my face get hot. "I'm sorry."

"Don't be," he laughs. "It's a good trade-off."

His hand finds its way up to my cheek. He leans down and kisses me, and his lips are an invitation I'm going to have to accept sooner or later. "If I didn't know you better, I'd think you were blushing."

But the fact is that he doesn't know me better. He doesn't really know me at all.

—

For the first time in weeks, we're not spending half the night in the garage. It's still early, but I tell him I'm tired and I want to go to bed. I'm not tired. I'm just hoping he'll follow me. After about fifteen minutes, I hear him come out of the shower and then he turns off the light and climbs in next to me. He kisses the side of my head and says good night and then laces his fingers through my mine like he always does; like he's reminding me that he's still here, or maybe vice versa.

I slide my hand under the fabric of his T-shirt, up his stomach until it's flat against the skin on his chest and I can feel his heart beating against my palm. I can just hear his breath hitch because he didn't see it coming. He's warm and solid and I want to touch every part of him. I should stop this, because I know where it's going. But I'm the one who started it, and really, I just don't want to.

"Sunshine." It's all he says.

He rests his hand on top of mine through the fabric of his shirt. "You can take it off if you want to," I tell him.

"I'd rather take off yours," he jokes.

"That too," I say, but I'm not joking. I feel him tense just slightly under my hand, but he doesn't move to do anything, and we lay there for a minute, just breathing and trying to read each other's thoughts.

"You have my permission," I whisper.

It isn't like I've never touched him and he's never touched me. Just never everywhere at once. I'm in one of his T-shirts, like always, and he pulls it up over my head and I let him because that's what I want. I want him to touch me. Here. Now. Everywhere. Always.

"I wish I could see you," he says.

"I'm glad you can't," I admit. Too many scars. I can blame them even if they aren't the real reason.

I'm more at peace with Josh than anywhere else in the world, and I want to run away before I ruin us both. But then his shirt is off, too, and his body is pressed against mine so that there's no space between us. He pushes my hair away, muttering something about "stupid hair always in your face," but he keeps his hand tangled in it, and then he kisses me, and that's what we do for a long time.

Somehow he leaves my body just enough to reach his nightstand to get a condom, which I think about telling him he doesn't need. Then he's leaning over me and kissing me again and I let myself focus on just that. Because it's real. It's true. One, real, amazing, true thing. And then his knee slips between mine, gently pushing them apart, and a moment later I can feel the pressure of him. I know the exact moment when he realizes— realizes one of the countless things I never told him. Because he stops right there. Suddenly eerily still. He's not kissing me anymore. He's staring at me, and his eyes are so close to mine that I think he can read my mind.

I know he's going to say something, but I don't want him to, because it will make me tell him things. He'll make me feel safe and safe is something I should never feel again.

There are a thousand words in his eyes, but all he says is, "Sunshine?" It's not my name. It's a question. Or maybe it's more than one, but I don't let him say anything else.

I reach around him, though I'm not sure this will even work, and I tilt my hips up and shove him toward me. And, for just a second, there's tearing and burning, and then it's done. I squeeze my eyes shut because pain is familiar and grounding and I'd rather give myself to that. I'm used to pain, and this really isn't so bad. It's the look on his face that I'm not used to—awe, confusion, wonder, and—please, please, please—don't let it be love.

"Are you okay?" He's inside me but he still doesn't move. His hands are on either side of my face, and he looks like he's scared of me.

"Yes," I whisper, but I don't know if it comes out. I don't know if I'm okay. It shouldn't be possible to be this close to another person. To let them crawl inside you.

Chapter 46

Josh

When it's over, we're both shaking, and for a moment I'm confused and comforted and loved and then I'm lost. I don't know what happened. Just that it did. And she's here, but she's not. And I want to be happy, but I can't, because she's crying underneath me. At first, it's just soft and barely there, and I hardly recognize what's happening because I've never seen her cry. Then her body starts racking with it, and it's so jagged and wrong. There's still barely any sound coming out, but it's the shaking that's almost worse, and it steals every undeserved ounce of joy I felt just the moment before.

I need to get away from here. I wish she would stop crying, because I don't think I can take it for one more second, and it's not like it's loud or melodramatic. It's not. It's just heartbreaking.

I don't know what I did, so I just hold her and whisper *I'm sorry*, because I don't know what else to do. *I'm sorry*. Again and again and again against her hair. I don't know how many times I say it or for how long, just that I can't stop. But she doesn't stop crying and I know that it's not enough.

—

She's gone in the morning, and I don't know if she's gone from the bed or the house or from everything.

She isn't at school. I called her phone three times, even though I'm not supposed to, but she didn't answer. I didn't expect her to. I wanted to text her but I couldn't think of any words that wouldn't sound desperate.

When I get home, she's waiting in my garage. She's on the counter where she used to sit and her chair is empty on the other side. I hit the button and the automatic door lowers, bringing all the dread of this moment down with it. I walk into the house, because I don't want to do this in my garage.

She's Nastya today. The hair, makeup, clothes, everything black like it is for school, except today it's for me. I shake my head. Nothing about her is real. I've had her sitting in front of me for months and I didn't see her. I didn't hear her. I didn't know her any better than everyone else. I feel like I've failed somehow. Failed me, failed her, failed us.

I don't say anything and she doesn't say anything. I start wondering if we may never speak again and then my mouth opens.

"Did I lose you?" It's not what I expected to ask, but I want the answer. Her face doesn't change, and I realize that I had forgotten what that blank expression even looked like on her.

"I lost you."

"Impossible," I say, but the word barely comes out.

"You don't want me." Her tone is flat and she has this weird calm about her that makes me want to scream.

I want to tell her that I don't remember what it's like not to want her, that maybe there isn't anything else I do want. I want to ask her who the hell she is to tell me what I do and don't want. But nothing will come out of my mouth, and maybe she thinks that means I'm agreeing with her.

"So this is over?" I ask.

"What's left?" This is where she finally looks in my eyes, and I know it's because she means it.

"You didn't tell me," I say, because I'm not ready to say there's nothing left.

"Tell you what?" She's playing dumb, and it insults us both.

"You know what."

"You didn't ask."

"*Ask?*" I think my voice goes up an octave because I can't believe this, and I feel a decade's worth of resolve shatter. "I didn't ask? Is that what you want? You want me to start asking questions? Now? I'm allowed? Because I don't think you want that, but hey, let's go for it. What the fuck happened to your hand?"

She flinches. Maybe because of the question. Maybe because I'm yelling now.

"No? Not that one? No good? Then how about what the hell happened last night?" Because I want this answer more than I ever wanted the other one.

She doesn't respond, which isn't even the slightest bit shocking, but I don't need her to, because I'm on a tear and I have no intention of stopping.

"Tell me! You're the one who came over here and insinuated yourself into every part of my life, and then you wait until I have every last thread of my existence wrapped around you and then you leave. Why? What is that about? Was it a joke? Were you bored? Thought it would be fun to fuck with me?"

"I'm ruined."

"What?" I don't even know what that means. "Because you were a virgin?" It sounds stupid, and I realize how much I hate that word. Maybe I'm stupid. Actually, I am stupid for ever assuming I knew anything about this girl. But she walks around with this gutter mouth spewing innuendos like she's talking about baking cookies and then I'm the prick for not realizing she's never done it before. Somehow, I'm to blame for everything here, and I don't even know what I did.

"Why then? Why did you sleep with me?" I hate the desperation in my voice.

"Because I knew you wanted to." Straight. Cold. Matter-of-fact. Empty. She knows it's a lie.

"Bullshit, Sunshine." There's no controlling my voice now. I am beyond pissed. "You lost your virginity because I wanted you to? Don't you *dare* put this on me. I *never* would have done that to you."

"You didn't do anything to me. I did it to you. I used you." The dead calm in her voice is infuriating.

"For what?" I'm shaking now because I'm so angry.

"It was the last thing about me that wasn't ruined. I just wanted to finish it." She's drawing circles on the floor with her toes.

"What the fuck does that even mean?"

Nothing. That's what I'm getting. That's what I'm worth to her.

"You're telling me that you used me to ruin you?" I'm forcing calm into my voice but I don't even know where I'm getting it from. Maybe the ice coming off her is starting to reach me. "That makes a lot of fucking sense." I laugh, and it's bitter. I walk across the room and my fist is through my bedroom door. The wood splinters into my hand. I see her cringe for a second before she remembers herself. Then the nothing expression returns and all that's left is Nastya.

"So what, then? Did I? Did I ruin you?"

She nods. And I laugh again because it's the only sound that will come out.

"Fucking amazing." I can't stop the laughing and I think I might be crazy. I throw my hands up because I'm done. "Congratulations, then. You wanted to be ruined? Well, you did your-self one better because you wrecked me, too, Sunshine. Now we're both worth shit."

She doesn't move. Just stares at the ground. Her hands are fists like mine.

I sit down because I think my knees are shaking now, too. I bend over and press my palms against my eyes. I can't see her, but I know she's still there.

"Get the fuck out of my house."

"I told you not to love me," she whispers, almost like she's saying it to herself.

"Believe me, Nastya. I don't."

She walks out and shuts the door silently behind her.

It's the first time I've ever said her name.

Nastya

Nastya. The word sounds like broken glass coming out of his mouth. Sleeping with Josh isn't what ruins me. This is what ruins me. His voice. His face. His horror at this whole fucked-up situation. He looked at me like he couldn't believe I was doing this, and I can't blame him because I couldn't believe it either. But I did it anyway, because that's what I do.

Chapter 47

Nastya

Everything is hell now and I deserve it, but I can handle pain if it's pain of my own choosing.

—

Drew tiptoes around me now and I avoid him. I won't put him in the middle of this. He belongs to Josh. I spend most of my time with Clay. Or alone. Being alone would be easier if I liked myself. But right now I don't. Not even a little.

Fourth and fifth periods are the worst, because that's when I have to see him, and I can't pretend that he never existed, like I try to every other moment of the day. As if that might help. As if anything might help. I could pretend that I don't watch him, that I have enough resolve and self-respect not to let him catch me staring, but I don't have the discipline. Every day I say I won't look, but I do. The only good thing about it is that he never catches me looking. Because he's never looking at me. And he shouldn't. I don't deserve him.

The world should be full of Josh Bennetts. But it's not. I had the only one.

And I threw him away.

—

One day Margot sits down at the kitchen table with me while I pretend to concentrate on reading a poem I haven't comprehended a word of. My homework is getting done more these days. I can't even tell you how many miles I run.

"It hasn't escaped me that apparently you live here again," she says.

I keep staring at the poem like the words will suddenly swim up from the paper and make their way into my brain.

"I'd ask you if you wanted to talk about it." She just barely smiles and she's trying, but it's pointless. Because everything is pointless right now. I'm pointless.

I even start going home on the weekends so no one will expect me at Sunday dinner. And maybe that's the only thing I do that's worth a damn.

No one asks me why I keep coming back all of a sudden. They just let me come.

I get another birthday present one weekend when I get home. Since I didn't take the phone, my mother gives me a camera. It's simpler, not as crazy as hers, but I don't think it's the camera she's giving me, anyway. She's giving me part of her. Trying to replace part of me. I don't know if it's a good idea or a bad idea, but I'm starting to get tired of judging and second-guessing everyone's motives, because I'm starting to grasp the real problem, and I know that it's me. I don't have Josh anymore. I've kind of lost Drew. I need my mother. I want the warmth of that unconditional love so much that I'm willing to ignore the price, and for the first time in almost three years maybe I can admit that, even if it's only in my head.

We don't talk yet, but maybe.

My mother shows me how to use the camera, and we wander around taking pictures of nothing and everything. She doesn't even drill me about format and composition. Sometimes my hand will stutter and ruin one, but we ignore it.

On Sundays, I work on teaching my dad how to make pancakes from scratch instead of a mix, because it's really just baking in a pan and it's something I can do.

Nothing is perfect. It's not even good yet, but maybe.

—

I miss him today. I miss him every day. I went to Home Depot tonight just to walk through the lumber aisles and try to breathe.

I'm back to hiding in the bathrooms at lunch. Clay props the door open for me again, but we pretend it doesn't mean anything.

My hands are turning soft again.

Josh will be eighteen next week.

Josh

"Who's it from?" I ask when Mrs. Leighton hands me the last present on the table. We've eaten dinner and done the whole cake thing. I skipped the wishing. Nothing in me wants to be here.

"It was on the porch this afternoon. It had a piece of paper taped on it, but all it said was your name. No card."

I rip open the paper, and now I want to disappear so I can be alone in this moment. I want to be allowed to see this without anyone seeing me.

I'm holding a simple black gallery frame in my hands. It's nothing special. The picture in the frame is what throws me, knocks me on the ground, and kicks me around a little bit.

When I pull off the rest of the wrapping paper, a photograph that had been stuck in the front of the frame falls to the floor. Drew picks it up and looks at it before handing it to me, and I can tell he wants to keep holding it.

I recognize the picture. It was in a photo album on the bookshelf in my living room. It's my mother with Amanda on her lap and they aren't looking at the camera. They're smiling at each other, but you can still see their faces. They're both beautiful, and I realize that I forgot that they were, like everything else I've lost to forgetting, because there's nobody left to remind me.

There are photographs all over my house. Everywhere. I didn't put all the people I loved away. They all still hang on the walls, mostly because they always have. I didn't put them there, but I didn't take them down, either. I left them where they were like nothing happened. But not this picture. This one has been tucked away in an album for years. I love this picture. I forgot that I did. And I can see this one. Not like the ones on the walls that I've walked by every day, so many times that they stopped registering a long time ago.

The picture in the frame is a perfectly rendered charcoal drawing, just like the photograph, only bigger. Even though it's black and white, I watch my mother's eyes crinkle with her smile and I see my sister breathe, and for a moment I think they're alive. It's Clay's work. There isn't a question. And there's only one person who could have given him that photograph. But she isn't here, either, because she left me, too.

She has no right to do this. To make it harder for me to hate her, because right now I need to hate her.

"I forgot how hot your mom was," Drew says, because he detests uncomfortable situations and his way of dissolving the tension is to remind us that he's an ass. And I love him for it.

Mrs. Leighton smacks Drew's arm. His father comes around

and smacks his head and then pulls Mrs. Leighton to him and kisses her hair.

And I go home alone.

—

It's been five weeks since she walked out of my house. I started counting the second the door closed. I wonder when I'll stop.

—

"So who's Corinthos having killed now?" Drew walks in after school and crashes on the other end of the couch. I switch the TV off because I'm not watching it anyway and I really just don't care.

"So," he asks, after waiting through the requisite fifteen seconds of silence, which is the maximum Drew can stand, "are you ever going to tell me what happened between you two?"

"No," I say, because it's true. Because it's the last thing I want to talk about. Because I might actually cry if I do, and honestly, because I really don't know what the hell happened. "I'm probably not."

Drew nods and doesn't argue. I know she's been avoiding him, too, even in Debate. "I miss having her around."

"Get used to it," I say, and I turn the TV back on.

Chapter 48

Nastya

I turn away from the mirror to catch Drew walking into the girls' bathroom in the back corner of the drama department. The drama teachers have planning this period and I've learned that this bathroom is almost always empty. So it's my favorite.

"I assume we're alone," he says, turning and locking the door. "You know this is like the fourth bathroom I've looked for you in. I was starting to fear for my safety."

"Seriously, Drew?" I whisper, and it's barely audible because I don't care if he locked the door and no one's around.

"I miss you," he says, like this is a valid excuse.

"You'll live."

"You miss me, too. Admit it, Nastypants."

He's right. I miss the crap out of him.

"What is that, anyway? Nastypants? You make me sound like I shit myself."

He looks down at my jeans as if he's considering this.

"I'm here to drag you out of your social abyss."

"You're here to ask me for a favor, so get on with it, because I don't like talking here."

"I need your bodyguard services this Friday."

"No, no, and no again. And wait. Hold on a second. No."

"What if I say please?"

"What if I say no?" He's trying to give me the look, but he and I are so far past the look that it's ridiculous. "You don't need me to get you through one night. Just tell everyone you're meeting me after. They'll buy it."

"No one will buy that after you and Josh. No one's going to believe I'd do that."

"There's nothing you wouldn't do."

"That's the *only* thing I wouldn't do, and everybody knows it. The only person in the world I wouldn't screw over is Josh."

"We're not talking about it, so stop bringing up his name and trying to insinuate him into this conversation."

"He is in this conversation whether I say his name or not."

He holds his hands up in surrender at the glare I shoot him. I will not talk about Josh.

"Fine. All I have to say is that I thought I had self-destructive tendencies, but you two make me look well-adjusted."

"Is he all right?"

"Actually I'm pretty sure he's the opposite of *all right*, but I'm also pretty sure that you knew that when you asked."

"What did he tell you?"

"Nope. Not playing this game. You're the one who made the rules. Not going to talk about Josh." He makes himself comfortable on the bathroom counter like we're in his kitchen at home. "Now, subject at hand. They don't need to think that I'm with you. I just need you to come and keep me in line. If you don't, I'll end up walking through the house, asking every single person if they've seen her. And then I'll probably say shitty things about her just to have an excuse to say her name or get her attention." He doesn't say her name now, but it's no secret who he's talking about. "You have to save me from myself. And save yourself from utter boredom and solitude in the process. Win-win."

There isn't any win for me in this situation. I'd rather staple my lips to my tongue than go to a party tonight. I climb up next to him on the counter and let out all the air in my lungs and he does the same.

"I should just go back to the way I was before," he says. "I used to be so awesome and she made me suck."

"If that's what you want, do it. Start tonight. You won't have any problem finding some girl willing to accompany you on the road back to soulless debauchery."

He doesn't respond, because he and I both know what he lost on that path already, and he hasn't forgiven himself for it. I don't know if there's another solution, but I try to offer him one.

"Isn't there another girl you can ask out? For real? Try to have a normal relationship? You messed everything up with Tierney, but you could actually try to learn from that and do it right this time." It's an asinine suggestion. If he told me to learn from my mistakes with Josh and put that knowledge to use with someone else, I'd dislocate his jaw. But it's all I've got to go with right now. "What about Tessa Walter?" I suggest.

He shakes his head. "Crazy eyes."

"Macy Singleton?"

"Laughs too loud."

"Audrey Lake?"

This time he glares at me like I've just suggested he date the Antichrist.

"She says *supposably*." If Drew Leighton were a woman, this would be his unforgivable thing.

"So why don't you just try again with Tierney?" She's the only one he really wants. I could name every girl in this school and he would find the flaw in every last one of them.

"I can't ask her to forgive me. I wouldn't respect her if she did. I don't deserve it."

I don't deserve it either. I'm not enough of a hypocrite to argue.

"Can't we just skip it? You don't have to go. You never even drink at these parties. Why would you want to hang out with a bunch of drunk assholes for no reason?" It's true. It took me a while to pick up on it, but once I did I never stopped noticing. Drew gets a drink as soon as he walks in and he carries it around the whole night, so everyone assumes he's drinking, but he never is.

"You noticed that, huh?" He's almost impressed. "You're the first one."

"I'm guessing there's a reason." I'm expecting him to say something about having to drive, but that's not what I get.

"Kara Matthews," he answers, like this explains everything, but he knows it doesn't, and I wait for him to give me the rest. "I don't even remember doing it. Tierney ripped me to shreds for hours that day, and she was right. She was right about every-thing she said about me, except the fact that I didn't care about her. But everything else she nailed me on. I got so lit that night that I would have screwed anyone at that party. I shit all over Tierney and everything and I don't even remember doing it."

"And you think if you weren't so drunk you wouldn't have done it?"

"No," he replies honestly. "I probably would have. But at least I'd know. If I was going to mess everything up, at least it would have been a conscious choice."

It makes perfect sense to me. He may not revel in the pain he caused himself, but at least he could say that he chose it. That's not the only thing that haunts him, though. There's a question there, too. The slim, slight possibility that, just maybe, he wouldn't have done it. Maybe if he hadn't been so wasted things might have turned out differently, and he would be with Tierney right now, not in a girls' bathroom being haunted by dead possibilities.

He shrugs in resignation. "I figure the next time I want to

completely destroy all chance of happiness, at least I'll remember doing it."

It'll make the self-loathing that much easier.

—

I could say that I have no idea why I agreed to this, but it would be a lie. I miss Drew, too. And I'm sick of myself. I'd rather drink flat beer and hang out with people who don't like me. No one at that party will hate me as much as I hate myself, so it'll be an improvement.

It's crowded already when we get to Kevin Leonard's house. The music is blaring, and I wonder how long this can possibly last before the neighbors call the police. I hope they do so I can leave, because I already regret it. I don't mind all the people. I actually do better with crowds and numbers, but the noise makes me edgy. I need the quiet to hear what's coming.

I follow Drew through the house, my fingers threaded through his belt loops so I don't lose him. He wants me on him tonight, I'm on him.

Damien Brooks finds us first and I can't stand him, but he's at least familiar.

"Drew!" He's already drunk. One word and it's evident. "Damn. I know you had her first, but I didn't think you'd go back there after Bennett. Man, you've got balls." He's laughing and congratulatory. Drew's laughing, too. I'm not even in the room. Oh, wait. I am, but you wouldn't know it the way they're talking. Good thing I don't give a shit.

Then Damien's eyes go wide like he's just discovered the atom or the concept of self-pleasure. "Have you guys been sharing her this whole time?"

Maybe I do give a shit. At least a little. Because I'm not listening to this anymore. I grab Drew's hand and start to pull away. I think he's had enough, too, because he doesn't fight me.

And then there's Tierney. The sniper I'm being used as a human shield against. I actually really like her, and I wish I wasn't the person being tasked with keeping Drew away from her. I don't blame her for wanting to hate Drew, but it doesn't mean she does. All of a sudden I wish they could just get their shit together, but my hypocrisy slaps me in the face before I can think any more on the subject.

We make it to the kitchen at the back of the house, where Kevin Leonard is manning a keg with a crowd surrounding it. They start chanting Drew's name like he's their god, and I guess if I were a teenage boy with no game, he'd be mine, too. It takes no time before we have cups full of warm beer and are fighting our way back out of the kitchen.

An hour and four and a half crap beers later, I'm leaning against a wall while Drew talks to a girl in a very tiny, very sparkly top, who has no problem shamelessly flirting with him in front of me. True to form, Drew is still carrying around the same half-full cup of beer he's had since we walked in. I'm not completely trashed, but I'm tired and I want to go home. I'm tipsy enough that my brain isn't bombarding me with a diatribe on how idiotic I am. Instead it's whispering that calling Josh wouldn't be so bad. Drunk dialing the perfect, incredible, wonderful boy I pissed all over might even be enough to win me a gold medal in selfishness. I don't get to fully explore that thought, though, because I'm back on duty.

Tierney starts walking in our direction and sparkly tank top girl walks away. Tierney's like that. No one really fucks with her, and I want to hug her and tell her I think she's sooooo awesome, so maybe I'm a little drunker than I thought. I didn't eat today, which might account for that. Rookie mistake.

I step over to put my half-full beer on a really ugly end table (I notice these things now); I don't need to drink any more.

Once I can pull Drew away from Tierney, I will have fulfilled my responsibilities and I can get him to take me home.

When I turn around, Drew isn't there. And neither is Tierney.

I start pushing my way through the throng of people, looking for either of them. I figure one will lead to the other, but it's not like I can walk around yelling their names and asking if anyone has seen them. I'm staying against the wall, out of the center of the chaos, when Kevin Leonard finds me.

"Enjoying the party?"

Huh? Is he expecting an answer? I give him a stupid thumbs-up and try to keep walking. Drew Leighton so owes me something for this. I start mentally making a list of what I want. There's only one thing on it so far, but I think it's out of his control.

"Wanna have sex with me?" Kevin asks. This was not the one thing on my list. I try to walk around him and his monstrous ego. He's obviously plastered and I'm getting more sober by the minute. I really want to go home and I want to kick Drew's ass. I'm not sure which of those things I want more right now and Kevin Leonard is still talking.

"We can go to my room. I blocked off the upstairs. No one will know."

I'll know, jackass. And I'll spend the rest of my days trying to block it from my memory.

"Come on, baby." Guess that's my answer. Real boys do call girls *baby*. Too bad I don't feel like laughing and I don't have time to choke him. "Please."

Does he think I'm looking for manners now? *Well, since you said please, I may have to reconsider my previous hell no stance on screwing you. I was just waiting for the good breeding to kick in.* I shake my head as definitively as I can and keep moving. Mercifully, he gives up and doesn't follow me.

He did give me an idea, though, because if I can't find Drew in the next ten minutes, I'm not waiting around to be propositioned again. I'll find another way home.

The next ten minutes are as fruitless as the last. I even give it another ten, just for shits and giggles, before I finally concede defeat. I walk the downstairs, and at least a few people have started to filter out, so it's not as jam-packed, but the music is still tattooing itself on my eardrums and splitting my brain. I shoot off a text to Drew asking where he is but I don't get any response. I send him another one telling him I'm sneaking upstairs to try to find a ride. I still don't get an answer.

I hang around the bottom of the stairs for a few minutes, and when Kara Matthews starts doing a beer bong in the kitchen, I use the distraction to duck under Kevin's makeshift barricade and sneak upstairs so I can use my phone.

I may be a little shitty right now, but even with a few beers in me, I never forget to watch my back. No one follows me, and I turn down the hall to the left and slip into one of the bedrooms. I stay against the wall until I can feel the light switch. The room is empty. The music is still blaring and I can just make out the muted chanting of Kara's name. I take out my phone, knowing there are only two people I can really call. Josh is the one I want to call, but I don't know if that's allowed anymore. There's Clay, who I'd have to text, but I could have done that from downstairs. I came up here for one reason and it's because I wanted to call Josh.

I dial and wait, but there isn't any answer. It doesn't go straight to voicemail. It just rings. When the recording finally kicks in, I hang up. It's too pathetic to think about leaving him a message. I flip the keyboard open to shoot Clay a text and see if he can pick me up, but before I can get the first word out, the door opens.

And Kevin Leonard is there.

"I thought you'd change your mind," he slurs, and I wonder how much he struggled to get it out. I'm about to shake my head again, but he's right in front of me now. And I'm not running away or saying no or pushing him. Because, really, I just don't care. If I want to ruin myself, then this is my chance. Josh is gone, like everything that was taken from me and everything I've thrown away since. There is no Josh Bennett for me anymore. There really isn't anything.

That's the only moment I have to think before his tongue is in my mouth and he tastes like piss beer and I probably do, too, and everything about this is disgusting, but I deserve it. He's grabbing my chest through my dress with one hand and running the other up my thigh. My arms are limp at my sides, and I close my eyes and just let him do it. He starts pulling my underwear down and then stops to get rid of my dress. He pulls it part of the way up, and I can feel the cold air on my inner thighs and against my stomach, reminding me that I should be used and thrown away, too.

Then his hand is between my legs, and I gag into his mouth when I feel his fingers. And maybe I've finally had enough and I won't choose this pain.

I break away from his mouth and his hand and pull my dress down. If there is such a thing as rock bottom, it's where I am right now. I can lie to myself. I can lie to Josh. But it's just that. A lie. I didn't destroy any part of me when I slept with him, even if I did destroy everything after. I knew that it wasn't true when I said it and I know it now. I don't regret one minute I ever spent with Josh. What I regret is every single second after. I regret ripping his heart out. I regret sending us both straight to hell.

If I let Kevin Leonard do this, if I let myself do this, then this here, now, will be what destroys the last good thing about me. This will be my unforgivable thing. I will never come back from it because there will be absolutely nothing left in me worth loving. And for once in my stupid, pissed-on life, I can't do it. Or, more importantly, maybe I won't.

I push my hand against his chest. Not violently. Just decisively. I shake my head at him. *No.* I try to look apologetic. I feel guilty. Am I supposed to feel bad in this situation? I don't really know the rules. I yank my dress down as far as it will go, but it doesn't feel like enough.

"What the fuck, Nastya?"

I shake my head again. I mouth the words *I can't* because I need to make sure he understands. He understands, but he doesn't care.

"You're really going to blue-ball me up here at my own fucking party?" I don't even have a chance to bend over and pull my underwear back up before he grabs me and kisses me again, and I don't need an invitation. I stomp on his foot and grab for the door, but my hands are shaking and it's locked and I can't make my fingers work fast enough. I get the lock flipped, but I don't have enough time to turn the doorknob. I should have gone at him harder, but I didn't think I needed to. I just wanted to let him know it wasn't happening and give myself enough of a window to make it to the door and get out. But it's not enough. His hand wraps around my arm, turning me to face him, and I grab his pinky finger and bend it back. I'm not in a position to take him down, and I just want to get away. That's all. I hear his finger crack, and his other hand immediately swings up and punches me. It's such a knee-jerk reaction, I'm not sure he even realizes what he's done. I catch the full force of his fist against my cheek and my balance is off, so the impact spins me face-first into the corner of the nightstand next to the bed. I can feel the blood running down from the corner of my eye, and I swipe it away. From this position, I flip over and try to buy myself a second by kicking him, but he grabs my ankle and drags me away from the door.

My underwear has worked its way down to my knees, the

panic is starting to push bile into my throat, and I feel myself stop breathing.

I'm panicking like this is a nightmare. He's laughing like it's a game.

"Come on. You came up here and made me think you were going to screw me. You could at least suck my dick." He doesn't even sound angry. It's like he's trying to convince me.

If I had any bad feelings about fighting dirty, they're gone now. The shit part is that I've never been as good at defending myself from the ground, and nothing is as easy as it was when I was practicing in a controlled situation. Nothing. Plus, the beer isn't helping, no matter how sober I suddenly feel.

I don't have the kubotan. It's in my purse under the seat in Drew's car, right next to my can of pepper spray, because I didn't have anywhere to clip it on my dress. I figured I was going to be stapled to Drew's side the entire night, anyway, so I didn't think I'd need it. Maybe the operative words there are *didn't think*.

The fact is that I don't want to use either of those things on Kevin Leonard. I just want to get out of this. I feel like I've set off a string of explosions and now I'm trying to outrun them.

It doesn't surprise me that putting myself in this stupid-ass situation is what it takes for me to finally decide not to completely incinerate what's left of my life. I'm such a fucking idiot. Maybe karma is just trying to give me what I said I wanted, but never really did. To wreck myself once and for all.

I can feel my cheek burning where he hit me, and the blood from the gash is running into my eye and I'm trying to focus, because I'm afraid at any moment I'm going to leave this room and be back in the trees, with dirt and blood in my mouth. And then I'll lose all control. I'll stop fighting completely. Kevin Leonard will be able to do whatever he wants, and I'll let him because I won't even be here anymore.

The focusing is almost impossible when my brain is split

between staying awake in this room and trying to fight him off. He's over me, pinning my arms and legs to the floor and pushing his mouth on me again. He has every one of my limbs immobilized. I can't even shift. I lean into him to give myself just enough leeway to tilt my head back and head-butt him because that's the only option I really have. I'm aiming for the bridge of his nose, but my position is off and my forehead cracks against his instead. It's a mistake, but he's so drunk that it's enough.

My head is screaming at me from the impact as his sweaty body falls on top of mine, crushing me with the weight of every bad decision I've made over the past three years.

"Dude! Forget it." There's saliva running down the side of his mouth.

The fight has gone out of him and I think it finally hits him, in his drunken stupor, what's going on, because he looks at me like he's just now seeing me bleeding from the head on the floor in this room with him. He leans back, and I haven't even had a moment to turn my body and free myself when the door abruptly opens and I'm looking up from the floor, underneath Kevin Leonard's body, at Drew Leighton's face.

"What the fuck, Leighton?" Kevin spits out. There's more embarrassment than venom in it, but I'm not excusing him any more than I'm excusing myself. He's still struggling to push himself off me, and I use the distraction to twist my hip and get the rest of the way free.

For a minute, or maybe just a second, Drew is frozen. There are so many emotions on his face that I can't sort them all now. Confusion, disgust, anger, guilt, fear, horror. I wonder how bad my face is to make his look like that.

Kevin is barely standing now, and I'm dizzily getting to my feet, my head still reeling from smashing into his. Before I even register what's happening, Drew's fist is in Kevin's face and he's down again. I look at Drew and he's shaking. There is something so wrong with the sight of Drew Leighton hitting someone. Drew Leighton is supposed to be sunny and irreverent and free of every care in the world. There isn't even a glimmer of violence in him. I wish he hadn't done it. I wish he hadn't seen this, because as crazy as I know it sounds, I feel like he's just lost his innocence.

Drew is standing in front of me, knuckles bleeding, with a look of such sheer despondence that I feel like I should comfort him. But I can't. Now that this is over, my adrenaline is starting to drop and I want to get away from here, because I smell like Kevin Leonard, and I'm starting to shake, too.

I lean against the wall to steady myself while Drew picks my phone up from the floor, shoving it in his pocket before looking back at me. He curses under his breath, pulling his sleeve over his wrist and trying to wipe the blood away from my eye. "Can you walk?" he whispers.

My expression tells him I can and that I don't appreciate the question. I don't say anything. We turn toward the door, and I realize that my underwear is still at my ankles. I just stand there, looking down at them. Drew turns to find out why I've stopped, his eyes following mine to my feet, and all of his muscles tense when he sees why I'm not coming. He stifles another curse as I bend over to pull them up because I can't look at his face right now.

"Stay behind me, okay?" His words are strained, and he sounds like he's in pain. He takes my hand so tightly, I think he might crush it and pulls me behind him so I'm blocked from view. I catch Tierney Lowell watching in the hall before I turn away. I drag my hair down around my face and lean into Drew's back like I'm wasted, just until we can get through everybody and out the door. And maybe wasted is exactly what I am.

My face is bleeding and swollen, but I don't even care. For the first time in forever, I make a choice not to shit all over my life and I can't even like myself for it because I made it five minutes too late.

At least no one can tell me it was random.

—

"Are you okay?" Drew waits until we've gotten in his car and driven away from the house to ask. I've hated that question for years.

"I'm fine," I say. "Your hand." My eyes go to his split knuckles, which are straining even more with his iron grip on the steering wheel.

"I don't give a shit about my hand," he bites out at me, and I instinctively recoil because I've never heard him raise his voice. "Sorry. I'm sorry." He pulls into the parking lot of a convenience store and parks the car. This whole situation is fucked up, and he says so at least three or four times.

"What happened?" He sounds like he doesn't really want the answer.

"Just a stupid situation that got out of hand."

"You think?" His tone is sharp.

"Are you pissed at me?" I ask.

"No, I'm pissed at me."

"Why?"

"Because it's my fault you were in that room in the first place. I finally bothered to look at my phone and got your text. I thought I'd find you sitting up there and waiting, not on the floor with Kevin Leonard on top of you." He takes a breath and lets it out, watching the lighted *R* on the store sign flicker in and out. "Josh is going to kill me."

"Josh isn't going to care."

"You know that isn't true, so don't say it. I don't have it in me to argue with you about it tonight." There is so much weight in his voice that I feel it physically pressing on me.

"If you knew what I did to Josh, you would hate me, too. He won't care, and I won't blame him for not caring."

"You're right. I don't know what you did to Josh. I have no idea what went on there because neither of you will tell me. I do know that whatever it was will not be enough to stop him from giving a shit about someone hurting you."

I flip down the visor and check the bruise on my face and the cut on my eye in the mirror. It's really not so bad, but my cheek and my forehead are already starting to swell, and I know it'll all look worse tomorrow.

"His pants were still on." He's tracing the logo on the steering wheel now.

I nod, even though he's not looking at me.

"So, he didn't—"

"No," I answer. I don't want to talk about Kevin Leonard anymore. "Did anybody else see?" I ask.

"I don't think so. Tierney did, but she was looking for us so—" He cuts himself off. "I don't think anyone else was paying attention."

We sit there, pretending to be mesmerized by the flashing lottery sign.

"I shouldn't have left you."

"You and Tierney?" I ask, ignoring the unspoken apology.

"I don't know." He shakes his head and turns the key in the ignition. "We need to get ice on your face."

Drew doesn't tell me where we're going. He doesn't ask where I want to go. He takes me where I need to go and maybe where he needs to go, too. He takes me to Josh's house.

The garage is closed when we get there, but Drew and I both have a key to the house. He turns his in the lock and pushes the door back for me. I walk inside and Drew follows. When we step into the dark of the foyer, it takes us a minute to process what we're hearing.

And then I wish on a thousand pennies that we didn't have that key.

Chapter 49

Josh

"What the hell, Drew? It's two in the morning." I look at his car in the driveway and it's empty. At first, I suspected he was bringing Sunshine back here because she was drunk, but there's no one in the car. "You already drop Nastya off?" I ask while he follows me into the family room. Calling her Nastya sounds wrong, but I don't feel right saying Sunshine out loud anymore.

"She's at home."

"So what's going on? Weren't you supposed to be home an hour ago?" I still don't get why he's here.

"Sarah's covering for me." Drew looks away like he doesn't want to tell me something, and it pisses me off because I'm sure it has something to do with Nastya getting shit-faced again at one of the parties he's always making her go to and I'm getting sick of it. When he turns back to me, though, I'm pretty sure I'm mistaken.

Everything I see in his face is wrong. The look he has now is so empty of everything I associate with Drew that it wakes me up all at once.

"Why? What happened?" He doesn't answer and I have to ask him again. "What happened, Drew?" I demand.

"I don't really know." His eyes are red and he looks like shit.

"In a second, I'm getting in the car and driving over there if you don't start giving me some answers that make sense."

"None of it makes *sense,* Josh." He shifts from defeated to pissed, and when he glares at me I think he's talking about more than Sunshine.

"You sound like her with the cryptic bullshit. Is she okay?"

"She said she was. Her face is messed-up, but she seems all right."

"What happened to her face?" My words are slow, and my voice comes out lower than I expect it to.

"Kevin Leonard."

"Kevin Leonard?" I feel like smashing Drew's face into the wall, at least until I can get to Kevin Leonard, and I don't even know what happened yet. "What did he do to her?" The words are forced. I'm struggling to control my anger long enough to find out what this is about, but I don't know how long I can do it.

"I don't know. Hit her. I think he was taking her clothes off. She really didn't tell me anything." Drew runs his hand through his hair again, and I notice that his knuckles are bleeding and there's blood on his shirt.

"How did she end up with him in the first place? Weren't you with her the whole time? Isn't that why you talked her into going with you?"

Drew studies the torn knuckles on his right hand but doesn't answer.

"Where the hell were you? You drag her to these parties, you get her drunk, and then you *leave her alone?*" I make sure the accusation is clear.

His head whips up and everything about him goes on the defensive.

"She's not helpless, Josh. In case you haven't noticed, she kind of does whatever she wants. I didn't drag her anywhere, and

I haven't gotten her drunk since the first night. She gets drunk all on her own now." He's trying to justify it to himself, but I can tell it isn't working.

"She hates being alone at those things. She wouldn't have walked away from you."

"She didn't." Guilt. He did ditch her. "She texted me, but I didn't hear it. She went upstairs where it was quiet so she could call you to get a ride. When I got up there, she was on the floor and he was on top of her." He tells me her face was bruised and bleeding, and when he gets to the part about her underwear around her ankles, he can't keep talking because he's trying not to cry, and if I weren't so disgusted with everyone in the world, I might actually be crying, too.

"You left her alone." I want to kill him. I want to blame him so I don't have to blame myself. I can't even think about the phone call.

"Yes, Josh! That's exactly what I did! I guilt-tripped her into coming with me and then I left her alone because I'm selfish. You don't think I know? Trust me, I know. I don't need you to remind me that I'm a prick. I've been reminded all fucking night, by her face and the blood and—" He runs his hand back through his hair as his voice cracks again, and I really hope he doesn't lose his shit because I can't see that. Not on top of everything else. Because, right now, I'm seeing her face and the blood, too, and I don't want to lose mine, either. "Just trust me," he says, "I know. Okay? I know."

His back is leaning against my kitchen counter, and I'm leaning against the wall across from him. Neither of us says anything for what seems like an hour even though it's probably less than a minute.

"She didn't tell you anything?"

"Not really." He shakes his head wearily. "The fucked-up

part is that she didn't even seem surprised. It was like she just expected it."

"Why didn't you bring her here?" I ask.

"I did." He levels his eyes at me and pauses to let this sink in, because in the shock of absorbing what happened to Sunshine, I've all but forgotten what I was doing while she was alone in a bedroom with Kevin Leonard. "Think real hard, Josh. We drove straight to your house about two hours ago. The garage was closed and the lights were off, so I thought you were asleep and I used my key. We walked into the house and guess what we heard?"

"She came in with you." It's not a question. It's a hand grenade.

"I thought seeing you was the only thing that would help her." The bitter-laced sarcasm is dripping from his voice, and I'm not sure which one of us he despises more at this moment.

"What did she say?" I ask, but it's quiet because I really don't want to know. All I've thought about since the day she walked out of here was the day she would walk back in. And tonight she did.

"Nothing. She hasn't said a word to me since we walked into your house."

"I need to see her." I don't want to see her. I don't want to face that she knows what I did. I don't want to face that I know what I did. But I need to see her. I need to see that she's still here and still okay, even if she hates me. Her hurt might kill me but I can survive her hate.

"No."

"No?"

"No." It's absolute.

"Who the fuck are you to say I can't see her?"

"Who the fuck are you to say you can?"

"What's that supposed to mean?"

"It means that she looked like hell when we walked into your house and she looked worse when we walked out."

I feel sick. Not figuratively sick. Sick like I might throw up right now. My face must tell him something, because his tone loses a little of its edge. Or maybe he's just tired of this whole shit night. "Josh, even if I did think it was okay, which I don't, because right now I think you're acting like me and I don't like you very much. But even if I did say you could see her, it's not up to me."

"She won't see me."

"She won't see you," he confirms. He won't offer me hope, and for the first time tonight, I feel grateful. "Are you ever going to tell me what happened between you two?" He hasn't stopped asking.

"No."

"Fine. Are you going to tell me what you were doing fucking Leigh?" His tone is as cold as his expression.

"I've been fucking Leigh for years." It's true. It's like second nature. Technically, nothing I did tonight was wrong. I didn't take advantage of anyone. I didn't cheat. I didn't leave Nastya alone with a drunk asshole. I can make all of the arguments that I want, to Drew, to Sunshine, to myself, but knowing how "not wrong" I was doesn't make me feel like any less of a prick.

I can even tell you why I did it. For the same reason I did it the first time and every time after. It was comforting and it made me feel normal. Leigh showed up, walked in and said hi, and like always, it was the easiest, most natural thing in the world. She sat on the couch and we watched television until she leaned over and kissed me. It was only a second before she pulled back and looked at me like she wanted to apologize. When I didn't say anything, she kissed me again and I let her because there wasn't a price to be paid or a choice to be made anymore. Nastya had made that choice for me.

Leigh picked up my hand and led me back to my room and

I went. For one night, I just wanted to pretend that there wasn't anyone to miss.

"You don't love her." It's an accusation, and if there was any humor at all in this situation, I would laugh, because I have no idea how Drew Leighton says this with a straight face. I want to hit him for it, and for so many other things, but there's a part of me that knows that I just don't need one more thing to be pissed at myself about tonight. Maybe I should hit him just to get him to hit me back, because that's what I deserve. I want him to hit me. I want him to beat my face in so I don't have to feel anything but that pain. The other is so much worse.

I walk to the opposite side of the room to put some distance between us, but he follows, sinking down onto the couch and sighing like this has been the longest night of his life. And I know that it probably has been, but I don't have any sympathy to offer him.

"This isn't really news, Drew. Why don't you just say whatever bullshit you want to say to me and then get out?"

"You love her."

"I think we just established that I don't."

"Not Leigh. Nastya. You love Nastya." I hate that word and it sounds all wrong coming from Drew's mouth. Drew, who makes a career of mocking it, of destroying girls for hoping for it. Drew, who has no right to judge me, but is sitting on my couch, with his feet on my coffee table, doing just that. Yet I don't deny what he says. I should deny it; deny it all night until I've convinced even myself that it could not possibly be true. That I couldn't really be so self-destructive as to fall in love with any girl, much less a girl who is cracked in a thousand places and who will leave me as soon as she's put back together again. But I guess the ability to think rationally has deserted me because I don't deny it at all. It's late. I'm tired and scared and hurt and so incredibly sorry, and I just can't think straight anymore tonight.

"She doesn't know that," I say finally, looking at Drew as if this might be an excuse for my behavior. As if it could make any of this less horrible. The words taste like the regret that is filling me up and spilling out of my mouth.

"Josh," he says, and when he does, all of the irreverence and sarcasm, all of the judgment and condescension are gone from his voice, and I hate him already for what he's going to say next.

"Everybody knows that."

Chapter 50

Nastya

It's a little after two o'clock in the morning. It's late, but it feels later, like this whole night has been so epic that nothing in the world is recognizable anymore. Drew left fifteen minutes ago, saying he'd be back in half an hour. He didn't mention where he was going, but he didn't need to. We both knew where he would end up.

I showered, and I'm trying to keep ice on my face, but really, I just want to go to bed, even if I won't sleep. I wonder if there are words I can write that will erase the images burned into my brain tonight; that will keep them from coming to find me. Not the ones with Kevin Leonard. The ones with Josh and that girl. The pictures I didn't even see. Pictures that are working like acid now, burning their way through every good memory and leaving only one behind. I already threw up once tonight at the thought of it, but as soon as the image invades my mind, my stomach convulses again, and I'm back in the bathroom, hung over the toilet and retching. But nothing comes up. There isn't anything left in me.

I flip the TV on downstairs and there's a knock on the door so soft that I almost miss it. I gave Drew my key to let himself back in, so I know it isn't him, but I have no idea who else would be here. I tiptoe to the door and look through the peephole to find Tierney Lowell on my front porch.

I have to take a minute to decide whether to open the door. Finally, I turn the dead bolt and face her. She's still dressed from the party and looks like she's been crying. I wonder if anyone came out of this night unscathed.

"Man, your face," she says almost immediately. "Sorry." She winces, and her discomfort at standing here with me is undeniable. "I don't want to wake anyone up."

I shake my head as I push the door back and motion for her to come in. We stare at each other for a minute. I know why she's here, but I'm waiting for her to ask. I wonder how she knew where I lived. Maybe Clay. She's been talking to him since they bonded over the art and science of bong construction. Her eyes move around the room, but she won't find what she's looking for.

"Is Drew here?"

I shake my head.

"Oh." There's no attempt to hide her disappointment. She takes a breath and her voice is sincere. "Are you okay?"

I'm going to start making people put a quarter in a jar every time they ask me that. I don't even know what okay means.

I nod.

"I just wanted to see if he was all right," she explains. "I don't think he's ever hit anybody before."

I don't think so, either.

"Is he all right?" There's no concealing the concern in her voice or the fact that she knows Drew well enough to realize that this is a valid question.

I don't nod or shake my head or even shrug. She has to ask him for that answer. I don't have it.

"He loves you," she says, reconciled.

I do nod for this, because I believe he does, but not in the way she thinks. I need to write a note to explain it to her because she deserves to know, but before the conversation can go any further, there's a key in the lock and Drew walks in. He stops dead when he sees Tierney, and if I could take a picture of the expression that passes between them, I would, and then I'd shove it in both their faces so they could never deny it again.

"I should go." She looks from Drew to me with misguided resignation before turning to leave.

I walk over to Drew and squeeze his hand, tilting my head toward the door, and he follows her out onto the porch.

Josh

Less than an hour after Drew leaves, I'm in her driveway. It's three thirty in the morning. Margot gets home in a few hours, and I wonder how Sunshine is going to explain her face. I grab my phone out of the cup holder and shove it in my pocket. I still haven't looked at it. I don't want to see her name on the display and all of the what-ifs lit up behind it. I can't face the reminder that if I had heard the phone, if I had picked it up, none of this would be happening.

Drew is standing on the porch watching Tierney Lowell's car disappear down the street. I walk past him and open the door so he won't have a chance to remind me that I'm not allowed to be here.

I don't even have time to prepare myself, because as soon as I walk in, she's there, standing in the kitchen. I've tried not to look at her for weeks. Seeing her now eviscerates me, rips me to pieces and sews me back together all wrong. I don't know if it's the cut by her eye or the bruise on her cheek or the expression on her face that does it, but I know that it's done because everything inside me hurts.

"Go home," Drew says from behind me, but I don't turn away because I can't stop looking at her.

"Just give us a minute." I don't know if I'm asking or telling.

"Not tonight, Josh," he says. It's not forceful, just defeated.

He's right. I should leave. She shouldn't have to deal with me on top of everything else. But I'm selfish. I want her to tell me she's okay, even if I know that she's not. I'll take lies right now if she'll give them to me.

"I just need one minute." I'm talking to Drew, but I'm looking at her. My voice is soft, but my tone isn't. I'm not going anywhere.

She nods to Drew, but he doesn't look convinced. He figures if he didn't keep Kevin Leonard away from her tonight, at least he can save her from having to deal with me.

"Go home, Drew," she says gently. "If your mom wakes up, she's going to be pissed. I'm good. I promise." It's such a lie, but it's so natural; it's like she's been telling it for years.

Drew still doesn't look happy, but he concedes. He walks over and hugs her just long enough to whisper "I'm sorry" in her ear, and then he leaves.

"Does it hurt?" It's a stupid question, asking a girl whose face is half swollen if it hurts, but it's the first thing I can think to say. She lifts the ice back up to her cheek and shakes her head.

"Not really."

We both stand there, looking at each other across the kitchen, with all the things we've done to hurt each other littering the path between us.

She puts the ice down and pulls a foil-covered plate off the top of the refrigerator. She removes the foil and puts the plate of sugar cookies on the table and tells me to sit.

"I know you said you were sick of them, but. . . ."

I did tell her I was sick of them. It was over a month ago.

She made like twelve batches in a week's time because she said she couldn't get the right balance between chewy and crunchy, and I said she was crazy because they all seemed exactly the same to me. I finally told her that until she made me something with chocolate in it, I would not be tasting another sugar cookie.

"Did you finally get it right?" I have no clue what the point of this conversation is, but she's my tangent girl, and I'll follow her if this is where she wants to go.

"I think so." She shrugs like it's really no big deal, even though we both know it was driving her insane. "You tell me."

She pushes the plate toward me. Her face is beat up. I just had sex with Leigh. We're sitting at her table, in the middle of the night, and she's making me critique her cookies.

"They taste," I say, trying not to talk with my mouth full, "exactly like the last eight hundred you made me try."

"I know they taste the same," she says, undeterred, "but are they too crunchy?"

I exhale slowly, putting the cookie down on the table.

"So we're going to talk about cookies." I nod robotically, picking up a napkin and twisting it around in my hands.

"I'm sorry I hurt you."

"What?" The words should have come from my mouth, but they didn't. They came from hers. I know she knows what I did tonight. All I can think is *Don't apologize to me. Please don't apologize to me.* Yesterday it would have been a blessing. Today it's a curse.

I want to tell her I'm sorry, too, but they're shit words and I'm a shit person.

"I'm so sorry I hurt you," she repeats as if I need to hear it again, and this time she throws the *so* in for good measure. Just to twist the knife.

"I'm the one who should be apologizing."

"You didn't do anything wrong."

I can't even believe that just came out of her mouth. It's worse than the apology.

"How can you say that? Everything that happened tonight was wrong. Everything! Every single thing!" I don't plan to raise my voice, but it happens, and maybe that's a good thing, because it sets her off, too.

"I know, Josh! What do you want me to say? That my heart broke a thousand times when I walked into your house tonight? That I came home and threw up, not because of what happened at that stupid party, but because I can't stop thinking about what you were doing with *that girl*? Is that what you want to hear? Because it's true!"

I know it's true. I know because the pain is all over her face and in her eyes and in her voice. I know because now it's making me as sick as she is and I can't do anything about it. It's done like everything else.

She gets up from the table and crosses the room, and I feel every inch of the space between us. "And you know what the worst part is?" she continues. "The worst part is that I'm not even allowed to be angry about it, because it's my fault. Is that what you need me to say? That I know it's all my fault? That none of this would have happened in the first place if I wasn't determined to destroy myself and everyone around me? Fine. It's all my fault! *Everything* is my fault, and no one knows it more than me. We're all in hell and I'm the one who put us here. I *know* and I'm *sorry*."

I stare at her for a minute because it's the first real feeling I've seen in her in forever. She's been an emotional black hole for weeks, but all of a sudden, the dead, flat calm is gone and she's as angry and frustrated and heartbroken as I am.

I stand up and take a step toward her. She looks at me like she doesn't know what the hell I'm doing. There's a mixture of fear and confusion on her face, and her eyes dart past me like those of a cornered animal looking for an opening to run. For just one second, she stops hiding the vulnerability that I always try to pretend doesn't exist. I should walk away and leave it alone, but I don't want to be in a room with her and not get to touch her one more time before everything goes back to shit again tomorrow.

"I'm going to walk over to you," I say, taking one step at a time in her direction like I'm talking down a jumper. "I'm going to put my arms around you and I'm going to hold you," I pause before taking the last step, "and you're going to let me."

"Why?" she asks, like it's the most insane thing she's ever heard and maybe, after tonight, it is.

"Because I need to."

I'm in front of her now and she doesn't back away, so I do what I said I would and put my arms around her. I feel her body soften just slightly against mine, but she doesn't move her arms or reciprocate. She doesn't forgive me and that's okay. I don't know if I forgive her, either.

When she does move, it's to bring her hand up to my chest and gently push me away. I lift my hand to her face, wishing I could erase the bruises and the hurt, but I stop just short of letting my fingers graze her skin and drop my hand back to my side. I wish she'd just let it go here, let me walk away without another word, but it never happens that way.

"I'd take it back if I could. I never should have hurt you." She keeps going back to that, and it's useless, because we can't undo anything at this point.

"I never should have let you," I say. It's true, and I knew it from the beginning. I shouldn't have let her hurt me. I should never have cared enough to make that possible. I even did what she wanted. I never told her that I loved her; but it didn't change anything. I loved her every day and I'm the one who suffered for it.

"I had to leave." There's pleading in her voice, begging me to understand something I don't. "I can't tell you the truth, and I know you want it. I would end up disappointing you, being the thing that's never enough, just like with everyone else."

"Leaving is the only thing you could have done to disappoint me." I would have lived every day without the truth, to keep her, even if it was wrong.

"It doesn't matter now," she says, and the regret of so much more than the past few weeks is etched on her face. She's accepting it. We can both be as sorry as we want, but too much has happened that we can't take back. Some things you just have to learn to live with. We both learned that lesson a long time ago.

"I'm going to beat the shit out of Kevin Leonard," I say finally, because I can do that one thing, even if it isn't nearly enough.

"Don't." There's determination in her voice.

"Why shouldn't I?"

"It's not a good enough reason."

"You are the only good reason." I may not be allowed to love her, but that doesn't mean I'll let anyone hurt her. Maybe that's ironic, since I'm the one who hurt her the most tonight.

"I don't want to be the reason for that. It's over and I want to forget it."

"How are you taking this so lightly? He could have raped you, and you act like nothing happened."

"Nothing did happen. Believe me, I've seen worse." She shrugs and it's maddening.

"Worse than being raped?" I look at her incredulously.

"Worse than almost being raped."

I drag my hand down my face in frustration.

"Enough with the cryptic, Sunshine! I'm sick of it. I'm sick of *this*!" I'm losing it all over again. I've done more yelling since I've known this girl than I have in the past ten years, and I can't seem to stop. "You say things like that all the time that make absolutely no sense! Like you want me to know something, but you won't tell me, so I'm just supposed to pick up random clues and figure it out. Guess what? I can't. I can't figure it out. I can't figure *you* out and I'm getting sick of trying."

I guess we didn't have to wait until tomorrow for everything to go to shit again. It's happening right now.

My hands are in my hair, and I can't stop walking around the room because I have so much pent-up aggression and I don't know where to put it. Now I understand the running. I think I could run out of here right now and not stop for miles. I take a breath and start again because I can't seem to stop talking, either.

"All I know is that something happened, or more likely, someone happened who fucked up your hand and did a job on the rest of you in the process, and I can't fix it."

"No one asked you to." The words are fierce and bitter. Her eyes turn almost feral. "Everyone wants to fix me. My parents want to fix me. My brother wants to fix me. My therapists want to fix me. You're supposed to be the person who doesn't want to fix me."

We're both exasperated now. We're both angry, and for some reason it's a relief. It makes me feel like, maybe, I'm not the only one in the room.

"I don't want to fix *you*. I want to fix *this*." I throw my arms out, but I don't even know what I'm referring to. Her? Me? The whole fucked-up world?

"What's the difference?"

What *is* the difference? I don't know. Maybe there isn't one. Maybe I do want to fix her. If I do, is that wrong? Does that make me the asshole in this scenario?

"I don't know," I answer, because it's the only thing I do know. I sit back down at the table and drop my head into my hands.

The emotions in this room are bouncing all over the place,

and I can't keep up. It's after four o'clock in the morning and I feel like my entire body has been wrung out, and I'm just done.

"I thought there was something wrong with you, too." Her voice is calmer and she sounds apologetic, like she thinks she's insulting me. But she isn't. "I thought you wouldn't care that I was wrong, because you just understood what it was like. I figured if I didn't ask you, you wouldn't ask me, and we could just pretend not to care what happened before. I guess it doesn't work that way." She half shrugs like she's known this all along, but she's finally coming to terms with it. "I just wanted one person who would look at me and not want to see someone else."

"Who looks at you like that?" I lift my head up and lower my hands so I can see her face, and I can't imagine anyone looking at this girl and wanting to see anything but her.

"Everyone who loves me."

"Who is it they want to see?

"A dead girl."

Chapter 51

Nastya

On Tuesday during fifth hour, Ms. McAllister continues the poetry unit. We covered the same lesson earlier in my class, and now I just get to listen in and try not to stare too much at the beautiful, priceless boy in the back row whose heart I stomped all over. I don't even know how long we ended up talking on Saturday morning. I know that we didn't resolve anything. There wasn't anything left to resolve. We had already put everything through the shredder and it was just gone.

I walk through the aisles, passing out a list of discussion questions on the poem "Renascence" by Edna St. Vincent Millay. I pass Ethan Hall's desk, and he checks out my face again. I've been able to do a good job covering it, but you can still make out the bruise.

"So you're beating your girlfriends now?" he directs at Drew. A hint of smug satisfaction crosses his face like he's telling me I got what I deserved for rejecting him. Maybe I did get what I deserved, but it wasn't for anything I did to him.

"No, that's your thing," Drew replies, unfazed.

"She did it in kickboxing."

I turn to catch Tierney Lowell glaring at Ethan. She's the only other person aside from Drew, Josh, and I who knows what happened with Kevin. I'm not surprised to hear her chime in. It's Drew she's defending, even if she won't admit it. I nod almost imperceptibly in thanks to her, because if he won't acknowledge it, I will.

When I pass Kevin Leonard's desk, he reaches out to grab my hand and say something. He looks embarrassed, but before he can touch me or open his mouth, Josh kicks the back of his chair. Hard. Kevin drops his hand and looks down at the paper in front of him, muttering "Sorry" under his breath, which I get the feeling is directed at Josh, not me.

Josh slides the handout across his desk when I place it there, but he makes no move to acknowledge me at all. I don't even exist. I'd trade my hand all over again to take back everything I did and hear him call me Sunshine.

"Who can explain what the poem is about?" Ms. McAllister asks to get started. She places the leftover handouts on top of a beautiful handmade oak podium that magically appeared in her room a week ago. It's a mystery where it came from.

"Trees," someone calls out.

"There are trees in the poem. That's not what it's *about*," she says.

"Aren't poems supposed to be short?" Trevor Mason asks. "Because this one was like a hundred pages long."

"Hyperbole, Mr. Mason," Ms. McAllister replies.

"Hyperbo-what?"

"Exaggeration, you tool," Tierney shoots at him, and then rolls her eyes, looking up to the ceiling before exhaling in defeat. "I'll just take the detention."

Ms. McAllister walks to her desk and fills out a detention slip.

"Who's the tool now?" Drew says, smirking at Tierney. He lifts his head to catch the glare of Ms. McAllister, who's still at her desk, pad of detention slips in hand. Then he glances back to Tierney. "Yeah, I know. Just give me one, too."

"Someone still needs to answer the question at hand." Ms. McAllister passes off the slips and returns to the front of the room.

Even if I wasn't watching the class, I would have been able to hear the collective turning of every head in the room when Josh's hand went up. Even Ms. McAllister looks like she doesn't quite know what to make of it.

"Josh?" she says tentatively.

He doesn't speak for a second, looking pained, like he already regrets drawing the attention.

"It's about the dream of second chances," he says finally. He hasn't raised his eyes from the paper on his desk, and I feel him looking at me without looking when he uses his grandfather's words. "The narrator doesn't respect the beauty of life and the world around her, so it crushes her into the ground, and once she's dead she realizes everything she took for granted and didn't see right in front of her while she was alive. She's begging for another chance to live again so she can appreciate it this time."

I've turned away from Josh to look at Ms. McAllister. She's watching him with an expression of pride and endearment that reminds me of the way I've seen Mrs. Leighton look at him. But I don't think Ms. McAllister's expression is as much about his answer as it is about the fact that he answered in the first place.

"And does she get that chance?" she asks Josh while I desperately focus on the poster of literary terms on the wall and wait for absolution. When it comes, I barely hear it.

"She does."

Josh

It's Wednesday before I see her again outside of school, and even there she hardly looks at me. Nothing has really changed except that, before last weekend, I felt more like a victim in all of this and, now, not so much.

It's already eleven. I've been in my garage for hours, but I haven't done much of anything. I reorganized the same tool chest twice, and now I'm sweeping up sawdust. I don't have the energy to do anything worthwhile, but I have a list that's just getting longer and I have to get started at some point. I've had more time over the last six weeks than I've had in months, and I haven't accomplished crap.

I go inside, make another cup of coffee, and carry it back out, resolving to start the initial cutting for the matching end table I promised I'd make Mrs. Leighton. And maybe I'm more tired than I thought, because when I open the door, the first thing I see is a set of pale white legs capped with black steel-toed boots swinging from the workbench.

"You know you're an addict. Caffeine's a bitch to break."

"Guess I won't break it then."

She nods and I want to ask her why she's here, but I'm glad she is, and for a few minutes, I want to pretend that everything is back to the way it used to be. Maybe that's what she wants, too.

"It'll stunt your growth, you know."

"Didn't know you were worried."

"Only about some parts." She smirks.

I smile for a minute, but it's weak, and I realize that I don't want to joke with her. Especially not like that. It makes me think of everything that happened that night and everything that's gone wrong since, and as much as I want to pretend everything is the way it was before, I'm just not a good enough liar.

"Helps keep me awake," I answer, not taking the bait.

"Why not just sleep?"

"Haven't been sleeping well," I say honestly.

"Maybe that's because of the caffeine. Vicious cycle."

"You don't drink it. Do you sleep well?"

"Point taken," she says faintly.

"Thank you." This conversation is so civilized, it's twisted.

She hops off the counter and walks over to me. The bruise on her face has faded, but it's not covered with makeup now, like it is at school, and I can still see it. I have to fight the urge to run my fingers over it and then run to Kevin Leonard's house and give him four more just like it.

"Here. Let me try it again." She reaches for the cup in my hand.

"If you're going to try it, you should at least put some shit in it first."

"Sounds appetizing."

"I drink it black. You won't. Your taste buds are opposed to anything that isn't sweet."

"Give it, jackass." I let go of the cup and she takes a mouthful while I watch her face contort at the bitterness. "Still gross."

"You get used to it." I shrug, taking the coffee back from her. She relinquishes it and shudders as if she's trying to expel the taste from her mouth. I have to try not to smile.

"I'd rather not." She scrunches up her nose and goes back to sitting on the counter. Her legs start swinging again, and I know how easy it would be to stay in this place and forget everything that's happened. But we'll always end up back where we were, because nothing's been resolved, and I'm not the one with the answers. Maybe, for once, I need to stop letting her dictate everything just because I want to keep her. I can't forget what she did and I can't expect her to forgive what I did, and I don't know where we go from here.

"It's not the same," I say, watching her write her name in the dust on the counter next to her. "We can't act like nothing happened . . . just pretend that it's all good."

"I know it isn't," she says, lifting her eyes to mine with something I might actually believe is hope. "But, maybe."

She ends up staying for the next two hours. She measures and marks the wood for me and I cut. We don't talk about us or Kevin Leonard or Leigh or lost hands or lost people or long-agos. We talk about furniture and tools and recipes and art competitions and debate. It's familiar and comfortable. There's something still hanging over us that we can't ignore forever, even if we do ignore it tonight. But, maybe.

It's after one in the morning when I drive her home, since she walked to my house. We sit in the truck, staring at her front door, because things shifted just a little bit in the other direction tonight, and neither of us is ready to let go of it yet. I reach my hand over and lay it, palm up, on the seat between us and she doesn't hesitate. She lays her left hand on mine and I close my fingers over it.

Chapter 52

Nastya

I'm not sure how long we sit in Josh's truck, holding hands, surrounded by darkness and unspoken regrets. But it's long enough to know that there are no stories or secrets in the world worth holding onto more than his hand.

Chapter 53

Nastya

I think a lot about all the little things that happened the day I was attacked and how any one of them might have changed everything. I wonder how many thousands of variables played a part in him finding me that day and if there are as many at work in my finding him.

—

Clay picks me up at eight in the morning, wearing a long-sleeved button-down shirt and dress pants, and not even remotely resembling the artfully unkempt mess I'm used to seeing. I doubt I look much like what he's used to seeing, either. I look more like Emilia today than I have in months. I don't know if it feels right, but it doesn't feel as wrong as it used to.

I look Clay up and down and cock my head to the side in appreciation.

"You too," he says, opening the car door for me. I'm not even sure why he's bringing me. He said he wanted me to see what I sat on my ass so long for, but I've seen it all already. I doubt it will look much different hanging on a wall.

The gallery opening is at nine, and all of the finalists have to be registered and checked in for interviews by ten. The drive is just over an hour, so we're fine. Clay's interview is at eleven, which gives me time to wander through the exhibits and check out his competition, though I can't even imagine how Clay Whitaker could ever have any.

"Here." Clay hooks an MP3 player up to the car stereo and hands it to me. "I figured we'd need music since we've exhausted all the good conversation topics. You can deejay."

I don't really want to deejay. I just want to lean my head against the window and close my eyes and pretend I'm on my way to an Italian restaurant in Brighton. I turn it on and flip to the first playlist and click on it. As long as it's not classical music or depressing love songs, we should be good.

I didn't go back to Josh's again after Wednesday night. When I let go of his hand and left his truck, I promised myself that the next time I stepped foot in his garage I would answer any question he wanted to ask, and I want to keep that promise.

I spend most of the drive trying to line the right words up in my head, rearranging them a hundred times, then finding new ones and starting all over again. When we pull in to the gallery an hour later, my cheeks are wet and I don't even remember when I started crying.

We get Clay checked in and then find the room where they're showing his work. It's one of the bigger rooms, and there are three artists sharing it. Clay's pictures are hung on the largest wall. I recognize most of them. Some are from his college portfolio. Some are the ones he's done of me. But it's hard to concentrate on any of them, because on the center of the wall I'm staring at, is something else entirely.

And it's overwhelming.

The centerpiece of the display is a sixteen-picture mosaic.

On each separate drawing is a part of my face and he's pieced them together like a puzzle. It's obvious that this is the reason I'm here. He hadn't shown it to me. I didn't even know he'd done it. It makes me want to run from the room.

A couple of people come in and comment on the drawings and ask questions to Clay and the two girls, named Sophie and Miranda, whose work is also on display here. I mostly try to face the wall and pretend I'm studying one of Sophie's paintings until Clay gets called for his interview.

Once he's gone, I venture out into the rest of the displays. I figure I can start at the rear of the gallery because most people haven't made their way there yet and it's quieter. I wander toward the back corner of the building into one of the smaller rooms.

For a moment, I don't know where I am. And for the third time in my life the world shifts under my feet and I just try to stay standing.

Because he's here.

It's his face. And it's not a nightmare. It's not a memory. He's here and real and looking at me. And I'm looking back. I'm standing in the middle of a moment that I've dreaded and hoped for since the day I remembered what he did to me.

The name on the wall next to the paintings is Aidan Richter, the school is the one in the next town over from Brighton, and the face in front of me belongs to the boy who killed me.

Everything in me turns on and shuts down at the same time. I am weak and strong. I am terrified and brave. I am lost and found. I am here and gone.

I'm afraid I'm going to stop breathing again.

He's older, like I am, but there is no mistaking it. I know his face like I know every one of the scars he gave me.

I want to run. I want to cry. I want to scream. I want to faint. I want to hurt him, break him, kill him. I want to ask him *why* as if there could ever possibly be a reason.

"Why?" It's a whisper and a scream.

I ask it, and not just in my head. That's the word I choose out of all of the thousands I could say to him. I ask the unanswerable question. Except that maybe it's not unanswerable. Maybe he's the only person in the world who can tell me.

I don't even know which *why* I'm asking. Why did you do it? Why was it me? Why are you here? Why am I here? Why?

He's looking at me like he's scared, and it's the only thing that could possibly make me happy at this moment. Good. Lots of people are scared of me. Girls at school. My parents. Even, sometimes, Josh Bennett. But this boy is the only one whose fear I want.

And I wonder if his presence here is a gift. Handed to me to even the score. God's version of making amends.

"You weren't supposed to remember." There isn't one thing about his voice that is the same. It's him, but not him. There isn't any rage or darkness gripping him. It's the same boy but not the same voice, not the same eyes, not the same madness.

"You weren't supposed to kill me."

"I didn't mean to."

"You didn't mean to?" My brain is wringing out the words, trying to find the meaning of them. But there isn't any. "How do you not mean to do what you did? You hit me in the face over and over again. You dragged me around by my hair and ripped it out of my head. You kicked me so hard and so many times that there wasn't a way to fix everything you broke. You murdered my hand. The bones were sticking out. All over the place. Do you remember it?" The last question is nothing more than a pathetic, strangled whisper.

"No." The word is almost an apology.

"No?" I don't remember what my hand looked like, either. I've only seen the pictures nobody wanted to show me. But he's the one who did it. He should have to remember.

"Not all of it. Pieces."

"Pieces? You did this to me and you don't even have the decency to remember?" I don't know where the word even comes from. I can't believe I'm talking to the boy who beat me to death about decency. I can't believe I'm talking to him at all. I'm supposed to be killing him.

"My brother killed himself."

"I'm sorry." *I'm sorry?* I said *I'm sorry* to this boy. I'm walking to school and smiling and saying hi all over again. No. I'm not. I'm not. I'm not. I forgive myself because it was automatic. I didn't mean it. I gave him the words but I won't give him sympathy. He's looking at me like he can't believe I said it, either. I think I'm insane. I don't know if this perverse conversation is real, but it must be because I don't think I could imagine this.

"I got home that day and I found him. Found his body." He's talking like he's rehearsed these words a thousand times in his head and he's just been waiting for the moment to say them.

And so he does.

He gives me the mythical why. He tells me the story. At least what he remembers of it and I think how ironic it is that I'm not supposed to remember, but I do, and the boy who is supposed to have all the answers has a mind full of blanks. But he spills everything in a mad rush like he's been holding onto it for years and wants to get it out before I stop him.

He tells me about his brother. About the girl his brother was in love with who went to the same school as me. The girl who broke up with his brother and who Aidan blamed for the suicide, even though he knows, now, that she wasn't the reason. The Russian girl. The Russian whore. The girl he went looking for that day. The girl he saw when he saw me. Just because I was there.

He pauses to take a breath and for a moment it's so quiet that I can hear the space between heartbeats. It's the quiet I've been searching for for three years and I find it with the boy who took it away.

And then he says the words. And it isn't possible for me to hate this boy more, but I do.

"I'm sorry. I'm so, so sorry."

My head wants to explode. This is not the way this is supposed to happen. He's not supposed to be apologizing. He's supposed to be evil and I'm supposed to hurt him.

My hands are fists without a purpose. I don't know where my breath comes from, just that it still comes. I can't hear any more of this. Because he's stealing my rage, and it's the only thing I have. He can't take that, too. He can't make me not hate him. I'll have nothing left.

He starts talking about his parents putting him in therapy after the suicide and about the guilt he lives under because he never told anybody about what he did to me. How he kept waiting and waiting to get caught but no one ever came for him. And he thought that he was being given a second chance, that I didn't die and he thought I was okay and it was some sort of new beginning. It was. Just to a shittier story.

Words. So many words. I don't need to know why he turned evil, just that he was. There is absolutely no part of me that wants to listen to him talk about his guilt and his therapy and his art and his healing. He doesn't get to feel better. He doesn't get to forgive himself. I won't give him permission.

And yet I don't think he does forgive himself. There is so much remorse and pain and self-loathing in his expression that I ache for him because I know what it feels like, and I hate myself for the aching.

He stops talking. I listened to every word he said, and it's my turn now. My turn to tell him everything I've needed to tell him since the day I remembered what he did to me. My turn to make him listen. But I don't get the chance. Clay walks in before

I can figure out which of the thousand words in my head I'm going to say first.

"There you are." Clay looks at me. "Did you make it all the way through already?"

He turns to Aidan Richter, who looks haunted and stares at me like I'm a specter. Some spirit from the past, come to claim what's owed.

"Hi," Clay says, and walks over to offer his hand. I want to grab it away and scream not to touch him. I know what those hands have done and I don't want them anywhere near Clay's. "Clay Whitaker. Your work?"

Clay glances around at the walls, which I've only now started to notice. This boy's art is so different from Clay's. There's nothing remotely similar at all. But it's amazing and I want to slap myself for thinking so. I despise him for the ability to create it.

And then I see it. And there are no words that exist to describe the hatred I feel for him. The painting. On the far side of one wall, all the way to the end, like a period or an afterthought. But it's not a painting. It's a memory that didn't happen.

I don't know anything about art, so I can't tell you that it's watercolor or acrylic or that it's on canvas or anything art-related at all. I can tell you that it's a painting of a hand, my hand, turned up and opened to the world, and that it reaches into my body and rips out everything that's left. Because in the palm, right in the center, is the pearl button I never reached.

Aidan Richter is gone and I'm still waiting.

I need to find him. He got to say everything and I said nothing. I won't let him absolve his guilt at my expense. He doesn't get to use me for that, too. He doesn't get to make me question everything I've believed for nearly three years and then walk away without listening to me.

I want my turn to scream at him. To ask him if he knows

that he's a murderer. If he knows that, even though I lived, it doesn't mean he didn't kill me. Just because they brought me back, it doesn't mean I wasn't dead. Just because they restarted it, it doesn't mean my heart didn't stop. It doesn't change anything he did. He killed the Brighton Piano Girl even if he didn't kill Emilia Ward. And I want to tell him. I want him to know what I know. I want him to hurt. I'm frantic with unsaid words.

Maybe no one found him before, but I know who he is now. I know his name. I can find him like he found me.

And when I do, it won't be random.

Chapter 54

Josh

When I get to Sunday dinner, I'm hoping she'll be there. She skipped it last weekend after everything that happened, and I don't blame her. I would have skipped it, too, if I wasn't desperate for even the slightest chance of seeing her.

My house is too quiet and my garage is too empty, so I came over here early. Dinner isn't ready, so Drew and I end up in his room because I don't feel like standing around being polite and making small talk. But I have nothing to talk to Drew about, either, and we just end up sitting here in stupid silence.

Maybe I should have stayed home. Sunshine never came back after we talked on Wednesday. I thought it was a turning point, but maybe I was just deluding myself again.

"Tell me what the hell happened between you two," Drew finally demands. "And don't say nothing. And don't say you don't know. I've gotten every evasive answer there is from both of you and I'm calling bullshit."

"I don't know." I look up at Drew and stop him before he can interrupt. "That's the absolute truth, whether you like it or not. I have no fucking idea. Everything was fine. Everything was good. And then it wasn't. All I know is that, for like five minutes, I think I was happy."

"Something had to have happened, Josh."

Something most definitely did happen. I wage an internal battle over whether to ask him the question that's in my head. I've always wondered how much she talks to Drew, how much goes on between them that I don't know about.

"Did she tell you she was a virgin?"

"What? *No way.*" He looks at me, disbelieving. "Seriously?"

I nod. He clearly didn't know any more than I did. I feel like I'm betraying her by telling him. But I have to tell someone. I have to try to understand. I feel like I'm drowning.

"How is that even possible? *She's* a virgin?"

"Not anymore," I answer.

"And that's what happened." He sobers. It's not even a question.

"That's what happened."

"Why would that break you up?" he asks, confused.

"I don't know. I don't get any of it. She said she was ruined and she was using me to ruin what was left."

"What's that supposed to mean?"

I just shake my head. I have no answers. I asked her the same thing and she never gave me any.

"That doesn't make any sense."

"Nothing about her has made sense since the day she got here. She just wanted to pretend it didn't matter. I did, too." It's the most I've ever said to anyone about her, and when I hear it come out of my mouth, I know how it sounds.

"You know she loves you, right?"

"She told you that?" I hate the hope in my voice.

"No, but—"

"I didn't think so." I don't want him taking pity on me with false hope. She either said it or she didn't. And she didn't. Then again, neither did I.

"Josh—"

Drew doesn't get a chance to finish because his mom calls us in for dinner, and I walk out before he can say anything else.

When we get to the kitchen, Mrs. Leighton hugs me and Drew walks away to pull a playlist up on the computer because it's his turn tonight. Everything is like normal.

And Sunshine isn't anywhere.

We're just about to bring the food to the table when Mr. Leighton calls out from the family room where he always watches the news before dinner. Mrs. Leighton yells back that it's time to eat and he needs to shut the TV off, but he calls her in again, and she must recognize something in his tone because she doesn't question it this time. She just goes, and we all follow.

And this is the moment before. The moment when everything is still familiar and understandable. The moment before everything shifts. I've had a few of these moments in my life. The moment I walk from the kitchen to the family room is one of them, the moment before I see the face on the television in the Leighton living room at Sunday dinner.

I don't even know why he called us in here until I follow everyone's eyes to the television screen. And then I know everything. I can't even hear what they're saying because the picture is screaming at me so loudly that it drowns out everything else. Mr. Leighton rewinds the DVR and turns it up, but I still barely process the words.

High school student Aidan Richter was arrested this afternoon after confessing to the brutal 2009 beating and attempted murder of then fifteen-year-old Emilia Ward, affectionately referred to by locals as the Brighton Piano Girl. The crime had gone unsolved for nearly three years until Richter, himself only sixteen at the time of the attack, arrived with his parents and attorney and surrendered himself into police custody earlier today. No other details have been released, and so far no comment has been made by either family. A press conference is scheduled to take place at 9:30 tomorrow morning.

"It's uncanny," Mr. Leighton says. But it's not and he knows it. There's nothing uncanny about it. It's like tumblers in a lock falling into place. Everything clicks.

brutal . . . beating . . . attempted murder . . . Emilia . . . Piano Girl

He pauses the TV on a split screen of a picture of the girl I have been looking at across my garage for months. Younger. No makeup. No black clothes. Smiling. Even with the dark hair and dark eyes, there is nothing dark about her. She's all light. Like sunshine.

"I remember seeing that on the news when it happened. It was a terrible story. It looks just like her," Mrs. Leighton says, and I wonder if she can't make herself believe it, or if she honestly doesn't.

"It is her."

We all turn, and standing in the entrance to the room is Sunshine's brother.

"I knocked, but no one answered the door," he says, but he's not really talking to us. He's staring at the TV. "Where is she?"

The Leightons look at him like he's a crazy person who just barged into their house. Their faces are carved in disbelief, but there's already so much shock in the room right now that it's hard to figure out the source of it.

"Asher, Nastya's brother," I say, answering a question no one asked and hearing how wrong that name sounds coming out of my mouth.

"Emilia's brother," he corrects. "Where is she? I need to bring her home." I know the home he's talking about isn't Margot's. He's taking her home to Brighton. He doesn't sound angry. Just tired. Like he's been living under all of this for such a long time and he just wants it to be over.

"She isn't here."

"Margot said she would be here. She said to try your house first" —he looks at me—"and if she wasn't there she'd be here for dinner." There's an uneasiness in his voice that matches his expression.

"She didn't come tonight," Mrs. Leighton says gently, and then turns her eyes, full of sympathy and questions, on me.

"Why don't you just track her phone?" I ask bitterly. Mostly because I can tell he's edgy and nervous and worried and he's making me all of those things, too.

"She left her phone on her bed," he answers, like he's starting to understand that she didn't just forget it.

Asher tells us what's happened since this afternoon in Brighton. As soon as her parents got the call from the police, he got in the car to pick her up so she wouldn't have to drive alone. In the meantime, they kept calling, trying to get hold of her, figuring they could get to her before it hit the news here. But no one's been able to reach her.

I pull my phone out of my pocket to check the messages. Nothing. I don't put it back. I just keep holding onto it, turning it over in my hands. Drew's doing the same thing. It makes us feel like we're doing something, willing them to ring, trying to figure out some way to help, even if it is useless. There isn't anybody to call and no one's going to call us and everyone here knows it. If she left and she didn't bring her phone, she did it for a reason— she doesn't want us knowing where she is.

The story on the news has changed, but we all keep looking at the television like there's something there. Like suddenly it's going to give us an answer. Maybe we just don't want to look at each other and see our own confusion reflected on someone else's face. I'm not confused. I actually feel like I understand something for the first time in months. Maybe I understand everything.

Asher walks out of the room to make a phone call, and once he does Drew looks at me. I can tell it's been killing him to wait. "Did she tell you?" he asks.

I should be able to say yes to that question. I should have made sure of that. I should have cared enough to make her tell me. Her secrets were an open secret between us and I allowed it. There was never a question that she wasn't telling me things. *Things.* How fucked up is that? Things. All things. Everything. But I knew that once she told me, I could never unhear it, and I was happier being ignorant.

I shake my head, and everyone's eyes are on me.

"How could she tell him? She doesn't talk," Sarah says.

Drew and I look at each other; and I don't know what's secret and what isn't anymore.

My phone rings and I grab it without looking at the caller ID, hoping it's her.

"Did you know this?" Clay asks, without even saying hello.

"No, I didn't," I say, but I don't have the energy to snap at him. Everyone assumes I should have known about this. I should have. But I didn't know anything.

"It is her, isn't it?" he asks, waiting for confirmation he doesn't need.

"It's her."

"I saw her with him yesterday."

"With who?"

"Aidan Richter. On the news. The kid who confessed."

"You *saw* her with him?" How is that possible?

"At the art competition. He was one of the finalists. When I got out of my interview, she was in the room with him."

"What were they doing?"

"I don't know. Standing there staring at each other. It was weird, but I just thought maybe he tried to talk to her and she didn't answer and it freaked him out."

"Is she okay?" The concern in his voice is genuine.

"I don't know. No one knows where she is." I'm not even sure how I get the words out without my voice breaking.

Asher walks back in while I'm still on the phone. "My parents called the credit card company."

I tell Clay to get over here and I hang up so I can hear what Asher is saying.

He tells us she used the card at a gas station on the northbound side of the turnpike just outside Brighton earlier today. He's going over to pick up some things from Margot's and then he's heading back there. It's beyond me what's so important that he has to pick it up before he goes looking for his sister, but I'm not in a position to put down people who love her. I said I loved her and look what I've done.

I haven't been able to interrupt him, because I'm trying to formulate my own thoughts before I drop-kick her brother with them.

"She was with him yesterday." My stomach twists when I say it. I'm afraid there are answers there I don't want to think about yet.

"What?" I don't know who says it. Maybe everybody.

"Aidan Richter. The kid who confessed. Clay said he saw them together at the art gallery. He was there." I force it out in one pained breath.

"Who the hell is Clay?" That wouldn't have been my first question if I were Asher, but I answer it, just now realizing how little her family really knows about her life here.

"He draws pictures of her. She went with him to a state competition yesterday. He said he found them in a room together, and when he saw the news today, he remembered him."

"Does he know anything else?" Asher asks, anxiously.

"I don't know. I told him to get over here."

Clay pulls up, and he's barely in the door before we bombard him with questions. He tells us what he knows, which isn't much. He was meeting with the judges while she looked around at the exhibits. When he found her after his interview, she was in a room with the Richter kid and they were staring at each other. He didn't hear anything, so he has no idea if they were speaking or not. Then Richter got called in for his interview and they didn't see him again. Clay drove her home at the end of the day and that was it.

"She was fine on the way home. She seemed fine. Not like she talks. She was upset in the morning on the way there, but in the afternoon, nothing unusual."

"Why was she upset?" I ask, because it's the first time he's mentioned it.

"I don't know. She looked out the window the whole time, and when we got there she was crying. She's been a mess ever since whatever happened between you two." He looks at me, but it's almost apologetic, like he didn't want to call either of us out, but he had to. "I wouldn't have said anything if this didn't happen."

"She was crying?" Asher looks like he doesn't understand. I guess she doesn't cry in front of him, either.

"Not like sobbing," Clay clarifies. "Just tears. I didn't even know until I looked at her. I wasn't going to call her on it. Who knows what goes on in her head?"

"Nobody," Asher says, and if it's possible, he looks more devastated than before.

"I thought you knew your sister," I say, throwing his words back at him because now I'm getting scared, and it's making me a dick.

"Nobody knows my sister," he says. And there isn't any argument for that.

We work out what we do and don't know at this point. We know a lot of things, just not the one thing we want to know. Where she is.

Basically what it comes down to is that no one has seen her since nine o'clock this morning and there's been no trace of her since she used her credit card at a gas station just after eleven right outside Brighton. There's nothing after that. But she's eighteen and she hasn't even been missing for twelve hours, so no one's going to look for her except us.

Asher has his parents on the phone the second we've sorted out Clay's story. While Asher talks to his mother, his father is calling the police station to let them know what happened between Sunshine and Aidan Richter yesterday. We're all wondering the same thing. The thing that no one is saying. If she went to Brighton, she went looking for him before he ever confessed. And if she was in Brighton at eleven o'clock and he turned himself in at three thirty—what happened in between?

Asher leaves, planning to stop at Margot's to pick up whatever it was he promised to bring his parents from his sister's room. Then he's heading straight back to Brighton. Margot's staying at her place on the off chance that Sunshine comes back this way.

Everyone knows I'm going, and Drew says he is, too. Asher gives us the address and the phone number to his parents' house and tells us he'll let them know we're coming. We decide to take our own cars in case we need to separate when we get there.

A few minutes later, I climb into my truck alone and head to Brighton. I spend the entire drive bargaining with everything I will ever have. I don't know how many times I say please. *Please give her back to me. Please not again. Just please.* My phone doesn't ring. It's the longest two hours of my life.

The room is full of controlled chaos. It reminds me of the day my mother and sister died. Phones ringing off the hook. Frantic calm. Poorly concealed fear. They're like zombie people. Empty. Haunted and endlessly waiting for something. I know what it looks like. These people were probably normal once. I think about how easily this could be the Leightons if it had been Sarah. How every normal family is one tragedy away from complete implosion.

There are photographs all over the room of a girl I should know, but don't. A girl in pastel dresses, with ribbons in her hair, smiling and playing the piano in more pictures than I can count. I feel like I'm mourning all over again, but this time it's for a girl I've never met.

Her parents are both on cell phones. The landline keeps ringing, but nobody answers it because the reporters keep calling. Finally, her father rips the cord out of the wall and then it's quiet. But not really.

Drew and I sit on the far side of the room. Separated physically and emotionally from the rest of the family. The rest of the family. Whether or not they acknowledge me, I am in that category also. She made sure of it, no matter how much I'd like to say otherwise. She's gone now, too. It fits.

Asher walks in not long after we arrive. He's carrying a stack of black-and-white composition books, the kind Ms. McAllister makes us use for creative writing. He puts them on the coffee table in the middle of the room. It's a hideous coffee table. I could make a better one. I think about offering.

I can only see the front of the book on the top of the pile. *Chemistry* is written in red marker on the cover. It's Sunshine's handwriting, and seeing it breaks me a little.

Her mother steps toward the stack of books like it's a bomb. "Is this them?"

Asher nods. He's pale and looks older than he did the first time I met him. Everyone here looks older than they should. Like they've seen too many horrible things and now they're just tired. I wonder if I look like that, too.

Nastya/Emilia/Sunshine. I don't know what to call her. Her mother picks up the book on top and opens it, flipping through the first few pages. "It's just chemistry notes," she says, relieved, but confused.

"Keep going, Mom." Asher sounds like he's delivering a deathblow.

A moment later her face contorts in the most wretched expression and her hand goes to her mouth, and I look away because just seeing it feels like an invasion. She looks exactly like Sunshine. Drew doesn't look away. He just stares at her. He looks older, too. I think it might have happened, just now, when he saw the look on this woman's face.

"It took her all of these to write this?" she asks to no one in particular. Her husband, Sunshine's father, the man who's been standing behind her the whole time, takes the book out of her hands, and she shakes her head at him. Not like she doesn't understand something, but like she's telling him no. She doesn't want him to look. It's like someone telling you not to look at a dead body, because if you look at it, you won't ever be able to not see it again. It will always be in your head and you won't ever close your eyes without the image being there. That's how she looks when she shakes her head at him. Like she's seen the body and she doesn't want him seeing it, too.

"No," Asher says. "It's all the same thing. In all of them. It just repeats like it's on a loop. Over and over and over again." His voice breaks on the third over and he starts to cry, but no one consoles him. They don't have any comfort to offer.

There's a knock at the door and a girl walks in. She doesn't say anything. She just walks straight over to Asher who doesn't move until she reaches him. Then he wraps his arms around her and folds her up until she's almost gone, and I miss Sunshine.

The mood in this room is so familiar. No one feels anything, but everyone keeps moving because there are so many things to do. But right now no one seems to know what they are.

The police said Aidan Richter is admitting to seeing her yesterday, but continues to deny having any contact with her today. No one knows whether or not it's true. There's nothing to go on. No place to even begin.

Finally they decide that Asher and Addison and Mr. Ward will take separate cars and go looking for her, even though they have no idea where to start. Asher was right. Nobody knows his sister, at least not the sister he has now.

Her mother is staying here to man the phone. They don't know what to tell Drew and me to do. We don't really know the area and we have no idea where she would go. We're just useless and waiting.

"You can wait in Emilia's room if you want," her mother offers. Everyone in this house calls her Emilia and it sounds more right than Nastya ever did.

Her room is insane, and I feel like I've walked into her mind. There are no walls. You can't see them. Every inch of space is covered with newspaper clippings, computer printouts, and handwritten notes on scraps of paper. They almost seem to move, to shimmer; swimming in and out of my vision like an optical illusion. Like her. I want to close my eyes but I can't. I just turn in a circle waiting for it to stop, but it goes on forever. I think I might run from the room, but now this is in my head, too. Like whatever dead body is hiding downstairs in those books.

We step in and get closer because you can't read any of it unless you're almost on top of the walls. Names. They're all names and origins and meanings. Some of them are from the newspaper, like the ones I've seen her cutting out at my house. Some were obviously printed off the internet. Others she's written herself.

I don't know how long we stare at the walls before Drew
speaks. "Where's Nastya?"

I look at him. I don't know. How would I know? But he's
looking at the walls, not me. He's searching for her name. I start
looking, too, but it's impossible.

"Your name means *salvation*," he says at one point, looking
at a handwritten scrap of paper taped up next to the window.

Salvation. Such a load of shit.

"Did she tell you that?" he asks.

"No." I never asked. I never asked a lot of things. "This is
pointless. We could look it up faster," I say, needing to look away.

Drew pulls out his phone and finds a baby name site on the
internet. He types Nastya in, and a second later, we have our
answer.

"Rebirth," he says. *"Resurrection.* Russian origin."

"I think that's why she picked it. The resurrection part. I
guess the Russian, too." Her mother is standing in the doorway.
She's pulled her hair back, and it makes the dark circles under
her eyes more noticeable.

"Why resurrection?" Drew asks.

"Because she died," her mother says, looking so much like
Sunshine that it unnerves me. "And she came back."

Her mother tells us what happened that day. I don't know if
we want to hear it, but she needs to tell it, so we listen. She
talks about the things we didn't hear on the news and the little
they know of Aidan Richter. She tells us about the part that
came after. The not remembering. Then, later, the not talking.
The surgeries and the physical therapy. The running and the self-
defense and the anger. Wanting to go back to school where no
one would know who she was. The Russian name her mother
didn't understand until now.

Then she talks about before. We hear story after story about a girl and a piano and a whole community who took ownership of her. Her eyes light up at the memory of it. But that's what it is—a memory. Like Sunshine said. I know what she's seeing. A dead girl.

And as I listen to these stories, in this shrine of a house, I start to understand why she left.

I feel like I learn more in one evening about the girl who has practically lived at my house for months than I have since the moment I met her. And I don't want to know any of it.

Her mother thanks us but I don't know why, and then she leaves to make more phone calls. I think she just needs something to do.

Drew lies back in Sunshine's bed, staring at the ceiling. I sit on the floor and lean against the wall. Every time I move I can hear paper crinkling against my back.

"I don't understand," he says, eventually.

"Don't understand what?" I ask. There are so many possible answers to that question.

"I don't get why he didn't rape her."

"What the fuck kind of a question is that?" I practically growl at him.

"I'm not trying to be a dick. I'm serious," he says, and I can tell he is being serious, and it's uncomfortable for him. All of this is uncomfortable for him. In the last few weeks, Drew has had to handle more emotionally charged, disturbing situations than he has in his whole life, and he's not equipped for it.

"Sorry," I apologize to him, because I am, for more than just biting his head off. He was going to have to start growing up at some point, but I feel bad that it had to be like this.

"I just don't get it. Gorgeous girl, alone, why doesn't he rape her? Why does he just beat the shit out of her and leave her there? It just doesn't make sense to me."

"Would it make sense if he had raped her?" I ask, because nothing about what happened to her makes sense.

"No. I guess I just want to understand why he did it. I want there to be a reason."

"Too much pain, rage, grief. Too much reality." There are so many things that can break you if there's nothing to hold you together.

"That's not an excuse," he says.

"No, it's not an excuse," I reply. "You asked for a reason. It's a reason. Just not a good one."

I can tell he's still struggling to understand, to make this fit into his view of the world, but it never will. And it shouldn't. It has no place in the world, no matter how often it happens.

I feel the clock cursing me with every minute that passes and I force myself not to look at it because I don't want to count them. I don't even know how long the silence persists before I have to say what's in my head because I don't want it in there anymore.

"I can't do this again," I tell him. Because I can't. I wasn't supposed to have to do this again. It was done. It was everybody. All of them. Gone. And then her. Why? What did I do that was so wrong? Why even give her to me, just to take her away? I know Drew wants to tell me not to let my mind go there, but he can't even make himself say the words. It's the only place left for my mind to go. "It's my fault. I never should have thought it was okay to love her."

He sighs, staring up at the ceiling. "It *is* okay, Josh. *She's* okay." He wants to believe it, but he doesn't, and it's worse than if he'd said nothing.

"No one is ever okay."

It's well after midnight, but no one is sleeping. We're on our third pot of coffee. I've made the last two, which is only right, since I've been the one drinking most of it.

Asher and Addison and Mr. Ward got back an hour ago. None of them said a word, but they didn't need to. If they had found anything, it would have spoken for itself. The quiet in this room is like a vise that just keeps tightening on us, little by little, until we're all suffocating from it. The piano hovers in the corner like a ghost, and I can't look at it, because now I know what it means, and it's haunting me, too.

Drew and I are at the dining room table. Mr. and Mrs. Ward are on one couch far enough away from each other that there's no danger of them touching. Addison is stretched out on the other couch with her head resting on Asher's lap, his hand mindlessly running through her hair.

The back door opens and it's a bomb detonating into the room. Everyone turns at once. And she's there.

No one moves. No one jumps up and runs to her or shrieks with joy. Everyone just stares, like we're all trying to make sure she's really here. She looks at all of us, her eyes passing over every battered face in the room until she reaches mine. And then there's nothing else. I can't move, but she does. And then she's right in front of me and all at once her mother says, "*Emilia,*" and Asher says, "*Em,*" and her father says, "*Milly,*" and Drew says, "*Nastya,*" and I say, "*Sunshine,*" and then she shatters.

All the pieces of all the girls go flying and I'm holding the one who's left.

My arms are wrapped around her, but I don't say anything. I don't think anything. I don't even know if I breathe. I'm so afraid that I am not going to be able to hold her together. I've seen her cry once before, but it was nothing like this. She is gone, disappeared into some otherworldly oblivion of pain. The sound. It's raw and primal and horrifying and I don't want to hear it. Her hand is pressed between my chest and her mouth, trying to stifle it, but it's not working. She won't stop shaking, always the shaking, and I'm begging in my head for her to stop. I can feel everyone in the room watching, but I can't think about them right now.

She's still standing, but she's not. All of her weight is on me. All of it. The weight of her body and her secrets and her tears and her pain and her regret and her loss, and I feel like I'm going to break, too, because it's too much. I don't want to know any of this. Now I understand why she spent so much time running. I want to run away, too. I want to drop her and fling the door open and not look back, because I can't do this. I'm not strong enough, not brave enough, not comforting enough. I'm not enough. I'm no one's salvation. Not even my own.

But I'm here and so is she and I can't let go. Maybe I don't need to save her forever. Maybe I can just save her right now, in this moment, and if I can do that, maybe it will save me and maybe that can be enough. I tighten my arms as if I can still the shaking with that alone. The crying has turned silent. Her face is buried against my chest. I'm watching the light reflect off her hair on top of her head and I focus on that, because I can't look around and see all of those faces asking me for answers I don't have.

Gradually, she calms. Her breathing slows and her body settles into mine and it steadies. Then I feel her take her own weight back, for just a moment, before she pulls away from me.

I loosen my arms and let her go, but my eyes stay on her. Her face goes blank, the way it was the first time I saw her, and I see every emotion being put away. It's like watching a video of an explosion played backward, every piece of debris being sucked back into place, like nothing ever happened.

I'm afraid to look away. Afraid she'll fall apart again. Afraid she'll disappear. Afraid. I never should have left my garage. I never should have let her in it.

Then she sees the pile of notebooks on the table and everything about her goes still. Her eyes won't leave them. They are a question and an answer all at once.

"How?" her mother asks, finally. Confused. Betrayed. Relieved. "You didn't remember."

I look at the faces of the people who love her, who haven't heard her voice in nearly two years. No one expects a response. But they get one.

"I remember everything," she whispers, and it's a confession and a curse.

The only other noise in the room is the sharp intake of her mother's breath at the sound of Sunshine's voice.

"Since when?" her father asks.

She pulls her eyes away from the notebooks to face him when she answers.

"Since the day I stopped talking."

Somehow, everyone eventually sleeps, scattered across the house on beds and floors and sofas. I end up on the twin bed in Sunshine's room, with her body curled up against mine, and I don't care how small the bed is, because she will never be close enough.

No one made any attempt to stop me when I climbed in with her. I think they all knew they couldn't prevent it. There was nothing in this house or on this earth that was going to keep me from being next to her.

Drew is on a makeshift bed on the floor because I don't think he wanted to be far away from her, either.

I listen to her breathing; the soft intake of air reminding me that she's here, her body pressed against mine, the way we've slept so many nights that I've lost count.

Sometime during the night, her mother comes in and looks at us on the bed together. Her expression is one of acceptance, if not understanding.

I watch her through the light filtering in from the hallway and I know she can see that I'm awake.

"What did you call her?" she asks, but I don't think it's her real question.

"Sunshine," I say, and she smiles like she believes it's perfect, and she may be the only person other than me who would think so.

"What is she to you?" she whispers. The real question and I know the answer even if I don't know how to say it.

Drew's muffled voice rises up from the floor before I can respond.

"Family," he says.

And he's right.

Chapter 55

Emilia

My parents leave the next morning for the news conference, and Asher goes to school, even though they told him he could skip today.

I walk Drew to his car, and I think I could hug him forever.

"I'll miss my Nastypants," he tells me.

"There will never come a day when I won't be your Nastypants." I smile and let go. "Tell Tierney to give you another chance. If you screw up this time, I'll take you down myself."

And then he's gone; and it's just me and Josh Bennett and all of the unasked questions.

I hand him one of the notebooks because it's the only way he'll know, and he looks at it like it's a viper.

"I don't ever want to know what's in those books," he says, and he won't take it out of my hands.

I tell him that I don't want to know what's in them either. But I do know and I need him to know too. So he reads it and his face tenses along with every other muscle in his body, and I can tell he's trying not to cry. And when I show him the pictures, he shoves his fist against his mouth and I think he wants to hit something, but there's nothing here to hit. When he gets to the one of my hand, the one with the bones coming through the skin in so many places it's hard to believe they ever put it back together again, he does cry. And I don't blame him.

I show him videos of me playing the piano and photo albums full of pictures and introduce him to the me he never met; but we don't say very much.

"You were really good," he says, his voice faint as it breaks the silence.

"I was fucking amazing," I try to joke, but it just comes out sad.

"You still are," he responds with quiet conviction, piercing me with his eyes the way he does when he wants to make sure I'm listening. "Every way that matters."

The silence returns and we sit on the couch, photo albums on our laps, staring at the wasted piano in the corner.

"I wish I could have saved you," he says finally. And this is what it always comes back to. Salvation. Him saving me. Me saving him. Impossibilities, because there is no such thing, and it's not what we ever needed from each other anyway.

"That's stupid," I echo his words from my birthday. "Because it's an impossible wish." I pick up his hand and he laces his fingers through mine, holding on tighter than he needs to. "You couldn't have saved me," I tell him. "You didn't even know me."

"I would have liked to."

"Mrs. Leighton told me you needed to be saved, too. But I can't do that either," I confess, and he looks at me skeptically because I never did tell him about that conversation. "I don't want you to save me and I can't save you," I say, because I need him to hear me say it, but also because I need to hear me say it.

He closes the photo album and lays it down on the coffee table and cringes because I've found that's what he does every time he looks at that coffee table. And then he turns and puts his hands on either side of my face and kisses me with a reverence

I may never understand. And maybe I'm a liar and I do need it, because being kissed by Josh Bennett is kind of like being saved. It's a promise and a memory of the future and a book of better stories.

When he stops, I'm still here, and he's still looking at me like he can't believe I am, and I want to keep that look forever.

"Emilia," he says, and when he does, it warms me to my soul. "Every day you save me."

Chapter 56

Josh

I say goodbye to her in her driveway two days after I got here. Two days after I learned the truth. Two days after I got her back. Two days to wrap my mind around losing her again.

I was planning on leaving tomorrow, but I know I have to leave today.

We're both leaning against the side of my truck, looking at the ground like it holds the secrets of the universe. Her hand is in a fist and she's tracing circles again with her foot, and I hate it because it reminds me of things I don't want to think about.

She told her parents that she was considering coming back with me, and they didn't like it, but they know her well enough to realize that telling her not to wouldn't accomplish much. And yet that's what I'm planning to do.

I take both of her hands and pull her in front of me, because I want to face her when I say everything I have to say. And maybe it's a mistake, because when I look at her now, I think, for just one second, that God doesn't hate me so much after all. But then I look again and all I can see is the goodbye all around us and I need to touch her one more time. If there has to be a last time I kiss her, I want to know that it's the last time. I trace the line of the scar by her hair. I don't know who moves first, but her lips are on mine and my hands are in her hair and we kiss each other with the regret and desperation of so many days I can't count them. Her body is crushed against mine, and I hold her there so tightly it's as if I'm trying to absorb her through sheer force of will.

But I can't, and when we stop, I rest my forehead against hers and start to say goodbye.

I know that if I don't talk now, I may never talk, and I'll just stay here until tomorrow and let her convince herself to come with me. And I'll convince myself that it's okay.

"I'm leaving today," I tell her, and I wait.

"Do you want me to go with you?" she asks so softly it's like she doesn't want me to hear it.

"Yes." It's honest, even if it goes against everything I'm going to say to her next. "But you shouldn't."

She nods like she's thought about it, too, and she knows it's true. But, like me, I don't think she wants to admit it.

She made me look at those pictures and read those notebooks, and now I know everything that she knows. But I don't know how to help her. I don't understand how she lived with that in her head every day and still held onto any thread of sanity.

"You should stay here and try to, I don't know, get better. Get better sounds stupid." It does sound stupid, but I don't know what won't sound stupid. *Get well? Heal? Fix things?* It's like she has a broken leg. Or she's a handyman. And I'm a shit for thinking it, but there's a part of me that knows that when she does get well, heal, fix things, she may not want me anymore. She may be so changed that we won't even know each other, if we ever did. And when that goodbye comes, it won't be temporary.

If none of this had ever happened, she would be still be here in Brighton where she belongs—the beautiful, talented, unattainable girl. And I'm a bastard, because I know the truth of her now, but I don't know how to regret it. Because to regret it would mean to regret that I ever met her and I can't make myself do that.

Part of us has always known that we were together because we were damaged. We had that life experience bond that neither of us ever wanted. And maybe when she's not so damaged anymore, I won't be enough for her. Maybe she'll want someone whose life isn't as tragic as hers. And that won't be me.

When I think about it, I want to rewind and go back to where I just said yes and leave it there. Yes, come with me. We'll play house and bake cookies and build chairs and life will be perfect. But I've started now; I'm in this and I can finish it.

"I'm going to say this and it probably won't sound good or eloquent or whatever and I'm probably going to ramble, but just let me say it, okay? Will you listen?"

Her eyes are soft on me. Her lips just barely turn up.

"You've listened to every word I've ever said. Even the ones I didn't say. I'll listen to anything, Josh." It's like a razor that slices through whatever is left holding me, and I just go.

"Maybe one day you'll come back. Maybe you never will and that'll suck, but you can't keep doing this. The blame and the self-loathing and the bullshit. I can't watch that. It makes me hate you for hating yourself. I don't want to lose you. But I'd rather lose you if it means you'll be happy. I think if you come back with me today, you'll never be okay. And I'll never be okay if you aren't. I need to know that there's a way for people like us to end up okay. I need to know that there even is such a thing as okay, or maybe not just okay, maybe even good, and it's out there and we just haven't found it yet. There's got to be a happier ending than this here. There's got to be a better story. Because we deserve one. *You* deserve one. Even if it doesn't end with you coming back to me."

The last part chokes me. Steals my air and burns my eyes. I'm kicking myself when I say it. I tell myself to shut up and keep her. Grab her and kiss her and tell her everything will be okay because I'll make it okay, good, even. Tell her that there's absolutely nothing wrong with her. Lie to her with every pretty lie I have. But I can't do it. I've done goodbyes before, and I can do this one, too. Somehow this one hurts worse than the others, because this one I could prevent if I wanted to, since I'm the one saying it. This goodbye comes with a choice the way none of the others ever did. And as much as I'm telling her to stay here, as much as I know she needs to stay here, I still want her to choose to come with me. To say fuck sanity and healing and closure. To say that I am the only thing she needs to be well and whole and alive. But we both know that's not true. She's going to say goodbye to me today and I have to let her, and neither of us knows if she's ever going to come back.

I've been trying to leave for twenty minutes, but I can't figure out how to say goodbye. Even now, I know that all the words I've given her today haven't been enough, because I haven't said the one thing that needs to be said the most. And if I want to leave here without regrets, I need to know that there are no more unsaid words left to haunt me.

"Wait." I catch her as she walks away, taking her hand and turning it over in mine, tracing the scars like I've done so many times before. She looks up, searching my face. Studying. The way she did when we first met. Trying to work out what I'm thinking.

I don't know how to say it—after all this time, I'm not even sure that I can—but I have to break her last rule, because if she knows nothing else, I need her to know this one thing.

"I love you, Sunshine," I tell her, before I lose my nerve. "And I don't give a shit whether you want me to or not."

Chapter 57

Emilia

I never realized that grief and self-pity weren't the same thing. I thought grieving was what I was doing all this time I had been feeling sorry for myself, but it wasn't. So for the first time in nearly three years, I let myself grieve.

—

Josh let me go. Or maybe I let him go. I'm not sure it matters. He left the day after Drew. He told me he loved me, but he wouldn't let me say it back, because he didn't want to hear it if I was lost to him. Then he kissed the palm of my left hand and gave it back to me and he got in his truck and he left.

I think the goodbye was harder on him, because he's used to losing people who die, but he's not used to losing people who walk away, and that's what I was doing. I don't know how long I'm going to stay. I don't even know if I'm going to go back at all. All I know is that it's time.

It's time for a lot of things, even if I can't make them happen all at once. And I'd like to, because patience has never been my thing.

I crawl into my mother's arms in a silent apology because

I don't know the words that will ever be enough. And when I speak, I tell her what I know is true: that I hate myself, that I am so very not okay, that I am afraid I'll feel like this forever and I don't know what to do. And then I tell her to make the phone call. I'll go.

I go to therapy nearly every day in the beginning. And I talk. And I talk. And I talk. And then I talk some more. And then I cry. And when I'm done crying, my parents come, and then my brother, and we try to find a way to crawl out of this hole together.

We finally found a therapist for me who doesn't have a lot of patience, either, and has no tolerance for my crap. I kind of love her. Because let's face it, when it comes to therapy, I don't need a kindergarten teacher; I need a drill sergeant. She gives me homework, which I actually do, and if and when I leave, we have a schedule for phone and weekend appointments. I know there really isn't an end in sight for me with the therapy. At least not for a while.

I even tried the group thing again, but only once, because I still don't like it. I still don't feel better just for knowing that shitty things happen to other people, too, and so I don't do that again. And I don't feel bad about it.

Yesterday, I sat down at the piano, but I didn't touch the keys. I think I'd like to keep that coffin closed. I'd like to remember that the last piece of music I played was beautiful and perfect, even if it wasn't. I won't even try to act like it doesn't still kill me; my lying skills haven't improved enough for that. I mourn it every day, and I wonder if I'll ever stop.

The nightmares haven't come back, but I expect them every night. All the secrets and stories are spit out of my head now. Everyone knows everything, so I guess the memories have nothing to hold over me anymore. I still itch for the notebooks like a sleeping pill before bed every night, but they're gone now. My

father helped me build a fire in the fire pit in the backyard and
he and my mother and Asher and I all took turns throwing them
in until the smoke was burning our eyes and we could blame the
tears on it. I'll never forget the words, but I won't write them
down again either.

I don't have the camera my mother gave me here, but we use
hers, and we take more pictures than we will ever need and try to
make new memories. We spread the proofs out over the kitchen
table, and I show her my favorite one and she shows me hers and
we print them and start a new wall together.

Aidan Richter is being held, but none of the lawyers will let
me talk to him, even though he's confessed. And maybe there
really isn't anything left to say. I've learned a lot about the why
of Aidan Richter. About the why of what happened that day.
How he came home. How he found his brother's body. How
reality became so unbearable in that moment that his mind just
shattered. They say he had a psychotic break. I know that's the
defense, but I don't want to hear it. I don't want to get it. Because
I can't excuse it. I can't forgive it. I won't. But my hate will never
be as clearly defined again, either. Aidan Richter wasn't prepared
for the shit life threw at him any more than I was. He just broke
in a very different way. I feel like everything I've spent the past
three years believing isn't quite as true as I thought it was. Like
the glass I've been looking through is coated in the dust of my
own perception and I haven't seen what's real. Because before it
was black and white, evil and not. And that's the most confusing
part—figuring out what's true.

For the nearly two years since I remembered, I've had a picture of evil in my head and it had his face. I spent that time planning to hurt him and feeling justified, like it was owed to me.
But when I came back to Brighton for him, I wasn't sure I could
do it. So I sat in the dirt. Under the trees. In the place where he

beat me. And I waited. I waited for the words. I waited for the courage. I waited to decide. But I waited too long; and he took that from me too.

I never did see him again after that day in the gallery. I never did get to make him listen. I'll be allowed to speak at his sentencing, whenever that is. I haven't decided if I will. I know there are still things to say, but I don't know what they are anymore, and there are days when I miss the silence.

Sometimes I wonder what ever became of the real Russian girl who I was supposed to be that day. I wonder if she heard about what happened and if she knows what part she played in it simply by existing.

One afternoon Josh calls, and in the understatement of the century, I tell him that I'm tired of being angry.

"Then don't be," he says, as if this is the most logical thing in the world. And maybe it is.

"But if I'm not angry, then isn't it the same as saying it's okay? Doesn't it mean I'm condoning it?"

"No. It means you're accepting it." He takes a breath and exhales. "I'm not telling you that you shouldn't be pissed. You should be furious. You're entitled to every ounce of anger you have." He stops speaking for a moment, and when he starts again his voice is quiet, and I can hear the tension coiling around his words. "I hate him too. You have no idea how much I want to kill him for what he did to you and if I thought it would make any part of this easier for you I would do it. So don't think that I don't believe your hatred is justified. But you always want choices and you have one now and I'd rather you choose to be happy. And I know that that sounds stupid. Maybe it sounds like the most impossible thing in the world, but it's still what I want. He took the fucking piano, Sunshine. He didn't take everything.

Look at your left hand. It's probably clenched in a fist right now, isn't it?"

I don't need to look. It is. He knows it.

"Now open it up and let it go."

And I do.

—

I think about the day I died and about the story Josh's grandfather told and three days later I write a letter to Aidan Richter for whenever they let him read it.

My name is Emilia Ward.

I have a list of nevers I started when I was fifteen. I will never be the Brighton Piano Girl again. I will never carry a child. I will never walk down the street in the middle of the afternoon without wondering if someone is waiting to kill me. I will never get back the months of my life that I spent in rehabilitation and in and out of hospitals, instead of in recitals and in and out of school. I will never get back the years I spent hating every last person in the world, including myself. I will never not know the meaning of the word pain.

I understand pain. I understand rage. You gave me the gift of that understanding. You understand it, too. I spent the past three years despising the person who did this to me, the person who stole my life and took my identity. I learned to despise myself in the process. I spent the last three years fortifying my rage, while you spent the last three years healing yours.

I will never forget what you did to me. I will never forgive it. I will never stop mourning what you stole from me. But I realize now I can't steal it back and I'm done spending every day trying to. I will never stop hating you, but I don't need to hurt you anymore. I think I can believe in spite of you; or maybe I can believe because of you. If you can heal your life, then maybe I can, too.

I don't know how they're going to punish you. I'm not even sure if I care. You and I both know how much was destroyed that day and nothing they do to you will ever be enough to fix it. So maybe I can't believe in forgiveness yet but I think I can believe in hope and I would like to believe in the dream of second chances. For both of us.

—

Nothing is perfect. It's not even good yet. But maybe.

And after five weeks, I go home.

Chapter 58

Emilia

I haven't gotten better. I'm not even close to okay. The only thing I've done is to decide to get better. But I think that may just be enough.

I'm trying to see the magic in everyday miracles now: the fact that my heart still beats, that I can lift my feet off the earth to walk and that there is something in me worthy of love. I know that bad things still happen. And sometimes I still ask myself why I am alive; but now, when I ask, I have an answer.

—

I get back on a Sunday morning, and that evening I walk into dinner at the Leighton house, unexpected but always welcome. I can tell the music is Sarah's, and it makes me smile because I still hate it, but not her. Everyone is laughing and helping and sniping, and other than the fact that Tierney Lowell is setting the table, everything is the same.

Seeing Josh is my homecoming. I didn't tell him I was coming back. He doesn't say anything when he sees me, and neither do I, because the fact that I'm here is an answer. We just look at each other and speak in the silence like we always have and no one interrupts the conversation.

"Hi—" Mrs. Leighton says, her eyes wide, when I walk into the kitchen without a stitch of black on me, carrying the same chocolate cake I brought the first time I had dinner here.

"Emilia." I fill the pause, because everyone is still trying to figure out what to call me. Except maybe Josh, who's always known.

"Emilia," she says, and hugs me. "You have a beautiful voice."

And maybe some things aren't the same.

—

No one follows us out when we leave. Josh pushes the door open and walks behind me onto the porch. Both of our cars are here, and I hadn't planned to go back to his house—not yet, anyway. I'm not sure what he's thinking or even where we stand. I have no idea how much has changed for him in the weeks I've been gone. Nothing, something, everything. I need to ask but the words don't come, and I just keep walking. His footsteps are only a breath behind mine, but I don't turn around. I'm not ready to face this moment even though it is as inevitable as every moment in my life that's led up to it.

So many things have shifted since the day I left here. I just can't figure out exactly how. I feel like I'm starting all over again for what? The third time? The fourth? I can't possibly know. I only hope that whatever life I start today will finally be the right one.

I stop when we reach his truck, but Josh keeps walking past it to my car. He leans back against the driver's side door, obviously making no attempt to open it. He looks exactly the same. I've been staring at him for the past two hours but I've hardly said a word to him, and the ones I have said have been meaningless. My voice was too much of a novelty over dinner, and I spent the evening in nonstop conversation with everyone but Josh. He said very little but he never stopped looking. Watching. Waiting for me to disappear.

He shoves his keys into his pocket and I expect his hand to follow them there, but he reaches out for my hand instead and pulls me into him. I think he's going to kiss me, but he doesn't. He wraps his arms around me, pressing me against his chest until I'm not even sure there are two of us anymore. I breathe him in and I know without even feeling it that he's doing the same.

"You came back," he whispers into my hair, his voice a mixture of gratitude and disbelief. It isn't a question, so I say nothing because there's nothing that needs to be said.

And that's when it comes. The question I feel destined to hear for the rest of my life—

"Are you okay?"

Only this may be the first time I haven't minded it. Because I finally feel free to answer.

"No."

"Will you be?" He pulls back slightly, just enough so that he can see my face and we are so close in this moment that I hate the words between us.

I don't nod. I don't tell him I think so. For the first time since the day I left my house humming a Haydn sonata with the world at my feet, I feel certain of something. No, I'm not okay. Maybe not even a little. But I will be. I am certain of that.

"Yes," I say, and it's as if I'm saying a thousand yeses. Yes, I came back. Yes, I love you. Yes, I want you to love me. Yes, I will be okay. Maybe not today or tomorrow or next week. But yes, one day, I will wake up and I will be okay. Yes.

And then he kisses me. Tentatively at first, waiting for something, but there isn't any need. I would kiss him forever.

I will kiss him forever. I know it like I know my own name. His hands cradle my face, holding me there like he always has. And with every brush of his lips against mine, I know what he's giving me and what I'm giving him and what it will cost us both.

And, for once, I am not afraid.

The tears come from every part of me, but I don't stop them or put them away, and I don't stop kissing him either. They are his tears and I'm surrendering them to him, releasing with them the last of my regrets. The regrets I saved for him, over him, about him and everything we did wrong. The worst of all my regrets.

He stops when he tastes my tears. Just looking at me as if my face alone will tell him where they came from and what they mean. And maybe it will but I'm waiting for him to ask. Waiting to see the look of confusion or reticence in his eyes, but it never comes. Instead he wipes the last tear away with the back of his fingers.

"No black shit," he says.

And I smile.

—

"Answer me something," Josh says, a month after I've gotten back. I'm in the chair in his garage and I'm doing homework, not woodworking, because I may never catch up. I could go inside and study in the air-conditioning, but I love this place. And being out here, breathing sawdust in Josh Bennett's garage with him, is worth any amount of sweat.

"I've answered everything, Josh. I don't think there are any questions left to ask."

"Just one," he says, laying down a screwdriver and coming over to lean against the workbench, opposite me. He pushes his boots out far enough so that they just touch mine.

I close the book and try not to smile at him, because I know what's coming. It's the question I've been waiting for him to ask since the day I got lost and ended up at his house in the middle of the night, before he even knew what the question was.

"What did you see when you died?" He has that tentative half smile, like he's almost embarrassed by what he's saying. "Because I'm guessing it wasn't the Sea of Tranquility."

And when I look at him, I'm not so sure it wasn't.

"Where did you go?" His voice drops just slightly, and he loses even the suggestion of a smile.

He's watching me like he's not sure he's allowed to ask the question, and he's not even sure he wants the answer. I can almost see his grandfather's words and Josh's doubts about them swimming in his head. On every side of me are the lights and the tools and the wood and the boots and the boy I want to see forever. And if my Sea of Tranquility were real, it would be this place, here, with him.

I don't say anything right away, because I just want one minute to look at his face before I give him my last secret.

And then I tell him.

"Your garage."

Acknowledgments

Thank you to God above all.

There aren't words to express the gratitude I owe to the two people who made the biggest sacrifice in the writing of this book—my two amazing girls. You make me smile every day and you are now and forever the greatest accomplishments of my life. Thank you for giving me time to live in my head for a while, even if it meant not enough playing and too much frozen food. I promise I don't love Josh Bennett more than you.

Thank you to my mother for the guilt trips, phone therapy, free babysitting, allowing me to live through adolescence, and for always being a friend. I love you. And thank you to my sisters. Just because.

Thank you to my in-laws for giving me a week that turned into thousands of words and a boy who turned into an incredible man.

Thank you to Carrie Bennefield, media specialist and beta reader extraordinaire, for all of your feedback and enthusiasm. And, most importantly, for not having me arrested for stalking you.

To Fred LeBaron, who has been a cheerleader for me since the first tweet I sent him—thank you for the advice, email heart-to-hearts, and not mocking me when you had to tell me how to find a Facebook message. I mean it when I say that everyone should be as awesome as you. Thank you, Jennifer Roberts-Hall and Kelly Moorhouse. Every author should be so lucky to have people like you championing their book. You have truly become friends.

Thank you to my agent, Emmanuelle Morgen, for all of your understanding, patience, and hard work, and to my editor, Amy Tannenbaum, whose enthusiasm for *TSoT* has been unfailing from the start. You are both wonderful.

Thank you so much to Judith Curr for believing in *The Sea of Tranquility* and the rest of the team at Atria: Hillary Tisman, Valerie Vennix, Taylor Dietrich, Nancy Singer, Jeanne Lee, Julia Scribner, and Isolde Sauer who have worked tirelessly behind the scenes to get this book into readers' hands.

I also want to take a moment to acknowledge the book bloggers who take the time to read and respectfully review books every day. The honest, thoughtful feedback you give is priceless. I owe a debt of gratitude to those who read this book very early on and helped it find an audience—Maryse; Aestas Book Blog; Mollie Kay Harper of Tough Critic Book Reviews; Reading, Eating & Dreaming; Lisa's Book Review, and any others I may have missed. Thank you, sincerely.

And an even bigger thank-you goes out to the readers who discovered *The Sea of Tranquility* and made it their mission to make sure others discovered it, too. I am and always will be humbled by your love for this book.

And lastly, only because every day begins and ends with him, thank you to my husband, Peter, the boy I've loved since I was seventeen. I will never forget what first love is like, because I married mine.

Life is short and TBR lists are long. I know that time is precious, and I thank you for spending yours with this book.

—*Katja*

The
Sea
of
Tranquility

KATJA MILLAY

A Readers Club Guide

Questions for Discussion

1. Various clues are presented to point to the fact that Nastya Kashnikov is not Emilia's real name. What are those clues? Did you pick up on them as you were reading?

2. At the beginning of the novel, Nastya has chosen to return to school. Considering how antisocial she is, why do you think she makes this choice?

3. As the book progresses, we learn how the injuries to Nastya's hand result in the loss of her ability to play the piano. In what ways does this loss affect her? In what other ways do the injuries to her hand affect her?

4. The themes of art and creation come up in many ways throughout the novel. Which characters are artistic? What role do you think that ability plays in the formation of their identities?

5. At one point Nastya says that she does not want to be dead, she just feels like she should be. Why do you think she feels that way? Do you think her feelings are valid?

6. Nastya explains that she doesn't dress the way she does because she particularly likes it. Why does she dress this way? What does she hope to accomplish? Is she successful? How do you feel about her decision?

7. Nastya is drawn to Drew from the moment they meet. Why do you think this is? How would you describe their friendship? Did you ever suspect that their relationship might turn into something more?

8. What does the Sea of Tranquility represent in the story? Does it have more than one meaning? How does it tie-in to Nastya's obsession with names?

9. At seventeen years old, Josh has lost every member of his family. How does he cope with those losses and his resulting grief? Do you think his response is natural? How do you think you would react under similar circumstances? Have you known anyone who has experienced this level of loss? If so, how was their reaction similar or different?

10. How did the alternating viewpoints enhance your understanding of the characters? How do you think the story would have been affected if told from only one point of view?

11. Nastya never explains when or why she began collecting names. When do you think she began? Why do you believe she started this hobby? Do you think she continues it beyond the close of the book? Do you believe that names have deeper meaning?

12. What are the driving forces behind Nastya's compulsive need to run? She explains that one of her therapists referred to it as a "healthy outlet." Do you believe it is?

13. Toward the end of the novel Nastya discovers that Josh has slept with Leigh. Why do you think he made that choice? Did it change how you felt about him? Was Nastya's reaction to that discovery what you would have expected? How do you think you would have reacted?

14. Why did Nastya feel the need to stop talking? Do you feel her choice was justified? Do you think you would be able to remain silent for more than a year knowing that you were physically able to speak?

15. How did the attack on Nastya affect her relationship with each of her family members?

16. Neither Josh nor Nastya wants a relationship with the other, but they each have very different reasons for feeling this way. What are those reasons? Do you believe they are valid?

17. Nastya writes the details of her attack in a series of notebooks every night before bed. What purpose does this serve for her? Was it effective?

18. Nastya forms relationships with three boys over the course of the novel. How do her friendships with Clay, Drew, and Josh vary? What purpose does each serve in her life?

19. What does Nastya mean when she tells Josh she's "ruined?" Why does she believe this about herself? Does her statement have multiple meanings? If so, what are they? Do you agree with her assessment?

20. Why does Nastya choose to cover up what transpired with Kevin Leonard at his party? Do you think her choice and her reaction to the situation fit her character? Did you agree with her decision? What would you have done?

21. Aidan Richter turns himself in after his confrontation with Nastya at the gallery. What do think drove him to do that? Do you think Nastya regrets not attacking him and getting her revenge when she had the chance? Do you think she forgives him? How did you feel when she saw his painting of her hand?

22. "The dream of second chances" becomes a recurring theme throughout the novel. Which characters receive a second chance, and in what way? Do you believe Aidan Richter gets a second chance? Does he deserve one?

23. Before the details of Nastya's attack are revealed, what did you believe had happened to her? What was your reaction when you learned what had actually occurred? Did your feelings toward her character change once you learned the truth? If yes, how so?

24. Nastya and Josh have life histories that result in them both seeming wise beyond their years. Yet in some ways they are still naïve and inexperienced. In what ways does each seem older than an average seventeen-year-old? In what ways does each seem younger?

25. In contrast, Drew has grown up somewhat sheltered. How do you think that affects the maturity of his choices and reactions?

26. The story leaves off with Josh and Nastya in his garage together. What do you think happens next? What does the future hold for them?

About the Author

Katja Millay grew up in Florida and graduated with a degree in film and television production from the Tisch School of the Arts at New York University. She has worked as a television producer and a film studies and screenwriting teacher. Currently she resides in Florida with her family. *The Sea of Tranquility* is her first book.

To learn more about
Katja Millay, visit her at:

Facebook

http://www.facebook.com/KatjaMillayAuthor

Twitter

@KatjaMillay

Goodreads

http://www.goodreads.com/katjamillay

Atria Books/Simon & Schuster Author Page

http://authors.simonandschuster.com/Katja-Millay/
410273682

THE VIKING CRITICAL LIBRARY

THE GRAPES OF WRATH

Text and Criticism

Born in Salinas, California, in 1902, JOHN STEINBECK grew up in a fertile agricultural valley about twenty-five miles from the Pacific Coast—and both valley and coast would serve as settings for some of his best fiction. In 1919, he went to Stanford University, where he intermittently enrolled in literature and writing courses until he left in 1925 without taking a degree. During the next five years, he supported himself as a laborer and journalist in New York City and then as a caretaker for a Lake Tahoe estate, all the time working on his first novel, *Cup of Gold* (1929). After marriage and a move to Pacific Grove, he published two California fictions, *The Pastures of Heaven* (1932) and *To a God Unknown* (1933), and worked on short stories later collected in *The Long Valley* (1938). Popular success and financial security came only with *Tortilla Flat* (1935), stories about Monterey's paisanos. A ceaseless experimenter throughout his career, Steinbeck changed courses regularly. Three powerful novels of the late 1930s focused on the California laboring class: *In Dubious Battle* (1936), *Of Mice and Men* (1937), and the book considered by many his finest, *The Grapes of Wrath* (1939). Early in the 1940s, Steinbeck became a filmmaker with *The Forgotten Village* (1941) and a serious student of marine biology with *Sea of Cortez* (1941). He devoted his services to the war, writing *Bombs Away* (1942) and the controversial play-novelette *The Moon Is Down* (1942). *Cannery Row* (1945), *The Wayward Bus* (1947), *The Pearl* (1947), *A Russian Journal* (1948), another experimental drama, *Burning Bright* (1950), and *The Log from the Sea of Cortez* (1951) preceded publication of the monumental *East of Eden* (1952), an ambitious saga of the Salinas Valley and his own family's history. The last decades of his life were spent in New York City and Sag Harbor with his third wife, with whom he traveled widely. Later books include *Sweet Thursday* (1954), *The Short Reign of Pippin IV: A Fabrication* (1957), *Once There Was a War* (1958), *The Winter of Our Discontent* (1961), *Travels with Charley in Search of America* (1962), *America and Americans* (1966), and the posthumously published *Journal of a Novel: The East of Eden Letters* (1969), *Viva Zapata!* (1975), *The Acts of King Arthur and His Noble Knights* (1976), and *Working*

Days: The Journals of The Grapes of Wrath (1989). He died in 1968, having won a Nobel Prize in 1962.

PETER LISCA has taught modern American literature at the University of North Carolina (Greensboro), the University of Washington, the University of Florida, and, as Fulbright professor, universities in Spain, Poland, Romania, and Argentina. He is the author of *The Wide World of John Steinbeck* and *John Steinbeck: Nature and Myth,* as well as numerous articles on Steinbeck and other authors.

KEVIN HEARLE has taught at California State University at Los Angeles, San Jose State University, the University of California at Santa Cruz, and Coe College. He is a founding member of the editorial board of *The Steinbeck Newsletter,* and the author of *Each Thing We Know Is Changed Because We Know It, And Other Poems.* His work has appeared in the volume *After* The Grapes of Wrath, and in *Steinbeck Quarterly, Yale Review, Western American Literature, Quarry West,* and *American Literature.*

JOHN STEINBECK

The Grapes
of Wrath

TEXT AND CRITICISM

EDITED BY Peter Lisca

UPDATED WITH Kevin Hearle

PENGUIN BOOKS

PENGUIN BOOKS
Published by the Penguin Group
Penguin Group (USA) Inc., 375 Hudson Street, New York, New York 10014, U.S.A.
Penguin Group (Canada), 90 Eglinton Avenue East, Suite 700, Toronto,
Ontario, Canada M4P 2Y3 (a division of Pearson Penguin Canada Inc.)
Penguin Books Ltd, 80 Strand, London WC2R 0RL, England
Penguin Ireland, 25 St Stephen's Green, Dublin 2, Ireland (a division of Penguin Books Ltd)
Penguin Group (Australia), 250 Camberwell Road, Camberwell,
Victoria 3124, Australia (a division of Pearson Australia Group Pty Ltd)
Penguin Books India Pvt Ltd, 11 Community Centre, Panchsheel Park, New Delhi – 110 017, India
Penguin Group (NZ), cnr Airborne and Rosedale Roads,
Albany, Auckland 1310, New Zealand (a division of Pearson New Zealand Ltd)
Penguin Books (South Africa) (Pty) Ltd, 24 Sturdee Avenue,
Rosebank, Johannesburg 2196, South Africa

Penguin Books Ltd, Registered Offices: 80 Strand, London WC2R 0RL, England

The Grapes of Wrath first published in the United States of America
by The Viking Press 1939
The Viking Critical Library *The Grapes of Wrath* published
by The Viking Press 1972
Published in Penguin Books 1977
This updated edition published in Penguin Books 1997

30 29 28 27 26 25 24 23 22 21

Copyright John Steinbeck, 1939
Copyright renewed John Steinbeck, 1967
Copyright © The Viking Press, Inc., 1972
Copyright © Kevin Hearle, 1997
All rights reserved

LIBRARY OF CONGRESS CATALOGING-IN-PUBLICATION DATA
Steinbeck, John, 1902–1968.
The grapes of wrath: text and criticism/John Steinbeck; edited by
Peter Lisca.—2nd ed. / updated with Kevin Hearle.
p.   cm. — (Viking critical library)
ISBN 0 14 02.4775 0 (pbk.)
1. Migrant agricultural laborers—California—Fiction. 2. Labor
camps—California—Fiction. 3. Steinbeck, John, 1902–1968. Grapes
of wrath. 4. Migrant agricultural laborers in literature. 5. Labor
camps in literature. 6. California—In literature. I. Lisca,
Peter. II. Hearle, Kevin, 1958–   . III. Title. IV. Series.
PS3537.T3234G8 1996
813'.52—dc20   96-137

Printed in the United States of America
Set in Electra

Contents

IV. CRITICISM

Editor's Preface to the Second Edition

Very few of those who read *The Grapes of Wrath* in 1939 could have
foreseen that this book, which dramatized the headlines and news-
reels of the day, which seemed so intimately connected with them
that its merits were debated not in literary terms but in those of
sociological research and political ideology, would continue to be
read long after the headlines had been forgotten. True, its depiction
of "the establishment" on one side and the dispossessed or victimized on the other has continued to find parallels down to the present
time. But if that were all it had to offer, *The Grapes of Wrath* would
be forgotten along with the headlines and the dozens of other "proletarian" novels of the 1930s. What distinguishes this one novel is
not only its greater authenticity of detail but also the genius of its
author, who, avoiding mere propaganda, was able to raise those details and themes to the level of lasting art while muting none of the
passionate human cry against injustice. Anyone who has used *The
Grapes of Wrath* in a classroom can testify to its viability, and this
second Viking Critical Library edition of the novel together with
historical and critical materials enriches our appreciation of its greatness. In fact, the response of students today leaves no doubt that as
literature, *The Grapes of Wrath* is experienced more completely now
than it was in 1939, when it was difficult to dissociate novel from
political tract, and to see Steinbeck's bold technical experiments as
something more than what one noted critic called "calculated
crudities."

Like all true works of art, *The Grapes of Wrath* reaches into universal human experience and hence is capable of communicating
across a chasm of ignorance about details of the intellectual and

social milieu from which it sprang. Once again, however, like all true art, it gains in stature when understood in relation to that milieu. Thus the study materials begin with two essays expressing various points of view about the conditions depicted in the novel, and they continue with another essay that samples reactions to the novel in Oklahoma, the state from which the Joads were uprooted. Together these essays comprise "The Social Context."

The second section of study materials—"The Creative Context"—consists of two essays, by major Steinbeck scholars, which set out the actual conditions under which the novel was conceived and written, and a letter by John Steinbeck himself, setting forth his intentions in writing the novel.

The third section of study materials—"Criticism"—presents a selection of essays on *The Grapes of Wrath*. Obviously, space does not allow the inclusion of many others perhaps equally worthwhile. The aim has been to offer the reader, in chronological order, some essays representing what these editors believe to be the more illuminating or provocative examinations of the novel right down to the most recent approaches. Regrettably, two or three excellent essays have not been included only because their length would prevent us representing the wider variety of writing about *The Grapes of Wrath*. The editors' introduction to this section presents a history of critical reactions to the novel, highlighting the major trends, with sufficient particulars to guide the reader further in some direction he might wish to pursue.

Additional material of interest includes maps of the route followed by the Joads, a Steinbeck chronology, topics for discussion and papers, and a selected bibliography for further study. The present text of the novel itself is that of the 1996 Library of America edition, which uses the first printing of the first edition of *The Grapes of Wrath*, corrected with reference to the original manuscript, typescript, and galleys. Those corrections are described in "A Note on the Text," which follows on page xix. All page references to *The Grapes of Wrath* in the essays printed here have been adjusted to the present text.

For assistance in the preparation of this second edition, I am very much indebted to Kevin Hearle.

To Robert DeMott, eminent Steinbeck scholar and friend, I am most deeply grateful for his early encouragement in this project, and his generous, sound advice. To Bett Adams, who, as my graduate assistant, helped me prepare the first edition and worked out the map of the Joads' journey retained here, I am still thankful. For her editorial labors on my behalf at Penguin Books, I thank Kristine Puopolo.

Impossible to specify for heartfelt thanks are those many Steinbeck scholars whom I have been privileged to know personally, and those many known to me only through their publications—from whom I have learned so much.

PETER LISCA

Chronology

1902   John Ernst Steinbeck born on February 27 in Salinas, California. His father, John Ernst, Sr., was a miller and was treasurer of Monterey County; his mother was formerly a schoolteacher. He was the third of four children, and the only son. Grew up in a semirural environment.

1919   Graduated from Salinas High School, a good student and athlete. Enrolled at Stanford University, but attended sporadically, dropping out to work on ranches, farms, and road-building gangs.

1924   Published two stories in *The Stanford Spectator*, "Fingers of Cloud" and "Adventures in Arcademy."

1925   Left Stanford without taking a degree. Went to New York, where he worked briefly as a reporter for the *American* and later as a laborer. Wrote short stories, but could find no publisher.

1926   Returned to California and continued to write, supporting himself by a variety of jobs, including caretaker of an isolated lodge near Lake Tahoe.

1929   Published first novel, *Cup of Gold*, a highly fictionalized biography of Henry Morgan, the buccaneer.

1930   Married Carol Henning and took up residence in a family cottage at Pacific Grove; continued to write, living mostly on a $25-a-month allowance from his father. Met Edward F.

Ricketts, commercial marine biologist, who became his close, influential friend and served as model for several of Steinbeck's characters.

1932   Moved to Los Angeles. Published *The Pastures of Heaven*.

1933   Returned to Pacific Grove. Published *To a God Unknown* and the first two parts of *The Red Pony*.

1934   "The Murder" chosen as an O. Henry Prize Story. His mother, Olive Hamilton Steinbeck, died.

1935   His father died. Published *Tortilla Flat* and was awarded the Commonwealth Club of California Gold Medal; realized his first financial success as author.

1936   Published *In Dubious Battle* and a series of articles on migrants ("The Harvest Gypsies") in *San Francisco News*. Traveled in Mexico.

1937   Published *Of Mice and Men*, the first of several of his novels to be chosen by the Book-of-the-Month Club. Also published *The Red Pony* (in three parts). Traveled in Europe. The play *Of Mice and Men* was produced in November and won the Drama Critics Circle Award for that season. Joined by Tom Collins, he traveled with Dust Bowl refugees between various migrant camps in California.

1938   Published *The Long Valley*, a collection of his short stories, and *Their Blood Is Strong*, a reprint of the migrant articles with a postscript.

1939   Published *The Grapes of Wrath*. Elected to the National Institute of Arts and Letters.

1940   Awarded the Pulitzer Prize for *The Grapes of Wrath*. Cruised the Gulf of California with Ricketts, collecting marine invertebrates. Wrote and helped film *The Forgotten Village*, a documentary, in Mexico. Received Social Work Today Award and American Booksellers Association Award.

1941   Published *Sea of Cortez*, with Ricketts, based on materials gathered in the Gulf of California.

1942 Published *The Moon Is Down* (also produced as a play) and *Bombs Away,* a documentary designed to encourage enlistments in the Army Air Corps. Divorced from Carol Henning.

1943 Married Gwyndolyn Conger, began residence in New York. Served as European war zone correspondent for the New York *Herald Tribune.*

1944 Wrote film story (unpublished) for *Lifeboat,* 20th Century–Fox. Thom, his first son, was born.

1945 Published *Cannery Row;* published *The Red Pony,* including a fourth part—"The Leader of the People"; published "The Pearl of the World" (same as *The Pearl*) in *Woman's Home Companion.* Wrote film story for *A Medal for Benny,* Paramount.

1946 Awarded the King Haakon (Norway) Liberty Cross for *The Moon Is Down.* Second son, John IV, was born.

1947 Published *The Pearl* and *The Wayward Bus.* Traveled in Russia with the photographer Robert Capa.

1948 Published *A Russian Journal,* with Robert Capa. Elected to American Academy of Arts and Letters. Edward Ricketts died. Divorced from Gwyndolyn Conger.

1950 Published *Burning Bright,* later produced as a play. Wrote film story for *Viva Zapata!* for 20th Century–Fox. Married Elaine Scott.

1951 Published *The Log from the* Sea of Cortez, containing the narrative portion from *Sea of Cortez* and a tribute to his deceased friend—"About Ed Ricketts."

1952 Published *East of Eden.* Traveled in Europe, sending reports to *Collier's.*

1954 Published *Sweet Thursday.*

1955 *Pipe Dream* (from *Sweet Thursday*) produced, a musical comedy by Rodgers and Hammerstein.

1956 "The Affair at 7, Rue de M——" chosen as an O. Henry Prize Story.

1957 Published *The Short Reign of Pippin IV*.

1958 Published *Once There Was a War*, a collection of his war dispatches.

1961 Published *The Winter of Our Discontent*, his last novel.

1962 Published *Travels with Charley*. Awarded the Nobel Prize for Literature.

1964 Appointed as a trustee of the John F. Kennedy Memorial Library. Awarded a Press Medal of Freedom and a United States Medal of Freedom.

1965– From November through April traveled in Europe and the
1966 Middle East, reporting his travels in "Letters to Alicia" (*Newsday*).

1966 Published *America and Americans*.

1966– From December through May reported from Vietnam on the
1967 American involvement, continuing his "Letters to Alicia."

1968 Suffered from coronary disease and died of a severe attack in New York City on December 20.

1969 *Journal of a Novel: The* East of Eden *Letters* published posthumously.

1975 *Steinbeck: A Life in Letters* published posthumously.

1976 *The Acts of King Arthur and His Nobel Knights* published posthumously.

1989 *Working Days: The Journals of* The Grapes of Wrath published posthumously.

1993 *Zapata* published posthumously.

A Note on the Text

The text used in this revised Viking Critical Library edition of *The Grapes of Wrath* differs from the text used in the first edition of the VCL. The present text follows the Library of America edition of *The Grapes of Wrath* (published in *The Grapes of Wrath and Other Writings*, 1996), which uses the first printing of the first edition of *The Grapes of Wrath*, corrected with reference to the original manuscript, typescript, and galleys. It corrects errors made by John Steinbeck's wife Carol in typing Steinbeck's manuscript, such as the accidental omission of whole lines and the misreading or mistyping of some words. In addition, the original wording has been restored at places where the Viking staff had thought it would be found objectionable and softened it. Typographical errors have also been corrected.

The lists below record, by page and line number, these corrections. The first list reports the transcription errors that have been corrected; the second list reports the places where censored passages have been restored. In each item, the reading of the present text comes first, followed by that of the first edition. The third list reports typographical errors made in the first printing that have been corrected.

Transcription errors in *The Grapes of Wrath*. 28.6–8, man . . . How] man. How 34.26, enslaved] ensnared 46.25, three] the 48.13, child] child's 48.19, Tommy?" . . . "Two] Tommy?" ¶ "Two 49.2, house . . . an'] house, an' 50.6, a couple-three] couple-three 50.34, han'] hand 51.17, went. Brought . . . wasn't] went. They wasn't

51.38, own words] words 53.20, said . . . Salt,] said. Salt, 53.31, wher-
ever] where 54.19, Casy . . . You're] Casy. "You're 55.22, preacher]
preachin' 55.29, knife . . . and] knife and 56.22, wasn't] was 59.27,
"You'd be] "You're 67.23, even give] give 69.11, come an'] come and
70.29, killer.' In . . . 'You] killer.' You 83.26, An' there . . . An' that]
An' that 97.9, film] flour 103.1, an'] and 107.39, go." . . . "Hardly]
go. Hardly 112.21–22, spareribs . . . wasn't] spareribs. ¶ "I wasn't
117.24, That] The 125.26, git] get 126.36, loose . . . "Need] loose.
"Need 131.37, "I—I] "I 142.26, really truly] really 144.22–24, jar . . .
screwed] jar and Tom screwed 147.12–14, He . . . An'] An' 147.16–
17, cried. "Why no!" ¶ "Oh] cried. ¶ "Why, no. Oh 148.12, 'em] cars
150.19, barely] hardly 156.9, from . . . mouth] from the mouth
156.38, know . . . syphilis] know—she has syphilis 164.5, They] Then
168.10, it . . . got] it. We got 168.19, idear] idea 168.25, you'll all]
you'll 169.14, s'pose] suppose 172.40, "Ready] "Reach 174.39,
comin'] gonna come 175.6, kinda folks] kinda fences 181.33, black
patches] patches 182.22, dusk] dark 190.32, An' he'll . . . look] An'
he'll look 191.26, fellas] folks 193.1, fust] first 194.2, then] they 198.5,
as a] as—as a 224.22, I . . . you] I can't tell you. I can't tell you
231.10, ferociously] frantically 238.24, through . . . holdings] through
their holdings 240.15, side] sides 241.39, moved cautiously] moved
244.31, kid] kids 248.1, wanta] want ta 252.35, wanta] want ta
253.19–20, was a-braggin' . . . High] was a braggin'. High 253.21,
says] say 256.34, wanta] want ta 265.14, wanta] want ta 266.6–11,
moment . . . "I] moment. "O.K.," he said. "I 267.27, gonna] goin' to
273.4, wanta] want ta 273.7, shush?] shh? 280.26, wanta] want ta
282.9, farmed] formed 292.13–15, rent." . . . hell!"] rent." ¶ "Rent,
hell!" 293.34, sheds] shade trees 294.34, wage] rate 309.6, play . . .
She] play." She 311.8, An'—did them] An'—them 313.25, roofed]
unroofed 315.19, Four been] Four 316.14, No,"] Nor," 322.12, on] of
322.31, But] But now 323.38, go] to 326.12, spoiled him . . . somepin]
spoiled somepin 326.31, if . . . rich] if I was rich, if I was rich 327.24,
back . . . A girl] back—a girl 352.16, woman you're] woman, you're
352.25–27, beat . . . He's] beat. He's 353.4, joke fell from] job fell on
358.8, "Gits] "Gets 359.31, unit.] units. 370.17, wanta] want ta
373.29, waved] moved 379.30, path] patch 384.28, ain't doin'] didn't
do 412.25, over an'] over 417.37, playin' it] playin' 421.4, wage] rate
426.33–36, Sharon. "You shouldn't . . . "You got] Sharon. She said,
"You got 434.12, night] night the 439.1, gonna] goin' to 439.19, outa]
inta 444.34–36, "Shucks!" . . . yawned.] "Shucks!" Ruthie yawned.

Censored passages in *The Grapes of Wrath*: 25.24, you . . . wasn't] you. They wasn't 25.27, out . . . 'em."] out in the grass." 38.33–34, no skin . . . ass.] nothing. 60.31, shit] crap 81.15, fuck] mess 85.35, fuckin'] messin' 121.29, Horseshit!] Baloney! 122.3, fuck] jump 156.33, Joan Crawford] So-and-So 180.25, shit] crap 187.20, shit] talk 191.14, fucked] fooled 195.19, shit] foul 207.27, ass] tail 226.18, up his ass] in his ear 238.27, fat-assed deputy] deputy 272.34, balls] overhalls 280.28, fat-ass deputies] deputies 287.29, fat-ass cops] cops 344.13, their ass] 'em.

The following is a list of typographical errors corrected, cited by page and line number: 19.18–19, forty-year old; 40.6, It; 61.16, said,; 62.18, Casey; 64.14, Start' em; 72.4, wouldn't; 72.9, couldn't; 75.30, a'plenty; 77.8, goin' without; 78.23, a' they; 82.23, Don't; 131.24, look; 138.7, mattresses; 141.1, hundred; 176.15, don't; 178.8, idea; 179.10, eyes; 190.36, "When; 198.16, go; 242.33, here here; 255.25, don't; 259.16, 'em; 266.36, Mike. is; 271.8, thinkin'.'; 271.17, out?'; 274.14, Tom,; 274.36, "Thank; 291.16, want to; 309.24, An; 310.15, it."; 315.18, tol',; 319.32, don't; 320.26, child; 328.33, don't; 357.9, Willy; 371.20, "O.K."; 377.11, jes'; 391.12, Don't . . . Don't; 391.38, sin now.; 392.9, on'; 401.29, headlight; 404.9, work, I; 404.29–30, Don' let; 425.20, matches,; 435.5, on the nose; 439.33, about him; 445.32, 'an; 450.26, where'; 450.33, don't.

I

THE GRAPES OF WRATH:
The Text

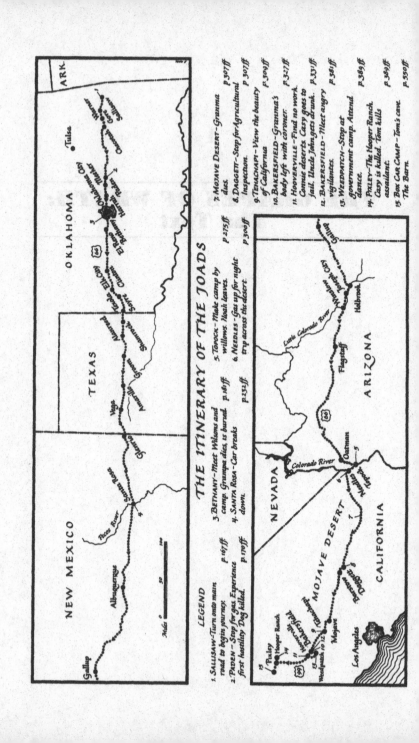

THE ITINERARY OF THE JOADS

LEGEND

1. SALLISAW—Turn onto main road to begin journey.
2. PADEN—Stop for gas. Experience first hostility. Dog killed.   p.167ff p.179ff
3. BETHANY—Meet Wilsons and camp. Grampa dies, is buried.   p.187ff
4. SANTA ROSA—Car breaks down.   p.232ff
5. TOPOCK—Make camp by willows. Noah leaves.   p.275ff
6. NEEDLES—Gas up for night trip across the desert.   p.305ff
7. MOJAVE DESERT—Gramma dies.   p.307ff
8. DAGGETT—Stop for Agricultural Inspection.   p.307ff
9. TEHACHAPI—View the beauty of California.   p.309ff
10. BAKERSFIELD—Gramma's body left with coroner.   p.3:17ff
11. HOOVERVILLE—Find no work. Connie deserts Casy goes to jail. Uncle John gets drunk.   p.331ff
12. BAKERSFIELD—Meet angry vigilantes.   p.361ff
13. WEEDPATCH—Stop at government camp. Attend dance.
14. PIXLEY—The Hooper Ranch. Casy is killed. Tom kills assailant.   p.389ff
15. BOX CAR CAMP—Tom's cave. The Barn.   p.389ff   p.550ff

CHAPTER 1

To the red country and part of the gray country of Oklahoma, the last rains came gently, and they did not cut the scarred earth. The plows crossed and recrossed the rivulet marks. The last rains lifted the corn quickly and scattered weed colonies and grass along the sides of the roads so that the gray country and the dark red country began to disappear under a green cover. In the last part of May the sky grew pale and the clouds that had hung in high puffs for so long in the spring were dissipated. The sun flared down on the growing corn day after day until a line of brown spread along the edge of each green bayonet. The clouds appeared, and went away, and in a while they did not try any more. The weeds grew darker green to protect themselves, and they did not spread any more. The surface of the earth crusted, a thin hard crust, and as the sky became pale, so the earth became pale, pink in the red country and white in the gray country.

In the water-cut gullies the earth dusted down in dry little streams. Gophers and ant lions started small avalanches. And as the sharp sun struck day after day, the leaves of the young corn became less stiff and erect; they bent in a curve at first, and then, as the central ribs of strength grew weak, each leaf tilted downward. Then it was June, and the sun shone more fiercely. The brown lines on the corn leaves widened and moved in on the central ribs. The weeds frayed and edged back toward their roots. The air was thin and the sky more pale; and every day the earth paled.

In the roads where the teams moved, where the wheels milled the ground and the hooves of the horses beat the ground, the dirt crust broke and the dust formed. Every moving thing lifted the dust into the air: a walking man lifted a thin layer as high as his waist, and a wagon lifted the dust as high as the fence tops, and an automobile boiled a cloud behind it. The dust was long in settling back again.

When June was half gone, the big clouds moved up out of Texas and the Gulf, high heavy clouds, rain-heads. The men in the fields looked up at the clouds and sniffed at them and held wet fingers up to sense the wind. And the horses were nervous while the clouds were up. The rain-heads dropped a little spattering and hurried on to some other country. Behind them the sky was pale again and the sun flared. In the dust there were drop craters where the rain had fallen, and there were clean splashes on the corn, and that was all.

A gentle wind followed the rain clouds, driving them on northward, a wind that softly clashed the drying corn. A day went by and the wind increased, steady, unbroken by gusts. The dust from the roads fluffed up and spread out and fell on the weeds beside the fields, and fell into the fields a little way. Now the wind grew strong and hard and it worked at the rain crust in the corn fields. Little by little the sky was darkened by the mixing dust, and the wind felt over the earth, loosened the dust, and carried it away. The wind grew stronger. The rain crust broke and the dust lifted up out of the fields and drove gray plumes into the air like sluggish smoke. The corn threshed the wind and made a dry, rushing sound. The finest dust did not settle back to earth now, but disappeared into the darkening sky.

The wind grew stronger, whisked under stones, carried up straws and old leaves, and even little clods, marking its course as it sailed across the fields. The air and the sky darkened and through them the sun shone redly, and there was a raw sting in the air. During a night the wind raced faster over the land, dug cunningly among the rootlets of the corn, and the corn fought the wind with its weakened leaves until the roots were freed by the prying wind and then each stalk settled wearily sideways toward the earth and pointed the direction of the wind.

The dawn came, but no day. In the gray sky a red sun appeared, a dim red circle that gave a little light, like dusk; and as that day advanced, the dusk slipped back toward darkness, and the wind cried and whimpered over the fallen corn.

Men and women huddled in their houses, and they tied handkerchiefs over their noses when they went out, and wore goggles to protect their eyes.

When the night came again it was black night, for the stars could not pierce the dust to get down, and the window lights could not even spread beyond their own yards. Now the dust was evenly mixed with the air, an emulsion of dust and air. Houses were shut tight, and cloth wedged around doors and windows, but the dust came in so thinly that it could not be seen in the air, and it settled like pollen on the chairs and tables, on the dishes. The people brushed it from their shoulders. Little lines of dust lay at the door sills.

In the middle of that night the wind passed on and left the land quiet. The dust-filled air muffled sound more completely than fog does. The people, lying in their beds, heard the wind stop. They awakened when the rushing wind was gone. They lay quietly and listened deep into the stillness. Then the roosters crowed, and their voices were muffled, and the people stirred restlessly in their beds and wanted the morning. They knew it would take a long time for the dust to settle out of the air. In the morning the dust hung like fog, and the sun was as red as ripe new blood. All day the dust sifted down from the sky, and the next day it sifted down. An even blanket covered the earth. It settled on the corn, piled up on the tops of the fence posts, piled up on the wires; it settled on roofs, blanketed the weeds and trees.

The people came out of their houses and smelled the hot stinging air and covered their noses from it. And the children came out of the houses, but they did not run or shout as they would have done after a rain. Men stood by their fences and looked at the ruined corn, drying fast now, only a little green showing through the film of dust. The men were silent and they did not move often. And the women came out of the houses to stand beside their men—to feel whether this time the men would break. The women studied the men's faces secretly, for the corn could go, as long as something else remained. The children stood near by, drawing figures in the dust with bare toes, and the children sent exploring senses out to see whether men and women would break. The children peeked at the faces of the men and women, and then drew careful lines in the dust with their toes. Horses came to the watering troughs and nuzzled the water to clear the surface dust. After a while the faces of the watching men lost their bemused perplexity and became hard and angry and resistant. Then the women knew that they were safe and that there was no break. Then they asked, What'll we do? And the men replied, I don't know. But it was all right. The women knew it was all right, and the watching children knew it was all right. Women and children knew deep in themselves that no misfortune was too great to bear if their men were whole. The women went into the houses to their work, and the children began to play, but cautiously at first. As the day went forward the sun became less red. It flared down on the dust-blanketed land. The men sat in the doorways of their houses; their hands were busy with sticks and little rocks. The men sat still—thinking—figuring.

CHAPTER 2

A huge red transport truck stood in front of the little roadside restaurant. The vertical exhaust pipe muttered softly, and an almost invisible haze of steel-blue smoke hovered over its end. It was a new truck, shining red, and in twelve-inch letters on its sides— OKLAHOMA CITY TRANSPORT COMPANY. Its double tires were new, and a brass padlock stood straight out from the hasp on the big back doors. Inside the screened restaurant a radio played, quiet dance music turned low the way it is when no one is listening. A small outlet fan turned silently in its circular hole over the entrance, and flies buzzed excitedly about the doors and windows, butting the screens. Inside, one man, the truck driver, sat on a stool and rested his elbows on the counter and looked over his coffee at the lean and lonely waitress. He talked the smart listless language of the roadsides to her. "I seen him about three months ago. He had a operation. Cut somepin out. I forget what." And she— "Doesn't seem no longer ago than a week I seen him myself. Looked fine then. He's a nice sort of a guy when he ain't stinko." Now and then the flies roared softly at the screen door. The coffee machine spurted steam, and the waitress, without looking, reached behind her and shut it off.

Outside, a man walking along the edge of the highway crossed over and approached the truck. He walked slowly to the front of it, put his hand on the shiny fender, and looked at the *No Riders* sticker on the windshield. For a moment he was about to walk on down the road, but instead he sat on the running board on the side away from the restaurant. He was not over thirty. His eyes were very dark brown and there was a hint of brown pigment in his eyeballs. His cheek bones were high and wide, and strong deep lines cut down his cheeks, in curves beside his mouth. His upper lip was long, and since his teeth protruded, the lips stretched to cover them, for this man kept his lips closed. His hands were hard, with broad fingers and nails as thick and ridged as little clam shells. The space between thumb and forefinger and the hams of his hands were shiny with callus.

The man's clothes were new—all of them, cheap and new. His gray cap was so new that the visor was still stiff and the button still on, not shapeless and bulged as it would be when it had served for a while all the various purposes of a cap—carrying sack, towel, handkerchief. His suit was of cheap gray hardcloth and so new that there were creases in the trousers. His blue chambray shirt was stiff and smooth with filler. The coat was too big, the trousers too short, for he was a tall man. The coat shoulder peaks hung down on his arms, and even then the sleeves were too short and the front of the coat flapped loosely over his stomach. He wore a pair of new tan shoes of the kind called "army last," hobnailed and with half-circles like horseshoes to protect the edges of the heels from wear. This man sat on the running board and took off his cap and mopped his face with it. Then he put on the cap, and by pulling started the future ruin of the visor. His feet caught his attention. He leaned down and loosened the shoelaces, and did not tie the ends again. Over his head the exhaust of the Diesel engine whispered in quick puffs of blue smoke.

The music stopped in the restaurant and a man's voice spoke from the loudspeaker, but the waitress did not turn him off, for she didn't know the music had stopped. Her exploring fingers had found a lump under her ear. She was trying to see it in a mirror behind the counter without letting the truck driver know, and so she pretended to push a bit of hair to neatness. The truck driver said, "They was a big dance in Shawnee. I heard somebody got killed or somepin. You hear anything?" "No," said the waitress, and she lovingly fingered the lump under her ear.

Outside, the seated man stood up and looked over the cowl of the truck and watched the restaurant for a moment. Then he settled back on the running board, pulled a sack of tobacco and a book of papers from his side pocket. He rolled his cigarette slowly and perfectly, studied it, smoothed it. At last he lighted it and pushed the burning match into the dust at his feet. The sun cut into the shade of the truck as noon approached.

In the restaurant the truck driver paid his bill and put his two nickels' change in a slot machine. The whirling cylinders gave him no score. "They fix 'em so you can't win nothing," he said to the waitress.

And she replied, "Guy took the jackpot not two hours ago. Three-eighty he got. How soon you gonna be back by?"

He held the screen door a little open. "Week-ten days," he said. "Got to make a run to Tulsa, an' I never get back soon as I think."

She said crossly, "Don't let the flies in. Either go out or come in."

"So long," he said, and pushed his way out. The screen door banged behind him. He stood in the sun, peeling the wrapper from a piece of gum. He was a heavy man, broad in the shoulders, thick in the stomach. His face was red and his blue eyes long and slitted from having squinted always at sharp light. He wore army trousers and high laced boots. Holding the stick of gum in front of his lips he called through the screen, "Well, don't do nothing you don't want me to hear about." The waitress was turned toward a mirror on the back wall. She grunted a reply. The truck driver gnawed down the stick of gum slowly, opening his jaws and lips wide with each bite. He shaped the gum in his mouth, rolled it under his tongue while he walked to the big red truck.

The hitch-hiker stood up and looked across through the windows. "Could ya give me a lift, mister?"

The driver looked quickly back at the restaurant for a second. "Didn' you see the *No Riders* sticker on the win'shield?"

"Sure—I seen it. But sometimes a guy'll be a good guy even if some rich bastard makes him carry a sticker."

The driver, getting slowly into the truck, considered the parts of this answer. If he refused now, not only was he not a good guy, but he was forced to carry a sticker, was not allowed to have company. If he took in the hitch-hiker he was automatically a good guy and also he was not one whom any rich bastard could kick around. He knew he was being trapped, but he couldn't see a way out. And he wanted to be a good guy. He glanced again at the restaurant. "Scrunch down on the running board till we get around the bend," he said.

The hitch-hiker flopped down out of sight and clung to the door handle. The motor roared up for a moment, the gears clicked in, and the great truck moved away, first gear, second gear, third gear, and then a high whining pick-up and fourth gear. Under the clinging man the highway blurred dizzily by. It was a mile to the first turn in the road, then the truck slowed down. The hitch-hiker stood up, eased the door open, and slipped into the seat. The driver looked over at him, slitting his eyes, and he chewed as though thoughts and impressions were being sorted and arranged by his jaws before they were finally filed away in his brain. His eyes began at the new cap, moved down the new clothes to the new shoes. The hitch-hiker squirmed his back against the seat in comfort, took off his cap, and swabbed his sweating forehead and chin with it. "Thanks, buddy," he said. "My dogs was pooped out."

"New shoes," said the driver. His voice had the same quality of secrecy and insinuation his eyes had. "You oughtn' to take no walk in new shoes—hot weather."

The hiker looked down at the dusty yellow shoes. "Didn't have no other shoes," he said. "Guy got to wear 'em if he got no others."

The driver squinted judiciously ahead and built up the speed of the truck a little. "Goin' far?"

"Uh-uh! I'd a walked her if my dogs wasn't pooped out."

The questions of the driver had the tone of a subtle examination. He seemed to spread nets, to set traps with his questions. "Lookin' for a job?" he asked.

"No, my old man got a place, forty acres. He's a cropper, but we been there a long time."

The driver looked significantly at the fields along the road where the corn was fallen sideways and the dust was piled on it. Little flints shoved through the dusty soil. The driver said, as though to himself, "A forty-acre cropper and he ain't been dusted out and he ain't been tractored out?"

" 'Course I ain't heard lately," said the hitch-hiker.

"Long time," said the driver. A bee flew into the cab and buzzed in back of the windshield. The driver put out his hand and carefully drove the bee into an air stream that blew it out of the window. "Croppers going fast now," he said. "One cat' takes and shoves ten families out. Cat's all over hell now. Tear in and shove the croppers out. How's your old man hold on?" His tongue and his jaws became busy with the neglected gum, turned it and chewed it. With each opening of his mouth his tongue could be seen flipping the gum over.

"Well, I ain't heard lately. I never was no hand to write, nor my old man neither." He added quickly, "But the both of us can, if we want."

"Been doing a job?" Again the secret investigating casualness. He looked out over the fields, at the shimmering air, and gathering his gum into his cheek, out of the way, he spat out the window.

"Sure have," said the hitch-hiker.

"Thought so. I seen your hands. Been swingin' a pick or an ax or a sledge. That shines up your hands. I notice all stuff like that. Take a pride in it."

The hitch-hiker stared at him. The truck tires sang on the road. "Like to know anything else? I'll tell you. You ain't got to guess."

"Now don't get sore. I wasn't gettin' nosy."

"I'll tell you anything. I ain't hidin' nothin'."

"Now don't get sore. I just like to notice things. Makes the time pass."

"I'll tell you anything. Name's Joad, Tom Joad. Old man is ol' Tom Joad." His eyes rested broodingly on the driver.

"Don't get sore. I didn't mean nothin'."

"I don't mean nothin' neither," said Joad. "I'm just tryin' to get along without shovin' nobody around." He stopped and looked out at the dry fields, at the starved tree clumps hanging uneasily in the heated distance. From his side pocket he brought out his tobacco and papers. He rolled his cigarette down between his knees, where the wind could not get at it.

The driver chewed as rhythmically, as thoughtfully, as a cow. He waited to let the whole emphasis of the preceding passage disappear and be forgotten. At last, when the air seemed neutral again, he said, "A guy that never been a truck skinner don't know nothin' what it's like. Owners don't want us to pick up nobody. So we got to set here an' just skin her along 'less we want to take a chance of gettin' fired like I just done with you."

" 'Preciate it," said Joad.

"I've knew guys that done screwy things while they're drivin' trucks. I remember a guy use' to make up poetry. It passed the time." He looked over secretly to see whether Joad was interested or amazed. Joad was silent, looking into the distance ahead, along the road, along the white road that waved gently, like a ground swell. The driver went on at last, "I remember a piece of poetry this here guy wrote down. It was about him an' a couple other guys goin' all over the world drinkin' and raisin' hell and screwin' around. I wisht I could remember how that piece went. This guy had words in it that Jesus H. Christ wouldn't know what they meant. Part was like this: 'An' there we spied a nigger, with a trigger that was bigger than a elephant's proboscis or the whanger of a whale.' That proboscis is a nose-like. With a elephant it's his trunk. Guy showed me in a dictionary. Carried that dictionary all over hell with him. He'd look in it while he's pulled up gettin' his pie an' coffee." He stopped, feeling lonely in the long speech. His secret eyes turned on his passenger. Joad remained silent. Nervously the driver tried to force him into participation. "Ever know a guy that said big words like that?"

"Preacher," said Joad.

"Well, it makes you mad to hear a guy use big words. 'Course with a preacher it's all right because nobody would fool around with a preacher anyway. But this guy was funny. You didn't give a damn when he said a big word 'cause he just done it for ducks. He wasn't puttin' on no dog." The driver was reassured. He knew at least that Joad was listening. He swung the great truck viciously around a bend and the tires shrilled. "Like I was sayin'," he continued, "guy that drives a truck does screwy things. He got to. He'd go nuts jus' settin' here an' the road sneakin' under the wheels. Fella says once that truck skinners eats all the time—all the time in hamburger joints along the road."

"Sure seem to live there," Joad agreed.

"Sure they stop, but it ain't to eat. They ain't hardly ever hungry. They're just goddamn sick of goin'—get sick of it. Joints is the only place you can pull up, an' when you stop you got to buy somepin so you can sling the bull with the broad behind the counter. So you get a cup of coffee and a piece pie. Kind of gives a guy a little rest." He chewed his gum slowly and turned it with his tongue.

"Must be tough," said Joad with no emphasis.

The driver glanced quickly at him, looking for satire. "Well, it ain't no goddamn cinch," he said testily. "Looks easy, jus' settin' here till you put in your eight or maybe your ten or fourteen hours. But the road gets into a guy. He's got to do somepin. Some sings an' some whistles. Company won't let us have no radio. A few takes a pint along, but them kind don't stick long." He said the last smugly. "I don't never take a drink till I'm through."

"Yeah?" Joad asked.

"Yeah! A guy got to get ahead. Why, I'm thinkin' of takin' one of them correspondence school courses. Mechanical engineering. It's easy. Just study a few easy lessons at home. I'm thinkin' of it. Then I won't drive no truck. Then I'll tell other guys to drive trucks."

Joad took a pint of whisky from his side coat pocket. "Sure you won't have a snort?" His voice was teasing.

"No, by God. I won't touch it. A guy can't drink liquor all the time and study like I'm goin' to."

Joad uncorked the bottle, took two quick swallows, re-corked it, and put it back in his pocket. The spicy hot smell of the whisky filled the cab. "You're all wound up," said Joad. "What's the matter—got a girl?"

"Well, sure. But I want to get ahead anyway. I been training my mind for a hell of a long time."

The whisky seemed to loosen Joad up. He rolled another cigarette and lighted it. "I ain't got a hell of a lot further to go," he said.

The driver went on quickly, "I don't need no shot," he said. "I train my mind all the time. I took a course in that two years ago." He patted the steering wheel with his right hand. "Suppose I pass a guy on the road. I look at him, an' after I'm past I try to remember ever'thing about him, kind a clothes an' shoes an' hat, an' how he walked an' maybe how tall an' what weight an' any scars. I do it pretty good. I can jus' make a whole picture in my head. Sometimes I think I ought to take a course to be a fingerprint expert. You'd be su'prised how much a guy can remember."

Joad took a quick drink from the flask. He dragged the last smoke from his raveling cigarette and then, with callused thumb and forefinger, crushed out the glowing end. He rubbed the butt to a pulp and put it out the window, letting the breeze suck it from his fingers. The big tires sang a high note on the pavement. Joad's dark quiet eyes became amused as he stared along the road. The driver waited and glanced uneasily over. At last Joad's long upper lip grinned up from his teeth and he chuckled silently, his chest jerked with the chuckles. "You sure took a hell of a long time to get to it, buddy."

The driver did not look over. "Get to what? How do you mean?"

Joad's lips stretched tight over his long teeth for a moment, and he licked his lips like a dog, two licks, one in each direction from the middle. His voice became harsh. "You know what I mean. You give me a goin'-over when I first got in. I seen you." The driver looked straight ahead, gripped the wheel so tightly that the pads of his palms bulged, and the backs of his hands paled. Joad continued, "You know where I come from." The driver was silent. "Don't you?" Joad insisted.

"Well—sure. That is—maybe. But it ain't none of my business. I mind my own yard. It ain't nothing to me." The words tumbled out now. "I don't stick my nose in nobody's business." And suddenly he was silent and waiting. And his hands were still white on the wheel. A grasshopper flipped through the window and lighted on top of the instrument panel, where it sat and began to scrape its wings with its angled jumping legs. Joad reached forward and crushed its hard skull-like head with his fingers, and he let it into the wind stream out the window. Joad chuckled again while he brushed the bits of broken insect from his fingertips. "You got me wrong, mister," he said. "I ain't keepin' quiet about it. Sure I been in McAlester. Been there four years. Sure these is the clothes they give me when I come out. I don't give a damn who know it. An' I'm goin' to my old man's place so I don't have to lie to get a job."

The driver said, "Well—that ain't none of my business. I ain't a nosy guy."

"The hell you ain't," said Joad. "That big old nose of yours been stickin' out eight miles ahead of your face. You had that big nose goin' over me like a sheep in a vegetable patch."

The driver's face tightened. "You got me all wrong—" he began weakly.

Joad laughed at him. "You been a good guy. You give me a lift. Well, hell! I done time. So what! You want to know what I done time for, don't you?"

"That ain't none of my affair."

"Nothin' ain't none of your affair except skinnin' this here bull-bitch along, an' that's the least thing you work at. Now look. See that road up ahead?"

"Yeah."

"Well, I get off there. Sure, I know you're wettin' your pants to know what I done. I ain't a guy to let you down." The high hum of the motor dulled and the song of the tires dropped in pitch. Joad got out his pint and took another short drink. The truck drifted to a stop where a dirt road opened at right angles to the highway. Joad got out and stood beside the cab window. The vertical exhaust pipe puttered up its barely visible blue smoke. Joad leaned toward the driver. "Homicide," he said quickly. "That's a big word—means I killed a guy. Seven years. I'm sprung in four for keepin' my nose clean."

The driver's eyes slipped over Joad's face to memorize it. "I never asked you nothin' about it," he said. "I mind my own yard."

"You can tell about it in every joint from here to Texola." He smiled. "So long, fella. You been a good guy. But look, when you been in stir a little while, you can smell a question comin' from hell to breakfast. You telegraphed yours the first time you opened your trap." He spatted the metal door with the palm of his hand. "Thanks for the lift," he said. "So long." He turned away and walked into the dirt road.

For a moment the driver stared after him, and then he called, "Luck!" Joad waved his hand without looking around. Then the motor roared up and the gears clicked and the great red truck rolled heavily away.

CHAPTER 3

The concrete highway was edged with a mat of tangled, broken, dry grass, and the grass heads were heavy with oat beards to catch on a dog's coat, and foxtails to tangle in a horse's fetlocks, and clover burrs to fasten in sheep's wool; sleeping life waiting to be spread and dispersed, every seed armed with an appliance of dispersal, twisting darts and parachutes for the wind, little spears and balls of tiny thorns, and all waiting for animals and for the wind, for a man's trouser cuff or the hem of a woman's skirt, all passive but armed with appliances of activity, still, but each possessed of the anlage of movement.

The sun lay on the grass and warmed it, and in the shade under the grass the insects moved, ants and ant lions to set traps for them, grasshoppers to jump into the air and flick their yellow wings for a second, sow bugs like little armadillos, plodding restlessly on many tender feet. And over the grass at the roadside a land turtle crawled, turning aside for nothing, dragging his high-domed shell over the grass. His hard legs and yellow-nailed feet threshed slowly through the grass, not really walking, but boosting and dragging his shell along. The barley beards slid off his shell, and the clover burrs fell on him and rolled to the ground. His horny beak was partly open, and his fierce, humorous eyes, under brows like fingernails, stared straight ahead. He came over the grass leaving a beaten trail behind him, and the hill, which was the highway embankment, reared up ahead of him. For a moment he stopped, his head held high. He blinked and looked up and down. At last he started to climb the embankment. Front clawed feet reached forward but did not touch. The hind feet kicked his shell along, and it scraped on the grass, and on the gravel. As the embankment grew steeper and steeper, the more frantic were the efforts of the land turtle. Pushing hind legs strained and slipped, boosting the shell along, and the horny head protruded as far as the neck could stretch. Little by little the shell slid up the embankment until at last a parapet cut straight across its line of march, the shoulder of the road, a concrete wall four inches high. As though they worked independently the hind legs pushed the shell against the wall. The head upraised and peered over the wall to the broad smooth plain of cement. Now the hands, braced on top of the wall, strained and lifted, and the shell came slowly up and rested its front end on the wall. For a moment the turtle rested. A red ant ran into the shell, into the soft skin inside the shell, and suddenly head and legs snapped in, and the armored tail clamped in sideways. The red ant was crushed between body and legs. And one head of wild oats was clamped into the shell by a front leg. For a long moment the turtle lay still, and then the neck crept out and the old humorous frowning eyes looked about and the legs and tail came out. The back legs went to work, straining like elephant legs, and the shell tipped to an angle so that the front legs could not reach the level cement plain. But higher and higher the hind legs boosted it, until at last the center of balance was reached, the front tipped down, the front legs scratched at the pavement, and it was up. But the head of wild oats was held by its stem around the front legs.

Now the going was easy, and all the legs worked, and the shell boosted along, waggling from side to side. A sedan driven by a forty-year-old woman approached. She saw the turtle and swung to the right, off the highway, the wheels screamed and a cloud of dust boiled up. Two wheels lifted for a moment and then settled. The car skidded back onto the road, and went on, but more slowly. The turtle had jerked into its shell, but now it hurried on, for the highway was burning hot.

And now a light truck approached, and as it came near, the driver saw the turtle and swerved to hit it. His front wheel struck the edge of the shell, flipped the turtle like a tiddly-wink, spun it like a coin, and rolled it off the highway. The truck went back to its course along the right side. Lying on its back, the turtle was tight in its shell for a long time. But at last its legs waved in the air, reaching for something to pull it over. Its front foot caught a piece of quartz and little by little the shell pulled over and flopped upright. The wild oat head fell out and three of the spearhead seeds stuck in the ground. And as the turtle crawled on down the embankment, its shell dragged dirt over the seeds. The turtle entered a dust road and jerked itself along, drawing a wavy shallow trench in the dust with its shell. The old humorous eyes looked ahead, and the horny beak opened a little. His yellow toe nails slipped a fraction in the dust.

CHAPTER 4

When Joad heard the truck get under way, gear climbing up to gear and the ground throbbing under the rubber beating of the tires, he stopped and turned about and watched it until it disappeared. When it was out of sight he still watched the distance and the blue air-shimmer. Thoughtfully he took the pint from his pocket, unscrewed the metal cap, and sipped the whisky delicately, running his tongue inside the bottle neck, and then around his lips, to gather in any flavor that might have escaped him. He said experimentally, "There we spied a nigger—" and that was all he could remember. At last he turned about and faced the dusty side road that cut off at right angles through the fields. The sun was hot, and no wind stirred the sifted dust. The road was cut with furrows where dust had slid and settled back into the wheel tracks. Joad took a few steps, and the flourlike dust spurted up in front of his new yellow shoes, and the yellowness was disappearing under gray dust.

He leaned down and untied the laces, slipped off first one shoe and then the other. And he worked his damp feet comfortably in the hot dry dust until little spurts of it came up between his toes, and until the skin on his feet tightened with dryness. He took off his coat and wrapped his shoes in it and slipped the bundle under his arm. And at last he moved up the road, shooting the dust ahead of him, making a cloud that hung low to the ground behind him.

The right of way was fenced, two strands of barbed wire on willow poles. The poles were crooked and badly trimmed. Whenever a crotch came to the proper height the wire lay in it, and where there was no crotch the barbed wire was lashed to the post with rusty baling wire. Beyond the fence, the corn lay beaten down by wind and heat and drought, and the cups where leaf joined stalk were filled with dust.

Joad plodded along, dragging his cloud of dust behind him. A little bit ahead he saw the high-domed shell of a land turtle, crawling slowly along through the dust, its legs working stiffly and jerkily. Joad stopped to watch it, and his shadow fell on the turtle. Instantly head and legs were withdrawn and the short thick tail clamped sideways into the shell. Joad picked it up and turned it over. The back was brown-gray, like the dust, but the underside of the shell was creamy yellow, clean and smooth. Joad shifted his bundle high under his arm and stroked the smooth undershell with his finger, and he pressed it. It was softer than the back. The hard old head came out and tried to look at the pressing finger, and the legs waved wildly. The turtle wetted on Joad's hand and struggled uselessly in the air. Joad turned it back upright and rolled it up in his coat with his shoes. He could feel it pressing and struggling and fussing under his arm. He moved ahead more quickly now, dragging his heels a little in the fine dust.

Ahead of him, beside the road, a scrawny, dusty willow tree cast a speckled shade. Joad could see it ahead of him, its poor branches curving over the way, its load of leaves tattered and scraggly as a molting chicken. Joad was sweating now. His blue shirt darkened down his back and under his arms. He pulled at the visor of his cap and creased it in the middle, breaking its cardboard lining so completely that it could never look new again. And his steps took on new speed and intent toward the shade of the distant willow tree. At the willow he knew there would be shade, at least one hard bar of absolute shade thrown by the trunk, since the sun had passed its zenith. The sun whipped the back of his neck now and made a little humming in his head. He could not see the base of the tree, for it grew out of a little swale that held water longer than the level places. Joad speeded his pace against the sun, and he started down the declivity. He slowed cautiously, for the bar of absolute shade was taken. A man sat on the ground, leaning against the trunk of the tree. His legs were crossed and one bare foot extended nearly as high as his head. He did not hear Joad approaching, for he was whistling solemnly the tune of "Yes, Sir, That's My Baby." His extended foot swung slowly up and down in the tempo. It was not dance tempo. He stopped whistling and sang in an easy thin tenor:

> "Yes, sir, that's my Saviour,
> Je—sus is my Saviour,
> Je—sus is my Saviour now.
> On the level
> 'S not the devil,
> Jesus is my Saviour now."

Joad had moved into the imperfect shade of the molting leaves
before the man heard him coming, stopped his song, and turned his
head. It was a long head, bony, tight of skin, and set on a neck as
stringy and muscular as a celery stalk. His eyeballs were heavy and
protruding; the lids stretched to cover them, and the lids were raw
and red. His cheeks were brown and shiny and hairless and his
mouth full—humorous or sensual. The nose, beaked and hard,
stretched the skin so tightly that the bridge showed white. There
was no perspiration on the face, not even on the tall pale forehead.
It was an abnormally high forehead, lined with delicate blue veins
at the temples. Fully half of the face was above the eyes. His stiff
gray hair was mussed back from his brow as though he had combed
it back with his fingers. For clothes he wore overalls and a blue shirt.
A denim coat with brass buttons and a spotted brown hat creased
like a pork pie lay on the ground beside him. Canvas sneakers, gray
with dust, lay near by where they had fallen when they were kicked
off.

The man looked long at Joad. The light seemed to go far into
his brown eyes, and it picked out little golden specks deep in the
irises. The strained bundle of neck muscles stood out.

Joad stood still in the speckled shade. He took off his cap and
mopped his wet face with it and dropped it and his rolled coat on
the ground.

The man in the absolute shade uncrossed his legs and dug with
his toes at the earth.

Joad said, "Hi. It's hotter'n hell on the road."

The seated man stared questioningly at him. "Now ain't you
young Tom Joad—ol' Tom's boy?"

"Yeah," said Joad. "All the way. Goin' home now."

"You wouldn't remember me, I guess," the man said. He smiled
and his full lips revealed great horse teeth. "Oh, no, you wouldn't
remember. You was always too busy pullin' little girls' pigtails when
I give you the Holy Sperit. You was all wropped up in yankin' that
pigtail out by the roots. You maybe don't recollect, but I do. The
two of you come to Jesus at once 'cause of that pigtail yankin'. Baptized both of you in the irrigation ditch at once. Fightin' an' yellin'
like a couple a cats."

Joad looked at him with drooped eyes, and then he laughed.
"Why, you're the preacher. You're the preacher. I jus' passed a rec-
ollection about you to a guy not an hour ago."

"I was a preacher," said the man seriously. "Reverend Jim Casy—was a Burning Busher. Used to howl out the name of Jesus to glory. And used to get an irrigation ditch so squirmin' full of repented sinners half of 'em like to drownded. But not no more," he sighed. "Just Jim Casy now. Ain't got the call no more. Got a lot of sinful idears—but they seem kinda sensible."

Joad said, "You're bound to get idears if you go thinkin' about stuff. Sure I remember you. You use ta give a good meetin'. I recollect one time you give a whole sermon walkin' around on your hands, yellin' your head off. Ma favored you more than anybody. An' Granma says you was just lousy with the spirit." Joad dug at his rolled coat and found the pocket and brought out his pint. The turtle moved a leg but he wrapped it up tightly. He unscrewed the cap and held out the bottle. "Have a little snort?"

Casy took the bottle and regarded it broodingly. "I ain't preachin' no more much. The sperit ain't in the people much no more; and worse'n that, the sperit ain't in me no more. 'Course now an' again the sperit gets movin' an' I rip out a meetin', or when folks sets out food I give 'em a grace, but my heart ain't in it. I on'y do it 'cause they expect it."

Joad mopped his face with his cap again. "You ain't too damn holy to take a drink, are you?" he asked.

Casy seemed to see the bottle for the first time. He tilted it and took three big swallows. "Nice drinkin' liquor," he said.

"Ought to be," said Joad. "That's fact'ry liquor. Cost a buck."

Casy took another swallow before he passed the bottle back. "Yes, sir!" he said. "Yes, sir!"

Joad took the bottle from him, and in politeness did not wipe the neck with his sleeve before he drank. He squatted on his hams and set the bottle upright against his coat roll. His fingers found a twig with which to draw his thoughts on the ground. He swept the leaves from a square and smoothed the dust. And he drew angles and made little circles. "I ain't seen you in a long time," he said.

"Nobody seen me," said the preacher. "I went off alone, an' I sat and figured. The sperit's strong in me, on'y it ain't the same. I ain't so sure of a lot of things." He sat up straighter against the tree. His bony hand dug its way like a squirrel into his overall pocket, brought out a black, bitten plug of tobacco. Carefully he brushed off bits of straw and gray pocket fuzz before he bit off a corner and settled the quid into his cheek. Joad waved his stick in negation when the plug was held out to him. The turtle dug at the rolled coat. Casy looked over at the stirring garment. "What you got there—a chicken? You'll smother it."

Joad rolled the coat up more tightly. "An old turtle," he said. "Picked him up on the road. An old bulldozer. Thought I'd take 'im to my little brother. Kids like turtles."

The preacher nodded his head slowly. "Every kid got a turtle some time or other. Nobody can't keep a turtle though. They work at it and work at it, and at last one day they get out and away they go—off somewheres. It's like me. I wouldn' take the good ol' gospel that was just layin' thereto my hand. I got to be pickin' at it an' workin' at it until I got it all tore down. Here I got the sperit some-times an' nothin' to preach about. I got the call to lead the people, an' no place to lead 'em."

"Lead 'em around and around," said Joad. "Sling 'em in the ir-rigation ditch. Tell 'em they'll burn in hell if they don't think like you. What the hell you want to lead 'em someplace for? Jus' lead 'em." The straight trunk shade had stretched out along the ground. Joad moved gratefully into it and squatted on his hams and made a new smooth place on which to draw his thoughts with a stick. A thick-furred yellow shepherd dog came trotting down the road, head low, tongue lolling and dripping. Its tail hung limply curled, and it panted loudly. Joad whistled at it, but it only dropped its head an inch and trotted fast toward some definite destination. "Goin' some-place," Joad explained, a little piqued. "Goin' for home maybe."

The preacher could not be thrown from his subject. "Goin' someplace," he repeated. "That's right, he's goin' someplace. Me— I don't know where I'm goin'. Tell you what—I use ta get the people jumpin' an' talkin' in tongues, an' glory-shoutin' till they just fell down an' passed out. An' some I'd baptize to bring 'em to. An' then—you know what I'd do? I'd take one of them girls out in the grass, an' I'd lay with her. Done it ever' time. Then I'd feel bad, an' I'd pray an' pray, but it didn't do no good. Come the nex' time, them an' me was full of the sperit, I'd do it again. I figgered there just wasn't no hope for me, an' I was a damned ol' hypocrite. But I didn't mean to be."

Joad smiled and his long teeth parted and he licked his lips. "There ain't nothing like a good hot meetin' for pushin' 'em over," he said. "I done that myself."

Casy leaned forward excitedly. "You see," he cried, "I seen it was that way, an' I started thinkin'." He waved his bony big-knuckled hand up and down in a patting gesture. "I got to thinkin' like this —'Here's me preachin' grace. An' here's them people gettin' grace so hard they're jumpin' an' shoutin'. Now they say layin' up with a girl comes from the devil. But the more grace a girl got in her, the quicker she wants to go out in the grass.' An' I got to thinkin' how in hell, s'cuse me, how can the devil get in when a girl is so full of the Holy Sperit that it's spoutin' out of her nose an' ears. You'd think that'd be one time when the devil didn't stand a snowball's chance in hell. But there it was." His eyes were shining with excitement. He worked his cheeks for a moment and then spat into the dust, and the gob of spit rolled over and over, picking up dust until it looked like a round dry little pellet. The preacher spread out his hand and looked at his palm as though he were reading a book. "An' there's me," he went on softly. "There's me with all them people's souls in my han'—responsible an' feelin' my responsibility—an' ever' time, I lay with one of them girls." He looked over at Joad and his face looked helpless. His expression asked for help.

Joad carefully drew the torso of a woman in the dirt, breasts, hips, pelvis. "I wasn't never a preacher," he said. "I never let nothin' get by when I could catch it. An' I never had no idears about it except I was goddamn glad when I got one."

"But you wasn't a preacher," Casy insisted. "A girl was just a girl to you. You could fuck 'em an' leave 'em. It wasn't nothin' to you. But to me they was holy vessels. I was savin' their souls. An' here with all that responsibility on me I'd just get 'em frothin' with the Holy Sperit, an' then I'd take 'em out an' screw 'em."

"Maybe I should of been a preacher," said Joad. He brought out his tobacco and papers and rolled a cigarette. He lighted it and squinted through the smoke at the preacher. "I been a long time without a girl," he said. "It's gonna take some catchin' up."

Casy continued, "It worried me till I couldn't get no sleep. Here I'd go to preachin' and I'd say, 'By God, this time I ain't gonna do it.' And right while I said it, I knowed I was."

"You should a got a wife," said Joad. "Preacher an' his wife stayed at our place one time. Jehovites they was. Slep' upstairs. Held meetin's in our barnyard. Us kids would listen. That preacher's missus took a godawful poundin' after ever' night meetin'."

"I'm glad you tol' me," said Casy. "I use to think it was jus' me. Finally it give me such pain I quit an' went off by myself an' give her a damn good thinkin' about." He doubled up his legs and scratched between his dry dusty toes. "I says to myself, 'What's gnawin' you? Is it the screwin'?' An' I says, 'No, it's the sin.' An' I says, 'Why is it that when a fella ought to be just about mule-ass proof against sin, an' all full up of Jesus, why is it that's the time a fella gets fingerin' his pants buttons?' " He laid two fingers down in his palm in rhythm, as though he gently placed each word there side by side. "I says, 'Maybe it ain't a sin. Maybe it's just the way folks is. Maybe we been whippin' the hell out of ourselves for nothin'.' An' I thought how some sisters took to beatin' theirselves with a three-foot shag of bobwire. An' I thought how maybe they liked to hurt themselves, an' maybe I liked to hurt myself. Well, I was layin' under a tree when I figured that out, and I went to sleep. And it come night, an' it was dark when I come to. They was a coyote squawkin' near by. Before I knowed it, I was sayin' out loud, 'The hell with it! There ain't no sin and there ain't no virtue. There's just stuff people do. It's all part of the same thing. And some of the things folks do is nice, and some ain't nice, but that's as far as any man got a right to say.' " He paused and looked up from the palm of his hand, where he had laid down the words.

Joad was grinning at him, but Joad's eyes were sharp and interested, too. "You give her a goin'-over," he said. "You figured her out."

Casy spoke again, and his voice rang with pain and confusion. "I says, 'What's this call, this sperit?' An' I says, 'It's love. I love people so much I'm fit to bust, sometimes.' An' I says, 'Don't you love Jesus?' Well, I thought an' thought, an' finally I says, 'No, I don't know nobody name' Jesus. I know a bunch of stories, but I only love people. An' sometimes I love 'em fit to bust, an' I want to make 'em happy, so I been preachin' somepin I thought would make 'em happy.' An' then—I been talkin' a hell of a lot. Maybe you wonder about me using bad words. Well, they ain't bad to me no more. They're jus' words folks use, an' they don't mean nothing bad with 'em. Anyways, I'll tell you one more thing I thought out; an' from a preacher it's the most unreligious thing, and I can't be a preacher no more because I thought it an' I believe it."

"What's that?" Joad asked.

Casy looked shyly at him. "If it hits you wrong, don't take no offense at it, will you?"

"I don't take no offense 'cept a bust in the nose," said Joad. "What did you figger?"

"I figgered about the Holy Sperit and the Jesus road. I figgered, 'Why do we got to hang it on God or Jesus? Maybe,' I figgered, 'maybe it's all men an' all women we love; maybe that's the Holy Sperit—the human sperit—the whole shebang. Maybe all men got one big soul ever'body's a part of.' Now I sat there thinkin' it, an' all of a suddent—I knew it. I knew it so deep down that it was true, and I still know it."

Joad's eyes dropped to the ground, as though he could not meet the naked honesty in the preacher's eyes. "You can't hold no church with idears like that," he said. "People would drive you out of the country with idears like that. Jumpin' an' yellin'. That's what folks like. Makes 'em feel swell. When Granma got to talkin' in tongues, you couldn't tie her down. She could knock over a full-growed deacon with her fist."

Casy regarded him broodingly. "Somepin I like to ast you," he said. "Somepin that been eatin' on me."

"Go ahead. I'll talk, sometimes."

"Well"—the preacher said slowly—"here's you that I baptized right when I was in the glory roof-tree. Got little hunks of Jesus jumpin' outa my mouth that day. You won't remember 'cause you was busy pullin' that pigtail."

"I remember," said Joad. "That was Susy Little. She bust my finger a year later."

"Well—did you take any good outa that baptizin'? Was your ways better?"

Joad thought about it. "No-o-o, can't say as I felt anything."

"Well—did you take any bad from it? Think hard."

Joad picked up the bottle and took a swig. "They wasn't nothing in it, good or bad. I just had fun." He handed the flask to the preacher.

He sighed and drank and looked at the low level of the whisky and took another tiny drink. "That's good," he said. "I got to worryin' about whether in messin' around maybe I done somebody a hurt."

Joad looked over toward his coat and saw the turtle, free of the cloth and hurrying away in the direction he had been following when Joad found him. Joad watched him for a moment and then got slowly to his feet and retrieved him and wrapped him in the coat again. "I ain't got no present for the kids," he said. "Nothin' but this ol' turtle."

"It's a funny thing," the preacher said. "I was thinkin' about ol' Tom Joad when you come along. Thinkin' I'd call in on him. I used to think he was a godless man but I liked him." He said confessingly, "But the only kind of men I ever really did like was godless men. How is Tom?"

"I don' know how he is. I ain't been home in four years."

"Didn't he write to you?"

Joad was embarrassed. "Well, Pa wasn't no hand to write for pretty, or to write for writin'. He'd sign up his name as nice as anybody, an' lick his pencil. But Pa never did write no letters. He always says what he couldn' tell a fella with his mouth wasn't worth leanin' on no pencil about."

"Been out travelin' around?" Casy asked.

Joad regarded him suspiciously. "Didn' you hear about me? I was in all the papers."

"No—I never. What?" He jerked one leg over the other and settled lower against the tree. The afternoon was advancing rapidly, and a richer tone was growing on the sun.

Joad said pleasantly, "Might's well tell you now an' get it over with. But if you was still preachin' I wouldn't tell, fear you get prayin' over me." He drained the last of the pint and flung it from him, and the flat brown bottle skidded lightly over the dust. "I been in McAlester them four years."

Casy swung around to him, and his brows lowered so that his tall forehead seemed even taller. "Ain't wantin' to talk about it, huh? I won't ask you no questions, if you done something bad——"

"I'd do what I done—again," said Joad. "I killed a guy in a fight. We was drunk at a dance. He got a knife in me, an' I killed him with a shovel that was layin' there. Knocked his head plumb to squash."

Casy's eyebrows resumed their normal level. "You ain't ashamed of nothin' then?"

"No," said Joad. "I ain't. I got seven years, account of he had a knife in me. Got out in four—parole."

"Then you ain't heard nothin' about your folks for four years?"

"Oh, I heard. Ma sent me a card two years ago, an' las' Christmas Granma sent a card. Jesus, the guys in the cell block laughed! Had a tree an' shiny stuff looks like snow. It says in po'try:

" 'Merry Christmus, purty child,
Jesus meek an' Jesus mild,
Underneath the Christmus tree
There's a gif' for you from me.'

"I guess Granma never read it. Prob'ly got it from a drummer an'
picked out the one with the mos' shiny stuff on it. The guys in my
cell block goddamn near died laughin'. Jesus Meek they called me
after that. Granma never meant it funny; she jus' figgered it was so
purty she wouldn' bother to read it. She lost her glasses the year I
went up. Maybe she never did find 'em."

"How they treat you in McAlester?" Casy asked.

"Oh, awright. You eat regular, an' get clean clothes, and there's
places to take a bath. It's pretty nice some ways. Makes it hard not
havin' no women." Suddenly he laughed. "They was a guy paroled,"
he said. " 'Bout a month he's back for breakin' parole. A guy ast him
why he bust his parole. 'Well, hell,' he says. 'They got no conveniences at my old man's place. Got no 'lectric lights, got no shower
baths. There ain't no books, an' the food's lousy.' Says he come back
where they got a few conveniences an' he eats regular. He says it
makes him feel lonesome out there in the open havin' to think what
to do next. So he stole a car an' come back." Joad got out his tobacco
and blew a brown paper free of the pack and rolled a cigarette. "The
guy's right, too," he said. "Las' night, thinkin' where I'm gonna
sleep, I got scared. An' I got thinkin' about my bunk, an' I wonder
what the stir-bug I got for a cell mate is doin'. Me an' some guys
had a strang band goin'. Good one. Guy said we ought to go on the
radio. An' this mornin' I didn' know what time to get up. Jus' laid
there waitin' for the bell to go off."

Casy chuckled. "Fella can get so he misses the noise of a saw
mill."

The yellowing, dusty, afternoon light put a golden color on the
land. The cornstalks looked golden. A flight of swallows swooped
overhead toward some waterhole. The turtle in Joad's coat began a
new campaign of escape. Joad creased the visor of his cap. It was
getting the long protruding curve of a crow's beak now. "Guess I'll
mosey along," he said. "I hate to hit the sun, but it ain't so bad
now."

Casy pulled himself together. "I ain't seen ol' Tom in a bug's
age," he said. "I was gonna look in on him anyways. I brang Jesus

to your folks for a long time, an' I never took up a collection nor nothin' but a bite to eat."

"Come along," said Joad. "Pa'll be glad to see you. He always said you got too long a pecker for a preacher." He picked up his coat roll and tightened it snugly about his shoes and turtle.

Casy gathered in his canvas sneakers and shoved his bare feet into them. "I ain't got your confidence," he said. "I'm always scared there's wire or glass under the dust. I don't know nothin' I hate so much as a cut toe."

They hesitated on the edge of the shade and then they plunged into the yellow sunlight like two swimmers hastening to get to shore. After a few fast steps they slowed to a gentle, thoughtful pace. The cornstalks threw gray shadows sideways now, and the raw smell of hot dust was in the air. The corn field ended and dark green cotton took its place, dark green leaves through a film of dust, and the bolls forming. It was spotty cotton, thick in the low places where water had stood, and bare on the high places. The plants strove against the sun. And distance, toward the horizon, was tan to invisibility. The dust road stretched out ahead of them, waving up and down. The willows of a stream lined across the west, and to the northwest a fallow section was going back to sparse brush. But the smell of burned dust was in the air, and the air was dry, so that mucus in the nose dried to a crust, and the eyes watered to keep the eyeballs from drying out.

Casy said, "See how good the corn come along until the dust got up. Been a dinger of a crop."

"Ever' year," said Joad. "Ever' year I can remember, we had a good crop comin', an' it never come. Grampa says she was good the first five plowin's, while the wild grass was still in her." The road dropped down a little hill and climbed up another rolling hill.

Casy said, "Ol' Tom's house can't be more'n a mile from here. Ain't she over that third rise?"

"Sure," said Joad. " 'Less somebody stole it, like Pa stole it."

"Your pa stole it?"

"Sure, got it a mile an' a half east of here an' drug it. Was a family livin' there, an' they moved away. Grampa an' Pa an' my brother Noah like to took the whole house, but she wouldn' come. They only got part of her. That's why she looks so funny on one end. They cut her in two an' drug her over with twelve head of horses and two mules. They was goin' back for the other half an' stick her together again, but before they got there Wink Manley come with his boys and stole the other half. Pa an' Grampa was pretty sore, but a little later them an' Wink got drunk together an' laughed their heads off about it. Wink, he says his house is at stud, an' if we'll bring our'n over an' breed 'em we'll maybe get a litter of crap houses. Wink was a great ol' fella when he was drunk. After that him an' Pa an' Grampa was friends. Got drunk together ever' chance they got."

"Tom's a great one," Casy agreed. They plodded dustily on down to the bottom of the draw, and then slowed their steps for the rise. Casy wiped his forehead with his sleeve and put on his flat-topped hat again. "Yes," he repeated, "Tom was a great one. For a godless man he was a great one. I seen him in meetin' sometimes when the sperit got into him just a little, an' I seen him take ten-twelve foot jumps. I tell you when ol' Tom got a dose of the Holy Sperit you got to move fast to keep from gettin' run down an' tromped. Jumpy as a stud horse in a box stall."

They topped the next rise and the road dropped into an old water-cut, ugly and raw, a ragged course, and freshet scars cutting into it from both sides. A few stones were in the crossing. Joad minced across in his bare feet. "You talk about Pa," he said. "Maybe you never seen Uncle John the time they baptized him over to Polk's place. Why, he got to plungin' an' jumpin'. Jumped over a feeny bush as big as a piana. Over he'd jump, an' back he'd jump, howlin' like a dog-wolf in moon time. Well, Pa seen him, an' Pa, he figgers he's the bes' Jesus-jumper in these parts. So Pa picks out a feeny bush 'bout twicet as big as Uncle John's feeny bush, and Pa lets out a squawk like a sow litterin' broken bottles, an' he takes a run at that feeny bush an' clears her an' bust his right leg. That took the sperit out of Pa. Preacher wants to pray it set, but Pa says, no, by God, he'd got his heart full of havin' a doctor. Well, they wasn't a doctor, but they was a travelin' dentist, an' he set her. Preacher give her a prayin' over anyways."

They plodded up the little rise on the other side of the water-cut. Now that the sun was on the wane some of its impact was gone, and while the air was hot, the hammering rays were weaker. The strung wire on crooked poles still edged the road. On the right-hand side a line of wire fence strung out across the cotton field, and the dusty green cotton was the same on both sides, dusty and dry and dark green.

Joad pointed to the boundary fence. "That there's our line. We didn't really need no fence there, but we had the wire, an' Pa kinda liked her there. Said it give him a feelin' that forty was forty. Wouldn't of had the fence if Uncle John didn' come drivin' in one night with six spools of wire in his wagon. He give 'em to Pa for a shoat. We never did know where he got that wire." They slowed for the rise, moving their feet in the deep soft dust, feeling the earth with their feet. Joad's eyes were inward on his memory. He seemed to be laughing inside himself. "Uncle John was a crazy bastard," he said. "Like what he done with that shoat." He chuckled and walked on.

Jim Casy waited impatiently. The story did not continue. Casy gave it a good long time to come out. "Well, what'd he do with that shoat?" he demanded at last, with some irritation.

"Huh? Oh! Well, he killed that shoat right there, an' he got Ma to light up the stove. He cut out pork chops an' put 'em in the pan, an' he put ribs an' a leg in the oven. He et chops till the ribs was done, an' he et ribs till the leg was done. An' then he tore into that leg. Cut off big hunks of her an' shoved 'em in his mouth. Us kids hung around slaverin', an' he give us some, but he wouldn' give Pa none. By an' by he et so much he throwed up an' went to sleep. While he's asleep us kids an' Pa finished off the leg. Well, when Uncle John woke up in the mornin' he slaps another leg in the oven. Pa says, 'John, you gonna eat that whole damn pig?' An' he says, 'I aim to, Tom, but I'm scairt some of her'll spoil 'fore I get her et, hungry as I am for pork. Maybe you better get a plate an' gimme back a couple rolls of wire.' Well, sir, Pa wasn't no fool. He jus' let Uncle John go on an' eat himself sick of pig, an' when he drove off he hadn't et much more'n half. Pa says, 'Whyn't you salt her down?' But not Uncle John; when he wants pig he wants a whole pig, an' when he's through, he don't want no pig hangin' around. So off he goes, and Pa salts down what's left."

Casy said, "While I was still in the preachin' sperit I'd a made a lesson of that an' spoke it to you, but I don't do that no more. What you s'pose he done a thing like that for?"

"I dunno," said Joad. "He jus' got hungry for pork. Makes me hungry jus' to think of it. I had jus' four slices of roastin' pork in four years—one slice ever' Christmas."

Casy suggested elaborately, "Maybe Tom'll kill the fatted calf like for the prodigal in Scripture."

Joad laughed scornfully. "You don't know Pa. If he kills a chicken most of the squawkin' will come from Pa, not the chicken. He don't never learn. He's always savin' a pig for Christmas and then it dies in September of bloat or somepin so you can't eat it. When Uncle John wanted pork he et pork. He had her."

They moved over the curving top of the hill and saw the Joad place below them. And Joad stopped. "It ain't the same," he said. "Looka that house. Somepin's happened. They ain't nobody there." The two stood and stared at the little cluster of buildings.

CHAPTER 5

They came in closed cars, and they felt the dry earth with their fingers, and sometimes they drove big earth augers into the ground for soil tests. The tenants, from their sunbeaten dooryards, watched uneasily when the closed cars drove along the fields. And at last the owner men drove into the dooryards and sat in their cars to talk out of the windows. The tenant men stood beside the cars for a while, and then squatted on their hams and found sticks with which to mark the dust.

In the open doors the women stood looking out, and behind them the children—corn-headed children, with wide eyes, one bare foot on top of the other bare foot, and the toes working. The women and the children watched their men talking to the owner men. They were silent.

Some of the owner men were kind because they hated what they had to do, and some of them were angry because they hated to be cruel, and some of them were cold because they had long ago found that one could not be an owner unless one were cold. And all of them were caught in something larger than themselves. Some of them hated the mathematics that drove them, and some were afraid, and some worshiped the mathematics because it provided a refuge from thought and from feeling. If a bank or a finance company owned the land, the owner man said, The Bank—or the Company—needs—wants—insists—must have—as though the Bank or the Company were a monster, with thought and feeling, which had enslaved them. These last would take no responsibility for the banks or the companies because they were men and slaves, while the banks were machines and masters all at the same time. Some of the owner men were a little proud to be slaves to such cold and powerful masters. The owner men sat in the cars and explained. You know the land is poor. You've scrabbled at it long enough, God knows.

The squatting tenant men nodded and wondered and drew figures in the dust, and yes, they knew, God knows. If the dust only wouldn't fly. If the top would only stay on the soil, it might not be so bad.

The owner men went on leading to their point: You know the land's getting poorer. You know what cotton does to the land; robs it, sucks all the blood out of it.

The squatters nodded—they knew, God knew. If they could only rotate the crops they might pump blood back into the land.

Well, it's too late. And the owner men explained the workings and the thinkings of the monster that was stronger than they were. A man can hold land if he can just eat and pay taxes; he can do that.

Yes, he can do that until his crops fail one day and he has to borrow money from the bank.

But—you see, a bank or a company can't do that, because those creatures don't breathe air, don't eat side-meat. They breathe profits; they eat the interest on money. If they don't get it, they die the way you die without air, without side-meat. It is a sad thing, but it is so. It is just so.

The squatting men raised their eyes to understand. Can't we just hang on? Maybe the next year will be a good year. God knows how much cotton next year. And with all the wars—God knows what price cotton will bring. Don't they make explosives out of cotton? And uniforms? Get enough wars and cotton'll hit the ceiling. Next year, maybe. They looked up questioningly.

We can't depend on it. The bank—the monster has to have profits all the time. It can't wait. It'll die. No, taxes go on. When the monster stops growing, it dies. It can't stay one size.

Soft fingers began to tap the sill of the car window, and hard fingers tightened on the restless drawing sticks. In the doorways of the sun-beaten tenant houses, women sighed and then shifted feet so that the one that had been down was now on top, and the toes working. Dogs came sniffing near the owner cars and wetted on all four tires one after another. And chickens lay in the sunny dust and fluffed their feathers to get the cleansing dust down to the skin. In the little sties the pigs grunted inquiringly over the muddy remnants of the slops.

The squatting men looked down again. What do you want us to do? We can't take less share of the crop—we're half starved now. The kids are hungry all the time. We got no clothes, torn an' ragged. If all the neighbors weren't the same, we'd be ashamed to go to meeting.

And at last the owner men came to the point. The tenant system won't work any more. One man on a tractor can take the place of twelve or fourteen families. Pay him a wage and take all the crop. We have to do it. We don't like to do it. But the monster's sick. Something's happened to the monster.

But you'll kill the land with cotton.

We know. We've got to take cotton quick before the land dies. Then we'll sell the land. Lots of families in the East would like to own a piece of land.

The tenant men looked up alarmed. But what'll happen to us? How'll we eat?

You'll have to get off the land. The plows'll go through the dooryard.

And now the squatting men stood up angrily. Grampa took up the land, and he had to kill the Indians and drive them away. And Pa was born here, and he killed weeds and snakes. Then a bad year came and he had to borrow a little money. An' we was born here. There in the door—our children born here. And Pa had to borrow money. The bank owned the land then, but we stayed and we got a little bit of what we raised.

We know that—all that. It's not us, it's the bank. A bank isn't like a man. Or an owner with fifty thousand acres, he isn't like a man either. That's the monster.

Sure, cried the tenant men, but it's our land. We measured it and broke it up. We were born on it, and we got killed on it, died on it. Even if it's no good, it's still ours. That's what makes it ours —being born on it, working it, dying on it. That makes ownership, not a paper with numbers on it.

We're sorry. It's not us. It's the monster. The bank isn't like a man.

Yes, but the bank is only made of men.

No, you're wrong there—quite wrong there. The bank is something else than men. It happens that every man in a bank hates what the bank does, and yet the bank does it. The bank is something more than men, I tell you. It's the monster. Men made it, but they can't control it.

The tenants cried, Grampa killed Indians, Pa killed snakes for the land. Maybe we can kill banks—they're worse than Indians and snakes. Maybe we got to fight to keep our land, like Pa and Grampa did.

And now the owner men grew angry. You'll have to go.

But it's ours, the tenant men cried. We——

No. The bank, the monster owns it. You'll have to go.

We'll get our guns, like Grampa when the Indians came. What then?

Well—first the sheriff, and then the troops. You'll be stealing if you try to stay, you'll be murderers if you kill to stay. The monster isn't men, but it can make men do what it wants.

But if we go, where'll we go? How'll we go? We got no money.

We're sorry, said the owner men. The bank, the fifty-thousand-acre owner can't be responsible. You're on land that isn't yours. Once over the line maybe you can pick cotton in the fall. Maybe you can go on relief. Why don't you go on west to California? There's work there, and it never gets cold. Why, you can reach out anywhere and pick an orange. Why, there's always some kind of crop to work in. Why don't you go there? And the owner men started their cars and rolled away.

The tenant men squatted down on their hams again to mark the dust with a stick, to figure, to wonder. Their sunburned faces were dark, and their sun-whipped eyes were light. The women moved cautiously out of the doorways toward their men, and the children crept behind the women, cautiously, ready to run. The bigger boys squatted beside their fathers, because that made them men. After a time the women asked, What did he want?

And the men looked up for a second, and the smolder of pain was in their eyes. We got to get off. A tractor and a superintendent. Like factories.

Where'll we go? the women asked.

We don't know. We don't know.

And the women went quickly, quietly back into the houses and herded the children ahead of them. They knew that a man so hurt and so perplexed may turn in anger, even on people he loves. They left the men alone to figure and to wonder in the dust.

After a time perhaps the tenant man looked about—at the pump put in ten years ago, with a goose-neck handle and iron flowers on the spout, at the chopping block where a thousand chickens had been killed, at the hand plow lying in the shed, and the patent crib hanging in the rafters over it.

The children crowded about the women in the houses. What we going to do, Ma? Where we going to go?

The women said, We don't know, yet. Go out and play. But don't go near your father. He might whale you if you go near him. And the women went on with the work, but all the time they watched the men squatting in the dust—perplexed and figuring.

The tractors came over the roads and into the fields, great crawlers moving like insects, having the incredible strength of insects. They crawled over the ground, laying the track and rolling on it and picking it up. Diesel tractors, puttering while they stood idle; they thundered when they moved, and then settled down to a droning roar. Snub-nosed monsters, raising the dust and sticking their snouts into it, straight down the country, across the country, through fences, through dooryards, in and out of gullies in straight lines. They did not run on the ground, but on their own roadbeds. They ignored hills and gulches, water courses, fences, houses.

The man sitting in the iron seat did not look like a man; gloved, goggled, rubber dust mask over nose and mouth, he was a part of the monster, a robot in the seat. The thunder of the cylinders sounded through the country, became one with the air and the earth, so that earth and air muttered in sympathetic vibration. The driver could not control it—straight across country it went, cutting through a dozen farms and straight back. A twitch at the controls could swerve the cat', but the driver's hands could not twitch because the monster that built the tractor, the monster that sent the tractor out, had somehow got into the driver's hands, into his brain and muscle, had goggled him and muzzled him—goggled his mind, muzzled his speech, goggled his perception, muzzled his protest. He could not see the land as it was, he could not smell the land as it smelled; his feet did not stamp the clods or feel the warmth and power of the earth. He sat in an iron seat and stepped on iron pedals. He could not cheer or beat or curse or encourage the extension of his power, and because of this he could not cheer or whip or curse or encourage himself. He did not know or own or trust or beseech the land. If a seed dropped did not germinate, it was no skin off his ass. If the young thrusting plant withered in drought or drowned in a flood of rain, it was no more to the driver than to the tractor.

He loved the land no more than the bank loved the land. He could admire the tractor—its machined surfaces, its surge of power, the roar of its detonating cylinders; but it was not his tractor. Behind

metaphor

the tractor rolled the shining disks, cutting the earth with blades—not plowing but surgery, pushing the cut earth to the right where the second row of disks cut it and pushed it to the left; slicing blades shining, polished by the cut earth. And pulled behind the disks, the harrows combing with iron teeth so that the little clods broke up and the earth lay smooth. Behind the harrows, the long seeders—twelve curved iron penes erected in the foundry, orgasms set by gears, raping methodically, raping without passion. The driver sat in his iron seat and he was proud of the straight lines he did not will, proud of the tractor he did not own or love, proud of the power he could not control. And when that crop grew, and was harvested, no man had crumbled a hot clod in his fingers and let the earth sift past his fingertips. No man had touched the seed, or lusted for the growth. Men ate what they had not raised, had no connection with the bread. The land bore under iron, and under iron gradually died; for it was not loved or hated, it had no prayers or curses.

At noon the tractor driver stopped sometimes near a tenant house and opened his lunch: sandwiches wrapped in waxed paper, white bread, pickle, cheese, Spam, a piece of pie branded like an engine part. He ate without relish. And tenants not yet moved away came out to see him, looked curiously while the goggles were taken off, and the rubber dust mask, leaving white circles around the eyes and a large white circle around nose and mouth. The exhaust of the tractor puttered on, for fuel is so cheap it is more efficient to leave the engine running than to heat the Diesel nose for a new start. Curious children crowded close, ragged children who ate their fried dough as they watched. They watched hungrily the unwrapping of the sandwiches, and their hunger-sharpened noses smelled the pickle, cheese, and Spam. They didn't speak to the driver. They watched his hand as it carried food to his mouth. They did not watch him chewing; their eyes followed the hand that held the sandwich. After a while the tenant who could not leave the place came out and squatted in the shade beside the tractor.

"Why, you're Joe Davis's boy!"

"Sure," the driver said.

"Well, what you doing this kind of work for—against your own people?"

"Three dollars a day. I got damn sick of creeping for my dinner

—and not getting it. I got a wife and kids. We got to eat. Three dollars a day, and it comes every day."

"That's right," the tenant said. "But for your three dollars a day fifteen or twenty families can't eat at all. Nearly a hundred people have to go out and wander on the roads for your three dollars a day. Is that right?"

And the driver said, "Can't think of that. Got to think of my own kids. Three dollars a day, and it comes every day. Times are changing, mister, don't you know? Can't make a living on the land unless you've got two, five, ten thousand acres and a tractor. Crop land isn't for little guys like us any more. You don't kick up a howl because you can't make Fords, or because you're not the telephone company. Well, crops are like that now. Nothing to do about it. You try to get three dollars a day someplace. That's the only way."

The tenant pondered. "Funny thing how it is. If a man owns a little property, that property is him, it's part of him, and it's like him. If he owns property only so he can walk on it and handle it and be sad when it isn't doing well, and feel fine when the rain falls on it, that property is him, and some way he's bigger because he owns it. Even if he isn't successful he's big with his property. That is so."

And the tenant pondered more. "But let a man get property he doesn't see, or can't take time to get his fingers in, or can't be there to walk on it—why, then the property is the man. He can't do what he wants, he can't think what he wants. The property is the man, stronger than he is. And he is small, not big. Only his possessions are big—and he's the servant of his property. That is so, too."

The driver munched the branded pie and threw the crust away. "Times are changed, don't you know? Thinking about stuff like that don't feed the kids. Get your three dollars a day, feed your kids. You got no call to worry about anybody's kids but your own. You get a reputation for talking like that, and you'll never get three dollars a day. Big shots won't give you three dollars a day if you worry about anything but your three dollars a day."

"Nearly a hundred people on the road for your three dollars. Where will we go?"

"And that reminds me," the driver said, "you better get out soon. I'm going through the dooryard after dinner."

"You filled in the well this morning."

"I know. Had to keep the line straight. But I'm going through the dooryard after dinner. Got to keep the lines straight. And—well, you know Joe Davis, my old man, so I'll tell you this. I got orders wherever there's a family not moved out—if I have an accident— you know, get too close and cave the house in a little—well, I might get a couple of dollars. And my youngest kid never had no shoes yet."

"I built it with my hands. Straightened old nails to put the sheathing on. Rafters are wired to the stringers with baling wire. It's mine. I built it. You bump it down—I'll be in the window with a rifle. You even come too close and I'll pot you like a rabbit."

"It's not me. There's nothing I can do. I'll lose my job if I don't do it. And look—suppose you kill me? They'll just hang you, but long before you're hung there'll be another guy on the tractor, and he'll bump the house down. You're not killing the right guy."

"That's so," the tenant said. "Who gave you orders? I'll go after him. He's the one to kill."

"You're wrong. He got his orders from the bank. The bank told him, 'Clear those people out or it's your job.' "

"Well, there's a president of the bank. There's a board of directors. I'll fill up the magazine of the rifle and go into the bank."

The driver said, "Fellow was telling me the bank gets orders from the East. The orders were, 'Make the land show profit or we'll close you up.' "

"But where does it stop? Who can we shoot? I don't aim to starve to death before I kill the man that's starving me."

"I don't know. Maybe there's nobody to shoot. Maybe the thing isn't men at all. Maybe, like you said, the property's doing it. Anyway I told you my orders."

"I got to figure," the tenant said. "We all got to figure. There's some way to stop this. It's not like lightning or earthquakes. We've got a bad thing made by men, and by God that's something we can change." The tenant sat in his doorway, and the driver thundered his engine and started off, tracks falling and curving, harrows combing, and the phalli of the seeder slipping into the ground. Across the dooryard the tractor cut, and the hard, foot-beaten ground was seeded field, and the tractor cut through again; the uncut space was ten feet wide. And back he came. The iron guard bit into the house-corner, crumbled the wall, and wrenched the little house from its foundation so that it fell sideways, crushed like a bug. And the driver was goggled and a rubber mask covered his nose and mouth. The tractor cut a straight line on, and the air and the ground vibrated with its thunder. The tenant man stared after it, his rifle in his hand. His wife was beside him, and the quiet children behind. And all of them stared after the tractor.

CHAPTER 6

The Reverend Casy and young Tom stood on the hill and looked down on the Joad place. The small unpainted house was mashed at one corner, and it had been pushed off its foundations so that it slumped at an angle, its blind front windows pointing at a spot of sky well above the horizon. The fences were gone and the cotton grew in the dooryard and up against the house, and the cotton was about the shed barn. The outhouse lay on its side, and the cotton grew close against it. Where the dooryard had been pounded hard by the bare feet of children and by stamping horses' hooves and by the broad wagon wheels, it was cultivated now, and the dark green, dusty cotton grew. Young Tom stared for a long time at the ragged willow beside the dry horse trough, at the concrete base where the pump had been. "Jesus!" he said at last. "Hell musta popped here. There ain't nobody livin' there." At last he moved quickly down the hill, and Casy followed him. He looked into the barn shed, deserted, a little ground straw on the floor, and at the mule stall in the corner. And as he looked in, there was a skittering on the floor and a family of mice faded in under the straw. Joad paused at the entrance to the tool-shed leanto, and no tools were there—a broken plow point, a mess of hay wire in the corner, an iron wheel from a hayrake and a rat-gnawed mule collar, a flat gallon oil can crusted with dirt and oil, and a pair of torn overalls hanging on a nail. "There ain't nothin' left," said Joad. "We had pretty nice tools. There ain't nothin' left."

Casy said, "If I was still a preacher I'd say the arm of the Lord had struck. But now I don't know what happened. I been away. I didn't hear nothin'." They walked toward the concrete well-cap, walked through cotton plants to get to it, and the bolls were forming on the cotton, and the land was cultivated.

"We never planted here," Joad said. "We always kept this clear. Why, you can't get a horse in now without he tromps the cotton." They paused at the dry watering trough, and the proper weeds that should grow under a trough were gone and the old thick wood of the trough was dry and cracked. On the well-cap the bolts that had held the pump stuck up, their threads rusty and the nuts gone. Joad

looked into the tube of the well and spat and listened. He dropped
a clod down the well and listened. "She was a good well," he said.
"I can't hear water." He seemed reluctant to go to the house. He
dropped clod after clod down the well. "Maybe they're all dead," he
said. "But somebody'd a told me. I'd a got word some way."

"Maybe they left a letter or something to tell in the house. Would
they of knowed you was comin' out?"

"I don' know," said Joad. "No, I guess not. I didn' know myself
till a week ago."

"Le's look in the house. She's all pushed out a shape. Something
knocked the hell out of her." They walked slowly toward the sagging
house. Two of the supports of the porch roof were pushed out so
that the roof flopped down on one end. And the house-corner was
crushed in. Through a maze of splintered wood the room at the
corner was visible. The front door hung open inward, and a low
strong gate across the front door hung outward on leather hinges.

Joad stopped at the step, a twelve-by-twelve timber. "Doorstep's
here," he said. "But they're gone—or Ma's dead." He pointed to the
low gate across the front door. "If Ma was anywheres about, that
gate'd be shut an' hooked. That's one thing she always done—seen
that gate was shut." His eyes were warm. "Ever since the pig got in
over to Jacobs' an' et the baby. Milly Jacobs was jus' out in the barn.
She come in while the pig was still eatin' it. Well, Milly Jacobs was
in a family way, an' she went ravin'. Never did get over it. Touched
ever since. But Ma took a lesson from it. She never lef' that pig gate
open 'less she was in the house herself. Never did forget. No—
they're gone—or dead." He climbed to the split porch and looked
into the kitchen. The windows were broken out, and throwing rocks
lay on the floor, and the floor and walls sagged steeply away from
the door, and the sifted dust was on the boards. Joad pointed to the
broken glass and the rocks. "Kids," he said. "They'll go twenty miles
to bust a window. I done it myself. They know when a house is
empty, they know. That's the fust thing kids do when folks move
out." The kitchen was empty of furniture, stove gone and the round
stovepipe hole in the wall showing light. On the sink shelf lay an old
beer opener and a broken fork with its wooden handle gone. Joad
slipped cautiously into the room, and the floor groaned under his
weight. An old copy of the Philadelphia *Ledger* was on the floor
against the wall, its pages yellow and curling. Joad looked into the
bedroom—no bed, no chairs, nothing. On the wall a picture of an

Indian girl in color, labeled Red Wing. A bed slat leaning against the wall, and in one corner a woman's high button shoe, curled up at the toe and broken over the instep. Joad picked it up and looked at it. "I remember this," he said. "This was Ma's. It's all wore out now. Ma liked them shoes. Had 'em for years. No, they've went—an' took ever'thing."

The sun had lowered until it came through the angled end windows now, and it flashed on the edges of the broken glass. Joad turned at last and went out and crossed the porch. He sat down on the edge of it and rested his bare feet on the twelve-by-twelve step. The evening light was on the fields, and the cotton plants threw long shadows on the ground, and the molting willow tree threw a long shadow.

Casy sat down beside Joad. "They never wrote you nothin'?" he asked.

"No. Like I said, they wasn't people to write. Pa could write, but he wouldn'. Didn't like to. It give him the shivers to write. He could work out a catalogue order as good as the nex' fella, but he wouldn' write no letters just for ducks." They sat side by side, staring off into the distance. Joad laid his rolled coat on the porch beside him. His independent hands rolled a cigarette, smoothed it and lighted it, and he inhaled deeply and blew the smoke out through his nose. "Somepin's wrong," he said. "I can't put my finger on her. I got an itch that somepin's wronger'n hell. Just this house pushed aroun' an' my folks gone."

Casy said, "Right over there the ditch was, where I done the baptizin'. You wasn't mean, but you was tough. Hung onto that little girl's pigtail like a bulldog. We baptize' you both in the name of the Holy Ghos', and still you hung on. Ol' Tom says, 'Hol' 'im under water.' So I shove your head down till you start to bubblin' before you'd let go a that pigtail. You wasn't mean, but you was tough. Sometimes a tough kid grows up with a big jolt of the sperit in him."

A lean gray cat came sneaking out of the barn and crept through the cotton plants to the end of the porch. It leaped silently up to the porch and crept low-belly toward the men. It came to a place between and behind the two, and then it sat down, and its tail stretched out straight and flat to the floor, and the last inch of it flicked. The cat sat and looked off into the distance where the men were looking.

Joad glanced around at it. "By God! Look who's here. Somebody stayed." He put out his hand, but the cat leaped away out of reach and sat down and licked the pads of its lifted paw. Joad looked at it, and his face was puzzled. "I know what's the matter," he cried. "That cat jus' made me figger what's wrong."

"Seems to me there's lots wrong," said Casy.

"No, it's more'n jus' this place. Whyn't that cat jus' move in with some neighbors—with the Rances. How come nobody ripped some lumber off this house? Ain't been nobody here for three-four months, an' nobody's stole no lumber. Nice planks on the barn shed, plenty good planks on the house, winda frames—an' nobody's took 'em. That ain't right. That's what was botherin' me, an' I couldn't catch hold of her."

"Well, what's that figger out for you?" Casy reached down and slipped off his sneakers and wriggled his long toes on the step.

"I don' know. Seems like maybe there ain't any neighbors. If there was, would all them nice planks be here? Why, Jesus Christ! Albert Rance took his family, kids an' dogs an' all, into Oklahoma City one Christmus. They was gonna visit with Albert's cousin. Well, folks aroun' here thought Albert moved away without sayin' nothin'—figgered maybe he got debts or some woman's squarin' off at him. When Albert come back a week later there wasn't a thing lef' in his house—stove was gone, beds was gone, winda frames was gone, an' eight feet of plankin' was gone off the south side of the house so you could look right through her. He come drivin' home just as Muley Graves was goin' away with three doors an' the well pump. Took Albert two weeks drivin' aroun' the neighbors' 'fore he got his stuff back."

Casy scratched his toes luxuriously. "Didn't nobody give him an argument? All of 'em jus' give the stuff up?"

"Sure. They wasn't stealin' it. They thought he lef' it, an' they jus' took it. He got all of it back—all but a sofa pilla, velvet with a pitcher of an Injun on it. Albert claimed Grampa got it. Claimed Grampa got Injun blood, that's why he wants that pitcher. Well, Grampa did get her, but he didn't give a damn about the pitcher on it. He jus' liked her. Used to pack her aroun' an' he'd put her wherever he was gonna sit. He never would give her back to Albert. Says, 'If Albert wants this pilla so bad, let him come an' get her. But he better come shootin', 'cause I'll blow his goddamn stinkin' head off if he comes messin' aroun' my pilla.' So finally Albert give up an' made Grampa a present of that pilla. It give Grampa idears, though.

He took to savin' chicken feathers. Says he's gonna have a whole damn bed of feathers. But he never got no feather bed. One time Pa got mad at a skunk under the house. Pa slapped that skunk with a two-by-four, and Ma burned all Grampa's feathers so we could live in the house." He laughed. "Grampa's a tough ol' bastard. Jus' set on that Injun pilla an' says, 'Let Albert come an' get her. Why,' he says, 'I'll take that squirt and wring 'im out like a pair of drawers.'"

The cat crept close between the men again, and its tail lay flat and its whiskers jerked now and then. The sun dropped low toward the horizon and the dusty air was red and golden. The cat reached out a gray questioning paw and touched Joad's coat. He looked around. "Hell, I forgot the turtle. I ain't gonna pack it all over hell." He unwrapped the land turtle and pushed it under the house. But in a moment it was out, headed southwest as it had been from the first. The cat leaped at it and struck at its straining head and slashed at its moving feet. The old, hard, humorous head was pulled in, and the thick tail slapped in under the shell, and when the cat grew tired of waiting for it and walked off, the turtle headed on southwest again.

Young Tom Joad and the preacher watched the turtle go—waving its legs and boosting its heavy, high-domed shell along toward the southwest. The cat crept along behind for a while, but in a dozen yards it arched its back to a strong taut bow and yawned, and came stealthily back toward the seated men.

"Where the hell you s'pose he's goin'?" said Joad. "I seen turtles all my life. They're always goin' someplace. They always seem to want to get there." The gray cat seated itself between and behind them again. It blinked slowly. The skin over its shoulders jerked forward under a flea, and then slipped slowly back. The cat lifted a paw and inspected it, flicked its claws out and in again experimentally, and licked its pads with a shell-pink tongue. The red sun touched the horizon and spread out like a jellyfish, and the sky above it seemed much brighter and more alive than it had been. Joad unrolled his new yellow shoes from his coat, and he brushed his dusty feet with his hand before he slipped them on.

The preacher, staring off across the fields, said, "Somebody's comin'. Look! Down there, right through the cotton."

Joad looked where Casy's finger pointed. "Comin' afoot," he said. "Can't see 'im for the dust he raises. Who the hell's comin' here?" They watched the figure approaching in the evening light,

and the dust it raised was reddened by the setting sun. "Man," said
Joad. The man drew closer, and as he walked past the barn, Joad
said, "Why, I know him. You know him—that's Muley Graves." And
he called, "Hey, Muley! How ya?"

The approaching man stopped, startled by the call, and then he
came on quickly. He was a lean man, rather short. His movements
were jerky and quick. He carried a gunny sack in his hand. His blue
jeans were pale at knee and seat, and he wore an old black suit coat,
stained and spotted, the sleeves torn loose from the shoulders in
back, and ragged holes worn through at the elbows. His black hat
was as stained as his coat, and the band, torn half free, flopped up
and down as he walked. Muley's face was smooth and unwrinkled,
but it wore the truculent look of a bad child, the mouth held tight
and small, the little eyes half scowling, half petulant.

"You remember Muley," Joad said softly to the preacher.

"Who's that?" the advancing man called. Joad did not answer.
Muley came close, very close, before he made out the faces. "Well,
I'll be damned," he said. "It's Tommy Joad. When'd you get out,
Tommy?" He dropped his sack to the ground.

"Two days ago," said Joad. "Took a little time to hitch-hike
home. An' look here what I find. Where's my folks, Muley? What's
the house all smashed up for, an' cotton planted in the dooryard?"

"By God, it's lucky I come by!" said Muley. " 'Cause ol' Tom
worried himself. When they was fixin' to move I was settin' in the
kitchen there. I jus' tol' Tom I wan't gonna move, by God. I tol' him
that, an' Tom says, 'I'm worryin' myself about Tommy. S'pose he
comes home an' they ain't nobody here. What'll he think?' I says,
'Whyn't you write down a letter?' An' Tom says, 'Maybe I will. I'll
think about her. But if I don't, you keep your eye out for Tommy
if you're still aroun'.' 'I'll be aroun',' I says. 'I'll be aroun' till hell
freezes over. There ain't nobody can run a guy name of Graves outa
this country.' An' they ain't done it, neither."

Joad said impatiently, "Where's my folks? Tell about you standin'
up to 'em later, but where's my folks?"

"Well, they was gonna stick her out when the bank come to
tractorin' off the place. Your grampa stood out here with a rifle, an'
he blowed the headlights off that cat', but she come on just the
same. Your grampa didn't wanta kill the guy drivin' that cat', an'
that was Willy Feeley, an' Willy knowed it, so he jus' come on, an'
bumped the hell outa the house. Ol' Tom jas' stood there a-cussin',

but it didn't do him no good. When he sees that cat' come a-bustin' through the house, an' give her a shake like a dog shakes a rat— well, it took somepin outa Tom. Kinda got into 'im. He ain't been the same ever since."

"Where is my folks?" Joad spoke angrily.

"What I'm tellin' you. Took three trips with your Uncle John's wagon. Took the stove an' the pump an' the beds. You should a seen them beds go out with all them kids an' your granma an' grampa settin' up against the headboard, an' your brother Noah settin' there smokin' a cigareet, an' spittin' la-de-da over the side of the wagon." Joad opened his mouth to speak. "They're all at your Uncle John's," Muley said quickly.

"Oh! All at John's. Well, what they doin' there? Now stick to her for a second, Muley. Jus' stick to her. In jus' a minute you can go on your own way. What they doin' there?"

"Well, they been choppin' cotton, all of 'em, even the kids an' your grampa. Gettin' money together so they can shove on west. Gonna buy a car and shove on west where it's easy livin'. There ain't nothin' here. Fifty cents a clean acre for choppin' cotton, an' folks beggin' for the chance to chop."

"An' they ain't gone yet?"

"No," said Muley. "Not that I know. Las' I heard was four days ago when I seen your brother Noah out shootin' jackrabbits, an' he says they're aimin' to go in about two weeks. John got his notice he got to get off. You jus' go on about eight miles to John's place. You'll find your folks piled in John's house like gophers in a winter burrow."

"O.K." said Joad. "Now you can ride on your own way. You ain't changed a bit, Muley. If you want to tell about somepin off northwest, you point your nose straight southeast."

Muley said truculently, "You ain't changed neither. You was a smart-aleck kid, an' you're still a smart aleck. You ain't tellin' me how to skin my life, by any chancet?"

Joad grinned. "No, I ain't. If you wanta drive your head into a pile a broken glass, there ain't nobody can tell you different. You know this here preacher, don't you, Muley? Rev. Casy."

"Why, sure, sure. Didn't look over. Remember him well." Casy stood up and the two shook hands. "Glad to see you again," said Muley. "You ain't been aroun' for a hell of a longtime."

"I been off a-askin' questions," said Casy. "What happened here? Why they kickin' folks off the lan'?"

Muley's mouth snapped shut so tightly that a little parrot's beak in the middle of his upper lip stuck down over his under lip. He scowled. "Them sons-a-bitches," he said. "Them dirty sons-a-bitches. I tell ya, men, I'm stayin'. They ain't gettin' rid a me. If they throw me off, I'll come back, an' if they figger I'll be quiet underground, why, I'll take a couple-three of the sons-a-bitches along for company." He patted a heavy weight in his side coat pocket. "I ain't a-goin'. My pa come here fifty years ago. An' I ain't a-goin'.''

Joad said, "What's the idear of kickin' the folks off?"

"Oh! They talked pretty about it. You know what kinda years we been havin'. Dust comin' up an' spoilin' ever'thing so a man didn't get enough crop to plug up an ant's ass. An' ever'body got bills at the grocery. You know how it is. Well, the folks that owns the lan' says, 'We can't afford to keep no tenants.' An' they says, 'The share a tenant gets is jus' the margin a profit we can't afford to lose.' An' they says, 'If we put all our lan' in one piece we can jus' hardly make her pay.' So they tractored all the tenants off a the lan'. All 'cept me, an' by God I ain't goin'. Tommy, you know me. You knowed me all your life."

"Damn right," said Joad, "all my life."

"Well, you know I ain't a fool. I know this land ain't much good. Never was much good 'cept for grazin'. Never should a broke her up. An' now she's cottoned damn near to death. If on'y they didn' tell me I got to get off, why, I'd prob'y be in California right now a-eatin' grapes an' a-pickin' an orange when I wanted. But them sons-a-bitches says I got to get off—an', Jesus Christ, a man can't, when he's tol' to!"

"Sure," said Joad. "I wonder Pa went so easy. I wonder Grampa didn' kill nobody. Nobody never tol' Grampa where to put his feet. An' Ma ain't nobody you can push aroun', neither. I seen her beat the hell out of a tin peddler with a live chicken one time 'cause he give her a argument. She had the chicken in one han', an' the ax in the other, about to cut its head off. She aimed to go for that peddler with the ax, but she forgot which han' was which, an' she takes after him with the chicken. Couldn' even eat that chicken when she got done. They wasn't nothing but a pair a legs in her han'. Grampa throwed his hip outa joint laughin'. How'd my folks go so easy?"

"Well, the guy that come aroun' talked nice as pie. 'You got to get off. It ain't my fault.' 'Well,' I says, 'whose fault is it? I'll go an' I'll nut the fella.' 'It's the Shawnee Lan' an' Cattle Company. I jus'' got orders.' 'Who's the Shawnee Lan' an' Cattle Company?' 'It ain't nobody. It's a company.' Got a fella crazy. There wasn't nobody you could lay for. Lot a the folks jus' got tired out lookin' for somepin to be mad at—but not me. I'm mad at all of it. I'm stayin'.''

A large red drop of sun lingered on the horizon and then dripped over and was gone, and the sky was brilliant over the spot where it had gone, and a torn cloud, like a bloody rag, hung over the spot of its going. And dusk crept over the sky from the eastern horizon, and darkness crept over the land from the east. The evening star flashed and glittered in the dusk. The gray cat sneaked away toward the open barn shed and passed inside like a shadow.

Joad said, "Well, we ain't gonna walk no eight miles to Uncle John's place tonight. My dogs is burned up. How's it if we go to your place, Muley? That's on'y about a mile."

"Won't do no good." Muley seemed embarrassed. "My wife an' the kids an' her brother all took an' went to California. They wasn't nothin' to eat. They wasn't as mad as me, so they went. Bought an ol' Chevy an' took what they could. Fella came a-passin' out han'bills say good wages in California. So they went. They wasn't nothin' to eat here."

The preacher stirred nervously. "You should of went too. You shouldn't of broke up the fambly."

"I couldn'," said Muley Graves. "Somepin jus' wouldn' let me."

"Well, by God, I'm hungry," said Joad. "Four solemn years I been eatin' right on the minute. My guts is yellin' bloody murder. What you gonna eat, Muley? How you been gettin' your dinner?"

Muley said ashamedly, "For a while I et frogs an' squirrels an' prairie dogs sometimes. Had to do it. But now I got some wire nooses on the tracks in the dry stream brush. Get rabbits, an' sometimes a prairie chicken. Skunks get caught, an' coons, too." He reached down, picked up his sack, and emptied it on the porch. Two cottontails and a jackrabbit fell out and rolled over limply, soft and furry.

"God Awmighty," said Joad, "it's more'n four years sence I've et fresh-killed meat."

Casy picked up one of the cottontails and held it in his hand. "You sharin' with us, Muley Graves?" he asked.

Muley fidgeted in embarrassment. "I ain't got no choice in the matter." He stopped on the ungracious sound of his own words. "That ain't like I mean it. That ain't. I mean"—he stumbled—"what I mean, if a fella's got somepin to eat an' another fella's hungry—

why, the first fella ain't got no choice. I mean, s'pose I pick up my rabbits an' go off somewheres an' eat 'em. See?"

"I see," said Casy. "I can see that. Muley sees somepin there, Tom. Muley's got a-holt of somepin, an' it's too big for him, an' it's too big for me."

Young Tom rubbed his hands together. "Who got a knife? Le's get at these here miserable rodents. Le's get at 'em."

Muley reached in his pants pocket and produced a large horn-handled pocket knife. Tom Joad took it from him, opened a blade, and smelled it. He drove the blade again and again into the ground and smelled it again, wiped it on his trouser leg, and felt the edge with his thumb.

Muley took a quart bottle of water out of his hip pocket and set it on the porch. "Go easy on that there water," he said. "That's all there is. This here well's filled in."

Tom took up a rabbit in his hand. "One of you go get some bale wire outa the barn. We'll make a fire with some a this broken plank from the house." He looked at the dead rabbit. "There ain't nothin' so easy to get ready as a rabbit," he said. He lifted the skin of the back, slit it, put his fingers in the hole, and tore the skin off. It slipped off like a stocking, slipped off the body to the neck, and off the legs to the paws. Joad picked up the knife again and cut off head and feet. He laid the skin down, slit the rabbit along the ribs, shook out the intestines onto the skin, and then threw the mess off into the cotton field. And the clean-muscled little body was ready. Joad cut off the legs and cut the meaty back into two pieces. He was picking up the second rabbit when Casy came back with a snarl of bale wire in his hand. "Now build up a fire and put some stakes up," said Joad. "Jesus Christ, I'm hungry for these here creatures!" He cleaned and cut up the rest of the rabbits and strung them on the wire. Muley and Casy tore splintered boards from the wrecked house-corner and started a fire, and they drove a stake into the ground on each side to hold the wire.

Muley came back to Joad. "Look out for boils on that jackrabbit," he said. "I don't like to eat no jackrabbit with boils." He took a little cloth bag from his pocket and put it on the porch.

Joad said, "The jack was clean as a whistle—Jesus God, you got salt too? By any chance you got some plates an' a tent in your pocket?" He poured salt in his hand and sprinkled it over the pieces of rabbit strung on the wire.

The fire leaped and threw shadows on the house, and the dry wood crackled and snapped. The sky was almost dark now and the stars were out sharply. The gray cat came out of the barn shed and trotted miaowing toward the fire, but, nearly there, it turned and went directly to one of the little piles of rabbit entrails on the ground. It chewed and swallowed, and the entrails hung from its mouth.

Casy sat on the ground beside the fire, feeding it broken pieces of board, pushing the long boards in as the flame ate off their ends. The evening bats flashed into the firelight and out again. The cat crouched back and licked its lips and washed its face and whiskers.

Joad held up his rabbit-laden wire between his two hands and walked to the fire. "Here, take one end, Muley. Wrap your end around that stake. That's good, now! Let's tighten her up. We ought to wait till the fire's burned down, but I can't wait." He made the wire taut, then found a stick and slipped the pieces of meat along the wire until they were over the fire. And the flames licked up around the meat and hardened and glazed the surfaces. Joad sat down by the fire, but with his stick he moved and turned the rabbit so that it would not become sealed to the wire. "This here is a party," he said. "Yes, sir, this sure as hell is a party. Salt, Muley's got, an' water an' rabbits. I wish he got a pot of hominy in his pocket. That's all I wish."

Muley said over the fire, "You fellas'd think I'm touched, the way I live."

"Touched, nothin'," said Joad. "If you're touched, I wisht ever'-body was touched."

Muley continued, "Well, sir, it's a funny thing. Somepin went an' happened to me when they tol' me I had to get off the place. Fust I was gonna go in an' kill a whole flock a people. Then all my folks all went away out west. An' I got wanderin' aroun'. Jus' walkin' aroun'. Never went far. Slep' wherever I was. I was gonna sleep here tonight. That's why I come. I'd tell myself, 'I'm lookin' after things so when all the folks come back it'll be all right.' But I knowed that wan't true. There ain't nothin' to look after. The folks ain't never comin' back. I'm jus' wanderin' aroun' like a damn ol' graveyard ghos'."

"Fella gets use' to a place, it's hard to go," said Casy. "Fella gets use' to a way a thinkin', it's hard to leave. I ain't a preacher no more, but all the time I find I'm prayin', not even thinkin' what I'm doin'."

Joad turned the pieces of meat over on the wire. The juice was dripping now, and every drop, as it fell in the fire, shot up a spurt of flame. The smooth surface of the meat was crinkling up and turn- ing a faint brown. "Smell her," said Joad. "Jesus, look down an' jus' smell her!"

Muley went on, "Like a damn ol' graveyard ghos'. I been goin' aroun' the places where stuff happened. Like there's a place over by our forty; in a gully they's a bush. Fust time I ever laid with a girl was there. Me fourteen an' stampin' an' jerkin' an' snortin' like a buck deer, randy as a billy goat. So I went there an' I laid down on the groun', an' I seen it all happen again. An' there's the place down by the barn where Pa got gored to death by a bull. An' his blood is right in that groun', right now. Mus' be. Nobody never washed it out. An' I put my han' on that groun' where my own pa's blood is part of it." He paused uneasily. "You fellas think I'm touched?"

Joad turned the meat, and his eyes were inward. Casy, feet drawn up, stared into the fire. Fifteen feet back from the men the fed cat was sitting, the long gray tail wrapped neatly around the front feet. A big owl shrieked as it went overhead, and the firelight showed its white underside and the spread of its wings.

"No," said Casy. "You ain't touched. You're lonely—but you ain't touched."

Muley's tight little face was rigid. "I put my han' right on the groun' where that blood is still. An' I seen my pa with a hole through his ches', an' I felt him shiver up against me like he done, an' I seen him kind of settle back an' reach with his han's an' his feet. An' I seen his eyes all milky with hurt, an' then he was still an' his eyes so clear—lookin' up. An' me a little kid settin' there, not cryin' nor nothin,' jus' settin' there." He shook his head sharply. Joad turned the meat over and over. "An' I went in the room where Joe was born. Bed wasn't there, but it was the room. An' all them things is true, an' they're right in the place they happened. Joe come to life right there. He give a big ol' gasp an' then he let out a squawk you could hear a mile, an' his granma standin' there says, 'That's a daisy, that's a daisy,' over an' over. An' her so proud she bust three cups that night."

Joad cleared his throat. "Think we better eat her now."

"Let her get good an' done, good an' brown, awmost black," said Muley irritably. "I wanta talk. I ain't talked to nobody. If I'm touched, I'm touched, an' that's the end of it. Like a ol' graveyard ghos' goin' to neighbors' houses in the night. Peters', Jacobs',

Rance's, Joad's; an' the houses all dark, standin' like miser'ble ratty boxes, but they was good parties an' dancin'. An' there was meetin's and shoutin' glory. They was weddin's, all in them houses. An' then I'd want to go in town an' kill folks. 'Cause what'd they take when they tractored the folks off the lan'? What'd they get so their 'margin a profit' was safe? They got Pa dyin' on the groun', an' Joe yellin' his first breath, an' me jerkin' like a billy goat under a bush in the night. What'd they get? God knows the lan' ain't no good. Nobody been able to make a crop for years. But them sons-a-bitches at their desks, they jus' chopped folks in two for their margin a profit. They jus' cut 'em in two. Place where folks live is them folks. They ain't whole, out lonely on the road in a piled-up car. They ain't alive no more. Them sons-a-bitches killed 'em." And he was silent, his thin lips still moving, his chest still panting. He sat and looked down at his hands in the firelight. "I—I ain't talked to nobody for a long time," he apologized softly. "I been sneakin' aroun' like a ol' grave-yard ghos'."

Casy pushed the long boards into the fire and the flames licked up around them and leaped up toward the meat again. The house cracked loudly as the cooler night air contracted the wood. Casy said quietly, "I gotta see them folks that's gone out on the road. I got a feelin' I got to see them. They gonna need help no preacher can give 'em. Hope of heaven when their lives ain't lived? Holy Sperit when their own sperit is downcast an' sad? They gonna need help. They got to live before they can afford to die."

Joad cried nervously, "Jesus Christ, le's eat this meat 'fore it's smaller'n a cooked mouse! Look at her. Smell her." He leaped to his feet and slid the pieces of meat along the wire until they were clear of the fire. He took Muley's knife from his pocket and sawed through a piece of meat until it was free of the wire. "Here's for the preacher," he said.

"I tol' you I ain't no preacher."

"Well, here's for the man, then." He cut off another piece. "Here, Muley, if you ain't too goddamn upset to eat. This here's jackrabbit. Tougher'n a bull-bitch." He sat back and clamped his long teeth on the meat and tore out a great bite and chewed it. "Jesus Christ! Hear her crunch!" And he tore out another bite ravenously.

Muley still sat regarding his meat. "Maybe I oughtn' to a-talked like that," he said. "Fella should maybe keep stuff like that in his head."

Casy looked over, his mouth full of rabbit. He chewed, and his muscled throat convulsed in swallowing. "Yes, you should talk," he said. "Sometimes a sad man can talk the sadness right out through his mouth. Sometimes a killin' man can talk the murder right out of his mouth an' not do no murder. You done right. Don't you kill nobody if you can help it." And he bit out another hunk of rabbit. Joad tossed the bones in the fire and jumped up and cut more off the wire. Muley was eating slowly now, and his nervous little eyes went from one to the other of his companions. Joad ate scowling like an animal, and a ring of grease formed around his mouth.

For a long time Muley looked at him, almost timidly. He put down the hand that held the meat. "Tommy," he said.

Joad looked up and did not stop gnawing the meat. "Yeah?" he said, around a mouthful.

"Tommy, you ain't mad with me talkin' about killin'people? You ain't huffy, Tom?"

"No," said Tom. "I ain't huffy. It's jus' somepin that happened."

"Ever'body knowed it wasn't no fault of yours," said Muley. "Ol' man Turnbull said he was gonna get you when ya come out. Says nobody can kill one a his boys. All the folks hereabouts talked him outa it, though."

"We was drunk," Joad said softly. "Drunk at a dance. I don' know how she started. An' then I felt that knife go in me, an' that sobered me up. Fust thing I see is Herb comin' for me again with his knife. They was this here shovel leanin' against the schoolhouse, so I grabbed it an' smacked 'im over the head. I never had nothing against Herb. He was a nice fella. Come a-bullin' after my sister Rosasharn when he was a little fella. No, I liked Herb."

"Well, ever'body tol' his pa that, an' finally cooled 'im down. Somebody says they's Hatfield blood on his mother's side in ol' Turnbull, an' he's got to live up to it. I don't know about that. Him an' his folks went on to California six months ago."

Joad took the last of the rabbit from the wire and passed it around. He settled back and ate more slowly now, chewed evenly, and wiped the grease from his mouth with his sleeve. And his eyes, dark and half closed, brooded as he looked into the dying fire. "Ever'body's goin' west," he said. "I got me a parole to keep. Can't leave the state."

"Parole?" Muley asked. "I heard about them. How do they work?"

"Well, I got out early, three years early. They's stuff I gotta do, or they send me back in. Got to report ever' so often."

"How they treat ya there in McAlester? My woman's cousin was in McAlester an' they give him hell."

"It ain't so bad," said Joad. "Like ever'place else. They give ya hell if ya raise hell. You get along O.K. les' some guard gets it in for ya. Then you catch plenty hell. I got along O.K. Minded my own business, like any guy would. I learned to write nice as hell. Birds an' stuff like that, too; not just word writin'. My ol' man'll be sore when he sees me whip out a bird in one stroke. Pa's gonna be mad when he sees me do that. He don't like no fancy stuff like that. He don't even like word writin'. Kinda scares 'im, I guess. Ever' time Pa seen writin', somebody took somepin away from 'im."

"They didn' give you no beatin's or nothin' like that?"

"No, I jus' tended my own affairs. 'Course you get goddamn good an' sick a-doin' the same thing day after day for four years. If you done somepin you was ashamed of, you might think about that. But, hell, if I seen Herb Turnbull comin' for me with a knife right now, I'd squash him down with a shovel again."

"Anybody would," said Muley. The preacher stared into the fire, and his high forehead was white in the settling dark. The flash of little flames picked out the cords of his neck. His hands, clasped about his knees, were busy pulling knuckles.

Joad threw the last bones into the fire and licked his fingers and then wiped them on his pants. He stood up and brought the bottle of water from the porch, took a sparing drink, and passed the bottle before he sat down again. He went on, "The thing that give me the mos' trouble was, it didn' make no sense. You don't look for no sense when lightnin' kills a cow, or it comes up a flood. That's jus' the way things is. But when a bunch of men take an' lock you up four years, it ought to have some meaning. Men is supposed to think things out. Here they put me in, an' keep me an' feed me four years. That ought to either make me so I won't do her again or else punish me so I'll be afraid to do her again"—he paused—"but if Herb or anybody else come for me, I'd do her again. Do her before I could figure her out. Specially if I was drunk. That sort of senselessness kind a worries a man."

Muley observed, "Judge says he give you a light sentence 'cause it wasn't all your fault."

Joad said, "They's a guy in McAlester—lifer. He studies all the time. He's sec'etary of the warden—writes the warden's letters an' stuff like that. Well, he's one hell of a bright guy an' reads law an' all stuff like that. Well, I talked to him one time about her, 'cause he reads so much stuff. An' he says it don't do no good to read books. Says he's read ever'thing about prisons now, an' in the old times; an' he says she makes less sense to him now than she did before he starts readin'. He says it's a thing that started way to hell an' gone back, an' nobody seems to be able to stop her, an' nobody got sense enough to change her. He says for God's sake don't read about her because he says for one thing you'll jus' get messed up worse, an' for another you won't have no respect for the guys that work the gover'ments."

"I ain't got a hell of a lot of respec' for 'em now," said Muley. "On'y kind a gover'ment we got that leans on us fellas is the 'safe margin a profit.' There's one thing that got me stumped, an' that's Willy Feeley—drivin' that cat', an' gonna be a straw boss on lan' his own folks used to farm. That worries me. I can see how a fella might come from some other place an' not know no better, but Willy belongs. Worried me so I went up to 'im and ast 'im. Right off he got mad. 'I got two little kids,' he says. 'I got a wife an' my wife's mother. Them people got to eat.' Gets madder'n hell. 'Fust an' on'y thing I got to think about is my own folks,' he says. 'What happens to other folks is their look-out,' he says. Seems like he's 'shamed, so he gets mad."

Jim Casy had been staring at the dying fire, and his eyes had grown wider and his neck muscles stood higher. Suddenly he cried, "I got her! If ever a man got a dose of the sperit, I got her! Got her all of a flash!" He jumped to his feet and paced back and forth, his head swinging. "Had a tent one time. Drawed as much as five hundred people ever' night. That's before either you fellas seen me." He stopped and faced them. "Ever notice I never took no collections when I was preachin' out here to folks—in barns an' in the open?"

"By God, you never," said Muley. "People around here got so use' to not givin' you money they got to bein' a little mad when some other preacher come along an' passed the hat. Yes, sir!"

"I took somepin to eat," said Casy. "I took a pair a pants when mine was wore out, an' a ol' pair a shoes when I was walkin' through to the groun', but it wasn't like when I had the tent. Some days there I'd take in ten or twenty dollars. Wasn't happy that-a-way, so I give her up, an' for a time I was happy. I think I got her now. I don' know if I can say her. I guess I won't try to say her—but maybe there's a place for a preacher. Maybe I can preach again. Folks out lonely on the road, folks with no lan', no home to go to. They got to have some kind of home. Maybe—" He stood over the fire. The hundred muscles of his neck stood out in high relief, and the firelight went deep into his eyes and ignited red embers. He stood and looked at the fire, his face tense as though he were listening, and the hands that had been active to pick, to handle, to throw ideas, grew quiet, and in a moment crept into his pockets. The bats flittered in and out of the dull firelight, and the soft watery burble of a night hawk came from across the fields.

Tom reached quietly into his pocket and brought out his tobacco, and he rolled a cigarette slowly and looked over it at the coals while he worked. He ignored the whole speech of the preacher, as though it were some private thing that should not be inspected. He said, "Night after night in my bunk I figgered how she'd be when I come home again. I figgered maybe Grampa or Granma'd be dead, an' maybe there'd be some new kids. Maybe Pa'd not be so tough. Maybe Ma'd set back a little an' let Rosasharn do the work. I knowed it wouldn't be the same as it was. Well, we'll sleep here I guess, an' come daylight we'll get on to Uncle John's. Leastwise I will. You think you're comin' along, Casy?"

The preacher still stood looking into the coals. He said slowly, "Yeah, I'm goin' with you. An' when your folks start out on the road I'm goin' with them. An' where folks are on the road, I'm gonna be with them."

"You'd be welcome," said Joad. "Ma always favored you. Said you was a preacher to trust. Rosasharn wasn't growed up then." He turned his head. "Muley, you gonna walk on over with us?" Muley was looking toward the road over which they had come. "Think you'll come along, Muley?" Joad repeated.

"Huh? No. I don't go no place, an' I don't leave no place. See that glow over there, jerkin' up an' down? That's prob'ly the super'ntendent of this stretch a cotton. Somebody maybe seen our fire."

Tom looked. The glow of light was nearing over the hill. "We ain't doin' no harm," he said. "We'll jus' set here. We ain't doin' nothin'."

Muley cackled. "Yeah! We're doin' somepin just' bein' here. We're trespassin'. We can't stay. They been tryin' to catch me for

two months. Now you look. If that's a car comin' we go out in the
cotton an' lay down. Don't have to go far. Then by God let 'em try
to fin' us! Have to look up an' down ever' row. Jus' keep your head
down."

Joad demanded, "What's come over you, Muley? You wasn't
never no run-an'-hide fella. You was mean."

Muley watched the approaching lights. "Yeah!" he said. "I was
mean like a wolf. Now I'm mean like a weasel. When you're huntin' somepin you're a hunter, an' you're strong. Can't nobody beat a hunter.
But when you get hunted—that's different. Somepin happens to you.
You ain't strong; maybe you're fierce, but you ain't strong. I been
hunted now for a long time. I ain't a hunter no more. I'd maybe
shoot a fella in the dark, but I don't maul nobody with a fence stake
no more. It don't do no good to fool you or me. That's how it is."

"Well, you go out an' hide," said Joad. "Leave me an' Casy tell
these bastards a few things." The beam of light was closer now, and
it bounced into the sky and then disappeared, and then bounced up
again. All three men watched.

Muley said, "There's one more thing about bein' hunted. You
get to thinkin' about all the dangerous things. If you're huntin' you
don't think about 'em, an' you ain't scared. Like you says to me, if
you get in any trouble they'll sen' you back to McAlester to finish
your time."

"That's right," said Joad. "That's what they tol' me, but settin'
here restin' or sleepin' on the groun'—that ain't gettin' in no trouble.
That ain't doin' nothin' wrong. That ain't like gettin' drunk or raisin'
hell."

Muley laughed. "You'll see. You jus' set here, an' the car'll come.
Maybe it's Willy Feeley, an' Willy's a deputy sheriff now. 'What you
doin' trespassin' here?' Willy says. Well, you always did know Willy
was full a shit, so you says, 'What's it to you?' Willy gets mad an'
says, 'You get off or I'll take you in.' An' you ain't gonna let no
Feeley push you aroun' 'cause he's mad an' scared. He's made a bluff
an' he got to go on with it, an' here's you gettin' tough an' you got
to go through—oh, hell, it's a lot easier to lay out in the cotton an'
let 'em look. It's more fun, too, 'cause they're mad an' can't do
nothin', an' you're out there a-laughin' at 'em. But you jus' talk to
Willy or any boss, an' you slug hell out of 'em an' they'll take you
in an' run you back to McAlester for three years."

"You're talkin' sense," said Joad. "Ever' word you say is sense.
But, Jesus, I hate to get pushed around! I lots rather take a sock at
Willy."

"He got a gun," said Muley. "He'll use it 'cause he's a deputy.
Then he either got to kill you or you got to get his gun away an' kill
him. Come on, Tommy. You can easy tell yourself you're foolin'
them lyin' out like that. An' it all just amounts to what you tell
yourself." The strong lights angled up into the sky now, and the even
drone of a motor could be heard. "Come on, Tommy. Don't have
to go far, jus' fourteen-fifteen rows over, an' we can watch what they
do."

Tom got to his feet. "By God, you're right!" he said. "I ain't got
a thing in the worl' to win, no matter how it comes out."

"Come on, then, over this way." Muley moved around the house
and out into the cotton field about fifty yards. "This is good," he
said. "Now lay down. You on'y got to pull your head down if they
start the spotlight goin'. It's kinda fun." The three men stretched
out at full length and propped themselves on their elbows. Muley
sprang up and ran toward the house, and in a few moments he came
back and threw a bundle of coats and shoes down. "They'd of taken
'em along just to get even," he said. The lights topped the rise and
bore down on the house.

Joad asked, "Won't they come out here with flashlights an' look
aroun' for us? I wisht I had a stick."

Muley giggled. "No, they won't. I tol' you I'm mean like a weasel.
Willy done that one night an' I clipped 'im from behint with a fence
stake. Knocked him colder'n a wedge. He tol' later how five guys
come at him."

The car drew up to the house and a spotlight snapped on.
"Duck," said Muley. The bar of cold white light swung over their
heads and crisscrossed the field. The hiding men could not see any
movement, but they heard a car door slam and they heard voices.
"Scairt to get in the light," Muley whispered. "Once-twice I've took
a shot at the headlights. That keeps Willy careful. He got somebody
with 'im tonight." They heard footsteps on wood, and then from
inside the house they saw the glow of a flashlight. "Shall I shoot
through the house?" Muley whispered. "They couldn't see where it
come from. Give 'em somepin to think about."

"Sure, go ahead," said Joad.

"Don't do it," Casy whispered. "It won't do no good. Jus' a waste. We got to get thinkin' about doin' stuff that means somepin."

A scratching sound came from near the house. "Puttin' out the fire," Muley whispered. "Kickin' dust over it." The car doors slammed, the headlights swung around and faced the road again. "Now duck!" said Muley. They dropped their heads and the spotlight swept over them and crossed and recrossed the cotton field, and then the car started and slipped away and topped the rise and disappeared.

Muley sat up. "Willy always tries that las' flash. He done it so often I can time 'im. An' he still thinks it's cute."

Casy said, "Maybe they left some fellas at the house. They'd catch us when we come back."

"Maybe. You fellas wait here. I know this game." He walked quietly away, and only a slight crunching of clods could be heard from his passage. The two waiting men tried to hear him, but he had gone. In a moment he called from the house, "They didn't leave nobody. Come on back." Casy and Joad struggled up and walked back toward the black bulk of the house. Muley met them near the smoking dust pile which had been their fire. "I didn' think they'd leave nobody," he said proudly. "Me knockin' Willy over an' takin' a shot at the lights once-twice keeps 'em careful. They ain't sure who it is, an' I ain't gonna let 'em catch me. I don't sleep near no house. If you fellas wanta come along, I'll show you where to sleep, where there ain't nobody gonna stumble over ya."

"Lead off," said Joad. "We'll folla you. I never thought I'd be hidin' out on my old man's place."

Muley set off across the fields, and Joad and Casy followed him. They kicked the cotton plants as they went. "You'll be hidin' from lots of stuff," said Muley. They marched in single file across the fields. They came to a water-cut and slid easily down to the bottom of it.

"By God, I bet I know," cried Joad. "Is it a cave in the bank?"

"That's right. How'd you know?"

"I dug her," said Joad. "Me an' my brother Noah dug her. Lookin' for gold we says we was, but we was jus' diggin' caves like kids always does." The walls of the water-cut were above their heads now. "Ought to be pretty close," said Joad. "Seems to me I remember her pretty close."

Muley said, "I've covered her with bresh. Nobody couldn't find her." The bottom of the gulch leveled off, and the footing was sand.

Joad settled himself on the clean sand. "I ain't gonna sleep in no cave," he said. "I'm gonna sleep right here." He rolled his coat and put it under his head.

Muley pulled at the covering brush and crawled into his cave. "I like it in here," he called. "I feel like nobody can come at me."

Jim Casy sat down on the sand beside Joad.

"Get some sleep," said Joad. "We'll start for Uncle John's at daybreak."

"I ain't sleepin'," said Casy. "I got too much to puzzle with." He drew up his feet and clasped his legs. He threw back his head and looked at the sharp stars. Joad yawned and brought one hand back under his head. They were silent, and gradually the skittering life of the ground, of holes and burrows, of the brush, began again; the gophers moved, and the rabbits crept to green things, the mice scampered over clods, and the winged hunters moved soundlessly overhead.

CHAPTER 7

In the towns, on the edges of the towns, in fields, in vacant lots, the used-car yards, the wreckers' yards, the garages with blazoned signs —Used Cars, Good Used Cars. Cheap transportation, three trailers. '27 Ford, clean. Checked cars, guaranteed cars. Free radio. Car with 100 gallons of gas free. Come in and look. Used Cars. No overhead.

A lot and a house large enough for a desk and chair and a blue book. Sheaf of contracts, dog-eared, held with paper clips, and a neat pile of unused contracts. Pen—keep it full, keep it working. A sale's been lost 'cause a pen didn't work.

Those sons-of-bitches over there ain't buying. Every yard gets 'em. They're lookers. Spend all their time looking. Don't want to buy no cars; take up your time. Don't give a damn for your time. Over there, them two people—no, with the kids. Get 'em in a car. Start 'em at two hundred and work down. They look good for one and a quarter. Get 'em rolling. Get 'em out in a jalopy. Sock it to 'em! They took our time.

Owners with rolled-up sleeves. Salesmen, neat, deadly, small intent eyes watching for weaknesses.

Watch the woman's face. If the woman likes it we can screw the old man. Start 'em on that Cad'. Then you can work 'em down to that '26 Buick. 'F you start on the Buick, they'll go for a Ford. Roll up your sleeves an' get to work. This ain't gonna last forever. Show 'em that Nash while I get the slow leak pumped up on that '25 Dodge. I'll give you a Hymie when I'm ready.

What you want is transportation, ain't it? No baloney for you. Sure the upholstery is shot. Seat cushions ain't turning no wheels over.

Cars lined up, noses forward, rusty noses, flat tires. Parked close together.

Like to get in to see that one? Sure, no trouble. I'll pull her out of the line.

Get 'em under obligation. Make 'em take up your time. Don't let 'em forget they're takin' your time. People are nice, mostly. They hate to put you out. Make 'em put you out, an' then sock it to 'em.

Cars lined up, Model T's, high and snotty, creaking wheel, worn bands. Buicks, Nashes, De Sotos.

Yes, sir. '22 Dodge. Best goddamn car Dodge ever made. Never wear out. Low compression. High compression got lots a sap for a while, but the metal ain't made that'll hold it for long. Plymouths, Rocknes, Stars.

Jesus, where'd that Apperson come from, the Ark? And a Chalmers and a Chandler—ain't made 'em for years. We ain't sellin' cars—rolling junk. Goddamn it, I got to get jalopies. I don't want nothing for more'n twenty-five, thirty bucks. Sell 'em for fifty, seventy-five. That's a good profit. Christ, what cut do you make on a new car? Get jalopies. I can sell 'em fast as I get 'em. Nothing over two hundred fifty. Jim, corral that old bastard on the sidewalk. Don't know his ass from a hole in the ground. Try him on that Apperson. Say, where is that Apperson? Sold? If we don't get some jalopies we got nothing to sell.

Flags, red and white, white and blue—all along the curb. Used Cars. Good Used Cars.

Today's bargain—up on the platform. Never sell it. Makes folks come in, though. If we sold that bargain at that price we'd hardly make a dime. Tell 'em it's jus' sold. Take out that yard battery before you make delivery. Put in that dumb cell. Christ, what they want for six bits? Roll up your sleeves—pitch in. This ain't gonna last. If I had enough jalopies I'd retire in six months.

Listen, Jim, I heard that Chevvy's rear end. Sounds like bustin' bottles. Squirt in a couple quarts of sawdust. Put some in the gears, too. We got to move that lemon for thirty-five dollars. Bastard cheated me on that one. I offer ten an' he jerks me to fifteen, an' then the son-of-a-bitch took the tools out. God Almighty! I wisht I had five hundred jalopies. This ain't gonna last. He don't like the tires? Tell 'im they got ten thousand in 'em, knock off a buck an' a half.

Piles of rusty ruins against the fence, rows of wrecks in back, fenders, grease-black wrecks, blocks lying on the ground and a pig weed growing up through the cylinders. Brake rods, exhausts, piled like snakes. Grease, gasoline.

See if you can't find a spark plug that ain't cracked. Christ, if I had fifty trailers at under a hundred I'd clean up. What the hell is he kickin' about? We sell 'em, but we don't push 'em home for him. That's good! Don't push 'em home. Get that one in the Monthly, I bet. You don't think he's a prospect? Well, kick 'im out. We got too much to do to bother with a guy that can't make up his mind. Take the right front tire off the Graham. Turn that mended side down. The rest looks swell. Got tread an' everything.

Sure! There's fifty thousan' in that ol' heap yet. Keep plenty oil in. So long. Good luck.

Lookin' for a car? What did you have in mind? See anything attracts you? I'm dry. How about a little snort a good stuff? Come on, while your wife's lookin' at that La Salle. You don't want no La Salle. Bearings shot. Uses too much oil. Got a Lincoln '24. There's a car. Run forever. Make her into a truck.

Hot sun on rusted metal. Oil on the ground. People are wandering in, bewildered, needing a car.

Wipe your feet. Don't lean on that car, it's dirty. How do you buy a car? What does it cost? Watch the children, now. I wonder how much for this one? We'll ask. It don't cost money to ask. We can ask, can't we? Can't pay a nickel over seventy-five, or there won't be enough to get to California.

God, if I could only get a hundred jalopies. I don't care if they run or not.

Tires, used, bruised tires, stacked in tall cylinders; tubes, red, gray, hanging like sausages.

Tire patch? Radiator cleaner? Spark intensifier? Drop this little pill in your gas tank and get ten extra miles to the gallon. Just paint it on—you got a new surface for fifty cents. Wipers, fan belts, gaskets? Maybe it's the valve. Get a new valve stem. What can you lose for a nickel?

All right, Joe. You soften 'em up an' shoot 'em in here. I'll close 'em, I'll deal 'em or I'll kill 'em. Don't send in no bums. I want deals.

Yes, sir, step in. You got a buy there. Yes, sir! At eighty bucks you got a buy.

I can't go no higher than fifty. The fella outside says fifty.

Fifty. Fifty? He's nuts. Paid seventy-eight fifty for that little number. Joe, you crazy fool, you tryin' to bust us? Have to can that guy. I might take sixty. Now look here, mister, I ain't got all day. I'm a business man but I ain't out to stick nobody. Got anything to trade?

Got a pair of mules I'll trade.

Mules! Hey, Joe, hear this? This guy wants to trade mules. Didn't nobody tell you this is the machine age? They don't use mules for nothing but glue no more.

Fine big mules—five and seven years old. Maybe we better look around.

Look around! You come in when we're busy, an' take up our time an' then walk out! Joe, did you know you was talkin' to pikers?

I ain't a piker. I got to get a car. We're goin' to California. I got to get a car.

Well, I'm a sucker. Joe says I'm a sucker. Says if I don't quit givin' my shirt away I'll starve to death. Tell you what I'll do—I can get five bucks apiece for them mules for dog feed.

I wouldn't want them to go for dog feed.

Well, maybe I can get ten or seven maybe. Tell you what we'll do. We'll take your mules for twenty. Wagon goes with 'em, don't it? An' you put up fifty, an' you can sign a contract to send the rest at ten dollars a month.

But you said eighty.

Didn't you never hear about carrying charges and insurance? That just boosts her a little. You'll get her all paid up in four-five months. Sign your name right here. We'll take care of ever'thing.

Well, I don't know——

Now, look here. I'm givin' you my shirt, an' you took all this time. I might a made three sales while I been talkin' to you. I'm disgusted. Yeah, sign right there. All right, sir. Joe, fill up the tank for this gentleman. We'll even give him gas.

Jesus, Joe, that was a hot one! What'd we give for that jalopy? Thirty bucks—thirty-five wasn't it? I got that team, an' if I can't get seventy-five for that team, I ain't a business man. An' I got fifty cash an' a contract for forty more. Oh, I know they're not all honest, but it'll surprise you how many kick through with the rest. One guy come through with a hundred two years after I wrote him off. I bet you this guy sends the money. Christ, if I could only get five hundred jalopies! Roll up your sleeves, Joe. Go out an' soften 'em, an' send 'em in to me. You get twenty on that last deal. You ain't doing bad.

Limp flags in the afternoon sun. Today's Bargain. '29 Ford pickup, runs good.

What do you want for fifty bucks—a Zephyr?

Horsehair curling out of seat cushions, fenders battered and hammered back. Bumpers torn loose and hanging. Fancy Ford roadster with little colored lights at fender guide, at radiator cap, and three behind. Mud aprons, and a big die on the gear-shift lever. Pretty girl on tire cover, painted in color and named Cora. Afternoon sun on the dusty windshields.

Christ, I ain't had time to go out an' eat! Joe, send a kid for a hamburger.

Spattering roar of ancient engines.

There's a dumb-bunny lookin' at that Chrysler. Find out if he got any jack in his jeans. Some a these farm boys is sneaky. Soften 'em up an' roll 'em in to me, Joe. You're doin' good.

Sure, we sold it. Guarantee? We guaranteed it to be an automobile. We didn't guarantee to wet-nurse it. Now listen here, you— you bought a car, an' now you're squawkin'. I don't give a damn if you don't make payments. We ain't got your paper. We turn that over to the finance company. They'll get after you, not us. We don't hold no paper. Yeah? Well you jus' get tough an' I'll call a cop. No, we did not switch the tires. Run 'im outa here, Joe. He bought a car, an' now he ain't satisfied. How'd you think if I bought a steak an' et half an' try to bring it back? We're runnin' a business, not a charity ward. Can ya imagine that guy, Joe? Say—looka there! Got a Elk's tooth! Run over there. Let 'em glance over that '36 Pontiac. Yeah.

Square noses, round noses, rusty noses, shovel noses, and the long curves of streamlines, and the flat surfaces before streamlining. Bargains Today. Old monsters with deep upholstery—you can cut her into a truck easy. Two-wheel trailers, axles rusty in the hard afternoon sun. Used Cars. Good Used Cars. Clean, runs good. Don't pump oil.

Christ, look at 'er! Somebody took nice care of 'er.

Cadillacs, La Salles, Buicks, Plymouths, Packards, Chevvies, Fords, Pontiacs. Row on row, headlights glinting in the afternoon sun. Good Used Cars.

Soften 'em up, Joe. Jesus, I wisht I had a thousand jalopies! Get 'em ready to deal, an' I'll close 'em.

Goin' to California? Here's jus' what you need. Looks shot, but they's thousan's of miles in her.

Lined up side by side. Good Used Cars. Bargains. Clean, runs good.

CHAPTER 8

The sky grayed among the stars, and the pale, late quarter-moon was insubstantial and thin. Tom Joad and the preacher walked quickly along a road that was only wheel tracks and beaten caterpillar tracks through a cotton field. Only the unbalanced sky showed the approach of dawn, no horizon to the west, and a line to the east. The two men walked in silence and smelled the dust their feet kicked into the air.

"I hope you're dead sure of the way," Jim Casy said. "I'd hate to have the dawn come an' us be way to hell an' gone somewhere." The cotton field scurried with waking life, the quick flutter of morning birds feeding on the ground, the scamper over the clods of disturbed rabbits. The quiet thudding of the men's feet in the dust, the squeak of crushed clods under their shoes, sounded against the secret noises of the dawn.

Tom said, "I could shut my eyes an' walk right there. On'y way I can go wrong is think about her. Jus' forget about her, an' I'll go right there. Hell, man, I was born right aroun' in here. I run aroun' here when I was a kid. They's a tree over there—look, you can jus' make it out. Well, once my old man hung up a dead coyote in that tree. Hung there till it was all sort of melted, an' then dropped off. Dried up, like. Jesus, I hope Ma's cookin' somepin. My belly's caved."

"Me too," said Casy. "Like a little eatin' tobacca? Keeps ya from gettin' too hungry. Been better if we didn' start so damn early. Better if it was light." He paused to gnaw off a piece of plug. "I was sleepin' nice."

"That crazy Muley done it," said Tom. "He got me clear jumpy. Wakes me up an' says, ' 'By, Tom. I'm goin' on. I got places to go.' An' he says, 'Better get goin' too, so's you'll be offa this lan' when the light comes.' He's gettin' screwy as a gopher, livin' like he does. You'd think Injuns was after him. Think he's nuts?"

"Well, I dunno. You seen that car come las' night when we had a little fire. You seen how the house was smashed. They's somepin purty mean goin' on. 'Course Muley's crazy, all right. Creepin'

aroun' like a coyote; that's boun' to make him crazy. He'll kill somebody purty soon an' they'll run him down with dogs. I can see it like
a prophecy. He'll get worse an' worse. Wouldn' come along with us,
you say?"

"No," said Joad. "I think he's scared to see people now. Wonder
he come up to us. We'll be at Uncle John's place by sunrise." They
walked along in silence for a time, and the late owls flew over toward
the barns, the hollow trees, the tank houses, where they hid from
daylight. The eastern sky grew fairer and it was possible to see the
cotton plants and the graying earth. "Damn' if I know how they're
all sleepin' at Uncle John's. He on'y got one room an' a cookin'
leanto, an' a little bit of a barn. Must be a mob there now."

The preacher said, "I don't recollect that John had a fambly. Just
a lone man, ain't he? I don't recollect much about him."

"Lonest goddamn man in the world," said Joad. "Crazy kind of
son-of-a-bitch, too—somepin like Muley, on'y worse in some ways.
Might see 'im anywheres—at Shawnee, drunk, or visitin' a widow
twenty miles away, or workin' his place with a lantern. Crazy.
Ever'body thought he wouldn't live long. A lone man like that don't
live long. But Uncle John's older'n Pa. Jus' gets stringier an' meaner
ever' year. Meaner'n Grampa."

"Look a the light comin'," said the preacher. "Silvery-like. Didn'
John never have no fambly?"

"Well, yes, he did, an' that'll show you the kind a fella he is—
set in his ways. Pa tells about it. Uncle John, he had a young wife.
Married four months. She was in a family way, too, an' one night
she gets a pain in her stomick, an' she says, 'You better go for a
doctor.' Well, John, he's settin' there, an' he says, 'You just got a
stomickache. You et too much. Take a dose a pain killer.' In the
night she wakes him up an' he gives her another dose a pain killer.
'You crowd up ya stomick an' ya get a stomickache,' he says. Nex'
noon she's outa her head, an' she dies at about four in the
afternoon."

"What was it?" Casy asked. "Poisoned from somepin she et?"

"No, somepin jus' bust in her. Ap—appendick or somepin. Well,
Uncle John, he's always been a easy-goin' fella, an' he takes it hard.
Takes it for a sin. For a long time he won't have nothin' to say to
nobody. Just walks aroun' like he don't see nothin', an' he prays
some. Took 'im two years to come out of it, an' then he ain't the
same. Sort of wild. Made a damn nuisance of hisself. Ever' time one

of us kids got worms or a gutache Uncle John brings a doctor out. Pa finally tol' him he got to stop. Kids all the time gettin' a gutache. He figures it's his fault his woman died. Funny fella. He's all the time makin' it up to somebody—givin' kids stuff, droppin' a sack a meal on somebody's porch. Give away about ever'thing he got, an' still he ain't very happy. Gets walkin' around alone at night sometimes. He's a good farmer, though. Keeps his lan' nice."

"Poor fella," said the preacher. "Poor lonely fella. Did he go to church much when his woman died?"

"No, he didn'. Never wanted to get close to folks. Wanted to be off alone. I never seen a kid that wasn't crazy about him. He'd come to our house in the night sometimes, an' we knowed he come 'cause jus' as sure as he come there'd be a pack a gum in the bed right beside ever' one of us. We thought he was Jesus Christ Awmighty."

The preacher walked along, head down. He didn't answer. And the light of the coming morning made his forehead seem to shine, and his hands, swinging beside him, flicked into the light and out again.

Tom was silent too, as though he had said too intimate a thing and was ashamed. He quickened his pace and the preacher kept step. They could see a little into gray distance ahead now. A snake wriggled slowly from the cotton rows into the road. Tom stopped short of it and peered. "Gopher snake," he said. "Let him go." They walked around the snake and went on their way. A little color came into the eastern sky, and almost immediately the lonely dawn light crept over the land. Green appeared on the cotton plants and the earth was gray-brown. The faces of the men lost their grayish shine. Joad's face seemed to darken with the growing light. "This is the good time," Joad said softly. "When I was a kid I used to get up an' walk around by myself when it was like this. What's that ahead?"

A committee of dogs had met in the road, in honor of a bitch. Five males, shepherd mongrels, collie mongrels, dogs whose breeds had been blurred by a freedom of social life, were engaged in complimenting the bitch. For each dog sniffed daintily and then stalked to a cotton plant on stiff legs, raised a hind foot ceremoniously and wetted, then went back to smell. Joad and the preacher stopped to watch, and suddenly Joad laughed joyously. "By God!" he said. "By God!" Now all dogs met and hackles rose, and they all growled and stood stiffly, each waiting for the others to start a fight. One dog mounted and, now that it was accomplished, the others gave way and watched with interest, and their tongues were out, and their tongues dripped. The two men walked on. "By God!" Joad said. "I think that up-dog is our Flash. I thought he'd be dead. Come, Flash!" He laughed again. "What the hell, if somebody called me, I wouldn' hear him neither. 'Minds me of a story they tell about Willy Feeley when he was a young fella. Willy was bashful, awful bashful. Well, one day he takes a heifer over to Graves' bull. Ever'body was out but Elsie Graves, and Elsie wasn't bashful at all. Willy, he stood there turnin' red an' he couldn' even talk. Elsie says, 'I know what you come for; the bull's out in back a the barn.' Well, they took the heifer out there an' Willy an' Elsie sat on the fence to watch. Purty soon Willy got feelin' purty fly. Elsie looks over an' says, like she don't know, 'What's a matter, Willy?' Willy's so randy he can't hardly set still. 'By God,' he says, 'by God, I wisht I was a-doin' that!' Elsie says, 'Why not, Willy? It's your heifer.' "

The preacher laughed softly. "You know," he said, "it's a nice thing not bein' a preacher no more. Nobody use' ta tell stories when I was there, or if they did I couldn' laugh. An' I couldn' cuss. Now I cuss all I want, any time I want, an' it does a fella good to cuss if he wants to."

A redness grew up out of the eastern horizon, and on the ground birds began to chirp, sharply. "Look!" said Joad. "Right ahead. That's Uncle John's tank. Can't see the win'mill, but there's his tank. See it against the sky?" He speeded his walk. "I wonder if all the folks are there." The hulk of the tank stood above a rise. Joad, hurrying, raised a cloud of dust about his knees. "I wonder if Ma—" They saw the tank legs now, and the house, a square little box, unpainted and bare, and the barn, low-roofed and huddled. Smoke was rising from the tin chimney of the house. In the yard was a litter, piled furniture, the blades and motor of the windmill, bedsteads, chairs, tables. "Holy Christ, they're fixin' to go!" Joad said. A truck stood in the yard, a truck with high sides, but a strange truck, for while the front of it was a sedan, the top had been cut off in the middle and the truck bed fitted on. And as they drew near, the men could hear pounding from the yard, and as the rim of the blinding sun came up over the horizon, it fell on the truck, and they saw a man and the flash of his hammer as it rose and fell. And the sun flashed on the windows of the house. The weathered boards were bright. Two red chickens on the ground flamed with reflected light.

"Don't yell," said Tom. "Let's creep up on 'em, like," and he walked so fast that the dust rose as high as his waist. And then he came to the edge of the cotton field. Now they were in the yard proper, earth beaten hard, shiny hard, and a few dusty crawling weeds on the ground. And Joad slowed as though he feared to go on. The preacher, watching him, slowed to match his step. Tom sauntered forward, sidled embarrassedly toward the truck. It was a Hudson Super-Six sedan, and the top had been ripped in two with a cold chisel. Old Tom Joad stood in the truck bed and he was nailing on the top rails of the truck sides. His grizzled, bearded face was low over his work, and a bunch of six-penny nails stuck out of his mouth. He set a nail and his hammer thundered it in. From the house came the clash of a lid on the stove and the wail of a child. Joad sidled up to the truck bed and leaned against it. And his father looked at him and did not see him. His father set another nail and drove it in. A flock of pigeons started from the deck of the tank house and flew around and settled again and strutted to the edge to look over; white pigeons and blue pigeons and grays, with iridescent wings.

Joad hooked his fingers over the lowest bar of the truck side. He looked up at the aging, graying man on the truck. He wet his thick lips with his tongue, and he said softly, "Pa."

"What do you want?" old Tom mumbled around his mouthful of nails. He wore a black, dirty slouch hat and a blue work shirt over which was a buttonless vest; his jeans were held up by a wide harness-leather belt with a big square brass buckle, leather and metal polished from years of wearing and his shoes were cracked and the soles swollen and boat-shaped from years of sun and wet and dust. The sleeves of his shirt were tight on his forearms, held down by the bulging powerful muscles. Stomach and hips were lean, and legs, short, heavy, and strong. His face, squared by a bristling pepper and salt beard, was all drawn down to the forceful chin, a chin thrust out and built out by the stubble beard which was not so grayed on the chin, and gave weight and force to its thrust. Over old Tom's un-whiskered cheek bones the skin was as brown as meerschaum, and wrinkled in rays around his eye-corners from squinting. His eyes were brown, black-coffee brown, and he thrust his head forward when he looked at a thing, for his bright dark eyes were failing. His lips, from which the big nails protruded, were thin and red.

He held his hammer suspended in the air, about to drive a set nail, and he looked over the truck side at Tom, looked resentful at being interrupted. And then his chin drove forward and his eyes looked at Tom's face, and then gradually his brain became aware of what he saw. The hammer dropped slowly to his side, and with his left hand he took the nails from his mouth. And he said wonderingly, as though he told himself the fact, "It's Tommy—" And then, still informing himself, "It's Tommy come home." His mouth opened again, and a look of fear came into his eyes. "Tommy," he said softly, "you ain't busted out? You ain't got to hide?" He listened tensely.

"Naw," said Tom. "I'm paroled. I'm free. I got my papers." He gripped the lower bars of the truck side and looked up.

Old Tom laid his hammer gently on the floor and put his nails in his pocket. He swung his leg over the side and dropped lithely to the ground, but once beside his son he seemed embarrassed and strange. "Tommy," he said, "we are goin' to California. But we was gonna write you a letter an' tell you." And he said, incredulously, "But you're back. You can go with us. You can go!" The lid of a coffee pot slammed in the house. Old Tom looked over his shoulder. "Le's supprise 'em," he said, and his eyes shone with excitement. "Your ma got a bad feelin' she ain't never gonna see you no more. She got that quiet look like when somebody died. Almost she don't want to go to California, fear she'll never see you no more." A stove lid clashed in the house again. "Le's supprise 'em," old Tom repeated. "Le's go in like you never been away. Le's jus' see what your ma says." At last he touched Tom, but touched him on the shoulder, timidly, and instantly took his hand away. He looked at Jim Casy.

Tom said, "You remember the preacher, Pa. He come along with me."

"He been in prison too?"

"No, I met 'im on the road. He been away."

Pa shook hands gravely. "You're welcome here, sir."

Casy said, "Glad to be here. It's a thing to see when a boy comes home. It's a thing to see."

"Home," Pa said.

"To his folks," the preacher amended quickly. "We stayed at the other place last night."

Pa's chin thrust out, and he looked back down the road for a moment. Then he turned to Tom. "How'll we do her?" he began excitedly. "S'pose I go in an' say, 'Here's some fellas want some breakfast,' or how'd it be if you jus' come in an' stood there till she seen you? How'd that be?" His face was alive with excitement.

"Don't le's give her no shock," said Tom. "Don't le's scare her none."

Two rangy shepherd dogs trotted up pleasantly, until they caught the scent of strangers, and then they backed cautiously away, watchful, their tails moving slowly and tentatively in the air, but their eyes and noses quick for animosity or danger. One of them, stretching his neck, edged forward, ready to run, and little by little he approached Tom's legs and sniffed loudly at them. Then he backed away and watched Pa for some kind of signal. The other pup was not so brave. He looked about for something that could honorably divert his attention, saw a red chicken go mincing by, and ran at it. There was the squawk of an outraged hen, a burst of red feathers, and the hen ran off, flapping stubby wings for speed. The pup looked proudly back at the men, and then flopped down in the dust and beat its tail contentedly on the ground.

"Come on," said Pa, "come on in now. She got to see you. I got to see her face when she sees you. Come on. She'll yell breakfast in a minute. I heard her slap the salt pork in the pan a good time ago." He led the way across the fine-dusted ground. There was no porch on this house, just a step and then the door; a chopping block beside the door, its surface matted and soft from years of chopping. The graining in the sheathing wood was high, for the dust had cut down the softer wood. The smell of burning willow was in the air, and, as the three men neared the door, the smell of frying side-meat and the smell of high brown biscuits and the sharp smell of coffee rolling in the pot. Pa stepped up into the open doorway and stood there blocking it with his wide short body. He said, "Ma, there's a coupla fellas jus' come along the road, an' they wonder if we could spare a bite."

Tom heard his mother's voice, the remembered cool, calm drawl, friendly and humble. "Let 'em come," she said. "We got a-plenty. Tell 'em they got to wash their han's. The bread is done. I'm jus' takin' up the side-meat now." And the sizzle of the angry grease came from the stove.

Pa stepped inside, clearing the door, and Tom looked in at his mother. She was lifting the curling slices of pork from the frying pan. The oven door was open, and a great pan of high brown biscuits stood waiting there. She looked out the door, but the sun was behind Tom, and she saw only a dark figure outlined by the bright yellow sunlight. She nodded pleasantly. "Come in," she said. "Jus' lucky I made plenty bread this morning."

Tom stood looking in. Ma was heavy, but not fat; thick with child-bearing and work. She wore a loose Mother Hubbard of gray cloth in which there had once been colored flowers, but the color was washed out now, so that the small flowered pattern was only a little lighter gray than the background. The dress came down to her ankles, and her strong, broad, bare feet moved quickly and deftly over the floor. Her thin, steel-gray hair was gathered in a sparse wispy knot at the back of her head. Strong, freckled arms were bare to the elbow, and her hands were chubby and delicate, like those of a plump little girl. She looked out into the sunshine. Her full face was not soft; it was controlled, kindly. Her hazel eyes seemed to have experienced all possible tragedy and to have mounted pain and suffering like steps into a high calm and a superhuman understanding. She seemed to know, to accept, to welcome her position, the citadel of the family, the strong place that could not be taken. And since old Tom and the children could not know hurt or fear unless she acknowledged hurt and fear, she had practiced denying them in herself. And since, when a joyful thing happened, they looked to see whether joy was on her, it was her habit to build up laughter out of inadequate materials. But better than joy was calm. Imperturbability could be depended upon. And from her great and humble position in the family she had taken dignity and a clean calm beauty. From her position as healer, her hands had grown sure and cool and quiet; from her position as arbiter she had become as remote and faultless in judgment as a goddess. She seemed to know that if she swayed the family shook, and if she ever really deeply wavered or despaired the family would fall, the family will to function would be gone.

She looked out into the sunny yard, at the dark figure of a man. Pa stood near by, shaking with excitement. "Come in," he cried. "Come right in, mister." And Tom a little shamefacedly stepped over the doorsill.

She looked up pleasantly from the frying pan. And then her hand sank slowly to her side and the fork clattered to the wooden floor. Her eyes opened wide, and the pupils dilated. She breathed heavily through her open mouth. She closed her eyes. "Thank God," she said. "Oh, thank God!" And suddenly her face was worried. "Tommy, you ain't wanted? You didn' bust loose?"

"No, Ma. Parole. I got the papers here." He touched his breast.

She moved toward him lithely, soundlessly in her bare feet, and her face was full of wonder. Her small hand felt his arm, felt the soundness of his muscles. And then her fingers went up to his cheek as a blind man's fingers might. And her joy was nearly like sorrow. Tom pulled his underlip between his teeth and bit it. Her eyes went wonderingly to his bitten lip, and she saw the little line of blood against his teeth and the trickle of blood down his lip. Then she knew, and her control came back, and her hand dropped. Her breath came out explosively. "Well!" she cried. "We come mighty near to goin' on without ya. An' we was wonderin' how in the worl' you could ever find us." She picked up the fork and combed the boiling grease and brought out a dark curl of crisp pork. And she set the pot of tumbling coffee on the back of the stove.

Old Tom giggled, "Fooled ya, huh, Ma? We aimed to fool ya, and we done it. Jus' stood there like a hammered sheep. Wisht Grampa'd been here to see. Looked like somebody'd beat ya between the eyes with a sledge. Grampa would a whacked 'imself so hard he'd a throwed his hip out—like he done when he seen Al take a shot at that grea' big airship the army got. Tommy, it come over one day, half a mile big, an' Al gets the thirty-thirty and blazes away at her. Grampa yells, 'Don't shoot no fledglin's, Al; wait till a growed-up one goes over,' an' then he whacked 'imself an' throwed his hip out."

Ma chuckled and took down a heap of tin plates from a shelf.

Tom asked, "Where is Grampa? I ain't seen the ol' devil."

Ma stacked the plates on the kitchen table and piled cups beside them. She said confidentially, "Oh, him an' Granma sleeps in the barn. They got to get up so much in the night. They was stumblin' over the little fellas."

Pa broke in, "Yeah, ever' night Grampa'd get mad. Tumble over Winfield, an' Winfield'd yell, an' Grampa'd get mad an' wet his drawers, an' that'd make him madder, an' purty soon ever'body in the house'd be yellin' their head off." His words tumbled out between chuckles. "Oh, we had lively times. One night when ever'body was yellin' an' a-cussin', your brother Al, he's a smart aleck now, he says, 'Goddamn it, Grampa, why don't you run off an' be a pirate?' Well, that made Grampa so goddamn mad he went for his gun. Al had ta sleep out in the fiel' that night. But now Granma an' Grampa both sleeps in the barn."

Ma said, "They can jus' get up an' step outside when they feel like it. Pa, run on out an' tell 'em Tommy's home. Grampa's a favorite of him."

"A course," said Pa. "I should of did it before." He went out the door and crossed the yard, swinging his hands high.

Tom watched him go, and then his mother's voice called his attention. She was pouring coffee. She did not look at him. "Tommy," she said hesitantly, timidly.

"Yeah?" His timidity was set off by hers, a curious embarrassment. Each one knew the other was shy, and became more shy in the knowledge.

"Tommy, I got to ask you—you ain't mad?"

"Mad, Ma?"

"You ain't poisoned mad? You don't hate nobody? They didn' do nothin' in that jail to rot you out with crazy mad?"

He looked sidewise at her, studied her, and his eyes seemed to ask how she could know such things. "No-o-o," he said. "I was for a little while. But I ain't proud like some fellas. I let stuff run off'n me. What's a matter, Ma?"

Now she was looking at him, her mouth open, as though to hear better, her eyes digging to know better. Her face looked for the answer that is always concealed in language. She said in confusion, "I knowed Purty Boy Floyd. I knowed his ma. They was good folks. He was full a hell, sure, like a good boy oughta be." She paused and then her words poured out. "I don' know all like this—but I know it. He done a little bad thing an' they hurt 'im, caught 'im an' hurt him so he was mad, an' the nex' bad thing he done was mad, an' they hurt 'im again. An' purty soon he was mean-mad. They shot at him like a varmint, an' he shot back, an' then they run him like a coyote, an' him a-snappin' an' a-snarlin', mean as a lobo. An' he was mad. He wasn't no boy or no man no more, he was jus' a walkin' chunk a mean-mad. But the folks that knowed him didn' hurt 'im. He wasn' mad at them. Finally they run him down an' killed 'im. No matter how they say it in the paper how he was bad—that's how it was." She paused and she licked her dry lips, and her whole face was an aching question. "I got to know, Tommy. Did they hurt you so much? Did they make you mad like that?"

Tom's heavy lips were pulled tight over his teeth. He looked down at his big flat hands. "No," he said. "I ain't like that." He paused and studied the broken nails, which were ridged like clam shells. "All the time in stir I kep' away from stuff like that. I ain' so mad."

She sighed, "Thank God!" under her breath.

He looked up quickly. "Ma, when I seen what they done to our house——"

She came near to him then, and stood close; and she said passionately, "Tommy, don't you go fightin' 'em alone. They'll hunt you down like a coyote. Tommy, I got to thinkin' an' dreamin' an' wonderin'. They say there's a hun'erd thousand of us shoved out. If we was all mad the same way, Tommy—they wouldn't hunt nobody down——" She stopped.

Tommy, looking at her, gradually drooped his eyelids, until just a short glitter showed through his lashes. "Many folks feel that way?" he demanded.

"I don' know. They're jus' kinda stunned. Walk aroun' like they was half asleep."

From outside and across the yard came an ancient creaking bleat. "Pu-raise Gawd fur vittory! Pu-raise Gawd fur vittory!"

Tom turned his head and grinned. "Granma finally heard I'm home. Ma," he said, "you never was like this before!"

Her face hardened and her eyes grew cold. "I never had my house pushed over," she said. "I never had my fambly stuck out on the road. I never had to sell—ever'thing— Here they come now." She moved back to the stove and dumped the big pan of bulbous biscuits on two tin plates. She shook flour into the deep grease to make gravy, and her hand was white with flour. For a moment Tom watched her, and then he went to the door.

Across the yard came four people. Grampa was ahead, a lean, ragged, quick old man, jumping with quick steps and favoring his right leg—the side that came out of joint. He was buttoning his fly as he came, and his old hands were having trouble finding the buttons, for he had buttoned the top button into the second buttonhole, and that threw the whole sequence off. He wore dark ragged pants and a torn blue shirt, open all the way down, and showing long gray underwear, also unbuttoned. His lean white chest, fuzzed with white hair, was visible through the opening in his underwear. He gave up the fly and left it open and fumbled with the underwear buttons, then gave the whole thing up and hitched his brown suspenders. His was a lean excitable face with little bright eyes as evil as a frantic child's eyes. A cantankerous, complaining, mischievous, laughing face. He fought and argued, told dirty stories. He was as lecherous as always. Vicious and cruel and impatient, like a frantic child, and the whole structure overlaid with amusement. He drank too much when he could get it, ate too much when it was there, talked too much all the time.

Behind him hobbled Granma, who had survived only because she was as mean as her husband. She had held her own with a shrill ferocious religiosity that was as lecherous and as savage as anything Grampa could offer. Once, after a meeting, while she was still speaking in tongues, she fired both barrels of a shotgun at her husband, ripping one of his buttocks nearly off, and after that he admired her and did not try to torture her as children torture bugs. As she walked she hiked her Mother Hubbard up to her knees, and she bleated her shrill terrible war cry: "Pu-raise Gawd fur vittory."

Granma and Grampa raced each other to get across the broad yard. They fought over everything, and loved and needed the fighting.

Behind them, moving slowly and evenly, but keeping up, came Pa and Noah—Noah the first-born, tall and strange, walking always with a wondering look on his face, calm and puzzled. He had never been angry in his life. He looked in wonder at angry people, wonder and uneasiness, as normal people look at the insane. Noah moved slowly, spoke seldom, and then so slowly that people who did not know him often thought him stupid. He was not stupid, but he was strange. He had little pride, no sexual urges. He worked and slept in a curious rhythm that nevertheless sufficed him. He was fond of his folks, but never showed it in any way. Although an observer could not have told why, Noah left the impression of being misshapen, his head or his body or his legs or his mind; but no misshapen member could be recalled. Pa thought he knew why Noah was strange, but Pa was ashamed, and never told. For on the night when Noah was born, Pa, frightened at the spreading thighs, alone in the house, and horrified at the screaming wretch his wife had become, went mad with apprehension. Using his hands, his strong fingers for forceps, he had pulled and twisted the baby. The midwife, arriving late, had found the baby's head pulled out of shape, its neck stretched, its body warped; and she had pushed the head back and molded the body with her hands. But Pa always remembered, and was ashamed. And he was kinder to Noah than to the others. In Noah's broad face, eyes too far apart, and long fragile jaw, Pa thought he saw the twisted, warped skull of the baby. Noah could do all that was required of him, could read and write, could work and figure, but he didn't seem to care; there was a listlessness in him toward things people wanted and needed. He lived in a strange silent house and looked out of it through calm eyes. He was a stranger to all the world, but he was not lonely.

The four came across the yard, and Grampa demanded, "Where is he? Goddamn it, where is he?" And his fingers fumbled for his pants button, and forgot and strayed into his pocket. And then he saw Tom standing in the door. Grampa stopped and he stopped the others. His little eyes glittered with malice. "Lookut him," he said. "A jailbird. Ain't been no Joads in jail for a hell of a time." His mind jumped. "Got no right to put 'im in jail. He done just what I'd do. Sons-a-bitches got not right." His mind jumped again. "An' ol' Turnbull, stinkin' skunk, braggin' how he'll shoot ya when ya come out. Says he got Hatfield blood. Well, I sent word to him. I says, 'Don't fuck around with no Joad. Maybe I got McCoy blood for all I know.' I says, 'You lay your sights anywheres near Tommy an' I'll take it an' I'll ram it up your ass,' I says. Scairt 'im, too."

Granma, not following the conversation, bleated, "Pu-raise Gawd fur vittory."

Grampa walked up and slapped Tom on the chest, and his eyes grinned with affection and pride. "How are ya, Tommy?"

"O.K." said Tom. "How ya keepin' yaself?"

"Full a piss an' vinegar," said Grampa. His mind jumped. "Jus' like I said, they ain't a gonna keep no Joad in jail. I says, 'Tommy'll come a-bustin' outa that jail like a bull through a corral fence.' An' you done it. Get outa my way, I'm hungry." He crowded past, sat down, loaded his plate with pork and two big biscuits and poured the thick gravy over the whole mess, and before the others could get in, Grampa's mouth was full.

Tom grinned affectionately at him. "Ain't he a heller?" he said. And Grampa's mouth was so full that he couldn't even splutter, but his mean little eyes smiled, and he nodded his head violently.

Granma said proudly, "A wicketer, cussin'er man never lived. He's goin' to hell on a poker, praise Gawd! Wants to drive the truck!" she said spitefully. "Well, he ain't goin' ta."

Grampa choked, and a mouthful of paste sprayed into his lap, and he coughed weakly.

Granma smiled up at Tom. "Messy, ain't he?" she observed brightly.

Noah stood on the step, and he faced Tom, and his wide-set eyes seemed to look around him. His face had little expression. Tom said, "How ya, Noah?"

"Fine," said Noah. "How a' you?" That was all, but it was a comfortable thing.

Ma waved the flies away from the bowl of gravy. "We ain't got room to set down," she said. "Jus' get yaself a plate an' set down wherever ya can. Out in the yard or someplace."

Suddenly Tom said, "Hey! Where's the preacher? He was right here. Where'd he go?"

Pa said, "I seen him, but he's gone."

And Granma raised a shrill voice, "Preacher? You got a preacher? Go git him. We'll have a grace." She pointed at Grampa. "Too late for him—he's et. Go git the preacher."

Tom stepped out on the porch. "Hey, Jim! Jim Casy!" he called. He walked out in the yard. "Oh, Casy!" The preacher emerged from under the tank, sat up, and then stood up and moved toward the house. Tom asked, "What was you doin', hidin'?"

"Well, no. But a fella shouldn' butt his head in where a fambly got fambly stuff. I was jus' settin' a-thinkin'."

"Come on in an' eat," said Tom. "Granma wants a grace."

"But I ain't a preacher no more," Casy protested.

"Aw, come on. Give her a grace. Won't do you no harm, an' she likes 'em." They walked into the kitchen together.

Ma said quietly, "You're welcome."

And Pa said, "You're welcome. Have some breakfast."

"Grace fust," Granma clamored. "Grace fust."

Grampa focused his eyes fiercely until he recognized Casy. "Oh, that preacher," he said. "Oh, he's all right. I always liked him since I seen him—" He winked so lecherously that Granma thought he had spoken and retorted, "Shut up, you sinful ol' goat."

Casy ran his fingers through his hair nervously. "I got to tell you, I ain't a preacher no more. If me jus' bein' glad to be here an' bein' thankful for people that's kind and generous, if that's enough—why, I'll say that kinda grace. But I ain't a preacher no more."

"Say her," said Granma. "An' get in a word about us goin' to California." The preacher bowed his head, and the others bowed their heads. Ma folded her hands over her stomach and bowed her head. Granma bowed so low that her nose was nearly in her plate of biscuit and gravy. Tom, leaning against the wall, a plate in his hand, bowed stiffly, and Grampa bowed his head sidewise, so that he could keep one mean and merry eye on the preacher. And on the preacher's face there was a look not of prayer, but of thought; and in his tone not supplication, but conjecture.

"I been thinkin'," he said. "I been in the hills, thinkin', almost you might say like Jesus went into the wilderness to think His way out of a mess of troubles."

"Pu-raise Gawd!" Granma said, and the preacher glanced over at her in surprise.

"Seems like Jesus got all messed up with troubles, and He couldn't figure nothin' out, an' He got to feelin' what the hell good is it all, an' what's the use fightin' an' figurin'. Got tired, got good an' tired, an' His sperit all wore out. Jus' about come to the conclusion, the hell with it. An' so He went off into the wilderness."

"A—men," Granma bleated. So many years she had timed her responses to the pauses. And it was so many years since she had listened to or wondered at the words used.

"I ain't sayin' I'm like Jesus," the preacher went on. "But I got tired like Him, an' I got mixed up like Him, an' I went into the wilderness like Him, without no campin' stuff. Nighttime I'd lay on my back an' look up at the stars; morning I'd set an' watch the sun come up; midday I'd look out from a hill at the rollin' dry country; evenin' I'd foller the sun down. Sometimes I'd pray like I always done. On'y I couldn' figure what I was prayin' to or for. There was the hills, an' there was me, an' we wasn't separate no more. We was one thing. An' there was me an' the hills an' there was the stars an' the black sky, an' we was all one thing. An' that one thing was holy."

"Hallelujah," said Granma, and she rocked a little, back and forth, trying to catch hold of an ecstasy.

"An' I got thinkin', on'y it wasn't thinkin', it was deeper down than thinkin'. I got thinkin' how we was holy when we was one thing, an' mankin' was holy when it was one thing. An' it on'y got unholy when one mis'able little fella got the bit in his teeth an' run off his own way, kickin' an' draggin' an' fightin'. Fella like that bust the holiness. But when they're all workin' together, not one fella for another fella, but one fella kind of harnessed to the whole shebang —that's right, that's holy. An' then I got thinkin' I don't even know what I mean by holy." He paused, but the bowed heads stayed down, for they had been trained like dogs to rise at the "amen" signal. "I can't say no grace like I use' ta say. I'm glad of the holiness of breakfast. I'm glad there's love here. That's all." The heads stayed down. The preacher looked around. "I've got your breakfast cold," he said; and then he remembered. "Amen," he said, and all the heads rose up.

"A—men," said Granma, and she fell to her breakfast, and broke down the soggy biscuits with her hard old toothless gums. Tom ate quickly, and Pa crammed his mouth. There was no talk until the food was gone, the coffee drunk; only the crunch of chewed food and the slup of coffee cooled in transit to the tongue. Ma watched the preacher as he ate, and her eyes were questioning, probing and understanding. She watched him as though he were suddenly a spirit, not human any more, a voice out of the ground.

The men finished and put down their plates, and drained the last of their coffee; and then the men went out, Pa and the preacher and Noah and Grampa and Tom, and they walked over to the truck, avoiding the litter of furniture, the wooden bedsteads, the windmill machinery, the old plow. They walked to the truck and stood beside it. They touched the new pine side-boards.

Tom opened the hood and looked at the big greasy engine. And Pa came up beside him. He said, "Your brother Al looked her over before we bought her. He says she's all right."

"What's he know? He's just a squirt," said Tom.

"He worked for a company. Drove truck last year. He knows quite a little. Smart aleck like he is. He knows. He can tinker an engine, Al can."

Tom asked, "Where's he now?"

"Well," said Pa, "he's a-billygoatin' aroun' the country. Tom-cattin' hisself to death. Smart-aleck sixteen-year-older, an' his nuts is just a-eggin' him on. He don't think of nothin' but girls and engines. A plain smart aleck. Ain't been in nights for a week."

Grampa, fumbling with his chest, had succeeded in buttoning the buttons of his blue shirt into the buttonholes of his underwear. His fingers felt that something was wrong, but did not care enough to find out. His fingers went down to try to figure out the intricacies of the buttoning of his fly. "I was worse," he said happily. "I was much worse. I was a heller, you might say. Why, they was a camp meetin' right in Sallisaw when I was a young fella a little bit older'n Al. He's just a squirt, an' punkin-soft. But I was older. An' we was to this here camp meetin'. Five hunderd folks there, an' a proper sprinklin' of young heifers."

"You look like a heller yet, Grampa," said Tom.

"Well, I am, kinda. But I ain't nowheres near the fella I was. Jus' let me get out to California where I can pick me an orange when I want it. Or grapes. There's a thing I ain't never had enough of. Gonna get me a whole big bunch a grapes off a bush, or whatever, an' I'm gonna squash 'em on my face an' let 'em run offen my chin."

Tom asked, "Where's Uncle John? Where's Rosasharn? Where's Ruthie an' Winfield? Nobody said nothin' about them yet."

Pa said, "Nobody asked. John gone to Sallisaw with a load a stuff to sell: pump, tools, chickens, an' all the stuff we brung over. Took Ruthie an' Winfield with 'im. Went 'fore daylight."

"Funny I never saw him," said Tom.

"Well, you come down from the highway, didn' you? He took the back way, by Cowlington. An' Rosasharn, she's nestin' with Connie's folks. By God! You don't even know Rosasharn's married to Connie Rivers. You 'member Connie. Nice young fella. An' Rosasharn's due 'bout three-four-five months now. Swellin' up right now. Looks fine."

"Jesus!" said Tom. "Rosasharn was just a little kid. An' now she's gonna have a baby. So damn much happens in four years if you're away. When ya think to start out west, Pa?"

"Well, we got to take this stuff in an' sell it. If Al gets back from his squirtin' aroun', I figgered he could load the truck an' take all of it in, an' maybe we could start out tomorra or day after. We ain't got so much money, an' a fella says it's damn near two thousan' miles to California. Quicker we get started, surer it is we get there. Money's a-dribblin' out all the time. You got any money?"

"On'y a couple dollars. How'd you get money?"

"Well," said Pa, "we sol' all the stuff at our place, an' the whole bunch of us chopped cotton, even Grampa."

"Sure did," said Grampa.

"We put ever'thing together—two hunderd dollars. We give seventy-five for this here truck, an' me an' Al cut her in two an' built on this here back. Al was gonna grind the valves, but he's too busy fuckin' aroun' to get down to her. We'll have maybe a hunderd an' fifty when we start. Damn ol' tires on this here truck ain't gonna go far. Got a couple of wore out spares. Pick stuff up along the road, I guess."

The sun, driving straight down, stung with its rays. The shadows of the truck bed were dark bars on the ground, and the truck smelled of hot oil and oilcloth and paint. The few chickens had left the yard to hide in the tool shed from the sun. In the sty the pigs lay panting, close to the fence where a thin shadow fell, and they complained shrilly now and then. The two dogs were stretched in the red dust under the truck, panting, their dripping tongues covered with dust. Pa pulled his hat low over his eyes and squatted down on his hams. And, as though this were his natural position of thought and observation, he surveyed Tom critically, the new but aging cap, the suit, and the new shoes.

"Did you spen' your money for them clothes?" he asked. "Them clothes are jus' gonna be a nuisance to ya."

"They give 'em to me," said Tom. "When I come out they give 'em to me." He took off his cap and looked at it with some admiration, then wiped his forehead with it and put it on rakishly and pulled at the visor.

Pa observed, "Them's a nice-lookin' pair a shoes they give ya."

"Yeah," Joad agreed. "Purty for nice, but they ain't no shoes to go walkin' aroun' in on a hot day." He squatted beside his father.

Noah said slowly, "Maybe if you got them side-boards all true on, we could load up this stuff. Load her up so maybe if Al comes in——"

"I can drive her, if that's what you want," Tom said. "I drove truck at McAlester."

"Good," said Pa, and then his eyes stared down the road. "If I ain't mistaken, there's a young smart aleck draggin' his tail home right now," he said. "Looks purty wore out, too."

Tom and the preacher looked up the road. And randy Al, seeing he was being noticed, threw back his shoulders, and he came into the yard with a swaying strut like that of a rooster about to crow. Cockily, he walked close before he recognized Tom; and when he did, his boasting face changed, and admiration and veneration shone in his eyes, and his swagger fell away. His stiff jeans, with the bottoms turned up eight inches to show his heeled boots, his three-inch belt with copper figures on it, even the red arm bands on his blue shirt and the rakish angle of his Stetson hat could not build him up to his brother's stature; for his brother had killed a man, and no one would ever forget it. Al knew that even he had inspired some admiration among boys of his own age because his brother had killed a man. He had heard in Sallisaw how he was pointed out: "That's Al Joad. His brother killed a fella with a shovel."

And now Al, moving humbly near, saw that his brother was not a swaggerer as he had supposed. Al saw the dark brooding eyes of his brother, and the prison calm, the smooth hard face trained to indicate nothing to a prison guard, neither resistance nor slavishness. And instantly Al changed. Unconsciously he became like his brother, and his handsome face brooded, and his shoulders relaxed. He hadn't remembered how Tom was.

Tom said, "Hello, Al. Jesus, you're growin' like a bean! I wouldn't of knowed you."

Al, his hand ready if Tom should want to shake it, grinned self-consciously. Tom stuck out his hand and Al's hand jerked out to meet it. And there was liking between these two. "They tell me you're a good hand with a truck," said Tom.

And Al, sensing that his brother would not like a boaster, said, "I don't know nothin' much about it."

Pa said, "Been smart-alecking aroun' the country. You look wore out. Well, you got to take a load of stuff into Sallisaw to sell."

Al looked at his brother Tom. "Care to ride in?" he said as casually as he could.

"No, I can't," said Tom. "I'll help aroun' here. We'll be—together on the road."

Al tried to control his question. "Did—did you bust out? Of jail?"

"No," said Tom. "I got paroled."

"Oh." And Al was a little disappointed.

CHAPTER 9

In the little houses the tenant people sifted their belongings and the belongings of their fathers and of their grandfathers. Picked over their possessions for the journey to the west. The men were ruthless because the past had been spoiled, but the women knew how the past would cry to them in the coming days. The men went into the barns and the sheds.

That plow, that harrow, remember in the war we planted mustard? Remember a fella wanted us to put in that rubber bush they call guayule? Get rich, he said. Bring out those tools—get a few dollars for them. Eighteen dollars for that plow, plus freight—Sears Roebuck.

Harness, carts, seeders, little bundles of hoes. Bring 'em out. Pile 'em up. Load 'em in the wagon. Take 'em to town. Sell 'em for what you can get. Sell the team and the wagon, too. No more use for anything.

Fifty cents isn't enough to get for a good plow. That seeder cost thirty-eight dollars. Two dollars isn't enough. Can't haul it all back—Well, take it, and a bitterness with it. Take the well pump and the harness. Take halters, collars, hames, and tugs. Take the little glass brow-band jewels, roses red under glass. Got those for the bay gelding. 'Member how he lifted his feet when he trotted?

Junk piled up in a yard.

Can't sell a hand plow any more. Fifty cents for the weight of the metal. Disks and tractors, that's the stuff now.

Well, take it—all junk—and give me five dollars. You're not buying only junk, you're buying junked lives. And more—you'll see—you're buying bitterness. Buying a plow to plow your own children under, buying the arms and spirits that might have saved you. Five dollars, not four. I can't haul 'em back— Well, take 'em for four. But I warn you, you're buying what will plow your own children under. And you won't see. You can't see. Take 'em for four. Now, what'll you give for the team and wagon? Those fine bays, matched they are, matched in color, matched the way they walk, stride to stride. In the stiff pull—straining hams and buttocks, split-second timed together. And in the morning, the light on them, bay light. They look over the fence sniffing for us, and the stiff ears swivel to hear us, and the black forelocks! I've got a girl. She likes to braid the manes and forelocks, puts little red bows on them. Likes to do it. Not any more. I could tell you a funny story about that girl and that off bay. Would make you laugh. Off horse is eight, near is ten, but might of been twin colts the way they work together. See? The teeth. Sound all over. Deep lungs. Feet fair and clean. How much? Ten dollars? For both? And the wagon— Oh, Jesus Christ! I'd shoot 'em for dog feed first. Oh, take 'em! Take 'em quick, mister. You're buying a little girl plaiting the forelocks, taking off her hair ribbon to make bows, standing back, head cocked, rubbing the soft noses with her cheek. You're buying years of work, toil in the sun; you're buying a sorrow that can't talk. But watch it, mister. There's a premium goes with this pile of junk and the bay horses—so beautiful—a packet of bitterness to grow in your house and to flower, some day. We could have saved you, but you cut us down, and soon you will be cut down and there'll be none of us to save you.

And the tenant men came walking back, hands in their pockets, hats pulled down. Some bought a pint and drank it fast to make the impact hard and stunning. But they didn't laugh and they didn't dance. They didn't sing or pick the guitars. They walked back to the farms, hands in pockets and heads down, shoes kicking the red dust up.

Maybe we can start again, in the new rich land—in California, where the fruit grows. We'll start over.

But you can't start. Only a baby can start. You and me—why, we're all that's been. The anger of a moment, the thousand pictures, that's us. This land, this red land, is us; and the flood years and the dust years and the drought years are us. We can't start again. The bitterness we sold to the junk man—he got it all right, but we have it still. And when the owner men told us to go, that's us; and when the tractor hit the house, that's us until we're dead. To California or any place—every one a drum major leading a parade of hurts, marching with our bitterness. And some day—the armies of bitterness will all be going the same way. And they'll all walk together, and there'll be a dead terror from it.

The tenant men scuffed home to the farms through the red dust. When everything that could be sold was sold, stoves and bedsteads, chairs and tables, little corner cupboards, tubs and tanks, still there were piles of possessions; and the women sat among them, turning them over and looking off beyond and back, pictures, square glasses, and here's a vase.

Now you know well what we can take and what we can't take. We'll be camping out—a few pots to cook and wash in, and mattresses and comforts, lantern and buckets, and a piece of canvas. Use that for a tent. This kerosene can. Know what that is? That's the stove. And clothes—take all the clothes. And—the rifle? Wouldn't go out naked of a rifle. When shoes and clothes and food, when even hope is gone, we'll have the rifle. When grampa came—did I tell you?—he had pepper and salt and a rifle. Nothing else. That goes. And a bottle for water. That just about fills us. Right up the sides of the trailer, and the kids can set in the trailer, and granma on a mattress. Tools, a shovel and saw and wrench and pliers. An ax, too. We had that ax forty years. Look how she's wore down. And ropes, of course. The rest? Leave it—or burn it up.

And the children came.

If Mary takes that doll, that dirty rag doll, I got to take my Injun bow. I got to. An' this roun' stick—big as me. I might need this stick. I had this stick so long—a month, or maybe a year. I got to take it. And what's it like in California?

The women sat among the doomed things, turning them over and looking past them and back. This book. My father had it. He liked a book. *Pilgrim's Progress.* Used to read it. Got his name in it. And his pipe—still smells rank. And this picture—an angel. I looked at that before the fust three come—didn't seem to do much good. Think we could get this china dog in? Aunt Sadie brought it from the St. Louis Fair. See? Wrote right on it. No, I guess not. Here's a letter my brother wrote the day before he died. Here's an old-time hat. These feathers—never got to use them. No, there isn't room.

How can we live without our lives? How will we know it's us without our past? No. Leave it. Burn it.

They sat and looked at it and burned it into their memories. How'll it be not to know what land's outside the door? How if you wake up in the night and know—and *know* the willow tree's not there? Can you live without the willow tree? Well, no, you can't. The willow tree is you. The pain on that mattress there—that dreadful pain—that's you.

And the children—if Sam takes his Injun bow an' his long roun' stick, I get to take two things. I choose the fluffy pilla. That's mine.

Suddenly they were nervous. Got to get out quick now. Can't wait. We can't wait. And they piled up the goods in the yards and set fire to them. They stood and watched them burning, and then frantically they loaded up the cars and drove away, drove in the dust. The dust hung in the air for a long time after the loaded cars had passed.

CHAPTER 10

When the truck had gone, loaded with implements, with heavy tools, with beds and springs, with every movable thing that might be sold, Tom hung around the place. He mooned into the barn shed, into the empty stalls, and he walked into the implement leanto and kicked the refuse that was left, turned a broken mower tooth with his foot. He visited places he remembered—the red bank where the swallows nested, the willow tree over the pig pen. Two shoats grunted and squirmed at him through the fence, black pigs, sunning and comfortable. And then his pilgrimage was over, and he went to sit on the doorstep where the shade was lately fallen. Behind him Ma moved about in the kitchen, washing children's clothes in a bucket; and her strong freckled arms dripped soapsuds from the elbows. She stopped her rubbing when he sat down. She looked at him a long time, and at the back of his head when he turned and stared out at the hot sunlight. And then she went back to her rubbing.

She said, "Tom, I hope things is all right in California."

He turned and looked at her. "What makes you think they ain't?" he asked.

"Well—nothing. Seems too nice, kinda. I seen the han'bills fellas pass out, an' how much work they is, an' high wages an' all; an' I seen in the paper how they want folks to come an' pick grapes an' oranges an' peaches. That'd be nice work, Tom, pickin' peaches. Even if they wouldn't let you eat none, you could maybe snitch a little ratty one sometimes. An' it'd be nice under the trees, workin' in the shade. I'm scared of stuff so nice. I ain't got faith. I'm scared somepin ain't so nice about it."

Tom said, "Don't roust your faith bird-high an' you won't do no crawlin' with the worms."

"I know that's right. That's Scripture, ain't it?"

"I guess so," said Tom. "I never could keep Scripture straight sence I read a book name' *The Winning of Barbara Worth.*"

Ma chuckled lightly and scrounged the clothes in and out of the bucket. And she wrung out overalls and shirts, and the muscles of her forearms corded out. "Your Pa's pa, he quoted Scripture all the time. He got it all roiled up, too. It was the *Dr. Miles' Almanac* he got mixed up. Used to read ever' word in that almanac out loud— letters from folks that couldn't sleep or had lame backs. An' later he'd give them people for a lesson, an' he'd say, 'That's a par'ble from Scripture.' Your Pa an' Uncle John troubled 'im some about it when they'd laugh." She piled wrung clothes like cord wood on the table. "They say it's two thousan' miles where we're goin'. How far ya think that is, Tom? I seen it on a map, big mountains like on a post card, an' we're goin' right through 'em. How long ya s'pose it'll take to go that far, Tommy?"

"I dunno," he said. "Two weeks, maybe ten days if we got luck. Look, Ma, stop your worryin'. I'm a-gonna tell you somepin about bein' in the pen. You can't go thinkin' when you're gonna be out. You'd go nuts. You got to think about that day, an' then the nex' day, about the ball game Sat'dy. That's what you got to do. Ol' timers does that. A new young fella gets buttin' his head on the cell door. He's thinkin' how long it's gonna be. Whyn't you do that? Jus' take ever' day."

"That's a good way," she said, and she filled up her bucket with hot water from the stove, and she put in dirty clothes and began punching them down into the soapy water. "Yes, that's a good way. But I like to think how nice it's gonna be, maybe, in California. Never cold. An' fruit ever'place, an' people just bein' in the nicest places, little white houses in among the orange trees. I wonder— that is, if we all get jobs an' all work—maybe we can get one of them little white houses. An' the little fellas go out an' pick oranges right off the tree. They ain't gonna be able to stand it, they'll get to yellin' so."

Tom watched her working, and his eyes smiled. "It done you good jus' thinkin' about it. I knowed a fella from California. He didn't talk like us. You'd of knowed he come from some far-off place jus' the way he talked. But he says they's too many folks lookin' for work right there now. An' he says the folks that pick the fruit live in dirty ol' camps an' don't hardly get enough to eat. He says wages is low an' hard to get any."

A shadow crossed her face. "Oh, that ain't so," she said. "Your father got a han'bill on yella paper, tellin' how they need folks to work. They wouldn' go to that trouble if they wasn't plenty work. Costs 'em good money to get them han'bills out. What'd they want ta lie for, an' costin' 'em money to lie?"

Tom shook his head. "I don' know, Ma. It's kinda hard to think why they done it. Maybe—" He looked out at the hot sun, shining on the red earth.

"Maybe what?"

"Maybe it's nice, like you says. Where'd Grampa go? Where'd the preacher go?"

Ma was going out of the house, her arms loaded high with the clothes. Tom moved aside to let her pass. "Preacher says he's gonna walk aroun'. Grampa's asleep here in the house. He comes in here in the day an' lays down sometimes." She walked to the line and began to drape pale blue jeans and blue shirts and long gray underwear over the wire.

Behind him Tom heard a shuffling step, and he turned to look in. Grampa was emerging from the bedroom, and as in the morning, he fumbled with the buttons of his fly. "I heerd talkin'," he said. "Sons-a-bitches won't let a ol' fella sleep. When you bastards get dry behin' the ears, you'll maybe learn to let a ol' fella sleep." His furious fingers managed to flip open the only two buttons on his fly that had been buttoned. And his hand forgot what it had been trying to do. His hand reached in and contentedly scratched under the testicles. Ma came in with wet hands, and her palms puckered and bloated from hot water and soap.

"Thought you was sleepin'. Here, let me button you up." And though he struggled, she held him and buttoned his underwear and his shirt and his fly. "You go aroun' a sight," she said, and let him go.

And he spluttered angrily, "Fella's come to a nice—to a nice—when somebody buttons 'em. I want ta be let be to button my own pants."

Ma said playfully, "They don't let people run aroun' with their clothes unbutton' in California."

"They don't, hey! Well, I'll show 'em. They think they're gonna show me how to act out there? Why, I'll go aroun' a-hangin' out if I wanta!"

Ma said, "Seems like his language gets worse ever' year. Showin' off, I guess."

The old man thrust out his bristly chin, and he regarded Ma with

his shrewd, mean, merry eyes. "Well, sir," he said, "we'll be a-startin'
'fore long now. An', by God, they's grapes out there, just a-hangin'
over inta the road. Know what I'm a-gonna do? I'm gonna pick me
a wash tub full a grapes, an' I'm gonna set in 'em, an' scrooge aroun',
an' let the juice run down my pants."

Tom laughed. "By God, if he lives to be two hundred you never
will get Grampa house broke," he said. "You're all set on goin', ain't
you, Grampa?"

The old man pulled out a box and sat down heavily on it. "Yes,
sir," he said. "An' goddamn near time, too. My brother went on out
there forty years ago. Never did hear nothin' about him. Sneaky son-
of-a-bitch, he was. Nobody loved him. Run off with a single-action
Colt of mine. If I ever run across him or his kids, if he got any out
in California, I'll ask 'em for that Colt. But if I know 'im, an' he got
any kids, he cuckoo'd 'em, an' somebody else is a-raisin' 'em. I sure
will be glad to get out there. Got a feelin' it'll make a new fella outa
me. Go right to work in the fruit."

Ma nodded. "He means it, too," she said. "Worked right up to
three months ago, when he throwed his hip out the last time."

"Damn right," said Grampa.

Tom looked outward from his seat on the doorstep. "Here comes
that preacher, walkin' aroun' from the back side a the barn."

Ma said, "Curiousest grace I ever heerd, that he give this
mornin'. Wasn't hardly no grace at all. Jus' talkin', but the sound of
it was like a grace."

"He's a funny fella," said Tom. "Talks funny all the time. Seems
like he's talkin' to hisself, though. He ain't tryin' to put nothin' over."

"Watch the look in his eye," said Ma. "He looks baptized. Got
that look they call lookin' through. He sure looks baptized. An' a-
walkin' with his head down, a-starin' at nothin' on the groun'. There
is a man that's baptized." And she was silent, for Casy had drawn
near the door.

"You gonna get sun-shook, walkin' around like that," said Tom.

Casy said, "Well, yeah—maybe." He appealed to them all suddenly, to Ma and Grampa and Tom. "I got to get goin' west. I got
to go. I wonder if I kin go along with you folks." And then he stood,
embarrassed by his own speech.

Ma looked to Tom to speak, because he was a man, but Tom
did not speak. She let him have the chance that was his right, and
then she said, "Why, we'd be proud to have you. 'Course I can't say

right now; Pa says all the men'll talk tonight and figger when we gonna start. I guess maybe we better not say till all the men come. John an' Pa an' Noah an' Tom an' Grampa an' Al an' Connie, they're gonna figger soon's they get back. But if they's room I'm pretty sure we'll be proud to have ya."

The preacher sighed. "I'll go anyways," he said. "Somepin's happening. I went up an' I looked, an' the houses is all empty, an' the lan' is empty, an' this whole country is empty. I can't stay here no more. I got to go where the folks is goin'. I'll work in the fiel's, an' maybe I'll be happy."

"An' you ain't gonna preach?" Tom asked.

"I ain't gonna preach."

"An' you ain't gonna baptize?" Ma asked.

"I ain't gonna baptize. I'm gonna work in the fiel's, in the green fiel's, an' I'm gonna be near to folks. I ain't gonna try to teach 'em nothin'. I'm gonna try to learn. Gonna learn why the folks walks in the grass, gonna hear 'em talk, gonna hear 'em sing. Gonna listen to kids eatin' mush. Gonna hear husban' an' wife a-poundin' the mattress in the night. Gonna eat with 'em an' learn." His eyes were wet and shining. "Gonna lay in the grass, open an' honest with anybody that'll have me. Gonna cuss an' swear an' hear the poetry of folks talkin'. All that's holy, all that's what I didn' understan'. All them things is the good things."

Ma said, "A-men."

The preacher sat humbly down on the chopping block beside the door. "I wonder what they is for a fella so lonely."

Tom coughed delicately. "For a fella that don't preach no more—" he began.

"Oh, I'm a talker!" said Casy. "No gettin' away from that. But I ain't preachin'. Preachin' is tellin' folks stuff. I'm askin' 'em. That ain't preachin', is it?"

"I don' know," said Tom. "Preachin's a kinda tone a voice, an' preachin's a way a lookin' at things. Preachin's bein' good to folks when they wanna kill ya for it. Las' Christmas in McAlester, Salvation Army come an' done us good. Three solid hours a cornet music, an' we set there. They was bein' nice to us. But if one of us tried to walk out, we'd a-drawed solitary. That's preachin'. Doin' good to a fella that's down an' can't smack ya in the puss for it. No, you ain't no preacher. But don't you blow no cornets aroun' here."

Ma threw some sticks into the stove. "I'll get you a bit now, but it ain't much."

Grampa brought his box outside and sat on it and leaned against the wall, and Tom and Casy leaned back against the house wall. And the shadow of the afternoon moved out from the house.

In the late afternoon the truck came back, bumping and rattling through the dust, and there was a layer of dust in the bed, and the hood was covered with dust, and the headlights were obscured with a red film. The sun was setting when the truck came back, and the earth was bloody in its setting light. Al sat bent over the wheel, proud and serious and efficient, and Pa and Uncle John, as befitted the heads of the clan, had the honor seats beside the driver. Standing in the truck bed, holding onto the bars of the sides, rode the others, twelve-year-old Ruthie and ten-year-old Winfield, grime-faced and wild, their eyes tired but excited, their fingers and the edges of their mouths black and sticky from licorice whips, whined out of their father in town. Ruthie, dressed in a real dress of pink muslin that came below her knees, was a little serious in her young-ladiness. But Winfield was still a trifle of a snot-nose, a little of a brooder back of the barn, and an inveterate collector and smoker of snipes. And whereas Ruthie felt the might, the responsibility, and the dignity of her developing breasts, Winfield was kid-wild and calfish. Beside them, clinging lightly to the bars, stood Rose of Sharon, and she balanced, swaying on the balls of her feet, and took up the road shock in her knees and hams. For Rose of Sharon was pregnant and careful. Her hair, braided and wrapped around her head, made an ash-blond crown. Her round soft face, which had been voluptuous and inviting a few months ago, had already put on the barrier of pregnancy, the self-sufficient smile, the knowing perfection-look; and her plump body—full soft breasts and stomach, hard hips and buttocks that had swung so freely and provocatively as to invite slapping and stroking—her whole body had become demure and serious. Her whole thought and action were directed inward on the baby. She balanced on her toes now, for the baby's sake. And the world was pregnant to her; she thought only in terms of reproduction and of motherhood. Connie, her nineteen-year-old husband, who had married a plump, passionate hoyden, was still frightened and bewildered at the change in her; for there were no more cat fights in bed, biting and scratching with muffled giggles and final tears. There was a balanced, careful, wise creature who smiled shyly but very firmly at him. Connie was proud and fearful of Rose of Sharon. Whenever he could, he put a hand on her or stood close, so that his body touched her at hip and shoulder, and he felt that this kept a relation that might be departing. He was a sharp-faced, lean young man of a Texas strain, and his pale blue eyes were sometimes dangerous and sometimes kindly, and sometimes frightened. He was a good hard worker and would make a good husband. He drank enough, but not too much; fought when it was required of him; and never boasted. He sat quietly in a gathering and yet managed to be there and to be recognized.

Had he not been fifty years old, and so one of the natural rulers of the family, Uncle John would have preferred not to sit in the honor place beside the driver. He would have liked Rose of Sharon to sit there. This was impossible, because she was young and a woman. But Uncle John sat uneasily, his lonely haunted eyes were not at ease, and his thin strong body was not relaxed. Nearly all the time the barrier of loneliness cut Uncle John off from people and from appetites. He ate little, drank nothing, and was celibate. But underneath, his appetites swelled into pressures until they broke through. Then he would eat of some craved food until he was sick; or he would drink jake or whisky until he was a shaken paralytic with red wet eyes; or he would raven with lust for some whore in Sallisaw. It was told of him that once he went clear to Shawnee and hired three whores in one bed, and snorted and rutted on their unresponsive bodies for an hour. But when one of his appetites was sated, he was sad and ashamed and lonely again. He hid from people, and by gifts tried to make up to all people for himself. Then he crept into houses and left gum under pillows for children; then he cut wood and took no pay. Then he gave away any possession he might have: a saddle, a horse, a new pair of shoes. One could not talk to him then, for he ran away, or if confronted hid within himself and peeked out of frightened eyes. The death of his wife, followed by months of being alone, had marked him with guilt and shame and had left an unbreaking loneliness on him.

But there were things he could not escape. Being one of the heads of the family, he had to govern; and now he had to sit on the honor seat beside the driver.

The three men on the seat were glum as they drove toward home over the dusty road. Al, bending over the wheel, kept shifting eyes from the road to the instrument panel, watching the ammeter needle, which jerked suspiciously, watching the oil gauge and the heat indicator. And his mind was cataloguing weak points and suspicious things about the car. He listened to the whine, which might be the rear end, dry; and he listened to tappets lifting and falling. He kept his hand on the gear lever, feeling the turning gears through it. And he had let the clutch out against the brake to test for slipping clutch plates. He might be a musking goat sometimes, but this was his responsibility, this truck, its running, and its maintenance. If something went wrong it would be his fault, and while no one would say it, everyone, and Al most of all, would know it was his fault. And so he felt it, watched it, and listened to it. And his face was serious and responsible. And everyone respected him and his responsibility. Even Pa, who was the leader, would hold a wrench and take orders from Al.

They were all tired on the truck. Ruthie and Winfield were tired from seeing too much movement, too many faces, from fighting to get licorice whips; tired from the excitement of having Uncle John secretly slip gum into their pockets.

And the men in the seat were tired and angry and sad, for they had got eighteen dollars for every movable thing from the farm: the horses, the wagon, the implements, and all the furniture from the house. Eighteen dollars. They had assailed the buyer, argued; but they were routed when his interest seemed to flag and he had told them he didn't want the stuff at any price. Then they were beaten, believed him, and took two dollars less than he had first offered. And now they were weary and frightened because they had gone against a system they did not understand and it had beaten them. They knew the team and the wagon were worth much more. They knew the buyer man would get much more, but they didn't know how to do it. Merchandising was a secret to them.

Al, his eyes darting from road to panel board, said, "That fella, he ain't a local fella. Didn' talk like a local fella. Clothes was different, too."

And Pa explained, "When I was in the hardware store I talked to some men I know. They say there's fellas comin' in jus' to buy up the stuff us fellas got to sell when we get out. They say these new fellas is cleaning up. But there ain't nothin' we can do about it. Maybe Tommy should of went. Maybe he could of did better."

John said, "But the fella wasn't gonna take it at all. We couldn' haul it back."

"These men I know told about that," said Pa. "Said the buyer fellas always done that. Scairt folks that way. We jus' don' know how to go about stuff like that. Ma's gonna be disappointed. She'll be mad an' disappointed."

Al said, "When ya think we're gonna go, Pa?"

"I dunno. We'll talk her over tonight an' decide. I'm sure glad Tom's back. That makes me feel good. Tom's a good boy."

Al said, "Pa, some fellas was talkin' about Tom, an' they says he's parole'. An' they says that means he can't go outside the State, or if he goes, an' they catch him, they send 'im back for three years."

Pa looked startled. "They said that? Seem like fellas that knowed? Not jus' blowin' off?"

"I don' know," said Al. "They was just a-talkin' there, an' I didn' let on he's my brother. I jus' stood an' took it in."

Pa said, "Jesus Christ, I hope that ain't true! We need Tom. I'll ask 'im about that. We got trouble enough without they chase the hell out of us. I hope it ain't true. We got to talk that out in the open."

Uncle John said, "Tom, he'll know."

They fell silent while the truck battered along. The engine was noisy, full of little clashings, and the brake rods banged. There was a wooden creaking from the wheels, and a thin jet of steam escaped through a hole in the top of the radiator cap. The truck pulled a high whirling column of red dust behind it. They rumbled up the last little rise while the sun was still half-face above the horizon, and they bore down on the house as it disappeared. The brakes squealed when they stopped, and the sound printed in Al's head—no lining left.

Ruthie and Winfield climbed yelling over the side walls and dropped to the ground. They shouted, "Where is he? Where's Tom?" And then they saw him standing beside the door, and they stopped, embarrassed, and walked slowly toward him and looked shyly at him.

And when he said, "Hello, how you kids doin'?" they replied softly, "Hello! All right." And they stood apart and watched him secretly, the great brother who had killed a man and been in prison. They remembered how they had played prison in the chicken coop and fought for the right to be prisoner.

Connie Rivers lifted the high tail-gate out of the truck and got down and helped Rose of Sharon to the ground; and she accepted it nobly, smiling her wise, self-satisfied smile, mouth tipped at the corners a little fatuously.

Tom said, "Why, it's Rosasharn. I didn' know you was comin' with them."

"We was walkin'," she said. "The truck come by an' picked us up." And then she said, "This is Connie, my husband." And she was grand, saying it.

The two shook hands, sizing each other up, looking deeply into each other; and in a moment each was satisfied, and Tom said, "Well, I see you been busy."

She looked down. "You do not see, not yet."

"Ma tol' me. When's it gonna be?"

"Oh, not for a long time! Not till nex' winter."

Tom laughed. "Gonna get 'im bore in a orange ranch, huh? In one a them white houses with orange trees all aroun'."

Rose of Sharon felt her stomach with both her hands. "You do not see," she said, and she smiled her complacent smile and went into the house. The evening was hot, and the thrust of light still flowed up from the western horizon. And without any signal the family gathered by the truck, and the congress, the family government, went into session.

The film of evening light made the red earth lucent, so that its dimensions were deepened, so that a stone, a post, a building had greater depth and more solidity than in the daytime light; and these objects were curiously more individual—a post was more essentially a post, set off from the earth it stood in and the field of corn it stood out against. And plants were individuals, not the mass of crop; and the ragged willow tree was itself, standing free of all other willow trees. The earth contributed a light to the evening. The front of the gray, paintless house, facing the west, was luminous as the moon is. The gray dusty truck, in the yard before the door, stood out magically in this light, in the overdrawn perspective of a stereopticon.

The people too were changed in the evening, quieted. They seemed to be a part of an organization of the unconscious. They obeyed impulses which registered only faintly in their thinking minds. Their eyes were inward and quiet, and their eyes, too, were lucent in the evening, lucent in dusty faces.

The family met at the most important place, near the truck. The house was dead, and the fields were dead; but this truck was the active thing, the living principle. The ancient Hudson, with bent and scarred radiator screen, with grease in dusty globules at the worn edges of every moving part, with hub caps gone and caps of red dust in their places—this was the new hearth, the living center of the family; half passenger car and half truck, high-sided and clumsy.

Pa walked around the truck, looking at it, and then he squatted down in the dust and found a stick to draw with. One foot was flat to the ground, the other rested on the ball and slightly back, so that one knee was higher than the other. Left forearm rested on the lower, left, knee; the right elbow on the right knee, and the right fist cupped for the chin. Pa squatted there, looking at the truck, his chin in his cupped fist. And Uncle John moved toward him and squatted down beside him. Their eyes were brooding. Grampa came out of the house and saw the two squatting together, and he jerked over and sat on the running board of the truck, facing them. That was the nucleus. Tom and Connie and Noah strolled in and squatted, and the line was a half-circle with Grampa in the opening. And then Ma came out of the house, and Granma with her, and Rose of Sharon behind, walking daintily. They took their places behind the squatting men; they stood up and put their hands on their hips. And the children, Ruthie and Winfield, hopped from foot to foot beside the women; the children squidged their toes in the red dust, but they made no sound. Only the preacher was not there. He, out of delicacy, was sitting on the ground behind the house. He was a good preacher and knew his people.

The evening light grew softer, and for a while the family sat and stood silently. Then Pa, speaking to no one, but to the group, made his report: "Got skinned on the stuff we sold. The fella knowed we couldn't wait. Got eighteen dollars only."

Ma stirred restively, but she held her peace.

Noah, the oldest son, asked, "How much, all added up, we got?"

Pa drew figures in the dust and mumbled to himself for a moment. "Hunderd fifty-four," he said. "But Al here says we gonna need better tires. Says these here won't last."

This was Al's first participation in the conference. Always he had stood behind with the women before. And now he made his report solemnly. "She's old an' she's ornery," he said gravely. "I gave the whole thing a good goin'-over 'fore we bought her. Didn' listen to the fella talkin' what a hell of a bargain she was. Stuck my finger in

the differential an' they wasn't no sawdust. Opened the gear box an'
they wasn't no sawdust. Test' her clutch an' rolled her wheels for
line. Went under her an' her frame ain't splayed none. She never
been rolled. Seen they was a cracked cell in her battery an' made
the fella put in a good one. The tires ain't worth a damn, but they're
a good size. Easy to get. She'll ride like a bull calf, but she ain't
shootin' no oil. Reason I says buy her is she was a pop'lar car.
Wreckin' yards is full a Hudson Super-Sixes, an' you can buy parts
cheap. Could a got a bigger, fancier car for the same money, but
parts too hard to get, an' too dear. That's how I figgered her anyways." The last was his submission to the family. He stopped speaking and waited for their opinions.

Grampa was still the titular head, but he no longer ruled. His
position was honorary and a matter of custom. But he did have the
right of first comment, no matter how silly his old mind might be.
And the squatting men and the standing women waited for him.
"You're all right, Al," Grampa said. "I was a squirt jus' like you, a-
fartin' aroun' like a dog-wolf. But when they was a job, I done it.
You've growed up good." He finished in the tone of a benediction,
and Al reddened a little with pleasure.

Pa said, "Sounds right-side-up to me. If it was horses we wouldn'
have to put the blame on Al. But Al's the on'y automobile fella
here."

Tom said, "I know some. Worked some in McAlester. Al's right.
He done good." And now Al was rosy with the compliment. Tom
went on, "I'd like to say—well, that preacher—he wants to go
along." He was silent. His words lay in the group, and the group was
silent. "He's a nice fella," Tom added. "We've knowed him a long
time. Talks a little wild sometimes, but he talks sensible." And he
relinquished the proposal to the family.

The light was going gradually. Ma left the group and went into
the house, and the iron clang of the stove came from the house. In
a moment she walked back to the brooding council.

Grampa said, "They was two ways a thinkin'. Some folks use' ta
figger that a preacher was poison luck."

Tom said, "This fella says he ain't a preacher no more."

Grampa waved his hand back and forth. "Once a fella's a
preacher, he's always a preacher. That's somepin you can't get shut
of. They was some folks figgered it was a good respectable thing to
have a preacher along. Ef somebody died, preacher buried 'em. Wed-

din' come due, or overdue, an' there's your preacher. Baby come, an' you got a christener right under the roof. Me, I always said they was preachers *an'* preachers. Got to pick 'em. I kinda like this fella. He ain't stiff."

Pa dug his stick into the dust and rolled it between his fingers so that it bored a little hole. "They's more to this than is he lucky, or is he a nice fella," Pa said. "We got to figger close. It's a sad thing to figger close. Le's see, now. There's Grampa an' Granma—that's two. An' me an' John an' Ma—that's five. An' Noah an' Tommy an' Al—that's eight. Rosasharn an' Connie is ten, an' Ruthie an' Winfiel' is twelve. We got to take the dogs 'cause what'll we do else? Can't shoot a good dog, an' there ain't nobody to give 'em to. An' that's fourteen."

"Not countin' what chickens is left, an' two pigs," said Noah.

Pa said, "I aim to get those pigs salted down to eat on the way. We gonna need meat. Carry the salt kegs right with us. But I'm wonderin' if we can all ride, an' the preacher too. An' kin we feed a extra mouth?" Without turning his head he asked, "Kin we, Ma?"

Ma cleared her throat. "It ain't kin we? It's will we?" she said firmly. "As far as 'kin,' we can't do nothin', not go to California or nothin'; but as far as 'will,' why, we'll do what we will. An' as far as 'will'—it's a long time our folks been here and east before, an' I never heerd tell of no Joads or no Hazletts, neither, ever refusin' food an' shelter or a lift on the road to anybody that asked. They's been mean Joads, but never that mean."

Pa broke in, "But s'pose there just ain't room?" He had twisted his neck to look up at her, and he was ashamed. Her tone had made him ashamed. "S'pose we jus' can't all get in the truck?"

"There ain't room now," she said. "There ain't room for more'n six, an' twelve is goin' sure. One more ain't gonna hurt; an' a man, strong an' healthy, ain't never no burden. An' any time when we got two pigs an' over a hunderd dollars, an' we wonderin' if we kin feed a fella—" She stopped, and Pa turned back, and his spirit was raw from the whipping.

Granma said, "A preacher is a nice thing to be with us. He give a nice grace this morning."

Pa looked at the face of each one for dissent, and then he said, "Want to call 'im over, Tommy? If he's goin', he ought ta be here."

Tom got up from his hams and went toward the house, calling, "Casy—oh, Casy!"

A muffled voice replied from behind the house. Tom walked to the corner and saw the preacher sitting back against the wall, looking at the flashing evening star in the light sky. "Calling me?" Casy asked.

"Yeah. We think long as you're goin' with us, you ought to be over with us, helpin' to figger things out."

Casy got to his feet. He knew the government of families, and he knew he had been taken into the family. Indeed his position was eminent, for Uncle John moved sideways, leaving space between Pa and himself for the preacher. Casy squatted down like the others, facing Grampa enthroned on the running board.

Ma went to the house again. There was a screech of a lantern hood and the yellow light flashed up in the dark kitchen. When she lifted the lid of the big pot, the smell of boiling side-meat and beet greens came out the door. They waited for her to come back across the darkening yard, for Ma was powerful in the group.

Pa said, "We got to figger when to start. Sooner the better. What we got to do 'fore we go is get them pigs slaughtered an' in salt, an' pack our stuff an' go. Quicker the better, now."

Noah agreed, "If we pitch in, we kin get ready tomorrow, an' we kin go bright the nex' day."

Uncle John objected, "Can't chill no meat in the heat a the day. Wrong time a year for slaughterin'. Meat'll be sof' if it don' chill."

"Well, le's do her tonight. She'll chill tonight some. Much as she's gonna. After we eat, le's get her done. Got salt?"

Ma said, "Yes. Got plenty salt. Got two nice kegs, too."

"Well, le's get her done, then," said Tom.

Grampa began to scrabble about, trying to get a purchase to arise. "Gettin' dark," he said. "I'm gettin' hungry. Come time we get to California I'll have a big bunch a grapes in my han' all the time, a-nibblin' off it all the time, by God!" He got up, and the men arose.

Ruthie and Winfield hopped excitedly about in the dust, like crazy things. Ruthie whispered hoarsely to Winfield, "Killin' pigs *and* goin' to California. Killin' pigs *and* goin'—all the same time."

And Winfield was reduced to madness. He stuck his finger against his throat, made a horrible face, and wobbled about, weakly shrilling, "I'm a ol' pig. Look! I'm a ol' pig. Look at the blood, Ruthie!" And he staggered and sank to the ground, and waved arms and legs weakly.

But Ruthie was older, and she knew the tremendousness of the time. "*And* goin' to California," she said again. And she knew this was the great time in her life so far.

The adults moved toward the lighted kitchen through the deep dusk, and Ma served them greens and side-meat in tin plates. But before Ma ate, she put the big round wash tub on the stove and started the fire to roaring. She carried buckets of water until the tub was full, and then around the tub she clustered the buckets, full of water. The kitchen became a swamp of heat, and the family ate hurriedly, and went out to sit on the doorstep until the water should get hot. They sat looking out at the dark, at the square of light the kitchen lantern threw on the ground outside the door, with a hunched shadow of Grampa in the middle of it. Noah picked his teeth thoroughly with a broom straw. Ma and Rose of Sharon washed up the dishes and piled them on the table.

And then, all of a sudden, the family began to function. Pa got up and lighted another lantern. Noah, from a box in the kitchen, brought out the bow-bladed butchering knife and whetted it on a worn little carborundum stone. And he laid the scraper on the chopping block, and the knife beside it. Pa brought two sturdy sticks, each three feet long, and pointed the ends with the ax, and he tied strong ropes, double half-hitched, to the middle of the sticks.

He grumbled, "Shouldn't of sold those single trees—all of 'em."

The water in the pots steamed and rolled.

Noah asked, "Gonna take the water down there or bring the pigs up here?"

"Pigs up here," said Pa. "You can't spill a pig and scald yourself like you can hot water. Water about ready?"

"Jus' about," said Ma.

"Aw right. Noah, you an' Tom an' Al come along. I'll carry the light. We'll slaughter down there an' bring 'em up here."

Noah took his knife, and Al the ax, and the four men moved down on the sty, their legs flickering in the lantern light. Ruthie and Winfield skittered along, hopping over the ground. At the sty Pa leaned over the fence, holding the lantern. The sleepy young pigs struggled to their feet, grunting suspiciously. Uncle John and the preacher walked down to help.

"All right," said Pa. "Stick 'em, an' we'll run 'em up and bleed an' scald at the house." Noah and Tom stepped over the fence. They slaughtered quickly and efficiently. Tom struck twice with the blunt head of the ax; and Noah, leaning over the felled pigs, found the great artery with his curving knife and released the pulsing streams of blood. Then over the fence with the squealing pigs. The preacher and Uncle John dragged one by the hind legs, and Tom and Noah the other. Pa walked along with the lantern, and the black blood made two trails in the dust.

At the house, Noah slipped his knife between tendon and bone of the hind legs; the pointed sticks held the legs apart, and the carcasses were hung from the two-by-four rafters that stuck out from the house. Then the men carried the boiling water and poured it over the black bodies. Noah slit the bodies from end to end and dropped the entrails out on the ground. Pa sharpened two more sticks to hold the bodies open to the air, while Tom with the scrubber and Ma with a dull knife scraped the skins to take out the bristles. Al brought a bucket and shoveled the entrails into it, and dumped them on the ground away from the house, and two cats followed him, mewing loudly, and the dogs followed him, growling lightly at the cats.

Pa sat on the doorstep and looked at the pigs hanging in the lantern light. The scraping was done now, and only a few drops of blood continued to fall from the carcasses into the black pool on the ground. Pa got up and went to the pigs and felt them with his hand, and then he sat down again. Granma and Grampa went toward the barn to sleep, and Grampa carried a candle lantern in his hand. The rest of the family sat quietly about the doorstep, Connie and Al and Tom on the ground, leaning their backs against the house wall, Uncle John on a box, Pa in the doorway. Only Ma and Rose of Sharon continued to move about. Ruthie and Winfield were sleepy now, but fighting it off. They quarreled sleepily out in the darkness. Noah and the preacher squatted side by side, facing the house. Pa scratched himself nervously, and took off his hat and ran his fingers through his hair. "Tomorra we'll get that pork salted early in the morning, an' then we'll get the truck loaded, all but the beds, an' nex' morning off we'll go." No one answered him. "Hardly is a day's work in all that," he said uneasily.

Tom broke in, "We'll be moonin' aroun' all day, lookin' for somepin to do." The group stirred uneasily. "We could get ready by daylight an' go," Tom suggested. Pa rubbed his knee with his hand. And the restiveness spread to all of them.

Noah said, "Prob'ly wouldn' hurt that meat to git her right down in salt. Cut her up, she'd cool quicker anyways."

It was Uncle John who broke over the edge, his pressures too great. "What we hangin' aroun' for? I want to get shut of this. Now we're goin', why don't we go?"

And the revulsion spread to the rest. "Whyn't we go? Get sleep on the way." And a sense of hurry crept into them.

Pa said, "They say it's two thousan' miles. That's a hell of a long ways. We oughta go. Noah, you an' me can get that meat cut up an' we can put all the stuff in the truck."

Ma put her head out of the door. "How about if we forget somepin, not seein' it in the dark?"

"We could look 'round after daylight," said Noah. They sat still then, thinking about it. But in a moment Noah got up and began to sharpen the bow-bladed knife on his little worn stone. "Ma," he said, "git that table cleared." And he stepped to a pig, cut a line down one side of the backbone and began peeling the meat forward, off the ribs.

Pa stood up excitedly. "We got to get the stuff together," he said. "Come on, you fellas."

Now that they were committed to going, the hurry infected all of them. Noah carried the slabs of meat into the kitchen and cut it into small salting blocks, and Ma patted the coarse salt in, laid it piece by piece in the kegs, careful that no two pieces touched each other. She laid the slabs like bricks, and pounded salt in the spaces. And Noah cut up the side-meat and he cut up the legs. Ma kept her fire going, and as Noah cleaned the ribs and the spines and leg bones of all the meat he could, she put them in the oven to roast for gnawing purposes.

In the yard and in the barn the circles of lantern light moved about, and the men brought together all the things to be taken, and piled them by the truck. Rose of Sharon brought out all the clothes the family possessed: the overalls, the thick-soled shoes, the rubber boots, the worn best suits, the sweaters and sheepskin coats. And she packed these tightly into a wooden box and got into the box and tramped them down. And then she brought out the print dresses and shawls, the black cotton stockings and the children's clothes— small overalls and cheap print dresses—and she put these in the box and tramped them down.

Tom went to the tool shed and brought what tools were left to go, a hand saw and a set of wrenches, a hammer and a box of assorted nails, a pair of pliers and a flat file and a set of rat-tail files.

And Rose of Sharon brought out the big piece of tarpaulin and spread it on the ground behind the truck. She struggled through the door with the mattresses, three double ones and a single. She piled them on the tarpaulin and brought arm-loads of folded ragged blankets and piled them up.

Ma and Noah worked busily at the carcasses, and the smell of roasting pork bones came from the stove. The children had fallen by the way in the late night. Winfield lay curled up in the dust outside the door; and Ruthie, sitting on a box in the kitchen where she had gone to watch the butchering, had dropped her head back against the wall. She breathed easily in her sleep, and her lips were parted over her teeth.

Tom finished with the tools and came into the kitchen with his lantern, and the preacher followed him. "God in a buckboard," Tom said, "smell that meat! An' listen to her crackle."

Ma laid the bricks of meat in a keg and poured salt around and over them and covered the layer with salt and patted it down. She looked up at Tom and smiled a little at him, but her eyes were serious and tired. "Be nice to have pork bones for breakfas'," she said.

The preacher stepped beside her. "Leave me salt down this meat," he said. "I can do it. There's other stuff for you to do."

She stopped her work then and inspected him oddly, as though he suggested a curious thing. And her hands were crusted with salt, pink with fluid from the fresh pork. "It's women's work," she said finally.

"It's all work," the preacher replied. "They's too much of it to split it up to men's or women's work. You got stuff to do. Leave me salt the meat."

Still for a moment she stared at him, and then she poured water from a bucket into the tin wash basin and she washed her hands. The preacher took up the blocks of pork and patted on the salt while she watched him. And he laid them in the kegs as she had. Only when he had finished a layer and covered it carefully and patted down the salt was she satisfied. She dried her bleached and bloated hands.

Tom said, "Ma, what stuff we gonna take from here?"

She looked quickly about the kitchen. "The bucket," she said.

"All the stuff to eat with: plates an' the cups, the spoons an' knives an' forks. Put all them in that drawer, an' take the drawer. The big fry pan an' the big stew kettle, the coffee pot. When it gets cool, take the rack outa the oven. That's good over a fire. I'd like to take the wash tub, but I guess there ain't room. I'll wash clothes in the bucket. Don't do no good to take little stuff. You can cook little stuff in a big kettle, but you can't cook big stuff in a little pot. Take the bread pans, all of 'em. They fit down inside each other." She stood and looked about the kitchen. "You jus' take that stuff I tol' you, Tom. I'll fix up the rest, the big can a pepper an' the salt an' the nutmeg an' the grater. I'll take all that stuff jus' at the last." She picked up a lantern and walked heavily into the bedroom, and her bare feet made no sound on the floor.

The preacher said, "She looks tar'd."

"Women's always tar'd," said Tom. "That's just the way women is, 'cept at meetin' once an' again."

"Yeah, but tar'der'n that. Real tar'd, like she's sick-tar'd."

Ma was just through the door, and she heard his words. Slowly her relaxed face tightened, and the lines disappeared from the taut muscular face. Her eyes sharpened and her shoulders straightened. She glanced about the stripped room. Nothing was left in it except trash. The mattresses which had been on the floor were gone. The bureaus were sold. On the floor lay a broken comb, an empty talcum powder can, and a few dust mice. Ma set her lantern on the floor. She reached behind one of the boxes that had served as chairs and brought out a stationery box, old and soiled and cracked at the corners. She sat down and opened the box. Inside were letters, clippings, photographs, a pair of earrings, a little gold signet ring, and a watch chain braided of hair and tipped with gold swivels. She touched the letters with her fingers, touched them lightly, and she smoothed a newspaper clipping on which there was an account of Tom's trial. For a long time she held the box, looking over it, and her fingers disturbed the letters and then lined them up again. She bit her lower lip, thinking, remembering. And at last she made up her mind. She picked out the ring, the watch charm, the earrings, dug under the pile and found one gold cuff link. She took a letter from an envelope and dropped the trinkets in the envelope. She folded the envelope over and put it in her dress pocket. Then gently and tenderly she closed the box and smoothed the top carefully with her fingers. Her lips parted. And then she stood up, took her lantern, and went back into the kitchen. She lifted the stove lid and laid the box gently among the coals. Quickly the heat browned the paper. A flame licked up and over the box. She replaced the stove lid and instantly the fire sighed up and breathed over the box.

Out in the dark yard, working in the lantern light, Pa and Al loaded the truck. Tools on the bottom, but handy to reach in case of a breakdown. Boxes of clothes next, and kitchen utensils in a gunny sack; cutlery and dishes in their box. Then the gallon bucket tied on behind. They made the bottom of the load as even as possible, and filled the spaces between boxes with rolled blankets. Then over the top they laid the mattresses, filling the truck in level. And last they spread the big tarpaulin over the load and Al made holes in the edge, two feet apart, and inserted little ropes, and tied it down to the side-bars of the truck.

"Now, if it rains," he said, "we'll tie it to the bar above, an' the folks can get underneath, out of the wet. Up front we'll be dry enough."

And Pa applauded. "That's a good idear."

"That ain't all," Al said. "First chance I git I'm gonna fin' a long plank an' make a ridge pole, an' put the tarp over that. An' then it'll be covered in, an' the folks'll be outa the sun, too."

And Pa agreed, "That's a good idear. Whyn't you think a that before?"

"I ain't had time," said Al.

"Ain't had time? Why, Al, you had time to coyote all over the country. God knows where you been this las' two weeks."

"Stuff a fella got to do when he's leavin' the country," said Al. And then he lost some of his assurance. "Pa," he asked. "You glad to be goin', Pa?"

"Huh? Well—sure. Leastwise—yeah. We had hard times here. 'Course it'll be all different out there—plenty work, an' ever'thing nice an' green, an' little white houses an' oranges growin' aroun'."

"Is it all oranges ever'where?"

"Well, maybe not ever'where, but plenty places."

The first gray of daylight began in the sky. And the work was done—the kegs of pork ready, the chicken coop ready to go on top. Ma opened the oven and took out the pile of roasted bones, crisp and brown, with plenty of gnawing meat left. Ruthie half awakened, and slipped down from the box, and slept again. But the adults stood around the door, shivering a little and gnawing at the crisp pork.

"Guess we oughta wake up Granma an' Grampa," Tom said. "Gettin' along on toward day."

Ma said, "Kinda hate to, till the las' minute. They need the sleep. Ruthie an' Winfield ain't hardly got no real rest neither."

"Well, they kin all sleep on top a the load," said Pa. "It'll be nice an' comf'table there."

Suddenly the dogs started up from the dust and listened. And then, with a roar, went barking off into the darkness. "Now what in hell is that?" Pa demanded. In a moment they heard a voice speaking reassuringly to the barking dogs and the barking lost its fierceness. Then footsteps, and a man approached. It was Muley Graves, his hat pulled low.

He came near timidly. "Morning, folks," he said.

"Why, Muley." Pa waved the ham bone he held. "Step in an' get some pork for yourself, Muley."

"Well, no," said Muley. "I ain't hungry, exactly."

"Oh, get it, Muley, get it. Here!" And Pa stepped into the house and brought out a hand of spareribs.

Muley took them. "I wasn't aiming to eat none a your stuff," he said. "I was jus' walkin' aroun', an' I thought how you'd be goin', an' I'd maybe say good-by."

"Goin' in a little while now," said Pa. "You'd a missed us if you'd come an hour later. All packed up—see?"

"All packed up." Muley looked at the loaded truck. "Sometimes I wisht I'd go an' fin' my folks."

Ma asked, "Did you hear from 'em out in California?"

"No," said Muley, "I ain't heard. But I ain't been to look in the post office. I oughta go in sometimes."

Pa said, "Al, go down, wake up Granma, Grampa. Tell 'em to come an' eat. We're goin' before long." And as Al sauntered toward the barn, "Muley, ya wanta squeeze in with us an' go? We'd try to make room for ya."

Muley took a bite of meat from the edge of a rib bone and chewed it. "Sometimes I think I might. But I know I won't," he said. "I know perfectly well the las' minute I'd run an' hide like a damn ol' graveyard ghos'."

Noah said, "You gonna die out in the fiel' some day, Muley."

"I know. I thought about that. Sometimes it seems pretty lonely, an' sometimes it seems all right, an' sometimes it seems good. It don't make no difference. But if ya come acrost my folks—that's really what I come to say—if ya come on any my folks in California, tell 'em I'm well. Tell 'em I'm doin' all right. Don't let on I'm livin' this way. Tell 'em I'll come to 'em soon's I git the money."

Ma asked, "An' will ya?"

"No," Muley said softly. "No, I won't. I can't go away. I got to stay now. Time back I might of went. But not now. Fella gits to thinkin', an' he gits to knowin'. I ain't never goin'."

The light of the dawn was a little sharper now. It paled the lanterns a little. Al came back with Grampa struggling and limping by his side. "He wasn't sleepin'," Al said. "He was settin' out back of the barn. They's somepin wrong with 'im."

Grampa's eyes had dulled, and there was none of the old meanness in them. "Ain't nothin' the matter with me," he said. "I jus' ain't a-goin'."

"Not goin'?" Pa demanded. "What you mean you ain't a-goin'? Why, here we're all packed up, ready. We got to go. We got no place to stay."

"I ain't sayin' for you to stay," said Grampa. "You go right on along. Me—I'm stayin'. I give her a goin'-over all night mos'ly. This here's my country. I b'long here. An' I don't give a goddamn if they's oranges an' grapes crowdin' a fella outa bed even. I ain't a-goin'. This country ain't no good, but it's my country. No, you all go ahead. I'll jus' stay right here where I b'long."

They crowded near to him. Pa said, "You can't, Grampa. This here lan' is goin' under the tractors. Who'd cook for you? How'd you live? You can't stay here. Why, with nobody to take care of you, you'd starve."

Grampa cried, "Goddamn it, I'm a ol' man, but I can still take care a myself. How's Muley here get along? I can get along as good as him. I tell ya I ain't goin', an' ya can lump it. Take Granma with ya if ya want, but ya ain't takin' me, an' that's the end of it."

Pa said helplessly, "Now listen to me, Grampa. Jus' listen to me, jus' a minute."

"Ain't a-gonna listen. I tol' ya what I'm a-gonna do."

Tom touched his father on the shoulder. "Pa, come in the house. I wanta tell ya somepin." And as they moved toward the house, he called, "Ma—come here a minute, will ya?"

In the kitchen one lantern burned and the plate of pork bones was still piled high. Tom said, "Listen, I know Grampa got the right to say he ain't goin', but he can't stay. We know that."

"Sure he can't stay," said Pa.

"Well, look. If we got to catch him an' tie him down, we li'ble to hurt him, an' he'll git so mad he'll hurt himself. Now we can't argue with him. If we could get him drunk it'd be all right. You got any whisky?"

"No," said Pa. "There ain't a drop a' whisky in the house. An' John got no whisky. He never has none when he ain't drinkin'."

Ma said, "Tom, I got a half a bottle soothin' sirup I got for Winfiel' when he had them earaches. Think that might work? Use ta put Winfiel' ta sleep when his earache was bad."

"Might," said Tom. "Get it, Ma. We'll give her a try anyways."

"I threw it out on the trash pile," said Ma. She took the lantern and went out, and in a moment she came back with a bottle half full of black medicine.

Tom took it from her and tasted it. "Don' taste bad," he said. "Make up a cup a black coffee, good an' strong. Le's see—says one teaspoon. Better put in a lot, coupla tablespoons."

Ma opened the stove and put a kettle inside, down next to the coals, and she measured water and coffee into it. "Have to give it to 'im in a can," she said. "We got the cups all packed."

Tom and his father went back outside. "Fella got a right to say what he's gonna do. Say, who's eatin' spareribs?" said Grampa.

"We've et," said Tom. "Ma's fixin' you a cup a coffee an' some pork."

He went into the house, and he drank his coffee and ate his pork. The group outside in the growing dawn watched him quietly, through the door. They saw him yawn and sway, and they saw him put his arms on the table and rest his head on his arms and go to sleep.

"He was tar'd anyways," said Tom. "Leave him be."

Now they were ready. Granma, giddy and vague, saying, "What's all this? What you doin' now, so early?" But she was dressed and agreeable. And Ruthie and Winfield were awake, but quiet with the pressure of tiredness and still half dreaming. The light was sifting rapidly over the land. And the movement of the family stopped. They stood about, reluctant to make the first active move to go. They were afraid, now that the time had come—afraid in the same way Grampa was afraid. They saw the shed take shape against the light, and they saw the lanterns pale until they no longer cast their circles of yellow light. The stars went out, few by few, toward the west. And still the family stood about like dream walkers, their eyes focused panoramically, seeing no detail, but the whole dawn, the whole land, the whole texture of the country at once.

Only Muley Graves prowled about restlessly, looking through the bars into the truck, thumping the spare tires hung on the back of the truck. And at last Muley approached Tom. "You goin' over the State line?" he asked. "You gonna break your parole?"

And Tom shook himself free of the numbness. "Jesus Christ, it's near sunrise," he said loudly. "We got to get goin'." And the others came out of their numbness and moved toward the truck.

"Come on," Tom said. "Le's get Grampa on." Pa and Uncle John and Tom and Al went into the kitchen where Grampa slept, his forehead down on his arms, and a line of drying coffee on the table. They took him under the elbows and lifted him to his feet, and he grumbled and cursed thickly, like a drunken man. Out the door they boosted him, and when they came to the truck Tom and Al climbed up, and, leaning over, hooked their hands under his arms and lifted him gently up, and laid him on top of the load. Al untied the tarpaulin, and they rolled him under and put a box under the tarp beside him, so that the weight of the heavy canvas would not be upon him.

"I got to get that ridge pole fixed," Al said. "Do her tonight when we stop." Grampa grunted and fought weakly against awakening, and when he was finally settled he went deeply to sleep again.

Pa said, "Ma, you an' Granma set in with Al for a while. We'll change aroun' so it's easier, but you start out that way." They got into the cab, and then the rest swarmed up on top of the load, Connie and Rose of Sharon, Pa and Uncle John, Ruthie and Winfield, Tom and the preacher. Noah stood on the ground, looking up at the great load of them sitting on top of the truck.

Al walked around, looking underneath at the springs. "Holy Jesus," he said, "them springs is flat as hell. Lucky I blocked under 'em."

Noah said, "How about the dogs, Pa?"

"I forgot the dogs," Pa said. He whistled shrilly, and one bouncing dog ran in, but only one. Noah caught him and threw him up on the top, where he sat rigid and shivering at the height. "Got to leave the other two," Pa called. "Muley, will you look after 'em some? See they don't starve?"

"Yeah," said Muley. "I'll like to have a couple dogs. Yeah! I'll take 'em."

"Take them chickens, too," Pa said.

Al got into the driver's seat. The starter whirred and caught, and whirred again. And then the loose roar of the six cylinders and a blue smoke behind. "So long, Muley," Al called.

And the family called, "Good-by, Muley."

Al slipped in the low gear and let in the clutch. The truck shuddered and strained across the yard. And the second gear took hold. They crawled up the little hill, and the red dust arose about them. "Chr-ist, what a load!" said Al. "We ain't makin' no time on this trip."

Ma tried to look back, but the body of the load cut off her view. She straightened her head and peered straight ahead along the dirt road. And a great weariness was in her eyes.

The people on top of the load did look back. They saw the house and the barn and a little smoke still rising from the chimney. They saw the windows reddening under the first color of the sun. They saw Muley standing forlornly in the dooryard looking after them. And then the hill cut them off. The cotton fields lined the road. And the truck crawled slowly through the dust toward the highway and the west.

CHAPTER 11

The houses were left vacant on the land, and the land was vacant because of this. Only the tractor sheds of corrugated iron, silver and gleaming, were alive; and they were alive with metal and gasoline and oil, the disks of the plows shining. The tractors had lights shining, for there is no day and night for a tractor and the disks turn the earth in the darkness and they glitter in the daylight. And when a horse stops work and goes into the barn there is a life and a vitality left, there is a breathing and a warmth, and the feet shift on the straw, and the jaws champ on the hay, and the ears and the eyes are alive. There is a warmth of life in the barn, and the heat and smell of life. But when the motor of a tractor stops, it is as dead as the ore it came from. The heat goes out of it like the living heat that leaves a corpse. Then the corrugated iron doors are closed and the tractor man drives home to town, perhaps twenty miles away, and he need not come back for weeks or months, for the tractor is dead. And this is easy and efficient. So easy that the wonder goes out of work, so efficient that the wonder goes out of land and the working of it, and with the wonder the deep understanding and the relation. And in the tractor man there grows the contempt that comes only to a stranger who has little understanding and no relation. For nitrates are not the land, nor phosphates and the length of fiber in the cotton is not the land. Carbon is not a man, nor salt nor water nor calcium. He is all these, but he is much more, much more; and the land is so much more than its analysis. That man who is more than his chemistry, walking on the earth, turning his plow point for a stone, dropping his handles to slide over an outcropping, kneeling in the earth to eat his lunch; that man who is more than his elements knows the land that is more than its analysis. But the machine man, driving a dead tractor on land he does not know and love, understands only chemistry; and he is contemptuous of the land and of himself. When the corrugated iron doors are shut, he goes home, and his home is not the land.

The doors of the empty houses swung open, and drifted back and forth in the wind. Bands of little boys came out from the towns to break the windows and to pick over the debris, looking for treasures. And here's a knife with half the blade gone. That's a good thing. And—smells like a rat died here. And look what Whitey wrote on the wall. He wrote that in the toilet in school, too, an' teacher made 'im wash it off.

When the folks first left, and the evening of the first day came, the hunting cats slouched in from the fields and mewed on the porch. And when no one came out, the cats crept through the open doors and walked mewing through the empty rooms. And then they went back to the fields and were wild cats from then on, hunting gophers and field mice, and sleeping in ditches in the daytime. When the night came, the bats, which had stopped at the doors for fear of light, swooped into the houses and sailed about through the empty rooms, and in a little while they stayed in dark room corners during the day, folded their wings high, and hung head-down among the rafters, and the smell of their droppings was in the empty houses.

And the mice moved in and stored weed seeds in corners, in boxes, in the backs of drawers in the kitchens. And weasels came in to hunt the mice, and the brown owls flew shrieking in and out again.

Now there came a little shower. The weeds sprang up in front of the doorstep, where they had not been allowed, and grass grew up through the porch boards. The houses were vacant, and a vacant house falls quickly apart. Splits started up the sheathing from the rusted nails. A dust settled on the floors, and only mouse and weasel and cat tracks disturbed it.

On a night the wind loosened a shingle and flipped it to the ground. The next wind pried into the hole where the shingle had been, lifted off three, and the next, a dozen. The midday sun burned through the hole and threw a glaring spot on the floor. The wild cats crept in from the fields at night, but they did not mew at the doorstep any more. They moved like shadows of a cloud across the moon, into the rooms to hunt the mice. And on windy nights the doors banged, and the ragged curtains fluttered in the broken windows.

CHAPTER 12

Highway 66 is the main migrant road. 66—the long concrete path across the country, waving gently up and down on the map, from Mississippi to Bakersfield—over the red lands and the gray lands, twisting up into the mountains, crossing the Divide and down into the bright and terrible desert, and across the desert to the mountains again, and into the rich California valleys.

66 is the path of a people in flight, refugees from dust and shrinking land, from the thunder of tractors and shrinking ownership, from the desert's slow northward invasion, from the twisting winds that howl up out of Texas, from the floods that bring no richness to the land and steal what little richness is there. From all of these the people are in flight, and they come into 66 from the tributary side roads, from the wagon tracks and the rutted country roads. 66 is the mother road, the road of flight.

Clarksville and Ozark and Van Buren and Fort Smith on 62, and there's an end of Arkansas. And all the roads into Oklahoma City, 66 down from Tulsa, 270 up from McAlester. 81 from Wichita Falls south, from Enid north. Edmond, McLoud, Purcell. 66 out of Oklahoma City; El Reno and Clinton, going west on 66. Hydro, Elk City, and Texola; and there's an end to Oklahoma. 66 across the Panhandle of Texas. Shamrock and McLean, Conway and Amarillo, the yellow. Wildorado and Vega and Boise, and there's an end of Texas. Tucumcari and Santa Rosa and into the New Mexican mountains to Albuquerque, where the road comes down from Santa Fe. Then down the gorged Rio Grande to Los Lunas and west again on 66 to Gallup, and there's the border of New Mexico.

And now the high mountains. Holbrook and Winslow and Flagstaff in the high mountains of Arizona. Then the great plateau rolling like a ground swell. Ashfork and Kingman and stone mountains again, where water must be hauled and sold. Then out of the broken sun-rotted mountains of Arizona to the Colorado, with green reeds on its banks, and that's the end of Arizona. There's California just over the river, and a pretty town to start it. Needles, on the river.

But the river is a stranger in this place. Up from Needles and over a burned range, and there's the desert. And 66 goes on over the terrible desert, where the distance shimmers and the black center mountains hang unbearably in the distance. At last there's Barstow, and more desert until at last the mountains rise up again, the good mountains, and 66 winds through them. Then suddenly a pass, and below the beautiful valley, below orchards and vineyards and little houses, and in the distance a city. And, oh, my God, it's over.

The people in flight streamed out on 66, sometimes a single car, sometimes a little caravan. All day they rolled slowly along the road, and at night they stopped near water. In the day ancient leaky radiators sent up columns of steam, loose connecting rods hammered and pounded. And the men driving the trucks and the overloaded cars listened apprehensively. How far between towns? It is a terror between towns. If something breaks—well, if something breaks we camp right here while Jim walks to town and gets a part and walks back and—how much food we got?

Listen to the motor. Listen to the wheels. Listen with your ears and with your hands on the steering wheel; listen with the palm of your hand on the gear-shift lever; listen with your feet on the floor boards. Listen to the pounding old jalopy with all your senses; for a change of tone, a variation of rhythm may mean—a week here? That rattle—that's tappets. Don't hurt a bit. Tappets can rattle till Jesus comes again without no harm. But that thudding as the car moves along—can't hear that—just kind of feel it. Maybe oil isn't gettin' someplace. Maybe a bearing's startin' to go. Jesus, if it's a bearing, what'll we do? Money's goin' fast.

And why's the son-of-a-bitch heat up so hot today? This ain't no climb. Le's look. God Almighty, the fan belt's gone! Here, make a belt outa this little piece a rope. Le's see how long—there. I'll splice the ends. Now take her slow—slow, till we can get to a town. That rope belt won't last long.

'F we can on'y get to California where the oranges grow before this here ol' jug blows up. 'F we on'y can.

And the tires—two layers of fabric worn through. On'y a four-ply tire. Might get a hunderd miles more outa her if we don't hit a rock an' blow her. Which'll we take—a hunderd, maybe, miles, or maybe spoil the tube? Which? A hunderd miles. Well, that's somepin you got to think about. We got tube patches. Maybe when she goes she'll only spring a leak. How about makin' a boot? Might get five hunderd more miles. Le's go on till she blows.

We got to get a tire, but, Jesus, they want a lot for a ol' tire. They look a fella over. They know he got to go on. They know he can't wait. And the price goes up.

Take it or leave it. I ain't in business for my health. I'm here a-sellin' tires. I ain't givin' 'em away. I can't help what happens to you. I got to think what happens to me.

How far's the nex' town?

I seen forty-two cars a you fellas go by yesterday. Where you all come from? Where all of you goin'?

Well, California's a big State.

It ain't that big. The whole United States ain't that big. It ain't that big. It ain't big enough. There ain't room enough for you an' me, for your kind an' my kind, for rich and poor together all in one country, for thieves and honest men. For hunger and fat. Whyn't you go back where you come from?

This is a free country. Fella can go where he wants.

That's what you think! Ever hear of the border patrol on the California line? Police from Los Angeles—stopped you bastards, turned you back. Says, if you can't buy no real estate we don't want you. Says, got a driver's license? Le's see it. Tore it up. Says you can't come in without no driver's license.

It's a free country.

Well, try to get some freedom to do. Fella says you're jus' as free as you got jack to pay for it.

In California they got high wages. I got a han'bill here tells about it.

Horseshit! I seen folks comin' back. Somebody's kiddin' you. You want that tire or don't ya?

Got to take it, but, Jesus, mister, it cuts into our money! We ain't got much left.

Well, I ain't no charity. Take her along.

Got to, I guess. Let's look her over. Open her up, look a' the casing—you son-of-a-bitch, you said the casing was good. She's broke damn near through.

The hell she is. Well—by George! How come I didn' see that?

You did see it, you son-of-a-bitch. You wanta charge us four bucks for a busted casing. I'd like to take a sock at you.

Now keep your shirt on. I didn' see it, I tell you. Here—tell ya what I'll do. I'll give ya this one for three-fifty.

You'll take a flying fuck at the moon! We'll try to make the nex' town.

Think we can make it on that tire?

Got to. I'll go on the rim before I'd give that son-of-a-bitch a dime.

What do ya think a guy in business is? Like he says, he ain't in it for his health. That's what business is. What'd you think it was? Fella's got— See that sign 'longside the road there? Service Club. Luncheon Tuesday, Colmado Hotel? Welcome, brother. That's a Service Club. Fella had a story. Went to one of them meetings an' told the story to all them business men. Says, when I was a kid my ol' man give me a haltered heifer an' says take her down an' git her serviced. An' the fella says, I done it, an' ever' time since then when I hear a business man talkin' about service, I wonder who's gettin' screwed. Fella in business got to lie an' cheat, but he calls it somepin else. That's what's important. You go steal that tire an' you're a thief, but he tried to steal your four dollars for a busted tire. They call that sound business.

Danny in the back seat wants a cup a water.

Have to wait. Got no water here.

Listen—that the rear end?

Can't tell.

Sound telegraphs through the frame.

There goes a gasket. Got to go on. Listen to her whistle. Find a nice place to camp an' I'll jerk the head off. But, God Almighty, the food's gettin' low, the money's gettin' low. When we can't buy no more gas—what then?

Danny in the back seat wants a cup a water. Little fella's thirsty.

Listen to that gasket whistle.

Chee-rist! There she went. Blowed tube an' casing all to hell. Have to fix her. Save that casing to make boots; cut 'em out an' stick 'em inside a weak place.

Cars pulled up beside the road, engine heads off, tires mended. Cars limping along 66 like wounded things, panting and struggling. Too hot, loose connections, loose bearings, rattling bodies.

Danny wants a cup of water.

People in flight along 66. And the concrete road shone like a mirror under the sun, and in the distance the heat made it seem that there were pools of water in the road.

Danny wants a cup a water.

He'll have to wait, poor little fella. He's hot. Nex' service station. *Service* station, like the fella says.

Two hundred and fifty thousand people over the road. Fifty thousand old cars—wounded, steaming. Wrecks along the road, abandoned. Well, what happened to them? What happened to the folks in that car? Did they walk? Where are they? Where does the courage come from? Where does the terrible faith come from?

And here's a story you can hardly believe, but it's true, and it's funny and it's beautiful. There was a family of twelve and they were forced off the land. They had no car. They built a trailer out of junk and loaded it with their possessions. They pulled it to the side of 66 and waited. And pretty soon a sedan picked them up. Five of them rode in the sedan and seven on the trailer, and a dog on the trailer. They got to California in two jumps. The man who pulled them fed them. And that's true. But how can such courage be, and such faith in their own species? Very few things would teach such faith.

The people in flight from the terror behind—strange things happen to them, some bitterly cruel and some so beautiful that the faith is refired forever.

CHAPTER 13

The ancient overloaded Hudson creaked and grunted to the highway at Sallisaw and turned west, and the sun was blinding. But on the concrete road Al built up his speed because the flattened springs were not in danger any more. From Sallisaw to Gore is twenty-one miles and the Hudson was doing thirty-five miles an hour. From Gore to Warner thirteen miles; Warner to Checotah fourteen miles; Checotah a long jump to Henrietta—thirty-four miles, but a real town at the end of it. Henrietta to Castle nineteen miles, and the sun was overhead, and the red fields, heated by the high sun, vibrated the air.

Al, at the wheel, his face purposeful, his whole body listening to the car, his restless eye jumping from the road to the instrument panel. Al was one with his engine, every nerve listening for weaknesses, for the thumps or squeals, hums and chattering that indicate a change that may cause a breakdown. He had become the soul of the car.

Granma, beside him on the seat, half slept, and whimpered in her sleep, opened her eyes to peer ahead, and then dozed again. And Ma sat beside Granma, one elbow out the window, and the skin reddening under the fierce sun. Ma looked ahead too, but her eyes were flat and did not see the road or the fields, the gas stations, the little eating sheds. She did not glance at them as the Hudson went by.

Al shifted himself on the broken seat and changed his grip on the steering wheel. And he sighed, "Makes a racket, but I think she's awright. God knows what she'll do if we got to climb a hill with the load we got. Got any hills 'tween here an' California, Ma?"

Ma turned her head slowly and her eyes came to life. "Seems to me they's hills," she said. " 'Course I dunno. But seems to me I heard they's hills an' even mountains. Big ones."

Granma drew a long whining sigh in her sleep.

Al said, "We'll burn right up if we got climbin' to do. Have to throw out some a' this stuff. Maybe we shouldn' a brang that preacher."

"You'll be glad a that preacher 'fore we're through," said Ma. "That preacher'll help us." She looked ahead at the gleaming road again.

Al steered with one hand and put the other on the vibrating gear-shift lever. He had difficulty in speaking. His mouth formed the words silently before he said them aloud. "Ma—" She looked slowly around at him, her head swaying a little with the car's motion. "Ma, you scared a goin'? You scared a goin' to a new place?"

Her eyes grew thoughtful and soft. "A little," she said. "Only it ain't like scared so much. I'm jus' a settin' here waitin'. When somepin happens that I got to do somepin—I'll do it."

"Ain't you thinkin' what's it gonna be like when we get there? Ain't you scared it won't be nice like we thought?"

"No," she said quickly. "No, I ain't. You can't do that. I can't do that. It's too much—livin' too many lives. Up ahead they's a thousan' lives we might live, but when it comes, it'll on'y be one. If I go ahead on all of 'em, it's too much. You got to live ahead 'cause you're so young, but—it's jus' the road goin' by for me. An' it's jus' how soon they gonna wanta eat some more pork bones." Her face tightened. "That's all I can do. I can't do no more. All the rest'd get upset if I done any more'n that. They all depen' on me jus' thinkin' about that."

Granma yawned shrilly and opened her eyes. She looked wildly about. "I got to git out, praise Gawd," she said.

"First clump a brush," said Al. "They's one up ahead."

"Brush or no brush, I got to git out, I tell ya." And she began to whine, "I got to git out. I got to git out."

Al speeded up, and when he came to the low brush he pulled up short. Ma threw the door open and half pulled the struggling old lady out beside the road and into the bushes. And Ma held her so Granma would not fall when she squatted.

On top of the truck the others stirred to life. Their faces were shining with sunburn they could not escape. Tom and Casy and Noah and Uncle John let themselves wearily down. Ruthie and Winfield swarmed down the side-boards and went off into the bushes. Connie helped Rose of Sharon gently down. Under the canvas, Grampa was awake, his head sticking out, but his eyes were drugged and watery and still senseless. He watched the others, but there was little recognition in his watching.

Tom called to him, "Want to come down, Grampa?"

The old eyes turned listlessly to him. "No," said Grampa. For a moment the fierceness came into his eyes. "I ain't a-goin', I tell you. Gonna stay like Muley." And then he lost interest again. Ma' came back, helping Granma up the bank to the highway.

"Tom," she said. "Get that pan a bones, under the canvas in back. We got to eat somepin." Tom got the pan and passed it around, and the family stood by the roadside, gnawing the crisp particles from the pork bones.

"Sure lucky we brang these along," said Pa. "Git so stiff up there can't hardly move. Where's the water?"

"Ain't it up with you?" Ma asked. "I set out that gallon jug."

Pa climbed the sides and looked under the canvas. "It ain't here. We must a forgot it."

Thirst set in instantly. Winfield moaned, "I wanta drink. I wanta drink." The men licked their lips, suddenly conscious of their thirst. And a little panic started.

Al felt the fear growing. "We'll get water first service station we come to. We need some gas too." The family swarmed up the truck sides; Ma helped Granma in and got in beside her. Al started the motor and they moved on.

Castle to Paden twenty-five miles and the sun passed the zenith and started down. And the radiator cap began to jiggle up and down and steam started to whish out. Near Paden there was a shack beside the road and two gas pumps in front of it; and beside a fence, a water faucet and a hose. Al drove in and nosed the Hudson up to the hose. As they pulled in, a stout man, red of face and arms, got up from a chair behind the gas pumps and moved toward them. He wore brown corduroys, and suspenders and a polo shirt; and he had a cardboard sun helmet, painted silver, on his head. The sweat beaded on his nose and under his eyes and formed streams in the wrinkles of his neck. He strolled toward the truck, looking truculent and stern.

"You folks aim to buy anything? Gasoline or stuff?" he asked.

Al was out already, unscrewing the steaming radiator cap with the tips of his fingers, jerking his hand away to escape the spurt when the cap should come loose. He looked over at the fat man. "Need some gas, mister."

"Got any money?"

"Sure. Think we're beggin'?"

The truculence left the fat man's face. "Well, that's all right, folks. He'p yourself to water." And he hastened to explain. "Road is full a people, come in, use water, dirty up the toilet, an' then, by God, they'll steal stuff an' don't buy nothin'. Got no money to buy with. Come beggin' a gallon gas to move on."

Tom dropped angrily to the ground and moved toward the fat man. "We're payin' our way," he said fiercely. "You got no call to give us a goin'-over. We ain't asked you for nothin'."

"I ain't," the fat man said quickly. The sweat began to soak through his short-sleeved polo shirt. "Jus' he'p yourself to water, and go use the toilet if you want."

Winfield had got the hose. He drank from the end and then turned the stream over his head and face, and emerged dripping. "It ain't cool," he said.

"I don' know what the country's comin' to," the fat man continued. His complaint had shifted now and he was no longer talking to or about the Joads. "Fifty-sixty cars a folks go by ever' day, folks all movin' west with kids an' househol' stuff. Where they goin'? What they gonna do?"

"Doin' the same as us," said Tom. "Goin' someplace to live. Tryin' to get along. That's all."

"Well, I don' know what the country's comin' to. I jus' don' know. Here's me tryin' to get along, too. Think any them big new cars stops here? No, sir! They go on to them yella-painted company stations in town. They don't stop no place like this. Most folks stops here ain't got nothin'."

Al flipped the radiator cap and it jumped into the air with a head of steam behind it, and a hollow bubbling sound came out of the radiator. On top of the truck, the suffering hound dog crawled timidly to the edge of the load and looked over, whimpering, toward the water. Uncle John climbed up and lifted him down by the scruff of the neck. For a moment the dog staggered on stiff legs, and then he went to lap the mud under the faucet. In the highway the cars whizzed by, glistening in the heat, and the hot wind of their going fanned into the service-station yard. Al filled the radiator with the hose.

"It ain't that I'm tryin' to git trade outa rich folks," the fat man went on. "I'm jus' tryin' to git trade. Why, the folks that stops here begs gasoline an' they trades for gasoline. I could show you in my back room the stuff they'll trade for gas an' oil: beds an' baby buggies an' pots an' pans. One family traded a doll their kid had for a gallon.

An' what'm I gonna do with the stuff, open a junk shop? Why, one fella wanted to gimme his shoes for a gallon. An' if I was that kinda fella I bet I could git—" He glanced at Ma and stopped.

Jim Casy had wet his head, and the drops still coursed down his high forehead, and his muscled neck was wet, and his shirt was wet. He moved over beside Tom. "It ain't the people's fault," he said. "How'd you like to sell the bed you sleep on for a tankful a gas?"

"I know it ain't their fault. Ever' person I talked to is on the move for a damn good reason. But what's the country comin' to? That's what I wanta know. What's it comin' to? Fella can't make a livin' no more. Folks can't make a livin' farmin'. I ask you, what's it comin' to? I can't figure her out. Ever'body I ask, they can't figure her out. Fella wants to trade his shoes so he can git a hunderd miles on. I can't figure her out." He took off his silver hat and wiped his forehead with his palm. And Tom took off his cap and wiped his forehead with it. He went to the hose and wet the cap through and squeezed it and put it on again. Ma worked a tin cup out through the side bars of the truck, and she took water to Granma and to Grampa on top of the load. She stood on the bars and handed the cup to Grampa, and he wet his lips, and then shook his head and refused more. The old eyes looked up at Ma in pain and bewilderment for a moment before the awareness receded again.

Al started the motor and backed the truck to the gas pump. "Fill her up. She'll take about seven," said Al. "We'll give her six so she don't spill none."

The fat man put the hose in the tank. "No, sir," he said. "I jus' don't know what the country's comin' to. Relief an' all."

Casy said, "I been walkin' aroun' in the country. Ever'body's askin' that. What we comin' to? Seems to me we don't never come to nothin'. Always on the way. Always goin' and goin'. Why don't folks think about that? They's movement now. People moving. We know why, an' we know how. Movin' 'cause they got to. That's why folks always move. Movin' 'cause they want somepin better'n what they got. An' that's the on'y way they'll ever git it. Wantin' it an' needin' it, they'll go out an' git it. It's bein' hurt that makes folks mad to fightin'. I been walkin' aroun' the country, an' hearin' folks talk like you."

The fat man pumped the gasoline and the needle turned on the pump dial, recording the amount. "Yeah, but what's it comin' to? That's what I want ta know."

Tom broke in irritably, "Well, you ain't never gonna know. Casy tries to tell ya an' you jest ast the same thing over. I seen fellas like you before. You ain't askin' nothin'; you're jus' singin' a kinda song. 'What we comin' to?' You don' wanta know. Country's movin' aroun', goin' places. They's folks dyin' all aroun'. Maybe you'll die pretty soon, but you won't know nothin'. I seen too many fellas like you. You don't want to know nothin'. Just sing yourself to sleep with a song— 'What we comin' to?' " He looked at the gas pump, rusted and old, and at the shack behind it, built of old lumber, the nail holes of its first use still showing through the paint that had been brave, the brave yellow paint that had tried to imitate the big company stations in town. But the paint couldn't cover the old nail holes and the old cracks in the lumber, and the paint could not be renewed. The imitation was a failure and the owner had known it was a failure. And inside the open door of the shack Tom saw the oil barrels, only two of them, and the candy counter with stale candies and licorice whips turning brown with age, and cigarettes. He saw the broken chair and the fly screen with a rusted hole in it. And the littered yard that should have been graveled, and behind, the corn field drying and dying in the sun. Beside the house the little stock of used tires and retreaded tires. And he saw for the first time the fat man's cheap washed pants and his cheap polo shirt and his paper hat. He said, "I didn' mean to sound off at ya, mister. It's the heat. You ain't got nothin'. Pretty soon you'll be on the road yourse'f. And it ain't tractors'll put you there. It's them pretty yella stations in town. Folks is movin'," he said ashamedly. "An' you'll be movin', mister."

The fat man's hand slowed on the pump and stopped while Tom spoke. He looked worriedly at Tom. "How'd you know?" he asked helplessly. "How'd you know we was already talkin' about packin' up an' movin' west?"

Casy answered him. "It's ever'body," he said. "Here's me that used to give all my fight against the devil 'cause I figgered the devil was the enemy. But they's somepin worse'n the devil got hold a the country, an' it ain't gonna let go till it's chopped loose. Ever see one a them Gila monsters take hold, mister? Grabs hold, an' you chop him in two an' his head hangs on. Chop him at the neck an' his head hangs on. Got to take a screw-driver an' pry his head apart to git him loose. An' while he's layin' there, poison is drippin' an' drippin' into the hole he's made with his teeth." He stopped and looked sideways at Tom.

The fat man stared hopelessly straight ahead. His hand started turning the crank slowly. "I dunno what we're comin' to," he said softly.

Over by the water hose, Connie and Rose of Sharon stood together, talking secretly. Connie washed the tin cup and felt the water with his finger before he filled the cup again. Rose of Sharon watched the cars go by on the highway. Connie held out the cup to her. "This water ain't cool, but it's wet," he said.

She looked at him and smiled secretly. She was all secrets now she was pregnant, secrets and little silences that seemed to have meanings. She was pleased with herself, and she complained about things that didn't really matter. And she demanded services of Connie that were silly, and both of them knew they were silly. Connie was pleased with her too, and filled with wonder that she was pregnant. He liked to think he was in on the secrets she had. When she smiled slyly, he smiled slyly too, and they exchanged confidences in whispers. The world had drawn close around them, and they were in the center of it, or rather Rose of Sharon was in the center of it with Connie making a small orbit about her. Everything they said was a kind of secret.

She drew her eyes from the highway. "I ain't very thirsty," she said daintily. "But maybe I *ought* to drink."

And he nodded, for he knew well what she meant. She took the cup and rinsed her mouth and spat and then drank the cupful of tepid water. "Want another?" he asked.

"Jus' a half." And so he filled the cup just half, and gave it to her. A Lincoln Zephyr, silvery and low, whisked by. She turned to see where the others were and saw them clustered about the truck. Reassured, she said, "How'd you like to be goin' along in that?"

Connie sighed, "Maybe—after." They both knew what he meant. "An' if they's plenty work in California, we'll git our own car. But them"—he indicated the disappearing Zephyr—"them kind costs as much as a good size house. I ruther have the house."

"I like to have the house *an'* one a them," she said. "But 'course the house would be first because—" And they both knew what she meant. They were terribly excited about the pregnancy.

"You feel awright?" he asked.

"Tar'd. Jus' tar'd ridin' in the sun."

"We *got* to do that or we won't never get to California."

"I know," she said.

The dog wandered, sniffing, past the truck, trotted to the puddle under the hose again and lapped at the muddy water. And then he moved away, nose down and ears hanging. He sniffed his way among the dusty weeds beside the road, to the edge of the pavement. He raised his head and looked across, and then started over. Rose of Sharon screamed shrilly. A big swift car whisked near, tires squealed. The dog dodged helplessly, and with a shriek, cut off in the middle, went under the wheels. The big car slowed for a moment and faces looked back, and then it gathered greater speed and disappeared. And the dog, a blot of blood and tangled, burst intestines, kicked slowly in the road.

Rose of Sharon's eyes were wide. "D'you think it'll hurt?" she begged. "Think it'll hurt?"

Connie put his arm around her. "Come set down," he said. "It wasn't nothin'."

"But I felt it hurt. I felt it kinda jar when I yelled."

"Come set down. It wasn't nothin'. It won't hurt." He led her to the side of the truck away from the dying dog and sat her down on the running board.

Tom and Uncle John walked out to the mess. The last quiver was going out of the crushed body. Tom took it by the legs and dragged it to the side of the road. Uncle John looked embarrassed, as though it were his fault. "I ought ta tied him up," he said.

Pa looked down at the dog for a moment and then he turned away. "Le's get outa here," he said. "I don' know how we was gonna feed 'im anyways. Just as well, maybe."

The fat man came from behind the truck. "I'm sorry, folks," he said. "A dog jus' don' last no time near a highway. I had three dogs run over in a year. Don't keep none, no more." And he said, "Don't you folks worry none about it. I'll take care of 'im. Bury 'im out in the corn field."

Ma walked over to Rose of Sharon, where she sat, still shuddering, on the running board. "You all right, Rosasharn?" she asked. "You feelin' poorly?"

"I—I seen that. Give me a start."

"I heard ya yip," said Ma. "Git yourself laced up, now."

"You suppose it might of hurt?"

"No," said Ma. " 'F you go to greasin' yourself an' feelin' sorry,

an' tuckin' yourself in a swalla's nest, it might. Rise up now, an' he'p
me get Granma comf'table. Forget that baby for a minute. He'll take
care a hisself."

"Where is Granma?" Rose of Sharon asked.

"I dunno. She's aroun' here somewheres. Maybe in the
outhouse."

The girl went toward the toilet, and in a moment she came out,
helping Granma along. "She went to sleep in there," said Rose of
Sharon.

Granma grinned. "It's nice in there," she said. "They got a patent toilet in there an' the water comes down. I like it in there," she
said contentedly. "Would of took a good nap if I wasn't woke up."

"It ain't a nice place to sleep," said Rose of Sharon, and she
helped Granma into the car. Granma settled herself happily. "Maybe
it ain't nice for purty, but it's nice for nice," she said.

Tom said, "Le's go. We got to make miles."

Pa whistled shrilly. "Now where'd them kids go?" He whistled
again, putting his fingers in his mouth.

In a moment they broke from the corn field, Ruthie ahead and
Winfield trailing her. "Eggs!" Ruthie cried. "I got sof' eggs." She
rushed close, with Winfield close behind. "Look!" A dozen soft,
grayish-white eggs were in her grubby hand. And as she held up her
hand, her eyes fell upon the dead dog beside the road. "Oh!" she
said. Ruthie and Winfield walked slowly toward the dog. They inspected him.

Pa called to them, "Come on, you, 'less you want to git left."

They turned solemnly and walked to the truck. Ruthie looked
once more at the gray reptile eggs in her hand, and then she threw
them away. They climbed up the side of the truck. "His eyes was
still open," said Ruthie in a hushed tone.

But Winfield gloried in the scene. He said boldly, "His guts was
just strowed all over—all over"—he was silent for a moment—
"strowed—all—over," he said, and then he rolled over quickly and
vomited down the side of the truck. When he sat up again his eyes
were watery and his nose running. "It ain't like killin' pigs," he said
in explanation.

Al had the hood of the Hudson up, and he checked the oil level.
He brought a gallon can from the floor of the front seat and poured
a quantity of cheap black oil into the pipe and checked the level
again.

Tom came beside him. "Want I should take her a piece?" he asked.

"I ain't tired," said Al.

"Well, you didn' get no sleep las' night. I took a snooze this morning. Get up there on top. I'll take her."

"Awright," Al said reluctantly. "But watch the oil gauge pretty close. Take her slow. An' I been watchin' for a short. Take a look a the needle now an' then. 'F she jumps to discharge it's a short. An' take her slow, Tom. She's overloaded."

Tom laughed. "I'll watch her," he said. "You can res' easy."

The family piled on top of the truck again. Ma settled herself beside Granma in the seat, and Tom took his place and started the motor. "Sure is loose," he said, and he put it in gear and pulled away down the highway.

The motor droned along steadily and the sun receded down the sky in front of them. Granma slept steadily, and even Ma dropped her head forward and dozed. Tom pulled his cap over his eyes to shut out the blinding sun.

Paden to Meeker is thirteen miles; Meeker to Harrah is fourteen miles; and then Oklahoma City—the big city. Tom drove straight on. Ma waked up and looked at the streets as they went through the city. And the family, on top of the truck, stared about at the stores, at the big houses, at the office buildings. And then the buildings grew smaller and the stores smaller. The wrecking yards and hot-dog stands, the out-city dance halls.

Ruthie and Winfield saw it all, and it embarrassed them with its bigness and its strangeness, and it frightened them with the fine-clothed people they saw. They did not speak of it to each other. Later—they would, but not now. They saw the oil derricks in the town, on the edge of the town; oil derricks black, and the smell of oil and gas in the air. But they didn't exclaim. It was so big and so strange it frightened them.

In the street Rose of Sharon saw a man in a light suit. He wore white shoes and a flat straw hat. She touched Connie and indicated the man with her eyes, and then Connie and Rose of Sharon giggled softly to themselves, and the giggles got the best of them. They covered their mouths. And it felt so good that they looked for other people to giggle at. Ruthie and Winfield saw them giggling and it looked such fun that they tried to do it too—but they couldn't. The giggles wouldn't come. But Connie and Rose of Sharon were breathless and red with stifling laughter before they could stop. It got so bad that they had only to look at each other to start over again.

The outskirts were wide spread. Tom drove slowly and carefully in the traffic, and then they were on 66—the great western road, and the sun was sinking on the line of the road. The windshield was bright with dust. Tom pulled his cap lower over his eyes, so low that he had to tilt his head back to see out at all. Granma slept on, the sun on her closed eyelids, and the veins on her temples were blue, and the little bright veins on her cheeks were wine-colored, and the old brown marks on her face turned darker.

Tom said, "We stay on this road right straight through."

Ma had been silent for a long time. "Maybe we better fin' a place to stop 'fore sunset," she said. "I got to get some pork a-boilin' an' some bread made. That takes time."

"Sure," Tom agreed. "We ain't gonna make this trip in one jump. Might's well stretch ourselves."

Oklahoma City to Bethany is fourteen miles.

Tom said, "I think we better stop 'fore the sun goes down. Al got to build that thing on the top. Sun'll kill the folks up there."

Ma had been dozing again. Her head jerked upright. "Got to get some supper a-cookin'," she said. And she said, "Tom, your pa tol' me about you crossin' the State line——"

He was a long time answering. "Yeah? What about it, Ma?"

"Well, I'm scairt about it. It'll make you kinda runnin' away. Maybe they'll catch ya."

Tom held his hand over his eyes to protect himself from the lowering sun. "Don't you worry," he said. "I figgered her out. They's lots a fellas out on parole an' they's more goin' in all the time. If I get caught for anything else out west, well, then they got my pitcher an' my prints in Washington. They'll sen' me back. But if I don't do no crimes, they won't give a damn."

"Well, I'm a-scairt about it. Sometimes you do a crime, an' you don't even know it's bad. Maybe they got crimes in California we don't even know about. Maybe you gonna do somepin an' it's all right, an' in California it ain't all right."

"Be jus' the same if I wasn't on parole," he said. "On'y if I get caught I get a bigger jolt'n other folks. Now you quit a-worryin'," he said. "We got plenty to worry about 'thout you figgerin' out things to worry about."

"I can't he'p it," she said. "Minute you cross the line you done a crime."

"Well, tha's better'n stickin' aroun' Sallisaw an' starvin' to death," he said. "We better look out for a place to stop."

They went through Bethany and out on the other side. In a ditch, where a culvert went under the road, an old touring car was pulled off the highway and a little tent was pitched beside it, and smoke came out of a stove pipe through the tent. Tom pointed ahead. "There's some folks campin'. Looks like as good a place as we seen." He slowed his motor and pulled to a stop beside the road. The hood of the old touring car was up, and a middle-aged man stood looking down at the motor. He wore a cheap straw sombrero, a blue shirt, and a black, spotted vest, and his jeans were stiff and shiny with dirt. His face was lean, the deep cheek-lines great furrows down his face so that his cheek bones and chin stood out sharply. He looked up at the Joad truck and his eyes were puzzled and angry.

Tom leaned out of the window. "Any law 'gainst folks stoppin' here for the night?"

The man had seen only the truck. His eyes focused down on Tom. "I dunno," he said. "We on'y stopped here 'cause we couldn' git no further."

"Any water here?"

The man pointed to a service-station shack about a quarter of a mile ahead. "They's water there they'll let ya take a bucket of."

Tom hesitated. "Well, ya 'spose we could camp down 'longside?"

The lean man looked puzzled. "We don't own it," he said. "We on'y stopped here 'cause this goddamn ol' trap wouldn' go no further."

Tom insisted. "Anyways you're here an' we ain't. You got a right to say if you wan' neighbors or not."

The appeal to hospitality had an instant effect. The lean face broke into a smile. "Why, sure, come on off the road. Proud to have ya." And he called, "Sairy, there's some folks goin' ta stay with us. Come on out an' say how d'ya do. Sairy ain't well," he added. The tent flaps opened and a wizened woman came out—a face wrinkled as a dried leaf and eyes that seemed to flame in her face, black eyes that seemed to look out of a well of horror. She was small and shuddering. She held herself upright by a tent flap, and the hand holding onto the canvas was a skeleton covered with wrinkled skin.

When she spoke her voice had a beautiful low timbre, soft and modulated, and yet with ringing overtones. "Tell 'em welcome," she said. "Tell 'em good an' welcome."

Tom drove off the road and brought his truck into the field and lined it up with the touring car. And people boiled down from the truck; Ruthie and Winfield too quickly, so that their legs gave way and they shrieked at the pins and needles that ran through their limbs. Ma went quickly to work. She untied the three-gallon bucket from the back of the truck and approached the squealing children. "Now you go git water—right down there. Ask nice. Say, 'Please, kin we git a bucket a water?' and say, 'Thank you.' An' carry it back together helpin', an' don't spill none. An' if you see stick wood to burn, bring it on." The children stamped away toward the shack.

By the tent a little embarrassment had set in, and social intercourse had paused before it started. Pa said, "You ain't Oklahomy folks?"

And Al, who stood near the car, looked at the license plates. "Kansas," he said.

The lean man said, "Galena, or right about there. Wilson, Ivy Wilson."

"We're Joads," said Pa. "We come from right near Sallisaw."

"Well, we're proud to meet you folks," said Ivy Wilson. "Sairy, these is Joads."

"I knowed you wasn't Oklahomy folks. You talk queer, kinda— that ain't no blame, you understan'."

"Ever'body says words different," said Ivy. "Arkansas folks says 'em different, and Oklahomy folks says 'em different. And we seen a lady from Massachusetts, an' she said 'em differentest of all. Couldn' hardly make out what she was sayin'."

Noah and Uncle John and the preacher began to unload the truck. They helped Grampa down and sat him on the ground and he sat limply, staring ahead of him. "You sick, Grampa?" Noah asked.

"You goddamn right," said Grampa weakly. "Sicker'n hell."

Sairy Wilson walked slowly and carefully toward him. "How'd you like ta come in our tent?" she asked. "You kin lay down on our mattress an' rest."

He looked up at her, drawn by her soft voice. "Come on now," she said. "You'll git some rest. We'll he'p you over."

Without warning Grampa began to cry. His chin wavered and

his old lips tightened over his mouth and he sobbed hoarsely. Ma rushed over to him and put her arms around him. She lifted him to his feet, her broad back straining, and she half lifted, half helped him into the tent.

Uncle John said, "He must be good an' sick. He ain't never done that before. Never seen him blubberin' in my life." He jumped up on the truck and tossed a mattress down.

Ma came out of the tent and went to Casy. "You been aroun' sick people," she said. "Grampa's sick. Won't you go take a look at him?"

Casy walked quickly to the tent and went inside. A double mattress was on the ground, the blankets spread neatly; and a little tin stove stood on iron legs, and the fire in it burned unevenly. A bucket of water, a wooden box of supplies, and a box for a table, that was all. The light of the setting sun came pinkly through the tent walls. Sairy Wilson knelt on the ground, beside the mattress, and Grampa lay on his back. His eyes were open, staring upward, and his cheeks were flushed. He breathed heavily.

Casy took the skinny old wrist in his fingers. "Feeling kinda tired, Grampa?" he asked. The staring eyes moved toward his voice but did not find him. The lips practiced a speech but did not speak it. Casy felt the pulse and he dropped the wrist and put his hand on Grampa's forehead. A struggle began in the old man's body, his legs moved restlessly and his hands stirred. He said a whole string of blurred sounds that were not words, and his face was red under the spiky white whiskers.

Sairy Wilson spoke softly to Casy. "Know what's wrong?"

He looked up at the wrinkled face and the burning eyes. "Do you?"

"I—think so."

"What?" Casy asked.

"Might be wrong. I wouldn' like to say."

Casy looked back at the twitching red face. "Would you say—maybe—he's workin' up a stroke?"

"I'd say that," said Sairy. "I seen it three times before."

From outside came the sounds of camp-making, wood chopping, and the rattle of pans. Ma looked through the flaps. "Granma wants to come in. Would she better?"

The preacher said, "She'll jus' fret if she don't."

"Think he's awright?" Ma asked.

Casy shook his head slowly. Ma looked quickly down at the struggling old face with blood pounding through it. She drew outside and her voice came through. "He's awright, Granma. He's jus' takin' a little res'."

And Granma answered sulkily, "Well, I want ta see him. He's a tricky devil. He wouldn't never let ya know." And she came scurrying through the flaps. She stood over the mattress and looked down. "What's the matter'th you?" she demanded of Grampa. And again his eyes reached toward her voice and his lips writhed. "He's sulkin'," said Granma. "I tol' you he was tricky. He was gonna sneak away this mornin' so he wouldn't have to come. An' then his hip got a-hurtin'," she said disgustedly. "He's jus' sulkin'. I seen him when he wouldn't talk to nobody before."

Casy said gently, "He ain't sulkin', Granma. He's sick."

"Oh!" She looked down at the old man again. "Sick bad, you think?"

"Purty bad, Granma."

For a moment she hesitated uncertainly. "Well," she said quickly, "why ain't you prayin'? You're a preacher, ain't you?"

Casy's strong fingers blundered over to Grampa's wrist and clasped around it. "I tol' you, Granma. I ain't a preacher no more."

"Pray anyway," she ordered. "You know all the stuff by heart."

"I can't," said Casy. "I don' know what to pray for or who to pray to."

Granma's eyes wandered away and came to rest on Sairy. "He won't pray," she said. "D'I ever tell ya how Ruthie prayed when she was a little skinner? Says, 'Now I lay me down to sleep. I pray the Lord my soul to keep. An' when she got there the cupboard was bare, an' so the poor dog got none. Amen.' That's jus' what she done." The shadow of someone walking between the tent and the sun crossed the canvas.

Grampa seemed to be struggling; all his muscles twitched. And suddenly he jarred as though under a heavy blow. He lay still and his breath was stopped. Casy looked down at the old man's face and saw that it was turning a blackish purple. Sairy touched Casy's shoulder. She whispered, "His tongue, his tongue, his tongue."

Casy nodded. "Get in front a Granma." He pried the tight jaws apart and reached into the old man's throat for the tongue. And as he lifted it clear, a rattling breath came out, and a sobbing breath was indrawn. Casy found a stick on the ground and held down the tongue with it, and the uneven breath rattled in and out.

Granma hopped about like a chicken. "Pray," she said. "Pray, you. Pray, I tell ya." Sairy tried to hold her back. "Pray, goddamn you!" Granma cried.

Casy looked up at her for a moment. The rasping breath came louder and more unevenly. "Our Father who art in Heaven, hallowed be Thy name——"

"Glory!" shouted Granma.

"Thy kingdom come, Thy will be done—on earth—as it is in Heaven."

"Amen."

A long gasping sigh came from the open mouth, and then a crying release of air.

"Give us this day—our daily bread—and forgive us—" The breathing had stopped. Casy looked down into Grampa's eyes and they were clear and deep and penetrating, and there was a knowing serene look in them.

"Hallelujah!" said Granma. "Go on."

"Amen," said Casy.

Granma was still then. And outside the tent all the noise had stopped. A car whished by on the highway. Casy still knelt on the floor beside the mattress. The people outside were listening, standing quietly intent on the sounds of dying. Sairy took Granma by the arm and led her outside, and Granma moved with dignity and held her head high. She walked for the family and held her head straight for the family. Sairy took her to a mattress lying on the ground and sat her down on it. And Granma looked straight ahead, proudly, for she was on show now. The tent was still, and at last Casy spread the tent flaps with his hands and stepped out.

Pa asked softly, "What was it?"

"Stroke," said Casy. "A good quick stroke."

Life began to move again. The sun touched the horizon and flattened over it. And along the highway there came a long line of huge freight trucks with red sides. They rumbled along, putting a little earthquake in the ground, and the standing exhaust pipes sputtered blue smoke from the Diesel oil. One man drove each truck, and his relief man slept in a bunk high up against the ceiling. But the trucks never stopped; they thundered day and night and the ground shook under their heavy march.

The family became a unit. Pa squatted down on the ground, and Uncle John beside him. Pa was the head of the family now. Ma stood behind him. Noah and Tom and Al squatted, and the preacher sat down, and then reclined on his elbow. Connie and Rose of Sharon walked at a distance. Now Ruthie and Winfield, clattering up with a bucket of water held between them, felt the change, and they slowed up and set down the bucket and moved quietly to stand with Ma.

Granma sat proudly, coldly, until the group was formed, until no one looked at her, and then she lay down and covered her face with her arm. The red sun set and left a shining twilight on the land, so that faces were bright in the evening and eyes shone in reflection of the sky. The evening picked up light where it could.

Pa said, "It was in Mr. Wilson's tent."

Uncle John nodded. "He loaned his tent."

"Fine friendly folks," Pa said softly.

Wilson stood by his broken car, and Sairy had gone to the mattress to sit beside Granma, but Sairy was careful not to touch her.

Pa called, "Mr. Wilson!" The man scuffed near and squatted down, and Sairy came and stood beside him. Pa said, "We're thankful to you folks."

"We're proud to help," said Wilson.

"We're beholden to you," said Pa.

"There's no beholden in a time of dying," said Wilson, and Sairy echoed him, "Never no beholden."

Al said, "I'll fix your car—me an' Tom will." And Al looked proud that he could return the family's obligation.

"We could use some help." Wilson admitted the retiring of the obligation.

Pa said, "We got to figger what to do. They's laws. You got to report a death, an' when you do that, they either take forty dollars for the undertaker or they take him for a pauper."

Uncle John broke in, "We never did have no paupers."

Tom said, "Maybe we got to learn. We never got booted off no land before, neither."

"We done it clean," said Pa. "There can't no blame be laid on us. We never took nothin' we couldn' pay; we never suffered no man's charity. When Tom here got in trouble we could hold up our heads. He only done what any man would a done."

"Then what'll we do?" Uncle John asked.

"We go in like the law says an' they'll come out for him. We on'y

got a hunderd an' fifty dollars. They take forty to bury Grampa an'
we won't get to California—or else they'll bury him a pauper." The
men stirred restively, and they studied the darkening ground in front
of their knees.

Pa said softly, "Grampa buried his pa with his own hand, done
it in dignity, an' shaped the grave nice with his own shovel. That
was a time when a man had the right to be buried by his own son
an' a son had the right to bury his own father."

"The law says different now," said Uncle John.

"Sometimes the law can't be foller'd no way," said Pa. "Not in
decency, anyways. They's lots a times you can't. When Floyd was
loose an' goin' wild, law said we got to give him up—an' nobody
give him up. Sometimes a fella got to sift the law. I'm sayin' now I
got the right to bury my own pa. Anybody got somepin to say?"

The preacher rose high on his elbow. "Law changes," he said,
"but 'got to's' go on. You got the right to do what you got to do."

Pa turned to Uncle John. "It's your right too, John. You got any
word against?"

"No word against," said Uncle John. "On'y it's like hidin' him in
the night. Grampa's way was t'come out a-shootin'."

Pa said ashamedly, "We can't do like Grampa done. We got to
get to California 'fore our money gives out."

Tom broke in, "Sometimes fellas workin' dig up a man an' then
they raise hell an' figger he been killed. The gov'ment's got more
interest in a dead man than a live one. They'll go hell-scrapin' tryin'
to fin' out who he was and how he died. I offer we put a note of
writin' in a bottle an' lay it with Grampa, tellin' who he is an' how
he died, an' why he's buried here."

Pa nodded agreement. "Tha's good. Wrote out in a nice han'.
Be not so lonesome too, knowin' his name is there with 'im, not jus'
a old fella lonesome underground. Any more stuff to say?" The circle
was silent.

Pa turned his head to Ma. "You'll lay 'im out?"

"I'll lay 'im out," said Ma. "But who's to get supper?"

Sairy Wilson said, "I'll get supper. You go right ahead. Me an'
that big girl of yourn."

"We sure thank you," said Ma. "Noah, you get into them kegs
an' bring out some nice pork. Salt won't be deep in it yet, but it'll
be right nice eatin'."

"We got a half sack a potatoes," said Sairy.

Ma said, "Gimme two half-dollars." Pa dug in his pocket and gave her the silver. She found the basin, filled it full of water, and went into the tent. It was nearly dark in there. Sairy came in and lighted a candle and stuck it upright on a box and then she went out. For a moment Ma looked down at the dead old man. And then in pity she tore a strip from her own apron and tied up his jaw. She straightened his limbs, folded his hands over his chest. She held his eyelids down and laid a silver piece on each one. She buttoned his shirt and washed his face.

Sairy looked in, saying, "Can I give you any help?"

Ma looked slowly up. "Come in," she said. "I like to talk to ya."

"That's a good big girl you got," said Sairy. "She's right in peelin' potatoes. What can I do to help?"

"I was gonna wash Grampa all over," said Ma, "but he got no other clo'es to put on. An' 'course your quilt's spoilt. Can't never get the smell a death from a quilt. I seen a dog growl an' shake at a mattress my ma died on, an' that was two years later. We'll wrop 'im in your quilt. We'll make it up to you. We got a quilt for you."

Sairy said, "You shouldn' talk like that. We're proud to help. I ain't felt so—safe in a long time. People needs—to help."

Ma nodded. "They do," she said. She looked long into the old whiskery face, with its bound jaw and silver eyes shining in the candlelight. "He ain't gonna look natural. We'll wrop him up."

"The ol' lady took it good."

"Why, she's so old," said Ma, "maybe she don't even rightly know what happened. Maybe she won't really truly know for quite a while. Besides, us folks takes a pride holdin' in. My pa used to say, 'Anybody can break down. It takes a man not to.' We always try to hold in." She folded the quilt neatly about Grampa's legs and around his shoulders. She brought the corner of the quilt over his head like a cowl and pulled it down over his face. Sairy handed her half-a-dozen big safety pins, and she pinned the quilt neatly and tightly about the long package. And at last she stood up. "It won't be a bad burying," she said. "We got a preacher to see him in, an' his folks is all aroun'." Suddenly she swayed a little, and Sairy went to her and steadied her. "It's sleep—" Ma said in a shamed tone. "No, I'm awright. We been so busy gettin' ready, you see."

"Come out in the air," Sairy said.

"Yeah, I'm all done here." Sairy blew out the candle and the two went out.

A bright fire burned in the bottom of the little gulch. And Tom, with sticks and wire, had made supports from which two kettles hung and bubbled furiously, and good steam poured out under the lids. Rose of Sharon knelt on the ground out of range of the burning heat, and she had a long spoon in her hand. She saw Ma come out of the tent, and she stood up and went to her.

"Ma," she said. "I got to ask."

"Scared again?" Ma asked. "Why, you can't get through nine months without sorrow."

"But will it—hurt the baby?"

Ma said, "They used to be a sayin', 'A chile born outa sorrow'll be a happy chile.' Isn't that so, Mis' Wilson?"

"I heard it like that," said Sairy. "An' I heard the other: 'Born outa too much joy'll be a doleful boy.'"

"I'm all jumpy inside," said Rose of Sharon.

"Well, we ain't none of us jumpin' for fun," said Ma. "You jes' keep watchin' the pots."

On the edge of the ring of firelight the men had gathered. For tools they had a shovel and a mattock. Pa marked out the ground— eight feet long and three feet wide. The work went on in relays. Pa chopped the earth with the mattock and then Uncle John shoveled it out. Al chopped and Tom shoveled, Noah chopped and Connie shoveled. And the hole drove down, for the work never diminished in speed. The shovels of dirt flew out of the hole in quick spurts. When Tom was shoulder deep in the rectangular pit, he said, "How deep, Pa?"

"Good an' deep. A couple feet more. You get out now, Tom, and get that paper wrote."

Tom boosted himself out of the hole and Noah took his place. Tom went to Ma, where she tended the fire. "We got any paper an' pen, Ma?"

Ma shook her head slowly, "No-o. That's one thing we didn' bring." She looked toward Sairy. And the little woman walked quickly to her tent. She brought back a Bible and a half pencil. "Here," she said. "They's a clear page in front. Use that an' tear it out." She handed book and pencil to Tom.

Tom sat down in the firelight. He squinted his eyes in concentration, and at last wrote slowly and carefully on the end paper in big clear letters: "This here is William James Joad, dyed of a stroke, old old man. His fokes bured him becaws they got no money to pay for funerls. Nobody kilt him. Jus a stroke an he dyed." He stopped. "Ma, listen to this here." He read it slowly to her.

"Why, that soun's nice," she said. "Can't you stick on somepin from Scripture so it'll be religious? Open up an' git a-sayin' somepin outa Scripture."

"Got to be short," said Tom. "I ain't got much room lef' on the page."

Sairy said, "How 'bout 'God have mercy on his soul'?"

"No," said Tom. "Sounds too much like he was hung. I'll copy somepin." He turned the pages and read, mumbling his lips, saying the words under his breath. "Here's a good short one," he said. " 'An' Lot said unto them, Oh, not so, my Lord.' "

"Don't mean nothin'," said Ma. "Long's you're gonna put one down, it might's well mean somepin."

Sairy said, "Turn to Psalms, over further. You kin always get somepin outa Psalms."

Tom flipped the pages and looked down the verses. "Now here *is* one," he said. "This here's a nice one, just blowed full a religion: 'Blessed is he whose transgression is forgiven, whose sin is covered.' How's that?"

"That's real nice," said Ma. "Put that one in."

Tom wrote it carefully. Ma rinsed and wiped a fruit jar and handed it to him. Tom tore the leaf carefully from the Bible and rolled it and put it in the fruit jar and he screwed the lid down tight on it. "Maybe the preacher ought to wrote it," he said.

Ma said, "No, the preacher wan't no kin." She took the jar from him and went into the dark tent. She unpinned the covering and slipped the fruit jar in under the thin cold hands and pinned the comforter tight again. And then she went back to the fire.

The men came from the grave, their faces shining with perspiration. "Awright," said Pa. He and John and Noah and Al went into the tent, and they came out carrying the long, pinned bundle between them. They carried it to the grave. Pa leaped into the hole and received the bundle in his arms and laid it gently down. Uncle John put out a hand and helped Pa out of the hole. Pa asked, "How about Granma?"

"I'll see," Ma said. She walked to the mattress and looked down at the old woman for a moment. Then she went back to the grave. "Sleepin'," she said. "Maybe she'd hold it against me, but I ain't a-gonna wake her up. She's tar'd."

Pa said, "Where at's the preacher? We oughta have a prayer."

Tom said, "I seen him walkin' down the road. He don't like to pray no more."

"Don't like to pray?"

"No," said Tom. "He ain't a preacher no more. He figgers it ain't right to fool people actin' like a preacher when he ain't a preacher. I bet he went away so nobody wouldn' ast him."

Casy had come quietly near, and he heard Tom speaking. "I didn' run away," he said. "I'll he'p you folks, but I won't fool ya."

Pa said, "Won't you say a few words? Ain't none of our folks ever been buried without a few words."

"I'll say 'em," said the preacher.

Connie led Rose of Sharon to the graveside, she reluctant. "You got to," Connie said. "It ain't decent not to. It'll jus' be a little."

The firelight fell on the grouped people, showing their faces and their eyes, dwindling on their dark clothes. All the hats were off now. The light danced, jerking over the people.

Casy said, "It'll be a short one." He bowed his head, and the others followed his lead. Casy said solemnly, "This here ol' man jus' lived a life an' jus' died out of it. I don' know whether he was good or bad, but that don't matter much. He was alive, an' that's what matters. An' now he's dead, an' that don't matter. Heard a fella tell a poem one time, an' he says 'All that lives is holy.' Got to thinkin', an' purty soon it means more than the words says. An' I wouldn' pray for a ol' fella that's dead. He's awright. He got a job to do, but it's all laid out for 'im an' there's on'y one way to do it. But us, we got a job to do, an' they's a thousan' ways, an' we don' know which one to take. An' if I was to pray, it'd be for the folks that don' know which way to turn. Grampa here, he got the easy straight. An' now cover 'im up and let 'im get to his work." He raised his head.

Pa said, "Amen," and the others muttered, "A-men." Then Pa took the shovel, half filled it with dirt, and spread it gently into the black hole. He handed the shovel to Uncle John, and John dropped in a shovelful. Then the shovel went from hand to hand until every man had his turn. When all had taken their duty and their right, Pa attacked the mound of loose dirt and hurriedly filled the hole. The women moved back to the fire to see to supper. Ruthie and Winfield watched, absorbed.

Ruthie said solemnly, "Grampa's down under there." And Winfield looked at her with horrified eyes. And then he ran away to the fire and sat on the ground and sobbed to himself.

Pa half filled the hole, and then he stood panting with the effort while Uncle John finished it. And John was shaping up the mound when Tom stopped him. "Listen," Tom said." 'F we leave a grave, they'll have it open in no time. We got to hide it. Level her off an' we'll strew dry grass. We got to do that."

Pa said, "I didn' think a that. It ain't right to leave a grave unmounded."

"Can't he'p it," said Tom. "They'd dig 'im right up, an' we'd get it for breakin' the law. You know what I get if I break the law."

"Yeah," Pa said. "I forgot that." He took the shovel from John and leveled the grave. "She'll sink, come winter," he said.

"Can't he'p that," said Tom. "We'll be a long ways off by winter. Tromp her in good, an' we'll strew stuff over her."

When the pork and potatoes were done the families sat about on the ground and ate, and they were quiet, staring into the fire. Wilson, tearing a slab of meat with his teeth, sighed with contentment. "Nice eatin' pig," he said.

"Well," Pa explained, "we had a couple shoats, an' we thought we might's well eat 'em. Can't get nothin' for them. When we get kinda use' ta movin' an' Ma can set up bread, why, it'll be pretty nice, seein' the country an' two kags a' pork right in the truck. How long you folks been on the road?"

Wilson cleared his teeth with his tongue and swallowed. "We ain't been lucky," he said. "We been three weeks from home."

"Why, God Awmighty, we aim to be in California in ten days or less."

Al broke in, "I dunno, Pa. With that load we're packin', we maybe ain't never gonna get there. Not if they's mountains to go over."

They were silent about the fire. Their faces were turned downward and their hair and foreheads showed in the firelight. Above the little dome of the firelight the summer stars shone thinly, and the heat of the day was gradually withdrawing. On her mattress, away from the fire, Granma whimpered softly like a puppy. The heads of all turned in her direction.

Ma said, "Rosasharn, like a good girl go lay down with Granma. She needs somebody now. She's knowin', now."

Rose of Sharon got to her feet and walked to the mattress and lay beside the old woman, and the murmur of their soft voices drifted to the fire. Rose of Sharon and Granma whispered together on the mattress.

Noah said, "Funny thing is—losin' Grampa ain't made me feel no different than I done before. I ain't no sadder than I was."

"It's just the same thing," Casy said. "Grampa an' the old place, they was jus' the same thing."

Al said, "It's a goddamn shame. He been talkin' what he's gonna do, how he gonna squeeze grapes over his head an' let the juice run in his whiskers, an' all stuff like that."

Casy said, "He was foolin', all the time. I think he knowed it. He knowed it. You fellas can make some kinda new life, but Grampa, his life was over an' he knowed it. An' Grampa didn' die tonight. He died the minute you took 'im off the place."

"You sure a that?" Pa cried. "Why no!"

"Oh, he was breathin'," Casy went on, "but he was dead. He was that place, an' he knowed it."

Uncle John said, "Did you know he was a-dyin'?"

"Yeah," said Casy. "I knowed it."

John gazed at him, and a horror grew in his face. "An' you didn' tell nobody?"

"What good?" Casy asked.

"We—we might of did somepin."

"What?"

"I don' know, but——"

"No," Casy said, "you couldn' a done nothin'. Your way was fixed an' Grampa didn' have no part in it. He didn' suffer none. Not after fust thing this mornin'. He's jus' stayin' with the lan'. He couldn' leave it."

Uncle John sighed deeply.

Wilson said, "We hadda leave my brother Will." The heads turned toward him. "Him an' me had forties side by side. He's older'n me. Neither one ever drove a car. Well, we went in an' we sol' ever'thing. Will, he bought a car, an' they give him a kid to show 'im how to use it. So the afternoon 'fore we're gonna start, Will an' Aunt Minnie go a-practicin'. Will, he comes to a bend in the road an' he yells 'Whoa' an' yanks back, an' he goes through a fence. An' he yells 'Whoa, you bastard' an' tromps down on the gas an' goes over into a gulch. An' there he was. Didn't have nothin' more to sell an' didn't have no car. But it were his own damn fault, praise God. He's so damn mad he won't come along with us, jus' set there a-cussin' an' a-cussin'."

"What's he gonna do?"

"I dunno. He's too mad to figger. An' we couldn' wait. On'y had eighty-five dollars to go on. We couldn' set an' cut it up, but we et it up anyways. Didn' go a hunderd mile when a tooth in the rear end bust, an' cost thirty dollars to get her fix', an' then we got to get a tire, an' then a spark plug cracked, an' Sairy got sick. Had ta stop ten days. An' now the goddamn car is bust again, an' money's gettin' low. I dunno when we'll ever get to California. 'F I could on'y fix a car, but I don' know nothin' about 'em."

Al asked importantly, "What's the matter?"

"Well, she jus' won't run. Starts an' farts an' stops. In a minute she'll start again, an' then 'fore you can git her goin', she peters out again."

"Runs a minute an' then dies?"

"Yes, sir. An' I can't keep her a-goin' no matter how much gas I give her. Got worse an' worse, an' now I cain't get her a-movin' a-tall."

Al was very proud and very mature, then. "I think you got a plugged gas line. I'll blow her out for ya."

And Pa was proud too. "He's a good hand with a car," Pa said.

"Well, I'll sure thank ya for a han'. I sure will. Makes a fella kinda feel—like a little kid, when he can't fix nothin'. When we get to California I aim to get me a nice car. Maybe she won't break down."

Pa said, "When we get there. Gettin' there's the trouble."

"Oh, but she's worth it," said Wilson. "Why, I seen han'bills how they need folks to pick fruit, an' good wages. Why, jus' think how it's gonna be, under them shady trees a-pickin' fruit an' takin' a bite ever' once in a while. Why, hell, they don't care how much you eat 'cause they got so much. An' with them good wages, maybe a fella can get hisself a little piece a land an' work out for extra cash. Why, hell, in a couple years I bet a fella could have a place of his own."

Pa said, "We seen them han'bills. I got one right here." He took out his purse and from it took a folded orange handbill. In black type it said, "Pea Pickers Wanted in California. Good Wages All Season. 800 Pickers Wanted."

Wilson looked at it curiously. "Why, that's the one I seen. The very same one. You s'pose—maybe they got all eight hunderd awready?"

Pa said, "This is jus' one little part a California. Why, that's the secon' biggest State we got. S'pose they did get all them eight hunderd. They's plenty places else. I rather pick fruit anyways. Like you says, under them trees an' pickin' fruit—why, even the kids'd like to do that."

Suddenly Al got up and walked to the Wilsons' touring car. He looked in for a moment and then came back and sat down.

"You can't fix her tonight," Wilson said.

"I know. I'll get to her in the morning."

Tom had watched his young brother carefully. "I was thinkin' somepin like that myself," he said.

Noah asked, "What you two fellas talkin' about?"

Tom and Al were silent, each waiting for the other. "You tell 'em," Al said finally.

"Well, maybe it's no good, an' maybe it ain't the same thing Al's thinking. Here she is, anyways. We got a overload, but Mr. an' Mis' Wilson ain't. If some of us folks could ride with them an' take some a their light stuff in the truck, we wouldn't break no springs an' we could git up hills. An' me an' Al both knows about a car, so we could keep that car a-rollin'. We'd keep together on the road an' it'd be good for ever'body."

Wilson jumped up. "Why, sure. Why, we'd be proud. We cer-tain'y would. You hear that, Sairy?"

"It's a nice thing," said Sairy. "Wouldn' be a burden on you folks?"

"No, by God," said Pa. "Wouldn't be no burden at all. You'd be helpin' us."

Wilson settled back uneasily. "Well, I dunno."

"What's a matter, don' you wanta?"

"Well, ya see—I on'y got 'bout thirty dollars lef', an' I won't be no burden."

Ma said, "You won't be no burden. Each'll help each, an' we'll all git to California. Sairy Wilson he'ped lay Grampa out," and she stopped. The relationship was plain.

Al cried, "That car'll take six easy. Say me to drive, an' Rosasharn an' Connie and Granma. Then we take the big light stuff an' pile her on the truck. An' we'll trade off ever' so often." He spoke loudly, for a load of worry was lifted from him.

They smiled shyly and looked down at the ground. Pa fingered the dusty earth with his fingertips. He said, "Ma favors a white house with oranges growin' around. They's a big pitcher on a calendar she seen."

Sairy said, "If I get sick again, you got to go on an' get there. We ain't a-goin' to burden."

Ma looked carefully at Sairy, and she seemed to see for the first time the pain-tormented eyes and the face that was haunted and shrinking with pain. And Ma said, "We gonna see you get through. You said yourself, you can't let help go unwanted."

Sairy studied her wrinkled hands in the firelight. "We got to get some sleep tonight." She stood up.

"Grampa—it's like he's dead a year," Ma said.

The families moved lazily to their sleep, yawning luxuriously. Ma sloshed the tin plates off a little and rubbed the grease free with a flour sack. The fire died down and the stars descended. Few passenger cars went by on the highway now, but the transport trucks thundered by at intervals and put little earthquakes in the ground. In the ditch the cars were barely visible under the starlight. A tied dog howled at the service station down the road. The families were quiet and sleeping, and the field mice grew bold and scampered about among the mattresses. Only Sairy Wilson was awake. She stared into the sky and braced her body firmly against pain.

CHAPTER 14

disoriented

The western land, nervous under the beginning change. The Western States, nervous as horses before a thunder storm. The great owners, nervous, sensing a change, knowing nothing of the nature of the change. The great owners, striking at the immediate thing, the widening government, the growing labor unity; striking at new taxes, at plans; not knowing these things are results, not causes. Results, not — _repeats_ causes; results, not causes. The causes lie deep and simply—the causes are a hunger in a stomach, multiplied a million times; a hunger in a single soul, hunger for joy and some security, multiplied a million times; muscles and mind aching to grow, to work, to create, multiplied a million times. The last clear definite function of man— muscles aching to work, minds aching to create beyond the single need—this is man. To build a wall, to build a house, a dam, and in the wall and house and dam to put something of Manself, and to Manself take back something of the wall, the house, the dam; to take hard muscles from the lifting, to take the clear lines and form from conceiving. For man, unlike any other thing organic or inorganic in the universe, grows beyond his work, walks up the stairs of his concepts, emerges ahead of his accomplishments. This you may say of man—when theories change and crash, when schools, philosophies, when narrow dark alleys of thought, national, religious, economic, grow and disintegrate, man reaches, stumbles forward, painfully, mistakenly sometimes. Having stepped forward, he may slip back, but only half a step, never the full step back. This you may say and know it and know it. This you may know when the bombs plummet out of the black planes on the market place, when prisoners are stuck like pigs, when the crushed bodies drain filthily in the dust. You may know it in this way. If the step were not being taken, if the stumbling-forward ache were not alive, the bombs would not fall, the throats would not be cut. Fear the time when the bombs stop falling while the bombers live—for every bomb is proof that the spirit has not died. And fear the time when the strikes stop while the great owners live—for every little beaten strike is proof that the step is being taken. And this you can know—fear the time when Manself will not suffer and die for a concept, for this one quality is the foundation of Manself, and this one quality is man, distinctive in the universe.

The Western States nervous under the beginning change. Texas and Oklahoma, Kansas and Arkansas, New Mexico, Arizona, California. A single family moved from the land. Pa borrowed money from the bank, and now the bank wants the land. The land company—that's the bank when it has land—wants tractors, not families on the land. Is a tractor bad? Is the power that turns the long furrows wrong? If this tractor were ours it would be good—not mine, but ours. If our tractor turned the long furrows of our land, it would be good. Not my land, but ours. We could love that tractor then as we have loved this land when it was ours. But this tractor does two things—it turns the land and turns us off the land. There is little difference between this tractor and a tank. The people are driven, intimidated, hurt by both. We must think about this.

One man, one family driven from the land; this rusty car creaking along the highway to the west. I lost my land, a single tractor took my land. I am alone and I am bewildered. And in the night one family camps in a ditch and another family pulls in and the tents come out. The two men squat on their hams and the women and children listen. Here is the node, you who hate change and fear revolution. Keep these two squatting men apart; make them hate, fear, suspect each other. Here is the anlage of the thing you fear. This is the zygote. For here "I lost my land" is changed; a cell is split and from its splitting grows the thing you hate—"We lost our land." The danger is here, for two men are not as lonely and perplexed as one. And from this first "we" there grows a still more dangerous thing: "I have a little food" plus "I have none." If from this problem the sum is "We have a little food," the thing is on its way, the movement has direction. Only a little multiplication now, and this land, this tractor are ours. The two men squatting in a ditch, the little fire, the side-meat stewing in a single pot, the silent, stone-eyed women; behind, the children listening with their souls to words their minds do not understand. The night draws down. The baby has a cold. Here, take this blanket. It's wool. It was my mother's blanket—take it for the baby. This is the thing to bomb. This is the beginning—from "I" to "we."

If you who own the things people must have could understand

this, you might preserve yourself. If you could separate causes from results, if you could know that Paine, Marx, Jefferson, Lenin, were results, not causes, you might survive. But that you cannot know. For the quality of owning freezes you forever into "I," and cuts you off forever from the "we."

The Western States are nervous under the beginning change. Need is the stimulus to concept, concept to action. A half-million people moving over the country; a million more restive, ready to move; ten million more feeling the first nervousness.

And tractors turning the multiple furrows in the vacant land.

Handwritten annotations:

Thomas Paine – wrote pamphlets
 – Revolutionary War
 – Against British government
 – "Common Sense"

Carl Marx – communist

Thomas Jefferson – President
 – Declaration of Independence

Vlatamin Lenin – Russian Revolutionary

□ what they are doing is just as much as our founding fathers

□ results of desparation
 – there needs could be met if they fight

Along 66 the hamburger stands—Al & Susy's Place—Carl's Lunch —Joe & Minnie—Will's Eats. Board-and-bat shacks. Two gasoline pumps in front, a screen door, a long bar, stools, and a foot rail. Near the door three slot machines, showing through the glass the wealth in nickels three bars will bring. And beside them, the nickel phonograph with records piled up like pies, ready to swing out to the turntable and play dance music, "Ti-pi-ti-pi-tin," "Thanks for the Memory," Bing Crosby, Benny Goodman. At one end of the counter a covered case; candy cough drops, caffeine sulphate called Sleepless, No-Doze; candy, cigarettes, razor blades, aspirin, Bromo-Seltzer, Alka-Seltzer. The walls decorated with posters, bathing girls, blondes with big breasts and slender hips and waxen faces, in white bathing suits, and holding a bottle of Coca-Cola and smiling—see what you get with a Coca-Cola. Long bar, and salts, peppers, mustard pots, and paper napkins. Beer taps behind the counter, and in back the coffee urns, shiny and steaming, with glass gauges showing the coffee level. And pies in wire cages and oranges in pyramids of four. And little piles of Post Toasties, corn flakes, stacked up in designs.

The signs on cards, picked out with shining mica: Pies Like Mother Used to Make. Credit Makes Enemies, Let's Be Friends. Ladies May Smoke But Be Careful Where You Lay Your Butts. Eat Here and Keep Your Wife for a Pet. IITYWYBAD?

Down at one end the cooking plates, pots of stew, potatoes, pot roast, roast beef, gray roast pork waiting to be sliced.

Minnie or Susy or Mae, middle-aging behind the counter, hair curled and rouge and powder on a sweating face. Taking orders in a soft low voice, calling them to the cook with a screech like a peacock. Mopping the counter with circular strokes, polishing the big shining coffee urns. The cook is Joe or Carl or Al, hot in a white coat and apron, beady sweat on white forehead, below the white cook's cap; moody, rarely speaking, looking up for a moment at each new entry. Wiping the griddle, slapping down the hamburger. He repeats Mae's orders gently, scrapes the griddle, wipes it down with burlap. Moody and silent.

Mae is the contact, smiling, irritated, near to outbreak; smiling while her eyes look on past—unless for truck drivers. There's the backbone of the joint. Where the trucks stop, that's where the customers come. Can't fool truck drivers, they know. They bring the custom. They know. Give 'em a stale cup a coffee an' they're off the joint. Treat 'em right an' they come back. Mae really smiles with all her might at truck drivers. She bridles a little, fixes her back hair so that her breasts will lift with her raised arms, passes the time of day and indicates great things, great times, great jokes. Al never speaks. He is no contact. Sometimes he smiles a little at a joke, but he never laughs. Sometimes he looks up at the vivaciousness in Mae's voice, and then he scrapes the griddle with a spatula, scrapes the grease into an iron trough around the plate. He presses down a hissing hamburger with his spatula. He lays the split buns on the plate to toast and heat. He gathers up stray onions from the plate and heaps them on the meat and presses them in with the spatula. He puts half the bun on top of the meat, paints the other half with melted butter, with thin pickle relish. Holding the bun on the meat, he slips the spatula under the thin pad of meat, flips it over, lays the buttered half on top, and drops the hamburger on a small plate. Quarter of a dill pickle, two black olives beside the sandwich. Al skims the plate down the counter like a quoit. And he scrapes his griddle with the spatula and looks moodily at the stew kettle.

Cars whisking by on 66. License plates. Mass., Tenn., R.I., N.Y., Vt., Ohio. Going west. Fine cars, cruising at sixty-five.

There goes one of them Cords. Looks like a coffin on wheels.

But, Jesus, how they travel!

See that La Salle? Me for that. I ain't a hog. I go for a La Salle.

'F ya goin' big, what's a matter with a Cad'? Jus' a little bigger, little faster.

I'd take a Zephyr myself. You ain't ridin' no fortune, but you got class an' speed. Give me a Zephyr.

Well, sir, you may get a laugh outa this—I'll take a Buick-Puick. That's good enough.

But, hell, that costs in the Zephyr class an' it ain't got the sap.

I don' care. I don' want nothin' to do with nothing of Henry Ford's. I don' like 'im. Never did. Got a brother worked in the plant. Oughta hear him tell.

Well, a Zephyr got sap.

The big cars on the highway. Languid, heat-raddled ladies, small nucleuses about whom revolve a thousand accouterments: creams, ointments to grease themselves, coloring matter in phials—black, pink, red, white, green, silver—to change the color of hair, eyes, lips, nails, brows, lashes, lids. Oils, seeds, and pills to make the bowels move. A bag of bottles, syringes, pills, powders, fluids, jellies to make their sexual intercourse safe, odorless, and unproductive. And this apart from clothes. What a hell of a nuisance!

Lines of weariness around the eyes, lines of discontent down from the corners of the mouth, breasts lying heavily in little hammocks, stomach and thighs straining against cases of rubber. And the mouths panting, the eyes sullen, disliking sun and wind and earth, resenting food and weariness, hating time that rarely makes them beautiful and always makes them old.

Beside them, little pot-bellied men in light suits and panama hats; clean, pink men with puzzled, worried eyes, with restless eyes. Worried because formulas do not work out; hungry for security and yet sensing its disappearance from the earth. In their lapels the insignia of lodges and service clubs, places where they can go and, by a weight of numbers of little worried men, reassure themselves that business is noble and not the curious ritualized thievery they know it is; that business men are intelligent in spite of the records of their stupidity; that they are kind and charitable in spite of the principles of sound business; that their lives are rich instead of the thin tiresome routines they know; and that a time is coming when they will not be afraid any more.

And these two, going to California; going to sit in the lobby of the Beverly-Wilshire Hotel and watch people they envy go by, to look at mountains—mountains, mind you, and great trees—he with his worried eyes and she thinking how the sun will dry her skin. Going to look at the Pacific Ocean, and I'll bet a hundred thousand dollars to nothing at all, he will say, "It isn't as big as I thought it would be." And she will envy plump young bodies on the beach. Going to California really to go home again. To say, "Joan Crawford was at the table next to us at the Trocadero. She's really a mess, but she does wear nice clothes." And he, "I talked to good sound business men out there. They don't see a chance till we get rid of that fellow in the White House." And, "I got it from a man in the know. —— has syphilis, you know—she was in that Warner picture. Man said she'd slept her way into pictures. Well, she got what she was looking for." But the worried eyes are never calm, and the pouting mouth is never glad. The big car cruising along at sixty.

I want a cold drink.

Well, there's something up ahead. Want to stop?

Do you think it would be clean?

Clean as you're going to find in this God-forsaken country.

Well, maybe the bottled soda will be all right.

The great car squeals and pulls to a stop. The fat worried man helps his wife out.

Mae looks at and past them as they enter. Al looks up from his griddle, and down again. Mae knows. They'll drink a five-cent soda and crab that it ain't cold enough. The woman will use six paper napkins and drop them on the floor. The man will choke and try to put the blame on Mae. The woman will sniff as though she smelled rotting meat and they will go out again and tell forever afterward that the people in the West are sullen. And Mae, when she is alone with Al, has a name for them. She calls them shitheels.

Truck drivers. That's the stuff.

Here's a big transport comin'. Hope they stop; take away the taste of them shitheels. When I worked in that hotel in Albuquerque, Al, the way they steal—ever' darn thing. An' the bigger the car they got, the more they steal—towels, silver, soap dishes. I can't figger it.

And Al, morosely, Where ya think they get them big cars and stuff? Born with 'em? You won't never have nothin'.

The transport truck, a driver and relief. How 'bout stoppin' for a cup a Java? I know this dump.

How's the schedule?

Oh, we're ahead!

Pull up, then. They's a ol' war horse in here that's a kick. Good Java, too.

The truck pulls up. Two men in khaki riding trousers, boots, short jackets, and shiny-visored military caps. Screen door—slam.

H'ya, Mae?

Well, if it ain't Big Bill the Rat! When'd you get back on this run?

Week ago.

The other man puts a nickel in the phonograph, watches the disk slip free and the turntable rise up under it. Bing Crosby's voice—golden. "Thanks for the memory, of sunburn at the shore—

You might have been a headache, but you never were a bore—"
And the truck driver sings for Mae's ears, you might have been a
haddock but you never was a whore—

Mae laughs. Who's ya frien', Bill? New on this run, ain't he?

The other puts a nickel in the slot machine, wins four slugs, and
puts them back. Walks to the counter.

Well, what's it gonna be?

Oh, cup a Java. Kinda pie ya got?

Banana cream, pineapple cream, chocolate cream—an' apple.

Make it apple. Wait— Kind is that big thick one?

Mae lifts it out and sniffs it. Banana cream.

Cut off a hunk; make it a big hunk.

Man at the slot machine says, Two all around.

Two it is. Seen any new etchin's lately, Bill?

Well, here's one.

Now, you be careful front of a lady.

Oh, this ain't bad. Little kid comes in late ta school. Teacher
says, "Why ya late?" Kid says, "Had a take a heifer down—get 'er
bred." Teacher says, "Couldn't your ol' man do it?" Kid says, "Sure
he could, but not as good as the bull."

Mae squeaks with laughter, harsh screeching laughter. Al, slicing
onions carefully on a board, looks up and smiles, and then looks
down again. Truck drivers, that's the stuff. Gonna leave a quarter
each for Mae. Fifteen cents for pie an' coffee an' a dime for Mae.
An' they ain't tryin' to make her, neither.

Sitting together on the stools, spoons sticking up out of the coffee mugs. Passing the time of day. And Al, rubbing down his griddle,
listening but making no comment. Bing Crosby's voice stops. The
turntable drops down and the record swings into its place in the pile.
The purple light goes off. The nickel, which has caused all this mechanism to work, has caused Crosby to sing and an orchestra to play
—this nickel drops from between the contact points into the box
where the profits go. This nickel, unlike most money, has actually
done a job of work, has been physically responsible for a reaction.

Steam spurts from the valve of the coffee urn. The compressor
of the ice machine chugs softly for a time and then stops. The electric fan in the corner waves its head slowly back and forth, sweeping
the room with a warm breeze. On the highway, on 66, the cars whiz
by.

They was a Massachusetts car stopped a while ago, said Mae.

Big Bill grasped his cup around the top so that the spoon stuck up between his first and second fingers. He drew in a snort of air with the coffee, to cool it. "You ought to be out on 66. Cars from all over the country. All headin' west. Never seen so many before. Sure some honeys on the road."

"We seen a wreck this mornin'," his companion said. "Big car. Big Cad', a special job and a honey, low, cream-color, special job. Hit a truck. Folded the radiator right back into the driver. Must a been doin' ninety. Steerin' wheel went right on through the guy an' lef' him a-wigglin' like a frog on a hook. Peach of a car. A honey. You can have her for peanuts now. Drivin' alone, the guy was."

Al looked up from his work. "Hurt the truck?"

"Oh, Jesus Christ! Wasn't a truck. One of them cut-down cars full a stoves an' pans an' mattresses an' kids an' chickens. Goin' west, you know. This guy come by us doin' ninety—r'ared up on two wheels just to pass us, an' a car's comin' so he cuts in an' whangs this here truck. Drove like he's blin' drunk. Jesus, the air was full a bed clothes an' chickens an' kids. Killed one kid. Never seen such a mess. We pulled up. Ol' man that's drivin' the truck, he jus' stan's there lookin' at that dead kid. Can't get a word out of 'im. Jus' rum-dumb. God Almighty, the road is full a them families goin' west. Never seen so many. Gets worse all a time. Wonder where the hell they all come from?"

"Wonder where they all go to," said Mae. "Come here for gas sometimes, but they don't hardly never buy nothin' else. People says they steal. We ain't got nothin' layin' around. They never stole nothin' from us."

Big Bill, munching his pie, looked up the road through the screened window. "Better tie your stuff down. I think you got some of 'em comin' now."

A 1926 Nash sedan pulled wearily off the highway. The back seat was piled nearly to the ceiling with sacks, with pots and pans, and on the very top, right up against the ceiling, two boys rode. On the top of the car, a mattress and a folded tent; tent poles tied along the running board. The car pulled up to the gas pumps. A dark-haired, hatchet-faced man got slowly out. And the two boys slid down from the load and hit the ground.

Mae walked around the counter and stood in the door. The man was dressed in gray wool trousers and a blue shirt, dark blue with sweat on the back and under the arms. The boys in overalls and nothing else, ragged patched overalls. Their hair was light, and it stood up evenly all over their heads, for it had been roached. Their faces were streaked with dust. They went directly to the mud puddle under the hose and dug their toes into the mud.

The man asked, "Can we git some water, ma'am?"

A look of annoyance crossed Mae's face. "Sure, go ahead." She said softly over her shoulder, "I'll keep my eye on the hose." She watched while the man slowly unscrewed the radiator cap and ran the hose in.

A woman in the car, a flaxen-haired woman, said, "See if you can't git it here."

The man turned off the hose and screwed on the cap again. The little boys took the hose from him and they upended it and drank thirstily. The man took off his dark, stained hat and stood with a curious humility in front of the screen. "Could you see your way to sell us a loaf of bread, ma'am?"

Mae said, "This ain't a grocery store. We got bread to make san'widges."

"I know, ma'am." His humility was insistent. "We need bread and there ain't nothin' for quite a piece, they say."

" 'F we sell bread we gonna run out." Mae's tone was faltering.

"We're hungry," the man said.

"Whyn't you buy a san'widge? We got nice san'widges, hamburgs."

"We'd sure admire to do that, ma'am. But we can't. We got to make a dime do all of us." And he said embarrassedly, "We ain't got but a little."

Mae said, "You can't get no loaf a bread for a dime. We only got fifteen-cent loafs."

From behind her Al growled, "God Almighty, Mae, give 'em bread."

"We'll run out 'fore the bread truck comes."

"Run out, then, goddamn it," said Al. And he looked sullenly down at the potato salad he was mixing.

Mae shrugged her plump shoulders and looked to the truck drivers to show them what she was up against.

She held the screen door open and the man came in, bringing a smell of sweat with him. The boys edged in behind him and they went immediately to the candy case and stared in—not with craving or with hope or even with desire, but just with a kind of wonder that such things could be. They were alike in size and their faces were alike. One scratched his dusty ankle with the toe nails of his other foot. The other whispered some soft message and then they straightened their arms so that their clenched fists in the overall pockets showed through the thin blue cloth.

Mae opened a drawer and took out a long waxpaper-wrapped loaf. "This here is a fifteen-cent loaf."

The man put his hat back on his head. He answered with inflexible humility, "Won't you—can't you see your way to cut off ten cents' worth?"

Al said snarlingly, "Goddamn it, Mae. Give 'em the loaf."

The man turned toward Al. "No, we want ta buy ten cents' worth of it. We got it figgered awful close, mister, to get to California."

Mae said resignedly, "You can have this for ten cents."

"That'd be robbin' you, ma'am."

"Go ahead—Al says to take it." She pushed the waxpapered loaf across the counter. The man took a deep leather pouch from his rear pocket, untied the strings, and spread it open. It was heavy with silver and with greasy bills.

"May soun' funny to be so tight," he apologized. "We got a thousan' miles to go, an' we don' know if we'll make it." He dug in the pouch with a forefinger, located a dime, and pinched in for it. When he put it down on the counter he had a penny with it. He was about to drop the penny back into the pouch when his eye fell on the boys frozen before the candy counter. He moved slowly down to them. He pointed in the case at big long sticks of striped peppermint. "Is them penny candy, ma'am?"

Mae moved down and looked in. "Which ones?"

"There, them stripy ones."

The little boys raised their eyes to her face and they stopped breathing; their mouths were partly opened, their half-naked bodies were rigid.

"Oh—them. Well, no—them's two for a penny."

"Well, gimme two then, ma'am." He placed the copper cent carefully on the counter. The boys expelled their held breath softly. Mae held the big sticks out.

"Take 'em," said the man.

They reached timidly, each took a stick, and they held them

down at their sides and did not look at them. But they looked at each other, and their mouth corners smiled rigidly with embarrassment.

"Thank you, ma'am." The man picked up the bread and went out the door, and the little boys marched stiffly behind him, the red-striped sticks held tightly against their legs. They leaped like chipmunks over the front seat and onto the top of the load, and they burrowed back out of sight like chipmunks.

The man got in and started his car, and with a roaring motor and a cloud of blue oily smoke the ancient Nash climbed up on the highway and went on its way to the west.

From inside the restaurant the truck drivers and Mae and Al stared after them.

Big Bill wheeled back. "Them wasn't two-for-a-cent candy," he said.

"What's that to you?" Mae said fiercely.

"Them was nickel apiece candy," said Bill.

"We got to get goin'," said the other man. "We're droppin' time." They reached in their pockets. Bill put a coin on the counter and the other man looked at it and reached again and put down a coin. They swung around and walked to the door.

"So long," said Bill.

Mae called, "Hey! Wait a minute. You got change."

"You go to hell," said Bill, and the screen door slammed.

Mae watched them get into the great truck, watched it lumber off in low gear, and heard the shift up the whining gears to cruising ratio. "Al—" she said softly.

He looked up from the hamburger he was patting thin and stacking between waxed papers. "What ya want?"

"Look there." She pointed at the coins beside the cups—two half-dollars. Al walked near and looked, and then he went back to his work.

"Truck drivers," Mae said reverently, "an' after them shitheels."

Flies struck the screen with little bumps and droned away. The compressor chugged for a time and then stopped. On 66 the traffic whizzed by, trucks and fine streamlined cars and jalopies; and they went by with a vicious whiz. Mae took down the plates and scraped the pie crusts into a bucket. She found her damp cloth and wiped the counter with circular sweeps. And her eyes were on the highway, where life whizzed by.

Al wiped his hands on his apron. He looked at a paper pinned to the wall over the griddle. Three lines of marks in columns on the paper. Al counted the longest line. He walked along the counter to the cash register, rang "No Sale," and took out a handful of nickels.

"What ya doin'?" Mae asked.

"Number three's ready to pay off," said Al. He went to the third slot machine and played his nickels in, and on the fifth spin of the wheels the three bars came up and the jack pot dumped out into the cup. Al gathered up the big handful of coins and went back of the counter. He dropped them in the drawer and slammed the cash register. Then he went back to his place and crossed out the line of dots. "Number three gets more play'n the others," he said. "Maybe I ought to shift 'em around." He lifted a lid and stirred the slowly simmering stew.

"I wonder what they'll do in California?" said Mae.

"Who?"

"Them folks that was just in."

"Christ knows," said Al.

"S'pose they'll get work?"

"How the hell would I know?" said Al.

She stared eastward along the highway. "Here comes a transport, double. Wonder if they stop? Hope they do." And as the huge truck came heavily down from the highway and parked, Mae seized her cloth and wiped the whole length of the counter. And she took a few swipes at the gleaming coffee urn too, and turned up the bottle-gas under the urn. Al brought out a handful of little turnips and started to peel them. Mae's face was gay when the door opened and the two uniformed truck drivers entered.

"Hi, sister!"

"I won't be a sister to no man," said Mae. They laughed and Mae laughed. "What'll it be, boys?"

"Oh, a cup a Java. What kinda pie ya got?"

"Pineapple cream an' banana cream an' chocolate cream an' apple."

"Give me apple. No, wait—what's that big thick one?"

Mae picked up the pie and smelled it. "Pineapple cream," she said.

"Well, chop out a hunk a that."

The cars whizzed viciously by on 66.

CHAPTER 16

Joads and Wilsons crawled westward as a unit: El Reno and Bridge-
port, Clinton, Elk City, Sayre, and Texola. There's the border, and
Oklahoma was behind. And this day the cars crawled on and on,
through the Panhandle of Texas. Shamrock and Alanreed, Groom
and Yarnell. They went through Amarillo in the evening, drove too
long, and camped when it was dusk. They were tired and dusty and
hot. Granma had convulsions from the heat, and she was weak when
they stopped.

That night Al stole a fence rail and made a ridge pole on the
truck, braced at both ends. That night they ate nothing but pan
biscuits, cold and hard, held over from breakfast. They flopped down
on the mattresses and slept in their clothes. The Wilsons didn't even
put up their tent.

Joads and Wilsons were in flight across the Panhandle, the rolling
gray country, lined and cut with old flood scars. They were in flight
out of Oklahoma and across Texas. The land turtles crawled through
the dust and the sun whipped the earth, and in the evening the heat
went out of the sky and the earth sent up a wave of heat from itself.

Two days the families were in flight, but on the third the land
was too huge for them and they settled into a new technique of
living; the highway became their home and movement their medium
of expression. Little by little they settled into the new life. Ruthie
and Winfield first, then Al, then Connie and Rose of Sharon, and,
last, the older ones. The land rolled like great stationary ground
swells. Wildorado and Vega and Boise and Glenrio. That's the end
of Texas. New Mexico and the mountains. In the far distance, waved
up against the sky, the mountains stood. And the wheels of the cars
creaked around, and the engines were hot, and the steam spurted
around the radiator caps. They crawled to the Pecos river, and
crossed at Santa Rosa. And they went on for twenty miles.

Al Joad drove the touring car, and his mother sat beside him, and
Rose of Sharon beside her. Ahead the truck crawled. The hot air
folded in waves over the land, and the mountains shivered in the

heat. Al drove listlessly, hunched back in the seat, his hand hooked easily over the cross-bar of the steering wheel; his gray hat, peaked and pulled to an incredibly cocky shape, was low over one eye; and as he drove, he turned and spat out the side now and then.

Ma, beside him, had folded her hands in her lap, had retired into a resistance against weariness. She sat loosely, letting the movement of the car sway her body and her head. She squinted her eyes ahead at the mountains. Rose of Sharon was braced against the movement of the car, her feet pushed tight against the floor, and her right elbow hooked over the door. And her plump face was tight against the movement, and her head jiggled sharply because her neck muscles were tight. She tried to arch her whole body as a rigid container to preserve her fetus from shock. She turned her head toward her mother.

"Ma," she said. Ma's eyes lighted up and she drew her attention toward Rose of Sharon. Her eyes went over the tight, tired, plump face, and she smiled. "Ma," the girl said, "when we get there, all you gonna pick fruit an' kinda live in the country, ain't you?"

Ma smiled a little satirically. "We ain't there yet," she said. "We don't know what it's like. We got to see."

"Me an' Connie don't want to live in the country no more," the girl said. "We got it all planned up what we gonna do."

For a moment a little worry came on Ma's face. "Ain't you gonna stay with us—with the family?" she asked.

"Well, we talked all about it, me an' Connie. Ma, we wanna live in a town." She went on excitedly, "Connie gonna get a job in a store or maybe a fact'ry. An' he's gonna study at home, maybe radio, so he can git to be a expert an' maybe later have his own store. An' we'll go to pitchers whenever. An' Connie says I'm gonna have a *doctor* when the baby's born; an' he says we'll see how times is, an' maybe I'll go to a hospiddle. An' we'll have a car, little car. An' after he studies at night, why—it'll be nice, an' he tore a page outa *Western Love Stories*, an' he's gonna send off for a course, 'cause it don't cost nothin' to send off. Says right on that clipping. I seen it. An', why—they even get you a job when you take that course—radios, it is—nice clean work, and a future. An' we'll live in town an' go to pitchers whenever, an'—well, I'm gonna have a 'lectric iron, an' the baby'll have all new stuff. Connie says all new stuff—white an'— Well, you seen in the catalogue all the stuff they got for a baby. Maybe right at first while Connie's studyin' at home it won't be so easy, but—well, when the baby comes, maybe he'll be all done studyin' an' we'll have a place, little bit of a place. We don't want nothin' fancy, but we want it nice for the baby—" Her face glowed with excitement. "An' I thought—well, I thought maybe we could all go in town, an' when Connie gets his store—maybe Al could work for him."

Ma's eyes had never left the flushing face. Ma watched the structure grow and followed it. "We don' want you to go 'way from us," she said. "It ain't good for folks to break up."

Al snorted, "Me work for Connie? How about Connie comes a-workin' for me? He thinks he's the on'y son-of-a-bitch can study at night?"

Ma suddenly seemed to know it was all a dream. She turned her head forward again and her body relaxed, but the little smile stayed around her eyes. "I wonder how Granma feels today," she said.

Al grew tense over the wheel. A little rattle had developed in the engine. He speeded up and the rattle increased. He retarded his spark and listened, and then he speeded up for a moment and listened. The rattle increased to a metallic pounding. Al blew his horn and pulled the car to the side of the road. Ahead the truck pulled up and then backed slowly. Three cars raced by, westward, and each one blew its horn and the last driver leaned out and yelled, "Where the hell ya think you're stoppin'?"

Tom backed the truck close, and then he got out and walked to the touring car. From the back of the loaded truck heads looked down. Al retarded his spark and listened to his idling motor. Tom asked, "What's a matter, Al?"

Al speeded the motor. "Listen to her." The rattling pound was louder now.

Tom listened. "Put up your spark an' idle," he said. He opened the hood and put his head inside. "Now speed her." He listened for a moment and then closed the hood. "Well, I guess you're right, Al," he said.

"Con-rod bearing, ain't it?"

"Sounds like it," said Tom.

"I kep' plenty oil in," Al complained.

"Well, it jus' didn' get to her. Drier'n a bitch monkey now. Well, there ain't nothin' to do but tear her out. Look, I'll pull ahead an' find a flat place to stop. You come ahead slow. Don't knock the pan out of her."

Wilson asked, "Is it bad?"

"Purty bad," said Tom, and walked back to the truck and moved slowly ahead.

Al explained, "I don' know what made her go out. I give her plenty of oil." Al knew the blame was on him. He felt his failure.

Ma said, "It ain't your fault. You done ever'thing right." And then she asked a little timidly, "Is it terrible bad?"

"Well, it's hard to get at, an' we got to get a new con-rod or else some babbitt in this one." He sighed deeply. "I sure am glad Tom's here. I never fitted no bearing. Hope to Jesus Tom did."

A huge red billboard stood beside the road ahead, and it threw a great oblong shadow. Tom edged the truck off the road and across the shallow roadside ditch, and he pulled up in the shadow. He got out and waited until Al came up.

"Now go easy," he called. "Take her slow or you'll break a spring too."

Al's face went red with anger. He throttled down his motor. "Goddamn it," he yelled, "I didn't burn that bearin' out! What d'ya mean, I'll bust a spring too?"

Tom grinned. "Keep all four feet on the groun'," he said. "I didn' mean nothin'. Jus' take her easy over this ditch."

Al grumbled as he inched the touring car down, and up the other side. "Don't you go givin' nobody no idear I burned out that bearin'." The engine clattered loudly now. Al pulled into the shade and shut down the motor.

Tom lifted the hood and braced it. "Can't even start on her before she cools off," he said. The family piled down from the cars and clustered about the touring car.

Pa asked, "How bad?" And he squatted on his hams.

Tom turned to Al. "Ever fitted one?"

"No," said Al, "I never. 'Course I had pans off."

Tom said, "Well, we got to tear the pan off an' get the rod out, an' we got to get a new part an' hone her an' shim her an' fit her. Good day's job. Got to go back to that las' place for a part, Santa Rosa. Albuquerque's about seventy-five miles on— Oh, Jesus, to-morra's Sunday! We can't get nothin' tomorra." The family stood silently. Ruthie crept close and peered into the open hood, hoping to see the broken part. Tom went on softly, "Tomorra's Sunday. Monday we'll get the thing an' prob'ly won't get her fitted 'fore Tuesday. We ain't got the tools to make it easy. Gonna be a job."

The shadow of a buzzard slid across the earth, and the family all looked up at the sailing black bird.

Pa said, "What I'm scairt of is we'll run outa money so we can't git there 't all. Here's all us eatin', an' got to buy gas an' oil. 'F we run outa money, I don' know what we gonna do."

Wilson said, "Seems like it's my fault. This here goddamn wreck's give me trouble right along. You folks been nice to us. Now you jus' pack up an' get along. Me an' Sairy'll stay, an' we'll figger some way. We don't aim to put you folks out none."

Pa said slowly, "We ain't a-gonna do it. No, sir. We got almost a kin bond. Grampa, he died in your tent."

Sairy said tiredly, "We been nothin' but trouble, nothin' but trouble."

Tom slowly made a cigarette, and inspected it and lighted it. He took off his ruined cap and wiped his forehead. "I got an idear," he said. "Maybe nobody gonna like it, but here she is: The nearer to California our folks get, the quicker they's gonna be money rollin' in. Now this here car'll go twicet as fast as that truck. Now here's my idear. You take out some a that stuff in the truck, an' then all you folks but me an' the preacher get in an' move on. Me an' Casy'll stop here an' fix this here car an' then we drive on, day an' night, an' we'll catch up, or if we don't meet on the road, you'll be a-workin' anyways. An' if you break down, why, jus' camp 'longside the road till we come. You can't be no worse off, an' if you get through, why, you'll all be a-workin', an' stuff'll be easy. Casy can give me a lif' with this here car, an' we'll come a-sailin'."

The gathered family considered it. Uncle John dropped to his hams beside Pa.

Al said, "Won't ya need me to give ya a han' with that con-rod?"

"You said your own se'f you never fixed one."

"That's right," Al agreed. "All ya got to have is a strong back. Maybe the preacher don' wanta stay."

"Well—whoever—I don' care," said Tom.

Pa scratched the dry earth with his forefinger. "I kind a got a notion Tom's right," he said. "It ain't goin' ta do no good all of us stayin' here. We can get fifty, a hunderd miles on 'fore dark."

Ma said worriedly, "How you gonna find us?"

"We'll be on the same road," said Tom. "Sixty-six right on through. Come to a place name' Bakersfiel'. Seen it on the map I got. You go straight on there."

"Yeah, but when we get to California an' spread out sideways off this road—?"

"Don't you worry," Tom reassured her. "We're gonna find ya. California ain't the whole world."

"Looks like an awful big place on the map," said Ma.

Pa appealed for advice. "John, you see any reason why not?"

"No," said John.

"Mr. Wilson, it's your car. You got any objections if my boy fixes her an' brings her on?"

"I don' see none," said Wilson. "Seems like you folks done ev-er'thing for us awready. Don' see why I cain't give your boy a han'."

"You can be workin', layin' in a little money, if we don' ketch up with ya," said Tom. "An' s'pose we all jus' lay aroun' here. There ain't no water here, an' we can't move this here car. But s'pose you all git out there an' git to work. Why, you'd have money, an' maybe a house to live in. How about it, Casy? Wanna stay with me an' gimme a lif'?"

"I wanna do what's bes' for you folks," said Casy. "You took me in, carried me along. I'll do whatever."

"Well, you'll lay on your back an' get grease in your face if you stay here," Tom said.

"Suits me awright."

Pa said, "Well, if that's the way she's gonna go, we better get a-shovin'. We can maybe squeeze in a hunderd miles 'fore we stop."

Ma stepped in front of him. "I ain't a-gonna go."

"What you mean, you ain't gonna go? You got to go. You got to look after the family." Pa was amazed at the revolt.

Ma stepped to the touring car and reached in on the floor of the back seat. She brought out a jack handle and balanced it in her hand easily. "I ain't a-gonna go," she said.

"I tell you, you got to go. We made up our mind."

And now Ma's mouth set hard. She said softly, "On'y way you gonna get me to go is whup me." She moved the jack handle gently again. "An' I'll shame you, Pa. I won't take no whuppin', cryin' an' a-beggin'. I'll light into you. An' you ain't so sure you can whup me anyways. An' if ya do get me, I swear to God I'll wait till you got your back turned, or you're settin' down, an' I'll knock you belly-up with a bucket. I swear to Holy Jesus' sake I will."

Pa looked helplessly about the group. "She sassy," he said. "I never seen her so sassy." Ruthie giggled shrilly.

The jack handle flicked hungrily back and forth in Ma's hand. "Come on," said Ma. "You made up your mind. Come on an' whup me. Jus' try it. But I ain't a-goin'; or if I do, you ain't never gonna get no sleep, 'cause I'll wait an' I'll wait, an' jus' the minute you take sleep in your eyes, I'll slap ya with a stick a stove wood."

"So goddamn sassy," Pa murmured. "An' she ain't young, neither."

The whole group watched the revolt. They watched Pa, waiting for him to break into fury. They watched his lax hands to see the fists form. And Pa's anger did not rise, and his hands hung limply at his sides. And in a moment the group knew that Ma had won. And Ma knew it too.

Tom said, "Ma, what's eatin' on you? What ya wanna do this-a-way for? What's the matter'th you anyways? You gone johnrabbit on us?"

Ma's face softened, but her eyes were still fierce. "You done this 'thout thinkin' much," Ma said. "What we got lef' in the worl'? Nothin' but us. Nothin' but the folks. We come out an' Grampa, he reached for the shovel-shelf right off. An' now, right off, you wanna bust up the folks——"

Tom cried, "Ma, we was gonna catch up with ya. We wasn't gonna be gone long."

Ma waved the jack handle. "S'pose we was camped, and you went on by. S'pose we got on through, how'd we know where to leave the word, an' how'd you know where to ask?" She said, "We got a bitter road. Granma's sick. She's up there on the truck a-pawin' for a shovel herself. She's jus' tar'd out. We got a long bitter road ahead."

Uncle John said, "But we could be makin' some money. We could have a little bit saved up, come time the other folks got there."

The eyes of the whole family shifted back to Ma. She was the power. She had taken control. "The money we'd make wouldn't do no good," she said. "All we got is the family unbroke. Like a bunch a cows, when the lobos are ranging, stick all together. I ain't scared while we're all here, all that's alive, but I ain't gonna see us bust up. The Wilsons here is with us, an' the preacher is with us. I can't say nothin' if they want to go, but I'm a-goin' cat-wild with this here piece a bar-arn if my own folks busts up." Her tone was cold and final.

Tom said soothingly, "Ma, we can't all camp here. Ain't no water here. Ain't even much shade here. Granma, she needs shade."

"All right," said Ma. "We'll go along. We'll stop first place they's water an' shade. An'—the truck'll come back an' take you in town to get your part, an' it'll bring you back. You ain't goin' walkin' along in the sun, an' I ain't havin' you out all alone, so if you get picked up there ain't nobody of your folks to he'p ya."

Tom drew his lips over his teeth and then snapped them open. He spread his hands helplessly and let them flop against his sides. "Pa," he said, "if you was to rush her one side an' me the other an' then the res' pile on, an' Granma jump down on top, maybe we can get Ma 'thout more'n two-three of us gets killed with that there jack handle. But if you ain't willin' to get your head smashed, I guess Ma's went an' filled her flush. Jesus Christ, one person with their mind made up can shove a lot of folks aroun'! You win, Ma. Put away that jack handle 'fore you hurt somebody."

Ma looked in astonishment at the bar of iron. Her hand trembled. She dropped her weapon on the ground, and Tom, with elaborate care, picked it up and put it back in the car. He said, "Pa, you jus' got set back on your heels. Al, you drive the folks on an' get 'em camped, an' then you bring the truck back here. Me an' the preacher'll get the pan off. Then, if we can make it, we'll run in Santa Rosa an' try an' get a con-rod. Maybe we can, seein' it's Sat'dy night. Get jumpin' now so we can go. Lemme have the monkey wrench an' pliers outa the truck." He reached under the car and felt the greasy pan. "Oh, yeah, lemme have a can, that ol' bucket, to catch the oil. Got to save that." Al handed over the bucket and Tom set it under the car and loosened the oil cap with a pair of pliers. The black oil flowed down his arm while he unscrewed the cap with his fingers, and then the black stream ran silently into the bucket. Al had loaded the family on the truck by the time the bucket was half full. Tom, his face already smudged with oil, looked out between the wheels. "Get back fast!" he called. And he was loosening the pan bolts as the truck moved gently across the shallow ditch and crawled away. Tom turned each bolt a single turn, loosening them evenly to spare the gasket.

The preacher knelt beside the wheels. "What can I do?"

"Nothin', not right now. Soon's the oil's out an' I get these here bolts loose, you can he'p me drop the pan off." He squirmed away under the car, loosening the bolts with a wrench and turning them out with his fingers. He left the bolts on each end loosely threaded to keep the pan from dropping. "Ground's still hot under here," Tom said. And then, "Say, Casy, you been awful goddamn quiet the las' few days. Why, Jesus! When I first come up with you, you was makin' a speech ever' half-hour or so. An' here you ain't said ten words the las' couple days. What's a matter—gettin' sour?"

Casy was stretched out on his stomach, looking under the car. His chin, bristly with sparse whiskers, rested on the back of one hand. His hat was pushed back so that it covered the back of his neck. "I done enough talkin' when I was a preacher to las' the rest a my life," he said.

"Yeah, but you done some talkin' sence, too."

"I'm all worried up," Casy said. "I didn' even know it when I was a-preachin' aroun', but I was doin' consid'able tom-cattin' aroun'. If I ain't gonna preach no more, I got to get married. Why, Tommy, I'm a-lustin' after the flesh."

"Me too," said Tom. "Say, the day I come outa McAlester I was smokin'. I run me down a girl, a hoor girl, like she was a rabbit. I won't tell ya what happened. I wouldn' tell nobody what happened."

Casy laughed. "I know what happened. I went a-fastin' into the wilderness one time, an' when I come out the same damn thing happened to me."

"Hell it did!" said Tom. "Well, I saved my money anyway, an' I give that girl a run. Thought I was nuts. I should a paid her, but I on'y got five bucks to my name. She said she didn' want no money. Here, roll in under here an' grab a-holt. I'll tap her loose. Then you turn out that bolt an' I turn out my end, an' we let her down easy. Careful that gasket. See, she comes off in one piece. They's on'y four cylinders to these here ol' Dodges. I took one down one time. Got main bearings big as a cantaloupe. Now—let her down—hold it. Reach up an' pull down that gasket where it's stuck—easy now. There!" The greasy pan lay on the ground between them, and a little oil still lay in the wells. Tom reached into one of the front wells and picked out some broken pieces of babbitt. "There she is," he said. He turned the babbitt in his fingers. "Shaft's up. Look in back an' get the crank. Turn her over till I tell you."

Casy got to his feet and found the crank and fitted it. "Ready?"

"Ready—now easy—little more—little more—right there."

Casy kneeled down and looked under again. Tom rattled the connecting-rod bearing against the shaft. "There she is."

"What ya s'pose done it?" Casy asked.

"Oh, hell, I don' know! This buggy been on the road thirteen years. Says sixty-thousand miles on the speedometer. That means a hunderd an' sixty, an' God knows how many times they turned the numbers back. Gets hot—maybe somebody let the oil get low—jus' went out." He pulled the cotter-pins and put his wrench on a bearing bolt. He strained and the wrench slipped. A long gash appeared on the back of his hand. Tom looked at it—the blood flowed evenly from the wound and met the oil and dripped into the pan.

"That's too bad," Casy said. "Want I should do that an' you wrap up your han'?"

"Hell, no! I never fixed no car in my life 'thout cuttin' myself. Now it's done I don't have to worry no more." He fitted the wrench again. "Wisht I had a crescent wrench," he said, and he hammered the wrench with the butt of his hand until the bolts loosened. He took them out and laid them with the pan bolts in the pan, and the cotter-pins with them. He loosened the bearing bolts and pulled out the piston. He put piston and connecting-rod in the pan. "There, by God!" He squirmed free from under the car and pulled the pan out with him. He wiped his hand on a piece of gunny sacking and inspected the cut. "Bleedin' like a son-of-a-bitch," he said. "Well, I can stop that." He urinated on the ground, picked up a handful of the resulting mud, and plastered it over the wound. Only for a moment did the blood ooze out, and then it stopped. "Bes' damn thing in the worl' to stop bleedin'," he said.

"Han'ful a spider web'll do it too," said Casy.

"I know, but there ain't no spider web, an' you can always get piss." Tom sat on the running board and inspected the broken bearing. "Now if we can on'y find a '25 Dodge an' get a used con-rod an' some shims, maybe we'll make her all right. Al must a gone a hell of a long ways."

The shadow of the billboard was sixty feet out by now. The afternoon lengthened away. Casy sat down on the running board and looked westward. "We gonna be in high mountains pretty soon," he said, and he was silent for a few moments. Then, "Tom!"

"Yeah?"

"Tom, I been watchin' the cars on the road, them we passed an' them that passed us. I been keepin' track."

"Track a what?"

"Tom, they's hunderds a families like us all a-goin' west. I watched. There ain't none of 'em goin' east—hunderds of 'em. Did you notice that?"

"Yeah, I noticed."

"Why—it's like—it's like they was runnin' away from soldiers. It's like a whole country is movin'."

"Yeah," Tom said. "They is a whole country movin'. We're movin' too."

"Well—s'pose all these here folks an' ever'body—s'pose they can't get no jobs out there?"

"Goddamn it!" Tom cried. "How'd I know? I'm jus' puttin' one foot in front a the other. I done it at Mac for four years, jus' marchin' in cell an' out cell an' in mess an' out mess. Jesus Christ, I thought it'd be somepin different when I come out! Couldn't think a nothin' in there, else you go stir happy, an' now can't think a nothin'." He turned on Casy. "This here bearing went out. We didn' know it was goin', so we didn' worry none. Now she's out an' we'll fix her. An' by Christ that goes for the rest of it! I ain't gonna worry. I can't do it. This here little piece of iron an' babbitt. See it? Ya see it? Well, that's the only goddamn thing in the world I got on my mind. I wonder where the hell Al is."

Casy said, "Now look, Tom. Oh, what the hell! So goddamn hard to say anything."

Tom lifted the mud pack from his hand and threw it on the ground. The edge of the wound was lined with dirt. He glanced over to the preacher. "You're fixin' to make a speech," Tom said. "Well, go ahead. I like speeches. Warden used to make speeches all the time. Didn't do us no harm an' he got a hell of a bang out of it. What you tryin' to roll out?"

Casy picked the backs of his long knotty fingers. "They's stuff goin' on and they's folks doin' things. Them people layin' one foot down in front of the other, like you says, they ain't thinkin' where they're goin', like you says—but they're all layin' 'em down the same direction, jus' the same. An' if ya listen, you'll hear a movin', an' a sneakin', an' a rustlin', an'—an' a res'lessness. They's stuff goin' on that the folks doin' it don't know nothin' about—yet. They's gonna come somepin outa all these folks goin' wes'—outa all their farms lef' lonely. They's comin' a thing that's gonna change the whole country."

Tom said, "I'm still layin' my dogs down one at a time."

"Yeah, but when a fence comes up at ya, ya gonna climb that fence."

"I climb fences when I got fences to climb," said Tom.

Casy sighed. "It's the bes' way. I gotta agree. But they's different kinda folks. They's folks like me that climbs fences that ain't even strang up yet—an' can't he'p it."

"Ain't that Al a-comin'?" Tom asked.

"Yeah. Looks like."

Tom stood up and wrapped the connecting-rod and both halves of the bearing in the piece of sack. "Wanta make sure I get the same," he said.

The truck pulled alongside the road and Al leaned out the window.

Tom said, "You was a hell of a long time. How far'd you go?"

Al sighed. "Got the rod out?"

"Yeah." Tom held up the sack. "Babbitt jus' broke down."

"Well, it wasn't no fault of mine," said Al.

"No. Where'd you take the folks?"

"We had a mess," Al said. "Granma got to bellerin', an' that set Rosasharn off an' she bellered some. Got her head under a mattress an' bellered. But Granma, she was just layin' back her jaw an' bayin' like a moonlight houn' dog. Seems like Granma ain't got no sense no more. Like a little baby. Don' speak to nobody, don' seem to reco'nize nobody. Jus' talks on like she's talkin' to Grampa."

"Where'd ya leave 'em?" Tom insisted.

"Well, we come to a camp. Got shade an' got water in pipes. Costs half a dollar a day to stay there. But ever'body's so goddamn tired an' wore out an' mis'able, they stayed there. Ma says they got to 'cause Granma's so tired an' wore out. Got Wilson's tent up an' got our tarp for a tent. I think Granma gone nuts."

Tom looked toward the lowering sun. "Casy," he said, "somebody got to stay with this car or she'll get stripped. You jus' as soon?"

"Sure. I'll stay."

Al took a paper bag from the seat. "This here's some bread an' meat Ma sent, an' I got a jug a water here."

"She don't forget nobody," said Casy.

Tom got in beside Al. "Look," he said. "We'll get back jus' as soon's we can. But we can't tell how long."

"I'll be here."

"Awright. Don't make no speeches to yourself. Get goin', Al."
The truck moved off in the late afternoon. "He's a nice fella," Tom
said. "He thinks about stuff all the time."

"Well, hell—if you been a preacher, I guess you got to. Pa'sall
mad about it costs fifty cents jus' to camp under a tree. He can't see
that noways. Settin' a-cussin'. Says nex' thing they'll sell ya a little
tank a air. But Ma says they gotta be near shade an' water 'cause a
Granma." The truck rattled along the highway, and now that it was
unloaded, every part of it rattled and clashed. The side-board of the
bed, the cut body. It rode hard and light. Al put it up to thirty-eight
miles an hour and the engine clattered heavily and a blue smoke of
burning oil drifted up through the floor boards.

"Cut her down some," Tom said. "You gonna burn her right
down to the hub caps. What's eatin' on Granma?"

"I don' know. 'Member the las' couple days she's been airy-nary,
sayin' nothin' to nobody? Well, she's yellin' an' talkin' plenty now,
on'y she's talkin' to Grampa. Yellin' at him. Kinda scary, too. You
can almos' see 'im a-settin' there grinnin' at her the way he always
done, a-fingerin' hisself an' grinnin'. Seems like she sees him a-settin'
there, too. She's jus' givin' him hell. Say, Pa, he give me twenty
dollars to hand you. He don' know how much you gonna need. Ever
see Ma stand up to 'im like she done today?"

"Not I remember. I sure did pick a nice time to get paroled. I
figgered I was gonna lay aroun' an' get up late an' eat a lot when I
come home. I was goin' out an' dance, an' I was gonna go tom-
cattin'—an' here I ain't had time to do none of them things."

Al said, "I forgot. Ma give me a lot a stuff to tell you. She says
don't drink nothin', an' don' get in no arguments, an' don't fight
nobody. 'Cause she says she's scairt you'll get sent back."

"She got plenty to get worked up about 'thout me givin' her no
trouble," said Tom.

"Well, we could get a couple beers, can't we? I'm jus' a-ravin' for
a beer."

"I dunno," said Tom. "Pa'd crap a litter of lizards if we buy
beers."

"Well, look, Tom. I got six dollars. You an' me could get a couple
pints an' go down the line. Nobody don't know I got that six bucks.
Christ, we could have a hell of a time for ourselves."

"Keep ya jack," Tom said. "When we get out to the coast you
an' me'll take her an' we'll raise hell. Maybe when we're workin'—"

He turned in the seat. "I didn' think you was a fella to go down the line. I figgered you was talkin' 'em out of it."

"Well, hell, I don't know nobody here. If I'm gonna ride aroun' much, I'm gonna get married. I'm gonna have me a hell of a time when we get to California."

"Hope so," said Tom.

"You ain't sure a nothin' no more."

"No, I ain't sure a nothin'."

"When ya killed that fella—did—did ya ever dream about it or anything? Did it worry ya?"

"No."

"Well, didn' ya never think about it?"

"Sure. I was sorry 'cause he was dead."

"Ya didn't take no blame to yourself?"

"No. I done my time, an' I done my own time."

"Was it—awful bad—there?"

Tom said nervously, "Look, Al. I done my time, an' now it's done. I don' wanna do it over an' over. There's the river up ahead, an' there's the town. Let's jus' try an' get a con-rod an' the hell with the res' of it."

"Ma's awful partial to you," said Al. "She mourned when you was gone. Done it all to herself. Kinda cryin' down inside of her throat. We could tell what she was thinkin' about, though."

Tom pulled his cap down low over his eyes. "Now look here, Al. S'pose we talk 'bout some other stuff."

"I was jus' tellin' ya what Ma done."

"I know—I know. But—I ruther not. I ruther jus'—lay one foot down in front a the other."

Al relapsed into an insulted silence. "I was jus' tryin' to tell ya," he said, after a moment.

Tom looked at him, and Al kept his eyes straight ahead. The lightened truck bounced noisily along. Tom's long lips drew up from his teeth and he laughed softly. "I know you was, Al. Maybe I'm kinda stir-nuts. I'll tell ya about it sometime maybe. Ya see, it's jus' somepin you wanta know. Kinda interestin'. But I got a kind a funny idear the bes' thing'd be if I forget about it for a while. Maybe in a little while it won't be that way. Right now when I think about it my guts gets all droopy an' nasty feelin'. Look here, Al, I'll tell ya one thing—the jail house is jus' a kind a way a drivin' a guy slowly nuts. See? An' they go nuts, an' you see 'em an' hear 'em, an' pretty soon you don' know if you're nuts or not. When they get to screamin' in the night sometimes you think it's you doin' the screamin'—an' sometimes it is."

Al said, "Oh! I won't talk about it no more, Tom."

"Thirty days is all right," Tom said. "An' a hunderd an' eighty days is all right. But over a year—I dunno. There's somepin about it that ain't like nothin' else in the worl'. Somepin screwy about it, somepin screwy about the whole idear a lockin' people up. Oh, the hell with it! I don' wanna talk about it. Look a the sun a-flashin' on them windas."

The truck drove to the service-station belt, and there on the right-hand side of the road was a wrecking yard—an acre lot surrounded by a high barbed-wire fence, a corrugated iron shed in front with used tires piled up by the doors, and price-marked. Behind the shed there was a little shack built of scrap, scrap lumber and pieces of tin. The windows were windshields built into the walls. In the grassy lot the wrecks lay, cars with twisted, stove-in noses, wounded cars lying on their sides with the wheels gone. Engines rusting on the ground and against the shed. A great pile of junk; fenders and truck sides, wheels and axles; over the whole lot a spirit of decay, of mold and rust; twisted iron, half-gutted engines, a mass of derelicts.

Al drove the truck up on the oily ground in front of the shed. Tom got out and looked into the dark doorway. "Don't see nobody," he said, and he called, "Anybody here?"

"Jesus, I hope they got a '25 Dodge."

Behind the shed a door banged. A specter of a man came through the dark shed. Thin, dirty, oily skin tight against stringy muscles. One eye was gone, and the raw, uncovered socket squirmed with eye muscles when his good eye moved. His jeans and shirt were thick and shiny with old grease, and his hands cracked and lined and cut. His heavy, pouting underlip hung out sullenly.

Tom asked, "You the boss?"

The one eye glared. "I work for the boss," he said sullenly. "Whatcha want?"

"Got a wrecked '25 Dodge? We need a con-rod."

"I don't know. If the boss was here he could tell ya—but he ain't here. He's went home."

"Can we look an' see?"

The man blew his nose into the palm of his hand and wiped his hand on his trousers. "You from hereabouts?"

"Come from east—goin' west."

"Look aroun' then. Burn the goddamn place down, for all I care."

"Looks like you don't love your boss none."

The man shambled close, his one eye flaring. "I hate 'im," he said softly. "I hate the son-of-a-bitch! Gone home now. Gone home to his house." The words fell stumbling out. "He got a way—he got a way a-pickin' a fella an' a-tearin' a fella. He—the son-of-a-bitch. Got a girl nineteen, purty. Says to me, 'How'd ya like ta marry her?' Says that right to me. An' tonight—says, 'They's a dance; how'd ya like to go?' Me, he says it to me!" Tears formed in his eye and tears dripped from the corner of the red eye socket. "Some day, by God —some day I'm gonna have a pipe wrench in my pocket. When he says them things he looks at my eye. An' I'm gonna, I'm gonna jus' take his head right down off his neck with that wrench, little piece at a time." He panted with his fury. "Little piece at a time, right down off'n his neck."

The sun disappeared behind the mountains. Al looked into the lot at the wrecked cars. "Over there, look, Tom! That there looks like a '25 or '26."

Tom turned to the one-eyed man. "Mind if we look?"

"Hell, no! Take any goddamn thing you want."

They walked, threading their way among the dead automobiles, to a rusting sedan, resting on flat tires.

"Sure it's a '25," Al cried. "Can we yank off the pan, mister?"

Tom kneeled down and looked under the car. "Pan's off awready. One rod's been took. Looks like one gone." He wriggled under the car. "Get a crank an' turn her over, Al." He worked the rod against the shaft. "Purty much froze with grease." Al turned the crank slowly. "Easy," Tom called. He picked a splinter of wood from the ground and scraped the cake of grease from the bearing and the bearing bolts.

"How is she for tight?" Al asked.

"Well, she's a little loose, but not bad."

"Well, how is she for wore?"

"Got plenty shim. Ain't been all took up. Yeah, she's O.K. Turn her over easy now. Get her down, easy—there! Run over the truck an' get some tools."

The one-eyed man said, "I'll get you a box a tools." He shuffled off among the rusty cars and in a moment he came back with a tin box of tools. Tom dug out a socket wrench and handed it to Al.

"You take her off. Don' lose no shims an' don' let the bolts get away, an' keep track a the cotter-pins. Hurry up. The light's gettin' dim."

Al crawled under the car. "We oughta get us a set a socket wrenches," he called. "Can't get in no place with a monkey wrench."

"Yell out if you want a hand," Tom said.

The one-eyed man stood helplessly by. "I'll help ya if ya want," he said. "Know what that son-of-a-bitch done? He come by an' he got on white pants. An' he says, 'Come on, le's go out to my yacht.' By God, I'll whang him some day!" He breathed heavily. "I ain't been out with a woman sence I los' my eye. An' he says stuff like that." And big tears cut channels in the dirt beside his nose.

Tom said impatiently, "Whyn't you roll on? Got no guards to keep ya here."

"Yeah, that's easy to say. Ain't so easy to get a job—not fora one-eye' man."

Tom turned on him. "Now look-a-here, fella. You got that eye wide open. An' ya dirty, ya stink. Ya jus' askin' for it. Ya like it. Lets ya feel sorry for yaself. 'Course ya can't get no woman with that empty eye flappin' aroun'. Put somepin over it an' wash ya face. You ain't hittin' nobody with no pipe wrench."

"I tell ya, a one-eye' fella got a hard row," the man said. "Can't see stuff the way other fellas can. Can't see how far off a thing is. Ever'thing's jus' flat."

Tom said, "Ya full a shit. Why, I knowed a one-legged whore one time. Think she was takin' two-bits in a alley? No, by God! She's gettin' half a dollar extra. She says, 'How many one-legged women you slep' with? None!' she says. 'O.K.,' she says. 'You got somepin pretty special here, an' it's gonna cos' ya half a buck extry.' An' by God, she was gettin' 'em, too, an' the fellas comin' out thinkin' they're pretty lucky. She says she's good luck. An' I knowed a hump-back in—in a place I was. Make his whole livin' lettin' folks rub his hump for luck. Jesus Christ, an' all you got is one eye gone."

The man said stumblingly, "Well, Jesus, ya see somebody edge away from ya, an' it gets into ya."

"Cover it up then, goddamn it. Ya stickin' it out like a cow's ass. Ya like to feel sorry for yaself. There ain't nothin' the matter with you. Buy yaself some white pants. Ya gettin' drunk an' cryin' in ya bed, I bet. Need any help, Al?"

"No," said Al. "I got this here bearin' loose. Jus' tryin' to work the piston down."

"Don' bang yaself," said Tom.

The one-eyed man said softly, "Think—somebody'd like—me?"

"Why, sure," said Tom. "Tell 'em ya dong's growed sence you los' your eye."

"Where at you fellas goin'?"

"California. Whole family. Gonna get work out there."

"Well, ya think a fella like me could get work? Black patch on my eye?"

"Why not? You ain't no cripple."

"Well—could I catch a ride with you fellas?"

"Christ, no. We're so goddamn full now we can't move. You get out some other way. Fix up one a these here wrecks an' go out by yaself."

"Maybe I will, by God," said the one-eyed man.

There was a clash of metal. "I got her," Al called.

"Well, bring her out, let's look at her." Al handed him the piston and connecting-rod and the lower half of the bearing.

Tom wiped the babbitt surface and sighted along it sideways. "Looks O.K. to me," he said. "Say, by God, if we had a light we could get this here in tonight."

"Say, Tom," Al said, "I been thinkin'. We got no ring clamps. Gonna be a job gettin' them rings in, specially underneath."

Tom said, "Ya know, a fella tol' me one time ya wrap some fine brass wire aroun' the ring to hol' her."

"Yeah, but how ya gonna get the wire off?"

"Ya don't get her off. She melts off an' don't hurt nothin'."

"Copper wire'd be better."

"It ain't strong enough," said Tom. He turned to the one-eyed man. "Got any fine brass wire?"

"I dunno. I think they's a spool somewheres. Where d'ya think a fella could get one a them black patches one-eye' fellas wear?"

"I don' know," said Tom. "Le's see if you can fin' that wire."

In the iron shed they dug through boxes until they found the spool. Tom set the rod in a vise and carefully wrapped the wire around the piston rings, forcing them deep into their slots, and where the wire was twisted he hammered it flat; and then he turned the piston and tapped the wire all around until it cleared the piston wall. He ran his finger up and down to make sure that the rings and wire were flush with the wall. It was getting dark in the shed. The one-eyed man brought a flashlight and shone its beam on the work.

"There she is!" said Tom. "Say—what'll ya take for that light?"

"Well, it ain't much good. Got fifteen cents' a new batteries. You can have her for—oh, thirty-five cents."

"O.K. An' what we owe ya for this here con-rod an' piston?"

The one-eyed man rubbed his forehead with a knuckle, and a line of dirt peeled off. "Well, sir, I jus' dunno. If the boss was here, he'd go to a parts book an' he'd find out how much is a new one, an' while you was workin', he'd be findin' out how bad you're hung up, an' how much jack ya got, an' then he'd—well, say it's eight bucks in the part book—he'd make a price a five bucks. An' if you put up a squawk, you'd get it for three. You say it's all me, but, by God, he's a son-of-a-bitch. Figgers how bad ya need it. I seen him git more for a ring gear than he give for the whole car."

"Yeah! But how much am I gonna give you for this here?"

" 'Bout a buck, I guess."

"Awright, an' I'll give ya a quarter for this here socket wrench. Make it twice as easy." He handed over the silver. "Thank ya. An' cover up that goddamn eye."

Tom and Al got into the truck. It was deep dusk. Al started the motor and turned on the lights. "So long," Tom called. "See ya maybe in California." They turned across the highway and started back.

The one-eyed man watched them go, and then he went through the iron shed to his shack behind. It was dark inside. He felt his way to the mattress on the floor, and he stretched out and cried in his bed, and the cars whizzing by on the highway only strengthened the walls of his loneliness.

Tom said, "If you'd tol' me we'd get this here thing an' get her in tonight, I'd a said you was nuts."

"We'll get her in awright," said Al. "You got to do her, though. I'd be scared I'd get her too tight an' she'd burn out, or too loose an' she'd hammer out."

"I'll stick her in," said Tom. "If she goes out again, she goes out. I got nothin' to lose."

Al peered into the dusk. The lights made no impression on the gloom; but ahead, the eyes of a hunting cat flashed green in reflection of the lights. "You sure give that fella hell," Al said. "Sure did tell him where to lay down his dogs."

"Well, goddamn it, he was askin' for it! Jus' a pattin' hisself 'cause he got one eye, puttin' all the blame on his eye. He's a lazy, dirty son-of-a-bitch. Maybe he can snap out of it if he knowed people was wise to him."

Al said, "Tom, it wasn't nothin' I done burned out that bearin'.'"

Tom was silent for a moment, then, "I'm gonna take a fall outa you, Al. You jus' scrabblin' ass over tit, fear somebody gonna pin some blame on you. I know what's a matter. Young fella, all full a piss an' vinegar. Wanta be a hell of a guy all the time. But, goddamn it, Al, don' keep ya guard up when nobody ain't sparrin' with ya. You gonna be all right."

Al did not answer him. He looked straight ahead. The truck rattled and banged over the road. A cat whipped out from the side of the road and Al swerved to hit it, but the wheels missed and the cat leaped into the grass.

"Nearly got him," said Al. "Say, Tom. You heard Connie talkin' how he's gonna study nights? I been thinkin' maybe I'd study nights too. You know, radio or television or Diesel engines. Fella might get started that-a-way."

"Might," said Tom. "Find out how much they gonna sock ya for the lessons, first. An' figger out if you're gonna study 'em. There was fellas takin' them mail lessons in McAlester. I never knowed one of 'em that finished up. Got sick of it an' left 'em slide."

"God Awmighty, we forgot to get somepin to eat."

"Well, Ma sent down plenty; preacher couldn' eat it all. Be some lef'. I wonder how long it'll take us to get to California."

"Christ, I don' know. Jus' plug away at her."

They fell into silence, and the dark came and the stars were sharp and white.

Casy got out of the back seat of the Dodge and strolled to the side of the road when the truck pulled up. "I never expected you so soon," he said.

Tom gathered the parts in the piece of sacking on the floor. "We was lucky," he said. "Got a flashlight, too. Gonna fix her right up."

"You forgot to take your dinner," said Casy.

"I'll get it when I finish. Here, Al, pull off the road a little more an' come hol' the light for me." He went directly to the Dodge and crawled under on his back. Al crawled under on his belly and directed the beam of the flashlight. "Not in my eyes. There, put her up." Tom worked the piston up into the cylinder, twisting and turning. The brass wire caught a little on the cylinder wall. With a quick push he forced it past the rings. "Lucky she's loose or the compression'd stop her. I think she's gonna work all right."

"Hope that wire don't clog the rings," said Al.

"Well, that's why I hammered her flat. She won't roll off. I think she'll jus' melt out an' maybe give the walls a brass plate."

"Think she might score the walls?"

Tom laughed. "Jesus Christ, them walls can take it. She's drinkin' oil like a gopher hole awready. Little more ain't gonna hurt none." He worked the rod down over the shaft and tested the lower half. "She'll take some shim." He said, "Casy!"

"Yeah."

"I'm takin' up this here bearing now. Get out to that crank an' turn her over slow when I tell ya." He tightened the bolts. "Now. Over slow!" And as the angular shaft turned, he worked the bearing against it. "Too much shim," Tom said. "Hold it, Casy." He took out the bolts and removed thin shims from each side and put the bolts back. "Try her again, Casy!" And he worked the rod again. "She's a little bit loose yet. Wonder if she'd be too tight if I took out more shim. I'll try her." Again he removed the bolts and took out another pair of the thin strips. "Now try her, Casy."

"That looks good," said Al.

Tom called, "She any harder to turn, Casy?"

"No, I don't think so."

"Well, I think she's snug here. I hope to God she is. Can't hone no babbitt without tools. This here socket wrench makes her a hell of a lot easier."

Al said, "Boss a that yard gonna be purty mad when he looks for that size socket an' she ain't there."

"That's his screwin'," said Tom. "We didn' steal her." He tapped the cotter-pins in and bent the ends out. "I think that's good. Look, Casy, you hold the light while me an' Al get this here pan up."

Casy knelt down and took the flashlight. He kept the beam on the working hands as they patted the gasket gently in place and lined the holes with the pan bolts. The two men strained at the weight of the pan, caught the end bolts, and then set in the others; and when they were all engaged, Tom took them up little by little until the pan settled evenly in against the gasket, and he tightened hard against the nuts.

"I guess that's her," Tom said. He tightened the oil tap, looked carefully up at the pan, and took the light and searched the ground. "There she is. Le's get the oil back in her."

They crawled out and poured the bucket of oil back in the crank case. Tom inspected the gasket for leaks.

"O.K., Al. Turn her over," he said. Al got into the car and stepped on the starter. The motor caught with a roar. Blue smoke poured from the exhaust pipe. "Throttle down!" Tom shouted. "She'll burn oil till that wire goes. Gettin' thinner now." And as the motor turned over, he listened carefully. "Put up the spark an' let her idle." He listened again. "O.K., Al. Turn her off. I think we done her. Where's that meat now?"

"You make a darn good mechanic," Al said.

"Why not? I worked in the shop a year. We'll take her good an' slow for a couple hunderd miles. Give her a chance to work in."

They wiped their grease-covered hands on bunches of weeds and finally rubbed them on their trousers. They fell hungrily on the boiled pork and swigged the water from the bottle.

"I like to starved," said Al. "What we gonna do now, go on to the camp?"

"I dunno," said Tom. "Maybe they'd charge us a extry half-buck. Le's go on an' talk to the folks—tell 'em we're fixed. Then if they wanta sock us extry—we'll move on. The folks'll wanta know. Jesus, I'm glad Ma stopped us this afternoon. Look around with the light, Al. See we don't leave nothin'. Get that socket wrench in. We may need her again."

Al searched the ground with the flashlight. "Don't see nothin'."

"All right. I'll drive her. You bring the truck, Al." Tom started the engine. The preacher got in the car. Tom moved slowly, keeping the engine at a low speed, and Al followed in the truck. He crossed the shallow ditch, crawling in low gear. Tom said, "These here Dodges can pull a house in low gear. She's sure ratio'd down. Good thing for us—I wanta break that bearin' in easy."

On the highway the Dodge moved along slowly. The 12-volt headlights threw a short blob of yellowish light on the pavement.

Casy turned to Tom. "Funny how you fellas can fix a car. Jus' light right in an' fix her. I couldn't fix no car, not even now when I seen you do it."

"Got to grow into her when you're a little kid," Tom said. "It ain't jus' knowin'. It's more'n that. Kids now can tear down a car 'thout even thinkin' about it."

A jackrabbit got caught in the lights and he bounced along ahead, cruising easily, his great ears flopping with every jump. Now and then he tried to break off the road, but the wall of darkness thrust him back. Far ahead bright headlights appeared and bore down on them. The rabbit hesitated, faltered, then turned and bolted toward the lesser lights of the Dodge. There was a small soft jolt as he went under the wheels. The oncoming car swished by.

"We sure squashed him," said Casy.

Tom said, "Some fellas like to hit 'em. Gives me a little shakes ever' time. Car sounds O.K. Them rings must a broke loose by now. She ain't smokin' so bad."

"You done a nice job," said Casy.

A small wooden house dominated the camp ground, and on the porch of the house a gasoline lantern hissed and threw its white glare in a great circle. Half a dozen tents were pitched near the house, and cars stood beside the tents. Cooking for the night was over, but the coals of the campfires still glowed on the ground by the camping places. A group of men had gathered to the porch where the lantern burned, and their faces were strong and muscled under the harsh white light, light that threw black shadows of their hats over their foreheads and eyes and made their chins seem to jut out. They sat on the steps, and some stood on the ground, resting their elbows on the porch floor. The proprietor, a sullen lanky man, sat in a chair on the porch. He leaned back against the wall, and he drummed his fingers on his knee. Inside the house a kerosene lamp burned, but its thin light was blasted by the hissing glare of the gasoline lantern. The gathering of men surrounded the proprietor.

Tom drove the Dodge to the side of the road and parked. Al drove through the gate in the truck. "No need to take her in," Tom said. He got out and walked through the gate to the white glare of the lantern.

The proprietor dropped his front chair legs to the floor and leaned forward. "You men wanta camp here?"

"No," said Tom. "We got folks here. Hi, Pa."

Pa, seated on the bottom step, said, "Thought you was gonna be all week. Get her fixed?"

"We was pig lucky," said Tom. "Got a part 'fore dark. We can get goin' fust thing in the mornin'."

"That's a pretty nice thing," said Pa. "Ma's worried. Ya Granma's off her chump."

"Yeah, Al tol' me. She any better now?"

"Well, anyways she's a-sleepin'."

The proprietor said, "If you wanta pull in here an' camp it'll cost you four bits. Get a place to camp an' water an' wood. An' nobody won't bother you."

"What the hell," said Tom. "We can sleep in the ditch right beside the road, an' it won't cost nothin'."

The owner drummed his knee with his fingers. "Deputy sheriff comes on by in the night. Might make it tough for ya. Got a law against sleepin' out in this State. Got a law about vagrants."

"If I pay you a half a dollar I ain't a vagrant, huh?"

"That's right."

Tom's eyes glowed angrily. "Deputy sheriff ain't your brother-'n-law by any chance?"

The owner leaned forward. "No, he ain't. An' the time ain't come yet when us local folks got to take no shit from you goddamn bums, neither."

"It don't trouble you none to take our four bits. An' when'd we get to be bums? We ain't asked ya for nothin'. All of us bums, huh? Well, we ain't askin' no nickels from you for the chance to lay down an' rest."

The men on the porch were rigid, motionless, quiet. Expression was gone from their faces; and their eyes, in the shadows under their hats, moved secretly up to the face of the proprietor.

Pa growled, "Come off it, Tom."

"Sure, I'll come off it."

The circle of men were quiet, sitting on the steps, leaning on the high porch. Their eyes glittered under the harsh light of the gas lantern. Their faces were hard in the hard light, and they were very still. Only their eyes moved from speaker to speaker, and their faces were expressionless and quiet. A lamp bug slammed into the lantern and broke itself, and fell into the darkness.

In one of the tents a child wailed in complaint, and a woman's soft voice soothed it and then broke into a low song, "Jesus loves you in the night. Sleep good, sleep good. Jesus watches in the night. Sleep, oh, sleep, oh."

The lantern hissed on the porch. The owner scratched in the V of his open shirt, where a tangle of white chest hair showed. He was watchful and ringed with trouble. He watched the men in the circle, watched for some expression. And they made no move.

Tom was silent for a long time. His dark eyes looked slowly up at the proprietor. "I don't wanta make no trouble," he said. "It's a hard thing to be named a bum. I ain't afraid," he said softly. "I'll go for you an' your deputy with my mitts—here now, or jump Jesus. But there ain't no good in it."

The men stirred, changed positions, and their glittering eyes moved slowly upward to the mouth of the proprietor, and their eyes watched for his lips to move. He was reassured. He felt that he had won, but not decisively enough to charge in. "Ain't you got half a buck?" he asked.

"Yeah, I got it. But I'm gonna need it. I can't set it out jus' for sleepin'."

"Well, we all got to make a livin'."

"Yeah," Tom said. "On'y I wisht they was some way to make her 'thout takin' her away from somebody else."

The men shifted again. And Pa said, "We'll get movin' smart early. Look, mister. We paid. This here fella is part a our folks. Can't he stay? We paid."

"Half a dollar a car," said the proprietor.

"Well, he ain't got no car. Car's out in the road."

"He came in a car," said the proprietor. "Ever'body'd leave their car out there an' come in an' use my place for nothin'."

Tom said, "We'll drive along the road. Meet ya in the morning. We'll watch for ya. Al can stay an' Uncle John can come with us—" He looked at the proprietor. "That awright with you?"

He made a quick decision, with a concession in it. "If the same number stays that come an' paid—that's awright."

Tom brought out his bag of tobacco, a limp gray rag by now, with a little damp tobacco dust in the bottom of it. He made a lean cigarette and tossed the bag away. "We'll go along pretty soon," he said.

Pa spoke generally to the circle. "It's dirt hard for folks to tear up an' go. Folks like us that had our place. We ain't shif'less. Till we got tractored off, we was people with a farm."

A young thin man, with eyebrows sunburned yellow, turned his head slowly. "Croppin'?" he asked.

"Sure we was sharecroppin'. Use' ta own the place."

The young man faced forward again. "Same as us," he said.

"Lucky for us it ain't gonna las' long," said Pa. "We'll get out west an' we'll get work an' we'll get a piece a growin' land with water."

Near the edge of the porch a ragged man stood. His black coat dripped torn streamers. The knees were gone from his dungarees. His face was black with dust, and lined where sweat had washed through. He swung his head toward Pa. "You folks must have a nice little pot a money."

"No, we ain't got no money," Pa said. "But they's plenty of us to work, an' we're all good men. Get good wages out there an' we'll put 'em together. We'll make out."

The ragged man stared while Pa spoke, and then he laughed, and his laughter turned to a high whinnying giggle. The circle of faces turned to him. The giggling got out of control and turned into coughing. His eyes were red and watering when he finally controlled the spasms. "You goin' out there—oh, Christ!" The giggling started again. "You goin' out an' get—good wages—oh, Christ!" He stopped and said slyly, "Pickin' oranges maybe? Gonna pick peaches?"

Pa's tone was dignified. "We gonna take what they got. They got lots a stuff to work in." The ragged man giggled under his breath.

Tom turned irritably. "What's so goddamn funny about that?"

The ragged man shut his mouth and looked sullenly at the porch boards. "You folks all goin' to California, I bet."

"I tol' you that," said Pa. "You didn' guess nothin'."

The ragged man said slowly, "Me—I'm comin' back. I been there."

The faces turned quickly toward him. The men were rigid. The hiss of the lantern dropped to a sigh and the proprietor lowered the front chair legs to the porch, stood up, and pumped the lantern until the hiss was sharp and high again. He went back to his chair, but he did not tilt back again. The ragged man turned toward the faces. "I'm goin' back to starve. I ruther starve all over at oncet."

Pa said, "What the hell you talkin' about? I got a han'bill says they got good wages, an' little while ago I seen a thing in the paper says they need folks to pick fruit."

The ragged man turned to Pa. "You got any place to go, back home?"

"No," said Pa. "We're out. They put a tractor past the house."

"You wouldn' go back then?"

" 'Course not."

"Then I ain't gonna fret you," said the ragged man.

" 'Course you ain't gonna fret me. I got a han'bill says they need men. Don't make no sense if they don't need men. Costs money for them bills. They wouldn' put 'em out if they didn' need men."

"I don' wanna fret you."

Pa said angrily, "You done some jackassin'. You ain't gonna shut up now. My han'bill says they need men. You laugh an' say they don't. Now, which one's a liar?"

The ragged man looked down into Pa's angry eyes. He looked sorry. "Han'bill's right," he said. "They need men."

"Then why the hell you stirrin' us up laughin'?"

" 'Cause you don't know what kind a men they need."

"What you talkin' about?"

The ragged man reached a decision. "Look," he said. "How many men they say they want on your han'bill?"

"Eight hunderd, an' that's in one little place."

"Orange color han'bill?"

"Why—yes."

"Give the name a the fella—says so and so, labor contractor?"

Pa reached in his pocket and brought out the folded handbill. "That's right. How'd you know?"

"Look," said the man. "It don't make no sense. This fella wants eight hundred men. So he prints up five thousand of them things an' maybe twenty thousan' people sees 'em. An' maybe two-three thousan' folks gets movin' account a this here han'bill. Folks that's crazy with worry."

"But it don't make no sense!" Pa cried.

"Not till you see the fella that put out this here bill. You'll see him, or somebody that's workin' for him. You'll be a-campin' by a ditch, you an' fifty other famblies. An' he'll come in. He'll look in your tent an' see if you got anything lef' to eat. An' if you got nothin', he says, 'Wanna job?' An' you'll say, 'I sure do, mister. I'll sure thank you for a chance to do some work.' An' he'll say, 'I can use you.' An' you'll say, 'When do I start?' An' he'll tell you where to go, an' what time, an' then he'll go on. Maybe he needs two hunderd men, so he talks to five hunderd, an' they tell other folks, an' when you get to the place, they's a thousan' men. This here fella says, 'I'm payin' twenty cents an hour.' An' maybe half a the men walk off. But they's still five hunderd that's so goddamn hungry they'll work for nothin' but biscuits. Well, this here fella's got a contract to pick them peaches or—chop that cotton. You see now? The more fellas he can get, an' the hungrier, less he's gonna pay. An' he'll get a fella with kids if he can, 'cause—hell, I says I wasn't gonna fret ya." The circle of faces looked coldly at him. The eyes tested his words. The ragged man grew self-conscious. "I says I wasn't gonna fret ya, an' here I'm a-doin' it. You gonna go on. You ain't goin' back." The silence hung on the porch. And the light hissed, and a halo of moths swung around and around the lantern. The ragged man went on nervously, "Lemme tell ya what to do when ya meet that fella says he got work. Lemme tell ya. Ast him what he's gonna pay. Ast him to write down what he's gonna pay. Ast him that. I tell you men you're gonna get fucked if you don't."

The proprietor leaned forward in his chair, the better to see the ragged dirty man. He scratched among the gray hairs on his chest. He said coldly, "You sure you ain't one of these here troublemakers? You sure you ain't a labor faker?"

And the ragged man cried, "I swear to God I ain't!"

"They's plenty of 'em," the proprietor said. "Goin' aroun' stirrin' up trouble. Gettin' folks mad. Chiselin' in. They's plenty of 'em. Time's gonna come when we string 'em all up, all them troublemakers. We gonna run 'em outa the country. Man wants to work, O.K. If he don't—the hell with him. We ain't gonna let him stir up trouble."

The ragged man drew himself up. "I tried to tell you fellas," he said. "Somepin it took me a year to find out. Took two kids dead, took my wife dead to show me. But I can't tell you. I should of knew that. Nobody couldn't tell me, neither. I can't tell ya about them little fellas layin' in the tent with their bellies puffed out an' jus' skin on their bones, an' shiverin' an' whinin' like pups, an' me runnin' aroun' tryin' to get work—not for money, not for wages!" he shouted. "Jesus Christ, jus' for a cup a flour an' a spoon a lard. An' then the coroner come. 'Them children died a heart failure,' he said. Put it on his paper. Shiverin', they was, an' their bellies stuck out like a pig bladder."

The circle was quiet, and mouths were open a little. The men breathed shallowly, and watched.

The ragged man looked around at the circle, and then he turned and walked quickly away into the darkness. The dark swallowed him, but his dragging footsteps could be heard a long time after he had gone, footsteps along the road; and a car came by on the highway, and its lights showed the ragged man shuffling along the road, his head hanging down and his hands in the black coat pockets.

The men were uneasy. One said, "Well—gettin' late. Got to get to sleep."

The proprietor said, "Prob'ly shif'less. They's so goddamn many shif'less fellas on the road now." And then he was quiet. And he tipped his chair back against the wall again and fingered his throat.

Tom said, "Guess I'll go see Ma for a minute, an' then we'll shove along a piece." The Joad men moved away.

Pa said, "S'pose he's tellin' the truth—that fella?"

The preacher answered, "He's tellin' the truth, awright. The truth for him. He wasn't makin' nothin' up."

"How about us?" Tom demanded. "Is that the truth for us?"

"I don' know," said Casy.

"I don' know," said Pa.

They walked to the tent, tarpaulin spread over a rope. And it was dark inside, and quiet. When they came near, a grayish mass stirred near the door and arose to person height. Ma came out to meet them.

"All sleepin'," she said. "Granma finally dozed off." Then she saw it was Tom. "How'd you get here?" she demanded anxiously. "You ain't had no trouble?"

"Got her fixed," said Tom. "We're ready to go when the rest is."

"Thank the dear God for that," Ma said. "I'm just a-twitterin' to go on. Wanta get where it's rich an' green. Wanta get there quick."

Pa cleared his throat. "Fella was jus' sayin'——"

Tom grabbed his arm and yanked it. "Funny what he says," Tom said. "Says they's lots a folks on the way."

Ma peered through the darkness at them. Inside the tent Ruthie coughed and snorted in her sleep. "I washed 'em up," Ma said. "Fust water we got enough of to give 'em a goin'-over. Lef' the buckets out for you fellas to wash too. Can't keep nothin' clean on the road."

"Ever'body in?" Pa asked.

"All but Connie an' Rosasharn. They went off to sleep in the open. Says it's too warm in under cover."

Pa observed querulously, "That Rosasharn is gettin' awful scary an' nimsy-mimsy."

"It's her fust," said Ma. "Her an' Connie sets a lot a store by it. You done the same thing."

"We'll go now," Tom said. "Pull off the road a little piece ahead. Watch out for us ef we don't see you. Be off right-han' side."

"Al's stayin'?"

"Yeah. Leave Uncle John come with us. 'Night, Ma."

They walked away through the sleeping camp. In front of one tent a low fitful fire burned, and a woman watched a kettle that cooked early breakfast. The smell of the cooking beans was strong and fine.

"Like to have a plate a them," Tom said politely as they went by.

The woman smiled. "They ain't done or you'd be welcome," she said. "Come aroun' in the daybreak."

"Thank you, ma'am," Tom said. He and Casy and Uncle John walked by the porch. The proprietor still sat in his chair, and the lantern hissed and flared. He turned his head as the three went by. "Ya runnin' outa gas," Tom said.

"Well, time to close up anyways."

"No more half-bucks rollin' down the road, I guess," Tom said.

The chair legs hit the floor. "Don't you go a-sassin' me. I 'member you. You're one of these here troublemakers."

"Damn right," said Tom. "I'm bolshevisky."

"They's too damn many of you kinda guys aroun'."

Tom laughed as they went out the gate and climbed into the Dodge. He picked up a clod and threw it at the light. They heard it hit the house and saw the proprietor spring to his feet and peer into the darkness. Tom started the car and pulled into the road. And he listened closely to the motor as it turned over, listened for knocks. The road spread dimly under the weak lights of the car.

CHAPTER 17

The cars of the migrant people crawled out of the side roads onto the great cross-country highway, and then took the migrant way to the West. In the daylight they scuttled like bugs to the westward; and as the dark caught them, they clustered like bugs near to shelter and to water. And because they were lonely and perplexed, because they had all come from a place of sadness and worry and defeat, and because they were all going to a new mysterious place, they huddled together; they talked together; they shared their lives, their food, and the things they hoped for in the new country. Thus it might be that one family camped near a spring, and another camped for the spring and for company, and a third because two families had pioneered the place and found it good. And when the sun went down, perhaps twenty families and twenty cars were there.

In the evening a strange thing happened: the twenty families became one family, the children were the children of all. The loss of home became one loss, and the golden time in the West was one dream. And it might be that a sick child threw despair into the hearts of twenty families, of a hundred people; that a birth there in a tent kept a hundred people quiet and awestruck through the night and filled a hundred people with the birth-joy in the morning. A family which the night before had been lost and fearful might search its goods to find a present for a new baby. In the evening, sitting about the fires, the twenty were one. They grew to be units of the camps, units of the evenings and the nights. A guitar unwrapped from a blanket and tuned—and the songs, which were all of the people, were sung in the nights. Men sang the words, and women hummed the tunes.

Every night a world created, complete with furniture—friends made and enemies established; a world complete with braggarts and with cowards, with quiet men, with humble men, with kindly men. Every night relationships that make a world, established; and every morning the world torn down like a circus.

At first the families were timid in the building and tumbling

become part of who they are

worlds, but gradually the technique of building worlds became their technique. Then leaders emerged, then laws were made, then codes came into being. And as the worlds moved westward they were more complete and better furnished, for their builders were more experienced in building them.

The families learned what rights must be observed—the right of privacy in the tent; the right to keep the past black hidden in the heart; the right to talk and to listen; the right to refuse help or to accept, to offer help or to decline it; the right of son to court and daughter to be courted; the right of the hungry to be fed; the rights of the pregnant and the sick to transcend all other rights.

emerged FOR survival

And the families learned, although no one told them, what rights are monstrous and must be destroyed: the right to intrude upon privacy, the right to be noisy while the camp slept, the right of seduction or rape, the right of adultery and theft and murder. These rights were crushed, because the little worlds could not exist for even a night with such rights alive.

And as the worlds moved westward, rules became laws, although no one told the families. It is unlawful to shit near the camp; it is unlawful in any way to foul the drinking water; it is unlawful to eat good rich food near one who is hungry, unless he is asked to share.

And with the laws, the punishments—and there were only two —a quick and murderous fight or ostracism; and ostracism was the worst. For if one broke the laws his name and face went with him, and he had no place in any world, no matter where created.

In the worlds, social conduct became fixed and rigid, so that a man must say "Good morning" when asked for it, so that a man might have a willing girl if he stayed with her, if he fathered her children and protected them. But a man might not have one girl one night and another the next, for this would endanger the worlds.

The families moved westward, and the technique of building the worlds improved so that the people could be safe in their worlds; and the form was so fixed that a family acting in the rules knew it was safe in the rules.

There grew up government in the worlds, with leaders, with elders. A man who was wise found that his wisdom was needed in every camp; a man who was a fool could not change his folly with his world. And a kind of insurance developed in these nights. A man with food fed a hungry man, and thus insured himself against hunger. And when a baby died a pile of silver coins grew at the door flap, for a baby must be well buried, since it has had nothing else of life. An old man may be left in a potter's field, but not a baby.

A certain physical pattern is needed for the building of a world —water, a river bank, a stream, a spring, or even a faucet unguarded. And there is needed enough flat land to pitch the tents, a little brush or wood to build the fires. If there is a garbage dump not too far off, all the better; for there can be found equipment—stove tops, a curved fender to shelter the fire, and cans to cook in and to eat from.

And the worlds were built in the evening. The people, moving in from the highways, made them with their tents and their hearts and their brains.

In the morning the tents came down, the canvas was folded, the tent poles tied along the running board, the beds put in place on the cars, the pots in their places. And as the families moved westward, the technique of building up a home in the evening and tearing it down with the morning light became fixed; so that the folded tent was packed in one place, the cooking pots counted in their box. And as the cars moved westward, each member of the family grew into his proper place, grew into his duties; so that each member, old and young, had his place in the car; so that in the weary, hot evenings, when the cars pulled into the camping places, each member had his duty and went to it without instruction: children to gather wood, to carry water; men to pitch the tents and bring down the beds; women to cook the supper and to watch while the family fed. And this was done without command. The families, which had been units of which the boundaries were a house at night, a farm by day, changed their boundaries. In the long hot light, they were silent in the cars moving slowly westward; but at night they integrated with any group they found.

Thus they changed their social life—changed as in the whole universe only man can change. They were not farm men any more, but migrant men. And the thought, the planning, the long staring silence that had gone out to the fields, went now to the roads, to the distance, to the West. That man whose mind had been bound with acres lived with narrow concrete miles. And his thought and his worry were not any more with rainfall, with wind and dust, with the thrust of the crops. Eyes watched the tires, ears listened to the clattering motors, and minds struggled with oil, with gasoline, with the thinning rubber between air and road. Then a broken gear was tragedy. Then water in the evening was the yearning, and food over the fire. Then health to go on was the need and strength to go on, and spirit to go on. The wills thrust westward ahead of them, and fears that had once apprehended drought or flood now lingered with anything that might stop the westward crawling.

The camps became fixed—each a short day's journey from the last.

And on the road the panic overcame some of the families, so that they drove night and day, stopped to sleep in the cars, and drove on to the West, flying from the road, flying from movement. And these lusted so greatly to be settled that they set their faces into the West and drove toward it, forcing the clashing engines over the roads.

But most of the families changed and grew quickly into the new life. And when the sun went down——

Time to look out for a place to stop.

And—there's some tents ahead.

The car pulled off the road and stopped, and because others were there first, certain courtesies were necessary. And the man, the leader of the family, leaned from the car.

Can we pull up here an' sleep?

Why, sure, be proud to have you. What State you from?

Come all the way from Arkansas.

They's Arkansas people down that fourth tent.

That so?

And the great question, How's the water?

Well, she don't taste so good, but they's plenty.

Well, thank ya.

No thanks to me.

But the courtesies had to be. The car lumbered over the ground to the end tent, and stopped. Then down from the car the weary people climbed, and stretched stiff bodies. Then the new tent sprang up; the children went for water and the older boys cut brush or wood. The fires started and supper was put on to boil or to fry. Early comers moved over, and States were exchanged, and friends and sometimes relatives discovered.

Oklahoma, huh? What county?

Cherokee.

Why, I got folks there. Know the Allens? They's Allens all over Cherokee. Know the Willises?

Why, sure.

And a new unit was formed. The dusk came, but before the dark was down the new family was of the camp. A word had been passed with every family. They were known people—good people.

I knowed the Allens all my life. Simon Allen, ol' Simon, had trouble with his first wife. She was part Cherokee. Purty as a black colt.

Sure, an' young Simon, he married a Rudolph, didn' he? That's what I thought. They went to live in Enid an' done well—real well.

Only Allen that ever done well. Got a garage.

When the water was carried and the wood cut, the children walked shyly, cautiously among the tents. And they made elaborate acquaintanceship gestures. A boy stopped near another boy and studied a stone, picked it up, examined it closely, spat on it, and rubbed it clean and inspected it until he forced the other to demand, What you got there?

And casually, Nothin'. Jus' a rock.

Well, what you lookin' at it like that for?

Thought I seen gold in it.

How'd you know? Gold ain't gold, it's black in a rock.

Sure, ever'body knows that.

I bet it's fool's gold, an' you figgered it was gold.

That ain't so, 'cause Pa, he's foun' lots a gold an' he tol' me how to look.

How'd you like to pick up a big ol' piece a gold?

Sa-a-ay! I'd git the bigges' old son-a-bitchin' piece a candy you ever seen.

I ain't let to swear, but I do, anyways.

Me too. Le's go to the spring.

And young girls found each other and boasted shyly of their popularity and their prospects. The women worked over the fire, hurrying to get food to the stomachs of the family—pork if there was money in plenty, pork and potatoes and onions. Dutch-oven biscuits or cornbread, and plenty of gravy to go over it. Side-meat or chops and a can of boiled tea, black and bitter. Fried dough in drippings if money was slim, dough fried crisp and brown and the drippings poured over it.

Those families which were very rich or very foolish with their money ate canned beans and canned peaches and packaged bread and bakery cake; but they ate secretly, in their tents, for it would not have been good to eat such fine things openly. Even so, children eating their fried dough smelled the warming beans and were unhappy about it.

When supper was over and the dishes dipped and wiped, the dark had come, and then the men squatted down to talk.

And they talked of the land behind them. I don' know what it's coming to, they said. The country's spoilt.

It'll come back though, on'y we won't be there.

Maybe, they thought, maybe we sinned some way we didn't know about.

Fella says to me, gov'ment fella, an' he says, she's gullied up on ya. Gov'ment fella. He says, if ya plowed 'cross the contour, she won't gully. Never did have no chance to try her. An' the new super' ain't plowin' 'cross the contour. Runnin' a furrow four miles long that ain't stoppin' or goin' aroun' Jesus Christ Hisself.

And they spoke softly of their homes: They was a little coolhouse under the win'mill. Use' ta keep milk in there ta cream up, an' watermelons. Go in there midday when she was hotter'n a heifer, an' she'd be jus' as cool, as cool as you'd want. Cut open a melon in there an' she'd hurt your mouth, she was so cool. Water drippin' down from the tank.

They spoke of their tragedies: Had a brother Charley, hair as yella as corn, an' him a growed man. Played the 'cordeen nice too. He was harrowin' one day an' he went up to clear his lines. Well, a rattlesnake buzzed an' them horses bolted an' the harrow went over Charley, an' the points dug into his guts an' his stomach, an' they pulled his face off an'—God Almighty!

They spoke of the future: Wonder what it's like out there?

Well, the pitchers sure do look nice. I seen one where it's hot an' fine, an' walnut trees an' berries; an' right behind, close as a mule's ass to his withers, they's a tall up mountain covered with snow. That was a pretty thing to see.

If we can get work it'll be fine. Won't have no cold in the winter. Kids won't freeze on the way to school. I'm gonna take care my kids don't miss no more school. I can read good, but it ain't no pleasure to me like with a fella that's used to it.

And perhaps a man brought out his guitar to the front of his tent. And he sat on a box to play, and everyone in the camp moved slowly in toward him, drawn in toward him. Many men can chord a guitar, but perhaps this man was a picker. There you have something—the deep chords beating, beating, while the melody runs on the strings like little footsteps. Heavy hard fingers marching on the frets. The man played and the people moved slowly in on him until the circle was closed and tight, and then he sang "Ten-Cent Cotton and Forty-Cent Meat." And the circle sang softly with him. And he sang "Why Do You Cut Your Hair, Girls?" And the circle sang. He wailed the song, "I'm Leaving Old Texas," that eerie song that was sung before the Spaniards came, only the words were Indian then.

And now the group was welded to one thing, one unit, so that in the dark the eyes of the people were inward, and their minds played in other times, and their sadness was like rest, like sleep. He sang the "McAlester Blues" and then, to make up for it to the older people, he sang "Jesus Calls Me to His Side." The children drowsed with the music and went into the tents to sleep, and the singing came into their dreams.

And after a while the man with the guitar stood up and yawned. Good night, folks, he said.

And they murmured, Good night to you.

And each wished he could pick a guitar, because it is a gracious thing. Then the people went to their beds, and the camp was quiet. And the owls coasted overhead, and the coyotes gabbled in the distance, and into the camp skunks walked, looking for bits of food— waddling, arrogant skunks, afraid of nothing.

The night passed, and with the first streak of dawn the women came out of the tents, built up the fires, and put the coffee to boil. And the men came out and talked softly in the dawn.

When you cross the Colorado river, there's the desert, they say. Look out for the desert. See you don't get hung up. Take plenty water, case you get hung up.

I'm gonna take her at night.

Me too. She'll cut the living Jesus outa you.

The families ate quickly, and the dishes were dipped and wiped. The tents came down. There was a rush to go. And when the sun arose, the camping place was vacant, only a little litter left by the people. And the camping place was ready for a new world in a new night.

But along the highway the cars of the migrant people crawled out like bugs, and the narrow concrete miles stretched ahead.

CHAPTER 18

The Joad family moved slowly westward, up into the mountains of New Mexico, past the pinnacles and pyramids of the upland. They climbed into the high country of Arizona, and through a gap they looked down on the Painted Desert. A border guard stopped them.

"Where you going?"

"To California," said Tom.

"How long you plan to be in Arizona?"

"No longer'n we can get acrost her."

"Got any plants?"

"No plants."

"I ought to look your stuff over."

"I tell you we ain't got no plants."

The guard put a little sticker on the windshield.

"O.K. Go ahead, but you better keep movin'."

"Sure. We aim to."

They crawled up the slopes, and the low twisted trees covered the slopes. Holbrook, Joseph City, Winslow. And then the tall trees began, and the cars spouted steam and labored up the slopes. And there was Flagstaff, and that was the top of it all. Down from Flagstaff over the great plateaus, and the road disappeared in the distance ahead. The water grew scarce, water was to be bought, five cents, ten cents, fifteen cents a gallon. The sun drained the dry rocky country, and ahead were jagged broken peaks, the western wall of Arizona. And now they were in flight from the sun and the drought. They drove all night, and came to the mountains in the night. And they crawled the jagged ramparts in the night, and their dim lights flickered on the pale stone walls of the road. They passed the summit in the dark and came slowly down in the late night, through the shattered stone debris of Oatman; and when the daylight came they saw the Colorado river below them. They drove to Topock, pulled up at the bridge while a guard washed off the windshield sticker. Then across the bridge and into the broken rock wilderness. And although they were dead weary and the morning heat was growing, they stopped.

Pa called, "We're there—we're in California!" They looked dully at the broken rock glaring under the sun, and across the river the terrible ramparts of Arizona.

"We got the desert," said Tom. "We got to get to the water and rest."

The road runs parallel to the river, and it was well into the morning when the burning motors came to Needles, where the river runs swiftly among the reeds.

The Joads and Wilsons drove to the river, and they sat in the cars looking at the lovely water flowing by, and the green reeds jerking slowly in the current. There was a little encampment by the river, eleven tents near the water, and the swamp grass on the ground. And Tom leaned out of the truck window. "Mind if we stop here a piece?"

A stout woman, scrubbing clothes in a bucket, looked up. "We don't own it, mister. Stop if you want. They'll be a cop down to look you over." And she went back to her scrubbing in the sun.

The two cars pulled to a clear place on the swamp grass. The tents were passed down, the Wilson tent set up, the Joad tarpaulin stretched over its rope.

Winfield and Ruthie walked slowly down through the willows to the reedy place. Ruthie said, with soft vehemence, "California. This here's California an' we're right in it!"

Winfield broke a tule and twisted it free, and he put the white pulp in his mouth and chewed it. They walked into the water and stood quietly, the water about the calves of their legs.

"We got the desert yet," Ruthie said.

"What's the desert like?"

"I don't know. I seen pitchers once says a desert. They was bones ever'place."

"Man bones?"

"Some, I guess, but mos'ly cow bones."

"We gonna get to see them bones?"

"Maybe. I don' know. Gonna go 'crost her at night. That's what Tom said. Tom says we get the livin' Jesus burned outa us if we go in daylight."

"Feels nice't an' cool," said Winfield, and he squidged his toes in the sand of the bottom.

They heard Ma calling, "Ruthie! Winfiel'! You come back." They turned and walked slowly back through the reeds and the willows.

The other tents were quiet. For a moment, when the cars came up, a few heads had stuck out between the flaps, and then were withdrawn. Now the family tents were up and the men gathered together.

Tom said, "I'm gonna go down an' take a bath. That's what I'm gonna do—before I sleep. How's Granma sence we got her in the tent?"

"Don' know," said Pa. "Couldn' seem to wake her up." He cocked his head toward the tent. A whining, babbling voice came from under the canvas. Ma went quickly inside.

"She woke up, awright," said Noah. "Seems like all night she was a-croakin' up on the truck. She's all outa sense."

Tom said, "Hell! She's wore out. If she don't get some res' pretty soon, she ain' gonna las'. She's jes' wore out. Anybody comin' with me? I'm gonna wash, an' I'm gonna sleep in the shade—all day long." He moved away, and the other men followed him. They took off their clothes in the willows and then they walked into the water and sat down. For a long time they sat, holding themselves with heels dug into the sand, and only their heads stuck out of the water.

"Jesus, I needed this," Al said. He took a handful of sand from the bottom and scrubbed himself with it. They lay in the water and looked across at the sharp peaks called Needles, and at the white rock mountains of Arizona.

"We come through them," Pa said in wonder.

Uncle John ducked his head under the water. "Well, we're here. This here's California, an' she don't look so prosperous."

"Got the desert yet," said Tom. "An' I hear she's a son-of-a-bitch."

Noah asked, "Gonna try her tonight?"

"What ya think, Pa?" Tom asked.

"Well, I don' know. Do us good to get a little res', 'specially Granma. But other ways, I'd kinda like to get acrost her an' get settled into a job. On'y got 'bout forty dollars left. I'll feel better when we're all workin', an' a little money comin' in."

Each man sat in the water and felt the tug of the current. The preacher let his arms and hands float on the surface. The bodies were white to the neck and wrists, and burned dark brown on hands and faces, with V's of brown at the collar bones. They scratched themselves with sand.

And Noah said lazily, "Like to jus' stay here. Like to lay here forever. Never get hungry an' never get sad. Lay in the water all life long, lazy as a brood sow in the mud."

And Tom, looking at the ragged peaks across the river and the Needles downstream: "Never seen such tough mountains. This here's a murder country. This here's the bones of a country. Wonder if we'll ever get in a place where folks can live 'thout fightin' hard scrabble an' rocks. I seen pitchers of a country flat an' green, an' with little houses like Ma says, white. Ma got her heart set on a white house. Get to thinkin' they ain't no such country. I seen pitchers like that."

Pa said, "Wait till we get to California. You'll see nice country then."

"Jesus Christ, Pa! This here *is* California."

Two men dressed in jeans and sweaty blue shirts came through the willows and looked toward the naked men. They called, "How's the swimmin'?"

"Dunno," said Tom. "We ain't tried none. Sure feels good to set here, though."

"Mind if we come in an' set?"

"She ain't our river. We'll len' you a little piece of her."

The men shucked off their pants, peeled their shirts, and waded out. The dust coated their legs to the knee; their feet were pale and soft with sweat. They settled lazily into the water and washed list-lessly at their flanks. Sun-bitten, they were, a father and a boy. They grunted and groaned with the water.

Pa asked politely, "Goin' west?"

"Nope. We come from there. Goin' back home. We can't make no livin' out there."

"Where's home?" Tom asked.

"Panhandle, come from near Pampa."

Pa asked, "Can you make a livin' there?"

"Nope. But at leas' we can starve to death with folks we know. Won't have a bunch a fellas that hates us to starve with."

Pa said, "Ya know, you're the second fella talked like that. What makes 'em hate you?"

"Dunno," said the man. He cupped his hands full of water and rubbed his face, snorting and bubbling. Dusty water ran out of his hair and streaked his neck.

"I like to hear some more 'bout this," said Pa.

"Me too," Tom added. "Why these folks out west hate ya?"

The man looked sharply at Tom. "You jus' goin' wes'?"

"Jus' on our way."

"You ain't never been in California?"

"No, we ain't."

"Well, don' take my word. Go see for yourself."

"Yeah," Tom said, "but a fella kind a likes to know what he's gettin' into."

"Well, if you truly wanta know, I'm a fella that's asked questions an' give her some thought. She's a nice country. But she was stole a long time ago. You git acrost the desert an' come into the country aroun' Bakersfield. An' you never seen such purty country—all orchards an' grapes, purtiest country you ever seen. An' you'll pass lan' flat an' fine with water thirty feet down, and that lan's layin' fallow. But you can't have none of that lan'. That's a Lan' and Cattle Company. An' if they don't want ta work her, she ain't gonna git worked. You go in there an' plant you a little corn, an' you'll go to jail!"

"Good lan', you say? An' they ain't workin' her?"

"Yes, sir. Good lan' an' they ain't! Well, sir, that'll get you a little mad, but you ain't seen nothin'. People gonna have a look in their eye. They gonna look at you an' their face says, 'I don't like you, you son-of-a-bitch.' Gonna be deputy sheriffs, an' they'll push you aroun'. You camp on the roadside, an' they'll move you on. You gonna see in people's face how they hate you. An'—I'll tell you somepin. They hate you 'cause they're scairt. They know a hungry fella gonna get food even if he got to take it. They know that fallow lan's a sin an' somebody' gonna take it. What the hell! You never been called 'Okie' yet."

Tom said, "Okie? What's that?"

"Well, Okie use' ta mean you was from Oklahoma. Now it means you're a dirty son-of-a-bitch. Okie means you're scum. Don't mean nothing itself, it's the way they say it. But I can't tell you nothin'. You got to go there. I hear there's three hunderd thousan' of our people there—an' livin' like hogs, 'cause ever'thing in California is owned. They ain't nothin' left. An' them people that owns it is gonna hang on to it if they got ta kill ever'body in the worl' to do it. An' they're scairt, an' that makes 'em mad. You got to see it. You got to hear it. Purtiest goddamn country you ever seen, but they ain't nice to you, them folks. They're so scairt an' worried they ain't even nice to each other."

Tom looked down into the water, and he dug his heels into the sand. "S'pose a fella got work an' saved, couldn' he get a little lan'?"

The older man laughed and he looked at his boy, and his silent boy grinned almost in triumph. And the man said, "You ain't gonna get no steady work. Gonna scrabble for your dinner ever' day. An' you gonna do her with people lookin' mean at you. Pick cotton, an' you gonna be sure the scales ain't honest. Some of 'em is, an' some of 'em ain't. But you gonna think all the scales is crooked, an' you don' know which ones. Ain't nothin' you can do about her anyways."

Pa asked slowly, "Ain't—ain't it nice out there at all?"

"Sure, nice to look at, but you can't have none of it. They's a grove of yella oranges—an' a guy with a gun that got the right to kill you if you touch one. They's a fella, newspaper fella near the coast, got a million acres——"

Casy looked up quickly, "Million acres? What in the worl' can he do with a million acres?"

"I dunno. He jus' got it. Runs a few cattle. Got guards ever'place to keep folks out. Rides aroun' in a bullet-proof car. I seen pitchers of him. Fat, sof' fella with little mean eyes an' a mouth like a asshole. Scairt he's gonna die. Got a million acres an' scairt of dyin'."

Casy demanded, "What in hell can he do with a million acres? What's he want a million acres for?"

The man took his whitening, puckering hands out of the water and spread them, and he tightened his lower lip and bent his head down to one shoulder. "I dunno," he said. "Guess he's crazy. Mus' be crazy. Seen a pitcher of him. He looks crazy. Crazy an' mean."

"Say he's scairt to die?" Casy asked.

"That's what I heard."

"Scairt God'll get him?"

"I dunno. Jus' scairt."

"What's he care?" Pa said. "Don't seem like he's havin' no fun."

"Grampa wasn't scairt," Tom said. "When Grampa was havin' the most fun, he come clostest to gettin' kil't. Time Grampa an' another fella whanged into a bunch a Navajo in the night. They was havin' the time a their life, an' same time you wouldn' give a gopher for their chance."

Casy said, "Seems like that's the way. Fella havin' fun, he don't give a damn; but a fella mean an' lonely an' old an' disappointed—he's scared of dyin'!"

Pa asked, "What's he disappointed about if he got a million acres?"

The preacher smiled, and he looked puzzled. He splashed a floating water bug away with his hand. "If he needs a million acres to
make him feel rich, seems to me he needs it 'cause he feels awful
poor inside hisself, and if he's poor in hisself, there ain't no million
acres gonna make him feel rich, an' maybe he's disappointed that
nothin' he can do'll make him feel rich—not rich like Mis' Wilson
was when she give her tent when Grampa died. I ain't tryin' to
preach no sermon, but I never seen nobody that's busy as a prairie
dog collectin' stuff that wasn't disappointed." He grinned. "Does
kinda soun' like a sermon, don't it?"

The sun was flaming fiercely now. Pa said, "Better scrunch down
under water. She'll burn the living Jesus outa you." And he reclined
and let the gently moving water flow around his neck. "If a fella's
willin' to work hard, can't he cut her?" Pa asked.

The man sat up and faced him. "Look, mister. I don' know ever'thing. You might go out there an' fall into a steady job, an' I'd be
a liar. An' then, you might never get no work, an' I didn' warn ya. I
can tell ya mos' of the folks is purty mis'able." He lay back in the
water. "A fella don' know ever'thing," he said.

Pa turned his head and looked at Uncle John. "You never was a
fella to say much," Pa said. "But I'll be goddamned if you opened
your mouth twicet sence we lef' home. What you think 'bout this
here?"

Uncle John scowled. "I don't think nothin' about it. We're a-goin'
there, ain't we? None of this here talk gonna keep us from goin'
there. When we get there, we'll get there. When we get a job we'll
work, an' when we don't get a job we'll set on our ass. This here talk
ain't gonna do no good no way."

Tom lay back and filled his mouth with water, and he spurted
it into the air and he laughed. "Uncle John don't talk much,
but he talks sense. Yes, by God! He talks sense. We goin' on tonight, Pa?"

"Might's well. Might's well get her over."

"Well, I'm goin' up in the brush an' get some sleep then." Tom
stood up and waded to the sandy shore. He slipped his clothes on
his wet body and winced under the heat of the cloth. The others
followed him.

In the water, the man and his boy watched the Joads disappear.
And the boy said, "Like to see 'em in six months. Jesus!"

The man wiped his eye corners with his forefinger. "I shouldn' of did that," he said. "Fella always wants to be a wise guy, wants to tell folks stuff."

"Well, Jesus, Pa! They asked for it."

"Yeah, I know. But like that fella says, they're a-goin' anyways. Nothin' won't be changed from what I tol' 'em, 'cept they'll be mis'-able 'fore they hafta."

Tom walked in among the willows, and he crawled into a cave of shade to lie down. And Noah followed him.

"Gonna sleep here," Tom said.

"Tom!"

"Yeah?"

"Tom, I ain't a-goin' on."

Tom sat up. "What you mean?"

"Tom, I ain't a-gonna leave this here water. I'm a-gonna walk on down this here river."

"You're crazy," Tom said.

"Get myself a piece a line. I'll catch fish. Fella can't starve beside a nice river."

Tom said, "How 'bout the fam'ly? How 'bout Ma?"

"I can't he'p it. I can't leave this here water." Noah's wideset eyes were half closed. "You know how it is, Tom. You know how the folks are nice to me. But they don't really care for me."

"You're crazy."

"No, I ain't. I know how I am. I know they're sorry. But— Well, I ain't a-goin'. You tell Ma—Tom."

"Now you look-a-here," Tom began.

"No. It ain't no use. I was in that there water. An' I ain't a-gonna leave her. I'm a-gonna go now, Tom—down the river. I'll catch fish an' stuff, but I can't leave her. I can't." He crawled back out of the willow cave. "You tell Ma, Tom." He walked away.

Tom followed him to the river bank. "Listen, you goddamn fool——"

"It ain't no use," Noah said. "I'm sad, but I can't he'p it. I got to go." He turned abruptly and walked downstream along the shore. Tom started to follow, and then he stopped. He saw Noah disappear into the brush, and then appear again, following the edge of the river. And he watched Noah growing smaller on the edge of the river, until he disappeared into the willows at last. And Tom took off his cap and scratched his head. He went back to his willow cave and lay down to sleep.

Under the spread tarpaulin Granma lay on a mattress, and Ma sat beside her. The air was stiflingly hot, and the flies buzzed in the shade of the canvas. Granma was naked under a long piece of pink curtain. She turned her old head restlessly from side to side, and she muttered and choked. Ma sat on the ground beside her, and with a piece of cardboard drove the flies away and fanned a stream of moving hot air over the tight old face. Rose of Sharon sat on the other side and watched her mother.

Granma called imperiously, "Will! Will! You come here, Will." And her eyes opened and she looked fiercely about. "Tol' him to come right here," she said. "I'll catch him. I'll take the hair off'n him." She closed her eyes and rolled her head back and forth and muttered thickly. Ma fanned with the cardboard.

Rose of Sharon looked helplessly at the old woman. She said softly, "She's awful sick."

Ma raised her eyes to the girl's face. Ma's eyes were patient, but the lines of strain were on her forehead. Ma fanned and fanned the air, and her piece of cardboard warned off the flies. "When you're young, Rosasharn, ever'thing that happens is a thing all by itself. It's a lonely thing. I know, I 'member, Rosasharn." Her mouth loved the name of her daughter. "You're gonna have a baby, Rosasharn, and that's somepin to you lonely and away. That's gonna hurt you, an' the hurt'll be lonely hurt, an' this here tent is alone in the worl', Rosasharn." She whipped the air for a moment to drive a buzzing blow fly on, and the big shining fly circled the tent twice and zoomed out into the blinding sunlight. And Ma went on, "They's a time of change, an' when that comes, dyin' is a piece of all dyin', and bearin' is a piece of all bearin', an' bearin' an' dyin' is two pieces of the same thing. An' then things ain't lonely any more. An' then a hurt don't hurt so bad, 'cause it ain't a lonely hurt no more, Rosasharn. I wisht I could tell you so you'd know, but I can't." And her voice was so soft, so full of love, that tears crowded into Rose of Sharon's eyes, and flowed over her eyes and blinded her.

"Take an' fan Granma," Ma said, and she handed the cardboard to her daughter. "That's a good thing to do. I wisht I could tell you so you'd know."

Granma, scowling her brows down over her closed eyes, bleated, "Will! You're dirty! You ain't never gonna get clean." Her little wrinkled claws moved up and scratched her cheek. A red ant ran up the curtain cloth and scrambled over the folds of loose skin on the old lady's neck. Ma reached quickly and picked it off, crushed it between thumb and forefinger, and brushed her fingers on her dress.

Rose of Sharon waved the cardboard fan. She looked up at Ma. "She—?" And the words parched in her throat.

"Wipe your feet, Will—you dirty pig!" Granma cried.

Ma said, "I dunno. Maybe if we can get her where it ain't so hot, but I dunno. Don't worry yourself, Rosasharn. Take your breath in when you need it, an' let it go when you need to."

A large woman in a torn black dress looked into the tent. Her eyes were bleared and indefinite, and the skin sagged to her jowls and hung down in little flaps. Her lips were loose, so that the upper lip hung like a curtain over her teeth, and her lower lip, by its weight, folded outward, showing her lower gums. "Mornin', ma'am," she said. "Mornin', an' praise God for victory."

Ma looked around. "Mornin'," she said.

The woman stooped into the tent and bent her head over Granma. "We heerd you got a soul here ready to join her Jesus. Praise God!"

Ma's face tightened and her eyes grew sharp. "She's tar'd, tha's all," Ma said. "She's wore out with the road an' the heat. She's jus' wore out. Get a little res', an' she'll be well."

The woman leaned down over Granma's face, and she seemed almost to sniff. Then she turned to Ma and nodded quickly, and her lips jiggled and her jowls quivered. "A dear soul gonna join her Jesus," she said.

Ma cried, "That ain't so!"

The woman nodded, slowly, this time, and put a puffy hand on Granma's forehead. Ma reached to snatch the hand away, and quickly restrained herself. "Yes, it's so, sister," the woman said. "We got six in Holiness in our tent. I'll go git 'em, an' we'll hol' a meetin'—a prayer an' grace. Jehovites, all. Six, countin' me. I'll go git 'em out."

Ma stiffened. "No—no," she said. "No, Granma's tar'd. She couldn't stan' a meetin'."

The woman said, "Couldn't stan' grace? Couldn' stan' the sweet breath of Jesus? What you talkin' about, sister?"

Ma said, "No, not here. She's too tar'd."

The woman looked reproachfully at Ma. "Ain't you believers, ma'am?"

"We always been Holiness," Ma said, "but Granma's tar'd, an' we been a-goin' all night. We won't trouble you."

"It ain't no trouble, an' if it was, we'd want ta do it for a soul a-soarin' to the Lamb."

Ma arose to her knees. "We thank ya," she said coldly. "We ain't gonna have no meetin' in this here tent."

The woman looked at her for a long time. "Well, we ain't a-gonna let a sister go away 'thout a little praisin'. We'll git the meetin' goin' in our own tent, ma'am. An' we'll forgive ya for your hard heart."

Ma settled back again and turned her face to Granma, and her face was still set and hard. "She's tar'd," Ma said. "She's on'y tar'd." Granma swung her head back and forth and muttered under her breath.

The woman walked stiffly out of the tent. Ma continued to look down at the old face.

Rose of Sharon fanned her cardboard and moved the hot air in a stream. She said, "Ma!"

"Yeah?"

"Whyn't ya let 'em hol' a meetin'?"

"I dunno," said Ma. "Jehovites is good people. They're howlers an' jumpers. I dunno. Somepin jus' come over me. I didn' think I could stan' it. I'd jus' fly all apart."

From some little distance there came the sound of the beginning meeting, a sing-song chant of exhortation. The words were not clear, only the tone. The voice rose and fell, and went higher at each rise. Now a response filled in the pause, and the exhortation went up with a tone of triumph, and a growl of power came into the voice. It swelled and paused, and a growl came into the response. And now gradually the sentences of exhortation shortened, grew sharper, like commands; and into the responses came a complaining note. The rhythm quickened. Male and female voices had been one tone, but now in the middle of a response one woman's voice went up and up in a wailing cry, wild and fierce, like the cry of a beast; and a deeper woman's voice rose up beside it, a baying voice, and a man's voice traveled up the scale in the howl of a wolf. The exhortation stopped, and only the feral howling came from the tent, and with it a thudding sound on the earth. Ma shivered. Rose of Sharon's breath was panting and short, and the chorus of howls went on so long it seemed that lungs must burst.

Ma said, "Makes me nervous. Somepin happened to me."

Now the high voice broke into hysteria, the gabbling screams of a hyena, the thudding became louder. Voices cracked and broke, and then the whole chorus fell to a sobbing, grunting undertone, and the slap of flesh and the thuddings on the earth; and the sobbing changed to a little whining, like that of a litter of puppies at a food dish.

Rose of Sharon cried softly with nervousness. Granma kicked the curtain off her legs, which lay like gray, knotted sticks. And Granma whined with the whining in the distance. Ma pulled the curtain back in place. And then Granma sighed deeply and her breathing grew steady and easy, and her closed eyelids ceased their flicking. She slept deeply, and snored through her half-open mouth. The whining from the distance was softer and softer until it could not be heard at all any more.

Rose of Sharon looked at Ma, and her eyes were blank with tears. "It done good," said Rose of Sharon. "It done Granma good. She's a-sleepin'."

Ma's head was down, and she was ashamed. "Maybe I done them good people wrong. Granma is asleep."

"Whyn't you ast our preacher if you done a sin?" the girl asked.

"I will—but he's a queer man. Maybe it's him made me tell them people they couldn' come here. That preacher, he's gettin' roun' to thinkin' that what people does is right to do." Ma looked at her hands, and then she said, "Rosasharn, we got to sleep. 'F we're gonna go tonight, we got to sleep." She stretched out on the ground beside the mattress.

Rose of Sharon asked, "How about fannin' Granma?"

"She's asleep now. You lay down an' rest."

"I wonder where at Connie is?" the girl complained. "I ain't seen him around for a long time."

Ma said, "Sh! Get some rest."

"Ma, Connie gonna study nights an' get to be somepin."

"Yeah. You tol' me about that. Get some rest."

The girl lay down on the edge of Granma's mattress. "Connie's got a new plan. He's thinkin' all a time. When he gets all up on 'lectricity he gonna have his own store, an' then guess what we gonna have?"

"What?"

"Ice—all the ice you want. Gonna have a ice box. Keep it full. Stuff don't spoil if you got ice."

"Connie's thinkin' all a time," Ma chuckled. "Better get some rest now."

Rose of Sharon closed her eyes. Ma turned over on her back and crossed her hands under her head. She listened to Granma's breathing and to the girl's breathing. She moved a hand to start a fly from her forehead. The camp was quiet in the blinding heat, but the noises of hot grass—of crickets, the hum of flies—were a tone that was close to silence. Ma sighed deeply and then yawned and closed her eyes. In her half-sleep she heard footsteps approaching, but it was a man's voice that started her awake.

"Who's in here?"

Ma sat up quickly. A brown-faced man bent over and looked in. He wore boots and khaki pants and a khaki shirt with epaulets. On a Sam Browne belt a pistol holster hung, and a big silver star was pinned to his shirt at the left breast. A loose-crowned military cap was on the back of his head. He beat on the tarpaulin with his hand, and the tight canvas vibrated like a drum.

"Who's in here?" he demanded again.

Ma asked, "What is it you want, mister?"

"What you think I want? I want to know who's in here."

"Why, they's jus' us three in here. Me an' Granma an' my girl."

"Where's your men?"

"Why, they went down to clean up. We was drivin' all night."

"Where'd you come from?"

"Right near Sallisaw, Oklahoma."

"Well, you can't stay here."

"We aim to get out tonight an' cross the desert, mister."

"Well, you better. If you're here tomorra this time I'll run you in. We don't want none of you settlin' down here."

Ma's face blackened with anger. She got slowly to her feet. She stooped to the utensil box and picked out the iron skillet. "Mister," she said, "you got a tin button an' a gun. Where I come from, you keep your voice down." She advanced on him with the skillet. He loosened the gun in the holster. "Go ahead," said Ma. "Scarin' women. I'm thankful the men folks ain't here. They'd tear ya to pieces. In my country you watch your tongue."

The man took two steps backward. "Well, you ain't in your country now. You're in California, an' we don't want you goddamn Okies settlin' down."

Ma's advance stopped. She looked puzzled. "Okies?" she said softly. "Okies."

"Yeah, Okies! An' if you're here when I come tomorra, I'll run ya in." He turned and walked to the next tent and banged on the canvas with his hand. "Who's in here?" he said.

Ma went slowly back under the tarpaulin. She put the skillet in the utensil box. She sat down slowly. Rose of Sharon watched her secretly. And when she saw Ma fighting with her face, Rose of Sharon closed her eyes and pretended to be asleep.

The sun sank low in the afternoon, but the heat did not seem to decrease. Tom awakened under his willow, and his mouth was parched and his body was wet with sweat, and his head was dissatisfied with his rest. He staggered to his feet and walked toward the water. He peeled off his clothes and waded into the stream. And the moment the water was about him, his thirst was gone. He lay back in the shallows and his body floated. He held himself in place with his elbows in the sand, and looked at his toes, which bobbed above the surface.

A pale skinny little boy crept like an animal through the reeds and slipped off his clothes. And he squirmed into the water like a muskrat, and pulled himself along like a muskrat, only his eyes and nose above the surface. Then suddenly he saw Tom's head and saw that Tom was watching him. He stopped his game and sat up.

Tom said, "Hello."

" 'Lo!"

"Looks like you was playin' mushrat."

"Well, I was." He edged gradually away toward the bank; he moved casually, and then he leaped out, gathered his clothes with a sweep of his arms, and was gone among the willows.

Tom laughed quietly. And then he heard his name called shrilly. "Tom, oh, Tom!" He sat up in the water and whistled through his teeth, a piercing whistle with a loop onthe end. The willows shook, and Ruthie stood looking at him.

"Ma wants you," she said. "Ma wants you right away."

"Awright." He stood up and strode through the water to the shore; and Ruthie looked with interest and amazement at his naked body.

Tom, seeing the direction of her eyes, said, "Run on now. Git!" And Ruthie ran. Tom heard her calling excitedly for Winfield as she went. He put the hot clothes on his cool, wet body and he walked slowly up through the willows toward the tent.

Ma had started a fire of dry willow twigs, and she had a pan of water heating. She looked relieved when she saw him.

"What's a matter, Ma?" he asked.

"I was scairt," she said. "They was a policeman here. He says we can't stay here. I was scairt he talked to you. I was scairt you'd hit him if he talked to you."

Tom said, "What'd I go an' hit a policeman for?"

Ma smiled. "Well—he talked so bad—I nearly hit him myself."

Tom grabbed her arm and shook her roughly and loosely, and he laughed. He sat down on the ground, still laughing. "My God, Ma. I knowed you when you was gentle. What's come over you?"

She looked serious. "I don' know, Tom."

"Fust you stan' us off with a jack handle, and now you try to hit a cop." He laughed softly, and he reached out and patted her bare foot tenderly. "A ol' hell-cat," he said.

"Tom."

"Yeah?"

She hesitated a long time. "Tom, this here policeman—he called us—Okies. He says, 'We don' want you goddamn Okies settlin' down.'"

Tom studied her, and his hand still rested gently on her bare foot. "Fella tol' about that," he said. "Fella tol' how they say it." He considered, "Ma, would you say I was a bad fella? Oughta be locked up—like that?"

"No," she said. "You been tried— No. What you ast me for?"

"Well, I dunno. I'd a took a sock at that cop."

Ma smiled with amusement. "Maybe I oughta ast you that, 'cause I nearly hit 'im with a skillet."

"Ma, why'd he say we couldn' stop here?"

"Jus' says they don' want no damn Okies settlin' down. Says he's gonna run us in if we're here tomorra."

"But we ain't use' ta gettin' shoved aroun' by no cops."

"I tol' him that," said Ma. "He says we ain't home now. We're in California, and they do what they want."

Tom said uneasily, "Ma, I got somepin to tell ya. Noah—he went on down the river. He ain't a-goin' on."

It took a moment for Ma to understand. "Why?" she asked softly.

"I don' know. Says he got to. Says he got to stay. Says for me to tell you."

"How'll he eat?" she demanded.

"I don' know. Says he'll catch fish."

Ma was silent a long time. "Family's fallin' apart," she said. "I don' know. Seems like I can't think no more. I jus' can't think. They's too much."

Tom said lamely, "He'll be awright, Ma. He's a funny kind a fella."

Ma turned stunned eyes toward the river. "I jus' can't seem to think no more."

Tom looked down the line of tents and he saw Ruthie and Winfield standing in front of a tent in decorous conversation with someone inside. Ruthie was twisting her skirt in her hands, while Winfield dug a hole in the ground with his toe. Tom called, "You, Ruthie!" She looked up and saw him and trotted toward him, with Winfield behind her. When she came up, Tom said, "You go get our folks. They're sleepin' down the willows. Get 'em. An' you, Winfiel'. You tell the Wilsons we're gonna get rollin' soon as we can." The children spun around and charged off.

Tom said, "Ma, how's Granma now?"

"Well, she got a sleep today. Maybe she's better. She's still a-sleepin'."

"Tha's good. How much pork we got?"

"Not very much. Quarter hog."

"Well, we got to fill that other kag with water. Got to take water along." They could hear Ruthie's shrill cries for the men down in the willows.

Ma shoved willow sticks into the fire and made it crackle up about the black pot. She said, "I pray God we gonna get some res'. I pray Jesus we gonna lay down in a nice place."

The sun sank toward the baked and broken hills to the west. The pot over the fire bubbled furiously. Ma went under the tarpaulin and came out with an apronful of potatoes, and she dropped them into the boiling water. "I pray God we gonna be let to wash some clothes. We ain't never been dirty like this. Don't even wash potatoes 'fore we boil 'em. I wonder why? Seems like the heart's took out of us."

The men came trooping up from the willows, and their eyes were full of sleep, and their faces were red and puffed with daytime sleep.

Pa said, "What's a matter?"

"We're goin'," said Tom. "Cop says we got to go. Might's well get her over. Get a good start an' maybe we'll be through her. Near three hunderd miles where we're goin'."

Pa said, "I thought we was gonna get a rest."

"Well, we ain't. We got to go. Pa," Tom said, "Noah ain't a-goin'. He walked on down the river."

"Ain't goin'? What the hell's the matter with him?" And then Pa caught himself. "My fault," he said miserably. "That boy's all my fault."

"No."

"I don't wanta talk about it no more," said Pa. "I can't—my fault."

"Well, we got to go," said Tom.

Wilson walked near for the last words. "We can't go, folks," he said. "Sairy's done up. She got to res'. She ain't gonna git acrost that desert alive."

They were silent at his words; then Tom said, "Cop says he'll run us in if we're here tomorra."

Wilson shook his head. His eyes were glazed with worry, and a paleness showed through his dark skin. "Jus' hafta do 'er, then. Sairy can't go. If they jail us, why, they'll hafta jail us. She got to res' an' get strong."

Pa said, "Maybe we better wait an' all go together."

"No," Wilson said. "You been nice to us; you been kin', but you can't stay here. You got to get on an' get jobs and work. We ain't gonna let you stay."

Pa said excitedly, "But you ain't got nothing."

Wilson smiled. "Never had nothin' when you took us up. This ain't none of your business. Don't you make me git mean. You got to go, or I'll get mean an' mad."

Ma beckoned Pa into the cover of the tarpaulin and spoke softly to him.

Wilson turned to Casy. "Sairy wants you should go see her."

"Sure," said the preacher. He walked to the Wilson tent, tiny and gray, and he slipped the flaps aside and entered. It was dusky and hot inside. The mattress lay on the ground, and the equipment was scattered about, as it had been unloaded in the morning. Sairy lay on the mattress, her eyes wide and bright. He stood and looked down at her, his large head bent and the stringy muscles of his neck tight along the sides. And he took off his hat and held it in his hand.

She said, "Did my man tell ya we couldn' go on?"

"Tha's what he said."

Her low, beautiful voice went on, "I wanted us to go. I knowed I wouldn' live to the other side, but he'd be acrost anyways. But he won't go. He don' know. He thinks it's gonna be all right. He don' know."

"He says he won't go."

"I know," she said. "An' he's stubborn. I ast you to come to say a prayer."

"I ain't a preacher," he said softly. "My prayers ain't no good."

She moistened her lips. "I was there when the ol' man died. You said one then."

"It wasn't no prayer."

"It was a prayer," she said.

"It wasn't no preacher's prayer."

"It was a good prayer. I want you should say one for me."

"I don' know what to say."

She closed her eyes for a minute and then opened them again. "Then say one to yourself. Don't use no words to it. That'd be awright."

"I got no God," he said.

"You got a God. Don't make no difference if you don' know what he looks like." The preacher bowed his head. She watched him apprehensively. And when he raised his head again she looked relieved. "That's good," she said. "That's what I needed. Somebody close enough—to pray."

He shook his head as though to awaken himself. "I don' understan' this here," he said.

And she replied, "Yes—you know, don't you?"

"I know," he said, "I know, but I don't understan'. Maybe you'll res' a few days an' then come on."

She shook her head slowly from side to side. "I'm jus' pain covered with skin. I know what it is, but I won't tell him. He'd be too sad. He wouldn' know what to do anyways. Maybe in the night, when he's a-sleepin'—when he waked up, it won't be so bad."

"You want I should stay with you an' not go on?"

"No," she said. "No. When I was a little girl I use' ta sing. Folks roun' about use' ta say I sung as nice as Jenny Lind. Folks use' ta come an' listen when I sung. An'—when they stood—an' me a-singin', why, me an' them was together more'n you could ever know. I was thankful. There ain't so many folks can feel so full up, so close, an' them folks standin' there an' me a-singin'. Thought maybe I'd sing in theaters, but I never done it. An' I'm glad. They wasn't nothin' got in between me an' them. An'—that's why I wanted you to pray. I wanted to feel that clostness, oncet more. It's the same thing, singin' an' prayin', jus' the same thing. I wisht you could a-heerd me sing."

He looked down at her, into her eyes. "Good-by," he said.

She shook her head slowly back and forth and closed her lips tight. And the preacher went out of the dusky tent into the blinding light.

The men were loading up the truck, Uncle John on top, while the others passed equipment up to him. He stowed it carefully, keeping the surface level. Ma emptied the quarter of a keg of salt pork into a pan, and Tom and Al took both little barrels to the river and washed them. They tied them to the running boards and carried water in buckets to fill them. Then over the tops they tied canvas to keep them from slopping the water out. Only the tarpaulin and Granma's mattress were left to be put on.

Tom said, "With the load we'll take, this ol' wagon'll boil her head off. We got to have plenty water."

Ma passed the boiled potatoes out and brought the half sack from the tent and put it with the pan of pork. The family ate standing, shuffling their feet and tossing the hot potatoes from hand to hand until they cooled.

Ma went to the Wilson tent and stayed for ten minutes, and then she came out quietly. "It's time to go," she said.

The men went under the tarpaulin. Granma still slept, her mouth wide open. They lifted the whole mattress gently and passed it up on top of the truck. Granma drew up her skinny legs and frowned in her sleep, but she did not awaken.

Uncle John and Pa tied the tarpaulin over the cross-piece, making a little tight tent on top of the load. They lashed it down to the side-bars. And then they were ready. Pa took out his purse and dug two crushed bills from it. He went to Wilson and held them out. "We want you should take this, an' '"—he pointed to the pork and potatoes—"an' that."

Wilson hung his head and shook it sharply. "I ain't a-gonna do it," he said. "You ain't got much."

"Got enough to get there," said Pa. "We ain't left it all. We'll have work right off."

"I ain't a-gonna do it," Wilson said. "I'll git mean if you try."

Ma took the two bills from Pa's hand. She folded them neatly and put them on the ground and placed the pork pan over them. "That's where they'll be," she said. "If you don' get 'em, somebody else will." Wilson, his head still down, turned and went to his tent; he stepped inside and the flaps fell behind him.

For a few moments the family waited, and then, "We got to go," said Tom. "It's near four, I bet."

The family climbed on the truck, Ma on top, beside Granma. Tom and Al and Pa in the seat, and Winfield on Pa's lap. Connie and Rose of Sharon made a nest against the cab. The preacher and Uncle John and Ruthie were in a tangle on the load.

Pa called, "Good-by, Mister and Mis' Wilson." There was no answer from the tent. Tom started the engine and the truck lumbered away. And as they crawled up the rough road toward Needles and the highway, Ma looked back. Wilson stood in front of his tent, staring after them, and his hat was in his hand. The sun fell full on his face. Ma waved her hand at him, but he did not respond.

Tom kept the truck in second gear over the rough road, to protect the springs. At Needles he drove into a service station, checked the worn tires for air, checked the spares tied to the back. He had the gas tank filled, and he bought two five-gallon cans of gasoline and a two-gallon can of oil. He filled the radiator, begged a map, and studied it.

The service-station boy, in his white uniform, seemed uneasy until the bill was paid. He said, "You people sure have got nerve."

Tom looked up from the map. "What you mean?"

"Well, crossin' in a jalopy like this."

"You been acrost?"

"Sure, plenty, but not in no wreck like this."

Tom said, "If we broke down maybe somebody'd give us a han'."

"Well, maybe. But folks are kind of scared to stop at night. I'd hate to be doing it. Takes more nerve than I've got."

Tom grinned. "It don't take no nerve to do somepin when there ain't nothin' else you can do. Well, thanks. We'll drag on." And he got in the truck and moved away.

The boy in white went into the iron building where his helper labored over a book of bills. "Jesus, what a hard-looking outfit!"

"Them Okies? They're all hard-lookin'."

"Jesus, I'd hate to start out in a jalopy like that."

"Well, you and me got sense. Them goddamn Okies got no sense and no feeling. They ain't human. A human being wouldn't live like they do. A human being couldn't stand it to be so dirty and miserable. They ain't a hell of a lot better than gorillas."

"Just the same I'm glad I ain't crossing the desert in no Hudson Super-Six. She sounds like a threshing machine."

The other boy looked down at his book of bills. And a big drop of sweat rolled down his finger and fell on the pink bills. "You know, they don't have much trouble. They're so goddamn dumb they don't know it's dangerous. And, Christ Almighty, they don't know any better than what they got. Why worry?"

"I'm not worrying. Just thought if it was me, I wouldn't like it."

"That's 'cause you know better. They don't know any better." And he wiped the sweat from the pink bill with his sleeve.

The truck took the road and moved up the long hill, through the broken, rotten rock. The engine boiled very soon and Tom slowed down and took it easy. Up the long slope, winding and twisting through dead country, burned white and gray, and no hint of life in it. Once Tom stopped for a few moments to let the engine cool, and then he traveled on. They topped the pass while the sun was still up, and looked down on the desert—black cinder mountains in the distance, and the yellow sun reflected on the gray desert. The little starved bushes, sage and greasewood, threw bold shadows on the sand and bits of rock. The glaring sun was straight ahead. Tom held his hand before his eyes to see at all. They passed the crest and coasted down to cool the engine. They coasted down the long sweep to the floor of the desert, and the fan turned over to cool the water in the radiator. In the driver's seat, Tom and Al and Pa, and Winfield on Pa's knee, looked into the bright descending sun, and their eyes were stony, and their brown faces were damp with perspiration. The burnt land and the black, cindery hills broke the even distance and made it terrible in the reddening light of the setting sun.

Al said, "Jesus, what a place. How'd you like to walk acrost her?"

"People done it," said Tom. "Lots a people done it; an' if they could, we could."

"Lots must a died," said Al.

"Well, we ain't come out exac'ly clean."

Al was silent for a while, and the reddening desert swept past. "Think we'll ever see them Wilsons again?" Al asked.

Tom flicked his eyes down to the oil gauge. "I got a hunch nobody ain't gonna see Mis' Wilson for long. Jus' a hunch I got."

Winfield said, "Pa, I wanta get out."

Tom looked over at him. "Might's well let ever'body out 'fore we settle down to drivin' tonight." He slowed the car and brought it to a stop. Winfield scrambled out and urinated at the side of the road. Tom leaned out. "Anybody else?"

"We're holdin' our water up here," Uncle John called.

Pa said, "Winfiel', you crawl up on top. You put my legs to sleep a-settin' on 'em." The little boy buttoned his overalls and obediently crawled up the back board and on his hands and knees crawled over Granma's mattress and forward to Ruthie.

The truck moved on into the evening, and the edge of the sun struck the rough horizon and turned the desert red.

Ruthie said, "Wouldn' leave you set up there, huh?"

"I didn' want to. It wasn't so nice as here. Couldn' lie down."

"Well, don' you bother me, a-squawkin' an' a-talkin'," Ruthie said, " 'cause I'm goin' to sleep, an' when I wake up, we gonna be there! 'Cause Tom said so! Gonna seem funny to see pretty country."

The sun went down and left a great halo in the sky. And it grew very dark under the tarpaulin, a long cave with light at each end— a flat triangle of light.

Connie and Rose of Sharon leaned back against the cab, and the hot wind tumbling through the tent struck the backs of their heads, and the tarpaulin whipped and drummed above them. They spoke together in low tones, pitched to the drumming canvas, so that no one could hear them. When Connie spoke he turned his head and spoke into her ear, and she did the same to him. She said, "Seems like we wasn't never gonna do nothin' but move. I'm so tar'd."

He turned his head to her ear. "Maybe in the mornin'. How'd you like to be alone now?" In the dusk his hand moved out and stroked her hip.

She said, "Don't. You'll make me crazy as a loon. Don't do that." And she turned her head to hear his response.

"Maybe—when ever'body's asleep."

"Maybe," she said. "But wait till they get to sleep. You'll make me crazy, an' maybe they won't get to sleep."

"I can't hardly stop," he said.

"I know. Me neither. Le's talk about when we get there; an' you move away 'fore I get crazy."

He shifted away a little. "Well, I'll get to studyin' nights right off," he said. She sighed deeply. "Gonna get one a them books that tells about it an' cut the coupon, right off."

"How long, you think?" she asked.

"How long what?"

"How long 'fore you'll be makin' big money an' we got ice?"

"Can't tell," he said importantly. "Can't really rightly tell. Fella oughta be studied up pretty good 'fore Christmus."

"Soon's you get studied up we could get ice an' stuff, I guess."

He chuckled. "It's this here heat," he said. "What you gonna need ice roun' Christmus for?"

She giggled. "Tha's right. But I'd like ice any time. Now don't. You'll get me crazy!"

The dusk passed into dark and the desert stars came out in the soft sky, stars stabbing and sharp, with few points and rays to them, and the sky was velvet. And the heat changed. While the sun was up, it was a beating, flailing heat, but now the heat came from below, from the earth itself, and the heat was thick and muffling. The lights of the truck came on, and they illuminated a little blur of highway ahead, and a strip of desert on either side of the road. And sometimes eyes gleamed in the lights far ahead, but no animal showed in the lights. It was pitch dark under the canvas now. Uncle John and the preacher were curled in the middle of the truck, resting on their elbows, and staring out the back triangle. They could see the two bumps that were Ma and Granma against the outside. They could see Ma move occasionally, and her dark arm moving against the outside.

Uncle John talked to the preacher. "Casy," he said, "you're a fella oughta know what to do."

"What to do about what?"

"I dunno," said Uncle John.

Casy said, "Well, that's gonna make it easy for me!"

"Well, you been a preacher."

"Look, John, ever'body takes a crack at me 'cause I been a preacher. A preacher ain't nothin' but a man."

"Yeah, but—he's—a *kind* of a man, else he wouldn' be a

preacher. I wanna ast you—well, you think a fella could bring bad luck to folks?"

"I dunno," said Casy. "I dunno."

"Well—see—I was married—fine, good girl. An' one night she got a pain in her stomach. An' she says, 'You better get a doctor.' An' I says, 'Hell, you jus' et too much.'" Uncle John put his hand on Casy's knee and he peered through the darkness at him. "She give me a *look*. An' she groaned all night, an' she died the next afternoon." The preacher mumbled something. "You see," John went on, "I kil't her. An' sence then I tried to make it up—mos'ly to kids. An' I tried to be good, an' I can't. I get drunk, an' I go wild."

"Ever'body goes wild," said Casy. "I do too."

"Yeah, but you ain't got a sin on your soul like me."

Casy said gently, "Sure I got sins. Ever'body got sins. A sin is somepin you ain't sure about. Them people that's sure about ever'-thing an' ain't got no sin—well, with that kind a son-of-a-bitch, if I was God I'd kick their ass right outa heaven! I couldn' stand 'em!"

Uncle John said, "I got a feelin' I'm bringin' bad luck to my own folks. I got a feelin' I oughta go away an' let 'em be. I ain't comf'-table bein' like this."

Casy said quickly, "I know this—a man got to do what he got to do. I can't tell you. I don't think they's luck or bad luck. On'y one thing in this worl' I'm sure of, an' that's I'm sure nobody got a right to mess with a fella's life. He got to do it all hisself. Help him, maybe, but not tell him what to do."

Uncle John said disappointedly, "Then you don' know?"

"I don' know."

"You think it was a sin to let my wife die like that?"

"Well," said Casy, "for anybody else it was a mistake, but if you think it was a sin—then it's a sin. A fella builds his own sins right up from the groun'."

"I got to give that a goin'-over," said Uncle John, and he rolled on his back and lay with his knees pulled up.

The truck moved on over the hot earth, and the hours passed. Ruthie and Winfield went to sleep. Connie loosened a blanket from the load and covered himself and Rose of Sharon with it, and in the heat they struggled together, and held their breaths. And after a time Connie threw off the blanket and the hot tunneling wind felt cool on their wet bodies.

On the back of the truck Ma lay on the mattress beside Granma, and she could not see with her eyes, but she could feel the struggling body and the struggling heart; and the sobbing breath was in her ear. And Ma said over and over, "All right. It's gonna be all right." And she said hoarsely, "You know the family got to get acrost. You know that."

Uncle John called, "You all right?"

It was a moment before she answered. "All right. Guess I dropped off to sleep." And after a time Granma was still, and Ma lay rigid beside her.

The night hours passed, and the dark was in against the truck. Sometimes cars passed them, going west and away; and sometimes great trucks came up out of the west and rumbled eastward. And the stars flowed down in a slow cascade over the western horizon. It was near midnight when they neared Daggett, where the inspection station is. The road was floodlighted there, and a sign illuminated, "keep right and stop." The officers loafed in the office, but they came out and stood under the long covered shed when Tom pulled in. One officer put down the license number and raised the hood.

Tom asked, "What's this here?"

"Agricultural inspection. We got to look over your stuff. Got any vegetables or seeds?"

"No," said Tom.

"Well, we got to look over your stuff. You got to unload."

Now Ma climbed heavily down from the truck. Her face was swollen and her eyes were hard. "Look, mister. We got a sick ol' lady. We got to get her to a doctor. We can't wait." She seemed to fight with hysteria. "You can't make us wait."

"Yeah? Well, we got to look you over."

"I swear we ain't got any thing!" Ma cried. "I swear it. An' Granma's awful sick."

"You don't look so good yourself," the officer said.

Ma pulled herself up the back of the truck, hoisted herself with huge strength. "Look," she said.

The officer shot a flashlight beam up on the old shrunken face. "By God, she is," he said. "You swear you got no seeds or fruits or vegetables, no corn, no oranges?"

"No, no. I swear it!"

"Then go ahead. You can get a doctor in Barstow. That's only eight miles. Go on ahead."

Tom climbed in and drove on.

The officer turned to his companion. "I couldn' hold 'em."

"Maybe it was a bluff," said the other.

"Oh, Jesus, no! You should of seen that ol' woman's face. That wasn't no bluff."

Tom increased his speed to Barstow, and in the little town he stopped, got out, and walked around the truck. Ma leaned out. "It's awright," she said. "I didn' wanta stop there, fear we wouldn' get acrost."

"Yeah! But how's Granma?"

"She's awright—awright. Drive on. We got to get acrost." Tom shook his head and walked back.

"Al," he said, "I'm gonna fill her up, an' then you drive some." He pulled to an all-night gas station and filled the tank and the radiator, and filled the crank case. Then Al slipped under the wheel and Tom took the outside, with Pa in the middle. They drove away into the darkness and the little hills near Barstow were behind them.

Tom said, "I don' know what's got into Ma. She's flighty as a dog with a flea up his ass. Wouldn' a took long to look over the stuff. An' she says Granma's sick; an' now she says Granma's awright. I can't figger her out. She ain't right. S'pose she wore her brains out on the trip."

Pa said, "Ma's almost like she was when she was a girl. She was a wild one then. She wasn' scairt of nothin'. I thought havin' all the kids an' workin' took it out a her, but I guess it ain't. Christ! When she got that jack handle back there, I tell you I wouldn' wanna be the fella took it away from her."

"I dunno what's got into her," Tom said. "Maybe she's jus' tar'd out."

Al said, "I won't be doin' no weepin' an' a-moanin' to get through. I got this goddamn car on my soul."

Tom said, "Well, you done a damn good job a pickin'. We ain't had hardly no trouble with her at all."

All night they bored through the hot darkness, and jackrabbits scuttled into the lights and dashed away in long jolt-ing leaps. And the dawn came up behind them when the lights of Mojave were ahead. And the dawn showed high mountains to the west. They filled the water and oil at Mojave and crawled into the mountains, and the dawn was about them.

Tom said, "Jesus, the desert's past! Pa, Al, for Christ sakes! The desert's past!"

"I'm too goddamn tired to care," said Al.

"Want me to drive?"

"No, wait awhile."

They drove through Tehachapi in the morning glow, and the sun came up behind them, and then—suddenly they saw the great valley below them. Al jammed on the brake and stopped in the middle of the road, and, "Jesus Christ! Look!" he said. The vineyards, the orchards, the great flat valley, greenand beautiful, the trees set in rows, and the farm houses.

And Pa said, "God Almighty!" The distant cities, the little towns in the orchard land, and the morning sun, golden on the valley. A car honked behind them. Al pulled to the side of the road and parked.

"I want ta look at her." The grain fields golden in the morning, and the willow lines, the eucalyptus trees in rows.

Pa sighed, "I never knowed they was anything like her." The peach trees and the walnut groves, and the dark green patches of oranges. And red roofs among the trees, and barns—rich barns. Al got out and stretched his legs.

He called, "Ma—come look. We're there!"

Ruthie and Winfield scrambled down from the car, and then they stood, silent and awestruck, embarrassed before the great valley. The distance was thinned with haze, and the land grew softer and softer in the distance. A windmill flashed in the sun, and its turning blades were like a little heliograph, far away. Ruthie and Winfield looked at it, and Ruthie whispered, "It's California."

Winfield moved his lips silently over the syllables. "There's fruit," he said aloud.

Casy and Uncle John, Connie and Rose of Sharon climbed down. And they stood silently. Rose of Sharon had started to brush her hair back, when she caught sight of the valley and her hand dropped slowly to her side.

Tom said, "Where's Ma? I want Ma to see it. Look, Ma! Come here, Ma." Ma was climbing slowly, stiffly, down the back board. Tom looked at her. "My God, Ma, you sick?" Her face was stiff and putty-like, and her eyes seemed to have sunk deep into her head, and the rims were red with weariness. Her feet touched the ground and she braced herself by holding the truck-side.

Her voice was a croak. "Ya say we're acrost?"

Tom pointed to the great valley. "Look!"

She turned her head, and her mouth opened a little. Her fingers
went to her throat and gathered a little pinch of skin and twisted
gently. "Thank God!" she said. "The fambly's here." Her knees
buckled and she sat down on the running board.

"You sick, Ma?"

"No, jus' tar'd."

"Didn' you get no sleep?"

"No."

"Was Granma bad?"

Ma looked down at her hands, lying together like tired lovers in
her lap. "I wisht I could wait an' not tell you. I wisht it could be
all—nice."

Pa said, "Then Granma's bad."

Ma raised her eyes and looked over the valley. "<u>Granma's dead.</u>"

They looked at her, all of them, and Pa asked, "When?"

"Before they stopped us las' night."

"So that's why you didn' want 'em to look."

"I was afraid we wouldn' get acrost," she said. "I tol' Granma we
couldn' he'p her. The fambly had ta get acrost. I tol' her, tol' her
when she was a-dyin'. We couldn' stop in the desert. There was the
young ones—an' Rosasharn's baby. I tol' her." She put up her hands
and covered her face for a moment. "She can get buried in a nice
green place," Ma said softly. "Trees aroun' an' a nice place. She got
to lay her head down in California."

The family looked at Ma with a little terror at her strength.

Tom said, "Jesus Christ! You layin' there with her all night long!"

"The fambly hadda get acrost," Ma said miserably.

Tom moved close to put his hand on her shoulder.

"Don' touch me," she said. "I'll hol' up if you don' touch me.
That'd get me."

Pa said, "We got to go on now. We got to go on down."

Ma looked up at him. "Can—can I set up front? I don' wanna
go back there no more—I'm tar'd. I'm awful tar'd."

They climbed back on the load, and they avoided the long stiff
figure covered and tucked in a comforter, even the head covered and
tucked. They moved to their places and tried to keep their eyes from
it—from the hump on the comfort that would be the nose, and the
steep cliff that would be the jut of the chin. They tried to keep their
eyes away, and they could not. Ruthie and Winfield, crowded in a

forward corner as far away from the body as they could get, stared at the tucked figure.

And Ruthie whispered, "Tha's Granma, an' she's dead."

Winfield nodded solemnly. "She ain't breathin' at all. She's awful dead."

And Rose of Sharon said softly to Connie, "She was a-dyin' right when we——"

"How'd we know?" he reassured her.

Al climbed on the load to make room for Ma in the seat. And Al swaggered a little because he was sorry. He plumped down beside Casy and Uncle John. "Well, she was ol'. Guess her time was up," Al said. "Ever'body got to die." Casy and Uncle John turned eyes expressionlessly on him and looked at him as though he were a curious talking bush. "Well, ain't they?" he demanded. And the eyes looked away, leaving Al sullen and shaken.

Casy said in wonder, "All night long, an' she was alone." And he said, "John, there's a woman so great with love—she scares me. Makes me afraid an' mean."

John asked, "Was it a sin? Is they any part of it you might call a sin?"

Casy turned on him in astonishment, "A sin? No, there ain't no part of it that's a sin."

"I ain't never done nothin' that wasn't part sin," said John, and he looked at the long wrapped body.

Tom and Ma and Pa got into the front seat. Tom let the truck roll and started on compression. And the heavy truck moved, snorting and jerking and popping down the hill. The sun was behind them, and the valley golden and green before them. Ma shook her head slowly from side to side. "It's purty," she said. "I wisht they could of saw it."

"I wisht so too," said Pa.

Tom patted the steering wheel under his hand. "They was too old," he said. "They wouldn't of saw nothin' that's here. Grampa would a been a-seein' the Injuns an' the prairie country when he was a young fella. An' Granma would a remembered an' seen the first home she lived in. They was too ol'. Who's really seein' it is Ruthie an' Winfiel'."

Pa said, "Here's Tommy talkin' like a growed-up man, talkin' like a preacher almos'."

And Ma smiled sadly. "He is. Tommy's growed way up—way up so I can't get aholt of 'im sometimes."

They popped down the mountain, twisting and looping, losing the valley sometimes, and then finding it again. And the hot breath of the valley came up to them, with hot green smells on it, and with resinous sage and tarweed smells. The crickets crackled along the road. A rattlesnake crawled across the road and Tom hit it and broke it and left it squirming.

Tom said, "I guess we got to go to the coroner, wherever he is. We got to get her buried decent. How much money might be lef', Pa?"

" 'Bout forty dollars," said Pa.

Tom laughed. "Jesus, are we gonna start clean! We sure ain't bringin' nothin' with us." He chuckled a moment, and then his face straightened quickly. He pulled the visor of his cap down low over his eyes. And the truck rolled down the mountain into the great valley.

CHAPTER 19

Once California belonged to Mexico and its land to Mexicans; and a horde of tattered feverish Americans poured in. And such was their hunger for land that they took the land—stole Sutter's land, Guerrero's land, took the grants and broke them up and growled and quarreled over them, those frantic hungry men; and they guarded with guns the land they had stolen. They put up houses and barns, they turned the earth and planted crops. And these things were possession, and possession was ownership.

The Mexicans were weak and fed. They could not resist, because they wanted nothing in the world as ferociously as the Americans wanted land.

. Then, with time, <u>the squatters were no longer squatters</u>, but owners; and their children grew up and had children on the land. And the hunger was gone from them, the feral hunger, the gnawing, tearing hunger for land, for water and earth and the good sky over it, for the green thrusting grass, for the swelling roots. They had these things so completely that they did not know about them any more. They had no more the stomach-tearing lust for a rich acre and a shining blade to plow it, for seed and a windmill beating its wings in the air. They arose in the dark no more to hear the sleepy birds' first chittering, and the morning wind around the house while they waited for the first light to go out to the dear acres. These things were lost, and crops were reckoned in dollars, and land was valued by principal plus interest, and crops were bought and sold before they were planted. Then crop failure, drought, and flood were no longer little deaths within life, but simple losses of money. And all their love was thinned with money, and all their fierceness dribbled away in interest until they were no longer farmers at all, but little shopkeepers of crops, little manufacturers who must sell before they can make. Then those farmers who were not good shopkeepers lost their land to good shopkeepers. No matter how clever, how loving a man might be with earth and growing things, he could not survive if he were not also a good shopkeeper. And as time went on, the business men had the farms, and the farms grew larger, but there were fewer of them.

Now farming became industry, and the owners followed Rome, although they did not know it. They imported slaves, although they did not call them slaves: Chinese, Japanese, Mexicans, Filipinos. They live on rice and beans, the business men said. They don't need much. They wouldn't know what to do with good wages. Why, look how they live. Why, look what they eat. And if they get funny—deport them.

And all the time the farms grew larger and the owners fewer. And there were pitifully few farmers on the land any more. And the imported serfs were beaten and frightened and starved until some went home again, and some grew fierce and were killed or driven from the country. And the farms grew larger and the owners fewer.

And the crops changed. Fruit trees took the place of grain fields, and vegetables to feed the world spread out on the bottoms: lettuce, cauliflower, artichokes, potatoes—stoop crops. A man may stand to use a scythe, a plow, a pitchfork; but he must crawl like a bug between the rows of lettuce, he must bend his back and pull his long bag between the cotton rows, he must go on his knees like a penitent across a cauliflower patch.

And it came about that owners no longer worked on their farms. They farmed on paper; and they forgot the land, the smell, the feel of it, and remembered only that they owned it, remembered only what they gained and lost by it. And some of the farms grew so large that one man could not even conceive of them any more, so large that it took batteries of bookkeepers to keep track of interest and gain and loss; chemists to test the soil, to replenish; straw bosses to see that the stooping men were moving along the rows as swiftly as the material of their bodies could stand. Then such a farmer really became a storekeeper, and kept a store. He paid the men, and sold them food, and took the money back. And after a while he did not pay the men at all, and saved bookkeeping. These farms gave food on credit. A man might work and feed himself; and when the work was done, he might find that he owed money to the company. And the owners not only did not work the farms any more, many of them had never seen the farms they owned.

And then the dispossessed were drawn west—from Kansas, Oklahoma, Texas, New Mexico; from Nevada and Arkansas families, tribes, dusted out, tractored out. Carloads, caravans, homeless and hungry; twenty thousand and fifty thousand and a hundred thousand and two hundred thousand. They streamed over the mountains, hungry and restless—restless as ants, scurrying to find work to do— to lift, to push, to pull, to pick, to cut—anything, any burden to bear, for food. The kids are hungry. We got no place to live. Like ants scurrying for work, for food, and most of all for land.

We ain't foreign. Seven generations back Americans, and beyond that Irish, Scotch, English, German. One of our folks in the Revolution, an' they was lots of our folks in the Civil War—both sides. Americans.

They were hungry, and they were fierce. And they had hoped to find a home, and they found only hatred. Okies—the owners hated them because the owners knew they were soft and the Okies strong, that they were fed and the Okies hungry; and perhaps the owners had heard from their grandfathers how easy it is to steal land from a soft man if you are fierce and hungry and armed. The owners hated them. And in the towns, the storekeepers hated them because they had no money to spend. There is no shorter path to a storekeeper's contempt, and all his admirations are exactly opposite. The town men, little bankers, hated Okies because there was nothing to gain from them. They had nothing. And the laboring people hated Okies because a hungry man must work, and if he must work, if he has to work, the wage payer automatically gives him less for his work; and then no one can get more.

And the dispossessed, the migrants, flowed into California, two hundred and fifty thousand, and three hundred thousand. Behind them new tractors were going on the land and the tenants were being forced off. And new waves were on the way, new waves of the dispossessed and the homeless, hardened, intent, and dangerous.

And while the Californians wanted many things, accumulation, social success, amusement, luxury, and a curious banking security, the new barbarians wanted only two things—land and food; and to them the two were one. And whereas the wants of the Californians were nebulous and undefined, the wants of the Okies were beside the roads, lying there to be seen and coveted: the good fields with water to be dug for, the good green fields, earth to crumble experimentally in the hand, grass to smell, oaten stalks to chew until the sharp sweetness was in the throat. A man might look at a fallow field and know, and see in his mind that his own bending back and his own straining arms would bring the cabbages into the light, and the golden eating corn, the turnips and carrots.

And a homeless hungry man, driving the roads with his wife beside him and his thin children in the back seat, could look at the fallow fields which might produce food but not profit, and that man could know how a fallow field is a sin and the unused land a crime against the thin children. And such a man drove along the roads and knew temptation at every field, and knew the lust to take these fields and make them grow strength for his children and a little comfort for his wife. The temptation was before him always. The fields goaded him, and the company ditches with good water flowing were a goad to him.

And in the south he saw the golden oranges hanging on the trees, the little golden oranges on the dark green trees; and guards with shotguns patrolling the lines so a man might not pick an orange for a thin child, oranges to be dumped if the price was low.

He drove his old car into a town. He scoured the farms for work. Where can we sleep the night?

Well, there's Hooverville on the edge of the river. There's a whole raft of Okies there.

He drove his old car to Hooverville. He never asked again, for there was a Hooverville on the edge of every town.

The rag town lay close to water; and the houses were tents, and weed-thatched enclosures, paper houses, a great junk pile. The man drove his family in and became a citizen of Hooverville—always they were called Hooverville. The man put up his own tent as near to water as he could get; or if he had no tent, he went to the city dump and brought back cartons and built a house of corrugated paper. And when the rains came the house melted and washed away. He settled in Hooverville and he scoured the countryside for work, and the little money he had went for gasoline to look for work. In the evening the men gathered and talked together. Squatting on their hams they talked of the land they had seen.

There's thirty thousan' acres, out west of here. Layin' there. Jesus, what I could do with that, with five acres of that! Why, hell, I'd have ever'thing to eat.

Notice one thing? They ain't no vegetables nor chickens nor pigs at the farms. They raise one thing—cotton, say, or peaches, or lettuce. 'Nother place'll be all chickens. They buy the stuff they could raise in the dooryard.

Jesus, what I could do with a couple pigs!

Well, it ain't yourn, an' it ain't gonna be yourn.

What we gonna do? The kids can't grow up this way.

In the camps the word would come whispering, There's work at Shafter. And the cars would be loaded in the night, the highways crowded—a gold rush for work. At Shafter the people would pile up, five times too many to do the work. A gold rush for work. They stole away in the night, frantic for work. And along the roads lay the temptations, the fields that could bear food.

That's owned. That ain't our'n.

Well, maybe we could get a little piece of her. Maybe—a little piece. Right down there—a patch. Jimson weed now. Christ, I could git enough potatoes off 'n that little patch to feed my whole family!

It ain't our'n. It got to have Jimson weeds.

Now and then a man tried; crept on the land and cleared a piece, trying like a thief to steal a little richness from the earth. Secret gardens hidden in the weeds. A package of carrot seeds and a few turnips. Planted potato skins, crept out in the evening secretly to hoe in the stolen earth.

Leave the weeds around the edge—then nobody can see what we're a-doin'. Leave some weeds, big tall ones, in the middle.

Secret gardening in the evenings, and water carried in a rusty can.

And then one day a deputy sheriff: Well, what you think you're doin'?

I ain't doin' no harm.

I had my eye on you. This ain't your land. You're trespassing.

The land ain't plowed, an' I ain't hurtin' it none.

You goddamned squatters. Pretty soon you'd think you owned it. You'd be sore as hell. Think you owned it. Get off now.

And the little green carrot tops were kicked off and the turnip greens trampled. And then the Jimson weed moved back in. But the cop was right. A crop raised—why, that makes ownership. Land hoed and the carrots eaten—a man might fight for land he's taken food from. Get him off quick! He'll think he owns it. He might even die fighting for the little plot among the Jimson weeds.

Did ya see his face when we kicked them turnips out? Why, he'd kill a fella soon's he'd look at him. We got to keep these here people down or they'll take the country. They'll take the country.

Outlanders, foreigners.

Sure, they talk the same language, but they ain't the same. Look how they live. Think any of us folks'd live like that? Hell, no!

In the evenings, squatting and talking. And an excited man: Whyn't twenty of us take a piece of lan'? We got guns. Take it an' say, "Put us off if you can." Whyn't we do that?

They'd jus' shoot us like rats.

Well, which'd you ruther be, dead or here? Under groun' or in a house all made of gunny sacks? Which'd you ruther for your kids, dead now or dead in two years with what they call malnutrition? Know what we et all week? Biled nettles an' fried dough! Know where we got the flour for the dough? Swep' the floor of a boxcar.

Talking in the camps, and the deputies, fat-assed men with guns slung on fat hips, swaggering through the camps: Give 'em somepin to think about. Got to keep 'em in line or Christ only knows what they'll do! Why, Jesus, they're as dangerous as niggers in the South! If they ever get together there ain't nothin' that'll stop 'em.

Quote: In Lawrenceville a deputy sheriff evicted a squatter, and the squatter resisted, making it necessary for the officer to use force. The eleven-year-old son of the squatter shot and killed the deputy with a .22 rifle.

Rattlesnakes! Don't take chances with 'em, an' if they argue, shoot first. If a kid'll kill a cop, what'll the men do? Thing is, get tougher'n they are. Treat 'em rough. Scare 'em.

What if they won't scare? What if they stand up and take it and shoot back? These men were armed when they were children. A gun is an extension of themselves. What if they won't scare? What if some time an army of them marches on the land as the Lombards did in Italy, as the Germans did on Gaul and the Turks did on Byzantium? They were land-hungry, ill-armed hordes too, and the legions could not stop them. Slaughter and terror did not stop them. How can you frighten a man whose hunger is not only in his own cramped stomach but in the wretched bellies of his children? You can't scare him—he has known a fear beyond every other.

In Hooverville the men talking: Grampa took his lan' from the Injuns.

Now, this ain't right. We're a-talkin' here. This here you're talkin' about is stealin'. I ain't no thief.

No? You stole a bottle of milk from a porch night before last.
An' you stole some copper wire and sold it for a piece of meat.

Yeah, but the kids was hungry.

It's stealin', though.

Know how the Fairfiel' ranch was got? I'll tell ya. It was all gov'-
ment lan', an' could be took up. Ol' Fairfiel', he went into San Francisco to the bars, an' he got him three hunderd stew bums. Them
bums took up the lan'. Fairfiel' kep' 'em in food an' whisky, an' then
when they'd proved the lan', ol' Fairfiel' took it from 'em. He used
to say the lan' cost him a pint of rotgut an acre. Would you say that
was stealin'?

Well, it wasn't right, but he never went to jail for it.

No, he never went to jail for it. An' the fella that put a boat
in a wagon an' made his report like it was all under water 'cause
he went in a boat—he never went to jail neither. An' the fellas
that bribed congressmen and the legislatures never went to jail
neither.

All over the State, jabbering in the Hoovervilles.

And then the raids—the swoop of armed deputies on the squatters' camps. Get out. Department of Health orders. This camp is a
menace to health.

Where we gonna go?

That's none of our business. We got orders to get you out of
here. In half an hour we set fire to the camp.

They's typhoid down the line. You want ta spread it all over?

We got orders to get you out of here. Now get! In half an hour
we burn the camp.

In half an hour the smoke of paper houses, of weed-thatched
huts, rising to the sky, and the people in their cars rolling over the
highways, looking for another Hooverville.

And in Kansas and Arkansas, in Oklahoma and Texas and New
Mexico, the tractors moved in and pushed the tenants out.

Three hundred thousand in California and more coming. And in
California the roads full of frantic people running like ants to pull,
to push, to lift, to work. For every manload to lift, five pairs of arms
extended to lift it; for every stomachful of food available, five mouths
open.

And the great owners, who must lose their land in an upheaval,
the great owners with access to history, with eyes to read history and

to know the great fact: when property accumulates in too few hands it is taken away. And that companion fact: when a majority of the people are hungry and cold they will take by force what they need. And the little screaming fact that sounds through all history: repression works only to strengthen and knit the repressed. The great owners ignored the three cries of history. The land fell into fewer hands, the number of the dispossessed increased, and every effort of the great owners was directed at repression. The money was spent for arms, for gas to protect the great holdings, and spies were sent to catch the murmuring of revolt so that it might be stamped out. The changing economy was ignored, plans for the change ignored; and only means to destroy revolt were considered, while the causes of revolt went on.

The tractors which throw men out of work, the belt lines which carry loads, the machines which produce, all were increased; and more and more families scampered on the highways, looking for crumbs from the great holdings, lusting after the land beside the roads. The great owners formed associations for protection and they met to discuss ways to intimidate, to kill, to gas. And always they were in fear of a principal—three hundred thousand—if they ever move under a leader—the end. Three hundred thousand, hungry and miserable; if they ever know themselves, the land will be theirs and all the gas, all the rifles in the world won't stop them. And the great owners, who had become through the might of their holdings both more and less than men, ran to their destruction, and used every means that in the long run would destroy them. Every little means, every violence, every raid on a Hooverville, every fat-assed deputy swaggering through a ragged camp put off the day a little and cemented the inevitability of the day.

The men squatted on their hams, sharp-faced men, lean from hunger and hard from resisting it, sullen eyes and hard jaws. And the rich land was around them.

D'ja hear about the kid in that fourth tent down?

No, I jus' come in.

Well, that kid's been a-cryin' in his sleep an' a-rollin' in his sleep. Them folks thought he got worms. So they give him a blaster, an' he died. It was what they call black-tongue the kid had. Comes from not gettin' good things to eat.

Poor little fella.

Yeah, but them folks can't bury him. Got to go to the county stone orchard.

Well, hell.

And hands went into pockets and little coins came out. In front of the tent a little heap of silver grew. And the family found it there.

Our people are good people; our people are kind people. Pray God some day kind people won't all be poor. Pray God some day a kid can eat.

And the associations of owners knew that some day the praying would stop.

And there's the end.

CHAPTER 20

The family, on top of the load, the children and Connie and Rose of Sharon and the preacher were stiff and cramped. They had sat in the heat in front of the coroner's office in Bakersfield while Pa and Ma and Uncle John went in. Then a basket was brought out and the long bundle lifted down from the truck. And they sat in the sun while the examination went on, while the cause of death was found and the certificate signed.

Al and Tom strolled along the street and looked in store windows and watched the strange people on the sidewalks.

And at last Pa and Ma and Uncle John came out, and they were subdued and quiet. Uncle John climbed up on the load. Pa and Ma got in the seat. Tom and Al strolled back and Tom got under the steering wheel. He sat there silently, waiting for some instruction. Pa looked straight ahead, his dark hat pulled low. Ma rubbed the side of her mouth with her fingers, and her eyes were far away and lost, dead with weariness.

Pa sighed deeply. "They wasn't nothin' else to do," he said.

"I know," said Ma. "She would a liked a nice funeral, though. She always wanted one."

Tom looked sideways at them. "County?" he asked.

"Yeah," Pa shook his head quickly, as though to get back to some reality. "We didn' have enough. We couldn' of done it." He turned to Ma. "You ain't to feel bad. We couldn' no matter how hard we tried, no matter what we done. We jus' didn' have it; embalming, an' a coffin an' a preacher, an' a plot in a graveyard. It would of took ten times what we got. We done the bes' we could."

"I know," Ma said. "I jus' can't get it outa my head what store she set by a nice funeral. Got to forget it." She sighed deeply and rubbed the side of her mouth. "That was a purty nice fella in there. Awful bossy, but he was purty nice."

"Yeah," Pa said. "He give us the straight talk, awright."

Ma brushed her hair back with her hand. Her jaw tightened. "We got to git," she said. "We got to find a place to stay. We got to get work an' settle down. No use a-lettin' the little fellas go hungry.

That wasn't never Granma's way. She always et a good meal at a funeral."

"Where we goin'?" Tom asked.

Pa raised his hat and scratched among his hair. "Camp," he said. "We ain't gonna spen' what little's lef' till we get work. Drive out in the country."

Tom started the car and they rolled through the streets and out toward the country. And by a bridge they saw a collection of tents and shacks. Tom said, "Might's well stop here. Find out what's doin', an' where at the work is." He drove down a steep dirt incline and parked on the edge of the encampment.

There was no order in the camp; little gray tents, shacks, cars were scattered about at random. The first house was nondescript. The south wall was made of three sheets of rusty corrugated iron, the east wall a square of moldy carpet tacked between two boards, the north wall a strip of roofing paper and a strip of tattered canvas, and the west wall six pieces of gunny sacking. Over the square frame, on untrimmed willow limbs, grass had been piled, not thatched, but heaped up in a low mound. The entrance, on the gunny-sack side, was cluttered with equipment. A five-gallon kerosene can served for a stove. It was laid on its side, with a section of rusty stovepipe thrust in one end. A wash boiler rested on its side against the wall; and a collection of boxes lay about, boxes to sit on, to eat on. A Model T Ford sedan and a two-wheel trailer were parked beside the shack, and about the camp there hung a slovenly despair.

Next to the shack there was a little tent, gray with weathering, but neatly, properly set up; and the boxes in front of it were placed against the tent wall. A stovepipe stuck out of the door flap, and the dirt in front of the tent had been swept and sprinkled. A bucketful of soaking clothes stood on a box. The camp was neat and sturdy. A Model A roadster and a little home-made bed trailer stood beside the tent.

And next there was a huge tent, ragged, torn in strips and the tears mended with pieces of wire. The flaps were up, and inside four wide mattresses lay on the ground. A clothes line strung along the side bore pink cotton dresses and several pairs of overalls. There were forty tents and shacks, and beside each habitation some kind of automobile. Far down the line a few children stood and stared at the newly arrived truck, and they moved cautiously toward it, little boys in overalls and bare feet, their hair gray with dust.

Tom stopped the truck and looked at Pa. "She ain't very purty," he said. "Want to go somewheres else?"

"Can't go nowheres else till we know where we're at," Pa said. "We got to ast about work."

Tom opened the door and stepped out. The family climbed down from the load and looked curiously at the camp. Ruthie and Winfield, from the habit of the road, took down the bucket and walked toward the willows, where there would be water; and the line of children parted for them and closed after them.

The flaps of the first shack parted and a woman looked out. Her gray hair was braided, and she wore a dirty, flowered Mother Hubbard. Her face was wizened and dull, deep gray pouches under blank eyes, and a mouth slack and loose.

Pa said, "Can we jus' pull up anywheres an' camp?"

The head was withdrawn inside the shack. For a moment there was quiet and then the flaps were pushed aside and a bearded man in shirt sleeves stepped out. The woman looked out after him, but she did not come into the open.

The bearded man said, "Howdy, folks," and his restless dark eyes jumped to each member of the family, and from them to the truck to the equipment.

Pa said, "I jus' ast your woman if it's all right to set our stuff anywheres."

The bearded man looked at Pa intently, as though he had said something very wise that needed thought. "Set down anywheres, here in this place?" he asked.

"Sure. Anybody own this place, that we got to see 'fore we can camp?"

The bearded man squinted one eye nearly closed and studied Pa. "You wanta camp here?"

Pa's irritation arose. The gray woman peered out of the burlap shack. "What you think I'm a-sayin'?" Pa said.

"Well, if you wanta camp here, why don't ya? I ain't a-stoppin' you."

Tom laughed. "He got it."

Pa gathered his temper. "I jus' wanted to know does anybody own it? Do we got to pay?"

The bearded man thrust out his jaw. "Who owns it?" he demanded.

Pa turned away. "The hell with it," he said. The woman's head popped back in the tent.

The bearded man stepped forward menacingly. "Who owns it?" he demanded. "Who's gonna kick us outa here? You tell *me*."

Tom stepped in front of Pa. "You better go take a good long sleep," he said. The bearded man dropped his mouth open and put a dirty finger against his lower gums. For a moment he continued to look wisely, speculatively at Tom, and then he turned on his heel and popped into the shack after the gray woman.

Tom turned on Pa. "What the hell was that?" he asked.

Pa shrugged his shoulders. He was looking across the camp. In front of a tent stood an old Buick, and the head was off. A young man was grinding the valves, and as he twisted back and forth, back and forth, on the tool, he looked up at the Joad truck. They could see that he was laughing to himself. When the bearded man had gone, the young man left his work and sauntered over.

"H'are ya?" he said, and his blue eyes were shiny with amusement. "I seen you just met the Mayor."

"What the hell's the matter with 'im?" Tom demanded.

The young man chuckled. "He's jus' nuts like you an' me. Maybe he's a little nutser'n me, I don' know."

Pa said, "I jus' ast him if we could camp here."

The young man wiped his greasy hands on his trousers. "Sure. Why not? You folks jus' come acrost?"

"Yeah," said Tom. "Jus' got in this mornin'."

"Never been in Hooverville before?"

"Where's Hooverville?"

"This here's her."

"Oh!" said Tom. "We jus' got in."

Winfield and Ruthie came back, carrying a bucket of water between them.

Ma said, "Le's get the camp up. I'm tuckered out. Maybe we can all rest." Pa and Uncle John climbed up on the truck to unload the canvas and the beds.

Tom sauntered to the young man, and walked beside him back to the car he had been working on. The valve-grinding brace lay on the exposed block, and a little yellow can of valve-grinding compound was wedged on top of the vacuum tank. Tom asked, "What the hell was the matter'th that ol' fella with the beard?"

The young man picked up his brace and went to work, twisting back and forth, grinding valve against valve seat. "The Mayor? Chris' knows. I guess maybe he's bull-simple."

"What's 'bull-simple'?"

"I guess cops push 'im aroun' so much he's still spinning."

Tom asked, "Why would they push a fella like that aroun'?"

The young man stopped his work and looked in Tom's eyes. "Chris' knows," he said. "You jus' come. Maybe you can figger her out. Some fellas says one thing, an' some says another thing. But you jus' camp in one place a little while, an' you see how quick a deputy sheriff shoves you along." He lifted a valve and smeared compound on the seat.

"But what the hell for?"

"I tell ya I don' know. Some says they don' want us to vote; keep us movin' so we can't vote. An' some says so we can't get on relief. An' some says if we set in one place we'd get organized. I don' know why. I on'y know we get rode all the time. You wait, you'll see."

"We ain't no bums," Tom insisted. "We're lookin' for work. We'll take any kind a work."

The young man paused in fitting the brace to the valve slot. He looked in amazement at Tom. "Lookin' for work?" he said. "So you're lookin' for work. What ya think ever'body else is lookin' for? Di'monds? What you think I wore my ass down to a nub lookin' for?" He twisted the brace back and forth.

Tom looked about at the grimy tents, the junk equipment, at the old cars, the lumpy mattresses out in the sun, at the blackened cans on fire-blackened holes where the people cooked. He asked quietly, "Ain't they no work?"

"I don' know. Mus' be. Ain't no crop right here now. Grapes to pick later, an' cotton to pick later. We're a-movin' on, soon's I get these here valves groun'. Me an' my wife an' my kid. We heard they was work up north. We're shovin' north, up aroun' Salinas."

Tom saw Uncle John and Pa and the preacher hoisting the tarpaulin on the tent poles and Ma on her knees inside, brushing off the mattresses on the ground. A circle of quiet children stood to watch the new family get settled, quiet children with bare feet and dirty faces. Tom said, "Back home some fellas come through with han'bills—orange ones. Says they need lots a people out here to work the crops."

The young man laughed. "They say they's three hunderd thousan' us folks here, an' I bet ever' dam' fam'ly seen them han'bills."

"Yeah, but if they don' need folks, what'd they go to the trouble puttin' them things out for?"

"Use your head, why don'cha?"

"Yeah, but I wanta know."

"Look," the young man said. "S'pose you got a job a work, an' there's jus' one fella wants the job. You got to pay 'im what he asts. But s'pose they's a hunderd men." He put down his tool. His eyes hardened and his voice sharpened. "S'pose they's a hunderd men wants that job. S'pose them men got kids, an' them kids is hungry. S'pose a lousy dime'll buy a box a mush for them kids. S'pose a nickel'll buy at leas' somepin for them kids. An' you got a hunderd men. Jus' offer 'em a nickel—why, they'll kill each other fightin' for that nickel. Know what they was payin', las' job I had? Fifteen cents an hour. Ten hours for a dollar an' a half, an' ya can't stay on the place. Got to burn gasoline gettin' there." He was panting with anger, and his eyes blazed with hate. "That's why them han'bills was out. You can print a hell of a lot of han'bills with what ya save payin' fifteen cents an hour for fiel' work."

Tom said, "That's stinkin'."

The young man laughed harshly. "You stay out here a little while, an' if you smell any roses, you come let me smell, too."

"But they is work," Tom insisted. "Christ Almighty, with all this stuff a-growin': orchards, grapes, vegetables—I seen it. They got to have men. I seen all that stuff."

A child cried in the tent beside the car. The young man went into the tent and his voice came softly through the canvas. Tom picked up the brace, fitted it in the slot of the valve, and ground away, his hand whipping back and forth. The child's crying stopped. The young man came out and watched Tom. "You can do her," he said. "Damn good thing. You'll need to."

"How 'bout what I said?" Tom resumed. "I seen all the stuff growin'."

The young man squatted on his heels. "I'll tell ya," he said quietly. "They's a big son-of-a-bitch of a peach orchard I worked in. Takes nine men all the year roun'." He paused impressively. "Takes three thousan' men for two weeks when them peaches is ripe. Got to have 'em or them peaches'll rot. So what do they do? They send out han'bills all over hell. They need three thousan', an' they get six thousan'. They get them men for what they wanta pay. If ya don'

wanta take what they pay, goddamn it, they's a thousan' men waitin'
for your job. So ya pick, an' ya pick, an' then she's done. Whole part
a the country's peaches. All ripe together. When ya get 'em picked,
ever' goddamn one is picked. There ain't another damn thing in that
part a the country to do. An' then them owners don' want you there
no more. Three thousan' of you. The work's done. You might steal,
you might get drunk, you might jus' raise hell. An' besides, you don'
look nice, livin' in ol' tents; an' it's a pretty country, but you stink it
up. They don' want you aroun'. So they kick you out, they move
you along. That's how it is."

Tom, looking down toward the Joad tent, saw his mother, heavy
and slow with weariness, build a little trash fire and put the cooking
pots over the flame. The circle of children drew closer, and the calm
wide eyes of the children watched every move of Ma's hands. An
old, old man with a bent back came like a badger out of a tent and
snooped near, sniffing the air as he came. He laced his arms behind
him and joined the children to watch Ma. Ruthie and Winfield stood
near to Ma and eyed the strangers belligerently.

Tom said angrily, "Them peaches got to be picked right now,
don't they? Jus' when they're ripe?"

" 'Course they do."

"Well, s'pose them people got together an' says, 'Let 'em rot.'
Wouldn' be long 'fore the price went up, by God!"

The young man looked up from the valves, looked sardonically
at Tom. "Well, you figgered out somepin, didn' you. Come right outa
your own head."

"I'm tar'd," said Tom. "Drove all night. I don't wanta start no
argument. An' I'm so goddamn tar'd I'd argue easy. Don' be smart
with me. I'm askin' you."

The young man grinned. "I didn' mean it. You ain't been here.
Folks figgered that out. An' the folks with the peach orchard figgered
her out too. Look, if the folks gets together, they's a leader—got to
be—fella that does the talkin'. Well, first time this fella opens his
mouth they grab 'im an' stick 'im in jail. An' if they's another leader
pops up, why, they stick 'im in jail."

Tom said, "Well, a fella eats in jail anyways."

"His kids don't. How'd you like to be in an' your kids starvin' to
death?"

"Yeah," said Tom slowly. "Yeah."

"An' here's another thing. Ever hear a' the blacklist?"

"What's that?"

"Well, you jus' open your trap about us folks gettin' together, an' you'll see. They take your pitcher an' send it all over. Then you can't get work nowhere. An' if you got kids——"

Tom took off his cap and twisted it in his hands. "So we take what we can get, huh, or we starve; an' if we yelp we starve."

The young man made a sweeping circle with his hand, and his hand took in the ragged tents and the rusty cars.

Tom looked down at his mother again, where she sat scraping potatoes. And the children had drawn closer. He said, "I ain't gonna take it. Goddamn it, I an' my folks ain't no sheep. I'll kick the hell outa somebody."

"Like a cop?"

"Like anybody."

"You're nuts," said the young man. "They'll pick you right off. You got no name, no property. They'll find you in a ditch, with the blood dried on your mouth an' your nose. Be one little line in the paper—know what it'll say? 'Vagrant foun' dead.' An' that's all. You'll see a lot of them little lines, 'Vagrant foun' dead.' "

Tom said, "They'll be somebody else foun' dead right 'longside of this here vagrant."

"You're nuts," said the young man. "Won't be no good in that."

"Well, what you doin' about it?" He looked into the grease-streaked face. And a veil drew down over the eyes of the young man.

"Nothin'. Where you from?"

"Us? Right near Sallisaw, Oklahoma."

"Jus' get in?"

"Jus' today."

"Gonna be aroun' here long?"

"Don't know. We'll stay wherever we can get work. Why?"

"Nothin'." And the veil came down again.

"Got to sleep up," said Tom. "Tomorra we'll go out lookin' for work."

"You kin try."

Tom turned away and moved toward the Joad tent.

The young man took up the can of valve compound and dug his finger into it. "Hi!" he called.

Tom turned. "What you want?"

"I wanta tell ya." He motioned with his finger, on which a blob of compound stuck. "I jus' wanta tell ya. Don' go lookin' for no trouble. 'Member how that bull-simple guy looked?"

"Fella in the tent up there?"

"Yeah—looked dumb—no sense?"

"What about him?"

"Well, when the cops come in, an' they come in all a time, that's how you wanta be. Dumb—don't know nothin'. Don't understan' nothin'. That's how the cops like us. Don't hit no cops. That's jus' suicide. Be bull-simple."

"Let them goddamn cops run over me, an' me do nothin'?"

"No, looka here. I'll come for ya tonight. Maybe I'm wrong. There's stools aroun' all a time. I'm takin' a chancet, an' I got a kid, too. But I'll come for ya. An' if ya see a cop, why, you're a goddamn dumb Okie, see?"

"Tha's awright if we're doin' anythin'," said Tom.

"Don' you worry. We're doin' somepin, on'y we ain't stickin' our necks out. A kid starves quick. Two-three days for a kid." He went back to his job, spread the compound on a valve seat, and his hand jerked rapidly back and forth on the brace, and his face was dull and dumb.

Tom strolled slowly back to his camp. "Bull-simple," he said under his breath.

Pa and Uncle John came toward the camp, their arms loaded with dry willow sticks, and they threw them down by the fire and squatted on their hams. "Got her picked over pretty good," said Pa. "Had ta go a long ways for wood." He looked up at the circle of staring children. "Lord God Almighty!" he said. "Where'd you come from?" All of the children looked self-consciously at their feet.

"Guess they smelled the cookin'," said Ma. "Winfiel', get out from under foot." She pushed him out of her way. "Got ta make us up a little stew," she said. "We ain't et nothin' cooked right sence we come from home. Pa, you go up to the store there an' get me some neck meat. Make a nice stew here." Pa stood up and sauntered away.

Al had the hood of the car up, and he looked down at the greasy engine. He looked up when Tom approached. "You sure look happy as a buzzard," Al said.

"I'm jus' gay as a toad in spring rain," said Tom.

"Looka the engine," Al pointed. "Purty good, huh?"

Tom peered in. "Looks awright to me."

"Awright? Jesus, she's wonderful. She ain't shot no oil nor nothin'." He unscrewed a spark plug and stuck his forefinger in the hole. "Crusted up some, but she's dry."

Tom said, "You done a nice job a pickin'. That what ya want me to say?"

"Well, I sure was scairt the whole way, figgerin' she'd bust down an' it'd be my fault."

"No, you done good. Better get her in shape, 'cause tomorra we're goin' out lookin' for work."

"She'll roll," said Al. "Don't you worry none about that." He took out a pocket knife and scraped the points of the spark plug.

Tom walked around the side of the tent, and he found Casy sitting on the earth, wisely regarding one bare foot. Tom sat down heavily beside him. "Think she's gonna work?"

"What?" asked Casy.

"Them toes of yourn."

"Oh! Jus' settin' here a-thinkin'."

"You always get good an' comf'table for it," said Tom.

Casy waggled his big toe up and his second toe down, and he smiled quietly. "Hard enough for a fella to think 'thout kinkin' hisself up to do it."

"Ain't heard a peep outa you for days," said Tom. "Thinkin' all the time?"

"Yeah, thinkin' all the time."

Tom took off his cloth cap, dirty now, and ruinous, the visor pointed as a bird's beak. He turned the sweat band out and removed a long strip of folded newspaper. "Sweat so much she's shrank," he said. He looked at Casy's waving toes. "Could ya come down from your thinkin' an' listen a minute?"

Casy turned his head on the stalk-like neck. "Listen all the time. That's why I been thinkin'. Listen to people a-talkin', an' purty soon I hear the way folks are feelin'. Goin' on all the time. I hear 'em an' feel 'em; an' they're beating their wings like a bird in a attic. Gonna bust their wings on a dusty winda tryin' ta get out."

Tom regarded him with widened eyes, and then he turned and looked at a gray tent twenty feet away. Washed jeans and shirts and a dress hung to dry on the tent guys. He said softly, "That was about what I was gonna tell ya. An' you seen awready."

"I seen," Casy agreed. "They's a army of us without no harness."

He bowed his head and ran his extended hand slowly up his forehead and into his hair. "All along I seen it," he said. "Ever' place we stopped I seen it. Folks hungry for side-meat, an' when they get it, they ain't fed. An' when they'd get so hungry they couldn' stan' it no more, why, they'd ast me to pray for 'em, an' sometimes I done it." He clasped his hands around drawn-up knees and pulled his legs in. "I use ta think that'd cut 'er," he said. "Use ta rip off a prayer an' all the troubles'd stick to that prayer like flies on flypaper, an' the prayer'd go a-sailin' off, a-takin' them troubles along. But it don' work no more."

Tom said, "Prayer never brought in no side-meat. Takes a shoat to bring in pork."

"Yeah," Casy said. "An' Almighty God never raised no wages. These here folks want to live decent and bring up their kids decent. An' when they're old they wanta set in the door an' watch the downing sun. An' when they're young they wanta dance an' sing an' lay together. They wanta eat an' get drunk and work. An' that's it— they wanta jus' fling their goddamn muscles aroun' an' get tired. Christ! What'm I talkin' about?"

"I dunno," said Tom. "Sounds kinda nice. When ya think you can get ta work an' quit thinkin' a spell? We got to get work. Money's 'bout gone. Pa give five dollars to get a painted piece of board stuck up over Granma. We ain't got much lef'."

A lean brown mongrel dog came sniffing around the side of the tent. He was nervous and flexed to run. He sniffed close before he was aware of the two men, and then looking up he saw them, leaped sideways, and fled, ears back, bony tail clamped protectively. Casy watched him go, dodging around a tent to get out of sight. Casy sighed. "I ain't doin' nobody no good," he said. "Me or nobody else. I was thinkin' I'd go off alone by myself. I'm a-eatin' your food an' a-takin' up room. An' I ain't give you nothin'. Maybe I could get a steady job an' maybe pay back some a the stuff you've give me."

Tom opened his mouth and thrust his lower jaw forward, and he tapped his lower teeth with a dried piece of mustard stalk. His eyes stared over the camp, over the gray tents and the shacks of weed and tin and paper. "Wisht I had a sack a Durham," he said. "I ain't had a smoke in a hell of a time. Use ta get tobacco in McAlester. Almost wisht I was back." He tapped his teeth again and suddenly he turned on the preacher. "Ever been in a jail house?"

"No," said Casy. "Never been."

"Don't go away right yet," said Tom. "Not right yet."

"Quicker I get lookin' for work—quicker I'm gonna find some."

Tom studied him with half-shut eyes and he put on his cap again. "Look," he said, "this ain't no lan' of milk an' honey like the preachers say. They's a mean thing here. The folks here is scared of us people comin' west; an' so they got cops out tryin' to scare us back."

"Yeah," said Casy. "I know. What you ask about me bein' in jail for?"

Tom said slowly, "When you're in jail—you get to kinda—sensin' stuff. Guys ain't let to talk a hell of a lot together—two maybe, but not a crowd. An' so you get kinda sensy. If somepin's gonna bust— if say a fella's goin' stir-bugs an' take a crack at a guard with a mop handle—why, you know it 'fore it happens. An' if they's gonna be a break or a riot, nobody don't have to tell ya. You're sensy about it. You know."

"Yeah?"

"Stick aroun'," said Tom. "Stick aroun' till tomorra anyways. Somepin's gonna come up. I was talkin' to a kid up the road. An' he's bein' jus' as sneaky an' wise as a dog coyote, but he's too wise. Dog coyote a-mindin' his own business an' innocent an' sweet, jus' havin' fun an' no harm—well, they's a hen roost clost by."

Casy watched him intently, started to ask a question, and then shut his mouth tightly. He waggled his toes slowly and, releasing his knees, pushed out his foot so he could see it. "Yeah," he said, "I won't go right yet."

Tom said, "When a bunch a folks, nice quiet folks, don't know nothin' about nothin'—somepin's goin' on."

"I'll stay," said Casy.

"An' tomorra we'll go out in the truck an' look for work."

"Yeah!" said Casy, and he waved his toes up and down and studied them gravely. Tom settled back on his elbow and closed his eyes. Inside the tent he could hear the murmur of Rose of Sharon's voice and Connie's answering.

The tarpaulin made a dark shadow and the wedge-shaped light at each end was hard and sharp. Rose of Sharon lay on a mattress and Connie squatted beside her. "I oughta help Ma," Rose of Sharon said. "I tried, but ever' time I stirred about I throwed up."

Connie's eyes were sullen. "If I'd of knowed it would be like this

I wouldn' of came. I'd a studied nights 'bout tractors back home an'
got me a three-dollar job. Fella can live awful nice on three dollars
a day, an' go to the pitcher show ever' night, too."

Rose of Sharon looked apprehensive. "You're gonna study nights
'bout radios," she said. He was long in answering. "Ain't you?" she
demanded.

"Yeah, sure. Soon's I get on my feet. Get a little money."

She rolled up on her elbow. "You ain't givin' it up!"

"No—no—'course not. But—I didn' know they was places like
this we got to live in."

The girl's eyes hardened. "You got to," she said quietly.

"Sure. Sure, I know. Got to get on my feet. Get a little money.
Would a been better maybe to stay home an' study 'bout tractors.
Three dollars a day they get, an' pick up extra money, too." Rose of
Sharon's eyes were calculating. When he looked down at her he saw
in her eyes a measuring of him, a calculation of him. "But I'm gonna
study," he said. "Soon's I get on my feet."

She said fiercely, "We got to have a house 'fore the baby comes.
We ain't gonna have this baby in no tent."

"Sure," he said. "Soon's I get on my feet." He went out of the
tent and looked down at Ma, crouched over the brush fire. Rose of
Sharon rolled on her back and stared at the top of the tent. And
then she put her thumb in her mouth for a gag and she cried silently.

Ma knelt beside the fire, breaking twigs to keep the flame up
under the stew kettle. The fire flared and dropped and flared and
dropped. The children, fifteen of them, stood silently and watched.
And when the smell of the cooking stew came to their noses, their
noses crinkled slightly. The sunlight glistened on hair tawny with
dust. The children were embarrassed to be there, but they did not
go. Ma talked quietly to a little girl who stood inside the lusting
circle. She was older than the rest. She stood on one foot, caressing
the back of her leg with a bare instep. Her arms were clasped behind
her. She watched Ma with steady small gray eyes. She suggested, "I
could break up some bresh if you want me, ma'am."

Ma looked up from her work. "You wanta get ast to eat, huh?"

"Yes, ma'am," the girl said steadily.

Ma slipped the twigs under the pot and the flame made a puttering sound. "Didn' you have no breakfast?"

"No, ma'am. They ain't no work hereabouts. Pa's in tryin' to sell
some stuff to git gas so's we can git 'long."

Ma looked up. "Didn' none of these here have no breakfast?"

The circle of children shifted nervously and looked away from the boiling kettle. One small boy said boastfully, "I did—me an' my brother did—an' them two did, 'cause I seen 'em. We et good. We're a-goin' south tonight."

Ma smiled. "Then you ain't hungry. They ain't enough here to go around."

The small boy's lip stuck out. "We et good," he said, and he turned and ran and dived into a tent. Ma looked after him so long that the oldest girl reminded her.

"The fire's down, ma'am. I can keep it up if you want."

Ruthie and Winfield stood inside the circle, comporting themselves with proper frigidity and dignity. They were aloof, and at the same time possessive. Ruthie turned cold and angry eyes on the little girl. Ruthie squatted down to break up the twigs for Ma.

Ma lifted the kettle lid and stirred the stew with a stick. "I'm sure glad some of you ain't hungry. That little fella ain't, anyways."

The girl sneered. "Oh, him! He was a-braggin'. He's always a-braggin'. High an' mighty. If he don't have no supper—know what he done? Las' night, come out an' says they got chicken to eat. Well, sir, I looked in whilst they was a-eatin' an' it was fried dough jus' like ever'body else."

"Oh!" And Ma looked down toward the tent where the small boy had gone. She looked back at the little girl. "How long you been in California?" she asked.

"Oh, 'bout six months. We lived in a gov'ment camp a while, an' then we went north, an' when we come back it was full up. That's a nice place to live, you bet."

"Where's that?" Ma asked. And she took the sticks from Ruthie's hand and fed the fire. Ruthie glared with hatred at the older girl.

"Over by Weedpatch. Got nice toilets an' baths, an' you kin wash clothes in a tub, an' they's water right handy, good drinkin' water; an' nights the folks plays music an' Sat'dy night they give a dance. Oh, you never seen anything so nice. Got a place for kids to play, an' them toilets with paper. Pull down a little jigger an' the water comes right in the toilet, an' they ain't no cops let to come look in your tent any time they want, an' the fella runs the camp is so polite, comes a-visitin' an' talks an' ain't high an' mighty. I wisht we could go live there again."

Ma said, "I never heard about it. I sure could use a wash tub, I tell you."

The girl went on excitedly, "Why, God Awmighty, they got hot water right in pipes, an' you get in under a shower bath an' it's warm. You never seen such a place."

Ma said, "All full now, ya say?"

"Yeah. Las' time we ast it was."

"Mus' cost a lot," said Ma.

"Well, it costs, but if you ain't got the money, they let you work it out—couple hours a week, cleanin' up, an' garbage cans. Stuff like that. An' nights they's music an' folks talks together an' hot water right in the pipes. You never seen nothin' so nice."

Ma said, "I sure wisht we could go there."

Ruthie had stood all she could. She blurted fiercely, "Granma died right on top a the truck." The girl looked questioningly at her. "Well, she did," Ruthie said. "An' the cor'ner got her." She closed her lips tightly and broke up a little pile of sticks.

Winfield blinked at the boldness of the attack. "Right on the truck," he echoed. "Cor'ner stuck her in a big basket."

Ma said, "You shush now, both of you, or you got to go away." And she fed twigs into the fire.

Down the line Al had strolled to watch the valve-grinding job. "Looks like you're 'bout through," he said.

"Two more."

"Is they any girls in this here camp?"

"I got a wife," said the young man. "I got no time for girls."

"I always got time for girls," said Al. "I got no time for nothin' else."

"You get a little hungry an' you'll change."

Al laughed. "Maybe. But I ain't never changed that notion yet."

"Fella I talked to while ago, he's with you, ain't he?"

"Yeah! My brother Tom. Better not fool with him. He killed a fella."

"Did? What for?"

"Fight. Fella got a knife in Tom. Tom busted 'im with a shovel."

"Did, huh? What'd the law do?"

"Let 'im off 'cause it was a fight," said Al.

"He don't look like a quarreler."

"Oh, he ain't. But Tom don't take nothin' from nobody." Al's voice was very proud. "Tom, he's quiet. But—look out!"

"Well—I talked to 'im. He didn' soun' mean."

"He ain't. Jus' as nice as pie till he's roused, an' then—look out." The young man ground at the last valve. "Like me to he'p you get them valves set an' the head on?"

"Sure, if you got nothin' else to do."

"Oughta get some sleep," said Al. "But, hell, I can't keep my han's out of a tore-down car. Jus' got to git in."

"Well, I'd admire to git a hand," said the young man. "My name's Floyd Knowles."

"I'm Al Joad."

"Proud to meet ya."

"Me too," said Al. "Gonna use the same gasket?"

"Got to," said Floyd.

Al took out his pocket knife and scraped at the block. "Jesus!" he said. "They ain't nothin' I love like the guts of a engine."

"How 'bout girls?"

"Yeah, girls too! Wisht I could tear down a Rolls an' put her back. I looked under the hood of a Cad' 16 one time an', God Awmighty, you never seen nothin' so sweet in your life! In Sallisaw—an' here's this 16 a-standin' in front of a restaurant, so I lifts the hood. An' a guy comes out an' says, 'What the hell you doin'?' I says, 'Jus' lookin'. Ain't she swell?' An' he jus' stands there. I don' think he ever looked in her before. Jus' stands there. Rich fella in a straw hat. Got a stripe' shirt on, an' eye glasses. We don' say nothin'. Jus' look. An' purty soon he says, 'How'd you like to drive her?'"

Floyd said, "The hell!"

"Sure—'How'd you like to drive her?' Well, hell, I got on jeans —all dirty. I says, 'I'd get her dirty.' 'Come on!' he says. 'Jus' take her roun' the block.' Well, sir, I set in that seat an' I took her roun' the block eight times, an', oh, my God Almighty!"

"Nice?" Floyd asked.

"Oh, Jesus!" said Al. "If I could of tore her down why—I'd a give—anythin'."

Floyd slowed his jerking arm. He lifted the last valve from its seat and looked at it. "You better git use' ta a jalopy," he said, " 'cause you ain't gonna drive no 16." He put his brace down on the running board and took up a chisel to scrape the crust from the block. Two stocky women, bare-headed and bare-footed, went by carrying a bucket of milky water between them. They limped against the weight of the bucket, and neither one looked up from the ground. The sun was half down in afternoon.

Al said, "You don't like nothin' much."

Floyd scraped harder with the chisel. "I been here six months," he said. "I been scrabblin' over this here State tryin' to work hard enough and move fast enough to get meat an' potatoes for me an' my wife an' my kid. I've run myself like a jackrabbit an'—I can't quite make her. There just ain't quite enough to eat no matter what I do. I'm gettin' tired, that's all. I'm gettin' tired way past where sleep rests me. An' I jus' don' know what to do."

"Ain't there no steady work for a fella?" Al asked.

"No, they ain't no steady work." With his chisel he pushed the crust off the block, and he wiped the dull metal with a greasy rag.

A rusty touring car drove down into the camp and there were four men in it, men with brown hard faces. The car drove slowly through the camp. Floyd called to them, "Any luck?"

The car stopped. The driver said, "We covered a hell of a lot a ground. They ain't a hand's work in this here county. We gotta move."

"Where to?" Al called.

"God knows. We worked this here place over." He let in his clutch and moved slowly down the camp.

Al looked after them. "Wouldn' it be better if one fella went alone? Then if they was one piece a work, a fella'd get it."

Floyd put down the chisel and smiled sourly. "You ain't learned," he said. "Takes gas to get roun' the country. Gas costs fifteen cents a gallon. Them four fellas can't take four cars. So each of 'em puts in a dime an' they get gas. You got to learn."

"Al!"

Al looked down at Winfield standing importantly beside him. "Al, Ma's dishin' up stew. She says come git it."

Al wiped his hands on his trousers. "We ain't et today," he said to Floyd. "I'll come give you a han' when I eat."

"No need 'less you wanta."

"Sure, I'll do it." He followed Winfield toward the Joad camp.

It was crowded now. The strange children stood close to the stew pot, so close that Ma brushed them with her elbows as she worked. Tom and Uncle John stood beside her.

Ma said helplessly, "I dunno what to do. I got to feed the fambly. What'm I gonna do with these here?" The children stood stiffly and looked at her. Their faces were blank, rigid, and their eyes went mechanically from the pot to the tin plate she held. Their eyes followed the spoon from pot to plate, and when she passed the steaming plate up to Uncle John, their eyes followed it up. Uncle John dug his spoon into the stew, and the banked eyes rose up with the spoon. A piece of potato went into John's mouth and the banked eyes were on his face, watching to see how he would react. Would it be good? Would he like it?

And then Uncle John seemed to see them for the first time. He chewed slowly. "You take this here," he said to Tom. "I ain't hungry."

"You ain't et today," Tom said.

"I know, but I got a stomickache. I ain't hungry."

Tom said quietly, "You take that plate inside the tent an' you eat it."

"I ain't hungry," John insisted. "I'd still see 'em inside the tent."

Tom turned on the children. "You git," he said. "Go on now, git." The bank of eyes left the stew and rested wondering on his face. "Go on now, git. You ain't doin' no good. There ain't enough for you."

Ma ladled stew into the tin plates, very little stew, and she laid the plates on the ground. "I can't send 'em away," she said. "I don' know what to do. Take your plates an' go inside. I'll let 'em have what's lef'. Here, take a plate in to Rosasharn." She smiled up at the children. "Look," she said, "you little fellas go an' get you each a flat stick an' I'll put what's lef' for you. But they ain't to be no fightin'." The group broke up with a deadly, silent swiftness. Children ran to find sticks, they ran to their own tents and brought spoons. Before Ma had finished with the plates they were back, silent and wolfish. Ma shook her head. "I dunno what to do. I can't rob the fambly. I got to feed the fambly. Ruthie, Winfiel', Al," she cried fiercely. "Take your plates. Hurry up. Git in the tent quick." She looked apologetically at the waiting children. "There ain't enough," she said humbly. "I'm a-gonna set this here kettle out, an' you'll all get a little tas', but it ain't gonna do you no good." She faltered, "I can't he'p it. Can't keep it from you." She lifted the pot and set it down on the ground. "Now wait. It's too hot," she said, and she went into the tent quickly so she would not see. Her family sat on the ground, each with his plate; and outside they could hear the children digging into the pot with their sticks and their spoons and their pieces of rusty tin. A mound of children smothered the pot from sight. They did not talk, did not fight or argue; but there was a quiet intentness in all of them, a wooden fierceness. Ma turned her back so she couldn't see. "We can't do that no more," she said. "We got to eat alone." There was the sound of scraping at the kettle, and then the mound of children broke and the children walked away and left the scraped kettle on the ground. Ma looked at the empty plates. "Didn' none of you get nowhere near enough."

Pa got up and left the tent without answering. The preacher smiled to himself and lay back on the ground, hands clasped behind his head. Al got to his feet. "Got to help a fella with a car."

Ma gathered the plates and took them outside to wash. "Ruthie," she called, "Winfiel'. Go get me a bucket a water right off." She handed them the bucket and they trudged off toward the river.

A strong broad woman walked near. Her dress was streaked with dust and splotched with car oil. Her chin was held high with pride. She stood a short distance away and regarded Ma belligerently. At last she approached. "Afternoon," she said coldly.

"Afternoon," said Ma, and she got up from her knees and pushed a box forward. "Won't you set down?"

The woman walked near. "No, I won't set down."

Ma looked questioningly at her. "Can I he'p you in any way?"

The woman set her hands on her hips. "You kin he'p me by mindin' your own children an' lettin' mine alone."

Ma's eyes opened wide. "I ain't done nothin'—" she began.

The woman scowled at her. "My little fella come back smellin' of stew. You give it to 'im. He tol' me. Don' you go a-boastin' an' a-braggin' 'bout havin' stew. Don' you do it. I got 'nuf troubles 'thout that. Come in ta me, he did, an' says, 'Whyn't we have stew?'" Her voice shook with fury.

Ma moved close. "Set down," she said. "Set down an' talk a piece."

"No, I ain't gonna set down. I'm tryin' to feed my folks, an' you come along with your stew."

"Set down," Ma said. "That was 'bout the las' stew we're gonna have till we get work. S'pose you was cookin' a stew an' a bunch a little fellas stood aroun' moonin', what'd you do? We didn't have enough, but you can't keep it when they look at ya like that."

The woman's hands dropped from her hips. For a moment her

eyes questioned Ma, and then she turned and walked quickly away, and she went into a tent and pulled the flaps down behind her. Ma stared after her, and then she dropped to her knees again beside the stack of tin dishes.

Al hurried near. "Tom," he called. "Ma, is Tom inside?"

Tom stuck his head out. "What you want?"

"Come on with me," Al said excitedly.

They walked away together. "What's a matter with you?" Tom asked.

"You'll find out. Jus' wait." He led Tom to the torn-down car. "This here's Floyd Knowles," he said.

"Yeah, I talked to him. How ya?"

"Jus' gettin' her in shape," Floyd said.

Tom ran his finger over the top of the block. "What kinda bugs is crawlin' on you, Al?"

"Floyd jus' tol' me. Tell 'im, Floyd."

Floyd said, "Maybe I shouldn', but—yeah, I'll tell ya. Fella come through an' he says they's gonna be work up north."

"Up north?"

"Yeah—place called Santa Clara Valley, way to hell an' gone up north."

"Yeah? Kinda work?"

"Prune pickin', an' pears an' cannery work. Says it's purty near ready."

"How far?" Tom demanded.

"Oh, Christ knows. Maybe two hundred miles."

"That's a hell of a long ways," said Tom. "How we know they's gonna be work when we get there?"

"Well, we don' know," said Floyd. "But they ain't nothin' here, an' this fella says he got a letter from his brother, an he's on his way. He says not to tell nobody, they'll be too many. We oughta get out in the night. Oughta get there an' get some work lined up."

Tom studied him. "Why we gotta sneak away?"

"Well, if ever'body gets there, ain't gonna be work for nobody."

"It's a hell of a long ways," Tom said.

Floyd sounded hurt. "I'm jus' givin' you the tip. You don' have to take it. Your brother here he'ped me, an' I'm givin' you the tip."

"You sure there ain't no work here?"

"Look, I been scourin' aroun' for three weeks all over hell, an' I ain't had a bit a work, not a single han'-holt. 'F you wanta look aroun' an' burn up gas lookin', why, go ahead. I ain't beggin' you. More that goes, the less chance I got."

Tom said, "I ain't findin' fault. It's jus' such a hell of a long ways. An' we kinda hoped we could get work here an' rent a house to live in."

Floyd said patiently, "I know ya jus' got here. They's stuff ya got to learn. If you'd let me tell ya, it'd save ya somepin. If ya don' let me tell ya, then ya got to learn the hard way. You ain't gonna settle down 'cause they ain't no work to settle ya. An' your belly ain't gonna let ya settle down. Now—that's straight."

"Wisht I could look aroun' first," Tom said uneasily.

A sedan drove through the camp and pulled up at the next tent. A man in overalls and a blue shirt climbed out. Floyd called to him, "Any luck?"

"There ain't a han'-turn of work in the whole darn country, not till cotton pickin'." And he went into the ragged tent.

"See?" said Floyd.

"Yeah, I see. But two hunderd miles, Jesus!"

"Well, you ain't settlin' down no place for a while. Might's well make up your mind to that."

"We better go," Al said.

Tom asked, "When is they gonna be work aroun' here?"

"Well, in a month the cotton'll start. If you got plenty money you can wait for the cotton."

Tom said, "Ma ain't a-gonna wanta move. She's all tar'd out."

Floyd shrugged his shoulders. "I ain't a-tryin' to push ya north. Suit yaself. I jus' tol' ya what I heard." He picked the oily gasket from the running board and fitted it carefully on the block and pressed it down. "Now," he said to Al, " 'f you want to give me a han' with that engine head."

Tom watched while they set the heavy head gently down over the head bolts and dropped it evenly. "Have to talk about it," he said.

Floyd said, "I don't want nobody but your folks to know about it. Jus' you. An' I wouldn't of tol' you if ya brother didn' he'p me out here."

Tom said, "Well, I sure thank ya for tellin' us. We got to figger it out. Maybe we'll go."

Al said, "By God, I think I'll go if the res' goes or not. I'll hitch there."

"An' leave the fambly?" Tom asked.

"Sure. I'd come back with my jeans plumb fulla jack. Why not?"

"Ma ain't gonna like no such thing," Tom said. "An' Pa, he ain't gonna like it neither."

Floyd set the nuts and screwed them down as far as he could with his fingers. "Me an' my wife come out with our folks," he said. "Back home we wouldn' of thought of goin' away. Wouldn' of thought of it. But, hell, we was all up north a piece and I come down here, an' they moved on, an' now God knows where they are. Been lookin' an' askin' about 'em ever since." He fitted his wrench to the engine-head bolts and turned them down evenly, one turn to each nut, around and around the series.

Tom squatted down beside the car and squinted his eyes up the line of tents. A little stubble was beaten into the earth between the tents. "No, sir," he said, "Ma ain't gonna like you goin' off."

"Well, seems to me a lone fella got more chance of work."

"Maybe, but Ma ain't gonna like it at all."

Two cars loaded with disconsolate men drove down into the camp. Floyd lifted his eyes, but he didn't ask them about their luck. Their dusty faces were sad and resistant. The sun was sinking now, and the yellow sunlight fell on the Hooverville and on the willows behind it. The children began to come out of the tents, to wander about the camp. And from the tents the women came and built their little fires. The men gathered in squatting groups and talked together.

A new Chevrolet coupé turned off the highway and headed down into the camp. It pulled to the center of the camp. Tom said, "Who's this? They don't belong here."

Floyd said, "I dunno—cops, maybe."

The car door opened and a man got out and stood beside the car. His companion remained seated. Now all the squatting men looked at the newcomers and the conversation was still. And the women building their fires looked secretly at the shiny car. The children moved closer with elaborate circuitousness, edging inward in long curves.

Floyd put down his wrench. Tom stood up. Al wiped his hands on his trousers. The three strolled toward the Chevrolet. The man who had got out of the car was dressed in khaki trousers and a flannel shirt. He wore a flat-brimmed Stetson hat. A sheaf of papers was held in his shirt pocket by a little fence of fountain pens and yellow pencils; and from his hip pocket protruded a notebook with metal covers. He moved to one of the groups of squatting men, and they looked up at him, suspicious and quiet. They watched him and did not move; the whites of their eyes showed beneath the irises, for they did not raise their heads to look. Tom and Al and Floyd strolled casually near.

The man said, "You men want to work?" Still they looked quietly, suspiciously. And men from all over the camp moved near.

One of the squatting men spoke at last. "Sure we wanta work. Where's at's work?"

"Tulare County. Fruit's opening up. Need a lot of pickers."

Floyd spoke up. "You doin' the hiring?"

"Well, I'm contracting the land."

The men were in a compact group now. An overalled man took off his black hat and combed back his long black hair with his fingers. "What you payin'?" he asked.

"Well, can't tell exactly, yet. 'Bout thirty cents, I guess."

"Why can't you tell? You took the contract, didn' you?"

"That's true," the khaki man said. "But it's keyed to the price. Might be a little more, might be a little less."

Floyd stepped out ahead. He said quietly, "I'll go, mister. You're a contractor, an' you got a license. You jus' show your license, an' then you give us an order to go to work, an' where, an' when, an' how much we'll get, an' you sign that, an' we'll all go."

The contractor turned, scowling. "You telling me how to run my own business?"

Floyd said, " 'F we're workin' for you, it's our business too."

"Well, you ain't telling me what to do. I told you I need men."

Floyd said angrily, "You didn' say how many men, an' you didn' say what you'd pay."

"Goddamn it, I don't know yet."

"If you don' know, you got no right to hire men."

"I got a right to run my business my own way. If you men want to sit here on your ass, O.K. I'm out getting men for Tulare County. Going to need a lot of men."

Floyd turned to the crowd of men. They were standing up now, looking quietly from one speaker to the other. Floyd said, "Twicet now I've fell for that. Maybe he needs a thousan' men. He'll get five thousan' there, an' he'll pay fifteen cents an hour. An' you poor bastards'll have to take it 'cause you'll be hungry. 'F he wants to hire men, let him hire 'em an' write it out an' say what he's gonna pay. Ast ta see his license. He ain't allowed to contract men without a license."

The contractor turned to the Chevrolet and called, "Joe!" His companion looked out and then swung the car door open and stepped out. He wore riding breeches and laced boots. A heavy pistol holster hung on a cartridge belt around his waist. On his brown shirt a deputy sheriff's star was pinned. He walked heavily over. His face was set to a thin smile. "What you want?" The holster slid back and forth on his hip.

"Ever see this guy before, Joe?"

The deputy asked "Which one?"

"This fella." The contractor pointed to Floyd.

"What'd he do?" The deputy smiled at Floyd.

"He's talkin' red, agitating trouble."

"Hm-m-m." The deputy moved slowly around to see Floyd's profile, and the color slowly flowed up Floyd's face.

"You see?" Floyd cried. "If this guy's on the level, would he bring a cop along?"

"Ever see 'im before?" the contractor insisted.

"Hmm, seems like I have. Las' week when that used-car lot was busted into. Seems like I seen this fella hangin' aroun'. Yep! I'd swear it's the same fella." Suddenly the smile left his face. "Get in the car," he said, and he unhooked the strap that covered the butt of his automatic.

Tom said, "You got nothin' on him."

The deputy swung around. "'F you'd like to go in too, you jus' open your trap once more. They was two fellas hangin' around that lot."

"I wasn't even in the State las' week," Tom said.

"Well, maybe you're wanted someplace else. You keep your trap shut."

The contractor turned back to the men. "You fellas don't want ta listen to these goddamn reds. Troublemakers—they'll get you in trouble. Now I can use all of you in Tulare County."

The men didn't answer.

The deputy turned back to them. "Might be a good idear to go," he said. The thin smile was back on his face. "Board of Health says we got to clean out this camp. An' if it gets around that you got reds out here—why, somebody might git hurt. Be a good idear if all you fellas moved on to Tulare. They isn't a thing to do aroun' here. That's jus' a friendly way a telling you. Be a bunch a guys down here, maybe with pick handles, if you ain't gone."

The contractor said, "I told you I need men. If you don't want to work—well, that's your business."

The deputy smiled. "If they don't want to work, they ain't a place for 'em in this county. We'll float 'em quick."

Floyd stood stiffly beside the deputy, and Floyd's thumbs were hooked over his belt. Tom stole a look at him, and then stared at the ground.

"That's all," the contractor said. "There's men needed in Tulare County; plenty of work."

Tom looked slowly up at Floyd's hands, and he saw the strings at the wrists standing out under the skin. Tom's own hands came up, and his thumbs hooked over his belt.

"Yeah, that's all. I don't want one of you here by tomorra morning."

The contractor stepped into the Chevrolet.

"Now, you," the deputy said to Floyd, "you get in that car." He reached a large hand up and took hold of Floyd's left arm. Floyd spun and swung with one movement. His fist splashed into the large face, and in the same motion he was away, dodging down the line of tents. The deputy staggered and Tom put out his foot for him to trip over. The deputy fell heavily and rolled, reaching for his gun. Floyd dodged in and out of sight down the line. The deputy fired from the ground. A woman in front of a tent screamed and then looked at a hand which had no knuckles. The fingers hung on strings against her palm, and the torn flesh was white and bloodless. Far down the line Floyd came in sight, sprinting for the willows. The deputy, sitting on the ground, raised his gun again and then, suddenly, from the group of men, the Reverend Casy stepped. He kicked the deputy in the neck and then stood back as the heavy man crumpled into unconsciousness.

The motor of the Chevrolet roared and it streaked away, churning the dust. It mounted to the highway and shot away. In front of her tent, the woman still looked at her shattered hand. Little droplets of blood began to ooze from the wound. And a chuckling hysteria began in her throat, a whining laugh that grew louder and higher with each breath.

The deputy lay on his side, his mouth open against the dust.

Tom picked up his automatic, pulled out the magazine and threw it into the brush, and he ejected the live shell from the chamber. "Fella like that ain't got no right to a gun," he said; and he dropped the automatic to the ground.

A crowd had collected around the woman with the broken hand, and her hysteria increased, a screaming quality came into her laughter.

Casy moved close to Tom. "You got to git out," he said. "You go down in the willas an' wait. He didn' see me kick 'im, but he seen you stick out your foot."

"I don' wanta go," Tom said.

Casy put his head close. He whispered, "They'll fingerprint you. You broke parole. They'll send you back."

Tom drew in his breath quietly. "Jesus! I forgot."

"Go quick," Casy said. " 'Fore he comes to."

"Like to have his gun," Tom said.

"No. Leave it. If it's awright to come back, I'll give ya four high whistles."

Tom strolled away casually, but as soon as he was away from the group he hurried his steps, and he disappeared among the willows that lined the river.

Al stepped over to the fallen deputy. "Jesus," he said admiringly, "you sure flagged 'im down!"

The crowd of men had continued to stare at the unconscious man. And now in the great distance a siren screamed up the scale and dropped, and it screamed again, nearer this time. Instantly the men were nervous. They shifted their feet for a moment and then they moved away, each one to his own tent. Only Al and the preacher remained.

Casy turned to Al. "Get out," he said. "Go on, get out—to the tent. You don't know nothin'."

"Yeah? How 'bout you?"

Casy grinned at him. "Somebody got to take the blame. I got no kids. They'll jus' put me in jail, an' I ain't doin' nothin' but set aroun'."

Al said, "Ain't no reason for——"

"Go on now," Casy said sharply. "You get outa this."

Al bristled. "I ain't takin' orders."

Casy said softly, "If you mess in this your whole fambly, all your folks, gonna get in trouble. I don' care about you. But your ma and your pa, they'll get in trouble. Maybe they'll send Tom back to McAlester."

Al considered it for a moment. "O.K.," he said, and he started away.

"Wait," Casy called. "Look, if they take me, you look aroun' an' when it's safe you give four high whistles. Then Tom'll know he can come back."

Al turned away again. "O.K.," he said. "I think you're a damn fool, though."

"Sure," said Casy. "Why not?"

The siren screamed again and again, and always it came closer. Casy knelt beside the deputy and turned him over. The man groaned and fluttered his eyes, and he tried to see. Casy wiped the dust off his lips. The families were in the tents now, and the flaps were down, and the setting sun made the air red and the gray tents bronze.

Tires squealed on the highway and an open car came swiftly into the camp. Four men, armed with rifles, piled out. Casy stood up and walked to them.

"What the hell's goin' on here?"

Casy said, "I knocked out your man there."

One of the armed men went to the deputy. He was conscious now, trying weakly to sit up.

"Now what happened here?"

"Well," Casy said, "he got tough an' I hit 'im, and he started shootin'—hit a woman down the line. So I hit 'im again."

"Well, what'd you do in the first place?"

"I talked back," said Casy.

"Get in that car."

"Sure," said Casy, and he climbed into the back seat and sat down. Two men helped the hurt deputy to his feet. He felt his neck gingerly. Casy said, "They's a woman down the row like to bleed to death from his bad shootin'."

"We'll see about that later. Mike, is this the fella that hit you?"

The dazed man stared sickly at Casy. "Don't look like him."

"It was me, all right," Casy said. "You got smart with the wrong fella."

Mike shook his head slowly. "You don't look like the right fella to me. By God, I'm gonna be sick!"

Casy said, "I'll go 'thout no trouble. You better see how bad that woman's hurt."

"Where's she?"

"That tent over there."

The leader of the deputies walked to the tent, rifle in hand. He spoke through the tent walls, and then went inside. In a moment he came out and walked back. And he said, a little proudly, "Jesus, what a mess a .45 does make! They got a tourniquet on. We'll send a doctor out."

Two deputies sat on either side of Casy. The leader sounded his horn. There was no movement in the camp. The flaps were down tight, and the people in their tents. The engine started and the car swung around and pulled out of the camp. Between his guards Casy sat proudly, his head up and the stringy muscles of his neck prominent. On his lips there was a faint smile and on his face a curious look of conquest.

When the deputies had gone, the people came out of the tents. The sun was down now, and the gentle blue evening light was in the camp. To the east the mountains were still yellow with sunlight. The women went back to the fires that had died. The men collected to squat together and to talk softly.

Al crawled from under the Joad tarpaulin and walked toward the willows to whistle for Tom. Ma came out and built her little fire of twigs.

"Pa," she said, "we ain't gonna have much. We et so late."

Pa and Uncle John stuck close to the camp, watching Ma peeling potatoes and slicing them raw into a frying pan of deep grease. Pa said, "Now what the hell made the preacher do that?"

Ruthie and Winfield crept close and crouched down to hear the talk.

Uncle John scratched the earth deeply with a long rusty nail. "He knowed about sin. I ast him about sin, an' he tol' me; but I don' know if he's right. He says a fella's sinned if he thinks he's sinned." Uncle John's eyes were tired and sad. "I been secret all my days," he said. "I done things I never tol' about."

Ma turned from the fire. "Don' go tellin', John," she said. "Tell 'em to God. Don' go burdenin' other people with your sins. That ain't decent."

"They're a-eatin' on me," said John.

"Well, don' tell 'em. Go down the river an' stick your head under an' whisper 'em in the stream."

Pa nodded his head slowly at Ma's words. "She's right," he said. "It gives a fella relief to tell, but it jus' spreads out his sin."

Uncle John looked up to the sun-gold mountains, and the mountains were reflected in his eyes. "I wisht I could run it down," he said. "But I can't. She's a-bitin' in my guts."

Behind him Rose of Sharon moved dizzily out of the tent. "Where's Connie?" she asked irritably. "I ain't seen Connie for a long time. Where'd he go?"

"I ain't seen him," said Ma. "If I see 'im, I'll tell 'im you want 'im."

"I ain't feelin' good," said Rose of Sharon. "Connie shouldn' of left me."

Ma looked up to the girl's swollen face. "You been a-cryin'," she said.

The tears started freshly in Rose of Sharon's eyes.

Ma went on firmly, "You git aholt on yaself. They's a lot of us here. You git aholt on yaself. Come here now an' peel some potatoes. You're feelin' sorry for yaself."

The girl started to go back in the tent. She tried to avoid Ma's stern eyes, but they compelled her and she came slowly toward the fire. "He shouldn' of went away," she said, but the tears were gone.

"You got to work," Ma said. "Set in the tent an' you'll get feelin' sorry about yaself. I ain't had time to take you in han'. I will now. You take this here knife an' get to them potatoes."

The girl knelt down and obeyed. She said fiercely, "Wait'll I see 'im. I'll tell 'im."

Ma smiled slowly. "He might smack you. You got it comin' with whinin' aroun' an' candyin' yaself. If he smacks some sense in you I'll bless 'im." The girl's eyes blazed with resentment, but she was silent.

Uncle John pushed his rusty nail deep into the ground with his broad thumb. "I got to tell," he said.

Pa said, "Well, tell then, goddamn it! Who'd ya kill?"

Uncle John dug with his thumb into the watch pocket of his blue jeans and scooped out a folded dirty bill. He spread it out and showed it. "Fi' dollars," he said.

"Steal her?" Pa asked.

"No, I had her. Kept her out."

"She was yourn, wasn't she?"

"Yeah, but I didn't have no right to keep her out."

"I don't see much sin in that," Ma said. "It's yourn."

Uncle John said slowly, "It ain't only the keepin' her out. I kep' her out to get drunk. I knowed they was gonna come a time when I got to get drunk, when I'd get to hurtin' inside so I got to get drunk. Figgered time wasn' yet, an' then—the preacher went an' give 'imself up to save Tom."

Pa nodded his head up and down and cocked his head to hear. Ruthie moved closer, like a puppy, crawling on her elbows, and Winfield followed her. Rose of Sharon dug at a deep eye in a potato with the point of her knife. The evening light deepened and became more blue.

Ma said, in a sharp matter-of-fact tone, "I don' see why him savin' Tom got to get you drunk."

John said sadly, "Can't say her. I feel awful. He done her so easy. Jus' stepped up there an' says, 'I done her.' An' they took 'im away. An' I'm a-gonna get drunk."

Pa still nodded his head. "I don't see why you got to tell," he said. "If it was me, I'd jus' go off an' get drunk if I had to."

"Come a time when I could a did somepin an' took the big sin off my soul," Uncle John said sadly. "An' I slipped up. I didn' jump on her, an'—an' she got away. Lookie!" he said. "You got the money. Gimme two dollars."

Pa reached reluctantly into his pocket and brought out the leather pouch. "You ain't gonna need no seven dollars to get drunk. You don't need to drink champagny water."

Uncle John held out his bill. "You take this here an' gimme two dollars. I can get good an' drunk for two dollars. I don' want no sin of waste on me. I'll spend whatever I got. Always do."

Pa took the dirty bill and gave Uncle John two silver dollars. "There ya are," he said. "A fella got to do what he got to do. Nobody don' know enough to tell 'im."

Uncle John took the coins. "You ain't gonna be mad? You know I got to?"

"Christ, yes," said Pa. "You know what you got to do."

"I wouldn' be able to get through this night no other way," he said. He turned to Ma. "You ain't gonna hold her over me?"

Ma didn't look up. "No," she said softly. "No—you go 'long."

He stood up and walked forlornly away in the evening. He walked up to the concrete highway and across the pavement to the grocery store. In front of the screen door he took off his hat, dropped it into the dust, and ground it with his heel in self-abasement. And he left his black hat there, broken and dirty. He entered the store and walked to the shelves where the whisky bottles stood behind wire netting.

Pa and Ma and the children watched Uncle John move away. Rose of Sharon kept her eyes resentfully on the potatoes.

"Poor John," Ma said. "I wondered if it would a done any good if—no—I guess not. I never seen a man so drove."

Ruthie turned on her side in the dust. She put her head close to Winfield's head and pulled his ear against her mouth. She whispered, "I'm gonna get drunk." Winfield snorted and pinched his mouth tight. The two children crawled away, holding their breath, their faces purple with the pressure of their giggles. They crawled around the tent and leaped up and ran squealing away from the tent. They ran to the willows, and once concealed, they shrieked with laughter. Ruthie crossed her eyes and loosened her joints; she staggered about, tripping loosely, with her tongue hanging out. "I'm drunk," she said.

"Look," Winfield cried. "Looka me, here's me, an' I'm Uncle John." He flapped his arms and puffed, he whirled until he was dizzy.

"No," said Ruthie. "Here's the way. Here's the way. *I'm* Uncle John. I'm awful drunk."

Al and Tom walked quietly through the willows, and they came on the children staggering crazily about. The dusk was thick now. Tom stopped and peered. "Ain't that Ruthie an' Winfiel'? What the hell's the matter with 'em?" They walked nearer. "You crazy?" Tom asked.

The children stopped, embarrassed. "We was—jus' playin'," Ruthie said.

"It's a crazy way to play," said Al.

Ruthie said pertly, "It ain't no crazier'n a lot of things."

Al walked on. He said to Tom, "Ruthie's workin' up a kick in the pants. She been workin' it up a long time. 'Bout due for it."

Ruthie mushed her face at his back, pulled out her mouth with her forefingers, slobbered her tongue at him, outraged him in every way she knew, but Al did not turn back to look at her. She looked at Winfield again to start the game, but it had been spoiled. They both knew it.

"Le's go down the water an' duck our heads," Winfield suggested. They walked down through the willows, and they were angry at Al.

Al and Tom went quietly in the dusk. Tom said, "Casy shouldn' of did it. I might of knew, though. He was talkin' how he ain't done nothin' for us. He's a funny fella, Al. All the time thinkin'."

"Comes from bein' a preacher," Al said. "They get all messed up with stuff."

"Where ya s'pose Connie was a-goin'?"

"Goin' to take a crap, I guess."

"Well, he was goin' a hell of a long way."

They walked among the tents, keeping close to the walls. At Floyd's tent a soft hail stopped them. They came near to the tent flap and squatted down. Floyd raised the canvas a little. "You gettin' out?"

Tom said, "I don' know. Think we better?"

Floyd laughed sourly. "You heard what that bull said. They'll burn ya out if ya don't. 'F you think that guy's gonna take a beatin' 'thout gettin' back, you're nuts. The pool-room boys'll be down here tonight to burn us out."

"Guess we better git, then," Tom said. "Where you a-goin'?"

"Why, up north, like I said."

Al said, "Look, a fella tol' me 'bout a gov'ment camp near here. Where's it at?"

"Oh, I think that's full up."

"Well, where's it at?"

"Go south on 99 'bout twelve-fourteen miles, an' turn east to Weedpatch. It's right near there. But I think she's full up."

"Fella says it's nice," Al said.

"Sure, she's nice. Treat ya like a man 'stead of a dog. Ain't no cops there. But she's full up."

Tom said, "What I can't understan's why that cop was so mean. Seemed like he was aimin' for trouble; seemed like he's pokin' a fella to make trouble."

Floyd said, "I don' know about here, but up north I knowed one a them fellas, an' he was a nice fella. He tol' me up there the deputies got to take guys in. Sheriff gets seventy-five cents a day for each prisoner, an' he feeds 'em for a quarter. If he ain't got prisoners, he don't make no profit. This fella says he didn' pick up nobody for a week, an' the sheriff tol' 'im he better bring in guys or give up his button. This fella today sure looks like he's out to make a pinch one way or another."

"We got to get on," said Tom. "So long, Floyd."

"So long. Prob'ly see you. Hope so."

"Good-by," said Al. They walked through the dark gray camp to the Joad tent.

The frying pan of potatoes was hissing and spitting over the fire. Ma moved the thick slices about with a spoon. Pa sat near by, hugging his knees. Rose of Sharon was sitting under the tarpaulin.

"It's Tom!" Ma cried. "Thank God."

"We got to get outa here," said Tom.

"What's the matter now?"

"Well, Floyd says they'll burn the camp tonight."

"What the hell for?" Pa asked. "We ain't done nothin'."

"Nothin' 'cept beat up a cop," said Tom.

"Well, we never done it."

"From what that cop said, they wanta push us along."

Rose of Sharon demanded, "You seen Connie?"

"Yeah," said Al. "Way to hell an' gone up the river. He's goin' south."

"Was—was he goin' away?"

"I don' know."

Ma turned on the girl. "Rosasharn, you been talkin' an' actin' funny. What'd Connie say to you?"

Rose of Sharon said sullenly, "Said it would a been a good thing if he stayed home an' studied up tractors."

They were very quiet. Rose of Sharon looked at the fire and her eyes glistened in the firelight. The potatoes hissed sharply in the frying pan. The girl sniffled and wiped her nose with the back of her hand.

Pa said, "Connie wasn' no good. I seen that a long time. Didn' have no guts, jus' too big for his balls."

Rose of Sharon got up and went into the tent. She lay down on the mattress and rolled over on her stomach and buried her head in her crossed arms.

"Wouldn' do no good to catch 'im, I guess," Al said.

Pa replied, "No. If he ain't no good, we don' want him."

Ma looked into the tent, where Rose of Sharon lay on her mattress. Ma said, "Sh. Don' say that."

"Well, he ain't no good," Pa insisted. "All the time a-sayin' what he's a-gonna do. Never doin' nothin'. I didn' wanta say nothin' while he's here. But now he's run out——"

"Sh!" Ma said softly.

"Why, for Christ's sake? Why do I got to shush? He run out, didn' he?"

Ma turned over the potatoes with her spoon, and the grease boiled and spat. She fed twigs to the fire, and the flames laced up and lighted the tent. Ma said, "Rosasharn gonna have a little fella an' that baby is half Connie. It ain't good for a baby to grow up with folks a-sayin' his pa ain't no good."

"Better'n lyin' about it," said Pa.

"No, it ain't," Ma interrupted. "Make out like he's dead. You wouldn' say no bad things about Connie if he's dead."

Tom broke in, "Hey, what is this? We ain't sure Connie's gone for good. We got no time for talkin'. We got to eat an' get on our way."

"On our way? We jus' come here." Ma peered at him through the firelighted darkness.

He explained carefully, "They gonna burn the camp tonight, Ma. Now you know I ain't got it in me to stan' by an' see our stuff burn up, nor Pa ain't got it in him, nor Uncle John. We'd come up a-fightin', an' I jus' can't afford to be took in an' mugged. I nearly got it today, if the preacher hadn' jumped in."

Ma had been turning the frying potatoes in the hot grease. Now she took her decision. "Come on!" she cried. "Le's eat this stuff. We got to go quick." She set out the tin plates.

Pa said, "How 'bout John?"

"Where is Uncle John?" Tom asked.

Pa and Ma were silent for a moment, and then Pa said, "He went to get drunk."

"Jesus!" Tom said. "What a time he picked out! Where'd he go?"

"I don' know," said Pa.

Tom stood up. "Look," he said, "you all eat an' get the stuff loaded. I'll go look for Uncle John. He'd of went to the store 'crost the road."

Tom walked quickly away. The little cooking fires burned in

front of the tents and the shacks, and the light fell on the faces of ragged men and women, on crouched children. In a few tents the light of kerosene lamps shone through the canvas and placed shadows of people hugely on the cloth.

Tom walked up the dusty road and crossed the concrete highway to the little grocery store. He stood in front of the screen door and looked in. The proprietor, a little gray man with an unkempt mustache and watery eyes, leaned on the counter reading a newspaper. His thin arms were bare and he wore a long white apron. Heaped around and in back of him were mounds, pyramids, walls of canned goods. He looked up when Tom came in, and his eyes narrowed as though he aimed a shotgun.

"Good evening," he said. "Run out of something?"

"Run out of my uncle," said Tom. "Or he run out, or something."

The gray man looked puzzled and worried at the same time. He touched the tip of his nose tenderly and waggled it around to stop an itch. "Seems like you people always lost somebody," he said. "Ten times a day or more somebody comes in here an' says, 'If you see a man named so an' so, an' looks like so an' so, will you tell 'im we went up north?' Somepin like that all the time."

Tom laughed. "Well, if you see a young snot-nose name' Connie, looks a little bit like a coyote, tell 'im to go to hell. We've went south. But he ain't the fella I'm lookin' for. Did a fella 'bout sixty years ol', black pants, sort of grayish hair, come in here an' get some whisky?"

The eyes of the gray man brightened. "Now he sure did. I never seen anything like it. He stood out front an' he dropped his hat an' stepped on it. Here, I got his hat here." He brought the dusty broken hat from under the counter.

Tom took it from him. "That's him, all right."

"Well, sir, he got couple pints of whisky an' he didn' say a thing. He pulled the cork an' tipped up the bottle. I ain't got a license to drink here. I says, 'Look, you can't drink here. You got to go outside.' Well, sir! He jus' stepped outside the door, an' I bet he didn't tilt up that pint more'n four times till it was empty. He throwed it away an' he leaned in the door. Eyes kinda dull. He says, 'Thank you, sir,' an' he went on. I never seen no drinkin' like that in my life."

"Went on? Which way? I got to get him."

"Well, it so happens I can tell you. I never seen such drinkin', so I looked out after him. He went north; an' then a car come along

an' lighted him up, an' he went down the bank. Legs was beginnin'
to buckle a little. He got the other pint open awready. He won't be
far—not the way he was goin'.''

Tom said, "Thank ya. I got to find him."

"You want ta take his hat?"

"Yeah! Yeah! He'll need it. Well, thank ya."

"What's the matter with him?" the gray man asked. "He wasn't
takin' pleasure in his drink."

"Oh, he's kinda—moody. Well, good night. An' if you see that
squirt Connie, tell 'im we've went south."

"I got so many people to look out for an' tell stuff to, I can't ever
remember 'em all."

"Don't put yourself out too much," Tom said. He went out
the screen door carrying Uncle John's dusty black hat. He crossed
the concrete road and walked along the edge of it. Below him in the
sunken field, the Hooverville lay; and the little fires flickered and the
lanterns shone through the tents. Somewhere in the camp a guitar
sounded, slow chords, struck without any sequence, practice chords.
Tom stopped and listened, and then he moved slowly along the side
of the road, and every few steps he stopped to listen again. He had
gone a quarter of a mile before he heard what he listened for. Down
below the embankment the sound of athick, tuneless voice, singing
drably. Tom cocked his head, the better to hear.

And the dull voice sang, "I've give my heart to Jesus, so Jesus
take me home. I've give my soul to Jesus, so Jesus is my home." The
song trailed off to a murmur, and then stopped. Tom hurried down
from the embankment, toward the song. After a while he stopped
and listened again. And the voice was close this time, the same slow,
tuneless singing, "Oh, the night that Maggie died, she called me to
her side, an' give to me them ol' red flannel drawers that Maggie
wore. They was baggy at the knees——"

Tom moved cautiously forward. He saw the black form sitting
on the ground, and he stole near and sat down. Uncle John tilted
the pint and the liquor gurgled out of the neck of the bottle.

Tom said quietly, "Hey, wait! Where do I come in?"

Uncle John turned his head. "Who you?"

"You forgot me awready? You had four drinks to my one."

"No, Tom. Don' try fool me. I'm all alone here. You ain't been
here."

"Well, I'm sure here now. How 'bout givin' me a snort?"

Uncle John raised the pint again and the whisky gurgled. He shook the bottle. It was empty. "No more," he said. "Wanta die so bad. Wanta die awful. Die a little bit. Got to. Like sleepin'. Die a little bit. So tar'd. Tar'd. Maybe—don' wake up no more." His voice crooned off. "Gonna wear a crown—a golden crown."

Tom said, "Listen here to me, Uncle John. We're gonna move on. You come along, an' you can go right to sleep up on the load."

John shook his head. "No. Go on. Ain't goin'. Gonna res' here. No good goin' back. No good to nobody—jus' a-draggin' my sins like dirty drawers 'mongst nice folks. No. Ain't goin'."

"Come on. We can't go 'less you go."

"Go ri' 'long. I ain't no good. I ain't no good. Jus' a-draggin' my sins, a-dirtyin' ever'body."

"You got no more sin'n anybody else."

John put his head close, and he winked one eye wisely. Tom could see his face dimly in the starlight. "Nobody don' know my sins, nobody but Jesus. He knows."

Tom got down on his knees. He put his hand on Uncle John's forehead, and it was hot and dry. John brushed his hand away clumsily.

"Come on," Tom pleaded. "Come on now, Uncle John."

"Ain't goin' go. Jus' tar'd. Gon' res' ri' here. Ri' here."

Tom was very close. He put his fist against the point of Uncle John's chin. He made a small practice arc twice, for distance; and then, with his shoulder in the swing, he hit the chin a delicate perfect blow. John's chin snapped up and he fell backwards and tried to sit up again. But Tom was kneeling over him and as John got one elbow up Tom hit him again. Uncle John lay still on the ground.

Tom stood up and, bending, he lifted the loose sagging body and boosted it over his shoulder. He staggered under the loose weight. John's hanging hands tapped him on the back as he went, slowly, puffing up the bank to the highway. Once a car came by and lighted him with the limp man over his shoulder. The car slowed for a moment and then roared away.

Tom was panting when he came back to the Hooverville, down from the road and to the Joad truck. John was coming to; he struggled weakly. Tom set him gently down on the ground.

Camp had been broken while he was gone. Al passed the bundles up on the truck. The tarpaulin lay ready to bind over the load.

Al said, "He sure got a quick start."

Tom apologized. "I had to hit 'im a little to make 'im come. Poor fella."

"Didn' hurt 'im?" Ma asked.

"Don' think so. He's a-comin' out of it."

Uncle John was weakly sick on the ground. His spasms of vomiting came in little gasps.

Ma said, "I lef' a plate a potatoes for you, Tom."

Tom chuckled. "I ain't just in the mood right now."

Pa called, "Awright, Al. Sling up the tarp."

The truck was loaded and ready. Uncle John had gone to sleep. Tom and Al boosted and pulled him up on the load while Winfield made a vomiting noise behind the truck and Ruthie plugged her mouth with her hand to keep from squealing.

"Awready," Pa said.

Tom asked, "Where's Rosasharn?"

"Over there," said Ma. "Come on, Rosasharn. We're a-goin'."

The girl sat still, her chin sunk on her breast. Tom walked over to her. "Come on," he said.

"I ain't a-goin'." She did not raise her head.

"You got to go."

"I want Connie. I ain't a-goin' till he comes back."

Three cars pulled out of the camp, up the road to the highway, old cars loaded with the camps and the people. They clanked up to the highway and rolled away, their dim lights glancing along the road.

Tom said, "Connie'll find us. I lef' word up at the store where we'd be. He'll find us."

Ma came up and stood beside him. "Come on, Rosasharn. Come on, honey," she said gently.

"I wanta wait."

"We can't wait." Ma leaned down and took the girl by the arm and helped her to her feet.

"He'll find us," Tom said. "Don' you worry. He'll find us." They walked on either side of the girl.

"Maybe he went to get them books to study up," said Rose of Sharon. "Maybe he was a-gonna surprise us."

Ma said, "Maybe that's jus' what he done." They led her to the truck and helped her up on top of the load, and she crawled under the tarpaulin and disappeared into the dark cave.

Now the bearded man from the weed shack came timidly to the

truck. He waited about, his hands clutched behind his back. "You gonna leave any stuff a fella could use?" he asked at last.

Pa said, "Can't think of nothin'. We ain't got nothin' to leave."

Tom asked, "Ain't ya gettin' out?"

For a long time the bearded man stared at him. "No," he said at last.

"But they'll burn ya out."

The unsteady eyes dropped to the ground. "I know. They done it before."

"Well, why the hell don't ya get out?"

The bewildered eyes looked up for a moment, and then down again, and the dying firelight was reflected redly. "I don' know. Takes so long to git stuff together."

"You won't have nothin' if they burn ya out."

"I know. You ain't leavin' nothin' a fella could use?"

"Cleaned out, slick," said Pa. The bearded man vaguely wandered away. "What's a matter with him?" Pa demanded.

"Cop-happy," said Tom. "Fella was sayin'—he's bull-simple. Been beat over the head too much."

A second little caravan drove past the camp and climbed to the road and moved away.

"Come on, Pa. Let's go. Look here, Pa. You an' me an' Al ride in the seat. Ma can get on the load. No. Ma, you ride in the middle. Al"—Tom reached under the seat and brought out a big monkey wrench—"Al, you get up behind. Take this here. Jus' in case. If anybody tries to climb up—let 'im have it."

Al took the wrench and climbed up the back board, and he settled himself cross-legged, the wrench in his hand. Tom pulled the iron jack handle from under the seat and laid it on the floor, under the brake pedal. "Awright," he said. "Get in the middle, Ma."

Pa said, "I ain't got nothin' in my han'."

"You can reach over an' get the jack handle," said Tom. "I hope to Jesus you don' need it." He stepped on the starter and the clanking flywheel turned over, the engine caught and died, and caught again. Tom turned on the lights and moved out of the camp in low gear. The dim lights fingered the road nervously. They climbed up to the highway and turned south. Tom said, "They comes a time when a man gets mad."

Ma broke in, "Tom—you tol' me—you promised me you wasn't like that. You promised."

"I know, Ma. I'm a-tryin'. But them deputies— Did you ever see a deputy that didn' have a fat ass? An' they waggle their ass an' flop their gun aroun'. Ma," he said, "if it was the law they was workin' with, why, we could take it. But it *ain't* the law. They're a-workin' away at our spirits. They're a-tryin' to make us cringe an' crawl like a whipped bitch. They tryin' to break us. Why, Jesus Christ, Ma, they comes a time when the on'y way a fella can keep his decency is by takin' a sock at a cop. They're workin' on our decency."

Ma said, "You promised, Tom. That's how Pretty Boy Floyd done. I knowed his ma. They hurt him."

"I'm a-tryin', Ma. Honest to God, I am. You don' want me to crawl like a beat bitch, with my belly on the groun', do you?"

"I'm a-prayin'. You got to keep clear, Tom. The fambly's breakin' up. You got to keep clear."

"I'll try, Ma. But when one a them fat asses gets to workin' me over, I got a big job tryin'. If it was the law, it'd be different. But burnin' the camp ain't the law."

The car jolted along. Ahead, a little row of red lanterns stretched across the highway.

"Detour, I guess," Tom said. He slowed the car and stopped it, and immediately a crowd of men swarmed about the truck. They were armed with pick handles and shotguns. They wore trench helmets and some American Legion caps. One man leaned in the window, and the warm smell of whisky preceded him.

"Where you think you're goin'?" He thrust a red face near to Tom's face.

Tom stiffened. His hand crept down to the floor and felt for the jack handle. Ma caught his arm and held it powerfully. Tom said, "Well—" and then his voice took on a servile whine. "We're strangers here," he said. "We heard about they's work in a place called Tulare."

"Well, goddamn it, you're goin' the wrong way. We ain't gonna have no goddamn Okies in this town."

Tom's shoulders and arms were rigid, and a shiver went through him. Ma clung to his arm. The front of the truck was surrounded by the armed men. Some of them, to make a military appearance, wore tunics and Sam Browne belts.

Tom whined, "Which way is it at, mister?"

"You turn right around an' head north. An' don't come back till the cotton's ready."

Tom shivered all over. "Yes, sir," he said. He put the car in reverse, backed around and turned. He headed back the way he had come. Ma released his arm and patted him softly. And Tom tried to restrain his hard smothered sobbing.

"Don' you mind," Ma said. "Don' you mind."

Tom blew his nose out the window and wiped his eyes on his sleeve. "The sons-of-bitches——"

"You done good," Ma said tenderly. "You done jus' good."

Tom swerved into a side dirt road, ran a hundred yards, and turned off his lights and motor. He got out of the car, carrying the jack handle.

"Where you goin'?" Ma demanded.

"Jus' gonna look. We ain't goin' north." The red lanterns moved up the highway. Tom watched them cross the entrance of the dirt road and continue on. In a few moments there came the sounds of shouts and screams, and then a flaring light arose from the direction of the Hooverville. The light grew and spread, and from the distance came a crackling sound. Tom got in the truck again. He turned around and ran up the dirt road without lights. At the highway he turned south again, and he turned on his lights.

Ma asked timidly, "Where we goin', Tom?"

"Goin' south," he said. "We couldn' let them bastards push us aroun'. We couldn'. Try to get aroun' the town 'thout goin' through it."

"Yeah, but where we goin'?" Pa spoke for the first time. "That's what I wanta know."

"Gonna look for that gov'ment camp," Tom said. "A fella said they don' let no fat-ass deputies in there. Ma—I got to get away from 'em. I'm scairt I'll kill one."

"Easy, Tom." Ma soothed him. "Easy, Tommy. You done good once. You can do it again."

"Yeah, an' after a while I won't have no decency lef'."

"Easy," she said. "You got to have patience. Why, Tom—us people will go on livin' when all them people is gone. Why, Tom, we're the people that live. They ain't gonna wipe us out. Why, we're the people—we go on."

"We take a beatin' all the time."

"I know." Ma chuckled. "Maybe that makes us tough. Rich fellas come up an' they die, an' their kids ain't no good, an' they die out.

But, Tom, we keep a-comin'. Don' you fret none, Tom. A different time's comin'."

"How do you know?"

"I don' know how."

They entered the town and Tom turned down a side street to avoid the center. By the street lights he looked at his mother. Her face was quiet and a curious look was in her eyes, eyes like the timeless eyes of a statue. Tom put out his right hand and touched her on the shoulder. He had to. And then he withdrew his hand. "Never heard you talk so much in my life," he said.

"Wasn't never so much reason," she said.

He drove through the side streets and cleared the town, and then he crossed back. At an intersection the sign said "99." He turned south on it.

"Well, anyways they never shoved us north," he said. "We still go where we want, even if we got to crawl for the right."

The dim lights felt along the broad black highway ahead.

CHAPTER 21

The moving, questing people were migrants now. Those families which had lived on a little piece of land, who had lived and died on forty acres, had eaten or starved on the produce of forty acres, had now the whole West to rove in. And they scampered about, looking for work; and the highways were streams of people, and the ditch banks were lines of people. Behind them more were coming. The great highways streamed with moving people. There in the Middle- and Southwest had lived a simple agrarian folk who had not changed with industry, who had not farmed with machines or known the power and danger of machines in private hands. They had not grown up in the paradoxes of industry. Their senses were still sharp to the ridiculousness of the industrial life.

And then suddenly the machines pushed them out and they swarmed on the highways. The movement changed them; the highways, the camps along the road, the fear of hunger and the hunger itself, changed them. The children without dinner changed them, the endless moving changed them. They were migrants. And the hostility changed them, welded them, united them—hostility that made the little towns group and arm as though to repel an invader, squads with pick handles, clerks and storekeepers with shotguns, guarding the world against their own people.

In the West there was panic when the migrants multiplied on the highways. Men of property were terrified for their property. Men who had never been hungry saw the eyes of the hungry. Men who had never wanted anything very much saw the flare of want in the eyes of the migrants. And the men of the towns and of the soft suburban country gathered to defend themselves; and they reassured themselves that they were good and the invaders bad, as a man must do before he fights. They said, These goddamned Okies are dirty and ignorant. They're degenerate, sexual maniacs. These goddamned Okies are thieves. They'll steal anything. They've got no sense of property rights.

And the latter was true, for how can a man without property know the ache of ownership? And the defending people said, They bring disease, they're filthy. We can't have them in the schools. They're strangers. How'd you like to have your sister go out with one of 'em?

The local people whipped themselves into a mold of cruelty. Then they formed units, squads, and armed them—armed them with clubs, with gas, with guns. We own the country. We can't let these Okies get out of hand. And the men who were armed did not own the land, but they thought they did. And the clerks who drilled at night owned nothing, and the little storekeepers possessed only a drawerful of debts. But even a debt is something, even a job is something. The clerk thought, I get fifteen dollars a week. S'pose a goddamn Okie would work for twelve? And the little storekeeper thought, How could I compete with a debtless man?

And the migrants streamed in on the highways and their hunger was in their eyes, and their need was in their eyes. They had no argument, no system, nothing but their numbers and their needs. When there was work for a man, ten men fought for it—fought with a low wage. If that fella'll work for thirty cents, I'll work for twenty-five.

If he'll take twenty-five, I'll do it for twenty.

No, me, I'm hungry. I'll work for fifteen. I'll work for food. The kids. You ought to see them. Little boils, like, comin' out, an' they can't run aroun'. Give 'em some windfall fruit, an' they bloated up. Me. I'll work for a little piece of meat.

And this was good, for wages went down and prices stayed up. The great owners were glad and they sent out more handbills to bring more people in. And wages went down and prices stayed up. And pretty soon now we'll have serfs again.

And now the great owners and the companies invented a new method. A great owner bought a cannery. And when the peaches and the pears were ripe he cut the price of fruit below the cost of raising it. And as cannery owner he paid himself a low price for the fruit and kept the price of canned goods up and took his profit. And the little farmers who owned no canneries lost their farms, and they were taken by the great owners, the banks, and the companies who also owned the canneries. As time went on, there were fewer farms. The little farmers moved into town for a while and exhausted their credit, exhausted their friends, their relatives. And then they too went on the highways. And the roads were crowded with men ravenous for work, murderous for work.

And the companies, the banks worked at their own doom and they did not know it. The fields were fruitful, and starving men moved on the roads. The granaries were full and the children of the poor grew up rachitic, and the pustules of pellagra swelled on their sides. The great companies did not know that the line between hunger and anger is a thin line. And money that might have gone to wages went for gas, for guns, for agents and spies, for blacklists, for drilling. On the highways the people moved like ants and searched for work, for food. And the anger began to ferment.

It was late when Tom Joad drove along a country road looking for the Weedpatch camp. There were few lights in the countryside. Only a sky glare behind showed the direction of Bakersfield. The truck jiggled slowly along and hunting cats left the road ahead of it. At a crossroad there was a little cluster of white wooden buildings.

Ma was sleeping in the seat and Pa had been silent and withdrawn for a long time.

Tom said, "I don' know where she is. Maybe we'll wait till daylight an' ast somebody." He stopped at a boulevard signal and another car stopped at the crossing. Tom leaned out. "Hey, mister. Know where the big camp is at?"

"Straight ahead."

Tom pulled across into the opposite road. A few hundred yards, and then he stopped. A high wire fence faced the road, and a wide-gated driveway turned in. A little way inside the gate there was a small house with a light in the window. Tom turned in. The whole truck leaped into the air and crashed down again.

"Jesus!" Tom said. "I didn' even see that hump."

A watchman stood up from the porch and walked to the car. He leaned on the side. "You hit her too fast," he said. "Next time you'll take it easy."

"What is it, for God's sake?"

The watchman laughed. "Well, a lot of kids play in here. You tell folks to go slow and they're liable to forget. But let 'em hit that hump once and they don't forget."

"Oh! Yeah. Hope I didn' break nothin'. Say—you got any room here for us?"

"Got one camp. How many of you?"

Tom counted on his fingers. "Me an' Pa an' Ma, Al an' Rosasharn an' Uncle John an' Ruthie an' Winfiel'. Them last is kids."

"Well, I guess we can fix you. Got any camping stuff?"

"Got a big tarp an' beds."

The watchman stepped up on the running board. "Drive down

the end of that line an' turn right. You'll be in Number Four Sanitary Unit."

"What's that?"

"Toilets and showers and wash tubs."

Ma demanded, "You got wash tubs—running water?"

"Sure."

"Oh! Praise God," said Ma.

Tom drove down the long dark row of tents. In the sanitary building a low light burned. "Pull in here," the watchman said. "It's a nice place. Folks that had it just moved out."

Tom stopped the car. "Right there?"

"Yeah. Now you let the others unload while I sign you up. Get to sleep. The camp committee'll call on you in the morning and get you fixed up."

Tom's eyes drew down. "Cops?" he asked.

The watchman laughed. "No cops. We got our own cops. Folks here elect their own cops. Come along."

Al dropped off the truck and walked around. "Gonna stay here?"

"Yeah," said Tom. "You an' Pa unload while I go to the office."

"Be kinda quiet," the watchman said. "They's a lot of folks sleeping."

Tom followed through the dark and climbed the office steps and entered a tiny room containing an old desk and a chair. The guard sat down at the desk and took out a form.

"Name?"

"Tom Joad."

"That your father?"

"Yeah."

"His name?"

"Tom Joad, too."

The questions went on. Where from, how long in the State, what work done. The watchman looked up. "I'm not nosy. We got to have this stuff."

"Sure," said Tom.

"Now—got any money?"

"Little bit."

"You ain't destitute?"

"Got a little. Why?"

"Well, the camp site costs a dollar a week, but you can work it out, carrying garbage, keeping the camp clean—stuff like that."

"We'll work it out," said Tom.

"You'll see the committee tomorrow. They'll show you how to use the camp and tell you the rules."

Tom said, "Say—what is this? What committee is this, anyways?"

The watchman settled himself back. "Works pretty nice. There's five sanitary units. Each one elects a Central Committee man. Now that committee makes the laws. What they say goes."

"S'pose they get tough," Tom said.

"Well, you can vote 'em out jus' as quick as you vote 'em in. They've done a fine job. Tell you what they did—you know the Holy Roller preachers all the time follow the people around, preachin' an' takin' up collections? Well, they wanted to preach in this camp. And a lot of the older folks wanted them. So it was up to the Central Committee. They went into meeting and here's how they fixed it. They say, 'Any preacher can preach in this camp. Nobody can take up a collection in this camp.' And it was kinda sad for the old folks, 'cause there hasn't been a preacher in since."

Tom laughed and then he asked, "You mean to say the fellas that runs the camp is jus' fellas—campin' here?"

"Sure. And it works."

"You said about cops——"

"Central Committee keeps order an' makes rules. Then there's the ladies. They'll call on your ma. They keep care of kids an' look after the sanitary units. If your ma isn't working, she'll look after kids for the ones that is working, an' when she gets a job—why, there'll be others. They sew, and a nurse comes out an' teaches 'em. All kinds of things like that."

"You mean to say they ain't no fat-ass cops?"

"No, sir. No cop can come in here without a warrant."

"Well, s'pose a fella is jus' mean, or drunk an' quarrelsome. What then?"

The watchman stabbed the blotter with a pencil. "Well, the first time the Central Committee warns him. And the second time they really warn him. The third time they kick him out of the camp."

"God Almighty, I can't hardly believe it! Tonight the deputies an' them fellas with the little caps, they burned the camp out by the river."

"They don't get in here," the watchman said. "Some nights the boys patrol the fences, 'specially dance nights."

"Dance nights? Jesus Christ!"

"We got the best dances in the county every Saturday night."

"Well, for Christ's sake! Why ain't they more places like this?"

The watchman looked sullen. "You'll have to find that out your-self. Go get some sleep."

"Good night," said Tom. "Ma's gonna like this place. She ain't been treated decent for a long time."

"Good night," the watchman said. "Get some sleep. This camp wakes up early."

Tom walked down the street between the rows of tents. His eyes grew used to the starlight. He saw that the rows were straight and that there was no litter about the tents. The ground of the street had been swept and sprinkled. From the tents came the snores of sleeping people. The whole camp buzzed and snorted. Tom walked slowly. He neared Number Four Sanitary Unit and he looked at it curiously, an unpainted building, low and rough. Under a roof, but open at the sides, the rows of wash trays. He saw the Joad truck standing near by, and went quietly toward it. The tarpaulin was pitched and the camp was quiet. As he drew near a figure moved from the shadow of the truck and came toward him.

Ma said softly, "That you, Tom?"

"Yeah."

"Sh!" she said. "They're all asleep. They was tar'd out."

"You ought to be asleep too," Tom said.

"Well, I wanted to see ya. Is it awright?"

"It's nice," Tom said. "I ain't gonna tell ya. They'll tell ya in the mornin'. Ya gonna like it."

She whispered, "I heard they got hot water."

"Yeah. Now you get to sleep. I don' know when you slep' las'."

She begged, "What ain't you a-gonna tell me?"

"I ain't. You get to sleep."

Suddenly she seemed girlish. "How can I sleep if I got to think about what you ain't gonna tell me?"

"No, you don't," Tom said. "First thing in the mornin' you get on your other dress an' then—you'll find out."

"I can't sleep with nothin' like that hangin' over me."

"You got to," Tom chuckled happily. "You jus' got to."

"Good night," she said softly; and she bent down and slipped under the dark tarpaulin.

Tom climbed up over the tail-board of the truck. He lay down on his back on the wooden floor and he pillowed his head on his crossed hands, and his forearms pressed against his ears. The night grew cooler. Tom buttoned his coat over his chest and settled back again. The stars were clear and sharp over his head.

It was still dark when he awakened. A small clashing noise brought him up from sleep. Tom listened and heard again the squeak of iron on iron. He moved stiffly and shivered in the morning air. The camp still slept. Tom stood up and looked over the side of the truck. The eastern mountains were blue-black, and as he watched, the light stood up faintly behind them, colored at the mountain rims with a washed red, then growing colder, grayer, darker, as it went up overhead, until at a place near the western horizon it merged with pure night. Down in the valley the earth was the lavender-gray of dawn.

The clash of iron sounded again. Tom looked down the line of tents, only a little lighter gray than the ground. Beside a tent he saw a flash of orange fire seeping from the cracks in an old iron stove. Gray smoke spurted up from a stubby smoke-pipe.

Tom climbed over the truck side and dropped to the ground. He moved slowly toward the stove. He saw a girl working about the stove, saw that she carried a baby on her crooked arm, and that the baby was nursing, its head up under the girl's shirtwaist. And the girl moved about, poking the fire, shifting the rusty stove lids to make a better draft, opening the oven door; and all the time the baby sucked, and the mother shifted it deftly from arm to arm. The baby didn't interfere with her work or with the quick gracefulness of her movements. And the orange fire licked out of the stove cracks and threw flickering reflections on the tent.

Tom moved closer. He smelled frying bacon and baking bread. From the east the light grew swiftly. Tom came near to the stove and stretched out his hands to it. The girl looked at him and nodded, so that her two braids jerked.

"Good mornin'," she said, and she turned the bacon in the pan.

The tent flap jerked up and a young man came out and an older man followed him. They were dressed in new blue dungarees and in dungaree coats, stiff with filler, the brass buttons shining. They were sharp-faced men, and they looked much alike. The younger man had a dark stubble beard and the older man a white stubble beard. Their heads and faces were wet, their hair dripped, water stood in drops on their stiff beards. Their cheeks shone with dampness. Together they stood looking quietly into the lightening east. They yawned together and watched the light on the hill rims. And then they turned and saw Tom.

"Mornin'," the older man said, and his face was neither friendly nor unfriendly.

"Mornin'," said Tom.

And, "Mornin'," said the younger man.

The water slowly dried on their faces. They came to the stove and warmed their hands at it.

The girl kept to her work. Once she set the baby down and tied her braids together in back with a string, and the two braids jerked and swung as she worked. She set tin cups on a big packing box, set tin plates and knives and forks out. Then she scooped bacon from the deep grease and laid it on a tin platter, and the bacon cricked and rustled as it grew crisp. She opened the rusty oven door and took out a square pan full of big high biscuits.

When the smell of the biscuits struck the air both of the men inhaled deeply. The younger said, "Kee-rist!" softly.

Now the older man said to Tom, "Had your breakfast?"

"Well, no, I ain't. But my folks is over there. They ain't up. Need the sleep."

"Well, set down with us, then. We got plenty—thank God!"

"Why, thank ya," Tom said. "Smells so darn good I couldn' say no."

"Don't she?" the younger man asked. "Ever smell anything so good in ya life?" They marched to the packing box and squatted around it.

"Workin' around here?" the young man asked.

"Aim to," said Tom. "We jus' got in las' night. Ain't had no chance to look aroun'."

"We had twelve days' work," the young man said.

The girl, working by the stove, said, "They even got new clothes." Both men looked down at their stiff blue clothes, and they smiled a little shyly. The girl set out the platter of bacon and the brown, high biscuits and a bowl of bacon gravy and a pot of coffee, and then she squatted down by the box too. The baby still nursed, its head up under the girl's shirtwaist.

They filled their plates, poured bacon gravy over the biscuits, and sugared their coffee.

The older man filled his mouth full, and he chewed and chewed and gulped and swallowed. "God Almighty, it's good!" he said, and he filled his mouth again.

The younger man said, "We been eatin' good for twelve days now. Never missed a meal in twelve days—none of us. Workin' an' gettin' our pay an' eatin'." He fell to again, almost frantically, and refilled his plate. They drank the scalding coffee and threw the grounds to the earth and filled their cups again.

There was color in the light now, a reddish gleam. The father and son stopped eating. They were facing to the east and their faces were lighted by the dawn. The image of the mountain and the light coming over it were reflected in their eyes. And then they threw the grounds from their cups to the earth, and they stood up together.

"Got to git goin'," the older man said.

The younger turned to Tom. "Lookie," he said. "We're layin' some pipe. 'F you wanta walk over with us, maybe we could get you on."

Tom said, "Well, that's mighty nice of you. An' I sure thank ya for the breakfast."

"Glad to have you," the older man said. "We'll try to git you workin' if you want."

"Ya goddamn right I want," Tom said. "Jus' wait a minute. I'll tell my folks." He hurried to the Joad tent and bent over and looked inside. In the gloom under the tarpaulin he saw the lumps of sleeping figures. But a little movement started among the bedclothes. Ruthie came wriggling out like a snake, her hair down over her eyes and her dress wrinkled and twisted. She crawled carefully out and stood up. Her gray eyes were clear and calm from sleep, and mischief was not in them. Tom moved off from the tent and beckoned her to follow, and when he turned, she looked up at him.

"Lord God, you're growin' up," he said.

She looked away in sudden embarrassment. "Listen here," Tom said. "Don't you wake nobody up, but when they get up, you tell 'em I got a chancet at a job, an' I'm a-goin' for it. Tell Ma I et breakfas' with some neighbors. You hear that?"

Ruthie nodded and turned her head away, and her eyes were little girl's eyes. "Don't you wake 'em up," Tom cautioned. He hurried back to his new friends. And Ruthie cautiously approached the sanitary unit and peeked in the open doorway.

The two men were waiting when Tom came back. The young woman had dragged a mattress out and put the baby on it while she cleaned up the dishes.

Tom said, "I wanted to tell my folks where-at I was. They wasn't awake." The three walked down the street between the tents.

The camp had begun to come to life. At the new fires the women worked, slicing meat, kneading the dough for the morning's bread. And the men were stirring about the tents and about the automobiles. The sky was rosy now. In front of the office a lean old man raked the ground carefully. He so dragged his rake that the tine marks were straight and deep.

"You're out early, Pa," the young man said as they went by.

"Yep, yep. Got to make up my rent."

The three went out the gate.

"Rent, hell!" the young man said. "He was drunk last Sat'dy night. Sung in his tent all night. Committee give him work for it." They walked along the edge of the oiled road; a row of walnut trees grew beside the way. The sun shoved its edge over the mountains.

Tom said, "Seems funny. I've et your food, an' I ain't tol' you my name—nor you ain't mentioned yours. I'm Tom Joad."

The older man looked at him, and then he smiled a little. "You ain't been out here long?"

"Hell, no! Jus' a couple days."

"I knowed it. Funny, you git outa the habit a mentionin' your name. They's so goddamn many. Jist fellas. Well, sir—I'm Timothy Wallace, an' this here's my boy Wilkie."

"Proud to know ya," Tom said. "You been out here long?"

"Ten months," Wilkie said. "Got here right on the tail a the floods las' year. Jesus! We had *a* time, *a* time! Goddamn near starve' to death." Their feet rattled on the oiled road. A truckload of men went by, and each man was sunk into himself. Each man braced himself in the truck bed and scowled down.

"Goin' out for the Gas Company," Timothy said. "They got a nice job of it."

"I could of took our truck," Tom suggested.

"No." Timothy leaned down and picked up a green walnut. He tested it with his thumb and then shied it at a blackbird sitting on a fence wire. The bird flew up, let the nut sail under it, and then settled back on the wire and smoothed its shining black feathers with its beak.

Tom asked, "Ain't you got no car?"

Both Wallaces were silent, and Tom, looking at their faces, saw that they were ashamed.

Wilkie said, "Place we work at is on'y a mile up the road."

Timothy said angrily, "No, we ain't got no car. We sol' our car. Had to. Run outa food, run outa ever'thing. Couldn' git no job. Fellas come aroun' ever' week, buyin' cars. Come aroun', an' if you're hungry, why, they'll buy your car. An' if you're hungry enough, they don't hafta pay nothin' for it. An'—we was hungry enough. Give us ten dollars for her." He spat into the road.

Wilkie said quietly, "I was in Bakersfiel' las' week. I seen her—a settin' in a use'-car lot—settin' right there, an' seventy-five dollars was the sign on her."

"We had to," Timothy said. "It was either us let 'em steal our car or us steal somepin from them. We ain't had to steal yet, but, goddamn it, we been close!"

Tom said, "You know, 'fore we lef' home, we heard they was plenty work out here. Seen han'bills askin' folks to come out."

"Yeah," Timothy said. "We seen 'em too. An' they ain't much work. An' wages is comin' down all a time. I git so goddamn tired jus' figgerin' how to eat."

"You got work now," Tom suggested.

"Yeah, but it ain't gonna las' long. Workin' for a nice fella. Got a little place. Works 'longside of us. But, hell—it ain't gonna las' no time."

Tom said, "Why in hell you gonna git me on? I'll make it shorter. What you cuttin' your own throat for?"

Timothy shook his head slowly. "I dunno. Got no sense, I guess. We figgered to get us each a hat. Can't do it, I guess. There's the place, off to the right there. Nice job, too. Gettin' thirty cents an hour. Nice frien'ly fella to work for."

They turned off the highway and walked down a graveled road, through a small kitchen orchard; and behind the trees they came to a small white farm house, a few sheds, and a barn; behind the barn a vineyard and a field of cotton. As the three men walked past the house a screen door banged, and a stocky sunburned man came down the back steps. He wore a paper sun helmet, and he rolled up his sleeves as he came across the yard. His heavy sunburned eyebrows were drawn down in a scowl. His cheeks were sunburned a beef red.

"Mornin', Mr. Thomas," Timothy said.

"Morning." The man spoke irritably.

Timothy said, "This here's Tom Joad. We wondered if you could see your way to put him on?"

Thomas scowled at Tom. And then he laughed shortly, and his brows still scowled. "Oh, sure! I'll put him on. I'll put everybody on. Maybe I'll get a hundred men on."

"We jus' thought—" Timothy began apologetically.

Thomas interrupted him. "Yes, I been thinkin' too." He swung around and faced them. "I've got some things to tell you. I been paying you thirty cents an hour—that right?"

"Why, sure, Mr. Thomas—but——"

"And I been getting thirty cents' worth of work." His heavy hard hands clasped each other.

"We try to give a good day of work."

"Well, goddamn it, this morning you're getting twenty-five cents an hour, and you take it or leave it." The redness of his face deepened with anger.

Timothy said, "We've give you good work. You said so yourself."

"I know it. But it seems like I ain't hiring my own men any more." He swallowed. "Look," he said. "I got sixty-five acres here. Did you ever hear of the Farmers' Association?"

"Why, sure."

"Well, I belong to it. We had a meeting last night. Now, do you know who runs the Farmers' Association? I'll tell you. The Bank of the West. That bank owns most of this valley, and it's got paper on everything it don't own. So last night the member from the bank told me, he said, 'You're paying thirty cents an hour. You'd better cut it down to twenty-five.' I said, 'I've got good men. They're worth thirty.' And he says, 'It isn't that,' he says. 'The wage is twenty-five now. If you pay thirty, it'll only cause unrest. And by the way,' he says, 'you going to need the usual amount for a crop loan next year?'" Thomas stopped. His breath was panting through his lips. "You see? The wage is twenty-five cents—and like it."

"We done good work," Timothy said helplessly.

"Ain't you got it yet? Mr. Bank hires two thousand men an' I hire three. I've got paper to meet. Now if you can figure some way out, by Christ, I'll take it! They got me."

Timothy shook his head. "I don' know what to say."

"You wait here." Thomas walked quickly to the house. The door slammed after him. In a moment he was back, and he carried a newspaper in his hand. "Did you see this? Here, I'll read it: 'Citizens, angered at red agitators, burn squatters' camp. Last night a band of citizens, infuriated at the agitation going on in a local squatters' camp, burned the tents to the ground and warned agitators to get out of the country.' "

Tom began, "Why, I—" and then he closed his mouth and was silent.

Thomas folded the paper carefully and put it in his pocket. He had himself in control again. He said quietly, "Those men were sent out by the Association. Now I'm giving 'em away. And if they ever find out I told, I won't have a farm next year."

"I jus' don't know what to say," Timothy said. "If they was agitators, I can see why they was mad."

Thomas said, "I watched it a long time. There's always red agitators just before a pay cut. Always. Goddamn it, they got me trapped. Now, what are you going to do? Twenty-five cents?"

Timothy looked at the ground. "I'll work," he said.

"Me too," said Wilkie.

Tom said, "Seems like I walked into somepin. Sure, I'll work. I got to work."

Thomas pulled a bandanna out of his hip pocket and wiped his mouth and chin. "I don't know how long it can go on. I don't know how you men can feed a family on what you get now."

"We can while we work," Wilkie said. "It's when we don't git work."

Thomas looked at his watch. "Well, let's go out and dig some ditch. By God," he said, "I'm a-gonna tell you. You fellas live in that government camp, don't you?"

Timothy stiffened. "Yes, sir."

"And you have dances every Saturday night?"

Wilkie smiled. "We sure do."

"Well, look out next Saturday night."

Suddenly Timothy straightened. He stepped close. "What you mean? I belong to the Central Committee. I got to know."

Thomas looked apprehensive. "Don't you ever tell I told."

"What is it?" Timothy demanded.

"Well, the Association don't like the government camps. Can't get a deputy in there. The people make their own laws, I hear, and you can't arrest a man without a warrant. Now if there was a big fight and maybe shooting—a bunch of deputies could go in and clean out the camp."

Timothy had changed. His shoulders were straight and his eyes cold. "What you mean?"

"Don't you ever tell where you heard," Thomas said uneasily. "There's going to be a fight in the camp Saturday night. And there's going to be deputies ready to go in."

Tom demanded, "Why, for God's sake? Those folks ain't bothering nobody."

"I'll tell you why," Thomas said. "Those folks in the camp are getting used to being treated like humans. When they go back to the squatters' camps they'll be hard to handle." He wiped his face again. "Go on out to work now. Jesus, I hope I haven't talked myself out of my farm. But I like you people."

Timothy stepped in front of him and put out a hard lean hand, and Thomas took it. "Nobody won't know who tol'. We thank you. They won't be no fight."

"Go on to work," Thomas said. "And it's twenty-five cents an hour."

"We'll take it," Wilkie said, "from you."

Thomas walked away toward the house. "I'll be out in a piece," he said. "You men get to work." The screen door slammed behind him.

The three men walked out past the little white-washed barn, and along a field edge. They came to a long narrow ditch with sections of concrete pipe lying beside it.

"Here's where we're a-workin'," Wilkie said.

His father opened the barn and passed out two picks and three shovels. And he said to Tom, "Here's your beauty."

Tom hefted the pick. "Jumping Jesus! If she don't feel good!"

"Wait'll about 'leven o'clock," Wilkie suggested. "See how good she feels then."

They walked to the end of the ditch. Tom took off his coat and dropped it on the dirt pile. He pushed up his cap and stepped into the ditch. Then he spat on his hands. The pick arose into the air and flashed down. Tom grunted softly. The pick rose and fell, and the grunt came at the moment it sank into the ground and loosened the soil.

Wilkie said, "Yes, sir, Pa, we got here a first-grade muckstick man. This here boy been married to that there little digger."

Tom said, "I put in time (*umph*). Yes, sir, I sure did (*umph*). Put in my years (*umph!*). Kinda like the feel (*umph!*)." The soil loosened ahead of him. The sun cleared the fruit trees now and the grape leaves were golden green on the vines. Six feet along and Tom stepped aside and wiped his forehead. Wilkie came behind him. The shovel rose and fell and the dirt flew out to the pile beside the lengthening ditch.

"I heard about this here Central Committee," said Tom. "So you're one of 'em."

"Yes, sir," Timothy replied. "And it's a responsibility. All them people. We're doin' our best. An' the people in the camp a-doin' their best. I wisht them big farmers wouldn' plague us so. I wisht they wouldn'."

Tom climbed back into the ditch and Wilkie stood aside. Tom said, "How 'bout this fight (*umph!*) at the dance, he tol' about (*umph*)? What they wanta do that for?"

Timothy followed behind Wilkie, and Timothy's shovel beveled the bottom of the ditch and smoothed it ready for the pipe. "Seems like they got to drive us," Timothy said. "They're scairt we'll organize, I guess. An' maybe they're right. This here camp is a organization. People there look out for theirselves. Got the nicest strang band in these parts. Got a little charge account in the store for folks that's hungry. Fi' dollars—you can git that much food an' the camp'll stan' good. We ain't never had no trouble with the law. I guess the big farmers is scairt of that. Can't throw us in jail—why, it scares 'em. Figger maybe if we can gove'n ourselves, maybe we'll do other things."

Tom stepped clear of the ditch and wiped the sweat out of his eyes. "You hear what that paper said 'bout agitators up north a Bakersfiel'?"

"Sure," said Wilkie. "They do that all a time."

"Well, I was there. They wasn't no agitators. What they call reds. What the hell is these reds anyways?"

Timothy scraped a little hill level in the bottom of the ditch. The sun made his white bristle beard shine. "They's a lot a fellas wanta know what reds is." He laughed. "One of our boys foun' out." He patted the piled earth gently with his shovel. "Fella named Hines—got 'bout thirty thousan' acres, peaches and grapes—got a cannery an' a winery. Well, he's all a time talkin' about 'them goddamn reds.' 'Goddamn reds is drivin' the country to ruin,' he says, an' 'We got to drive these here red bastards out.' Well, they were a young fella jus' come out west here, an' he's listenin' one day. He kinda scratched his head an' he says, 'Mr. Hines, I ain't been here long. What is these goddamn reds?' Well, sir, Hines says, 'A red is any son-of-a-bitch that wants thirty cents an hour when we're payin' twenty-five!' Well, this young fella he thinks about her, an' he scratches his head, an' he says, 'Well, Jesus, Mr. Hines. I ain't a son-of-a-bitch, but if that's what a red is—why, I want thirty cents an hour. Ever'body does. Hell, Mr. Hines, we're all reds.' " Timothy drove his shovel along the ditch bottom, and the solid earth shone where the shovel cut it.

Tom laughed. "Me too, I guess." His pick arced up and drove down, and the earth cracked under it. The sweat rolled down his forehead and down the sides of his nose, and it glistened on his neck. "Damn it," he said, "a pick is a nice tool (*umph*), if you don' fight it (*umph*). You an' the pick (*umph*) workin' together (*umph*)."

In line, the three men worked, and the ditch inched along, and the sun shone hotly down on them in the growing morning.

When Tom left her, Ruthie gazed in at the door of the sanitary unit for a while. Her courage was not strong without Winfield to boast for. She put a bare foot in on the concrete floor, and then withdrew it. Down the line a woman came out of a tent and started a fire in a tin camp stove. Ruthie took a few steps in that direction, but she could not leave. She crept to the entrance of the Joad tent and looked in. On one side, lying on the ground, lay Uncle John, his mouth open and his snores bubbling spittily in his throat. Ma and Pa were covered with a comfort, their heads in, away from the light. Al was on the far side from Uncle John, and his arm was flung over his eyes. Near the front of the tent Rose of Sharon and Winfield lay, and there was the space where Ruthie had been, beside Winfield. She squatted down and peered in. Her eyes remained on Winfield's tow head; and as she looked, the little boy opened his eyes and stared out at her, and his eyes were solemn. Ruthie put her finger to her lips and beckoned with her other hand. Winfield rolled his eyes over to Rose of Sharon. Her pink flushed face was near to him, and her mouth was open a little. Winfield carefully loosened the blanket and slipped out. He crept out of the tent cautiously and joined Ruthie. "How long you been up?" he whispered.

She led him away with elaborate caution, and when they were safe, she said, "I never been to bed. I was up all night."

"You was not," Winfield said. "You're a dirty liar."

"Awright," she said. "If I'm a liar I ain't gonna tell you nothin' that happened. I ain't gonna tell how the fella got killed with a stab knife an' how they was a bear come in an' took off a little chile."

"They wasn't no bear," Winfield said uneasily. He brushed up his hair with his fingers and he pulled down his overalls at the crotch.

"All right—they wasn't no bear," she said sarcastically. "An' they ain't no white things made outa dish-stuff, like in the catalogues."

Winfield regarded her gravely. He pointed to the sanitary unit. "In there?" he asked.

"I'm a dirty liar," Ruthie said. "It ain't gonna do me no good to tell stuff to you."

"Le's go look," Winfield said.

"I already been," Ruthie said. "I already set on 'em. I even pee'd in one."

"You never neither," said Winfield.

They went to the unit building, and that time Ruthie was not afraid. Boldly she led the way into the building. The toilets lined one side of the large room, and each toilet had its compartment with a door in front of it. The porcelain was gleaming white. Hand basins lined another wall, while on the third wall were four shower compartments.

"There," said Ruthie. "Them's the toilets. I seen 'em in the catalogue." The children drew near to one of the toilets. Ruthie, in a burst of bravado, boosted her skirt and sat down. "I tol' you I been here," she said. And to prove it, there was a tinkle of water in the bowl.

Winfield was embarrassed. His hand twisted the flushing lever. There was a roar of water. Ruthie leaped into the air and jumped away. She and Winfield stood in the middle of the room and looked at the toilet. The hiss of water continued in it.

"You done it," Ruthie said. "You went an' broke it. I seen you."

"I never. Honest I never."

"I seen you," Ruthie said. "You jus' ain't to be trusted with no nice stuff."

Winfield sunk his chin. He looked up at Ruthie and his eyes filled with tears. His chin quivered. And Ruthie was instantly contrite.

"Never you mind," she said. "I won't tell on you. We'll pretend like she was already broke. We'll pretend we ain't even been in here." She led him out of the building.

The sun lipped over the mountain by now, shone on the corrugated-iron roofs of the five sanitary units, shone on the gray tents and on the swept ground of the streets between the tents. And the camp was waking up. The fires were burning in camp stoves, in the stoves made of kerosene cans and of sheets of metal. The smell of smoke was in the air. Tent flaps were thrown back and people moved about in the streets. In front of the Joad tent Ma stood looking up and down the street. She saw the children and came over to them.

"I was worryin'," Ma said. "I didn' know where you was."

"We was jus' lookin'," Ruthie said.

"Well, where's Tom? You seen him?"

Ruthie became important. "Yes, ma'am. Tom, he got me up an' he tol' me what to tell you." She paused to let her importance be apparent.

"Well—what?" Ma demanded.

"He said tell you—" She paused again and looked to see that Winfield appreciated her position.

Ma raised her hand, the back of it toward Ruthie. "What?"

"He got work," said Ruthie quickly. "Went out to work." She looked apprehensively at Ma's raised hand. The hand sank down again, and then it reached out for Ruthie. Ma embraced Ruthie's shoulders in a quick convulsive hug, and then released her.

Ruthie stared at the ground in embarrassment, and changed the subject. "They got toilets over there," she said. "White ones."

"You been in there?" Ma demanded.

"Me an' Winfiel'," she said; and then, treacherously, "Winfiel', he bust a toilet."

Winfield turned red. He glared at Ruthie. "She pee'd in one," he said viciously.

Ma was apprehensive. "Now what did you do? You show me." She forced them to the door and inside. "Now what'd you do?"

Ruthie pointed. "It was a-hissin' and a-swishin'. Stopped now."

"Show me what you done," Ma demanded.

Winfield went reluctantly to the toilet. "I didn' push it hard," he said. "I jus' had aholt of this here, an'—" The swish of water came again. He leaped away.

Ma threw back her head and laughed, while Ruthie and Winfield regarded her resentfully. "Tha's the way she works," Ma said. "I seen them before. When you finish, you push that."

The shame of their ignorance was too great for the children. They went out the door, and they walked down the street to stare at a large family eating breakfast.

Ma watched them out of the door. And then she looked about the room. She went to the shower closets and looked in. She walked to the wash basins and ran her finger over the white porcelain. She turned the water on a little and held her finger in the stream, and jerked her hand away when the water came hot. For a moment she regarded the basin, and then, setting the plug, she filled the bowl a little from the hot faucet, a little from the cold. And then she washed her hands in the warm water, and she washed her face. She was brushing water through her hair with her fingers when a step sounded on the concrete floor behind her. Ma swung around. An elderly man stood looking at her with an expression of righteous shock.

He said harshly, "How you come in here?"

Ma gulped, and she felt the water dripping from her chin and soaking through her dress. "I didn' know," she said apologetically. "I thought this here was for folks to use."

The elderly man frowned on her. "For men folks," he said sternly. He walked to the door and pointed to a sign on it: MEN. "There," he said. "That proves it. Didn' you see that?"

"No," Ma said in shame, "I never seen it. Ain't they a place where I can go?"

The man's anger departed. "You jus' come?" he asked more kindly.

"Middle of the night," said Ma.

"Then you ain't talked to the Committee?"

"What committee?"

"Why, the Ladies' Committee."

"No, I ain't."

He said proudly, "The Committee'll call on you purty soon an' fix you up. We take care of folks that jus' come in. Now, if you want a ladies' toilet, you jus' go on the other side of the building. That side's yourn."

Ma said uneasily, "Ya say a ladies' committee—comin' to my tent?"

He nodded his head. "Purty soon, I guess."

"Thank ya," said Ma. She hurried out, and half ran to the tent.

"Pa," she called. "John, git up! You, Al. Git up an' git washed." Startled sleepy eyes looked out at her. "All of you," Ma cried. "You git up an' git your face washed. An' comb your hair."

Uncle John looked pale and sick. There was a red bruised place on his chin.

Pa demanded, "What's the matter?"

"The Committee," Ma cried. "They's a committee—a ladies' committee a-comin' to visit. Git up now, an' git washed. An' while we was a-sleepin' an' a-snorin', Tom's went out an' got work. Git up, now."

They came sleepily out of the tent. Uncle John staggered a little, and his face was pained.

"Git over to that house and wash up," Ma ordered. "We got to get breakfus' an' be ready for the Committee." She went to a little pile of split wood in the camp lot. She started a fire and put up her cooking irons. "Pone," she said to herself. "Pone an' gravy. That's quick. Got to be quick." She talked on to herself, and Ruthie and Winfield stood by, wondering.

The smoke of the morning fires arose all over the camp, and the mutter of talk came from all sides.

Rose of Sharon, unkempt and sleepy-eyed, crawled out of the tent. Ma turned from the cornmeal she was measuring in fistfuls. She looked at the girl's wrinkled dirty dress, at her frizzled uncombed hair. "You got to clean up," she said briskly. "Go right over and clean up. You got a clean dress. I washed it. Git your hair combed. Git the seeds out a your eyes." Ma was excited.

Rose of Sharon said sullenly, "I don' feel good. I wisht Connie would come. I don't feel like doin' nothin' 'thout Connie."

Ma turned full around on her. The yellow cornmeal clung to her hands and wrists. "Rosasharn," she said sternly, "you git upright. You jus' been mopin' enough. They's a ladies' committee a-comin', an' the fambly ain't gonna be frawny when they get here."

"But I don' feel good."

Ma advanced on her, mealy hands held out. "Git," Ma said. "They's times when how you feel got to be kep' to yourself."

"I'm a-goin' to vomit," Rose of Sharon whined.

"Well, go an' vomit. 'Course you're gonna vomit. Ever'body does.

Git it over an' then you clean up, an' you wash your legs an' put on them shoes of yourn." She turned back to her work. "An' braid your hair," she said.

A frying pan of grease sputtered over the fire, and it splashed and hissed when Ma dropped the pone in with a spoon. She mixed flour with grease in a kettle and added water and salt and stirred the gravy. The coffee began to turn over in the gallon can, and the smell of coffee rose from it.

Pa wandered back from the sanitary unit, and Ma looked critically up. Pa said, "Ya say Tom's got work?"

"Yes, sir. Went out 'fore we was awake. Now look in that box an' get you some clean overhalls an' a shirt. An', Pa, I'm awful busy. You git in Ruthie an' Winfiel's ears. They's hot water. Will you do that? Scrounge aroun' in their ears good, an' their necks. Get 'em red an' shinin'."

"Never seen you so bubbly," Pa said.

Ma cried, "This here's the time the fambly got to get decent. Comin' acrost they wasn't no chancet. But now we can. Th'ow your dirty overhalls in the tent an' I'll wash 'em out."

Pa went inside the tent, and in a moment he came out with pale blue, washed overalls and shirt on. And he led the sad and startled children toward the sanitary unit.

Ma called after him, "Scrounge aroun' good in their ears."

Uncle John came to the door of the men's side and looked out, and then he went back and sat on the toilet a long time and held his aching head in his hands.

Ma had taken up a panload of brown pone and was dropping spoons of dough in the grease for a second pan when a shadow fell on the ground beside her. She looked over her shoulder. A little man dressed all in white stood behind her—a man with a thin, brown, lined face and merry eyes. He was lean as a picket. His white clean clothes were frayed at the seams. He smiled at Ma. "Good morning," he said.

Ma looked at his white clothes and her face hardened with sus-. picion. "Mornin'," she said.

"Are you Mrs. Joad?"

"Yes."

"Well, I'm Jim Rawley. I'm camp manager. Just dropped by to see if everything's all right. Got everything you need?"

Ma studied him suspiciously. "Yes," she said.

Rawley said, "I was asleep when you came last night. Lucky we had a place for you." His voice was warm.

Ma said simply, "It's nice. 'Specially them wash tubs."

"You wait till the women get to washing. Pretty soon now. You never heard such a fuss. Like a meeting. Know what they did yesterday, Mrs. Joad? They had a chorus. Singing a hymn tune and rubbing clothes all in time. That was something to hear, I tell you."

The suspicion was going out of Ma's face. "Must a been nice. You're the boss?"

"No," he said. "The people here worked me out of a job. They keep the camp clean, they keep order, they do everything. I never saw such people. They're making clothes in the meeting hall. And they're making toys. Never saw such people."

Ma looked down at her dirty dress. "We ain't clean yet," she said. "You jus' can't keep clean a-travelin'."

"Don't I know it," he said. He sniffed the air. "Say—is that your coffee smells so good?"

Ma smiled. "Does smell nice, don't it? Outside it always smells nice." And she said proudly, "We'd take it in honor 'f you'd have some breakfus' with us."

He came to the fire and squatted on his hams, and the last of Ma's resistance went down. "We'd be proud to have ya," she said. "We ain't got much that's nice, but you're welcome."

The little man grinned at her. "I had my breakfast. But I'd sure like a cup of that coffee. Smells so good."

"Why—why, sure."

"Don't hurry yourself."

Ma poured a tin cup of coffee from the gallon can. She said, "We ain't got sugar yet. Maybe we'll get some today. If you need sugar, it won't taste good."

"Never use sugar," he said. "Spoils the taste of good coffee."

"Well, I like a little sugar," said Ma. She looked at him suddenly and closely, to see how he had come so close so quickly. She looked for motive on his face, and found nothing but friendliness. Then she looked at the frayed seams on his white coat, and she was reassured.

He sipped the coffee. "I guess the ladies'll be here to see you this morning."

"We ain't clean," Ma said. "They shouldn't be comin' till we get cleaned up a little."

"But they know how it is," the manager said. "They came in the same way. No, sir. The committees are good in this camp because they do know." He finished his coffee and stood up. "Well, I got to go on. Anything you want, why, come over to the office. I'm there all the time. Grand coffee. Thank you." He put the cup on the box with the others, waved his hand, and walked down the line of tents. And Ma heard him speaking to the people as he went.

Ma put down her head and she fought with a desire to cry.

Pa came back leading the children, their eyes still wet with pain at the ear-scrounging. They were subdued and shining. The sun-burned skin on Winfield's nose was scrubbed off. "There," Pa said. "Got dirt an' two layers a skin. Had to almost lick 'em to make 'em stan' still."

Ma appraised them. "They look nice," she said. "He'p yaself to pone an' gravy. We got to get stuff outa the way an' the tent in order."

Pa served plates for the children and for himself. "Wonder where Tom got work?"

"I dunno."

"Well, if he can, we can."

Al came excitedly to the tent. "What a place!" he said. He helped himself and poured coffee. "Know what a fella's doin'? He's buildin' a house trailer. Right over there, back a them tents. Got beds an' a stove—ever'thing. Jus' live in her. By God, that's the way to live! Right where you stop—tha's where you live."

Ma said, "I ruther have a little house. Soon's we can, I want a little house."

Pa said, "Al—after we've et, you an' me an' Uncle John'll take the truck an' go out lookin' for work."

"Sure," said Al. "I like to get a job in a garage if they's any jobs. Tha's what I really like. An' get me a little ol' cut-down Ford. Paint her yella an' go a-kyoodlin' aroun'. Seen a purty girl down the road. Give her a big wink, too. Purty as hell, too."

Pa said sternly, "You better get you some work 'fore you go a-tom-cattin'."

Uncle John came out of the toilet and moved slowly near. Ma frowned at him.

"You ain't washed—" she began, and then she saw how sick and weak and sad he looked. "You go on in the tent an' lay down," she said. "You ain't well."

He shook his head. "No," he said. "I sinned, an' I got to take my punishment." He squatted down disconsolately and poured himself a cup of coffee.

Ma took the last pones from the pan. She said casually, "The manager of the camp come an' set an' had a cup a coffee."

Pa looked over slowly. "Yeah? What's he want awready?"

"Jus' come to pass the time," Ma said daintily. "Jus' set down an' had coffee. Said he didn' get good coffee so often, an' smelt our'n."

"What'd he want?" Pa demanded again.

"Didn' want nothin'. Come to see how we was gettin' on."

"I don' believe it," Pa said. "He's probably a-snootin' an' a-smellin' aroun'."

"He was not!" Ma cried angrily. "I can tell a fella that's snootin' aroun' quick as the nex' person."

Pa tossed his coffee grounds out of his cup.

"You got to quit that," Ma said. "This here's a clean place."

"You see she don't get so goddamn clean a fella can't live in her," Pa said jealously. "Hurry up, Al. We're goin' out lookin' for a job."

Al wiped his mouth with his hand. "I'm ready," he said.

Pa turned to Uncle John. "You a-comin'?"

"Yes, I'm a-comin'."

"You don't look so good."

"I ain't so good, but I'm comin'."

Al got in the truck. "Have to get gas," he said. He started the engine. Pa and Uncle John climbed in beside him and the truck moved away down the street.

Ma watched them go. And then she took a bucket and went to the wash trays under the open part of the sanitary unit. She filled her bucket with hot water and carried it back to her camp. And she was washing the dishes in the bucket when Rose of Sharon came back.

"I put your stuff on a plate," Ma said. And then she looked closely at the girl. Her hair was dripping and combed, and her skin was bright and pink. She had put on the blue dress printed with little white flowers. On her feet she wore the heeled slippers of her wedding. She blushed under Ma's gaze. "You had a bath," Ma said.

Rose of Sharon spoke huskily. "I was in there when a lady come in an' done it. Know what you do? You get in a little stall-like, an' you turn handles, an' water comes a-floodin' down on you—hot water or col' water, jus' like you want it—an' I done it!"

"I'm a-goin' to myself," Ma cried. "Jus' soon as I get finish' here. You show me how."

"I'm a-gonna do it ever' day," the girl said. "An' that lady—she seen me, an' she seen about the baby, an'—know what she said? Said they's a nurse comes ever' week. An' I'm to go see that nurse an' she'll tell me jus' what to do so's the baby'll be strong. Says all the ladies here do that. An' I'm a-gonna do it." The words bubbled out. "An'—know what—? Las' week they was a baby borned an' the whole camp give a party, an' they give clothes, an' they give stuff for the baby—even give a baby buggy—wicker one. Wasn't new, but they give it a coat a pink paint, an' it was jus' like new. An' they give the baby a name, an' had a cake. Oh, Lord!" She subsided, breathing heavily.

Ma said, "Praise God, we come home to our own people. I'm a-gonna have a bath."

"Oh, it's nice," the girl said.

Ma wiped the tin dishes and stacked them. She said, "We're Joads. We don't look up to nobody. Grampa's grampa, he fit in the Revolution. We was farm people till the debt. And then—them people. They done somepin to us. Ever' time they come seemed like they was a-whippin' me—all of us. An' in Needles, that police. He done somepin to me, made me feel mean. Made me feel ashamed. An' now I ain't ashamed. These folks is our folks—is our folks. An' that manager, he come an' set an' drank coffee, an' he says, 'Mrs. Joad' this, an' 'Mrs. Joad' that—an' 'How you gettin' on, Mrs. Joad?' " She stopped and sighed. "Why, I feel like people again." She stacked the last dish. She went into the tent and dug through the clothes box for her shoes and a clean dress. And she found a little paper package with her earrings in it. As she went past Rose of Sharon, she said, "If them ladies comes, you tell 'em I'll be right back." She disappeared around the side of the sanitary unit.

Rose of Sharon sat down heavily on a box and regarded her wedding shoes, black patent leather and tailored black bows. She wiped the toes with her finger and wiped her finger on the inside of her skirt. Leaning down put a pressure on her growing abdomen. She sat up straight and touched herself with exploring fingers, and she smiled a little as she did it.

Along the road a stocky woman walked, carrying an apple box of dirty clothes toward the wash tubs. Her face was brown with sun, and her eyes were black and intense. She wore a great apron, made from a cotton bag, over her gingham dress, and men's brown oxfords were on her feet. She saw that Rose of Sharon caressed herself, and she saw the little smile on the girl's face.

"So!" she cried, and she laughed with pleasure. "What you think it's gonna be?"

Rose of Sharon blushed and looked down at the ground, and then peeked up, and the little shiny black eyes of the woman took her in. "I don' know," she mumbled.

The woman plopped the apple box on the ground. "Got a live tumor," she said, and she cackled like a happy hen. "Which'd you ruther?" she demanded.

"I dunno—boy, I guess. Sure—boy."

"You jus' come in, didn' ya?"

"Las' night—late."

"Gonna stay?"

"I don' know. 'F we can get work, guess we will."

A shadow crossed the woman's face, and the little black eyes grew fierce. " 'F you can git work. That's what we all say."

"My brother got a job already this mornin'."

"Did, huh? Maybe you're lucky. Look out for luck. You can't trus' luck." She stepped close. "You can only git one kind a luck. Cain't have more. You be a good girl," she said fiercely. "You be good. If you got sin on you—you better watch out for that there baby." She squatted down in front of Rose of Sharon. "They's scandalous things goes on in this here camp," she said darkly. "Ever' Sat'dy night they's dancin', an' not only squar' dancin', neither. They's some does clutch-an'-hug dancin'! I seen 'em."

Rose of Sharon said guardedly, "I like dancin', squar' dancin'." And she added virtuously, "I never done that other kind."

The brown woman nodded her head dismally. "Well, some does. An' the Lord ain't lettin' it get by, neither; an' don' you think He is."

"No, ma'am," the girl said softly.

The woman put one brown wrinkled hand on Rose of Sharon's knee, and the girl flinched under the touch. "You let me warn you now. They ain't but a few deep down Jesus-lovers lef'. Ever' Sat'dy night when that there strang ban' starts up an' should be a-playin' hymnody, they're a-reelin'—yes, sir, a-reelin'. I seen 'em. Won' go near, myself, nor I don' let my kin go near. They's clutch-an'-hug, I tell ya." She paused for emphasis and then said, in a hoarse whisper, "They do more. They give a stage play oncet." She backed away and cocked her head to see how Rose of Sharon would take such a revelation.

"Actors?" the girl said in awe.

"No, sir!" the woman exploded. "Not *actors*, not them already damn' people. Our own kinda folks. Our own people. An' they was little children didn' know no better, in it, an' they was pertendin' to be stuff they wasn't. I didn' go near. But I hearn 'em talkin' what they was a-doin'. The devil was jus' a-struttin' through this here camp."

Rose of Sharon listened, her eyes and mouth open. "Oncet in school we give a Chris' chile play—Christmas."

"Well—I ain' sayin' tha's bad or good. They's good folks thinks a Chris' chile is awright. But—well, I wouldn' care to come right out flat an' say so. But this here wasn' no Chris' chile. This here was sin an' delusion an' devil stuff. Struttin' an' paradin' an' speakin' like they're somebody they ain't. An' dancin' an' clutchin' an' a-huggin'."

Rose of Sharon sighed.

"An' not jus' a few, neither," the brown woman went on. "Gettin' so's you can almos' count the deep-down lamb-blood folks on your toes. An' don' you think them sinners is puttin' nothin' over on God, neither. No, sir, He's a-chalkin' 'em up sin by sin, an' He's drawin' His line an' addin' 'em up sin by sin. God's a-watchin', an' I'm a-watchin'. He's awready smoked two of 'em out."

Rose of Sharon panted, "Has?"

The brown woman's voice was rising in intensity. "I seen it. Girl a-carryin' a little one, jes' like you. An' she play-acted, an' she hug-danced. And"—the voice grew bleak and ominous—"she thinned out and she skinnied out, an'—she dropped that baby, dead."

"Oh, my!" The girl was pale.

"Dead and bloody. 'Course nobody wouldn' speak to her no more. She had a go away. Can't tech sin 'thout catchin' it. No, sir. An' they was another, done the same thing. An' she skinnied out, an'—know what? One night she was gone. An' two days, she's back. Says she was visitin'. But—she ain't got no baby. Know what I think?

I think the manager, he took her away to drop her baby. He don' believe in sin. Tol' me hisself. Says the sin is bein' hungry. Says the sin is bein' cold. Says—I tell ya, he tol' me hisself—can't see God in them things. Says them girls skinnied out 'cause they didn' git 'nough food. Well, I fixed him up." She rose to her feet and stepped back. Her eyes were sharp. She pointed a rigid forefinger in Rose of Sharon's face. "I says, 'Git back!' I says. I says, 'I knowed the devil was rampagin' in this here camp. Now I know who the devil is. Git back, Satan,' I says. An', by Chris', he got back! Tremblin' he was, an' sneaky. Says, 'Please!' Says, 'Please don' make the folks unhappy.' I says, 'Unhappy? How 'bout their soul? How 'bout them dead babies an' them poor sinners ruint 'count of play-actin'?' He jes' looked, an' he give a sick grin an' went away. He knowed when he met a real testifier to the Lord. I says, 'I'm a-helpin' Jesus watch the goin's-on. An' you an' them other sinners ain't gittin' away with it.'" She picked up her box of dirty clothes. "You take heed. I warned you. You take heed a that pore chile in your belly an' keep outa sin." And she strode away titanically, and her eyes shone with virtue.

Rose of Sharon watched her go, and then she put her head down on her hands and whimpered into her palms. A soft voice sounded beside her. She looked up, ashamed. It was the little white-clad manager. "Don't worry," he said. "Don't you worry."

Her eyes blinded with tears. "But I done it," she cried. "I hug-danced. I didn' tell her. I done it in Sallisaw. Me an' Connie."

"Don't worry," he said.

"She says I'll drop the baby."

"I know she does. I kind of keep my eye on her. She's a good woman, but she makes people unhappy."

Rose of Sharon sniffled wetly. "She knowed two girls los' their baby right in this here camp."

The manager squatted down in front of her. "Look!" he said. "Listen to me. I know them too. They were too hungry and too tired. And they worked too hard. And they rode on a truck over bumps. They were sick. It wasn't their fault."

"But she said——"

"Don't worry. That woman likes to make trouble."

"But she says you was the devil."

"I know she does. That's because I won't let her make people miserable." He patted her shoulder. "Don't you worry. She doesn't know." And he walked quickly away.

Rose of Sharon looked after him; his lean shoulders jerked as he walked. She was still watching his slight figure when Ma came back, clean and pink, her hair combed and wet, and gathered in a knot. She wore her figured dress and the old cracked shoes; and the little earrings hung in her ears.

"I done it," she said. "I stood in there an' let warm water come a-floodin' an' a-flowin' down over me. An' they was a lady says you can do it ever' day if you want. An'—did them ladies' committee come yet?"

"Uh-uh!" said the girl.

"An' you jus' set there an' didn' redd up the camp none!" Ma gathered up the tin dishes as she spoke. "We got to get in shape," she said. "Come on, stir! Get that sack and kinda sweep along the groun'." She picked up the equipment, put the pans in their box and the box in the tent. "Get them beds neat," she ordered. "I tell ya I ain't never felt nothin' so nice as that water."

Rose of Sharon listlessly followed orders. "Ya think Connie'll be back today?"

"Maybe—maybe not. Can't tell."

"You sure he knows where-at to come?"

"Sure."

"Ma—ya don' think—they could a killed him when they burned—?"

"Not him," Ma said confidently. "He can travel when he wants —jackrabbit-quick an' fox-sneaky."

"I wisht he'd come."

"He'll come when he comes."

"Ma——"

"I wisht you'd get to work."

"Well, do you think dancin' an' play-actin' is sins an'll make me drop the baby?"

Ma stopped her work and put her hands on her hips. "Now what you talkin' about? You ain't done no play-actin'."

"Well, some folks here done it, an' one girl, she dropped her baby—dead—an' bloody, like it was a judgment."

Ma stared at her. "Who tol' you?"

"Lady that come by. An' that little fella in white clothes, he come by an' he says that ain't what done it."

Ma frowned. "Rosasharn," she said, "you stop pickin' at yourself. You're jest a-teasin' yourself up to cry. I don' know what's come at you. Our folks ain't never did that. They took what come to 'em dry-eyed. I bet it's that Connie give you all them notions. He was jes' too big for his overhalls." And she said sternly, "Rosasharn, you're jest one person, an' they's a lot of other folks. You git to your proper place. I knowed people built theirself up with sin till they figgered they was big mean shucks in the sight a the Lord."

"But, Ma——"

"No. Jes' shut up an' git to work. You ain't big enough or mean enough to worry God much. An' I'm gonna give you the back a my han' if you don' stop this pickin' at yourself." She swept the ashes into the fire hole and brushed the stones on its edge. She saw the committee coming along the road. "Git workin'," she said. "Here's the ladies comin'. Git a-workin' now, so's I can be proud." She didn't look again, but she was conscious of the approach of the committee.

There could be no doubt that it was the committee; three ladies, washed, dressed in their best clothes: a lean woman with stringy hair and steel-rimmed glasses, a small stout lady with curly gray hair and a small sweet mouth, and a mammoth lady, big of hock and buttock, big of breast, muscled like a dray-horse, powerful and sure. And the committee walked down the road with dignity.

Ma managed to have her back turned when they arrived. They stopped, wheeled, stood in a line. And the great woman boomed, "Mornin', Mis' Joad, ain't it?"

Ma whirled around as though she had been caught off guard. "Why, yes—yes. How'd you know my name?"

"We're the committee," the big woman said. "Ladies' Committee of Sanitary Unit Number Four. We got your name in the office."

Ma flustered, "We ain't in very good shape yet. I'd be proud to have you ladies come an' set while I make up some coffee."

The plump committee woman said, "Give our names, Jessie. Mention our names to Mis' Joad. Jessie's the Chair," she explained.

Jessie said formally, "Mis' Joad, this here's Annie Littlefield an' Ella Summers, an' I'm Jessie Bullitt."

"I'm proud to make your acquaintance," Ma said. "Won't you set down? They ain't nothin' to set on yet," she added. "But I'll make up some coffee."

"Oh, no," said Annie formally. "Don't put yaself out. We jes' come to call an' see how you was, an' try to make you feel at home."

Jessie Bullitt said sternly, "Annie, I'll thank you to remember I'm Chair."

"Oh! Sure, sure. But next week I am."

"Well, you wait'll next week then. We change ever' week," she explained to Ma.

"Sure you wouldn' like a little coffee?" Ma asked helplessly.

"No, thank you." Jessie took charge. "We gonna show you 'bout the sanitary unit fust, an' then if you wanta, we'll sign you up in the Ladies' Club an' give you duty. 'Course you don' have to join."

"Does—does it cost much?"

"Don't cost nothing but work. An' when you're knowed, maybe you can be 'lected to this committee," Annie interrupted. "Jessie, here, is on the committee for the whole camp. She's a big committee lady."

Jessie smiled with pride. " 'Lected unanimous," she said. "Well, Mis' Joad, I guess it's time we tol' you 'bout how the camp runs."

Ma said, "This here's my girl, Rosasharn."

"How do," they said.

"Better come 'long too."

The huge Jessie spoke, and her manner was full of dignity and kindness, and her speech was rehearsed.

"You shouldn' think we're a-buttin' into your business, Mis' Joad. This here camp got a lot of stuff ever'body uses. An' we got rules we made ourself. Now we're a-goin' to the unit. That there, ever'body uses, an' ever'body got to take care of it." They strolled to the roofed section where the wash trays were, twenty of them. Eight were in use, the women bending over, scrubbing the clothes, and the piles of wrung-out clothes were heaped on the clean concrete floor. "Now you can use these here any time you want," Jessie said. "The on'y thing is, you got to leave 'em clean."

The women who were washing looked up with interest. Jessie said loudly, "This here's Mis' Joad an' Rosasharn, come to live." They greeted Ma in a chorus, and Ma made a dumpy little bow at them and said, "Proud to meet ya."

Jessie led the committee into the toilet and shower room.

"I been here awready," Ma said. "I even took a bath."

"That's what they're for," Jessie said. "An' they's the same rule. You got to leave 'em clean. Ever' week they's a new committee to swab out oncet a day. Maybe you'll git on that committee. You got to bring your own soap."

"We got to get some soap," Ma said. "We're all out."

Jessie's voice became almost reverential. "You ever used this here kind?" she asked, and pointed to the toilets.

"Yes, ma'am. Right this mornin'."

Jessie sighed. "Tha's good."

Ella Summers said, "Jes' las' week——"

Jessie interrupted sternly, "Mis' Summers—I'll tell."

Ella gave ground. "Oh, awright."

Jessie said, "Las' week, when you was Chair, you done it all. I'll thank you to keep out this week."

"Well, tell what that lady done," Ella said.

"Well," said Jessie, "it ain't this committee's business to go a-blabbin', but I won't pass no names. Lady come in las' week, an' she got in here 'fore the committee got to her, an' she had her ol' man's pants in the toilet, an' she says, 'It's too low, an' it ain't big enough. Bust your back over her,' she says. 'Why couldn' they stick her higher?'" The committee smiled superior smiles.

Ella broke in, "Says, 'Can't put 'nough in at oncet.'" And Ella weathered Jessie's stern glance.

Jessie said, "We got our troubles with toilet paper. Rule says you can't take none away from here." She clicked her tongue sharply. "Whole camp chips in for toilet paper." For a moment she was silent, and then she confessed. "Number Four is usin' more than any other. Somebody's a-stealin' it. Come up in general ladies' meetin'. 'Ladies' side, Unit Number Four is usin' too much.' Come right up in meetin'!"

Ma was following the conversation breathlessly. "Stealin' it— what for?"

"Well," said Jessie, "we had trouble before. Las' time they was three little girls cuttin' paper dolls out of it. Well, we caught them. But this time we don't know. Hardly put a roll out 'fore it's gone. Come right up in meetin'. One lady says we oughta have a little bell that rings ever' time the roll turns oncet. Then we could count how many ever'body takes." She shook her head. "I jes' don' know," she said. "I been worried all week. Somebody's a-stealin' toilet paper from Unit Four."

From the doorway came a whining voice, "Mis' Bullitt." The committee turned. "Mis' Bullitt, I hearn what you says." A flushed, perspiring woman stood in the doorway. "I couldn' git up in meetin', Mis' Bullitt. I jes' couldn'. They'd a-laughed or somepin."

"What you talkin' about?" Jessie advanced.

"Well, we-all—maybe—it's us. But we ain't a-stealin', Mis' Bullitt."

Jessie advanced on her, and the perspiration beaded out on the flustery confessor. "We can't he'p it, Mis' Bullitt."

"Now you tell what you're tellin'," Jessie said. "This here unit's suffered a shame 'bout that toilet paper."

"All week, Mis' Bullitt. We couldn' he'p it. You know I got five girls."

"What they been a-doin' with it?" Jessie demanded ominously.

"Jes' usin' it. Hones', jes' usin' it."

"They ain't got the right! Four-five sheets is enough. What's the matter'th 'em?"

The confessor bleated, "Skitters. All five of 'em. We been low on money. They et green grapes. They all five got the howlin' skitters. Run out ever' ten minutes." She defended them, "But they ain't stealin' it."

Jessie sighed. "You should a tol'," she said. "You got to tell. Here's Unit Four been sufferin' shame 'cause you never tol'. Anybody can git the skitters."

The meek voice whined, "I jes' can't keep 'em from eatin' them green grapes. An' they're a-gettin' worse all a time."

Ella Summers burst out, "The Aid. She oughta git the Aid."

"Ella Summers," Jessie said, "I'm a-tellin' you for the las' time, you ain't the Chair." She turned back to the raddled little woman. "Ain't you got no money, Mis' Joyce?"

She looked ashamedly down. "No, but we might git work any time."

"Now you hol' up your head," Jessie said. "That ain't no crime. You jes' waltz right over t' the Weedpatch store an' git you some grocteries. The camp got twenty dollars' credit there. You git yourself fi' dollars' worth. An' you kin pay it back to the Central Committee when you git work. Mis' Joyce, you knowed that," she said sternly. "How come you let your girls git hungry?"

"We ain't never took no charity," Mrs. Joyce said.

"This ain't charity, an' you know it," Jessie raged. "We had all that out. They ain't no charity in this here camp. We won't have no charity. Now you waltz right over an' git you some grocteries, an' you bring the slip to me."

Mrs. Joyce said timidly, "S'pose we can't never pay? We ain't had work for a long time."

"You'll pay if you can. If you can't, that ain't none of our business, an' it ain't your business. One fella went away, an' two months later he sent back the money. You ain't got the right to let your girls git hungry in this here camp."

Mrs. Joyce was cowed. "Yes, ma'am," she said.

"Git you some cheese for them girls," Jessie ordered. "That'll take care a them skitters."

"Yes, ma'am." And Mrs. Joyce scuttled out of the door.

Jessie turned in anger on the committee. "She got no right to be stiff-necked. She got no right, not with our own people."

Annie Littlefield said, "She ain't been here long. Maybe she don't know. Maybe she's took charity one time-another. No," Annie said, "don't you try to shut me up, Jessie. I got a right to pass speech." She turned half to Ma. "If a body's ever took charity, it makes a burn that don't come out. This ain't charity, but if you ever took it, you don't forget it. I bet Jessie ain't ever done it."

"No, I ain't," said Jessie.

"Well, I did," Annie said. "Las' winter; an' we was a-starvin'—me an' Pa an' the little fellas. An' it was a-rainin'. Fella tol' us to go to the Salvation Army." Her eyes grew fierce. "We was hungry—they made us crawl for our dinner. They took our dignity. They—I hate 'em! An'—maybe Mis' Joyce took charity. Maybe she didn' know this ain't charity. Mis' Joad, we don't allow nobody in this camp to build theirself up that-a-way. We don't allow nobody to give nothing to another person. They can give it to the camp, an' the camp can pass it out. We won't have no charity!" Her voice was fierce and hoarse. "I hate 'em," she said. "I ain't never seen my man beat before, but them—them Salvation Army done it to 'im."

Jessie nodded. "I heard," she said softly, "I heard. We got to take Mis' Joad aroun'."

Ma said, "It sure is nice."

"Le's go to the sewin' room," Annie suggested. "Got two machines. They's a-quiltin', an' they're makin' dresses. You might like ta work over there."

When the committee called on Ma, Ruthie and Winfield faded imperceptibly back out of reach.

"Whyn't we go along an' listen?" Winfield asked.

Ruthie gripped his arm. "No," she said. "We got washed for them sons-a-bitches. I ain't goin' with 'em."

Winfield said, "You tol' on me 'bout the toilet. I'm a-gonna tell what you called them ladies."

A shadow of fear crossed Ruthie's face. "Don' do it. I tol' 'cause I knowed you didn' really break it."

"You did not," said Winfield.

Ruthie said, "Le's look aroun'." They strolled down the line of tents, peering into each one, gawking self-consciously. At the end of the unit there was a level place on which a croquet court had been set up. Half a dozen children played seriously. In front of a tent an elderly lady sat on a bench and watched. Ruthie and Winfield broke into a trot. "Leave us play," Ruthie cried. "Leave us get in."

The children looked up. A pig-tailed little girl said, "Nex' game you kin."

"I wanta play now," Ruthie cried.

"Well, you can't. Not till nex' game."

Ruthie moved menacingly out on the court. "I'm a-gonna play." The pig-tails gripped her mallet tightly. Ruthie sprang at her, slapped her, pushed her, and wrested the mallet from her hands. "I says I was gonna play," she said triumphantly.

The elderly lady stood up and walked onto the court. Ruthie scowled fiercely and her hands tightened on the mallet. The lady said, "Let her play—like you done with Ralph las' week."

The children laid their mallets on the ground and trooped silently off the court. They stood at a distance and looked on with expressionless eyes. Ruthie watched them go. Then she hit a ball and ran after it. "Come on, Winfiel'. Get a stick," she called. And then she looked in amazement. Winfield had joined the watching children, and he too looked at her with expressionless eyes. Defiantly she hit the ball again. She kicked up a great dust. She pretended to have a good time. And the children stood and watched. Ruthie lined up two balls and hit both of them, and she turned her back on the watching eyes, and then turned back. Suddenly she advanced on them, mallet in hand. "You come an' play," she demanded. They moved silently back at her approach. For a moment she stared at them, and then she flung down the mallet and ran crying for home. The children walked back on the court.

Pigtails said to Winfield, "You can git in the nex' game."

The watching lady warned them, "When she comes back an'

wants to be decent, you let her. You was mean yourself, Amy." The game went on, while in the Joad tent Ruthie wept miserably.

The truck moved along the beautiful roads, past orchards where the peaches were beginning to color, past vineyards with the clusters pale and green, under lines of walnut trees whose branches spread half across the road. At each entrance-gate Al slowed; and at each gate there was a sign: "No help wanted. No trespassing."

Al said, "Pa, they's boun' to be work when them fruits gets ready. Funny place—they tell ya they ain't no work 'fore you ask 'em." He drove slowly on.

Pa said, "Maybe we could go in anyways an' ask if they know where they's any work. Might do that."

A man in blue overalls and a blue shirt walked along the edge of the road. Al pulled up beside him. "Hey, mister," Al said. "Know where they's any work?"

The man stopped and grinned, and his mouth was vacant of front teeth. "No," he said. "Do you? I been walkin' all week, an' I can't tree none."

"Live in that gov'ment camp?" Al asked.

"Yeah!"

"Come on, then. Git up back, an' we'll all look." The man climbed over the side-boards and dropped in the bed.

Pa said, "I ain't got no hunch we'll find work. Guess we got to look, though. We don't even know where-at to look."

"Shoulda talked to the fellas in the camp," Al said. "How you feelin', Uncle John?"

"I ache," said Uncle John. "I ache all over, an' I got it comin'. I oughta go away where I won't bring down punishment on my own folks."

Pa put his hand on John's knee. "Look here," he said, "don' you go away. We're droppin' folks all the time—Grampa an' Granma dead, Noah an' Connie—run out, an' the preacher—in jail."

"I got a hunch we'll see that preacher agin," John said.

Al fingered the ball on the gear-shift lever. "You don' feel good enough to have no hunches," he said. "The hell with it. Le's go back an' talk, an' find out where they's some work. We're jus' huntin' skunks under water." He stopped the truck and leaned out the window and called back, "Hey! Lookie! We're a-goin' back to the camp an' try an' see where they's work. They ain't no use burnin' gas like this."

The man leaned over the truck side. "Suits me," he said. "My dogs is wore clean up to the ankle. An' I ain't even got a nibble."

Al turned around in the middle of the road and headed back.

Pa said, "Ma's gonna be purty hurt, 'specially when Tom got work so easy."

"Maybe he never got none," Al said. "Maybe he jus' went lookin', too. I wisht I could get work in a garage. I'd learn that stuff quick, an' I'd like it."

Pa grunted, and they drove back toward the camp in silence.

When the committee left, Ma sat down on a box in front of the Joad tent, and she looked helplessly at Rose of Sharon. "Well—" she said, "well—I ain't been so perked up in years. Wasn't them ladies nice?"

"I get to work in the nursery," Rose of Sharon said. "They tol' me. I can find out all how to do for babies, an' then I'll know."

Ma nodded in wonder. "Wouldn' it be nice if the menfolks all got work?" she asked. "Them a-workin', an' a little money comin' in?" Her eyes wandered into space. "Them a-workin', an' us a-workin' here, an' all them nice people. Fust thing we get a little ahead I'd get me a little stove—nice one. They don' cost much. An' then we'd get a tent, big enough, an' maybe secon'-han' springs for the beds. An' we'd use this here tent jus' to eat under. An' Sat'dy night we'll go to the dancin'. They says you can invite folks if you want. I wisht we had some frien's to invite. Maybe the men'll know somebody to invite."

Rose of Sharon peered down the road. "That lady that says I'll lose the baby—" she began.

"Now you stop that," Ma warned her.

Rose of Sharon said softly, "I seen her. She's a-comin' here, I think. Yeah! Here she comes. Ma, don' let her——"

Ma turned and looked at the approaching figure.

"Howdy," the woman said. "I'm Mis' Sandry—Lisbeth Sandry. I seen your girl this mornin'."

"Howdy do," said Ma.

"Are you happy in the Lord?"

"Pretty happy," said Ma.

"Are you saved?"

"I been saved." Ma's face was closed and waiting.

"Well, I'm glad," Lisbeth said. "The sinners is awful strong aroun' here. You come to a awful place. They's wicketness all around about. Wicket people, wicket goin's-on that a lamb'-blood Christian jes' can't hardly stan'. They's sinners all around us."

Ma colored a little, and shut her mouth tightly. "Seems to me they's nice people here," she said shortly.

Mrs. Sandry's eyes stared. "Nice!" she cried. "You think they're nice when they's dancin' an' huggin'? I tell ya, ya eternal soul ain't got a chancet in this here camp. Went out to a meetin' in Weedpatch las' night. Know what the preacher says? He says, 'They's wicketness in that camp.' He says, 'The poor is tryin' to be rich.' He says, 'They's dancin' an' huggin' when they should be wailin' an' moanin' in sin.' That's what he says. 'Ever'body that ain't here is a black sinner,' he says. I tell you it made a person feel purty good to hear 'im. An' we knowed we was safe. We ain't danced."

Ma's face was red. She stood up slowly and faced Mrs. Sandry. "Git!" she said. "Git out now, 'fore I git to be a sinner a-tellin' you where to go. Git to your wailin' an' moanin'."

Mrs. Sandry's mouth dropped open. She stepped back. And then she became fierce. "I thought you was Christians."

"So we are," Ma said.

"No, you ain't. You're hell-burnin' sinners, all of you! An' I'll mention it in meetin', too. I can see your black soul a-burnin'. I can see that innocent chile in that there girl's belly a-burnin'."

A low wailing cry escaped from Rose of Sharon's lips. Ma stooped down and picked up a stick of wood.

"Git!" she said coldly. "Don' you never come back. I seen your kind before. You'd take the little pleasure, wouldn' you?" Ma advanced on Mrs. Sandry.

For a moment the woman backed away and then suddenly she threw back her head and howled. Her eyes rolled up, her shoulders and arms flopped loosely at her side, and a string of thick ropy saliva ran from the corner of her mouth. She howled again and again, long deep animal howls. Men and women ran up from the other tents, and they stood near—frightened and quiet. Slowly the woman sank to her knees and the howls sank to a shuddering, bubbling moan. She fell sideways and her arms and legs twitched. The white eyeballs showed under the open eyelids.

A man said softly, "The sperit. She got the sperit." Ma stood looking down at the twitching form.

The little manager strolled up casually. "Trouble?" he asked. The crowd parted to let him through. He looked down at the woman. "Too bad," he said. "Will some of you help get her back to her tent?" The silent people shuffled their feet. Two men bent over and lifted the woman, one held her under the arms and the other took her feet. They carried her away, and the people moved slowly after them. Rose of Sharon went under the tarpaulin and lay down and covered her face with a blanket.

The manager looked at Ma, looked down at the stick in her hand. He smiled tiredly. "Did you clout her?" he asked.

Ma continued to stare after the retreating people. She shook her head slowly. "No—but I would a. Twicet today she worked my girl up."

The manager said, "Try not to hit her. She isn't well. She just isn't well." And he added softly, "I wish she'd go away, and all her family. She brings more trouble on the camp than all the rest together."

Ma got herself in hand again. "If she comes back, I might hit her. I ain't sure. I won't let her worry my girl no more."

"Don't worry about it, Mrs. Joad," he said. "You won't ever see her again. She works over the newcomers. She won't ever come back. She thinks you're a sinner."

"Well, I am," said Ma.

"Sure. Everybody is, but not the way she means. She isn't well, Mrs. Joad."

Ma looked at him gratefully, and she called, "You hear that, Rosasharn? She ain't well. She's crazy." But the girl did not raise her head. Ma said, "I'm warnin' you, mister. If she comes back, I ain't to be trusted. I'll hit her."

He smiled wryly. "I know how you feel," he said. "But just try not to. That's all I ask—just try not to." He walked slowly away toward the tent where Mrs. Sandry had been carried.

Ma went into the tent and sat down beside Rose of Sharon. "Look up," she said. The girl lay still. Ma gently lifted the blanket from her daughter's face. "That woman's kinda crazy," she said. "Don't you believe none of them things."

Rose of Sharon whispered in terror, "When she said about burnin', I—felt burnin'."

"That ain't true," said Ma.

"I'm tar'd out," the girl whispered. "I'm tar'd a things happenin'. I wanta sleep. I wanta sleep."

"Well, you sleep, then. This here's a nice place. You can sleep."

"But she might come back."

"She won't," said Ma. "I'm a-gonna set right outside, an' I won't let her come back. Res' up now, 'cause you got to get to work in the nu'sery purty soon."

Ma struggled to her feet and went to sit in the entrance to the tent. She sat on a box and put her elbows on her knees and her chin in her cupped hands. She saw the movement in the camp, heard the voices of the children, the hammering on an iron rim; but her eyes were staring ahead of her.

Pa, coming back along the road, found her there, and he squatted near her. She looked slowly over at him. "Git work?" she asked.

"No," he said, ashamed. "We looked."

"Where's Al and John and the truck?"

"Al's fixin' somepin. Had ta borry some tools. Fella says Al got to fix her there."

Ma said sadly, "This here's a nice place. We could be happy here awhile."

"If we could get work."

"Yeah! If you could get work."

He felt her sadness, and studied her face. "What you a-mopin' about? If it's sech a nice place why have you got to mope?"

She gazed at him, and she closed her eyes slowly. "Funny, ain't it. All the time we was a-movin' an' shovin', I never thought none. An' now these here folks been nice to me, been awful nice; an' what's the first thing I do? I go right back over the sad things—that night Grampa died an' we buried him. I was all full up of the road, and bumpin' and movin', an' it wasn't so bad. But I come out here, an' it's worse now. An' Granma—an' Noah walkin' away like that! Walkin' away jus' down the river. Them things was part of all, an' now they come a-flockin' back. Granma a pauper, an' buried a pauper. That's sharp now. That's awful sharp. An' Noah walkin' away down the river. He don' know what's there. He jus' don' know. An' we don' know. We ain't never gonna know if he's alive or dead. Never gonna know. An' Connie sneakin' away. I didn' give 'em brain room before, but now they're a-flockin' back. An' I oughta be glad 'cause we're in a nice place." Pa watched her mouth while she talked. Her eyes were closed. "I can remember how them mountains was, sharp as ol' teeth beside the river where Noah walked. I can remember how the stubble was on the groun' where Grampa lies. I can remember the choppin' block back home with a feather caught on it, all criss-crossed with cuts, an' black with chicken blood."

Pa's voice took on her tone. "I seen the ducks today," he said. "Wedgin' south—high up. Seems like they're awful dinky. An' I seen the blackbirds a-settin' on the wires, an' the doves was on the fences." Ma opened her eyes and looked at him. He went on, "I seen a little whirlwin', like a man a-spinnin' acrost a fiel'. An' the ducks drivin' on down, wedgin' on down to the southward."

Ma smiled. "Remember?" she said. "Remember what we'd always say at home? 'Winter's a-comin' early,' we said, when the ducks flew. Always said that, an' winter come when it was ready to come. But we always said, 'She's a-comin' early.' I wonder what we meant."

"I seen the blackbirds on the wires," said Pa. "Settin' so close together. An' the doves. Nothin' sets so still as a dove—on the fence wires—maybe two, side by side. An' this little whirlwin'—big as a man, an' dancin' off acrost a fiel'. Always did like the little fellas, big as a man."

"Wisht I wouldn't think how it is home," said Ma. "It ain't our home no more. Wisht I'd forget it. An' Noah."

"He wasn't ever right—I mean—well, it was my fault."

"I tol' you never to say that. Wouldn' a lived at all, maybe."

"But I should a knowed more."

"Now stop," said Ma. "Noah was strange. Maybe he'll have a nice time by the river. Maybe it's better so. We can't do no worryin'. This here is a nice place, an' maybe you'll get work right off."

Pa pointed at the sky. "Look—more ducks. Big bunch. An' Ma, 'Winter's a-comin' early.' "

She chuckled. "They's things you do, an' you don' know why."

"Here's John," said Pa. "Come on an' set, John."

Uncle John joined them. He squatted down in front of Ma. "We didn' get nowheres," he said. "Jus' run aroun'. Say, Al wants to see ya. Says he got to git a tire. Only one layer a cloth lef', he says."

Pa stood up. "I hope he can git her cheap. We ain't got much lef'. Where is Al?"

"Down there, go the nex' cross-street an' turn right. Says gonna blow out an' spoil a tube if we don' get a new one." Pa strolled away, and his eyes followed the giant V of ducks down the sky.

Uncle John picked a stone from the ground and dropped it from his palm and picked it up again. He did not look at Ma. "They ain't no work," he said.

"You didn' look all over," Ma said.

"No, but they's signs out."

"Well, Tom musta got work. He ain't been back."

Uncle John suggested, "Maybe he went away—like Connie, or like Noah."

Ma glanced sharply at him, and then her eyes softened. "They's things you know," she said. "They's stuff you're sure of. Tom's got work, an' he'll come in this evenin'. That's true." She smiled in satisfaction. "Ain't he a fine boy!" she said. "Ain't he a good boy!"

The cars and trucks began to come into the camp, and the men trooped by toward the sanitary unit. And each man carried clean overalls and shirt in his hand.

Ma pulled herself together. "John, you go find Pa. Get to the store. I want beans an' sugar an'—a piece of fryin' meat an' carrots an'—tell Pa to get somepin nice—anything—but nice—for tonight. Tonight—we'll have—somepin nice."

The migrant people, scuttling for work, scrabbling to live, looked always for pleasure, dug for pleasure, manufactured pleasure, and they were hungry for amusement. Sometimes amusement lay in speech, and they climbed up their lives with jokes. And it came about in the camps along the roads, on the ditch banks beside the streams, under the sycamores, that the story teller grew into being, so that the people gathered in the low firelight to hear the gifted ones. And they listened while the tales were told, and their participation made the stories great.

I was a recruit against Geronimo——

And the people listened, and their quiet eyes reflected the dying fire.

Them Injuns was cute—slick as snakes, an' quiet when they wanted. Could go through dry leaves, an' make no rustle. Try to do that sometime.

And the people listened and remembered the crash of dry leaves under their feet.

Come the change of season an' the clouds up. Wrong time. Ever hear of the army doing anything right? Give the army ten chances, an' they'll stumble along. Took three regiments to kill a hundred braves—always.

And the people listened, and their faces were quiet with listening. The story tellers, gathering attention into their tales, spoke in great rhythms, spoke in great words because the tales were great, and the listeners became great through them.

They was a brave on a ridge, against the sun. Knowed he stood out. Spread his arms an' stood. Naked as morning, an' against the sun. Maybe he was crazy. I don' know. Stood there, arms spread out; like a cross he looked. Four hunderd yards. An' the men—well, they raised their sights an' they felt the wind with their fingers; an' then they jus' lay there an' couldn' shoot. Maybe that Injun knowed somepin. Knowed we couldn' shoot. Jes' laid there with the rifles cocked, an' didn' even put 'em to our shoulders. Lookin' at him. Head-band, one feather. Could see it, an' naked as the sun. Long time we laid there an' looked, an' he never moved. An' then the captain got mad. "Shoot, you crazy bastards, shoot!" he yells. An' we jus' laid there. "I'll give you to a five-count, an' then mark you down," the captain says. Well, sir—we put up our rifles slow, an' ever' man hoped somebody'd shoot first. I ain't never been so sad in my life. An' I laid my sights on his belly, 'cause you can't stop a Injun no other place—an'—then. Well, he jest plunked down an' rolled. An' we went up. An' he wasn' big—he'd looked so grand— up there. All tore to pieces an' little. Ever see a cock pheasant, stiff and beautiful, ever' feather drawed an' painted, an' even his eyes drawed in pretty? An' bang! You pick him up—bloody an' twisted, an' you spoiled him—you spoiled somepin better'n you; an' eatin' him don't never make it up to you, 'cause you spoiled somepin in yaself, an' you can't never fix it up.

And the people nodded, and perhaps the fire spurted a little light and showed their eyes looking in on themselves.

Against the sun, with his arms out. An' he looked big—as God.

And perhaps a man balanced twenty cents between food and pleasure, and he went to a movie in Marysville or Tulare, in Ceres or Mountain View. And he came back to the ditch camp with his memory crowded. And he told how it was:

They was this rich fella, an' he makes like he's poor, an' they's this rich girl, an' she purtends like she's poor too, an' they meet in a hamburg' stan'.

Why?

I don't know why—that's how it was.

Why'd they purtend like they's poor?

Well, they're tired of bein' rich.

Horseshit!

You want to hear this, or not?

Well, go on then. Sure, I wanta hear it, but if I was rich I'd git so many pork chops—I'd cord 'em up aroun' me like wood, an' I'd eat my way out. Go on.

Well, they each think the other one's poor. An' they git arrested an' they git in jail, an' they don' git out 'cause the other one'd find out the first one is rich. An' the jail keeper, he's mean to 'em 'cause he thinks they're poor. Oughta see how he looks when he finds out. Jes' nearly faints, that's all.

What they git in jail for?

Well, they git caught at some kind a radical meetin' but they ain't radicals. They jes' happen to be there. An' they don't each one wanta marry fur money, ya see.

So the sons-of-bitches start lyin' to each other right off.

Well, in the pitcher it was like they was doin' good. They're nice to people, you see.

I was to a show oncet that was me, an' more'n me; an' my life, an' more'n my life, so ever'thing was bigger.

Well, I git enough sorrow. I like to git away from it.

Sure—if you can believe it.

So they got married, an' then they foun' out, an' all them people that's treated 'em mean. They was a fella had been uppity, an' he nearly fainted when this fella come in with a plug hat on. Jes' nearly fainted. An' they was a newsreel with them German soldiers kickin' up their feet—funny as hell.

And always, if he had a little money, a man could get drunk. The hard edges gone, and the warmth. Then there was no loneliness, for a man could people his brain with friends, and he could find his enemies and destroy them. Sitting in a ditch, the earth grew soft under him. Failures dulled and the future was no threat. And hunger did not skulk about, but the world was soft and easy, and a man could reach the place he started for. The stars came down wonderfully close and the sky was soft. Death was a friend, and sleep was death's brother. The old times came back—dear and warm. A girl with pretty feet, who danced one time at home. A horse—a long time ago. A horse and a saddle. And the leather was carved. When was that? Ought to find a girl to talk to. That's nice. Might lay with her, too. But warm here. And the stars down so close, and sadness and pleasure so close together, really the same thing. Like to stay drunk all the time. Who says it's bad? Who dares to say it's bad? Preachers—but they got their own kinda drunkenness. Thin, barren women, but they're too miserable to know. Reformers—but they don't bite deep enough into living to know. No—the stars are close and dear and I have joined the brotherhood of the worlds. And everything's holy—everything, even me.

A harmonica is easy to carry. Take it out of your hip pocket, knock it against your palm to shake out the dirt and pocket fuzz and bits of tobacco. Now it's ready. You can do anything with a harmonica:

thin reedy single tone, or chords, or melody with rhythm chords. You can mold the music with curved hands, making it wail and cry like bagpipes, making it full and round like an organ, making it as sharp and bitter as the reed pipes of the hills. And you can play and put it back in your pocket. It is always with you, always in your pocket. And as you play, you learn new tricks, new ways to mold the tone with your hands, to pinch the tone with your lips, and no one teaches you. You feel around—sometimes alone in the shade at noon, sometimes in the tent door after supper when the women are washing up. Your foot taps gently on the ground. Your eyebrows rise and fall in rhythm. And if you lose it or break it, why, it's no great loss. You can buy another for a quarter.

A guitar is more precious. Must learn this thing. Fingers of the left hand must have callus caps. Thumb of the right hand a horn of callus. Stretch the left-hand fingers, stretch them like a spider's legs to get the hard pads on the frets.

This was my father's box. Wasn't no bigger'n a bug first time he give me C chord. An' when I learned as good as him, he hardly never played no more. Used to set in the door, an' listen an' tap his foot. I'm tryin' for a break, an' he'd scowl mean till I get her, an' then he'd settle back easy, an' he'd nod. "Play," he'd say. "Play nice." It's a good box. See how the head is wore. They's many a million songs wore down that wood an' scooped her out. Some day she'll cave in like a egg. But you can't patch her nor worry her no way or she'll lose tone. Play her in the evening, an' they's a harmonica player in the nex' tent. Makes it pretty nice together.

The fiddle is rare, hard to learn. No frets, no teacher.

Jes' listen to a ol' man an' try to pick it up. Won't tell how to double. Says it's a secret. But I watched. Here's how he done it.

Shrill as a wind, the fiddle, quick and nervous and shrill.

She ain't much of a fiddle. Give two dollars for her. Fella says they's fiddles four hundred years old, and they git mellow like whisky. Says they'll cost fifty-sixty thousan' dollars. I don' know. Soun's like a lie. Harsh ol' bastard, ain't she? Wanta dance? I'll rub up the bow with plenty rosin. Man! Then she'll squawk. Hear her a mile.

These three in the evening, harmonica and fiddle and guitar. Playing a reel and tapping out the tune, and the big deep strings of the guitar beating like a heart, and the harmonica's sharp chords and the skirl and squeal of the fiddle. People have to move close. They can't help it. "Chicken Reel" now, and the feet tap and a young lean buck takes three quick steps, and his arms hang limp. The square closes up and the dancing starts, feet on the bare ground, beating dull, strike with your heels. Hands 'round and swing. Hair falls down, and panting breaths. Lean to the side now.

Look at that Texas boy, long legs loose, taps four times for ever' damn step. Never seen a boy swing aroun' like that. Look at him swing that Cherokee girl, red in her cheeks an' her toe points out. Look at her pant, look at her heave. Think she's tired? Think she's winded? Well, she ain't. Texas boy got his hair in his eyes, mouth's wide open, can't get air, but he pats four times for ever' darn step, an' he'll keep a-going' with the Cherokee girl.

The fiddle squeaks and the guitar bongs. Mouth-organ man is red in the face. Texas boy and the Cherokee girl, pantin' like dogs an' a-beatin' the groun'. Ol' folks stan' a-pattin' their han's. Smilin' a little, tappin' their feet.

Back home—in the schoolhouse, it was. The big moon sailed off to the westward. An' we walked, him an' me—a little ways. Didn' talk 'cause our throats was choked up. Didn' talk none at all. An' purty soon they was a haycock. Went right to it and laid down there. Seein' the Texas boy an' that girl a-steppin' away into the dark— think nobody seen 'em go. Oh, God! I wisht I was a-goin' with that Texas boy. Moon'll be up 'fore long. I seen that girl's ol' man move out to stop 'em, an' then he didn'. He knowed. Might as well stop the fall from comin', and might as well stop the sap from movin' in the trees. An' the moon'll be up 'fore long.

Play more—play the story songs—"As I Walked through the Streets of Laredo."

The fire's gone down. Be a shame to build her up. Little ol' moon'll be up 'fore long.

Beside an irrigation ditch a preacher labored and the people cried. And the preacher paced like a tiger, whipping the people with his voice, and they groveled and whined on the ground. He calculated them, gauged them, played on them, and when they were all squirm-ing on the ground he stooped down and of his great strength he picked each one up in his arms and shouted, Take 'em, Christ! and threw each one in the water. And when they were all in, waist deep in the water, and looking with frightened eyes at the master, he knelt down on the bank and he prayed for them; and he prayed that all men and women might grovel and whine on the ground. Men and women, dripping, clothes sticking tight, watched; then gurgling and sloshing in their shoes they walked back to the camp, to the tents, and they talked softly in wonder:

We been saved, they said. We're washed white as snow. We won't never sin again.

And the children, frightened and wet, whispered together:

We been saved. We won't sin no more.

Wisht I knowed what all the sins was, so I could do 'em.

The migrant people looked humbly for pleasure on the roads.

On Saturday morning the wash tubs were crowded. The women washed dresses, pink ginghams and flowered cottons, and they hung them in the sun and stretched the cloth to smooth it. When afternoon came the whole camp quickened and the people grew excited. The children caught the fever and were more noisy than usual. About mid-afternoon child bathing began, and as each child was caught, subdued, and washed, the noise on the playground gradually subsided. Before five, the children were scrubbed and warned about getting dirty again; and they walked about, stiff in clean clothes, miserable with carefulness.

At the big open-air dance platform a committee was busy. Every bit of electric wire had been requisitioned. The city dump had been visited for wire, every tool box had contributed friction tape. And now the patched, spliced wire was strung out to the dance floor, with bottle necks as insulators. This night the floor would be lighted for the first time. By six o'clock the men were back from work or from looking for work, and a new wave of bathing started. By seven, dinners were over, men had on their best clothes: freshly washed overalls, clean blue shirts, sometimes the decent blacks. The girls were ready in their print dresses, stretched and clean, their hair braided and ribboned. The worried women watched the families and cleaned up the evening dishes. On the platform the string band practiced, surrounded by a double wall of children. The people were intent and excited.

In the tent of Ezra Huston, chairman, the Central Committee of five men went into meeting. Huston, a tall spare man, wind-blackened, with eyes like little blades, spoke to his committee, one man from each sanitary unit.

"It's goddamn lucky we got the word they was gonna try to bust up the dance!" he said.

The tubby little representative from Unit Three spoke up. "I think we oughta squash the hell out of 'em, an' show 'em."

"No," said Huston. "That's what they want. No, sir. If they can git a fight goin', then they can run in the cops an' say we ain't orderly. They tried it before—other places." He turned to the sad dark boy from Unit Two. "Got the fellas together to go roun' the fences an' see nobody sneaks in?"

The sad boy nodded. "Yeah! Twelve. Tol' 'em not to hit nobody. Jes' push 'em out ag'in."

Huston said, "Will you go out an' find Willie Eaton? He's chairman a the entertainment, ain't he?"

"Yeah."

"Well, tell 'im we wanta see 'im."

The boy went out, and he returned in a moment with a stringy Texas man. Willie Eaton had a long fragile jaw and dust-colored hair. His arms and legs were long and loose, and he had the gray sunburned eyes of the Panhandle. He stood in the tent, grinning, and his hands pivoted restlessly on his wrists.

Huston said, "You heard about tonight?"

Willie grinned. "Yeah!"

"Did anything 'bout it?"

"Yeah!"

"Tell what you done."

Willie Eaton grinned happily. "Well, sir, ordinary ent'tainment committee is five. I got twenty more—all good strong boys. They're a-gonna be a-dancin' an' a-keepin' their eyes open an' their ears open. First sign—any talk or argament, they close in tight. Worked her out purty nice. Can't even see nothing. Kinda move out, an' the fella will go out with 'em."

"Tell 'em they ain't to hurt the fellas."

Willie laughed gleefully. "I tol' 'em," he said.

"Well, tell 'em so they know."

"They know. Got five men out to the gate lookin' over the folks that comes in. Try to spot 'em 'fore they git started."

Huston stood up. His steel-colored eyes were stern. "Now you look here, Willie. We don't want them fellas hurt. They's gonna be deputies out by the front gate. If you blood 'em up, why—them deputies'll git you."

"Got that there figgered out," said Willie. "Take 'em out the back way, into the fiel'. Some a the boys'll see they git on their way."

"Well, it soun's awright," Huston said worriedly. "But don't you let nothing happen, Willie. You're responsible. Don' you hurt them fellas. Don' you use no stick nor no knife or arn, or nothing like that."

"No, sir," said Willie. "We won't mark 'em."

Huston was suspicious. "I wisht I knowed I could trus' you, Willie. If you got to sock 'em, sock 'em where they won't bleed."

"Yes, sir!" said Willie.

"You sure of the fellas you picked?"

"Yes, sir."

"Awright. An' if she gits outa han', I'll be in the right-han' corner, this way on the dance floor."

Willie saluted in mockery and went out.

Huston said, "I dunno. I jes' hope Willie's boys don't kill nobody. What the hell the deputies want to hurt the camp for? Why can't they let us be?"

The sad boy from Unit Two said, "I lived out at Sunlan' Lan' an' Cattle Company's place. Honest to God, they got a cop for ever' ten people. Got one water faucet for 'bout two hundred people."

The tubby man said, "Jesus, God, Jeremy. You ain't got to tell me. I was there. They got a block of shacks—thirty-five of 'em in a row, an' fifteen deep. An' they got ten crappers for the whole she-bang. An', Christ, you could smell 'em a mile. One of them deputies give me the lowdown. We was settin' aroun', an' he says, 'Them goddamn gov'ment camps,' he says. 'Give people hot water, an' they gonna want hot water. Give 'em flush toilets, an' they gonna want 'em.' He says, 'You give them goddamn Okies stuff like that an' they'll want 'em.' An' he says, 'They hol' red meetin's in them gov'-ment camps. All figgerin' how to git on relief,' he says."

Huston asked, "Didn' nobody sock him?"

"No. They was a little fella, an' he says, 'What you mean, relief?'

" 'I mean relief—what us taxpayers put in an' you goddamn Okies takes out.'

" 'We pay sales tax an' gas tax an' tobacco tax,' this little guy says. An' he says, 'Farmers get four cents a cotton poun' from the gov'ment—ain't that relief?' An' he says, 'Railroads an' shippin' com-panies draws subsidies—ain't that relief?'

" 'They're doin' stuff got to be done,' this deputy says.

" 'Well,' the little guy says, 'how'd your goddamn crops get picked if it wasn't for us?' " The tubby man looked around.

"What'd the deputy say?" Huston asked.

"Well, the deputy got mad. An' he says, 'You goddamn reds is all the time stirrin' up trouble,' he says. 'You better come along with me.' So he takes this little guy in, an' they give him sixty days in jail for vagrancy."

"How'd they do that if he had a job?" asked Timothy Wallace.

The tubby man laughed. "You know better'n that," he said. "You know a vagrant is anybody a cop don't like. An' that's why they hate this here camp. No cops can get in. This here's United States, not California."

Huston sighed. "Wisht we could stay here. Got to be goin' 'fore long. I like this here. Folks gits along nice; an', God Awmighty, why can't they let us do it 'stead of keepin' us miserable an' puttin' us in jail? I swear to God they gonna push us into fightin' if they don't quit a-worryin' us." Then he calmed his voice. "We jes' got to keep peaceful," he reminded himself. "The committee got no right to fly off'n the handle."

The tubby man from Unit Three said, "Anybody that thinks this committee got all cheese an' crackers ought to jes' try her. They was a fight in my unit today—women. Got to callin' names, an' then got to throwin' garbage. Ladies' Committee couldn' handle it, an' they come to me. Want me to bring the fight in this here committee. I tol' 'em they got to handle women trouble theirselves. This here committee ain't gonna mess with no garbage fights."

Huston nodded. "You done good," he said.

And now the dusk was falling, and as the darkness deepened the practicing of the string band seemed to grow louder. The lights flashed on and two men inspected the patched wire to the dance floor. The children crowded thickly about the musicians. A boy with a guitar sang the "Down Home Blues," chording delicately for himself, and on his second chorus three harmonicas and a fiddle joined him. From the tents the people streamed toward the platform, men in their clean blue denim and women in their ginghams. They came near to the platform and then stood quietly waiting, their faces bright and intent under the light.

Around the reservation there was a high wire fence, and along the fence, at intervals of fifty feet, the guards sat in the grass and waited.

Now the cars of the guests began to arrive, small farmers and their families, migrants from other camps. And as each guest came through the gate he mentioned the name of the camper who had invited him.

The string band took a reel tune up and played loudly, for they were not practicing any more. In front of their tents the Jesus-lovers sat and watched, their faces hard and contemptuous. They did not speak to one another, they watched for sin, and their faces condemned the whole proceeding.

At the Joad tent Ruthie and Winfield had bolted what little dinner they had, and then they started for the platform. Ma called them back, held up their faces with a hand under each chin, and looked into their nostrils, pulled their ears and looked inside, and sent them to the sanitary unit to wash their hands once more. They dodged around the back of the building and bolted for the platform, to stand among the children, close-packed about the band.

Al finished his dinner and spent half an hour shaving with Tom's razor. Al had a tight-fitting wool suit and a striped shirt, and he bathed and washed and combed his straight hair back. And when the washroom was vacant for a moment, he smiled engagingly at himself in the mirror, and he turned and tried to see himself in profile when he smiled. He slipped his purple arm-bands on and put on his tight coat. And he rubbed up his yellow shoes with a piece of toilet paper. A late bather came in, and Al hurried out and walked recklessly toward the platform, his eye peeled for girls. Near the dance floor he saw a pretty blond girl sitting in front of a tent. He sidled near and threw open his coat to show his shirt.

"Gonna dance tonight?" he asked.

The girl looked away and did not answer.

"Can't a fella pass a word with you? How 'bout you an' me dancin'?" And he said nonchalantly, "I can waltz."

The girl raised her eyes shyly, and she said, "That ain't nothin' —anybody can waltz."

"Not like me," said Al. The music surged, and he tapped one foot in time. "Come on," he said.

A very fat woman poked her head out of the tent and scowled at him. "You git along," she said fiercely. "This here girl's spoke for. She's a-gonna be married, an' her man's a-comin' for her."

Al winked rakishly at the girl, and he tripped on, striking his feet to the music and swaying his shoulders and swinging his arms. And the girl looked after him intently.

Pa put down his plate and stood up. "Come on, John," he said; and he explained to Ma, "We're a-gonna talk to some fellas about gettin' work." And Pa and Uncle John walked toward the manager's house.

Tom worked a piece of store bread into the stew gravy on his plate and ate the bread. He handed his plate to Ma, and she put it in the bucket of hot water and washed it and handed it to Rose of Sharon to wipe. "Ain't you goin' to the dance?" Ma asked.

"Sure," said Tom. "I'm on a committee. We're gonna entertain some fellas."

"Already on a committee?" Ma said. "I guess it's 'cause you got work."

Rose of Sharon turned to put the dish away. Tom pointed at her. "My God, she's a-gettin' big," he said.

Rose of Sharon blushed and took another dish from Ma. "Sure she is," Ma said.

"An' she's gettin' prettier," said Tom.

The girl blushed more deeply and hung her head. "You stop it," she said, softly.

"'Course she is," said Ma. "Girl with a baby always gets prettier."

Tom laughed. "If she keeps a-swellin' like this, she gonna need a wheelbarra to carry it."

"Now you stop," Rose of Sharon said, and she went inside the tent, out of sight.

Ma chuckled, "You shouldn' ought to worry her."

"She likes it," said Tom.

"I know she likes it, but it worries her, too. And she's a-mournin' for Connie."

"Well, she might's well give him up. He's prob'ly studyin' to be President of the United States by now."

"Don't worry her," Ma said. "She ain't got no easy row to hoe."

Willie Eaton moved near, and he grinned and said, "You Tom Joad?"

"Yeah."

"Well, I'm Chairman the Entertainment Committee. We gonna need you. Fella tol' me 'bout you."

"Sure, I'll play with you," said Tom. "This here's Ma."

"Howdy," said Willie.

"Glad to meet ya."

Willie said, "Gonna put you on the gate to start, an' then on the floor. Want ya to look over the guys when they come in, an' try to spot 'em. You'll be with another fella. Then later I want ya to dance an' watch."

"Yeah! I can do that awright," said Tom.

Ma said apprehensively, "They ain't no trouble?"

"No, ma'am," Willie said. "They ain't gonna be no trouble."

"None at all," said Tom. "Well, I'll come 'long. See you at the dance, Ma." The two young men walked quickly away toward the main gate.

Ma piled the washed dishes on a box. "Come on out," she called, and when there was no answer, "Rosasharn, you come out."

The girl stepped from the tent, and she went on with the dish-wiping.

"Tom was on'y jollyin' ya."

"I know. I didn't mind; on'y I hate to have folks look at me."

"Ain't no way to he'p that. Folks gonna look. But it makes folks happy to see a girl in a fambly way—makes folks sort of giggly an' happy. Ain't you a-goin' to the dance?"

"I was—but I don' know. I wisht Connie was here." Her voice rose. "Ma, I wisht he was here. I can't hardly stan' it."

Ma looked closely at her. "I know," she said. "But, Rosasharn—don' shame your folks."

"I don' aim to, Ma."

"Well, don't you shame us. We got too much on us now, without no shame."

The girl's lip quivered. "I—I ain' goin' to the dance. I couldn'—Ma—he'p me!" She sat down and buried her head in her arms.

Ma wiped her hands on the dish towel and she squatted down in front of her daughter, and she put her two hands on Rose of Sharon's hair. "You're a good girl," she said. "You always was a good girl. I'll take care a you. Don't you fret." She put an interest in her tone. "Know what you an' me's gonna do? We're a-goin' to that dance, an' we're a-gonna set there an' watch. If anybody says to come dance—why, I'll say you ain't strong enough. I'll say you're poorly. An' you can hear the music an' all like that."

Rose of Sharon raised her head. "You won't let me dance?"

"No, I won't."

"An' don' let nobody touch me."

"No, I won't."

The girl sighed. She said desperately, "I don' know what I'm a-gonna do, Ma. I jus' don' know. I don' know."

Ma patted her knee. "Look," she said. "Look here at me. I'm a-gonna tell ya. In a little while it ain't gonna be so bad. In a little

while. An' that's true. Now come on. We'll go get washed up, an'
we'll put on our nice dress an' we'll set by the dance." She led Rose
of Sharon toward the sanitary unit.

Pa and Uncle John squatted with a group of men by the porch
of the office. "We nearly got work today," Pa said. "We was jus' a
few minutes late. They awready got two fellas. An', well, sir, it was
a funny thing. They's a straw boss there, an' he says, 'We jus' got
some two-bit men. 'Course we could use twenty-cent men. We can
use a lot a twenty-cent men. You go to your camp an' say we'll put
a lot a fellas on for twenty cents.'"

The squatting men moved nervously. A broad-shouldered man,
his face completely in the shadow of a black hat, spatted his knee
with his palm. "I know it, goddamn it!" he cried. "An' they'll git
men. They'll git hungry men. You can't feed your fam'ly on twenty
cents an hour, but you'll take anything. They got you goin' an'
comin'. They jes' auction a job off. Jesus Christ, pretty soon they're
gonna make us pay to work."

"We would of took her," Pa said. "We ain't had no job. We sure
would a took her, but they was them guys in there, an' the way they
looked, we was scairt to take her."

Black Hat said, "Get crazy thinkin'! I been workin' for a fella,
an' he can't pick his crop. Cost more jes' to pick her than he can git
for her, an' he don' know what to do."

"Seems to me—" Pa stopped. The circle was silent for him.
"Well—I jus' thought, if a fella had a acre. Well, my woman she
could raise a little truck an' a couple pigs an' some chickens. An' us
men could get out an' find work, an' then go back. Kids could maybe
go to school. Never seen sech schools as out here."

"Our kids ain't happy in them schools," Black Hat said.

"Why not? They're pretty nice, them schools."

"Well, a raggedy kid with no shoes, an' them other kids with
socks on, an' nice pants, an' them a-yellin' 'Okie.' My boy went to
school. Had a fight evr' day. Done good, too. Tough little bastard.
Ever' day he got to fight. Come home with his clothes tore an' his
nose bloody. An' his ma'd whale him. Made her stop that. No need
ever'body beatin' the hell outa him, poor little fella. Jesus! He give
some a them kids a goin'-over, though—them nice-pants sons-a-
bitches. I dunno. I dunno."

Pa demanded, "Well, what the hell am I gonna do? We're outa

money. One of my boys got a short job, but that won't feed us. I'm a-gonna go an' take twenty cents. I got to."

Black Hat raised his head, and his bristled chin showed in the light, and his stringy neck where the whiskers lay flat like fur. "Yeah!" he said bitterly. "You'll do that. An' I'm a two-bit man. You'll take my job for twenty cents. An' then I'll git hungry an' I'll take my job back for fifteen. Yeah! You go right on an' do her."

"Well, what the hell can I do?" Pa demanded. "I can't starve so's you can get two bits."

Black Hat dipped his head again, and his chin went into the shadow. "I dunno," he said. "I jes' dunno. It's bad enough to work twelve hours a day an' come out jes' a little bit hungry, but we got to figure all a time, too. My kid ain't gettin' enough to eat. I can't think all the time, goddamn it! It drives a man crazy." The circle of men shifted their feet nervously.

Tom stood at the gate and watched the people coming in to the dance. A floodlight shone down into their faces. Willie Eaton said, "Jes' keep your eyes open. I'm sendin' Jule Vitela over. He's half Cherokee. Nice fella. Keep your eyes open. An' see if you can pick out the ones."

"O.K.," said Tom. He watched the farm families come in, the girls with braided hair and the boys polished for the dance. Jule came and stood beside him.

"I'm with you," he said.

Tom looked at the hawk nose and the high brown cheek bones and the slender receding chin. "They says you're half Injun. You look all Injun to me."

"No," said Jule. "Jes' half. Wisht I was a full-blood. I'd have my lan' on the reservation. Them full-bloods got it pretty nice, some of 'em."

"Look a them people," Tom said.

The guests were moving in through the gateway, families from the farms, migrants from the ditch camps. Children straining to be free and quiet parents holding them back.

Jule said, "These here dances done funny things. Our people got nothing, but jes' because they can ast their frien's to come here to the dance, sets 'em up an' makes 'em proud. An' the folks respects 'em 'count of these here dances. Fella got a little place where I was a-workin'. He come to a dance here. I ast him myself, an' he come. Says we got the only decent dance in the county, where a man can take his girls an' his wife. Hey! Look."

Three young men were coming through the gate—young working men in jeans. They walked close together. The guard at the gate questioned them, and they answered and passed through.

"Look at 'em careful," Jule said. He moved to the guard. "Who ast them three?" he asked.

"Fella named Jackson, Unit Four."

Jule came back to Tom. "I think them's our fellas."

"How ya know?"

"I dunno how. Jes' got a feelin'. They're kinda scared. Foller 'em an' tell Willie to look 'em over, an' tell Willie to check with Jackson, Unit Four. Get him to see if they're all right. I'll stay here."

Tom strolled after the three young men. They moved toward the dance floor and took their positions quietly on the edge of the crowd. Tom saw Willie near the band and signaled him.

"What cha want?" Willie asked.

"Them three—see—there?"

"Yeah."

"They say a fella name' Jackson, Unit Four, ast 'em."

Willie craned his neck and saw Huston and called him over. "Them three fellas," he said. "We better get Jackson, Unit Four, an' see if he ast 'em."

Huston turned on his heel and walked away; and in a few moments he was back with a lean and bony Kansan. "This here's Jackson," Huston said. "Look, Jackson, see them three young fellas—?"

"Yeah."

"Well, did you ast 'em?"

"No."

"Ever see 'em before?"

Jackson peered at them. "Sure. Worked at Gregorio's with 'em."

"So they knowed your name."

"Sure. I worked right beside 'em."

"Awright," Huston said. "Don't you go near 'em. We ain't gonna th'ow 'em out if they're nice. Thanks, Mr. Jackson."

"Good work," he said to Tom. "I guess them's the fellas."

"Jule picked 'em out," said Tom.

"Hell, no wonder," said Willie. "His Injun blood smelled 'em. Well, I'll point 'em out to the boys."

A sixteen-year-old boy came running through the crowd. He stopped, panting, in front of Huston. "Mista Huston," he said. "I been like you said. They's a car with six men parked down by the euc'lyptus trees, an' they's one with four men up that north-side road. I ast 'em for a match. They got guns. I seen 'em."

Huston's eyes grew hard and cruel. "Willie," he said, "you sure you got ever'thing ready?"

Willie grinned happily. "Sure have, Mr. Huston. Ain't gonna be no trouble."

"Well, don't hurt 'em. 'Member now. If you kin, quiet an' nice, I kinda like to see 'em. Be in my tent."

"I'll see what we kin do," said Willie.

Dancing had not formally started, but now Willie climbed onto the platform. "Choose up your squares," he called. The music stopped. Boys and girls, young men and women, ran about until eight squares were ready on the big floor, ready and waiting. The girls held their hands in front of them and squirmed their fingers. The boys tapped their feet restlessly. Around the floor the old folks sat, smiling slightly, holding the children back from the floor. And in the distance the Jesus-lovers sat with hard condemning faces and watched the sin.

Ma and Rose of Sharon sat on a bench and watched. And as each boy asked Rose of Sharon as partner, Ma said, "No, she ain't well." And Rose of Sharon blushed and her eyes were bright.

The caller stepped to the middle of the floor and held up his hands. "All ready? Then let her go!"

The music snarled out "Chicken Reel," shrill and clear, fiddle skirling, harmonicas nasal and sharp, and the guitars booming on the bass strings. The caller named the turns, the squares moved. And they danced forward and back, hands 'round, swing your lady. The caller, in a frenzy, tapped his feet, strutted back and forth, went through the figures as he called them.

"Swing your ladies an' a dol ce do. Join han's roun' an' away we go." The music rose and fell, and the moving shoes beating in time on the paltform sounded like drums. "Swing to the right an' a swing to lef'; break, now—break—back to—back," the caller sang the high vibrant monotone. Now the girls' hair lost the careful combing. Now perspiration stood out on the foreheads of the boys. Now the experts showed the tricky inter-steps. And the old people on the edge of the floor took up the rhythm, patted their hands softly, and tapped their feet; and they smiled gently and then caught one another's eyes and nodded.

Ma leaned her head close to Rose of Sharon's ear. "Maybe you wouldn' think it, but your Pa was as nice a dancer as I ever seen, when he was young." And Ma smiled. "Makes me think of ol' times," she said. And on the faces of the watchers the smiles were of old times.

"Up near Muskogee twenty years ago, they was a blin' man with a fiddle——"

"I seen a fella oncet could slap his heels four times in one jump."

"Swedes up in Dakota—know what they do sometimes? Put pepper on the floor. Gits up the ladies' skirts an' makes 'em purty lively—lively as a filly in season. Swedes do that sometimes."

In the distance, the Jesus-lovers watched their restive children. "Look on sin," they said. "Them folks is ridin' to hell on a poker. It's a shame the godly got to see it." And their children were silent and nervous.

"One more roun' an' then a little res'," the caller chanted. "Hit her hard, 'cause we're gonna stop soon." And the girls were damp and flushed, and they danced with open mouths and serious reverent faces, and the boys flung back their long hair and pranced, pointed their toes, and clicked their heels. In and out the squares moved, crossing, backing, whirling, and the music shrilled.

Then suddenly it stopped. The dancers stood still, panting with fatigue. And the children broke from restraint, dashed on the floor, chased one another madly, ran, slid, stole caps, and pulled hair. The dancers sat down, fanning themselves with their hands. The members of the band got up and stretched themselves and sat down again. And the guitar players worked softly over their strings.

Now Willie called, "Choose again for another square, if you can." The dancers scrambled to their feet and new dancers plunged forward for partners. Tom stood near the three young men. He saw them force their way through, out on the floor, toward one of the forming squares. He waved his hand at Willie, and Willie spoke to the fiddler. The fiddler squawked his bow across the strings. Twenty young men lounged slowly across the floor. The three reached the square. And one of them said, "I'll dance with this here."

A blond boy looked up in astonishment. "She's my partner."

"Listen, you little son-of-a-bitch——"

Off in the darkness a shrill whistle sounded. The three were walled in now. And each one felt the grip of hands. And then the wall of men moved slowly off the platform.

Willie yelped, "Le's go!" The music shrilled out, the caller intoned the figures, the feet thudded on the platform.

A touring car drove to the entrance. The driver called, "Open up. We hear you got a riot."

The guard kept his position. "We got no riot. Listen to that music. Who are you?"

"Deputy sheriffs."

"Got a warrant?"

"We don't need a warrant if there's a riot."

"Well, we got no riots here," said the gate guard.

The men in the car listened to the music and the sound of the caller, and then the car pulled slowly away and parked in a crossroad and waited.

In the moving squad each of the three young men was pinioned, and a hand was over each mouth. When they reached the darkness the group opened up.

Tom said, "That sure was did nice." He held both arms of his victim from behind.

Willie ran over to them from the dance floor. "Nice work," he said. "On'y need six now. Huston wants to see these here fellers."

Huston himself emerged from the darkness. "These the ones?"

"Sure," said Jule. "Went right up an' started it. But they didn' even swing once."

"Let's look at 'em." The prisoners were swung around to face him. Their heads were down. Huston put a flashlight beam in each sullen face. "What did you wanta do it for?" he asked. There was no answer. "Who the hell tol' you to do it?"

"Goddarn it, we didn' do nothing. We was jes' gonna dance."

"No, you wasn't," Jule said. "You was gonna sock that kid."

Tom said, "Mr. Huston, jus' when these here fellas moved in, somebody give a whistle."

"Yeah, I know! The cops come right to the gate." He turned back. "We ain't gonna hurt you. Now who tol' you to come bus' up our dance?" He waited for a reply. "You're our own folks," Huston said sadly. "You belong with us. How'd you happen to come? We know all about it," he added.

"Well, goddamn it, a fella got to eat."

"Well, who sent you? Who paid you to come?"

"We ain't been paid."

"An' you ain't gonna be. No fight, no pay. Ain't that right?"

One of the pinioned men said, "Do what you want. We ain't gonna tell nothing."

Huston's head sank down for a moment, and then he said softly, "O.K. Don't tell. But looka here. Don't knife your own folks. We're tryin' to get along, havin' fun an' keepin' order. Don't tear all that down. Jes' think about it. You're jes' harmin' yourself.

"Awright, boys, put 'em over the back fence. An' don't hurt 'em. They don't know what they're doin'."

The squad moved slowly toward the rear of the camp, and Huston looked after them.

Jule said, "Le's jes' take one good kick at their ass."

"No, you don't!" Willie cried. "I said we wouldn'."

"Jes' one nice little kick," Jule pleaded. "Jes' loft 'em over the fence."

"No, sir," Willie insisted.

"Listen, you," he said, "we're lettin' you off this time. But you take back the word. If'n ever this here happens again, we'll jes' natcherally kick the hell outa whoever comes; we'll bust ever' bone in their body. Now you tell your boys that. Huston says you're our kinda folks—maybe. I'd hate to think it."

They neared the fence. Two of the seated guards stood up and moved over. "Got some fellas goin' home early," said Willie. The three men climbed over the fence and disappeared into the darkness.

And the squad moved quickly back toward the dance floor. And the music of "Ol' Dan Tucker" skirled and whined from the string band.

Over near the office the men still squatted and talked, and the shrill music came to them.

Pa said, "They's change a-comin'. I don' know what. Maybe we won't live to see her. But she's a-comin'. They's a res'less feelin'. Fella can't figger nothin' out, he's so nervous."

And Black Hat lifted his head up again, and the light fell on his bristly whiskers. He gathered some little rocks from the ground and shot them like marbles, with his thumb. "I don' know. She's a-comin' awright, like you say. Fella tol' me what happened in Akron, Ohio. Rubber companies. They got mountain people in 'cause they'd work cheap. An' these here mountain people up an' joined the union. Well, sir, hell jes' popped. All them storekeepers and legioners an' people like that, they get drillin' an' yellin', 'Red!' An' they're gonna run the union right outa Akron. Preachers git a-preachin' about it, an' papers a-yowlin', an' they's pick handles put out by the rubber companies, an' they're a-buyin' gas. Jesus, you'd think them mountain boys was reg'lar devils!" He stopped and found some more rocks to shoot. "Well, sir—it was las' March, an' one Sunday five thousan' of them mountain men had a turkey shoot outside a town. Five thousan' of 'em jes' marched through town with their rifles. An' they had their turkey shoot, an' then they marched back. An' that's all they done. Well, sir, they ain't been no trouble sence then. These here citizens committees give back the pick handles, an' the store-keepers keep their stores, an' nobody been clubbed nor tarred an' feathered, an' nobody been killed." There was a long silence, and then Black Hat said, "They're gettin' purty mean out here. Burned that camp an' beat up folks. I been thinkin'. All our folks got guns. I been thinkin' maybe we ought to git up a turkey shootin' club an' have meetin's ever' Sunday."

The men looked up at him, and then down at the ground, and their feet moved restlessly and they shifted their weight from one leg to the other.

CHAPTER 25

The spring is beautiful in California. Valleys in which the fruit blossoms are fragrant pink and white waters in a shallow sea. Then the first tendrils of the grapes, swelling from the old gnarled vines, cascade down to cover the trunks. The full green hills are round and soft as breasts. And on the level vegetable lands are the mile-long rows of pale green lettuce and the spindly little cauliflowers, the gray-green unearthly artichoke plants.

And then the leaves break out on the trees, and the petals drop from the fruit trees and carpet the earth with pink and white. The centers of the blossoms swell and grow and color: cherries and apples, peaches and pears, figs which close the flower in the fruit. All California quickens with produce, and the fruit grows heavy, and the limbs bend gradually under the fruit so that little crutches must be placed under them to support the weight.

Behind the fruitfulness are men of understanding and knowledge and skill, men who experiment with seed, endlessly developing the techniques for greater crops of plants whose roots will resist the million enemies of the earth: the molds, the insects, the rusts, the blights. These men work carefully and endlessly to perfect the seed, the roots. And there are the men of chemistry who spray the trees against pests, who sulphur the grapes, who cut out disease and rots, mildews and sicknesses. Doctors of preventive medicine, men at the borders who look for fruit flies, for Japanese beetle, men who quarantine the sick trees and root them out and burn them, men of knowledge. The men who graft the young trees, the little vines, are the cleverest of all, for theirs is a surgeon's job, as tender and delicate; and these men must have surgeons' hands and surgeons' hearts to slit the bark, to place the grafts, to bind the wounds and cover them from the air. These are great men.

Along the rows, the cultivators move, tearing the spring grass and turning it under to make a fertile earth, breaking the ground to hold the water up near the surface, ridging the ground in little pools for the irrigation, destroying the weed roots that may drink the water away from the trees.

And all the time the fruit swells and the flowers break out in long clusters on the vines. And in the growing year the warmth grows and the leaves turn dark green. The prunes lengthen like little green bird's eggs, and the limbs sag down against the crutches under the weight. And the hard little pears take shape, and the beginning of the fuzz comes out on the peaches. Grape blossoms shed their tiny petals and the hard little beads become green buttons, and the buttons grow heavy. The men who work in the fields, the owners of the little orchards, watch and calculate. The year is heavy with produce. And men are proud, for of their knowledge they can make the year heavy. They have transformed the world with their knowledge. The short, lean wheat has been made big and productive. Little sour apples have grown large and sweet, and that old grape that grew among the trees and fed the birds its tiny fruit has mothered a thousand varieties, red and black, green and pale pink, purple and yellow; and each variety with its own flavor. The men who work in the experimental farms have made new fruits: nectarines and forty kinds of plums, walnuts with paper shells. And always they work, selecting, grafting, changing, driving themselves, driving the earth to produce.

And first the cherries ripen. <u>Cent and a half a pound</u>. Hell, we can't pick 'em for that. Black cherries and red cherries, full and sweet, and the birds eat half of each cherry and the yellowjackets buzz into the holes the birds made. And on the ground the seeds drop and dry with black shreds hanging from them.

The purple prunes soften and sweeten. My God, we can't pick them and dry and sulphur them. We can't pay wages, no matter what wages. And the purple prunes carpet the ground. And first the skins wrinkle a little and swarms of flies come to feast, and the valley is filled with the odor of sweet decay. The meat turns dark and the crop shrivels on the ground.

And the pears grow yellow and soft. Five dollars a ton. Five dollars for forty fifty-pound boxes; trees pruned and sprayed, orchards cultivated—pick the fruit, put it in boxes, load the trucks, deliver the fruit to the cannery—forty boxes for five dollars. We can't do it. And the yellow fruit falls heavily to the ground and splashes on the ground. The yellowjackets dig into the soft meat, and there is a smell of ferment and rot.

Then the grapes—we can't make good wine. People can't buy good wine. Rip the grapes from the vines, good grapes, rotten grapes, wasp-stung grapes. Press stems, press dirt and rot.

But there's mildew and formic acid in the vats.

Add sulphur and tannic acid.

The smell from the ferment is not the rich odor of wine, but the smell of decay and chemicals.

Oh, well. It has alcohol in it, anyway. They can get drunk.

The little farmers watched debt creep up on them like the tide. They sprayed the trees and sold no crop, they pruned and grafted and could not pick the crop. And the men of knowledge have worked, have considered, and the fruit is rotting on the ground, and the decaying mash in the wine vats is poisoning the air. And taste the wine—no grape flavor at all, just sulphur and tannic acid and alcohol.

This little orchard will be a part of a great holding next year, for the debt will have choked the owner.

This vineyard will belong to the bank. Only the great owners can survive, for they own the canneries too. And four pears peeled and cut in half, cooked and canned, still cost fifteen cents. And the canned pears do not spoil. They will last for years.

The decay spreads over the State, and the sweet smell is a great sorrow on the land. Men who can graft the trees and make the seed fertile and big can find no way to let the hungry people eat their produce. Men who have created new fruits in the world cannot create a system whereby their fruits may be eaten. And the failure hangs over the State like a great sorrow.

The works of the roots of the vines, of the trees, must be destroyed to keep up the price, and this is the saddest, bitterest thing of all. Carloads of oranges dumped on the ground. The people came for miles to take the fruit, but this could not be. How would they buy oranges at twenty cents a dozen if they could drive out and pick them up? And men with hoses squirt kerosene on the oranges, and they are angry at the crime, angry at the people who have come to take the fruit. A million people hungry, needing the fruit—and kerosene sprayed over the golden mountains.

And the smell of rot fills the country.

Burn coffee for fuel in the ships. Burn corn to keep warm, it makes a hot fire. Dump potatoes in the rivers and place guards along the banks to keep the hungry people from fishing them out. Slaughter the pigs and bury them, and let the putrescence drip down into the earth.

There is a crime here that goes beyond denunciation. There is a sorrow here that weeping cannot symbolize. There is a failure here that topples all our success. The fertile earth, the straight tree rows, the sturdy trunks, and the ripe fruit. And children dying of pellagra must die because a profit cannot be taken from an orange. And coroners must fill in the certificates—died of malnutrition—because the food must rot, must be forced to rot.

The people come with nets to fish for potatoes in the river, and the guards hold them back; they come in rattling cars to get the dumped oranges, but the kerosene is sprayed. And they stand still and watch the potatoes float by, listen to the screaming pigs being killed in a ditch and covered with quicklime, watch the mountains of oranges slop down to a putrefying ooze; and in the eyes of the people there is the failure; and in the eyes of the hungry there is a growing wrath. In the souls of the people the grapes of wrath are filling and growing heavy, growing heavy for the vintage.

★ you have to look to the SYSTEMS (root causes)

— The problem can't be solved by attacking one person due to it not being just one persons fault, rather the systems

CHAPTER 26

In the Weedpatch camp, on an evening when the long, barred clouds hung over the set sun and inflamed their edges, the Joad family lingered after their supper. Ma hesitated before she started to do the dishes.

"We got to do somepin," she said. And she pointed at Winfield. "Look at 'im," she said. And when they stared at the little boy, "He's a-jerkin' an' a-twistin' in his sleep. Lookut his color." The members of the family looked at the earth again in shame. "Fried dough," Ma said. "<u>One month we been here</u>. An' Tom had five days' work. An' the rest of you scrabblin' out ever' day, an' no work. An' scairt to talk. An' the money gone. You're scairt to talk it out. Ever' night you jus' eat, an' then you get wanderin' away. Can't bear to talk it out. Well, you got to. Rosasharn ain't far from due, an' lookut her color. You got to talk it out. Now don't none of you get up till we figger somepin out. One day' more grease an' two days' flour, an' ten potatoes. You set here an' get busy!"

They looked at the ground. Pa cleaned his thick nails with his pocket knife. Uncle John picked at a splinter on the box he sat on. Tom pinched his lower lip and pulled it away from his teeth.

He released his lip and said softly, "We been a-lookin', Ma. Been walkin' out sence we can't use the gas no more. Been goin' in ever' gate, walkin' up to ever' house, even when we knowed they wasn't gonna be nothin'. Puts a weight on ya. Goin' out lookin' for somepin you know you ain't gonna find."

Ma said fiercely, "You ain't got the right to get discouraged. This here fambly's goin' under. You jus' ain't got the right."

Pa inspected his scraped nail. "We gotta go," he said. "We didn' wanta go. It's nice here, an' folks is nice here. We're feared we'll have to go live in one a them Hoovervilles."

"Well, if we got to, we got to. First thing is, we got to eat."

Al broke in. "I got a tankful a gas in the truck. I didn' let nobody get into that."

Tom smiled. "This here Al got a lot of sense along with he's randy-pandy."

"Now you figger," Ma said. "I ain't watchin' this here fambly starve no more. One day' more grease. That's what we got. Come time for Rosasharn to lay in, she got to be fed up. You figger!"

"This here hot water an' toilets—" Pa began.

"Well, we can't eat no toilets."

Tom said, "They was a fella come by today lookin' for men to go to Marysville. Pickin' fruit."

"Well, why don' we go to Marysville?" Ma demanded.

"I dunno," said Tom. "Didn' seem right, somehow. He was so anxious. Wouldn' say how much the pay was. Said he didn' know exactly."

Ma said, "We're a-goin' to Marysville. I don' care what the pay is. We're a-goin'."

"It's too far," said Tom. "We ain't got the money for gasoline. We couldn' get there. Ma, you say we got to figger. I ain't done nothin' but figger the whole time."

Uncle John said, "Feller says they's cotton a-comin' in up north, near a place called Tulare. That ain't very far, the feller says."

"Well, we got to git goin', an' goin' quick. I ain't a-settin' here no longer, no matter how nice." Ma took up her bucket and walked toward the sanitary unit for hot water.

"Ma gets tough," Tom said. "I seen her a-gettin' mad quite a piece now. She jus' boils up."

Pa said with relief, "Well, she brang it into the open, anyways. I been layin' at night a-burnin' my brains up. Now we can talk her out, anyways."

Ma came back with her bucket of steaming water. "Well," she demanded, "figger anything out?"

"Jus' workin' her over," said Tom. "Now s'pose we jus' move up north where that cotton's at. We been over this here country. We know they ain't nothin' here. S'pose we pack up an' shove north. Then when the cotton's ready, we'll be there. I kinda like to get my han's aroun' some cotton. You got a full tank, Al?"

"Almos'—'bout two inches down."

"Should get us up to that place."

Ma poised a dish over the bucket. "Well?" she demanded.

Tom said, "You win. We'll move on, I guess. Huh, Pa?"

"Guess we got to," Pa said.

Ma glanced at him. "When?"

"Well—no need waitin'. Might's well go in the mornin'."

"We got to go in the mornin'. I tol' you what's lef'."

"Now, Ma, don' think I don' wanta go. I ain't had a good gutful to eat in two weeks. 'Course I filled up, but I didn' take no good from it."

Ma plunged the dish into the bucket. "We'll go in the mornin'," she said.

Pa sniffled. "Seems like times is changed," he said sarcastically. "Time was when a man said what we'd do. Seems like women is tellin' now. Seems like it's purty near time to get out a stick."

Ma put the clean dripping tin dish out on a box. She smiled down at her work. "You get your stick, Pa," she said. "Times when they's food an' a place to set, then maybe you can use your stick an' keep your skin whole. But you ain't a-doin' your job, either a-thinkin' or a-workin'. If you was, why, you could use your stick, an' women folks'd sniffle their nose an' creep-mouse aroun'. But you jus' get you a stick now an' you ain't lickin' no woman you're a-fightin', 'cause I got a stick all laid out too."

Pa grinned with embarrassment. "Now it ain't good to have the little fellas hear you talkin' like that," he said.

"You get some bacon inside the little fellas 'fore you come tellin' what else is good for 'em," said Ma.

Pa got up in disgust and moved away, and Uncle John followed him.

Ma's hands were busy in the water, but she watched them go, and she said proudly to Tom, "He's all right. He ain't beat. I was scairt he wouldn' get mad. He's good an' mad. Look how he walks a-heelin' down with his feet. He's like as not to take a smack at me."

Tom laughed. "You jus' a-treadin' him on?"

"Sure," said Ma. "Take a man, he can get worried an' worried, an' it eats out his liver, an' purty soon he'll jus' lay down and die with his heart et out. But if you can take an' make 'im mad, why, he'll be awright. Pa, he didn' say nothin', but he's mad now. He'll show me now. He's awright."

Al got up. "I'm gonna walk down the row," he said.

"Better see the truck's ready to go," Tom warned him.

"She's ready."

"If she ain't, I'll turn Ma on ya."

"She's ready." Al strolled jauntily along the row of tents.

Tom sighed. "I'm a-gettin' tired, Ma. How 'bout makin' me mad?"

"You got more sense, Tom. I don' need to make you mad. I got to lean on you. Them others—they're kinda strangers, all but you. You won't give up, Tom."

The joke fell from him. "I don' like it," he said. "I wanta go out like Al. An' I wanta get mad like Pa, an' I wanta get drunk like Uncle John."

Ma shook her head. "You can't, Tom. I know. I knowed from the time you was a little fella. You can't. They's some folks that's just theirself an' nothin' more. There's Al—he's jus' a young fella after a girl. You wasn't never like that, Tom."

"Sure I was," said Tom. "Still am."

"No you ain't. Ever'thing you do is more'n you. When they sent you up to prison I knowed it. You're spoke for."

"Now, Ma—cut it out. It ain't true. It's all in your head."

She stacked the knives and forks on top of the plates. "Maybe. Maybe it's in my head. Rosasharn, you wipe up these here an' put 'em away."

The girl got breathlessly to her feet and her swollen middle hung out in front of her. She moved sluggishly to the box and picked up a washed dish.

Tom said, "Gettin' so tightful it's a-pullin' her eyes wide."

"Don't you go a-jollyin'," said Ma. "She's doin' good. You go 'long an' say goo'-by to anybody you wan'."

"O.K.," he said. "I'm gonna see how far it is up there."

Ma said to the girl, "He ain't sayin' stuff like that to make you feel bad. Where's Ruthie an' Winfiel'?"

"They snuck off after Pa. I seen 'em."

"Well, leave 'em go."

Rose of Sharon moved sluggishly about her work. Ma inspected her cautiously. "You feelin' pretty good? Your cheeks is kinda saggy."

"I ain't had milk like they said I ought."

"I know. We jus' didn' have no milk."

Rose of Sharon said dully, "Ef Connie hadn' went away, we'd a had a little house by now, with him studyin' an' all. Would a got milk like I need. Would a had a nice baby. This here baby ain't gonna be no good. I ought a had milk." She reached in her apron pocket and put something into her mouth.

Ma said, "I seen you nibblin' on somepin. What you eatin'?"

"Nothin'."

"Come on, what you nibblin' on?"

"Jus' a piece a slack lime. Foun' a big hunk."

"Why, tha's jus' like eatin' dirt."

"I kinda feel like I wan' it."

Ma was silent. She spread her knees and tightened her skirt. "I know," she said at last. "I et coal oncet when I was in a fambly way. Et a big piece a coal. Granma says I shouldn'. Don' you say that about the baby. You got no right even to think it."

"Got no husban'! Got no milk!"

Ma said, "If you was a well girl, I'd take a whang at you. Right in the face." She got up and went inside the tent. She came out and stood in front of Rose of Sharon, and she held out her hand. "Look!" The small gold earrings were in her hand. "These is for you."

The girl's eyes brightened for a moment, and then she looked aside. "I ain't pierced."

"Well, I'm a-gonna pierce ya." Ma hurried back into the tent. She came back with a cardboard box. Hurriedly she threaded a needle, doubled the thread and tied a series of knots in it. She threaded a second needle and knotted the thread. In the box she found a piece of cork.

"It'll hurt. It'll hurt."

Ma stepped to her, put the cork in back of the ear lobe and pushed the needle through the ear, into the cork.

The girl twitched. "It sticks. It'll hurt."

"No more'n that."

"Yes, it will."

"Well, then. Le's see the other ear first." She placed the cork and pierced the other ear.

"It'll hurt."

"Hush!" said Ma. "It's all done."

Rose of Sharon looked at her in wonder. Ma clipped the needles off and pulled one knot of each thread through the lobes.

"Now," she said. "Ever' day we'll pull one knot, and in a couple weeks it'll be all well an' you can wear 'em. Here—they're your'n now. You can keep 'em."

Rose of Sharon touched her ears tenderly and looked at the tiny spots of blood on her fingers. "It didn' hurt. Jus' stuck a little."

"You oughta been pierced long ago," said Ma. She looked at the girl's face, and she smiled in triumph. "Now get them dishes all done up. Your baby gonna be a good baby. Very near let you have a baby without your ears was pierced. But you're safe now."

"Does it mean somepin?"

"Why, 'course it does," said Ma. " 'Course it does."

Al strolled down the street toward the dancing platform. Outside a neat little tent he whistled softly, and then moved along the street. He walked to the edge of the grounds and sat down in the grass.

The clouds over the west had lost the red edging now, and the cores were black. Al scratched his legs and looked toward the evening sky.

In a few moments a blond girl walked near; she was pretty and sharp-featured. She sat down in the grass beside him and did not speak. Al put his hand on her waist and walked his fingers around.

"Don't," she said. "You tickle."

"We're goin' away tomorra," said Al.

She looked at him, startled. "Tomorra? Where?"

"Up north," he said lightly.

"Well, we're gonna git married, ain't we?"

"Sure, sometime."

"You said purty soon!" she cried angrily.

"Well, soon is when soon comes."

"You promised." He walked his fingers around farther. "Git away," she cried. "You said we was."

"Well, sure we are."

"An' now you're goin' away."

Al demanded, "What's the matter with you? You in a fambly way?"

"No, I ain't."

Al laughed. "I jus' been wastin' my time, huh?"

Her chin shot out. She jumped to her feet. "You git away from me, Al Joad. I don' wanta see you no more."

"Aw, come on. What's the matter?"

"You think you're jus'—hell on wheels."

"Now wait a minute."

"You think I got to go out with you. Well, I don't! I got lots a chances."

"Now wait a minute."

"No, sir—you git away."

Al lunged suddenly, caught her by the ankle, and tripped her. He grabbed her when she fell and held her and put his hand over her angry mouth. She tried to bite his palm, but he cupped it out over her mouth, and he held her down with his other arm. And in a moment she lay still, and in another moment they were giggling together in the dry grass.

"Why, we'll be a-comin' back purty soon," said Al. "An' I'll have a pocketful a jack. We'll go down to Hollywood an' see the pitchers."

She was lying on her back. Al bent over her. And he saw the bright evening star reflected in her eyes, and he saw the black cloud reflected in her eyes. "We'll go on the train," he said.

"How long ya think it'll be?" she asked.

"Oh, maybe a month," he said.

The evening dark came down and Pa and Uncle John squatted with the heads of families out by the office. They studied the night and the future. The little manager, in his white clothes, frayed and clean, rested his elbows on the porch rail. His face was drawn and tired.

Huston looked up at him. "You better get some sleep, mister."

"I guess I ought. Baby born last night in Unit Three. I'm getting to be a good midwife."

"Fella oughta know," said Huston. "Married fella got to know."

Pa said, "We're a-gittin' out in the mornin'."

"Yeah? Which way you goin'?"

"Thought we'd go up north a little. Try to get in the first cotton. We ain't had work. We're outa food."

"Know if they's any work?" Huston asked.

"No, but we're sure they ain't none here."

"They will be, a little later," Huston said. "We'll hold on."

"We hate to go," said Pa. "Folks been so nice here—an' the toilets an' all. But we got to eat. Got a tank of gas. That'll get us a little piece up the road. We had a bath ever' day here. Never was so clean in my life. Funny thing—use ta be I on'y got a bath ever' week an' I never seemed to stink. But now if I don't get one ever' day I stink. Wonder if takin' a bath so often makes that?"

"Maybe you couldn't smell yourself before," the manager said.

"Maybe. I wisht we could stay."

The little manager held his temples between his palms. "I think there's going to be another baby tonight," he said.

"We gonna have one in our fambly 'fore long," said Pa. "I wisht we could have it here. I sure wisht we could."

Tom and Willie and Jule the half-breed sat on the edge of the dance floor and swung their feet.

"I got a sack of Durham," Jule said. "Like a smoke?"

"I sure would," said Tom. "Ain't had a smoke for a hell of a time." He rolled the brown cigarette carefully, to keep down the loss of tobacco.

"Well, sir, we'll be sorry to see you go," said Willie. "You folks is good folks."

Tom lighted his cigarette. "I been thinkin' about it a lot. Jesus Christ, I wisht we could settle down."

Jule took back his Durham. "It ain't nice," he said. "I got a little girl. Thought when I come out here she'd get some schoolin'. But hell, we ain't in one place hardly long enough. Jes' gits goin' an' we got to drag on."

"I hope we don't get in no more Hoovervilles," said Tom. "I was really scairt, there."

"Deputies push you aroun'?"

"I was scairt I'd kill somebody," said Tom. "Was on'y there a little while, but I was a-stewin' aroun' the whole time. Depity come in an' picked up a frien', jus' because he talked outa turn. I was jus' stewin' all the time."

"Ever been in a strike?" Willie asked.

"No."

"Well, I been a-thinkin' a lot. Why don' them depities get in here an' raise hell like ever' place else? Think that little guy in the office is a-stoppin' 'em? No, sir."

"Well, what is?" Jule asked.

"I'll tell ya. It's 'cause we're all a-workin' together. Depity can't pick on one fella in this camp. He's pickin' on the whole darn camp. An' he don't dare. All we got to do is give a yell an' they's two hunderd men out. Fella organizin' for the union was a-talkin' out on the road. He says we could do that any place. Jus' stick together. They ain't raisin' hell with no two hunderd men. They're pickin' on one man."

"Yeah," said Jule, "an' suppose you got a union? You got to have leaders. They'll jus' pick up your leaders, an' where's your union?"

"Well," said Willie, "we got to figure her out some time. I been out here a year, an' wages is goin' right on down. Fella can't feed his fam'ly on his work now, an' it's gettin' worse all the time. It ain't gonna do no good to set aroun' an' starve. I don' know what to do. If a fella owns a team a horses, he don't raise no hell if he got to feed 'em when they ain't workin'. But if a fella got men workin' for him, he jus' don' give a damn. Horses is a hell of a lot more worth than men. I don' understan' it."

"Gits so I don' wanta think about it," said Jule. "An' I got to think about it. I got this here little girl. You know how purty she is. One week they give her a prize in this camp 'cause she's so purty. Well, what's gonna happen to her? She's gettin' spindly. I ain't gonna stan' it. She's so purty. I'm gonna bust out."

"How?" Willie asked. "What you gonna do—steal some stuff an' git in jail? Kill somebody an' git hung?"

"I don' know," said Jule. "Gits me nuts thinkin' about it. Gits me clear nuts."

"I'm a-gonna miss them dances," Tom said. "Them was some of the nicest dances I ever seen. Well, I'm gonna turn in. So long. I'll be seein' you someplace." He shook hands.

"Sure will," said Jule.

"Well, so long." Tom moved away into the darkness.

In the darkness of the Joad tent Ruthie and Winfield lay on their mattress, and Ma lay beside them. Ruthie whispered, "Ma!"

"Yeah? Ain't you asleep yet?"

"Ma—they gonna have croquet where we're goin'?"

"I don' know. Get some sleep. We want to get an early start."

"Well, I wisht we'd stay here where we're sure we got croquet."

"Sh!" said Ma.

"Ma, Winfiel' hit a kid tonight."

"He shouldn' of."

"I know. I tol' 'im, but he hit the kid right in the nose an', Jesus, how the blood run down!"

"Don' talk like that. It ain't a nice way to talk."

Winfield turned over. "That kid says we was Okies," he said in an outraged voice. "He says he wasn't no Okie 'cause he come from Oregon. Says we was goddamn Okies. I socked him."

"Sh! You shouldn'. He can't hurt you callin' names."

"Well, I won't let 'im," Winfield said fiercely.

"Sh! Get some sleep."

Ruthie said, "You oughta seen the blood run down—all over his clothes."

Ma reached a hand from under the blanket and snapped Ruthie on the cheek with her finger. The little girl went rigid for a moment, and then dissolved into sniffling, quiet crying.

In the sanitary unit Pa and Uncle John sat in adjoining compartments. "Might's well get in a good las' one," said Pa. "It's sure nice. 'Member how the little fellas was so scairt when they flushed 'em the first time?"

"I wasn't so easy myself," said Uncle John. He pulled his overalls neatly up around his knees. "I'm gettin' bad," he said. "I feel sin."

"You can't sin none," said Pa. "You ain't got no money. Jus' sit tight. Cos' you at leas' two bucks to sin, an' we ain't got two bucks amongst us."

"Yeah! But I'm a-thinkin' sin."

"Awright. You can think sin for nothin'."

"It's jus' as bad," said Uncle John.

"It's a whole hell of a lot cheaper," said Pa.

"Don't you go makin' light of sin."

"I ain't. You jus' go ahead. You always gets sinful jus' when hell's a-poppin'."

"I know it," said Uncle John. "Always was that way. I never tol' half the stuff I done."

"Well, keep it to yaself."

"These here nice toilets gets me sinful."

"Go out in the bushes then. Come on, pull up ya pants an' le's get some sleep." Pa pulled his overall straps in place and snapped the buckle. He flushed the toilet and watched thoughtfully while the water whirled in the bowl.

It was still dark when Ma roused her camp. The low night lights shone through the open doors of the sanitary unit. From the tents along the road came the assorted snores of the campers.

Ma said, "Come on, roll out. We got to be on our way. Day's not far off." She raised the screechy shade of the lantern and lighted the wick. "Come on, all of you."

The floor of the tent squirmed into slow action. Blankets and comforts were thrown back and sleepy eyes squinted blindly at the light. Ma slipped on her dress over the underclothes she wore to bed. "We got no coffee," she said. "I got a few biscuits. We can eat 'em on the road. Jus' get up now, an' we'll load the truck. Come on now. Don't make no noise. Don' wanta wake the neighbors."

It was a few moments before they were fully aroused. "Now don' you get away," Ma warned the children. The family dressed. The men pulled down the tarpaulin and loaded up the truck. "Make it nice an' flat," Ma warned them. They piled the mattress on top of the load and bound the tarpaulin in place over its ridge pole.

"Awright, Ma," said Tom. "She's ready."

Ma held a plate of cold biscuits in her hand. "Awright. Here. Each take one. It's all we got."

Ruthie and Winfield grabbed their biscuits and climbed up on the load. They covered themselves with a blanket and went back to sleep, still holding the cold hard biscuits in their hands. Tom got into the driver's seat and stepped on the starter. It buzzed a little, and then stopped.

"Goddamn you, Al!" Tom cried. "You let the battery run down."

Al blustered, "How the hell was I gonna keep her up if I ain't got gas to run her?"

Tom chuckled suddenly. "Well, I don' know how, but it's your fault. You got to crank her."

"I tell you it ain't my fault."

Tom got out and found the crank under the seat. "It's my fault," he said.

"Gimme that crank." Al seized it. "Pull down the spark so she don't take my arm off."

"O.K. Twist her tail."

Al labored at the crank, around and around. The engine caught, spluttered, and roared as Tom choked the car delicately. He raised the spark and reduced the throttle.

Ma climbed in beside him. "We woke up ever'body in the camp," she said.

"They'll go to sleep again."

Al climbed in on the other side. "Pa 'n' Uncle John got up top," he said. "Goin' to sleep again."

Tom drove toward the main gate. The watchman came out of the office and played his flashlight on the truck. "Wait a minute."

"What ya want?"

"You checkin' out?"

"Sure."

"Well, I got to cross you off."

"O.K."

"Know which way you're goin'?"

"Well, we're gonna try up north."

"Well, good luck," said the watchman.

"Same to you. So long."

The truck edged slowly over the big hump and into the road. Tom retraced the road he had driven before, past Weedpatch and west until he came to 99, then north on the great paved road, toward Bakersfield. It was growing light when he came into the outskirts of the city.

Tom said, "Ever' place you look is restaurants. An' them places all got coffee. Lookit that all-nighter there. Bet they got ten gallons a coffee in there, all hot!"

"Aw, shut up," said Al.

Tom grinned over at him. "Well, I see you got yaself a girl right off."

"Well, what of it?"

"He's mean this mornin', Ma. He ain't good company."

Al said irritably, "I'm goin' out on my own purty soon. Fella can make his way lot easier if he ain't got a fambly."

Tom said, "You'd have yaself a fambly in nine months. I seen you playin' aroun'."

"Ya crazy," said Al. "I'd get myself a job in a garage an' I'd eat in restaurants——"

"An' you'd have a wife an' kid in nine months."

"I tell ya I wouldn'."

Tom said, "You're a wise guy, Al. You gonna take some beatin' over the head."

"Who's gonna do it?"

"They'll always be guys to do it," said Tom.

"You think jus' because you——"

"Now you jus' stop that," Ma broke in.

"I done it," said Tom. "I was a-badgerin' him. I didn' mean no harm, Al. I didn' know you liked that girl so much."

"I don't like no girls much."

"Awright, then, you don't. You ain't gonna get no argument out of me."

The truck came to the edge of the city. "Look a them hot-dog stan's—hunderds of 'em," said Tom.

Ma said, "Tom! I got a dollar put away. You wan' coffee bad enough to spen' it?"

"No, Ma. I'm jus' foolin'."

"You can have it if you wan' it bad enough."

"I wouldn' take it."

Al said, "Then shut up about coffee."

Tom was silent for a time. "Seems like I got my foot in it all the time," he said. "There's the road we run up that night."

"I hope we don't never have nothin' like that again," said Ma. "That was a bad night."

"I didn' like it none either."

The sun rose on their right, and the great shadow of the truck ran beside them, flicking over the fence posts beside the road. They ran on past the rebuilt Hooverville.

"Look," said Tom. "They got new people there. Looks like the same place."

Al came slowly out of his sullenness. "Fella tol' me some a them people been burned out fifteen-twenty times. Says they jus' go hide down the willows an' then they come out an' build 'em another weed shack. Jus' like gophers. Got so use' to it they don't even get mad no more, this fella says. They jus' figger it's like bad weather."

"Sure was bad weather for me that night," said Tom. They moved up the wide highway. And the sun's warmth made them shiver. "Gettin' snappy in the mornin'," said Tom. "Winter's on the way. I jus' hope we can get some money 'fore it comes. Tent ain't gonna be nice in the winter."

Ma sighed, and then she straightened her head. "Tom," she said, "we gotta have a house in the winter. I tell ya we got to. Ruthie's awright, but Winfiel' ain't so strong. We got to have a house when the rains come. I heard it jus' rains cats aroun' here."

"We'll get a house, Ma. You res' easy. You gonna have a house."

"Jus' so's it's got a roof an' a floor. Jus' to keep the little fellas off'n the groun'."

"We'll try, Ma."

"I don' wanna worry ya now."

"We'll try, Ma."

"I jus' get panicky sometimes," she said. "I jus' lose my spunk."

"I never seen you when you lost it."

"Nights I do, sometimes."

There came a harsh hissing from the front of the truck. Tom

grabbed the wheel tight and he thrust the brake down to the floor. The truck bumped to a stop. Tom sighed. "Well, there she is." He leaned back in the seat. Al leaped out and ran to the right front tire.

"Great big nail," he called.

"We got any tire patch?"

"No," said Al. "Used it all up. Got patch, but no glue stuff."

Tom turned and smiled sadly at Ma. "You shouldn' a tol' about that dollar," he said. "We'd a fixed her some way." He got out of the car and went to the flat tire.

Al pointed to a big nail protruding from the flat casing. "There she is!"

"If they's one nail in the county, we run over it."

"Is it bad?" Ma called.

"No, not bad, but we got to fix her."

The family piled down from the top of the truck. "Puncture?" Pa asked, and then he saw the tire and was silent.

Tom moved Ma from the seat and got the can of tire patch from underneath the cushion. He unrolled the rubber patch and took out the tube of cement, squeezed it gently. "She's almos' dry," he said. "Maybe they's enough. Awright, Al. Block the back wheels. Le's get her jacked up."

Tom and Al worked well together. They put stones behind the wheels, put the jack under the front axle, and lifted the weight off the limp casing. They ripped off the casing. They found the hole, dipped a rag in the gas tank and washed the tube around the hole. And then, while Al held the tube tight over his knee, Tom tore the cement tube in two and spread the little fluid thinly on the rubber with his pocket knife. He scraped the gum delicately. "Now let her dry while I cut a patch." He trimmed and beveled the edge of the blue patch. Al held the tube tight while Tom put the patch tenderly in place. "There! Now bring her to the running board while I tap her with a hammer." He pounded the patch carefully, then stretched the tube and watched the edges of the patch. "There she is! She's gonna hold. Stick her on the rim an' we'll pump her up. Looks like you keep your buck, Ma."

Al said, "I wisht we had a spare. We got to get us a spare, Tom, on a rim an' all pumped up. Then we can fix a puncture at night."

"When we get money for a spare we'll get us some coffee an' side-meat instead," Tom said.

The light morning traffic buzzed by on the highway, and the sun grew warm and bright. A wind, gentle and sighing, blew in puffs from the southwest, and the mountains on both sides of the great valley were indistinct in a pearly mist.

Tom was pumping at the tire when a roadster, coming from the north, stopped on the other side of the road. A brown-faced man dressed in a light gray business suit got out and walked across to the truck. He was bareheaded. He smiled, and his teeth were very white against his brown skin. He wore a massive gold wedding ring on the third finger of his left hand. A little gold football hung on a slender chain across his vest.

"Morning," he said pleasantly.

Tom stopped pumping and looked up. "Mornin'."

The man ran his fingers through his coarse, short, graying hair. "You people looking for work?"

"We sure are, mister. Lookin' even under boards."

"Can you pick peaches?"

"We never done it," Pa said.

"We can do anything," Tom said hurriedly. "We can pick anything there is."

The man fingered his gold football. "Well, there's plenty of work for you about forty miles north."

"We'd sure admire to get it," said Tom. "You tell us how to get there, an' we'll go a-lopin'."

"Well, you go north to Pixley, that's thirty-five or -six miles, and you turn east. Go about six miles. Ask anybody where the Hooper ranch is. You'll find plenty of work there."

"We sure will."

"Know where there's other people looking for work?"

"Sure," said Tom. "Down at the Weedpatch camp they's plenty lookin' for work."

"I'll take a run down there. We can use quite a few. Remember now, turn east at Pixley and keep straight east to the Hooper ranch."

"Sure," said Tom. "An' we thank ya, mister. We need work awful bad."

"All right. Get along as soon as you can." He walked back across the road, climbed into his open roadster, and drove away south.

Tom threw his weight on the pump. "Twenty apiece," he called. "One—two—three—four—" At twenty Al took the pump, and then Pa and then Uncle John. The tire filled out and grew plump and smooth. Three times around, the pump went. "Let 'er down an' le's see," said Tom.

Al released the jack and lowered the car. "Got plenty," he said. "Maybe a little too much."

They threw the tools into the car. "Come on, le's go," Tom called. "We're gonna get some work at last."

Ma got in the middle again. Al drove this time.

"Now take her easy. Don't burn her up, Al."

They drove on through the sunny morning fields. The mist lifted from the hilltops and they were clear and brown, with black-purple creases. The wild doves flew up from the fences as the truck passed. Al unconsciously increased his speed.

"Easy," Tom warned him. "She'll blow up if you crowd her. We got to get there. Might even get in some work today."

Ma said excitedly, "With four men a-workin' maybe I can get some credit right off. Fust thing I'll get is coffee, 'cause you been wanting that, an' then some flour an' bakin' powder an' some meat. Better not get no side-meat right off. Save that for later. Maybe Sat'dy. An' soap. Got to get soap. Wonder where we'll stay." She babbled on. "An' milk. I'll get some milk 'cause Rosasharn, she ought to have milk. The lady nurse says that."

A snake wriggled across the warm highway. Al zipped over and ran it down and came back to his own lane.

"Gopher snake," said Tom. "You oughtn't to done that."

"I hate 'em," said Al gaily. "Hate all kinds. Give me the stomach-quake."

The forenoon traffic on the highway increased, salesmen in shiny coupés with the insignia of their companies painted on the doors, red and white gasoline trucks dragging clinking chains behind them, great square-doored vans from wholesale grocery houses, delivering produce. The country was rich along the roadside. There were orchards, heavy leafed in their prime, and vineyards with the long green crawlers carpeting the ground between the rows. There were melon patches and grain fields. White houses stood in the greenery, roses growing over them. And the sun was gold and warm.

In the front seat of the truck Ma and Tom and Al were overcome with happiness. "I ain't really felt so good for a long time," Ma said. " 'F we pick plenty peaches we might get a house, pay rent even, for a couple months. We got to have a house."

Al said, "I'm a-gonna save up. I'll save up an' then I'm a-goin' in a town an' get me a job in a garage. Live in a room an' eat in restaurants. Go to the movin' pitchers ever' damn night. Don' cost much. Cowboy pitchers." His hands tightened on the wheel.

The radiator bubbled and hissed steam. "Did you fill her up?" Tom asked.

"Yeah. Wind's kinda behind us. That's what makes her boil."

"It's a awful nice day," Tom said. "Use' ta work there in Mc-Alester an' think all the things I'd do. I'd go in a straight line way to hell an' gone an' never stop nowheres. Seems like a long time ago. Seems like it's years ago I was in. They was a guard made it tough. I was gonna lay for 'im. Guess that's what makes me mad at cops. Seems like ever' cop got his face. He use' ta get red in the face. Looked like a pig. Had a brother out west, they said. Use' ta get fellas paroled to his brother, an' then they had to work for nothin'. If they raised a stink, they'd get sent back for breakin' parole. That's what the fellers said."

"Don' think about it," Ma begged him. "I'm a-gonna lay in a lot a stuff to eat. Lot a flour an' lard."

"Might's well think about it," said Tom. "Try to shut it out, an' it'll whang back at me. They was a screwball. Never tol' you 'bout him. Looked like Happy Hooligan. Harmless kinda fella. Always was gonna make a break. Fellas all called him Hooligan." Tom laughed to himself.

"Don' think about it," Ma begged.

"Go on," said Al. "Tell about the fella."

"It don't hurt nothin', Ma," Tom said. "This fella was always gonna break out. Make a plan, he would; but he couldn' keep it to hisself an' purty soon ever'body knowed it, even the warden. He'd make his break an' they'd take 'im by the han' an' lead 'im back. Well, one time he drawed a plan where he's goin' over. 'Course he showed it aroun', an' ever'body kep' still. An' he hid out, an' ever'-body kep' still. So he's got himself a rope somewheres, an' he goes over the wall. They's six guards outside with a great big sack, an' Hooligan comes quiet down the rope an' they jus' hol' the sack out an' he goes right inside. They tie up the mouth an' take 'im back inside. Fellas laughed so hard they like to died. But it busted Hooligan's spirit. He jus' cried an' cried, an' moped aroun' an' got sick. Hurt his feelin's so bad. Cut his wrists with a pin an' bled to death 'cause his feelin's was hurt. No harm in 'im at all. They's all kinds a screwballs in stir."

"Don' talk about it," Ma said. "I knowed Purty Boy Floyd's ma. He wan't a bad boy. Jus' got drove in a corner."

The sun moved up toward noon and the shadow of the truck grew lean and moved in under the wheels.

"Mus' be Pixley up the road," Al said. "Seen a sign a little back." They drove into the little town and turned eastward on a narrower road. And the orchards lined the way and made an aisle.

"Hope we can find her easy," Tom said.

Ma said, "That fella said the Hooper ranch. Said anybody'd tell us. Hope they's a store near by. Might get some credit, with four men workin'. I could get a real nice supper if they'd gimme some credit. Make up a big stew maybe."

"An' coffee," said Tom. "Might even get me a sack a Durham. I ain't had no tobacca of my own for a long time."

Far ahead the road was blocked with cars, and a line of white motorcycles was drawn up along the roadside. "Mus' be a wreck," Tom said.

As they drew near a State policeman, in boots and Sam Browne belt, stepped around the last parked car. He held up his hand and Al pulled to a stop. The policeman leaned confidentially on the side of the car. "Where you going?"

Al said, "Fella said they was work pickin' peaches up this way."

"Want to work, do you?"

"Damn right," said Tom.

"O.K. Wait here a minute." He moved to the side of the road and called ahead. "One more. That's six cars ready. Better take this batch through."

Tom called, "Hey! What's the matter?"

The patrol man lounged back. "Got a little trouble up ahead. Don't you worry. You'll get through. Just follow the line."

There came the splattering blast of motorcycles starting. The line of cars moved on, with the Joad truck last. Two motorcycles led the way, and two followed.

Tom said uneasily, "I wonder what's a matter."

"Maybe the road's out," Al suggested.

"Don' need four cops to lead us. I don' like it."

The motorcycles ahead speeded up. The line of old cars speeded up. Al hurried to keep in back of the last car.

"These here is our own people, all of 'em," Tom said. "I don' like this."

Suddenly the leading policemen turned off the road into a wide graveled entrance. The old cars whipped after them. The motorcycles roared their motors. Tom saw a line of men standing in the ditch beside the road, saw their mouths open as though they were yelling, saw their shaking fists and their furious faces. A stout woman ran toward the cars, but a roaring motorcycle stood in her way. A high wire gate swung open. The six old cars moved through and the gate closed behind them. The four motorcycles turned and sped back in the direction from which they had come. And now that the motors were gone, the distant yelling of the men in the ditch could be heard. Two men stood beside the graveled road. Each one carried a shotgun.

One called, "Go on, go on. What the hell are you waiting for?" The six cars moved ahead, turned a bend and came suddenly on the peach camp.

There were fifty little square, flat-roofed boxes, each with a door and a window, and the whole group in a square. A water tank stood high on one edge of the camp. And a little grocery store stood on the other side. At the end of each row of square houses stood two men armed with shotguns and wearing big silver stars pinned to their shirts.

The six cars stopped. Two bookkeepers moved from car to car. "Want to work?"

Tom answered, "Sure, but what is this?"

"That's not your affair. Want to work?"

"Sure we do."

"Name?"

"Joad."

"How many men?"

"Four."

"Women?"

"Two."

"Kids?"

"Two."

"Can all of you work?"

"Why—I guess so."

"O.K. Find house sixty-three. Wages five cents a box. No bruised fruit. All right, move along now. Go to work right away."

The cars moved on. On the door of each square red house a number was painted. "Sixty," Tom said. "There's sixty. Must be down that way. There, sixty-one, sixty-two— There she is."

Al parked the truck close to the door of the little house. The family came down from the top of the truck and looked about in bewilderment. Two deputies approached. They looked closely into each face.

"Name?"

"Joad," Tom said impatiently. "Say, what is this here?"

One of the deputies took out a long list. "Not here. Ever see these here? Look at the license. Nope. Ain't got it. Guess they're O.K."

"Now you look here. We don't want no trouble with you. Jes' do your work and mind your own business and you'll be all right." The two turned abruptly and walked away. At the end of the dusty street they sat down on two boxes and their position commanded the length of the street.

Tom stared after them. "They sure do wanta make us feel at home."

Ma opened the door of the house and stepped inside. The floor was splashed with grease. In the one room stood a rusty tin stove and nothing more. The tin stove rested on four bricks and its rusty stovepipe went up through the roof. The room smelled of sweat and grease. Rose of Sharon stood beside Ma. "We gonna live here?"

Ma was silent for a moment. "Why, sure," she said at last. "It ain't so bad once we wash it out. Get her mopped."

"I like the tent better," the girl said.

"This got a floor," Ma suggested. "This here wouldn' leak when it rains." She turned to the door. "Might as well unload," she said.

The men unloaded the truck silently. A fear had fallen on them. The great square of boxes was silent. A woman went by in the street, but she did not look at them. Her head was sunk and her dirty gingham dress was frayed at the bottom in little flags.

The pall had fallen on Ruthie and Winfield. They did not dash away to inspect the place. They stayed close to the truck, close to the family. They looked forlornly up and down the dusty street. Winfield found a piece of baling wire and he bent it back and forth until it broke. He made a little crank of the shortest piece and turned it around and around in his hands.

Tom and Pa were carrying the mattresses into the house when

a clerk appeared. He wore khaki trousers and a blue shirt and a black necktie. He wore silver-bound eyeglasses, and his eyes, through the thick lenses, were weak and red, and the pupils were staring little bull's eyes. He leaned forward to look at Tom.

"I want to get you checked down," he said. "How many of you going to work?"

Tom said, "They's four men. Is this here hard work?"

"Picking peaches," the clerk said. "Piece work. Give five cents a box."

"Ain't no reason why the little fellas can't help?"

"Sure not, if they're careful."

Ma stood in the doorway. "Soon's I get settled down I'll come out an' help. We got nothin' to eat, mister. Do we get paid right off?"

"Well, no, not money right off. But you can get credit at the store for what you got coming."

"Come on, let's hurry," Tom said. "I wanta get some meat an' bread in me tonight. Where de we go, mister?"

"I'm going out there now. Come with me."

Tom and Pa and Al and Uncle John walked with him down the dusty street and into the orchard, in among the peach trees. The narrow leaves were beginning to turn a pale yellow. The peaches were little globes of gold and red on the branches. Among the trees were piles of empty boxes. The pickers scurried about, filling their buckets from the branches, putting the peaches in the boxes, carrying the boxes to the checking station; and at the stations, where the piles of filled boxes waited for the trucks, clerks waited to check against the names of the pickers.

"Here's four more," the guide said to a clerk.

"O.K. Ever picked before?"

"Never did," said Tom.

"Well, pick careful. No bruised fruit, no windfalls. Bruise your fruit an' we won't check 'em. There's some buckets."

Tom picked up a three-gallon bucket and looked at it. "Full a holes on the bottom."

"Sure," said the near-sighted clerk. "That keeps people from stealing them. All right—down in that section. Get going."

The four Joads took their buckets and went into the orchard. "They don't waste no time," Tom said.

"Christ Awmighty," Al said. "I ruther work in a garage."

Pa had followed docilely into the field. He turned suddenly on Al. "Now you jus' quit it," he said. "You been a-hankerin' an' a-complainin' an' a-bullblowin'. You get to work. You ain't so big I can't lick you yet."

Al's face turned red with anger. He started to bluster.

Tom moved near to him. "Come on, Al," he said quietly. "Bread an' meat. We got to get 'em."

They reached for the fruit and dropped them in the buckets. Tom ran at his work. One bucket full, two buckets. He dumped them in a box. Three buckets. The box was full. "I jus' made a nickel," he called. He picked up the box and walked hurriedly to the station. "Here's a nickel's worth," he said to the checker.

The man looked into the box, turned over a peach or two. "Put it over there. That's out," he said. "I told you not to bruise them. Dumped 'em outa the bucket, didn't you? Well, every damn peach is bruised. Can't check that one. Put 'em in easy or you're working for nothing."

"Why—goddamn it——"

"Now go easy. I warned you before you started."

Tom's eyes drooped sullenly. "O.K.," he said. "O.K." He went quickly back to the others. "Might's well dump what you got," he said. "Yours is the same as mine. Won't take 'em."

"Now, what the hell!" Al began.

"Got to pick easier. Can't drop 'em in the bucket. Got to lay 'em in."

They started again, and this time they handled the fruit gently. The boxes filled more slowly. "We could figger somepin out, I bet," Tom said. "If Ruthie an' Winfiel' or Rosasharn jus' put 'em in the boxes, we could work out a system." He carried his newest box to the station. "Is this here worth a nickel?"

The checker looked them over, dug down several layers. "That's better," he said. He checked the box in. "Just take it easy."

Tom hurried back. "I got a nickel," he called. "I got a nickel. On'y got to do that there twenty times for a dollar."

They worked on steadily through the afternoon. Ruthie and Winfield found them after a while. "You got to work," Pa told them. "You got to put the peaches careful in the box. Here, now, one at a time."

The children squatted down and picked the peaches out of the extra bucket, and a line of buckets stood ready for them. Tom carried the full boxes to the station. "That's seven," he said. "That's eight. Forty cents we got. Get a nice piece of meat for forty cents."

The afternoon passed. Ruthie tried to go away. "I'm tar'd," she whined. "I got to rest."

"You got to stay right where you're at," said Pa.

Uncle John picked slowly. He filled one bucket to two of Tom's. His pace didn't change.

In mid-afternoon Ma came trudging out. "I would a come before, but Rosasharn fainted," she said. "Jes' fainted away."

"You been eatin' peaches," she said to the children. "Well, they'll blast you out." Ma's stubby body moved quickly. She abandoned her bucket quickly and picked into her apron. When the sun went down they had picked twenty boxes.

Tom set the twentieth box down. "A buck," he said. "How long do we work?"

"Work till dark, long as you can see."

"Well, can we get credit now? Ma oughta go in an' buy some stuff to eat."

"Sure. I'll give you a slip for a dollar now." He wrote on a strip of paper and handed it to Tom.

He took it to Ma. "Here you are. You can get a dollar's worth of stuff at the store."

Ma put down her bucket and straightened her shoulders. "Gets you, the first time, don't it?"

"Sure. We'll all get used to it right off. Roll on in an' get some food."

Ma said, "What'll you like to eat?"

"Meat," said Tom. "Meat an' bread an' a big pot a coffee with sugar in. Great big piece a meat."

Ruthie wailed, "Ma, we're tar'd."

"Better come along in, then."

"They was tar'd when they started," Pa said. "Wild as rabbits they're a-gettin'. Ain't gonna be no good at all 'less we can pin 'em down."

"Soon's we get set down, they'll go to school," said Ma. She trudged away, and Ruthie and Winfield timidly followed her.

"We got to work ever' day?" Winfield asked.

Ma stopped and waited. She took his hand and walked along holding it. "It ain't hard work," she said. "Be good for you. An' you're helpin' us. If we all work, purty soon we'll live in a nice house. We all got to help."

"But I got so tar'd."

"I know. I got tar'd too. Ever'body gets wore out. Got to think about other stuff. Think about when you'll go to school."

"I don't wanta go to no school. Ruthie don't, neither. Them kids that goes to school, we seen 'em, Ma. Snots! Calls us Okies. We seen 'em. I ain't a-goin'."

Ma looked pityingly down on his straw hair. "Don' give us no trouble right now," she begged. "Soon's we get on our feet, you can be bad. But not now. We got too much, now."

"I et six of them peaches," Ruthie said.

"Well, you'll have the skitters. An' it ain't close to no toilet where we are."

The company's store was a large shed of corrugated iron. It had no display window. Ma opened the screen door and went in. A tiny man stood behind the counter. He was completely bald, and his head was blue-white. Large, brown eyebrows covered his eyes in such a high arch that his face seemed surprised and a little frightened. His nose was long and thin, and curved like a bird's beak, and his nostrils were blocked with light brown hair. Over the sleeves of his blue shirt he wore black sateen sleeve protectors. He was leaning on his elbows on the counter when Ma entered.

"Afternoon," she said.

He inspected her with interest. The arch over his eyes became higher. "Howdy."

"I got a slip here for a dollar."

"You can get a dollar's worth," he said, and he giggled shrilly. "Yes, sir. A dollar's worth. One dollar's worth." He waved his hand at the stock. "Any of it." He pulled his sleeve protectors up neatly.

"Thought I'd get a piece of meat."

"Got all kinds," he said. "Hamburg, like to have some hamburg? Twenty cents a pound, hamburg."

"Ain't that awful high? Seems to me hamburg was fifteen las' time I got some."

"Well," he giggled softly, "yes, it's high, an' same time it ain't high. Time you go on in town for a couple poun's of hamburg, it'll cos' you 'bout a gallon gas. So you see it ain't really high here, 'cause you got no gallon a gas."

Ma said sternly, "It didn' cos' you no gallon a gas to get it out here."

He laughed delightedly. "You're lookin' at it bass-ackwards," he said. "We ain't a-buyin' it, we're a-sellin' it. If we was buyin' it, why, that'd be different."

Ma put two fingers to her mouth and frowned with thought. "It looks all full a fat an' gristle."

"I ain't guaranteein' she won't cook down," the storekeeper said. "I ain't guaranteein' I'd eat her myself; but they's lots of stuff I wouldn' do."

Ma looked up at him fiercely for a moment. She controlled her voice. "Ain't you got some cheaper kind a meat?"

"Soup bones," he said. "Ten cents a pound."

"But them's jus' bones."

"Them's jes' bones," he said. "Make nice soup. Jes' bones."

"Got any boilin' beef?"

"Oh, yeah! Sure. That's two bits a poun'."

"Maybe I can't get no meat," Ma said. "But they want meat. They said they wanted meat."

"Ever'body wants meat—needs meat. That hamburg is purty nice stuff. Use the grease that comes out a her for gravy. Purty nice. No waste. Don't throw no bone away."

"How—how much is side-meat?"

"Well, now you're gettin' into fancy stuff. Christmas stuff. Thanksgivin' stuff. Thirty-five cents a poun'. I could sell you turkey cheaper, if I had some turkey."

Ma sighed. "Give me two pounds hamburg."

"Yes, ma'am." He scooped the pale meat on a piece of waxed paper. "An' what else?"

"Well, some bread."

"Right here. Fine big loaf, fifteen cents."

"That there's a twelve-cent loaf."

"Sure, it is. Go right in town an' get her for twelve cents. Gallon a gas. What else can I sell you, potatoes?"

"Yes, potatoes."

"Five pounds for a quarter."

Ma moved menacingly toward him. "I heard enough from you. I know what they cost in town."

The little man clamped his mouth tight. "Then go git 'em in town."

Ma looked at her knuckles. "What is this?" she asked softly. "You own this here store?"

"No. I jus' work here."

"Any reason you got to make fun? That help you any?" She regarded her shiny wrinkled hands. The little man was silent. "Who owns this here store?"

"Hooper Ranches, Incorporated, ma'am."

"An' they set the prices?"

"Yes, ma'am."

She looked up, smiling a little. "Ever'body comes in talks like me, is mad?"

He hesitated for a moment. "Yes, ma'am."

"An' that's why you make fun?"

"What cha mean?"

"Doin' a dirty thing like this. Shames ya, don't it? Got to act flip, huh?" Her voice was gentle. The clerk watched her, fascinated. He didn't answer. "That's how it is," Ma said finally. "Forty cents for meat, fifteen for bread, quarter for potatoes. That's eighty cents. Coffee?"

"Twenty cents the cheapest, ma'am."

"An' that's the dollar. Seven of us workin, an' that's supper." She studied her hand. "Wrap 'em up," she said quickly.

"Yes, ma'am," he said. "Thanks." He put the potatoes in a bag and folded the top carefully down. His eyes slipped to Ma, and then hid in his work again. She watched him, and she smiled a little.

"How'd you get a job like this?" she asked.

"A fella got to eat," he began; and then, belligerently, "A fella got a right to eat."

"What fella?" Ma asked.

He placed the four packages on the counter. "Meat," he said. "Potatoes, bread, coffee. One dollar, even." She handed him her slip of paper and watched while he entered the name and the amount in a ledger. "There," he said. "Now we're all even."

Ma picked up her bags. "Say," she said. "We got no sugar for the coffee. My boy Tom, he wants sugar. Look!" she said. "They're a-workin' out there. You let me have some sugar an' I'll bring the slip in later."

The little man looked away—took his eyes as far from Ma as he could. "I can't do it," he said softly. "That's the rule. I can't. I'd get in trouble. I'd get canned."

"But they're a-workin' out in the field now. They got more'n a dime comin'. Gimme ten cents' of sugar. Tom, he wanted sugar in his coffee. Spoke about it."

"I can't do it, ma'am. That's the rule. No slip, no groceries. The manager, he talks about that all the time. No, I can't do it. No, I can't. They'd catch me. They always catch fellas. Always. I can't."

"For a dime?"

"For anything, ma'am." He looked pleadingly at her. And then his face lost its fear. He took ten cents from his pocket and rang it up in the cash register. "There," he said with relief. He pulled a little bag from under the counter, whipped it open and scooped some sugar into it, weighed the bag, and added a little more sugar. "There you are," he said. "Now it's all right. You bring in your slip an' I'll get my dime back."

Ma studied him. Her hand went blindly out and put the little bag of sugar on the pile in her arm. "Thanks to you," she said quietly. She started for the door, and when she reached it, she turned about. "I'm learnin' one thing good," she said. "Learnin' it all a time, ever' day. If you're in trouble or hurt or need—go to poor people. They're the only ones that'll help—the only ones." The screen door slammed behind her.

The little man leaned his elbows on the counter and looked after her with his surprised eyes. A plump tortoise-shell cat leaped up on the counter and stalked lazily near to him. It rubbed sideways against his arms, and he reached out with his hand and pulled it against his cheek. The cat purred loudly, and the tip of its tail jerked back and forth.

Tom and Al and Pa and Uncle John walked in from the orchard when the dusk was deep. Their feet were a little heavy against the road.

"You wouldn' think jus' reachin' up an' pickin'd get you in the back," Pa said.

"Be awright in a couple days," said Tom. "Say, Pa, after we eat I'm a-gonna walk out an' see what all that fuss is outside the gate. It's been a-workin' on me. Wanta come?"

"No," said Pa. "I like to have a little while to jus' work an' not think about nothin'. Seems like I jus' been beatin' my brains to death for a hell of a long time. No, I'm gonna set awhile, an' then go to bed."

"How 'bout you, Al?"

Al looked away. "Guess I'll look aroun' in here, first," he said.

"Well, I know Uncle John won't come. Guess I'll go her alone. Got me all curious."

Pa said, "I'll get a hell of a lot curiouser 'fore I'll do anything about it—with all them cops out there."

"Maybe they ain't there at night," Tom suggested.

"Well, I ain't gonna find out. An' you better not tell Ma where you're a-goin'. She'll jus' squirt her head off worryin'."

Tom turned to Al. "Ain't you curious?"

"Guess I'll jus' look aroun' this here camp," Al said.

"Lookin' for girls, huh?"

"Mindin' my own business," Al said acidly.

"I'm still a-goin'," said Tom.

They emerged from the orchard into the dusty street between the red shacks. The low yellow light of kerosene lanterns shone from some of the doorways, and inside, in the half-gloom, the black shapes of people moved about. At the end of the street a guard still sat, his shotgun resting against his knee.

Tom paused as he passed the guard. "Got a place where a fella can get a bath, mister?"

The guard studied him in the half-light. At last he said, "See that water tank?"

"Yeah."

"Well, there's a hose over there."

"Any warm water?"

"Say, who in hell you think you are, J. P. Morgan?"

"No," said Tom. "No, I sure don't. Good night, mister."

The guard grunted contemptuously. "Hot water, for Christ's sake. Be wantin' tubs next." He stared glumly after the four Joads.

A second guard came around the end house. "'S'matter, Mack?"

"Why, them goddamn Okies. 'Is they warm water?' he says."

The second guard rested his gun butt on the ground. "It's them gov'ment camps," he said. "I bet that fella been in a gov'ment camp. We ain't gonna have no peace till we wipe them camps out. They'll be wantin' clean sheets, first thing we know."

Mack asked, "How is it out at the main gate—hear anything?"

"Well, they was out there yellin' all day. State police got it in hand. They're runnin' the hell outa them smart guys. I heard they's a long lean son-of-a-bitch spark-pluggin' the thing. Fella says they'll get him tonight, an' then she'll go to pieces."

"We won't have no job if it comes too easy," Mack said.

"We'll have a job, all right. These goddamn Okies! You got to watch 'em all the time. Things get a little quiet, we can always stir 'em up a little."

"Have trouble when they cut the rate here, I guess."

"We sure will. No, you needn' worry about us havin' work—not while Hooper's snubbin' close."

The fire roared in the Joad house. Hamburger patties splashed and hissed in the grease, and the potatoes bubbled. The house was full of smoke, and the yellow lantern light threw heavy black shadows on the walls. Ma worked quickly about the fire while Rose of Sharon sat on a box resting her heavy abdomen on her knees.

"Feelin' better now?" Ma asked.

"Smell a cookin' gets me. I'm hungry, too."

"Go set in the door," Ma said. "I got to have that box to break up anyways."

The men trooped in. "Meat, by God!" said Tom. "And coffee. I smell her. Jesus, I'm hungry! I et a lot of peaches, but they didn' do no good. Where can we wash, Ma?"

"Go down to the water tank. Wash down there. I jus' sent Ruthie an' Winfiel' to wash." The men went out again.

"Go on now, Rosasharn," Ma ordered. "Either you set in the door or else on the bed. I got to break that box up."

The girl helped herself up with her hands. She moved heavily to one of the mattresses and sat down on it. Ruthie and Winfield came in quietly, trying by silence and by keeping close to the wall to remain obscure.

Ma looked over at them. "I got a feelin' you little fellas is lucky they ain't much light," she said. She pounced at Winfield and felt his hair. "Well, you got wet, anyway, but I bet you ain't clean."

"They wasn't no soap," Winfield complained.

"No, that's right. I couldn' buy no soap. Not today. Maybe we can get soap tomorra." She went back to the stove, laid out the plates, and began to serve the supper. Two patties apiece and a big potato. She placed three slices of bread on each plate. When the meat was all out of the frying pan she poured a little of the grease on each plate. The men came in again, their faces dripping and their hair shining with water.

"Leave me at her," Tom cried.

They took the plates. They ate silently, wolfishly, and wiped up the grease with the bread. The children retired into the corner of the room, put their plates on the floor, and knelt in front of the food like little animals.

Tom swallowed the last of his bread. "Got any more, Ma?"

"No," she said. "That's all. You made a dollar, an' that's a dollar's worth."

"That?"

"They charge extry out here. We got to go in town when we can."

"I ain't full," said Tom.

"Well, tomorra you'll get in a full day. Tomorra night—we'll have plenty."

Al wiped his mouth on his sleeve. "Guess I'll take a look around," he said.

"Wait, I'll go with you." Tom followed him outside. In the darkness Tom went close to his brother. "Sure you don' wanta come with me?"

"No. I'm gonna look aroun' like I said."

"O.K.," said Tom. He turned away and strolled down the street. The smoke from the houses hung low to the ground, and the lanterns threw their pictures of doorways and windows into the street. On the doorsteps people sat and looked out into the darkness. Tom could see their heads turn as their eyes followed him down the street. At the street end the dirt road continued across a stubble field, and the black lumps of haycocks were visible in the starlight. A thin blade of moon was low in the sky toward the west, and the long cloud of the milky way trailed clearly overhead. Tom's feet sounded softly on the dusty road, a dark path against the yellow stubble. He put his hands in his pockets and trudged along toward the main gate. An embankment came close to the road. Tom could hear the whisper of water against the grasses in the irrigation ditch. He climbed up the bank and looked down on the dark water, and saw the stretched reflections of the stars. The State road was ahead. Car lights swooping past showed where it was. Tom set out again toward it. He could see the high wire gate in the starlight.

A figure stirred beside the road. A voice said, "Hello—who is it?"

Tom stopped and stood still. "Who are you?"

A man stood up and walked near. Tom could see the gun in his hand. Then a flashlight played on his face. "Where you think you're going?"

"Well, I thought I'd take a walk. Any law against it?"

"You better walk some other way."

Tom asked, "Can't I even get out of here?"

"Not tonight you can't. Want to walk back, or shall I whistle some help an' take you?"

"Hell," said Tom, "it ain't nothin' to me. If it's gonna cause a mess, I don't give a darn. Sure, I'll go back."

The dark figure relaxed. The flash went off. "Ya see, it's for your own good. Them crazy pickets might get you."

"What pickets?"

"Them goddamn reds."

"Oh," said Tom. "I didn' know 'bout them."

"You seen 'em when you come, didn' you?"

"Well, I seen a bunch a guys, but they was so many cops I didn' know. Thought it was a accident."

"Well, you better git along back."

"That's O.K. with me, mister." He swung about and started back. He walked quietly along the road a hundred yards, and then he stopped and listened. The twittering call of a raccoon sounded near the irrigation ditch and, very far away, the angry howl of a tied dog. Tom sat down beside the road and listened. He heard the high soft laughter of a night hawk and the stealthy movement of a creeping animal in the stubble. He inspected the skyline in both directions, dark frames both ways, nothing to show against. Now he stood up and walked slowly to the right of the road, off into the stubble field, and he walked bent down, nearly as low as the haycocks. He moved slowly and stopped occasionally to listen. At last he came to the wire fence, five strands of taut barbed wire. Beside the fence he lay on his back, moved his head under the lowest strand, held the wire up with his hands and slid himself under, pushing against the ground with his feet.

He was about to get up when a group of men walked by on the edge of the highway. Tom waited until they were far ahead before he stood up and followed them. He watched the side of the road for tents. A few automobiles went by. A stream cut across the fields, and the highway crossed it on a small concrete bridge. Tom looked over the side of the bridge. In the bottom of the deep ravine he saw a tent and a lantern was burning inside. He watched it for a moment,

saw the shadows of people against the canvas walls. Tom climbed a
fence and moved down into the ravine through brush and dwarf
willows; and in the bottom, beside a tiny stream, he found a trail. A
man sat on a box in front of the tent.

"Evenin'," Tom said.

"Who are you?"

"Well—I guess, well—I'm jus' goin' past."

"Know anybody here?"

"No. I tell you I was jus' goin' past."

A head stuck out of the tent. A voice said, "What's the matter?"

"Casy!" Tom cried. "Casy! For Chris' sake, what you doin'
here?"

"Why, my God, it's Tom Joad! Come on in, Tommy. Come on
in."

"Know him, do ya?" the man in front asked.

"Know him? Christ, yes. Knowed him for years. I come west with
him. Come on in, Tom." He clutched Tom's elbow and pulled him
into the tent.

Three other men sat on the ground, and in the center of the
tent a lantern burned. The men looked up suspiciously. A dark-faced,
scowling man held out his hand. "Glad to meet ya," he said. "I heard
what Casy said. This the fella you was tellin' about?"

"Sure. This is him. Well, for God's sake! Where's your folks?
What you doin' here?"

"Well," said Tom, "we heard they was work this-a-way. An' we
come, an' a bunch a State cops run us into this here ranch an' we
been a-pickin' peaches all afternoon. I seen a bunch a fellas yellin'.
They wouldn' tell me nothin', so I come out here to see what's goin'
on. How'n hell'd you get here, Casy?"

The preacher leaned forward and the yellow lantern light fell on
his high pale forehead. "Jail house is a kinda funny place," he said.
"Here's me, been a-goin' into the wilderness like Jesus to try find out
somepin. Almost got her sometimes, too. But it's in the jail house I
really got her." His eyes were sharp and merry. "Great big ol' cell,
an' she's full all a time. New guys come in, and guys go out. An'
'course I talked to all of 'em."

" 'Course you did," said Tom. "Always talk. If you was up on
the gallows you'd be passin' the time a day with the hangman. Never
seen sech a talker."

The men in the tent chuckled. A wizened little man with a wrinkled face slapped his knee. "Talks all the time," he said. "Folks kinda likes to hear 'im, though."

"Use' ta be a preacher," said Tom. "Did he tell that?"

"Sure, he told."

Casy grinned. "Well, sir," he went on, "I begin gettin' at things. Some a them fellas in the tank was drunks, but mostly they was there 'cause they stole stuff; an' mostly it was stuff they needed an' couldn' get no other way. Ya see?" he asked.

"No," said Tom.

"Well, they was nice fellas, ya see. What made 'em bad was they needed stuff. An' I begin to see, then. It's need that makes all the trouble. I ain't got it worked out. Well, one day they give us some beans that was sour. One fella started yellin', an' nothin' happened. He yelled his head off. Trusty come along an' looked in an' went on. Then another fella yelled. Well, sir, then we all got yellin'. And we all got on the same tone, an' I tell ya, it jus' seemed like that tank bulged an' give and swelled up. By God! Then somepin happened! They come a-runnin', and they give us some other stuff to eat—give it to us. Ya see?"

"No," said Tom.

Casy put his chin down on his hands. "Maybe I can't tell you," he said. "Maybe you got to find out. Where's your cap?"

"I come out without it."

"How's your sister?"

"Hell, she's big as a cow. I bet she got twins. Gonna need wheels under her stomach. Got to holdin' it with her han's, now. You ain' tol' me what's goin' on."

The wizened man said, "We struck. This here's a strike."

"Well, fi' cents a box ain't much, but a fella can eat."

"Fi' cents?" the wizened man cried. "Fi' cents! They payin' you fi' cents?"

"Sure. We made a buck an' a half."

A heavy silence fell in the tent. Casy stared out the entrance, into the dark night. "Lookie, Tom," he said at last. "We come to work there. They says it's gonna be fi' cents. They was a hell of a lot of us. We got there an' they says they're payin' two an' a half cents. A fella can't even eat on that, an' if he got kids— So we says we won't take it. So they druv us off. An' all the cops in the worl' come down on us. Now they're payin' you five. When they bust this here strike—ya think they'll pay five?"

"I dunno," Tom said. "Payin' five now."

"Lookie," said Casy. "We tried to camp together, an' they druv us like pigs. Scattered us. Beat the hell outa fellas. Druv us like pigs. They run you in like pigs, too. We can't las' much longer. Some people ain't et for two days. You goin' back tonight?"

"Aim to," said Tom.

"Well—tell the folks in there how it is, Tom. Tell 'em they're starvin' us an' stabbin' theirself in the back. 'Cause sure as cow-flops she'll drop to two an' a half jus' as soon as they clear us out."

"I'll tell 'em," said Tom. "I don' know how. Never seen so many guys with guns. Don' know if they'll even let a fella talk. An' folks don' pass no time of day. They jus' hang down their heads an' won't even give a fella a howdy."

"Try an' tell 'em, Tom. They'll get two an' a half, jus' the minute we're gone. You know what two an' a half is—that's one ton of peaches picked an' carried for a dollar." He dropped his head. "No —you can't do it. You can't get your food for that. Can't eat for that."

"I'll try to get to tell the folks."

"How's your ma?"

"Purty good. She liked that gov'ment camp. Baths an' hot water."

"Yeah—I heard."

"It was pretty nice there. Couldn' find no work, though. Had a leave."

"I'd like to go to one," said Casy. "Like to see it. Fella says they ain't no cops."

"Folks is their own cops."

Casy looked up excitedly. "An' was they any trouble? Fightin', stealin', drinkin'?"

"No," said Tom.

"Well, if a fella went bad—what then? What'd they do?"

"Put 'im outa the camp."

"But they wasn' many?"

"Hell, no," said Tom. "We was there a month, an' on'y one."

Casy's eyes shone with excitement. He turned to the other men. "Ya see?" he cried. "I tol' you. Cops cause more trouble than they stop. Look, Tom. Try an' get the folks in there to come on out. They can do it in a couple days. Them peaches is ripe. Tell 'em."

"They won't," said Tom. "They're a-gettin' five, an' they don' give a damn about nothin' else."

"But jus' the minute they ain't strikebreakin' they won't get no five."

"I don' think they'll swalla that. Five they're a-gettin'. Tha's all they care about."

"Well, tell 'em anyways."

"Pa wouldn' do it," Tom said. "I know 'im. He'd say it wasn't none of his business."

"Yes," Casy said disconsolately. "I guess that's right. Have to take a beatin' 'fore he'll know."

"We was outa food," Tom said. "Tonight we had meat. Not much, but we had it. Think Pa's gonna give up his meat on account a other fellas? An' Rosasharn oughta get milk. Think Ma's gonna wanta starve that baby jus' 'cause a bunch a fellas is yellin' outside a gate?"

Casy said sadly, "I wisht they could see it. I wisht they could see the on'y way they can depen' on their meat— Oh, the hell! Get tar'd sometimes. God-awful tar'd. I knowed a fella. Brang 'im in while I was in the jail house. Been tryin' to start a union. Got one started. An' then them vigilantes bust it up. An' know what? Them very folks he been tryin' to help tossed him out. Wouldn' have nothin' to do with 'im. Scared they'd get saw in his comp'ny. Says, 'Git out. You're a danger on us.' Well, sir, it hurt his feelin's purty bad. But then he says, 'It ain't so bad if you know.' He says, 'French Revolution—all them fellas that figgered her out got their heads chopped off. Always that way,' he says. 'Jus' as natural as rain. You ain't doin' it for fun no way. Doin' it 'cause you have to. 'Cause it's you. Look a Washington,' he says. 'Fit the Revolution, an' after, them sons-a-bitches turned on him. An' Lincoln the same. Same folks yellin' to kill 'em. Natural as rain.'"

"Don't soun' like no fun," said Tom.

"No, it don't. This fella in jail, he says, 'Anyways, you do what you can. An',' he says, 'the on'y thing you got to look at is that ever' time they's a little step fo'ward, she may slip back a little, but she never slips clear back. You can prove that,' he says, 'an' that makes the whole thing right. An' that means they wasn't no waste even if it seemed like they was.'"

"Talkin'," said Tom. "Always talkin'. Take my brother Al. He's out lookin' for a girl. He don't care 'bout nothin' else. Couple days he'll get him a girl. Think about it all day an' do it all night. He don't give a damn 'bout steps up or down or sideways."

"Sure," said Casy. "Sure. He's jus' doin' what he's got to do. All of us like that."

The man seated outside pulled the tent flap wide. "Goddamn it, I don' like it," he said.

Casy looked out at him. "What's the matter?"

"I don' know. I jus' itch all over. Nervous as a cat."

"Well, what's the matter?"

"I don' know. Seems like I hear somepin, an' then I listen an' they ain't nothin' to hear."

"You're jus' jumpy," the wizened man said. He got up and went outside. And in a second he looked into the tent. "They's a great big ol' black cloud a-sailin' over. Bet she's got thunder. That's what's itchin' him—'lectricity." He ducked out again. The other two men stood up from the ground and went outside.

Casy said softly, "All of 'em's itchy. Them cops been sayin' how they're gonna beat the hell outa us an' run us outa the county. They figger I'm a leader 'cause I talk so much."

The wizened face looked in again. "Casy, turn out that lantern an' come outside. They's somepin."

Casy turned the screw. The flame drew down into the slots and popped and went out. Casy groped outside and Tom followed him. "What is it?" Casy asked softly.

"I dunno. Listen!"

There was a wall of frog sounds that merged with silence. A high, shrill whistle of crickets. But through this background came other sounds—faint footsteps from the road, a crunch of clods up on the bank, a little swish of brush down the stream.

"Can't really tell if you hear it. Fools you. Get nervous," Casy reassured them. "We're all nervous. Can't really tell. You hear it, Tom?"

"I hear it," said Tom. "Yeah, I hear it. I think they's guys comin' from ever' which way. We better get outa here."

The wizened man whispered, "Under the bridge span—out that way. Hate to leave my tent."

"Le's go," said Casy.

They moved quietly along the edge of the stream. The black span was a cave before them. Casy bent over and moved through. Tom behind. Their feet slipped into the water. Thirty feet they moved, and their breathing echoed from the curved ceiling. Then they came out on the other side and straightened up.

A sharp call, "There they are!" Two flashlight beams fell on the men, caught them, blinded them. "Stand where you are." The voices came out of the darkness. "That's him. That shiny bastard. That's him."

Casy stared blindly at the light. He breathed heavily."Listen," he said. "You fellas don' know what you're doin'. You're helpin' to starve kids."

"Shut up, you red son-of-a-bitch."

A short heavy man stepped into the light. He carried a new white pick handle.

Casy went on, "You don' know what you're a-doin'.''

The heavy man swung with the pick handle. Casy dodged down into the swing. The heavy club crashed into the side of his head with a dull crunch of bone, and Casy fell sideways out of the light.

"Jesus, George. I think you killed him."

"Put the light on him," said George. "Serve the son-of-a-bitch right." The flashlight beam dropped, searched and found Casy's crushed head.

Tom looked down at the preacher. The light crossed the heavy man's legs and the white new pick handle. Tom leaped silently. He wrenched the club free. The first time he knew he had missed and struck a shoulder, but the second time his crushing blow found the head, and as the heavy man sank down, three more blows found his head. The lights danced about. There were shouts, the sound of running feet, crashing through brush. Tom stood over the prostrate man. And then a club reached his head, a glancing blow. He felt the stroke like an electric shock. And then he was running along the stream, bending low. He heard the splash of footsteps following him. Suddenly he turned and squirmed up into the brush, deep into a poison-oak thicket. And he lay still. The footsteps came near, the light beams glanced along the stream bottom. Tom wriggled up through the thicket to the top. He emerged in an orchard. And still he could hear the calls, the pursuit in the stream bottom. He bent low and ran over the cultivated earth; the clods slipped and rolled under his feet. Ahead he saw the bushes that bounded the field, bushes along the edges of an irrigation ditch. He slipped through the fence, edged in among vines and blackberry bushes. And then he lay still, panting hoarsely. He felt his numb face and nose. The nose was crushed, and a trickle of blood dripped from his chin. He lay still on his stomach until his mind came back. And then he crawled slowly over the edge of the ditch. He bathed his face in the cool water, tore off the tail of his blue shirt and dipped it and held it against his torn cheek and nose. The water stung and burned.

The black cloud had crossed the sky, a blob of dark against the stars. The night was quiet again.

Tom stepped into the water and felt the bottom drop from under his feet. He threshed the two strokes across the ditch and pulled himself heavily up the other bank. His clothes clung to him. He moved and made a slopping noise; his shoes squished. Then he sat down, took off his shoes and emptied them. He wrung the bottoms of his trousers, took off his coat and squeezed the water from it.

Along the highway he saw the dancing beams of the flashlights, searching the ditches. Tom put on his shoes and moved cautiously across the stubble field. The squishing noise no longer came from his shoes. He went by instinct toward the other side of the stubble field, and at last he came to the road. Very cautiously he approached the square of houses.

Once a guard, thinking he heard a noise, called, "Who's there?"

Tom dropped and froze to the ground, and the flashlight beam passed over him. He crept silently to the door of the Joad house. The door squalled on its hinges. And Ma's voice, calm and steady and wide awake:

"What's that?"

"Me. Tom."

"Well, you better get some sleep. Al ain't in yet."

"He must a foun' a girl."

"Go on to sleep," she said softly. "Over under the window."

He found his place and took off his clothes to the skin. He lay shivering under his blanket. And his torn face awakened from its numbness, and his whole head throbbed.

It was an hour more before Al came in. He moved cautiously near and stepped on Tom's wet clothes.

"Sh!" said Tom.

Al whispered, "You awake? How'd you get wet?"

"Sh," said Tom. "Tell you in the mornin'."

Pa turned on his back, and his snoring filled the room with gasps and snorts.

"You're col'," Al said.

"Sh. Go to sleep." The little square of the window showed gray against the black of the room.

Tom did not sleep. The nerves of his wounded face came back to life and throbbed, and his cheek bone ached, and his broken nose bulged and pulsed with pain that seemed to toss him about, to shake him. He watched the little square window, saw the stars slide down over it and drop from sight. At intervals he heard the footsteps of the watchmen.

At last the roosters crowed, far away, and gradually the window lightened. Tom touched his swollen face with his fingertips, and at his movement Al groaned and murmured in his sleep.

The dawn came finally. In the houses, packed together, there was a sound of movement, a crash of breaking sticks, a little clatter of pans. In the graying gloom Ma sat up suddenly. Tom could see her face, swollen with sleep. She looked at the window, for a long moment. And then she threw the blanket off and found her dress. Still sitting down, she put it over her head and held her arms up and let the dress slide down to her waist. She stood up and pulled the dress down around her ankles. Then, in bare feet, she stepped carefully to the window and looked out, and while she stared at the growing light, her quick fingers unbraided her hair and smoothed the strands and braided them up again. Then she clasped her hands in front of her and stood motionless for a moment. Her face was lighted sharply by the window. She turned, stepped carefully among the mattresses, and found the lantern. The shade screeched up, and she lighted the wick.

Pa rolled over and blinked at her. She said, "Pa, you got more money?"

"Huh? Yeah. Paper wrote for sixty cents."

"Well, git up an' go buy some flour an' lard. Quick, now."

Pa yawned. "Maybe the store ain't open."

"Make 'em open it. Got to get somepin in you fellas. You got to get out to work."

Pa struggled into his overalls and put on his rusty coat. He went sluggishly out the door, yawning and stretching.

The children awakened and watched from under their blanket, like mice. Pale light filled the room now, but colorless light, before the sun. Ma glanced at the mattresses. Uncle John was awake, Al slept heavily. Her eyes moved to Tom. For a moment she peered at him, and then she moved quickly to him. His face was puffed and

blue, and the blood was dried black on his lips and chin. The edges
of the torn cheek were gathered and tight.

"Tom," she whispered, "what's the matter?"

"Sh!" he said. "Don't talk loud. I got in a fight."

"Tom!"

"I couldn' help it, Ma."

She knelt down beside him. "You in trouble?"

He was a long time answering. "Yeah," he said. "In trouble. I
can't go out to work. I got to hide."

The children crawled near on their hands and knees, staring
greedily. "What's the matter'th him, Ma?"

"Hush!" Ma said. "Go wash up."

"We got no soap."

"Well, use water."

"What's the matter'th Tom?"

"Now you hush. An' don't you tell nobody."

They backed away and squatted down against the far wall, knowing they would not be inspected.

Ma asked, "Is it bad?"

"Nose busted."

"I mean the trouble?"

"Yeah. Bad!"

Al opened his eyes and looked at Tom. "Well, for Chris' sake!
What was you in?"

"What's a matter?" Uncle John asked.

Pa clumped in. "They was open all right." He put a tiny bag of
flour and his package of lard on the floor beside the stove. " 'S'a
matter?" he asked.

Tom braced himself on one elbow for a moment, and then he
lay back. "Jesus, I'm weak. I'm gonna tell ya once. So I'll tell all of
ya. How 'bout the kids?"

Ma looked at them, huddled against the wall. "Go wash ya face."

"No," Tom said. "They got to hear. They got to know. They
might blab if they don' know."

"What the hell is this?" Pa demanded.

"I'm a-gonna tell. Las' night I went out to see what all the yellin'
was about. An' I come on Casy."

"The preacher?"

"Yeah, Pa. The preacher, on'y he was a-leadin' the strike. They
come for him."

Pa demanded, "Who come for him?"

"I dunno. Same kinda guys that turned us back on the road that night. Had pick handles." He paused. "They killed 'im. Busted his head. I was standin' there. I went nuts. Grabbed the pick handle." He looked bleakly back at the night, the darkness, the flashlights, as he spoke. "I—I clubbed a guy."

Ma's breath caught in her throat. Pa stiffened. "Kill 'im?" he asked softly.

"I—don't know. I was nuts. Tried to."

Ma asked, "Was you saw?"

"I dunno. I dunno. I guess so. They had the lights on us."

For a moment Ma stared into his eyes. "Pa," she said, "break up some boxes. We got to get breakfas'. You got to go to work. Ruthie, Winfiel'. If anybody asts you—Tom is sick—you hear? If you tell—he'll—get sent to jail. You hear?"

"Yes, ma'am."

"Keep your eye on 'em, John. Don' let 'em talk to nobody." She built the fire as Pa broke the boxes that had held the goods. She made her dough, put a pot of coffee to boil. The light wood caught and roared its flame in the chimney.

Pa finished breaking the boxes. He came near to Tom. "Casy—he was a good man. What'd he wanta mess with that stuff for?"

Tom said dully, "They come to work for fi' cents a box."

"That's what we're a-gettin'."

"Yeah. What we was a-doin' was breakin' strike. They give them fellas two an' a half cents."

"You can't eat on that."

"I know," Tom said wearily. "That's why they struck. Well, I think they bust that strike las' night. We'll maybe be gettin' two an' a half cents today."

"Why, the sons-a-bitches——"

"Yeah! Pa. You see? Casy was still a—good man. Goddamn it, I can't get that pitcher outa my head. Him layin' there—head jus' crushed flat an' oozin'. Jesus!" He covered his eyes with his hand.

"Well, what we gonna do?" Uncle John asked.

Al was standing up now. "Well, by God, I know what I'm gonna do. I'm gonna get out of it."

"No, you ain't, Al," Tom said. "We need you now. I'm the one. I'm a danger now. Soon's I get on my feet I got to go."

Ma worked at the stove. Her head was half turned to hear. She put grease in the frying pan, and when it whispered with heat, she spooned the dough into it.

Tom went on, "You got to stay, Al. You got to take care a the truck."

"Well, I don' like it."

"Can't help it, Al. It's your folks. You can help 'em. I'm a danger to 'em."

Al grumbled angrily. "I don' know why I ain't let to get me a job in a garage."

"Later, maybe." Tom looked past him, and he saw Rose of Sharon lying on the mattress. Her eyes were huge—opened wide. "Don' worry," he called to her. "Don' you worry. Gonna get you some milk today." She blinked slowly, and didn't answer him.

Pa said, "We got to know, Tom. Think ya killed this fella?"

"I don' know. It was dark. An' somebody smacked me. I don' know. I hope so. I hope I killed the bastard."

"Tom!" Ma called. "Don' talk like that."

From the street came the sound of many cars moving slowly. Pa stepped to the window and looked out. "They's a whole slew a new people comin' in," he said.

"I guess they bust the strike, awright," said Tom. "I guess you'll start at two an' a half cents."

"But a fella could work at a run, an' still he couldn' eat."

"I know," said Tom. "Eat win'fall peaches. That'll keep ya up."

Ma turned the dough and stirred the coffee. "Listen to me," she said. "I'm gettin' cornmeal today. We're a-gonna eat cornmeal mush. An' soon's we get enough for gas, we're movin' away. This ain't a good place. An' I ain't gonna have Tom out alone. No, sir."

"Ya can't do that, Ma. I tell you I'm jus' a danger to ya."

Her chin was set. "That's what we'll do. Here, come eat this here, an' then get out to work. I'll come out soon's I get washed up. We got to make some money."

They ate the fried dough so hot that it sizzled in their mouths. And they tossed the coffee down and filled their cups and drank more coffee.

Uncle John shook his head over his plate. "Don't look like we're a-gonna get shet of this here. I bet it's my sin."

"Oh, shut up!" Pa cried. "We ain't got the time for your sin. Come on now. Le's get out to her. Kids, you come he'p. Ma's right. We got to go outa here."

When they were gone, Ma took a plate and a cup to Tom. "Better eat a little somepin."

"I can't, Ma. I'm so darn sore I couldn' chew."

"You better try."

"No, I can't, Ma."

She sat down on the edge of his mattress. "You got to tell me," she said. "I got to figger how it was. I got to keep straight. What was Casy a-doin'? Why'd they kill 'im?"

"He was jus' standin' there with the lights on 'im."

"What'd he say? Can ya 'member what he says?"

Tom said, "Sure. Casy said, 'You got no right to starve people.' An' then this heavy fella called him a red son-of-a-bitch. An' Casy says, 'You don' know what you're a-doin'.' An' then this guy smashed 'im."

Ma looked down. She twisted her hands together. "Tha's what he said—'You don' know what you're doin' '?"

"Yeah!"

Ma said, "I wisht Granma could a heard."

"Ma—I didn' know what I was a-doin', no more'n when you take a breath. I didn' even know I was gonna do it."

"It's awright. I wisht you didn' do it. I wisht you wasn' there. But you done what you had to do. I can't read no fault on you." She went to the stove and dipped a cloth in the heating dishwater. "Here," she said. "Put that there on your face."

He laid the warm cloth over his nose and cheek, and winced at the heat. "Ma, I'm a-gonna go away tonight. I can't go puttin' this on you folks."

Ma said angrily, "Tom! They's a whole lot I don' un'erstan'. But goin' away ain't gonna ease us. It's gonna bear us down." And she went on, "They was the time when we was on the lan'. They was a boundary to us then. Ol' folks died off, an' little fellas come, an' we was always one thing—we was the fambly—kinda whole and clear. An' now we ain't clear no more. I can't get straight. They ain't nothin' keeps us clear. Al—he's a-hankerin' an' a-jibbitin' to go off on his own. An' Uncle John is jus' a-draggin' along. Pa's lost his place. He ain't the head no more. We're crackin' up, Tom. There ain't no fambly now. An' Rosasharn—" She looked around and found the girl's wide eyes. "She gonna have her baby an' they won't be no fambly. I don' know. I been a-tryin' to keep her goin'. Winfiel'—

what's he gonna be, this-a-way? Gettin' wild, an' Ruthie too—like animals. Got nothin' to trus'. Don' go, Tom. Stay an' help."

"O.K.," he said tiredly. "O.K. I shouldn', though. I know it."

Ma went to her dishpan and washed the tin plates and dried them. "You didn' sleep."

"No."

"Well, you sleep. I seen your clothes was wet. I'll hang 'em by the stove to dry." She finished her work. "I'm goin' now. I'll pick. Rosasharn, if anybody comes, Tom's sick, you hear? Don' let nobody in. You hear?" Rose of Sharon nodded. "We'll come back at noon. Get some sleep, Tom. Maybe we can get outa here tonight." She moved swiftly to him. "Tom, you ain't gonna slip out?"

"No, Ma."

"You sure? You won't go?"

"No, Ma. I'll be here."

"Awright. 'Member, Rosasharn." She went out and closed the door firmly behind her.

Tom lay still—and then a wave of sleep lifted him to the edge of unconsciousness and dropped him slowly back and lifted him again.

"You—Tom!"

"Huh? Yeah!" He started awake. He looked over at Rose of Sharon. Her eyes were blazing with resentment. "What you want?"

"You killed a fella!"

"Yeah. Not so loud! You wanta rouse somebody?"

"What da I care?" she cried. "That lady tol' me. She says what sin's gonna do. She tol' me. What chance I got to have a nice baby? Connie's gone, an' I ain't gettin' good food. I ain't gettin' milk." Her voice rose hysterically. "An' now you kill a fella. What chance that baby got to get bore right? I know—gonna be a freak—a freak! I never done no dancin'."

Tom got up. "Sh!" he said. "You're gonna get folks in here."

"I don' care. I'll have a freak! I didn' dance no hug-dance."

He went near to her. "Be quiet."

"You get away from me. It ain't the first fella you killed, neither." Her face was growing red with hysteria. Her words blurred. "I don' wanta look at you." She covered her head with her blanket.

Tom heard the choked, smothered cries. He bit his lower lip and studied the floor. And then he went to Pa's bed. Under the edge of the mattress the rifle lay, a lever-action Winchester .38, long and heavy. Tom picked it up and dropped the lever to see that a cartridge was in the chamber. He tested the hammer on half-cock. And then he went back to his mattress. He laid the rifle on the floor beside him, stock up and barrel pointing down. Rose of Sharon's voice thinned to a whimper. Tom lay down again and covered himself, covered his bruised cheek with the blanket and made a little tunnel to breathe through. He sighed, "Jesus, oh, Jesus!"

Outside, a group of cars went by, and voices sounded.

"How many men?"

"Jes' us—three. Whatcha payin'?"

"You go to house twenty-five. Number's right on the door."

"O.K., mister. Whatcha payin'?"

"Two and a half cents."

"Why, goddamn it, a man can't make his dinner!"

"That's what we're payin'. There's two hundred men coming from the South that'll be glad to get it."

"But, Jesus, mister!"

"Go on now. Either take it or go on along. I got no time to argue."

"But——"

"Look. I didn' set the price. I'm just checking you in. If you want it, take it. If you don't, turn right around and go along."

"Twenty-five, you say?"

"Yes, twenty-five."

Tom dozed on his mattress. A stealthy sound in the room awakened him. His hand crept to the rifle and tightened on the grip. He drew back the covers from his face. Rose of Sharon was standing beside his mattress.

"What you want?" Tom demanded.

"You sleep," she said. "You jus' sleep off. I'll watch the door. They won't nobody get in."

He studied her face for a moment. "O.K.," he said, and he covered his face with the blanket again.

In the beginning dusk Ma came back to the house. She paused on the doorstep and knocked and said, "It's me," so that Tom would not be worried. She opened the door and entered, carrying a bag. Tom awakened and sat up on his mattress. His wound had dried and tightened so that the unbroken skin was shiny. His left eye was drawn nearly shut. "Anybody come while we was gone?" Ma asked.

"No," he said. "Nobody. I see they dropped the price."

"How'd you know?"

"I heard folks talkin' outside."

Rose of Sharon looked dully up at Ma.

Tom pointed at her with his thumb. "She raised hell, Ma. Thinks all the trouble is aimed right smack at her. If I'm gonna get her upset like that I oughta go 'long."

Ma turned on Rose of Sharon. "What you doin'?"

The girl said resentfully, "How'm I gonna have a nice baby with stuff like this?"

Ma said, "Hush! You hush now. I know how you're a-feelin', an' I know you can't he'p it, but you jus' keep your mouth shut."

She turned back to Tom. "Don't pay her no mind, Tom. It's awful hard, an' I 'member how it is. Ever'thing is a-shootin' right at you when you're gonna have a baby, an' ever'thing anybody says is a insult, an' ever'thing's against you. Don't pay no mind. She can't he'p it. It's jus' the way she feels."

"I don' wanta hurt her."

"Hush! Jus' don' talk." She set her bag down on the cold stove. "Didn' hardly make nothin'," she said. "I tol' you, we're gonna get outa here. Tom, try an' wrassle me some wood. No—you can't. Here, we got on'y this one box lef'. Break it up. I tol' the other fellas to pick up some sticks on the way back. Gonna have mush an' a little sugar on."

Tom got up and stamped the last box to small pieces. Ma carefully built her fire in one end of the stove, conserving the flame under one stove hole. She filled a kettle with water and put it over the flame. The kettle rattled over the direct fire, rattled and wheezed.

"How was it pickin' today?" Tom asked.

Ma dipped a cup into her bag of cornmeal. "I don' wanta talk about it. I was thinkin' today how they use' to be jokes. I don' like it, Tom. We don't joke no more. When they's a joke, it's a mean bitter joke, an' they ain't no fun in it. Fella says today, 'Depression is over. I seen a jackrabbit, an' they wasn't nobody after him.' An' another fella says, 'That ain't the reason. Can't afford to kill jackrabbits no more. Catch 'em and milk 'em an' turn 'em loose. One you seen prob'ly gone dry.' That's how I mean. Ain't really funny, not funny like that time Uncle John converted an Injun an' brang him home, an' that Injun et his way clean to the bottom of the bean bin, an' then backslid with Uncle John's whisky. Tom, put a rag with col' water on your face."

The dusk deepened. Ma lighted the lantern and hung it on a nail. She fed the fire and poured cornmeal gradually into the hot water. "Rosasharn," she said, "can you stir the mush?"

Outside there was a patter of running feet. The door burst open and banged against the wall. Ruthie rushed in. "Ma!" she cried. "Ma. Winfiel' got a fit!"

"Where? Tell me!"

Ruthie panted, "Got white an' fell down. Et so many peaches he skittered hisself all day. Jus' fell down. White!"

"Take me!" Ma demanded. "Rosasharn, you watch that mush."

She went out with Ruthie. She ran heavily up the street behind the little girl. Three men walked toward her in the dusk, and the center man carried Winfield in his arms. Ma ran up to them. "He's mine," she cried. "Give 'im to me."

"I'll carry 'im for you, ma'am."

"No, here, give 'im to me." She hoisted the little boy and turned back; and then she remembered herself. "I sure thank ya," she said to the men.

"Welcome, ma'am. The little fella's purty weak. Looks like he got worms."

Ma hurried back, and Winfield was limp and relaxed in her arms. Ma carried him into the house and knelt down and laid him on a mattress. "Tell me. What's the matter?" she demanded. He opened his eyes dizzily and shook his head and closed his eyes again.

Ruthie said, "I tol' ya, Ma. He skittered all day. Ever' little while. Et too many peaches."

Ma felt his head. "He ain't fevered. But he's white and drawed out."

Tom came near and held the lantern down. "I know," he said. "He's hungered. Got no strength. Get him a can a milk an' make him drink it. Make 'im take milk on his mush."

"Winfiel'," Ma said. "Tell how ya feel."

"Dizzy," said Winfield, "jus' a-whirlin' dizzy."

"You never seen sech skitters," Ruthie said importantly.

Pa and Uncle John and Al came into the house. Their arms were full of sticks and bits of brush. They dropped their loads by the stove. "Now what?" Pa demanded.

"It's Winfiel'. He needs some milk."

"Christ Awmighty! We all need stuff!"

Ma said, "How much'd we make today?"

"Dollar forty-two."

"Well, you go right over'n get a can a milk for Winfiel'."

"Now why'd he have to get sick?"

"I don't know why, but he is. Now you git!" Pa went grumbling out the door. "You stirrin' that mush?"

"Yeah." Rose of Sharon speeded up the stirring to prove it.

Al complained, "God Awmighty, Ma! Is mush all we get after workin' till dark?"

"Al, you know we got to git. Take all we got for gas. You know."

"But, God Awmighty, Ma! A fella needs meat if he's gonna work."

"Jus' you sit quiet," she said. "We got to take the bigges' thing an' whup it fust. An' you know what that thing is."

Tom asked, "Is it about me?"

"We'll talk when we've et," said Ma. "Al, we got enough gas to go a ways, ain't we?"

" 'Bout a quarter tank," said Al.

"I wisht you'd tell me," Tom said.

"After. Jus' wait."

"Keep a-stirrin' that mush, you. Here, lemme put on some coffee. You can have sugar on your mush or in your coffee. They ain't enough for both."

Pa came back with one tall can of milk. " 'Leven cents," he said disgustedly.

"Here!" Ma took the can and stabbed it open. She let the thick stream out into a cup, and handed it to Tom. "Give that to Winfiel'."

Tom knelt beside the mattress. "Here, drink this."

"I can't. I'd sick it all up. Leave me be."

Tom stood up. "He can't take it now, Ma. Wait a little."

Ma took the cup and set it on the window ledge. "Don't none of you touch that," she warned. "That's for Winfiel'."

"I ain't had no milk," Rose of Sharon said sullenly. "I oughta have some."

"I know, but you're still on your feet. This here little fella's down. Is that mush good an' thick?"

"Yeah. Can't hardly stir it no more."

"Awright, le's eat. Now here's the sugar. They's about one spoon each. Have it on ya mush or in ya coffee."

Tom said, "I kinda like salt an' pepper on mush."

"Salt her if you like," Ma said. "The pepper's out."

The boxes were all gone. The family sat on the mattresses to eat their mush. They served themselves again and again, until the pot was nearly empty. "Save some for Winfiel'," Ma said.

Winfield sat up and drank his milk, and instantly he was ravenous. He put the mush pot between his legs and ate what was left and scraped at the crust on the sides. Ma poured the rest of the canned milk in a cup and sneaked it to Rose of Sharon to drink secretly in a corner. She poured the hot black coffee into the cups and passed them around.

"Now will you tell what's goin' on?" Tom asked. "I wanta hear."

Pa said uneasily, "I wisht Ruthie an' Winfiel' didn' hafta hear. Can't they go outside?"

Ma said, "No. They got to act growed up, even if they ain't. They's no help for it. Ruthie—you an' Winfiel' ain't ever to say what you hear, else you'll jus' break us to pieces."

"We won't," Ruthie said. "We're growed up."

"Well, jus' be quiet, then." The cups of coffee were on the floor. The short thick flame of the lantern, like a stubby butterfly's wing, cast a yellow gloom on the walls.

"Now tell," said Tom.

Ma said, "Pa, you tell."

Uncle John slupped his coffee. Pa said, "Well, they dropped the price like you said. An' they was a whole slew a new pickers so goddamn hungry they'd pick for a loaf a bread. Go for a peach, an' somebody'd get it first. Gonna get the whole crop picked right off. Fellas runnin' to a new tree. I seen fights—one fella claims it's his tree, 'nother fella wants to pick off'n it. Brang these here folks from as far's El Centro. Hungrier'n hell. Work all day for a piece a bread. I says to the checker, 'We can't work for two an' a half cents a box,' an' he says, 'Go on, then, quit. These fellas can.' I says, 'Soon's they get fed up they won't.' An' he says, 'Hell, we'll have these here peaches in 'fore they get fed up.'" Pa stopped.

"She was a devil," said Uncle John. "They say they's two hunderd more men comin' in tonight."

Tom said, "Yeah! But how about the other?"

Pa was silent for a while. "Tom," he said, "looks like you done it."

"I kinda thought so. Couldn' see. Felt like it."

"Seems like the people ain't talkin' 'bout much else," said Uncle John. "They got posses out, an' they's fellas talkin' up a lynchin'—'course when they catch the fella."

Tom looked over at the wide-eyed children. They seldom blinked their eyes. It was as though they were afraid something might happen in the split second of darkness. Tom said, "Well—this fella that done it, he on'y done it after they killed Casy."

Pa interrupted, "That ain't the way they're tellin' it now. They're sayin' he done it fust."

Tom's breath sighed out, "Ah-h!"

"They're workin' up a feelin' against us folks. That's what I heard. All them drum-corpse fellas an' lodges an' all that. Say they're gonna get this here fella."

"They know what he looks like?" Tom asked.

"Well—not exactly—but the way I heard it, they think he got hit. They think—he'll have——"

Tom put his hand up slowly and touched his bruised cheek.

Ma cried, "It ain't so, what they say!"

"Easy, Ma," Tom said. "They got it cold. Anything them drum-corpse fellas say is right if it's against us."

Ma peered through the ill light, and she watched Tom's face, and particularly his lips. "You promised," she said.

"Ma, I—maybe this fella oughta go away. If—this fella done somepin wrong, maybe he'd think, 'O.K. Le's get the hangin' over. I done wrong an' I got to take it.' But this fella didn' do nothin' wrong. He don' feel no worse'n if he killed a skunk."

Ruthie broke in, "Ma, me an' Winfiel' knows. He don' have to go this-fella'in' for us."

Tom chuckled. "Well, this fella don' want no hangin', 'cause he'd do it again. An' same time, he don't aim to bring trouble down on his folks. Ma—I got to go."

Ma covered her mouth with her fingers and coughed to clear her throat. "You can't," she said. "They wouldn' be no way to hide out. You couldn' trus' nobody. But you can trus' us. We can hide you, an' we can see you get to eat while your face gets well."

"But, Ma——"

She got to her feet. "You ain't goin'. We're a-takin' you. Al, you back the truck against the door. Now, I got it figgered out. We'll put one mattress on the bottom, an' then Tom gets quick there, an' we take another mattress an' sort of fold it so it makes a cave, an' he's in the cave; and then we sort of wall it in. He can breathe out the end, ya see. Don't argue. That's what we'll do."

Pa complained, "Seems like the man ain't got no say no more. She's jus' a heller. Come time we get settled down, I'm a-gonna smack her."

"Come that time, you can," said Ma. "Roust up, Al. It's dark enough."

Al went outside to the truck. He studied the matter and backed up near the steps.

Ma said, "Quick now. Git that mattress in!"

Pa and Uncle John flung it over the end gate. "Now that one." They tossed the second mattress up. "Now—Tom, you jump up there an' git under. Hurry up."

Tom climbed quickly, and dropped. He straightened one mattress and pulled the second on top of him. Pa bent it upwards, stood it sides up, so that the arch covered Tom. He could see out between the side-boards of the truck. Pa and Al and Uncle John loaded quickly, piled the blankets on top of Tom's cave, stood the buckets against the sides, spread the last mattress behind. Pots and pans, extra clothes, went in loose, for their boxes had been burned. They were nearly finished loading when a guard moved near, carrying his shotgun across his crooked arm.

"What's goin' on here?" he asked.

"We're goin' out," said Pa.

"What for?"

"Well—we got a job offered—good job."

"Yeah? Where's it at?"

"Why—down by Weedpatch."

"Let's have a look at you." He turned a flashlight in Pa's face, in Uncle John's, and in Al's. "Wasn't there another fella with you?"

Al said, "You mean that hitch-hiker? Little short fella with a pale face?"

"Yeah. I guess that's what he looked like."

"We jus' picked him up on the way in. He went away this mornin' when the rate dropped."

"What did he look like again?"

"Short fella. Pale face."

"Was he bruised up this mornin'?"

"I didn' see nothin'," said Al. "Is the gas pump open?"

"Yeah, till eight."

"Git in," Al cried. "If we're gonna get to Weedpatch 'fore mornin' we gotta ram on. Gettin' in front, Ma?"

"No, I'll set in back," she said. "Pa, you set back here too. Let Rosasharn set in front with Al an' Uncle John."

"Give me the work slip, Pa," said Al. "I'll get gas an' change if I can."

The guard watched them pull along the street and turn left to the gasoline pumps.

"Put in two," said Al.

"You ain't goin' far."

"No, not far. Can I get change on this here work slip?"

"Well—I ain't supposed to."

"Look, mister," Al said. "We got a good job offered if we get there tonight. If we don't, we miss out. Be a good fella."

"Well, O.K. You sign her over to me."

Al got out and walked around the nose of the Hudson. "Sure I will," he said. He unscrewed the water cap and filled the radiator.

"Two, you say?"

"Yeah, two."

"Which way you goin'?"

"South. We got a job."

"Yeah? Jobs is scarce—reg'lar jobs."

"We got a frien'," Al said. "Job's all waitin' for us. Well, so long." The truck swung around and bumped over the dirt street into the road. The feeble headlights jiggled over the way, and the right headlight blinked on and off from a bad connection. At every jolt the loose pots and pans in the truck-bed jangled and crashed.

Rose of Sharon moaned softly.

"Feel bad?" Uncle John asked.

"Yeah! Feel bad all a time. Wisht I could set still in a nice place. Wisht we was home an' never come. Connie wouldn' a went away if we was home. He would a studied up an' got someplace." Neither Al nor Uncle John answered her. They were embarrassed about Connie.

At the white painted gate to the ranch a guard came to the side of the truck. "Goin' out for good?"

"Yeah," said Al. "Goin' north. Got a job."

The guard turned his flashlight on the truck, turned it up into the tent. Ma and Pa looked stonily down into the glare. "O.K." The guard swung the gate open. The truck turned left and moved toward 101, the great north-south highway.

"Know where we're a-goin'?" Uncle John asked.

"No," said Al. "Jus' goin', an' gettin' goddamn sick of it."

"I ain't so tur'ble far from my time," Rose of Sharon said threateningly. "They better be a nice place for me."

The night air was cold with the first sting of frost. Beside the road the leaves were beginning to drop from the fruit trees. On the load, Ma sat with her back against the truck side, and Pa sat opposite, facing her.

Ma called, "You all right, Tom?"

His muffled voice came back, "Kinda tight in here. We all through the ranch?"

"You be careful," said Ma. "Might git stopped."

Tom lifted up one side of his cave. In the dimness of the truck the pots jangled. "I can pull her down quick," he said. " 'Sides, I don' like gettin' trapped in here." He rested up on his elbow. "By God, she's gettin' cold, ain't she?"

"They's clouds up," said Pa. "Fellas says it's gonna be an early winter."

"Squirrels a-buildin' high, or grass seeds?" Tom asked. "By God, you can tell weather from anythin'. I bet you could find a fella could tell weather from a old pair of underdrawers."

"I dunno," Pa said. "Seems like it's gittin' on winter to me. Fella'd have to live here a long time to know."

"Which way we a-goin'?" Tom asked.

"I dunno. Al, he turned off lef'. Seems like he's goin' back the way we come."

Tom said, "I can't figger what's best. Seems like if we get on the main highway they'll be more cops. With my face this-a-way, they'd pick me right up. Maybe we oughta keep to back roads."

Ma said, "Hammer on the back. Get Al to stop."

Tom pounded the front board with his fist; the truck pulled to a stop on the side of the road. Al got out and walked to the back. Ruthie and Winfield peeked out from under their blanket.

"What ya want?" Al demanded.

Ma said, "We got to figger what to do. Maybe we better keep on the back roads. Tom says so."

"It's my face," Tom added. "Anybody'd know. Any cop'd know me."

"Well, which way you wanta go? I figgered north. We been south."

"Yeah," said Tom, "but keep on back roads."

Al asked, "How 'bout pullin' off an' catchin' some sleep, goin' on tomorra?"

Ma said quickly, "Not yet. Le's get some distance fust."

"O.K." Al got back in his seat and drove on.

Ruthie and Winfield covered up their heads again. Ma called, "Is Winfiel' all right?"

"Sure, he's awright," Ruthie said. "He been sleepin'."

Ma leaned back against the truck side. "Gives ya a funny feelin' to be hunted like. I'm gittin' mean."

"Ever'body's gittin' mean," said Pa. "Ever'body. You seen that fight today. Fella changes. Down that gov'ment camp we wasn' mean."

Al turned right on a graveled road, and the yellow lights shuddered over the ground. The fruit trees were gone now, and cotton plants took their place. They drove on for twenty miles through the cotton, turning, angling on the country roads. The road paralleled a bushy creek and turned over a concrete bridge and followed the stream on the other side. And then, on the edge of the creek the lights showed a long line of red boxcars, wheelless; and a big sign on the edge of the road said, "Cotton Pickers Wanted." Al slowed down. Tom peered between the side-bars of the truck. A quarter of a mile past the boxcars Tom hammered on the car again. Al stopped beside the road and got out again.

"Now what ya want?"

"Shut off the engine an' climb up here," Tom said.

Al got into the seat, drove off into the ditch, cut lights and engine. He climbed over the tail gate. "Awright," he said.

Tom crawled over the pots and knelt in front of Ma. "Look," he said. "It says they want cotton pickers. I seen that sign. Now I been tryin' to figger how I'm gonna stay with you, an' not make no trouble. When my face gets well, maybe it'll be awright, but not now. Ya see them cars back there. Well, the pickers live in them. Now maybe they's work there. How about if you get work there an' live in one of them cars?"

"How 'bout you?" Ma demanded.

"Well, you seen that crick, all full a brush. Well, I could hide in that brush an' keep outa sight. An' at night you could bring me out somepin to eat. I seen a culvert, little ways back. I could maybe sleep in there."

Pa said, "By God, I'd like to get my hands on some cotton! There's work I un'erstan'."

"Them cars might be a purty place to stay," said Ma. "Nice an' dry. You think they's enough brush to hide in, Tom?"

"Sure. I been watchin'. I could fix up a little place, hide away. Soon's my face gets well, why, I'd come out."

"You gonna scar purty bad," said Ma.

"Hell! Ever'body got scars."

"I picked four hunderd poun's oncet," Pa said. " 'Course it was a good heavy crop. If we all pick, we could get some money."

"Could get some meat," said Al. "What'll we do right now?"

"Go back there, an' sleep in the truck till mornin'," Pa said. "Git work in the mornin'. I can see them bolls even in the dark."

"How 'bout Tom?" Ma asked.

"Now you jus' forget me, Ma. I'll take me a blanket. You look out on the way back. They's a nice culvert. You can bring me some bread or potatoes, or mush, an' just leave it there. I'll come get it."

"Well!"

"Seems like good sense to me," said Pa.

"It is good sense," Tom insisted. "Soon's my face gets a little better, why, I'll come out an' go to pickin'."

"Well, awright," Ma agreed. "But don' you take no chancet. Don' you let nobody see you for a while."

Tom crawled to the back of the truck. "I'll jus' take this here blanket. You look for that culvert on the way back, Ma."

"Take care," she begged. "You take care."

"Sure," said Tom. "Sure I will." He climbed the tail board, stepped down the bank. "Good night," he said.

Ma watched his figure blur with the night and disappear into the bushes beside the stream. "Dear Jesus, I hope it's awright," she said.

Al asked, "You want I should go back now?"

"Yeah," said Pa.

"Go slow," said Ma. "I wanta be sure an' see that culvert he said about. I got to see that."

Al backed and filled on the narrow road, until he had reversed his direction. He drove slowly back to the line of boxcars. The truck lights showed the cat-walks up to the wide car doors. The doors were dark. No one moved in the night. Al shut off his lights.

"You and Uncle John climb up back," he said to Rose of Sharon. "I'll sleep in the seat here."

Uncle John helped the heavy girl to climb up over the tail board. Ma piled the pots in a small space. The family lay wedged close together in the back of the truck.

A baby cried, in long jerking cackles, in one of the boxcars. A dog trotted out, sniffing and snorting, and moved slowly around the Joad truck. The tinkle of moving water came from the streambed.

Cotton Pickers Wanted—placards on the road, handbills out, orange-colored handbills—Cotton Pickers Wanted.

Here, up this road, it says.

The dark green plants stringy now, and the heavy bolls clutched in the pod. White cotton spilling out like popcorn.

Like to get our hands on the bolls. Tenderly, with the fingertips.

I'm a good picker.

Here's the man, right here.

I aim to pick some cotton.

Got a bag?

Well, no, I ain't.

Cost ya a dollar, the bag. Take it out o' your first hunderd and fifty. Eighty cents a hunderd first time over the field. Ninety cents second time over. Get your bag there. One dollar. 'F you ain't got the buck, we'll take it out of your first hunderd and fifty. That's fair, and you know it.

Sure it's fair. Good cotton bag, last all season. An' when she's wore out, draggin', turn 'er aroun', use the other end. Sew up the open end. Open up the wore end. And when both ends is gone, why, that's nice cloth! Makes a nice pair a summer drawers. Makes nightshirts. And well, hell—a cotton bag's a nice thing.

Hang it around your waist. Straddle it, drag it between your legs. She drags light at first. And your fingertips pick out the fluff, and the hands go twisting into the sack between your legs. Kids come along behind; got no bags for the kids—use a gunny sack or put it in your ol' man's bag. She hangs heavy, some, now. Lean forward, hoist 'er along. I'm a good hand with cotton. Finger-wise, boll-wise. Jes' move along talkin', an' maybe singin' till the bag gets heavy. Fingers go right to it. Fingers know. Eyes see the work—and don't see it.

Talkin' across the rows——

They was a lady back home, won't mention no names—had a nigger kid all of a sudden. Nobody knowed before. Never did hunt

out the nigger. Couldn' never hold up her head no more. But I
started to tell—she was a good picker.

Now the bag is heavy, boost it along. Set your hips and tow it
along, like a work horse. And the kids pickin' into the old man's sack.
Good crop here. Gets thin in the low places, thin and stringy. Never
seen no cotton like this here California cotton. Long fiber, bes' damn
cotton I ever seen. Spoil the lan' pretty soon. Like a fella wants to
buy some cotton lan'—Don' buy her, rent her. Then when she's
cottoned on down, move someplace new.

Lines of people moving across the fields. Finger-wise. Inquisitive
fingers snick in and out and find the bolls. Hardly have to look.

Bet I could pick cotton if I was blind. Got a feelin' for a cotton
boll. Pick clean, clean as a whistle.

Sack's full now. Take her to the scales. Argue. Scale man says
you got rocks to make weight. How 'bout him? His scales is fixed.
Sometimes he's right, you got rocks in the sack. Sometimes you're
right, the scales is crooked. Sometimes both; rocks an' crooked
scales. Always argue, always fight. Keeps your head up. An' his head
up. What's a few rocks? Jus' one, maybe. Quarter pound? Always
argue.

Back with the empty sack. Got our own book. Mark in the
weight. Got to. If they know you're markin', then they don't cheat.
But God he'p ya if ya don' keep your own weight.

This is good work. Kids runnin' aroun'. Heard 'bout the cotton-
pickin' machine?

Yeah, I heard.

Think it'll ever come?

Well, if it comes—fella says it'll put han' pickin' out.

Come night. All tired. Good pickin', though. Got three dollars,
me an' the ol' woman an' the kids.

The cars move to the cotton fields. The cotton camps set up.
The screened high trucks and trailers are piled high with white fluff.
Cotton clings to the fence wires, and cotton rolls in little balls along
the road when the wind blows. And clean white cotton, going to the
gin. And the big, lumpy bales standing, going to the compress. And
cotton clinging to your clothes and stuck to your whiskers. Blow your
nose, there's cotton in your nose.

Hunch along now, fill up the bag 'fore dark. Wise fingers seeking
in the bolls. Hips hunching along, dragging the bag. Kids are tired,

now in the evening. They trip over their feet in the cultivated earth. And the sun is going down.

Wisht it would last. It ain't much money, God knows, but I wisht it would last.

On the highway the old cars piling in, drawn by the handbills.

Got a cotton bag?

No.

Cost ya a dollar, then.

If they was on'y fifty of us, we could stay awhile, but they's five hunderd. She won't last hardly at all. I knowed a fella never did git his bag paid out. Ever' job he got a new bag, an' ever' fiel' was done 'fore he got his weight.

Try for God's sake ta save a little money! Winter's comin' fast. They ain't no work at all in California in the winter. Fill up the bag 'fore it's dark. I seen that fella put two clods in.

Well, hell. Why not? I'm jus' balancin' the crooked scales.

Now here's my book, three hunderd an' twelve poun's.

Right!

Jesus, he never argued! His scales mus' be crooked. Well, that's a nice day anyways.

They say a thousan' men are on their way to this field. We'll be fightin' for a row tomorra. We'll be snatchin' cotton, quick.

Cotton Pickers Wanted. More men picking, quicker to the gin.

Now into the cotton camp.

Side-meat tonight, by God! We got money for side-meat! Stick out a han' to the little fella, he's wore out. Run in ahead an' git us four poun' of side-meat. The ol' woman'll make some nice biscuits tonight, ef she ain't too tired.

The boxcars, twelve of them, stood end to end on a little flat beside the stream. There were two rows of six each, the wheels removed. Up to the big sliding doors slatted planks ran for cat-walks. They made good houses, water-tight and draftless, room for twenty-four families, one family in each end of each car. No windows, but the wide doors stood open. In some of the cars a canvas hung down in the center of the car, while in others only the position of the door made the boundary.

The Joads had one end of an end car. Some previous occupant had fitted up an oil can with a stovepipe, had made a hole in the wall for the stovepipe. Even with the wide door open, it was dark in the ends of the car. Ma hung the tarpaulin across the middle of the car.

"It's nice," she said. "It's almost nicer than anything we had 'cept the gov'ment camp."

Each night she unrolled the mattresses on the floor, and each morning rolled them up again. And every day they went into the fields and picked the cotton, and every night they had meat. On a Saturday they drove into Tulare, and they bought a tin stove and new overalls for Al and Pa and Winfield and Uncle John, and they bought a dress for Ma and gave Ma's best dress to Rose of Sharon.

"She's so big," Ma said. "Jus' a waste of good money to get her a new dress now."

The Joads had been lucky. They got in early enough to have a place in the boxcars. Now the tents of the late-comers filled the little flat, and those who had the boxcars were oldtimers, and in a way aristocrats.

The narrow stream slipped by, out of the willows, and back into the willows again. From each car a hard-beaten path went down to the stream. Between the cars the clothes lines hung, and every day the lines were covered with drying clothes.

In the evening they walked back from the fields, carrying their folded cotton bags under their arms. They went into the store which stood at the crossroads, and there were many pickers in the store, buying their supplies.

"How much today?"

"We're doin' fine. We made three and a half today. Wisht she'd keep up. Them kids is gettin' to be good pickers. Ma's worked 'em up a little bag for each. They couldn' tow a growed-up bag. Dump into ours. Made bags outa a couple old shirts. Work fine."

And Ma went to the meat counter, her forefinger pressed against her lips, blowing on her finger, thinking deeply. "Might get some pork chops," she said. "How much?"

"Thirty cents a pound, ma'am."

"Well, lemme have three poun's. An' a nice piece a boilin' beef. My girl can cook it tomorra. An' a bottle a milk for my girl. She dotes on milk. Gonna have a baby. Nurse-lady tol' her to eat lots a milk. Now, le's see, we got potatoes."

Pa came close, carrying a can of sirup in his hands. "Might get this here," he said. "Might have some hotcakes."

Ma frowned. "Well—well, yes. Here, we'll take this here. Now —we got plenty lard."

Ruthie came near, in her hands two large boxes of Cracker Jack, in her eyes a brooding question, which on a nod or a shake of Ma's head might become tragedy or joyous excitement. "Ma?" She held up the boxes, jerked them up and down to make them attractive.

"Now you put them back——"

The tragedy began to form in Ruthie's eyes. Pa said, "They're on'y a nickel apiece. Them little fellas worked good today."

"Well—" The excitement began to steal into Ruthie's eyes. "Awright."

Ruthie turned and fled. Halfway to the door she caught Winfield and rushed him out the door, into the evening.

Uncle John fingered a pair of canvas gloves with yellow leather palms, tried them on and took them off and laid them down. He moved gradually to the liquor shelves, and he stood studying the labels on the bottles. Ma saw him. "Pa," she said, and motioned with her head toward Uncle John.

Pa lounged over to him. "Gettin' thirsty, John?"

"No, I ain't."

"Jus' wait till cotton's done," said Pa. "Then you can go on a hell of a drunk."

" 'Tain't sweatin' me none," Uncle John said. "I'm workin' hard an' sleepin' good. No dreams nor nothin'."

"Jus' seen you sort of droolin' out at them bottles."

"I didn' hardly see 'em. Funny thing. I wanta buy stuff. Stuff I don't need. Like to git one a them safety razors. Thought I'd like to have some a them gloves over there. Awful cheap."

"Can't pick no cotton with gloves," said Pa.

"I know that. An' I don't need no safety razor, neither. Stuff settin' out there, you jus' feel like buyin' it whether you need it or not."

Ma called, "Come on. We got ever'thing." She carried a bag. Uncle John and Pa each took a package. Outside Ruthie and Winfield were waiting, their eyes strained, their cheeks puffed and full of Cracker Jack.

"Won't eat no supper, I bet," Ma said.

People streamed toward the boxcar camp. The tents were lighted. Smoke poured from the stovepipes. The Joads climbed up their cat-walk and into their end of the boxcar. Rose of Sharon sat on a box beside the stove. She had a fire started, and the tin stove was wine-colored with heat. "Did ya get milk?" she demanded.

"Yeah. Right here."

"Give it to me. I ain't had any sence noon."

"She thinks it's like medicine."

"That nurse-lady says so."

"You got potatoes ready?"

"Right there—peeled."

"We'll fry 'em," said Ma. "Got pork chops. Cut up them potatoes in the new fry pan. And th'ow in a onion. You fellas go out an' wash, an' bring in a bucket a water. Where's Ruthie an' Winfiel'? They oughta wash. They each got Cracker Jack," Ma told Rose of Sharon. "Each got a whole box."

The men went out to wash in the stream. Rose of Sharon sliced the potatoes into the frying pan and stirred them about with the knife point.

Suddenly the tarpaulin was thrust aside. A stout perspiring face looked in from the other end of the car. "How'd you all make out, Mis' Joad?"

Ma swung around. "Why, evenin', Mis' Wainwright. We done good. Three an' a half. Three fifty-seven, exact."

"We done four dollars."

"Well," said Ma. " 'Course they's more *of* you."

"Yeah. Jonas is growin' up. Havin' pork chops, I see."

Winfield crept in through the door. "Ma!"

"Hush a minute. Yes, my men jus' loves pork chops."

"I'm cookin' bacon," said Mrs. Wainwright. "Can you smell it cookin'?"

"No—can't smell it over these here onions in the potatoes."

"She's burnin'!" Mrs. Wainwright cried, and her head jerked back.

"Ma," Winfield said.

"What? You sick from Cracker Jack?"

"Ma—Ruthie tol'."

"Tol' what?"

" 'Bout Tom."

Ma stared. "Tol'?" Then she knelt in front of him. "Winfiel', who'd she tell?"

Embarrassment seized Winfield. He backed away. "Well, she on'y tol' a little bit."

"Winfiel'! Now you tell what she said."

"She—she didn' eat all her Cracker Jack. She kep' some, an' she et jus' one piece at a time, slow, like she always done, an' she says, 'Bet you wisht you had some lef'.'"

"Winfiel'!" Ma demanded. "You tell now." She looked back nervously at the curtain. "Rosasharn, you go over an' talk to Mis' Wainwright so she don' listen."

"How 'bout these here potatoes?"

"I'll watch 'em. Now you go. I don' want her listenin' at that curtain." The girl shuffled heavily down the car and went around the side of the hung tarpaulin.

Ma said, "Now, Winfiel', you tell."

"Like I said, she et jus' one little piece at a time, an' she bust some in two so it'd las' longer."

"Go on, hurry up."

"Well, some kids come aroun', an' 'course they tried to get some, but Ruthie, she jus' nibbled an' nibbled, an' wouldn' give 'em none. So they got mad. An' one kid grabbed her Cracker Jack box."

"Winfiel', you tell quick about the other."

"I am," he said. "So Ruthie got mad an' chased 'em, an' she fit one, an' then she fit another, an' then one big girl up an' licked her.

Hit 'er a good one. So then Ruthie cried, an' she said she'd git her big brother, an' he'd kill that big girl. An' that big girl said, Oh, yeah? Well, she got a big brother too." Winfield was breathless in his telling. "So then they fit, an' that big girl hit Ruthie a good one, an' Ruthie said her brother'd kill that big girl's brother. An' that big girl said how about if her brother kil't our brother. An' then—an' then, Ruthie said our brother already kil't two fellas. An'—an'—that big girl said, 'Oh, yeah? You're jus' a little smarty liar.' An' Ruthie said, Oh, yeah? Well, our brother's a-hidin' right now from killin' a fella, an' he can kill that big girl's brother too. An' then they called names an' Ruthie throwed a rock, an' that big girl chased her, an' I come home."

"Oh, my!" Ma said wearily. "Oh! My dear sweet Lord Jesus asleep in a manger! What we goin' to do now?" She put her forehead in her hand and rubbed her eyes. "What we gonna do now?" A smell of burning potatoes came from the roaring stove. Ma moved automatically and turned them.

"Rosasharn!" Ma called. The girl appeared around the curtain. "Come watch this here supper. Winfiel', you go out an' you fin' Ruthie an' bring her back here."

"Gonna whup her, Ma?" he asked hopefully.

"No. This here you couldn' do nothin' about. Why, I wonder, did she haf' to do it? No. It won't do no good to whup her. Run now, an' find her an' bring her back."

Winfield ran for the car door, and he met the three men tramping up the cat-walk, and he stood aside while they came in.

Ma said softly, "Pa, I got to talk to you. Ruthie tol' some kids how Tom's a-hidin'."

"What?"

"She tol'. Got in a fight an' tol'."

"Why, the little bitch!"

"No, she didn' know what she was a-doin'. Now look, Pa. I want you to stay here. I'm goin' out an' try to fin' Tom an' tell him. I got to tell 'im to be careful. You stick here, Pa, an' kinda watch out for things. I'll take 'im some dinner."

"Awright," Pa agreed.

"Don' you even mention to Ruthie what she done. I'll tell her."

At that moment Ruthie came in, with Winfield behind her. The little girl was dirtied. Her mouth was sticky, and her nose still dripped a little blood from her fight. She looked shamed and frightened. Winfield triumphantly followed her. Ruthie looked fiercely about, but she went to a corner of the car and put her back in the corner. Her shame and fierceness were blended.

"I tol' her what she done," Winfield said.

Ma was putting two chops and some fried potatoes on a tin plate. "Hush, Winfiel'," she said. "They ain't no need to hurt her feelings no more'n what they're hurt."

Ruthie's body hurtled across the car. She grabbed Ma around the middle and buried her head in Ma's stomach, and her strangled sobs shook her whole body. Ma tried to loosen her, but the grubby fingers clung tight. Ma brushed the hair on the back of her head gently, and she patted her shoulders. "Hush," she said. "You didn' know."

Ruthie raised her dirty, tear-stained, bloody face. "They stoled my Cracker Jack!" she cried. "That big son-of-a-bitch of a girl, she belted me—" She went off into hard crying again.

"Hush!" Ma said. "Don' talk like that. Here. Let go. I'm a-goin' now."

"Whyn't ya whup her, Ma? If she didn't git snotty with her Cracker Jack 'twouldn' a happened. Go on, give her a whup."

"You jus' min' your business, mister," Ma said fiercely. "You'll git a whup yourself. Now leggo, Ruthie."

Winfield retired to a rolled mattress, and he regarded the family cynically and dully. And he put himself in a good position of defense, for Ruthie would attack him at the first opportunity, and he knew it. Ruthie went quietly, heart-brokenly to the other side of the car.

Ma put a sheet of newspaper over the tin plate. "I'm a-goin' now," she said.

"Ain't you gonna eat nothin' yourself?" Uncle John demanded.

"Later. When I come back. I wouldn' want nothin' now." Ma walked to the open door; she steadied herself down the steep, cleated cat-walk.

On the stream side of the boxcars, the tents were pitched close together, their guy ropes crossing one another, and the pegs of one at the canvas line of the next. The lights shone through the cloth, and all the chimneys belched smoke. Men and women stood in the doorways talking. Children ran feverishly about. Ma moved majestically down the line of tents. Here and there she was recognized as she went by. "Evenin', Mis' Joad."

"Evenin'."

"Takin' somepin out, Mis' Joad?"

"They's a frien'. I'm takin' back some bread."

She came at last to the end of the line of tents. She stopped and looked back. A glow of light was on the camp, and the soft overtone of a multitude of speakers. Now and then a harsher voice cut through. The smell of smoke filled the air. Someone played a harmonica softly, trying for an effect, one phrase over and over.

Ma stepped in among the willows beside the stream. She moved off the trail and waited, silently, listening to hear any possible follower. A man walked down the trail toward the camp, boosting his suspenders and buttoning his jeans as he went. Ma sat very still, and he passed on without seeing her. She waited five minutes and then she stood up and crept on up the trail beside the stream. She moved quietly, so quietly that she could hear the murmur of the water above her soft steps on the willow leaves. Trail and stream swung to the left and then to the right again until they neared the highway. In the gray starlight she could see the embankment and the black round hole of the culvert where she always left Tom's food. She moved forward cautiously, thrust her package into the hole, and took back the empty tin plate which was left there. She crept back among the willows, forced her way into a thicket, and sat down to wait. Through the tangle she could see the black hole of the culvert. She clasped her knees and sat silently. In a few moments the thicket crept to life again. The field mice moved cautiously over the leaves. A skunk padded heavily and unself-consciously down the trail, carrying a faint effluvium with him. And then a wind stirred the willows delicately, as though it tested them, and a shower of golden leaves coasted down to the ground. Suddenly a gust boiled in and racked the trees, and a cricking downpour of leaves fell. Ma could feel them on her hair and on her shoulders. Over the sky a plump black cloud moved, erasing the stars. The fat drops of rain scattered down, splashing loudly on the fallen leaves, and the cloud moved on and unveiled the stars again. Ma shivered. The wind blew past and left the thicket quiet, but the rushing of the trees went on down the stream. From back at the camp came the thin penetrating tone of a violin feeling about for a tune.

Ma heard a stealthy step among the leaves far to her left, and she grew tense. She released her knees and straightened her head, the better to hear. The movement stopped, and after a long moment began again. A vine rasped harshly on the dry leaves. Ma saw a dark figure creep into the open and draw near to the culvert. The black round hole was obscured for a moment, and then the figure moved back. She called softly, "Tom!" The figure stood still, so still, so low to the ground that it might have been a stump. She called again, "Tom, oh, Tom!" Then the figure moved.

"That you, Ma?"

"Right over here." She stood up and went to meet him.

"You shouldn' of came," he said.

"I got to see you, Tom. I got to talk to you."

"It's near the trail," he said. "Somebody might come by."

"Ain't you got a place, Tom?"

"Yeah—but if—well, s'pose somebody seen you with me—whole fambly'd be in a jam."

"I got to, Tom."

"Then come along. Come quiet." He crossed the little stream, wading carelessly through the water, and Ma followed him. He moved through the brush, out into a field on the other side of the thicket, and along the plowed ground. The blackening stems of the cotton were harsh against the ground, and a few fluffs of cotton clung to the stems. A quarter of a mile they went along the edge of the field, and then he turned into the brush again. He approached a great mound of wild blackberry bushes, leaned over and pulled a mat of vines aside. "You got to crawl in," he said.

Ma went down on her hands and knees. She felt sand under her, and then the black inside of the mound no longer touched her, and she felt Tom's blanket on the ground. He arranged the vines in place again. It was lightless in the cave.

"Where are you, Ma?"

"Here. Right here. Talk soft, Tom."

"Don't worry. I been livin' like a rabbit some time."

She heard him unwrap his tin plate.

"Pork chops," she said. "And fry potatoes."

"God Awmighty, an' still warm."

Ma could not see him at all in the blackness, but she could hear him chewing, tearing at the meat and swallowing.

"It's a pretty good hide-out," he said.

Ma said uneasily, "Tom—Ruthie tol' about you." She heard him gulp.

"Ruthie? What for?"

"Well, it wasn' her fault. Got in a fight, an' says her brother'll

lick that other girl's brother. You know how they do. An' she tol'
that her brother killed a man an' was hidin'."

Tom was chuckling. "With me I was always gonna get Uncle
John after 'em, but he never would do it. That's jus' kid talk, Ma.
That's awright."

"No, it ain't," Ma said. "Them kids'll tell it aroun' an' then the
folks'll hear, an' they'll tell aroun', an' pretty soon, well, they liable
to get men out to look, jus' in case. Tom, you got to go away."

"That's what I said right along. I was always scared somebody'd
see you put stuff in <u>that culvert,</u> an' then they'd watch."

"I know. But I wanted you near. I was scared for you. I ain't
seen you. Can't see you now. How's your face?"

"Gettin' well quick."

"Come clost, Tom. Let me feel it. Come clost." He crawled near.
Her reaching hand found his head in the blackness and her fingers
moved down to his nose, and then over his left cheek. "You got a
bad scar, Tom. An' your nose is all crooked."

"Maybe tha's a good thing. Nobody wouldn't know me, maybe.
If my prints wasn't on record, I'd be glad." He went back to his
eating.

"Hush," she said. "Listen!"

"It's the wind, Ma. Jus' the wind." The gust poured down the
stream, and the trees rustled under its passing.

She crawled close to his voice. "I wanta touch ya again, Tom.
It's like I'm blin', it's so dark. <u>I wanta remember, even if it's on'y my
fingers that remember</u>. You got to go away, Tom."

"Yeah! I knowed it from the start."

"We made purty good," she said. "I been squirrelin' money away.
Hol' out your han', Tom. I got seven dollars here."

"I ain't gonna take ya money," he said. "I'll get 'long all right."

"Hol' out ya han', Tom. I ain't gonna sleep none if you got no
money. Maybe you got to take a bus, or somepin. I want you should
go a long ways off, three-four hunderd miles."

"I ain't gonna take it."

"Tom," she said sternly. "You take this money. You hear me?
You got no right to cause me pain."

"You ain't playin' it fair," he said.

"I thought maybe you could go to a big city. Los Angeles, maybe.
They wouldn' never look for you there."

"Hm-m," he said. "Lookie, Ma. I been all day an' all night hidin' alone. Guess who I been thinkin' about? Casy! He talked a lot. Used ta bother me. But now I been thinkin' what he said, an' I can remember—all of it. Says one time he went out in the wilderness to find his own soul, an' he foun' he didn' have no soul that was his'n. Says he foun' he jus' got a little piece of a great big soul. Says a wilderness ain't no good, 'cause his little piece of a soul wasn't no good 'less it was with the rest, an' was whole. Funny how I remember. Didn' think I was even listenin'. But I know now a fella ain't no good alone."

"He was a good man," Ma said.

Tom went on, "He spouted out some Scripture once, an' it didn' soun' like no hell-fire Scripture. He tol' it twicet, an' I remember it. Says it's from the Preacher."

"How's it go, Tom?"

"Goes, 'Two are better than one, because they have a good reward for their labor. For if they fall, the one will lif' up his fellow, but woe to him that is alone when he falleth, for he hath not another to help him up.' That's part of her."

"Go on," Ma said. "Go on, Tom."

"Jus' a little bit more. 'Again, if two lie together, then they have heat: but how can one be warm alone? And if one prevail against him, two shall withstand him, and a three-fold cord is not quickly broken.'"

"An' that's Scripture?"

"Casy said it was. Called it the Preacher."

"Hush—listen."

"On'y the wind, Ma. I know the wind. An' I got to thinkin', Ma—most of the preachin' is about the poor we shall have always with us, an' if you got nothin', why, jus' fol' your hands an' to hell with it, you gonna git ice cream on gol' plates when you're dead. An' then this here Preacher says two get a better reward for their work."

"Tom," she said. "What you aimin' to do?"

He was quiet for a long time. "I been thinkin' how it was in that gov'ment camp, how our folks took care a theirselves, an' if they was a fight they fixed it theirself; an' they wasn't no cops wagglin' their guns, but they was better order than them cops ever give. I been a-wonderin' why we can't do that all over. Throw out the cops that ain't our people. All work together for our own thing—all farm our own lan'."

[margin note, left: → practical solidarity]

[margin note, bottom: ↑ working together | one big soul | all connected]

"Tom," Ma repeated, "what you gonna do?"

"What Casy done," he said. *imitation solidarity*

"But they killed him."

"Yeah," said Tom. "He didn' duck quick enough. He wasn' doing nothin' against the law, Ma. I been thinkin' a hell of a lot, thinkin' about our people livin' like pigs, an' the good rich lan' layin' fallow, or maybe one fella with a million acres, while a hunderd thousan' good farmers is starvin'. An' I been wonderin' if all our folks got together an' yelled, like them fellas yelled, only a few of 'em at the Hooper ranch——"

Ma said, "Tom, they'll drive you, an' cut you down like they done to young Floyd."

"They gonna drive me anyways. They drivin' all our people."

"You don't aim to kill nobody, Tom?"

"No. I been thinkin', long as I'm a outlaw anyways, maybe I could— Hell, I ain't thought it out clear, Ma. Don' worry me now. Don' worry me."

They sat silent in the coal-black cave of vines. Ma said, "How'm I gonna know 'bout you? They might kill ya an' I wouldn' know. They might hurt ya. How'm I gonna know?"

Tom laughed uneasily, "Well, maybe like Casy says, a fella ain't got a soul of his own, but on'y a piece of a big one—an' then——"

"Then what, Tom?"

"Then it don' matter. Then I'll be all aroun' in the dark. I'll be ever'where—wherever you look. Wherever they's a fight so hungry people can eat, I'll be there. Wherever they's a cop beatin' up a guy, I'll be there. If Casy knowed, why, I'll be in the way guys yell when they're mad an'—I'll be in the way kids laugh when they're hungry an' they know supper's ready. An' when our folks eat the stuff they raise an' live in the houses they build—why, I'll be there. See? God, I'm talkin' like Casy. Comes of thinkin' about him so much. Seems like I can see him sometimes."

"I don' un'erstan'," Ma said. "I don' really know."

"Me neither," said Tom. "It's jus' stuff I been thinkin' about. Get thinkin' a lot when you ain't movin' aroun'. You got to get back, Ma."

"You take the money then."

He was silent for a moment. "Awright," he said.

"An', Tom, later—when it's blowed over, you'll come back. You'll find us?"

"Sure," he said. "Now you better go. Here, gimme your han'."
He guided her toward the entrance. Her fingers clutched his wrist.
He swept the vines aside and followed her out. "Go up to the field
till you come to a sycamore on the edge, an' then cut acrost the
stream. Good-by."

"Good-by," she said, and she walked quickly away. Her eyes were
wet and burning, but she did not cry. Her footsteps were loud and
careless on the leaves as she went through the brush. And as she
went, out of the dim sky the rain began to fall, big drops and few,
splashing on the dry leaves heavily. Ma stopped and stood still in the
dripping thicket. She turned about—took three steps back toward
the mound of vines; and then she turned quickly and went back
toward the boxcar camp. She went straight out to the culvert and
climbed up on the road. The rain had passed now, but the sky was
overcast. Behind her on the road she heard footsteps, and she turned
nervously. The blinking of a dim flashlight played on the road. Ma
turned back and started for home. In a moment a man caught up
with her. Politely, he kept his light on the ground and did not play
it in her face.

"Evenin'," he said.

Ma said, "Howdy."

"Looks like we might have a little rain."

"I hope not. Stop the pickin'. We need the pickin'."

"I need the pickin' too. You live at the camp there?"

"Yes, sir." Their footsteps beat on the road together.

"I got twenty acres of cotton. Little late, but it's ready now.
Thought I'd go down and try to get some pickers."

"You'll get 'em awright. Season's near over."

"Hope so. My place is only a mile up that way."

"Six of us," said Ma. "Three men an' me an' two little fellas."

"I'll put out a sign. Two miles—this road."

"We'll be there in the mornin'."

"I hope it don't rain."

"Me too," said Ma. "Twenty acres won' las' long."

"The less it lasts the gladder I'll be. My cotton's late. Didn' get
it in till late."

"What you payin', mister?"

"Ninety cents."

"We'll pick. I hear fellas say nex' year it'll be seventy-five or even
sixty."

"That's what I hear."

"They'll be trouble," said Ma.

"Sure. I know. Little fella like me can't do anything. The Association sets the wage, and we got to mind. If we don't—we ain't got a farm. Little fella gets crowded all the time."

They came to the camp. "We'll be there," Ma said. "Not much pickin' lef'." She went to the end boxcar and climbed the cleated walk. The low light of the lantern made gloomy shadows in the car. Pa and Uncle John and an elderly man squatted against the car wall.

"Hello," Ma said. "Evenin', Mr. Wainwright."

He raised a delicately chiseled face. His eyes were deep under the ridges of his brows. His hair was blue-white and fine. A patina of silver beard covered his jaws and chin. "Evenin', ma'am," he said.

"We got pickin' tomorra," Ma observed. "Mile north. Twenty acres."

"Better take the truck, I guess," Pa said. "Get in more pickin'."

Wainwright raised his head eagerly. "S'pose we can pick?"

"Why, sure. I walked a piece with the fella. He was comin' to get pickers."

"Cotton's nearly gone. Purty thin, these here seconds. Gonna be hard to make a wage on the seconds. Got her pretty clean the fust time."

"Your folks could maybe ride with us," Ma said. "Split the gas."

"Well—that's frien'ly of you, ma'am."

"Saves us both," said Ma.

Pa said, "Mr. Wainwright—he's got a worry he come to us about. We was a-talkin' her over."

"What's the matter?"

Wainwright looked down at the floor. "Our Aggie," he said. "She's a big girl—near sixteen, an' growed up."

"Aggie's a pretty girl," said Ma.

"Listen 'im out," Pa said.

"Well, her an' your boy Al, they're a-walkin' out ever' night. An' Aggie's a good healthy girl that oughta have a husban', else she might git in trouble. We never had no trouble in our family. But what with us bein' so poor off, now, Mis' Wainwright an' me, we got to worryin'. S'pose she got in trouble?"

Ma rolled down a mattress and sat on it. "They out now?" she asked.

"Always out," said Wainwright. "Ever' night."

"Hm. Well, Al's a good boy. Kinda figgers he's a dung-hill rooster these days, but he's a good steady boy. I couldn' want for a better boy."

"Oh, we ain't complainin' about Al as a fella! We like him. But what scares Mis' Wainwright an' me—well, she's a growed-up woman-girl. An' what if we go away, or you go away, an' we find out Aggie's in trouble? We ain't had no shame in our family."

Ma said softly, "We'll try an' see that we don't put no shame on you."

He stood up quickly. "Thank you, ma'am. Aggie's a growed-up woman-girl. She's a good girl—jes' as nice an' good. We'll sure thank you, ma'am, if you'll keep shame from us. It ain't Aggie's fault. She's growed up."

"Pa'll talk to Al," said Ma. "Or if Pa won't, I will."

Wainwright said, "Good night, then, an' we sure thank ya." He went around the end of the curtain. They could hear him talking softly in the other end of the car, explaining the result of his embassy.

Ma listened a moment, and then, "You fellas," she said. "Come over an' set here."

Pa and Uncle John got heavily up from their squats. They sat on the mattress beside Ma.

"Where's the little fellas?"

Pa pointed to a mattress in the corner. "Ruthie, she jumped Winfiel' an' bit 'im. Made 'em both lay down. Guess they're asleep. Rosasharn, she went to set with a lady she knows."

Ma sighed. "I foun' Tom," she said softly. "I—sent 'im away. Far off."

Pa nodded slowly. Uncle John dropped his chin on his chest. "Couldn' do nothin' else," Pa said. "Think he could, John?"

Uncle John looked up. "I can't think nothin' out," he said. "Don't seem like I'm hardly awake no more."

"Tom's a good boy," Ma said; and then she apologized, "I didn' mean no harm a-sayin' I'd talk to Al."

"I know," Pa said quietly. "I ain't no good any more. Spen' all my time a-thinkin' how it use' ta be. Spen' all my time thinkin' of home, an' I ain't never gonna see it no more."

"This here's purtier—better lan'," said Ma.

"I know. I never even see it, thinkin' how the willow's los' its leaves now. Sometimes figgerin' to mend that hole in the south fence. Funny! Woman takin' over the fambly. Woman sayin' we'll do this here, an' we'll go there. An' I don' even care."

"Woman can change better'n a man," Ma said soothingly. "Woman got all her life in her arms. Man got it all in his head. Don' you mind. Maybe—well, maybe nex' year we can get a place."

"We got nothin', now," Pa said. "Comin' a long time—no work, no crops. What we gonna do then? How we gonna git stuff to eat? An' I tell you Rosasharn ain't so far from due. Git so I hate to think. Go diggin' back to a ol' time to keep from thinkin'. Seems like our life's over an' done."

"No, it ain't," Ma smiled. "It ain't, Pa. An' that's one more thing a woman knows. I noticed that. Man, he lives in jerks—baby born an' a man dies, an' that's a jerk—gets a farm an' loses his farm, an' that's a jerk. Woman, it's all one flow, like a stream, little eddies, little waterfalls, but the river, it goes right on. Woman looks at it like that. We ain't gonna die out. People is goin' on—changin' a little, maybe, but goin' right on."

"How can you tell?" Uncle John demanded. "What's to keep ever'thing from stoppin'; all the folks from jus' gittin' tired an' layin' down?"

Ma considered. She rubbed the shiny back of one hand with the other, pushed the fingers of her right hand between the fingers of her left. "Hard to say," she said. "Ever'thing we do—seems to me is aimed right at goin' on. Seems that way to me. Even gettin' hungry—even bein' sick; some die, but the rest is tougher. Jus' try to live the day, jus' the day."

Uncle John said, "If on'y she didn' die that time——"

"Jus' live the day," Ma said. "Don' worry yaself."

"They might be a good year nex' year, back home," said Pa.

Ma said, "Listen!"

There were creeping steps on the cat-walk, and then Al came in past the curtain. "Hullo," he said. "I thought you'd be sleepin' by now."

"Al," Ma said. "We're a-talkin'. Come set here."

"Sure—O.K. I wanta talk too. I'll hafta be goin' away pretty soon now."

"You can't. We need you here. Why you got to go away?"

"Well, me an' Aggie Wainwright, we figgers to get married, an'

I'm gonna git a job in a garage, an' we'll have a rent' house for a while, an'—" He looked up fiercely. "Well, we are, an' they ain't nobody can stop us!"

They were staring at him. "Al," Ma said at last, "we're glad. We're awful glad."

"You are?"

"Why, 'course we are. You're a growed man. You need a wife. But don' go right now, Al."

"I promised Aggie," he said. "We got to go. We can't stan' this no more."

"Jus' stay till spring," Ma begged. "Jus' till spring. Won't you stay till spring? Who'd drive the truck?"

"Well——"

Mrs. Wainwright put her head around the curtain. "You heard yet?" she demanded.

"Yeah! Jus' heard."

"Oh, my! I wisht—I wisht we had a cake. I wisht we had—a cake or somepin."

"I'll set on some coffee an' make up some pancakes," Ma said. "We got sirup."

"Oh, my!" Mrs. Wainwright said. "Why—well. Look, I'll bring some sugar. We'll put sugar in them pancakes."

Ma broke twigs into the stove, and the coals from the dinner cooking started them blazing. Ruthie and Winfield came out of their bed like hermit crabs from shells. For a moment they were careful; they watched to see whether they were still criminals. When no one noticed them, they grew bold. Ruthie hopped all the way to the door and back on one foot, without touching the wall.

Ma was pouring flour into a bowl when Rose of Sharon climbed the cat-walk. She steadied herself and advanced cautiously. "What's a matter?" she asked.

"Why, it's news!" Ma cried. "We're gonna have a little party 'count a Al an' Aggie Wainwright is gonna get married."

Rose of Sharon stood perfectly still. She looked slowly at Al, who stood there flustered and embarrassed.

Mrs. Wainwright shouted from the other end of the car, "I'm puttin' a fresh dress on Aggie. I'll be right over."

Rose of Sharon turned slowly. She went back to the wide door, and she crept down the cat-walk. Once on the ground, she moved slowly toward the stream and the trail that went beside it. She took the way Ma had gone earlier—into the willows. The wind blew more steadily now, and the bushes whished steadily. Rose of Sharon went down on her knees and crawled deep into the brush. The berry vines cut her face and pulled at her hair, but she didn't mind. Only when she felt the bushes touching her all over did she stop. She stretched out on her back. And she felt the weight of the baby inside of her.

In the lightless car, Ma stirred, and then she pushed the blanket back and got up. At the open door of the car the gray starlight penetrated a little. Ma walked to the door and stood looking out. The stars were paling in the east. The wind blew softly over the willow thickets, and from the little stream came the quiet talking of the water. Most of the camp was still asleep, but in front of one tent a little fire burned, and people were standing about it, warming themselves. Ma could see them in the light of the new dancing fire as they stood facing the flames, rubbing their hands; and then they turned their backs and held their hands behind them. For a long moment Ma looked out, and she held her hands clasped in front of her. The uneven wind whisked up and passed, and a bite of frost was in the air. Ma shivered and rubbed her hands together. She crept back and fumbled for the matches beside the lantern. The shade screeched up. She lighted the wick, watched it burn blue for a moment and then put up its yellow, delicately curved ring of light. She carried the lantern to the stove and set it down while she broke the brittle dry willow twigs into the fire box. In a moment the fire was roaring up the chimney.

Rose of Sharon rolled heavily over and sat up. "I'll git right up," she said.

"Whyn't you lay a minute till it warms?" Ma asked.

"No, I'll git."

Ma filled the coffee pot from the bucket and set it on the stove, and she put on the frying pan, deep with fat, to get hot for the pones. "What's over you?" she said softly.

"I'm a-goin' out," Rose of Sharon said.

"Out where?"

"Goin' out to pick cotton."

"You can't," Ma said. "You're too far along."

"No, I ain't. An' I'm a-goin'."

Ma measured coffee into the water. "Rosasharn, you wasn't to the pancakes las' night." The girl didn't answer. "What you wanta pick cotton for?" Still no answer. "Is it 'cause of Al an' Aggie?" This time Ma looked closely at her daughter. "Oh. Well, you don' need to pick."

"I'm goin'."

"Awright, but don' you strain yourself."

"Git up, Pa! Wake up, git up!"

Pa blinked and yawned. "Ain't slep' out," he moaned. "Musta been on to eleven o'clock when we went down."

"Come on, git up, all a you, an' wash."

The inhabitants of the car came slowly to life, squirmed up out of the blankets, writhed into their clothes. Ma sliced salt pork into her second frying pan. "Git out an' wash," she commanded.

A light sprang up in the other end of the car. And there came the sound of the breaking of twigs from the Wainwright end. "Mis' Joad," came the call. "We're gettin' ready. We'll be ready."

Al grumbled, "What we got to be up so early for?"

"It's on'y twenty acres," Ma said. "Got to get there. Ain't much cotton lef'. Got to be there 'fore she's picked." Ma rushed them dressed, rushed the breakfast into them. "Come on, drink your coffee," she said. "Got to start."

"We can't pick no cotton in the dark, Ma."

"We can *be* there when it gets light."

"Maybe it's wet."

"Didn' rain enough. Come on now, drink your coffee. Al, soon's you're through, better get the engine runnin'."

She called, "You near ready, Mis' Wainwright?"

"Jus' eatin'. Be ready in a minute."

Outside, the camp had come to life. Fires burned in front of the tents. The stovepipes from the boxcars spurted smoke.

Al tipped up his coffee and got a mouthful of grounds. He went down the cat-walk spitting them out.

"We're awready, Mis' Wainwright," Ma called. She turned to Rose of Sharon. "You shouldn' come."

"I'm a-goin' out."

"Lemme look 't your eyes." Ma stared into the girl's nervous bright eyes. "You ain't goin'," she said. "You got to stay."

The girl set her jaw. "I'm a-goin'," she said. "Ma, I got to go."

"Well, you got no cotton sack. You can't pull no sack."

"I'll pick into your sack."

"I wisht you wouldn'."

"I'm a-goin'."

Ma sighed. "I'll keep my eye on you. Wisht we could have a doctor." Rose of Sharon moved nervously about the car. She put on a light coat and took it off. "Take a blanket," Ma said. "Then if you wanta res', you can keep warm." They heard the truck motor roar up behind the boxcar. "We gonna be first out," Ma said exultantly. "Awright, get your sacks. Ruthie, don' you forget them shirts I fixed for you to pick in."

Wainwrights and Joads climbed into the truck in the dark. The dawn was coming, but it was slow and pale.

"Turn lef'," Ma told Al. "They'll be a sign out where we're goin'." They drove along the dark road. And other cars followed them, and behind, in the camp, the cars were being started, the families piling in; and the cars pulled out on the highway and turned left.

A piece of cardboard was tied to a mailbox on the right-hand side of the road, and on it, printed with blue crayon, "Cotton Pickers Wanted." Al turned into the entrance and drove out to the barnyard. And the barnyard was full of cars already. An electric globe on the end of the white barn lighted a group of men and women standing near the scales, their bags rolled under their arms. Some of the women wore the bags over their shoulders and crossed in front.

"We ain't so early as we thought," said Al. He pulled the truck against a fence and parked. The families climbed down and went to join the waiting group, and more cars came in from the road and parked, and more families joined the group. Under the light on the barn end, the owner signed them in.

"Hawley?" he said. "H-a-w-l-e-y? How many?"

"Four. Will——"

"Will."

"Benton——"

"Benton."

"Amelia——"

"Amelia."

"Claire——"

"Claire. Who's next? Carpenter? How many?"

"Six."

He wrote them in the book, with a space left for the weights. "Got your bags? I got a few. Cost you a dollar." And the cars poured into the yard. The owner pulled his sheep-lined leather jacket up around his throat. He looked at the driveway apprehensively. "This twenty isn't gonna take long to pick with all these people," he said.

Children were climbing into the big cotton trailer, digging their toes into the chicken-wire sides. "Git off there," the owner cried. "Come on down. You'll tear that wire loose." And the children climbed slowly down, embarrassed and silent. The gray dawn came. "I'll have to take a tare for dew," the owner said. "Change it when the sun comes out. All right, go out when you want. Light enough to see."

The people moved quickly out into the cotton field and took their rows. They tied the bags to their waists and they slapped their hands together to warm stiff fingers that had to be nimble. The dawn colored over the eastern hills, and the wide line moved over the rows. And from the highway the cars still moved in and parked in the barnyard until it was full, and they parked along the road on both sides. The wind blew briskly across the field. "I don't know how you all found out," the owner said. "There must be a hell of a grapevine. The twenty won't last till noon. What name? Hume? How many?"

The line of people moved out across the field, and the strong steady west wind blew their clothes. Their fingers flew to the spilling bolls, and flew to the long sacks growing heavy behind them.

Pa spoke to the man in the row to his right. "Back home we might get rain out of a wind like this. Seems a little mite frosty for rain. How long you been out here?" He kept his eyes down on his work as he spoke.

His neighbor didn't look up. "I been here nearly a year."

"Would you say it was gonna rain?"

"Can't tell, an' that ain't no insult, neither. Folks that lived here all their life can't tell. If the rain can git in the way of a crop, it'll rain. Tha's what they say out here."

Pa looked quickly at the western hills. Big gray clouds were coasting over the ridge, riding the wind swiftly. "Them looks like rainheads," he said.

His neighbor stole a squinting look. "Can't tell," he said. And all down the line of rows the people looked back at the clouds. And then they bent lower to their work, and their hands flew to the cotton. They raced at the picking, raced against time and cotton weight, raced against the rain and against each other—only so much cotton to pick, only so much money to be made. They came to the other side of the field and ran to get a new row. And now they faced into the wind, and they could see the high gray clouds moving over the sky toward the rising sun. And more cars parked along the roadside, and new pickers came to be checked in. The line of people moved frantically across the field, weighed at the end, marked their cotton, checked the weights into their own books, and ran for new rows.

At eleven o'clock the field was picked and the work was done. The wire-sided trailers were hooked on behind wire-sided trucks, and they moved out to the highway and drove away to the gin. The cotton fluffed out through the chicken wire and little clouds of cotton blew through the air, and rags of cotton caught and waved on the weeds beside the road. The pickers clustered disconsolately back to the barnyard and stood in line to be paid off.

"Hume, James. Twenty-two cents. Ralph, thirty cents. Joad, Thomas, ninety cents. Winfield, fifteen cents." The money lay in rolls, silver and nickels and pennies. And each man looked in his own book as he was being paid. "Wainwright, Agnes, thirty-four cents. Tobin, sixty-three cents." The line moved past slowly. The families went back to their cars, silently. And they drove slowly away.

Joads and Wainwrights waited in the truck for the driveway to clear. And as they waited, the first drops of rain began to fall. Al put his hand out of the cab to feel them. Rose of Sharon sat in the middle, and Ma on the outside. The girl's eyes were lusterless again.

"You shouldn' of came," Ma said. "You didn' pick more'n ten-fifteen pounds." Rose of Sharon looked down at her great bulging belly, and she didn't reply. She shivered suddenly and held her head high. Ma, watching her closely, unrolled her cotton bag, spread it over Rose of Sharon's shoulders, and drew her close.

At last the way was clear. Al started his motor and drove out into the highway. The big infrequent drops of rain lanced down and splashed on the road, and as the truck moved along, the drops became smaller and closer. Rain pounded on the cab of the truck so loudly that it could be heard over the pounding of the old worn motor. On the truck bed the Wainwrights and Joads spread their cotton bags over their heads and shoulders.

Rose of Sharon shivered violently against Ma's arm, and Ma cried, "Go faster, Al. Rosasharn got a chill. Gotta get her feet in hot water."

Al speeded the pounding motor, and when he came to the boxcar camp, he drove down close to the red cars. Ma was spouting orders before they were well stopped. "Al," she commanded, "you an' John an' Pa go into the willows an' c'lect all the dead stuff you can. We got to keep warm."

"Wonder if the roof leaks."

"No, I don' think so. Be nice an' dry, but we got to have wood. Got to keep warm. Take Ruthie an' Winfiel' too. They can get twigs. This here girl ain't well." Ma got out, and Rose of Sharon tried to follow, but her knees buckled and she sat down heavily on the running board.

Fat Mrs. Wainwright saw her. "What's a matter? Her time come?"

"No, I don' think so," said Ma. "Got a chill. Maybe took col'. Gimme a han', will you?" The two women supported Rose of Sharon. After a few steps her strength came back—her legs took her weight.

"I'm awright, Ma," she said. "It was jus' a minute there."

The older women kept hands on her elbows. "Feet in hot water," Ma said wisely. They helped her up the cat-walk and into the boxcar.

"You rub her," Mrs. Wainwright said. "I'll get a far' goin'." She used the last of the twigs and built up a blaze in the stove. The rain poured now, scoured at the roof of the car.

Ma looked up at it. "Thank God we got a tight roof," she said. "Them tents leaks, no matter how good. Jus' put on a little water, Mis' Wainwright."

Rose of Sharon lay still on a mattress. She let them take off her shoes and rub her feet. Mrs. Wainwright bent over her. "You got pain?" she demanded.

"No. Jus' don' feel good. Jus' feel bad."

"I got pain killer an' salts," Mrs. Wainwright said. "You're welcome to 'em if you want 'em. Perfec'ly welcome."

The girl shivered violently. "Cover me up, Ma. I'm col'." Ma brought all the blankets and piled them on top of her. The rain roared down on the roof.

Now the wood-gatherers returned, their arms piled high with sticks and their hats and coats dripping. "Jesus, she's wet," Pa said. "Soaks you in a minute."

Ma said, "Better go back an' get more. Burns up awful quick. Be dark purty soon." Ruthie and Winfield dripped in and threw their sticks on the pile. They turned to go again. "You stay," Ma ordered. "Stan' up close to the fire an' get dry."

The afternoon was silver with rain, the roads glittered with water. Hour by hour the cotton plants seemed to blacken and shrivel. Pa and Al and Uncle John made trip after·trip into the thickets and brought back loads of dead wood. They piled it near the door, until the heap of it nearly reached the ceiling, and at last they stopped and walked toward the stove. Streams of water ran from their hats to their shoulders. The edges of their coats dripped and their shoes squished as they walked.

"Awright, now, get off them clothes," Ma said. "I got some nice coffee for you fellas. An' you got dry overhalls to put on. Don' stan' there."

The evening came early. In the boxcars the families huddled together, listening to the pouring water on the roofs.

CHAPTER 29

Over the high coast mountains and over the valleys the gray clouds marched in from the ocean. The wind blew fiercely and silently, high in the air, and it swished in the brush, and it roared in the forests. The clouds came in brokenly, in puffs, in folds, in gray crags; and they piled in together and settled low over the west. And then the wind stopped and left the clouds deep and solid. The rain began with gusty showers, pauses and downpours; and then gradually it settled to a single tempo, small drops and a steady beat, rain that was gray to see through, rain that cut midday light to evening. And at first the dry earth sucked the moisture down and blackened. For two days the earth drank the rain, until the earth was full. Then puddles formed, and in the low places little lakes formed in the fields. The muddy lakes rose higher, and the steady rain whipped the shining water. At last the mountains were full, and the hillsides spilled into the streams, built them to freshets, and sent them roaring down the canyons into the valleys. The rain beat on steadily. And the streams and the little rivers edged up to the bank sides and worked at willows and tree roots, bent the willows deep in the current, cut out the roots of cottonwoods and brought down the trees. The muddy water whirled along the bank sides and crept up the banks until at last it spilled over, into the fields, into the orchards, into the cotton patches where the black stems stood. Level fields became lakes, broad and gray, and the rain whipped up the surfaces. Then the water poured over the highways, and cars moved slowly, cutting the water ahead, and leaving a boiling muddy wake behind. The earth whispered under the beat of the rain, and the streams thundered under the churning freshets.

When the first rain started, the migrant people huddled in their tents, saying, It'll soon be over, and asking, How long's it likely to go on?

And when the puddles formed, the men went out in the rain with shovels and built little dikes around the tents. The beating rain worked at the canvas until it penetrated and sent streams down. And then the little dikes washed out and the water came inside, and the streams wet the beds and the blankets. The people sat in wet clothes. They set up boxes and put planks on the boxes. Then, day and night, they sat on the planks.

Beside the tents the old cars stood, and water fouled the ignition wires and water fouled the carburetors. The little gray tents stood in lakes. And at last the people had to move. Then the cars wouldn't start because the wires were shorted; and if the engines would run, deep mud engulfed the wheels. And the people waded away, carrying their wet blankets in their arms. They splashed along, carrying the children, carrying the very old, in their arms. And if a barn stood on high ground, it was filled with people, shivering and hopeless.

Then some went to the relief offices, and they came sadly back to their own people.

They's rules—you got to be here a year before you can git relief. They say the gov'ment is gonna help. They don' know when.

And gradually the greatest terror of all came along.

They ain't gonna be no kinda work for three months.

In the barns, the people sat huddled together; and the terror came over them, and their faces were gray with terror. The children cried with hunger, and there was no food.

Then the sickness came, pneumonia, and measles that went to the eyes and to the mastoids.

And the rain fell steadily, and the water flowed over the highways, for the culverts could not carry the water.

Then from the tents, from the crowded barns, groups of sodden men went out, their clothes slopping rags, their shoes muddy pulp. They splashed out through the water, to the towns, to the country stores, to the relief offices, to beg for food, to cringe and beg for food, to beg for relief, to try to steal, to lie. And under the begging, and under the cringing, a hopeless anger began to smolder. And in the little towns pity for the sodden men changed to anger, and anger at the hungry people changed to fear of them. Then sheriffs swore in deputies in droves, and orders were rushed for rifles, for tear gas, for ammunition. Then the hungry men crowded the alleys behind the stores to beg for bread, to beg for rotting vegetables, to steal when they could.

Frantic men pounded on the doors of the doctors; and the doctors were busy. And sad men left word at country stores for the coroner to send a car. The coroners were not too busy. The coroners' wagons backed up through the mud and took out the dead.

And the rain pattered relentlessly down, and the streams broke their banks and spread out over the country.

Huddled under sheds, lying in wet hay, the hunger and the fear bred anger. Then boys went out, not to beg, but to steal; and men went out weakly, to try to steal.

The sheriffs swore in new deputies and ordered new rifles; and the comfortable people in tight houses felt pity at first, and then distaste, and finally hatred for the migrant people.

In the wet hay of leaking barns babies were born to women who panted with pneumonia. And old people curled up in corners and died that way, so that the coroners could not straighten them. At night frantic men walked boldly to hen roosts and carried off the squawking chickens. If they were shot at, they did not run, but splashed sullenly away; and if they were hit, they sank tiredly in the mud.

The rain stopped. On the fields the water stood, reflecting the gray sky, and the land whispered with moving water. And the men came out of the barns, out of the sheds. They squatted on their hams and looked out over the flooded land. And they were silent. And sometimes they talked very quietly.

No work till spring. No work.

And if no work—no money, no food.

Fella had a team of horses, had to use 'em to plow an' cultivate an' mow, wouldn' think a turnin' 'em out to starve when they wasn't workin'.

Them's horses—we're men.

The women watched the men, watched to see whether the break had come at last. The women stood silently and watched. And where a number of men gathered together, the fear went from their faces, and anger took its place. And the women sighed with relief, for they knew it was all right—the break had not come; and the break would never come as long as fear could turn to wrath.

Tiny points of grass came through the earth, and in a few days the hills were pale green with the beginning year.

CHAPTER 30

In the boxcar camp the water stood in puddles, and the rain splashed in the mud. Gradually the little stream crept up the bank toward the low flat where the boxcars stood.

On the second day of the rain Al took the tarpaulin down from the middle of the car. He carried it out and spread it over the nose of the truck, and he came back into the car and sat down on his mattress. Now, without the separation, the two families in the car were one. The men sat together, and their spirits were damp. Ma kept a little fire going in the stove, kept a few twigs burning, and she conserved her wood. The rain poured down on the nearly flat roof of the boxcar.

On the third day the Wainwrights grew restless. "Maybe we better go 'long," Mrs. Wainwright said.

And Ma tried to keep them. "Where'd you go an' be sure of a tight roof?"

"I dunno, but I got a feelin' we oughta go along." They argued together, and Ma watched Al.

Ruthie and Winfield tried to play for a while, and then they too relapsed into sullen inactivity, and the rain drummed down on the roof.

On the third day the sound of the stream could be heard above the drumming rain. Pa and Uncle John stood in the open door and looked out on the rising stream. At both ends of the camp the water ran near to the highway, but at the camp it looped away so that the highway embankment surrounded the camp at the back and the stream closed it in on the front. And Pa said, "How's it look to you, John? Seems to me if that crick comes up, she'll flood us."

Uncle John opened his mouth and rubbed his bristling chin. "Yeah," he said. "Might at that."

Rose of Sharon was down with a heavy cold, her face flushed and her eyes shining with fever. Ma sat beside her with a cup of hot milk. "Here," she said. "Take this here. Got bacon grease in it for strength. Here, drink it!"

Rose of Sharon shook her head weakly. "I ain't hungry."

Pa drew a curved line in the air with his finger. "If we was all to get our shovels an' throw up a bank, I bet we could keep her out. On'y have to go from up there down to there."

"Yeah," Uncle John agreed. "Might. Dunno if them other fellas'd wanta. They'd maybe ruther move somewheres else."

"But these here cars is dry," Pa insisted. "Couldn' find no dry place as good as this. You wait." From the pile of brush in the car he picked a twig. He ran down the cat-walk, splashed through the mud to the stream and he set his twig upright on the edge of the swirling water. In a moment he was back in the car. "Jesus, ya get wet through," he said.

Both men kept their eyes on the little twig on the water's edge. They saw the water move slowly up around it and creep up the bank. Pa squatted down in the doorway. "Comin' up fast," he said. "I think we oughta go talk to the other fellas. See if they'll help ditch up. Got to git outa here if they won't." Pa looked down the long car to the Wainwright end. Al was with them, sitting beside Aggie. Pa walked into their precinct. "Water's risin'," he said. "How about if we throwed up a bank? We could do her if ever'body helped."

Wainwright said, "We was jes' talkin'. Seems like we oughta be gettin' outa here."

Pa said, "You been aroun'. You know what chancet we got a gettin' a dry place to stay."

"I know. But jes' the same——"

Al said, "Pa, if they go, I'm a-goin' too."

Pa looked startled. "You can't, Al. The truck— We ain't fit to drive that truck."

"I don' care. Me an' Aggie got to stick together."

"Now you wait," Pa said. "Come on over here." Wainwright and Al got to their feet and approached the door. "See?" Pa said, pointing. "Jus' a bank from there an' down to there." He looked at his stick. The water swirled about it now, and crept up the bank.

"Be a lot a work, an' then she might come over anyways," Wainwright protested.

"Well, we ain't doin' nothin', might's well be workin'. We ain't gonna find us no nice place to live like this. Come on, now. Le's go talk to the other fellas. We can do her if ever'body helps."

Al said, "If Aggie goes, I'm a-goin' too."

Pa said, "Look, Al, if them fellas won't dig, then we'll all hafta go. Come on, le's go talk to 'em." They hunched their shoulders and ran down the cat-walk to the next car and up the walk into its open door.

Ma was at the stove, feeding a few sticks to the feeble flame. Ruthie crowded close beside her. "I'm hungry," Ruthie whined.

"No, you ain't," Ma said. "You had good mush."

"Wisht I had a box a Cracker Jack. There ain't nothin' to do. Ain't no fun."

"They'll be fun," Ma said. "You jus' wait. Be fun purty soon. Git a house an' a place, purty soon."

"Wisht we had a dog," Ruthie said.

"We'll have a dog; have a cat, too."

"Yella cat?"

"Don't bother me," Ma begged. "Don't go plaguin' me now, Ruthie. Rosasharn's sick. Jus' you be a good girl a little while. They'll be fun." Ruthie wandered, complaining, away.

From the mattress where Rose of Sharon lay covered up there came a quick sharp cry, cut off in the middle. Ma whirled and went to her. Rose of Sharon was holding her breath and her eyes were filled with terror.

"What is it?" Ma cried. The girl expelled her breath and caught it again. Suddenly Ma put her hand under the covers. Then she stood up. "Mis' Wainwright," she called. "Oh, Mis' Wainwright!"

The fat little woman came down the car. "Want me?"

"Look!" Ma pointed at Rose of Sharon's face. Her teeth were clamped on her lower lip and her forehead was wet with perspiration, and the shining terror was in her eyes.

"I think it's come," Ma said. "It's early."

The girl heaved a great sigh and relaxed. She released her lip and closed her eyes. Mrs. Wainwright bent over her.

"Did it kinda grab you all over—quick? Open up an' answer me." Rose of Sharon nodded weakly. Mrs. Wainwright turned to Ma. "Yep," she said. "It's come. Early, ya say?"

"Maybe the fever brang it."

"Well, she oughta be up on her feet. Oughta be walkin' aroun'."

"She can't," Ma said. "She ain't got the strength."

"Well, she oughta." Mrs. Wainwright grew quiet and stern with efficiency. "I he'ped with lots," she said. "Come on, le's close that door, nearly. Keep out the draf'." The two women pushed on the heavy sliding door, boosted it along until only a foot was open. "I'll git our lamp, too," Mrs. Wainwright said. Her face was purple with excitement. "Aggie," she called. "You take care of these here little fellas."

Ma nodded, "Tha's right. Ruthie! You an' Winfiel' go down with Aggie. Go on now."

"Why?" they demanded.

" 'Cause you got to. Rosasharn gonna have her baby."

"I wanta watch, Ma. Please let me."

"Ruthie! You git now. You git quick." There was no argument against such a tone. Ruthie and Winfield went reluctantly down the car. Ma lighted the lantern. Mrs. Wainwright brought her Rochester lamp down and set it on the floor, and its big circular flame lighted the boxcar brightly.

Ruthie and Winfield stood behind the brush pile and peered over. "Gonna have a baby, an' we're a-gonna see," Ruthie said softly. "Don't you make no noise now. Ma won't let us watch. If she looks this-a-way, you scrunch down behin' the brush. Then we'll see."

"There ain't many kids seen it," Winfield said.

"There ain't no kids seen it," Ruthie insisted proudly. "On'y us."

Down by the mattress, in the bright light of the lamp, Ma and Mrs. Wainwright held conference. Their voices were raised a little over the hollow beating of the rain. Mrs. Wainwright took a paring knife from her apron pocket and slipped it under the mattress. "Maybe it don't do no good," she said apologetically. "Our folks always done it. Don't do no harm, anyways."

Ma nodded. "We used a plow point. I guess anything sharp'll work, long as it can cut birth pains. I hope it ain't gonna be a long one."

"You feelin' awright now?"

Rose of Sharon nodded nervously. "Is it a-comin'?"

"Sure," Ma said. "Gonna have a nice baby. You jus' got to help us. Feel like you could get up an' walk?"

"I can try."

"That's a good girl," Mrs. Wainwright said. "That *is* a good girl. We'll he'p you, honey. We'll walk with ya." They helped her to her feet and pinned a blanket over her shoulders. Then Ma held her arm from one side, and Mrs. Wainwright from the other. They walked her to the brush pile and turned slowly and walked her back, over and over; and the rain drummed deeply on the roof.

Ruthie and Winfield watched anxiously. "When's she gonna have it?" he demanded.

"Sh! Don't draw 'em. We won't be let to look."

Aggie joined them behind the brush pile. Aggie's lean face and yellow hair showed in the lamplight, and her nose was long and sharp in the shadow of her head on the wall.

Ruthie whispered, "You ever saw a baby bore?"

"Sure," said Aggie.

"Well, when's she gonna have it?"

"Oh, not for a long, long time."

"Well, how long?"

"Maybe not 'fore tomorrow mornin'."

"Shucks!" said Ruthie. "Ain't no good watchin' now, then. Oh! Look!"

The walking women had stopped. Rose of Sharon had stiffened, and she whined with pain. They laid her down on the mattress and wiped her forehead while she grunted and clenched her fists. And Ma talked softly to her. "Easy," Ma said. "Gonna be all right—all right. Jus' grip ya han's. Now, then, take your lip outa your teeth. Tha's good—tha's good." The pain passed on. They let her rest awhile, and then helped her up again, and the three walked back and forth, back and forth between the pains.

Pa stuck his head in through the narrow opening. His hat dripped with water. "What ya shut the door for?" he asked. And then he saw the walking women.

Ma said, "Her time's come."

"Then—then we couldn' go 'f we wanted to."

"No."

"Then we got to buil' that bank."

"You got to."

Pa sloshed through the mud to the stream. His marking stick was four inches down. Twenty men stood in the rain. Pa cried, "We got to build her. My girl got her pains." The men gathered around him.

"Baby?"

"Yeah. We can't go now."

A tall man said, "It ain't our baby. We kin go."

"Sure," Pa said. "You can go. Go on. Nobody's stoppin' you. They's only eight shovels." He hurried to the lowest part of the bank and drove his shovel into the mud. The shovelful lifted with a suck-

ing sound. He drove it again, and threw the mud into the low place
on the stream bank. And beside him the other men ranged themselves. They heaped the mud up in a long embankment, and those
who had no shovels cut live willow whips and wove them in a mat
and kicked them into the bank. Over the men came a fury of work,
a fury of battle. When one man dropped his shovel, another took it
up. They had shed their coats and hats. Their shirts and trousers
clung tightly to their bodies, their shoes were shapeless blobs of mud.
A shrill scream came from the Joad car. The men stopped, listened
uneasily, and then plunged to work again. And the little levee of
earth extended until it connected with the highway embankment on
either end. They were tired now, and the shovels moved more
slowly. And the stream rose slowly. It edged above the place where
the first dirt had been thrown.

Pa laughed in triumph. "She'd come over if we hadn' a built
up!" he cried.

The stream rose slowly up the side of the new wall, and tore at
the willow mat. "Higher!" Pa cried. "We got to git her higher!"

The evening came, and the work went on. And now the men
were beyond weariness. Their faces were set and dead. They worked
jerkily, like machines. When it was dark the women set lanterns in
the car doors, and kept pots of coffee handy. And the women ran
one by one to the Joad car and wedged themselves inside.

The pains were coming close now, twenty minutes apart. And
Rose of Sharon had lost her restraint. She screamed fiercely under
the fierce pains. And the neighbor women looked at her and patted
her gently and went back to their own cars.

Ma had a good fire going now, and all her utensils, filled with
water, sat on the stove to heat. Every little while Pa looked in the
car door. "All right?" he asked.

"Yeah! I think so," Ma assured him.

As it grew dark, someone brought out a flashlight to work by.
Uncle John plunged on, throwing mud on top of the wall.

"You take it easy," Pa said. "You'll kill yaself."

"I can't he'p it. I can't stan' that yellin'. It's like—it's like
when——"

"I know," Pa said. "But jus' take it easy."

Uncle John blubbered, "I'll run away. By God, I got to work or
I'll run away."

Pa turned from him. "How's she stan' on the last marker?"

The man with the flashlight threw the beam on the stick. The rain cut whitely through the light. "Comin' up."

"She'll come up slower now," Pa said. "Got to flood purty far on the other side."

"She's comin' up, though."

The women filled the coffee pots and set them out again. And as the night went on, the men moved slower and slower, and they lifted their heavy feet like draft horses. More mud on the levee, more willows interlaced. The rain fell steadily. When the flashlight turned on faces, the eyes showed staring, and the muscles on the cheeks were welted out.

For a long time the screams continued from the car, and at last they were still.

Pa said, "Ma'd call me if it was bore." He went on shoveling the mud sullenly.

The stream eddied and boiled against the bank. Then, from up the stream there came a ripping crash. The beam of the flashlight showed a great cottonwood toppling. The men stopped to watch. The branches of the tree sank into the water and edged around with the current while the stream dug out the little roots. Slowly the tree was freed, and slowly it edged down the stream. The weary men watched, their mouths hanging open. The tree moved slowly down. Then a branch caught on a stump, snagged and held. And very slowly the roots swung around and hooked themselves on the new embankment. The water piled up behind. The tree moved and tore the bank. A little stream slipped through. Pa threw himself forward and jammed mud in the break. The water piled against the tree. And then the bank washed quickly down, washed around ankles, around knees. The men broke and ran, and the current worked smoothly into the flat, under the cars, under the automobiles.

Uncle John saw the water break through. In the murk he could see it. Uncontrollably his weight pulled him down. He went to his knees, and the tugging water swirled about his chest.

Pa saw him go. "Hey! What's the matter?" He lifted him to his feet. "You sick? Come on, the cars is high."

Uncle John gathered his strength. "I dunno," he said apologetically. "Legs give out. Jus' give out." Pa helped him along toward the cars.

When the dike swept out, Al turned and ran. His feet moved heavily. The water was about his calves when he reached the truck.

He flung the tarpaulin off the nose and jumped into the car. He stepped on the starter. The engine turned over and over, and there was no bark of the motor. He choked the engine deeply. The battery turned the sodden motor more and more slowly, and there was no cough. Over and over, slower and slower. Al set the spark high. He felt under the seat for the crank and jumped out. The water was higher than the running board. He ran to the front end. Crank case was under water now. Frantically he fitted the crank and twisted around and around, and his clenched hand on the crank splashed in the slowly flowing water at each turn. At last his frenzy gave out. The motor was full of water, the battery fouled by now. On slightly higher ground two cars were started and their lights on. They floundered in the mud and dug their wheels down until finally the drivers cut off the motors and sat still, looking into the headlight beams. And the rain whipped white streaks through the lights. Al went slowly around the truck, reached in, and turned off the ignition.

When Pa reached the cat-walk, he found the lower end floating. He stepped it down into the mud, under water. "Think ya can make it awright, John?" he asked.

"I'll be awright. Jus' go on."

Pa cautiously climbed the cat-walk and squeezed himself in the narrow opening. The two lamps were turned low. Ma sat on the mattress beside Rose of Sharon, and Ma fanned her still face with a piece of cardboard. Mrs. Wainwright poked dry brush into the stove, and a dank smoke edged out around the lids and filled the car with a smell of burning tissue. Ma looked up at Pa when he entered, and then quickly down.

"How—is she?" Pa asked.

Ma did not look up at him again. "Awright, I think. Sleepin'."

The air was fetid and close with the smell of the birth. Uncle John clambered in and held himself upright against the side of the car. Mrs. Wainwright left her work and came to Pa. She pulled him by the elbow toward the corner of the car. She picked up a lantern and held it over an apple box in the corner. On a newspaper lay a blue shriveled little mummy.

"Never breathed," said Mrs. Wainwright softly. "Never was alive."

Uncle John turned and shuffled tiredly down the car to the dark end. The rain whished softly on the roof now, so softly that they could hear Uncle John's tired sniffling from the dark.

Pa looked up at Mrs. Wainwright. He took the lantern from her hand and put it on the floor. Ruthie and Winfield were asleep on their own mattress, their arms over their eyes to cut out the light.

Pa walked slowly to Rose of Sharon's mattress. He tried to squat down, but his legs were too tired. He knelt instead. Ma fanned her square of cardboard back and forth. She looked at Pa for a moment, and her eyes were wide and staring, like a sleepwalker's eyes.

Pa said, "We—done—what we could."

"I know."

"We worked all night. An' a tree cut out the bank."

"I know."

"You can hear it under the car."

"I know. I heard it."

"Think she's gonna be all right?"

"I dunno."

"Well—couldn' we—of did nothin'?"

Ma's lips were stiff and white. "No. They was on'y one thing to do—ever—an' we done it."

"We worked till we dropped, an' a tree— Rain's lettin' up some." Ma looked at the ceiling, and then down again. Pa went on, compelled to talk. "I dunno how high she'll rise. Might flood the car."

"I know."

"You know ever'thing."

She was silent, and the cardboard moved slowly back and forth.

"Did we slip up?" he pleaded. "Is they anything we could of did?"

Ma looked at him strangely. Her white lips smiled in a dreaming compassion. "Don't take no blame. Hush! It'll be awright. They's changes—all over."

"Maybe the water—maybe we'll have to go."

"When it's time to go—we'll go. We'll do what we got to do. Now hush. You might wake her."

Mrs. Wainwright broke twigs and poked them in the sodden, smoking fire.

From outside came the sound of an angry voice. "I'm goin' in an' see the son-of-a-bitch myself."

And then, just outside the door, Al's voice, "Where you think you're goin'?"

"Goin' in to see that bastard Joad."

"No, you ain't. What's the matter'th you?"

"If he didn't have that fool idear about the bank, we'd a got out. Now our car is dead."

"You think ours is burnin' up the road?"

"I'm a-goin' in."

Al's voice was cold. "You're gonna fight your way in."

Pa got slowly to his feet and went to the door. "Awright, Al. I'm comin' out. It's awright, Al." Pa slid down the cat-walk. Ma heard him say, "We got sickness. Come on down here."

The rain scattered lightly on the roof now, and a new-risen breeze blew it along in sweeps. Mrs. Wainwright came from the stove and looked down at Rose of Sharon. "Dawn's a-comin' soon, ma'am. Whyn't you git some sleep? I'll set with her."

"No," Ma said. "I ain't tar'd."

"In a pig's eye," said Mrs. Wainwright. "Come on, you lay down awhile."

Ma fanned the air slowly with her cardboard. "You been frien'ly," she said. "We thank you."

The stout woman smiled. "No need to thank. Ever'body's in the same wagon. S'pose we was down. You'd a give us a han'."

"Yes," Ma said, "we would."

"Or anybody."

"Or anybody. Use' ta be the fambly was fust. It ain't so now. It's anybody. Worse off we get, the more we got to do."

"We couldn' a saved it."

"I know," said Ma.

Ruthie sighed deeply and took her arm from over her eyes. She looked blindly at the lamp for a moment, and then turned her head and looked at Ma. "Is it bore?" she demanded. "Is the baby out?"

Mrs. Wainwright picked up a sack and spread it over the apple box in the corner.

"Where's the baby?" Ruthie demanded.

Ma wet her lips. "They ain't no baby. They never was no baby. We was wrong."

"Shucks!" Ruthie said. Winfield stirred uneasily.

Ma said, "Hush now an' go to sleep. You wake up Winfiel'."

Ruthie yawned. "I wisht it had a been a baby."

Mrs. Wainwright sat down beside Ma and took the cardboard from her and fanned the air. Ma folded her hands in her lap, and her tired eyes never left the face of Rose of Sharon, sleeping in exhaustion. "Come on," Mrs. Wainwright said. "Jus' lay down. You'll be right beside her. Why, you'd wake up if she took a deep breath, even."

"Awright, I will." Ma stretched out on the mattress beside the sleeping girl. And Mrs. Wainwright sat on the floor and kept watch.

Pa and Al and Uncle John sat in the car doorway and watched the steely dawn come. The rain had stopped, but the sky was deep and solid with cloud. As the light came, it was reflected on the water. The men could see the current of the stream, slipping swiftly down, bearing black branches of trees, boxes, boards. The water swirled into the flat where the boxcars stood. There was no sign of the embankment left. On the flat the current stopped. The edges of the flood were lined with yellow foam. Pa leaned out the door and placed a twig on the cat-walk, just above the water line. The men watched the water slowly climb to it, lift it gently and float it away. Pa placed another twig an inch above the water and settled back to watch.

"Think it'll come inside the car?" Al asked.

"Can't tell. They's a hell of a lot of water got to come down from the hills yet. Can't tell. Might start up to rain again."

Al said, "I been a-thinkin'. If she come in, ever'thing'll get soaked."

"Yeah."

"Well, she won't come up more'n three-four feet in the car 'cause she'll go over the highway an' spread out first."

"How you know?" Pa asked.

"I took a sight on her, off the end of the car." He held his hand. " 'Bout this far up she'll come."

"Awright," Pa said. "What about it? We won't be here."

"We got to be here. Truck's here. Take a week to get the water out of her when the flood goes down."

"Well—what's your idear?"

"We can tear out the side-boards of the truck an' build a kinda platform in here to pile our stuff an' to set up on."

"Yeah? How'll we cook—how'll we eat?"

"Well, it'll keep our stuff dry."

The light grew stronger outside, a gray metallic light. The second little stick floated away from the cat-walk. Pa placed another one higher up. "Sure climbin'," he said. "I guess we better do that."

Ma turned restlessly in her sleep. Her eyes started wide open. She cried sharply in warning, "Tom! Oh, Tom! Tom!"

Mrs. Wainwright spoke soothingly. The eyes flicked closed again and Ma squirmed under her dream. Mrs. Wainwright got up and walked to the doorway. "Hey!" she said softly. "We ain't gonna git out soon." She pointed to the corner of the car where the apple box was. "That ain't doin' no good. Jus' cause trouble an' sorra. Couldn' you fellas kinda—take it out an' bury it?"

The men were silent. Pa said at last, "Guess you're right. Jus' cause sorra. 'Gainst the law to bury it."

"They's lots a things 'gainst the law that we can't he'p doin'."

"Yeah."

Al said, "We oughta git them truck sides tore off 'fore the water comes up much more."

Pa turned to Uncle John. "Will you take an' bury it while Al an' me git that lumber in?"

Uncle John said sullenly, "Why do I got to do it? Why don't you fellas? I don' like it." And then, "Sure. I'll do it. Sure, I will. Come on, give it to me." His voice began to rise. "Come on! Give it to me."

"Don' wake 'em up," Mrs. Wainwright said. She brought the apple box to the doorway and straightened the sack decently over it.

"Shovel's standin' right behin' you," Pa said.

Uncle John took the shovel in one hand. He slipped out the doorway into the slowly moving water, and it rose nearly to his waist before he struck bottom. He turned and settled the apple box under his other arm.

Pa said, "Come on, Al. Le's git that lumber in."

In the gray dawn light Uncle John waded around the end of the car, past the Joad truck; and he climbed the slippery bank to the highway. He walked down the highway, past the boxcar flat, until he came to a place where the boiling stream ran close to the road, where the willows grew along the road side. He put his shovel down, and holding the box in front of him, he edged through the brush until he came to the edge of the swift stream. For a time he stood watching it swirl by, leaving its yellow foam among the willow stems. He held the apple box against his chest. And then he leaned over and set the box in the stream and steadied it with his hand. He said fiercely, "Go down an' tell 'em. Go down in the street an' rot an' tell 'em that way. That's the way you can talk. Don' even know if you was a boy or a girl. Ain't gonna find out. Go on down now, an' lay in the street. Maybe they'll know then." He guided the box gently out into the current and let it go. It settled low in the water, edged sideways, whirled around, and turned slowly over. The sack floated away, and the box, caught in the swift water, floated quickly away, out of sight, behind the brush. Uncle John grabbed the shovel and went rapidly back to the boxcars. He sloshed down into the water and waded to the truck, where Pa and Al were working, taking down the one-by-six planks.

Pa looked over at him. "Get it done?"

"Yeah."

"Well, look," Pa said. "If you'll he'p Al, I'll go down the store an' get some stuff to eat."

"Get some bacon," Al said. "I need some meat."

"I will," Pa said. He jumped down from the truck and Uncle John took his place.

When they pushed the planks into the car door, Ma awakened and sat up. "What you doin'?"

"Gonna build up a place to keep outa the wet."

"Why?" Ma asked. "It's dry in here."

"Ain't gonna be. Water's comin' up."

Ma struggled up to her feet and went to the door. "We got to git outa here."

"Can't," Al said. "All our stuff's here. Truck's here. Ever'thing we got."

"Where's Pa?"

"Gone to get stuff for breakfas'."

Ma looked down at the water. It was only six inches down from the floor by now. She went back to the mattress and looked at Rose of Sharon. The girl stared back at her.

"How you feel?" Ma asked.

"Tar'd. Jus' tar'd out."

"Gonna get some breakfas' into you."

"I ain't hungry."

Mrs. Wainwright moved beside Ma. "She looks all right. Come through it fine."

Rose of Sharon's eyes questioned Ma, and Ma tried to avoid the question. Mrs. Wainwright walked to the stove.

"Ma."

"Yeah? What you want?"

"Is—it—all right?"

Ma gave up the attempt. She kneeled down on the mattress.

"You can have more," she said. "We done ever'thing we knowed."

Rose of Sharon struggled and pushed herself up. "Ma!"

"You couldn' he'p it."

The girl lay back again, and covered her eyes with her arms. Ruthie crept close and looked down in awe. She whispered harshly, "She sick, Ma? She gonna die?"

" 'Course not. She's gonna be awright. Awright."

Pa came in with his armload of packages. "How is she?"

"Awright," Ma said. "She's gonna be awright."

Ruthie reported to Winfield. "She ain't gonna die. Ma says so."

And Winfield, picking his teeth with a splinter in a very adult manner, said, "I knowed it all the time."

"How'd you know?"

"I won't tell," said Winfield, and he spat out a piece of the splinter.

Ma built the fire up with the last twigs and cooked the bacon and made gravy. Pa had brought store bread. Ma scowled when she saw it. "We got any money lef'?"

"Nope," said Pa. "But we was so hungry."

"An' you got store bread," Ma said accusingly.

"Well, we was awful hungry. Worked all night long."

Ma sighed. "Now what we gonna do?"

As they ate, the water crept up and up. Al gulped his food and he and Pa built the platform. Five feet wide, six feet long, four feet above the floor. And the water crept to the edge of the doorway, seemed to hesitate a long time, and then moved slowly inward over the floor. And outside, the rain began again, as it had before, big heavy drops splashing on the water, pounding hollowly on the roof.

Al said, "Come on now, let's get the mattresses up. Let's put the blankets up, so they don't git wet." They piled their possessions up on the platform, and the water crept over the floor. Pa and Ma, Al and Uncle John, each at a corner, lifted Rose of Sharon's mattress, with the girl on it, and put it on top of the pile.

And the girl protested, "I can walk. I'm awright." And the water crept over the floor, a thin film of it. Rose of Sharon whispered to Ma, and Ma put her hand under the blanket and felt her breast and nodded.

In the other end of the boxcar, the Wainwrights were pounding, building a platform for themselves. The rain thickened, and then passed away.

Ma looked down at her feet. The water was half an inch deep on the car floor by now. "You, Ruthie—Winfiel'!" she called distractedly. "Come get on top of the pile. You'll get cold." She saw them safely up, sitting awkwardly beside Rose of Sharon. Ma said suddenly, "We got to git out."

"We can't," Pa said. "Like Al says, all our stuff's here. We'll pull off the boxcar door an' make more room to set on."

The family huddled on the platforms, silent and fretful. The water was six inches deep in the car before the flood spread evenly over the embankment and moved into the cotton field on the other side. During that day and night the men slept soddenly, side by side on the boxcar door. And Ma lay close to Rose of Sharon. Sometimes Ma whispered to her and sometimes sat up quietly, her face brooding. Under the blanket she hoarded the remains of the store bread.

The rain had become intermittent now—little wet squalls and quiet times. On the morning of the second day Pa splashed through the camp and came back with ten potatoes in his pockets. Ma watched him sullenly while he chopped out part of the inner wall of the car, built a fire, and scooped water into a pan. The family ate the steaming boiled potatoes with their fingers. And when this last food was gone, they stared at the gray water; and in the night they did not lie down for a long time.

When the morning came they awakened nervously. Rose of Sharon whispered to Ma.

Ma nodded her head. "Yes," she said. "It's time for it." And then she turned to the car door, where the men lay. "We're a-gettin' outa here," she said savagely, "gettin' to higher groun'. An' you're comin' or you ain't comin', but I'm takin' Rosasharn an' the little fellas outa here."

"We can't!" Pa said weakly.

"Awright, then. Maybe you'll pack Rosasharn to the highway, anyways, an' then come back. It ain't rainin' now, an' we're a-goin'."

"Awright, we'll go," Pa said.

Al said, "Ma, I ain't goin'."

"Why not?"

"Well—Aggie—why, her an' me——"

Ma smiled. " 'Course," she said. "You stay here, Al. Take care of the stuff. When the water goes down—why, we'll come back. Come quick, 'fore it rains again," she told Pa. "Come on, Rosasharn. We're goin' to a dry place."

"I can walk."

"Maybe a little, on the road. Git your back bent, Pa."

Pa slipped into the water and stood waiting. Ma helped Rose of Sharon down from the platform and steadied her across the car. Pa took her in his arms, held her as high as he could, and pushed his way carefully through the deep water, around the car, and to the highway. He set her down on her feet and held onto her. Uncle John carried Ruthie and followed. Ma slid down into the water, and for a moment her skirts billowed out around her.

"Winfiel', set on my shoulder. Al—we'll come back soon's the water's down. Al—" She paused. "If—if Tom comes—tell him we'll be back. Tell him be careful. Winfiel'! Climb on my shoulder—there! Now, keep your feet still." She staggered off through the breast-high water. At the highway embankment they helped her up and lifted Winfield from her shoulder.

They stood on the highway and looked back over the sheet of water, the dark red blocks of the cars, the trucks and automobiles deep in the slowly moving water. And as they stood, a little misting rain began to fall.

"We got to git along," Ma said. "Rosasharn, you feel like you could walk?"

"Kinda dizzy," the girl said. "Feel like I been beat."

Pa complained, "Now we're a-goin', where we goin'?"

"I dunno. Come on, give your han' to Rosasharn." Ma took the girl's right arm to steady her, and Pa her left. "Goin' someplace where it's dry. Got to. You fellas ain't had dry clothes on for two days." They moved slowly along the highway. They could hear the rushing of the water in the stream beside the road. Ruthie and Winfield marched together, splashing their feet against the road. They went slowly along the road. The sky grew darker and the rain thickened. No traffic moved along the highway.

"We got to hurry," Ma said. "If this here girl gits good an' wet —I don' know what'll happen to her."

"You ain't said where-at we're a-hurryin' to," Pa reminded her sarcastically.

The road curved along beside the stream. Ma searched the land and the flooded fields. Far off the road, on the left, on a slight rolling hill a rain-blackened barn stood. "Look!" Ma said. "Look there! I bet it's dry in that barn. Le's go there till the rain stops."

Pa sighed. "Prob'ly get run out by the fella owns it."

Ahead, beside the road, Ruthie saw a spot of red. She raced to it. A scraggly geranium gone wild, and there was one rain-beaten blossom on it. She picked the flower. She took a petal carefully off and stuck it on her nose. Winfield ran up to see.

"Lemme have one?" he said.

"No, sir! It's all mine. I foun' it." She stuck another red petal on her forehead, a little bright-red heart.

"Come on, Ruthie! Lemme have one. Come on, now." He grabbed at the flower in her hand and missed it, and Ruthie banged him in the face with her open hand. He stood for a moment, surprised, and then his lips shook and his eyes welled.

The others caught up. "Now what you done?" Ma asked. "Now what you done?"

"He tried to grab my fl'ar."

Winfield sobbed, "I—on'y wanted one—to—stick on my nose."

"Give him one, Ruthie."

"Leave him find his own. This here's mine."

"Ruthie! You give him one."

Ruthie heard the threat in Ma's tone, and changed her tactics. "Here," she said with elaborate kindness. "I'll stick on one for you." The older people walked on. Winfield held his nose near to her. She wet a petal with her tongue and jabbed it cruelly on his nose. "You little son-of-a-bitch," she said softly. Winfield felt for the petal with his fingers, and pressed it down on his nose. They walked quickly after the others. Ruthie felt how the fun was gone. "Here," she said. "Here's some more. Stick some on your forehead."

From the right of the road there came a sharp swishing. Ma cried, "Hurry up. They's a big rain. Le's go through the fence here. It's shorter. Come on, now! Bear on, Rosasharn." They half dragged the girl across the ditch, helped her through the fence. And then the storm struck them. Sheets of rain fell on them. They plowed through the mud and up the little incline. The black barn was nearly obscured by the rain. It hissed and splashed, and the growing wind drove it along. Rose of Sharon's feet slipped and she dragged between her supporters.

"Pa! Can you carry her?"

Pa leaned over and picked her up. "We're wet through anyways," he said. "Hurry up. Winfiel'—Ruthie! Run on ahead."

They came panting up to the rain-soaked barn and staggered into the open end. There was no door in this end. A few rusty farm tools lay about, a disk plow and a broken cultivator, an iron wheel. The rain hammered on the roof and curtained the entrance. Pa gently set Rose of Sharon down on an oily box. "God Awmighty!" he said.

Ma said, "Maybe they's hay inside. Look, there's a door." She swung the door on its rusty hinges. "They is hay," she cried. "Come on in, you."

It was dark inside. A little light came in through the cracks between the boards.

"Lay down, Rosasharn," Ma said. "Lay down an' res'. I'll try to figger some way to dry you off."

Winfield said, "Ma!" and the rain roaring on the roof drowned his voice. "*Ma!*"

"What is it? What you want?"

"Look! In the corner."

Ma looked. There were two figures in the gloom; a man who lay on his back, and a boy sitting beside him, his eyes wide, staring at the newcomers. As she looked, the boy got slowly up to his feet and came toward her. His voice croaked. "You own this here?"

"No," Ma said. "Jus' come in outa the wet. We got a sick girl. You got a dry blanket we could use an' get her wet clothes off?"

The boy went back to the corner and brought a dirty comfort and held it out to Ma.

"Thank ya," she said. "What's the matter'th that fella?"

The boy spoke in a croaking monotone. "Fust he was sick—but now he's starvin'."

"What?"

"Starvin'. Got sick in the cotton. He ain't et for six days."

Ma walked to the corner and looked down at the man. He was about fifty, his whiskery face gaunt, and his open eyes were vague and staring. The boy stood beside her. "Your pa?" Ma asked.

"Yeah! Says he wasn' hungry, or he jus' et. Give me the food. Now he's too weak. Can't hardly move."

The pounding of the rain decreased to a soothing swish on the roof. The gaunt man moved his lips. Ma knelt beside him and put her ear close. His lips moved again.

"Sure," Ma said. "You jus' be easy. He'll be awright. You jus' wait'll I get them wet clo'es off'n my girl."

Ma went back to the girl. "Now slip 'em off," she said. She held the comfort up to screen her from view. And when she was naked, Ma folded the comfort about her.

The boy was at her side again explaining, "I didn' know. He said he et, or he wasn' hungry. Las' night I went an' bust a winda an' stoled some bread. Made 'im chew 'er down. But he puked it all up, an' then he was weaker. Got to have soup or milk. You folks got money to git milk?"

Ma said, "Hush. Don' worry. We'll figger somepin out."

Suddenly the boy cried, "He's dyin', I tell you! He's starvin' to death, I tell you."

"Hush," said Ma. She looked at Pa and Uncle John standing helplessly gazing at the sick man. She looked at Rose of Sharon huddled in the comfort. Ma's eyes passed Rose of Sharon's eyes, and then came back to them. And the two women looked deep into each other. The girl's breath came short and gasping.

She said "Yes."

Ma smiled. "I knowed you would. I knowed!" She looked down at her hands, tight-locked in her lap.

Rose of Sharon whispered, "Will—will you all—go out?" The rain whisked lightly on the roof.

Ma leaned forward and with her palm she brushed the tousled hair back from her daughter's forehead, and she kissed her on the forehead. Ma got up quickly. "Come on, you fellas," she called. "You come out in the tool shed."

Ruthie opened her mouth to speak. "Hush," Ma said. "Hush and git." She herded them through the door, drew the boy with her; and she closed the squeaking door.

For a minute Rose of Sharon sat still in the whispering barn. Then she hoisted her tired body up and drew the comfort about her. She moved slowly to the corner and stood looking down at the wasted face, into the wide, frightened eyes. Then slowly she lay down beside him. He shook his head slowly from side to side. Rose of Sharon loosened one side of the blanket and bared her breast. "You got to," she said. She squirmed closer and pulled his head close. "There!" she said. "There." Her hand moved behind his head and supported it. Her fingers moved gently in his hair. She looked up and across the barn, and her lips came together and smiled mysteriously.

II

The Social Context

Frank J. Taylor

Frank J. Taylor was a newspaperman on several West Coast papers and the San Francisco Bureau of the Associated Press. He was assistant manager of the New York Globe and manager of the Washington Bureau of the Scripps-Howard newspapers. After 1924, he devoted his time to writing books and doing articles for nationally known magazines. He died in 1972.

CALIFORNIA'S GRAPES OF WRATH

Californians are wrathy over *The Grapes of Wrath*, John Steinbeck's best-selling novel of migrant agricultural workers. Though the book is fiction, many readers accept it as fact.

By implication, it brands California farmers with unbelievable cruelty in their dealings with refugees from the "dust bowl." It charges that they deliberately lured a surplus of workers westward to depress wages, deputized peace officers to hound the migrants ever onward, burned the squatters' shacktowns, stomped down gardens and destroyed surplus foods in a conspiracy to force the refugees to work for starvation wages, allowed children to hunger and mothers to bear babies unattended in squalor. It implies that hatred of the migrants is fostered by the land barons who use the "Bank of the West" (obviously the Bank of America) and the "Farmers Association" (the Associated Farmers) to gobble up the lands of the small farmers and concentrate them in a few large holdings.

Originally published in *Forum* CII (November 1939), 232–38.

These are a few of the sins for which Steinbeck indicts California farmers. It is difficult to rebut fiction, which requires no proof, with facts, which do require proof.

The experiences of the Joad family, whose misfortunes in their trek from Oklahoma to California Steinbeck portrays so graphically, are not typical of those of the real migrants I found in the course of two reportorial tours of the agricultural valleys. I made one inquiry during the winter of 1937–38, following the flood which Steinbeck describes; I made another at the height of the harvest this year.

Along three thousand miles of highways and byways, I was unable to find a single counterpart of the Joad family. Nor have I discovered one during fifteen years of residence in the Santa Clara Valley (the same valley where John Steinbeck now lives), which is crowded each summer with transient workers harvesting the fruit crops. The lot of the "fruit tramp" is admittedly no bed of roses, but neither is it the bitter fate described in *The Grapes of Wrath*.

NO JOADS HERE

The Joad family of nine, created by Steinbeck to typify the "Okie" migrants, is anything but typical. A survey made for the Farm Security Administration revealed that thirty was the average age of migrant adults, that the average family had 2.8 children.

Steinbeck's Joads, once arrived in the "land of promise," earned so little that they faced slow starvation. Actually, no migrant family hungers in California unless it is too proud to accept relief. Few migrants are.

There is no red tape about getting free food or shelter.

The FSA maintains warehouses in eleven strategically located towns, where the grant officer is authorized to issue 15 days' rations to any migrant who applies, identifies himself by showing his driver's license, and answers a few simple questions about his family, his earnings, and his travels. In emergencies, the grant officer may issue money for clothing, gasoline, or medical supplies. The food includes standard brands of a score of staple products, flour, beans, corn meal, canned milk and tomatoes, dried fruit, and other grocery items. Before the 15 days are up, the grant officer or his assistant visits the migrant family in camp, and, if the need still exists, the ration is renewed repeatedly until the family finds work.

Shelter is provided by the FSA (a unit of the Federal Resettlement Administration) at model camps which Steinbeck himself represents as satisfactory. The one at Shafter is typical. A migrant family is assigned to a wooden platform on which a tent may be pitched; if the family lacks a tent, the camp has some to lend. The rent is a dime a day, and the migrant who wants to save the money can work it out by helping to clean up camp. The dime goes into a community benefit fund, administered by a committee. Camp facilities include toilets, showers and laundry tubs, with hot and cold running water, a community house. These thirteen camps cost around $190,000 apiece, and each accommodates some three hundred families. Last summer there were vacant platforms, though in winter there is a shortage of space.

Various relief organizations divide the responsibility of providing food and shelter for California's migrants. Federal authorities, working through the FSA, assume the burden for the first year. After a migrant family has been in the State a year, it becomes eligible for State relief. After three years, it becomes a county charge. State relief for agricultural workers averages $51 a month in California, as compared with $21 in Oklahoma, less for several neighboring States. The U.S. Farm Placement Service notes that WPA wages in California are $44 per month, in Oklahoma $32. California old-age pensions are $32 per month, Oklahoma's $20. These are U.S. Social Security Board figures. Records of the FSA grant offices indicate that many migrants earned under $200 a year back home—or less than one third the relief allowance in California. Thus thousands of Okies, having discovered this comparative bonanza, urge their kinsfolk to join them in California, where the average migrant family earns $400 during the harvest season and is able, after the first lean year, to draw an equal sum for relief during eight months of enforced idleness.

WAGES, HEALTH CONDITIONS

The advantages of life in California for migrant workers are not limited to the salubrious climate and largess.

When the harvest is on, the base wage for agricultural workers on California farms is $2.10 per day with board, as compared to $1.00 in Oklahoma, $1.35 in Texas, and 65 cents in Arkansas. These figures are from the U.S. Bureau of Agricultural Economics. Cotton pickers in California's San Joaquin Valley are paid 90 cents per 100 pounds.

In Oklahoma, the pay is 65 cents a hundred, in Arkansas and Texas 60 cents, California has 180 separate crops to harvest, and some crop is ripening somewhere in the State every month of the year. A fortunate migrant may work eight to ten months each year. Back home he was lucky to work three months.

Another advantage of life in California is the free medical service. Few of the migrants had ever seen the inside of a hospital or employed a doctor, dentist, or nurse before they came to California. Each FSA camp has a full-time nurse and a part-time doctor to serve the migrant families without charge. Medical supplies, too, are free.

At the Shafter camp, I asked how many babies had been born in camp this year.

"None," the manager replied. "The mothers all go to Kern General Hospital."

At the hospital, supported by Kern County, I learned that, of 727 children born to migrant mothers in the County during the first 5 months of this year, 544 were delivered in the hospital, without charge. In fact, under State law, no general hospital may refuse a mother in labor. Yet in the Steinbeck book a camp manager is obliged to act as midwife.

It is a fortunate break, not only for the migrants but for the Californians as well, that the incoming streams of dilapidated "jalopies," piled high with beds and utensils, converge at Bakersfield, seat of Kern County. As large as Massachusetts (and wealthy, thanks to oil), Kern County maintains a remarkable health service under the direction of Dr. Joe Smith, who believes that an ill person is a menace to others and that it is the County's duty to make him well. Dr. Smith's eighteen nurses, each with a car, spend most of their time in schools and labor camps, checking the health and diet of children. Any migrant family needing medical service can have it free at Kern General, and some with contagious diseases receive it against their will.

Kern County, strategically located, is California's front-line defense against epidemics. Few migrant families manage to cross the huge area without at least one examination. Other counties to the north likewise employ nurses to visit the migrant camps, but they are not as selfishly altruistic as is Kern. Though resisting the nurses' attentions at first, the migrants are now eager for them.

One of the accusations in the Steinbeck novel is that State and County peace officers hound the migrants from camp to camp, to push them into strikebreaking jobs. But inquiry reveals that officers invade camps only when appealed to by health officials.

The health officer of Madera County found a group of migrants camped atop a huge manure pile. "It's warmer here," they protested, when he ordered them to move. Only when he invoked police authority would they budge.

One health deputy discovered a case of smallpox in a camp. Telling the family to stay indoors, he hurried to town for vaccine. When he came back, the entire camp had evaporated into the night, and, before all the exposed migrants could be traced and rounded up into isolation camps, health officers of the neighboring counties had to cope with over six hundred cases of smallpox.

Investigating a typhus outbreak, a health officer found that several families had chopped holes in their cabin floors for toilets, without digging pits. In Santa Clara County, migrants were found camping around a polluted well. One of them explained, "The folks that was here before us used it," and they stayed on until deputy sheriffs removed them forcibly.

Outside nearly every agricultural community, from El Centro on the Mexican border to Redding near the Oregon line, is a shantytown or squatter camp. These are frightful places in which to live, devoid of adequate sanitation, often without pure water. Local authorities can do little about these rural slums, because they are outside city limits.

The most unsanitary squatter camp was that in the river bottom just north of Bakersfield, where squatters had made themselves at home on property of the Kern County Land Company, one of the State's major land "barons." The land company offered no objection to the squatter camp, but the citizens of Bakersfield did when the migrants' children came over the line to school and epidemics of flu, skin diseases, chicken pox, and other ailments depleted the classrooms. There were threats of vigilante action from irate parents, but what happened was quite different. Deputies from the County health office surveyed the camp, discovered that most of the occupants were employed and could afford to rent homes, that some of them had been there seven years. After six months of patient persuasion, all but twenty-six families were induced to move to town. When the twenty-six refused to budge, the health officer had their flimsy shacks moved to higher ground. They are still there. The vacated shacks were pushed into a pile and burned by order of the health department. That is the prosaic story behind the lurid burning of Bakersfield's "Hooverville," as dramatized in *The Grapes of Wrath* (280).

THE GREAT MIGRATION

The great flood of the winter of 1937–38, with which Steinbeck drowned the last hopes of the Joad family, hit the migrants hardest in Madera County, where thousands of them worked in the cotton fields. Near Firebaugh, the San Joaquin River rose in its rampage to wash out eight hundred campers. It was after dark one Saturday night when a deputy sheriff reported the plight of these unfortunates to Dr. Lee A. Stone, the wiry old health officer, an ex-Southerner formerly on the staff of the U.S. Public Health Service. Dr. Stone mobilized all the trucks and cars he could find, hurried to the scene, moved the eight hundred refugees thirty miles through the blinding rain to the little city of Madera, and sheltered them in the schools. Then he raised funds by phone for temporary quarters.

Discovering that most of his unexpected guests had but recently come to California, he hit on the idea of returning them to their kinsfolk in Oklahoma, Arkansas, and Texas. When he had raised the necessary funds to buy railroad tickets, he hurried over with the news.

They listened in stony silence.

Finally, one of the men spoke up. "Thanks, Doc," he drawled. "Here we be and here we stay and we ain't a gonna leave the promised land."

"No sirree, we ain't a gonna leave California," chorused the rest. And they didn't.

Almost all the counties in the San Joaquin and Sacramento Valleys have standing offers of free transportation back home for any migrant family. Not one family in a hundred has accepted.

No one knows how many migrants have poured into California since the last census was taken, because the count was not started until 1935, when the State Department of Agriculture instructed the plant-quarantine inspectors at the border to check and report incoming farm workers. To date, 285,000 of them have been reported, but the count is incomplete because many thousands have ridden in on freight trains.

The migrants' trek dates back to 1925, when cotton first became a major crop in California. Some authorities think that almost a hundred thousand families have moved into the State, mostly from the dust-bowl area. This would mean half a million individuals, a migration exceeding the gold rush of pioneer days. Others who have studied the trek of the Okies—so called because forty-two out of every hundred migrants come from Oklahoma—place the figure at three hundred thousand.

In either case, it is a tremendous lump of impoverished population for the people of the Great Interior Valley to assimilate. It is as if the entire population of Cincinnati were to visit Cleveland and, once there, decide to remain indefinitely as star boarders. And it has taken the combined resources of the State, the counties, the federal government, and the individual farmers to meet the emergency. Madera County, for instance, which had 15,000 residents when the invasion started, now has double that population; and most of the newcomers are public charges part of each year. Kern County has a population of 130,000 persons, of whom 35,000 are on relief. The County hospital budget has increased from $100,000 in 1926 to the present figure of $970,000, all of which except some $8,000, contributed by the federal government for the aid of crippled children, is paid by Kern's taxpayers.

CALIFORNIA'S SPECIAL PROBLEM

Owing to the peculiarities of agriculture in the Far West, the farmers of California are as hopelessly dependent on the migrant workers as the migrants are dependent on the farmers for jobs. For California agriculture differs from farming elsewhere in several ways.

Most California crops are so extremely perishable that they must be harvested on the day of ripening—not a day earlier or a day later. This is true of fresh fruits, such as peaches, apricots, and pears, which must be picked, packed, iced, and shipped to the hour. It is true also of field crops like lettuce, tomatoes, melons. Asparagus is actually harvested twice a day. Timely and uninterrupted handling of these perishables means the difference between a $300,000,000 yearly income and a multimillion expense for intensive planting, cultivating, irrigating, spraying, thinning, and harvesting. Most of the California farmers' customers live two to three thousand miles distant, beyond two mountain ranges, and it costs as much to deliver the foodstuffs to them in good condition as it does to battle the perennial droughts, the insects, the vagaries of soil and atmosphere in the struggle to grow the crops. Including nonperishables, the annual take from the soil totals around $600,000,000 and is the State's main livelihood.

Another peculiarity of California agriculture is the manner in which it is broken up into "deals," to use the local term for crops. There are about 180 deals in all, and they, too, are often migrant. The lettuce deal begins in midwinter in Imperial Valley, near the Mexican border; it migrates first to Arizona, then to the Salinas Valley, which from April to November is the country's salad bowl. Melon, tomato, spinach, fresh-pea deals likewise follow the sun north each spring and summer. Navel oranges ripen in midwinter south of the Tehachapi range, Valencias in midsummer north of these mountains. The peach deal trails the apricot deal; then comes the prune deal, the grape deal, and finally cotton.

California is a long, slender State, broken up into a score of agricultural "islands." In the San Diego island, the growers concentrate on avocados and bulbs. The Santa Clara Valley is the prune and apricot island. The Sacramento Valley produces nine tenths of the country's canned peaches. There are three grape islands, two lettuce islands, an asparagus island behind the dikes of the delta country— a sort of little Netherlands. There is a cotton belt in the San Joaquin Valley. In all these highly specialized, intensively cultivated regions, harvest time comes with a vengeance.

For generations, transient workers have appeared by the thousands at harvest time.

The Mexicans pitched their tents in orchards or made camp in rude summertime shelters. They picked the fruit, collected their wages, and faded over the horizon to the next crop. They were good workers, with an instinctive touch for ripening fruit and melons, and better help than the Orientals who preceded them. In 1934, the migrations of these Mexican workers ended abruptly, as their new agrarian government back home offered each returning family a slice of a confiscated estate.

The exodus of the Mexicans coincided with the influx of dust-bowl refugees. For a time, the Okies were the answer to the farmers' prayers. They still are, for that matter, except that there are now too many of them for the available jobs and they have brought with them serious social problems.

Three years ago the University of California assigned Dr. R. L. Adams, Professor of Agricultural Economics, to survey the State's farm-labor requirements. Dr. Adams says the crops require 144,700 workers in the peak months, over and above the year-round hired hands. By midwinter this demand has fallen off to 59,000. In May, it is back to a hundred thousand; in August it is 134,000. Thus there are at times nearly 86,000 more workers than jobs, even if there is no labor surplus. Today there is a surplus of fifty to seventy thousand workers, even at the harvest peak. Early this year the influx was tapering off, but in June 1,600 more agricultural workers were at the border than in June a year earlier.

HOUSING: A STUMBLING BLOCK

Unlike the Mexicans, the Okies do not disappear over the horizon at the end of each harvest. They linger on in the flimsy shelters intended only for the rainless California summer. When rains come, in the fall, the camp sites are seas of mud; rubbish and filth accumulate; and the farmers are taken to task for the facilities provided for their unwelcome guests. Hence the migrant-worker problem is essentially a housing problem.

The FSA has sought a solution in low-price cottages, costing $1,000 to $1,500 per unit and renting for $8.20 per month, including heat, light, and water. Each is surrounded by a half-acre of land for a garden. These cottages are snapped up as soon as they are completed, but there are not enough of them, and they are usable only for workers who have ceased to be migrants. FSA has another answer, a portable motorized camp—platforms, Diesel-powered electric plant, laundry tubs and showers—so designed that it may be loaded on trucks and shifted with the crops and the demand for harvest hands. First tried out this summer, it may be the migrant camp of the future.

The farmers, who have added ten thousand cabins to the shelters provided for migrant workers in the last three years, look askance at the FSA camps. Because of the perishable nature of their crops, California farmers live in terror of strikes. The federal camps are feared as hotbeds of radical activities, a fear that dates back to 1931, when communists undertook to organize the fruit workers and dispatched squads of agitators to drag workers from their ladders and intimidate their families. I found no evidence to justify this alarm.

The Okies I talked with were oblivious to class struggle; all they asked was more work.

On many of the larger farms, such as the Tagus, the Hoover, the DiGiorgio ranches, the owners provide housing as good as FSA demonstration communities and for less.

On the Tagus Ranch, H. C. Merritt offers two hundred permanent families neat little cottages for $3.00 to $5.00 per month, including a plot of ground for a garden. Some of the first white migrants chopped up the partitions between the rooms and used them for firewood, although free wood was provided for the chopping. When he protested, the Okies explained they preferred to live in one-room houses. Now Tagus families are graduated from one-room to three-room houses as they qualify for them.

Mr. Merritt's attitude toward federal camps is typical. "If my workmen live on the ranch and I tell them to be on hand at eight in the morning to pick peaches, they're on hand," he said. "If they're in a federal camp, I don't know whether they'll be here or not. While I'm looking for other pickers, the peaches drop on the ground, and a year's work is gone."

STUBBORN INDIVIDUALISTS

An inference of *The Grapes of Wrath* is that most of the California farmlands are in great holdings, operated by corporations or land "barons." The State has 6,732,390 acres devoted to crops, and the 1935 census shows that 1,738,906 are in farms less than 100 acres in extent, 3,068,742 are in farms of 100 to 1,000 acres, and 1,924,742 are in farms of over 1,000.

An insinuation of *The Grapes of Wrath* is that wages are forced down by the Associated Farmers and the Bank of America, acting in conspiracy. Actually, neither the Association nor the Bank concerns itself with wages. Rates of pay are worked out through the farmer co-operatives in each crop or through local groups, such as the San Joaquin Regional Council, which agrees each spring on a base wage. California farmers pay higher wages than those of any State but Connecticut, according to the U.S. Farm Placement Bureau.

This same federal organization conducted an inquiry into the charge, aired in *The Grapes of Wrath*, that California farmers had distributed handbills through the dust-bowl area, offering jobs to lure a surplus of migrant labor to the State. Only two cases were unearthed, one by a labor contractor in Santa Barbara County, another by an Imperial Valley contractor. The licenses of both have since been revoked. At the Associated Farmers head office in San Francisco, I saw hundreds of clippings from Midwest newspapers—publicity inspired by the Association—advising migrants *not* to come to California.

The problem of connecting migrant workers who want jobs with farmers who need help is serious. A rumor will sweep like wildfire through migrant camps, of jobs in some valley hundreds of miles distant. Two days later that valley is swamped with so many workers that the harvest which ordinarily would last a month is finished in a week. The U.S. Department of Labor, working with the State Employment Office, now maintains job-information services in eighty-one towns and cities. At any of these offices, migrant workers may check on job prospects in any other area. But most workers still prefer to take a chance.

California's big question—what is going to happen to these people—is still unanswered.

East of Visalia, the FSA is attempting an experiment in cooperative farming. On the 530-acre Mineral King ranch, purchased with federal funds, twenty above-average migrant families were set to work raising cotton, alfalfa, and poultry and running a dairy. At the end of the first year, the farm showed a profit of $900 per family, more than twice the average family's earning from following the crops.

At Casa Grande, Arizona, the FSA has another co-operative farm, of 4,000 acres, with sixty families working it.

Co-operative farms, directed by trained men from universities, produce good crops and good livings; but the Okies are rugged individualists. "I'm not going to have any damn government telling me what I'm going to plant," exploded one of the Mineral King farmers, as he packed his family in the car and took to the road again. And so, in spite of the good intentions of the Farm Security Administration, the Governor's Committee on Unemployment, the Simon J. Lubin Society, the John Steinbeck Committee, and other organizations, the highly individualistic newcomers probably will work out their own destiny in their own way.

For a glimpse of how they may do it, visit Salinas, in the lettuce island, which saw its first invasion eight years ago. The first Okies in the area squatted in squalor outside the town until an enterprising wheat farmer divided his ranch into half-acre lots, which he offered at $250 apiece, $5.00 down, $5.00 a month. The Okies snapped them up and strutted around, proud of their property ownership. Today, in Little Oklahoma City, as the community is called, one can envisage the whole process of assimilation—the ancient trailer resting on its axles, a lean-to or tent alongside it, in the front a wooden shack and, sometimes, a vine-covered cottage. Off to the south, some of the Okies are living in neat little three- to five-room cottages. The Okies of Little Oklahoma City are fortunate. They muscled into the lettuce-packing game and now have virtually a monopoly around Salinas, earning from 50 to 60 cents an hour for eight or nine months of the year. In that one community, three thousand migrants have achieved a respectable standard of living. Their children are intermarrying with the natives. Outwardly, they are Californians.

What they have done can be done by others. Their accomplishment is a challenge to shiftless Okies and an answer to the broad accusations hurled so heedlessly in *The Grapes of Wrath*.

Carey McWilliams

Carey McWilliams practiced law, served as Commissioner of Immigration and Housing for the state of California, and was for twenty years the editor of The Nation. *In addition to writing such in-depth investigations of American socioeconomic issues as* Factories in the Field, Ill Fares the Land, Brethren Under the Skin, *and* Witchhunt: The Revival of Heresy, *he also wrote numerous books on California, a biography of Ambrose Bierce, and an autobiography. He died in 1980.*

CALIFORNIA PASTORAL

On December 6, 1939, the LaFollette Committee hearings opened in San Francisco in an atmosphere of tension, defiance, and considerable truculence. No sooner had Senator LaFollette announced that the committee was in session than Phil Bancroft, Associated Farmers leader, arose and demanded that the Senator cease "giving aid and comfort to the Communists," and that he return to Wisconsin and mind his own business. During the first week that the committee was in session, the Associated Farmers held their annual convention at Stockton, with over 2,000 members in attendance. Open defiance of the committee was voiced throughout the convention. John Steinbeck was warmly denounced as the arch-enemy, defamer, and slanderer of migratory farm labor in California, while I was tenderly referred to as "Agricultural Pest No. 1 in California, outranking pear blight and boll weevil."

Reprinted from *Antioch Review* II (March 1942), 103–21.

The impact of the "dust bowl" migration upon the rural economy of California was graphically outlined in an opening statement to the committee prepared by Henry H. Fowler, its chief counsel. Between January 1, 1933, and June 1, 1939—the years of greatest migration to California—approximately 180 agricultural strikes had occurred in the state. Strikes had taken place in 34 out of the 58 counties of California—in every important agricultural county and in connection with every major crop. The national significance of these strikes can perhaps best be appraised in light of the realization that California produces about 40 per cent of the fruits and vegetables consumed in the United States.

In concluding his statement, Mr. Fowler pointed out that "California agriculture has and is suffering from employer-employee strife far out of proportion to the number of workers employed in comparison with the remainder of the country." Comparative figures amply justify this conclusion. Normally employing only 4.4 per cent of the nation's agricultural workers, California has been the scene of from 34.3 to 100 per cent of the annual strikes among agricultural workers. The importance of the strikes themselves can be variously illustrated. Approximately 89,276 workers were involved in 113 out of the total of 180 strikes recorded during this period. Civil and criminal disturbances occurred in connection with 65 out of 180 strikes; arrests of one type or another were reported in 39 strikes; property damage occurred in 11; evictions and deportations were noted in 15. The year 1937, which marked the height of the dust-bowl migration, was also the year during which 14 so-called "violent" strikes occurred. During their first years in California, the Joads did not contribute notably to the tranquility of the state. As bearing on the favorite question of whether *The Grapes of Wrath* accurately described conditions in California, I have selected three typical "incidents" investigated by the LaFollette Committee. The facts are, in each case, all recorded in the transcript of the hearing. These vignettes of "rural life in California," in the years from 1933 to 1939, tell the story of the reception accorded Tom Joad and his fellow migrants in California. The Associated Farmers of California are still smarting from the inconsiderate manner in which the LaFollette Committee came along in 1939 and verified the general picture of conditions in the state as set forth in *The Grapes of Wrath* and *Factories in the Field*. Let the record, then, speak for itself.

THE OKIES PICK 'COTS

Yolo and Solano counties lie in the Sacramento Valley, in northern California. There are no large towns or population centers in either county. For years migrants have trooped into the area each season to work in the apricot orchards around Winters—a small stream of migrants in April to thin the groves, a river of migrants for the harvest period which begins in July and lasts for about thirty days. Not only is the picking season short, but the 'cots are a precarious crop. In the morning they are likely to be "a bit on the green tinge," but by afternoon or the next morning they may be too ripe to pick. For the shippers and canners are fastidious, and with a market pretty thoroughly controlled, they can deal with the growers in an arbitrary and high-handed manner. If the market happens to be glutted, they simply refuse to receive any more apricots that day and the crop rots in the field.

In the early summer of 1937, about 3,500 or 4,000 migrants, most of them recent recruits from the dust bowl, were camped in the Winters district. Some of them had moved into the growers' camps; others were camped along the highways; a large group were huddled together in a squatter camp. Most of them were living in roadside camps with a "good many people sleeping out on the roads." One large grower had occasion to visit the major migrant camp in the community. "Conditions," he testified, "were awful. There were many families there. There were broken-down cars and there were pieces of tents, and they were going to march on the town." Robert Blum, a reporter for the Oakland *Tribune*, also visited the camp. "I wouldn't want to live there myself," was his comment. Everyone agreed that there was a surplus of workers in the area; perhaps 200 or 250 more families had moved in than could possibly hope to find employment.

"Trouble," had been anticipated. The growers had been "tipped off" that Henry Wells and Donald Bingham, organizers for Local 20241, Agricultural Workers Union, affiliated at that time with the American Federation of Labor, were about to invade the district. Before any union demands were presented, however, the machinery had been set in motion "to control the situation." In the month of June, 1937, 47 persons were sworn in as deputy sheriffs in Yolo County and 27 of these were deputized on June 7—weeks before the strike occurred. In Solano County twelve deputies were sworn in, making an emergency force, for the two counties, of 59 men. The funds to pay for the salaries and supplies of this improvised force naturally came from the general funds of the two counties. Units of the Associated Farmers had existed in both counties since 1934; but because of the fact that the apricot district overlapped their boundaries, an emergency organization, known as the Yosolano Associated Farmers, was formed.

On June 21, 1937 the growers of the district met in the American Legion hall, in Winters, to fix the rate for picking. The practice of joint action among growers on wage rates is, of course, quite common throughout California. At this meeting a union organizer appeared and presented the demands of the workers: 40 cents an hour; union recognition; job stewards; and yearly vacations for permanent employees. It must be remembered that 4,000 people had moved into the district for the season. No one knows from what distances they had traveled; some of them, however, had driven 400 or 500 miles. These workers had not only paid their own transportation expenses but, as usually happens, they had arrived some weeks in advance of the season. Nor were they to be blamed for having anticipated the season, for no one can tell in advance the precise day or week when the 'cots will be ripe. After traveling considerable distances and waiting days and even weeks for the season to start, these workers could anticipate about three weeks employment. Naturally they wanted to make as much as they could during this brief period.

The demand for a nickel an hour increase was denied and the rate for the season was fixed at 35 cents an hour. The demand, according to the union organizer, was "turned down flat." Out of 4,000 workers, the union had a paid-up membership of about 500, a total membership of perhaps a thousand. For a few days prior to June 22, the union had been holding meetings on the property of Mr. John Storland, a small grower. Typical of many small growers in California, Mr. Storland was inclined to sympathize with the workers; he even had the quaint notion that they had a right to hold public meetings. To make possible the exercise of this right, he had donated a corner of his property for union meetings. But his fellow-growers in the community did not agree with Mr. Storland. They sent two delegations to interview him. On the first visit, they protested gently but firmly against the use of his property for strike meetings; on their second call, they protested "more forcibly, more vigorously," and informed Mr. Storland that he would have "to take the consequences" if further meetings were permitted.

On June 22, 1937, the strike started. Picket lines were established at one or two of the orchards and the appearance of these pickets was the signal for the Associated Farmer machine to swing into action. On that day a total of 16 strikers were arrested. Those who were arrested were told that the action against them would be dismissed if they would agree "to leave this locality for at least a distance of twenty miles" and not return. A large delegation of fruit growers then called upon the Board of Supervisors of Solano County and demanded action. The chairman of the Board was, as might be expected, an officer and director of the Associated Farmers of Solano County. The growers got instant and double-barrelled action: first, an emergency anti-camping ordinance was adopted; and second, an apricot patrol of deputy sheriffs was created. Prior to the time the patrol was established and on the day when the first special deputies were sworn in, the Board of Supervisors of Yolo County had adopted an interesting resolution:

> Whereas, the County of Yolo has already exceeded the amount budgeted for relief of employable and unemployable indigents; therefore be it,
> Resolved: That from this date no relief will be given unemployed employables or transient indigents in the county.

The suspension and cessation of relief during the apricot picking season was designed, of course, to insure acceptance of the wage rate previously established by the growers. Taking advantage of the ordinance against public camping, the sheriff, accompanied by his hastily recruited army of deputies, moved on the migrant camp and told the workers that "they would have to get out—it was the order of the Board." And move they did, in all directions. In many instances the county had to provide gasoline, out of public funds, to enable the stranded migrants "to move on."

In the meantime, general headquarters had been established in the city hall at Winters. No one seems to have raised any question or to have even considered the propriety of using public property for a strike-breaking center. Not only was the apricot patrol policing the orchards during all this time, but martial law, in effect, had been decreed throughout the area. Let Mr. Blum, a reporter for the Oakland *Tribune*, describe what he observed:

> Throughout the morning of the 23d, groups of special deputies—that is, nonuniformed deputies—were patrolling the town of Winters, the main street and adjacent streets and along the railroad tracks, in groups of two or three; questioning persons whom they might have encountered along the sidewalks or walking along the roadways, and I was close to several of these groups. They would stop these people and ask them what they were doing, and if they were looking for work. If they said they were looking for work, they would walk back with them to the City Hall, where this employment committee or employment headquarters was located. If they said they weren't looking for work or could not explain their presence in town satisfactorily, they were told that if they did not leave town or accept work they would be faced with being jailed.

Mr. L. M. Ireland, an insurance salesman, was one of the special deputy sheriffs. "At that time," said Mr. Ireland, "the fruit was just about ready to fall on the ground, and we knew—I had lived in Winters all my life—and I knew that if this fruit did fall on the ground it wasn't going to hurt the farmers but the whole business community as well." So Mr. Ireland, insurance salesman, joined up with the vigilantes. One morning while he was acting as a deputy, a farmer came to town and asked help in getting some pickers. Mr. Ireland and another deputy got busy at once. They interviewed several stragglers on Main Street and marched them off to G.H.Q. and then called at the home of a prospective worker. Asked if he wanted to work, he answered: "Who the hell's business is it?" For this unforgivable piece of *lèse majesté*, he was promptly placed under arrest and taken to the calaboose. Mr. Ireland thought that the whole affair had been handled with remarkable decorum and propriety, since the sheriff had cautioned the deputies "to be exceptionally careful about hurting any person or trying not to make anybody peeved."

While the strike was in progress, Mr. John T. Dudley, secretary of the Industrial Union Council of Sacramento, was asked to visit Winters, observe conditions, and report back to the Council. By the time Mr. Dudley arrived on the scene, the strike was virtually at an end and the migrants were being evicted from their camp. Realizing that there was nothing much to be accomplished in Winters, Mr. Dudley and his committee started to return to Sacramento. But as they were leaving, the sheriff and his posse picked them up and took them to the courthouse. A crowd of three or four hundred people quickly gathered, and stared through the windows into the room where the sheriff was quizzing Mr. Dudley. Members of the mob, at the open windows and the doors, swung ropes about and shouted: "Bring 'em out! We'll tar and feather them! Let's get them out and hang them!" When Mr. Dudley asked permission to use the telephone, "some big heavy-set fellow with a deputy sheriff's badge yelled very loudly: 'Don't let that bastard use the phone!' " The sheriff refused to accord the party a safe escort out of the county and decided to lock them up in jail overnight. Fearing a possible suit for false arrest, he managed the next morning to browbeat Mr. Dudley into pleading guilty to a charge of vagrancy and then released him. I would merely emphasize that this little episode occurred in the county courthouse, in the presence of the sheriff and of the chairman of the Board of Supervisors.

The strike was broken; the migrants were scattered; the 'cots were picked. But the victory had to be officially reported, solemnly memorialized, and formally chronicled. The scene of the victory rites was the annual meeting of the Associated Farmers of California, December 6, 1937, at which the president of the Yolo County unit, praising the action in the 'cots, said that "the strength of any army depends upon what happens under fire. Yolo County unit proved itself this year during the apricot strike at Winters." *Business Week*, in its issue of July 17, 1937, neatly summed up the situation as follows:

Yolo County has an ordinance which forbids picketing. Solano County hurriedly enacted an ordinance forbidding itinerant pickers to camp on public property, for reasons of public health. Since the only camp ground available is on the property of the farmers, unemployed pickers could only move on. And the deputy sheriffs saw to it that they did just that, even providing enough gasoline, in some cases, to take them out of the two counties. The strike faded, the apricots were picked, and the farmers were delighted to have found an effective method to break strikes.

Tom Joad had had his first taste of industrialized agriculture; glorious Yosolano had triumphed over 4,000 destitute pickers; peace was restored.

Despite its usual acumen, *Business Week* neglected to praise one aspect of this action—its cheapness. Through the good work of the staff of the LaFollette Committee, it is possible to set forth an accounting:

Expended by the City of Winters for telephone calls, meals for special officers, and "sundries"	\$ 135.10
Expended by the County of Yolo for special deputies during the scrimmage	667.48
Expended by the County of Solano for the same purpose	1,187.25
Expended by the County of Solano for gas and oil used as part of the technique to evict migrants	46.26
Total	\$2,036.09

In addition to the public funds spent in breaking this strike, the growers themselves contributed a niggardly pittance of \$185.36; otherwise the entire cost of the action fell upon the general taxpayers of the community. But if the nickel an hour increase had been granted, it would have cost the growers, for the season, about \$66,600. The saving was, therefore, substantial; the community itself had been taxed to support the vigilantism of the Associated Farmers. It will also be noted that the scrimmage itself was not at all unlike a somewhat similar episode described in *The Grapes of Wrath*.

STORM TROOPERS IN STANISLAUS

The principal town in Stanislaus County, in the San Joaquin Valley, is Modesto. It is a pleasant little place with urban pretensions. There are nice homes on well-shaded streets; a junior college; a highly developed civic life. There are good stores; good hotels; a good newspaper. There are six important canneries, any number of dry-yards, and an airport in Modesto. Okies and Arkies began to drift into the community around 1933 and 1934, but they found it difficult to settle in the town itself. So they moved out near the airport and attempted to shift for themselves. There a large land company subdivided a tract of land near the airport and sold tiny lots to migrants. Soon there were two thriving communities: Little Oklahoma on one side of a canal bank, and Little Arkansas on the other. The two settlements today constitute a good-sized community. But the migrants are not a part of Modesto; they even have their own shopping center. Visiting Little Oklahoma one can see the migrant settlement pattern in its several phases: first the tent or trailer parked on a lot; then a lean-to or shack on the rear of the lot (later to be used as a garage); and finally the little one- or two-room frame shack built by the occupants. Here the "folks" have settled. On some of the streets in Little Oklahoma all the residents are from the same county or small town in Oklahoma. The settlement is something of a mess but the inhabitants have done their best to make it a decent community and to invest it with even a few of the airs of a typical California town.

Here, in Little Oklahoma, lives my friend, Mrs. Lawler—a kind, hospitable, friendly woman. Her husband used to be a farmer, and later an oil worker in Oklahoma. The Lawlers have three children, a boy and a girl and an older daughter now happily married to a "Californian." The first year they were in Little Oklahoma, the daughter was returning home from school one afternoon when a neighbor boy, passing her on a bicycle, shouted: "Get out of the way, you damned Okie!" This made the girl feel "right bad." For the boy was himself an Okie, only he had lived in California for several years and this made him a kind of Californian—a native son by adoption. Mrs. Lawler, like most of the women in Little Oklahoma, works in the canneries at night. Standing at the vats or bins during the warm humid mid-summer nights, it gets pretty suffocating. The atmosphere is thick and soggy; the foreladies keep pushing the help hard. But once the Lawlers had a break. A movie company on location near Modesto needed some extras for the filming of Dodge City. Mr. and Mrs. Lawler and some of their neighbors got bit-parts in the picture. If you have seen the picture, you will remember Mrs. Lawler. She is the woman who stands at the street corner and, as the herd of wild steers comes stampeding through the town, rushes out in front of the herd, picks up a youngster, and dashes to cover. "Not a bit afraid of cattle," she was so cool and daring in the picture that she gave the cameraman the thrill of his life. For she waited until the very last second before making her famous dash to save the child. It was the big moment in the picture and Mrs. Lawler made $50 out of her brief but endlessly exciting career as an actress. When the picture was shown in Modesto, Mrs. Lawler and her neighbors were there to see it; they were also present when *The Grapes of Wrath* was shown. Mrs. Lawler liked it almost as much as *Dodge City*, only "the little hurts are the worst and I could have told them so much about that."

Most of the families in Little Oklahoma and Little Arkansas are on relief, or working on WPA projects, part of the year. There just isn't enough work. You can't make a living in the canneries and it is "a killing and back-breaking" job anyway.

I have other friends in Modesto but I had better not mention their names. They are the kind of people who want to see you at night, "but not downtown." They are always eager to tell what they know; what they have observed; to furnish names and dates. They are as furtive as Negroes in the Deep South. They will talk above a whisper, but they don't want to be quoted. They are teachers, and lawyers, and housewives, and janitors, and clerks. If any of them were to say publicly what they have told me in private, they would have to leave Modesto. They all remember the excitement when Fred Hogue, of the Associated Farmers, organized a private army. Senator LaFollette and Senator Thomas heard about this episode and were truly amazed. I mentioned it during the course of a Town Meeting of the Air broadcast in March, 1940, but not many people would believe that such an episode had occurred.

The Associated Farmers had organized in Stanislaus County in 1936. Most of the money for the organization had come from the banks, hotels, oil companies, farm implement houses, and the canneries. There had been a riot of cannery workers in Stockton during 1937 and Stockton is only thirty miles or so from Modesto. The Associated Farmers were afraid that the Okie women might decide to join the union. So they decided to stage a "mobilization." Three thousand people assembled in the football stadium at the junior college and at the conclusion of the meeting rose and repeated the following pledge: "We pledge ourselves for law and order and the right to work." The speakers at the meeting included the sheriff, the city attorney, an official of the Associated Farmers, the president of the Retail Merchants Association, the president of the Chamber of Commerce, the president of one of the canneries, and representing "the farmers," Roy Pike, manager of the El Solyo Ranch—one of the largest farm-factories in California. But no one spoke on behalf of labor; no one spoke on behalf of the Okies, although the meeting was being held for their benefit. The meeting was quite successful for, as Mr. Pike observed, "the hangers-on around several of the canneries in Modesto, who have been present for over a week in relation to the threatened strike, were absent the next morning." The leading citizens had mobilized; the little people were put in their place.

Senator Thomas questioned Mr. Hogue about this meeting and also about the plans for a citizens' army which had been prepared by the Associated Farmers. The Associated Farmers were to raise an army of 600 men; the business interests in Modesto were to raise and to drill a similar force. Both groups were organized in such a way that they could be mobilized on two hours' notice. The "third order of business" in the Manual of Instructions was as follows:

> Organize Drill Squads and arrange to meet with them twice a week for at least three weeks until all hands become accustomed to the things expected of them because of their volunteering for and undertaking the important responsibility of their enrollment as Special Deputies under the Sheriff of Stanislaus County.

Another portion of the Manual stated:

> Each Captain in charge of four Sergeants; each Sergeant in charge of four Corporals; and each Corporal in charge of four Privates.

Here is Senator Thomas' comment, at the conclusion of this part of the investigation:

> Mr. Hogue, I have never seen a military organization put down on paper any more definitely than that plan which you have provided here.

In reporting on the work of the Associated Farmers of Stanislaus County, at the annual convention on December 6, 1937, Mr. Hogue was quoted as follows:

The Associated Farmers have 700 contributing members in the county and their assessment to the State organization has been paid. No labor difficulties. Approximately 6,000 cannery workers are employed in the county and the canneries are run on the "open-shop" basis. Due to the work of the Associated Farmers, labor organizers coming in were unable to make headway.

The officials of the Associated Farmers testified before Senator LaFollette that this army of 1,200 men had never actually been drilled. My Modesto friends, who were in a position to know the facts, later told me that the armies—the businessmen's unit and the "farmer" unit—drilled for several weeks at the junior college.

THE JOADS ON STRIKE

Madera is one of the principal "cotton counties" in the San Joaquin Valley. Although California produces only about 3 per cent of the cotton grown in the United States, the crop is one of the most profitable products raised in the state. California cotton growers, in 1938, received about $23,476,000, with some $3,350,000 additional in the form of A.A.A. benefit payments. Cotton in California is an irrigated crop: its yields are about three times as great as the national average yield per acre. Cotton can be grown in California for less cost per pound than elsewhere in the United States and commands a somewhat better price by reason of its long fibre quality. A hundred pounds of seed cotton in California contain more lint than the same amount of cotton grown elsewhere. Most of the cotton grown in the state used to be shipped to Japan. Despite the obvious advantages which cotton growers in California enjoy over those in other areas, they receive the same Triple A subsidies. As a consequence, cotton is a "racket" crop in California; it is grown for the Triple A payments. In 1938, $3,356,361 in Triple A payments were divided among 8,700 cotton growers in the state. Of these cotton growers, 204 members of the Associated Farmers received $1,107,544.72. To state it another way, 2.34 per cent of the cotton growers received 33 per cent of the total benefit payments. The people in the San Joaquin Valley will tell you that cotton is the curse of the valley. It exhausts the soil, makes for an unbalanced farm economy, and breeds poverty. But it is a highly profitable crop for a few hundred growers.

It takes 35,000 workers to pick the cotton crop in California. There are few single men or single women in the fields; large families are always preferred. The beginning of the dust-bowl migration to California can be traced back to the early '20s when cotton became an important crop. As long as cotton has been grown in the state, families have come west each fall from Oklahoma, Texas, and Arkansas to work in the fields. The cotton growers, however, preceded the cotton pickers, from the South to California. Many former Texas, Georgia, and Mississippi growers moved west to California when it was discovered that cotton could be grown there with such marked advantages. Once re-established in California, they naturally sent back to Texas and Oklahoma for their labor. They also brought their prejudices with them when they moved to California. One grower, testifying at the LaFollette hearings, told the Senator:

> I am a southerner, born in Georgia, and when a big buck nigger gets up on a platform and walks backward and forward and says, "I haven't worked for a year, I have eat jail food, and have been in the fighting and can do it," that kind of gets under my skin.

Most of these large cotton growers are, of course, migrants themselves. But this circumstance has not predisposed them as a group to regard the plight of the Joads in California with any particular sympathy.

In March and April, 1939, I was in the San Joaquin Valley, inspecting labor camps. There are some 470 cotton camps in the valley. According to a formula used by the growers, each cabin in a cotton camp is theoretically supposed to account for 800 pounds of cotton a day during the picking season. Since the average worker can only pick about 200 pounds a day, it follows that each cabin must contain about four active pickers. Overcrowding is inevitable. The cabins are all one-room frame shacks and I have frequently found as many as eight and ten people living in one cabin. Some of the cotton camps are quite large; as many as 2,000 pickers will sometimes be found in a single camp. There are Negro camps, Mexican camps, and White-American camps. In some of the camps, particularly those operated by Mexican labor contractors, it is not uncommon to see open gambling, cock fights, and occasionally, to discover a contractor who is operating a *bagnio* with six or seven bedraggled Mexican prostitutes. Most of the camps should ordinarily be vacant in March or April since the cotton picking is over by January. But in the spring of 1939 the camps were 40 per cent occupied. Most of the occupants told me that they had been stranded at the end of the season and had to stay on in the camp. With scarcely an exception, they were all on relief, and in many cases the growers were getting $5 a month rent for the cabins from the State Relief Administration. Most of the large cotton camps are located miles away from the nearest major highway, and some of them, in the winter and spring, are islands in a sea of mud and water. There is a characteristic odor about a cotton camp that defies description. For days after an inspection trip of this kind, I could still imagine that the odor of the camps somehow clung to my clothes.

One day in May, 1939, I received a long distance telephone call from Governor Culbert L. Olson. Workers in Madera County were threatening to picket the offices of the State Relief Administration in protest against a rate of 20 cents an hour which had been established by the growers as the prevailing wage for cotton chopping. Prior to the time that Governor Olson was elected, the State Relief Administration followed the practice of denying relief whenever employment was available in the fields, regardless of what wage might be offered. The Governor, in this case, had promised the workers a hearing to determine whether they should be forced off relief to chop cotton at 20 cents an hour. He asked me to conduct the hearing. Two days later I opened the hearing in the Memorial Hall in Madera. Workers swarmed all over the place: they packed the hall; they stood in the doorways; they sat perched on the window ledges. Shortly after I arrived, a delegation of eight or ten cotton growers entered the hall. When they walked into the already crowded hall, a path was opened for them like that through which Moses crossed the Red Sea. I have never felt, before or since, such a sharply drawn class line. The growers were disdainful and contemptuous; the workers ominously quiet. The very idea of the hearing was anathema to the growers; the workers, on the other hand, enjoyed every moment of the hearing and listened intently to the testimony. Throughout the hearing—the first of its kind ever conducted in California—perfect order was maintained, with the workers showing a tendency to laugh good-naturedly at the description of their own sorry plight.

The story they had to tell was undeniably impressive. Working ten hours a day in the fields chopping cotton, they had to pay their own transportation expenses to and from work, sometimes commuting ten and fifteen miles each way. For the miserable shacks in which most of them lived, rents averaged about $8 or $10 a month. Utility charges were high; food was high. Under these circumstances, no man could support a family on 20 cents an hour. Average earnings for the season, at this rate, would actually be less than the meager allowances they received on relief. All of the growers who testified agreed that the rate was too low, but they contended it was the most they could afford to pay. At the conclusion of the hearing, I recommended to the Governor that no worker should be cut off relief unless afforded 27½ cents an hour in fields of "clean" cotton, or 30 cents an hour in fields of "dirty" cotton. The rates recommended were meager, but a strike was avoided at the time. It was quite apparent to me then that, with feeling running high among the migrants, there would be trouble in the fall when cotton picking started. Seldom have the Associated Farmers of California been as wild with rage as they were over the wage-rate hearing in Madera. The Governor's office was bombarded with letters, telegrams, and petitions of protest. Meetings were held throughout the state to condemn the idea of wage-rate hearings. An increase of 7½ cents an hour was enough to convince the Associated Farmers that I intended, alone and singlehanded, to "sovietize" California agriculture.

One of the reasons that this incident had occurred in Madera County was the fact that dust-bowl migrants had been pouring into the county since 1933. The population of the county had nearly doubled—between 1935 and 1938. Migrants discovered, of course, that there was no place for them in the rural economy of the region except as farm workers. There were no homesteads to be claimed, no free lands awaiting settlement. The price of good farm land in the county was utterly beyond the reach of the average migrant family. Stranded in the community, migrants had to seek relief. Resentment between "residents" and "newcomers" rapidly developed. A great portion of the population of the county actually came from the same areas in the South and Southwest; they were all citizens, all farmers, all "White-Americans." They shared to a considerable degree the same prejudices, the same taboos, the same aspirations. Yet the residents vehemently contended that they were "the people of Madera County"; and by inference that the Okies were "aliens."

This feeling was so pronounced that in the summer of 1939 a sign appeared in the foyer of a motion picture theatre in a San Joaquin Valley town, reading: "Negroes and Okies Upstairs."

Basically the social antagonism that divided Madera County into two warring camps—about equal in numbers but with the "residents" in almost exclusive possession of the symbols of authority and prestige—can be traced to the economic relationships involved in large-scale cotton operations in California. Over 50 per cent of the large-scale cotton farms in the United States are located in Arizona and California. There is one company, in California, which operates, through lessees, 10,000 acres of cotton land. Industrialized agriculture frequently involves a division of tasks or of functions. As Professor Clark Kerr has pointed out, a six-fold division of functions may be found in cotton production in California: ownership, financing, custom-work, supervision, labor, and management. Most of the operators are lessees; the land owners are banks, insurance companies, large land companies. Financing is handled through the cotton-ginning companies to a large extent. Custom-work implies that the "operator" or "lessee" may, and frequently does, contract with a "custom contractor" to supply the machinery needed for certain operations. Supervision is supplied by foremen, superintendents, or labor contractors. The actual manual labor is performed by migrant workers. Management may be obtained through a general farm manager who may supervise or manage several different operations at the same time. It frequently happens, therefore, that the land owner is far removed from actual farm operations and that even the operator or lessee has no interest, other than a purely speculative interest, in the land itself. Under this pattern of operations, the operator or lessee can usually be found sitting behind a desk in an air-cooled office in the nearest town.

The "controls" of a system of this kind are usually traceable to the cotton-ginning company, which stands behind the cotton grower. In California one concern, Anderson, Clayton and Company, gins about 35 per cent of the total cotton production. The company operates 46 cotton-ginning plants in the San Joaquin Valley, 28 in Arizona. Needless to say, the company has long been one of the patron saints of the Associated Farmers. The company has its affiliates and subsidiaries: Western Production Company, the Interstate Cotton and Oil Company, and the San Joaquin Cotton and Oil Company. The company made loans in 1939 totaling more than $6,500,000 to approximately 1,986 California cotton growers. When a cotton operator desires a loan, the company exercises a direct control over the budget. If a particular budget is "out of line" on labor costs, the company simply refuses to make a loan until the item in question is corrected. The amount of the loan is advanced in a series of installments or allotments. The chattel mortgage used to secure the loan provides that the money to be advanced by the company is to be used by the mortgagor as the company at its exclusive discretion shall direct. The grower must agree to gin his crop at one of the company's gins; he must also agree to sell his cotton seed to the company as well as the cotton oil. When the all-important matter of securing an advance to cover picking costs arises, the grower must negotiate with the company to the best of his ability. The company will want to know what rate the grower intends to pay for cotton-picking labor. If this rate is out of line, he will not get an advance. The actual relationship is not that of 1,986 independent cotton growers, but of 1,986 operators raising cotton for Anderson, Clayton and Company. The control that the cotton-ginning companies exercise over wage rates was clearly brought out during the LaFollette Committee hearings:

Senator LaFollette: Now, then, suppose a farmer or a grower desired to pay higher wages than that set by the bureau, what would be the policy as far as the request for advancing money was concerned?

Mr. Jensen [of Anderson, Clayton and Company]: Well, if such a grower—I really don't know—we don't encounter that, that I know of, Senator.

To understand the role that the cotton-ginning companies play in this situation it is necessary to remember that they are only incidentally interested in the price of cotton. They make money out of ginning rates, warehouse rates; out of the by-products, the seed, the oil, the cotton-cake. But they must induce others to raise cotton and they must recruit workers to pick cotton. The only reason Anderson, Clayton and Company does not raise most of the cotton in California is simply that it is cheaper for them to get someone else to do it. They are willing to allow a margin of profit for the grower—most of which is squeezed out of labor—provided the genuinely lucrative phases of the business remain their exclusive prerogative.

Disregarding the organized action of the workers in the spring, the cotton growers met in August, 1939, and fixed a uniform rate of 75 cents a hundred pounds for cotton picking. Immediately workers began to hold protest meetings throughout the San Joaquin Valley. They had not been consulted about this rate; nor were they given an opportunity to express their views on the fairness of the rate before it was established. Thus once again Governor Olson decided to intervene. A committee of seven was appointed to hold a hearing and to recommend a fair rate. The hearing this time was held in Fresno. The growers were not in attendance; they had decided to boycott the hearing. Witness after witness paraded to the stand to tell us why he could not make a living on "75 cents a hundred." Bert Wilson, who farmed for forty years in Oklahoma, told us that "a man cain't make a living under $1.25 a hundred. Groceries is too high. We sleep on the ground, put our babies on the ground, and these farmers will ask us to pick for eighty cents and we cain't do it. I have a little cabin that rents for $4 a month, about 12 × 12, and six in the family—we just cain't bed up like dogs." John Stevens had raised cotton in Oklahoma for twenty years before coming to California in 1938. An elderly man, he had a wife and six children to support. For weeks before the hearing, the family had been living on "a little meat, some gravy, light bread and coffee," and camping in a tent. When he arrived in California, in April, 1938, Stevens "went to picking peas. Then I went to the cherries over east of Stockton. Then I came back over to Hollister to the fruit and couldn't get in there. Too many people there. Worked then in the garlic and then back to Sacramento for the hops, and then the tomatoes and then back to the hops and the peas, and then the cotton." The previous year, 1938, he had managed to get about 30 days work "in the cotton. You would go into the field where there's 160 acres and there would be a man for every row from the start. It don't last long and you are all the time moving. You can't make nothing —there are too many people and it keeps you on the move."

Here in brief is what we discovered at this hearing: thousands of migrant families, stranded throughout the San Joaquin Valley, hopefully regarded the cotton-picking season, from September to January, as the one employment opportunity by which they might earn enough to keep off relief during the winter. Without consulting these workers, *all* of the cotton growers of the valley had agreed upon a wage rate. Insofar as the growers were concerned, they were practicing collective bargaining—among themselves. But this same right they refused to concede to others. Professor Clark Kerr has some pointed comments to make about this method of determining wage rates:

> The effectiveness of fixing the rates is increased by the inelasticity of the supply curve of labor. There is little alternate employment immediately available and channels for relief are partly closed. The supply curve in part of its range apparently also may be a backward sloping one. Farmers and government officials consistently report that raising the wages means that the workers quit earlier in the day and do not bring their children with them, and thus it takes longer to get the work done. A supply curve with this negative slope invites wage fixation and at comparatively low levels, *since lowering the rate may actually increase, rather than decrease,* the supply of labor. Also, the labor supply is constantly composed of new workers coming into the area for reasons in addition to the prospective level of wages offered there and having little connection with those who went before or who came after. Individual employers likewise may never face the same workers again. [Italics added by McWilliams.]

Nothing so strikingly illustrates the cul-de-sac into which the migrants had drifted in California, than the curious circumstance that a lowered wage rate, in this case, might possibly attract more workers than a rate fixed at a subsistence level. The more migrants, the less work; the lower the rate, the more migrants in the field.

Since our board had no power to enforce its recommendations, it had merely the effect of delaying for a week or so the strike of cotton pickers that had already been voted. Headquarters for the strike were established in Madera and there, in the city park, the strikers assembled nearly every night. There was little formal organization about the strike and practically no experienced leadership. With about 30,000 workers involved, the maximum that were out on strike was never more than 8,000 or 10,000 workers. But in certain counties, such as Madera, the strike was amazingly effective. The production of cotton began to decline rapidly. Within a week after the strike was called, it had become about 90 per cent effective in Madera County. Since the LaFollette Committee investigators had, by October, 1939, arrived in California there was little violence at the outset of the strike. But, when the strike began to be effective, the growers, in the words of one of their spokesmen, "decided to squeeze the core out of the boil."

On the morning of October 21, 1939, an army began to converge from all directions upon the public park in Madera. Wearing arm bands with the letters "AFC" (Associated Farmers of California), over six hundred men, armed with clubs, pick handles, rubber hose, and auto cranks, rushed into the park and proceeded to break up an orderly strike meeting. Standing on the edge of the park and obviously enjoying the affray was Sheriff W. O. Justice ("With Out" Justice, the migrants called him) of Madera County. Scores of strikers were injured and were treated at the hospital; among those receiving a minor injury was an investigator of the LaFollette Committee! Called as witness before the LaFollette Committee, the sheriff freely admitted that assaults were committed in his presence and that he had made not a single arrest. At first he testified that he could not identify the assailants. But Senator LaFollette then produced a photograph, taken at the time, which showed the sheriff in company with the ringleaders of the mob. With the utmost reluctance, the sheriff was then forced to identify, one after another, eight or ten people in the picture. Having forced him to admit then that he did know who the leaders of the mob were, the Senator then asked him if he intended to arrest them. The answer was a prompt and unequivocal "No." Yet before the strike was over, he had arrested 142 strikers for purely technical offenses, such as peaceful picketing and parading without a permit. Bail had been fixed in these cases as high as $2,500. Not a single grower was arrested although admittedly they had paraded without a permit, committed assaults, and fomented a riot. The record of this incident, in the LaFollette Committee transcript (Volume 51), is as clear a case of the unequal enforcement of the law as that committee ever exposed.

After the riot on October 21, the strike soon collapsed. Governor Olson sent personal representatives to Madera to address later strike meetings and these meetings were not disturbed. But the strike itself had, in the meantime, been broken. Gradually the Joads drifted into the fields to pick cotton at six-bits a hundred; the gins were soon running at full capacity; and a bumper crop was harvested.

These notes by no means exhaust the LaFollette Committee transcript, but they will serve to illustrate, perhaps, the fact that Mr. Steinbeck, in *The Grapes of Wrath*, was not relying upon his imagination. One of the incidents I have described took place *after* the publication of the novel at a time when the Associated Farmers, by every resource at their disposal, were attempting to convince the public that there was not a shred of truth in the book. Had some of the leaders of the organization been trying out for parts in the picture, they could not have acted more in character than they did.

Martin Shockley

Martin S. Shockley has taught at The Citadel, the University of Oklahoma, Carleton College, Evansville College, and the University of North Texas. He is co-author of Reading and Writing, and editor of Southwest Writers Anthology. His articles have appeared in Studies in Philology, American Literature, and College English. His most recent publication is Last Round-Up.

THE RECEPTION OF
THE GRAPES OF WRATH
IN OKLAHOMA

Most of us remember the sensational reception of The Grapes of Wrath (1939), Mr. Westbrook Pegler's column about the vile language of the book, Raymond Clapper's column recommending the book to economic royalists, Mr. Frank J. Taylor's article in the Forum attacking factual inaccuracies (this volume, 457–68), and the editorial in Collier's charging communistic propaganda. Many of us also remember that the Associated Farmers of Kern County, California, denounced the book as "obscene sensationalism" and "propaganda in its vilest form," that the Kansas City Board of Education banned the book from Kansas City libraries, and that the Library Board of East St. Louis banned it and ordered the librarian to burn the three copies which the library owned. These items were carried in the Oklahoma

Reprinted from American Literature XV (January 1944), 351–61. By permission of the publisher.

press. The *Forum's* article was even reprinted in the Sunday section of the Oklahoma City *Daily Oklahoman* on October 29, 1939, with the editor's headnote of approval.

With such publicity, *The Grapes of Wrath* sold sensationally in Oklahoma bookstores. Most stores consider it their best seller, excepting only *Gone With the Wind.* One bookstore in Tulsa reported about one thousand sales. Mr. Hollis Russell of Stevenson's Bookstore in Oklahoma City told me, "People who looked as though they had never read a book in their lives came in to buy it."

Of thirty libraries answering my letter of inquiry, only four, including one state college library, do not own at least one copy of the book, and the Tulsa Public Library owns twenty-eight copies. Most libraries received the book soon after publication in the spring of 1939. Librarians generally agreed that the circulation of *The Grapes of Wrath* was second only to that of *Gone With the Wind,* although three librarians reported equal circulation for the two books, and one (Oklahoma Agricultural and Mechanical College) reported *The Grapes of Wrath* their most widely circulated volume. The librarians often added that many private copies circulated widely in their communities, and some called attention to the extraordinary demand for rental copies. A few libraries restricted circulation to "adults only." About half the libraries mentioned long waiting lists, Miss Sue Salmon of the Duncan Public Library reporting that "Even as late as the spring of 1940 we counted 75 people waiting." Mrs. Virginia Harrison of A. and M. College stated that the four copies there "were on waiting list practically the entire time up to March 19, 1941." After over two hundred students had signed the waiting list for the two copies in the University of Oklahoma library, faculty members donated several additional copies to the library.

The Grapes of Wrath was reviewed throughout Oklahoma to large and curious audiences. A high-school English teacher wrote that he had reviewed the book three times, at a ladies' culture club, at a faculty tea, and at a meeting of the Junior Chamber of Commerce, receiving comments ranging from one lady's opinion that Ma Joad was a "magnificent character," to a lawyer's remark that "Such people should be kept in their place." When Professor J. P. Blickensderfer reviewed the book in the library at the University of Oklahoma, so many people were turned away for lack of standing room that he repeated the review two weeks later, again to a packed audience.

Much of what has passed in Oklahoma for criticism of *The Grapes of Wrath* has been little or nothing more than efforts to prove or to disprove the factual accuracy of Steinbeck's fiction. One of the minority supporters of the truth of Steinbeck's picture of the Okies has been Professor O. B. Duncan, Head of the Department of Sociology at A. and M. College. In an interview widely printed in Oklahoma newspapers, Professor Duncan discussed the economic and social problems which are involved.

> The farm migrant as described in Steinbeck's *Grapes of Wrath*, Duncan said, was the logical consequence of privation, insecurity, low income, inadequate standards of living, impoverishment in matters of education and cultural opportunities and a lack of spiritual satisfaction.
>
> "I have been asked quite often if I could not dig up some statistics capable of refuting the story of the *Grapes of Wrath*," Duncan related. "It cannot be done, for all the available data proved beyond doubt that the general impression given by Steinbeck's book is substantially reliable."[1]

Billed as "The one man, who above all others, should know best the farm conditions around Sallisaw," Mr. Houston Ward, county agent for Sequoyah County, of which Sallisaw is the county seat, spoke over radio station WKY in Oklahoma City on March 16, 1940, under the sponsorship of the State Agriculture Department. Under the headline "Houston B. Ward 'Tells All' About *The Grapes of Wrath*," the press quoted Mr. Ward on these inaccuracies:

> "Locating Sallisaw in the dust bowl region; having Grandpaw Joad yearning for enough California grapes to squish all over his face when in reality Sallisaw is in one of the greatest grape growing regions in the nation; making the tractor as the cause of the farmer's dispossession when in reality there are only 40 tractors in all Sequoyah county. . . . People in Sequoyah county are so upset by these obvious errors in the book and picture, they are inclined to overlook the moral lesson the book teaches," Ward said.[2]

Numerous editorials in Oklahoma newspapers have refuted or debunked Steinbeck by proving that not all Oklahomans are Joads, and that not all Oklahoma is dust bowl. The following editorial, headed "GRAPES OF WRATH? OBSCENITY AND INACCURACY," is quoted from the Oklahoma City *Times*, May 4, 1939:

> How book reviewers love to have their preconceived notions about any given region corroborated by a morbid, filthily-worded novel! It is said that *Grapes of Wrath*, by John Steinbeck, shows symptoms of becoming a best seller, by kindness of naive, ga-ga reviewers. It pictures Oklahoma with complete and absurd untruthfulness, hence has what it takes. That American literary tradition is still in its nonage . . . is amply proved by the fact that goldfish-swallowing critics who know nothing about the region or people pictured in a novel accept at face value even the most inaccurate depiction, by way of alleged regional fiction. No, the writer of these lines has not read the book. This editorial is based upon hearsay, and that makes it even, for that is how Steinbeck knows Oklahoma.

Mr. W. M. Harrison, editor of the Oklahoma City *Times*, devoted his column, "The Tiny Times," to a review of the book on May 8, 1939. He wrote:

> Any reader who has his roots planted in the red soil will boil with indignation over the bedraggled, bestial characters that will give the ignorant east convincing confirmation of their ideas of the people of the southwest. . . . If you have children, I'd advise against leaving the book around home. It has *Tobacco Road* looking as pure as Charlotte Brontë, when it comes to obscene, vulgar, lewd, stable language.

Usually the editors consider the book a disgrace to the state, and when they do not deny its truth they seek compensation. One editor wrote:

> Oklahoma may come in for some ridicule in other states because of such movie mistakes as *Oklahoma Kid* and such literature as the current *Grapes of Wrath*. Nationally we may rank near the bottom in the number of good books purchased, and in the amount we pay our teachers. But when

the biggest livestock and Four H club show comes along each
year the nation finds out that somebody amounts to something in Oklahoma.[3]

On September 25, 1941, during the Oklahoma State Fair, the
Daily Oklahoman, of Oklahoma City, carried a large cartoon showing
the Oklahoma farmer proudly and scornfully reclining atop a heap
of corn, wheat, and pumpkins, jeering at a small and anguished
Steinbeck holding a copy of *The Grapes of Wrath*. The caption:
"Now eat every gol-durn word of it."

Considerable resentment toward the state of California was felt
in Oklahoma because California had stigmatized Oklahoma by call-
ing all dust bowl migrants—even those from Arkansas and Texas—
"Okies." One lengthy newspaper editorial was headed "So California
Wants Nothing But Cream"[4] and another "It's Enough to Justify a
Civil War."[5] On June 13, 1939, the *Daily Oklahoman* carried under
a streamer headline a long article on the number of Californians on
Oklahoma's relief rolls. In Tulsa, employees of the Mid Continent
Petroleum Company organized the Oklahoma's California Hecklers
Club, the stated purpose being to "make California take back what
she's been dishing out." The club's motto was "A heckle a day will
keep a Californian at bay." A seven-point program was adopted, beginning, "Turn the other cheek, but have a raspberry in it," and
ending, "Provide Chamber of Commerce publicity to all Californians
who can read."[6] The Stillwater *Gazette* in editorial approval wrote
of the club: "*The Grapes of Wrath* have soured and this time it's the
Californians who'll get indigestion."[7]

Numerous letters from subscribers have appeared in newspapers
throughout Oklahoma. Some are apologetic, some bitter, some violent. A few have defended Steinbeck, sympathized with the Joads,
and praised *The Grapes of Wrath*. Some take the book as text for
economic, social, or political preachments. Miss Mary E. Lemon, of
Kingfisher, wrote:

> To many of us John Steinbeck's novel, *The Grapes of Wrath*,
> has sounded the keynote of our domestic depression, and put
> the situation before us in an appealing way. When the small
> farmers and home owners—the great masses upon which our
> national stability depends—were being deprived of their
> homes and sent roaming about the country, knocking from

pillar to post; when banks were bursting with idle money, and insurance companies were taking on more holdings and money than they knew what to do with, Steinbeck attempted a sympathetic exposition of this status.[8]

Mr. P. A. Oliver, of Sallisaw, wrote no less emphatically:

The Grapes of Wrath was written to arouse sympathy for the millions of poor farmers and tenants who have been brought to miserable ruin because of the development of machinery. . . . The people are caught in the inexorable contradiction of capitalism. As machinery is more and more highly developed, more and more workers are deprived of wages, of buying power. As buying power is destroyed, markets are destroyed. As the millions of workers are replaced by machinery in the industrial centers, the markets over the world collapse. The collapse of world markets destroyed the market for the cotton and vegetables produced by the poor farmers and tenants of Sequoyah county. Sequoyah county is a part of the world and hence suffered along with the rest of the capitalistic world in the collapse of capitalistic business. The day of free enterprise is done. The day of the little farmer is done. had it not been for government spending, every farmer in the United States, every banker, every lawyer, every doctor, and all other professional workers and wage earners would long since have joined the Joads on the trail of tears. Better do some serious thinking before you ridicule the Joads.[9]

From September 22 to 25, 1940, a Congressional committee headed by Representative Tolan of California held hearings in Oklahoma's capitol investigating the problem of migratory workers. Apparently Oklahoma viewed with suspicion this intrusion, for as early as August 16, a newspaper editorial stated that

Anticipating an attempt to "smear" Oklahoma, Governor Phillips is marshalling witnesses and statistics to give the state's version of the migration. He has called on Dr. Henry G. Bennett and faculty members of the Oklahoma A. and M. college to assist in the presentation. Oklahoma has a right to resent any undue reflections on the state. If the hearing develops into a mud-slinging contest, Oklahoma citizens have a few choice puddles from which to gather ammunition for an attack on the ham-and-egg crackpot ideas hatched on the western coast.[10]

On September 9 the *Daily Oklahoman* of Oklahoma City carried a story giving the names of the members of the committee which the governor had appointed to prepare his report. The paper stated that "Governor Phillips announced his intention to refute the 'Okies' story when the committee of congressmen come here to study conditions causing the migration." During the hearings, front-page stories kept Oklahomans alert to Steinbeck's guilt. On September 20 the *Daily Oklahoman* reported with apparent relief that "The fictional Joad family of *The Grapes of Wrath* could be matched by any state in the union, according to testimony." Next morning the same paper's leading editorial on "Mechanized Farms and 'Okies' " stated that mechanized farming was not responsible for conditions represented in *The Grapes of Wrath*. The editorial concluded, "It is a disagreeable fact, but one that cannot be ignored by men earnestly seeking the truth wherever found, that two of the chief factors that produce 'Okies' are AAA and WPA."

Under the heading " 'Grapes' Story Arouses Wrath of Governor," the Oklahoma City *Times* on October 2, 1939, printed the story of a correspondence between His Excellency Leon C. Phillips, Governor of Oklahoma, and an unnamed physician of Detroit, Michigan. The unnamed physician wrote, as quoted in the paper:

> "Is it at all conceivable that the state of Oklahoma, through its corporations and banks, is dispossessing farmers and share-croppers . . . ? I am wondering whether you, my dear governor, have read the book in question." To which the governor warmly replied: "I have not read the thing. I do not permit myself to get excited about the works of any fiction writer. In Oklahoma we have as fine citizens as even your state could boast. . . . I would suggest you go back to reading detective magazines. . . ."

The following news item is quoted from the Stillwater *Gazette* of March 23, 1940:

Thirty-six unemployed men and women picketed Oklahoma's state capitol for two hours Saturday calling on Governor Phillips to do something about conditions portrayed in John Steinbeck's novel, *The Grapes of Wrath*. One of their signs stated "Steinbeck told the truth." Eli Jaffee, president of the Oklahoma City Workers' Alliance, said that "we are the Okies who didn't go to California, and we want jobs." Phillips refused to talk with the group. He said that he considered that the novel and the movie version of the book presented an exaggerated and untrue picture of Oklahoma's tenant farmer problems as well as an untruthful version of how migrants are received in California.

If His Excellency the Governor had been reticent as a critic of literature, the Honorable Lyle Boren, Congressman from Oklahoma, was no way abashed. The following speech, reprinted from the *Congressional Record*, was published in the *Daily Oklahoman*, January 24, 1940:

Mr. Speaker, my colleagues, considerable has been said in the cloakrooms, in the press and in various reviews about a book entitled *The Grapes of Wrath*. I cannot find it possible to let this dirty, lying, filthy manuscript go heralded before the public without a word of challenge or protest.

I would have my colleagues in Congress, who are concerning themselves with the fundamental economic problems of America, know that Oklahoma, like other States in the Union, has its economic problems, but that no Oklahoma economic problem has been portrayed in the low and vulgar lines of this publication. As a citizen of Oklahoma, I would have it known that I resent, for the great State of Oklahoma, the implications in that book. . . .

I stand before you today as an example in my judgment, of the average son of the tenant farmer of America. If I have in any way done more in the sense of personal accomplishment than the average son of the tenant farmer of Oklahoma, it has been a matter of circumstance, and I know of a surety that the heart and brain and character of the average tenant farmer of Oklahoma cannot be surpassed and probably not equalled by any other group.

Today, I stand before this body as a son of a tenant farmer, labeled by John Steinbeck as an "Okie." For myself, for my dad and my mother, whose hair is silvery in the service of building the State of Oklahoma, I say to you, and to every honest, square-minded reader in America, that the painting Steinbeck made in his book is a lie, a black, infernal creation of a twisted, distorted mind.

Some have blasphemed the name of Charles Dickens by making comparisons between his writing and this. I have no doubt but that Charles Dickens accurately portrayed certain economic conditions in his country and in his time, but this book portrays only John Steinbeck's unfamiliarity with facts and his complete ignorance of his subject. . . .

Take the vulgarity out of this book and it would be blank from cover to cover. It is painful to me to further charge that if you take the obscene language out, its author could not sell a copy. . . .

I would have you know that there is not a tenant farmer in Oklahoma that Oklahoma needs to apologize for. I want to declare to my nation and to the world that I am proud of my tenant-farmer heritage, and I would to Almighty God that all citizens of America could be as clean and noble and fine as the Oklahomans that Steinbeck labeled "Okies." The only apology that needs to be made is by the State of California for being the parent of such offspring as this author. . . .

Just nine days after Congressman Boren's speech had appeared in print, a long reply by Miss Katharine Maloney, of Coalgate, appeared on the Forum page of the Oklahoma City *Times*. I quote a few brief excerpts from Miss Maloney's letter:

If Boren read *The Grapes of Wrath*, which I have cause to believe he did not, he would not label John Steinbeck a "damnable liar." John Steinbeck portrayed the characters in his book just as they actually are. . . . Why, if Boren wants to bring something up in congress, doesn't he do something to bring better living conditions to the tenant farmer? . . . This would make a better platform for a politician than the book. . . .

Not only politics, but the pulpit as well were moved by the book. One minister in Wewoka was quoted as praising it as a "truthful book of literary as well as social value, resembling in power and beauty of style the King James version of the Bible."[11] His was decidedly a minority opinion. The other extreme may be represented by the Reverend W. Lee Rector, of Ardmore, who considered *The Grapes of Wrath* a "heaven-shaming and Christ-insulting book." As reported in the press, the Reverend Mr. Rector stated:

"The projection of the preacher of the book into a role of hypocrisy and sexuality discounts the holy calling of God-called preachers. . . . The sexual roles that the author makes the preacher and young women play is so vile and misrepresentative of them as a whole that all readers should revolt at the debasement the author makes of them." The pastor complained that the book's masterly handling of profanity tends to "popularize iniquity" and that the book is "100 percent false to Christianity. We protest with all our heart against the Communistic base of the story. . . . As does Communism, it shrewdly inveighs against the rich, the preacher, and Christianity. Should any of us Ardmore preachers attend the show which advertises this infamous book, his flock should put him on the spot, give him his walking papers, and ask God to forgive his poor soul."[12]

Other Oklahomans resented the filming of the story. Mr. Reo M'Vickn wrote the following letter, which was published in the Oklahoma City *Times* on January 26, 1940:

After reading the preview of *Grapes of Wrath* (*Look*, January 16) I think the state of Oklahoma as a whole should take definite steps to prevent the use of the name of our state in such a production. They are trying to disgrace Oklahoma and I for one am in favor of stopping them before they get started.

Oklahoma Chambers of Commerce had already tried to stop the filming of the picture. The following story is taken from the Oklahoma City *Times*, August 7, 1939:

Neither Stanley Draper, secretary-manager of the Oklahoma City Chamber of Commerce, nor Dr. J. M. Ashton, research director of the State Chamber of Commerce, wants Twentieth Century Fox Corporation to make *Grapes of Wrath* in the "dust bowl." . . . Enough fault was found with the facts in Joseph [*sic*] Steinbeck's book on the "okies." . . . So the two Chamber of Commerce men think someone should protest the inaccurate and unfair treatment the state seems to be about to receive in the filming of the picture. Draper is going to suggest the mayor of Oklahoma City protest, and Ashton will ask the governor to do likewise. . . .

On September 1, 1941, the *Daily Oklahoman* carried a four-column headline, "Lions to Attack 'Okie' Literature." The news story described the nature of the attack:

Those who write smart and not so complimentary things about Oklahoma and Okies had better watch out, because the 3-A district governor of Oklahoma Lions clubs and his cabinet, at their first session here Sunday, discussed an all-out counter-offensive. . . . The district governor and a dozen members of his cabinet agreed in their meeting at the Skirvin hotel that something should be done to offset *Grapes of Wrath* publicity. . . .[13]

The opinions and incidents which I have presented are representative, by no means inclusive. There are, I should say, two main bodies of opinion, one that this is an honest, sympathetic, and artistically powerful presentation of economic, social, and human problems; the other, the great majority, that this is a vile, filthy book, an outsider's malicious attempt to smear the state of Oklahoma with outrageous lies. The latter opinion, I may add, is frequently accompanied by the remark: "I haven't read a word of it, but I know it's all a dirty lie."

The reception of *The Grapes of Wrath* in Oklahoma suggests many interesting problems, particularly pertinent to contemporary regional literature in America. Any honest literary interpretation of a region seems to offend the people of that region. Ellen Glasgow, though herself a Virginian, has been received in her native state with a coolness equal to the warmth with which Virginians have welcomed Thomas Nelson Page. Romanticizers of the Old South are local literary lions, while authors who treat contemporary problems are renegades who would ridicule their own people for the sake of literary notoriety.

A tremendous provincial self-consciousness expresses itself in fierce resentment of "outsiders who meddle in our affairs." One consistent theme in the writings of Oklahomans who attacked *The Grapes of Wrath* was that this book represents us unfairly; it will give us a lot of unfavorable publicity, and confirm the low opinion of us that seems to prevail outside the state. Rarely did someone say, "We should do something about those conditions; we should do something to help those people." Generally they said, "We should deny it vigorously; all Oklahomans are not Okies."

Properly speaking, *The Grapes of Wrath* is not a regional novel; but it has regional significance; it raises regional problems. Economic collapse, farm tenantry, migratory labor are not regional problems; they are national or international in scope, and can never be solved through state or regional action. But the Joads represent a regional culture which, as Steinbeck shows us, is now rapidly disintegrating as the result of extra-regional forces. It may well be that powerful extra-regional forces operating in the world today foreshadow the end of cultural regionalism as we have known it in America.

NOTES

1. Oklahoma City *Times*, Feb. 5, 1940.
2. *Ibid.*, March 16, 1940.
3. *Ibid.*, Dec. 5, 1939.
4. *Ibid.*, Nov. 28, 1938.
5. *Ibid.*, Aug. 6, 1938.
6. Stillwater *Gazette*, April 26, 1940.
7. *Ibid.*
8. Oklahoma City *Times*, Dec. 22, 1939.
9. Sallisaw *Democrat-American*, March 28, 1940.
10. *Payne County News* (Stillwater), Aug. 16, 1940.
11. Letter in my possession.
12. Oklahoma City *Times*, March 30, 1940.
13. The governor of district 3-A of the Lions clubs of Oklahoma is Dr. Joseph H. Marshburn, Professor of English in the University of Oklahoma.

III

The Creative Context

Jackson J. Benson

Jackson J. Benson has taught at San Diego State University. He has received two National Endowment for the Humanities fellowships, and published nine books, including the biography The True Adventures of John Steinbeck, Writer, *which won the PEN West Award for non-fiction. His most recent book is* Wallace Stegner: His Life and Work.

THE BACKGROUND TO THE COMPOSITION
OF *THE GRAPES OF WRATH*

. . . Years ago, when I first read John Steinbeck's *The Grapes of Wrath*, I noticed the second part of the novel's dedication, "To TOM who lived it," and it added a certain excitement to the novel. I thought, as perhaps most readers also thought, that the dedication referred to some real-life counterpart of the novel's central character, Tom Joad. And in thinking about the novel, I began to consider it, in part, a testimony to a friendship. Through the years I have had it in my mind's eye that Steinbeck traveled to Oklahoma and hooked up with a family, the Joads, which had been dusted off of its farm

This excerpt is reprinted from *Critical Essays on Steinbeck's* The Grapes of Wrath (G. K. Hall & Co.), edited by John Ditsky. Copyright © 1989 by John Ditsky. The essay is condensed from material published as "John Steinbeck and Farm Labor Unionization: The Background of *In Dubious Battle*" (with Anne Loftis) in *American Literature* 5 (April 1976): 151–232, and from *The True Adventures of John Steinbeck, Writer* (Viking Press) by Jackson J. Benson. Copyright © 1984 by Jackson J. Benson. By permission of John Ditsky.

and was headed West. I saw the writer becoming a companion to the older son, while the family made its way in an old battered car made into a truck, across the desert and mountains into California. And in my imagination I saw John Steinbeck, squatting on his heels with a tin cup in his hand in front of a roadside campfire, probing the heart and mind of a Tom Joad dressed in overalls and looking a little like Henry Fonda.

But it didn't happen that way. First, contrary to the story that has become part of American folklore, John did not travel to Oklahoma and then make a trip back to California with a migrant family. He made four trips to the Central Valley, and on one occasion drove on from Bakersfield over the Tehachapi Mountains through the Mojave to the state line near Needles. When he came back, he talked about the "Okies," and his friends assumed he had gone all the way to Oklahoma. John loved being mysterious, and several years later when acquaintances would mention the "Oklahoma trip," he would only smile, without comment. Many years later he began to talk of the trip with the migrants from Oklahoma as if he had actually made it.[1]

Second, the Tom in the dedication did not refer to a real-life Tom Joad or to a migrant at all, but to Tom Collins, the manager of the Arvin Sanitary Camp. Collins was a very unusual man who would provide a great deal of background information for Steinbeck about the migrants, their customs, speech, and behavior, and at the same time, he also would make a considerable contribution to the spirit of the novel, its attitudes and values.

When John, accompanied by Eric Thomsen, arrived at Arvin on his first research trip to the Valley, it was just nightfall and raining. The wheels of his car threw up muddy water as he drove by the rows of dripping tents to the canvas shelter that was the temporary office. Inside, sitting at a littered table and surrounded by a throng of people who had come in to stand out of the rain, was Tom Collins, a small man in a damp, frayed, white suit. As John recalls the scene,

> The crowding people looked at him all the time. Just stood and looked at him. He had a small moustache, his graying, black hair stood up on his head like the quills of a frightened porcupine, and his large, dark eyes, tired beyond sleepiness, the kind of tired that won't let you sleep even if you have the time and a bed.

Thomsen introduced John to Tom, and the latter invited them to his own tent for coffee. It was made, but not drunk, for reports kept coming in from all over the muddy camp: there was an epidemic, and every kind of winter disease had developed—measles, whooping cough, mumps, pneumonia. And this one man was trying to do everything in this gathering of two thousand people because there was no one else to help. Even if the residents wanted to help, they couldn't for lack of knowledge. Back and forth he went, nursing, advising, settling arguments, and doing whatever he could to help the suffering, console the worried families, and keep the peace until morning should finally come.[2]

This was Steinbeck's introduction to the man who became the most important single source for his novel. Later, during three additional trips to various parts of California, Collins would accompany the writer. In John's words, "[we] sat in the ditches with the migrant workers, lived and ate with them. We heard a thousand miseries and a thousand jokes. We ate fried dough and sow belly, worked with the sick and the hungry, listened to complaints and little triumphs."

It was not only Collins's endurance and capacity for work that attracted Steinbeck's admiration, but his love for people, no matter how poor or how ignorant, and his very large capacity for acceptance. Collins's background was that of a man who had trained for a time for the priesthood and then quit to become a teacher. After teaching for the Navy in Alaska and Guam, he started his own school for delinquent boys, and when that enterprise went bankrupt, he found a job as head of the Federal Transient Service Facility (the Depression era soup kitchens) in Los Angeles.[3] He was an idealist, a utopian reformer, a romantic, and, at his worst, something of a con artist; at the same time he was also a good administrator, a compassionate man, and experienced enough not to be too surprised at the foolish and stupid things that men do both to themselves and to each other.

After leaving the Federal Transient Service, he worked for the Resettlement Administration and Farm Security Administration from 1935 to 1941. He was very good at this work, and this period no doubt became the high-water mark of his life. Although he was not an administrator who could make decisions about the camps as a whole, he probably had more impact on the camp program than any other individual, for he was the first camp manager and designed the way the camps would actually operate. After his tenure at the

Marysville camp, he had become so well regarded by his superiors that he was assigned to open most of the camps as they were built and to train new managers.[4]

Collins made the camps work by giving most of the day-to-day responsibility for running the camps to the residents themselves. He established a simple democracy, in which the camp was governed by a camp committee made up of one representative from each of the sections of the camp. Each unit elected its representatives to this town council, as well as electing representatives to various operating committees that dealt with fire, recreation, children's playground, and children's welfare, and the governing board of the Women's Club. (This club, which figures prominently in the government camp section of the novel, was later called the "Good Neighbors Society.") The camp committee at Weedpatch had the primary responsibility for setting up the rules and enforcing them, a job it took seriously.[5]

Tact is probably the key quality that made Collins so successful as a manager. He was conscious of the fact that those who came to the camp had been pushed around, insulted, and looked down upon, and he made every effort to allay their natural hostility and suspicion and restore their sense of self-worth by treating each resident with dignity. Milan Dempster, who came into the camp program as a manager in 1937, recalls that both Collins and Robert Hardie, who replaced Collins at Weedpatch, were extremely sensitive to the temper of the people in the camps, constantly cultivating a sense of their instincts and ways.[6]

Taking charge of the initial planning and organization for one camp after another as each opened, Collins would usually work with two hundred to a thousand people, many of them ignorant of basic sanitation, many of them either hostile and suspicious or worn out and desperate, to help them mold themselves into a cohesive, self-governing society. Even though this was a society of migrants, a society whose members were always changing, the residents achieved a continuity, always passing on from the old residents to the new the spirit of what Collins called "the good neighbor." It was an old-fashioned virtue that both Collins and his Okies could believe in.

Steinbeck spent several days with Collins on this first visit, carefully observing the operations of the camp, following Collins in his work, mingling with and talking to the campers—blending in with ordinary people inconspicuously and talking to them convincingly about their own interests were two of the author's major talents. He attended a camp committee meeting, watched the Good Neighbors Society welcome new arrivals, and went to one of the weekend camp dances. Since it was part of Collins's job to keep track of conditions at nearby squatters' camps, Steinbeck also accompanied him on these trips and visited nearby farms, where he not only gathered material for his *News* articles, but also stored away bits and pieces of material that he would later use in *The Grapes of Wrath*.

One of the squatters' camps they visited was just north of Arvin at Lamont where they talked to the young son of the chairman of the Weedpatch Camp Committee who was a fugitive from the law, staying away from his family for fear of bringing them trouble. Dewey Russell, a manager of the camp after Collins, has said that Collins told him that the model for the Joad family was that of Sherm Eastom, the camp committee chairman at the time Steinbeck visited Weedpatch. Collins also told Russell that the model for Tom Joad was "the son [of Eastom] who was a fugitive, lived under another name, out in Lamont."[7]

• • •

In the words of a friend and neighbor who saw Steinbeck on his return from his trip to the Valley, the writer came back with "a pile of material" given to him by Collins "on the Okies and the government camp he managed, with observations and dialogue."[8] This stack of material was composed of copies of Collins's camp reports, a rich vein of detailed information that John would use for his *News* articles and in *The Grapes of Wrath*. These reports, which were sent to the Farm Security Administration sometimes weekly, sometimes biweekly, were often very long, running to twelve, fourteen, even twenty pages. They included observations, statistics, and anecdotes covering almost every aspect of camp life, as well as some information about migrant life outside the camp. In the reports there are many discussions of the kinds of items one would expect—of the physical facilities and what was needed (at Weedpatch it was spraying equipment for the insects, and shade trees), of supplies (they were always running short of toilet paper), of efforts at make-do (Collins showed the baseball team how to make a baseball out of an old golf ball he had), and of social activities (the weekly dances are frequently mentioned).[9]

But there was also a great deal of material that one might not expect. Collins apparently fancied himself a social scientist, for he presents numerous surveys, lists, polls, and investigations. He seems to have counted everything countable, including the number of campers per bed each month. There are classifications of campers by occupation and state of origin, and lists of the kinds and years of cars in the camp. He kept a log of all the visitors and took surveys of work opportunities, attitudes of nearby farmers, and conditions in local squatters' camps. He counted the sick, those who had jobs, and those who caused trouble. He also investigated (by inviting himself to dinner) the diets of the campers.

In addition to the lists and statistics, which are probably more interesting to us today than they were to the officials at Farm Security Administration headquarters who had to read them, he told of his own experiences with various campers, sometimes at great length. He also included the words to some forty songs sung by the migrants, ranging from "It's the Wrong Way to Whip the Devil" to "The Lily of Hill Billy Valley" and "Why Do You Bob Your Hair, Girls?" But of all the miscellaneous matter that Collins put into his reports, the most interesting items, as well as the most useful to those such as Steinbeck who tapped the reports for material, are the narratives. These run from short anecdotes, which Collins usually included at the end of the reports under the title "Bits of Migrant Wisdom," to long stories with their own titles ("A Bird of Prey," "A Romance," "We Commit a Mortal Sin"), which might run to several pages. Collins had an ear for voice and intonation, for colorful dialogue, phonetically spelled to reproduce migrant dialects:

> All wimen shuda be in bed and tucked under by 8 oclock. Aint no good womn afoot and aloose after that air hour less she be agoin to cherch.
>
> Kaint see how cum folks kinda hate us migrants. The Good Book says as how Jesus went from place to place when he wus on erf. Aint it so Jesus wus a migrant?
>
> Gawd is good to us farm lab'rs. When we aint got wuk and every'thing luks blue he sends us a new baby ter keep us happy.

In writing *The Grapes of Wrath* Steinbeck used Collins's reports as a kind of handbook of migrant attitudes and behavior, describing as they do ways of speaking, patterns of reaction, and conditions of life and work in various settings. In the novel there are names, characters, incidents, and pieces of dialogue that have direct ties to the reports, and bits and pieces of Collins's color are sprinkled here and there. For example, Gramma's "ancient creaking bleat" in the first part of the book, "Pu-raise Gawd fur Vittory! Pu-raise Gawd fur Vittory!" (104) when she hears of Tom Joad's return home from prison, is taken exactly from Collins's report of the favorite expression of a woman that he employed as a part-time housekeeper. This woman, called the "Holy One" by Collins, appears to be the model for the woman in the novel who causes so much grief to others through her religious fanaticism (420–24) (Collins employed her to keep her away from the camp and out of trouble).

Quite naturally, many of the anecdotes adapted from Collins's reports appear in the section of the novel that is set in the government camp (389–493). And many of these relate to the sanitary facilities of the camp, which were new and strange to most of these people who, by and large, had grown up and lived all their lives on the same poor farm without flush toilets, showers, or modern laundry tubs. Less directly, almost every major scene or incident that appears in the camp section of the novel—such as the Joad arrival in camp, the camp committee meeting, and the dance—has its roots in one or more descriptions in the reports.

Beyond such connections between Collins's material and Steinbeck's novel, there were deeper influences flowing from the camp manager to the author, influences of emotion and attitude, which are difficult to measure or locate precisely. Both men had faith that our democratic institutions, through the pressure of an enlightened citizenry, could and would correct the inequities that appeared to be tearing the fabric of society apart. Although they hated the abuses of capitalism and favored labor unionizing, they really didn't see the problem in political terms. They saw it as a matter of attitude.

But most important, at least when assessed from the point of view of the novel and its qualities, both Collins and Steinbeck had an idealized view of the common man and attributed somewhat more dignity, wisdom, and courage to the migrants than they actually as a whole probably possessed—or at least more than most observers would be inclined to assign to them. While Steinbeck's idealism was usually moderated by a rather skeptical view of individual human nature, Collins sometimes lapsed into an uncritical sentimentality.

His camp reports reveal a vision of the migrants as a sort of displaced American yeomanry, blessed with old-time American virtues, but misunderstood and abused for a rural simplicity that clashed with the sophistication of their new surroundings. There was no doubt more truth in this view than in the contrary position, widely held in parts of California, that the migrants were little more than animals and need not be treated any better. Nevertheless, Collins's position in reaction to the abuse of the migrants, which he resented so deeply, was in its own way extreme: seldom do the reports ever mention migrant misbehavior that was seriously reprehensible. All migrant misbehavior seems to be of a minor nature, and always it is subject to treatment by education. By and large, the reports picture a people who are quaint: they are the salt of the earth, the charming subjects of a study in folklore. Over and over again Collins notes that once they can get themselves clean and settled, they are happy, and their happiness is stabilized and their dignity restored by participation in the representative government of the camp.

Collins had a great faith in a kind of basic Jacksonian democracy that he felt was not only the natural preference of the migrants but also the natural condition toward which all men aspired or should aspire. The problem was that society at large was in error insofar as it did not emulate the society that he had helped to create in his camps. For Collins, the camps were indeed a "demonstration." They gave flesh to the vision of man's possible social perfection, wherein all men were "good neighbors," responsive to each other's needs, and responsible citizens in a democratic society that was responsive to the general welfare.

Some of these ideas held by Collins no doubt rubbed off on Steinbeck, for good or ill, as we seem to be able to detect in the general tenor and value system of the novel. But, since Steinbeck was leaning toward, if not in fact already possessing, many of these values, there is no way to tell how much came from Collins, and there is little in Collins's vision that was original except in its application to the migrants. The utopian, visionary-Romantic was not an uncommon figure in his time—both popular and serious literature frequently featured it. What we seem to be dealing with here is not just influence, in the strictest sense, but the transmission and reinforcement of feelings and attitudes by the man who Steinbeck felt was closest to the Dust Bowl migrants. In this sense, the most important contribution by Collins to *The Grapes of Wrath* may well have been to the spirit at the heart of the novel, rather than to the details and color of its surface. It was Steinbeck's gift to make both the details on the surface and the vision beneath it both believable and moving.

• • •

In September of 1936, Helen Horn, an employee of the F.S.A.'s Division of Information in San Francisco, wrote to Collins, asking, "How did you like John Steinbeck and isn't it slick that the San Francisco News will let him do a series? That ought to do us a lot of good unless they start adulterating the copy which they promised they won't." Steinbeck, in the meantime, was sorting out his experiences with Thomsen and Collins, organizing the background material he had gathered, and shuffling through Collins's reports for usable material. The background information that he had gathered earlier in the summer was the basis for a short summary of the migrant situation in California that appeared in the September 12th *Nation*, about a week and a half after his return from Weedpatch.[10] He wrote to Collins soon after he returned:

> I want to thank you for one of the very fine experiences of a life. But I think you know exactly how I feel about it. I hope I can be of some kind of help. On the other hand I don't want to be presumptuous. In the articles I shall be very careful to try to do some good and no harm.[11]

During the last weeks of the month, he finished his series for the *News*, called *The Harvest Gypsies*, an excellent example of what we today would call "investigative, advocacy reporting." Under the circumstances of Steinbeck's emotional commitment at the time, it was a tribute to his self-control that the articles were so calm and carefully presented. The articles, seven of them, trace the background of migrant labor in California, identify the new migrants from the Dust Bowl, describe the living conditions of the squatters' camps, discuss the large corporate farm structure of much of California's agriculture and large grower-migrant labor relations, examine the government camp program, and make recommendations for the future.

At the end of September he went back to Weedpatch to talk

again to Collins and observe life at the camp. A week later he wrote to his literary agents, "I just returned yesterday from the strike area of Salinas and from my migrants in Bakersfield. This thing is dangerous. Maybe it will be patched up for a while, but I look for the lid to blow off in a few weeks. Issues are very sharp here now. . . . My material drawer is chock full."[12] The Salinas lettuce strike, which he refers to here, had started about the first of September, and although Steinbeck did not profess much love for his hometown during these years, he was both hurt and angered at the outrageous vigilantism that swept through the area and within a month crushed the strike.

This strike was a major test case of its time and was much on the minds of all those concerned with farm labor, employers and employees, throughout the state. The way it was handled set a very frightening precedent. The usual fears of Red revolutionaries and economic displacement led Salinas to place its police and judicial powers, extralegally, in the hands of a retired army officer, who declared his own version of martial law and formed a local militia to resist the strike and scatter the strikers. Civil rights were voided and an internment camp set up, and neither the county nor state governments interfered to any significant extent in one of the largest vigilante actions ever to take place in California.

Steinbeck's letters suggest that he was furious, but also depressed by the easy abandonment of Constitutional principles by the average citizen in response to the fear spread by large growers motivated by greed. The parallel to Hitler's methods used in the recent past to take over Germany was a strong one, and Steinbeck was only one among many who feared that the hysteria and the bullyboy tactics inspired by the wealthy in Salinas might spread across the country.

Closer to home, however, the novelist, who had seen the hopelessness of migrant families in their makeshift camps, riddled with disease and existing often on the edge of starvation, felt that the defeat of the strikers was a defeat for all the migrants. Actually, while this was true in principle perhaps, the workers in Salinas were a slightly different group, more akin to the professional pickers he had pictured in *In Dubious Battle* than the Dust Bowl migrants near Bakersfield who were the subjects of his *San Francisco News* articles. Yet, it was the bringing together in his own mind of these two extremes, the brutality and blind selfishness of the Salinas strike with the helpless misery of the most unfortunate of the Okies, that ap-

parently created the drama that was the main stimulus for the first
version of the book that would become *The Grapes of Wrath*.

This first draft, called "L'Affaire Lettuceberg," was planned as
another strike novel. It would combine the material to be drawn from
Collins's accounts of the Dust Bowl migrants with the Salinas strike,
focusing on the outrageous behavior of the growers and vigilantes.
Carol, John's first wife, recalls it as a satire filled with caricatures of
Salinas "fat cats."[13]

For a time, however, John's efforts to get his "big book," as he
began calling it, under way were stalled by an anger so deep that it
poisoned his thinking. Out of frustration, he wrote a satirical allegory
called "The Great Pig Sticking," which, having partially relieved his
feelings of outrage, he threw into the stove. By the end of the year,
he was able to get a start on his novel, but in January he wrote his
agent, Elizabeth Otis, "The new book has struck a bad snag. Heaven
knows how long it will take to write. The subject is so huge that it
scares me to death. And I'm not going to rush it. It must be worked
out with great care."

But outside events now conspired to delay the writing. *Of Mice
and Men* was published in February 1937—a book about another
kind of farm laborer, the bindlestiff—and its selection by the Book-
of-the-Month Club and sale to Hollywood gave the Steinbecks
enough money to go to Europe. On the way back, during the summer of 1937, Steinbeck stopped off at the George Kaufman farm in
Pennsylvania where he and Kaufman worked on the stage script of
the short novel. John did not like New York—he felt, as he said later,
that he had achieved a kind of "fifth-rate celebrity" and was suspicious that being wined and dined in the big city would somehow
corrupt him. What he didn't say, and what must have been the case,
was that he felt in his bones that high living at this moment was
totally inappropriate to what was on his mind and the task ahead.

His book was much on his mind, and he was impatient with the
playwriting. He wrote Tom Collins from New York:

Dear Tom:
Your letter was waiting when we got in [to New York from
Europe]. Be home in about a month. Then in the house
about two weeks and then I'm going to visit you for a while.
Let me know where Gridley is and how to find you. I've got
to get the smell of drawing rooms out of my nose. A squat-

ter's camp is a wonderful place for that. So I'll be seeing you pretty soon and will be very glad to. . . .

> Sincerely,
> John S.
> (8/37)

And then later on a postcard he wrote, "In a few weeks I want to go up to your camp to see you. I'll bring blankets and stay a while if I may."

As soon as possible after the script for *Of Mice and Men* was finished, and even though Kaufman wanted him to stay to help stage the play on Broadway, John, with his wife, left on the train for Chicago. There, they bought a car and then drove back to California, following the migrants' route along through Oklahoma and then through the Central Valley. Back home, the conflict between new-found wealth and celebrity, on the one hand, and compassion for the plight of "his" migrants, on the other, once again came to the fore as he prepared to return to the field. His battered old Chevy would have been appropriate, but he could hardly mingle among the desperately poor migrants in a new car. So he bought an old bakery wagon and piled his blankets and cooking gear in the back.

Many years later, in a somewhat similar situation when he was outfitting "Rocinante" for the voyage he took with Charley to rediscover America, he compared the pickup with its camper to the pie wagon he took to the Central Valley. In both instances he wanted to get out among the people without being conspicuous. About the end of October 1937, he left his home in Los Gatos and headed east to Stockton, then north through Sacramento, Marysville, and on to the government camp at Gridley, where Tom Collins was the manager.

•   •   •   •

John stayed in town for a couple of days, coming into the camp frequently to visit with Tom and talk to the campers. Then, Tom and John went out together for a few days to work in the hop fields and to stay the night on a ranch here and a squatters' camp there. During this period John wrote a card posted from the Gridley camp to Larry Powell, his first bibliographer:

Dear Larry:
I have to write this sitting in a ditch. Carol forwarded your
letter. . . . I'll be home in two or three weeks. I'm out
working—may go south to pick a little cotton. All this—needless to say is *not* for publication—migrants are going south
now and I'll probably go along. I enjoy it a lot.

Very flattering article—thanks.
Sincerely,
John

This was the trip that Steinbeck's Los Gatos friends thought was
being made to Oklahoma. Actually, he and Tom Collins traveled in
the pie wagon south, down Highway 99 to Stockton, Fresno, and
Arvin, staying a few days at Collins's old camp with the idea of joining up with the migrants to pick cotton. But Steinbeck and Collins
found the situation around Bakersfield chaotic and dangerous, ready
to explode. Attracted by the cotton harvest, 70,000 migrants had
gathered in the San Joaquin Valley during the end of the summer.
There was no work, because the crop was late, and due to the vast
surplus of labor, not much chance of work once the crop came in.
So most of these people found themselves stuck in the Valley with
no opportunity to get money and no resources with which they could
either continue to live in the Valley or move elsewhere. They
roamed the countryside like wild animals, trying to find some means
of subsistence.

Steinbeck and Collins continued their survey of conditions by
driving on to Barstow and following Highway 66 to Needles at the
state line, and from there, going on to Brawley, in the Imperial
Valley, by way of Blythe and El Centro. After a trip of about four
weeks, Steinbeck came home from the south, stopping by to see his
sister Esther in Watsonville (the pie wagon in genteel company
proved embarrassing—his brother-in-law was a conservative farmer).
Home in Los Gatos before Thanksgiving, he started to work again
on his manuscript, writing steadily in ink in a large bookkeeping
ledger and at the end of each day counting his words and entering
the total in a column at the back. He was very troubled by what he
had seen, and working like an accountant (his father's occupation)
was part of his self-discipline.

In the meantime, the thousands of transients in the Central

Valley were, in the words of Carey McWilliams, herded about like
cattle and "permitted to eke out an existence in the fantastic hope
that they would ultimately disperse, vanish into the sky or march
over the mountains and into the sea or be swallowed up by the rich
and fertile earth. But they did not move, and with the winter season
came heavy rains and floods. Soon a major crisis was admitted to
exist, with over 50,000 workers destitute and starving."[14] The people
at various social agencies knew what was happening but were frustrated by an inability to act. After beating back the temporary challenge of union organizing in the early and middle thirties, the large
growers and their corporate allies had once again assumed almost
absolute power in the state's agriculture industry. By putting tremendous pressure on both the state's administration and the
Congress, they were able to use their opposition to any sort of government aid for migrant workers to insure a "go slow" policy. They
were afraid that help for the workers would encourage them to stay
where they were not needed, and they opposed aid on the grounds
that it would give the workers enough independence so that they
might try once again to organize.

At the height of the floods around Visalia, the Farm Security
Administration was called in to provide relief, but for many, it was
too little and too late. For the frustrated F.S.A. administrators, it was
a heartbreaking struggle. Conditions were so bad that field-workers
trying to get food to the migrants and to rescue the sick could not
get the supplies in where they were needed. Powerful trucks borrowed from the National Guard, fitted with tire chains, slipped, slid
into ditches, and bogged down in the mire. In the sea of mud that
confronted them, rescuers could not even find the stranded and half-
buried enclaves of migrants who had hidden themselves here and
there across thousands of square miles of drenched farmlands to escape the wrath of local authorities. The F.S.A. realized it was not
only fighting the elements in order to save lives, but it was fighting
a political battle as well. To make any progress with the problem
over the long haul, it would have to rally public opinion.

Steinbeck had letters from Fred Soule, at F.S.A. Information,
and Tom Collins describing the situation in the Valley. Soule asked
him if he couldn't go down to the flood area and help by reporting
what was going on. This is how John described his mission to his
agent, Elizabeth Otis:

I must go to Visalia. Four thousand families, drowned out of their tents are really starving to death. The resettlement administration of the government asked me to write some news stories. The newspapers won't touch the stuff but they will under my byline. The locals are fighting the government bringing in food and medicine. I'm going to try to break the story hard enough so that food and drugs can get moving. Shame and a hatred of publicity will do the job to the miserable local bankers. . . . Talk about Spanish children. The death of children by starvation in our valleys is simply staggering. I've got to do it. If I can sell the articles I'll use the proceeds for serum and such. Codliver oil would give the live kids a better chance.

(2/14/38)

Collins had been pulled away from his camp-manager post to join other F.S.A. personnel in the stricken area who were administering relief. After receiving his letter, Steinbeck wrote back: "Will you write as soon as you get this letting me know where you can be found at various times of the day or night? And Tom—please don't tell anyone I am coming. My old feud with the ass[ociated] farmers is stirring again and I don't want my movements traced." One of the reasons it has been so difficult for scholars to discover the details concerning Steinbeck's trips among the migrants is that he worked hard at the time to conceal them. From the time that *In Dubious Battle* and "The Harvest Gypsies" were published until several years after the publication of *The Grapes of Wrath*, Steinbeck had a genuine fear of retribution by the Associated Farmers for his pro-farm labor writings. He had seen what he believed to be evidence of intimidation by violence, blackmail, and extortion on the part of the Associated Farmers and other grower organizations and believed that they were capable of anything. Indeed, he and others familiar with the union movement in California were convinced that several "unsolved" murders of union leaders had been carried out by law enforcement officers at the behest of wealthy landowners. So it is not an exaggeration to say that since he had already become a symbol of the fight to help the dispossessed, he had some justification to fear for his life and was acting with courage, both in his direct actions to aid the migrants and in his determination to write his novel.

In mid-February of 1938, Steinbeck went to Visalia and spent about ten days in the company of Collins, helping in whatever way he could. As he wrote his agents, "I've tied into the thing from the first and I must get down there and see if I can't do something to help knock these murderers on the heads" (2/38). In an unpublished autobiographical novel, Collins described some of their experiences:

When we reached the flooded areas we found John's old pie truck useless, so we set out on foot. We walked most of the first night and we were very tired. . . . For forty-eight hours, and without food or sleep, we worked among the sick and half-starved people, dragging some from torn and ragged tents, floored with inches of water, stagnant water, to the questionable shelter of a higher piece of ground. We couldn't speak to one another because we were too tired, yet we worked together as cogs in an intricate piece of machinery. [At two o'clock in the morning they both just collapsed in the muddy fields and slept.]

. . . [At dawn] I found John lying on his back. He was a mass of mud and slime. His face was a mucky mask punctuated with eyes, a nose and a mouth. He was close beside me, so I knew it was John. How long we had slept in that mire we knew not. . . . [It began to rain again. Ahead of them, some yards away, they spied another tent.] We frightened the little children we found in the tent, the two little children. . . . We must have looked like men from some far-away planet to those two children, the sunken cheeks—the huge lump on the bed—they frightened John and me. Inside the tent was dry because it was on high land, but it was an island in a sea of mud and water all around it. Everything under that bit of canvas was dry—everything—the makeshift stove was without heat; all shapes of cans were empty; pans, pots and kettles—all were dry. Everything, for there was not a morsel of food—not a crumb of bread.

"Mommy has been like that a long time. She won't get up. Mommy won't listen to us. She won't get up." Such was the greeting cried to us by the two little children.

Mommy couldn't get up. She was the lump on the old bed. Mommy was ill and she hadn't eaten for some time. She had skimped and skimped so that the children would have a bite. . . .

"How far is it to the nearest store? Is there an old car near here? Is the store East or West?" But the children only stared as John threw the questions to them. Well did he know that the big food trucks could never get off the roads and travel two miles or more over the muddy, drowned fields to that tent! So John faded into the early morning. . . .

[Sometime later John returned.] John and I sat on the dirt floor. We sat there and the five of us ate the food which John had obtained from the little store some muddy distance away. We sat there and ate a bite—a bite that was a banquet. . . .

Then names and ages of our new-found friends for delivery to the government agency which would succor the isolated family, and we were off again to find other mothers and children out there in that vast wilderness of mud and deep water.[15]

After more than a week, John went into town to clean up and rest. With Collins and several other relief workers, he went to a restaurant to get his first solid, cooked meal in many days. He had two breakfasts of steak and eggs, much to the dismay of one of the workers, Sis Reamer (the very same woman who took John years earlier to meet Cicil McKiddy), who was very angry that he could bear to eat so well, considering that they were surrounded by people who were starving. This reaction would seem to foreshadow a conflict that would envelope John for the rest of his life; while conservatives like the Associated Farmers would continue to denounce him as a Communist, liberals would attack him for his lack of total commitment to the welfare of the poor. He cared deeply about the poor, but his commitment was to writing, not to political solutions.[16]

* * *

John went home for only two days and was back again in the flood area. Returning from this second trip, he wrote to Elizabeth:

Just got back from another week in the field. The floods have aggravated the starvation and sickness. I went down for Life this time. Fortune wanted me to do an article for them but I don't. I don't like the audience. The Life sent me down with a photographer from its staff and we took a lot of pictures of the people. They guarantee not to use it if they change it and will send me the proofs. They paid my expenses and will put up money for the help of some of these people. . . .

It is the most heartbreaking thing in the world. If Life does use the stuff there will be lots of pictures and swell ones. It will give you an idea of the kind of people they are and the kind of faces. I break myself every time I go out because the argument that one person's effort can't really do anything doesn't seem to apply when you come on a bunch of starving children and you have a little money. I can't rationalize it for myself anyway. So don't get me a job for a slick [magazine]. I want to put a tag of shame on the greedy bastards who are responsible for this but I can best do it through newspapers.

(2/38)

But *Life* did not print the article, apparently because he would not let them edit it and some of the language was too liberal for the editors to swallow. The irony was that the big money magazine, *Fortune*, got someone else to do an article which, even though it was sympathetic to the migrants, *was* published.[17]

John's experiences in the flood had a profound effect on him. They would eventually lead to the dramatic final scenes of his finished novel, but in the meantime they sat in the back of his mind, like a conscience prodding him toward a deeper, more significant creation than the one he was presently working on. He was not satisfied with the tenor and direction of "L'Affaire Lettuceberg," and when he was nearly finished with the draft in early May of 1938, he revealed his doubts to his agent, telling her that if she thought it was no good, then he would "burn it up and forget it."

When he began the project, almost two years earlier, he had the idea that he had gained enough monetary security so that he could take several years to write a long, complex novel which he would attempt to make an important work of art. Soon afterward, however, he was pulled by his sympathies toward launching a satirical attack on those responsible for the horrors of migrant life and the terrors of vigilante violence. For these many months he had been drawn by his emotions in one direction, and by his artistic aspirations in another, yet he was unwilling to recognize that he could fulfill one goal or the other but probably not both. Now that the draft was nearly completed, he claimed, in a letter to his agent, that "I don't care about its literary excellence . . . only whether it does the job I want it to do. . . . It is a mean, nasty book and if I could make it nastier I would" (5/2/38).

But in the end, the artist won out over the propagandist. Carol, as committed as she was to the cause of the underdog, hated the draft and argued against it. John himself found that he could not stomach it, and writing once again to his agent, Elizabeth Otis, explained why he had decided to burn it, after all: "Not once in the writing of it have I felt the curious warm pleasure that comes when work is going well. My whole work drive has been aimed at making people understand each other and then I deliberately write this book, the aim of which is to cause hatred through partial understanding" (5/38). The most persuasive argument against "L'Affaire Lettuce-berg" would not have been possible damage to his reputation, which he cared little about, but, following his traumatic struggle to save lives in the mud of the San Joaquin Valley, that a cheap treatment would not do justice to the dignity of his subject.

So he started all over. This time the book would focus on the migrants themselves, rather than on his hatred of those who had persecuted them. By the first of June he was well on his way and pleased with his progress, writing to Elizabeth Otis that "it is a nice thing to be working and believing in my work again" and "I don't yet understand what happened or why the bad book should have cleared the air so completely for this one. I am simply glad that it is so" (6/1/38).

There was something in John's makeup that seemed to make it impossible for him to slowly plan, develop, and then deliberately write a long work of fiction. The excitement of the material and emotion would cook in his mind, so that the pressure built to a point that slow, careful composition became impossible. When at last he found his true direction and began writing the final draft of *The Grapes of Wrath*, he made it a long sprint, rather than a marathon run, and the strain very nearly destroyed him. From the beginning of June to the end of October, he wrote the manuscript, and then during November and early December, he revised and made corrections. Although he repeatedly told himself to slow down, the pace gradually quickened until, during the last weeks, he was working day and night. It was a remarkable period of work: in six months he wrote a 200,000-word novel that was highly complex in structure, detailed in fabric, and quite varied in tone and style.

In early September he reported to Elizabeth Otis that

> Carol is typing ms (2nd draft) and I'm working on first. I can't tell when I will be done but Carol will have second done almost at the same time I have first. And—this is a secret— the 2nd draft is so clear and good that it, carefully and clearly corrected, will be what I submit. Carol's time is too valuable to do purely stenographic work.
>
>   (9/10/38)

Carol was in fact writing the revision, that is, correcting errors and editing for contradictions and awkwardness, while John was doing the initial draft. In the same letter he reported that his wife had come up with a brilliant idea for the title of the new book. "The grapes of wrath" from "The Battle Hymn of the Republic" gave the book a dynamic focus, and the words of the hymn could be applied in numerous ways to the novel's contents:

> I . . . like it better all the time. I think it is Carol's best title so far. I like it because it is a march and this book is a kind of march—because it is in our own revolutionary tradition and because in reference to this book it has a large meaning. And I like it because people know the Battle Hymn who don't know the Star Spangled Banner.

He particularly liked the title because it gave an American stamp to his material. From previous experience he knew that there would be those who would try to smear the book as foreign-spirited, and he wanted to blunt such an attack from the outset because he felt very strongly that what he was describing was an American phenomenon. . . .

NOTES

1. Interview, Mrs. Carol (Steinbeck) Brown, 20 July 1970; interview, Mrs. Gwyndolyn Steinbeck, 6 March 1971.
2. John Steinbeck, "Foreword" to Windsor Drake (Tom Collins), "Bring-

ing in the Sheaves," *Journal of Modern Literature* 5 (April 1976): 211–13.

3. Interview, Patricia Collins Olson, 14 April 1974.

4. F.S.A./Wash.

5. Arvin Migratory Labor Camp Reports, F.S.A./San Bruno.

6. Interview, Milan Dempster, 16 June 1971.

7. Interview (by John Berthelsen), Dewey Russell.

8. Interview, Reginald Loftus, 23 June 1971.

9. The material in this and the following paragraphs has been taken from the Arvin Migratory Labor Camp Reports, Lubin Collection, Bancroft Library, University of California, Berkeley.

10. "Dubious Battle in California," 302–304.

11. August 1936.

12. October 1936. Special Collections, Stanford University Libraries.

13. Interview, Mrs. Carol (Steinbeck) Brown, 31 May 1974.

14. McWilliams, *Factories*, 315.

15. Windsor Drake (Tom Collins), "From *Bringing in the Sheaves*," *Journal of Modern Literature* 5 (April 1976): 221–24.

16. Ibid.; interview, Francis Whitaker, 18 October 1976.

17. "I Wonder Where We Can Go Now," *Fortune* (April 1939).

Robert DeMott

Robert DeMott teaches at Ohio University. He is the author of Steinbeck's Reading, *and the editor of* Working Days: The Journals of The
Grapes of Wrath, *which was chosen as a New York Times* Outstanding Book *in 1989. His recent essays are collected in* Steinbeck's Type-
writer, *and his recent poetry in* News of Loss. *He is a member of the
editorial board of* The Steinbeck Newsletter, *and coedited (with Elaine
Steinbeck) two volumes in the Library of America Steinbeck series.*

"WORKING DAYS AND HOURS": STEINBECK'S WRITING OF *THE GRAPES OF WRATH*

I wrote *The Grapes of Wrath* in one hundred days, but many years
of preparation preceded it. I take a hell of a long time to get
started. The actual writing is the last process.[1]

John Steinbeck's masterpiece *The Grapes of Wrath* (1939) had a
complex foreground and grew through an eventful process of ac-
cretion and experimentation. In one way or another, from August
1936, when Steinbeck discovered the plight of the Dust Bowl refu-

Reprinted from *Studies in American Fiction* 18:1 (Spring 1990), 3–15. Copyright
Northeastern University, 1990. This essay is condensed and revised from the Intro-
duction to *Working Days: The Journals of* The Grapes of Wrath by John Steinbeck,
edited by Robert DeMott (Viking Press, 1989). Introduction copyright © 1989 by
Robert DeMott. By permission of Viking Penguin, a division of Penguin Books USA
Inc. and *Studies in American Fiction*.

gees in California, a subject he told Louis Paul was "like nothing in the world," through October of 1939, when he vowed to put behind him "that part of my life that made the *Grapes*," the "Matter of the Migrants" was Steinbeck's major artistic preoccupation.[2] "The writer can only write about what he admires," Steinbeck claimed, "and since our race admires gallantry, the writer will deal with it where he finds it. He finds it in the struggling poor now. (Steinbeck, "Interview," this volume, 540.) From the moment Steinbeck entered the fray, he prophesied that the presence of the heroic, pioneer-stock Oklahoma migrants would change the fabric of California life. He had little foresight, however, about what his own role in that change would be, how difficult realizing his vision would become, or the degree to which his writing labors would change him.

Between 1936 and 1938 Steinbeck's engagement with his material evolved through at least four major stages of writing: (1) A seven-part series of investigative reports, "The Harvest Gypsies," which appeared October 5–12, 1936, in the San Francisco *News*. (These were reprinted in the spring of 1938 as a pamphlet, *Their Blood Is Strong*, published by the Simon J. Lubin Society with a preface by John Barry.) (2) An unfinished novel, "The Oklahomans," which apparently belonged to late 1937 and which has not survived. (3) A "vicious" 70,000-word anti-vigilante satire, "L'Affaire Lettuceberg," which he finished between February and May of 1938 and then destroyed. And (4) *The Grapes of Wrath*, which was written in one hundred days between late May and late October of 1938.

The ecologically minded Steinbeck wasted little of this material; aspects of setting, conflict, characterization, and theme established in the first three stages found their way into *The Grapes of Wrath*. Each stage shared a fixed core of opposing elements: on one side, the tyranny of California's industrialized agricultural system; on the other side, the innate dignity and resilience of the victimized American migrants. As Steinbeck unequivocally reminded San Francisco *News* columnist John Barry, "every effort I can bring to bear is and has been at the call of the common working people to the end that they may eat what they raise, wear what they weave, use what they produce, and in every way and in completeness share in the works of their hands and their heads. And the reverse is also true. I am actively opposed to any man or group who, through financial or political control of means of production and distribution, is able to control and dominate the lives of workers."[3]

Each stage of composition differs, however, in tone, style, and execution, so that by the time Steinbeck wrote his celebrated novel, his vision and his control had matured greatly. When Steinbeck witnessed the flooding and starvation at Visalia in February and March of 1938, his attitude toward the workers' plight deepened drastically. It was no longer possible for him to record those experiences in a cool, journalistic manner, as he had done in "The Harvest Gypsies." Stronger emotions were required to do the subject justice. At first it was blind anger in the case of "L'Affaire"; then, when that unbridled ferociousness seemed to trivialize both his talent and his subject, he called up in its place every ounce of moral indignation and compassion. Thus, besides providing the setting for the final chapters of *The Grapes of Wrath*, Steinbeck's wounding at Visalia opened the floodgates of his attention, created the compelling justification of the novel, provided its haunting spiritual urgency, and rooted it in the deepest well springs of democratic fellow-feeling. In short, Visalia made all the difference between cranking out a cheap revenge tract and writing a novel of tragic ennoblement.

During the writing of his 200,000-word novel, Steinbeck also kept a journal to record his struggle with the book and with the times from which it emerged. Ninety-nine entries spanning the summer and fall of 1938 constitute the true history of the making of *The Grapes of Wrath*. The entries comprise Steinbeck's attempt "to map the actual working days and hours" of his novel and therefore provide an unparalleled account of the shapings and seizings, the naked slidings, of his creative psyche. Steinbeck's private diary reveals self-doubts, whining, paranoia, and reversals; it also shows dedication, resourcefulness, integrity, and endurance. Taken together, this twin, double-voiced, parallel construction (the public *The Grapes of Wrath* on one side and the private *Working Days* on the other) enacts the process of Steinbeck's humanistic belief and embodies the shape of his artistic faith.

Unlike the sprawling entries on symbolism and philosophy that mark Steinbeck's daily log for his 1952 novel *East of Eden* (the entries were published posthumously in 1969 as *Journal of a Novel: The East of Eden Letters*), here Steinbeck is working in a different mode, more focused and sharp, less self-reflexive and expansive, but no less revealing about his habitual literary concerns. Readers accustomed to the tone of familiarity and camaraderie of *Journal of a Novel* (the entries were daily letters to Pascal Covici) will find this "diary of a book" limited in intention and scope, and hermetic (even claustro-phobic) in tone and attitude. Here, for instance, is his fifth entry, written on June 3, 1938, when he was a couple of days into the novel's composition:

> Duke arrived yesterday. Left this morning. [Indecipherable] showed up this morning. Had to kick them out. Simply can't have people around on working days. Carol spending the day down on the peninsula. Telephone ringing pretty badly. Suggested *The Long Valley* as title for shorts. Irritated today. People want to come to see me next Monday. Can't be. Just want to sit. Day not propitious. Have a loose feeling that makes me nervous. Will get to work and try to forget all the bothers. I get nuts if not protected from all the outside stuff. Dinner tonight at Tolertons'. I like them very much. Must make note of work progress at the end of this day. I want to finish my stint if possibly I can. Impulses to do other things. Wind blowing over me, etc. But must continue for the sake of discipline. Well, the stint is done but I think I'll try to finish out the chapter tomorrow. Be about one more page. Lionel Smith came over. Bob C. and Margery Bailey coming down tomorrow night. Glad I got done. I hate to break the discipline.

Brief and staccato, these daily notes helped regulate his discipline in the face of an inordinate number of interruptions (some worthwhile, most merely bothersome) that his growing public fame as the author of *In Dubious Battle*, *Of Mice and Men*, and *Their Blood Is Strong* had brought him. (An agent for Selznick International Pictures set the tone of the summer by requesting an "advanced reading" of the unwritten novel "to review its motion picture possibilities"; exasperated, Steinbeck directed his agents to reply that "the book will not be for sale!")

Despite the "leisurely" pace he hoped to establish for his novel, Steinbeck could hardly wait to address the day's fictive project before his concentration waned.

> Now to the day's work and now Muley comes in and the reason for the desertion becomes apparent. Also the night comes with sleeping in the darkening plain and stars. And

after that I think a small inter chapter or maybe a large one
dealing with the equipment of migration. Well here goes for
Muley. Well that is done. I like Muley. He is a fine hater.
Must write a few letters now.

Steinbeck's covenant with the fiction-making process took precedence over incendiary sociological or political demands. He was writing a novel, not a journalistic tract. On July 6, just launched into
Chapter 13, he stated:

> Now the land work starts again. Now the crossing and I must
> get into it the feeling of movement and of life. . . . Make the
> people live. Make them live. But my people must be more
> than people. They must be an over-essence of people. . . . It
> is the first day and night. And it has in it the first commu-
> nication with other migrants. This is important, very impor-
> tant. . . . I simply must get this book done before anything
> else. No matter what other things are going on. And I can't
> leave. I must get back to the Joad family on their movement
> to the west. And now the time has come to go to work. . . .
> Work is the only good thing.

Maintaining his work intensity was paramount. Without looking
back, Steinbeck overcame the disappointing "L'Affaire Lettuceberg," and within a week, or perhaps ten days at the most, he started
headlong on the new, unnamed manuscript, which was not actually
entitled *The Grapes of Wrath* until early September by Carol Steinbeck, who was typing the novel. However, his work on "L'Affaire"
was not wasted because it cleared the way for *The Grapes* by purging
his unchecked anger and the desire for his own brand of artistic
vengeance. Naturally, following the events he witnessed at Visalia,
Steinbeck's partisanship for the migrants and his sense of indignation at California's labor situation carried over to the new book, but
they were given a more articulate, and therefore believable, shape.
The whole process of passing through a "bad" book proved beneficial.[4]

The epic scale and technical plan of *Grapes* apparently crystal-
lized between May 15 and May 25 of 1938. During that time, perhaps the most fertile germinative moment in Steinbeck's writing life,
the organizational form of the novel, with its alternating chapters of

exposition and narrative, leaped to life in his mind. Steinbeck was not an elite literary practitioner, but he achieved in *The Grapes of Wrath* a compelling combination of individual style, visual realism, and rambunctious, symphonic form that was at once accessible and experimental, documentarian and fictive, expository and lyrical. He envisioned the novel whole, all the way down to the subversive last scene "ready for so long" (Rose of Sharon giving her breast to a starving man), which became both the propelling image of the book and the imaginative climax toward which the entire novel moved.[5]

Indeed, except for a few after-thoughts and insertions, *The Grapes of Wrath* was written with remarkably pre-ordained motion and directed passion. Steinbeck apparently did not work from a formal outline (nothing of the kind has ever turned up); rather, he sketched out the novel in his head in aggregate first, followed by a brief planning session each day. While Steinbeck vacillated about his ability to execute the plan, he showed few reservations about the plan itself. On June 10 he wrote in his work diary:

> With luck I should be finished with this first draft in October sometime and then God knows what I'll do. I'll surely be ready for a rest. Sometimes now I get a little bit tired just with the multitude of this story but the movement is so fascinating that I don't stay tired. And the leisurely pace is good too. This must be a good book. It simply must. I haven't any choice. It must be far and away the best thing I've ever attempted—slow but sure, piling detail on detail until a picture and an experience emerge. Until the whole throbbing thing emerges. And I can do it. I feel very strong to do it. Today for instance into the picture is the evening and the cooking of the rabbits and the discussion of prison and punishment. And the owls and the cat catches a mouse and they sit on the sloping porch. And tomorrow the beginning of the used car yard if I am finished with this scene. Better make this scene three pages instead of two. Because there can never be too much of background. Well to work on the characters. Friday's work is done and I think pretty good work. . . .

From the outset Steinbeck possessed an intuitive sense of rightness concerning the direction his book and his characters would take.

Indeed, *The Grapes of Wrath* embodies the form of his attention: in the entire handwritten manuscript of 165 12" × 18" ledger pages, the number of deletions and emendations are so few and infrequent as to be nearly nonexistent.[6] Despite his late stretch-drive doubts, and the refrain of self-deprecation that sounds throughout the work diary, the truth is that in writing *The Grapes of Wrath* Steinbeck was creating with the full potency of his imaginative powers. His ability to execute a work of its reach and magnitude so flawlessly places him among the premier creative talents of his age. From the vantage point of history, the venture stands as one of those happy occasions when a writer simply wrote better than he thought he could.

Steinbeck set out immediately to establish a unified work rhythm, a "single track mind" that would allow him to complete the enormous task in approximately five months. Though he had written steadily throughout the 1930s (he published eleven books and limited editions in the first eight years of the decade), the work never seemed to get easier. Averaging 2000 words a day (some days as few as 800, some days, when the juices were flowing, as many as 2200), Steinbeck began the novel unhurriedly to keep its "tempo" under control, hoping at the same time to keep alive the large rhythmic structure of the novel. This he accomplished by listening to Tchaikovsky's ballet *The Swan Lake*, Stravinsky's "very fine" *Symphony of Psalms*, and Beethoven's symphonies and sonatas. Music set a mood conducive to writing and established a rhythm for the day's work. Even more important, classical music provided Steinbeck with structural and lyric analogies for his fiction.[7] The contrapuntal form of the novel, with its alternating chapters, its consonant combination of major chords, is deeply rooted in the attentiveness, the tonal acuity, of Steinbeck's ear.

Even with musical inspiration, however, Steinbeck's anxiety escalated during the late summer, his pace became increasingly frenetic, and his work became a chore. That he completed the novel within the time he had allotted testifies to his discipline, resilience, will power, and singleness of purpose. His story of making his novel is a dramatic testimony to triumph over intrusions, obstacles, and self-inflicted doubts. Nearly each day brought unsolicited requests for his name and new demands on his time, including unscheduled visitors, unanticipated disruptions, and reversals. Domestic relations with Carol were frequently strained, even hostile (Steinbeck apparently subscribed to the theory that sexual intercourse dissipated the creative drive). Throughout the summer a procession of house guests trooped to Los Gatos, including his sisters, Beth Ainsworth and Mary Dekker, and long-time friends Carlton "Duke" Sheffield, Ed Ricketts, and Ritch and Tal Lovejoy, plus new acquaintances, such as Wallace and Martha Ford, Broderick Crawford, Charlie Chaplin, and Pare Lorentz.

As if that were not enough to erode the novelist's initial composure and solitude, the Steinbecks' tiny house on Greenwood Lane was besieged with the noise of neighborhood building, which nearly drove them to distraction. By mid-summer, hoping for permanent sanctuary, they began looking at secluded real estate, finally settling on the Biddle Ranch, a 47-acre spread in the Santa Cruz Mountains above Los Gatos. Even though it was the most stunning location they had ever seen, its original homestead was in utter disrepair, so besides buying the land the Steinbecks would also have to build a new house, and that too became the source of additional frustrations and distractions. They did not move there until November of 1938, the month after *Grapes* was finished (all final corrections of the typescript and galley proofs took place at the Biddle Ranch), but preparations for its purchase took up a great deal of Steinbeck's time and energy from mid-July onward: "Friday I took off to consider my progress, and instead got caught in all the details of the new ranch. And I grow frightened of this property. It is so much. One person or two have not the right to have so much."

Although Steinbeck insisted on effacing his own presence in *The Grapes of Wrath*, the fact is that it was a very personal book, invested with biographical import. In a general way, the "plodding" pace of Steinbeck's writing schedule informed the slow, "crawling" movement of the Joads' journey, while the harried beat of his own life gave the proper "feel" and tone to the beleaguered Joads. Specifically, aspects of Steinbeck's life bore directly on manuscript decisions. For instance, on July 12, confused by increasing distractions and lured by the possibility of owning the Biddle Ranch, Steinbeck did not know which "general" chapter he would use next. During the planning session of Wednesday morning, July 13, he settled on what would become Chapter 14, one of the most important theoretical chapters in the novel and perhaps the most significant summation of organismal philosophy Steinbeck had yet written. The first half of the chapter augurs changes in the Western states' socioeconomic basis, and includes a paean to the universal human capacity for creation: "For man, unlike any other thing organic or inorganic in the universe, grows beyond his work, walks up the stairs of his concepts, emerges ahead of his accomplishments" (151). The second half of the chapter expresses the central core of Steinbeck's mature Phalanx theory, the creation of an aggregate, dynamic "We" from distinct, myriad selves. The summary quality of this chapter suggests that Steinbeck intended to use it later in the novel as a kind of climactic crescendo. Instead he inserted it at the mid-point of the novel for several reasons: its dithyrambic tone and heightened language re-awakened his flagging attention; its optimistic, theoretical values restored focus and clarity to the narrative line; its extolment of creativity, based on humanity's willingness to "suffer and die for a concept," provided an immediate reminder that his own compositional process could be endured for the sake of the cause he espoused; and its concern for families who had lost their land may have partly assuaged his guilt, if not his sense of irony, as he was about to make the biggest property purchase of his life.

Emerging ahead of his accomplishments seemed to Steinbeck insurmountable at times that summer, because major interruptions kept occurring, any one of which might have sidetracked a less dedicated writer. August proved the most embattled time of all. Early in the month Steinbeck noted in his journal: "There are now four things or five rather to write through—throat, bankruptcy, Pare, ranch, and the book."[8] His litany of woes included Carol's painful tonsil operation, which temporarily incapacitated her; the bankruptcy of Steinbeck's publisher, Covici-Friede, which threatened the end of steady royalty payments and an uncertain publishing future for the novel he was writing; Pare Lorentz's offer to involve Steinbeck in making a film version of *In Dubious Battle*; the purchase of the Biddle Ranch, which Carol wanted badly and Steinbeck felt compelled to buy for her (they argued over the pressure this caused); and the book itself, still untitled (and therefore still without "being"), which now seemed more recalcitrant than ever (Fensch, *Conversations*, 21–27). Except for the making of the film, all these dilemmas resolved themselves, though not always quickly enough for Steinbeck. On August 16, in the middle of what he called a "Bad, Lazy Time," he lamented:

Demoralization complete and seemingly unbeatable. So many things happening that I can't not be interested. . . . All this is more excitement than our whole lives put together. All crowded into a month. . . . My many weaknesses are beginning to show their heads. I simply must get this thing out of my system. I'm not a writer. I've been fooling myself and other people. I wish I were. This success will ruin me as sure as hell. It probably won't last, and that will be all right. I'll try to go on with work now. Just a stint every day does it, I keep forgetting.

Although Steinbeck did not believe writing was a team sport, the fact is *The Grapes of Wrath* profited from the involvement of other people, primarily Tom Collins, who kept Steinbeck supplied with much of the basic field information he needed to make his novel accurate and detailed, and Carol Steinbeck, who besides typing the novel, served her husband in most other imaginable capacities. By dedicating the novel to them, Steinbeck properly acknowledged their contributions. What is not widely known, however, is the importance of filmmaker Pare Lorentz. His documentary film *The River* (1937) directly influenced the style of Steinbeck's novel (especially the catalogue of towns along Route 66 in Chapter 12); his martial rendition of Julia Ward Howe's "Battle Hymn of the Republic" at the end of his radio drama *Ecce Homo!* (May, 1938) may have given Carol Steinbeck the idea for the novel's title, *The Grapes of Wrath*. More than that, Lorentz provided moral support when Steinbeck was floundering with the novel and was personally depressed.

On the weekend of August 20, Lorentz arrived in Los Gatos (Steinbeck had not seen him since Spring). As the newly appointed director of the United States Film Service, Lorentz was supervising filming of the Grand Coulee Dam construction scenes for his cinematic *Ecce Homo!* Lorentz was one of the other major American artists working with the bleak subject of the displacement of the "Common Man," so it should come as no surprise that the novelist considered the filmmaker a spiritual ally: "You know what I think of Pare. I'll back him and work with him to the limit. And he's about the *only* man I would do a picture with."[9] They discussed further a full-length dramatic film of *In Dubious Battle*, then rushed off to visit Charlie Chaplin in Pebble Beach, where they stayed up all night, drinking and talking about the state of Depression America. Most of all, Lorentz, a man of exceptional vision and shared sympathies (they were both Rooseveltian New Dealers), made Steinbeck feel less depressed about the "temper" of the "country at large" and about the novelist's own accomplishments, praising the technique and theme of Steinbeck's new book as "monumental."[10] Rescued from his crisis of conscience by Lorentz's prediction that the book would be "among the greatest novels of the age," Steinbeck rebounded.

In early October, rebuked often enough by his wife's example and by her words (Ma Joad's indomitableness owes much to Carol's spirit), Steinbeck roused himself from "self-indulgence" and "laziness" to mount the final drive. The last five chapters of the novel came to him so abundantly that he had more material than he could use. A few days from the end Steinbeck was so tired he nearly collapsed. He was again assailed with "grave doubts" about his "run-of-the-mill" book. And then, in one of those magical transferences artists are heir to in moments of extreme exhaustion or receptivity, Steinbeck believed that Tom Joad, his fictive alter ego, not only floated above the novel's "last pages . . . like a spirit," but he imagined that Joad actually entered the novelist's work space, the private chamber of his soul: "Tom! Tom! Tom!" Steinbeck wrote on October 20. "I know. It wasn't him. Yes, I think I can go on now. In fact, I feel stronger. Much stronger. Funny where the energy comes from. Now to work, only now it isn't work anymore." With that visitation, that benediction, Steinbeck arrived at the intersection of novel and journal, a luminous point where the life of the writer and the creator of life merge. The terms of the complex investment fulfilled, Steinbeck needed only three more days to complete *The Grapes of Wrath*.

Finally, sometime around noon on Wednesday, October 26, Steinbeck, "so dizzy" he could "hardly see the page," completed the last 775 words of the novel: "Finished this day—and I hope to God it's good." At the bottom of the concluding manuscript page, Steinbeck, whose writing was normally minuscule, scrawled in letters an inch-and-a-half high, "*END#*." It should have been cause for joyous celebration, but between bouts of bone-weary tiredness and nervous exhaustion, he felt only numbness and maybe a little of the mysterious satisfaction that comes from having given his all.

Steinbeck had no grasp of the effectiveness of his novel or its potential popularity, and he warned Covici—by now at Viking Press—against a large first printing. Following a four-day recuperation in San Francisco, the Steinbecks moved to their new Brush Road home (still under construction) on the old Biddle Ranch property, where Carol finished typing the 751-page typescript, and together they made "routine" final corrections. The only "clean" copy of the book was sent to his New York agents, McIntosh and Otis, on December 7, 1938, roughly six months after he sat down to write the novel. Elizabeth Otis' visit to Los Gatos in late December of 1938 to smooth out some of Steinbeck's "rough" language (especially the dozen instances of "fuck," "shit," "screw," and "fat ass"), its enthusiastic reception at Viking (spoiled briefly by the wrangling that ensued over the controversial ending) all struck the novelist, by then suffering from severely painful sciatica and tonsillitis, as anticlimactic.

Right after the novel officially appeared on April 14, 1939 (there were several advance printings before that, however, designed to take maximum advantage of the controversial subject), Steinbeck took off for the Middle West to work as an "Assistant Cameraman" for Lorentz, who was then filming Paul de Kruif's *The Fight for Life* at Chicago's Maternity Hospital. Steinbeck appreciated the anonymity that came from long hours of hard work in a strange city, and the challenge of learning the nuts and bolts of a new artistic medium, but there was still an element of "pure escapism" in his trip. It was a pattern Steinbeck would repeat several times over the next few years. Though he was not aware of it then, he had closed the door on an entire chapter of his life. The unabated sales, the frenzied public clamor, and the vicious personal attacks over *The Grapes of Wrath* confirmed his worst fears about the fruits of success and pushed the tensions between the Steinbecks to the breaking point, a condition exacerbated by Steinbeck's growing romantic attachment to a younger woman, Gwyn Conger, and his repeated absences in Mexico and Hollywood.

Steinbeck did not quit writing as he once threatened to do, but by the early 1940s, no longer content to be the chronicler of Depression-era subjects, he went afield to find new roots, new sources, new forms. Between 1940 and 1943, for example, Steinbeck's artistic quest resulted in unpublished poetry (a suite of twenty-five love poems for Gwyn), an unfinished satire ("The God in the Pipes"), and a completed novel written in first-person point of view, which was an unprecedented technical choice for Steinbeck (*Lifeboat*; only marginally the basis for Hitchcock's 1944 film). His restless "ranges and searches" also led to one of his most important publications, the collaborative travel and marine biology book, *Sea of Cortez: A Leisurely Journal of Travel and Research* (with Edward

F. Ricketts). During this period he also wrote a documentary film script, *The Forgotten Village*; a play-novel, *The Moon Is Down*; a patriotic documentary book, *Bombs Away: The Story of a Bomber Team*; and war journalism for the New York *Herald Tribune* (later collected as *Once There Was a War*). Clearly, he had energy to spare, though it no longer went into epic structures like *The Grapes of Wrath* but into the "foundation of some new discipline. . . ."

Many "have speculated," his biographer writes, "about what happened to change Steinbeck after *The Grapes of Wrath*. One answer is that what happened was the writing of the novel itself."[11] Here, surely, is a private tragedy, a cautionary tale, to parallel the tragic aspects of his fiction: an isolated individual writer composed a novel that extolled a social group's capacity for survival in a hostile economic world but was himself so nearly tractored under in the process that the unique qualities (the angle of vision, the vital signature, the moral indignation) that made his art exemplary in the first place could never be repeated with the same integrated force. If *The Grapes of Wrath* permanently changed the literary landscape of American fiction and altered the public's awareness about the socio-economic nightmare caused by the Dust Bowl, the Depression, and the corporate farm industry, the book also changed Steinbeck permanently. In his journal Steinbeck had the prescience to commit to words the inside narrative of his most focused years. Laboring over *The Grapes of Wrath* meant Steinbeck would never be the same writer again. His change from 1930s social realist to 1940s experimentalist was not caused by a bankruptcy of talent or even a failure of nerve. Rather, it was the backlash of an unprecedented success, a repugnant "posterity," that turned Steinbeck so painfully self-conscious, and so deeply disgusted with the imposed limits of proletarian subject matter and form, he could never again return to the "Matter of the Migrants," even though his critical audience clamored for him to do so, and turned hostile when he refused.

NOTES

1. John Steinbeck in Caskie Stinett, *Back to Abnormal* (New York: Bernard Geis Associates, 1963), p. 96.
2. In *Steinbeck: A Life in Letters* (New York: Viking Press, 1975), p. 129.
3. John Barry's San Francisco *News* column, "Ways of the World" (July 13, 1938), p. 14, reprinted in *Working Days*, pp. 151–52.

4. After destroying "L'Affaire," Steinbeck told his agent, Elizabeth Otis, on June 1st, ". . . it is a nice thing to be working and believing in my work again. I hope I can keep the drive all fall. I like it. I only feel whole and well when it is this way. I don't yet understand what happened or why the bad book should have cleared the air so completely for this one. I am simply glad that it is so." In Steinbeck, *Letters*, p. 167.

5. Jackson J. Benson in *Looking for Steinbeck's Ghost* (Norman: University of Oklahoma Press, 1988), pp. 71–72, offers a wholly new source for Steinbeck's final scene. A man named Kilkenny, who Steinbeck met in a hobo camp near Berkeley in the early 1920s, "told a story about himself in Oregon when he was fourteen, saved from death by exposure and starvation by being given the breast of a nursing farmer's wife. The writer gave Kilkenny some money and told him, 'I can use that.' "

6. For a textual study, see Roy S. Simmonds' careful examination, "The Original Manuscript," in the special *Grapes of Wrath* issue of *San Jose Studies*, XVI (Winter, 1990). See also "Note on the Texts" in the Library of America, *The Grapes of Wrath and Other Writings*, pp. 1051–1055.

7. In writing *The Grapes*, he said, "I have worked in a musical technique . . . and have tried to use the forms and the mathematics of music rather than those of prose. . . . In composition, in movement, in tone and in scope it is symphonic." John Steinbeck, letter to Merle Armitage (February 17, 1939); courtesy of University of Virginia Library.

8. See also his complaint to Elizabeth Otis: "My book crawls along day after day at about the same pace as the people in it. I hope it isn't a tiresome book. It might well be and I won't know it until it is finished and into type. With all the mess and illness and everything I only lost five working days and that isn't so bad. . . ." Letter, August [10 & 11], 1938; courtesy of Department of Special Collections, Stanford University Library.

9. John Steinbeck to Elizabeth Otis, Letter [August 4 and 5, 1938]; courtesy of Department of Special Collections, Stanford University Library. Steinbeck's imbibement of Lorentz's stylistic influence is reported in a letter to Joseph Henry Jackson. See DeMott, *Steinbeck's Reading*, p. 142.

10. Annie Laurie Williams to John Steinbeck, Letter (September 9, 1938); courtesy of Rare Book and Manuscript Library, Columbia University.

11. Benson, *True Adventures*, p. 392.

John Steinbeck

After the publication of The Grapes of Wrath, *Steinbeck found himself besieged with requests for guest appearances, speeches, and interviews. Being very shy and suspicious of the effects of publicity on the integrity of his work, he acceded to very few of these demands. When asked by his friend Joseph Henry Jackson of the San Francisco Chronicle, however, he sent the following suggestion for the kind of questions and answers he would prefer in such an interview.*

SUGGESTION FOR AN INTERVIEW WITH JOSEPH HENRY JACKSON

Q. Why did you choose the migration from the dust bowl to California as the theme for a novel?

A. Well, whether a writer knows it or not, or wants it or not, he simply sets down what the people of his own time are doing, thinking, wanting. He can't help that. It is all the writer knows. I have set down what a large section of our people are doing and wanting, and symbolically what all people of all time are doing and wanting. This migration is the outward sign of the want.

Q. And what, in all time, are all people doing and wanting?

A. They use different symbols in different times but universally, people want comfort and security and out of these a relationship with one another. In the growth of our country the symbol of these things was new land. That was the security. The writer sets down the desire of his own time, the action of the people toward attaining that desire, the obstacles to attainment and the struggle to overcome the obstacles.

Q. In the growing American literature there was no such cleavage between so called classes as seems to be at the core of present-day writing. Can you account for that?

A. Easily. Before the country was settled, the whole drive of the country by both rich and poor was to settle it. To this end they worked together. The menaces were Indians, weather, loneliness and the quality of the unknown. But this phase ended. When there was no longer unlimited land for everyone, then battles developed for what there was. And then as always, those few who had financial resources and financial brains had little difficulty acquiring the land in larger and larger blocks. I speak in terms of land, but the same applies of course to all resources, minerals, timber, etc. This condition left the great people in their original desire for the security symbol, land, but this time the menace (as they say in Hollywood) had changed. It was no longer Indians and weather and loneliness, it had become the holders of the land. In this discussion I am ignoring justice and law although it is pretty impossible to acquire half a million acres of land justly and lawfully. Now, since the people go on with their struggle, the writer still sets down that struggle and still sets down the opponents. The opponents or rather the obstacles to the desired end right now happen to be those individuals and groups of financiers who by the principle of ownership withhold security from the mass of the people. And since this is so, this is the material the writer deals in.

Q. And do you think that by removing this principle of ownership, the people will gain their desire?

A. To a certain extent. But the greatness of the human lies in the fact that he never attains his desire. His desire keeps bounding ahead of his attainment and his search is endless. Out of this he has grown stronger slowly and constantly during the ages. There is little question in my mind that the principle of private ownership of means of production is not long with us. This is not in terms of what I think is right or wrong or good or bad, but in terms of what is inevitable. The province of the writer is to set down what is and what may come of it with as little confusion and as little nonsense as possible. The human like any other life form will tolerate an un-healthful condition for some time and then will either die or will overcome the condition either by mutation or by destroying the un-healthful condition. Since there seems little tendency for the human race to become extinct, and since one cannot through biological mu-tation overcome the necessity for eating, I judge that the final method will be the one chosen.

Q. During the middle period of American writing, many books were written about owners and financiers, in a word about the con-trollers of financial destiny, the empire builders and such. Lately there are no such books. Books are written about the poor. Can you account for this?

A. Boileau said that Kings, Gods, and Heroes only were fit sub-jects for literature. The writer can only write about what he admires. Present-day kings aren't very inspiring, the gods are on a vacation and about the only heroes left are the scientists and the poor. In the time you speak of, the time of the empire builders, those giants may have been outrageous but they had courage. When they did a thing they took the credit or the blame. Rockefeller at Leadville earned the hatred of the whole country for shooting miners. But at present there are no heroic giants. Ownership is hidden in interlocking di-rectorates, labor spying and labor war is carried on by agents pro-vocateurs, owners hide under the names of proxies and corporation titles. In a word, they have ceased being Heroes and have become cowardly and contemptible. And as such they have become, in Boi-leau's sense, unworthy of literature. But the poor are still in the open. When they make a struggle it is an heroic struggle with star-vation, death or imprisonment the penalty if they lose. And since our race admires gallantry, the writer will deal with it where he finds it. He finds it in the struggling poor now. When the rich are hurt they show a tendency to jump off office buildings, or, as several doctors have assured me, to become sexually impotent.

Q. Then you admire the migrant people you describe in this book? Will you tell me why?

A. I admire them intensely. Because they are brave, because al-though the technique of their life is difficult and complicated, they meet it with increasing strength, because they are kind, humorous and wise, because their speech has the metaphor and flavor and imagery of poetry, because they can resist and fight back and because I believe that out of those qualities will grow a new system and a new life which will be better than anything we have had before.

IV

Criticism

Editors' Introduction:
The Pattern of Criticism

The hysterical reaction that *The Grapes of Wrath* aroused in part of the American public, and notably in its politicians and self-appointed guardians of morality, was reflected in book reviews and literary essays. Most of these were emotional reactions to the social message of the novel. Curiously, as public excitement over the novel subsided, so too did literary interest, and there would be fewer critical essays on *The Grapes of Wrath* for the next fifteen years. To be sure, the novel was not ignored in literary histories and in surveys of American fiction, some of which contain valuable insights: for example, Harry Thornton Moore's chapter in his pioneer study of Steinbeck (1939), the twenty pages in Joseph Warren Beach's *American Fiction, 1920–1940* (reprinted in Tedlock and Wicker), and the briefer considerations by Harry Slochower, Floyd Stovall, and others.* But the current standing of a piece of literature is indicated to a large extent by its ability to sustain a dialogue among critics. It is therefore significant that in those first fifteen years there appeared in literary journals fewer than half a dozen essays devoted to a critical analysis of *The Grapes of Wrath*. Only two of these, by Frederic Carpenter (this volume, 562–71) and by Chester E. Eisinger (reprinted in Donohue) made a measurable contribution to our understanding of

This essay, in a slightly different form, was presented at the University of Connecticut conference on *The Grapes of Wrath*, May 3, 1969. It appeared in the first edition of this volume for the first time. The current version has been updated by Kevin Hearle.
* For complete bibliographical information about materials mentioned in this essay, consult the Bibliography at the end of this volume.

the novel. By contrast, in the equal space of time between 1954 and 1969 there appeared at least forty essays, short and long, on *The Grapes of Wrath*, most of which considered some technical aspect of the novel. For these and other reasons to be made clear, 1954 is a useful point of demarcation in an account of how the novel was received by critics.

One of the most striking aspects of critical writing about *The Grapes of Wrath* in its first fifteen years was its assertive nature. There was little analysis or detailed explication. This was true whether the topic of discussion was the novel's total impact, its use of interchapters, the nature of its social message, or whatever. The assertions concerning the characters' credibility and effectiveness were particularly extreme. There was Malcolm Cowley's statement that "in the Joad family, everyone from Grampa—'full a' piss an' vinegar,' as he says of himself—down to the two brats, Ruthie and Winfield, is a distinct and living person." And, there was Edmund Wilson's statement (reprinted in Donohue) that "it is as if human sentiments and speeches had been assigned to a flock of lemmings on their way to throw themselves into the sea." It is toward one of these two poles that almost all assertions gravitated. Thus Joseph Warren Beach: ". . . it is notable as a work of fiction by virtue of the fact that all social problems are so effectively dramatized in individual situations and characters." But the great majority of commentators agreed with Wilson. Harry Thornton Moore, who published the first book on Steinbeck the same year as *The Grapes of Wrath*, found Casy the most real character in the book, yet even Casy was "nevertheless . . . something of a contrivance, a sounding board." Arthur Hobson Quinn, as late as 1951, found all but Ma Joad to be "puppets with differentiating traits." Alfred Kazin, who thought Steinbeck's people in general were at least "always on the verge of becoming human," withheld this charity from the Joads, whom he called "symbolic marionettes." Similar assertions were made by Max Eastman, John S. Kennedy (reprinted in Tedlock and Wicker), W. M. Frohock, and Kenneth Burke, to name only well-known figures.

The voices of moderation were few. Harry Slochower said simply that Steinbeck was "more successful in his picture of the general forces that surround his people than in the creation of characters who react to them." And those attempting to understand the particular nature and purpose of Steinbeck's characterization were even fewer. Kenneth Burke, alone, among those critics agreeing with Wilson, offered a rationale for his opinion: ". . . most of the characters derive their role, which is to say their personality, purely from their relationship to the basic situation." Reacting to Wilson's strong statements, Stanley Edgar Hyman suggested (reprinted in Tedlock and Wicker) that by the same logic one could prove that "because Shakespeare packed *Hamlet* with images of disease and decay he thought of all people as diseased." Hyman went on to point toward a thematic use of these images in *The Grapes of Wrath*. Leon Whipple observed that ". . . on the whole Steinbeck is interested in people as symbols in his design" and "of necessity he makes inarticulate people articulate, but within the conventions we must grant a novelist."

This same pattern of polarity, with few opinions in between, is observed in another aspect of the novel to receive much critical attention—its interchapters. As late as 1951, Frederick J. Hoffman, a well-known and respected scholar, stated that these interchapters in *The Grapes of Wrath* are "perhaps some of the most wretched violations of aesthetic taste observable in modern American fiction. . . . A study of the style, rhetoric, and intellectual content of the fifteen chapters reveals Steinbeck's writing at its worst and his mind at its most confused. . . ." Although this judgment was not unique, no other commentator of significance quite reached this height of invective. Malcolm Cowley simply found most of the interchapters "too shrill, too evangelistic." At the other pole, we have such statements as Harry Thornton Moore's, that the interchapters are, in some respect, the best parts of the book, and Joseph Warren Beach's approval of them as, in the most part, "ingenious and effective means of dramatizing the thought of a whole group of people." Although Beach did not use the word, he described some of these interchapters in terms of cinematic montage techniques. Howard Baker found these chapters a "brilliant structural effect," imposing form on an "intrinsically formless narrative." Slochower found them necessary "because his characters by themselves, *do not know* and therefore cannot 'tell' the wider meaning of their story."

Incomplete as these attempts were, at least, unlike the opinions about the characters, they sometimes moved toward analytic understanding. Certainly not all critics stopped with Bernard de Voto, who found these interchapters "necessary because no one could have stood the painfulness of the story without some tranquilizing relief"!

It may be noted in passing that not all qualified readers found *The Grapes of Wrath* so moving. Harry Thornton Moore observed that the novel lacked the "compulsion of participation" necessary; that Steinbeck had assembled "all the ingredients for a great book, and then failed to provide it with a proportioned and intensified drama." Maxwell Geismar (reprinted in Donohue) thought the novel lacked the art and realism of certain previous Steinbeck books and was a return to glamour and theatrics, that it was sentimental and distorted. And Arthur Hobson Quinn, in 1951, recorded that "the final impression left by the novel is not of the author's indignation so much as of his cleverness as a contriver of effects." Puzzled by the novel's continuing popularity in the face of what he took to be true opinions like those above, Bernard Bowron (reprinted in French, *Companion*) set out to solve this mystery. He discovered that the novel's appeal lay not in its social message, or its characters, or its techniques (which he dismissed as "calculated crudities"), but in the simple fact that *The Grapes of Wrath* was another example of the "Wagons West" romance, complete with tarpaulin-covered trucks, campfires, natural hazards, and hostile Indians cleverly disguised as state troopers and deputized vigilantes. The novel, said Bowron, "appeals to any grown man who just wants to go camping," and it was finally dismissed as "a triumph of literary engineering."

As might be expected, the vehement polarity of opinion concerning another aspect of the novel, its sociological message, gradually subsided as the proletarian thirties gave way to the national unity of the forties. Also, the excellent article by Carey McWilliams, "California Pastoral" (this volume, 469–89), based on the LaFollette committee investigations, put a permanent lid on potboiling attempts to discredit the novel by an attack on its facts. One need quote only from Elizabeth Monroe to recall the kind of reaction which was soon to disappear, although it broke out briefly again in one essay as late as 1959. Miss Monroe objected to *The Grapes of Wrath* particularly because it is a novel "that preaches class warfare and hate," and because the only sin the novel recognizes is "the desire to possess" things. In the less extreme terms of another reviewer, Steinbeck was "arousing the poor . . . to courage, endurance, organization and revolt." The full weight of such statements cannot be appreciated unless it is kept in mind that in that era such terms were impossible to dissociate from international Communism.

In this context of opinion about the novel's sociological message, the very early essay by Frederic I. Carpenter (1941), "The Philosophical Joads," (this volume, 562–71) takes on real significance. Carpenter's analysis made two important points. First, that *The Grapes of Wrath* is not spontaneously irresponsible in its observations about American life, but has sure roots in our native American tradition: the mystical transcendentalism of Emerson, the earthy democracy of Whitman, and the pragmatic instrumentalism of William James. Carpenter leaned heavily on this. "To repeat," he said: "this group idea of *The Grapes of Wrath* is that of American Transcendentalism. . . . For the first time in history, *The Grapes of Wrath* brings together and makes real three great skeins of American thought." Secondly, and this is more implicit in the essay than explicit, Carpenter suggested that the novel's form and technique are intimately related to this content—the "imaginative realization of these old ideas in new and concrete forms."

Six years later, Chester E. Eisinger found a fourth "skein of American thought" in the novel—Jeffersonian agrarianism. It is interesting that Eisinger's perception of this element in *The Grapes of Wrath* led him to question the novel's accomplishment. "It remains to inquire," he summed up, "if agrarianism, its form and substance, is the part of the Jeffersonian tradition that we should preserve." And he went on to suggest that technological progress had made agrarianism impractical and undesirable. Eisinger's analysis, although it overstates somewhat, and Carpenter's essay were the most valuable contributions made in fifteen years to our understanding of the novel's social content.

In these same fifteen years there appeared no essays of comparable value analyzing the technical or formal aspects of *The Grapes of Wrath*. B. R. McElderry's essay (reprinted in French, *Companion*) in 1944 was a valiant attempt to give the novel critical respectability, but the method could not succeed. To bring short passages from a variety of critical essays by a variety of writers on drama, poetry, and fiction into momentary contact with the novel as if they were touchstones was not to examine "*The Grapes of Wrath* in the Light of Modern Critical Theory," but to light a match in the Marabar caves. For example, he quoted from Edmund Wilson's essay describing *The Grapes of Wrath* as "mere sentimental optimism" and then went on to say that although this is a valid charge, "I do not believe it is a very important one."

Finally, it is curious that although some reviewers and several

subsequent critics made general remarks concerning certain similarities of the novel to the Bible, no essay appeared in which this
similarity was explored further. In his study of Steinbeck, Moore
remarked in passing that "the exodus of the dispossessed looking for
their promised land" had a familiar ring, and suggested that Tom
Joad may be "the Joshua to come." Moore also noted the biblical
flavor of the prose style, but concluded lamely, "It may have been
partly deliberate in a general way (certainly there is no intricate
matching of episode with episode)." Except for some observations
concerning the symbolism of the novel's ending, no critic pushed
beyond this point. Yet it was precisely with an exploration of this
symbolism that productive analysis of *The Grapes of Wrath* was to
begin its second fifteen years in the winepress of criticism.

This period began in 1955 with Warren French's spirited attack
(reprinted in French, *Companion*) on Bowron's thesis that *The
Grapes of Wrath* owed its popularity to its exploitation of the "Wagons West" romance. French disposed of the superficial similarities
judged so significant by Bowron and also pointed out in detail the
basic differences, suggesting that both *The Grapes of Wrath* and the
"Wagons West" romances were examples of an older, journey motif
which included such variants as the Hebrew *Exodus*, the *Odyssey*,
and *Pilgrim's Progress*. This observation was elaborated by subsequent critics.

A year later Martin Shockley's ground-breaking essay, "Christian
Symbolism in *The Grapes of Wrath*" (reprinted in Tedlock and
Wicker), provoked a flurry of attacks and counterattacks to the number of eight exchanges over a six-year period. Reacting against the
denial of Casy as a Christ figure by novelist Alan Paton and theolo-
gian Liston Pope, Shockley stated: "I propose an interpretation of
The Grapes of Wrath in which Casy represents a contemporary
adaptation of the Christ image, and in which the meaning of the
book is revealed through a sequence of Christian symbols." Earlier
critics had pointed to some possible parallels to the Bible, usually
the Old Testament, but Shockley was the first to make so bold and
inclusive a statement. Actually, his observations on the novel's biblical language and the western exodus do not add much to what
Moore had pointed out sixteen years earlier. But the similarities he
drew between Christ and Casy in terms of words and deeds were
central and well supported. He also saw Tom Joad as a disciple and

pointed to Rosasharn's last action as representing the "resurrective aspect of Christ," the "multifoliate rose" image of T. S. Eliot.

Unfortunately, although Shockley had declared that Casy is a Christ "innocent of Paulism, of Catholicism, of Puritanism," he had to resort to Unitarianism and Albert Schweitzer to make a "Christian" statement out of Casy's words, "All that lives is holy" and "Maybe all men got one big soul ever'body's a part of." It may have been this weakness in his argument which prompted Eric W. Carlson's attack (reprinted in Donohue). "In *The Grapes of Wrath*," said Carlson, "a few loose biblical analogies may be identified, but these are not primary to the structure of the novel, and to contend that they give it an 'essentially and thoroughly Christian' meaning is to distort Steinbeck's intention and its primary framework of *non-*Christian symbolism." The theme of the novel, said Carlson, is not specifically Christian because: a) it is not an expression of humility and resignation; b) it has its origins in the people, not a body of religious concepts and beliefs. The social theme can resemble Christianity only "after doctrine, dogma, sacrament, ritual, miracle, and theism itself have been stripped away, leaving only the idealized brotherhood of man and the Unitarian Oversoul. . . . Christianity without Christ is hardly Christianity." The ideas of "resurrection and redemption are conspicuously absent." According to Carlson, not even the ending of the novel is Christian symbolism, but a culminating expression of "the main theme of the novel: the prime function of life is to nourish life." Finally, the novel's "epic naturalism is neither romantic, nor mystic, nor Christian. . . . it is a humanistic integration of the knowledge of man made available by modern science, philosophy, and art."

Shockley and Carlson, along with your editor Lisca, in his "*The Grapes of Wrath* as Fiction," (this volume, 572–88) proposed the central arguments which were to be elaborated and qualified by several subsequent critics. Some, such as de Schweinitz, attempted to mediate by pointing out that one side was using the word "Christian" less rigidly than the other; that the novel is not an "*illustration*" of Hebraism or Christianity but "strongly and pervasively *recalls* them." But Walter F. Taylor (reprinted in Donohue) in 1959 insisted that the novel was not only *not* Christian or Hebraic, but positively anti-religious: "He has only hijacked part of the Christian story in order to turn it to the illustration of profoundly non-Christian meanings." Two years earlier, George Bluestone (reprinted in Davis, *Steinbeck*) had also questioned the novel's supposed "Christian" theme, but with more pertinence and less hysteria. He had pointed out that throughout the novel there is "suspicion of a theology not rooted in ordinary human needs," and that Ma Joad, who is most furious at the religious fanatics, "represents the state of natural grace to which Casy aspires." Bluestone also pointed out the ironic implications of little Ruthie's prayer, as it is recalled by Granma: "Now I lay me down to sleep. I pray the Lord my soul to keep. An' when she got there the cupboard was bare, an' so the poor dog got none."

Others, for example Crockett, Moseley, Dougherty, Dunn (all four reprinted in Donohue), Browning, Slade, Pollock (reprinted in French, *Companion*), and Cannon (reprinted in Donohue) came to Shockley's aid. Some brought with them more flexible interpretations of the Bible to fit the words and actions of Tom and Casy. Others brought new parallels, such as Tom's being a Moses figure or even a St. Paul, or the number of Joads corresponding to the 12 disciples, or 12 tribes of Israel, or Ma Joad's being a Deborah, or Casy's being really an Aaron figure, or Rosasharn's milk being a symbol not of communion but of the manna which the Jews ate in the wilderness. Etcetera!

This growing wild flood of biblical criticism crested in 1963 with the appearance of Joseph Fontenrose's chapter on the novel and J. P. Hunter's essay, "Steinbeck's Wine of Affirmation in *The Grapes of Wrath*." Fontenrose provided such a wealth of detailed, convincing parallels with both the Old and New Testament as to make any further doubt about their organic relationship to the novel irresponsible. Fontenrose further provided a larger scheme within which these symbols and references could be assimilated. He proposed that the book's "concluding theme that family interests must be subordinate to the common welfare, that all individual souls are part of one great soul, corresponds to Jesus' rejection of family ties for the kingdom of heaven's sake: 'For whosoever shall do the will of my father which is in heaven, the same is my brother, and sister, and mother.'" "In no Steinbeck novel," said Fontenrose, "do the biological and mythical strands fit so neatly together as in *The Grapes of Wrath*." And, going beyond the biblical parallels, "Jesus is a dying god, and the dying god is the year spirit, the rituals of whose cult are entwined in this novel with rituals of migration and colony-founding."

To this, J. P. Hunter added even more specific biblical parallels, such as, for example, the Joads climbing into the truck two by two while Noah stands on the ground watching. He further strengthened the observation made by your editor Lisca, French, and Fontenrose that the book's major theme is the "conversion to a wider concern" which is emphasized by a pattern of Old and New Testament references. Thus the ending of the novel becomes truly organic because it is Rosasharn, who had been the most self-centered, who now, out of necessity, adopts the human race as her family. For Hunter the book's ending telescopes the Old Testament deluge, the New Testament stable, and the continuing act of communion; Mount Ararat, Bethlehem, and California.

The culmination to which these two critics bring this material is so impressive that it is difficult to see what could follow them in this vein. And it is precisely this impasse which is admitted in Agnes Donohue's "The Endless Journey to No End" (in Donohue): "Enough has been made," she says, "of the biblical analogues in *The Grapes of Wrath*. . . . What Steinbeck suggests is richly symbolic, a mixture of myth and scripture." She sees the journey motif "as a complex symbol of fallen man's compulsive but doomed search for Paradise and ritual reenactment of the Fall. More than an historical, biblical, or sociological exodus, the journey of the Joads is a deeply mythical hegira of the human spirit in a fallen world. . . ."

This changing conception of the book's action, from social document to "Wagons West" romance to biblical analogue to "deeply mythical hegira of the human spirit," is reflected also in corresponding changes at other critical points. Editor Peter Lisca's essay on *The Grapes of Wrath* pointed out some of the techniques whereby the interchapters are closely knit into the fiber of the novel. Hunter and French supported this attempt through their discussions of these chapters' thematic contribution to the whole. Through the work of Bluestone and Griffin and Freedman (this volume, 589-602), criticism has moved from the mere repetition of Wilson's charge about Steinbeck's "animalism" to a careful analysis of the symbolic meaning and thematic function of the animals and animal tropes in the novel. Bluestone in 1957 carefully noted not only the wide range of themes which are "accompanied by, or expressed in terms of, zoological images," but also he plotted a curve of their incidence and matched this neatly to the curve of the novel's plot. Working together on the assumption that "dominant motifs are of central importance in the form and meaning of certain works of fiction" (an assumption critics had made very infrequently about the work of Steinbeck), Griffin and Freedman classified the various tropes and put them into categories according to their function; for example, "metonymic" and "epitome." Their work demonstrated, in fact, that certain parts of *The Grapes of Wrath* cannot be understood without some analysis of the particular animal imagery involved, which often creates and not merely illustrates meaning. The two critics concluded that "Steinbeck's intricate and masterful manipulation of the various references to machines and animals is an essential factor in the stature of *The Grapes of Wrath* as one of the monuments of twentieth-century American literature."

Concerning the novel's themes, French, in his 1961 study of Steinbeck, demonstrated in detail an earlier thesis that the main theme is "the education of the heart," the movement of the Joads from regarding themselves as a "self-important family unit" to their regarding themselves "as a part of a vast human family." In this respect, French rightly compared Steinbeck to Hawthorne, for in this light *The Grapes of Wrath* is not a political or sociological novel, but a moral one, substantially more than "a period piece about a troublesome past era." Later, in an essay written specifically for the first edition of this book (this volume, 603–15), John R. Reed pointed out how masterfully Steinbeck transforms the naturalistic and even vulgar details of poverty into aesthetically effective and meaningful contributions.

But it must not be assumed from these last examples that recognition of the technical and thematic accomplishment of Steinbeck's greatest novel has proceeded smoothly up to the present. On the occasion of Steinbeck's being awarded the Nobel Prize for Literature in 1962, Arthur Mizener (reprinted in Donohue) objected to this award, repeating that even *The Grapes of Wrath*, his best book, is "watered down by tenth-rate philosophizing," "sentimentality," and "thoroughly unbelievable, manipulated characters." The most methodical effort to deny the accomplishment of this great novel came in an article by Walter Fuller Taylor, who found many pernicious ideas which are "not organically necessary to the social message" of the novel. "For under cover of a pious social objective a number of other and quite different meanings are slipped past the reader's guard: those of hostility, bitterness, and contempt toward the middle classes, of antagonism toward religion in its organized forms, of the enjoyment of a Tobacco-Road sort of slovenliness, of an easy-going promiscuity and animalism in sex, of Casy's curious transcendental mysticism [apparently on a par with the other vices], of a tolerance that at first seems all-inclusive but that actually extends only so far as Steinbeck's personal preferences." Worse yet, perhaps, the novel is rife with "vulgarity in deed and word."

Clearly, as Taylor's arguments demonstrate, such attempts to discredit the novel are hysterical. And, although some famous critics, such as Harold Bloom (in Bloom, *Steinbeck* and *Grapes*) and Leslie Fiedler (in Shillinglaw), still seem to misconstrue much, if not all, of Steinbeck's accomplishment—as late as 1990, Fiedler was comparing *The Grapes of Wrath* unfavorably to Margaret Mitchell's *Gone With the Wind*—there continue to be a healthy number of critics who consider Steinbeck's works to be worthy of their serious consideration.

As literary studies in the United States underwent a metamorphosis in the 1970s and 1980s, Steinbeck critics, although rarely in the vanguard of change, developed a number of important reference materials on Steinbeck and *The Grapes of Wrath*. In fact, perhaps the most universally heralded developments in criticism on *The Grapes of Wrath* in the last twenty-five years have been the publication of Jackson Benson's magnificent biography, *The True Adventures of John Steinbeck, Writer*, and of Robert DeMott's edition of *Working Days*, Steinbeck's journal covering the writing of *The Grapes of Wrath*. Also notable are DeMott's *Steinbeck's Reading* and its two supplements, which are important resources for those interested in tracing influences on Steinbeck. The bibliographies by Robert Harmon and Tetsumaro Hayashi are, of course, indispensable.

Steinbeck critics also continued to produce sound, textual analyses in the tradition of the New Critics. John Ditsky, in an essay (this volume, 654–63), used a thorough analysis of the symbolic, mythic and structural components of the novel's ending to ably sum up and put to rest the old controversy as to its appropriateness. Mary Ann Caldwell (in Davis, *Grapes*) and Phyllis T. Dircks focused on Steinbeck's use of the interchapters. Essays examining a single symbol or set of symbols included Carl Bredahl's essay on beverages (reprinted in Hayashi, *Grapes*), Stuart Burns's essay (reprinted in Davis, *Grapes*) in which an analysis of the turtle as symbol leads to a conclusion that the novel's ending is essentially pessimistic, and Ramona Lucius's essay on light and dark as symbols in both the novel and the

film. The host of articles examining Steinbeck's use of biblical allusions continued with Tamara Rombold's article, and Tetsumaro Hayashi's essay in *Kyushu American Literature* (Japan). Meanwhile,
Kathleen Farr Elliott derived an article from having apparently
solved the mystery as to what "IITYWYBAD" means, and Helen
Lojek (reprinted in Hayashi, *Grapes*) and Patrick Shaw (this volume,
616–24) contributed, respectively, character studies of Jim Casy
and Tom Joad. Essays tracing influences on Steinbeck included those
by John Timmerman (in Noble), Richard Astro (in Astro), Warren
French (in Hayashi, *Arthurian*), Duane Carr (reprinted in Hayashi,
Grapes), and Patrick B. Mullen. Studies of the Joads' journey included Reloy Garcia's essay (reprinted in Hayashi, *Grapes*), Agnes
Donohue's essay (in Donohue) on Steinbeck and Hawthorne, and
the aforementioned piece by Patrick Shaw. John Conder's essay (this
volume, 625–42) on Steinbeck's development of the subgenre of
naturalist fiction proved to be an excellent refinement of the fairly
common studies of Steinbeck's debt to John Dos Passos.

A number of critics continued the by now traditional focus on
Steinbeck as social critic. Anne Loftis (in Shillinglaw) and William
Howarth (in Wyatt, *New*) focused on the relationship between Steinbeck's source material and the novel. Sylvia Cook (in Hayashi,
Grapes) examined the relationship between Steinbeck's biological
perspective, the Depression, and the political vision of his novels.
The concept and dynamics of community were examined by Peter
Lisca (in Ditsky). Richard Pressman (in Hayashi, *Grapes*) devoted an
interesting few pages to the strange absence of the Communist party
from *The Grapes of Wrath*. And James P. Degnan (in Astro and Hayashi) focused on Steinbeck's critique of land monopolization.

The reception of the novel also continued to interest critics. In
essays that paralleled Shockley's article (this volume, 490–501), Susan Shillinglaw (in Hayashi, *Years*) and Gerald Haslam examined the
reception of *The Grapes of Wrath* in California. Following in the
footsteps of Jean-Paul Sartre, who in 1946 had written about Steinbeck's reputation in France, Roy Simmonds detailed Steinbeck's reputation in Britain (in Ditsky, *Critical*), and Maurice Mendelson wrote
an essay on the high esteem in which Steinbeck was held by critics
in what was then the Soviet Union. Similarly, M. R. Satyanarayana
provided an update on a decade of Steinbeck criticism in India, and
Thomas Wendel informed readers that Steinbeck was Finland's most
popular American author.

Eventually, however, the revolutions that had swept over English departments at universities across the country found their way into the pages of *Steinbeck Quarterly*, and into books on Steinbeck. Although not all Steinbeck critics have been comfortable with the insights provided by feminism, new historicism, ethnic studies, discourse analysis, and postmodernism, to name but a few of the contemporary schools of literary criticism, most book-length studies of Steinbeck's work in general, and of *The Grapes of Wrath* in particular, have included significant essays from at least one of the newer schools of criticism. And if the experience of the past twenty years is any indication, Steinbeck's works are not equally amenable to every new method of literary analysis. For example, if the quantity and quality of the essays are reliable guides, then the search for postmodern narrative self-consciousness seems to be most rewarded by analysis of *East of Eden*; although recently there have also been interesting articles applying this approach to *Sea of Cortez, Cannery Row*, and *Sweet Thursday*. To date, despite the success of Howard Levant's formalist approach to Steinbeck, *The Grapes of Wrath* has been curiously immune to the postmodernist approach. Somewhat similarly, ethnic studies have provided a variety of important insights into *Tortilla Flat, In Dubious Battle, East of Eden*, and *Viva Zapata!*; however, with the exception of one chapter on the figure of the Indian in Louis Owens's monograph, *The Grapes of Wrath* has not been especially fertile territory for ethnic studies. *The Grapes of Wrath* has, however, yielded a brilliant but fairly difficult Bakhtinian analysis of the dialogism of its discourses by Louis Owens and Hector Torres. Related articles by other critics on *The Winter of Our Discontent* and *The Pastures of Heaven* strongly suggest that discourse analysis may yet provide a wealth of new information on the whole range of Steinbeck's work.

Interdisciplinary approaches to *The Grapes of Wrath* have also proved influential in recent years. Christopher Salter used the novel as the basis for a lesson on social geography (reprinted in Ditsky, *Critical*), and Deborah Schneer (in Shillinglaw) applied the principles of object relations theories of psychology to an analysis of the "ruling class" in Steinbeck's novel. Studies of the value of performance in coming to an understanding of Steinbeck's work included one chapter in Joseph Millichap's *Steinbeck and Film*, Mimi Reisel Gladstein's article (in Ditsky, *Critical*) comparing the depiction of Ma Joad in the book and the film, the aforementioned essay by Ramona Lucius,

Peter Whitebrook's *Staging Steinbeck*, Robert Morsberger's general essay (in Benson, *Short*) on Steinbeck's understanding and use of dramatic techniques, and the script and production information from Frank Galati's adaptation of Steinbeck's novel to the stage. And Pare Lorentz, who was a major influence on Steinbeck's views on documentary film and through that on *The Grapes of Wrath*, included a critique of Ford's film in his *Movies 1927–41: Lorentz on Film*.

Historians have also continued to put *The Grapes of Wrath* in new perspective. Donald Worster's *Dust Bowl*, Walter J. Stein's *California and the Dust Bowl Migration*, Cletus Daniel's *A History of California Farm Workers, 1870–1941*, and James N. Gregory's *The Dust Bowl Migration and Okie Culture in California* all provide significant background for an understanding of the social conditions to which Steinbeck was responding. Worster's *Rivers of Empire* and his essay "Hydraulic Society in California" (in *Under Western Skies*) were notable for their analysis of the interaction between economies of scale, arid landscape, and the exploitation of laborers.

Closely related to the work of historians has been the work of new historicist critics. David Cassuto's essay on water in *The Grapes of Wrath* applies a neo-Marxist spin on new historicism, and in an essay (this volume, 643–53) from his excellent monograph study of *The Grapes of Wrath*, Louis Owens reveals how an understanding of the manipulation of biblical analogies in the development of American nationalist mythology informs Steinbeck's use of biblical allusions, and how Steinbeck's understanding of the role tenant farmers played in the process leading up to their own displacement desentimentalizes the Joads. David Wyatt's chapter on Steinbeck in *The Fall into Eden* and Owens's *John Steinbeck's Re-Vision of America* perform much the same function of recontextualization for Steinbeck's canon as a whole.

Although all of these newer schools, especially a not very theoretical version of new historicism, have made solid contributions to Steinbeck criticism, the new approach which arguably has been most influential in Steinbeck studies to date has been feminism. Beginning with Sandra Beatty's and Mimi Reisel Gladstein's general essays on Steinbeck's depiction of women (in Hayashi, *Women*), feminist critics soon began to undertake analyses of specific female characters and of questions of gender in individual works by Steinbeck. Gladstein alone has written essays on Ma Joad and Rosasharn as "indestructible women" (reprinted in Bloom, *Grapes*), on the similarities between Ma Joad and Hemingway's Pilar in *For Whom the Bell Tolls*, and on the disparity between the women Steinbeck knew and those he portrayed in his fiction (in Noble). Gladstein's aforementioned article comparing Steinbeck's depiction of Ma Joad to the character as presented in John Ford's film offers a particularly good approach to illustrating Ma Joad's centrality to the novel for readers who might otherwise be resistant to feminist readings. John Ditsky, in a perhaps seminal essay (in Hayashi, *Years*), develops an illuminating argument about the Steinbeck canon as a whole based on Steinbeck's gendering as female both the process and result of his writing. A number of critics, including Charlotte Hadella and Abby Werlock, have written important feminist articles on other Steinbeck works, but nothing specifically on *The Grapes of Wrath*. Feminist studies focusing exclusively on *The Grapes of Wrath* include: Warren Motley's important essay which traces Steinbeck's views of matriarchy and patriarchy to his reading of Briffault, Joan Hedrick's solid critique (in Davis, *Grapes*) of Ma Joad as an unrealistic Earth Mother figure whose very strength may obviate the need for real political change, and Nellie McKay's essay (this volume, 664–81) on the importance of gender roles to an understanding of *The Grapes of Wrath*.

Slowly at first, but more and more surely, utilizing the work of their predecessors, literary critics have added to our understanding and appreciation of what is certainly one of the great American novels. This process is not yet complete. Each time the present editors have discussed *The Grapes of Wrath* with students they have come away with something new and valuable, some fresh observation made possible through the different knowledge and experience of their own time and age. As you read the following essays, perhaps you will find that some particular point significant in your own understanding of the novel seems not to have been noticed by these critics. That will be the beginning of your own contribution.

Frederic I. Carpenter

Frederic I. Carpenter taught at the University of Chicago, Harvard, and the University of California at Berkeley. He was editorial adviser for College English *and editor of* New England Quarterly. *His publications include* Emerson Handbook, American Literature and the Dream, The American Myth, *two books on Robinson Jeffers, and one on Eugene O'Neill. He died in 1991.*

THE PHILOSOPHICAL JOADS

A popular heresy has it that a novelist should not discuss ideas—especially not abstract ideas. Even the best contemporary reviewers concern themselves with the entertainment value of a book (will it please their readers?), and with the impression of immediate reality which it creates. *The Grapes of Wrath*, for instance, was praised for its swift action and for the moving sincerity of its characters. But its mystical ideas and the moralizing interpretations intruded by the author between the narrative chapters were condemned. Presumably the book became a best seller in spite of these; its art was great enough to overcome its philosophy.

But in the course of time a book is also judged by other standards. Aristotle once argued that poetry should be more "philosophical" than history; and all books are eventually weighed for their content of wisdom. Novels that have become classics do more than

Reprinted from *College English* II (January 1941), 315–25. By permission of the National Council of Teachers of English and Frederic I. Carpenter.

tell a story and describe characters; they offer insight into men's motives and point to the springs of action. Together with the moving picture, they offer the criticism of life.

Although this theory of art may seem classical, all important modern novels—especially American novels—have clearly suggested an abstract idea of life. *The Scarlet Letter* symbolized "sin," *Moby-Dick* offered an allegory of evil. *Huck Finn* described the revolt of the "natural individual" against "civilization," and *Babbitt* (like Emerson's "Self-reliance") denounced the narrow conventions of "society." Now *The Grapes of Wrath* goes beyond these to preach a positive philosophy of life and to damn that blind conservatism which fears ideas.

I shall take for granted the narrative power of the book and the vivid reality of its characters: modern critics, both professional and popular, have borne witness to these. The novel is a best seller. But it also has ideas. These appear abstractly and obviously in the interpretative interchapters. But more important is Steinbeck's creation of Jim Casy, "the preacher," to interpret and to embody the philosophy of the novel. And consummate is the skill with which Jim Casy's philosophy has been integrated with the action of the story, until it motivates and gives significance to the lives of Tom Joad, and Ma, and Rose of Sharon. It is not too much to say that Jim Casy's ideas determine and direct the Joads's actions.

Beside and beyond their function in the story, the ideas of John Steinbeck and Jim Casy possess a significance of their own. They continue, develop, integrate, and realize the thought of the great writers of American history. Here the mystical transcendentalism of Emerson reappears, and the earthy democracy of Whitman, and the pragmatic instrumentalism of William James and John Dewey. And these old philosophies grow and change in the book until they become new. They coalesce into an organic whole. And, finally, they find embodiment in character and action, so that they seem no longer ideas, but facts. The enduring greatness of *The Grapes of Wrath* consists in its imaginative realization of these old ideas in new and concrete forms. Jim Casy translates American philosophy into words of one syllable, and the Joads translate it into action.

I

"Ever know a guy that said big words like that?" asks the truck driver in the first narrative chapter of *The Grapes of Wrath*. "Preacher," replies Tom Joad. "Well, it makes you mad to hear a guy use big words. Course with a preacher it's all right because nobody would fool around with a preacher anyway." But soon afterward Tom meets Jim Casy and finds him changed. "I was a preacher," said the man seriously, "but not no more." Because Casy has ceased to be an orthodox minister and no longer uses big words, Tom Joad plays around with him. And the story results.

But although he is no longer a minister, Jim Casy continues to preach. His words have become simple and his ideas unorthodox. "Just Jim Casy now. Ain't got the call no more. Got a lot of sinful idears—but they seem kinda sensible" (23). A century before, this same experience and essentially these same ideas had occurred to another preacher: Ralph Waldo Emerson had given up the ministry because of his unorthodoxy. But Emerson had kept on using big words. Now Casy translates them: "Why do we got to hang it on God or Jesus? Maybe it's all men an' all women we love; maybe that's the Holy Sperit—the human sperit— the whole shebang. Maybe all men got one big soul ever'body's a part of" (27). And so the Emersonian oversoul comes to earth in Oklahoma.

Unorthodox Jim Casy went into the Oklahoma wilderness to save his soul. And in the wilderness he experienced the religious feeling of identity with nature which has always been the heart of transcendental mysticism: "There was the hills, an' there was me, an' we wasn't separate no more. We was one thing. An' that one thing was holy." Like Emerson, Casy came to the conviction that holiness, or goodness, results from this feeling of unity: "I got to thinkin' how we was holy when we was one thing, an' mankin' was holy when it was one thing."

Thus far Jim Casy's transcendentalism has remained vague and apparently insignificant. But the corollary of this mystical philosophy is that any man's self-seeking destroys the unity or "holiness" of nature: "An' it [this one thing] on'y got unholy when one mis'able little fella got the bit in his teeth, an' run off his own way. . . . Fella like that bust the holiness" (83). Or, as Emerson phrased it, while discussing Nature: "The world lacks unity because man is disunited with himself. . . . Love is its demand." So Jim Casy preaches the religion of love.

He finds that this transcendental religion alters the old standards: "Here's me that used to give all my fight against the devil 'cause I figured the devil was the enemy. But they's somepin worse'n the devil got hold a the country" (129). Now, like Emerson, he almost welcomes "the dear old devil." Now he fears not the lusts of the flesh but rather the lusts of the spirit. For the abstract lust of possession isolates a man from his fellows and destroys the unity of nature and the love of man. As Steinbeck writes: "The quality of owning freezes you forever into 'I,' and cuts you off forever from the 'we'" (153). Or, as the Concord farmers in Emerson's poem "Hamatreya" had exclaimed: " 'Tis mine, my children's and my name's," only to have "their avarice cooled like lust in the chill of the grave." To a preacher of the oversoul, possessive egotism may become the unpardonable sin.

If a society has adopted "the quality of owning" (as typified by absentee ownership) as its social norm, then Protestant nonconformity may become the highest virtue, and even resistance to authority may become justified. At the beginning of his novel Steinbeck had suggested this, describing how "the faces of the watching men lost their bemused perplexity and became hard and angry and resistant. Then the women knew that they were safe . . . their men were whole" (7). For this is the paradox of Protestantism: when men resist unjust and selfish authority, they themselves become "whole" in spirit.

But this American ideal of nonconformity seems negative: how can men be sure that their Protestant rebellion does not come from the devil? To this there has always been but one answer—faith: faith in the instincts of the common man, faith in ultimate social progress, and faith in the direction in which democracy is moving. So Ma Joad counsels the discouraged Tom: "Why, Tom, we're the people that live. They ain't gonna wipe us out. Why, we're the people—we go on" (280). And so Steinbeck himself affirms a final faith in progress: "when theories change and crash, when schools, philosophies . . . grow and disintegrate, man reaches, stumbles forward. . . . Having stepped forward, he may slip back, but only half a step, never the full step back" (151). Whether this be democratic faith, or mere transcendental optimism, it has always been the motive force of our American life and finds reaffirmation in this novel.

II

Upon the foundation of this old American idealism Steinbeck has built. But the Emersonian oversoul had seemed very vague and very ineffective—only the individual had been real, and he had been concerned more with his private soul than with other people. *The Grapes of Wrath* develops the old idea in new ways. It traces the transformation of the Protestant individual into the member of a social group—the old "I" becomes "we." And it traces the transformation of the passive individual into the active participant—the idealist becomes pragmatist. The first development continues the poetic thought of Walt Whitman; the second continues the philosophy of William James and John Dewey.

"One's-self I sing, a simple separate person," Whitman had proclaimed. "Yet utter the word Democratic, the word En-Masse." Other American writers had emphasized the individual above the group. Even Whitman celebrated his "comrades and lovers" in an essentially personal relationship. But Steinbeck now emphasizes the group above the individual and from an impersonal point of view. Where formerly American and Protestant thought has been separatist, Steinbeck now faces the problem of social integration. In his novel the "mutually repellent particles" of individualism begin to cohere.

"This is the beginning," he writes, "from 'I' to 'we.' " This is the beginning, that is, of reconstruction. When the old society has been split and the Protestant individuals wander aimlessly about, some new nucleus must be found, or chaos and nihilism will follow. "In the night one family camps in a ditch and another family pulls in and the tents come out. The two men squat on their hams and the women and children listen. Here is the node." Here is the new nucleus. "And from this first 'we' there grows a still more dangerous thing: 'I have a little food' plus 'I have none.' If from this problem the sum is 'We have a little food,' the thing is on its way, the movement has direction" (152). A new social group is forming, based on the word "en masse." But here is no socialism imposed from above; here is a natural grouping of simple separate persons.

By virtue of his wholehearted participation in this new group the individual may become greater than himself. Some men, of course, will remain mere individuals, but in every group there must be leaders, or "representative men." A poet gives expression to the group

idea, or a preacher organizes it. After Jim Casy's death, Tom is chosen to lead. Ma explains: "They's some folks that's just theirself an'
nothin' more. There's Al [for instance] he's jus' a young fella after a
girl. You wasn't never like that, Tom" (353). Because he has been
an individualist, but through the influence of Casy and of his group
idea has become more than himself, Tom becomes "a leader of the
people." But his strength derives from his increased sense of participation in the group.

From Jim Casy, and eventually from the thought of Americans
like Whitman, Tom Joad has inherited this idea. At the end of the
book he sums it up, recalling how Casy "went out in the wilderness
to find his own soul, an' he foun' he didn't have no soul that was
his'n. Says he foun' he jus' got a little piece of a great big soul. Says
a wilderness ain't no good 'cause his little piece of a soul wasn't no
good 'less it was with the rest, an' was whole" (418). Unlike Emerson,
who had said goodbye to the proud world, these latterday Americans
must live in the midst of it. "I know now," concludes Tom, "a fella
ain't no good alone."

To repeat: this group idea is American, not Russian; and stems
from Walt Whitman, not Karl Marx. But it does include some elements that have usually seemed sinful to orthodox Anglo-Saxons.
"Of physiology from top to toe I sing," Whitman had declared, and
added a good many details that his friend Emerson thought unnecessary. Now the Joads frankly discuss anatomical details and joke
about them. Like most common people, they do not abscond or
conceal. Sometimes they seem to go beyond the bounds of literary
decency: the unbuttoned antics of Grandpa Joad touch a new low
in folk-comedy. The movies (which reproduced most of the realism
of the book) could not quite stomach this. But for the most part they
preserved the spirit of the book, because it was whole and healthy.

In Whitman's time almost everyone deprecated this physiological
realism, and in our own many readers and critics still deprecate it.
Nevertheless, it is absolutely necessary—both artistically and logically. In the first place, characters like the Joads do act and talk that
way—to describe them as genteel would be to distort the picture.
And, in the second place, Whitman himself had suggested the necessity of it: just as the literature of democracy must describe all
sorts of people, "en masse," so it must describe all of the life of the
people. To exclude the common or "low" elements of individual life
would be as false as to exclude the common or low elements of

society. Either would destroy the wholeness of life and nature. Therefore, along with the dust-driven Joads, we must have Grandpa's dirty drawers.

But beyond this physiological realism lies the problem of sex. And this problem is not one of realism at all. Throughout this turbulent novel an almost traditional reticence concerning the details of sex is observed. The problem here is rather one of fundamental morality, for sex had always been a symbol of sin. *The Scarlet Letter* reasserted the authority of an orthodox morality. Now Jim Casy questions that orthodoxy. On this first meeting with Tom he describes how, after sessions of preaching, he had often lain with a girl and then felt sinful afterward. This time the movies repeated his confession, because it is central to the motivation of the story. Disbelief in the sinfulness of sex converts Jim Casy from a preacher of the old morality to a practitioner of the new.

But in questioning the old morality Jim Casy does not deny morality. He doubts the strict justice of Hawthorne's code: "Maybe it ain't a sin. Maybe it's just the way folks is. Maybe we been whippin' the hell out of ourselves for nothin' " (26). But he recognizes that love must always remain responsible and purposeful. Al Joad remains just "a boy after a girl." In place of the old, Casy preaches the new morality of Whitman, which uses sex to symbolize the love of man for his fellows. Jim Casy and Tom Joad have become more responsible and more purposeful than Pa Joad and Uncle John ever were: they love people so much that they are ready to die for them. Formerly the only unit of human love was the family, and the family remains the fundamental unit. The tragedy of *The Grapes of Wrath* consists in the breakup of the family. But the new moral of this novel is that the love of all people—if it be unselfish—may even supersede the love of family. So Casy dies for his people, and Tom is ready to, and Rose of Sharon symbolically transmutes her maternal love to a love of all people. Here is a new realization of "the word democratic, the word en-masse."

III

"An' I got to thinkin', Ma—most of the preachin' is about the poor we shall have always with us, an' if you got nothin', why, jus' fol' your hands an' to hell with it, you gonna git ice cream on gol' plates when you're dead. An' then this here Preacher says two get a better reward for their work" (418).

Catholic Christianity had always preached humility and passive obedience. Protestantism preached spiritual nonconformity, but kept its disobedience passive. Transcendentalism sought to save the individual but not the group. ("Are they *my* poor?" asked Emerson.) Whitman sympathized more deeply with the common people and loved them abstractly, but trusted that God and democracy would save them. The pragmatic philosophers first sought to implement American idealism by making thought itself instrumental. And now Steinbeck quotes scripture to urge popular action for the realization of the old ideals.

In the course of the book Steinbeck develops and translates the thought of the earlier pragmatists. "Thinking," wrote John Dewey, "is a kind of activity which we perform at specific need." And Steinbeck repeats: "Need is the stimulus to concept, concept to action" (153). The cause of the Okies' migration is their need, and their migration itself becomes a kind of thinking—an unconscious groping for the solution to a half-formulated problem. Their need becomes the stimulus to concept.

In this novel a kind of pragmatic thinking takes place before our eyes: the idea develops from the predicament of the characters, and the resulting action becomes integral with the thought. The evils of absentee ownership produce the mass migration, and the mass migration results in the idea of group action: "A half-million people moving over the country. . . . And tractors turning the multiple furrows in the vacant land" (153).

But what good is generalized thought? And how is future action to be planned? Americans in general, and pragmatists in particular, have always disagreed in answering these questions. William James argued that thought was good only in so far as it satisfied a particular need and that plans, like actions, were "plural"—and should be conceived and executed individually. But Charles Sanders Peirce, and the transcendentalists before him, had argued that the most generalized thought was best, provided it eventually resulted in effective action. The problems of mankind should be considered as a unified whole, monistically.

Now Tom Joad is a pluralist—a pragmatist after William James. Tom said, "I'm still layin' my dogs down one at a time." Casy replied: "Yeah, but when a fence comes up at ya, ya gonna climb that fence."

"I climb fences when I got fences to climb," said Tom. But Jim Casy believes in looking far ahead and seeing the thing as a whole: "But they's different kinda folks. They's folks like me that climbs fences that ain't even strang up yet" (175). Which is to say that Casy is a kind of transcendental pragmatist. His thought seeks to generalize the problems of the Okies and to integrate them with the larger problem of industrial America. His solution is the principle of group action guided by conceptual thought and functioning within the framework of democratic society and law.

And at the end of the story Tom Joad becomes converted to Jim Casy's pragmatism. It is not important that the particular strike should be won, or that the particular need should be satisfied; but it is important that men should think in terms of action, and that they should think and act in terms of the whole rather than the particular individual. "For every little beaten strike is proof that the step is being taken" (151). The value of an idea lies not in its immediate but in its eventual success. That idea is good which works—in the long run.

But the point of the whole novel is that action is an absolute essential of human life. If need and failure produce only fear, disintegration follows. But if they produce anger, then reconstruction may follow. The grapes of wrath must be trampled to make manifest the glory of the Lord. At the beginning of the story Steinbeck described the incipient wrath of the defeated farmers. At the end he repeats the scene. "And where a number of men gathered together, the fear went from their faces, and anger took its place. And the women sighed with relief . . . the break would never come as long as fear could turn to wrath" (434). Then wrath could turn to action.

IV

To sum up: the fundamental idea of *The Grapes of Wrath* is that of American transcendentalism: "Maybe all men got one big soul ever'body's a part of" (27). From this idea it follows that every individual will trust those instincts which he shares with all men, even when these conflict with the teachings of orthodox religion and of existing society. But his self-reliance will not merely seek individual freedom, as did Emerson. It will rather seek social freedom or mass democracy, as did Whitman. If this mass democracy leads to the abandonment of genteel taboos and to the modification of some traditional ideas of morality, that is inevitable. But whatever happens, the American will act to realize his ideals. He will seek to make himself whole—i.e., to join himself to other men by means of purposeful actions for some goal beyond himself.

But at this point the crucial question arises—and it is "crucial" in every sense of the word. What if this self-reliance leads to death? What if the individual is killed before the social group is saved? Does the failure of the individual action invalidate the whole idea? "How'm I gonna know about you?" Ma asks. "They might kill ya an' I wouldn't know."

The answer has already been suggested by the terms in which the story has been told. If the individual has identified himself with the oversoul, so that his life has become one with the life of all men, his individual death and failure will not matter. From the old transcendental philosophy of identity to Tom Joad and the moving pictures may seem a long way, but even the movies faithfully reproduced Tom's final declaration of transcendental faith: "They might kill ya," Ma had objected.

"Tom laughed uneasily, 'Well, maybe like Casy says, a fella ain't got a soul of his own, but on'y a piece of a big one—an' then—'

" 'Then what, Tom?'

" 'Then it don' matter. Then I'll be aroun' in the dark. I'll be ever'where—wherever you look. Wherever they's a fight so hungry people can eat, I'll be there. Wherever they's a cop beating up a guy, I'll be there. If Casy knowed, why, I'll be in the way guys yell when they're mad an'—I'll be in the way kids laugh when they're hungry an' they know supper's ready. An' when our folks eat the stuff they raise an' live in the houses they build—why, I'll be there. See?' " (419).

For the first time in history, *The Grapes of Wrath* brings together and makes real three great skeins of American thought. It begins with the transcendental oversoul, Emerson's faith in the common man, and his Protestant self-reliance. To this it joins Whitman's religion of the love of all men and his mass democracy. And it combines these mystical and poetic ideas with the realistic philosophy of pragmatism and its emphasis on effective action. From this it develops a new kind of Christianity—not otherworldly and passive, but earthly and active. And Oklahoma Jim Casy and the Joads think and do all these philosophical things.

Peter Lisca

Peter Lisca has taught at the Woman's College of the University of North Carolina, the University of Washington, and the University of Florida. He is the author of The Wide World of John Steinbeck *and* John Steinbeck: Nature and Myth, *as well as numerous articles appearing in* PMLA, Modern Fiction Studies, Twentieth Century Literature, *and various collections of essays.*

THE GRAPES OF WRATH AS FICTION

When *The Grapes of Wrath* was published in April of 1939 there was little likelihood of its being accepted and evaluated as a piece of fiction. Because of its nominal subject, it was too readily confused with such high-class reporting as Ruth McKenny's *Industrial Valley*, the WPA collection of case histories called *These Are Our Lives*, and Dorothea Lange and Paul S. Taylor's *An American Exodus*. The merits of *The Grapes of Wrath* were debated as social documentation rather than fiction. In addition to incurring the disadvantages of its historical position, coming as a kind of climax to the literature of the Great Depression, Steinbeck's novel also suffered from the perennial vulnerability of all social fiction to an attack on its facts and intentions.

The passage of eighteen years has done very little to alter this initial situation. Except for scattered remarks, formal criticism of *The*

Reprinted from *PMLA*, LXXII (March 1957), 269–309. By permission of the Modern Language Association. Copyright © 1957 by the Modern Language Association.

Grapes of Wrath is still pretty much limited to a chapter by Joseph Warren Beach (reprinted in Tedlock and Wicker), a chapter by Harry Thornton Moore, a few paragraphs by Kenneth Burke, part of a chapter by the French critic Claude-Edmonde Magny (reprinted in Tedlock and Wicker), and an essay by B. R. McElderry, Jr. (reprinted in French, *Companion*). In a period of such intensive analysis of the techniques of fiction as the past fifteen years, the dearth of critical material on *The Grapes of Wrath* must indicate an assumption on the part of critics that this novel cannot sustain such analysis. The present paper is an attempt to correct this assumption by exploring some of the techniques by which John Steinbeck was able to give significant form to his sprawling materials and prevent his novel of social protest from degenerating into propaganda.

The ideas and materials of *The Grapes of Wrath* presented Steinbeck with a problem of structure similar to that of Tolstoy's in writing *War and Peace*. Tolstoy's materials were, roughly, the adventures of the Bezukhov, Rostov, and Bolkonski families on the one hand, and the Napoleonic Wars on the other. And while the plot development brought these two blocks of material together, there was enough about the Napoleonic Wars left over so that the author had to incorporate it in separate philosophic interchapters. Steinbeck's materials were similar. There were the adventures of the Joads, the Wilsons, and the Wainwrights; there was also the Great Depression. And like Tolstoy, he had enough material left over to write separate philosophic interchapters.

In the light of this basic analogy, Percy Lubbock's comments on the structural role of these two elements in *War and Peace* become significant for an understanding of structure in *The Grapes of Wrath*: "I can discover no angle at which the two stories will appear to unite and merge in a single impression. Neither is subordinated to the other, and there is nothing above them . . . to which they are both related. Nor are they placed together to illustrate a contrast; nothing *results* from their juxtaposition. Only from time to time, upon no apparent principle and without a word of warning, one of them is dropped and the other is resumed."[1] In these few phrases Lubbock has defined the aesthetic conditions not only for *War and Peace* but for any other piece of fiction whose strategies include an intercalary construction—*The Grapes of Wrath*, for example. The test is whether anything *results* from this kind of structure.

Counting the opening description of the drought and the penultimate chapter on the rains, pieces of straightforward description allowable even to strictly "scenic" novels (Lubbock's term for materials presented entirely from the reader's point of view), there are in *The Grapes of Wrath* sixteen interchapters, making up roughly seventy-nine pages—almost one sixth of the book. In none of these chapters do the Joads, Wilsons, or Wainwrights appear.

These interchapters have two main functions. First, by presenting the social background they serve to amplify the pattern of action created by the Joad family. Thus, for example, Chapter i presents in panoramic terms the drought which forces the Joads off their land; Chapters vii and ix depict, respectively, the buying of jalopies for the migration and the selling of household goods; Chapter xi describes at length a decaying and deserted house which is the prototype of all the houses abandoned in the Dust Bowl. In thirteen such chapters almost every aspect of the Joads's adventures is enlarged and seen as part of the social climate. The remaining interchapters have the function of providing such historical information as the development of land ownership in California, the consequent development of migrant labor, and certain economic aspects of the social lag. These three informative chapters make up fewer than twenty of the novel's four-hundred-fifty-odd pages. Scattered through the sixteen interchapters are occasional paragraphs whose purpose is to present, with choric effect, the philosophy or social message to which the current situation gives rise. For the most part these paragraphs occur in four chapters—ix, xi, xiv, and xix.

While all of these various materials are obviously ideologically related to the longer narrative section of the novel (three hundred seventy-five pages), there remains the problem of their aesthetic integration with the book as a whole. Even a cursory reading will show that there is a general correspondence between the material of each interchapter and that of the current narrative portion. The magnificent opening description of the drought sets forth the condition which gives rise to the novel's action; Highway 66 is given a chapter as the Joads begin their trek on that historic route; the chapters dealing with migrant life appear interspersed with the narrative of the Joads's actual journey; the last interchapter, xxix, describes the rain in which the action of the novel ends.

A more careful reading will make evident that this integration of the interchapters into a total structure goes far beyond this merely complementary juxtaposition. There is in addition an intricate inter-

weaving of specific details. Like the anonymous house in the interchapter (v), one corner of the Joad house has been knocked off its
foundation by a tractor (41). The man who in the interchapter threatens the tractor driver with his rifle becomes Grampa Joad, except
that whereas the anonymous tenant does not fire, Grampa shoots
out both headlights (42, 48). The tractor driver in the interchapter,
Joe Davis, is a family acquaintance of the anonymous tenants, as
Willy is an acquaintance of the Joads in the narrative chapter (39,
48). The jalopy sitting in the Joads's front yard is the same kind of
jalopy described in the used-car lot of Chapter vii. Chapter viii ends
with Al Joad driving off to sell a truckload of household goods. Chapter ix is an interchapter describing anonymous farmers selling such
goods, including many items which the Joads themselves are selling
—pumps, farming tools, furniture, a team and wagon for ten dollars.
In the following chapter Al Joad returns with an empty truck, having
sold everything for eighteen dollars—including ten dollars for a team
and wagon. Every interchapter is tied into the book's narrative portion by this kind of specific cross reference, which amplifies the
Joads's typical actions to the level of a communal experience.

Often, this interlocking of details becomes thematic or symbolic.
The dust which is mentioned twenty-seven times in the four pages
of Chapter i comes to stand not only for the land itself but also for
the basic situation out of which the novel's action develops. Everything which moves on the ground, from insects to trucks, raises a
proportionate amount of dust: "a walking man lifted a thin layer as
high as his waist" (5). When Tom returns home after four years in
prison and gets out of the truck which had given him a ride, he steps
off the highway and performs the symbolic ritual of taking off his
new, prison-issue shoes and carefully working his bare feet into the
dust. He then moves off across the land, "making a cloud that hung
low to the ground behind him" (20).

One of the novel's most important symbols, the turtle, is presented in what is actually the first interchapter (iii). And while this
chapter is a masterpiece of realistic description (often included as
such in Freshman English texts), it is also obvious that the turtle is
symbolic and its adventures prophetic allegory. "Nobody can't keep
a turtle though," says Jim Casy. "They work at it and work at it, and
at last one day they get out and away they go . . ." (24). The indom-
itable life force that drives the turtle drives the Joads, and in the
same direction—southwest. As the turtle picks up seeds in its shell

and drops them on the other side of the road, so the Joads pick up life in Oklahoma and carry it across the country to California. (As Grandfather in "The Leader of the People" puts it, "We carried life out here and set it down the way those ants carry eggs.") As the turtle survives the truck's attempts to smash it on the highway and as it crushes the red ant which runs into its shell, so the Joads endure the perils of their journey.

This symbolic value is retained and further defined when the turtle enters specifically into the narrative. Its incident with the red ant (19) is echoed one hundred and ninety-one pages later when another red ant runs over "the folds of loose skin" on Granma's neck and she reaches up with her "little wrinkled claws"; Ma Joad picks it off and crushes it (210). In Chapter iii the turtle is seen "dragging his high-domed shell across the grass." In the next chapter, Tom sees "the high-domed shell of a land turtle" and picking up the turtle, carries it with him (20). It is only when he is convinced that his family has left the land that he releases the turtle, which travels "southwest as it had been from the first," a direction which is repeated in the next two sentences. The first thing which Tom does after releasing the turtle is to put on his shoes, which he had taken off when he left the highway and stepped onto the land (47). Thus, not only the turtle but also Tom's connection with it is symbolic, as symbolic as Lennie's appearance in *Of Mice and Men* with a dead mouse in his pocket.

In addition to this constant knitting together of the two kinds of chapters, often the interchapters are further assimilated into the narrative portion by incorporating in themselves the techniques of fiction. The general conflict between small farmers and the banks, for example, is presented as an imaginary dialogue, each speaker personifying the sentiments of his group. And although neither speaker is a "real" person, both are dramatically differentiated and their arguments embody details particular to the specific social condition. This kind of dramatization is also evident in such chapters as those concerning the buying of used cars, the selling of household goods, the police intimidation of migrants, and others.

Because Steinbeck's subject in *The Grapes of Wrath* is not the adventures of the Joad family so much as the social conditions which occasion them, these interchapters serve a vital purpose. As Percy Lubbock has pointed out, the purely "scenic" technique "is out of the question . . . whenever the story is too big, too comprehensive, too widely ranging to be treated scenically, with no opportunity for general and panoramic survey. . . . These stories, therefore, which will not naturally accommodate themselves to the reader's point of view, and the reader's alone, we regard as rather pictorial than dramatic—meaning that they call for some narrator, somebody who *knows*, to contemplate the facts and create an impression of them [254-255]."

Steinbeck's story certainly is "big," "comprehensive," and "wide ranging." But although he tried to free his materials by utilizing what Lubbock calls "pictorial" as well as "scenic" techniques, he also took pains to keep these techniques from breaking the novel in two parts. The cross reference of detail, the interweaving symbols, and the dramatization are designed to make the necessary "pictorial" sections of the novel tend toward the "scenic." Conversely, an examination of the narrative portion of *The Grapes of Wrath* will reveal that its techniques make the "scenic" tend toward the "pictorial." Steinbeck worked from both sides to make the two kinds of chapters approach each other and fuse into a single impression.

That the narrative portion of *The Grapes of Wrath* tends toward the "pictorial" can be seen readily if the book is compared to another of Steinbeck's social novels, *In Dubious Battle*, which has a straightforward plot development and an involving action. Of course things happen in *The Grapes of Wrath*, and what happens not only grows out of what has gone before but grows into what will happen in the future. But while critics have perceived that plot is not the organizational principle of the novel, they have not attempted to relate this fact to the novel's materials as they are revealed through other techniques, assuming instead that this lack of plot constitutes one of the novel's major flaws. Actually, this lack of an informing plot is instrumental in at least two ways. It could reasonably be expected that the greatest threat to the novel's unity would come from the interchapters' constant breaking up of the narrative line of action. But the very fact that *The Grapes of Wrath* is *not* organized by a unifying plot works for absorbing these interchapters smoothly into its texture. A second way in which this tendency of the "scenic" toward the "pictorial" is germane to the novel's materials becomes evident when it is considered that Steinbeck's subject is not an action so much as a situation. Description, therefore, must often substitute for narration.

This substitution of the static for the dynamic also gives us an insight into the nature and function of the novel's characters, who often have been called "puppets," "symbolic marionettes," and "symbols," but seldom real people. While there are scant objective grounds for determining whether a novel's characters are "real," one fruitful approach is to consider fictional characters not only in relation to life but in relation to the *rest* of the fiction of which they are a part.

In his Preface to *The Forgotten Village*, which immediately followed *The Grapes of Wrath*, Steinbeck comments on just these relationships.

> A great many documentary films have used the generalized method, that is, the showing of a condition or an event as it affects a group of people. The audience can then have a personalized reaction from imagining one member of that group. I have felt that this was the more difficult observation from the audience's viewpoint. It means very little to know that a million Chinese are starving unless you know one Chinese who is starving. In *The Forgotten Village* we reversed the usual process. Our story centered on one family in one small village. We wished our audience to know this family very well, and incidentally to like it, as we did. Then, from association with this little personalized group, the larger conclusion concerning the racial group could be drawn with something like participation.[2]

This is precisely the strategy in *The Grapes of Wrath*. Whatever value the Joads have as individuals is "incidental" to their primary function as a "personalized group." Kenneth Burke has pointed out that "most of the characters derive their role, which is to say their personality, purely from their relationship to the basic situation." But what he takes to be a serious weakness is actually one of the book's greatest accomplishments. The characters are so absorbed into the novel's "basic situation" that the reader's response goes beyond sympathy for individuals to moral indignation about their social condition. This is, of course, precisely Steinbeck's intention. And certainly the Joads are admirably suited for this purpose. This conception of character is parallel to the fusing of the "scenic" and "pictorial" techniques in the narrative and interchapters.

Although the diverse materials of *The Grapes of Wrath* made organization by a unifying plot difficult, nevertheless the novel does have structural form. The action progresses through three successive movements, and its significance is revealed by an intricate system of themes and symbols.

The Grapes of Wrath is divided into thirty consecutive chapters with no larger grouping; but even a cursory reading reveals that the novel is made up of three major parts: the drought, the journey, and California. The first section ends with Chapter x (116). It is separated from the second section, the journey, by *two* interchapters. The first of these chapters presents a final picture of the deserted land—"The houses were left vacant on the land, and the land was vacant because of this." The second interchapter is devoted to Highway 66. It is followed by Chapter xiii which begins the Joads's journey on that historic highway—"The ancient overloaded Hudson creaked and grunted to the highway at Sallisaw and turned west, and the sun was blinding" (124). The journey section extends past the geographical California border, across the desert to Bakersfield (124-230). This section ends with Chapter xviii—"And the truck rolled down the mountain into the great valley"—and the next chapter begins the California section by introducing the reader to labor conditions in that state. Steinbeck had this tripartite division in mind as early as September of 1937, when he told one interviewer that he was working on "the first of three related longer novels."[3]

This structure has its roots in the Old Testament. The novel's three sections correspond to the oppression in Egypt, the exodus, and the sojourn in the land of Canaan, which in both accounts is first viewed from the mountains. The parallel is not worked out in detail, but the grand design is there: the plagues (erosion), the Egyptians (banks), the exodus (journey), and the hostile tribes of Canaan (Californians).

This Biblical structure is supported by a continuum of symbols and symbolic actions. The most pervasive symbolism is that of grapes. The novel's title, taken from "The Battle Hymn of the Republic" ("He is trampling out the vintage where the grapes of wrath are stored"), is itself a reference to Revelation: "And the angel thrust in his sickle into the earth, and gathered the vine of the earth, and cast it into the great winepress of the wrath of God" (xiv.19). Similarly in Deuteronomy: "Their grapes are grapes of gall, their clusters are bitter. Their wine is the poison of serpents" (xxxii.32); in Jeremiah: "The fathers have eaten sour grapes, and their children's teeth are set on edge" (xxxi.29). Sometimes these aspects of the symbol are stated in the novel's interchapters: "In the souls of the people the grapes of wrath are filling and growing heavy, growing heavy for the vintage" (349).

But Steinbeck also uses grapes for symbols of plenty, as the one huge cluster of grapes which Joshua and Oshea bring back from their first excursion into the rich land of Canaan, a cluster so huge that "they bare it between two on a staff" (Num. xiii.23). It is this meaning of grapes that is frequently alluded to by Grampa Joad: "Gonna get me a whole big bunch a grapes off a bush, or whatever, an' I'm gonna squash 'em on my face an' let 'em run offen my chin" (85). Although Grampa dies long before the Joads get to California, he is symbolically present through the anonymous old man in the barn (stable), who is saved from starvation by Rosasharn's breasts: "This thy stature is like to a palm tree, and thy breasts to clusters of grapes" (Cant. vii.7).[4] Rosasharn's giving of new life to the old man is another reference to the orthodox interpretation of Canticles: "I [Christ] am the rose of Sharon, and the lily of the valleys" (ii.1); and to the Gospels: "take, eat; this is my body." Still another important Biblical symbol is Jim Casy (Jesus Christ), who will be discussed in another connection.

Closely associated with this latter symbolic meaning of grapes and the land of Canaan is Ma Joad's frequent assertion that "We are the people." She has not been reading Carl Sandburg; she has been reading her Bible. As Sairy tells Tom when he is looking for a suitable verse to bury with Grampa, "Turn to Psalms, over further. You kin always get somepin outa Psalms" (144). And it is from Psalms that Ma gets her phrase: "For he is our God; and we are the people of his pasture, and the sheep of his hand" (xcv.7). They are the people who pick up life in Oklahoma (Egypt) and carry it to California (Canaan) as the turtle picks up seeds and as the ants pick up their eggs in "The Leader of the People." These parallels to the Hebrews of Exodus are all brought into focus when, near the end of the novel, Uncle John sets Rose of Sharon's stillborn child in an old apple crate (like Moses in the basket), sets the box in a stream "among the willow stems" and floats it toward the town saying, "Go down an' tell 'em" (446).

As the Israelites developed a code of laws in their exodus, so do the migrants: "The families learned what rights must be observed— the right of privacy in the tent . . . the right of the hungry to be fed; the rights of the pregnant and the sick to transcend all other rights" (195). Chapter xvii can be seen as the "Deuteronomy" of *The Grapes of Wrath*. It is this kind of context which makes of the Joads's journey "out west" an archetype of mass migration.[5]

The novel's Biblical structure and symbolism are supported by Steinbeck's skillful use of an Old Testament prose. The extent to which he succeeded in re-creating the epic dignity of this prose can be demonstrated by arranging a typical passage from the novel according to phrases, in the manner of the Bates Bible, leaving the punctuation intact except for capitals.

> The tractors had lights shining,
> For there is no day and night for a tractor
> And the disks turn the earth in the darkness
> And they glitter in the daylight.
>
> And when a horse stops work and goes into the barn
> There is a life and a vitality left,
> There is a breathing and a warmth,
> And the feet shift on the straw,
> And the jaws champ on the hay,
> And the ears and the eyes are alive.
> There is a warmth of life in the barn,
> And the heat and smell of life.
>
> But when the motor of a tractor stops,
> It is as dead as the ore it came from.
> The heat goes out of it
> Like the living heat that leaves a corpse. (117)

The parallel grammatical structure of parallel meanings, the simplicity of diction, the balance, the concrete details, the summary sentences, the reiterations—all are here. Note also the organization: four phrases for the tractor, eight for the horse, four again for the tractor. Except for the terms of machinery, this passage might be one of the psalms.

It is this echo—more, this pedal point—evident even in the most obviously "directed" passages, which supports their often simple philosophy, imbuing them with a dignity which their content alone could not sustain. The style gives them their authority:

Burn coffee for fuel in the ships. Burn corn to keep warm,
it makes a hot fire. Dump potatoes in the rivers and place
guards along the banks to keep the hungry people from fishing them out. Slaughter the pigs and bury them, and let the
putrescence drip down into the earth.

There is a crime here that goes beyond denunciation.
There is a sorrow here that weeping cannot symbolize. There
is a failure here that topples all our success. The fertile earth,
the straight tree rows, the sturdy trunks, and the ripe fruit.
And children dying of pellagra must die because a profit cannot be taken from an orange. (348)

These passages are not complex philosophy, but they may well
be profound. The Biblical resonance which gives them authority is
used discreetly, is never employed on the trivial and particular, and
its recurrence has a cumulative effect.

There are many other distinct prose styles in the interchapters
of *The Grapes of Wrath*, and each is just as functional in its place.
There is, for example, the harsh, staccato prose of Chapter vii, which
is devoted to the sale of used cars.

Cadillacs, La Salles, Buicks, Plymouths, Packards, Chevvies,
Fords, Pontiacs. Row on row, headlights glinting in the afternoon sun. Good Used Cars.

Soften 'em up, Joe. Jesus, I wisht I had a thousand jalopies!
Get 'em ready to deal, and I'll close 'em.

Goin' to California? Here's jus' what you need. Looks
shot, but they's thousan's of miles in her.

Lined up side by side. Good Used Cars. Bargains. Clean,
runs good. (68)

A good contrast to this prose style is offered by Chapter ix, which
presents the loss and despair of people forced to abandon their
household goods. Here the prose style itself takes on their dazed
resignation.

The women sat among the doomed things, turning them over
and looking past them and back. This book. My father had
it. He liked a book. *Pilgrim's Progress*. Used to read it. Got
his name in it. And his pipe—still smells rank. And this

picture—an angel. I looked at that before the fust three
come—didn't seem to do much good. Think we could get
this china dog in? Aunt Sadie brought it from the St. Louis
Fair. See? Wrote right on it. No, I guess not. Here's a letter
my brother wrote the day before he died. Here's an old-time
hat. These feathers—never got to use them. No, there isn't
room. (90)

At times, as in the description of a folk dance in Chapter xxiii,
the prose style becomes a veritable chameleon: "Look at that Texas
boy, long legs loose, taps four times for ever' damn step. Never see
a boy swing aroun' like that. Look at him swing that Cherokee girl,
red in her cheeks an' her toe points out" (329). No other American
novel has succeeded in forging and making instrumental so many
prose styles.

This rapid shifting of prose style and technique has value as
Americana and contributes to a "realism" far beyond that of literal
reporting. Also, this rapid shifting is important because it tends to
destroy any impression that these interchapters are, as a group, a
separate entity. They are a group only in that they are not a direct
part of the narrative. They have enough individuality of subject matter, prose style, and technique to keep the novel from falling into
two parts, and to keep the reader from feeling that he is now reading
"the other part."

In addition to the supporting Biblical structure and context, the
interchapters and narrative section are held together by an interweaving of two opposing themes which make up the "plot" of *The
Grapes of Wrath*. One of these, the negative one, concerns itself with
the increasingly straitened circumstances of the Joads. At the beginning of their journey they have $154, their household goods, two
barrels of pork, a serviceable truck, and their good health. As the
novel progresses they become more and more impoverished until at
the end they are destitute, without food, sick, their truck and goods
abandoned in the mud, without shelter, and without hope of work.
This economic decline is paralleled by a disintegration of the family's
morale. The Joads start off as a cheerful group full of hope and will
power and by the end of the novel are spiritually bankrupt. As Steinbeck had noted about the migrants around Bakersfield three years
earlier, they "feel that paralyzed dullness with which the mind pro-
tects itself against too much sorrow and too much pain."[6] When the

Joads enter their first Hooverville they catch a glimpse of the deterioration which lies ahead of them. They see filthy tin and rug shacks littered with trash, the children dirty and diseased, the heads of families "bull-simple" from being roughed-up too often, all spirit gone and in its place a whining, passive resistance to authority. Although the novel ends before the Joads come to this point, in the last chapter they are well on their way.

And as the family group declines morally and economically, so the family unit itself breaks up. Grampa dies before they are out of Oklahoma and lies in a nameless grave; Granma is buried a pauper; Noah deserts the family; Connie deserts Rosasharn; the baby is born dead; Tom becomes a fugitive; Al is planning to leave as soon as possible; Casy is killed; and they are forced to abandon the Wilsons.

These two negative or downward movements are balanced by two positive or upward movements. Although the primitive family unit is breaking up, the fragments are going to make up a larger group. The sense of a communal unit grows steadily through the narrative—the Wilsons, the Wainwrights—and is pointed to again and again in the interchapters: "One man, one family driven from the land; this rusty car creaking along the highway to the west. I lost my land, a single tractor took my land. I am alone and I am bewildered. And in the night one family camps in a ditch and another family pulls in and the tents come out. The two men squat on their hams and the women and children listen. . . . For here 'I lost my land' is changed; a cell is split and from its splitting grows the thing you [owners] hate—'We lost *our* land' " (152). Oppression and intimidation only serve to strengthen the social group; the relief offered by a federal migrant camp only gives them a vision of the democratic life they can attain by cooperation, which is why the local citizens are opposed to these camps.

Another of the techniques by which Steinbeck develops this theme of unity can be illustrated by the Joads's relationship with the Wilson family of Kansas, which they meet just before crossing the Oklahoma border. This relationship is developed not so much by explicit statement, as in the interchapters, as by symbols. Grampa Joad, for example, dies in the Wilsons' tent and is buried in one of the Wilsons' blankets. Furthermore, the epitaph which is buried with Grampa (in Oklahoma soil) is written on a page torn from the Wilsons' Bible—that page usually reserved for family births, marriages, and deaths. In burying this page with Grampa the Wilsons symbolize not only their adoption of the Joads, but their renouncing of hope for continuing their own family line. Also, note it is the more destitute Wilson family which embraces the Joads. Steinbeck makes of the two families' relationship a microcosm of the migration's total picture, its human significance.

This growing awareness on the part of the people en masse is paralleled by the education and conversion of Tom and Casy. At the beginning of the book, Tom's attitude is individualistic. He is looking out for himself. As he puts it, "I'm still laying my dogs down one at a time," and "I climb fences when I got fences to climb" (175). His first real lesson comes when Casy strikes out against the trooper to save his friend and then gives himself up in his place (264). The section immediately following is that of the family's stay in a federal migrant camp, and here Tom's education is advanced still further. By the time Casy is killed, Tom is ready for his conversion, which he seals by revenging his mentor. While Tom is hiding out in the cave after having struck the vigilante, he has time to think of Casy and his message, so that in his last meeting with his mother, in which he asserts his spiritual unity with all men, it is evident that he has moved from material and personal resentment to ethical indignation, from particulars to principles. It is significant that this last meeting between mother and son should take place under conditions reminiscent of the prenatal state. The entrance to the cave is covered with black vines and the interior is damp and completely dark, so that the contact of mother and son is actually physical rather than visual; she gives him food. When Tom comes out of the cave after announcing his conversion it is as though he were reborn. When Tom says, "An' when our folks eat the stuff they raise an' live in the houses they build—why, I'll be there" (419), he is paraphrasing Isaiah: "And they shall build houses and inhabit them, they shall not build and another inhabit; they shall not plant and another eat" (lxv, 21–22).

The development of Jim Casy is similar to that of Tom. He moves from Bible-belt evangelism to social prophecy. At the beginning of the book he has already left preaching and has returned from "in the hills, thinkin', almost you might say like Jesus went into the wilderness to think His way out of a mess of troubles" (83). But although Casy is already approaching his revelation of the Over-Soul, it is only through his experiences with the Joads that he is able to complete his vision. As Tom moves from material resentment to ethical indignation, so Casy moves from the purely speculative to the pragmatic. Both move from stasis to action. Casy's Christlike development is complete when he dies saying, "You don' know what you're a-doin' " (386). Those critics are reading superficially who, like Elizabeth N. Monroe, think that Steinbeck "expects us to admire Casy, an itinerant preacher, who, over-excited from his evangelistic revivals, is in the habit of taking one or another of the girls in his audience to lie in the grass." Actually, Casy himself perceives the incongruity of this behavior, which is why he goes "into the wilderness" and renounces his Bible-belt evangelism for a species of social humanism, and his congregation for the human race. His development, like that of Tom, is symbolic of the changing social condition which is the novel's essential theme, paralleling the development of the Joad family as a whole, which is, again, but a "personalized group." Casy resembles Ralph Waldo Emerson more than he does Lewis's Elmer Gantry or Caldwell's Semon Dye. For like Emerson, Casy discovers the Over-Soul through intuition and rejects his congregation in order to preach to the world.[7]

Because these themes of education and conversion are not the central, involving action of the novel, but grow slowly out of a rich and solid context, the development of Tom and Casy achieves an authority lacking in most proletarian fiction. The novel's thematic organization also makes it possible for Steinbeck successfully to incorporate the widest variety of materials and, with the exception of romantic love, to present a full scale of human emotions.

This ability of Steinbeck's thematic structure to absorb incidents organically into its context is important for an understanding of the novel's last scene, of which there has been much criticism. The novel's materials do make a climactic ending difficult. The author faced three pitfalls: a *deus ex machina* ending; a summing up, moral essay; and simply a new level of horror. But the novel's thematic treatment of material made it possible for Steinbeck to end on a high point, to bring his novel to a symbolic climax without doing violence to credulity, structure, or theme.

This climax is prepared for by the last interchapter, which parallels in terms of rain the opening description of the drought. The last paragraphs of these chapters are strikingly similar:

The women studied the men's faces secretly. . . . After a while the faces of the watching men lost their bemused perplexity and became hard and angry and resistant. Then the women knew that they were safe and that there was no break. (7)

The women watched the men, watched to see whether the break had come at last. . . . And where a number of men gathered together, the fear went from their faces, and anger took its place. And the women sighed with relief, for they knew it was all right—the break had not come. (434)

With this latter paragraph, a recapitulation of the novel's two main themes as they are worked out in three movements, *The Grapes of Wrath* is brought full circle. The last chapter compactly reenacts the whole drama of the Joads's journey in one uninterrupted continuity of suspense. The rain continues to fall; the little mud levee collapses; Rosasharn's baby is born dead; the boxcar must be abandoned; they take to the highway in search of food and find instead a starving man. Then the miracle happens. As Rose of Sharon offers her breast to the old man the novel's two counter themes are brought together in a symbolic paradox. Out of her own need she gives life; out of the profoundest depth of despair comes the greatest assertion of faith.[8]

Steinbeck's great achievement in *The Grapes of Wrath* is that while minimizing what seem to be the most essential elements of fiction—plot and character—he was able to create a well-made and emotionally compelling novel out of materials which in most other hands have resulted in sentimental propaganda.

NOTES

1. *The Craft of Fiction* (New York: Peter Smith, 1945), p. 33.
2. New York: The Viking Press, 1941.
3. Joseph Henry Jackson, "John Steinbeck: A Portrait," *Sat. Rev. of Lit.*, xvi (Sept. 25, 1937), 18.
4. One of the oddest interpretations of this scene is that of Harry Slochower, who uses this incident to explain the novel's title: "The grapes have turned to 'wrath,' indicated by the fact that the first milk of the mother is said to be bitter."
5. Bernard Bowron fails to perceive this larger significance of the Joads's

journey and attempts to make far too much out of some obvious similarities to the Covered Wagon genre.

6. "The Harvest Gypsies."

7. Further parallels between Casy and Christ: see Martin Shockley's "Christian Symbolism in *The Grapes of Wrath*" (reprinted in Tedlock and Wicker).

8. For parallels to this scene see Maupassant's "Idylle"; Byron's *Childe Harold*, can. iv, st. 148–151; Rubens' painting of old Cimon taking milk from the breast of Pero; and an 18th-century play called *The Grecian's Daughter*, discussed in Maurice W. Disher's *Blood and Thunder* (London: Frederick Muller Ltd., 1949), p. 23. See also Celeste T. Wright (reprinted in Donohue).

Robert J. Griffin and
William A. Freedman

Robert J. Griffin has taught at Yale University, California State University, Hayward, and City College of San Francisco. He has written an essay on Sinclair Lewis published in American Winners of the Nobel Prize, *edited* Twentieth Century Interpretation of Arrowsmith, *and published various articles in* College English, Yale Review, Studies in English Literature, Kansas City Review, *and* The Nation.

William A. Freedman has taught at Brooklyn College of the City University of New York and the University of Haifa. He is the author of Laurence Sterne and the Origins of the Musical Novel, *and of poems and articles in a variety of journals and little magazines including* Antioch Review, APR, Novel, Modern Fiction Studies, Studies in English Literature, *and* Studies in Romanticism.

MACHINES AND ANIMALS:
PERVASIVE MOTIFS IN
THE GRAPES OF WRATH

Once the hubbub over John Steinbeck's "propaganda tract" began to die down—there are still those who refuse to let it die completely—critics began to pay serious attention to *The Grapes of Wrath* as a work of art.[1] Such aspects of the novel as its characterization (whether or not the Joads are "cardboard figures"), the prose

Reprinted from *Journal of English and Germanic Philology*, LXII (April 1963), 569–80. By permission of the publisher.

style (actually the several prose styles, but particularly the poetic effectiveness of the descriptive passages), and the interrelationship of the different kinds of chapters[2] have been discussed at some length. In this paper we should like to concentrate on two pervasive motifs in the novel, namely, the crucially important motifs of *machines* and *animals* which contribute considerably to structure and thematic content. We may call these two the "dominant motifs," but we must remember that extracting these elements is necessarily an act of oversimplification; it is only through their complex relationships with subsidiary motifs and devices, and with the more straightforward narration and exposition and argumentation, that they provide major symbols integral to the art and substance of the novel.[3] With this qualification in mind, we may proceed to a consideration of machines and animals as sources of tropes, as signs and underscoring devices, and ultimately as persistent symbols.

Very few of the tropes of the novel—the metaphors, similes, and allusions—make use of machinery as such. "Tractored out" is of course a prominent figure of speech repeated several times to express the Okies' plight in being forced from their plots of land by the mechanical monstrosity of industrialized farming ("tractored off" also appears a couple of times). But otherwise about the only instance of a metaphorical use of machinery is a single simile late in the novel: the weary men trying to build a bank of earth to hold back the floor "worked jerkily, like machines" (440). There are a good many metaphors applied to mechanical apparatuses—that is, tropes in which machinery is characterized by some nonmechanical phenomenon as the vehicle of the metaphor. Generally this metaphorical characterization of machines emphasizes animalism or the bestial side of human affairs, as the seeders are said to rape the land. Fundamentally these metaphors appear designed to contribute to a general sense of tragedy or disaster indicated by such secondary motifs as the blood tropes—"the sun was as red as ripe new blood" (7), "the earth was bloody in [the sun's] setting light" (97)—and the frequent recurrence of "cut"—"the sun cut into the shade" (10), "the road was cut with furrows" (20).

While there are very few machine tropes, animal tropes abound. Often animals are used to characterize the human sex drive: Muley Graves (whose name is not inappropriate here) refers to himself during his first experience as "snortin' like a buck deer, randy as a billygoat" (54); young, virile Al Joad has been "a-billygoatin' aroun' the country. Tom-cattin' hisself to death" (84). And the sexuality of animals several times appears as the vehicle of a metaphor: Casy refers to a participant in a revival meeting as "jumpy as a stud horse in a box stall" (31). Animal tropes frequently serve to denote violence or depravity in human behavior: fighting "like a couple of cats" (22); a tractor hitting a share-cropper's cabin "give her a shake like a dog shakes a rat" (49); Muley used to be "mean like a wolf" but now is "mean like a weasel" (60); and Ma Joad describes Purty Boy Floyd's career as comparable to a maddened animal at bay—"they shot at him like a varmint, an' he shot back, an' then they run him like a coyote, an' him a-snappin' an' a-snarlin', mean as a lobo" (78). Animal tropes may simply indicate a harmless playfulness or swagger: Winfield Joad is "kid-wild and calfish" (97), and Al acts like "a dung-hill rooster" (422). But the most frequent and significant use of the numerous animal tropes is to characterize the Okies' plight: the Joads are forced off their forty acres, forced to live "piled in John's house like gophers in a winter burrow" (49); then they begin an abortive trip toward what they hope will prove to be a "New Canaan" in California, and Casy uses this tacit analogy to describe the impersonal, industrial economy from which they are fleeing:

> Ever see one a them Gila monsters take hold, mister? Grabs hold, an' you chop him in two an' his head hangs on. Chop him at the neck an' his head hangs on. Got to take a screwdriver an' pry his head apart to git him loose. An' while he's layin' there, poison is drippin' an' drippin' into the hole he's made with his teeth. (129)

Casy argues that the wrong results from men not staying "harnessed" together in a common effort ("mankin' was holy when it was one thing"); one man can get "the bit in his teeth an' run off his own way, kickin' an' draggin' an' fightin' " (83). Consequently the roads to California are "full of frantic people running like ants" (237—the "ants" simile appears again, for instance, on 284). In California the Okies work, when they can get work, "like draft horses" (441); they are driven "like pigs" (383) and forced to live "like pigs" (419). Casy has been observing and listening to the Okies in their misfortunes, and he knows their fear and dissatisfaction and restlessness: "I hear 'em an' feel 'em; an' they're beating their wings like a bird in a attic. Gonna bust their wings on a dusty winda tryin' ta get out" (249).

It should be noted that the animalistic references to people are not as a rule unfavorable ("randy as a billygoat" is scarcely a pejorative in Steinbeck's lusty lexicon). The few derogatory animal tropes are almost all applied to the exploiters (banks, land companies, profiteers) and not to the exploited (the Joads and the other Okies). That these latter must behave like the lower animals is not their fault. Their animalism is the result of the encroachments of the machine economy. Machines, then, are frequently depicted as evil objects: they "tear in and shove the croppers out" (12); "one man on a tractor can take the place of twelve or fourteen families" (36); so the Okies must take to the road, seeking a new home, lamenting, "I lost my land, a single tractor took my land" (152). Farming has become a mechanized industry, and Steinbeck devotes an entire chapter (nineteen) to the tragic results:

> The tractors which throw men out of work, the belt lines which carry loads, the machines which produce, all were increased; and more and more families scampered on the highways, looking for crumbs from the great holdings, lusting after the land beside the roads. The great owners formed associations for protection and they met to discuss ways to intimidate, to kill, to gas. (238)

The Okies are very aware of the evils brought about by mechanization. Reduced to picking cotton for bare-subsistence wages, they realize that even this source of income may soon go. One asks, "Heard 'bout the cotton-pickin' machine?" (407).

The Joads find themselves living—trying to live—in an age of machinery. Machines or mechanized devices quite naturally play important roles in the symbolism of the novel. ("Symbolism" is here understood to mean the employment of concrete images—objects and events—to embody or suggest abstract qualities or concepts.) Some machines serve as "interior" symbols; they are, that is, recognized as symbolic by characters in the novel. Still others, largely because of the frequency with which or crucial contexts in which they appear, can be seen by the careful reader to take on symbolic significance. The "huge red transport truck" of chapter two, for example, can be seen as a sort of epitome of the mechanical-industrial economy—the bigness, the newness, the mobility, the massive efficiency, even the inhumanity *(No Riders)* and lack of trust—"a brass padlock stood straight out from the hasp on the big back doors" (9). It is a mobile era in which one must accommodate to the mass mechanization in order to survive. Farmers can no longer hope to get by with a team and a wagon. And Steinbeck finds in the used-car business (chapter seven), preying on the need to move out and move quickly, an apt representation for the exploitation of those who have not yet been able to accommodate: "In the towns, on the edges of the towns, in fields, in vacant lots, the used-car yards, the wreckers' yards, the garages with blazoned signs—Used Cars, Good Used Cars, Cheap transportation" (64). The Joads' makeshift truck aptly represents their predicament—their need to move, their inability to move efficiently or in style, their over-all precariousness: "The engine was noisy, full of little clashings, and the brake rods banged. There was a wooden creaking from the wheels, and a thin jet of steam escaped through a hole in the top of the radiator cap" (100).⁴ Steinbeck makes overt the symbolic nature of this truck; when the members of the family meet for their final council before migrating, they meet near the truck: "The house was dead, and the fields were dead; but this truck was the active thing, the living principle" (101). Here, as throughout the novel, the Joads' predicament is a representative instance of the predicaments of thousands. Highway 66 is the "main migrant road" (chapter twelve), and on this "long concrete path" move the dispossessed, the "people in flight": "In the day ancient leaky radiators sent up columns of steam, loose connecting rods hammered and pounded. And the men driving the trucks and the overloaded cars listened apprehensively. How far between towns? It is a terror between towns. If something breaks—well, if something breaks we camp right here while Jim walks to town and gets a part and walks back" (120). Along this route the dispossessed farmers find that they are not alone in their troubles. The independent, small-scale service station operator is being squeezed out of his livelihood just as the farmers have been; Tom tells the poor operator that he too will soon be a part of the vast moving (129). And the various types of vehicles moving along Route 66 are obvious status symbols. Some have "class an' speed"; these are the insolent chariots of the exploiters. Others are the beat-up, overloaded conveyors of the exploited in search of a better life. The reactions of those who are better-off to the sad vehicles of the Okies are representative of their lack of understanding and sympathy:

> "Jesus, I'd hate to start out in a jalopy like that."
> "Well, you and me got sense. Them goddamn Okies got no sense and no feeling. They ain't human. A human being wouldn't live like they do. A human being couldn't stand it to be so dirty and miserable. They ain't a hell of a lot better than gorillas." (221)

The Okies are conscious of vehicles as status symbols and automatically distrust anyone in a better car. When a new Chevrolet pulls into the laborers' camp, the laborers automatically know that it brings trouble. Similarly the condition of the Okies' vehicles provides perfect parallels for their own sad state. As the Joads are trying to move ahead without being able to ascertain exactly where they are headed—"even if we got to crawl"—so their truck's "dim lights felt along the broad black highway ahead" (281). As the Joads' condition worsens, so naturally does that of their truck (e.g., "the right headlight blinked on and off from a bad connection"—401). In the development of the novel their vehicles are so closely identified with the Okies that a statement of some damage to the vehicles becomes obviously symbolic of other troubles for the owners. When the disastrous rains come, "beside the tents the old cars stood, and water fouled the ignition wires and water fouled the carburetors" (433). The disastrousness of the ensuing flood is quite clearly signaled by mention of the "trucks and automobiles deep in the slowly moving water" (450).

As the Okies' vehicles provide an accurate index to their circumstances, so do the animals they own, particularly their pets. The deserted cat that Tom and Casy find when they survey the Joads' deserted farm represents the forlorn state of the dispossessed (see 45–47—the cat actually foreshadows the appearance of Muley Graves with his tales of lonely scavengering). The dogs that appear when Tom and Casy reach Uncle John's place are indicative of human behavior in the face of new circumstances (one sniffs cautiously up to examine the strangers, while the other seeks some adequate excuse for avoiding the possible danger—75). After the company's tractors move in and the share-croppers are "shoved off" their land, the pets that they left behind must fend for themselves and thus gradually revert to the primitive state of their ancestors—a reversion not unlike the desperate measures that the Okies are driven to by adversity and animosity: "The wild cats crept in from the fields at night, but they did not mew at the doorstep any more. They moved like shadows of a cloud across the moon, into the rooms to hunt the mice" (118). The Joads take a dog with them on their flight to California, but he is not prepared to adjust to the new, fast, mechanized life thrust upon him; when his owners stop for gas and water, he wanders out to the great highway—"A big swift car whisked near, tires squealed. The dog dodged helplessly, and with a shriek, cut off in the middle, went under the wheels" (131). The owner of the dilapidated independent service station comments on the sad scene, "A dog jus' don' last no time near a highway. I had three dogs run over in a year. Don't keep none, no more" (131). After the Joads have been in California for a while and discover the grim facts of life for them there, they move on to another "Hooverville" camp of migrants. They find their fellow job-seekers hungry, fearful, and distrustful; the single pet there vividly expresses the general attitude or atmosphere of the place: "A lean brown mongrel dog came sniffing around the side of the tent. He was nervous and flexed to run. He sniffed close before he was aware of the two men, and then looking up he saw them, leaped sideways, and fled, ears back, bony tail clamped protectively" (250). Yet having pets is indicative of the love and sympathy of which man is capable when in favorable circumstances. The simple, "natural" Joads never lose their appreciation for pets. When their fortunes are at their lowest ebb, Ma still holds hopes for a pleasant future: " 'Wisht we had a dog,' Ruthie said. [Ma replied] 'We'll have a dog; have a cat, too' " (437).

Pets, then, serve as symbolic indices to human situations; and other animal symbols are used to excellent advantage. One of Steinbeck's favorite devices is the use of epitome—the description of some object or event, apart from the main movement of the narrative, which symbolically sums up something central to the meaning of the narrative. Toward the end of The Grapes of Wrath the migrants are gathered about a fire, telling stories, and one of them recounts an experience of a single Indian brave whom they were forced to shoot—epitomizing the indomitability and dignity of man, and foreshadowing Casy's fate.[5]

We have already noted the use of animals for symbolic foreshadowing (for instance, the dispossessed cat and Muley Graves).[6] Probably Steinbeck's most famous use of the symbolic epitome is the land turtle.[7] The progress of the Okies, representative of the perseverance of "Manself," is neatly foreshadowed in the description of the turtle's persistent forward movement: he slowly plods his way, seeking to prevail in the face of adversities, and he succeeds in spite of insects, such obstacles as the highway, motorists swerving to hit him (though some swerve to avoid hitting him), Tom's imprisoning him for a while in his coat, the attacks of a cat, and so on. Steinbeck does not leave discernment of the rich parallels wholly to the reader's imagination. There are, for instance, similarities between Tom's progress along the dirt road and the turtle's: "And as the turtle crawled on down the embankment, its shell dragged dirt over the seeds . . . drawing a wavy shallow trench in the dust with its shell" (19); and "Joad plodded along, dragging his cloud of dust behind him . . . dragging his heels a little in the fine dust" (20—at this point in the novel Tom has not yet begun to sow the seeds of new growth among the downtrodden Okies). Casy remarks on the indomitability of the turtle, and its similarity to himself: "Nobody can't keep a turtle though. They work at it and work at it, and at last one day they get out and away they go—off somewheres. It's like me" (24). But at this point in the novel Casy is not altogether like the turtle, for he has not yet discovered the goal to which he will devote himself unstintingly: " 'Goin' someplace,' he repeated. 'That's right, he's goin' someplace. Me—I don't know where I'm goin' ' " (24).[8]

Animal epitomes, such as the turtle and the "lean gray cat," occur several times at crucial points. And frequently a person's character will be represented by his reaction to or treatment of lower animals. As Tom and Casy walk along the dusty road a gopher snake wriggles across their path; Tom peers at it, sees that it is harmless, and says, "Let him go" (71). Tom is not cruel or vicious, but he does recognize the need to prevent or put down impending disaster. Later, a "rattlesnake crawled across the road and Tom hit it and broke it and left it squirming" (230). The exploitation of the Okies is symbolized by the grossly unfair price paid a share-cropper for the matched pair of bay horses he is forced to sell. In this purchase of the bays, the exploiters are buying a part of the croppers' history, their loves and labors; and a swelling bitterness is part of the bargain: "You're buying years of work, toil in the sun; you're buying a sorrow that can't talk. But watch it, mister" (89).

Animals convey symbolic significance throughout the novel. When the Okies are about to set out on what they are aware will be no pleasure jaunt to California—though they scarcely have any idea how dire will be the journey and the life at the end of it—an ominous "shadow of a buzzard slid across the earth, and the family all looked up at the sailing black bird" (168). In the light of the more obvious uses of animals as epitomes or omens, it is easy to see that other references to animals, which might otherwise seem incidental, are intentionally parallel to the actions or troubles of people. Here is a vivid parallel for the plight of the share-cropper, caught in the vast, rapid, mechanized movement of the industrial economy (the great highway is persistently the bearer of symbolic phenomena):

A jackrabbit got caught in the lights and he bounced along ahead, cruising easily, his great ears flopping with every jump. Now and then he tried to break off the road, but the wall of darkness thrust him back. Far ahead bright headlights appeared and bore down on them. The rabbit hesitated, faltered, then turned and bolted toward the lesser lights of the Dodge. There was a small soft jolt as he went under the wheels. The oncoming car swished by. (186)

As the weary Okies gather in a Hooverville to try to find some way out of the disaster they have flown into, moths circle frantically about the single light: "A lamp bug slammed into the lantern and broke itself, and fell into darkness" (187). While the wary mongrel at the camp represents the timorous doubts of the Okies, the arrogant skunks that prowl about at night are reminiscent of the imperious deputies and owners who intimidate the campers. The Okies are driven like animals, forced to live like animals, and frequently the treatment they receive from their short-term employers is not as good as that given farm animals:

Fella had a team of horses, had to use 'em to plow an' cultivate an' mow, wouldn' think a turnin' 'em out to starve when they wasn't workin'.

Them's horses—we're men. (434)

We have seen that both machines and animals serve as effective symbolic devices in The Grapes of Wrath. Frequently the machine and animal motifs are conjoined to afford a doubly rich imagery or symbolism. Thus the banks are seen as monstrous animals, but *mechanical* monsters: "the banks were machines and masters all at the same time" (34). The men for whom the share-croppers formerly worked disclaim responsibility: "It's the monster. The bank isn't like a man" (36). The tractors that the banks send in are similarly monstrous—"snub-nosed monsters, raising the dust and sticking their snouts into it, straight down the country, across the country, through fences, through dooryards, in and out of gullies in straight lines" (38). And the man driving the tractor is no longer a man; he is "a part of the monster, a robot in the seat" (38). Their inability to stop these monsters represents the frantic frustration of the dispossessed; Grampa Joad tries to shoot a tractor, and does get one of its headlights, but the monster keeps on moving across their land (48). The new kind of mechanical farming is contrasted with the old kind of personal contact with the land. The new kind is easy and efficient: "So easy that the wonder goes out of work, so efficient that the wonder goes out of land and the working of it, and with the wonder the deep understanding and the relation" (117).

We have seen that machines are usually instruments or indices of misfortune in Steinbeck's novel. But to assume that machinery is automatically or necessarily bad for Steinbeck would be a serious mistake. Machines are *instruments*, and in the hands of the right people they can be instruments of good fortune. When the turtle tries to cross the highway, one driver tries to smash him, while another swerves to miss him (19)[9]; it depends on who is behind the wheel. Al's relationship with the truck is indicative of the complex problems of accommodating in a machine age. He knows about motors, so he can take care of the truck and put it to good use. He is admitted to a place of responsibility in the family council because of his up-to-date ability. He becomes "the soul of the car" (124). The young people are more in tune with the machines of their times, whereas the older ones are not prepared to accommodate to the exigencies of the industrial economy:

Casy turned to Tom. "Funny how you fellas can fix a car. Jus' light right in an' fix her. I couldn't fix no car, not even now when I seen you do it."

"Got to grow into her when you're a little kid," Tom said.

"It ain't jus' knowin'. It's more'n that. Kids now can tear
down a car 'thout even thinkin' about it." (185)

The tractors that shove the croppers off their land are not inherently
evil; they are simply the symptoms of unfair exploitation. In one of
the interchapters (fourteen) Steinbeck expresses the thought that the
machines are in themselves of neutral value:

Is a tractor bad? Is the power that turns the long furrows
wrong? If this tractor were ours it would be good—not mine,
but ours. If our tractor turned the long furrows of our land,
it would be good. Not my land, but ours. We could love that
tractor then as we have loved this land when it was ours. But
this tractor does two things—it turns the land and turns us
off the land. There is little difference between this tractor
and a tank. The people are driven, intimidated, hurt by both.
(152)

Machinery, like the science and technology that can develop bigger
and better crops (see 346–49), is not enough for progress; there must
be human understanding and cooperation. The Okies—through a
fault not really their own—have been unable to adjust to the machinery of industrialization. Toward the very last of the novel Ma
pleads with Al not to desert the family, because he is the only one
left qualified to handle the truck that has become so necessary a part
of their lives. As the flood creeps up about the Joads, the truck is
inundated, put out of action. But the novel ends on a hopeful note
of human sharing, and we may surmise that the Okies (or at least
their children) can eventually assimilate themselves into a machine-
oriented society.

Some critics have noted Steinbeck's preoccupation with animal
images and symbols, and labeled his view of man as "biological."[10]
This label is a gross oversimplification, responsible for a good deal of
misreading of Steinbeck's work. The animal motif in *Grapes* does
not at all indicate that man is or ought to be exactly like the lower
animals. The Okies crawl across the country like ants, live like pigs,
and fight amongst themselves like cats, mainly because they have
been forced into this animalistic existence. Man can plod on in his
progress like the turtle, but he can also become conscious of his goals
and deliberately employ new devices in attaining those goals. Man's

progress need not be blind; for he can couple human knowledge with human love, and manipulate science and technology to make possible the betterment of himself and all his fellows. Steinbeck does not present a picture of utopia in his novel, but the dominant motifs do indicate that such a society is possible.

It has been a fundamental assumption of this study that dominant motifs are of central importance in the form and meaning of certain works of fiction. In this particular case we would contend that Steinbeck's intricate and masterful manipulation of the various references to machines and animals is an essential factor in the stature of *The Grapes of Wrath* as one of the monuments of twentieth-century American literature. By their very pervasiveness—the recurrence of the components that constitute the motifs—the references contribute significantly to the unity of the work; they help, for instance, to bind together the Joad chapters with those which generalize the meaning that the Joads' story illustrates. Certain animals and machines play important parts on the literal level of the story, and these and others serve to underscore principal developments or "themes" in the novel. Certain animals and machines are recognizably symbolic within the context of the story, and still others (the epitomes for example) can be discerned as much more meaningful than their overt, apparently incidental mention might at first seem to indicate. Both the interior and the more subtle symbols— as reinforced by the recurrence of related allusions or figures of speech—are interwoven and played off against one another to such an extent that the overall meaning is not merely made more vivid: it is considerably enriched. A consideration of these motifs does not begin to exhaust the richness of the book; but this discussion can, we hope, contribute to a fuller understanding of Steinbeck's novel as a consummate complex work of art.

NOTES

1. For discussion of the criticism about Steinbeck's work, see Peter Lisca, *The Wide World of John Steinbeck*, and E. W. Tedlock, Jr., and C. V. Wicker, *Steinbeck and His Critics*. Lisca's treatment of the criticism serves as his introductory chapter and centers on the lamentable preoccupation with Steinbeck's social and philosophical attitudes and the consequent neglect of his artistry. Tedlock and Wicker's is likewise introductory and similarly oriented, closing with the hopeful convic-

tion that "future critics will find him to be an artist with an artist's intentions, methods, and stature" (p. xli). Another comprehensively excellent study of the novels is Warren French, *John Steinbeck* (New York, 1975).

2. See Lisca (572–88 of this volume) for discussion of Steinbeck's success at integrating different kinds of chapters into a unified though complex structure.

3. A really thorough exegesis of the novel would have to describe the many secondary devices interwoven with the major motifs: the significance of clothing, e.g., particularly hats—the gradual metamorphosis of the cheap new cap Tom gets on leaving prison, Uncle John's defacement of his old hat as he prepares to lose himself in drink, etc. The Biblical allusions—though not a "motif" in our sense—are of course an essential part of the novel.

4. Of course it is inevitable that the poor condition of the Joads' truck parallels their own predicament; they cannot afford anything better. But the point is that the truck becomes so accurate an index that the author can use it for metonymic expression of the owners' plight; deterioration of the truck expresses deterioration of the family. A symbol is not the less a symbol because it functions well at the literal level.

5. "They was a brave on a ridge, against the sun. Knowed he stood out. Spread his arms an' stood." Finally the soldiers are prevailed upon to shoot him down. "An' he wasn' big—he'd looked so grand—up there. All tore to pieces an' little. Ever see a cock pheasant, stiff and beautiful, ever' feather drawed an' painted, an' even his eyes drawed in pretty? An'. bang! You pick him up—bloody and twisted, an' you spoiled somepin better'n you; . . . you spoiled somepin in yaself, an' you can't never fix it up" (325).

6. There are in *Grapes* numerous instances of foreshadowing which do not participate in either of the dominant motifs. For example, Rose of Sharon's gesture of human sharing at the end of the novel is foreshadowed in Tom's first meal in the government camp: a mother breast-feeding her child invites him to share the breakfast she is cooking (289).

7. Kenneth Burke has called the turtle a "mediating material object for tying together Tom, Casy, and the plot, a kind of externalizing vessel, or 'symbol.' "

8. The case of the turtle is an excellent example of the intricate interrelationships of the Joads' story and the interchapters (i.e., those which do not deal directly with the Joad plot). All of chapter three is devoted to descriptions of the turtle's slow, apparently unwitting but nonetheless definite progress. Yet, under analysis this chapter, like that on the

used-car lots, for instance, proves to be an integral part of the "symbolic structure" of the novel.

9. Steinbeck makes frequent use of such contrasts or juxtapositions. The cheerfulness of the Saturday night dance at the government camp, for example, is effectively juxtaposed with the harsh grumbling of the hyperreligious campers who do not attend (329).

10. See e.g., Edmund Wilson. Peter Lisca (*The Wide World of John Steinbeck*) has tried to dispel this misconception of Steinbeck's biologism—as has Frederick Bracher. While there are still those who prefer to view *Grapes* as a primarily sociological document, the oversimplification of Steinbeck's "biological view" has been pretty well quashed in recent criticism.

John R. Reed

John R. Reed has taught at the University of Cincinnati, the University of Connecticut, and Wayne State University. He is the author of numerous books, including Dickens and Thackeray: Punishment and Forgiveness, Victorian Will, *and two recent volumes of poetry,* Great Lake *and* Life Sentences.

THE GRAPES OF WRATH
AND THE ESTHETICS OF INDIGENCE

The representative from Oklahoma, Lyle H. Boren, addressing the 76th Congress of the United States in 1940, angrily dismissed *The Grapes of Wrath* as a false and foul novel. "Take the vulgarity out of this book," he said, "and it would be blank from cover to cover."[1] For a time, much of the criticism of Steinbeck's most popular novel pointed to the unsavoriness of its details and the crudeness of its speech. In recent years, however, few critics have concerned themselves with what now appears as rather tame language. But Steinbeck's use of rough language and his descriptions of some crude features of indigent life are thematically important.

Walter Fuller Taylor described *The Grapes of Wrath* as a "parable" rather than a realistic novel. He felt that any reader who accepted the novel, accepted "a concept of sexual promiscuity, a

This essay, in slightly different form, was presented at the University of Connecticut's conference on *The Grapes of Wrath*, May 3, 1969. Printed here for the first time by permission of the author.

humorous tolerance of the Tobacco-Road way of life." For Taylor, the pernicious philosophy behind the novel was that "the only values lie in the experiences of the moment, the only valid end of living is the continued renewing of the life of the life cells."[2] Edmund Wilson, too, had seen Steinbeck's philosophy as essentially biological with nothing to oppose the "vision of man's hating and destroying himself except an irreducible faith in life."

A series of critics have, however, traced a broader and more organized moral purpose in the imagery, allusions, and motifs of *The Grapes of Wrath*. These various approaches do not all agree, and so Agnes McNeill Donohue concludes that "as a storyteller with an American Puritan background Steinbeck seems to be mixing freely Old and New Testament imagery, Hebraic, Christian, archetypal and mythic symbols to enrich, fertilize, and extend his meaning." For her, Steinbeck's meaning is that man is a fallen creature journeying to a false Eden that reveals only his own corrupt heart.

My interest is not with such extensions of Steinbeck's meaning, but with the methods by which he was able to transform the image of the poor by associating their earthy life of the soil with emerging ideals and the abstractions and broad hopes that those ideals bring. Steinbeck himself, in accepting the Nobel Prize for Literature in 1962, said that the writer "is charged with exposing our many grievous faults and failures, with dredging up to the light our dark and dangerous dreams, for the purpose of improvement." But he added that a writer must also "celebrate man's proven capacity for greatness of heart and spirit," and he asserted: "I hold that a writer who does not passionately believe in the perfectibility of man has no dedication nor any membership in literature."[3]

It is my feeling that *The Grapes of Wrath* does not represent, as Maxwell Geismer has it (*Writers in Crisis*), "the dubious nuptials of 'Tobacco Road' with the *Ladies' Home Journal*," but signifies instead a marriage of man's "faults and failures" with his own "greatness of heart and spirit." It is in the use of indigence and its concomitants that Steinbeck makes evident man's capacity for moral transformation.

Early in *The Grapes of Wrath* the truck driver who gives Tom Joad a ride observes Tom's work-glazed hands, commenting, "I notice all stuff like that. Take a pride in it" (13). Whether or not we can take this as Steinbeck's conscious clue to be on the alert for revelatory details, we certainly will recall the author's own observation of Tom's hands only a few pages before when he described them as "hard, with broad fingers and nails as thick and ridged as little clam shells. The space between thumb and forefinger and the hams of his hands were shiny with callus" (9). We may remember this description soon after when we learn of the land turtle with "high-domed shell" who creeps determinedly forward on "hard legs and yellow-nailed feet" and who has "brows like fingernails" (18). Such alerts to the association of simple details can, I believe, be taken as hints for the proper reading of Steinbeck's novel. Details which seem gratuitous at the beginning of the novel are gradually transformed to meaningful adjuncts of a higher mode of existence. This transformation results from a growing emphasis upon human dignity and an increasingly broad and symbolic fictional context.

When Tom first encounters Casy their manners and conversation are a peculiar combination of vulgarity and elevation. Steinbeck observes that Tom does not wipe the whiskey bottle after Casy has taken his swallow, but explains that Tom refrained from this hygienic gesture out of "politeness" (23). Steinbeck describes Casy's "gob of spit" in detail while the ex-preacher marvels at how "the more grace a girl got in her, the quicker she wants to go out in the grass" (25). Yet these superficially crude musings mask an inchoate nobility that reveals itself when Casy says "There ain't no sin and there ain't no virtue. There's just stuff people do. It's all part of the same thing" (26). And that thing is what Casy calls "the Holy Sperit—the human sperit" when he wonders if "maybe all men got one big soul ever'body's a part of" (27).

Notwithstanding the Reverend Mr. W. Lee Rector's assertion that the novel "tends to 'popularize iniquity,'"[4] Casy and Tom's concerns become less personal and more universal as their energies are channeled away from sensual gratification toward the achievement of an ideal. In fact, there is little actual description of sexual activity in *The Grapes of Wrath*, and when it occurs, it is discreet. Steinbeck is not writing a mere apology for the sensuous life. Primarily he is opposing the full-bloodedness of the Joads to the mechanical existence against which they must struggle.

The vitality of the Okies is demonstrated in their faults, but more nobly in their love for the land, which has ancestral and personal value. "Place where folks live is them folks," Muley says, refusing to leave the land that is, by law, no longer his (55). Unlike the Okies, the tractor operator "could not see the land as it was, he could not smell the land as it smelled; his feet did not stamp the clods or feel the warmth and power of the earth" (38). Perhaps in their attachment to the earth and their preservation of primary emotions the Okies are vulgar, but the vulgarity that led Casy to sport in the grass with consenting girls filled with the Holy Sperit, is perhaps nobler than the machines that come onto the land, "orgasms set by gears, raping methodically, raping without passion" (39). In contrast to the Okies, the landowners in California had lost their passion for the earth "and all their love was thinned with money, and all their fierceness dribbled away in interest until they were no longer farmers at all" (231). One dispossessed farmer provides us with Steinbeck's meaning. "If a man owns a little property," he says, "that property is him, it's part of him, and it's like him," and "even if he isn't successful he's big with his property." "But let a man get property he doesn't see" and the property becomes stronger than the man "and he is small, not big" (40). There is dignity in love, not in volume or power.

Steinbeck is not romanticizing the passions of the Okies, as the constant animal imagery indicates; he is simply demonstrating that they retain a sensuous and vital force that has gone out of the business and managerial classes. Like Thoreau, Steinbeck believes that the less encumbered a man is by possessions, the more easily will he find his own soul. Possessions, for Steinbeck, are accretions that smother the spiritual life, as his often-quoted picture of middle-class tourists indicates. It is worth quoting again. "Languid, heat-raddled ladies, small nucleuses about whom revolve a thousand accouterments: creams, ointments to grease themselves, coloring matter in phials—black, pink, red, white, green, silver—to change the color of hair, eyes, lips, nails, brows, lashes, lids. Oils, seeds, and pills to make the bowels move. A bag of bottles, syringes, pills, powders, fluids, jellies to make their sexual intercourse safe, odorless, and unproductive" (155–56). The "little pot-bellied" husbands of these women are associated less with failures of the sensuous life and more with failures of the spirit, for their many organizations and societies are born of anxiety and designed to "reassure themselves that business is noble and not the curious ritualized thievery they know it is" (156).

These representatives of the acquisitive middle class do not display the crude faults of the Okies, but neither do they reveal a capacity for the greatness of heart and spirit that Steinbeck confers on his ostensibly ignoble migrants. It is Casy who expresses the traditional paradox emerging from this contrast. If a man "needs a million acres to make him feel rich," he says, "seems to me he needs it 'cause he feels awful poor inside hisself," and no amount of land will make him "rich like Mis' Wilson was when she give her tent when Grampa died" (207).

It is safe to charge that Steinbeck used crude language in *The Grapes of Wrath*. But it is worth noticing that this language is used colorfully and acutely by the migrants, less precisely, but just as crudely, by small business people, and cruelly and colorlessly by the secure community. The Joads and other migrants use raw language in the form of conventional expletives or as metaphor—for example, one disillusioned migrant's description of a certain millionaire as a "fat, sof' fella with little mean eyes an' a mouth like a ass-hole" (206). This language appears in the novel because it is the migrants' idiom as Casy realizes when he justifies his own forms of speech. "Maybe you wonder about me using bad words. Well, they ain't bad to me no more. They're jus' words folks use, an' they don't mean nothing bad with 'em" (26).[5]

This kind of language is humorous, splenetic, even fierce without being vicious; it is direct and forceful. More reprehensible is the subtlety and cruelty of the secure community's foul language. The police and associates of the dominant classes use the same crude expletives as the migrants, but their community at large has viler pejoratives. Soon after arriving in California the Joads learn what Okies are. "Well, Okie use' ta mean you was from Oklahoma. Now it means you're a dirty son-of-a-bitch. Okie means you're scum. Don't mean nothing itself, it's the way they say it" (205). Language means less than the spirit in which it is used. Casy sees the innocence of the Okies' raw talk, while we are forced to recognize the malice of their antagonists. Earthy speech, under these circumstances, becomes an insignia of honor.

Whereas the language of the Okies remains largely the same (though with an increasing use of words like "holy," "love," and "dignity") and only our attitude toward it changes, the quality of migrant life, as well as our attitude toward it, changes. Early in the novel the character of indigent life is indicated by Tom's anecdotes about Grampa (30, 46), Uncle John (31), and Willy's heifer (72), and incidents like the time "the pig got in over to Jacobs' an' et the baby" (44). But these references to an earthy way of life do not remain mere random details. Instead they assume their place in a broad pattern of transformation. Occasional shocking details occur later in the novel—as in one man's description of how his brother was killed when a harrow ran over him "an' the points dug into his guts an' his stomach, an' they pulled his face off an'—God almighty!" (199). But when they appear, these later details no longer indicate a crude and earthy attitude toward life so much as the hardships that men who work the soil must endure. From being offensive details, they become evidence of strength.

Just as derogatory language becomes more vile in the mouths of the middle class than among the migrants, so unpleasant details are more savage in the established community. The man who was run over by a harrow died for his land and his brother in telling the story is appalled by the details; Tom knocked a man's head "plumb to squash," but it was in self-defense (28). The deputy sheriff who fired his pistol at Floyd Knowles, however, showed no consideration for the human life around him. When he shot, "a woman in front of a tent screamed and then looked at a hand which had no knuckles. The fingers hung on strings against her palm, and the torn flesh was white and bloodless" (264). This is an unpleasant detail, but its purpose is considerably different from the others. This detail is an indictment.

Steinbeck was not using the details of indigent and oppressed existence in order to gain an effect by shock. He had already done that in a series of articles written for the *San Francisco News* and later published with an added epilogue as a pamphlet entitled *Their Blood Is Strong*. Peter Lisca remarks that "actually, the extremes of poverty, injustice, and suffering depicted in these articles are nowhere equaled in *The Grapes of Wrath*."[6] And indeed nowhere in *The Grapes of Wrath* is there a description so disgusting and moving as one in *Their Blood Is Strong* that pictures a three-year-old child with "a gunny sack tied about his middle for clothing" suffering "the swollen belly caused by malnutrition. . . . He sits on the ground in the sun in front of the house, and the little black fruit flies buzz in circles and land on his closed eyes and crawl up his nose until he weakly brushes them away. They try to get at the mucus in the eye-corners. This child seems to have the reactions of a baby much younger. The first year he had a little milk, but he has had none since." In his novel, Steinbeck modified such details and carefully selected those that he used. Because such details are judiciously spaced, Rose of Sharon's "blue shriveled little mummy" (442) has more impact, and the conditions that produced it appear more unjust and repulsive.

Other details are presented with equal economy and with the same sort of accretive transformation. They reveal the movement of mind among the Joads and the Okies from self-concern to a broader, more exalted consciousness. Early in the novel, the hard-pressed Oklahoma farmers speculate on the future. "Maybe next year will be a good year. God knows how much cotton next year. And with all the wars—God knows what price cotton will bring. Don't they make explosives out of cotton? And uniforms? Get enough wars and cotton'll hit the ceiling" (35). It is evident that these people are not above profiting from the sufferings of others, though they themselves will soon confront the uniforms and explosives their cotton goes to produce. Like their exploiters, they find it easy to overlook the consequences for others of their own prosperity. That is because they are not forced to experience the terror of war, just as the rich are not obliged to experience the anguish of poverty. It requires a sharp and painful uprooting to expand the consciousness of the poor. Steinbeck warns that "the quality of owning freezes you forever into 'I' and cuts you off forever from the 'we'" (153). The migrants, having lost everything, inadvertently discover the meaning of their transformation from I to We, and in this transformation they achieve their highest dignity, for they become aware of abstractions that bind together lives that are otherwise squalid and debased.

It is in Chapter Ten, the chapter in which the Joads actually set out on their journey, that the transforming process becomes evident. Grampa's consistent vulgarity is touched by sentiment when he declares that he will not leave the land (113). The simple migration to the West is touched by glory in Casy's ambition to learn what the people really are (96). The first hint of movement from I to We is signaled in the Joads' admitting Casy as a member of the family, though he has nothing more than his spirit to offer. But Ma already senses what Casy stands for. Hearing Casy explain how he "got thinkin' how we was holy when we was one thing, an' mankin' was holy when it was one thing," Ma feels he is "suddenly a spirit, not human any more, a voice out of the ground" (83, 84). Casy, the wandering, homeless preacher, becomes the attendant spirit of these wandering and homeless people, and it is this human spirit of idealism that will leaven and transform commonplace people like the Joads. Now the ancient Hudson truck becomes not merely a conveyance, but a "living principle" (102); it is "the new hearth, the living center of the family" (102). Given this sanctification of the truck, Steinbeck's elaborate descriptions of how to select vehicles (102-103) and how to fix them (172) become more than repair manual entries for migrants. The commonplace details of indigent life magnify in importance because of their consequences. "Eyes watched the tires, ears listened to the clattering motors, and minds struggled with oil, with gasoline, with the thinning rubber between air and road. Then a broken gear was tragedy" (196-97). Similarly, death and killing are transformed in value. When Casy and Tom share Muley's rabbits, the elaborate description of how Tom skins and prepares the animals may appear unnecessary and even offensive (52), but not much later a similar description of the killing and preparing of two pigs is of crucial importance, since survival of the Joad family will depend upon this activity (105). Suddenly the anecdote of Uncle John's wasteful consumption of pork takes on ominous significance (32). Food is no longer a subject for jokes. From Tom's homicidal act of defense, to the killing of rabbits and pigs, and to Casy's advice to Muley not to kill anyone if he can help it (56), death is generally associated with survival among the migrants.[7]

Still, on both large and small scale, the migrants' attitude toward death is more considerate than the attitude of the classes above them. Compare, for example, the crime of murder that put Tom in jail with the crime of the California landowners. "There is a crime here that goes beyond denunciation. There is a sorrow here that weeping cannot symbolize. There is a failure here that topples all our success. The fertile earth, the straight tree rows, the sturdy trunks, and the ripe fruit. And children dying of pellagra must die because a profit cannot be taken from an orange. And coroners must fill in the certificates—died of malnutrition—because the food must rot, must be forced to rot" (348-49). When the vigilantes murder Casy, it is difficult not to observe that "Casy's crushed head" (386) resembles Herb Turnbull's head that Tom had knocked "plumb to squash." Tom once more reacts defensively when he strikes down Casy's murderer. The identical act that was initially an unfortunate event in Tom's case, becomes an outright premeditated murder on the part of the vigilante, and is instantly transformed to a gesture of liberation by Tom. As with other details in the novel, all value is conferred by the meaning that surrounds them.

The difference in attitudes toward death is particularized in the death of the Joad dog. The animal is killed by "a big swift car," which slows momentarily after the accident and then speeds away, apparently because the occupants are indifferent to, or ashamed of, "the blot of blood and tangled, burst intestines" kicking slowly in the road (131). Like the crime of the great landowners, this involves a pointless extinguishing of life. As Winfield remarks, "It ain't like killin' pigs" (132).

In *Their Blood Is Strong*, Steinbeck regarded the destruction of dignity as one of the most regrettable results of the migrant's life. "A man herded about, surrounded by armed guards, starved, and forced to live in filth, loses his dignity; that is, he loses his valid position in regard to society, and consequently his whole ethics toward society." Dignity is also a central question in *The Grapes of Wrath*. As the vulgar details of their way of life assume a part in a developing pattern and are exalted by identification with an ideal, so references to pride and dignity among the Okies become more prominent.

The shift of emphasis from physical to spiritual concerns becomes obvious with the death of the earthy old Grampa. The family does not want to take charity and have Grampa buried by the State. On the other hand, they cannot afford the expense of a burial. Pa laments the time when a son could bury his parents "in dignity," and decides that the family will bury Grampa themselves, because "sometimes the law can't be foller'd no way . . . not in decency, anyways" (141). Even "Granma moved with dignity and held her head high" when Grampa died (139). The clumsy and sometimes humorous details of the burial are dignified by Casy's clear identification of Grampa with the land the Joads are leaving. His death becomes a symbolic gesture and, significantly enough, it is at this point that the Joads and the Wilsons decide to combine their forces and travel together, taking another large step from I to We.

Gradually the movement West is enlarged and ennobled. Just before Grampa's death, the ennoblement had been signaled by Steinbeck's questions, "Where does the courage come from? Where does the terrible faith come from?" (123). But after Grampa's death the concern for unity of purpose, preservation of the individual will, and maintenance of dignity become dominant and the Okies are no longer mere travelers, but "a moving, questing people" (282). They have "changed their social life—changed as in the whole universe only man can change" (196).

It is important then that men maintain their dignity and pride and that they be able to transform the meanness of their lives—the indignities and humiliations of poverty and abuse—into something larger and more significant. Consequently, Steinbeck praises the government camps because they encourage dignity, pride, and decency. The Hoovervilles and company camps make men feel debased, but, as Pa reflects later, "Down that gov'ment camp we wasn' mean" (403).[8]

Bearing upon this issue is another very important aspect of the novel. If it is assumed that men must, at any cost, maintain their dignity, then it is worthwhile to consider what the cost may be. At the end of the first chapter, the women of families that are being driven off the land find consolation in the "hard and angry and resistant" look that replaces the "bemused perplexity" of their men and they realize that they are "safe and that there was no break" (7). And near the end of the novel, the women again "sighed with relief, for they knew it was all right—the break had not come; and the break would never come as long as fear could turn to wrath" (434). It is man's capacity to transform perplexity and fear to wrath and resistance that Steinbeck means to describe through his selection of apparently unconnected details of indigent life.

The Okies are not strangers to violence. Tom's crime, for example, is not shameful, but honored by his brother Al (86), and Pa Joad declares, "When Tom here got in trouble we could hold up our heads" (140). Steinbeck constantly refers to the essentially violent attitudes of the Okies. The first reaction of the dispossessed farmers is to ask who they can kill to protect themselves. "The tenants cried, Grampa killed Indians, Pa killed snakes for the land. Maybe we can kill banks—they're worse than Indians and snakes" (36). Even Ma, who is first described as being "remote and faultless in judgment as a goddess" whose "imperturbability could be depended upon" (76), declares that only by force will she tolerate the separation of her family (169). Moreover, Ma is tempted to hit a policeman (215), threatens to strike Mrs. Sandry, who has been tormenting Rose of Sharon (320), and generally manifests a tendency to "boil up" as Tom puts it (351).[9]

Steinbeck carefully shows that the Okies live in a climate of toughness and violence and are prepared to respond violently to protect themselves. It is worth recalling the title of Steinbeck's pamphlet, *Their Blood Is Strong*, in which he notes that the migrants are only "gypsies by force of circumstance." More correctly, "they are descendants of men who crossed into the Middle West, who won their lands by fighting." In *The Grapes of Wrath*, Steinbeck describes these migrants as "the new barbarians" who, unlike the Californians, were "hardened, intent, and dangerous" and "wanted only two things—land and food." Accordingly, the owners hated the migrants for perhaps they "had heard from their grandfathers how easy it is to steal land from a soft man if you are fierce and hungry and armed" (233). But the migrants become still more dangerous if they can preserve and venerate their dignity; what Steinbeck calls their Manself, and which he defines as the capacity to "suffer and die for a concept"—important because "this one quality is man, distinctive in the universe" (152). Even intimations of violence can be ennobled. It is not mere familiarity with and acceptance of violence as a remedy that the dominant class must fear from the migrants, but their elevation of that violence to a controlled, disciplined and idealized weapon.

Just as crudities of behavior are transformed to noble simplicities, and banal details are transformed to life-and-death essentials; and just as killing a rabbit to satisfy a brief hunger becomes killing pigs to sustain a family, thereby foreshadowing the severe needs to come; so Tom's crime and the random violence of the migrants are transformed to righteous anger, a power ready for disciplined use. Tom feels shamed when Ma prevents him from responding violently to the insolent bullying of vigilantes (280), but Ma has learned the important lesson of containing force until it can be effectively used. When Tom kicks a deputy sheriff to prevent him from shooting Floyd Knowles, Casy insists upon assuming the blame. This is an act of serious importance, for it represents the substitution of an idea for a response and of one I for another—the largest step toward disciplining the powers of the people. And Casy knows what his act signifies: "Between his guards Casy sat proudly, his head up and the stringy muscles of his neck prominent. On his lips there was a faint smile and on his face a curious look of conquest" (267). Casy has both preserved his dignity and achieved a higher end; moreover, occurring at a moment of jeopardy, his act assumes greater significance. Yet it is only one of several important preparations for the final cancellation of I in favor of We. When Rose of Sharon witnesses a similar jeopardy, she discards outmoded notions of shame and self in favor of a selfless dignity by offering what she can of herself for

another, and, like Casy, "her lips came together and smiled mysteriously" (453). It is the smile of an even higher conquest.

Peter Lisca was correct in emphasizing the essentially integrated
nature of *The Grapes of Wrath*, but this integration surely does not
depend upon a Biblical structure. I do not feel that *The Grapes of
Wrath* requires the network of Hebraic, Christian, archetypal and
mythic allusions and symbols that can be found in it to convey its
meaning. If that were so, Steinbeck might be guilty of what Alfred
Kazin described as the left-wing writer's folly, which "was to assume
that artistry was something *added* to the concern" for social questions. If Biblical allusion, in itself, were an important artistic feature,
popular rewritings of the Twenty-third Psalm that appeared during
the Thirties might be valued as noble poems rather than cutting
satires.

> Depression is my shepherd; I am in want.
> He maketh me to lie down on park benches; He leadeth me
>   beside still factories.
> He restoreth the bread lines; He leadeth me in the paths of
>   destruction for his Party's sake.
> Yea, though I walk through the Valley of Unemployment, I
>   fear every evil; for thou art with me; the Politicians and
>   Profiteers they frighten me.
> Thou preparest a reduction in mine salary before me in the
>   presence of mine creditors; Thou anointest mine income
>   with taxes; my expenses runneth over mine income.
> Surely unemployment and poverty will follow me all the days
>   of the Republican administration; and I shall dwell in a
>   mortgaged house forever.[10]

Rose of Sharon's act, though dignified by various religious and
mythic allusions, needs only its own power to demonstrate nobility.
The transformation of her nature in a moment of crisis merely epitomizes the general movement of the novel from concerns of the
flesh to concerns of the spirit.

It is easy to agree with Eric Carlson, who claims that "Steinbeck's
search for spiritual values looks inside human experience, nature,
and the life process," and that his "naturalism goes beyond both the
mechanistic determinism of Dreiser and the mystic dualism of traditional Christianity" and "lifts the biology of stimulus-response to

the biology of spirit." *The Grapes of Wrath*, which was denounced as filthy, crude, and ill-made, is in fact none of these. It is not ill-made because Steinbeck, through selection and restraint,[11] transformed the potentially offensive details of indigent life into an esthetically sound artistic creation. Details develop and expand in meaning and function to achieve a thematic ecology, and the final, emblematic tableau, arrested at the moment between life and death, unites animal necessity with the high achievements of the human spirit.

NOTES

1. Part of Boren's speech is reproduced on pp. 497–98 of this book.
2. *Mississippi Quarterly* XII (Summer 1959), pp. 136–144.
3. Reprinted in *The Viking Portable Steinbeck* (revised edition), pp. 690–692.
4. Reported in Shockley's essay, p. 490 of this book.
5. Later, when he has decided to join the Joads heading for California, Casy explains that he wants to learn what the people are all about. "Gonna lay in the grass, open an' honest with anybody that'll have me. Gonna cuss an' swear an' hear the poetry of folks talkin'. All that's holy, all that's what I didn' understan'. All them things is the good things" (96). The same sentiment would probably apply to the waitress Mae's term for tourists. "She calls them shitheels" (157).
6. *The Wide World of John Steinbeck*, p. 145.
7. Al Joad, however, the person least capable of recognizing the consequences of his own acts, purposely swerves the truck to try to kill a cat on the road (183).
8. See also *The Grapes of Wrath* (307) for an amplification of this sentiment.
9. According to an earlier passage (50–51), Ma has been given to violent behavior in previous incidents.
10. Quoted in Donald W. Whisenhunt's "The Bard in the Depression: Texas Style," *Journal of Popular Culture* (Winter 1968), pp. 375–376.
11. Steinbeck rewrote the novel, feeling that he had been too severe on the landowners and big companies. He sought to be fair in his rendering of the situation and apparently this attempt at restraint had an effect upon his style.

Patrick W. Shaw

Patrick W. Shaw has taught at the University of Missouri at Rolla, Louisiana State University, and Texas Tech University. He is the author of Willa Cather and the Art of Conflict, *and has contributed essays to* American Literature, Southern Studies, American Notes and Queries, Mark Twain Journal, American Imago, *and* Studies in Contemporary Satire.

TOM'S OTHER TRIP:
PSYCHO-PHYSICAL QUESTING IN
THE GRAPES OF WRATH

Many critics have examined the Oklahoma-to-California journey which is the heart of John Steinbeck's *The Grapes of Wrath*. A detailed summary of these commentaries is unnecessary, but some brief mention of the literal journey is required as introduction to the literal-nonliteral parallels which are the basis of the present discussion. In general the substantive journey is explained in terms of the questing knight and the biblical exodus, the influences of Malory and the Old Testament upon Steinbeck being commonly acknowledged. Moreover, since Steinbeck uses Route 66 as his most important unifying device, the attention given the Oklahoma–California

Reprinted from *Steinbeck Quarterly* 16.1–2 (Winter–Spring 1983), 17–25. By permission of founder/editor, Professor Tetsumaro Hayashi, of the *Steinbeck Quarterly* and the author.

trip is warranted on grounds of narrative structure if for no other reason. Despite its significance, however, the geographical trip may well not be the quintessential journey in the novel. Speaking more specifically of Hawthorne and Melville than of Steinbeck, Harry Levin notes that "against the received opinions that Americans are uniformly pragmatic and utilitarian, [American writers] would set a transcendental world view."[1] This is precisely what Steinbeck does. In keeping with the independent, perhaps even rebellious, tradition that forms the context of Levin's comment, Steinbeck offers the expected and obvious pragmatism, but only so that the subtle transcendental view is emphasized by contrast. Against the mundane reality of the blacktop, Steinbeck sets Tom Joad's spiritual migration, which though directly related to the literal journey, is nonetheless more revealing of Steinbeck's holistic design and moral intent.

This is hardly meant to suggest that Tom's transcendentalism has gone unnoted or that a nonliteral form of travel has not been appreciated. Tetsumaro Hayashi recently summarized Tom's journey as being "never merely a passage from place to place, but an urgent quest for discovery."[2] And more than two decades ago Peter Lisca noted Tom's move from an "individualistic" attitude to "ethical indignation"—that is, from selfish unawareness to transcendental humanitarianism.[3] Others have seen this same progression in Tom, have recognized Tom as another of Steinbeck's fictional advocates of a teleological world view. What has remained unappreciated, perhaps, are the close parallels which Steinbeck develops between Tom's literal journey and his psychological journey, the psycho-physical quest motif. Steinbeck very carefully orchestrates Tom's progression from a singular, self-centered individual to a person who has abandoned self almost entirely.

Steinbeck emphasizes Tom's growth by having him travel through five different stages of psychological development, just as he travels in five different states of the union. The mere cleverness of the matching numbers little concerns Steinbeck, certainly. He is more interested in the pervasive significance of the changes that occur in Tom in relation to the changes in his environment, his family, and society as a whole. Tom is indeed the pragmatist, a man of the naturalistic world responding to stimuli; but ultimately he manages a quantum jump onto the plane of spiritual awareness—a jump which at first appears unforeshadowed in the narrative design but which in fact is made possible by the very actions that surround Tom. It is this integration of the real and the transcendent that most concerns Steinbeck.

Stage one of Tom's life is, in effect, all those years he has existed before the reader encounters him. When Tom first appears in the novel, stage one of his psychological development is coming to completion, paralleling the termination of his life in Oklahoma. Steinbeck chooses to dwell neither on Tom's life in his native state nor on the psychological state that is about to conclude; but in the intercalary chapters concerning the recent past of Oklahoma agriculture and in the cocky, strutting character of Al Joad (who epitomizes the pre-prison Tom), Steinbeck marks the psycho-social road Tom has travelled to his present condition of isolated selfishness. Tom is quite literally alone when first introduced, "a man walking along the edge of the highway" (9), trying futilely, as time will tell, to reach his former home near Sallisaw. The McAlester prison from which Tom has just been paroled emblematizes the barriers which have isolated him, but significantly Tom is not embittered by the experience; he is, in fact, noticeably phlegmatic about it all. Neither Tom nor the reader can at this early stage articulate the ramifications of this attitude, but later Tom's inability or refusal to be bitter stands as an early indication of his innate balance, his native "goodness," that leads ultimately to his spiritual awakening. Ironically, Tom has even found some solace in the camaraderie experienced at McAlester, a feeling which itself presages Tom's later awareness that his true incarceration was self-inflicted and had little to do with physical barriers, whether they be prison walls or state lines. In short, Tom's corporeal release foreshadows the spiritual emancipation he will soon experience.

Goaded by the pragmatic reality of tired feet and an innate desire to re-establish human contact, Tom solicits a ride with the truck driver. The trucker, however, is a mechanical man, a representative of the oppressive capitalist system and is himself imprisoned by mistrust and suspicion. Although he claims to have "been training my mind for a hell of a long time" (15), the discipline has conditioned him to look for the worst in his fellow humans. He scrutinizes with Sherlockian care, but he remains blindly trapped in a prison symbolized by his padlocked rig and its "No Riders" warning. The trucker stands as a reminder of Tom's imprisoned state and is a prelude to what Tom soon will not be: a man confined either literally or symbolically by the state and dumb to the obligations of his own humanity. Unlike the driver, Tom will discover, without long training or objective scrutiny, the psychic country to which no red truck or dilapidated Hudson can carry him. Tom's ride with the driver is predictably short, and after sharing only a few quick miles with him, Tom is back on the dusty road alone, his first post-prison effort at human contact unsuccessful. His imminent meeting with Jim Casy will prove more rewarding.

The second phase of Tom's psychological journey commences when he meets Casy, not on the asphalt highway but in the natural dust of the Oklahoma field. This second stage is distinguished from the first in that now for the first time Tom establishes a voluntary, heartfelt human relationship. His friendship with Casy is not forced upon him by the vagaries of birth, the demands of mutual imprisonment, or the necessity of the moment. Like Tom, Casy has been wandering both literally and psychologically. He has abandoned his restrictive fundamentalist preaching and is now poised on the outskirts of socialistic transcendentalism. Tom, who has no real devotion to orthodox piety, hardly recalls Casy from his preaching days; but now that Casy has rejected the hypocritical backwoods Calvinism, Tom readily embraces him as a companion. Although Tom cannot articulate why, he relates to the spiritual uncertainty that Casy is experiencing, for Casy himself has travelled the rough road of spiritual turmoil. At the moment of meeting, both men are unshod, a condition that evokes both their natural proximity to the soil and their vulnerability to the "wire or glass under the dust" (30), unlike the recently departed trucker who rides high, separated from nature by rubber and concrete and safe from guns and clubs that strike in the night.

Years later, in *Travels with Charley*, Steinbeck would regret "that America has succumbed to the super highway, the high-tension line, and national television,"[4] thus isolating itself spiritually and physically from nature; but with Tom and Casy he retains (at least temporarily) his belief in individual, cosmic progress, not in terms of goods packaged, trucked, and sold, but in terms of pragmatic humanism. Therefore, when Tom meets Casy he forms the first ties that will eventually cause him to move from a surly isolato to a selfless prophet. Appropriately, Casy both initiates and terminates Tom's socializing process, for he is with Tom from the moment of their meeting in the Oklahoma field to his own death beside the

California stream. He guides Tom through or at least into the remaining states and stages of his development.

After meeting Casy, Tom releases the turtle he recently captured in the road. Whatever else the much-discussed turtle signifies, it suggests the biological dead end that stands in direct contrast to Tom's progressive journey into humanitarianism. Like the turtle, Tom is admirable for his devotion to getting things done, his one-step-at-a-time persistence. In contrast to the turtle, however, Tom is capable of learning from experience, acquiring awareness, and realizing the existence of values and worlds beyond his own immediate needs and goals. Steinbeck believed (at least in 1939 and with the influence of Ed Ricketts) that all organisms possess the potential for growth in the biological or Darwinian sense, possess the genetic possibility of adaptation, until they reach the point at which their genetic mutations fail them or condition them for environments that no longer exist. Yet the uniqueness of the human animal, for Steinbeck, is the potential for progress beyond mere physical adaptability, the potential to transcend the biological limitations and rise to spiritual, moral elevations. Thus superficially Tom may seem, like the turtle, to be responding instinctively—biologically or genetically as it were; may seem to be approaching the dead end suggested by the walled-in terrapin. The rural life of the individual dirt farmer has been tractored out by banks, and the peculiar lifestyle of the tenant farmer appears moribund. But Tom rises above the economic, intellectual narrowness that dooms the other dirt farmers. He attains a form of cosmic, humanistic awareness that distinguishes him from the others of his class and from the lowly turtle. Appropriately, when he meets Casy and intuitively realizes the change that is about to occur, he dissociates himself from the creature that no longer emblematizes his future. "I ain't gonna pack it all over hell" (47), Tom says, ironically suggesting the alternate state to which he could have descended had he remained turtlelike in his ambitions.

Tom, then, crosses the border of the first of his psychic states when he meets Casy. He moves from isolato to companion, the second stage of his psycho-spiritual journey. The stage will technically last throughout the remainder of the novel, for Casy and Tom stay together; but more importantly, the second stage will soon be subsumed, will last independently only for the period of time required for Tom and Casy to stroll the country lane to Uncle John's house. In this brief walk, however, the Casy-Tom relationship is permanently established, thereby illustrating the power of their natural camaraderie and spiritual affinity.

Tom enters the third stage of his psychological journey by the simple act of taking his place in the family circle, quietly and without fanfare. Merely by joining the family Tom acquires a multiplicity of roles—son, brother, nephew, grandson, and brother-in-law. Paradoxically, however, Tom remains insulated. He is loyal and loving within the family unit, and even persuades the other members to adopt his new friend Casy—whom, significantly, they neither understand nor appreciate apart from his past fundamentalism; but Tom's humanitarian concern, his compassion does not yet extend beyond the limited confines of the family unit. In short, he is still walled in. Tom assures Ma that he "ain' so mad" (78) as a result of his imprisonment in McAlester, yet throughout the journey to California his attitude toward nonfamily members remains surly and threatening, as witnessed by the episode with the gas-station operator near Paden, Oklahoma (126), and the encounter with the one-eyed garage worker near Santa Rosa, New Mexico (179). Tom tolerates only those persons who move within the family unit or who directly benefit the Joad cause—like the Wilsons. Otherwise he is Neanderthal in his singular defense of the family group.

Tom's devotion to and trust in the family, however, will prove misplaced. From the very beginning of the California trip the family is disintegrating, and ultimately the family betrays Tom. In discussing the literal fragmentation of the family, Lisca notes that the family's disintegration parallels its moral and economic decline and says that "although the primitive family unit is breaking up, the fragments are going to make up a larger group."[5] Lisca's point is that the family breakup is a "positive" factor in the narrative, for each fragment will eventually serve as a nucleus for new family formations. This may well be the case, though actually Steinbeck neither shows any such new formations nor clearly implies that such a possibility exists—particularly not for Noah and Rose of Sharon's stillborn baby. And, lest we forget, a member of the family betrays Tom and another member of the family resents and opposes his very presence. What the breaking up of the family and the actions of Ruthie and Rose of Sharon do indicate is that Tom is perforce being driven into the open, is literally having the protective (and insulating) wall torn from around him piece by piece. Tom is able to make his cosmic leap only by losing himself *and* his family, and the dissolution of the family unit is a natural process which forces Tom to confront the larger issues that lead to his transcendence.

The transcendentalist must first be self-reliant before he can perform humanitarian deeds, for the concept of the Oversoul requires not only social consciousness but individual worth and responsibility. This self-reliance is what Tom is moving toward by way of the family disintegration. His assuredness is not the isolated individualism of surly truculence, but self-esteem tempered by the fire of humanitarian zeal, the flame of humiliation, and the knowledge of wrong actions.

Thus the fourth stage of Tom's psychic journey has commenced by the time the Joads reach California. Here necessity forces Tom to live within the larger social unit of the migrant camps and periodically to leave his family, which in any event is rapidly disintegrating. In the Hooverville near Bakersfield the family continues to come apart, yet at the same time Tom is establishing the first friendly relationship with persons outside the family travelling unit, a growth illustrated by his association with Floyd Knowles (260). Then, in the government camp at Weedpatch, Tom's commitment to nonfamily members increases, as seen in his working relationship with the Wallaces (292) and in his appointment to the peacekeeping committee at the Saturday night party (336). Tom is finally directing his energies toward socially constructive activities, not dissipating them in the peevish violence of the angry animal, the attitude which in the past has imprisoned him both literally and spiritually. Tom will soon kill Casy's murderer in much the same fashion as he killed Herb Turnbull; but the paramount distinction between these two killings is that Tom's motive has shifted from mere self-preservation or ego-demand to the preservation of others and their ideas. This is the essence of Steinbeck's pragmatic humanism: to do what one must do, but for the right reasons.

The bludgeoning is an epiphany for Tom, and with it he enters the fifth and final stage of his psycho-social journey. All along Tom has possessed the pragmatic part of Steinbeck's dialectic, but only upon Casy's death does he acquire the humanist element once and for all, the insight necessary for discerning right reasons. Throughout the narrative he has been inching toward the humane consciousness that Casy has advocated; but after Casy dies, Tom truly understands and begins to think in terms of the transcendental ideas, realizing that his soul is "on'y a piece of a big one" (419). The utterance certainly lacks the eloquence of Emerson, but is a far cry from Tom's earlier pragmatic avowal: "I'm just tryin' to get along without shovin' nobody around" (13). With his new awareness, Tom relinquishes his self-serving individuality and moves beyond the mundane struggle simply to feed himself and his kin. He perceives the larger social, humanitarian issues that such struggles symbolize, and his commitment henceforth is not limited to the Joad family nor to any single group but to the concept of humankind. He has combined pragmatics with metaphysics.

Steinbeck emphasizes this cardinal change in his protagonist by means of the implicit comparisons between Tom and his brother Al and between Tom and Ma. Steinbeck places these comparisons strategically, locating Tom's killing of the vigilante between distinct allusions to Al and the conversation with Ma.

Only minutes before Casy is murdered and Tom makes his ultimate commitment by killing the murderer, Tom talks about Al:

> Take my brother Al. He's out lookin' for a girl. He don't care 'bout nothin' else. Couple days he'll get him a girl. Think about it all day an' do it all night. He don't give a damn 'bout steps up or down or sideways. (384–85)

Al represents the early Tom, as Steinbeck's several allusions to Al's "tomcatting" suggest. But Tom, bereft of family and without sexual companionship, transcends the simple biological lust that drives his brother. The primordial urge to reproduce his own biological image has been replaced by a far higher calling. Tom will soon take the "step up," and his thoughts of his brother at this critical moment stress how far Tom has come since he was like Al. Al's journey covers mere geography; Tom's is through psychological space, over spiritual distances.

In his last conversation with Ma, just after the killing, Tom tries to explain the step that he has taken. Ma, however, remains the steadfast pragmatist, unable to conceptualize the ideas Tom wants to articulate for her. Tom hopes to explain Casy's actions and the meaning of the Oversoul; but when he is finished Ma says quite succinctly: "I don' un'erstan', . . . I don' really know" (419). She loves Tom, wants to minister to his bodily needs, and is greatly concerned about his future safety. But she cannot share his philosophical awakenings. Their journey commences with the dawn, for the sun is "blinding" when they turn west at Sallisaw. Tom's journey ends (or actually begins) with a different kind of dawn. For Ma, however, there remain only the twilight demands of here and now. She is devoted to the doctrine of *carpe diem*, telling Uncle John to "Jus' live the day" (423). She can feed the body, as she so graphically demonstrates by proxy when she silently directs Rose of Sharon to offer her breast to the starving old man, but a true cosmic spiritual awareness escapes her. In comparison to Tom's transcendence, Ma remains ignorant, a fact symbolized by the "gloom" of the barn in which we last see her.

Some accuse Steinbeck of making a puppet of Tom, making him jump in and assume Casy's transcendentalist mantle without any preliminary structural or artistic design. On the contrary, Steinbeck's narrative purpose is quite intricate, though definitely discernible. Practically every action in the novel foreshadows Tom's final transformation. His journey from Oklahoma to California is but the facade for his more important psychic journey from isolato to prophet. In the beginning, Tom is an outlaw on probation. In the conclusion he is still an outlaw, but it is an outlawry as different from the original kind as drought is from flood—as different, one might say, as young Hester Prynne's "A" is from mature Hester's "A." In both the geographical and spiritual sojourn Tom operates within five states; and though he does not literally discover the Eden that he and his family imagined, he does discover the enlightened state of awareness that is his salvation. By recognizing the dual forms of journeying that Tom simultaneously experiences, we recognize commensurately the art of Steinbeck's holistic narrative and the power of his humanistic relativism.

NOTES

1. *The Power of Blackness* (New York: Vintage Books, 1958), p. 8.
2. Tetsumaro Hayashi (ed.), *Steinbeck's Travel Literature: Essays in Criticism* (Muncie, Indiana: Steinbeck Society of America, 1980), p. vi.
3. Peter Lisca, *The Wide World of John Steinbeck* (New Brunswick, New Jersey: Rutgers University Press, 1958), p. 173.
4. Richard Astro, "Travels with Steinbeck: The Laws of Thought and the Laws of Things," in *Steinbeck's Travel Literature: Essays in Criticism*, p. 9.
5. Lisca, *The Wide World of John Steinbeck*, p. 172.

John J. Conder

John J. Conder has taught at the University of Wisconsin, Madison, and Vanderbilt University. He is the author of A Formula of His Own: Henry Adams's Literary Experiment *and* Naturalism in American Fiction: The Classic Phase.

STEINBECK AND NATURE'S SELF:
THE GRAPES OF WRATH

Both Dreiser and Dos Passos saw the self as a product of mechanisms and hence incapable of freedom, and both postulated the existence of a second self beyond the limitations of determinism. Dreiser arrived late at the notion and, borrowing it wholesale from Brahmanic thought, barely tested its meaning, save to see it as the source of man's freedom. Although Dos Passos never developed a version of such a self, he early found its existence and suppression the cause of man's misery and, in elaborating on that theme, he was able to enlarge a cluster of themes and attitudes associated with a second self—in particular those associated with its relationship to society and to nature. In *The Grapes of Wrath*, Steinbeck renders his version of a second self in man and brings to mature development that cluster of themes and attitudes. Significantly, he brings them to maturity within a framework of determinism and so harmonizes authentic freedom and determinism in a way that Dos Passos never could do, since the second self, the true source of man's freedom, remains forever an embryo in his pages.

The interchapters of Steinbeck's novel create a network of interlocking determinisms through their emphasis on the operations of abstract, impersonal forces in the lives of the Oklahomans. Chapter 5 is especially effective both in capturing the poignancy of the human situation created by such forces and in pointing to the kind of deterministic force underlying the others in the novel. In one fleeting episode a nameless Oklahoman who threatens the driver of a bulldozer leveling his house is told that armed resistance is futile, for the driver acts in the service of the bank, and "the bank gets orders from the East." The Oklahoman cries, "But where does it stop? Who can we shoot?" "I don't know," the driver replies. "Maybe there's nobody to shoot. Maybe the thing isn't men at all. Maybe . . . the property's doing it" (41). Or at least the Bank, the monster requiring "profits all the time" in order to live and dwarfing in size and power even the owner men, who feel "caught in something larger than themselves" (35, 34).

The vision that appears here has a name: economic determinism. This view does not say that man has no free will. One might indeed find among a group of bank presidents a corporate Thoreau who prefers jail (or unemployment) to following the demands of the system. It merely asserts that most men charged with the operation of an economic structure will act according to rules requiring the bank's dispossession of its debtors when a disaster renders them incapable of meeting payments on their mortgaged property. Far from denying free will, such determinism fully expects and provides for the willed resistance of the Oklahomans. The police take care of that. Nor is this vision without its moral component, though neither the police nor the owner men can be held individually responsible. "Some of the owner men were kind," Steinbeck writes, "because they hated what they had to do, and some of them were angry because they hated to be cruel, and some of them were cold because they had long ago found that one could not be an owner unless one were cold" (34). These anonymous men are not devil figures but individuals performing functions within a system, so the work indicts the system rather than individuals who act in its service. In the case of the Oklahomans, the indictment is founded on a fundamental irony: societies, designed to protect men from nature's destructive features—here a drought—complete nature's destructive work, expelling men from the dust bowl into which nature's drought has temporarily transformed their farms.

But the expulsion of the Oklahomans is not the only inexorable consequence of the operation of economic force. These men, women, and children who "clustered like bugs near to shelter and to water" (194) automatically create in their camps a society within the larger society, acting according to the same instinctual dictate that initially made the Joad family, seeking self-preservation, seem "a part of an organization of the unconscious" (101). "Although no one told them," the families instinctively learned "what rights are monstrous and must be destroyed" (195)—the "rights" of rape, adultery, and the like—and which must be preserved. Instinct welds the group "to one thing, one unit" (200); and the contempt, fear, and hostility they encounter as they traveled the highways "like ants and searched for work, for food" reinforce the bonds of group solidarity by releasing an anger whose ferment "changed them . . . united them" all the more (284, 282). Here is the basis of that much-remarked-on shift in the novel from farmer to migrant, from "I" to "we," from family to group.

This emphasis upon the spontaneous development of a social group is not limited to the interchapters; but it is there that Steinbeck notes not only the inevitability of its development but, more important, the concurrent emergence of a group consciousness and the inevitable future consequences that its emergence entails. Economic determinism thus spawns responses that are biologically determined. Of course the scope of Steinbeck's biological determinism is sharply limited. He states with certainty but two simple facts: that the "anlage of movement" (18) possessed by the oatbeards, foxtails, and clover burrs of chapter 3 has its counterpart in the anlage of "two squatting men" discussing their common plight, and that the realization of the potential in such anlage is inevitable. As the narrative voice proclaims to the owner men: "Here is the anlage of the thing you fear. This is the zygote. For here 'I lost my land' is changed; a cell is split and from its splitting grows the thing you hate— 'We lost *our* land' " (152). Thus, forces that destroy one community create another by stimulating the communal anlage inherent in instinct, which sets the primary goals of life—in the Oklahomans' case, survival.

But in a novel that so beautifully portrays society as a system of interrelated forces, there is more to the matter than what has just been described. If economic determinism breeds biological determinism, biological determinism in turn spawns an inevitable social conflict that in time becomes an historically determined sequence of events with predictable outcome. Although there are references to it elsewhere, chapter 19 most clearly transforms this economic determinism into an historical one. It describes armed Californians, who earlier had stolen land from Mexicans, guarding the stolen land. Following the pattern of the Romans ("although they did not know it"), "they imported slaves, although they did not call them slaves: Chinese, Japanese, Mexicans, Filipinos" (232). Later appear the dispossessed Oklahomans of the East, "like ants scurrying for work, for food, and most of all for land" (233). When the slaves rebel, Steinbeck, using repetition, emphasizes the cause-effect relationship between the migrants' condition and their rebellion against it. "The great owners, striking at the immediate thing, the widening government, the growing labor unity; . . . not knowing these things are results, not causes. Results, not causes; results, not causes. The causes lie deep and simply" (151). And that he believes these causes compel the appearance of the effect proceeding from them—that is, believes the causes determine that effect's emergence—becomes clear in chapter 19 when he associates "the inevitability of the day" (238) when the owners must lose their land with their violent temporizing: "Only means to destroy revolt were considered, while the causes of revolt went on" (238).

But now some observations about the relation of the interchapters and the plot of *The Grapes of Wrath* are needed in order to show that Steinbeck's determinism can embrace freedom of the will because his literary structure creates a statistical determinism. The interchapters display the growth of a group consciousness controlled by instinct's response to the dynamic of economic forces. This emphasis is carried into the story in a variety of ways, most notably through Ma's insistence on keeping the family together. But in the story proper, instinct does not rule each person with equal power. The instinctual power that drives the group in the interchapters is unequally distributed among its individual members. Grampa's resistance to leaving Oklahoma testifies to the power of age to overcome the instinct to survive. And age is not the only force limiting the role of instinct in individual lives. Attached to his land, Muley Graves refuses to leave it in order to depart for California. He makes a choice that reduces him to "a ol' graveyard ghos'" (55) living by night as a trespasser on land once his own. Noah finds the hardships of the journey greater than the comfort derived from the group and leaves, last seen walking by a river into the greenery of the surrounding countryside to an unknown future. Connie, angry that he did not remain to work for the bank (and thus aid in the Oklahomans' dispossession), abandons his pregnant wife Rosasharn.

In the plot, then, free will plays a major role. Even those who remain with the group make numerous free choices to assure its survival, as Ma's words about the need to get to California testify: "It ain't kin we? It's will we?" (104). This emphasis on choice and free will sets limits on the rule of instinct, limits that avoid reducing the individual to the level of a will-less animal, a mere pawn of instinct. Man's possession of instincts roots him in nature, but he is different from other things in nature, as Steinbeck makes clear by describing in chapter 14 man's willingness to "die for a concept" as the "one quality [that] is the foundation of Manself . . . distinctive in the universe" (151). And this emphasis on man's uniqueness in nature, so inextricably related to his will, in turn limits the scope of the novel's historical determinism, which is based on Steinbeck's biological determinism. Even in the group that will give history its future shape, there are individuals who will depart from the historical patterns which that group is aborning.

Seen in this way, Steinbeck's determinism does not at first sight seem a far cry from Dos Passos's, at least insofar as the economic base that underlies their respective deterministic outlooks issues in a statistical determinism for each writer. But Steinbeck's interchapters are a technical innovation that create a significant expansion and difference of vision, first appearances notwithstanding. Steinbeck gains two major advantages from them. First, by creating this preserve for rendering abstract social forces, he releases a considerable number of other chapters—his plot chapters—for portraying characters as developing states of consciousness rather than as those fragments of force which they seem to be in *Manhattan Transfer*. He thereby can *emphasize* the existence of free will in his novel. Just by making freely willed decisions the basis of his statistical determinism, in other words, he gives will a role more prominent than the one it plays in Dos Passos's work, where chance prevails and will is nugatory.

The second advantage is of far greater importance because it shows Steinbeck's idiosyncratic way of harmonizing determinism and freedom. In addition to portraying abstract forces operating on a grand scale in space and time, those chapters also are instrumental in showing the change in the group from an organism biologically determined by instinct and externally determined by social forces to an organism that achieves rationality and hence a freedom of will capable of transcending the bonds of determinism. The interchapters are indispensable because they dramatize Steinbeck's belief that a group is a living organism possessing a life of its own independent of the individuals who comprise it, and the implementation of that view is a part of the novel's genius.

Steinbeck clarifies his view of a group in *Log from the Sea of Cortez*, a collaboration of sorts, where in a passage specifically written by him he uses marine analogies to explain his sense of the normal relation of an individual to the group of which he is a part:

There are colonies of pelagic tunicates which have taken a shape like the finger of a glove. Each member of the colony is an individual animal, but the colony is another individual animal, not at all like the sum of its individuals. Some of the colonists, girdling the open end, have developed the ability, one against the other, of making a pulsing movement very like muscular action. Others of the colonists collect the food and distribute it, and the outside of the glove is hardened and protected against contact. Here are two animals, and yet the same thing. . . . So a man of individualistic reason, if he must ask, "Which is the animal, the colony or the individual?" must abandon his particular kind of reason and say, "Why, it's two animals and they aren't alike any more than the cells of my body are like me. I am much more than the sum of my cells and, for all I know, they are much more than the division of me." There is no quietism in such acceptance, but rather the basis for a far deeper understanding of us and our world. (*Log*, 167–68)

This quotation stresses the individuality of the group and the uniqueness, apart from it, of its component elements. In the following quotation Steinbeck introduces an added dimension in the larger animal, here a school of fish:

> And this larger animal, the school, seems to have a nature
> and drive and ends of its own. . . . If we can think in this
> way, it will not seem so unbelievable . . . that it seems to be
> directed by a school intelligence. . . . We suspect that when
> the school is studied as an animal rather than as a sum of
> unit fish, it will be found that certain units are assigned spe-
> cial functions to perform; that weaker or slower units may
> even take their place as placating food for the predators for
> the sake of the security of the school as an animal. (*Log*, 243)

Biology thus seems to confirm the eternal copresence of the one
and the many. Applying the thrust of the thought of this passage to
the relation of the human individual to his group, one can account
for this phenomenon, the purposiveness of the larger animal independent of the individuals composing it, only by assuming that
individual men have a dual nature, both a group identity and a personal one independent of it but not necessarily in conflict with it.

More must be made of this observation, but in order to do so
precisely, it is necessary to restate the earlier relation established
between interchapters and plot, using now not the language of determinism and free will but language taken from Steinbeck's quotation above. The content of the interchapters and the content of the
plot of *The Grapes of Wrath* relate to each other as the larger animal
(the migrant group) to the individuals composing it. The plot portrays members of the school in their rich individuality, whereas the
interchapters show the formation of the larger animal that they com-
pose, a formation that takes place both on a de facto level (by virtue
of circumstance, a physical group is formed) and on an instinctive
one, which endows the animal with life. By virtue of the instinct for
self-preservation, in the camps twenty families become one large
family, sharing a single instinct. The animal can come to life on this
instinctual level because the animal's anlage is in the separate family,
the basic unit through which man fulfills his needs, and the instinctual sense of unity is strengthened by a common set of threatening
circumstances issuing in shared emotions: first fear, then anger. In
this condition, the "school intelligence" directing its drives is instinctual alone, and hence the human group is more like the school of
fish to which Steinbeck refers. Guided solely by instinct, the human
group–animal achieves a measure of protection from a hostile social
environment, but with instinct alone, it can no more transcend the

social determinism of the body politic than the turtle (which in the novel symbolizes it in this condition) can transcend the machinations of the drivers eager to squash it. Chance alone can save the group or the turtle as both walk, like Tom, one step ahead of the other, living from day to day.

But the group changes, and in this respect the plot goes one step further than the interchapters, which halt with the fermenting of the grapes of wrath. For the plot shows the emergence of a rational group consciousness, first in Casy, then in Tom, whose final talk with his mother, representing the principle of family, discloses that his own consciousness has transcended such limitations. In fact it is mainly in Tom that the group develops a head for its body; for he survives the murdered Casy, and he was from the beginning more clearly a member of the de facto group than Casy, who owned no land. And by stressing how the animal that is the group achieves rational consciousness and (hence) freedom, Steinbeck harmonizes freedom and determinism in his most important way. The group determined by instinct and circumstance in the interchapters achieves both rational self-awareness and freedom in the person of a member who substitutes the consciousness of a group for a private consciousness and thus gives the group access to the faculty of human will. Tom thus enables it to move from instinct to reason and to that freedom which reasoned acts of the will provide. By having the group consciousness mature in the plot section of his novel, Steinbeck thus unites it to the interchapters structurally and harmonizes his novel philosophically.

And he provides a triumph for the group within the context of determinism, for their attainment of rational group consciousness is itself a determined event because such potential is inherent in the species. Their achieved freedom of will as a group thus is the final term of a socially determined sequence of events that leads to the group's creation, and the group's exercise of it to attain its ends fulfills the historical determinism of the novel. Yet this is not the only hope in these pages, for the prospective triumph of the group provides hope for the triumph of the individual as a whole person.

The Grapes of Wrath is the story of the exploitation of a dispossessed group, and it is difficult not to feel that it will always engender sympathies for the dispossessed of the earth wherever and whenever they might appear. But the novel's indictment of society for what it does to individuals should have an equally enduring appeal; for here its message goes beyond the conditions of oppressed groups and addresses individuals in all strata of complex societies. The condition of individual Oklahomans in fact is an extreme representation of the condition of social man, and in the capacity of individual Oklahomans to change lies the hope for social man.

The migrants' achievement of rational freedom speaks for more than freedom for the group. It tells readers of a vital difference in kinds of freedom. Steinbeck has written, "I believe that man is a double thing—a group animal and at the same time an individual. And it occurs to me that he cannot successfully be the second until he has fulfilled the first." Only the fulfilled group self can create a successful personal self; only freedom exercised by a personal self in harmony with a group self can be significant.

This aspect of the novel's vision depends upon Steinbeck's fuller conception of an individual's two selves. One is his social self definable by the role he plays in society and by the attitudes he has imbibed from its major institutions. The other is what is best called his species self. It contains all the biological mechanisms—his need for sexual expression, for example—that link him to other creatures in nature. And by virtue of the fact that he is thus linked to the natural world, he can feel a sense of unity with it in its inanimate as well as its animate forms. But the biological element in this self also connects him to the world of man, for it gives him an instinctive sense of identification with other members of his species, just as the members of other species have an instinctive sense of oneness with their own kind.

The species self thus has connections to nonhuman and human nature, and Steinbeck refers to the latter connection when he speaks of man as a "group animal." He views a healthy personal identity as one in which the species self in both its aspects can express itself through the social self of the individual. But society thwarts, or seeks to thwart, the expression of that self. It seeks not only to cut man off from his awareness of his connections to nonhuman nature, it seeks also to sever him from the group sense of oneness with the human species that the individual's species self possesses. Ironically, therefore, purely social man loses a sense of that unity with others which society presumably exists to promote.

The novel's social criticism rests on this view, and its emphasis on grotesques, purely social beings cut off from their connections to nature, both human and nonhuman, portrays an all-too-familiar image of modern man. In too many instances, by imposing mechanical rhythms on human nature, society creates half-men. Its repeated attempts to distort the individual's identity is emphasized by numerous dichotomies between social demands and instinct. Tom tries to comprehend the meaning of his imprisonment for killing in self-defense. Casy tries to understand the meaning of his preaching sexual abstinence when he cannot remain chaste himself. And the point is made by the basic events that set the story moving. A mechanical monster, indifferent to the maternal instincts of the Ma Joads who exercise their species selves in the interest of family solidarity, expels families from their land. The social mechanism thus tries to thwart the demands of the group aspect of the self to remain together. And the same mechanism is responsible for sowing what has become a dust bowl with cotton, rendering it permanently useless for agriculture, thus showing its indifference—nay, hostility—to the connections with nature that the species self feels.

This suppression of the species self is not rigorously foreordained for every individual, and hence the novel's determinism does not rest on the universality of its occurrence. Ma's personality remains undistorted from the novel's beginning to its end. Her intense commitment to the family proceeds from a very live species self; and though she must enlarge her vision to include more than her family, her insistence that Casy join the family on its westward exodus and numerous demonstrations of her concern for others outside her immediate family bear witness that her vision is not all that limited to begin with. But such suppression is nonetheless widespread, and indeed a sufficient number of people must be transformed into grotesques if social structures are to perpetuate themselves. They thereby make many men grotesques and subject all men to economic determinism. Thus the attention to grotesques is part of the pattern of economic determinism in the novel; such determinism can only prevail under conditions guaranteeing with statistical certainty that society can distort man's nature.

The novel singles out two social institutions that assure the creation of grotesques: religion and the law. Lizbeth Sandry is the major representative of a grotesque created by religion. Her intolerance of dancing represents her intolerance of sex, and such intolerance displays religion's warping influence on human instinct. She arouses Ma's ire by warning Rosasharn, "If you got sin on you—you better watch out for that there baby" (308). Her religious views, importing a supernatural mandate into the realm of nature, impose on natural behavior value judgments (like "sin") designed to thwart the normal expression of the species self. This divorce between her social and species selves, indicated by her views, makes Lizbeth Sandry much like one of Sherwood Anderson's grotesques, as all social selves alienated from the species self must be.

Uncle John and Connie's wife, Rosasharn, carry into the family Lizbeth Sandry's fanaticism. Uncle John's felt sense of guilt over his wife's death impels him to blame all the family misfortunes on what he takes to be his sin: his failure to summon a doctor when she complained of physical ailments. His exaggerated sense of sin fails to take into account his own human nature (his natural fallibility) and circumstance; for his reluctance to call a doctor doubtlessly depended on strained finances. His compulsive references to that sin make him as much a grotesque as Lizbeth Sandry, his grotesquerie compounded by his need for wild drinking bouts to escape the sin.

Not only does he become a grotesque, but his obsession with sin blinds Uncle John to the true cause of the family's misfortunes and so shows that religion can indeed be an opiate of the people useful for sustaining an unjust social structure. In this sense Rosasharn is like him, for she has been affected by Lizbeth Sandry's sense of sin. Of course, Rosasharn's sense of sin does not transform her into the grotesque that Uncle John has become. It illustrates that selfishness noted by other critics, for throughout most of the novel she thinks only of herself and her unborn baby, to the total exclusion of the problems of other people. But her view of Tom's killing a deputy, which is one illustration of her selfishness (she shows concern only for her baby, not for her brother), also points to the larger consequences of Uncle John's obsession with sin. She tells Tom, "That lady tol' me. She says what sin's gonna do. . . . An' now you kill a fella. What chance that baby got to get bore right?" (393). Like Uncle John's explanation for family misfortunes, her view of the real enough threat to her unborn child deflects the source of that threat into a theological realm inaccessible to man, the realm of the devil who tempts man's fallen nature to sin, rather than assigning it to the realm of the accessible and the real, the social forces responsible for the deaths of Casy, the deputy, and her own child.

If religion enforces a split between man's two selves, suppressing one and thus deforming the other, so do most social institutions.

Hence the law motif is central to the novel, law being the second (and more important) institution that Steinbeck indicts in his defense of the self; for it is law that holds society's other institutions together and, supported by police power, gives them their governing authority.

References to the law appear in a variety of contexts, but their meaning is best embodied in the opposition between law and fundamental human needs, those " 'got to's' " (141) to which Casy refers that compel men to say, "They's lots a things 'gainst the law that we can't he'p doin' " (446). Burying Grampa, for example, in defiance of local edict. But there are more important illustrations of how the law thwarts the expression of man's nature, even when it does not manage to distort it. Tom finds no meaning, at the novel's outset, in a system that imprisons him for killing in self-defense, and he discovers the true meaning of the system only after he kills the deputy who murders Casy—a nice bit of symmetry that illustrates his growth in awareness as he perceives, like Casy, that his second killing is also an instinctual response, one of self-defense against the true assaulter, the system, which so thwarts man's instinctual life that it leaves him no choice other than to strike back. This line of meaning is echoed by others: by Ma, who says of Purty Boy Floyd, "He wan't a bad boy. Jus' got drove in a corner" (367); by the nameless owner men who tell the tenants early in the novel, "You'll be stealing if you try to stay, you'll be murderers if you kill to stay" (37). And it is implicit in Tom's own position at the beginning of the plot: to leave the state violates the conditions of his parole, yet to stay means to break up the family and to face unemployment and possible starvation.

Under such circumstances, it is not surprising to discover that the true prison in The Grapes of Wrath is the world outside the prison walls, the real point of Tom's story of a man who deliberately violated parole to return to jail so that he could enjoy the "conveniences" (among them good food) so conspicuously absent in his home (29). "Here's me, been a-goin' into the wilderness like Jesus to try to find out somepin," Casy says. "Almost got her sometimes, too. But it's in the jail house I really got her" (381). He discovers his proper relationship to men there because it is the place of the free: of men who exercised the natural rights of nature's self only to be imprisoned by the society that resents their exercise. And in fact he can see how the law violates self because he has already seen how religion does. Without the revelations of the wilderness, he would not have had the revelation of the jailhouse; the first is indispensable to the second. Together, they make him the touchstone for understanding the novel's philosophy of self and for measuring the selves of the novel's other characters.

Just as the species self is the ultimate source of freedom for a group, it is the same for an individual. If man can recognize that he is a part of nature by virtue of that self's existence—if he can affirm for this aspect of a naturalistic vision—he can liberate himself from the condition of being a grotesque and, in recognizing his oneness with others, escape the tentacles of economic determinism as well. This is the novel's philosophy of self, and Casy's life is its lived example, both in his thought and in his practice.

Casy has arrived at the vision that man is a part of nature in the novel's opening pages, the discrepancy between his religious preachment and his sexual practice prompting his withdrawal from society to go to the hills in order to comprehend his true relation to the world and leading to his Emersonian sense of connection with nonhuman nature: " 'There was the hills, an' there was me, an' we wasn't separate no more' " (83). Casy has thus found his deepest nature, that self which is connected even to nonhuman nature, and so he has taken the first vital step toward his liberation. In his way of recovering this self, Casy should be measured less by Emerson than by Thoreau, who went to the woods "to drive life into a corner" and discovered that "not till we are lost . . . , not till we have lost the world, do we begin to find ourselves, and realize where we are and the infinite extent of our relations" (Walden, chapters 2 and 8). For Thoreau, as for Casy and Steinbeck, a true knowledge of the relationship between one's self and the external world can only be derived from an empirical study of the structure of physical reality. Such empiricism imparts the knowledge that man does relate to the whole and inspires, in Steinbeck's words written elsewhere, "the feeling we call religious," the sense of unity between self and outside world that makes "a Jesus, a St. Augustine, a St. Francis, a Roger Bacon, a Charles Darwin, and an Einstein." Writing of his own interest "in relationships of animal to animal" (Log, 217–18), Steinbeck later gave a clue to the general source of the religious vision at which Casy has arrived at the beginning of The Grapes of Wrath:

If one observes in this relational sense, it seems apparent that
species are only commas in a sentence, that each species is
at once the point and the base of a pyramid, that all life is
relational to the point where an Einsteinian relativity seems
to emerge. And then not only the meaning but the feeling
about species grows misty. One merges into another, groups
melt into ecological groups until the time when what we
know as life meets and enters what we think of as nonlife:
barnacle and rock, rock and earth, earth and tree, tree and
rain and air. And the units nestle into the whole and are
inseparable from it. (*Log*, 218)

Any reader of "Song of Myself" would know instantly what Casy
and Steinbeck mean. This sense of relationship inspires reverence
not for an unknowable God outside of nature but for knowable nature in all its forms; for if one feels united to "the hills," one is clearly
in a position to take the next step and feel reverence for nature in
its animate forms, and especially in the form known as the human
species to which all men belong. And Casy has clearly taken this step
as well, as his subsequent remarks on the holiness of man testify. "I
got thinkin' how we was holy when we was one thing, an' mankin'
was holy when it was one thing." Such human holiness and the
consequent sense of human solidarity it engenders come from each
man feeling he is "kind of harnessed to the whole shebang" (83),
to all of nature. In finding his deepest self, then, Casy has run against
the grain of his old social self to embrace a naturalistic religious view
which, from Steinbeck's angle of vision, more surely inspires that
sense of brotherly love preached by Christianity than Christianity
does. A passage from *The Log from the Sea of Cortez* aptly represents
the religious view of the novel:

Why do we so dread to think of our species as a species? Can
it be that we are afraid of what we may find? That human
self-love would suffer too much and that the image of God
might prove to be a mask? This could be only partly true, for
if we could cease to wear the image of a kindly, bearded,
interstellar dictator, we might find ourselves true images of
his kingdom, our eyes the nebulae, and universes in our cells.
(*Log*, 266)

By descending into his species self, Casy abandons the arrogance of social man who thinks of himself only in terms of his distinctiveness in nature. Specifically, he abandons his social self as preacher and the limitations which it imposes on creating significant relationships with the world outside. As a preacher he necessarily divorced himself from his species self, with its instinctual need for sexual expression, because of Christianity's sexual ethic. Or, rather, since in fact he did act on these instincts, it is more accurate to say that the Christian sexual ethic cut him off from the knowledge that his species self is his better self. Not only does it promote a sense of connection with nature which a Christian sense of man's uniqueness denies—more important, it promotes a sense of connection with all of mankind suppressed by Christianity's parochialism, its division of the world between those who possess the truth and those who live in outer darkness.

Casy's reverence for nature (which also inspires a reverence for human life) allows him to escape character deformations visible in other figures in the novel. Such reverence is markedly absent in men who use their cars to try to run a turtle down, just as it is absent in Al, who swerves his car to squash a snake. When Al becomes "the soul of the car" (124), of course, he is helping his family in their and his time of need, and to that extent the promptings of his species self are very much with him. But its larger sympathies are blunted because the social means by which he is forced to help his family, the automobile on which he must rely, tarnishes him with the taint of "mechanical man," a phrase Steinbeck uses to describe the social man divorced from his species self, and thus accounts for his squashing the snake. In the car he loses contact with that aspect of the species self which reveres life in all its forms, and by so much he becomes a warped victim of society.

Casy escapes this kind of warping because he has established a relationship to the whole, to nonhuman nature. But he also escapes the warping of an Uncle John or a Lizbeth Sandry because he is empirical in establishing a relation to the parts, to the members of the human community which must be man's first concern, as he makes clear when he says, "I ain't gonna preach" and "I ain't gonna baptize":

> I'm gonna work in the fiel's, in the green fiel's, an' I'm gonna
> be near to folks. I ain't gonna try to teach 'em nothin'. I'm

gonna try to learn. Gonna learn why the folks walks in the
grass, gonna hear 'em talk, gonna hear 'em sing. Gonna listen
to kids eatin' mush. Gonna hear husban' an' wife a-poundin'
the mattress in the night. Gonna eat with 'em an' learn. . . .
All that's holy, all that's what I didn' understan'. All them
things is the good things. (96)

Like Thoreau, Casy has reason to believe that most men "have
somewhat hastily concluded that it is the chief end of man here to
'glorify God and enjoy him forever' " (*Walden,* chapter 2). But his
empiricism, not oddly at all, makes him accept in others the very
religious view he has already rejected, for such might prove to be
the true expression of another's nature. Here he is best measured by
Emerson, the Emerson who proclaimed, "Obey thyself," when he
tells Uncle John, "I know this—a man got to do what he got to do,"
or when he says of Uncle John's obsession: "For anybody else it was
a mistake, but if you think it was a sin—then it's a sin" (224).

And he follows Emerson in another way. Casy's interest in the
parts shows that, like Emerson, he cannot rest satisfied with a religious "high," the feeling of oneness with "the all" that he has already
experienced at the novel's opening and that Emerson experienced
as "a transparent eyeball" (*Nature:* 1836). Like Emerson, he must
translate the insight derived from that experience into ethical terms
on the level of practical action. Having concluded that the devil
whom most men should fear is society ("they's somepin worse'n the
devil got hold a the country" [129]), he not surprisingly discovers the
level of practical action by which he can relate to them in a prison,
whose inmates are there mainly " 'cause they stole stuff; an' mostly
it was stuff they needed an' couldn' get no other way. . . . It's need
that makes all the trouble" (382). Since society cannot provide man's
basic needs, Casy will help to secure them and, in the process, he
brings his species self into relation with men by adopting a social
one that permits its expression. He becomes a strike organizer.

Casy's new personal identity is thus an expression of a larger self
which, as Emerson knew, can be realized in a diverse number of
concrete social forms, though such self-realization earns the world's
displeasure. Members of the family who remain in the group thus
move toward that larger self when they abandon older views of theological sin as a causal factor in human affairs and approximate Casy's newer view in their words and actions. Uncle John displays this

movement, his escape from the ranks of the grotesque, when he floats Rosasharn's stillborn baby to the town, admonishing it to "go down in the street an' rot an' tell 'em that way" (446), just as Rosasharn does when she breastfeeds the old man in the novel's closing paragraph. Her gesture acknowledges the truth of Uncle John's words, that the sin that killed her baby was social and not theological in origin. The same gesture shows her overcoming a solipsism engendered by her pregnancy by enlarging the sympathies of her species self to embrace more than the child that society denied her. That gesture, finally, is the perfect one to signal the awakening of nature's self, the self growing from that human biological nature which mothers and fathers the species.

The novel thus suggests the desirability of a society based not on absolutes imported supernaturally into nature by systems derived from a priori thinking, but one whose institutions accommodate themselves to subjective absolutes. In this way Steinbeck's novel expands the naturalistic vision of *Manhattan Transfer*. It develops the theme only subordinate in the earlier novel: man and nature are one, not two. But *The Grapes of Wrath* is also a logical and satisfying conclusion to naturalism prior to Dos Passos. If man's connections to nonhuman nature seemed a source of savagery for Crane, nonetheless, at the last, nature in "The Open Boat" was just nature—a vast system for man to interpret for his own benefit, could he but escape the complicated social fabric to see that the primary purpose of societies is to aid him in creating such interpretations. Even in *McTeague*, brute nature is not entirely without its redeeming values: it alone provides McTeague with the sixth sense to flee the city that so twists the lives of the people in Norris's pages. Because the novel is so completely deterministic, however, nature is not used as an avenue of escape. In its form as sexual drive, it instead contributes to McTeague's destruction. But for Steinbeck, nature did become a viable avenue of escape when he developed a religious vision based on the feeling resulting from empirically ascertainable knowledge, the knowledge that man is related to the vast system called Nature. This vision is implicit in Dreiser's view of a creative spirit, but unlike Dreiser, Steinbeck postulates no unknowable purpose in this spirit possibly running at cross-purposes to man's own. He escapes the tentacles of determinism that hold Dreiser's men and women in thrall because he does not unravel the Hobbesian dilemma; because he does not reduce consciousness to temperament or instinct; because he instead makes consciousness in the service of man's instinct the center of man's freedom. Like Emerson, and Dreiser at the last, he assumes that if nature's spirit has purpose, man as part of it can give it expression and direction by realizing his own purpose. To attain knowledge of this ability is to begin to meet the demands of spring.

Louis Owens

Louis Owens has taught at the University of Pisa, California State University, Northridge, the University of California at Santa Cruz, and the University of New Mexico. He is the author of two book-length studies of American Indian fiction, and four novels. His work in Steinbeck criticism includes John Steinbeck's Re-Vision of America, *numerous articles, and* The Grapes of Wrath: Trouble in the Promised Land.

THE AMERICAN JOADS

That Steinbeck should keep the Bible firmly in both the background and the foreground of this great American novel is essential, for he is writing not simply about an isolated historical and sociological event—the Dust Bowl and the "Okie" migration—but about a nation founded solidly upon a biblical consciousness, as the novel's title indicates. From the first writings of the colonial founders, America was the New Canaan or New Jerusalem, and the colonists, such as William Bradford's pilgrims at Plymouth, were the chosen people who consciously compared themselves to the Israelites. Their leaders were repeatedly likened to Moses, for they, too, had fled from persecution and religious bondage in England and Europe for the new promise of a place called America. Thus Bradford, in *Of Plymouth*

Reprinted from The Grapes of Wrath: *Trouble in the Promised Land* by Louis D. Owens. Copyright © 1989 by G. K. Hall & Co. Reprinted by permission of Twayne Publishers, an imprint of Simon & Schuster Macmillan.

Plantation (1620–50), felt compelled to compare his pilgrims to "Moyses & the Isralits when they went out of Egipte."[1] Out of this acutely biblical consciousness arose what has come to be called the American myth, a kind of national consciousness with which Steinbeck was fascinated throughout his life.

Within this mode of thought, if America was the New Eden, within the wilderness of that Eden lurked the Serpent. Almost at once, in their battle to wrest a continent away from wilderness and from the inhabitants of that wilderness, the colonists imagined themselves embroiled in a desperate struggle with Satan. They saw themselves as the Army of Christ. The Indian in the forest, in resisting the colonists' invasion, appeared to be in league with Satan himself. In his book *The Wonder-Working Providence of Sion's Savior in New England*, describing without compunction the beheading of Pequot Indians, Captain Edward Johnson, in 1653, exhorted the Puritans to "take up your arms and march manfully on till all opposers of Christ's kingly power be abolished."[2]

In *The Grapes of Wrath* Jim Casy has spent his life prior to our meeting with him as just such a Calvinistic fire-and-brimstone fundamentalist embattled with Satan, as he tells Tom Joad: "Here's me that used to give all my fight against the devil 'cause I figured the devil was the enemy. But they's somepin worse'n the devil got hold a the country" (129). It is in the wilderness that Casy has his revelation about man and God, and quickly he moves from Calvinism to a kind of transcendentalism, from that pattern of thought which places the earth under man's dominion and looks at wilderness as the unreclaimed haunt of Satan to that philosophy which makes man inseparable from the natural world and finds in wilderness a direct relationship with truth.

From his past battle with the devil to his declaration that "There was the hills, an' there was me, an' we wasn't separate no more" (83), Casy has taken an enormous stride away from what Steinbeck defines in this novel as the short-sighted and destructive historical pattern of American thought and settlement. Within the Christ-like Casy, commitment to man and to nature becomes a single driving force toward a unity with what Steinbeck and Ricketts in *The Log from the Sea of Cortez* defined mystically as "the whole thing, known and unknowable."

The settlement of America may be seen as a process of ever westward expansion in search of that Eden which seemed to recede always before the eyes of the first colonists. The process became one of despoiling the Garden in the search for the Garden until, finally, Americans stood at the edge of the Pacific, having slaughtered and driven from their lands the original inhabitants, having deforested enormous portions of the continent, and having fought and gouged with all other claimants to the continent in order to reach the western shore. Surely, if there were ever to be a Garden it must be at the western edge. And the beauty and fecundity of California seemed to fulfill that promise. Still, Americans were left with a feeling of loss, emptiness, summed up in Walt Whitman's great poem, "Facing West from California's Shores," in which he concludes with a parenthetic question that resounds throughout American history and American literature: "But where is what I started for so long ago? / And why is it yet unfound?"

Whitman's question is central to *The Grapes of Wrath*. Grampa exclaims, "Gonna get me a whole big bunch of grapes off a bush, or whatever, an' I'm gonna squash 'em on my face an' let 'em run offen my chin" (85). And the faceless, representative owner voices of chapter 5 advise the evicted tenants, "Why don't you go on west to California? There's work there, and it never gets cold. Why, you can reach out anywhere and pick an orange" (37). Both Grampa's dream of grapes and the owners' vague visions of plenty underscore the crucial association between California and the biblical Canaan. And when the Joads arrive at Tehachapi Pass and look down on the fertile San Joaquin Valley, often referred to as the Great Central Valley, California indeed seems to be the New Canaan, the Promised Land sought after for nearly four centuries:

They drove through Tehachapi in the morning glow, and the sun came up behind them, and then—suddenly they saw the great valley below them. Al jammed on the brake and stopped in the middle of the road, and, "Jesus Christ! Look!" he said. The vineyards, the orchards, the great flat valley, green and beautiful, the trees set in rows, and the farm houses. And Pa said, "God Almighty!" The distant cities, the little towns in the orchard land, and the morning sun, golden on the valley. . . .
    Ruthie and Winfield scrambled down from the car, and then they stood, silent and awestruck, embarrassed before the great valley. The distance was thinned with haze, and the

land grew softer and softer in the distance. A windmill flashed in the sun, and its turning blades were like a little heliograph, far away. Ruthie and Winfield looked at it, and Ruthie said, "It's California." (227)

It is Winfield who puts the valley into perspective and locates it firmly within the American dream of Eden rediscovered: " 'There's fruit,' he said aloud" (227).

When a rattlesnake crawls across the road and Tom drives over it and crushes it as the family starts down into the valley, the way has been cleared for entry into the Garden; the serpent—the symbolic evil of this Promised Land—has at long last been removed. To emphasize the quintessentially American idea of a new beginning, a kind of return to the Garden, Steinbeck has Tom laugh and say, "Jesus, are we gonna start clean! We sure ain't bringin' nothin' with us" (230). With these words, Tom defines the most dangerous flaw within the dream of America as the new beginning: the Joads, like the Dutch sailors who look longingly at the continent at the end of F. Scott Fitzgerald's *The Great Gatsby*, and like all of us, are indeed bringing their pasts with them. This Garden is inhabited by flawed men, men who, like Tom with his scar at the novel's end, are marked. The Eden- and Canaan-like valley that spreads so wonderfully beneath the Joads will prove to be filled with hatred, violence, greed, and corruption—the fruits of man's wisdom and knowledge lying rotting in the fields and orchards. It is a heavily ironic entrance into the Promised Land.

Steinbeck's use of and fascination with what has been termed the American Myth—the myth of this continent as the new Eden and the American as the new Adam—appear again and again throughout his fiction. *Cup of Gold* (1929), Steinbeck's first novel, offers a fictionalized account of the pirate Henry Morgan's conquest of Panama. The primary symbol of this new world in the novel is the chalice or golden cup that suggests the Holy Grail. Purity, promise, and innocence all come together in the symbol of the Grail but, as Steinbeck's conqueror discovers, the New World—America—loses its innocence in the process of being discovered. In *The Pastures of Heaven* (1932), Steinbeck's early episodic novel, the author makes a small California valley a microcosm for America and the people of that valley, with their fatal insistence upon a kind of illusory innocence, microcosmic Americans. Characters in that novel

(Steinbeck's second published though third written) look upon the valley called Pastures of Heaven and they dream of starting over in all innocence, of leaving their flawed selves and the fallen world behind. Steinbeck's message in the novel, of course, is that such illusions of innocence are impossible to realize and dangerous to harbor. Fallen man brings his own flaws into Eden.

Throughout his career, Steinbeck was obsessed with America as a subject. The myths deeply ingrained in our national consciousness and the patterns of thought that have carried us from wilderness to world power appear again and again in Steinbeck's writing, not only in such obvious studies of the nation as *America and Americans* or *Travels with Charley*, but also throughout the novels.

In *The Short Reign of Pippin IV* (1957), Steinbeck, like Henry James before him, but on a lighter note, takes a young "ideal" American to France in order to contrast the public and private moralities of the two nations. Four years later, in his final novel, *The Winter of Our Discontent*, Steinbeck turns his scrutiny squarely upon his own nation in a dark study of the American conscience. Here, Steinbeck evokes American history in the name of his protagonist, Ethan Allen Hawley, who lives in a home with "Adam" decorations. Again Steinbeck creates in Ethan a character who refuses, as long as possible, to recognize humanity's flaws. And in the most allegorical of his major novels, *East of Eden* (1952), Steinbeck creates an explicit American Adam in the character of Adam Trask, who, in a self-destructive search for his own unfallen Eden, flees from his Calvinistic, Jehovah-like father on the eastern seaboard and settles in the Salinas Valley in California.

Steinbeck recognized deep within the American and the universally human psyche a need to believe in the possibility of beginning anew, of returning symbolically from the exile of maturation and experience to a lost Eden and lost innocence. The original English colonists saw America very consciously as this new Eden, and Americans have ever since translated that dream of recovering Eden into the American dream, the dream of shedding the past and starting over. For Walt Whitman this meant an outright denial of original sin, a chance to proclaim himself Adam—the representative American—newly born into innocence. For Benjamin Franklin it meant a chance to create oneself in the pattern of one's imagination, free of any burden of guilt. It is no coincidence that, as a boy, Fitzgerald's Gatsby wrote notes to himself reminiscent of Benjamin

Franklin's *Autobiography*. It is this refusal to see the evil we do and the belief in an Eden just west of the next mountain range that Steinbeck saw as the most dangerous flaw in the dream. In *East of Eden*, Adam Trask refuses to see the evil within his wife or within others. He is doomed by that self-willed innocence.

In *The Grapes of Wrath*, Steinbeck evokes this pattern of American thought and American expansion, a pattern that begins with thoughts of a new Eden and moves inexorably westward. This is the illusory hope voiced by a representative migrant in one of the novel's interchapters: "Maybe we can start again, in the new rich land—in California, where the fruit grows. We'll start over" (89). The impossibility of such a dream is made clear in the answering voice: "But you can't start. Only a baby can start. . . . The bitterness we sold to the junk man—he got it all right, but we have it still. And when the owner men told us to go, that's us; and when the tractor hit the house, that's us until we're dead. To California or any place—every one a drum major leading a parade of hurts marching with our bitterness" (89).

Steinbeck takes pains to place the Joads and the Dust Bowl migrants as a whole securely within this pattern of American history and simultaneously to avoid the sin with which he has often been charged: sentimentalizing his characters. Certainly Steinbeck makes it clear that the sharecroppers are victimized by an inhuman economic monster—personified by the enormous, impersonal tractors raping the land—that tears at the roots of the agrarian life Thomas Jefferson so highly prized for Americans. When Steinbeck causes his representative migrant voice to plead with the owners for a chance to remain on the land, however, he qualifies the celebrated Jeffersonian agrarianism and love-for-the-land in this novel by tainting the sharecroppers' wish: "Get enough wars and cotton'll hit the ceiling" (35), the cropper argues. While the reader is likely to sympathize with the powerless tenant farmer, the tenants' willingness to accept war and death as the price for a chance to remain on their farms and thus further "cotton out" the land is difficult to admire on any level.

Steinbeck goes a step further, to make it clear that the migrants are firmly fixed in a larger, even more damning American pattern. Though the tenants have tried to persuade the owners to let them hang on, hoping for a war to drive up cotton prices, the tenant voice also warns the owners: "But you'll kill the land with cotton." And the owners reply: "We know. We've got to take cotton quick before the land dies. Then we'll sell the land. Lots of families in the East would like to own a piece of land" (36). It is the westering pattern of American history laid bare: people arrive on the Atlantic seaboard seeking Eden only to discover a rocky and dangerous paradise with natives who aggressively resent the "discovery" of their land; Eden must lie ever to the west, over the next hill, across the next plain; then only the Pacific Ocean is there and, along with Jody's grandfather in Steinbeck's *The Red Pony*, we end up shaking our fists at the Pacific because it stopped us, and broke the pattern of displacement. As long as we believe there is a Garden to the west we feel justified in using up and abandoning the place we inhabit today. Tomorrow we will pick up and go, always in the direction of the setting sun, always with the belief that we can put the past behind us, that the ends will be justified by the means. We believe that such acts as passing out smallpox-infested blankets to Indian tribes and the massacre at Wounded Knee and, finally, the theft of the continent from the Indians can be put behind us in the quest for new land and new self.

That the croppers are part of this pattern becomes even more evident when the representative tenant voice informs us that their fathers had to "kill the Indians and drive them away." And when the tenant voice adds, "Grampa killed Indians, Pa killed snakes for the land" (36), Steinbeck is attempting to ensure that we hear a powerful echo of the Puritan forebears who wrested the wilderness from the serpent Satan and his Indian servants, killing and displacing the original inhabitants of the New Canaan.

It is difficult to feel excessive sorrow for these ignorant men who are quite willing to barter death to maintain their place in the destructive pattern of American expansion—a pattern that has ravaged a continent. That Steinbeck thought long about the American phenomenon of destroying the Garden in the search for the Garden is suggested in his declaration (recorded more than a decade later in *Journal of a Novel*, the journal he kept while writing his great investigation of the American myth, *East of Eden*) that "people dominate the land, gradually. They strip it and rob it. Then they are forced to try to replace what they have taken out" [39].

Although Steinbeck makes it clear that man draws sustenance from close contact with the earth, through touching it and feeling a part of it, and in spite of Tom Joad's final wish that the people will one day "all farm our own lan' " (418), Steinbeck is not making a case for Jeffersonian agrarianism in this novel. Jeffersonian agrarianism, as defined succinctly by Chester E. Eisinger in his influential essay "Jeffersonian Agrarianism in *The Grapes of Wrath*," was "essentially democratic: it insisted on the widespread ownership of property, on political and economic independence, on individualism; it created a society in which every individual had status; it made the dignity of man something more than a political slogan." Drawing parallels between Thomas Jefferson's insistence upon the small farmer as the foundation of an ideal society and the philosophy developed in *The Grapes of Wrath*, Eisinger suggests that "Steinbeck was concerned with democracy, and looked upon agrarianism as a way of life that would enable us to realize the full potentialities of the creed."

The "essentially inhuman and unproductive nature of the machine age," according to this reading of the novel, is destroying "a way of life that was based on the retention of the land." Such a reading, while persuasive, leads even Eisinger to question the value of agrarianism itself: "It remains to inquire if agrarianism, its form and substance, is the part of the Jeffersonian tradition that we should preserve." The Jeffersonian ideal is bankrupt, the critic declares, and thus Steinbeck's conclusions in the novel are of dubious value.

If we look more closely at attitudes toward America and, in particular, the small farmer in *The Grapes of Wrath*, it should become clear that Steinbeck, too, saw fully illuminated the "bankruptcy of Jefferson's ideal." By carefully and precisely placing the tenants within the historical pattern that has led to the destruction of the land, Steinbeck is making it obvious that agrarianism alone is insufficient. In fact, the ideal of the independent small farmer, the Jeffersonian image of the heroic individualist wresting an isolated living from the soil, is very firmly scuttled in *The Grapes of Wrath*. Muley Graves points to an aspect of this failure when he tells Tom and Casy, "I know this land ain't much good. Never was much good 'cept for grazin'. Never should a broke her up. An' now she's cottoned damn near to death" (50).

The small farmers of this novel proudly proclaim their grandparents' theft of the land from the Indians, freely acknowledging that murder was their grandparents' tool. They argue that they should be allowed to stay on and raise more cotton because war will boost the price of cotton. Then they tell the owners that they will kill the land with cotton. These small farmers are far from anyone's ideal. They are clearly a part of a system that has failed and in the process has violated the continent. Steinbeck sends them on the road so they may discover a new relationship with their fellow man and with the land itself. The Jeffersonian ideal is one of individuals working the land on isolated farms; Steinbeck's ideal is one of all men working together, committed to man and land, to "the whole thing." It is, in fact, precisely the dangerous idea of man as isolated and independent that Steinbeck is attempting to expose. He is no Jeffersonian.

Once the Joads and their fellow migrants have reached California, they can go no farther. The Joads are the representative migrants, and the migrants are the representative Americans. The migrants' westward journey is America's, a movement that encapsulates the directionality of the American experience. The horrors confronting the migrants to the California Eden have been brought on by all of us, Steinbeck implies; no one is innocent. When, near the novel's conclusion, Uncle John places Rose of Sharon's stillborn baby in an apple box and releases it upon the flood waters with the words, "Go down an' tell 'em" (446), Steinbeck is emphasizing the new consciousness. This Moses—in the Edenically suggestive apple box—is stillborn because the people have no further need for a Moses. There is no Promised Land and nowhere else to go, no place for a Moses to lead his chosen people. The American myth of the Eden ever to the west is shattered, the dangers of the myth exposed. The new leader will be an everyman, a Tom Joad, who crawls into a cave of vines—the womb of the earth—to experience his rebirth, who emerges committed not to leading the people somewhere but to making this place, this America, the garden it might be. This is the Tom who, early in the novel, says to Casy, "What the hell you want to lead 'em someplace for? Jus' lead 'em" (24).

At the novel's end, Tom has become such a leader, one who will not lead the people "someplace" but will lead them toward a new understanding of the place they inhabit here and now. For the same reason, Steinbeck has left Noah behind at the Colorado River, the boundary of this garden, because, in spite of the impending flood, there is no place for a Noah in the new country. Two symbols of mankind's new beginnings from the Bible are rejected in the exclusion of Noah and the stillborn Moses. Through these two rather heavy-handed allusions, Steinbeck is declaring that there is no second chance, no starting over.

The Grapes of Wrath is Steinbeck's jeremiad, his attempt to ex-

pose not only the actual, historical suffering of a particular segment
of our society, but also the pattern of thought, the mind-set, that has
led to far more than this one isolated tragedy. In this novel, with the
Bible very much in mind, Steinbeck sets out to expose the fatal
dangers of the American myth of a new Eden, and to illuminate a
path toward a new consciousness of commitment instead of displacement. And in making his argument, Steinbeck is careful not to sen-
timentalize his fictional creations, careful to emphasize the shared
guilt and responsibility—a new sensibility, not sentimentality, is
Steinbeck's answer.

In spite of howls of outrage from the states at the opposite ends
of the novel's journey—both Oklahoma and California—however,
and in spite of his care to avoid sentimentalizing his characters,
America took the Joads to heart, forming out of *The Grapes of Wrath*
a new American archetype of oppression and endurance. And in
spite of his care to make the Joads and the migrants as a whole far
less than perfect, and to place his protagonists squarely within the
destructive pattern of American expansion, as soon as the novel was
published critics who read less carefully than they should have began
to accuse Steinbeck of sentimentality in his portrayal of the downtrodden migrants. Edmund Wilson was one of the first influential
critics to take such a position, declaring that in this novel Steinbeck
learned much from films, "and not only from the documentary pictures of Pare Lorentz, but also from the sentimental symbolism of
Hollywood."[3] Bernard De Voto had anticipated Wilson when he
complained that the novel's ending was "symbolism gone sentimental." Still a third major American critic, R. W. B. Lewis, found Steinbeck's fiction "mawkish" and "constitutionally unequipped to deal
with the more sombre reality a man must come up against. . . ."

There is much in *The Grapes of Wrath* to ward off such accusations if a reader goes beyond mere surface story. In addition to
showing the reader the tenant farmers' willingness to continue to
use up the land with cotton and their eagerness for war, Steinbeck
consistently shows us the flaws in his characters. As Steinbeck
scholar Warren French pointed out long ago, Steinbeck takes care
to undercut the nobility and "goodness" of the migrants. Although
Casy, in sacrificing himself for the people, and Tom, in dedicating
his life to the same cause, move close to heroism, no one in the
novel is seen through a sentimental lens.

One of the most obvious examples of Steinbeck's care to avoid sentimentality can be found in the novel's final chapter. Just before the Joads reach the barn and discover the starving man and young boy, Ruthie discovers a "scraggly geranium gone wild." Plucking the flower, she sticks one of the petals onto her forehead, "a little bright-red heart." With this symbol of delicate beauty and love surviving amidst the devastation of ravaged and ravaging nature, Steinbeck could have left his reader with a soft and sentimental portrait-in-miniature of hope. Instead, he deftly undercuts the sentimentalism of the moment through the verisimilitude of his characters. "Come on, Ruthie!" the girl's younger brother, Winfield, begins at once to whine, "Lemme have one." Ruthie, in keeping with the character the reader has come to expect, "banged him in the face with her open hand" (451). A moment later she "wet a petal with her tongue and jabbed it cruelly on his nose. 'You little son-of-a-bitch,' she said softly" (451). In the children's attraction toward the bright-red petals Steinbeck illuminates an image of the enduring life-force and the wellspring of hope in the novel. In Ruthie's convincing cruelty the author refuses to allow his characters to succumb to the potential sentimentalism inherent in the image. The romantic symbol and its ironic deflation prepare for the novel's emotional and critically controversial finale.

NOTES

1. William Bradford, *Of Plymouth Plantation*, ed. Harvey Wish (New York: Capricorn Books, 1962), 36.
2. Edward Johnson, *Johnson's Wonder-Working Providence*, ed. J. Franklin Jameson (New York: Barnes & Noble, 1959), 30.
3. Edmund Wilson, *The Boys in the Back Room: Notes on California Novelists* (San Francisco: Colt Press, 1941), 61.

John Ditsky

John Ditsky has taught at Wayne State University, the University of Detroit, Mercy, and the University of Windsor. He is the author of Essays on East of Eden, John Steinbeck: Life, Work, and Criticism, numerous essays on Steinbeck's work, and three books of poetry. He has also been the editor of Critical Essays on Steinbeck's The Grapes of Wrath, the poetry editor of The University of Windsor Review, and a founding member of the editorial board of The Steinbeck Newsletter.

THE ENDING OF *THE GRAPES OF WRATH*: A FURTHER COMMENTARY

The current revival of interest in Steinbeck, prompted in part by the efforts of the Steinbeck Society, has thus far not included adequate reconsideration of what was—at the time of the book's first appearance—a matter of some controversy: the value and meaning of the final scene in The Grapes of Wrath. Perhaps a greater liberty in the presentation of sex is responsible for this neglect of what was once a crucial problem for Steinbeck's critics; at any rate, it is clear enough that the matter remains unsettled, however relatively ignored at present, and as deserving of attention as ever—if not necessarily for the reasons once advanced. With initial sympathy for the

Reprinted from Critical Essays on Steinbeck's The Grapes of Wrath (G. K. Hall & Co., 1989), edited by John Ditsky. Copyright © 1989 by John Ditsky. By permission of John Ditsky.

author's presumed intentions as a critical approach, therefore, I have made a series of reflections upon the function of that ending scene within the book as a whole, particularly insofar as that scene may be considered the book's culmination: the apotheosis of the concept of the group-man explicated in *The Red Pony*. Furthermore, it is an appropriate time to weigh the general cultural significance of Steinbeck's work as an American novelist, and this scene is central to such a purpose.

I am speaking, then, of that final scene (449–53) in which, on the third day of their entrapment by flood, the surviving Joads—Ma, Pa, Uncle John, Ruthie, Winfield, and Rose of Sharon—leave their boxcar refuge and, under Ma's direction, move to new quarters in a nearby barn where they find a boy and his starving father—to whom Rose of Sharon, who has just lost her own baby, is seen giving her breast as the novel closes. A number of observations will follow, divided only partially arbitrarily into general topics: the Bible and religion; myth and the ritual moment; the role of woman; the new community.

I

Steinbeck has constructed this final scene as an emergence from the shadow of death: a resurrection of the group-man in an Easter of the human spirit. Thus the biblical quality of the scene is appropriate (one thinks of both the Eden and Flood narratives), as is the occasionally biblical-sounding prose ("On the morning of the second day . . ." [449]). It is astonishing that Steinbeck manages to control this scene at all—to keep it working within the demands of the conventional novel form while allowing it to ascend into the simultaneously expressionistic. The reduction to simplicities is totally apt; the scene represents a re-Genesis, mankind deliberately re-creating itself in the image of God ("manself" divinized).

Joseph Fontenrose comments at length upon the Mosaic and Messianic parallels in *The Grapes of Wrath*, developing the prior work of Peter Lisca, Celeste Wright, and Martin Shockley, all of whom have noted the eucharistic nature of Rose of Sharon's act. Calling the deserter Connie the group's Judas, Fontenrose notes the fact that the new social organism is itself in its infancy at the book's end, and that Rose of Sharon is imitating primitive adoption ceremonials as she foster-mothers mankind. In effect, he concludes of the ending scene, "The Joads' intense feelings of family loyalty have been transcended; they have expanded to embrace all men." More than this, even by her name Rose of Sharon reminds us of biblical imagery of fertility and promise. Song of Solomon 2, which begins "I am the Rose of Sharon, and the lily of the valleys," goes on to guarantee that "the winter is past, the rain is over and gone," and that the vines will soon put forth "the tender grape." The "beloved" who is described there as feeding among the lilies—a figuratively real event in the novel—completes a relationship traditionally interpreted as that of Christ and His Church, God and His people. Add the other possibilities of Mary (addressed as "Mystical rose") and of the soul, and the potential meanings begin to ripple outward in profusion. Rose of Sharon's act accomplishes, through the influx of divine spirit, a kind of virgin birth of anonymous man—a man who, because of the mystical overtones of the moment, becomes representative Man (as standing for all of mankind), and potentially a version of the Son of Man (for the necessity of playing the Christ-role is emphasized throughout the novel).

As water implies baptism, the flood implies a new start—a re-Creation. Just as there was only one "tree" in the original Eden, there can be no "shame" in the discovery of the knowledge of good and evil in the new Eden. Steinbeck's Testament ends with a fusing of the significant actions of the Old and the New: the snake has been run over by a truck, anticipating the woman's heel; now there is only the "stuff people do," as Casy puts it (26), and the need for intellectualization has been obviated by direct experience. Rose of Sharon's action communicates an immediate redemption of a "chosen" people.

In these religious terms, therefore, the scene is almost devoid of sexuality—for all its sexual implications. Prurient interest remains in the eye of the beholder, and shame to him who thinks it evil. Sex exists here in its most abstracted, perfected sense; implicitly, however, it is within the understanding of the women, Ma and Rose of Sharon, who look "deep into each other" (453) before Rose of Sharon assents to Ma's request, unasked with words. What ensues is an almost philosophically justified use of sexual powers: right use of the body's intimate reproductive faculties to promote Life itself. Thus the ingredients for a possible dirty joke become the elements of an almost passive ritual. It is the reversing of, but also the concomitant of, the joyful flowing of life in the earlier scene of zestful copulation on the moving truck—with Connie and Rose of Sharon finding brief joy in their corner of the moving community, while Granma experiences her death struggle in another (224-25). Both the truck scene and the final tableau share a vitality so significant that both are accompanied by meaningful exchanges, of gifts paid for by losses: death (Granma, the baby) for life.

Finally, the final scene completes a turning-outward into society of energies that, in Greek or Faulknerian tragedy, might have turned into unproductive incestual frustrations. In the new familial system, older terminology is replaced by simpler concepts of "male" and "female" roles, and only the presence of external, social demands legitimizes what might otherwise have become sexual anarchy.

II

There is nothing remarkable in that a moral or religious progress, whose Christ-referents are ample, should end in an epiphany of sorts—miracle-plus-vision. The biblical, even medieval, instinct would have been to erect a shrine. Steinbeck constructs a kind of canopy over this final scene by rendering it as a tableau. The supposed improbability of this final act ignores the fact that the Joad family had long since been wrenched out of the conventional, traditional mores of viable family units. This is especially so after the dead child is set adrift without its sex even being determined. At this juncture, there has finally been a complete break with the past; and a transfer from the normal and specifically literal to the extraordinary and symbolic has been made possible. Thus a showing-forth ensues: a mixed action which shepherds and Magi might attend.

Therefore, Rose of Sharon becomes statuary, as worn mother and starving man fuse in a lasting composition. Steinbeck's endowment of the ordinarily human with exceptional qualities on extraordinary occasions is made possible by his exterior presentation during all other times—the result of his deliberately scientific, empirical approach to human nature, itself premised on the belief that humanity can never understand itself until it first understands the animal within the human. It is not, as Edmund Wilson phrased it in his classic missing-of-the-point, that Steinbeck tends "to present human life in animal terms," but that Steinbeck sees humanity as above the animal when it demonstrates the intelligence required to grasp its real situation and act accordingly—or when, driven by an evolutionary process to discover radical methods of survival as a species, it finds the instinctive understanding to make changes for the better. It is not, then, that Rose of Sharon "must offer her milk" to a starving stranger, as Wilson has it, out of an animal "loyalty to life itself." Rather, it is that people like the Joads finally understand what they will have to do for themselves if society should continue to fail to recognize their humanity; and Rose of Sharon's gesture is its admission. To say, as Wilson did, that "Mr. Steinbeck almost always in his fiction is dealing with the lower animals or with humans so rudimentary that they are almost on the animal level . . ." is to display a peculiar distance from reality in the speaker himself.

Of course, Wilson was writing at the end of a decade—the thirties—when writers commonly described human beings out of a preconceived notion of human worth rather than by trying, as Steinbeck did, to decide what was truly human by observation. This approach by Steinbeck, when at his best, shows dehumanized human material straining upward towards its own ideal—precisely what occurs at the ending of *The Grapes of Wrath*. Negative interpretations such as Wilson's should not be allowed to obscure the validity of Steinbeck's ruthlessly honest (not "sentimental") questioning of the human condition: "What am I? What are the limitations inherent in my mode of existence?" Not only are Steinbeck's methods interestingly predictive of logical positivism and structuralism, but his approach to anthropology has become increasingly widespread as well. Rose of Sharon can be said to have pointed the way; extending the Mosaic parallels of the novel, we can say that with her act, mankind has been to the mountain to see the Promised Land—rather than the "mirage" of the Joads' first sight of California. Thus she can be said to have acquired monumentality, the quality of significant statuary, in her final scene.

Again, Theodore Pollock (reprinted in French, *Companion*) correctly noted that the supposedly sentimental gesture under discussion occurs after the "human sacrifice" of Rose of Sharon's baby. But Rose of Sharon is openly abandoning, however intellectually and temporarily, conventional folk expectations about the attainment of futurity—the bearing of children to "carry on"—in order to establish futurity in societal, or "group," terms. Though Warren French footnotes Pollock's argument by drawing literal parallels of scene— "drought and downpour"—with Eliot's *The Waste Land*, he does not take the argument far enough. Surely this dead infant, prophet of solidarity and "wrath," can also be paralleled with the same year-myth of "human sacrifice" that Eliot exploits, with all its suggestions of Nature-appeasement—and in a similar texture of spring's ironics. The exploration of Steinbeck's awareness and employment of myth has barely begun, in other words.

III

Folk-sensitivity to mythic elements is also central to Steinbeck's consideration of the role of women, particularly in the evolving group-family. Earlier in the novel, Rose of Sharon and Granma are established as linked together, as poles of womanhood on the Ma-axis, when well-meaning Jehovites offer a service for the dying Granma in a nearby tent. The fervor of sympathy causes the men and women of the sect to join in a "feral howling," making "a thudding sound on the earth." Though Ma shivers in testimony to the power of the experience, Granma joins her whining with the whining she hears (like a dog joining a siren's wail), and Rose of Sharon's breath comes in short pants. When the service concludes, Granma sinks into restful sleep, and Rose of Sharon acknowledges that "It done Granma good" (212). Like the final rain-dance scene in the earlier *To a God Unknown*, in which the joyful people don animal skins and roll in the mud in an ecstasy of celebration of the land's fecundity, this scene involves the three adult women of *The Grapes of Wrath* in an act of tribute to a power older than organized medicine and a ritual prior to established religions. Out of this power and ritual emerges the final scene, in which Rose of Sharon, once she sees what is wanted of her, similarly reacts with "short and gasping" breaths (453).

Rose of Sharon repeatedly emphasizes the damage being done to her ability to function as wife and mother by the events of the novel. Found nibbling "a piece of slack lime," she wails "Got no husban'! Got no milk!" (354) and predicts "This here baby ain't gonna be no good." Her willingness to perform within woman's conventional biological roles is dealt serious and seemingly permanent damage by the losses of Connie and the baby, both arguably the result of the evils of the social structure whose failure has produced the dramatic tension of the book. Miraculously, both are restored when she encounters a man in specific need of, as his boy puts it, "soup or milk" (453). Gently caressing the hair of the man as she feeds him, she smiles "mysteriously"—having pulled off the splendid trick of mothering an anonymous beloved.

"Women's always tar'd," Tom had said of his mother early in the novel. "That's just the way women is . . ." (110). But when the family is under way, and the possibility of the "folks" being "busted up" arises, Ma revolts, raising a jack handle against Pa and shaming him out of absolute control of the family unit (169-70). It is a successful revolt, one that Ma justifies in a later scene:

> Pa sniffled. "Seems like times is changed," he said sarcastically. "Time was when a man said what we'd do. Seems like women is tellin' now. Seems like it's purty near time to get out a stick."
>
> Ma . . . smiled down at her work. "You get your stick, Pa," she said. "Times when they's food an' a place to set, then maybe you can use your stick an' keep your skin whole. But you ain't a-doin' your job, either a-thinkin' or a-workin'. If you was, why you could use your stick, an' women folks'd sniffle their nose an' creep-mouse aroun'. . . ." (352)

When the male-dominated society fails, woman asserts her centrality in human affairs, and control is hers to exercise. This latter-day reflection of the effects of the frontier on woman allows Ma the privilege of speaking *for* the group: "Why, we're the people—we go on," she tells Tom in a celebrated passage (280).

Implicit within this final scene, then, is the completion of a sociological change—the development of a sort of Moynihan-syndrome of absent father and ruling mother—that has been seen coming throughout the novel. The stage of menopause becomes a sort of substitute for the distinctions of sex: a masculine authority allows Ma to take the reins of government away from Pa; Rose of Sharon, however, remains a functioning biological woman on her side of the barrier of age. However, the change is not quite this simple, for while woman is assigned new roles *within* the revised familial structure, man is given certain new functions of leadership and strength *outside of* it—that is, within the evolving group structure of the family-at-large. If this is less than clear in the cases of Pa and Uncle John, it is decidedly so for Tom, who inherits the mantle of Casy's philosophical/ethical authority (with Ma's blessings) and his stance as Christ, as divinized manhood.

For Rose of Sharon herself, her final action is also the personal attainment of maturity. The relative lack of full emotional growth in both her and Connie is perhaps most clearly seen when Connie frightens her by putting "Soon's I get on my feet" ahead of thoughts of how her baby is to be born, and she responds by putting "her thumb in her mouth for a gag" and crying silently (252). Yet she is still developing within her role of woman, and when Connie deserts his moral responsibilities for the chance of making money, Rose of Sharon achieves her full womanhood through Other-commitment. The split between Connie and Rose of Sharon mirrors the conflict within society at large, between the materialistic success-ethic and what used to be called the Life-force.

Rose of Sharon had been frightened by the prediction of a woman at the government camp that "hug-dancing" and play-acting (she had been in a "Chris' chile play" at school) would cause her to lose her baby, as had happened to another girl like her. She is consoled by the "white-clad" (and presumably angelic?) camp-manager, who gives a factual answer, and by Ma, who argues that Rose of Sharon isn't big enough to attract God's attention (307-12). Ironically enough, she acquires epic dimension after the predicted loss of her baby occurs—in a final balletic stasis, a frozen hug-dance with a stranger, a second Christ-child play if ever there was one.

The boy whose father Rose of Sharon nurses explains that the father's hunger was aggravated by his having given his own food to his son. When after this initial sacrificial act, the son took more immediate measures to obtain food—he "stoled some bread" for his father, the most revolutionary action in the final scene (but only in conventional legal terms)—the father had "puked it all up" (453). Neither protective self-sacrifice nor violent seizure are successful, therefore; only the return to woman, to the feminine principle, provides the answer: not inward or outward force, but a balanced exchange. Ironically, this hungry, wet, and "beat" Rose of Sharon still smiles mysteriously as she gives of herself. Is she satisfied? (She is certainly relieved, for it is the anxiety caused by her milk's arrival that has spurred Ma, and thus the family, out of their boxcar coffin and back into movement [449].) Thus this sharing of resources involves a simple, if unconventional, realignment of needs and assets. Rose of Sharon's "mysterious" smile is the outward sign of the discovery of a timeless truth: the simplicity and goodness of cycles, the rightness of necessity, the perfectness of circles. "You go to," she says, and the new order leaps into being. She has regained the "self-sufficient smile, the knowing perfection-look," of her early pregnancy (97). Because she is wiser than before, her idea of fulfillment has been altered forever.

IV

Warren French described the ending of the novel in terms of the Joads' initiation: "Their education is completed." This is precisely so. Steinbeck has taken that hackneyed expression of the Depression generation, "The School of Hard Knocks," and its politer antecedent, "The School of Life," and made them a figurative dramatic structure for the whole novel. There are dropouts aplenty, but enough survivors are present for the graduation: the rebirth of Rose of Sharon, swaddled in a dirty blanket, nursing instead of being nursed, giving instead of taking. She is a Louvre of mixed subjects: a Nativity, a *Mona Lisa*, an immense and heroic Delacroix. Most of all, however, she is a tableau of quasi-Christian giving, the paradox of exchange among those with no possessions whose doctrinal source in the New Testament apparently so fascinated Steinbeck.

It is a fundamentally conservative gesture, of course—this rewiring of circuits accomplishing a restoration of power. It is precisely the common man's commonsense answer to the enormity of the Depression and the absurdities of the system that allowed it to happen at all, and then permitted it to go on. It is the perfect refutation of the values inherent in the classic examples of capitalistic unreason: fruit rotting on the vine; crops plowed under; the killing of little pigs.

In Steinbeck, the real is neither inflated nor cosmetically altered, but idealized: the "real" persons simply fade away at the end, and out of identity-consciousness. In the "true" pop-culture version of the same elements, the Playmate of the Month, every mole airbrushed away, descends into the gutter or the hands of a trembling wino in a 42nd Street old-magazine shop. How ironic that in the boob-culture that is America, objections should have been raised on the fittingness of such a scene of wish-fulfillment as this one, in which tableaux of the Nativity and the Pietà are superimposed upon a vision of breast-attainment. Indeed, the scene is in this respect ideal, taking its leap into the transcendental by virtue of its very elemental qualities—satisfying the national craving with a contact as aesthetically electric (hence disquieting, even as it is satisfying) as the touch of God and Adam on the Sistine Chapel ceiling: the perfect stranger finding solace of suck at the breast of the husbandless wife and childless mother. What a forbidden, what a necessary, nourishment!

The new society posited at the close has been in obvious development throughout the book. Its growth as idea has been organic, involving the pruning of the unfit. Its utopian vision is the last and most telling avatar of the "westering" urge so central to Steinbeck's Americanism, the ultimate submersion of the human in the "natural"; it is motion in quest of a dream and harmonic stasis. But in realistic terms, Utopia was the government camp, already glimpsed as the token of what might have been: in strict American literary tradition, it is that experimental unit of agrarian democracy, the land-based model community.

"There the story ends *in medias res*," Fontenrose concludes by way of setting up something of a straw man. For in truth, the narrative of the Joads has nowhere to go after Rose of Sharon draws the camera in to focus upon that mysterious smile, then holds the pose while the camera backs away—by means of a helicopter shot, say—to make it clear that she has become the world's true center. In terms of contemporary American culture, it is Woman picking up the pieces of the American dream and holding the man-caused shards together, the seams invisible. The power to work this miracle is implied in Rose of Sharon's smile. It is an Eastern smile, a smile of understanding, in this ultimate Western book. She has got it all now. All the lines of narrative come to focus in her; like light, they prism in her:

> For he hath regarded the low estate of his handmaiden: for, behold, from henceforth all generations shall call me blessed. . . .
> He hath filled the hungry with good things; and the rich he hath sent empty away. . . . (*Luke* I: 48 and 53)

Nellie Y. McKay

Nellie Y. McKay has taught at the University of Wisconsin, Madison. She is the author of Jean Toomer: A Study of His Literary Life and Work, *the editor of* Critical Essays on Toni Morrison, *co-editor of the* Norton Anthology of African-American Literature, *and a contributor to* New Literary History *and* The Columbia History of the American Novel.

From "HAPPY[?]-WIFE-AND-MOTHERDOM": THE PORTRAYAL OF MA JOAD IN JOHN STEINBECK'S *THE GRAPES OF WRATH*

. . . The centrality of women to the action of *The Grapes of Wrath* is clear from the beginning. For one thing, not only among the Joads, the main characters in this novel, but in all the families in crisis, the children look to the women for answers to their immediate survival: "What we going to do, Ma? Where we going to go?" (37) the anonymous children ask. In male-dominated sex-gender systems, children depend on their mothers for parenting, and their stability rests mainly on the consistency and reliability with which women meet their needs. There is no question that in this model the woman/wife/mother makes the most important contributions to family stability. This chapter does not challenge Steinbeck's understanding of the value of women's roles in the existing social order. I attempt, however, to place his vision of those roles within the framework of an American consciousness that has long been nourished by gender myths that associated women with nature, and thus primarily with the biological and cultural functions of motherhood and mothering, whereas men occupy a separate masculine space that affords them independence and autonomy. By adopting Robert Briffault's theory that matriarchy is a cohesive, nonsexually dominating system,[1] Steinbeck assures us that the family can survive by returning to an earlier stage of collective, nonauthoritarian security while the larger society moves toward a socialistic economy. As he sees it, in times of grave familial or community need, a strong, wise woman like Ma Joad has the opportunity (or perhaps the duty) to assert herself and still maintain her role as selfless nurturer of the group. In this respect, she is leader and follower, wise and ignorant, and simple and complex, simultaneously,[2] In short, she is the woman for all seasons, the nonintrusive, indestructible "citadel" on whom everyone else can depend.

This idealistic view of womanhood is especially interesting because, although there are qualities in Steinbeck's work that identify him with the sentimental and romantic traditions, as a writer with sympathies toward socialism he also saw many aspects of American life in the light of harsh realism. His reaction to the plight of the Oklahoma farmers in this novel moved him to a dramatic revision of the frontier patriarchal myth of individual, white-male success through unlimited access to America's abundant and inexhaustible expanses of land. He begins with the equivalent of a wide-lens camera view that portrays the once-lush land grown tired and almost unyielding from overuse, and then follows that up with vivid descriptions of farmers being brutally dispossessed by capitalist greed from the place they thought belonged to them. His instincts are also keen in the matter of character development; unanticipated circumstances alter the worldview that many of the people in the novel previously held, and their changes are logical. As they suffer, the Joads, in particular the mother and her son Tom (the other Joad men never develop as fully), gradually shed their naïveté and achieve a sound political consciousness of class and economic oppression. This is a difficult education for them, but one which they eventually accept. Through it all, without the unshakable strength and wisdom of the mother, who must at times assert her will to fill the vacuum of her husband's incapability, nothing of the family, as they define it, would survive. Still, she never achieves an identity of her own, or recognizes the political reality of women's roles within a male-dominated system. She is never an individual in her own right. Even when she becomes fully aware of class discrimination and understands that the boundaries of the biological family are much too narrow a structure from which to challenge the system they struggle against, she continues to fill the social space of the invincible woman/wife/mother.

Critics identify two distinct narrative views of women in Steinbeck's writings. In one, in novels such as *To a God Unknown* (1933) and *The Grapes of Wrath* (1939), the image is positive and one-dimensional, with female significance almost completely associated with the maternal roles that Kolodny and others decry. In the other, for example *Tortilla Flat* (1935), *Of Mice and Men* (1937), *East of Eden* (1952), and several of the short stories in *The Long Valley* (1938), the portraiture is socially negative. Whores, hustlers, tramps, or madams are the outstanding roles that define the majority of these women. More graphically stated by one critic, these women "seem compelled to choose between homemaking and whoredom."[3] Interestingly, in spite of their questionable behavior, women within this group are often described as "big-breasted, big-hipped, and warm," thus implying the maternal types. In his post-1943 fiction, after he moved to New York City, sophisticated women characters who are jealous, vain, and cunning—the opposite of the women in his earlier works—appear (as negative portrayals) in Steinbeck's work. Furthermore, Steinbeck's "positive" women are impressively "enduring," but never in their own self-interests. Their value resides in the manner in which they are able to sustain their nurturing and reproductive capabilities for the benefit of the group. As Mimi Reisel Gladstein notes,

> they act as the nurturing and reproductive machinery of the group. Their optimistic significance lies, not in their individual spiritual triumph, but in their function as perpetuators of the species. They are not judged by any biblical or traditional sense of morality. (79)

In conjunction with their ability to endure and to perpetuate the species, they are also the bearers of "knowledge—both of their husbands and of men generally," knowledge which enables them to "come . . . [closer than men] to an understanding of the intricacies of human nature and the profundities of life in general."[4]

Since its publication in 1939, *The Grapes of Wrath*, one of Steinbeck's most celebrated works, has been the subject of a variety of controversial appraisals. Seen by some, including Levant, as "an attempted prose epic, a summation of national experience at a given time," others belabor its ideological and technical flaws. The disagreements it continues to raise speak well for the need to continue to evaluate its many structural and thematic strands.

The novel opens on a note that explodes the American pastoral of the seventeenth and eighteenth centuries that Kolodny describes in her work. The lush and fertile lands that explorers in Virginia and the Carolinas saw give way to the Oklahoma Dust Bowl, where ". . . dawn came, but no day. In the gray sky a red sun appeared, a dim red circle that gave a little light, like dusk; and as that day advanced, the dusk slipped back toward darkness, and the wind cried and whimpered over the fallen corn" (6). The impotence and confusion of a bewildered group of displaced people replace the assuredness and confidence of the nation's early settlers. In this world where nature is gone awry, and human control lies in the hands of men greedy for wealth and in possession of new technology that enhances their advantages, the men, women, and children who have, until now, lived on the land are helpless against an unspeakable chaos.

Feeling completely out of control in a situation they cannot comprehend, the men stand in silence by their fences or sit in the doorways of the houses they will soon leave, space that echoes loudly with their impotent unspoken rage, for they are without power or influence to determine their destinies. Even more outrageous for them is their profound sense of alienation. Armed with rifles, and willing to fight for what they consider rightfully theirs, there is no one for them to take action against. They can only stare helplessly at the machines that demolish their way of life. They do not understand why they no longer have social value outside of their disintegrating group, and they do not know how to measure human worth in terms of abstract economic principles. "One man on a tractor can take the place of twelve or fourteen families," the representatives of the owner men explain to the uncomprehending displaced farmers.

That some of their own people assist the invaders leaves them more befuddled.

> "Well, what you doing this kind of work for—against your own people?"

a farmer asks the tractor-driver son of an old acquaintance. The man replies:

> [for] "three dollars a day. . . . I got a wife and kids. We got to eat . . . and it comes every day."
>   "But for your three dollars a day fifteen or twenty families can't eat at all,"

the farmer rebuts, and continues:

> "Nearly a hundred people have to go out and wander on the roads for your three dollars a day. Is that right?" . . . And the driver [says], "Can't think of that. Got to think of my own kids. Three dollars a day, and it comes every day. Times are changing, mister, don't you know? Can't make a living on the land unless you've got two, five, ten thousand acres and a tractor. Crop land isn't for little guys like us any more. . . . You try to get three dollars a day someplace. That's the only way." (40)

The quality of the frustration and level of the ineffectiveness that the men feel is displayed in the actions of Grampa, the patriarch of the Joad clan. He fires a futile shot at the advancing tractor but succeeds only in "blow[ing] the headlights off that cat', . . . [while] she come on just the same" (48). The march of technology and the small farmers' distress go hand in hand.

Deprived of traditional assertive masculine roles, for the most part, the helpless, silent men seldom move; only their hands are engaged—uselessly—"busy," with sticks and little rocks as they survey the ruined crops, their ruined homes, their ruined way of life, "thinking—figuring," and finding no solution to the disintegration rapidly enveloping them. Nor do the women/wives/mothers precipitously intrude on their shame. They are wise in the ways of mothering their men; of understanding the depth of their hurt and confusion, and in knowing that at times their greatest contribution to the healing of the others' psychic wounds lies in their supportive silence. "They knew that a man so hurt and so perplexed may turn in anger, even on people he loves. They left the men alone to figure and to wonder in the dust" (37). Secretly, unobtrusively, because they are good women, they study the faces of their men to know if this time they would "break." Also furtively, the children watch the faces of the men and the women. When the men's faces changed from "bemused perplexity" (7) to anger and resistance, although they still did not know what they would do, the women and children knew they were "safe"—for "no misfortune was too great to bear if their men were whole" (7).

In the face of such disaster, enforced idleness is the lot of men. Their work comes to a halt. The women, however, remain busy, for the housewife's traditional work, from which society claims she derives energy, purpose, and fulfillment, goes on. In addition, as conditions worsen and the men further internalize impotence, the women know they will be responsible for making the crucial decisions to lead their families through the adjustment period ahead. Critic Joan Hedrick explains the dynamics of the division of labor in sex-gender-differentiated systems this way, rather than as women's "nature":

> Though there are no crops to be harvested, there are clothes to mend, cornmeal to stir, side-meat to cut up for dinner. In a time of unemployment, women embody continuity, not out of some mythic identity as the Great Mother, but simply because their work, being in the private sphere of the family, has not been taken away. . . .

According to critics Richard Astro and Warren Motley, Steinbeck's philosophy of women was deeply influenced by his readings of Robert Briffault's *The Mothers: The Matriarchal Theory of Social Origins* (1931), a work they include in a group that "strove to heal the . . . post-Darwinian split between scientific thinking and ethical experience." Although Briffault saw matriarchy (historically antecedent to patriarchy) as a primitive and regressive order, he felt it described a "relationship based on cooperation rather than power," and fostered an "equalitarian" society to which "authority" and "domination" were foreign. As Motley sees it, Steinbeck did not believe that matriarchy was regressive, but he was convinced that the shock of dispossession undermined the patriarchal authority (based on male economic dominance) of the Joad men and the other farmers to such an extent that they were forced to turn back to matriarchy, the more positive social organization force, epitomized by Ma Joad's "high calm," "superhuman understanding," and selfless concern for her family, as the hope for a better future. Matriarchy, divested of the threat of authority and domination over men, was a system that suited Steinbeck's purpose in this novel.

The Grapes of Wrath delineates the tragedy of an agrarian family in a world in which capitalist greed and the demands of rapidly advancing technology supersede human needs and extenuating financial circumstances. Different in their attitudes from other white groups who seek the American Dream in social and economic mobility, the hard-working Joads, once tenant farmers, now reduced to share-cropper status, lived contentedly on the land in a community of like others, for three generations. They asked little of anyone outside of their world. Solid Americans, as they understand that term, they wanted only to live and let live. For instance, oblivious to the implications of his racial politics, the tenant man proudly explains his family's contributions to the pioneer history of white America. His grandfather arrived in frontier Oklahoma territory in his youth, when his worldly possessions amounted to salt, pepper, and a rifle. But before long, he successfully staked out a claim for his progeny:

> Grampa took up the land, and he had to kill the Indians and drive them away. And Pa was born here, and he killed weeds and snakes. . . . An' we [the third succeeding generation] was born here. . . . And Pa had to borrow money. The bank owned the land then, but we stayed and we got a little bit of what we raised. (36)

Unfortunately, the irony of their helplessness in confrontation with the power of the banks, with the absent, large land owners, and with the great crawling machines versus the fate of the Indians (to the farmer, of no greater concern than the comparison he makes of them to snakes or weeds) completely escapes the present generation. The subsequent education in class politics might have come sooner and been less psychologically devastating to the Joads and their friends if they had been able to recognize the parallels between racial and economic hegemony.

Three characters drive the action in *The Grapes of Wrath*: Jim Casy, a country preacher turned political activist; Tom Joad, the eldest son, ex-convict, and moral conscience of the family; and the indestructible Ma Joad, who holds center stage. At times she assumes mythic proportions, but her portraiture is also realistic and she acts with wisdom. Impressionistically, she is firmly planted in the earth, but she is more dependable than the land, which could not withstand the buffeting of nature or the persistent demands of small farmers or the evil encroachment of technology and corporate power. Her position is established at the beginning of the novel:

> Ma was heavy, but not fat; thick with child-bearing and work. . . . her strong, broad bare feet moved quickly and deftly over the floor. . . . Her full face was not soft; it was controlled, kindly. *Her hazel eyes seemed to have experienced all possible tragedy and to have mounted pain and suffering like steps into a high calm and a superhuman understanding. She seemed to know, to accept, to welcome her position, the citadel of the family.* (76—italics mine)

Unless she admitted hurt or fear or joy, the family did not know those emotions; and better than joy they loved her calm. They could depend on her "imperturbability." When Tom, Jr., returns from prison to find no homestead, the house pushed off its foundations, fences gone, and other signs of living vanished, his first thought is "They're gone—or Ma's dead" (44). He knows that under no circumstances would she permit the place to fall into such ruin if she were there. His is not a casual observation, but a statement fraught with anxiety. As Nancy Chodorow points out, in the sex-gender system, the absent mother is always the source of discomfiture for her children. Tom Joad closely associates the physical deterioration of his home with a missing mother, a signal for him of the catastrophe of which he is yet unaware.[5]

There is no question that Steinbeck had, as Howard Levant stresses, "profound respect" and "serious intentions" for the materials in *The Grapes of Wrath*. His sympathies are with a group of people who, though politically and economically unaggressive by other traditional American standards, represented an important core in the national life.[6] His portrayal of the misfortunes and downfall of this family constitutes a severe critique of a modern economic system that not only devalues human lives on the basis of class but, in so doing, that violates the principles of the relationship between hard work and reward and the sanctity of white family life on which the country was founded. In light of the brutal social and economic changes, and the disruptions of white family stability, there is no doubt that Steinbeck saw strong women from traditional working-class backgrounds as instrumental in a more humane transformation of the social structure. Of necessity, women are essential to any novel in which the conventional family plays a significant role. Here, he gives the same significance to the destruction of a family-centered way of life that one group had shaped and perpetrated for generations as he does to the economic factors that precipitated such a dire situation. Furthermore, through female characters in *The Grapes of Wrath*, Steinbeck's sensitivities to the values of female sensibilities demonstrate a point of view that supports the idea of humanitarian, large-scale changes that would make America, as a nation, more responsive to larger social needs.

In this respect, in spite of the grim reality of the lives of the Joads and their neighbors, *The Grapes of Wrath* is optimistic in favor of massive social change. We can trace this optimism from the beginning of the book, in which, unlike traditional plots of the naturalistic novels of its day, events unfold through the consciousness of the characters in such a way as to permit them to envision themselves exercising free will and exerting influence on their social world. In addition, as a result of his economic politics, Steinbeck reinforces the idea that the situation is not the dilemma of an isolated family, but of an entire group of people of a particular class. If sufficiently politicized, they can and will act. The novel chronicles the misfortunes and political education of the Joad family, but they represent the group from which they come, and share the feelings of their like-others. For example, also at the beginning, an unnamed farmer, recognizing his individual impotence in the face of capitalism and the technological monster, protests: "We've got a bad thing made by men, and by God that's something *we* can change" (41— italics mine). While neither he nor his fellow farmers can comprehend the full meaning of that statement at the time, the end of the novel suggests that those who survive will come to realize that group action can have an effect on the monstrous ideology that threatens their existence. But first they must survive; and the women are at the center of making that survival possible.

The first mention of Ma Joad in the novel occurs when Tom, recently released from jail after serving four of a seven-year sentence for killing a man in self-defense, returns to the homestead to find it in ruin. During his absence, he had almost no contact with his family, for, as Tom observes to his friend Casy: "they wasn't people to write" (45). Two years earlier, however, his mother sent him a Christmas card, and, the following year, the grandmother did the same. His mother's appears to have been appropriate; his grandmother's, a card with a "tree an' shiny stuff [that] looks like snow," with an embarrassing message in "po'try," was not:

> Merry Christmas, purty child,
> Jesus meek an' Jesus mild,
> Underneath the Christmas tree
> There's a gif' for you from me. (29)

Tom recalls the teasing of his cellmates who saw the card. Subsequently, they call him "Jesus Meek."

Given the living situation within the Joad community—the hard work and frustration over the yield of the land and the absence of genteel rituals, especially in such hard times—the fact that both women sent Christmas cards to the incarcerated young man is testimony to the quality of their commitment to mothering. Granma's card, however, is not appropriate for the young man confined involuntarily among men for whom only masculine symbols and behavior are acceptable. Nevertheless, Tom does not hold this against her. He understands and accepts her impulse and her motive. He believes she liked the card for its shiny exterior and that she never read the message, perhaps because, having lost her glasses several years before, she could not see to read. Symbolically, Granma may have good intentions, but she lacks the perception to fill successfully the present or future needs of her family. Later, when both grandparents die enroute to California, the family realizes that they were too old to make the transition from one way of life to another. On the other hand, although there is no mention of the nature of Ma Joad's card, we can assume that it was not a cause of embarrassment for her son. She is the woman of wisdom who knows how to use her talents to comfort her family in its moments of greatest distress. The differences in the two Christmas cards set the stage for understanding that Ma Joad is the woman who will be the significant force in the life of the family in the difficult times ahead.

Critics of Steinbeck's women often note that the first time we come face to face with Ma Joad she is engaged in the most symbolic act of mothering—feeding her family. I add that the second time we see her, she is washing clothes with her arms, up to her elbows, in soapsuds, and the third time, she is trying to dress the cantankerous grandfather who is by now incapable of caring for his own basic needs. Occurring in quick succession on a busy morning, these are the housewife's most important tasks: feeding the family, keeping them clean, and tending to the needs of those too young or too old to do so for themselves. In these earliest scenes with Ma Joad, the family is making its final preparations for the journey to California, and women's work not only goes on almost uninterruptedly, but increases in intensity. The adults, though full of apprehensions, have high hopes that steady work and a return to stability await them at the end of the trip. They have seen handbills calling for laborers to come to California to reap the harvests of a rich and fruitful land. They believe the handbills, for who would go to the expense of print-ing misrepresentations of the situation?

Although at all times the Joads have very little or almost no money; and, while in Oklahoma, no realistic appraisal of how long the trip to California will take in their dilapidated vehicle; and, in California, no assurances of how soon they will find work or a place to settle or know the nature of their future; an interesting aspect of Ma Joad's mothering psychology surfaces in different locations. On one hand, through most of the novel, she insists that her consider-ations are mainly for her family; on the other, she is willing to share the little food she has, to nurture whoever else is in need and comes along her way. We see this for the first time in Oklahoma, on first meeting her. Tom and his friend Casy arrive just as she completes the breakfast preparations on the day before the long, uncertain jour-ney begins. Before she recognizes who they are, she invites them to partake of her board. Most notably, evidence of her largesse occurs again under more stressful circumstances, when she feeds a group of hungry children in California, although there is not sufficient food even for her family.

Another extension of Ma Joad's mothering precipitates her into a new and unaccustomed position of power within the family when she insists that Casy, with no family of his own, but who wishes to travel with them, be taken along. This is her first opportunity to assert herself outside of her housewife's role, to claim leadership in important decision making, whereas previously only the men officiated. Casy travels with the Joads only because Ma Joad overrides the objections of her husband, whose concerns for their space needs, and the small amount of money and little food they have, lead him to think it unwise to take an extra person, especially an outsider to the family, on the trip. Questioned on the matter, Ma replies:

> "It ain't kin we? It's will we? . . . As far as 'kin,' we can't do nothin', not go to California or nothin'; but as far as 'will,' why, we'll do what we will." (104)

When the conversation ends, Casy has been accepted and she has gained new authority. She accepts this unpretentiously and with an absence of arrogance that will accompany her actions each time she finds it necessary to assert her will in the weeks and months ahead. And always, she asserts herself only for the good of the family. Two incidents that illustrate the group's understanding and acceptance of her wisdom and good judgment are especially noteworthy in this context. One occurs when the car breaks down during the journey and she refuses to agree to split up the family in order to hasten the arrival of some of its members in California. When her husband insists that separating is their better alternative, she openly defies him and, armed with a jack handle, challenges him to "whup" her first to gain her obedience to his will (169).[7] The second incident takes place in California, when, after weeks of the group's unsuccessful search for work and a decent place to settle down, she chides the men for capitulating to despair. "You ain't got the right to get discouraged," she tells them, "this here fambly's goin' under. You jus' ain't got the right" (350).

But these situations, in which Ma's voice carries, also illustrate the tensions between men and women, in sex-gender-role systems, when women move into space traditionally designated to men. Each time Ma asserts her leadership she meets with Pa's resentment, for, regardless of her motives, he perceives that she usurps his authority. In the first instance, when Casy is accepted into the group, "Pa turned back, and his spirit was raw from the whipping" her ascendancy represented to him (104). She, mindful of her role, leaves the family council and goes back to the house, to women's place, and women's work. But nothing takes place in her absence, the family waits for her return before continuing with their plans, "for [she] was powerful in the group" (105). During the trip (when Ma challenges Pa to "whup" her), after several suspenseful minutes, as the rest of the group watch his hands, the fists never form: After his effort to break the tension with humor, Tom says, "one person with their mind made up can shove a lot of folks aroun'!" (171). But again she is the victor and the "eyes of the whole family shifted back to Ma. She was the power. She had taken control" (170). Finally, in California, when Ma has her way once more in spite of Pa's opposition, and the family will move from a well-kept camp that had been a temporary respite from the traumas of the journey and their stay in Hooverville, but that placed them in an area in which they could find no work,

> Pa sniffled. "Seems like times is changed," he said sarcastically. "Time was when a man said what we'd do. Seems like women is tellin' now. Seems like it's purty near time to get out a stick." (352)

But he makes no attempt to beat her, for she quickly reminds him that men have the "right" to beat their women only when they (the men) are adequately performing their masculine roles.

> "You get your stick, Pa," she said. "Times when they's food an' a place to set, then maybe you can use your stick an' keep your skin whole. But you ain't a-doin' your job, either a-thinkin' or a-workin'. If you was, why, you could use your stick, an' women folks'd sniffle their nose an' creep-mouse aroun'. But you jus' get you a stick now an' you ain't lickin' no woman; you're a fightin', 'cause I got a stick all laid out too." (352)

In each of the instances mentioned here, once the decision is made and Ma's wise decision carries, she returns to women's place and/or displays stereotypical women's emotions. After her first confrontation with Pa over Casy, she hastens to tend the pot of "boiling side-meat and beet greens" to feed her family. Following the second, after she has challenged Pa to a fight and wins, she looks at the bar of iron and her hand trembles as she drops it on the ground. Finally, when she rouses the family from despair, she immediately resumes washing the breakfast dishes, "plunging" her hands into the bucket of water. And, to emphasize her selflessness, as her angry husband leaves the scene, she registers pride in her achievement, but not for herself. "He's all right," she notes to Tom. "He ain't beat. He's like as not to take a smack at me." Then she explains the aim of her "sassiness."

> "Take a man, he can get worried an' worried, an' it eats out his liver, an' purty soon he'll jus' lay down and die with his heart et out. But if you can take an' make 'im mad, why, he'll be awright. Pa, he didn't say nothin', but he's mad now. He'll show me now. He's awright. (352)

Only once does Ma come face to face with the issue of gender roles, and the possibilities of recognizing women's oppression within the conventions of the patriarchal society, and that is in her early relationships with Casy, when, in her psychological embrace of him, he is no longer a stranger, or even a friend, he becomes one of the male members of the family. He thanks her for her decision to let him accompany them to California by offering to "salt down" the meat they will carry with them. To this offer, she is quick to point out that the task is "women's work" that need not concern him. It is interesting that the only crack in the ideology of a gender-based division of labor to occur in the novel is in Casy's reply to Ma, and his subsequent actions: "It's all work. . . . They's too much of it to split it up to men's or women's work. . . . Leave me salt the meat" (109). Although she permits him to do it, apparently, she learns nothing from the encounter, for it never becomes a part of her thinking. On the other hand, Casy's consciousness of the politics of class is in formation before we meet him in the novel and he is the only character in the book to realize that women are oppressed by the division of labor based on the differentiation of sex-gender roles.

If the wisdom that Steinbeck attributes to women directs Ma to step outside of her traditional role in times of crisis, as noted above, her actions immediately after also make it clear that she is just as willing to retreat to wifehood and motherdom. In this, she supports Steinbeck's championing of Briffault's theory that, in matriarchy, women do not seek to have authority over men. In her case, not even equality of place is sought, only the right to lead, for the good of the group, when her man is incapable of doing so. And Steinbeck suggests why women are better equipped to lead in time of great social stress: They are closer to nature and to the natural rhythms of the earth. When family morale is at its lowest point, Ma continues to nurture confidence: "Man, he lives in jerks—" she says, "baby born an' a man dies, an' that's a jerk—gets a farm an' loses his farm, an' that's a jerk." But women are different. They continue on in spite of the difficulties. "Woman, it's all one flow, like a stream, little eddies, little waterfalls, but the river, it goes right on. Woman looks at it like that" (423). In times of crisis, Steinbeck suggests, the survival of the family and, by extension, the social order, depends on the wisdom and strength of the mother, whose interests are always those of her husband and children.

The long trek from Oklahoma to California provides many instances that demonstrate Ma's selfless nurturing, her wisdom, her leadership abilities, and, above all, her centeredness in the family. An important illustration of the latter occurs at the time of the death of the grandmother on the long night in which the family makes an incredibly precarious desert crossing into California. Lying with the dead old woman all night to conceal this partially unforeseen mishap from the rest of the group, Ma Joad's only thought during the ordeal is: "The fambly hadda get acrost" (228). Alone with her secret of the true state of the old woman's condition, her considerations for the other members of the family, in this case particularly for the future of the younger children and for her daughter's unborn child, take precedence over the tremendous emotional cost to herself. Her determination to protect the family is almost ferocious, as she stands up to the officials at the agricultural inspection station on the California border to prevent them from discovering the dead woman by making a thorough check of the contents of the truck.

> Now Ma climbed heavily down from the truck. Her face was swollen and her eyes were hard. "Look, mister. We got a sick ol' lady. We got to get her to a doctor. We can't wait." She seemed to fight with hysteria. "You can't make us wait." (225)

Her apparent distress over the welfare of the old woman's health is convincing. One inspector perfunctorily waves the beam of his flashlight into the interior of the vehicle, and decides to let them pass.

"I couldn' hold 'em" he tells his companion. "Maybe it was a bluff," the other replied, to which the first responded: "Oh, Jesus, no! You should of seen that ol' woman's face. That wasn't no bluff" (226). Ma is so intent on keeping the death a secret, even from the rest of the group as long as their overall situation remains threatening, that, when they arrive in the next town, she assures Tom that Granma is "awright—awright," and she implores him to "[d]rive on. We got to get acrost" (226). She absorbs the trauma of the death in herself, and only after they have arrived safely on the other side of the desert does she give the information to the others. Even then she refuses the human touch that would unleash her own emotional vulnerability. The revelation of this act to protect the family is one of the most powerful scenes in the novel. The members of the family, already almost fully dependent on her emotional stamina, look at her "with a little terror at her strength" (228). Son Tom moves toward her in speechless admiration and attempts to put his hand on her shoulder to comfort her. " 'Don' touch me,' she said. 'I'll hol' up if you don' touch me. That'd get me' " (228). And Casy, the newest member of the family, can only say: "there's a woman so great with love—she scares me" (229).

In Steinbeck's vision of a different and more humane society than capitalistic greed spawned, he also believed that efforts like Ma Joad's, to hold the family together in the way she always knew it (individualism as a viable social dynamic), were doomed to failure. Although she is unconscious of it at the time, her initial embrace of Casy is a step toward a redefinition of family, and, by the time the Joads arrive in California, other developments have already changed the situation. Both Grampa and Granma are dead. Soon after, son Noah, feeling himself a burden on the meager resources at hand, wanders away. In addition, Casy is murdered for union activities; Al, whose mechanical genius was invaluable during the trip, is ready to marry and leave; Connie, Rose of Sharon's husband, deserts, and her baby is stillborn; and Tom, in an effort to avenge Casy's death, becomes a fugitive from the law and decides to become a union organizer, to carry on Casy's work. Through these events, first Tom, and then Ma, especially through Tom's final conversation with her, achieve an education in the politics of class oppression, and realize that the system that diminishes one family to the point of its physical and moral disintegration can only be destroyed through the cooperative efforts of those of the oppressed group. "Use' ta be the fambly was fust. It ain't so now. It's anybody," Ma is forced to admit toward the end of the novel (444).

But, although the structure of the traditional family changes to meet the needs of a changing society, in this novel at least, Steinbeck sees "happy-wife-and-motherdom" as the central role for women, even for those with other significant contributions to make to the world at large. Ma Joad's education in the possibilities of class action do not extend to an awareness of women's lives and identities beyond the domestic sphere, other than that which has a direct relationship on the survival of the family. The conclusion of the novel revises the boundaries of that family. In this scene, unable physically to supply milk from her own breasts to save the old man's life, she initiates her daughter into the sisterhood of "mothering the world," of perpetuating what Nancy Chodorow calls "The Reproduction of Mothering." Ma Joad is the epitome of the Earth Mother. Critics note that Steinbeck need give her no first name, for she is the paradigmatic mother, and this is the single interest of her life. The seventeenth- and eighteenth-century metaphor of the fecund, virgin American land (women) gives way to that of the middle-aged mother (earth), "thick with child-bearing and work," but Steinbeck holds onto the stereotypical parallels between woman and nature. In our typical understanding of that word, Ma may not be happy in her role, but "her face . . . [is] controlled and kindly" and she fully accepts her place. Having "experienced all possible tragedy and . . . mounted pain and suffering like steps into a high calm," she fulfills her highest calling in the realm of wife and motherdom.

NOTES

1. Cited from Motley.
2. Mimi Reisel Gladstein, *The Indestructible Woman in Faulkner, Hemingway, and Steinbeck* (Ann Arbor, MI: University of Michigan Research Press, 1986), p. 79.
3. Peter Lisca, *The Wide World of John Steinbeck* (New Brunswick, NJ: Rutgers University Press, 1958), pp. 206–7. Quoted from Beatty in Hayashi's *Women*, p. 1.
4. Sandra Falkenberg, "A Study of Female Characterization in Steinbeck's Fiction," in *Steinbeck Quarterly*, Vol. 8 (2), Spring 1975, pp. 50–6.
5. Nancy Chodorow, *The Reproduction of Motherhood: Psychoanalysis and the Sociology of Gender* (Berkeley: University of California Press, 1978).

6. See Annette Kolodny, *The Lay of the Land: Metaphor as Experience and History in American Life and Letters* (Chapel Hill: University of North Carolina Press, 1975), pp. 26–28 for an account of the high regard men like Thomas Jefferson had for the small farmer. In spite of the benefits of large-scale farming, he advocated the independent, family-size farm, and believed that those who tilled the earth gained "substantial and genuine virtue."

7. Ma Joad's challenge to her husband is that she be "whupped," not beaten. A woman may be beaten if her husband thinks she deserves it, and she accepts it without resistance. To be whipped indicates that she will fight back, and that he must win the fight in order to claim that he has whipped her.

Mimi Reisel Gladstein

Mimi Reisel Gladstein has taught at Universidad Central de Venezuela, Universidad Complutence de Madrid, and the University of Texas, El Paso. She is the author of The Ayn Rand Companion, The Indestructible Woman in Faulkner, Hemingway, and Steinbeck, *and essays in* College English, San Jose Studies, Steinbeck Quarterly, *and numerous collections of Steinbeck criticism.*

THE GRAPES OF WRATH: STEINBECK AND THE ETERNAL IMMIGRANT

The many conferences and publications honoring the fiftieth anniversary of *The Grapes of Wrath* in 1989 give strong indication of the durability of John Steinbeck's world-famous novel. There are still a few holdouts such as Leslie Fiedler, who fudges his condemnation of this "problematic middlebrow book" by allowing the "ambiguous, archetypal final scene" to "redeem" the work, but even hardened Steinbeck-basher Harold Bloom concedes that "no canonical standards worthy of human respect could exclude *The Grapes of Wrath* from a serious reader's esteem." And while expressing his reservations, Bloom is still "grateful for the novel's continued existence."

If further assurance is needed, and I think it is not, of the book's continued and continuing significance, the success of the Steppen-

Reprinted from *John Steinbeck: The Years of Greatness, 1936-1939*, edited by Tetsumaro Hayashi. Copyright © 1993 by The University of Alabama Press. By permission of The University of Alabama Press.

wolf Theatre Company production of *The Grapes of Wrath* in Chicago, La Jolla, London, and on Broadway adds evidence of the ability of the story to capture new audiences. Frank Galati's adaptation of Steinbeck's novel has elicited a chorus of praise from critics, each with his or her own explanation of the reason why Steinbeck's timely tale of a problem in the 1930s continues to engage us in the 1990s. To this end, the *USA Today* article about the production was headlined "New *Grapes* Still Bears Fruit."[1] Terry Kinney, the actor who plays Jim Casy in the Steppenwolf production, sees parallels between the problem of the homeless in New York's East Village and the story of the Joads. A review by David Patrick Stearns connects Steinbeck's "surprisingly timely message" with how "we deal with holocaust."[2] Like Kinney, Mimi Kramer, in her review in the *New Yorker*, claims that *The Grapes of Wrath* is about homelessness, but what she describes is a more general homelessness, which, in her opinion, characterizes all great American epics, including *Gone with the Wind*, *Moby-Dick*, and on another level *The Wizard of Oz*.[3] Alan Brinkley's response to his own question of "Why Steinbeck's Okies Speak to Us Today" is that Steinbeck's message is of the importance of a "transcendent community" that Brinkley links to both modern radicalism and conservatism, citing former President George Bush's "thousand points of light" as a contemporary expression of a call to transcendent community.[4]

Kinney, Stearns, Kramer, and Brinkley all posit acceptable explanations for the lasting quality of Steinbeck's novel. Each of their theories adds its own illumination to Steinbeck's story. And this is appropriate, because Steinbeck described *The Grapes of Wrath* as a five-layered book, explaining that "a reader will find as many as he can and won't find more than he has in himself."[5]

I would like to suggest yet a different layer in Steinbeck's novel, a layer that, at Steinbeck's suggestion, I found in myself. It is a layer that, like the other layers, readers have found in themselves; it explains a significant portion of the book's continuing and universal appeal, because if *The Grapes of Wrath* is about homelessness, if it is about the exploitation of an underclass by the power structure, and if it is the American equivalent of the exodus from Egypt, as various writers have suggested, it is also the story of a quintessential American experience.

And it is more than that. For while the immigrant's experience can be categorized on a personal level and also be seen as a national paradigm, it is not just in America that *The Grapes of Wrath* endures. Steinbeck's pages communicate to a worldwide audience, as the Third International Steinbeck Congress and the Steinbeck Conference held in October 1989 in Moscow illustrate. And while there are as many reasons for the novel's worldwide appeal as there are for its American appeal, perhaps the theme of the eternal immigrant is another reason why the story of the Joads speaks to such varying audiences. For the problems faced by immigrants are international. Peoples move, boundaries change, economic and political problems create migrations. The Oklahomans in California are like the Chinese in Malaysia, the Indians in South Africa, the Turkish in Germany, or the Algerians in France. Professor Jin Young Choi, speaking on "Steinbeck Studies in Korea" on the first day of the Third International Steinbeck Congress, commented on the parallels between Steinbeck's Okies and Korean farmers who moved to Manchuria. Her evocation of the empathy with which the Korean psyche, educated by the experiences of Korean immigrants in China, Japan, and Manchuria, is keyed to the suffering of the displaced provides yet another piece of evidence in the case I wish to build. My thesis, then, is that the Joads gain much of their literary cachet from the similarities of the problems suffered by immigrants everywhere. Their experience is universal.

At first, when Steinbeck was writing his "Harvest Gypsies" series of articles for the *San Francisco News,* neither he nor the editorial staff of that newspaper saw the Dust Bowl migrants as analogous to the previous groups of immigrants who had been exploited by California's agricultural industry. Because they were American citizens, Steinbeck expected that the newcomers would be treated differently from the immigrant or foreign labor that California had imported in the past. In his newspaper series, Steinbeck describes them as "the best American stock, intelligent, resourceful, and if given a chance, socially responsible." The editorial that accompanied his articles stated, "They cannot be handled as the Japanese, Mexicans, and Filipinos." These prophesies proved false.

Putting aside the question of whether or not these opinions are, in themselves, nationalistic or racist, for purposes of this discussion, the significant fact is that by the time Steinbeck finished *The Grapes of Wrath,* less than three years later, he had learned that xenophobia does not discriminate between migrants and immigrants, between light skin and dark. What he saw in the years between the publication of the articles and the completion of the novel found its way into his fictional narrative and clearly illustrated that, in terms of what they encountered in California, this "best American stock" was treated the same as any immigrant stock.

Steinbeck's awareness of this is communicated both subtly and pointedly. In chapter 19, one of the interchapters where he expresses the mood of the Californians during this period and their hostile attitude toward drought refugees, his narration leaves little doubt that the Oklahomans are perceived as aliens, not countrymen. Steinbeck depicts a scene where a deputy sheriff tramples the small, secret garden of one of the migrant workers. We enter the sheriff's thoughts as he kicks off the heads of turnip greens. "Outlanders," he thinks, "foreigners" (235). His reason recoils from this untruth, but it is no match for his emotions, which rationalize his actions by explaining, "Sure, they talk the same language, but they ain't the same" (236).

The sheriff is one individual, but in the narrative Steinbeck also imagines the thought patterns of the general community. In these passages is more evidence that the newcomers are considered foreigners. To excuse their brutality toward the migrants, the citizens who run the communities project a possible uprising among the Okies. In their collective paranoia, they fear that the farm laborers might retaliate against their harsh treatment, might march against their oppressors as "the Lombards did in Italy, as the Germans did on Gaul and the Turks did on Byzantium" (236). Clearly, the images in the Californians' minds equate the Okies with foreigners.

Chapter 19 is one of the most clearly articulated instances in which Steinbeck's narrative demonstrates that he understood that the Oklahomans were more immigrant than migrant in the minds of his fellow Californians. But he also develops the idea dramatically through his narrative. In the Joad family scenes, he shows us the Joads experiencing what immigrants have borne throughout history.

To fully develop parallels between the Joad family experiences and the experiences of immigrant groups throughout the world, I would need a book-length manuscript. For the purposes of this essay, I have chosen to illustrate parallels to one or two immigrant groups, hoping that in the variety of my examples, the particular will establish the universal.[6]

At the heart of every immigrant's experience is a dream—a vision of hope that is embodied in his or her destination. Americans have long seen their country as the land of opportunity, and the vision carried in the hearts of most immigrants who have come here is of the *goldeneh medina*, a place where the streets are paved with gold. For every immigrant is impelled by the expectation of a better life at his or her journey's end. What else but such a vision could entice Haitians to brave stormy seas on rickety rafts, the Vietnamese boat people, the Marielitos, Mexican boys to allow themselves to be locked into suffocating boxcars? Similarly, the Joads embark upon a hazardous journey, their overburdened truck like a rickety raft, the Arizona and California deserts seas of sand rather than water. The gold at the end of their journey is embodied in the orange groves of California rather than the imagined gold-paved streets of New York. Ma's vision is of a place "never cold. An' fruit ever' place, an' people just bein' in the nicest places, little white houses in among the orange trees. . . . An' the little fellas go out an' pick oranges right off the tree" (93). Ma's dream vision, where gold/oranges hang on the trees (lie in the streets) just for the taking, is an archetypal immigrant fantasy.

For Ma the oranges represent more than gold; they represent the luxury and nourishment of the Promised Land. In her vision, oranges are abundant "ever' place" and readily accessible, "right off the tree." Orange trees do not grow in Oklahoma, so oranges are also a bit of a delicacy. For my father, who was raised in Poland, the symbol was bananas, a great luxury in that cold country. When he was told that bananas were sold at five cents a stalk in Nicaragua, the country he first immigrated to, he thought it must be a land of unimagined luxury and abundance.

For Grampa Joad, in the novel, the synecdoche is more biblical. California is where he can "get me a whole big bunch a grapes" and "squash 'em on my face an' let 'em run offen my chin" (85). Fruit, be it oranges, grapes, or bananas, is a universal symbol for abundance and luxury. Maybe that is why the horn of plenty is filled with it.

The immigrant's dream is often unrealistic, and extravagant expectations can lead to bitter disappointment. Steinbeck foreshadows this in his novel. Even Ma, who acts as the cheerleader for the venture, has her moments of doubt. She says to Tom, "I'm scared of stuff so nice. I ain't got faith. I'm scared somepin ain't so nice about it" (92). Faced with the reality of pulling up roots and leaving his and his ancestors' home ground, Grampa rejects his promised luxury: "I don't give a goddamn if they's oranges an' grapes crowdin' a fella outa bed even" (113). The dream turns to ashes as the nourishing oranges and grapes become "winfall" peaches that, rather than providing sustenance, cause "the skitters." My father's bitter lesson came when, having bought several stalks of five-cent bananas at the dock the minute his boat landed, he discovered that a stalk of bananas cost only two cents in the city.

It is characteristic of the immigrant experience that immigrants garner no credit for either family or nationality contributions to the history and culture of the country into which they travel. This is a truth Italian-Americans know well. It mattered not that the Americas were both discovered by and named for Italians: Columbus's and Vespucci's countrymen were not greeted warmly nor treated well as immigrants. As one Italian immigrant noted, they were only expected to perform "all the manual and menial work the older Americans spurned."[7] Steinbeck also notes that past contributions have no bearing on present treatment when he has the general voice of the migrants explain, "One of our folks in the Revolution, an' they was lots of our folks in the Civil War—both sides" (233). Ma also boasts about the Joad lineage: "We're Joads. We don't look up to nobody. Grampa's grampa, he fit in the Revolution" (307). These credentials are ignored by the Californians.

Another aspect of the immigrant experience that echoes from the pages of The Grapes of Wrath is the propensity for finding a derogatory term with which to label the new arrival. Contemporary sociology books define this as an "ethnophaulism."[8] The term carries with it deprecatory stereotypes and negative images. And the world learned the term "Okies" from Steinbeck. The term became so well known that my immigrant father was bemused when I brought home what he referred to jokingly as an "Okie" to marry. He expected a rube, driving a laden-down jalopy. The image of the "Okie" as beaten-down loser was so pervasive that the Board of Regents of the University of Oklahoma came up with the idea of creating a championship football team as an antidote for the statewide depression caused by Steinbeck's book.[9]

In the novel, Tom first hears the word from a man who, returning from California, tells him, "You never been called 'Okie' yet." Tom doesn't know what the word means. He asks, "Okie? What's that?" The man responds, "Well, Okie use' ta mean you was from Oklahoma. Now it means you're a dirty son-of-a-bitch. Okie means you're scum" (205). Tom's reaction to the term is like that of the young protagonist in an autobiographical short story by Chicano writer John Rechy. In "El Paso del Norte" Rechy speaks of the hatred in Texas for Mexicans. In grammar school his protagonist is called "Mexicangreaser, Mexicangreaser." The boy is perplexed and says, "Well, yes, my mother did do an awful lot of frying but we never put any grease on our hair and so it bothered me."[10] Each immigrant group has experienced its share of such epithets, complete with the stereotypes that accompany them. The effect is soul-withering. Even the redoubtable Ma is unnerved by the epithet. Her interchange with the policeman who first uses the term on her illustrates both the negative effect of the name-calling and the fact that Ma sees herself as coming from a different country than his.

The policeman begins by saying to Ma, "We don't want none of you settlin' down here." Ma's response is anger. She picks up an iron skillet and advances on the man. When he loosens his gun, she rejoins, "Go ahead. . . . Scarin' women. I'm thankful the men folks ain't here. They'd tear you to pieces. *In my country* [emphasis mine] you watch your tongue." It is at this point that the man responds, "Well, *you ain't in your country* [emphasis mine] now. You're in California, an' we don't want you goddamn Okies settlin' down" (213–14). Note that both Ma and the policeman see themselves as coming from different countries, not as citizens of the same country. At this point in the interchange Ma's advance is stopped. It is not the gun that stops her, but the effect of the name-calling: "She looked puzzled. 'Okies?' she said softly. 'Okies' " (214). When the man leaves, Ma has to fight with her face to keep from breaking down. The effect is so devastating that Rose of Sharon pretends to be asleep (214).

Hungarians have been called "hunkies," Bohemians "bohunks," Chinese "chinks," and Italians "dagos." Ethnophaulisms exist for every kind of immigrant, regardless of race or country of origin. In scenes such as the one between Ma and the policeman, Steinbeck shows that he understands the effects of this kind of name-calling. He shows his Californians behaving toward the new arrivals in ways that are typical of the in-group's behavior toward the out-group. He is particularly adept at underlining the distance between the behavior of the out-group and the way that behavior is perceived by the in-group. This he does with caustic dramatic irony. In one instance, the reader has just finished a scene in which the Joads act unusually compassionately and charitably. They, who have so few resources, give part of what they have to people who are neither kin nor longtime friends. Pa takes "two crushed bills" from his purse and leaves them, together with a half sack of potatoes and a quarter of a keg of salt pork that Ma has put by, for the Wilsons (219). After this remarkable act of charity, their next stop is a service station in Needles. The service station attendant does not see the Joads that Steinbeck has just shown the reader. He sees only their determination, which he translates into hardness, describing them to his helper as "a hard-looking outfit." His helper provides the stereotype: "Them Okies? They're all hard-lookin'" (221). Then he goes on to make statements that reveal the depth of his prejudice, a prejudice expressed toward this group of Anglo-American migrants, but one remarkably similar to the prejudices expressed toward many immigrant groups.

One of the cruel ironies of the treatment of immigrant groups is that they are paid lower wages, given poorer working conditions, limited to uninhabitable living quarters, and then despised as being subhuman because they live as they do. Steinbeck has his service station boy say, "Them goddamn Okies got no sense and no feeling. They ain't human. A human being wouldn't live like they do. A human being couldn't stand it to be so dirty and miserable. They ain't a hell of a lot better than gorillas" (221). The universality of this kind of negative stereotyping is almost too obvious for commentary. It is the kind of thinking that allows the killing of "gooks" because they aren't seen as human, the lynching of "niggers" because they are seen as an inferior species.

Steinbeck shows numerous instances of the Okies being treated as less than human. Although Floyd, a man the Joads meet in the first Hooverville camp, does little more than ask the contractor about his license and pay scale, the deputy shoots at Floyd when he runs from possible incarceration. Only the most blatant disregard for the bystanders could produce such a response by the deputies, as lawmen are taught to hold their fire in a crowd. Steinbeck's narrative makes it clear that Floyd is dodging in and out of sight in a crowd of people when the deputy fires (264). The result is horrible. A woman's hand is shattered. This has no effect on the deputy, who "raised his gun again" (264). At this point, Casy kicks him in the neck. The woman is hysterical, with blood oozing from her wound. When the rest of the deputy's group arrives and Casy tells them that the deputy hit a woman, they show no interest in her. Even when Casy says, "They's a woman down the row like to bleed to death from his bad shootin'," their response is: "We'll see about that later" (266). After Casy reminds them a third time, they finally go to take a look. Their behavior, which up to this point is totally devoid of responsibility, is compounded by insensitivity and lack of humanity. They do not see a woman, another human being. They only see the "mess a .45 does make" (267).

Because of their powerlessness and because they are seen as less than human, immigrants are often housed apart and in dehumanizing facilities. This has been true since medieval times, when immigrants were relegated to the outskirts of the city, the most dangerous area in those days because it was most vulnerable to attack. In an ironic reversal, today's most dangerous areas are the inner cities, where ghettos are most often located. This "segregation" or "ghettoization" is called "spatial segregation" in contemporary sociological studies. Steinbeck's Okies are subjected to this "spatial segregation." They are not allowed to settle where they like but are shunted to the Hoovervilles, impermanent shantytowns of tents and shacks. And even these miserable communities are seen as threatening by the xenophobic citizens. The first Hooverville the Joads stay in is burned so its inhabitants must move on. The burning of ghettos, or shtetls, was common, and was sometimes responsible for creating immigrants, as in the fictional Anatevka of *Fiddler on the Roof*, which had many real-life analogues.

When the migrant workers are given housing by the companies that hire them, the living conditions are appalling. Universally, living conditions and working conditions that immigrant and migrant workers must endure are disgraceful. The burning to death of the young garment workers who were locked up in the loft is a historical instance of the abusive working conditions immigrants suffered. When the Joads go to pick peaches, they are, for all intents and purposes, locked in. A police escort ushers them in, a guard with a shotgun sits at the end of each street (377), and when Tom tries to go outside the camp for a walk, a guard with a gun tells him he cannot leave the compound (380). The image is of a work camp—as in the Netherlands, where the Moluccans were housed in the concentration camps abandoned by the Nazis.

The house the Joads are assigned is one room for eight people, a room that smells of sweat and grease. Nor have the facilities for laboring immigrants changed much. If anything, they are worse. In a 1981 study, migrant housing is called "grotesque" and "nightmarish." The reporter says it is difficult to write about "without seeming to be melodramatic."[11] Brent Ashabrenner, in a 1985 book about Haitians, Jamaicans, and Guatemalans who, with their families, are the contemporary Okies of Florida and the South, reports similar conditions.[12]

Steinbeck leaves his immigrant family devastated by death, desertion, and flood. The last scene—Rose of Sharon's selfless act of giving—used to fill me with impatience. How ridiculous to expect that this woman, whose lack of proper nutrition and care has produced a dead baby, should have enough nourishment to sustain a dying man. What a paltry symbolic act. And yet, history has proved Steinbeck's impulse unerring. For, as Ma prophesied, the people do go on. The Okies have survived. James Gregory, in his recently published *American Exodus*, charts the durability of the Okie subculture in California today.[13]

Faced with seemingly insurmountable obstacles, immigrants the world over not only survive, but prevail. Michael Dukakis, the son of Greek immigrants, ran for president of the United States. Alberto Fujimori, son of Japanese immigrants to Peru, won the Peruvian presidency. Roberto Villareal, who as a boy picked cotton with his Mexican immigrant family in the fields of Texas, is now chairman of the Department of Political Science at the University of Texas at El Paso, my university. *The Grapes of Wrath* speaks to me, because *The Grapes of Wrath* speaks of me, an immigrant, who with my family experienced the pains and promise of immigration, an experience Steinbeck wrote of so tellingly in his story of the Joads.

NOTES

1. Stephen Schaefer, "New *Grapes* Still Bears Fruit," *USA Today*, March 23, 1990, p. 4D.
2. David Patrick Stearns, "Steppenwolf's Gritty Honesty Dazzles in Clear, Classic Style," *USA Today*, March 23, 1990, p. 4D.
3. Mimi Kramer, "Tender Grapes," *New Yorker*, April 2, 1990, pp. 87–88.
4. Alan Brinkley, "Why Steinbeck's Okies Speak to Us Today," *New York Times*, March 18, 1990, sec. 2, p. 13.
5. Elaine Steinbeck and Robert Wallsten, eds., *Steinbeck: A Life in Letters* (New York: Viking Press, 1975), pp. 178–79.
6. To establish the universal character of the immigrant experience,

among the works consulted but not cited are: Thomas D. Boswell and James R. Curtis, *The Cuban-American Experience* (Totawa, N.J.: Rowman & Allanheld Publishers, 1984); Francesco Cordasco and Eugene Bucchioni, *The Puerto Rican Experience* (Totawa, N.J.: Rowman & Littlefield, 1973); Thomas H. Holloway, *Immigrants on the Land* (Chapel Hill: University of North Carolina Press, 1980); Woo Moo Hurh and Kwang Chung Kim, *Korean Immigrants in America* (Teaneck, N.J.: Fairleigh Dickinson University Press, 1984); Constantine M. Panunzio, *The Soul of an Immigrant* (New York: Arno Press and *New York Times*, 1969); Sherman C. Bezalel, *The Jew within American Society* (Detroit: Wayne State University Press, 1961); Barbara Miller Solomon, *Ancestors and Immigrants* (Cambridge: Harvard University Press, 1956).

7. Michael A. Musmanno, *The Story of the Italians in America* (Garden City, N.Y.: Doubleday, 1965), p. 6.
8. Vincent N. Parrillo, *Strangers to These Shores: Race and Ethnic Relations in the United States*, 2d ed. (New York: John Wiley & Sons, 1985), pp. 64–65. Parrillo defines ethnophaulism as "the language of prejudice, the verbal picture of a negative stereotype."
9. George Lynn Cross, *Presidents Can't Punt* (Norman: University of Oklahoma Press, 1977), p. 7.
10. John Rechy, "El Paso del Norte," in *New Writing in the USA*, ed. Donald Allen and Robert Creeley (Middlesex, England: Penguin Books, 1967), p. 211.
11. Ronald L. Goldfarb, *Migrant Farm Workers: A Caste of Despair* (Ames: Iowa State University Press, 1981), p. 40.
12. Brent Ashabrenner, *Dark Harvest: Migrant Farm Workers in America* (New York: Dodd, Mead & Co., 1985).
13. James N. Gregory, *American Exodus: The Dust Bowl Migration and Okie Culture in California* (New York: Oxford University Press, 1989).

Topics for Discussion and Papers

1. After finishing his first reading of the manuscript, Steinbeck's longtime editor had doubts about the ending. In a letter, Pascal Covici told Steinbeck, "It seems to us that the last few pages need building up. The incident needs leading up to, so that the meeting with the starving man is not so much an accident or chance encounter, but more an integral part of the saga of the Joad family." Covici also suggested that the ending not be so abrupt, "so that the symbolism of the gesture is more apparent in relation to the book as a whole." Steinbeck replied that he could not make the changes, adding, "It is casual—there is no fruity climax, it is not more important than any other part of the book—if there is a symbol, it is a survival symbol not a love symbol, it must be an accident, it must be a stranger, and it must be quick. . . . The fact that the Joads don't know him, don't care about him, have no ties to him—that is the emphasis. The giving of the breast has no more sentiment than the giving of a piece of bread." Discuss, point by point, the merits of the objections raised by Covici. Is Steinbeck's justification in his reply convincing? Where would you amplify or disagree with either argument? Be sure to refer to the essays by Shockley, Ditsky, and Owens in your consideration of these questions.

2. Although it is always interesting to have an author's statements about his or her own work, it would be uncritical to confuse these statements with the work itself. Choose one or two of Steinbeck's own questions and answers about his philosophy and intentions included in the list he sent to Joseph Henry Jackson

(540), and examine the novel for the degree to which it embodies these statements.

3. If you were asked by someone who had not read the novel, "What is it about?" what would you write down in one sentence? Compare your sentence with those of others. If the sentences are strikingly different—as they are likely to be—how do you account for their diversity? Try to make a case for your sentence against those of others. Do your disagreements indicate a failure of communication on the part of the novel? What can you conclude about the novel from this experiment?

4. George Miron, in a pamphlet called *The Truth about John Steinbeck and the Migrants*, states that he can think "of no other novel which advances the idea of class war and promotes hatred of class against class . . . more than does *The Grapes of Wrath*." Is this the kind of impression the novel leaves with you? In opposition to the above statement, consider that of Stanley Edgar Hyman in "Some Notes on John Steinbeck": "Actually, as a careful reading makes clear, the central message of *The Grapes of Wrath* is an appeal to the owning class to behave, to become enlightened, rather than to the working class to change its own conditions." Consider Benson's essay (505), and the story it tells of Steinbeck's earlier manuscript, *L'Affaire Lettuceberg*.

5. Compare the view of agricultural and migrant conditions in Frank J. Taylor's article with that in the article by Carey McWilliams. Which is the more convincing? Why? Pursue this topic further in the following sources: Carey McWilliams, *Factories in the Field*; Donald Worster, *Dust Bowl*; Walter J. Stein, *California and the Dust Bowl Migration*; Paul S. Taylor, *On the Ground in the Thirties*; Cletus E. Daniel, *A History of California Farm Workers, 1870–1941*; and James N. Gregory, *American Exodus: The Dust Bowl Migration and Okie Culture in California*.

6. In their introduction, "The Pattern of Criticism," your editors state that "the hysterical reaction which *The Grapes of Wrath* aroused in part of the American public [as evidenced in Shockley's essay in this volume, in Shillinglaw in Hayashi, *Years*, and in Haslam] was reflected in book reviews." Consult the *Book Review Digest* and select some reviews which, judging from the excerpt presented there, promise to be "hysterical" and report on them. On what grounds was the book most objected to?

7. *The Grapes of Wrath* also provided the impetus for a number of

other novelists and one prominent filmmaker to respond to what they saw as Steinbeck's project. Compare *The Grapes of Wrath* to any of the following works: Ruth Comfort Mitchell's *Of Human Kindness*, Marshall V. Hartranft's *The Grapes of Gladness: California's Refreshing and Inspiring Answer to John Steinbeck's "Grapes of Wrath,"* or Preston Sturges's film *Sullivan's Travels.* Pursue this topic further in the following sources: Shillinglaw, "California Answers *The Grapes of Wrath*" (in Hayashi, *Years*) for the books, and Hearle, "Sturges and *The Grapes of Wrath: Sullivan's Travels* as Documentary Comedy" for the film.

8. *The Grapes of Wrath* is sometimes compared to Harriet Beecher Stowe's *Uncle Tom's Cabin* in its immediate social repercussions. What were the long-term social repercussions, if any, from Steinbeck's novel? Pursue this topic further, by doing research on social conditions among post–World War II migrant farmworkers in the following sources: Donald Worster, *Rivers of Empire*; Ronald L. Goldfarb, *Migrant Farm Workers: A Caste of Despair*; and Brent Ashabrenner, *Dark Harvest: Migrant Farmworkers in America*. Discuss how Steinbeck's book and Stowe's book differ in the means by which they achieved their social effects. Do you think that Stowe's book would be as effective today? Why or why not?

9. Steinbeck wrote two other novels in the 1930s dealing with migrant workers: *In Dubious Battle* and *Of Mice and Men*. The latter is very different from *The Grapes of Wrath* in that it deals much more with individuals, although of course they may be seen as representative. *In Dubious Battle* is a novel about a strike of migrant workers and resembles *The Grapes of Wrath* in its attention to large groups of people. Yet the two novels, although they share this trait, are very different in other respects—prose style, structure, characterization, use of symbolism, etc.—and in their total effects. Compare one or more aspects of both novels in some detail.

10. Assuming that the information in the essay by Carey McWilliams is correct, use this essay to "prove" or "disprove" as many facts, incidents, and conditions as you can in *The Grapes of Wrath*.

11. A number of early critics, and even a few readers at Steinbeck's publishers, remarked on the vulgarity of *The Grapes of Wrath*, and Steinbeck's works have for years been continually among

the most frequently banned books in America. Make a list of passages which might have been found offensive. How do they compare to similar passages in contemporary fiction? Does there seem to be some effective purpose for each passage? What is their cumulative contribution to the novel? Consult Reed's essay.

12. In her essay, "*The Grapes of Wrath*: Steinbeck and the Eternal Immigrant," Mimi Reisel Gladstein gives one argument for the book's contemporary relevance. Are there others? Do you feel that this relevance to our own time is coincidental or that the novel has some universal or enduring qualities which will continue to keep it relevant to contemporary life? What are these qualities and how are they achieved?

13. What was your initial reaction to the interchapters in *The Grapes of Wrath*? Did they "interfere" with your reading of the novel, or did they contribute to your participation and enjoyment? If they interfered, do the arguments in your editor Peter Lisca's essay, "*The Grapes of Wrath* as Fiction," convince you of their centrality to the novel or that you might enjoy them on a second reading of the book? If you enjoyed them, do that essay's arguments satisfactorily explain your enjoyment? Consider also DeMott's essay on Steinbeck's writing process and the development of the book's structure, and Conder's essay on how the novel's structure establishes tension between individual free will and "statistical determinism."

14. As noted in the introduction to the critical essays, much discussion of the novel has revolved around its characters. Some reviewers and critics have found them to be mere puppets, animalistic, unreal; others have praised them for their human qualities. Where do Shaw and McKay stand on this? Where do you stand? What kinds of details can you present to support your opinion? Is it possible to logically argue this point at all? What kinds of evidence can be agreed on? Furthermore, it is clear that most contemporary readers have no difficulty in accepting the book's characters as real, moving human beings. What might be some of the reasons for this shift in appreciation? Consider the social context and the possible effects of mass communications media.

15. Assuming that *The Grapes of Wrath* is essentially accurate in its depiction of economic, political, sociological conditions in

Oklahoma, en route, and in California, how fair is the novel in assigning blame for these conditions? To appreciate Steinbeck's ideas about blame, you might want to consider Steinbeck's ideas in *The Log from the Sea of Cortez* about nonteleological thinking.

16. Commentators have made much of the book's biblical symbolism. How much of this was apparent to you on a first reading? Although it is impossible to question that this symbolism is ubiquitous in *The Grapes of Wrath*, what is the effect of its presence? Would the novel be appreciably diminished if the biblical symbolism were completely removed? How? Be sure to consider the viewpoints expressed by Lisca, Ditsky, and Owens.

17. In 1936, Steinbeck wrote for the *San Francisco News* a series of eight articles on migrant labor in California. These were reprinted together with an epilogue by Steinbeck in 1938 by the Simon J. Lubin Society of California in a pamphlet called *Their Blood Is Strong* (reprinted in French, *Companion*; and as *The Harvest Gypsies*). Also in 1936, Steinbeck wrote an essay for *The Nation* (September 13) called "Dubious Battle in California," again on the subject of migrant labor. Read one or both of these works in conjunction with the DeMott and Benson essays reprinted here, and comment on the use of this material in *The Grapes of Wrath*. What observations did he not use in the novel? Why?

18. Compare Steinbeck's articles on migrant labor (detailed in the preceding question) with those by McWilliams and Frank J. Taylor in this volume. Could Steinbeck have written *The Grapes of Wrath* without doing his own research?

19. It has been charged sometimes by critics that *The Grapes of Wrath* is "sentimental." Look up several definitions of the term in dictionaries and literary handbooks. Do you agree that this term can be applied to the novel's characters and plot? To the interchapters? Just what are the specific sentimental incidents and aspects of characters in the novel? Do you agree with Owens's claim that the Joads and the other migrants aren't sentimentalized, because Steinbeck implicates the Okies in the process that leads to their displacement? Why do you agree or disagree? Is it possible to have sentimental elements and still be a great novel?

20. Griffin and Freedman in "Machines and Animals: Pervasive Mo-

tifs in *The Grapes of Wrath*" point to the novel's concern with mechanized agriculture. Gather evidence from the novel for a summary of Steinbeck's views on the subject. Is he really against mechanized agriculture per se? Is he really for a return to the horse and plow? In modern literature, mechanization is often linked with determinism, or at least with a decrease in the efficacy of individual free will. Consider the evidence from Griffin and Freedman's essay, and test it against Conder's notions of the tension between free will and determinism in *The Grapes of Wrath*.

21. McKay's essay claims that Steinbeck "holds onto the stereotypical parallels between woman and nature," and she gives a number of examples of Steinbeck depicting women as more "natural" than men. Consider the many descriptions in the novel of nature and landscape. Do the parallels work both ways? Is nature "feminized" in *The Grapes of Wrath*? Consider other stereotypical parallels and dualities (natural vs. artificial, natural vs. mechanical, Man vs. Nature, etc.) in the novel. Are the constituent parts of these pairs gendered in *The Grapes of Wrath*? If so, are they masculine or feminine? Why? Compare Steinbeck's use of gendering to that of other American novelists of the 1930s, and to that of novelists of today.

22. McKay notes that Ma Joad, despite being the emotional center of the family and its strongest member, cannot imagine for herself any role in the world larger than, or other than, wife and mother. Authors, however, are capable of having imaginations which are larger than those of their characters. What evidence, if any, is there in *The Grapes of Wrath* that Steinbeck believed women could play important roles outside the family structure?

23. Most attention to the novel's characters focuses on the adults and their sometimes symbolic roles—Jim Casey, Tom, Granma, Grampa, and Ma Joad. There are in the novel, however, not only the Joad children, but those of other migrants. Looking at the children in the novel, what can be said of their reality as children? What is their contribution to the novel's direction? Consider the end of Owens's essay.

24. John Ford's movie version of *The Grapes of Wrath* is recognized as a classic American film, yet it departs from Steinbeck's novel in a number of significant ways. View the film and compare it to Steinbeck's book. Pursue this topic further in the following

sources: George Bluestone, *"The Grapes of Wrath"* in *Novels into Film* (reprinted in Davis, *Steinbeck*); Mimi Reisel Gladstein, "From Heroine to Supporting Player: The Diminution of Ma Joad" (in Ditsky, *Critical*); Joseph R. Millichap, *Steinbeck and Film*; and Leslie Gossage, "The Artful Propaganda of John Ford's 'The Grapes of Wrath' " (in Wyatt, *New*).

25. It is tempting when talking about a long and impressive novel to call it "epic." Look up the term in some literary handbooks. Does *The Grapes of Wrath* seem to embody any of these characteristics? Does it embody enough of them to be called an epic?

Bibliography

WORKS BY JOHN STEINBECK

For information concerning articles, poems, letters, speeches, separate publication of short stories, etc., by Steinbeck, consult the Hayashi bibliographies cited below. Those items marked with an asterisk are available from Penguin Books.

Fiction

* *Cup of Gold.* New York: Robert M. McBride & Co., 1929.
* *The Pastures of Heaven.* New York: Brewer, Warren & Putnam, 1932.
* *To a God Unknown.* New York: Robert O. Ballou, 1933.
* *Tortilla Flat.* New York: Covici-Friede, 1935.
* *In Dubious Battle.* New York: Covici-Friede, 1936.
* *The Red Pony.* New York: Covici-Friede, 1937; The Viking Press, 1945 [included in *The Long Valley*, 1938].
* *Of Mice and Men.* New York: Covici-Friede, 1937.
* *The Long Valley.* New York: The Viking Press, 1938.
* *The Grapes of Wrath.* New York: The Viking Press, 1939.
* *The Moon Is Down.* New York: The Viking Press, 1942.
* *Cannery Row.* New York: The Viking Press, 1945.
* *The Wayward Bus.* New York: The Viking Press, 1947.
* *The Pearl.* New York: The Viking Press, 1947.
* *Burning Bright.* New York: The Viking Press, 1950.
* *East of Eden.* New York: The Viking Press, 1952.
* *Sweet Thursday.* New York: The Viking Press, 1954.
* *The Short Reign of Pippin IV.* New York: The Viking Press, 1957.
* *The Winter of Our Discontent.* New York: The Viking Press, 1961.

Nonfiction

Their Blood Is Strong (pamphlet). San Francisco: Simon J. Lubin Society of California, Inc., 1938. [Articles published in *San Francisco News*, October 5–12, 1936, as "The Harvest Gypsies."] Reprinted in French, *Companion*, pp. 53–92, and as *The Harvest Gypsies*. Berkeley: Heyday Books, 1988.

Sea of Cortez: A Leisurely Journal of Travel and Research (in collaboration with Edward F. Ricketts). New York: The Viking Press, 1941.

Bombs Away: The Story of a Bomber Team. New York: The Viking Press, 1942.

A Russian Journal (with pictures by Robert Capa). New York: The Viking Press, 1948.

* *The Log from the Sea of Cortez*. New York: The Viking Press, 1951. [The narrative portion of *Sea of Cortez* and a tribute, "About Ed Ricketts."]

* *Once There Was a War*. New York: The Viking Press, 1958. [Steinbeck's wartime dispatches published in the *New York Herald Tribune*, June–December, 1943.]

* *Travels with Charley in Search of America*. New York: The Viking Press, 1962.

America and Americans. New York: The Viking Press, 1966.

* *Journal of a Novel: The* East of Eden *Letters* (posthumous). New York: The Viking Press, 1969.

* *Working Days: The Journals of* The Grapes of Wrath (posthumous, edited by Robert DeMott). New York: The Viking Press, 1989.

Plays

Of Mice and Men. New York: Covici-Friede, 1937.

The Moon Is Down. New York: The Viking Press, 1943.

Burning Bright. New York: The Viking Press, 1951.

Pipe Dream (musical comedy by Richard Rodgers and Oscar Hammerstein II based on *Sweet Thursday*). New York: The Viking Press, 1956.

Translation

The Acts of King Arthur and His Noble Knights: From the Winchester Manuscripts of Thomas Malory and Other Sources (posthumous, edited by Chase Horton). New York: Farrar, Straus and Giroux, 1976.

Letters and Interviews

* *Steinbeck: A Life in Letters* (posthumous, edited by Elaine Steinbeck and Robert Wallsten). New York: The Viking Press, 1975.

Letters to Elizabeth: A Selection of Letters from John Steinbeck to Elizabeth Otis (posthumous, edited by Florian J. Shasky and Susan F. Riggs).

San Francisco: Book Club of California, 1978.

Steinbeck and Covici: The Story of a Friendship (posthumous, edited by Thomas Fensch). Middlebury: Paul S. Eriksson, Publisher, 1979.

John Steinbeck on Writing (posthumous, edited by Tetsumaro Hayashi). Steinbeck Essay Series, No. 2. Muncie: Steinbeck Research Institute, Ball State University, 1988.

Film Stories and Scripts

The Forgotten Village (documentary). Herbert Kline, producer, 1941. Story and script. New York: The Viking Press, 1941.

Lifeboat. 20th Century–Fox Film Corp., 1944. Story. Unpublished.

A Medal for Benny. Paramount Studios, 1945. Story, with Jack Wagner. *Best Film Plays—1945,* edited by John Gassner and Dudley Nichols. New York: Crown, 1946.

The Pearl (from his novel). RKO, 1947. Script. Unpublished.

The Red Pony (from his stories). Feldman Group Productions and Lewis Milestone Productions, 1949. Script. Unpublished.

* *Zapata* (posthumous, edited by Robert Morsberger, and including: "Zapata: A Narrative, in Dramatic Form, of the Life of Emiliano Zapata" and film script of *Viva Zapata!*). 20th Century–Fox Film Corp., 1949. New York: The Viking Press, 1993.

CRITICISM

The following bibliography does not attempt to be complete, but the section on *The Grapes of Wrath* does include citations for most books and for the more important articles not included in those books. For your convenience, this bibliography has been designed to be used in conjunction with the descriptive listing of essays in your "Editors' Introduction: The Pattern of Criticism" (547–61). Each critical essay mentioned in that introduction is either listed individually in this bibliography, or the book in which it appears is cited parenthetically in the introduction, and that book is, in turn, included in this bibliography. If you require a comprehensive bibliography, Tetsumaro Hayashi has compiled the three most complete sources for bibliographic information on the whole range of Steinbeck's work; however, for material through 1989, the most complete bibliography of criticism and ephemera related solely to *The Grapes of Wrath* is *The Grapes of Wrath: A Fifty Year Bibliographic Survey* by Robert B. Harmon and John F. Early. For bibliographic information on current criticism of Steinbeck and *The Grapes of Wrath,* the regularly updated Modern Language Association (MLA) bibliography, in either the CD-ROM or on-line versions, is the leading source.

ON STEINBECK, GENERAL

Books

Astro, Richard. *John Steinbeck and Edward F. Ricketts: The Shaping of a Novelist.* Minneapolis: University of Minnesota Press, 1973.

———, and Tetsumaro Hayashi, eds. *Steinbeck: The Man and His Work.* Corvallis: Oregon State University Press, 1971.

Benson, Jackson J. *Looking for Steinbeck's Ghost.* Norman, University of Oklahoma Press, 1988.

———. *The True Adventures of John Steinbeck, Writer.* New York: Viking Press, 1984.

———, ed. *The Short Novels of John Steinbeck: Critical Essays with a Checklist to Steinbeck Criticism.* Durham, NC: Duke University Press, 1990.

Bloom, Harold, ed. *John Steinbeck.* Modern Critical Views. New York: Chelsea House Publishers, 1987.

Coers, Donald V., Paul D. Ruffin, and Robert J. DeMott. *After The Grapes of Wrath: Essays on John Steinbeck in Honor of Tetsumaro Hayashi.* Athens: Ohio University Press, 1995.

Crouch, Steve. *Steinbeck Country.* Palo Alto, CA: American West Publishing, 1973; Portland, OR: Graphic Arts Center Publishing, 1987.

Davis, Robert Murray. *Steinbeck: A Collection of Critical Essays.* Twentieth Century Views. Englewood Cliffs, NJ: Prentice-Hall, 1972.

DeMott, Robert. *Steinbeck's Reading: A Catalogue of Books Owned and Borrowed.* New York: Garland Publishing Co., 1984.

Ditsky, John. *John Steinbeck: Life, Work, and Criticism.* Fredericton, New Brunswick, Canada: York Press, 1985.

Fensch, Thomas C. *Conversations with John Steinbeck.* Jackson: University Press of Mississippi, 1988.

Ferrell, Keith. *John Steinbeck: The Voice of the Land.* New York: M. Evans, 1988.

Fontenrose, Joseph. *John Steinbeck: An Introduction and Interpretation.* American Authors and Critics Series. New York: Barnes and Noble, 1963; New York: Holt, Rinehart and Winston, 1967.

French, Warren. *John Steinbeck.* Twayne's United States Authors Series. New York: Twayne, 1961; New York: G. K. Hall, 1975.

Harmon, Robert B. *Steinbeck Bibliographies: An Annotated and Indexed Guide to Bibliographic Information Sources.* Metuchen, NJ: Scarecrow Press, 1987.

Hayashi, Tetsumaro. *A New Steinbeck Bibliography (1927–1971).* Metuchen, NJ: Scarecrow Press, 1967.

———. *A New Steinbeck Bibliography (1971–1981).* Metuchen, NJ: Scarecrow Press, 1983.

———. *Steinbeck and the Arthurian Theme*. Steinbeck Monograph Series. 5. Muncie, IN: Steinbeck Society of America, Ball State University, 1975.

———. *A Student's Guide to Steinbeck's Literature: Primary and Secondary Sources*. Steinbeck Bibliography Series. 1. Muncie, IN: Steinbeck Research Center, 1986, and 1989.

———, ed. *John Steinbeck: The Years of Greatness, 1936–1939*. Tuscaloosa: University of Alabama Press, 1993.

———, ed. *A New Study Guide to Steinbeck's Major Works with Critical Explications*. Metuchen, NJ: Scarecrow Press, 1993.

———, ed. *Steinbeck's Literary Dimension*. Metuchen, NJ: Scarecrow Press, 1973.

———, ed. *Steinbeck's Women: Essays in Criticism*. Steinbeck Monograph Series. 9. Muncie, IN: Steinbeck Society of America, Ball State University, 1979.

———, and Reloy Garcia, eds. *Steinbeck's Literary Dimension: A Guide to Comparative Studies, Series II*. Metuchen, NJ: Scarecrow Press, 1991.

———, Yasuo Hashiguchi, and Richard F. Peterson, eds. *John Steinbeck: East and West*. Steinbeck Monograph Series. 8. Muncie, IN: Steinbeck Society of America, 1988.

———, and Kenneth D. Swan, eds. *Steinbeck's Prophetic Vision of America*. Upland, IN: Taylor University for the Steinbeck Society of America, 1976.

Jones, Lawrence William. *John Steinbeck as Fabulist*. Steinbeck Monograph Series. 3. Marston La France, ed. Muncie, IN: Steinbeck Society of America, 1973.

Levant, Howard. *The Novels of John Steinbeck*. Columbia: University of Missouri Press, 1975.

Lisca, Peter. *John Steinbeck: Nature and Myth*. New York: Crowell, 1978.

———. *The Wide World of John Steinbeck*. New Brunswick, NJ: Rutgers University Press, 1958.

McCarthy, Paul. *John Steinbeck*. New York: Frederick Ungar Publishing, 1980.

Marks, Lester J. *Thematic Design in the Novels of John Steinbeck*. The Hague: Mouton, 1969.

Millichap, Joseph R. *Steinbeck and Film*. New York: Frederick Ungar Publishing, 1983.

Moore, Harry T. *The Novels of John Steinbeck: A First Critical Study*. Chicago: Normandie House, 1939; Port Washington, NY: Kennikat Press, 1968.

Noble, Donald R. *The Steinbeck Question: New Essays in Criticism*. Troy, NY: Whitston Publishing Company, 1993.

Owens, Louis. *John Steinbeck's Re-Vision of America*. Athens: University of Georgia Press, 1985.

Parini, Jay. *John Steinbeck: A Biography*. New York: Henry Holt, 1995.

Pearson, Pauline, comp. *Guide to Steinbeck Country*. Salinas, CA: John Steinbeck Library, 1984.

Pratt, John Clark. *John Steinbeck: A Critical Essay*. Grand Rapids, MI: William B. Eerdmans, 1970.

Sheffield, Carlton A. *Steinbeck: The Good Companion*. Portola Valley, CA: American Lives Foundation, 1983.

Simmonds, Roy S. *Steinbeck's Literary Achievement*. Steinbeck Monograph Series. 6. Muncie, IN: Steinbeck Society of America, Ball State University, 1976.

Stoddard, Martin. *California Writers: Jack London, John Steinbeck, the Tough Guys*. New York: St. Martin's Press, 1983.

Tedlock, E. W., Jr., and C. V. Wicker, eds. *Steinbeck and His Critics: A Record of Twenty-five Years*. Albuquerque: University of New Mexico Press, 1957.

Timmerman, John. *John Steinbeck's Fiction: The Aesthetics of the Road Taken*. Norman: University of Oklahoma Press, 1986.

Valjean, Nelson. *John Steinbeck, The Errant Knight: An Intimate Biography of His California Years*. San Francisco: Chronicle Books, 1975.

Essays

Astro, Richard. "John Steinbeck." *A Literary History of the American West*, 424–46. Fort Worth: Texas Christian University Press, 1987.

Beaugrande, Robert Alain de. "A Rhetorical Theory of Audience Response." *Rhetoric 78: Proceedings of "Theory of Rhetoric: An Interdisciplinary Conference."* Ed. Robert L. Brown, Jr., and Martin Steinmann, Jr., 9–20. University of Minnesota Center for Advanced Studies in Language, Style, and Literary Theory, 1979.

Bedford, R. C. "Steinbeck's Nonverbal Invention." *Steinbeck Quarterly* 18.3–4 (1985): 70–78.

Benson, Jackson J. "Through a Political Glass, Darkly: The Example of John Steinbeck." *Studies in American Fiction* 12.1 (1984): 45–59.

Britch, Carroll, and Cliff Lewis. "Shadow of the Indian in the Fiction of John Steinbeck." *MELUS: The Journal of the Society for the Study of the Multi-Ethnic Literature of the United States* 11.2 (1984): 39–58.

Covici, Pascal, Jr. "John Steinbeck and the Language of Awareness." *The Thirties: Fiction, Poetry, Drama*. Ed. Warren French, 47–54. Deland, FL: Everett Edwards Press, 1967.

DeMott, Robert. "Steinbeck's Reading: First Supplement." *Steinbeck Quarterly* 17.3–4 (1984): 97–103.

———. "Steinbeck's Reading: Second Supplement." *Steinbeck Quarterly* 22.1 (1989): 4–8.

Ditsky, John. "The Devil in Music: Unheard Themes in Steinbeck's Fiction." *Steinbeck Quarterly* 25.3–4 (1992): 80–86.

———. "John Steinbeck—Yesterday, Today, and Tomorrow." *Steinbeck Quarterly* 23.1 (1990): 5–16.

Eastman, Max. "John Steinbeck—Genevieve Tabouis." *The American Mercury* LIV (June 1942): 754–56.

Fortune magazine. "I Wonder Where We Can Go Now." (April 1939).

French, Warren. "John Steinbeck and American Literature." *San Jose Studies* 13.2 (1987): 35–48.

Frohock, W. M. "John Steinbeck: The Utility of Wrath." *The Novel of Violence in America*, 124–43. Dallas: Southern Methodist University Press, 1958.

Geismar, Maxwell. "John Steinbeck." *American Moderns: From Rebellion to Conformity*, 151–56, 164–67. New York: Hill and Wang, 1958.

Hoffman, Frederick J. *The Modern Novel in America, 1900–1950*, 160–68. Chicago: Henry Regnery, 1951.

Hyman, Stanley Edgar. "John Steinbeck: Of Invertebrates and Men." *The Promised End: Essays and Reviews, 1942–1962*, 17–22. Cleveland and New York: World, 1963.

Kazin, Alfred. *On Native Grounds: An Interpretation of Modern American Prose Literature*, 393–99. New York: Harcourt, Brace, 1942.

Lewis, Richard W. B. "John Steinbeck: The Fitful Daemon." *The Young Rebel in American Literature*. Ed. Carl Bode, 121–41. London: Heinemann, 1959; New York: Frederick Praeger, 1960.

Lisca, Peter. "Steinbeck and Hemingway: Suggestions for a Comparative Study." *Steinbeck Quarterly* II (Spring 1969): 9–17.

———. "Steinbeck's Image of Man and His Decline as a Writer." *Modern Fiction Studies* X (Spring 1966): 3–10.

McCarthy, Kevin M. "The Name Is the Game." *The Linguistic Connection.* Ed. Jean Casagrande, 161–70. Lanham, MD: University Press of America, 1983.

Mendelson, Maurice. "From *The Grapes of Wrath* to *The Winter of Our Discontent.*" *Twentieth-Century American Literature: A Soviet View.* Trans. Ronald Vroon, 411–26. Moscow: Progress Publishers, 1976.

Owens, Louis. "A Garden of My Land: Landscape and Dreamscape in John Steinbeck's Fiction." *Steinbeck Quarterly* 23.3–4 (1990): 78–88.

———. "Reconsideration: 'Grandpa Killed Indians, Pa Killed Snakes': Steinbeck and the American Indian." *MELUS: The Journal of the Society for the Study of the Multi-Ethnic Literature of the United States* 15.2 (1988): 85–92.

Quinn, Arthur Hobson. "Steinbeck." *The Literature of the American People*, 958–61. New York: Appleton-Century-Crofts, 1951.

Sartre, Jean-Paul. "American Novelists in French Eyes." *Atlantic Monthly* CLXXVIII (August 1946): 114–18.

Satyanarayana, M. R. "Steinbeck Criticism in India: 1968–78." *Steinbeck Quarterly* XIV. 1–2 (1981): 52–56.

Schmidt, Gary D. "Steinbeck's 'Breakfast': A Reconsideration." *Western American Literature* 26.4 (1992): 303–11.

Siefker, Donald L., comp. "Cumulative Index to Volumes I–X (1968–1977.)" *Steinbeck Quarterly* XI.2 (1978): 36–61.

———, comp. "Cumulative Index to Volumes XI–XX (1978–1987.)" *Steinbeck Quarterly*. Steinbeck Bibliography Series. 2. (1989): 10–41.

Slochower, Harry. "John Dos Passos and John Steinbeck: Contrasting Notions of the Communal Personality." *Byrdcliffe Afternoons*, 11–27. Woodstock, NY: Overlook Press, January, 1940.

———. "The Promise of America: John Steinbeck." *No Voice Is Wholly Lost*, 299–306. New York: Creative Age Press, 1945. Reprinted as *Literature and Philosophy Between Two World Wars: The Problem in a War Culture*, 299–308. New York: Citadel Press, 1964.

Stoneback, H. R. "Songs of 'Anger and Survival': John Steinbeck on Woody Guthrie." *Steinbeck Quarterly* 23.1–2 (1990): 34–42.

Wendel, Thomas. "John Steinbeck: Finland's Favorite American Author." *Steinbeck Newsletter* (Winter 1990): 4–5.

Whipple, Thomas K. "Steinbeck: Through a Glass, Though Brightly." *Study Out the Land*, 40–44. Berkeley: University of California Press, 1943.

Yarmus, Marcia. "John Steinbeck's Toponymic Preferences." *From Oz to the Onion Patch*. Ed. Edward Callary, 147–60. DeKalb, IL: North Central Name Society, 1986.

ON THE GRAPES OF WRATH

Books

Bloom, Harold, ed. *John Steinbeck's* The Grapes of Wrath. Modern Critical Views. New York: Chelsea House Publishers, 1988.

Davis, Robert Con, ed. The Grapes of Wrath: *A Collection of Critical Essays*. Englewood Cliffs, NJ: Prentice-Hall, 1982.

Ditsky, John, ed. *Critical Essays on Steinbeck's* The Grapes of Wrath. Boston: G. K. Hall, 1989.

Donohue, Agnes McNeill, comp. *A Casebook on* The Grapes of Wrath. New York: Crowell, 1968.

French, Warren, ed. *A Companion to* The Grapes of Wrath. New York: Viking Penguin, 1963; Penguin Books, 1989.

———, ed. *Filmguide to "The Grapes of Wrath."* Bloomington: Indiana University Press, 1973.

Galati, Frank. *John Steinbeck's* The Grapes of Wrath. New York: Penguin Books, 1991.

Harmon, Robert B., and John F. Early. The Grapes of Wrath: *A Fifty Year Bibliographic Survey.* San Jose: Steinbeck Research Center, 1990.

Hayashi, Tetsumaro, ed. *Steinbeck's* The Grapes of Wrath: *Essays in Criticism.* Steinbeck Essay Series. 3. Muncie, IN: Steinbeck Research Center, 1990.

Miron, George. *The Truth about John Steinbeck and the Migrants.* Los Angeles: Haynes Corporation, 1939.

Owens, Louis. The Grapes of Wrath: *Trouble in the Promised Land.* Boston: Twayne Publishers, 1989.

Shillinglaw, Susan, ed. The Grapes of Wrath: *A Special Issue.* Proceedings from "*The Grapes of Wrath,* 1939–1989: An Interdisciplinary Forum," March 16–18, 1989, San Jose State University. *San Jose Studies* XVI. 1 (1990).

Whitebrook, Peter. *Staging Steinbeck: Dramatising* The Grapes of Wrath. London: Cassell, 1989.

Worster, Donald. *Dust Bowl: The Southern Plains in the 1930s.* New York: Oxford University Press, 1979.

Wyatt, David, ed. *New Essays on* The Grapes of Wrath. New York: Cambridge University Press, 1990.

Essays

Baker, Howard. "In Praise of the Novel: The Fiction of Huxley, Steinbeck, & Others." *Southern Review* V (1939–1940): 778–800.

Balogun, F. Odun. "Naturalist Proletarian Prose Epics: *Petals of Blood* and *The Grapes of Wrath.*" *Journal of English* (Yemen) 11 (1983): 88–106.

Beck, William J., and Edward Erickson. "The Emergence of Class Consciousness in *Germinal* and *The Grapes of Wrath.*" *Comparatist: Journal of the Southern Comparative Literature Association* 12 (May 1988): 44–57.

Benson, Jackson J. "Environment as Meaning and the Great Central Valley." *Steinbeck Quarterly* 10.1–2 (1977): 12–20.

Bristol, Horace. "John Steinbeck and *The Grapes of Wrath.*" *Steinbeck Newsletter* (Fall 1988): 6–8.

Browning, Chris. "Grape Symbolism in *The Grapes of Wrath.*" *Discourse* XI (Winter 1968): 129–40.

Burke, Kenneth. *The Philosophy of Literary Form,* 91 and *passim.* Baton Rouge: Louisiana State University Press, 1941.

Cassuto, David. "Turning Wine into Water: Water as Privileged Signifier in *The Grapes of Wrath*." *Papers on Language and Literature: A Journal for Scholars and Critics of Language and Literature* 29.1 (1993): 67–95.

Davis, Robert Murray. "The World of John Steinbeck's Joads." *World Literature Today: A Literary Quarterly of the University of Oklahoma* 64.3 (1990): 401–404.

De Voto, Bernard. "American Novels: 1939." *Atlantic Monthly* CLXV (January 1949): 66–74.

Dircks, Phyllis T. "Steinbeck's Statement on the Inner Chapters of *The Grapes of Wrath*." *Steinbeck Quarterly* 24.3–4 (1991): 86–94.

Ek, Grete. "A 'Speaking Picture' in John Steinbeck's *The Grapes of Wrath*." *American Studies in Scandinavia* 10 (1978): 111–15.

Elliott, Kathleen Farr. "Steinbeck's 'IITYWYBAD.' " *Steinbeck Quarterly* 6.2 (1973): 53–54.

Evans, Thomas G. "Impersonal Dilemmas: The Collision of Modernist and Popular Traditions in Two Political Novels, *The Grapes of Wrath* and *Ragtime*." *South Atlantic Review* 52.1 (1987): 71–85.

Gladstein, Mimi R. "Ma Joad and Pilar: Significantly Similar." *Steinbeck Quarterly* 14.3–4 (1981): 93–104.

"*The Grapes of Wrath*." *Columbia Literary History of the United States*. Ed. Emory Elliott, 726, 753–54, 859, 864, 868. New York: Columbia University Press, 1988.

Greene, Suzanne Ellery. "*The Grapes of Wrath*." *Books for Pleasure: Popular Fiction, 1914–1945*, 116, 120, 125, 127–28, 138–39, 143–45, 151–52. Bowling Green, OH: Bowling Green University Popular Press, 1974.

Haslam, Gerald. "*The Grapes of Wrath*: A Book That Stretched My Soul" and "What about the Okies?" *The Other California: The Great Central Valley in Life and Letters*, 87–95, 105–23. Reno: University of Nevada Press, 1994.

Hayashi, Tetsumaro. "Steinbeck's Use of Old Testament Motifs in *The Grapes of Wrath*." *Kyushu American Literature* 29 (1988): 1–11.

Hearle, Kevin. "Sturges and *The Grapes of Wrath*: 'Sullivan's Travels' as Documentary Comedy." *Steinbeck Newsletter* (Summer 1994): 5–7.

Heavilin, Barbara Anne. "Hospitality, the Joads, and the Stranger Motif: Structural Symmetry in John Steinbeck's *The Grapes of Wrath*." *South Dakota Review* 29.2 (1991): 142–52.

Henderson, George. "John Steinbeck's Spatial Imagination in *The Grapes of Wrath*." *California History* 68.4 (1989): 210–23.

Hunter, J. P. "Steinbeck's Wine of Affirmation in *The Grapes of Wrath*." *Essays in Modern American Literature*. Ed. Richard E. Langford, Guy Owen, William Taylor, 76–89. Deland, FL: Stetson University Press, 1963.

Kaida, Koichi. "The Cave Experience in *The Grapes of Wrath.*" *Kyushu American Literature* 28 (1987): 67–69.

Krim, Arthur. "*Fruchte des Zorns: The Grapes of Wrath* in Wartime Germany." *Steinbeck Newsletter* (Summer 1994): 1–4.

——. "John Steinbeck and Highway 66." *Steinbeck Newsletter* (Summer 1991): 8–9.

Lorentz, Pare. "*The Grapes of Wrath.*" *Movies 1927–1941: Lorentz on Film.* Norman: University of Oklahoma Press, 1986.

Lucius, Ramona. "Let There Be Darkness: Reversed Symbols of Light and Dark in *The Grapes of Wrath.*" *Pleiades* 12.1 (1991): 50–58.

McCarthy, Paul Eugene. "The Joads and Other Rural Families in Depression Fiction." *South Dakota Review* 19.3 (1981): 51–68.

Maine, Barry. "Steinbeck's Debt to Dos Passos." *Steinbeck Quarterly* 23.1–2 (1990): 17–26.

Motley, Warren. "From Patriarchy to Matriarchy: Ma Joad's Role in *The Grapes of Wrath.*" *American Literature* 54.3 (1982): 397–412.

Mullen, Patrick B. "American Folklife and *The Grapes of Wrath.*" *Journal of American Culture* 1.4 (1978): 742–53.

Owens, Louis, and Hector Torres. "Dialogic Structure and Levels of Discourse in Steinbeck's *The Grapes of Wrath.*" *Arizona Quarterly* 45.4 (1989): 75–94.

Parfit, Michael. "The Dust Bowl." *Smithsonian* 19.3 (1989): 44–57.

Paton, Alan, and Liston Pope. "The Novelist and Christ." *Saturday Review* XXXVII (December 4, 1954): 15–16, 56–59.

Rombold, Tamara. "Biblical Inversion in *The Grapes of Wrath.*" *College Literature* 14.2 (1987): 146–66.

Salter, Christopher L. "John Steinbeck's *The Grapes of Wrath* as a Primer for Cultural Geography." *Humanistic Geography and Literature: Essays on the Experience of Place,* 142–58. London: Croom Helm, 1981; Totowa, NJ: Barnes and Noble, 1981.

Slade, Leonard A. "The Use of Biblical Allusions in *The Grapes of Wrath.*" *College Language Association Journal* XI (March 1968): 241–47.

Terkel, Studs. "The Dust Bowl Revisited: 'We Still See Their Faces.'" *San Francisco Review of Books* 13 (Spring 1989): 24, 29.

Timmerman, John H. "The Squatters Circle in *The Grapes of Wrath.*" *Studies in American Fiction* 17.2 (1989): 203–11.

Trachtenberg, Stanley. "John Steinbeck and the Fate of Protest." *North Dakota Quarterly* 41 (Spring 1973): 5–11.

Werlock, Abby H. P. "Poor Whites: Joads and Snopeses." *San Jose Studies* 18.1 (1992): 61–71.

White, Ray Lewis. "*The Grapes of Wrath* and the Critics of 1939." *RALSJ* 13.2 (1983): 134–64.

Worster, Donald. "I Never Knowed They Was Anything Like Her." *Rivers of Empire: Water, Aridity & the Growth of the American West*, 213–33. New York: Pantheon, 1985.

———. "Hydraulic Society in California." *Under Western Skies: Nature and History in the American West*, 53–63. New York: Oxford University Press, 1992.

Wyatt, David. "Steinbeck's Lost Gardens." *The Fall into Eden: Landscape and Imagination in California*. New York: Cambridge University Press, 1986.